Donna Gillespie's epic masterpiece
THE LIGHT BEARER

On the day of her birth, Auriane received a mysterious amulet from a priestess—and a double-edged prophecy of doom and glory. The daughter of a Germanic tribal chieftain, Auriane witnessed unspeakable horrors committed against her people by ruthless invaders. And when tragedy tore her family apart, she took the oath of a warrior—and vowed revenge. Tales of her brilliant swath of conquest carried as far as Rome, to the renowned statesman Marcus Julianus—who felt his destiny intertwined with Auriane's . . . and wore about his neck an identical amulet . . .

"There are no flat passages in *The Light Bearer*, only a fast-flowing stream that erupts into a full-scale torrent in the book's conclusion." —*The Washington Post Book World*

"An intriguing recording of everyday detail, national issues, and more importantly, religion and psychology."
—*Publishers Weekly* (starred review)

"Gillespie spent eleven years bringing this magnificent book to completion . . . replete with excitement . . . Gillespie's love of the written word is evident."
—*Marina Times*

"A time capsule journey into a world of richly embroidered adventure . . . a treasure. Phrases never sit static on the pages . . . they are fluid grace points that translate instantly into living, active images in the reader's imagination."
—*Northwest Florida Daily News*

THE LIGHT BEARER

DONNA GILLESPIE

JOVE BOOKS, NEW YORK

THE LIGHT BEARER

A Jove Book / published by arrangement with
the author

PRINTING HISTORY
Berkley trade paperback edition published September 1994
Jove edition / November 1996

The Putnam Berkley World Wide Web site address is
http://www.berkley.com/berkley

ISBN: 0-515-11966-0

A JOVE BOOK®
Jove Books are published by The Berkley Publishing Group,
200 Madison Avenue, New York, New York 10016.
JOVE and the "J" design are trademarks
belonging to Jove Publications, Inc.

PRINTED IN THE UNITED STATES OF AMERICA

10 9 8 7 6 5 4 3 2 1

For my parents

Acknowledgments

I would like to thank my writing instructor, Leonard Bishop, a brilliant and inspiring teacher who made me believe I could write a novel. And I would also like to thank Joe Capello, whose constant encouragement helped me through all those times when completing this book seemed impossible. And I owe a great debt to Donna Levin, for all her timely advice, and to Bruce Hartford, for all those times that he drove across town to help me out of my latest computer crisis. Others whose help was indispensable were my editor, Susan Allison, and my agent, Robert Stricker.

I am also grateful to the following people for their friendship and support over the years, and their insightful critiques of the manuscript: Victoria Micu, Marilyn Day, Trisha Johnson-Reece, Christine Gross, Phyllis Holliday, Suzanne Juergensen, William Buford, Lynn Allen, Julie Whelly, Robert Hunt, Brad Newsham, Karen Caronna, Gloria Suffin, Margaret Cuthbert, Leigh Anne Varney, Donal Brown. And I'm greatly indebted to the San Francisco Public Library, which became a second home through the years, and to the Goethe Institute.

The Northern Frontier~
The Chatti and Neighboring Tribes

THE SACRED EARTH

CHAPTER I

It was a wolf-ridden night. Early spring in the wastes of Germania was not kind to creatures of warm blood. Wind, snow and stars ruled here, not man. Night wind played the land like a bone flute, its desolate tones gently rising and falling with the hills. This country was home to the Chattians, the most warlike of the Germanic tribes dwelling beyond the Rhine, and the most independent of their all-conquering neighbor to the south, Imperial Rome. To the Roman world this was the sunless side of the Rhine, ruled by spells and dreams, where limbs of trees might spring to life and reach down to strangle a man, where bottomless bogs waited with gaped mouths, eager to swallow their bones.

On this night the skin doors of the rude dwellings of the Chattians were dropped shut against spirits and elves. But at the hall of their first war-leader, Baldemar, the smoke-hole was pulled open, the doorskin torn off. For within, his young wife, Athelinda, writhed on a rush mat, losing a grim struggle to push out her first child. The women thralls who served her unfastened the gates of the animal pens as well, and unbraided their thick blond hair—for anything knotted, closed or bound might hold the child back.

As Roman historians reckoned time, this was the eleventh year of the reign of the lame Emperor Claudius—or two years before Claudius' wife Agrippina sent him the dish of poisoned mushrooms that ushered in the rule of her son Nero. But to the Chattians, who knew only the wheel of the seasons and daily

3

struggle with the earth, the intrigues of the Roman court would have seemed a village madman's tale. The tribe knew too well, however, the Roman soldiers of the frontier, who lately kidnapped a hundred of their young warriors to be trained for the Roman army. Baldemar on this night was encamped three days' ride to the south near the confluence of the Rhine and Main, poised to attack the great Roman fortress of Mogontiacum in retaliation for these frequent abductions. And so he left his fierce old mother Hertha, mistress of the wide fields ringed about the Village of the Boar, to receive the child into the clan.

Hertha first sent to the Village for the midwife Sigdrifa, who used all her arts to no avail. When Sigdrifa decided no mortal woman could safely deliver Athelinda, the midwife waited until Hertha dozed with the exhausted Athelinda cradled in her arms, then slunk off into the night — Sigdrifa had no wish to be held to account by one so protective of his honor as Baldemar for the death of his wife. And so as dawn tinted blue the last stubborn patches of old snow, Hertha ordered Mudrin, youngest of the thralls, to travel to the lodge of Thrusnelda, a holy woman said to be able to sing a child from the womb.

But Mudrin got no farther than the threshold when she stopped abruptly as if some enchantment froze her heart. The basket she carried as a gift for the medicine-woman slid from her hands; honeyed hazelnuts, baked apples and dried plums rolled out onto the earthen floor.

Hertha gave her a pitiless look. "Mudrin, you shy at your own footfall! What is it!"

Then Hertha noticed what she had not before. The whole of the homestead was oddly still — and it was the unholy quiet of the burial ground. The field thralls had not yet come forth from their huts, though she knew they rose as usual with the mournful baying of the hound-keeper's horn. Even the wild things of the forest hushed their twitterings and rustlings. The wind itself ceased its keening, and seemed to listen. From the yard she heard a dog's growl give way to a whine, as though the beast's anger turned to fear.

Hertha rose. "Mudrin! Speak! What do you gape at!"

Hertha made her way to the door, her spine stiff with disdain. She was dressed scarcely differently from the thralls — all the women wore a shift of fine wool woven into a plaid of many hues of brown; the loose garment was girded with a rope, and draped with a heavy cloak of rough undyed wool. The sole sign of

Hertha's rank was the silver fibula inset with garnets that secured her cloak; the thralls' cloaks were fastened with thorns. Yet anyone could have seen at once that Hertha was the one who was free and noble. Her black eyes were harsh with pride, betraying a ferocious soul too great for her withered body. She had the look of one who would be transfixed by a spear before she allowed an enemy to come near the stores, or perish of starvation before she would consent to share meat with one who failed to avenge a murdered kinsman. "Speak, or I'll have your tongue!"

Mudrin was still silent. Fredemund, one of the loom-women, came grumbling up behind the younger woman, moving minimally, painfully; her middle was thick as a barrel.

"Mother of the gods!" Fredemund exclaimed softly. "Mudrin, what mischief have you done!"

"No sacrilege!" Mudrin took an ill-planned step backward and stepped on a chicken that flapped noisily into the air, then crashed into a willow-withy screen. Her voice was a whelp's whine. "I committed no sacrilege!"

Hertha swept past them and looked out.

Where forest gave way to field, before the broken stone wall, she saw the solitary form of a woman. No horse, no snapped branch, no stirring of sparrows announced this traveler's coming; she might have materialized there from the world of ghosts. Her hooded cloak was strikingly white against the forest gloom. With grave steps the woman began to move toward them, swaying slightly like some image of the gods carried in a procession. At her back a raven erupted from the forest, arced upward and gave a raw cry, as though in attendance upon her.

"*Ramis,*" Hertha exclaimed softly.

"Fredemund," Mudrin whispered, "draw the door."

"Be still!" Hertha commanded. "You'll not keep her out. She sees right through to your very bones."

No common priestess of the settlements could have evoked in them such dread. The multitudes of Holy Ones whom they saw every day, crowded about the village sanctuaries or attending the divine springs and hallowed groves scattered over their lands, inspired respect but not terror—for these mingled often with the people, and no tales were spread of their awesome gifts. But Ramis was one of a dark, reclusive sisterhood called the Holy Nine, the most feared prophetesses of all the northern tribes. It was said they could raise their own from the dead and foretell the fall of nations. They conversed with the Fates as familiarly as they spoke with their own kin. Their veins ran not with blood but ichor. Ramis was answerable only to their highest one, a prophetess called the Veleda, whose title meant "the One Who Sees." The Veleda dwelled hidden away from all humanity in a lofty pinewood tower on the River Lippe and handed down her oracles through servants. It was death to look on her face, but Ramis, it was said, once ascended that tower and lived.

"She cannot be here," Mudrin whispered to Fredemund. "She is with Baldemar and the army."

"It's not difficult to travel so far so quickly when you lope through the wood in the shape of a black wolf," Fredemund answered darkly.

"You chuttering hens—I warn you for the final time to silence!" Hertha cried out in a ringing voice that betrayed her own unease. In ordinary times Hertha feared nothing and no one. But Ramis could not be halted, frightened into obedience, bartered with, or understood. Hertha felt she faced an armed stranger in the dark. Had the great prophetess come to curse them all, or to save Athelinda? Or had she been drawn by the destiny of the child? It was whispered in the village that Ramis sometimes stole firstborn children to raise as apprentices. What better one to steal than the firstborn of Baldemar?

Now Ramis was close enough that they could see her face, austere as bone, with its fine brow, smooth as the moon, and the grim hollows of her cheeks; Hertha could with disturbing ease imagine the skull beneath the skin. Ramis' eyes were mild and gray-blue, opaque as river ice, but with a darkness underneath hinting at the black water surging beneath the ice. Her mouth was severe and neatly formed; on a gentler woman it might have been beautiful but on Ramis' face it was a finely chiseled instrument. Though she was not much past middle years, she seemed never to have been young; imagining her as a maiden was as difficult as imagining the grand and gnarled oak as a sapling.

In her right hand was a staff of hazelwood; its brass knob was inset with glowing stones of amber. The thralls felt their hearts clutch at the sight of it, for this was the staff of condemnation: When Ramis broke it at the Law-Assembly, she sentenced the accused man to death. But that staff was not more dreadful than those supple hands, adept at drawing ropes taut about human necks. Ramis was a sacrificing priestess and to her fell the sacred duty of offering a human life to the gods in the spring rites held at the edge of the bog. Though the one who gave his life always did so willingly, still to look on those hands was to gaze on a source of terrifying mystery. The hood of her cloak and her hairy calfskin boots were lined with white cat fur. White cats were sacred to the goddess she served, whose many names changed with the place and season but who was most often called Fria, the Lady. A circlet of silver lay on Ramis' head; from it hung a delicately worked crescent moon.

Ramis halted before the door and inclined her head. Mudrin and Fredemund quietly panicked, not realizing what was wrong.

"The axhead!" Hertha reminded them. "Mudrin, quickly, dig it out."

It was the custom of the people to bury an axhead in the earth of the doorway with the blade facing the sky, to give protection against lightning. But a tribal priestess could not come near any implement fashioned of iron, for this metal was too profane and new; its presence was jarring to the subtle powers of the Holy Ones, passed down from the age of giants when implements were fashioned only of living stone.

Mudrin dug it out with a broken potsherd. Ramis stepped gracefully through.

"Greetings to the noble Hertha and blessing on this house." Ramis' voice, at least, inspired no terror; it was womanly and kind, though with a hint of power held back.

"Greetings, High One." Hertha smiled wanly. "Stay as long as we please you. Honor us by sharing our meat and mead."

Ramis inclined her head in acknowledgment, then wordlessly she walked toward Athelinda. As she passed over the threshing floor, then down the long hearthfire, past the tall grain-storage jars and the brightly painted warriors' shields mounted along the walls, Hertha followed at a respectful distance. Mudrin and Fredemund sought safety behind Athelinda's warp-weight loom. From Ramis drifted the scent of fertile earth mingled with spikenard and thyme.

The only sounds in the hallowed silence were the flitting of birds in the thatch of the roof and the soft jingling of the many sickle-shaped tools of bronze that hung at Ramis' belt. When she came to the bed of sheepskins on which Athelinda lay, she withdrew a leather pouch from her cloak and ordered the thralls to put the herbs it contained into a bronze vessel and boil them with goat's milk. Then she drew back the hood of her cloak, revealing unbound hair of dark blond with long streaks of silver, and sat on the weaving stool next to Athelinda.

Hertha felt in one moment a burden fit for an ox had been taken from her shoulders. The Holy Nine were the best midwives in the land. Perhaps Ramis *had* come only to save Athelinda. How she knew she was needed here was known only by the ghosts.

At the sight of her, Athelinda made a mewling sound and struggled weakly to get away. But Ramis put a gentle palm on her forehead and intoned the words of a birth-charm in a voice full of powerful comfort. Terror eased from Athelinda's pain-fogged eyes.

Ramis' hands then traveled with brisk confidence over Athelinda's swollen body, moving through a succession of tasks with light, swift grace. First she determined the position of the child, probing deftly for what was wrong. Then she massaged Athelinda's belly with an ointment of hen's grease, dittany, and hollyhock, stroking her hips, her back, beseeching her body to release the child. When the draught she had ordered the thralls to prepare was poured out into a clay vessel, she put it to Athelinda's dry lips. Ramis' presence seemed to reawaken the fire in Athelinda's eyes, as though an extinguished torch were touched by one that burned brightly.

Then Ramis dragged the laboring woman to her feet while carefully supporting her weight, and forced her to take staggering steps. Athelinda's copper-colored hair was soaked with her exertions; it swung limply down. For long moments Ramis walked with her this way; Hertha guessed she was shifting the child's position. When Ramis was satisfied she had done so, she helped Athelinda into a crouching position over a bed of straw. After long moments of insistent manipulations of Ramis' hands, the child came all at once.

Ramis caught the glistening, red creature in her strong hands. Mudrin's eyes blurred with tears. Those hands that so skillfully took life at the edge of the bog now just as skillfully preserved it.

As Ramis raised the child up, Hertha saw something flickering in the priestess's eye that she had not thought possible there—a vulnerable look, the look of a mother, overfull with love.

With gentle triumph Ramis proclaimed, "A girl child is born to the clan." After saving aside the birth-string so it could later be ceremonially buried, she laid the little creature on her mother's breast.

"You have blessed us," Hertha said with exaggerated graciousness—she did not want to seem ungrateful by betraying her unease. A girl child was more likely to be stolen away for an apprentice. "Mudrin! Fredemund!" She clapped her hands. "Prepare for the oracle."

A priestess was called to every birth to prophesy the future of the child; all counted it an honor they had one so august as Ramis to perform this common rite. Fredemund, moving stiffly as an old mare, spread a white linen cloth before the hearthfire. Mudrin found her birdbone flute and, with a child's animal spirits, began to play while walking round the hearthfire, weaving an intricate net of notes through which harmful spirits could not pass.

Ramis shook out her silver and bronze hair until it hung down like a second cloak, nearly as long, laid over the first. The prophetess then placed her staff at the edge of the white cloth and settled herself behind it, sitting cross-legged. She waited until she saw the babe take milk. No oracle would be given before a child was put to the breast, to protect the newborn in case the parents were terrified of its fate and wanted to cast it out. For once a child took food it became a member of the clan, and to kill it then would be the most heinous crime of all, the murder of kin.

"Tell us first," Hertha ventured as she settled beside Athelinda, "what ancestor is born among us? Whose name shall she bear?"

Ramis watched approvingly as the babe began to suck. "There is but one name for her, my lady. She must be called Auriane."

Hertha's eyes flashed, but she stifled her fury. They had been betrayed. And a name, once given, could not be taken back. With cautious affront she protested: "But . . . that is not a name of our family! You have given her a priestess-name!"

"I have given her the name that is hers."

Athelinda spoke; in her exhaustion she feared nothing and no one. "It is the right of the mother and father to name the child!"

Hertha glared at Athelinda, astonished by her spirited rashness. If Ramis were goaded to wrath she might curse the cattle with disease or blast the fields for a generation.

But Ramis only answered Athelinda mildly, "I am her mother and father."

Athelinda pressed the child's cheek to hers and shut her eyes. Tears seeped from beneath her dark lashes. "You thief of children! You shall not have her!"

"Athelinda! Silence yourself or fall into darkness!" Hertha hissed.

"Hertha! Be at peace!" Ramis interrupted in her clear, commanding alto. "I do not hear those words. They are spoken not to me but to the specter of all the evils she has known." Ramis turned to Athelinda, her voice now soft as fleece, "Athelinda, take heed. The child is neither yours *nor* mine, truly, and these things are not to be feared. Life flows through this little one and carries her along, as it flows through you and me. Would you try and dam the river of the gods? You cannot stop a name, no more than you can stop the night."

With a quick gesture Ramis flung agaric onto the fire, causing it to jump. But it settled back at once as though it knew its master. Mudrin's notes on the bone flute shifted in tone; now they were warm, low, and enticing as she lured the spirits of foreknowing.

Ramis withdrew from her robe a linen bag that contained twenty-four polished sticks of beechwood; on each was burned a runic letter painted with red lead. She began casting them three at a time onto the white cloth, collecting them up and throwing them down in a sure, rapid rhythm, gathering information about the life of the child in the order that they fell. As she divined she hummed a strong amelodic tune that blended chillingly with Mudrin's aching notes on the bone flute. Ramis paused only once and smiled a bare smile, as if a thing she had suspected had been confirmed. Then just as swiftly she returned the rune-sticks to the cloth bag, tied it up again, and returned it to her cloak.

The thralls crept closer, full of some dim sense that this oracle would be a disturbing one. Hertha found Athelinda's limp hand and held to it tightly.

Ramis bowed her head, humming still; her voice rose in pitch and intensified until it seemed it would shake ghosts from the air. When slowly she raised her head again, it seemed to Hertha her features were melted by the firelight and music and remolded into ancient shape. In the smoky gloom that face was a stark mask with two nether pits for eyes. She was a woman of a thousand winters, fashioned of rocks and rime. Her hair was long grass, her bones were stone, her mind, a field of stars. Her lids eased closed; her head gently rolled back. The fire seemed to swell and subside with her breathing. Her humming faded away, and Mudrin let her last flute note evaporate on the air.

Ramis had fallen into a deep trance; her eyes were peacefully shut. When she spoke at last, her voice was tired and drawn; the words seemed to drift from her like smoke.

"We are the spirits of forest and grove. We hum with one voice: This child is mine. But she shall not know it for a long time. She will resist us mightily, and from this will come her sorrow.

"The fate of this one is fearsome and surpassingly strange. But such things come, at turnings of the times."

Ramis was silent for an uncomfortably long time, and Hertha shivered, shifting closer to Athelinda and the nursing child for comfort; Ramis' silence was a black chasm crowded with demons.

Then Ramis began to cough, though no smoke from the hearthfire was carried in her direction; they realized she envisioned fire in her mind. When she spoke again, her words seemed some surging lay of tragedy sung to the beat of a funereal drum.

"In her time will be war and more war, until the Wolf-Men of the South break into our lands in great numbers to devastate and burn. The dead will lie unquiet, their bleached bones buried in snow. The Fates will weave with our entrails. Dead children will be our crop. Mothers and fathers will bury daughters and sons, and holy groves will be devoured by fire. Victorious wolf! Beware your victory, for the wheel never stops turning."

Hertha felt a low pulse of alarm. The meaning in the words was unmistakable: Within the lifetime of the girl there would be some great and terrible war with Rome. *The Fates grant me death by that day,* she prayed.

"But this one who has come will be a thorn in the paw of the Great Wolf. She will bring shame down on the posturing mighty. Great will be her luck in war."

Hertha tautened in disbelief. *What sort of child had they brought forth?* She had heard many birth oracles and usually they promised such common things as a fruitful marriage, an honorable life, a gift of land or cattle, or vengeance won against an enemy of the clan. Hertha looked at the girl as if for an explanation, but the child's blank surprised eyes revealed nothing.

"This one newly born has come to close wounds. She will bring disruption to the ancient order, then turn round at the last and give everything to save it. She will endure a great trial by ordeal in a foreign land. But for this there is no knowing, for we are masters of our fates, though few of us know it, and she will die or live by her own designing.

"And then I see darkness, the darkness needed to bring the light. She will be led to slaughter her own . . . but by this same act she will save her own."

A chill hand clamped round Hertha's heart.

To slaughter *her own?* Which one of us is this baby going to murder? What foul trick have the Fates played on us? How could Ramis bless such a scourge?

She wondered if this was a normal child, conceived in the regular way. Tales of women raped by demons had gone round frequently of late. The children of these horrid couplings *looked* human enough at first, Hertha reminded herself uneasily. Then she chided herself for believing thralls' tales.

"Bring her to me now," Ramis said softly, her eyes still closed. As Fredemund held the baby before Ramis, the priestess drew forth an amulet; it seemed no more than a pouch of black leather strung from a thong. She adjusted the thong for the tiny neck.

"Many will seek her life but this child must live. I give her the most powerful protection I can give. In this pouch is the sacred earth called the *aurr,* the pure soil taken from the tracks of the cart of the Nameless One when she journeys over the earth in spring. This child must be named for the Sacred Mold, for her whole life is a sacrifice to earth. I will that the protection of earth be always with you, Auriane."

She opened the pouch, took a bit of the earth within, wet it with her spittle and daubed it on the forehead of the child, tracing the form of the rune of long life. Then she bound it up again and placed the black leather amulet about the child's neck.

What were they to do? Hertha wondered frantically. Should a child be raised who will be "led to slaughter her own"? She thought of sending a message at once to Baldemar. But did he still live? She felt caught in a whirlpool, sucked down into darkness.

"You have asked of Baldemar," Ramis said suddenly.

Hertha drew in a breath. She had spoken no word aloud. Instinctively she dropped her gaze, as if to conceal her thoughts from Ramis' remorselessly searching mind.

"Bright is his fortune and for long, all is well. Tomorrow he will scatter the Wolf-Men, and from this day he will thrive. More battle-friends will be won to him than to any other . . . they fling themselves into the fray like the foaming wave onto the shore.

"He will be called the Feeder of Wolves, the great Breaker of Rings. He will be called the Protector of the Land . . ."

Hertha turned to smile with relief at Athelinda, but Fredemund had taken Auriane from her and the young mother was sinking quickly into sleep.

". . . His hall will glitter like the heavens with treasure from his many victories—"

Ramis had been speaking smoothly and easily; abruptly she stopped. Hertha looked up quickly to examine her face. Ramis'

expression was no longer peaceful; her features delicately contracted into a look of horror.

When Ramis spoke oracles she walked a winding path; often
she was as startled as her listeners by what was suddenly visible
beyond a sharp turn. And now she seemed unwilling to speak on.
It was as though she wished to protect them from something and
wrestled with herself because she knew she could not. A prophecy
could not be held back because it was unpleasant, for this would
violate sacred law. An oracle was an emanation of all nature, and
in nature beauty and terror were braided together.

"What is it!" Hertha whispered. The flames crackled angrily.
Auriane started to cry.

When Ramis spoke at last, her voice was dry as the sound of an
adder in the grass; there was a faint rattle in her throat.

"Baldemar will fall victim at the last to the greatest crime of all
humanity. And *she who just came forth* will be the one to do the
deed."

When Ramis was gone, Hertha roused Athelinda.

" . . . not have the child!" Athelinda moaned as she fitfully
awakened. "She shall not!" Life for Athelinda had been cold and
hard as an iron blade. She had weathered deadly winters that
halved the herds and pruned away the tribe's aged and ill; she had
braved enemy spears while accompanying the grain wagons that
trailed the native army. She had endured the hatred of her mother's
kin when she married Baldemar because she had broken the
ancient law by traveling to her husband's land to live instead of
having her husband come to her. And she had suffered the
bleakness of spirit Baldemar's long absences brought—this land's
gentle summer was the raiding season, and annually he decamped
in spring, not to return until the time of rattling leaves. Athelinda
wanted this child to be the one creature in the Three Worlds that
was hers alone; she and the girl would be bound in common need,
and by a love known only to a mother and daughter who sit at the
same loom.

"Athelinda, take heed! You fell off asleep, you missed the worst
of it! This monster must be gotten rid of, named and fed or not.
Athelinda, you spawned a murderer of kin!"

"What foul madness do you speak?"

"Your daughter will kill *my* son!"

"I heard no such thing."

"Of course not! You slept through it!"

"I do not believe you, wicked woman! What demon possesses you!"

"Give me that child. I'll do to it what it deserves!"

"Ramis is sometimes wrong. I did not hear it—and I don't believe it!"

"Athelinda! Mother love has robbed you of your wits! We all must agree to it. The child was born, lived for a day, became sickly, and died. If Mudrin and Fredemund say anything to anyone, they die for it. Now hand the brat to me. It goes into the bogs!"

Athelinda struggled to sit up. She had a fine, supple strength not always visible, but when it came, it flashed to the fore quick as a cat-strike. She was an avenging sylph with eyes that burned hot as a midsummer fire.

"You are monstrous! She has taken food! Harm her and you commit the very crime of which you accuse the child. Even if Ramis *did* say it I don't believe it, and you are moonstruck to listen, for it is nonsense. Name a time when it has happened among us. You cannot. And that is because it *could* not happen. All nature would rise against a child before it could lay a hand upon a parent. Leave this child be, or I will go in arms to the next Law-Assembly and tell the tale of your crime before all our kinsmen and you shall stand judgment for it!"

"Athelinda! You would not speak against the mother of your husband!"

"I would and I will, if the mother of my husband murders my child."

And so Athelinda prevailed that day, and the child lived. As the seasons turned and Auriane grew, she felt a sense of dread in Hertha's presence that she could never understand, as though she knew somehow what had passed on that day between her mother and grandmother.

The oracle Athelinda heard in a fog of childbed pain was soon distorted in her mind and half forgotten. What she remembered most clearly was Ramis' betrayal: She gave the child a priestess-name.

The child will not be one, Athelinda promised herself. The life of a priestess is barren and grim with fearful magic, and they have no home to call their own. This child will live close to the hearth of her kin, and I'll see she marries someone near—she will weave with me and stay by me.

And so Athelinda took Baldemar's first sword, one he cast aside in his youth, and placed it in Auriane's cradle, hidden beneath the straw. She thought by doing this she would stunt any oracular powers that might develop in the child. Iron would pin her to the earth, to the everyday life of woman and man.

And so all through her earliest days Auriane slept over a sword.

CHAPTER II

Six summers passed. This was the fourth year of the reign of Nero. Dusty evening settled upon the Subura, the saddest and poorest district of the imperial city of Rome. All the flies in the Empire, it was said, bred in this festering sink nestled between two great hills crowned with senatorial mansions. In the Subura prostitutes could be lured from shadowed places for the cost of a cup of boiled peas, and beggar children lamed by their masters so they could better incite pity fought with snake charmers and acrobats to wrest a few copper coins from citizens hurrying to the shops. Here thieves, tomb robbers, charioteers and poisoners felt at ease drinking toasts with idle young noblemen come for a night's adventure. Each dawn illumined fresh corpses in the street.

In the dank gloom of a Subura fuller's shop, one of the poorer establishments where human urine was used to lift the grime from the clothes, a boy called Endymion was offered for sale by his master, a fuller named Lucius Grannus, who had decided this was a boy no reasonable man could restrain. He was fathered by a mad dog, Grannus maintained, and nursed by Nemesis herself in one of her foulest moods. Grannus meant to pass the boy on to someone who would work him to death as he deserved. It was Lucius Grannus who gave him the name Endymion—that was what he called every boy he set to the task of hauling the cleaned clothes in from the vats.

This was the third time in as many years that Endymion had

been sold. Each time his lot became more miserable. His back was crisscrossed with scars and welts from Grannus' beatings; at night he wrapped his feet in rags because Grannus would not buy shoes. As he stood before the buyer, his wrists bound tightly with cord, he formed a resolution that terrified him, but he knew the time had come.

He had always known that when he judged himself grown tall enough and sturdy enough in body to survive the life of a fugitive, he would run for freedom. Now he was nearly as tall as Grannus, and the muscles of his arms were supple and hard from lifting loads too great for a boy. When this new master led him into the streets he would break and run: the swarms of idlers, beggars and tenement dwellers crowding the vendors' stalls would flow about him and make pursuit difficult. He would not be given a better chance. It must be so. He felt himself quickly dying, and he was not yet fourteen years old.

Wretched as this life was, it was not this that finally drove him to risk the hazards of escape. It was the knowledge that all about him behind high walls were storehouses of books, forever beyond his reach.

By a cruel trick of fortune Endymion knew of books and reading. In fact, this ragged boy knew as well as the most learned scholar in the city the writings of the Stoic philosopher Seneca. This came about because his fourth master, a bootmaker, on learning Endymion could write in a neat, clear hand, had hired him out to a scriptorium—a hall where slave scribes laboriously copied the books bound for the bookstalls. Endymion did not remember who taught him to read; at times he caught a shadowed memory of a shimmering woman who emanated kindness, but always she dissolved in white mist; he supposed her to be a literate slave nurse who had charge of him for a time before he was sold away.

It happened that this scriptorium produced chiefly the works of Seneca, whose steady stream of treatises, tragedies and works of poetry were more than enough to keep twenty slaves employed. The words of the great philosopher became as familiar to the boy as the beat of blood in the temple, the rhythm of breathing. They lived in his mind like the words of parents might have, had his parents kept him, or the commands of a priestess or priest at a child's first visit to the temple of the family's patron god. One day he would be comforted by some phrase of the philosopher's, then the next he was not certain he knew what it meant. He had heard love described as a sort of sweet torment, and he decided philosophy was the same. That the other slaves of the scriptorium were not so affected made him wonder sometimes if he were mad.

The master of the scriptorium rid himself of the boy when Endymion began to insert his own words into the manuscripts. Once after he obediently copied ". . . *the wise man is not owned by what he owns, and so is happy. And the swiftest course to happiness is to possess little or nothing,"* he added, *"Then why are not slaves, who possess nothing, the happiest and wisest of men?"*

The master of the scriptorium had him soundly beaten. Shortly after, he was sold to a ropemaker who passed him on to the mule driver who sold him to Lucius Grannus.

But the half-understood ideas penned in a waking dream followed him here to the fuller's shop, beckoning him to the world's edge, shredding his peace, threatening with death while they promised luminous life.

All the cautions Endymion had heard throughout his life battered his ears then. Slaves in Rome cannot escape. Not your master but the whole city is your jailer. No door will open to you and every hand is lifted against you—or held out for the reward when you are captured.

"He comes with a warning, now," Lucius Grannus was saying to Terentius, who had come to buy. Grannus was a shaggy brute with bright obtuse eyes and a look of sluggish petulance. He had begun life as a field slave on an estate in Gaul and had earned his freedom by performing as a wrestler. "He's vicious, and he thieves," Grannus went on. "So don't slink off and complain of me to the magistrate, I break no law in selling him—I've told you his vices."

At this, Terentius narrowed his eyes skeptically. He had already determined that Grannus would sell a spavined donkey to his own mother. But the boy would do, he thought, in spite of Lucius Grannus. He approved of that wild and unbroken look in the boy's dark eyes. Terentius sought intractable slaves no one else wanted. The more spirited they were, he maintained, the longer they lasted turning the wheel of the great crane that his own employer, a contractor in the service of the Imperial Ministry of Works, used for raising mammoth blocks of travertine. It was the docile ones, Terentius always argued, who succumbed first.

Terentius took Endymion's chin in a sunburnt hand and wrenched the boy's head to one side as though inspecting an animal for soundness. Endymion felt molten rage spurt through his limbs.

Not now, he cautioned himself. Be still a little longer. In a few moments I will either be free and an animal no longer, or in Hades.

"What did he thieve?" Terentius was forced to shout to be heard over the din from the street: The barks of hawkers vied with the moans of tavern songs and the hollow ricocheting shrieks from a cheap bathhouse across the narrow street.

"Books," Grannus answered aggressively, sensing Terentius doubted all he said.

"*Books?* The wretch *reads?*"

Grannus grinned. "He can turn the wheel all day and read Greek love poems to you at night. Like getting two for one price, is it not?" Grannus' laughter made Terentius think of a panting dog.

Endymion coughed. "He is diseased!" Terentius exclaimed.

"Not so. It's only the sulfur fumes." Grannus indicated the whole shop with a gesture of a hairy hand. "They all cough." Behind him the Syrian slaves whose task was to tread the clothes in the vats were seated on a bench, noisily lapping an evening meal of beans and cabbage and vinegar water—they seemed more like animals feeding at a manger than humans taking a meal. Over them an owl was carved into the wall, the symbol of Minerva, the patroness of fullers. Terentius guessed the raw patches on the treaders' legs were caused by the urine, which was collected from the public tanks set out in front of every tenement for the fullers' use. Now that the sinister liquid was undisturbed, the two great vats in which the clothes were trod looked like squares of black marble marking a tomb. In the dimly lit room beyond, other slaves still worked, draping tunics and togas on wickerwork frames and spreading them over burning pots of sulfur; the thick foul smoke made him feel he had come upon a fissure to the underworld. Terentius was grateful he worked beneath the sun.

"He's comely. Quite the proud young colt," said Terentius, noticing how carefully the boy watched him, the somber eyes flickering with restless intelligence. Terentius gathered up some of Endymion's silken black hair and fondled it. This hair is too long for a slave, Terentius thought; it would only breed lice. When his hand moved lazily down, drawn to the boy's thigh, Endymion pulled sharply back. "Not trained for other duties, I see," Terentius said affably. "All right, I'll give you fifty. I've five more to look at today; I'm a man in a hurry."

"I said I'd sell him, not give him as a gift." Grannus put a hand the size of a frying pan around Endymion's shoulders and pretended to lead the boy away. "Well, my boy, your fortunes have

turned. Looks like you get to live out your life romping in piss
after all. You're lucky *I* have you—this man's so loath to part with
his money the only meat you'd get from him is the roasted flesh
of the boys that get crushed under the slipped blocks."

"Come back here, Grannus, you mule. Sixty. Sixty—and not
one sesterce more. I could get a skilled mason for that. And there
better not be anything else wrong with him. Wait, and what is
this?"

Terentius fumbled in Endymion's dirty tunic and held up an
amulet about the boy's neck, holding it close to the smoking
Medusa lamp suspended from the ceiling. "What sort of amulet is
this? It's an odd one."

"Who knows or cares? I won't charge you extra for it."

Terentius held it to his nose. "Smells like dirt. He's got a bag of
dirt around his neck. I want it off him. It's some witchery and it's
filthy."

Grannus pulled a small knife from his belt and reached for the
thong on which the amulet was hung. Endymion's eyes flared.

"You will not touch it!" The boy's clear young voice pulled both
of them up short like a hard yank on a rein. Even the Syrian
treaders looked up briefly before resuming their contented feeding. Terentius laughed aloud; it was to him as though a donkey
discovered powers of speech and issued a command.

The black leather amulet had hung around Endymion's neck
always. He guessed his father or mother must have put it there,
those shadowy parents who must have been. Who else would have
done so? All he had of a family was this pathetic bit of evidence
that once, he must have had one. Protecting it was a reflex of
survival, like protecting his own heart.

Grannus' bristly cheeks reddened. "Here's one last lesson in
manners!" He took up his leather strap and lashed it hard across
the boy's face.

The boy's soul was dry tinder, bursting into flame. Endymion
erupted into motion without thought, feeling he vaulted out over a
dark chasm. Perhaps he would clear it, perhaps not—he no longer
cared.

He raised his bound hands and struck the hanging Medusa lamp,
sloshing hot oil into Grannus' face. The fuller yelped. While
Grannus was still blinded, he kicked him with one determined
blow to the back of the knee, toppling him into the urine-filled vat.
Then while Terentius watched, immobilized with surprise, Endy

mion sprang for the open door, swift and direct as the arrow from the bow.

"Whoreson! Spawn of a snake!" Grannus shouted, sputtering, as he struggled up, his mane of hair plastered to his head by the liquid of the vats. "Ajax! Syphax!" he cried out to his two sturdily built doorkeepers. "Get him! Or I'll see you whipped to the bone!"

As he pulled himself out, soaked and dripping, he said to Terentius while waving a hand in angry dismissal, "On your way! Out of my shop. I'll not sell him now. I want him crucified!" Then Grannus sprinted out after them, a loud squishing noise from his sodden sandals accompanying every stride.

As Endymion burst into the crowded street, the first rush of freedom made him feel like a young god. The sluggish air of the Subura, reeking of burnt garlic and dung, seemed to him fresh and bracing as a sea wind. His feet pounding the lava cobbles of the street seemed to shout "I can live!" His blood surged in a joyous torrent. With every sense he thought: And this is *how* I will live—I will outrun and I will outthink whatever comes for me.

He heard behind him sharp quick shouts and frantic scuffling. He half turned once to see Ajax and Syphax, followed by Grannus, in vigorous pursuit.

"Runaway!" Grannus bellowed as he ran. "Friends! Neighbors! Help! Runaway boy!" After a moment's hesitation—the thought of parting with any sum was painful to him—he shouted out, "Reward! Fifty sesterces!"

The neighbors and idlers who saw the boy erupt from the door of Lucius Grannus' shop knew at once that this was a runaway. But for long moments no one stirred from their place: Half looked on in wine-soaked apathy, while the rest would not aid Grannus because they despised him: All had heard the reports that the fuller was in the habit of returning worn clothes for garments given to him new, while occasionally passing a once-washed toga to an obliging Praetor's clerk so that no one dared prosecute in the courts. But after a moment two brown-skinned boys, sons of an Ethiopian freedman, became excited by the reward; they sprinted after Endymion, eager as young hounds.

Endymion knew he had somehow to free his hands—he ran too awkwardly with them bound. The street sheltered him as he knew it would; to the regular chaos of the Subura was added crowds of poor free workers with sacks of tools slung on their shoulders, returning at evening to their tenement rooms, and ranks of haughty attendants accompanying the occasional wealthy man in his litter

as he returned from the law courts, as well as schoolchildren
singing or fighting as they moved through the street, and ragged
lines of priests and priestesses of Cybele, striking blunted swords
against shields with less fire and energy now as they departed their
temple than when they set out in the morning.

Endymion darted between two donkeys daintily picking their
way over the cobbles, both laden with great baskets of plums
projecting precariously on either side. One reared, pitching plums
into the street. As his pursuers stumbled and slipped in them,
Endymion forced a path through a crowd about a barber's shop. In
the short moments when he was concealed, he skidded to a stop
and thrust his hands into a sausage vendor's brazier. He ground his
teeth in agony as the glowing charcoal singed his flesh as well as
the cord.

He looked up and met the eyes of Ajax and Syphax, no farther
off than the width of the street. They burst forward with renewed
energy. Endymion forced himself to calmness. Once more he put
his hands into the brazier.

The sausage vendor turned and came for him, shouting. Ajax
lunged at him, seizing the cloth of his tunic. Endymion jerked his
hands apart with all his strength. The cord broke.

The boy dropped to the street and rapidly rolled over once; the
cloth of his tunic ripped. All Ajax got was a torn bit of it as the boy
scrambled up again. Sausages tumbled into the street, to be
snatched up instantly by beggar children who fell on them like a
flock of crows. Endymion shot forward again in a frenzied run.

He dashed round an auctioneer's platform, struggling through
knots of people, stepping on feet, nearly knocking a public
notice-writer off his ladder as the man posted a notice for an
exhibition of gladiators. Then he was caught and slowed by a
playful group of prostitutes with gold hoops in their ears, their
silken shifts and shawls vibrant as parrot feathers. They grasped
him by the waist, slowing him, fondling him aggressively. He
looked back and saw Grannus' head bobbing above the crowd as
the fuller swiftly gained ground. And ahead, the throng grew
thicker. The first blush of freedom had faded, and now dull terror
crept in. The crowds were an evil mire, hindering him, holding
him, sucking him down.

"You won the race, my beautiful Adonis—now come for your
prize!" one of the prostitutes said in her rich, liquid voice,
laughing as she struggled to lift him up.

"Is this a capon or a young rooster?" another cried gaily. "Let's see! Hold him there!"

"A hundred sesterces for the runaway!" came Grannus' gasping shout, alarmingly close at hand.

Endymion struck and kicked and bit, struggling against plush arms, mischievous hands, cushioned hips and breasts, enveloped in their dusky scents of cinnamon and damp flesh, becoming entangled in their jingling bracelets, until finally the prostitutes pushed him away in disgust, deciding he was too obnoxious to bother with. When he looked back again, he saw the number of pursuers had grown to twenty and more, their ranks swelled by the increased reward: Anyone fleet of foot who was able to leave his work and give chase had done so. Their tunics were all tucked up to their waists and the people made way for them as they might for stampeding beasts. Their fierce shouts pierced his mind like knives. Endymion felt himself a wriggling piece of live bait, inciting the hungry city to snap its jaws round him, mangle him and swallow him down. Soon it would be as if he had never lived. Even the high tenements darkening the street seemed to lean close, squeezing him to hold him and slow him.

How quick, brutal, and fragile is life. You are born, you live a few years in wild hope, then you are dragged back into the night. You might have breathed on a little longer, had you not dared think yourself a human creature instead of an engine of muscle and bone.

He saw to his left a twisting alley with steeply ascending steps, flanked by a tannery and a vendor of portrait busts. It led in the direction of the Old Forum, where fewer in the throng would know his face. He streaked into it, taking the steps five at a time, his sandals slipping on well-worn stone. He began to panic when after several turns the alley did not open into another street. Behind him the many feet of the bounty-hunters tapped furiously on the steps. Then the alley ended abruptly in a tenement's high windowless wall.

After a moment of plummeting into unfathomable terror, he saw a covered way half concealed in foliage, a tunnel of ivy between the tenement and the back of a great-house.

He dashed into it and found himself suddenly amidst a gayer, gentler world of sculpted box hedges, perfumed air, and flower-edged walkways that were a homage to geometry. A serene pool mirrored a troupe of dancing bronze Pans. Again he felt the hand of death on his neck. He blundered into the private garden of a great mansion. Now he was truly trapped.

The doorkeeper, a broadly built Thracian slave, strode close and looked down on him, huge fists on his hips. "What do you want, boy?"

Endymion glanced swiftly about. In a shadowy peristyle, lit by the shivering flames of a row of wall sconces, he saw a series of pale paintings depicting the mysteries of Isis. He deduced from this that most likely this was a woman's house, for Isis was the deity beloved of wealthy matrons.

"Message for the mistress!" he announced with all the confidence he could muster. "It's most urgent. I ran the whole distance!"

The doorkeeper frowned, uncertainty in his face. "Is it her mother? How does she fare?"

"Not well! Not well at all!" Success! the boy thought. He takes me for a slave-messenger. "In fact, she is dying!"

The footsteps of Grannus and his hungry pack reached the alley's end.

"Good lad! Quickly, in there!" The Thracian indicated a door that must have been the entrance to his mistress's chambers. Endymion sprinted for it. At that moment Grannus, Ajax and the rest crowded dumb-faced into the entrance of the garden.

From the chamber came a high, thin scream.

"Calf-brain! That was a runaway!" Grannus shouted to the doorkeeper as he roughly shoved him aside and charged on. A half-dozen slaves of the household rushed forward to stop this human herd from invading the lady's chamber, but Grannus got through.

Grannus stopped in the doorway of the dim, tapestried bedroom and had just enough time to see, caught in the grillwork of a balcony that overlooked the street, cloth torn from the tunic he had provided the boy fluttering in the wind, mocking him. Then the lady struck, stabbing him with one of her long sharp hairpins, penetrating the flesh of his upper arm to the bone.

The boy would pay for this, too.

Endymion had won himself a moment to think. He did not deceive himself into believing Grannus would give up the chase. Indeed, at that moment, Grannus was redoubling his efforts; in the next street he paid a small sum to a public crier, who moved toward the Old Forum, calling out, "Boy, dark hair, dark eyes, and comely, ran off from Grannus' fuller's shop! Amulet of black leather about his neck! Boy—" in his penetrating singsong cry.

Endymion ran up Mercury Street, knowing he had to inform the one true friend of his short life of his fate. Then he would go and hide in the Great Drain, and tomorrow, the gods willing, he would escape from the city. He stopped halfway down the short steep street and cast a pebble at the shuttered first story window of Pollio's bakery shop. Within moments a man with drifting white hair, an unobtrusive ghost, materialized in the doorway and began descending the stone steps with timid care, as though he feared he might step in something unpleasant. The old man's testing glance flicked from side to side, stopping suddenly at the sight of the boy. His smile was as the boy imagined a hermit's would be: tentative and shy from lack of use.

"Lycas," Endymion cried, embracing him with boyish vigorousness. "I've run away."

"Creon! You have not!" Lycas grasped the boy's shoulders, frail desperation in his hands. "That is children's foolishness!"

"You've fallen two names behind. It's *Endymion* now. And it's true."

"It is death, boy," he whispered, thrusting his face into Endymion's, transfixing the boy with bleary eyes. "Book learning is to blame for this. Books are worse than wine, I say. You read one and you need another—there's no end to it. What ails you that you cannot content yourself with just living on under the sun? Grannus at least did not beat you every day."

"I—" he began, and stopped, seeing no use in telling Lycas he wanted to be a philosopher as Seneca was. He already believes I'm half mad, the boy thought. Why worry him more by proving it to him? "I want to . . . to belong to no one but the gods."

"The rats in the slaves' prison belong to no one. Is it so glorious? And they say those rats are large enough to take a hound. By sunfall tomorrow, you'll know if it's true."

"Lycas, it's been done and cannot be undone. Can you get me some crusts and oil and maybe a—Lycas, you are ill."

"The same illness. It has settled on the lungs."

"What is being done for it?"

"Nothing this time. I'm too old to be worth treating. For certain it's the Island for me this time." When masters did not want to pay for the treatment of sick slaves often they abandoned them on the tiny Island of Aesculapius that broke the brownish-yellow waters of the Tiber.

"That is against the law!"

"Ha! You have not changed! When you grow up you'll realize a law is but words, my boy. One bribe is worth a hundred laws. Pollio does as he wills."

"Then I *shall* live—if only to return and punish him for that!" Something dark and brilliant flashed in the boy's eyes then, and it frightened the old man, for it was a passion that might challenge kings. Such determination could only bring trouble into the life of a slave.

"A pity all this is, my poor . . . what name did you say? . . . *Endymion*. You would have been tall, and comelier than Paris. Here, take these, my boy." Lycas fumbled with a pouch that hung from the thong that girded his tunic.

"Your grain tokens! I can't—"

"Spargus can always steal me more." He pressed them into Endymion's hand. "Now be careful where you barter them. You don't want stolen grain tokens added to your troubles. Now stay away from—"

From the street both heard the cheerful melodic call of the crier, "Boy, fair of feature, dark hair, dark eyes, run off from Grannus' shop . . ."

"Nemesis!" Endymion whispered, looking swiftly up and down Mercury Street. "Get inside, quickly, you must not be seen with me. Curses on all this. Curses on all life. Lycas, one day I will help you. I promise it as I live, and I swear it on this amulet. I do not know how I'll do it, but I will." He gave Lycas a quick clumsy embrace and was off.

Lycas felt misery welling in his chest as he watched the boy bound up the street in springing strides. What would become of that poor haunted child? His only flaw was that perverse urge to question the natural order of things. The old man was ashamed, he loved that boy so much. Love was a useless and troublesome emotion for a slave.

As Endymion struggled through the throng in the Via Sacra, making slow progress toward the Great Drain, he was forced to halt at a crossroad, for some sort of procession approached, making its way toward the Palace. He heard the rhythmic tramp of the way-clearers' feet, the snap of their whips, and a soft chorus of cries of *"Clarissimus,"* or "Illustrious One," the crowd's traditional salutation for a great man. The boy felt a start of panic as he realized his progress would be barred for many moments, but as there was no sign anywhere of either Grannus or the crier, he calmed his fears.

Before him, beneath the shimmering disk of the moon, loomed the Palace of the Caesars; dusk washed it a uniform shade of blue-white so that it seemed a single floating form, at once delicate and awesome, a haunting testament to power on earth. Its multitude of shivering lamps alight in tier upon tier of moon-pale colonnades made it appear an earthly firmament ablaze with stars, which seemed fitting to the boy since gods dwelled there. Sweet spicy scents that slowed the limbs drifted from the Palace, filling him with heavy pleasurable sensations as though the multitude of delights to be known within could send out their own intoxicating vapor. A debilitating longing, stinging, bittersweet, settled on him as he thought of all that was housed within: more books than he could read in a lifetime and wise ministers who used philosophy to decide the fates of distant nations.

Then the procession came abreast of him, and he could see the Palace no more. Three ranks of red-liveried attendants were followed by friends and clients on foot, all robed in purest white. Above them a grand litter gently swayed, shouldered by eight Bithynian bearers; the covered chair was strewn with rose-garlands flung at it by admirers. Endymion guessed there was some great banquet tonight at the Palace, and this litter bore the guest of honor.

Then he saw a second litter behind the first; it was this one that caused him to take a quick breath. It was starkly plain, not even curtained, leaving its occupant visible to the people.

A bolt of excitement shot through him. *Seneca.* Of course. Who else would be carried about in such a shabby litter? The chair came closer, and now he recognized the living face behind the portrait busts everywhere on view. The boy supposed that as First Advisor to the Emperor, the great philosopher dined nightly at the Palace. Very likely, every day at dusk he passed this way.

All thought of danger fled Endymion's mind. He fought his way through the press of people, desperate to get close. He pushed his way between a Tuscan farmer and a silk merchant, then suddenly found himself nearly in the litter's path.

Seneca was reading as he was borne along, squinting as he held a bronze hand lamp close to a bookroll, his nobly proportioned bald head bowed.

The statues of him do not do him justice, the boy thought. They do not capture those eyes, how they seem to love the world, how they teem with enough knowledge to fill the bookrolls of a dozen rich men's libraries. Or all the patient kindliness in that face, or that visible firmness of purpose. I can hear him declaring aloud a slave is a man, not an animal to be beaten, that the bloody contests of the arena are wrong; I see him looking with dark scorn at those who call him foolish or mad.

Was the philosopher reading from one of his own works, perhaps a copy that he, Endymion, had penned? What grand thoughts upon the nature of the universe flickered through that magically complex mind even as he gazed upon him?

Endymion did not hear the cry behind him, "Boy, dark hair, dark eyes, black amulet about his neck . . ."

Then the biting stench of urine enveloped him. Unnoticed, Grannus had slipped up close behind him. With him was a man of the Vigiles, the city's police-firemen, in leather armor and steel cap; from one of his hands hung a coiled length of rope. The boy spun around, but too late; the rope snapped about him, binding his arms to his sides. A second rope slid over his wrists, burning his flesh. Someone kicked him from behind, and he fell into the path of the litter bearers of the philosopher. He muffled a moan, refusing to cry out, enraged that his one lapse of attention had brought about his destruction. The Fates used his love of philosophy to bait him like an animal.

"*Got* the little hellion!" Grannus exclaimed through heaving laughter. "It pays a man to keep his body in soldier's condition. A small cross is all we'll need for this one." He kicked the boy in the stomach.

But Endymion managed somehow to struggle up. The litter's progress was halted while the bearer who had half stumbled over the boy righted himself. For one instant the gazes of boy and philosopher met.

And in Seneca's eyes, something jumped. It was, for a quick sharp moment that seemed full enough to hold a life, as though they knew one another. The old man felt he turned a corner into some timeless place and collided with himself as a child. How well Seneca knew that look of ardent young eyes brimming with questions that would drive one to madness if not followed to their end.

Even Grannus paused, put off balance by the oddness of the moment.

And Endymion spoke. It was a grave impertinence for a slave to speak to anyone freeborn if not addressed first, and to address a man with the rank of Senator was a criminal act. But rank is of little importance to one so close to being dragged out of the world, and he had a boy's pure trust in a hero whom he imagined to be all-knowing.

"Please, I beg your kindness," he began; there was such self-possession in his tone that Seneca saw clearly how he would look as a man.

"I would be a learned man, as you are. I . . . I know by heart your treatise *On the Brevity of Life* and your essay *On Anger.* Speak for me and you shall not regret it! I will serve you all your days."

"Rabid pup!" Grannus shouted, jerking him away. "Stuff a rag in his mouth!"

Seneca met the boy's eyes for an instant more, quite evidently moved by his plight. He raised his right hand, ordering the bearers not to move.

Then a man of the crowd cried out to Seneca. "*Clarissimus!* Did Socrates own five hundred cedarwood tables and twelve estates and forty million in gold—and half the isle of Britannia?"

Seneca's glance shifted warily about. *Not this again.*

"Read us an ode!" came another strident voice. "I've been in the country of late—I haven't heard the latest in brazen, shameless flattery!"

Seneca scowled at his tormentors, looking like some disgruntled river god.

In these days it seemed to the philosopher the people let no opportunity pass to make sport of him, and the taunts stung all the more because somewhere in the stillness of his mind he suspected he deserved them. He *was* rich enough to ransom an emperor. And he had written lyrics in praise of Nero's mother Agrippina that made him queasy to recall. Now people pointed to the boy, nodding and smiling knowingly. And saying what? That Seneca was so much the slave of passion that he could not make the short journey to the Palace without pausing to secure a boy for the night's dalliance?

When Seneca turned back to Endymion, it seemed to the boy a curtain dropped in the philosopher's eyes. With a sharp gesture of his hand Seneca motioned his bearers to move on.

Endymion felt no pain as Grannus struck him across the mouth—for the pain inside was worse. The world's heart was ripped open; within was nothing but worms and rot. The great man was ruled not by his philosophy, but by others' opinions, like any common shopkeeper. Endymion guessed that even the philosopher's reading in public was merely for show—the people expected him to have a bookroll always in hand. As Grannus kicked the boy to the ground once more, Endymion felt as though his soul had been crushed under horses. If all good did not rest in Seneca, then where was it? Not in any man, surely. He knew then that even if the Fates softened toward him and granted him long life, never again would he be able to see another, not even an emperor or king, as greater than he was.

The thought made him feel the desolation of one adrift on the night sea.

As Grannus and the patrolman of the Vigiles led the boy down Mercury Street, and to his execution, a voice arresting as a trumpet fanfare brought all three to a halt.

"Lucius Grannus! Stand there!"

Spitting a curse, Grannus turned round. Unknown to the fuller and the boy, the call of the crier had attracted the attention of another man as well—the guest of honor borne in the first litter.

The garlanded litter had been set down. Its occupant, a man of late middle years, approached them at the stately, unhurried pace of one accustomed to making others wait. His face, possessed in his youth of an ascetic handsomeness, had long since settled into pleasant and comfortable softness; retreating black and silver hair accentuated a formidable forehead. He had the look about him of one who neglected the body for the mind—his complexion was pallid; his hands were cushioned and dead-white. A once-firm body was beginning to go gently to fat, and about his eyes were deeply engraved lines from long nights of squinting over faded manuscripts by lamplight, reading the great works or dictating books of his own. Though there was a hint of indulgence about his eyes—he had the look of one who would deliberate long before issuing a punishment and then worry over it later—he was quite obviously the sort of man only a fool would attempt to deceive— when roused, as he was now, those eyes had the ruthless directness of a hawk's. His toga was immaculately white; on the tunic beneath was just visible the broad purple stripe of a senator. He had the barest limp, which somehow only added to his dignity.

As the crowd shrank back to give him room, they exchanged looks of simple disbelief. What could such a man as *that* care for the doings of a fuller and a boy? For this was Marcus Arrius Julianus, one of the half-dozen most influential men of the Senate; his ancestry, rich with illustrious names, could be traced to the time of the First Punic War. Any citizen in the crowd could have recited to a traveler from afar all there was to know about this man. He was one of Seneca's dearest friends. Lately he had returned from the province of Upper Germania, where he had served as military governor at the fortress of Mogontiacum on the Rhine until he was called home for the honor of a consulship, which meant he was nominally co-ruler, for a short time, with Nero, though in reality it was an empty honor, for Nero shared power with no one. A master of many disciplines, he was as familiar with the arts of the architect-engineer as he was with military strategy, the history of nations, and the natural sciences. He was celebrated as the greatest living authority on the savage Germanic tribes, the Chattians, Hermundures and their neighbors, and had completed thirty volumes of a proposed fifty-volume work on their customs and beliefs. It was well-known he fervently wished to retire but that Nero's military council would not allow it—and that the cause was a renegade Chattian chieftain named Baldemar, who had been terrorizing the frontier towns of Gaul for a decade. This Baldemar sent no emissaries, refused to give hostages and would not negotiate—clearly a war was needed to control him. But Nero would not order a campaign—he needed all his resources to pay for his sumptuous stage plays and extended days of chariot races—and both Nero and his council firmly believed Marcus Arrius Julianus the only commander able to control the Chattian chieftain through diplomacy. Because of Baldemar, it was commonly said, old Julianus would likely die in the barbarous wastes of Germania.

"He's coming for *you,* Grannus!" called out a voice in the crowd. "It's that toga full of moth holes you gave him for one washed just once!" A raw burst of laughter came from the curious who paused to watch. As Marcus Arrius Julianus approached the boy the soft hissing call, *"Clarissimus!"* followed him like a wake.

"Grannus smells like a goat's behind!"

"You're supposed to wash the *clothes* in it, Grannus, the *clothes!"*

The Senator suppressed a displeased look as the mild breeze brought him the first scent of Grannus. He nodded at the boy. "Turn him around," he said with soft finality. "I want to see him."

"He's mine, fair and paid for, most noble one," Grannus said, bowing awkwardly, too many times, his red lips stretched into a broad smile. "He's uncommonly vicious—you'd not want him!"

Marcus Julianus ignored Grannus. Gravely the Senator lifted the boy's chin. Grannus seethed with irritation, too intimidated to protest. Endymion met the older man's worried but gentle eyes for a moment, then cast his own down, faintly embarrassed because he did not know what was expected of him. Then carefully, solemnly, and almost as if he feared it, Julianus drew the amulet from the boy's tunic, and turned the pouch of black leather over in his hands. Endymion was aware of tension in the older man's face, as of profound emotion under tight control. During all this, Grannus lowered his shaggy head and made a rough sound in the back of his throat—he was a hound held in check while a larger hound snatched his bone.

"My good man, you are mistaken," Marcus Julianus said finally in a voice of smooth dismissal. "The slave is mine. But to avoid inconveniencing you over the error, I will buy him from you. Nestor!" he called to an immaculately groomed freedman-secretary who smelled of hyacinthus oil. The Senator nodded curtly at Grannus. "Pay him. The whole purse. At once."

Nestor dropped a purse heavy with coins of gold into Grannus' cupped hands. Grannus started when he peered inside. He would not have gotten as much in gold had he sold his entire shop. Greed warred briefly with his eagerness to see the boy punished. Then he grinned, displaying yellowed horse teeth, first at Marcus Arrius Julianus and then at the crowd, as though to say, "Ha! I got the best of this situation, after all!"

He pushed the boy, still bound, in the direction of his new master.

The crowd did not know what to make of this, but gossip would not be stopped for lack of information. So as the story was told and retold in every tavern, the motive of this strange scene was attributed to lust, in spite of the fact that Marcus Arrius Julianus was one of the few aristocrats of whom no stories whatever filtered down of a passion for young boys.

"Take this slave to the house," a bewildered Endymion heard his new master say briskly to the freedman. "Prepare him and give him clean clothes."

On the following day Endymion, dressed in a tunic of finest linen, paced restively in the writing room of the senatorial mansion of Marcus Arrius Julianus. He felt wary as a sentinel. As he waited for the great man to find a moment to speak to him, he examined the room in a sort of lucid daze. Atop a cypress writing table was a silver wine service; he realized with dismay that each of its heavy, masterfully crafted cups cost three times what he himself was worth. But the fact that he recognized the cup's bas-relief as the death of Dido from the *Aeneid* gave him a fleeting sense of belonging. Behind the table was a water clock in milky aquamarine glass plated with gold. *How elegantly the wealthy mark the hour—a slave need know only day and night.* Everywhere was a profusion of books, stuffed hurriedly into niches in the wall, or allowed to spill onto the floor with extravagant carelessness. He marveled that he did not snatch up those nearest and begin greedily reading, and would have liked to believe he had attained some of the philosophers' ability to control the passions, but his pitiless good sense told him that, in truth, the sharp unease he felt was dampening his lust for books. *What in the name of all-wise Minerva was wanted of him?*

This great-house was a labyrinthine paradise of interlocking gardens and chill, skylit rooms splashed with iridescent panoramas of ancient days that alternated with dim, sumptuously padded chambers aglow with the low sheen of dark precious woods and gold, rooms crowded with the mysteries of smooth-worn family treasures, thrown casually together with a magically sculpted Aphrodite by Praxiteles or Skopas, or the priceless bronzes it was fashionable to collect in these times. This was an earthly Elysium teeming with all those things the true philosopher was not supposed to want. The mansion was built into the side of the Esquiline Hill; from the balcony of the writing room he could see the reeking Subura far below—the steady flow of people and animals in its principal street put him in mind of a dirty, sluggish river. He wondered once if he had been lifted up to the sky in some cruel jest of the gods; soon they would tire of this sport and drop him back into the slime.

When Marcus Arrius Julianus entered at last, at the fourth hour of morning, Endymion rose quickly from his place, grimly ready to face whatever might come. He bowed, uttering the word *"Clarissimus"* with boyish dignity.

"Raise yourself up. You bow too low for a free man."

"You are freeing me? Why?"

The face of Marcus Julianus looked more wan and worn in the thin glare of the morning light. He signaled to the boy to sit, and then he settled himself facing him, moving ponderously as if his leg gave him pain.

"No, I am not freeing you," he said patiently. "I *cannot* free you, because you were never a slave. I went through that stage-act of buying you only to divert the crowd from the truth. I know of but one way to tell you this, and that is to tell you directly. But first, take a good draught of this."

He took up a flagon, poured unwatered wine into one of the weighty silver cups, then held it out to the boy. Endymion hesitated a moment, his mind unsettled with questions, then he took it. The contents were so strikingly superior to any wine he had ever tasted—the most delicate fruit of autumn, he thought, musky silk—that he doubted at first that it *was* wine.

Marcus Arrius Julianus seized him with gentle, demanding eyes.

"You are my son."

The words struck him first like a blow that is not seen coming. His mind was a brilliant blank. Slowly the boy shook his head as he cautiously tested the words on his reasoning mind, as if he were not certain he could bear the weight of them. He felt he hovered precariously between the two existences, the highest and the lowest, separated by a chasm of night.

In one moment he felt he sensed the truth with some deep knowing, the instant he first saw this man, but it simply had not come to light in his waking thoughts. There was a rightness to it, the feel of a lock sliding in place in the dark.

And in the next, he decided this old man must have simply gone mad, and even felt a stirring of pity for him. He leapt back to the familiarity of the lowest.

"I . . . I beg your pardon, but I am Endymion, lately a slave of a fuller. I appreciate your kindnesses but—"

"No," Julianus continued with soft insistence. He put an all-encompassing hand about the boy's shoulder. In his eye was a fervent look, blurred with pain.

"You are *not* Endymion. Your name is the same as mine. The death masks in the atrium are *your* ancestors. You are heir to this house and to all within it, as well as to lands stretching from Africa to Gaul—it would take a procurator a year to properly sort out everything you own. You are heir to a tradition that goes back to the foundation of this city. You must awaken to this! You must at once stop thinking of yourself as a slave."

"Why do you tell me this? It cannot be true."

"You prove it by your very skepticism—an obnoxious family trait. I beg you, listen! I know it is hard to let go what feels right and is well-known, even if it be an evil thing that brings misery.

But you must believe. When you were six, I gave you out to a baker's wife to raise and let it be known that you died in the summer fever. It was necessary, to save you from one who would still seek your life today, should she learn you are alive."

The boy guessed he referred to Agrippina, the mother of Nero, who in Nero's youth murdered anyone whom she judged a threat to her son's sovereignty, either by poison, a treason charge, or an arranged accident in the street.

"But why would she be so roused to wrath by a mere child?"

"Her astrologer Archimedes poisoned her mind against you. There was not a babe born in those times that she did not have its horoscope cast. Archimedes told her that it was quite clearly in your chart that 'the fate of the whole country would one day rest in your hands.' Rightly or wrongly, she read that as an imperial destiny.

"And so we—your mother and I—hid you away, in hope that one day her power would be broken and we could bring you out again."

A faint hoarseness came to his voice then. "But the baker . . . lost you. You either ran off or were stolen away—he could not say which. I tried every way I knew to trace you, but the streets had swallowed you up. Your mother made offerings every day at the Temple of Juno to no avail. I never thought to see you alive again."

"But . . . how can you be so *certain?* I was little when last you saw me."

"I would know you now by your eyes alone, which are so like your dear mother's it near reduces me to mourning joy just to look at you. You have as well her proud chin. But this" —he drew the amulet from the boy's tunic, handling it with reverence, as if it were a pearl—"would make me swear by my life."

"It's a bag of dirt."

"It *is* a bag of dirt. And there is not another like it anywhere, except in the far wastes of the north where winter lasts half through summer. In Germania once I gave audience to a tribal prophetess, a Chattian woman called Ramis—a strange and disturbing woman, that was. She came to petition for the life of ten of her tribesmen condemned to die, and when I granted her wish, she gave me this—although it is against their law to give it to foreigners. I am not certain why she gave it to me. It is earth taken from their most sacred ground, called the *aurr*, and, know well, there is powerful magic in these things. She said, as I recall, that it 'brings the wearer to his own true destiny,' whatever that might mean. Perhaps she meant just this, Marcus—that it would return you to me."

The boy faintly withdrew at the sound of the new name—it belonged to one highborn, and it sounded absurd and wrong to him, almost like mockery. Then gradually the truth of it settled softly about him, and he accepted it. For a long time he sat without moving, carefully trying on this new life in his mind. These things could not happen. But they had. Before nothing was possible. Now what was not possible? The worm in the earth had become a man.

"My mother . . . she is not living, is she?"

"She died of grief a year after you were lost." His father turned away, his voice coming with effort. "It is mad perhaps . . . but when midnight closes round, I feel her spirit strongly about the family altar. She was . . . most brilliantly learned. There, in those niches, are her works—a tragic drama, several medical treatises, and her five books of narrative poetry."

It was almost unbearable to know he had had a mother and that she had grieved for him while he lived almost in distance of a cry. The boy rose and moved to the books, those fragile traces of her life, and put a reverential hand on one of the volumes. *Mother. Brilliantly learned. I see your face! . . . Wise brow . . . proud chin . . . and your eyes—wells of gentle mystery, the eyes of Minerva.*

She, then, must have been the vision in white who taught him to read; she was no wraith; she had a heart and blood and salt tears. In the garden was a sudden ruffling of leaves, as though they were brushed by spectral garments; he sensed a spirit in the wind that was wild, protective, sad, and he wondered if it was her ghost, gladdened at his return.

"Your rescue must, for a time, be a close-kept secret," his father continued. "Nero's mother still murders for her son, but her power is declining. She has long been at war with Seneca and the Guards, and slowly she is losing. But the city is still infested with her spies. We'll have to hide you here. All who see you and all your tutors must be loyal to us and sworn to secrecy."

The word *tutors* bore him up once more on a wave of joyful amazement. He would be educated. He should have expected as much, but he had not had time to think through to the end everything now given him. The universe of stars and sea and land and history would become his own country. He would be a philosopher. He would become what he had thought Seneca was, before this day.

The elder Julianus talked on a short time more, enumerating the deeds of his family, answering his son's rapidly multiplying questions, then abruptly he took his leave, not wanting to overburden the boy at this first meeting. And in the following days the Senator began the process of preparing his son for this new life, effecting the transformation, as the old man put it, from human animal to young man. A tutor in speech took Marcus in hand, helping rid him of the accent of the Subura, schooling him in the idioms and vocabulary of his class. The house steward instructed him in the rudiments of deportment: He was taught the right and wrong ways of draping the *toga praetexta* worn by aristocratic boys, the proper way a man reclines at table, the elaborate ceremony that accompanied the reception of visitors. And through it all, Marcus thought: While I am being taught the polite way to address an augur or pronounce the titles of my friend's friends, below me in the muddy streets, Lycas is dying. We are bound to one another. My own good fortune must be his. *I must speak for him.*

When a month passed, the chief steward announced to Marcus Julianus the Elder that the boy had become just civilized enough to be allowed to dine with him.

Have I the right to speak for Lycas? Marcus wondered, full of nameless apprehension as he readied himself. *I say that I do, whatever the judgment of this world.*

They dined in the modest *triclinium* by the kitchens, not the grand dining hall that overlooked the fountains, which was reserved for official banquets. Marcus Julianus the Elder was settled already on the first couch when young Marcus entered; the boy took a place opposite him, on the third couch. The old man noted with approval how deftly his son managed the oyster spoon, how sparing the boy was with wine.

Twice Marcus heard the hour called, and the sun reddened and sank, lazily setting fire to all that was gold in the room, while the boy sought for the proper moment to ask what he must. When he thought his father had spun out enough battle tales to render the old man as affable and receptive as he might ever be, he spoke.

"Father"—he began, cautiously testing the word; he had not yet used it often enough, and it felt like an awkward bundle he nearly dropped—"there is a man I would have brought here. He will die if he is left where he is, and he has been friend and father to me.

He is the slave of the baker Pollio, and his name is Lycas." Marcus paused, sensing a delicate tension in the silence as though he had committed some small breach of manners.

A servant interrupted with the third course; the heavy silver platters descended swiftly, silently as if on hawks' wings. Before them was filleted turbot mixed with goose liver, drizzled with a sauce of honey, oil, pounded pepper, lovage, and marjoram.

"Pollio?" His father gave him a bemused, formal smile and shook his head. "I am sorry, that fellow is not our friend. He is the client of that doddering curmudgeon Publilius who opposes me in the Senate every chance he is given. I will purchase nothing from him, neither his bread nor his slaves."

"But Father, Lycas will die." Marcus raised himself slightly on his couch. He was surprised at how quickly fear vanished once the parrying began; in its place was only a bright, hard resolve. "Cannot a feud be set aside for a day for such a grave purpose as this?"

Julianus smiled tolerantly, but his eyes sharpened in irritation. "It is not right for a boy to so question his father, but I will allow it this once because you are ignorant. Do not misunderstand me, your fine sentiments do you great honor. But there's more to this matter, Marcus—that baker's been accused of forgery and is due to go before the magistrate. To have dealings with a man such as that does no good for the family name. You are unschooled in these matters. *You must not ask such a thing.* Now let us eat this fine turbot before it grows unacceptably cold!"

But Marcus rose from his couch, left the table, and crossed to the mullioned window. There was a moment of turbulent silence. When he turned round to face his father, the elder Julianus started at the change in him—the boy's eyes were alight with such passion and brilliance he might have drawn a sword against an advancing enemy.

"I am unschooled in many things, and you are quite right, I do not know the ways of the highborn," he said softly. "But this is a matter beyond high and low and all the estates of society, it is a matter of . . . of love, a love that is natural to all, and it is the same, rich *or* poor. I gave my *word* to him—I know enough of honor to know a man must stand by his word. And as for Pollio, he has not yet made his case before the magistrate. *The man who judges before the other party is heard is unjust, even if his judgment is right.*"

Julianus stared at his son through the delicately rising steam, trapped between outrage and astonishment. Were not those last words taken from one of Seneca's dramas?

With no training he weaves the words of the philosopher with rhetoric, as if it were the natural thing to do. And such strength, such well-tempered fire in the voice. And how dare he.

"Enough!" The Senator's anger was beginning to break loose from its tight bonds. His clenched hands betrayed his desire to rise up and seize his son by the shoulders—but the old man stayed on his couch. A commander sits. A subordinate stands. "You gave your *word*, you say. You're but a boy, you must *ungive* it. A boy has no such right, while his father lives." He gave the boy his stormiest glare. "I find you willful and filled with ingratitude. My reply is *no*—and I will hear no more on it!"

Marcus did not move; he met the elder Julianus' eyes boldly, quietly, trembling faintly as if facing his father required great physical effort, but he showed no sign of the terrified submission the Senator expected.

"Do you respect nothing and no one? Again I say it, *no!*"

The boy looked away. His voice when he finally spoke was full of effort and pain.

"Then I do not want all these things, however fine." He removed the chalcedony ring his father had given him and laid it on the dining table. "And I want no place in this world. I think in most matters you are a good man. But in this matter you are ruled by pride and anger. What am I to do? Forget him and walk on, as if he were not suffering almost in my shadow? Among the highborn, you live by your philosophy. When one lowborn is at your mercy, you cast it aside. Lycas knows better how to live than you—he would never set pride over filial love. I am not your son. I am Lycas' son."

Marcus then turned and started bravely for the door. For a moment his father watched him, horrified, unable to move, knowing at once this was no child's game, but a show of strength of mind far beyond his years.

The boy has been seized by a demon. It cannot be. He truly means to return to the streets.

"Wait there!" Julianus cried out. "You are quite mad! Do you really think I'm going to sit here while my newfound son bludgeons me with Stoic philosophy, then vanishes once more? Halt!"

The boy did not slow.

"Perhaps—oh, curses on you!—perhaps something can be arranged."

Marcus paused before the richly carved door.

"I . . . I will do it secretly. I'll get someone neutral in this matter to buy this fellow in his own name, and then he can turn round and sell him to me. Come now, back to your place. I will not have to pay a teacher of rhetoric for long; I see you're already formidably adept at persuasion! Look how you've made a beggar out of me! Where do you come by such thoughts? You are utterly confounding. You really meant to leave, did you not?"

Marcus visibly relaxed and smiled awkwardly, a boy once more. A fleeting look of shame and fledgling affection for his father came into his face. "Not willingly, Father. But yes, I would have left." He hesitated. "Father, I *am* grateful. What you said of ingratitude—it is not true."

Marcus came back wearily; when he was settled once more, his father reached across the table and put a clumsy but protective hand over his. After a space of comfortable silence Julianus said with a new darkness in his voice, "Fine son that you are, I fear you'll not live long. You've little or no notion of what you've fallen into. You've come aboard a golden ship, you see, but know this: It's one that's slowly sinking."

Julianus was silent while a mute servant came in to light the many-branched bronze lamp suspended low over the dining table. Almost as an afterthought the Senator started to pick delicately at the meal. Marcus could not eat; the boy looked away from the growing cluster of little flames, out into the swift-gathering gloom, and shuddered at how close he had come to spending this night shivering in the Great Drain, struggling against the damp to snatch a little sleep.

When they were alone once more, Julianus continued, his tone resonant with warning, "I mean not to frighten you, but there is something you must know at once. You see, you are a slave still, in spite of all—only now, to that lyric-scribbling brute in the Palace. Nero is outgrowing his old tutor, Seneca—and when he outgrows people he kills them. Already he has poisoned his foster brother and suffocated his first wife in her steambath, and I fear that someday soon, when he gathers up the courage and finds a way to make it look like someone else did it, he'll murder his own mother. And Seneca, who has long been my friend, is not separate in Nero's mind from me. Soon he will turn on *us*, if not this year, then the next, and if I am away or no longer living, *you will bear it alone.* You must learn to curb that stubbornness, or drag yourself and all our family to our doom. You must learn to flatter and to bend. And it is not, I fear, your nature to do so.''

Marcus briefly met his father's eyes, then looked off again, thinking it better not to say: Surely there were ways other than flattery to ensure the survival of those you must protect. Why cannot they be preserved with truth, as the philosophers suggest?

Julianus saw the resistance still very much alive in the boy's eyes, though settled now into a low-banked fire. And he found himself thinking once more of Archimedes' prediction that one day the fate of the country would rest in his son's hands.

"You *must.* It is a greater lesson than any tutor's. One day you will be the prow of the ship. One day you will stand in the Senate instead of me. All the lessons in literature and music and philosophy will not serve you so well as this one. *Learn to bend.* Or perish.''

GERMANIA

CHAPTER III

It was midsummer, the height of the raiding season.

The valley was sacred to Wodan, god of the spear. It lay in the wilder part of Chattian lands, where tawny mountain cats slunk over sandstone escarpments and scrub pines made a stubborn stand in sandy soil. The god's sad, wise presence seemed everywhere—in the quiet bold eyes of a fawn, the incantation of a brook that had dug its way into this valley for millennia, in the moody sky, which, to the south, was a fierce, joyous blue and, to the north, frowning with thunderclouds.

Among the stalks of yarrow a hare hesitated, upright on its haunches. Its free forepaws seemed to ask a question. Its black eyes were fixed on everything and nothing.

Nearby was another pair of eyes—these were steady, gray, and full of patience, clear as the mountain pools whose striking clarity conceals great depth. They saw the hare and nothing else. These eyes belonged to Auriane, who had lived now through sixteen summers.

She sat a dun-colored pony. One tanned arm drew back the string of a bow that Baldemar had made for her. As she took aim she imagined herself a hunting cat, aware only of the sun's nurturing warmth, the fine movement of her hands on a weapon that, like a cat's claw, seemed not separate from her body. Her hair was pulled back into a single careless braid matted with bark and leaf. It was closer in color to the coat of a chestnut horse than the

45

many hues of blond so common among her people. Though her finely molded cheek and high, clean brow were a close copy of Athelinda's, Auriane's features were a sturdier rendering of her mother's. She wore a sleeveless tunic of bearskin that made her appear one more furry predator of the wild. Strung on a thong around her throat was a Roman silver denarius.

In her gamebag were three hares taken already. Auriane was glad of them; Hertha was less cruel to her when she brought home fresh meat.

The flowery air of midsummer brought drowsy contentment, and she gave no thought whatever to raids. She had heard the gruesome tales told around winter hearthfires and she knew this system of valleys was often used by their tribal enemies as an entry gate to Chattian lands, but she had the boundless confidence of a child who has never been grievously hurt. The name of Baldemar always served better than any fortress, and no raiding band ever dared come near her family's hall.

In the moment before she let the arrow fly, she squinted, imitating Baldemar.

An animal sense warned her to look up. She stifled a cry.

At the rim of the valley where ground mist rolled down like smoke, blotting out the spires of pines, she saw one flash of red, then another—the deep bloodred of warriors' tunics. And then she saw dozens of them, massed together as they ran, appearing, disappearing, moving swiftly into the heart of her people's lands, where their rich fields lay, and their herds of sheep and cattle. She knew at once these were warriors of the Hermundures, their ancestral enemies from the southeast.

A raid.

Arrow was returned to quiver and she wheeled the pony around, giving him a hard kick with her heels. The pony, whom she named Brunwin, lunged forward and settled into a choppy gallop, dodging thickets, hurdling fallen logs, losing his grip on the stony ground, running on a track roughly parallel to the raiders above. She knew she must outdistance them and sound the alarm before they reached the farmlands and villages. To do this, she must reach the ford in Antelope River before them—which would not prove too difficult if the pony kept his pace.

She leaned far over the pony's bristly mane, holding back a raw cry of joy. She felt like a racehorse released, eager to test speed to the limit. Here was adventure that was not mere child's imaginings. Always she felt a pull to be at the center of the fray, as if all life existed there. She would never go round a ditch or high wall if she thought she could send her pony over it. There was a strain of madness in the family, she often heard Hertha say, that skipped only Hertha herself. Baldemar had it in great measure and he had passed it on to Auriane.

She felt, too, the brash pride of the young: *I saw them first, and I will be first with the alarm.* She called on Epona, goddess of horses, and prayed the heron feather affixed to Brunwin's bridle would make him swift. It was, she thought, a cowardly time to strike: The most celebrated warriors of her people were not yet returned from their last foray, an attack on a detachment of Roman soldiers erecting a line of wooden watchtowers on the Taunus Mountain, which lay deep in the territories her people claimed as their own.

The signal towers had been burned and the Romans driven off—though she knew they would return; they were persistent as flies. But the warriors had not broken camp because Wido—the second powerful chieftain of the tribe and her father's enemy—delayed them with an endless dispute over the spoil, haggling over every last silver horse bit or ivory-handled dagger that had been taken. "He waits to see what I want," Baldemar reported to Athelinda in a runner's message, "and it becomes what he wants." Because of Wido's petty greed, she thought, her people's fields and villages were left vulnerable, protected by the old, the very young, and the farm women whose knowledge of weapons did not extend beyond hurling pots and stones.

Girl and pony shot through the deep shade of a stand of olive-gray beeches, galloping almost soundlessly over a sandy forest floor and into a muddy meadow divided by a melancholy line of willows. The path sloped steeply downward into Wolf's Head Bog, and for the first time this place did not fill her with spirit-terror; she knew only the excitement of the race. Here nature's corpse was laid out rotting. The brackish pools to either side of the narrow path were graves, crowded with the remains of generations of men given in the spring sacrifice or convicted of great crimes and drowned by the Assembly of the Moon. At night their spirits took the form of the fire that played over the water, the baleful will-o'-the-wisps, beckoning anyone who ventured close to join them in restless death. She whipped past the maternal bulk of the Initiation Stone, half hidden among tall ferns, where Athelinda brought her for her ceremonies of womanhood; it was still stained with her first moon blood. Near it was a cluster of smooth, faceless wooden images of the goddess Fria, springing like mischievous mushrooms from the damp. *Lady of the Bog,* she prayed silently, *protect me from the wrath of the living and of the dead.*

The pony scrambled up a steep slope and clattered onto drier ground. As they whipped past the tortured shape of the Lightning Oak, she averted her eyes. In that corpse of a tree, her grandmother told her, were imprisoned the souls of all the wretches who let kinsmen lie unavenged. When she was still so young she was not allowed to ride alone, Hertha brought her there and cuffed her until she memorized the words: *"If one of our own is slain, I must draw blood in return, even if it takes to the end of my days. Vengeance is holy, it gives life to the clan!"*

As they struggled up the long fir-clad rise, she judged herself close enough to the villages to sound the alarm. Taking up the cattle horn that hung at her belt, she blew three urgent blasts—the signal for a raid.

And to her surprise, from ahead she heard an eruption of answering shouts. As she flashed past a break in the trees, she saw, far ahead of her, a second band of warriors, at least a hundred in number, just as they crowned the rise that concealed Antelope River and disappeared. She felt a first spasm of fear: They would reach the ford before her, and she would be trapped on the wrong side of the river. She was a girl alone. They would cut her throat and pitch her into a bog for hunting in territory they claimed as their own. Or they would take her as a slave, and she would live out her life as some warrior's prize, a miserable creature no better than his cattle or sheep.

Then from behind her came still more warriors' cries. A third band followed her. How came there to be so many? The three bands seemed almost to run in formation. The men behind were perhaps meant to hold the ford, or to serve as a reserve force. Something about this was sinister and wrong. Hermundures never raided in such numbers, nor with such foreplanning. And what war band would agree to *follow* another? It would bring too much shame. Among both her own people and the Hermundures, warriors fought all their lives for the coveted places at the head of the charge.

Again she lifted the horn to her lips and blew three blasts, knowing as she did so she might be giving up her life in warning, for she signaled her own position. But life left little choice in these matters. The safety she would have won by silence was the safety of a *niding*, the strongest term of condemnation in use among the tribes, which roughly meant: "wretch who loses his soul through betraying his kin."

And this time she heard the answering horns of her people, carrying on her warning to the remotest parts of Chattian lands. The droning and trilling increased, moaning through the wood, sounding near then far, until the horns became so numerous they melted into one powerful disharmonious tone. Her spirit rose with the horns and she was seized suddenly with a fierce love of all this country. She felt her mind a great wing stretched out protectively over the land.

Brunwin struggled up a path cut long ago through the scrub pine and at last gained the top of the ridge. She looked down. At first she saw only the gleaming serpent-shape of the river, molten in the sun. Then she saw them, three hundred and more, swarming in a dark knot, bristling with a thicket of upright spears. The sight was fascinating and terrifying at once, like coming upon a nest of wasps. Some forded the river in thin files while others milled behind. She pulled Brunwin to a halt, fearful they would see her.

But then a slingstone slashed through the boughs from above and grazed the pony's rump, searing flesh and bringing blood. Auriane looked up. A warrior left to serve as a sentry had climbed a pine. She watched, paralyzed by the sight of him, as he took aim a second time.

Brunwin kicked out once, nearly throwing her over his head. Then he bolted. His belly low to the ground, with strenuous strides he flung her toward the busy ford. She clung to his mane, knowing bit and rein were useless now. Brunwin would not slow until he reached his own shed in the horse pens of the hall of Baldemar. Branches lashed her face. Dark patches of sweat appeared on the pony's neck. Then they broke free, onto the wide, treeless bank of the river.

She shut her eyes. They saw her. Sharp barking shouts were raised. With a grim innocence she thought: And so, death comes. Except for Hertha's torments, life was kind and good. Why should anyone expect to live long?

Her one hope was that they would consider a lone girl on a bolting pony not worth their trouble while greater plunder waited beyond the river. Brunwin had just enough wit left to know to stay away from them; as he galloped he edged to the right. Four of the warriors broke from the band, shouting and laughing in the tribal tongue, and darted across her path. One playfully cast a spear that missed.

But a firm command in a strange tongue called them back. More surprising to her still, the four obeyed.

Brunwin's hooves broke the river into showers of crystal; as he lunged through knee-deep water, she heard bits of a shouted argument.

". . . a pretty wench . . . spirited and proud. . . ."

"This one's *mine*, you lust-maddened brigand!"

"Take one of mine if you're so in need! We're already found out, there's no time!"

"We're doubly found out, if you let her live! Get her!"

Auriane gained the stone-strewn far bank. A spear was aimed in earnest. It ripped through the side of her bearskin tunic and tore flesh near her ribs. The pain was like scalding water but her panic quickly numbed it.

Then the pony's right shoulder pitched sharply down. He struggled up with Auriane clinging to the side of his neck, skittered sideways, then settled into a lurching canter that was painfully slow. With a fresh seizure of dread, Auriane realized he had slipped on a stone and lamed himself.

From behind came the sound of leather-clad feet slapping the ground in rapid rhythm, followed by splashing as they struck the water. She looked back. Three warriors raced each other in their eagerness to catch and kill her. Each was lightly armed with one short spear. Two had hair of dirty yellow, menacingly long, trailing in the wind. The third was smaller in stature with hair that was unusually dark. He pulled slightly ahead with a grin on his face that was fixed and triumphant like a skull's.

Fright froze her muscles. She cried out jumbled words to Fria, hardly knowing what words she spoke, and managed to lash the trailing end of the rein across Brunwin's rump, but her hardy mount, terrified as she, was already doing his best. The pony followed no path, struggling and crashing through the underbrush, while she bowed her head to avoid being struck from his back by low-hanging branches. For the moment at least, the thick forest rendered their spears useless. She prayed they would become discouraged and give up the chase.

She looked back to see if they gained ground. They had. She felt her bones go limp. Her soul slid quietly toward death, not protesting, feeling a dull throbbing acceptance, a muddy sense of punishment deserved, dragging her down.

It was meant to be. Was I not cursed from birth? Hertha knows it. Could I not always see my evil reflected in her eyes? The earth purges itself on me. My own cursedness coughed up these fiends. Why struggle? Why not slip from Brunwin's back . . . and into the talons of the Fates?

The forest broke; they burst in on the side path of a narrow field of einkorn wheat. Here she sensed human presences. On the field's far side was a humble thatched house smeared with brilliant clay; it resembled a misshapen hornet's nest. A crone named Herwig lived there with her thralls, the grandmother of a vast family scattered over all their lands. But now there was only evil stillness about—the house and all who sheltered there had taken to the underground storage pits called *souterrains* at the first sounding of the horns. Some, doubtless, hid in the field. She screamed out the old woman's name, even though she knew her voice would not carry far enough. From the door of the thatched house a curious cow thrust her head. Auriane's tears of hopelessness were blown off by the wind.

One fair-haired runner dropped back, exhausted. The remaining two gained a horse length. She realized Brunwin's staggering canter would take her through the great Ash Grove, the holiest precinct in all their lands, a place she would never enter willingly for fear of rousing the dread, brooding spirit of the Ash. Hope surged again. Surely they would fear to follow her there.

Another spear was cast. It arced above her, piercing the ground ahead of her, standing upright as a boundary pole. She looked back and saw that one of the remaining runners meant to come no closer to the dread grove; he slowed, then cast his spear before turning back. But the dark-haired warrior seemed not to know an ash from an apple tree, or care. He ran with the frenzied energy of a dog closing on game, powerful strides pulling him steadily closer. His broad chest strained against the close-fitting red tunic. The muscles of his upper arms seemed ready to burst the warrior's ring that encircled them. He meant to have her.

With one hand she sought beneath her tunic for Ramis' amulet of sacred earth, the *aurr*, and pressed it to her breast. She thought she felt it quicken and grow warm. *Sacred earth, flesh and mind of Fria, keep me on the path to my fate,* she prayed. But perhaps her fate was to die.

When she came alongside the upright spear, she acted without thought, grappling with it desperately, then managing to pull it up, nearly unseating herself. From behind she heard a sputtered curse.

The spear felt heavy and awkward in her hand. Athelinda had taught her spear-casting along with the many arts of the homestead, for a woman must be able to defend field and hall in time of raids. But the spears she used were lighter, and not iron tipped, and she cast them at nothing more fearsome than posts.

I've enraged him—now he will kill me cruelly and slowly. But he has one spear—if he misses, I'm armed and he's not. Surely he will think of that. I've never killed a man, only hares—I cannot! Yet it is done every day. Will his ghost pursue me off the world's edge? I know *my* ghost would pursue *him*. Does Baldemar consider these things before he slays? I will not live to ask him.

The sky disappeared behind a rippling canopy of ash boughs. She was swallowed up in holy gloom. The warrior of the Hermundures was but four horse lengths behind; his heaving breath was rasping and loud in this hushed place. *Why had he no fear?* "Should any man enter the Ash Grove who was not called in by its Spirit," the Holy Ones warned, "he will not walk out again in human shape."

We will become sparrows. Or both of us will be imprisoned in a tree, living a life of tiresome sameness, our feet embedded in earth, our leafy hair touching the sky. My mother and father will never guess what became of me.

The ash trees watched her dourly, too venerable and aged to react swiftly to this intrusion. Where were the grove's priestesses and priests? No one ever told her if they too sought cover in a raid. Hollow silence pooled in the bluish deeps between austere trunks; gauzy shafts of light occasionally illumined the forest floor. The slender pillars of this temple stood free and alone: The Ash was proud and let nothing grow beneath it—any hapless plant that tried was strangled by its roots or killed by its shade.

Brunwin staggered pitifully, and she knew he must rest or die. His coat was now wholly soaked and his wheezing hurt her to hear.

It is time. I must *try* to save myself, or I disgrace all my kin.

She pulled hard on the reins, but the pony would not slow. So she raised herself up and sprang from his back while keeping a good grip on the reins with one hand and holding the spear aloft in the other. She fell hard. Brunwin reared, his body twisting round as he came to the end of the rein. The warrior slowed in surprise. He danced lightly toward her, balancing the spear, deftly taking aim. She saw he was fair of face and full of brash confidence.

She moved behind an ash tree, careful not to injure it by

touching the gray-green bark, dragging the pony with her. Sick terror rose in her throat. The warrior approached with caution, gracefully dancing sideways round the tree. She did not understand why he was so determined to slay her rather than take her alive; it was one more element of the raid that was both horrifying and peculiar. She sensed he thought no more of her life than he might of an animal to be slaughtered; the random malice of a troll flickered in his eyes.

As she moved too, careful to keep the tree between them, she was dimly aware of a dark, low hum on a bone pipe, a persistent sound that rose and grew stronger until it poured into the air around like some warm liquid. Her eye just caught the movement of a priestly robe, spectral and white, far back in the labyrinth of trunks.

The Holy Ones *were* here, watching, marking all she did. Her cry for help died before it formed in her throat. They would give no aid, for she had stumbled out of daily life and into mythic life. "What passes in the Ash Grove," they would say, "is a sign for what will pass in the world." Her fate would be read as a portent. They would watch with detachment to see if she lived or died, then interpret the future from her final writhings. She was numbed by how suddenly all that protected her vanished: her family's fame, her numerous kin, and her father's many Companions—the boldest warriors of the tribe. She was a girl alone, stripped naked for death.

The dark-haired warrior lunged unexpectedly to the left, and the tree no longer shielded her. His spear-arm snapped out. The weapon was skillfully aimed and powerfully thrown.

Swifter than thought, she dropped into a heap on the forest floor. Had she not, the spear would have torn through her chest. She heard it sink deep into the flesh of an ash at her back. From the warrior came a low husky laugh. He is a madman, she thought. He struck an ash tree to the heart and yet he feels no terror.

Before she had time to scramble to her feet, he was sprinting toward her to take her with his hunting knife.

The sound of running feet held her transfixed. She saw a quick vision of her blood splattered on the bark. He was all the enemies she ever feared: the ogre with its swampy breath, the stooped shadow of a lurking man-thing seen at dusk beyond the last field, the Romans with their terrifying relentlessness, the guest-murderers of the winter tales.

But in the next instant she felt a powerful stillness gathering within, as if there were a holy grove in her heart. It seemed a spirit far older than her own took possession of her—it might have been an ancestor who worshipped here, or the vast soul of the Ash itself. A dark steady strength flooded into her limbs.

I can live if I will it. Arise and fight. The blood on the bark is not mine but his.

She sprang up with collected grace. Almost playfully, as though she were testing her skill rather than fighting for her life, she centered the spear's weight in her palm and drew her arm back, eyes on his heart. She whipped forward.

It was a hard straight throw. But he was alarmingly quick and he dodged it; she succeeded only in tearing off part of his tunic. He slowed for a moment, face contracted in pain from the flesh wound she made, looking back once to see if her spear fell close enough to be retrieved. It had not. He raised the hunting knife and lunged for her.

But she was already gone, darting like a deer to the tree in which his spear was lodged. He ran hard, meaning to fall on her before she got it free.

Working feverishly, she disengaged it. As she spun round, he sprang, knife bared like a single tearing tooth. He grinned. His hair was sweat-darkened. Distended nostrils gulped in air.

Fria, lady of Night, I am your servant, let me live!

She cast the spear with all her strength—it was the last leap of a festival dancer before she drops into exhaustion. The spear seemed to jump lightly from her hand, glad to be free.

It struck high in his chest, pitching him backward. He staggered a few steps, seizing the spear in both hands as if he could not believe it was embedded in his body.

Her joy was mingled with dread as the eyes of the warrior of the Hermundures became sky-blank, his gaped mouth stopped in place—a mouth no longer, but a frightful hole. He fell heavily to his knees, then sank quietly to his side. The blood pulsed out in a low fountain, darkening his tunic, reddening the ground. For long moments she stood very still, her breathing labored, not yet believing the struggle was done.

She edged toward him and almost humbly knelt down. The huge nostrils that moments ago grabbed at air as if with a strong fist now reached for it with a slack hand.

One fluttery breath eased out and he took no more.

I killed. Earth will collect in an empty skull where once a mind had been. A body carefully tended all the days of his life is set by me on a course of rot. A spirit is ripped from its housing and set adrift. However commonly it is done, still it is an awesome part to take.

The wind all day had been still, but now it rose purposefully, rushing through the boughs like swiftly running water. She sensed the nearness of Wodan, keeper of souls, and above him, all-enveloping Fria, setting the wind.

Was this kill your gift? she asked the gods. The wind surged harder until it was a roaring torrent and she heard a whispered *yes* in the wild dance of green above.

And then a passage was flung open to dreams she had had many times, of battle and the sword. In one, she stood before a grave mound by moonlight. Her head was bowed, and she touched white lips to the cold steel of a sword encrusted with mold, and she knew it was Baldemar's. In another she stood armed as a warrior on the palisade of a fort, the enemies of all their lives arrayed before her, the remnants of her people behind her, waiting for doom. The visions unsettled her and she forced them from her mind.

At last she rose, and set about searching for small round stones to pile on the corpse. The warrior was enemy spirit now, and she must prevent his ghost from stalking the villages. After a short struggle she removed the spear from his chest. It was family treasure and must be preserved, for with it she had taken her first enemy. Then she cut a lock of his hair for use as an amulet. Finally she set about stripping the body. She found strange things.

She took first his hunting knife. But the belt in which it had been sheathed made her pause. It had odd signs carved into it, and they were not runes. From his tunic she took a moist sponge and a rolled sheet of something thin as a leaf with more of these strange signs written over a curious drawing of radiating weblike lines. But she had no time to puzzle over these things. From beyond the grove she heard the distant thunder of cattle driven off and women's screams. The Hermundures were striking on every side. Athelinda would be half mad from fear for her safety. Quickly she put all she found into her gamebag.

She heard the crackle of leaves behind her.

She turned and saw Hylda, most ancient of the Ash Priestesses, approaching in dreamy silence. Her mouth was set in a simple line, revealing as much as a toad's. The wind kept her silver hair in ghostly motion. Her skin was the color of a hazelnut; her eyes were like a deer's, liquid and mournful. The wind tugged at her clothes; she was like some fragile autumn leaf no longer getting nourishment from the tree, locked in a last struggle with the wind that tried to tear it from its twig. She held a torch in one hand.

"Let the fire cleanse!" Her voice was one Auriane would expect of a dwarf, sweet and high.

Auriane watched numbly, unable to speak. Hylda brushed the torch so close past Auriane's face she nearly singed her hair. Then the old priestess walked nine times round the body, humming all the while, passing the fire close over the corpse. She stopped, studying the body, and Auriane knew she saw ruptures in the world about in the angle of an arm, the contortion of the trunk.

"He died with open eyes," Hylda said finally, nodding knowingly. "It is great evil, great evil. It means the dead watch us." The old woman gestured delicately. "It means an enemy rises from within."

She looked sharply at Auriane. "When this man broke into my grove, he became all enemies, even those that rise from within. And you, Auriane, are his slayer."

Hylda's eyes seemed to stare inward as she solemnly touched her staff to Auriane's left shoulder, then to her right. Auriane leaned away slightly, wondering if madness had taken the old woman.

She has spoken too long with trees. She's grown a heart of bark.

"Your lot is to protect your people with your own body, to be a living shield as long as your spirit is clothed in flesh," Hylda went on in her tremulous voice. "Any weapon you touch is blessed. Any weapon you wield has thrice the war-luck in your hand. The oracle commands you: Marry the god, and victory will be your fate."

She felt a jump in her chest; it was excitement and terror. To "marry the god" meant to join the shield maidens, a small but greatly revered order of priestesses who lived and fought with the warriors and performed the rites that sent them to the Sky Hall when they were slain. Then came a sense of being both surprised and not surprised. A part of her rebelled, seized suddenly with a blind need for the comfort of farm and hearth.

No, I cannot live such a harsh grim life. But Hylda need not know.

"Who is the enemy who rises from within?" Auriane asked carefully.

"You will know him. He was always there in seed form. He falls now on fertile soil."

Auriane looked at Hylda with a worried frown. "But this cannot be. I am to marry Witgern when I am twenty."

"To *that* I have no answer. I know only what I read in the dead man's eyes."

A new eruption of war cries wrested Auriane's attention away. Auriane moved off slowly, not wanting to show disrespect. "My lady . . . , I must go. My mother is alone!" She took up the pony's rein and began to lead him off.

"Go then, but never forget," Hylda admonished, following Auriane. For an instant their gazes fully met, and Auriane was aware of a dry, spidery spirit that yearned to seize her and suck in a strong young soul. Hylda wagged a withered finger. *"You have more kin in this grove than in any hall* . . . and they will claim you one day."

Auriane hurried on, half dragging Brunwin. She *would* forget. I will turn my back on this. I will deny the kill was my own.

She looked round once and saw more Holy Ones emerging from the gloom, their cloaks white as swans; as they flocked round the body, dove-soft sounds came from them, and she knew they spoke excitedly of the rare omen.

Many saw, then. They will not let me hide from this. But I will not live that life—I refuse!

To the east and west she saw the angry smoke of free-running fires. The Hermundures were burning all in their path—fields, sheds, houses. She was alarmed by how close they had penetrated to her father's hall. But once she was home she would be nestled in safety. It had always been so.

In her impatience she mounted the weary pony again and Brunwin broke into a limping trot, fighting the rein in his panic. Finally they jolted down the familiar rocky path over Axhead Hill, then the birch forest fell away and they passed a welcome sight: the neat pile of stones that marked the boundary line of her family's lands. Here was safety, and the world's center. She blew one more horn blast, more from joy than in warning. The pony raised his head eagerly and began to gallop; he knew this field of ripening barley. They flashed past her mother's apple trees, then crossed the fallow field that next year would be planted with flax. Its north side was girded by a fence of human bones.

Only Baldemar had such a fence; it was constructed of the bones of Roman soldiers slain in a lifetime of battles on the border. Auriane winced as Brunwin rushed at it—he was lame and should not jump—but the sturdy pony insisted. He burst forward, cleared the low fence and landed in soft dung.

Then came long rows of cattle sheds of varying heights, and

beyond, the field thralls' huts, appearing like a cluster of modest haystacks hugging the shadows of the tall pines. The silence all about roused her apprehension and anger. There was no reason for driving the cattle off to safety and hiding in the souterrains. Who—god or man—would dare strike this farm?

And then she came to the open gate in the low palisade that ringed the precincts of the hall itself. Two tall poles flanked it; atop one was affixed the skull of a mountain cat, the totem animal of the Chattians, from which they took their name. Atop the other was the skull, spine and loose dried hide of the stallion offered last autumn in the yearly horse sacrifice. Both were possessed of such terrible holiness that she scarce dared look upon them.

When they cantered through, they left a wake of chickens fluttering up in panic. As the pony threaded his way among the dome-shaped clay kilns in the yard, Auriane saw the glowing vessels being fired within had been abandoned. Why had the kilns been deserted in such haste? Where were Mudrin and Fredemund? Athelinda's mead shed, too, was empty of life.

Beyond lay the hall itself. Its long low shape with its drooping cover of thatch made her think of some great brooding beast crouched at the forest's edge. The hall was for certain a living thing, a creature of old comfortable habits and scents that loved her in return for her love.

The wide entranceway was built in the center of one long side of the hall. Athelinda was there, struggling with a goat that refused to come out. Her mother saw her and released the goat, who promptly wheeled about and returned to the hall. On her back sleeping in a sling was Arnwulf, the baby born this year at the time of the first lambs. Two other babes born since Auriane's birth had died young of the sicknesses of children.

Brunwin lurched to a halt and Auriane dropped to the ground. She drew in a breath at the sight of her mother.

The sight of her mother's pale lips, of that finely made face so taut and drawn, and the beaten look in her eyes made Auriane feel that the earth was giving way beneath her.

To Auriane, Athelinda had always been a supple but stable force, all-powerful but benign; when she was younger she believed her mother's touch caused cows to bring forth milk and set the farm in motion as the mind of Fria set the stars. Her mother had no limits upon her; she spun tales from the rich stuff of her mind with the same ease that she spun wool. That strength was unexpected—she seemed, at first look, fragile as a glass vessel.

THE LIGHT BEARER 59

But Auriane had seen her rise at midnight and battle her way through waist-deep snow to assist a frightened, sweating mare in the foaling barn, or walk with dignified calm to the center of a hostile Assembly to spiritedly make the case of a wronged kinsman. Fredemund said out of her hearing, "Behold the pretty bird—but beware the sharp beak!" Athelinda's hair was dark bronze like her own, but her mother's was calmed and controlled in a neat braided knot secured with a boar's tusk comb—that knot that Auriane once imagined somehow held the world together.

"Auriane!" A brief look of relief gave way to anger. "Where have you been? Did you not hear the horns? Perhaps you forgot where you live. Perhaps you forgot you have a family. While you were out dancing with elves, the house of your father's brother was burned. They'll be burning here next!"

Auriane said nothing, shocked to silence by the sight of her mother's dress torn near the knee. It was the finest she owned, dyed scarlet by her own hand with madder root—and to see it gaping open was horrifying beyond reason, as if she saw her mother's flesh torn. Her twisted torque of silver and her serpent arm rings, which normally made her look bright and noble, today seemed to weight her down like a yoke. Her doeskin shoes inset with beads of amber, which were her pride, she had let become caked with mud from the souterrains.

"Mother . . . , I am sorry—" she began haltingly and stopped, suddenly feeling too frail inside. Finally she realized what her mother had said.

"*Theudobald's* hall?" she whispered, feeling as though all her blood drained from her body. "But it cannot be. How could they dare?" She felt she fought for balance on moving earth. "You're mad to think they would come here! How can you say it?"

"Watch whom you're calling mad, saucy child. It has happened! Now help me push the animals out—they'll be burned alive."

Auriane met her gaze numbly for a moment, slowly shaking her head in denial. Then she lost her strength all at once and rushed to her mother, embracing her tightly, breaking easily through Athelinda's anger, for love as always was too close beneath the surface. "Mother, what is happening to us?" Auriane's soft wail was muffled in her mother's cloak.

"The gods know," Athelinda said with bitter calm, patiently stroking Auriane's hair. "The earth delivers up monsters, the enemy knows no law, the Wheel of Yule spins backward and nidings are crowned as kings." She put an arm about Auriane and they walked toward the open door. "Perhaps it's world's end. He lives longest who knows when to hide."

They entered the cozy gloom of the hall. It smelled as always of tanned hides, fresh-mown hay and day-old leek-and-venison stew, mingled today with the smell of wet ash from the freshly doused hearth fire. Auriane began with a calf, pushing on the creature's haunches to coax it outside to safety. Athelinda herded chickens with a broom, striking at them with motions that were frantic and sad, her eyes bright and intent.

Auriane looked at her. "Mother, there is something else. *What is it?*"

Athelinda hesitated and then said, "A message came this morning from your father. He's gotten an order—an *order*, if you can believe it—from the Roman Governor. As if we were his subjects! Marcus Julianus, king over the whole world—" Athelinda was abruptly silent, as if she decided at the last moment to spare her daughter the truth.

"Mother, tell me. I am not a child!"

"Very well then. He wants you married to one of the sons of Wido."

Auriane made the peculiar discovery that the heart could feel nausea. She gave the calf an overly rough shove that speedily propelled it into the yard.

"How dare he?" she whispered. Suddenly no enemy in the forest seemed so frightful as the Romans with their dark purposes and invisible snares.

"They dare anything that suits their purpose."

"I am far too young!"

"Not to *them*. I have heard it said that in Rome they marry girl children of twelve."

"But . . . what of Witgern?" Chickens pecked at her feet. "This cannot be. I'm to marry Witgern, the Holy Ones have given their blessing on it!" She said nothing of Hylda and the oracle, for it was too unsettling to the order of the world and this day was plagued already with too much disorder. "There was an outcry, I hope, at this monstrous insult to Witgern's family?"

Athelinda's silence was more eloquent than any reply. Finally she said, "A meeting of the Assembly was called to settle the question. Geisar convinced them this was the one certain way to end the warring between your father and Wido."

"That priest is Wido's pet dog! I guessed it before! Was the Assembly with us?"

"Not nearly enough so. That in itself is odd. But then Wido has more new Companions than rotted meat has flies. Their voices were louder than ours. So many Companions—soon, with them, Wido shall have whatever he wants. Now help with the animals, have you not the wit to work and talk at the same time!"

Auriane obligingly began dragging a cow by its bell rope. "What did Father do?"

"He soundly chastised them. He said we would be fools to back down and allow the Romans to usurp the right of parents, and furthermore he said he would make war on the Assembly itself if he had to, to prevent this loathsome means of settling a fight that was never his," Athelinda said between heaving breaths as she recaptured the goat that escaped earlier. "And then he strode off, followed, of course, by his Companions and all the kin of Witgern."

"Loathsome means! Well said!" Auriane smiled with satisfaction as she imagined Baldemar thundering the words. "Father is right in what he said—Wido's always the one to begin the disputes. But something is troubling here. The Romans have always *encouraged* us to war among ourselves. Why suddenly do they want peace between Father and Wido, and marriage, unless there is some common cause between Wido and the Governor?"

Athelinda set her broom upright and gave Auriane the forbidding look that would have sent Mudrin off whimpering. "Do not even *speak* those words. Wido is a scoundrel and a horsethief but no Chattian chief has *ever* betrayed us to the Romans. That is different. Where is your pride in your people?" The sharpness in her voice awakened Arnwulf, and he began softly to cry.

"I have pride, Mother. But you cannot escape from a trap if you do not know how that trap is made." The cow butted her, taking advantage of the fact that she was not paying attention. "The Romans do not like to lose face. They would not give such an order unless they planned to enforce it."

"That is why Baldemar is sending Witgern here at once. It won't be a proper marriage, of course, you're far too young, only an oath of promising—you'll be married at the proper time when you're twenty. But it *will* prevent the Assembly from marrying you to anyone else."

Witgern here at once? Auriane thought, disliking the idea suddenly. She had nothing against Witgern himself, but Hylda's words were beginning to stir in her blood like some slow-acting draught. Marriage to *anyone* began to feel like a fence about a wild place. But, of course, marriage to Witgern is what must be.

They pushed out four ewes, the last of the animals. And Athelinda noticed for the first time what lay in the yard next to Brunwin's saddlecloth.

"Auriane, what is all that? Whose spear is that? What's in that gamebag?"

"I killed one of the raiders." She said it without enthusiasm; she no longer cared.

"Fria, Mother of Us All, have mercy, you could have been killed!" Her mother edged toward the enemy spear, then stood in silence, her expression strangely sad.

"What is it, Mother?"

"Nothing. I just did not expect this . . . so soon. No, don't ask me what I mean. Everyone's underground but you. Go now!"

"Mother," Auriane protested, "if they do burn . . . *here*, father's weapons must be gotten out."

Athelinda made a despairing gesture. "My daughter is mad. That cursed sword in the cradle's to blame for this! There isn't time!"

"There must be time!" Auriane darted back into the hall and made her way to the high-seat, over which the weapons were mounted. She hesitated before the sword of Baldemar's youth, with which he took his first man—she had always feared to touch it because she was taught that in it lived the soul of every enemy it had slain. As her hand closed round the bone handle, she was certain she felt a kick of angry life within. In one moment there was something strangely familiar in the weapon's feel, as if she had been reunited with a lost limb. Then she took up the hunting spear with which Baldemar felled his first boar, and started for the door. But before she stepped out, she looked thoroughly about, from her sleeping-hides to the looms, to the dead hearthfire to the beloved walls, full of a sense of pinched and painful longing, not letting herself fully know it might well be a final look. Then she concealed Brunwin as best she could in the juniper bushes behind the cowsheds and hurried to the souterrain.

Because the hall of Baldemar had many dependents, two souterrains had been dug into the earth behind the mead shed. Each was cut deep and wide enough to shelter twenty people. Wattlework hurdles were fitted over them; these were carefully covered with brushwood to disguise their presence. In peaceful times these rectangular pits were used for storage, but in time of raids they became places of refuge.

Auriane knelt by the nearest of them and handed the weapons down to Athelinda. Then she lowered herself into the earthy dark, finding with her feet the notches cut into the soil and clinging to roots as she descended. She pulled the frame in place, then dropped the rest of the way. The rank smell of many bodies enveloped her. She settled between Athelinda and a mead cask. No one spoke. Speckled light filtered through the interlace of hazel-wood branches above. After a time Athelinda held a skin of mead to the baby's parted lips—he must not awaken and cry now. Arnwulf seemed to drink in his sleep.

Auriane gradually discerned Hertha's resolute profile in the half-light. Her grandmother sat rigidly erect on a small wooden bench, holding her counting stick before her like a spear, in stiff denial of her helplessness. Auriane saw something pathetic in those relentlessly judging eyes, the beaked outline of that commanding nose, held up like some small blunt weapon against the world. Set before her grandmother was a chest filled with the treasures of a lifetime. Hertha was remote from them and it was more than silence; it had the quality of one who readied herself for death. Indeed, Auriane saw, she even wore her finest cloak and the saffron-dyed dress that she meant to be buried with, and her arms glowed with her richest rings. Auriane found it almost brought her to tears, even though Hertha never had any love for her.

"What of Charis?" Auriane whispered finally to her mother. Charis was Theudobald's wife. "And the baby?"

"No one has seen them," Athelinda replied.

Hertha addressed Athelinda in a whisper that Auriane knew she was meant to overhear. "For the good of us all, she *should* marry one of Wido's sons. Nothing but ill comes from that child."

"I will not speak of this now!" Athelinda's sharply whispered reply concealed a note of pleading.

Mother does not put her down soundly enough, Auriane thought miserably. I know she fears Hertha, who knows the magic of raising the dead, but she should not bow down. And how dare Hertha speak *of* me and not *to* me, as if I were a dog!

"Nothing but ill, I say," Hertha whispered on as if Athelinda had not spoken. "Why *not* use her to make a peaceful alliance? I feel sorry for Witgern, if you would know the truth. He knows he's getting a bride with demon's blood and dares not protest!"

"I will not listen to this!" Athelinda whispered with more spirit.

Soon I will burst into flame when Hertha talks so! Auriane thought. I do not care if she curses me nine times and I die. I am a child like any other, aren't I? *Why has she always despised me so?* Mother, I think you know more than you tell.

Hertha could never let Athelinda's words be the last. "Our haughty princess thinks to refuse, I'll wager. Once again, she escapes up a tree. Once again, Athelinda, you're too much the feather-hearted fool to use the axe."

Unknown to Hertha this last taunt worked against her purpose, for her words reminded Auriane of the generosity of Baldemar's love. Once when Auriane was seven, she had scrambled up a pine tree to escape Hertha's birch rod, and for a day she refused to come down, struggling against hunger and exhaustion so she would not fall out of the tree. Hertha had shouted threats until she became hoarse and finally sent for Garn, a field thrall, to cut down Auriane's tree with an axe. But Athelinda dispatched a messenger to Baldemar, who left a victory feast and came at once, arriving at the same time as the axe. Auriane was ready to go down with the tree. But Baldemar rode up with fifteen slightly embarrassed Companions and coaxed her down with a wise word or two. Hertha shouted at him to punish her, saying Auriane had trampled the seed corn, galloping over it with her pony—which she had not—and helped a thrall escape who Hertha planned to punish with a hundred lashes, which was true. But Baldemar forbade it, and Auriane always remembered his words: *"Better a spirit that does not quite fit in this world than one that is broken."*

Athelinda said nothing in reply to Hertha; she just moved closer to Auriane and put a reassuring arm about her daughter's shoulders. For long, no one spoke and the silence above began to madden Auriane; it was like the indrawn breath of a dragon. In the unnatural quiet she felt closely the presence of the Hermundures. Sadly she looked at Arnwulf.

Poor fragile nestling. Why do the gods make us so helpless? We cannot fly, nor have we claws—we are pushed naked into a world that would devour us at every turn.

Now Auriane could see the thralls in the gloom. Mudrin, Fredemund and the five women who worked the looms sat on a ledge of earth, the place of greater honor. Beneath them on the moist ground were the field thralls, pressed close together. Garn, who was chief over them, sat a little apart. The field thralls farmed their separate plots and were required to hand over half of what they produced to the tribe. Among them was a former Chattian warrior who disgraced himself by dropping his weapons in battle and running off—for this, the Assembly condemned him to slavery. There were five women of the Hermundures, taken during the repeated skirmishes between the tribes that erupted over the disputed ownership of salt springs. And then there were the two Romans. One was a Gallic slave trader caught by her father's men with a cartload of Chattian children bound for the slave markets. The Assembly had not sacrificed him to Wodan because they felt such an offering unworthy. The other Roman was Decius.

It was Decius who fascinated her, for he was a captive Roman legionary soldier. There before her, tamed and close, was one of that terrifying race of men who built stone dwellings like mountains and enslaved all the peoples in their path. Often she studied Decius in secret, watching him as he pulled weeds from his miserable plot or threw mock spears at imaginary targets to keep his body youthful and strong. She searched for signs of unusual mettle and strength, and was sharply disappointed when she found none. Decius was just a man. He threw a spear no farther than a Chattian warrior, and his courage was no greater; he was even smaller in stature than most of their men. Decius revealed to her none of the war mysteries of the all-conquering tribe of the South.

The only thing extraordinary about Decius was his arrogance. When she observed him, he stared back with far more boldness than anyone would expect from a thrall. It was a look that said, "I am better than you, even enslaved." Even now he seemed to watch all about him with amused contempt—as though her people were unruly children who had somehow upset the natural order of things and temporarily got the better of him. He learned as little of their language as possible, as though the Chattian language defiled the tongue. He kept his hair clipped short and his face shaved in the Roman fashion, and Auriane knew it was because he did not want to look like them. He scorned mead, preferring wine so poor it looked like brown river mud. Once she had caught him seated before his hut, holding up a thin, rolled sheet and staring at it intently; she wondered if he had gone into some kind of trance. She described what she had seen to Baldemar, who patiently explained that the language of the Romans was marvelous; every word in it could be represented by a series of marks, not unlike runes, and what Decius had been doing was called *reading*. For nights after hearing this, Auriane had hardly been able to sleep, considering this. With this talking paper you could hear the words of someone a great distance away, or even a thousand years dead. But it seemed a thing that could breed confusion: How did a person who could perform this reading know precisely what was meant when he could not hear the musical tones of the voice?

Then she tensed with excitement. Why had she not thought of this at once? The letters on the belt she took from the slain warrior must be in the language of the Romans. She must seek out Decius and get him to interpret the words.

Decius saw her watching him and grinned. It was a smile that snagged her and held her; it was playful and scornful and made her want to strike him across the face. He was young still, not much past twenty, and had the sort of face she imagined made life easier in cities: smooth, finely made but not overly so, formed like a boy's, yet with the resolution of a man's, with swift, impenetrable eyes that were adept at keeping the world at bay, but could not conceal the unaccountable sadness lurking underneath.

She summoned a mildly haughty glare—she did not want him to think himself capable of upsetting her overmuch—but he only broadened his grin.

Then from above, they heard the wail of a child, the quavering singsong cry of one who has given up all hope of help and given in to a world of dread.

"Mother, that is Thusko. He is alive!" Thusko was the child of Theudobald and Charis, and her own cousin. He had somehow escaped the attack on his home and wandered to the one other place familiar to him. From the sound of his broken cries they guessed he ran stumbling and falling toward the abandoned hall, thinking he ran to safety.

While Auriane cast about for some means of safely signaling to the boy, Athelinda shot from her place, scrambled up the dirt wall and dragged aside the wattlework hurdle, not even pausing to take Arnwulf from her back.

"Mother, no!" Auriane called out softly. She tried to grasp Athelinda's foot but lost her hold.

Hertha roused herself from her fiercely private meditation. "Foolish woman! I command you, Athelinda, come back!"

"Ignorant barbarian sow!" This voice was Decius'. Fortunately for himself he spoke in Latin—or Auriane would have been at his throat with a hunting knife.

But Athelinda was gone. She followed the white-blond head of Thusko as he ran in a ragged path beyond the feed-troughs.

Auriane now had such a strong sense of the enemy about she

imagined she smelled their sweat and blood. *Mother,* she cried in her mind, you walk into the open jaws of a serpent!

She heard her mother's fast footsteps grow fainter.

And then the silence was pierced by a single trilling war cry, penetrating as an iron needle thrust into the brain. It ignited others, and the air was chaotic with cries. Then abruptly the war trill ceased, and from every side came the sound of bodies crashing through brush to the accompaniment of soul-shredding shrieks as hundreds of warriors climbed the low palisade and broke in on the yard, entrapping Athelinda in their midst. Auriane heard cracking pottery, the snorts and neighs of terrified horses, and the pitiful yelps of guard dogs as the Hermundures killed them with clubs.

Soon after came the crisp crackling sound of fire eagerly devouring brushwood. The sound gathered force quickly, erupting into a hot rush of noise as if a pillar of fire were sucked up to the sky. And Auriane knew the hall of Baldemar was burning.

Then she heard Athelinda's scream. It was full throated at first, then became a stifled moan, as if someone covered her mouth. The sound sent wildfire through her veins.

She withdrew Baldemar's sword from its sheath and sprang to her feet. Swiftly she began to climb out, struggling a little with the sword's awkward weight.

But a man's hand shot over her mouth and an iron arm encircled her waist, holding her firmly. She writhed furiously, but gradually her captor succeeded in dragging her back.

It was Decius. "Crazed whelp!" came his casually commanding voice in her ear as he spoke between gritted teeth, half in Latin, half in badly pronounced Chattian. "You can throw *your* life away if you want, but you'll not throw away mine!"

Hertha rose stiffly. "Do not touch her, thrall!" Her voice was a cat's spit-and-hiss. "How *dare* you lay a hand on a free woman. I'll see you flogged and drowned!"

With great effort Decius wrestled Auriane down and pinned her arms behind her back; then he eased himself on top of her, using his weight to hold her down. Above them a horse's hoof tore through the brush; instinctively all covered their heads. Decius recovered himself first. Long ago he learned to cover panic with calculated glibness. "Ah, the minds of savages," he said with elaborate amusement between gasps for breath, as Auriane thrashed beneath him, "I've given up trying to puzzle them out. By Jupiter's thunderbolts, they fairly *lust* for the chance to throw themselves on each other's weapons!" He added, grinning down at Auriane, "By the way, my pugnacious pet, that's a *sword*, not a garden hoe."

Auriane nearly succeeded in pitching him off, but he kept his seat. "My apologies, venerable old woman," Decius said to Hertha, but used the wrong word and unwittingly said, "venerable ogress." Hertha withdrew sharply as if Decius flung poison in her face, then slowly she advanced on him, counting stick brandished. Decius went on easily, still grinning, "But *surely* you see—as long as I'm still of sound mind, I cannot be expected to idly sit by while this battle-crazed filly reveals our hiding place."

He looked down again at Auriane. "And as long as we're on the matter, here's another bit of badly needed advice. A smarter bitch would have picked up the *spear*, not the sword—then you wouldn't have to get in so close."

Hertha's counting stick cracked against Decius' back. As he wrenched about to fend her off, Auriane bit his hand down to the bone.

"Daughter of Hades!" Decius cried, shaking Auriane off as he might a rabid mutt. She got free and clambered up again, sword in hand. This time she managed to force her head past the wattlework frame before Decius recovered himself and got a secure grip on her ankles. But in the moment before he succeeded in dragging her back again, Auriane saw a scene that would shatter her peace forever.

At first she saw only the fire. It was some torch wielded by the Giants, thrust into her face, searing her skin. A great yellow column of flame snaked as if to underworld music, unashamedly devouring the seat of the chief of chiefs as if it were any other dwelling, gathering all the more power because of the great spirit that lived in that hall. The furious yellow demon ate her cradle; her mother's loom, her father's high seat, the wood floor where she took her first steps.

Then she saw the Hermundures. It seemed all three bands converged upon this place—this must have been their destination from the start. They were a plague of red crawling things, swarming everywhere, seeming animated by one mind. Their dirty yellow hair swung free; their faces gleamed with sweat. Some rode wild-eyed horses with boars' tusks affixed to the bridles; bulging sacks of treasure and rich pelts were slung from their shoulders. Others threw fresh brands on the fire or cast spears at the fleeing sheep, slaughtering them for sport. One led a captive thrall woman by her hair. Some sang drunken war songs while performing a clumsy loping dance. At a distance a group of them whipped a great herd of cattle amassed from several homesteads.

Then a low rolling coil of dense smoke was chased off by a gust of wind—and she saw Athelinda.

Her mother lay on her back on the ground. Arnwulf was nowhere about. Athelinda's hair had been torn from its plait and it fanned out about her like a silken coverlet. The linen shift she wore had been slashed open down the front with one stroke of a sword. Her bare legs were startlingly white against the dark soil. White legs, black earth—this was a picture that ever after would intrude on Auriane's mind at unexpected times and she would try to hold the image, to keep at bay the memory of what she saw next.

One of the warriors approached her mother on all fours like some stealthy wolf; then he lowered himself slowly over her limp body. A hard knot of nausea formed in Auriane's stomach as she realized he meant to lock together with her as animals did. Her mother's legs, white as bleached bone, and the warrior's, tawny and muscular, were pressed together. He sank into her, making her flesh his flesh, stabbing at her center, befouling the temple that was her mother.

Where were the gods? The demon-warrior's mouth was fastened to her mother's neck and Auriane imagined he sucked the blood from her, drinking in her nobility, stealing her power, taking the elixir that would give him the luck of all her ancestors. He would leave her a husk, with nothing left in her but his poison seed.

Auriane struck out, blind and crazed as a dog with the mouth-foaming disease, her mind shapeless with rage as she raked rigid fingers over the ground and grabbed at roots. She longed to put out her eyes, to put out every torch, to put out all life, and to return to chaos. She hated all weakness, even Athelinda's.

The sight melted her mind into a new shape. *If her mother was prey to whatever comes, then so was she.* Readiness for battle would follow her even into sleep.

Decius was braced for her struggles, his hands tight about her ankles. Gradually he dragged her down once more. Then exhaustion overcame her and she collapsed next to him in a limp heap. Though it ceased to be necessary, he kept a secure grip on her.

Hertha's eyes were glassy as if she would not touch the world more, even with her sight. She gazed with a vaguely accusing look at the torn place in the wattlework hurdle, as if it were a living thing responsible for their plight.

For long moments all was still in the souterrain. At last the shouts above became more infrequent and they knew the raiders retreated, ebbing off like a storm tide, leaving sad wreckage in their wake. Finally there was only the roar of the fire and woeful silence.

Auriane drew herself up by force of will, pushing Decius away when he tried to help her climb out.

The bodies of animals were strewn everywhere as if blown about by a powerful wind. The hall of Baldemar was a raging furnace. Auriane ran over broken crockery and fell down beside her mother.

She covered Athelinda's naked legs with her cloak. Her mother turned her head weakly, and her lips moved. Auriane felt she leapt from bottomless cavern to sunny meadow. Her mother lived.

She pressed her cheek to her mother's, shaking with hard sobs, not realizing she moaned aloud, "I should have come . . . I could have saved you . . . I am cursed!"

From behind her she heard Hertha. "Auriane!" That voice was a serrated blade sawing at Auriane's heart. "Do not touch her! She must be cleansed by sacrifice!"

Auriane looked round. Thusko stood near Hertha, hiding his face in her cloak. The boy was unharmed. But Arnwulf lay lifeless in her grandmother's arms. The warrior who attacked her mother, she quickly realized, must have first hurled the child to the ground, and to his death.

Auriane tore Arnwulf from Hertha's arms and turned round, fearful Athelinda would see him. *She must not know yet,* Auriane thought. Let her be stronger before she knows.

She crushed Arnwulf to her chest, as if her determination and her body's warmth might restore the small body to life. There was so little difference between those eyes shut in sleep and in death. It could not be. The mercilessness of the day was unending. She sank to her knees holding him, and seasons might have passed full of unvoiced shrieks of fury, and pleas to the gods to give her back her brother, her home, her childhood.

She was aware that Decius paused, lingering behind the other thralls, watching her for a time. She had no words for him. And she knew vaguely that behind her, Hertha was slowly, deliberately unbraiding her hair, while uttering a prayer commonly spoken during final rites. But Auriane cared for nothing more in the world. Her mind was reaching for her brother's soul and finding only emptiness.

As the sun sank, flaring at the tops of the pines, twelve Oak Priestesses from the temple-lodge below the Village of the Boar came soundlessly from the forest. These priestesses were skilled medicine women, come to see who lived and who needed their ministrations. Fearful pity showed in many faces. Their long hair, never cut in their lives, were so many lustrous manes of bright gold, dark gold, chestnut and sienna, nearly sweeping the ground. The bronze sickles, strike-a-lights, multiple knives and balls of crystal slung from their belts made a delicate music. They looked at Hertha with alarm, whispering purposefully among themselves. But they dared not interfere with a woman of her rank.

Hertha stood facing the flames, palms outstretched, her hair loosened and streaming down. Auriane in her misery made nothing of this.

The Oak Priestesses flocked around Athelinda. Thrusnelda, their silver-haired First Priestess, had tears in her eyes as she smoothed the hair from Athelinda's forehead. Then four of them gently lifted her and laid her on a straw mat. They meant to carry her to the Oak Lodge, where they would heal her with herbs and ritual magic.

They took Arnwulf from Auriane with difficulty; her arms were locked about him. He must be prepared for the rites of cremation and the urn burial of his ashes. Thrusnelda tried to get Auriane to follow her, but she could not move. Her soul was cold and heavy as a standing stone. She sat very still, fascinated by the fire.

"Daughter, there will be wolves," Thrusnelda said, all intrusive benevolence as she put her padded hands on Auriane's shoulders, sheltering Auriane with her motherly bulk. She smelled of the thousand herbs dried and stored in her lodge. "This ground is unhallowed, and night comes. You must come with us."

Auriane gave no sign she heard. "Auriane," Thrusnelda tried again, gently still, but with more urgency. *"Your grandmother prepares to do a thing you should not see.* Come with us now, I beg you, in the name of the spirit of the Oak."

"What can I see more horrible than what I have seen already?" Auriane said then. "Let me be, please. Wolves will not come while the fire burns."

"I knew your mother and grandmother as babes and I do not know what is best?" Thrusnelda allowed herself the smallest display of irritability. Then she shrugged. "Stay then, and come when you are ready." The old priestess left bread and mead for her, then removed her own cloak and put it about Auriane's shoulders. Four of the holy women then lifted the mat on which Athelinda lay and bore her off.

After a time Auriane could not help but notice Hertha. Her masses of dove-gray hair collected about her then unfurled like some flag of surrender as she began walking with grave, measured steps toward the blazing hall. Her face was rigid with purpose.

Auriane realized she meant to walk into the flames.

The sight thrust Auriane back into the world. She leapt up. *"No!"* Her cry was a long forlorn howl.

Auriane ran until she was abreast of her grandmother. She thought the raging heat would melt the features from her face. She could not bear another death.

She seized Hertha's arm. Hertha recoiled and fought her off savagely. Her grandmother's hair lashed Auriane across the face.

"Your touch fouls! Demon child, stand off from me!"

"Grandmother! Despise me if you will, but stay with us! Too much already has been taken from us!"

Auriane was ashamed of her quavering voice, but she struggled on. "There is no greater sign of ill omen than the death of a mother. In doing this, you harm Baldemar grievously and give aid to Wido. At least, think of your son!"

Hertha looked at her, those sallow eyes nearly emptied of life. Gusts of heated wind filled her linen dress and caused it to dance lightly like some frolicksome ghost. Her lips were parched; that voice was the hissing sigh of a bellows. "Silence! You know nothing of life and death and harm. The gods have fled from this hall, ignorant child, or these calamities could not have come to pass. *I*, at least, am not fool enough to live on without honor."

To her amazement, Auriane found her fear of her grandmother suddenly vanished. It was as though this single day drove her from childhood, and she saw Hertha as she truly was: not august and terrifying, but a brittle, bitter girl grown old, to whom life was a series of punishments alleviated only by occasional opportunities to inflict punishment on others.

"Grandmother, you desert us all! Your answer to our weakness is to weaken us more!" Auriane cried angrily over the roar of the flames, dimly astonished at her own presumption. "It is wicked of you, wicked and cowardly! Honor can be reclaimed. You know Baldemar will avenge this, swiftly and surely as thunderclap follows lightning. What is this nonsense about honor? They murdered his son! They outraged his wife! He will lay waste to their whole country!"

A lethal light flashed in Hertha's eyes. "And who will avenge *him*, fool, when he dies by a kinswoman's hand?"

"What are you saying? Who has said these things? *What* kinswoman?"

"Arnwulf's murder can be avenged, but no one in heaven or earth will be able to avenge Baldemar's. For who can take vengeance on their own? It is the greatest curse that can be laid on a clan—for vengeance cannot cleanse it. What passed today is the first sign of this curse."

Auriane sensed the beast that had tracked her all her life was finally poised to spring.

Hertha went on with triumph in her eyes, "He will die by *your* hand. *Yours,* Auriane, and so it has been foretold!"

"You're utterly mad! Demons possess you! I cannot believe such loathsome words come from your mouth! Do you not see how I love him! Athelinda does not love him more!"

But her grandmother was sealed once more in her tower of silence. Hertha wrestled free of Auriane and resumed her processional walk toward the burning hall. Auriane followed for a time, vigorously shaking her head, her voice a shriek.

"Grandmother, no!" she repeated until she thought the heat would boil her blood. Hertha never slowed. Her step seemed almost eager, as if she joined a fiery lover. She was a demoness whose will was stronger than fire.

At the last she was a wriggling black thing against molten gold, more worm than human, and to Auriane it seemed she danced in delight. A sense of doom settled over her as she watched Hertha's form swaying, thinning, thickening in the blast of heat, rippling like an eel under water.

Auriane felt her chest collapse. A savage guilt battered her heart, as if she pushed Hertha into the fire herself. *So that is why she despised me always,* Auriane thought. But why is she so *certain* I will commit a crime too horrible to name that she walks into flames?

Auriane retreated from the heat and returned to the place where her mother's blood stained the ground. She felt herself tied to the tail of a dragon, lashed first one way, then the other—first her mother, then Arnwulf, and now this—and with this last blow she felt all the struggle run out of her. The sun seemed to wane in grief as she fell among the potsherds, tumbling into lurid dreams where elves and giants danced on the corpse of her family, a world where only fire and the sword were real.

CHAPTER IV

The following morning, while the hillsides still smoked from the raiders' fires, Witgern and twenty of Baldemar's Companions galloped noisily into the yard. Where the hall of Baldemar once stood was a charred and glowing midden, hotter than a forge; here and there a living flame still stirred, seeming to taunt them. The young Companions rode round it, staring in dazed disbelief.

The Hermundures have gone mad, Witgern thought. How had jackals summoned the mettle to maul a lion? Surely they know that when Baldemar punishes them he will be a scythe leveling ripe wheat.

One of the young Companions, fearing the fiery hall was a sign from the gods that all who served Baldemar were cursed, stole off alone into the wood and used his bridle reins to hang himself from a pine.

Finally Witgern saw Auriane. The sight tripped his heart. She lay curled on her side, asleep or dead in the shadow of a watering trough for kine. The others saw her, too, but they kept a discreet distance so that Witgern could approach her alone.

Witgern was tall and strongly made, with thick red-gold hair that settled at his shoulders, and morose blue eyes in an earnest face that was clean shaven. It was the face of one who might compose songs when he was alone, a countenance that made it difficult to believe he had performed the bloody deeds attributed to him. But they were true enough. Though Witgern had seen only twenty-four summers, he alone vied with Sigwulf, a seasoned warrior, for the coveted position at Baldemar's right hand in the charge. His wolfskin cloak was fastened with the tusk of a boar that had fatally gored four warriors before Witgern brought it down alone. His horse's bridle was adorned with the bronze medallions of two Roman cavalry Centurions he slew in a single foray—a feat Baldemar himself had not matched. But Witgern was shrouded in a stubborn melancholy that mystified his fellows, for it seemed there was no gift of the Fates he missed: His father's herds were second in size to Baldemar's, and his mother's fields were nearly as vast as Hertha's. He knew a different tale for every day of the moon; he could down nine horns of mead and still stand upright, and rarely did he lose a spear-casting contest; he even somehow managed to win consistently at dice. And beyond this, Baldemar intended to grant him the greatest gift he could give—his only daughter.

Two spotted dogs edged close to him, fangs bared. Witgern beat them back with a barrel stave and knelt down beside Auriane.

His first thought embarrassed him because it did not seem it should be his first: *Cover her!* They should not see my wife-to-be in this state, bare of her fine ornaments, and her clothes shredded by dogs. Is my great prize still alive? How Sigwulf would rejoice if my one chance of a clan-tie to Baldemar was torn from me.

He put a hesitant hand to her throat to feel for her pulse. *She lived.* He felt a wild rush of relief, followed by a giddiness he was certain was love.

That summery innocence. No wonder Wido wanted her in his family more than he wanted a thousand rings of silver. But this wonder belonged solely to him.

He tore a bit of cloth from his own tunic, dipped it into the water of the trough, and gently wiped the blood from her face.

Look away, you rogues, and do not despise me for having the great good fortune to *love* the woman to whom I am to be married. Do not think I don't hear your thoughts; Witgern carries on like some coddled prince who drinks wine from fountains! Love's a luxury only the pampered peoples of the south can afford!

He quickly determined that Auriane was bruised and exhausted but not hurt. At least, she had no great wounds of the flesh. As she opened her eyes and withdrew from him in the instinctive way of maltreated beasts, *then* he saw her wound—a mauled soul that would never again trust the world to be gentle and fair. He forgot himself for a moment and felt a sharp sadness for her. There was in her look that haunted grief he saw often in the faces of those who outlived all their children, watching every one fall victim to the Roman plague. The Fates shredded everyone's peace soon enough, but they had gotten to her so young.

She struggled to sit up, but she did not crawl close to him for comfort as he wished. She was sealed in wary solitude, as if she stood alone on a citadel. While staring at the fire, she told him in a few toneless words of Hertha's suicide, Arnwulf's death and the outrage suffered by her mother.

Witgern knew then just how great a catastrophe this was. Many of the tribespeople and even some of his fellow Companions would see this as a sign Baldemar was no longer fit to lead them in battle; they might desert him for a younger man. A chief's growing weakness was like a rotting center beam of a house—it was a thing to be anxiously watched. The plundering Hermundures might have given Wido his fondest wish—to lead the army alone. And Witgern was not certain even the sacred rite of vengeance could cleanse the stain of that blackest of curses, the voluntary death of a mother. The Holy Ones would doubtless require a lavish gift of appeasement from Baldemar, to be paid to Wodan through his priest.

Witgern even feared for his own life. Baldemar in his great grief might hold *him* partly accountable, simply because he had come too late. Such things happened among them—misfortune's cause was sometimes held to be the curse of those who were near.

Witgern realized Auriane watched him gravely, readying herself to speak difficult words. "Witgern, look at me," she said urgently. "Your mind is far off to the south."

"You are easy enough to look upon!" Witgern smiled, anxious to tease her down from her citadel. Her solemnity made him feel something was required of him that he did not know how to give. He took her hand. "You are beauteous beyond sun and moon, even when you've rolled all day in the mud!"

"No pretty words on this day, Witgern. Please, I cannot bear it."

Witgern suddenly felt uncomfortable. Now what problem was *she* going to present to him?

The soft gray eyes held him fast. "Witgern, I dare not wait—I must tell it now. I cannot marry you."

At first Witgern felt nothing. *"What is this?"* he said softly. He looked round hurriedly once, fearful the others overheard, then dropped his voice to a taut whisper. "What monstrous thing are you saying?" Slowly, a creeping coldness came into his stomach.

That will of hers, that rogue will, immovable as a standing stone—what could stand against it? It was Baldemar's will, born again.

"What have I done that you should cast me off?" He released her hand. But he sensed Auriane felt his pain, and he knew remorse was undermining her. *Very good. I'll appeal to that kindliness.*

"Nothing!" She looked restively down. "It . . . it is not my wish to be cruel. Please, I beg you, do not think ill of me!"

"How could I think ill of you?" he whispered, while inside, suddenly he hated her. Two fellow Companions heard sharp whispered words and turned to look at them. Witgern warned them away with a scowl.

"As the gods live, if I *could* marry, I would marry you."

"Just tell me what I've done!"

"Witgern, it has nothing whatever to do with you. It is because of my mother."

"Curses on Helle. I thought Athelinda liked me."

"Not that." She turned away, her face flushed scarlet in the heat, her eyes glistening. "My mother married and was happy. She thought she could raise children in . . . in a slaughtering pen. And look what became of her and her children! Over there, you can still see what is left of her loom. Witgern, hear me please! I cannot farm and bear children on a battlefield. I cannot stay here trussed like kine, never knowing the day of slaughter. I . . . I must go to the gate and *meet* the slaughterer—"

"Poor child. Of course you think so now—"

"You know me little, Witgern. If you will not heed my heart, perhaps you'll listen to the judgment of the gods. As the raid began, I fell into my fate." She recounted the tale of the Ash Grove slaying, finding it easier to tell than she expected—all fear of Hylda's oracle had been burned away in the fire. "I am meant to be 'a living shield.' . . . What is that but a shield maiden, consecrated to unmarried life in the service of the god? What I will, Witgern, is what the gods intend. So it was said, too, of Baldemar in his youth. The sign of a shield maiden, all say, is that she cannot sleep on settled land. It is the truth, Witgern. . . . There is a fatal restiveness in the heart. . . ."

Witgern dropped his head into his hands. "You cannot do this to me!"

As he spoke the words, he realized she very well could. They had not yet taken the oath and shared the horn. The cursed marriage she could wriggle out of, without violating ancient law. And as for Baldemar, when had he ever denied her what she wanted? It was not so much that he indulged this daughter who for so long was his only child; it was that uncanny *complicity* between them—what one wanted always somehow seemed to echo what the other had already planned. She was his heir in far more than name.

Nor did it surprise him as much as it might; her family tended to produce warlike women. A maternal aunt, Freydis of the Swift Spear, lived as a shield maiden, having dedicated her life to vengeance after the Romans massacred all her children.

But he knew he must mount a vigorous fight or he would despise himself as a weakling. "You shame me and you bring grave insult to my family. For certain, Baldemar will not allow me to be used so! I warn you, I mean to bring a complaint before him!"

He knew at once he made a grave mistake. In her eyes an iron gate clanged shut.

"I thought better of you, Witgern. I am not a dog to be threatened with a stick. And should anyone force me, in your family or mine, I will take my own life."

Witgern's insides were a swamp of misery. He was stripped of everything—the eminence of her mother's mothers and her father's fathers, their rich wealth in fields and cattle, the glow that would be about his name should he win such a wife—and he was left only with the shame, the throbbing shame. In that moment he would have welcomed the death sentence of Baldemar.

"Very well, then," he said, getting stiffly to his feet. "I will be humiliated before the Companions. I will become 'the wretched Baldemar's daughter spurned.' Make me a laughingstock. What is it to you?"

"I would be no fit wife! I would be a madwoman! But you do not care over-much do you? As long as I appeared to be a fit wife? As long as your praises are sung when the feast is done? I praise this disaster, then, if only because it brought forth your true nature before I bound myself to you!"

"Curses on you and on all life!"

Witgern spun round, kicking up a spray of dirt and stones, and strode off into the pines. Auriane watched his retreating back, feeling suddenly isolated in winter cold while insidious doubt crept in, beckoning, beckoning with promise of a life of harvest feasts, warmth overflowing, fellowship about the loom. But it is not so, she reminded herself. The promise of warmth is a cruel sham. There is no settled ground. Who loves me must love what I love, honor and freedom, freedom from . . . the dark armed menace beyond the pines.

Another young Companion, the amiable red-bearded Thorgild, helped her rise, and the whole party of them accompanied her to the village, leaving Witgern to his mortification and rage. They were sharply curious about this rift between Witgern and the daughter of their chief, but custom demanded they ask no questions.

Witgern paused beneath the gently swaying body of the Companion who had hanged himself.

No one must know she has done this to me, no one must know. . . .

He considered taking his own life then, regarding the dead man with horror mingled with envy. Shivering, he cut his own horse's reins, knotted them and threw them over a branch. *No. I cannot. I've lived well, I deserve a better death.*

He clung to the corpse's ankles and cried bitterly. After a time one of the half-wild spotted dogs approached, challenging him with threatening barks. And Witgern was seized with an idea, borne off passionately by what seemed the one solution to his dilemma.

There are injuries that disqualify a man forever from making a noble marriage. *If I could manage it so all men thought I suffered some accident, and that it was the Fates who spurned me, not Baldemar's daughter.* . . .

Blindness. But in only one eye. No priestess or priest will join a maid of rank to a man half blind—it is too ill-omened. The bride and groom must be whole at the time of their union, or the match will breed only disaster. Yes. I'll say to Maragin, Thorgild, Coniaric and the others that one of the dogs got me.

He lured the spotted dog close with a ration of dried venison. When the beast came close enough he slashed at it with his sword and finally cut its throat. *There. This would confirm the truth of his story.*

Then, after an awful moment of hesitation, he pierced his right eye. The blood was rich and warm. His eye was full of fire. He sank to his knees, stifling a cry. But the agony was small, he thought, beside the shame he would have felt at being publicly cast off by Baldemar's daughter.

• • •

In every village and grove across their lands, the people cried out for vengeance. By the time Witgern and his party returned to the southern camp of the Chattian army, the warriors gathered there were like a half-broken horse ready to bolt at the barest touch of the whip. Why did Baldemar not mount the attack while the blood of their kinsmen was still fresh on the ground? Four days had elapsed since the raid, and still Baldemar remained mysteriously quiet, keeping to his tent, making no move to lead them against the raiders. The camp turned many anxious glances toward the great black tent of aurochs hides that was Baldemar's. How could he remain passive in the face of this monstrous attack on himself? Perhaps age eroded the sharpness of his mind—Baldemar *was* seven harsh winters older than Wido. Or perhaps grief had hamstrung his will to fight.

The Chattian army was camped on the wind-protected slope of Sheepshead Hill, a site uncomfortably close to the Roman border. Because they expected war at once, none dispersed after the last campaign; rather, the camp was swollen with new arrivals. Whole families crowded in; geese, pigs, goats and sturdy blond children darted among the haphazardly spaced tents. The Chattian army, though more disciplined than most tribal hordes, still would hardly have been termed an army by Roman reckoning; it was too disorderly in its habits and too impetuous in its aims. They were more a loose collection of warriors grouped by clan, each seeking individual glory. They marched and they camped in no order, some sleeping under the sky, others living under lean-tos made of their cloaks, men temporarily melted into one in time of need by the fire of a Baldemar or the promises of quick wealth of a Wido. When the summer raiding was done and the spoil divided, they retreated to their farms and their festivals and feasting and brawling. They had one feature, however, for which the Romans praised them: The Chattians alone possessed an organized system of food supply. A train of provisions carts followed the army on the march; these were stocked, managed and defended by a party of battle-trained women from one group of families who inherited this duty from their mothers and grandmothers. A woman called Romilda was chief over them now. Other tribal armies foraged and looted as they marched and were forced to retreat when the food supply dwindled. The Chattians' grain supply, coupled with their readiness to give strict obedience to their chiefs—another custom rare in the north—made them a formidable foe to Roman and barbarian alike.

On his first day Witgern wasted no time in crossing the path of Geisar, First Priest of Wodan, who officiated at important marriages. Witgern now wore over his eye a fine-looking black patch covered with silken cloth. As he expected, Geisar promptly declared him unfit for marriage to Auriane because he was maimed. Witgern listened to this with hushed sadness, all the while despising himself for his playacting.

Witgern expected in spite of everything that Baldemar would summon him at once—he *was* first at the scene. He thought Baldemar would be eager to question him. When he did not, Witgern began to imagine Baldemar *did* hold him to account. By the second day Witgern convinced himself Baldemar meant to condemn him to death. He was isolated with his accumulating fears and only dimly aware of the increasing chaos all about him.

When seven days passed, the whole of the camp began to raise the driving chant to the sky: *"Give us vengeance! Baldemar, lead us out!"* as they milled about, shaking polished weapons above their heads, colliding with the roaming children and animals. By late afternoon Witgern saw an alarming sight: Wido mounted one of the provisions carts and began haranguing the throng, intending to take advantage of Baldemar's inactivity. Witgern watched dispiritedly from the back of the crowd, close enough to see Wido's crone's chin jutting out and the energetic chopping gestures of his hands. Some of Wido's words reached Witgern's ears.

"The gods know a man's end before he knows it himself and they send us signs! When Wodan takes a man's mother and takes also his son . . ." Witgern heard before Wido's voice was obscured by a new outburst of chanting.

That viper tongue wags as always, Witgern thought. But what was disturbing was that on this day the people seemed to be listening closely to him, as if Wido were *not* a cattle thief with the bones of murdered guests beneath his hall. Normally, when Wido ranted on about Baldemar, he attracted a miserable collection of malcontents. But on this day a good half of the army—a mixture of the poor swordless farmers, the wealthier men with longswords at their sides, and even some of Baldemar's Companions— pressed close, eyes intent upon Wido.

Lust for vengeance, Witgern concluded, has robbed them of their wits.

Witgern fought his way closer and saw a thing that alarmed him more. In the short time he had been in the camp, Wido seemed to have attracted a good hundred or so new men to his own force of Companions. They were arrayed behind him now, dressed similarly in dark brown tunics and marten skin cloaks. Among them he saw some with faces marked in woad-blue with the Chaucian tribal sign, some with the torques of the Bructeres, others with hair pulled tightly into Suebian knots — and he realized these were men lured from neighboring tribes. Where did Wido get the gold to pay them all? The only honorable way was through raiding, and Wido was too slothful to organize frequent forays — he was more the hyena, picking at the kills of others.

And still throughout this day, Baldemar summoned none of his Companions. The great black tent on the hilltop was not without its visitors, however. Witgern saw a steady stream of thralls, poor farmers, foreign traders, brigands and wanderers ushered there for questioning. But what did Baldemar need to know, Witgern wondered angrily, other than that the raiders were Hermundures?

Baldemar, you are making a mortal mistake. Do you not hear them crying out for you? You will lose them forever.

"Every moment we delay shames us more!" Wido's voice rose to an ecstatic screech.

"Hail Wido, greatest of chiefs!" Wido's Companions bellowed in response.

Witgern slept fitfully that night, trying to stop his ears. The shouting and chanting had become feasting and celebration. He wondered if the common lot of people were half mad already, just awaiting the coming of someone a little madder than themselves to ignite them to frenzy. He expected by dawn to hear Wido proclaimed a living god.

But just as the night sky turned leaden gray, the summons finally came. Witgern was to report to Baldemar's tent at once.

It is death. I am certain of it.

He arrayed himself in his finest war gear, splashed well water on his face, and tried not to let his mind clutch at life. He told himself the shuddering of his hands was due to the sharp cold of dawn.

Perhaps my ghost can serve his dead mother and murdered child.

He saw that Wido had resumed his fevered shouting along with the first cocks' crows. The rascal must have slept in that cart, Witgern thought.

I pray Baldemar does not speak of Auriane—but, of course, he will. Will he guess I maimed myself? Remember that wretched saying, *"Where you see but a footprint, Baldemar sees the whole man."* Somehow, he'll *know*. Curses on Helle.

As Witgern made his way along the irregular avenue between the common tents, his gaze on that great forbidding tent atop the hill, a hairy hand reached from behind a deerhide lean-to, snapped round his arm and pulled him to a halt.

"Hail, friend! If you're still anyone's friend. You've abandoned everyone. And how come he's summoned you and none of us?"

"Sigwulf, you mead-soaked mountebank—let me be!" The very sight of Sigwulf was a taunt. *He has his pick of the wellborn daughters. His hall will crawl with children, his casks will teem with mead while mine will be empty.*

Sigwulf was coarsely built with muscular features, a great irregular nose that looked like some clay model partly smashed with a fist, and toughened skin that seemed to have weathered as many storms as the hide of his tent. His tangled black beard threatened to break any comb not fashioned of iron. The bones of some small bird he recently consumed clung to it now. Those black eyes always simmered at low heat, ready to burst into flames at the barest insult. All said his courage approached madness. He was a creature of impulse rather than reflection, and for this reason Witgern rarely had much to say to him.

Sigwulf squinted at Witgern. "By Helle, Witgern, I don't know whether to clap you on the back or sacrifice a horse to you!" Sigwulf grinned a too-broad grin that begged Witgern to acknowledge his cleverness.

Witgern greeted the remark with a bored glare. In the last day he had heard too many tepid witticisms likening his face to that of Wodan, their one-eyed god. "If you have words for me," Witgern said sourly, "say them."

"Help us! That's all I have to say. The burden's on you alone. Tell him the Weasel's shamelessly courting them day and night. Tell him his men are clamoring for a word with him. Must I sell myself into slavery so he'll summon me?" Sigwulf pulled Witgern closer. The smell of sour mead made Witgern want to retch. "Did you know Geisar betrayed us? That priest can't hear the god anymore for the clink of silver. He stripped the furs from our backs."

"The god's gift? Well, tell me, how much?"

"A thousand head of cattle, a thousand of sheep, and a thousand rings of beaten gold, all to be dumped into the Rhine. The gold's for Hertha, I suppose. Never did a mother do her son so ill."

"You're drunk. Watch that impious tongue, I say—before someone rips it out." Witgern half turned, then muttered to himself, "Son of a black dog. Wido could lose all his cattle to sickness and all his kin, and Geisar would require of him one hen, one clay vessel, and a bone pin. We are ruined."

"Witgern, I am sorry for your plight, truly," Sigwulf said then. Though sincerely meant, the words came out as a mocking imitation of frankness—Sigwulf would rather roast on a spit than show gentleness. "I never coveted all the love he gives you, you must know it, and I do not even *want* his precious daughter. I promise I'll refuse her if he offers her to me."

With a mighty effort that left him trembling, Witgern restrained himself from delivering a blow to Sigwulf's face. He said softly, "If you've a wise tongue in your head, you'll shut your mouth about that."

They then heard one startling horn blast from the base of the hill, followed by crashing arhythmic music rudely reverberating through the dawn hush of the valley. Witgern straightened and looked down at the base of the hill. "Curses on Helle!" he cried out.

Just beyond the haphazardly spaced tents of the Companions, Wido had mounted a horse and hoisted up a boar standard. Right before the eyes of Baldemar's Companions he was forming up the army. Men were pulling down tents, hastily covering firepits over with earth, loading pack horses with war gear and gathering up spears, all the while shouting out insults to the Hermundures and striking swords against shields, a noxious noise meant to drive off evil spirits sent by the enemy. The men were brilliant with the colors of war in their fittings of burnished bronze, their blood-colored cloaks, their wickerwork shields splashed with raw yellow and blue paint. Witgern looked quickly to the narrow neck of the valley and saw that even Romilda's wagons were positioned to move.

He left Sigwulf abruptly, filled with a wild sadness that made him forget his own circumstances. *This is no fit end for you, Baldemar! Stop him!*

Witgern hesitated before Baldemar's tent, intimidated at first by its brooding bulk. It seemed the spirits of night lingered about it still, defying the sallow light of morning. The cat skull mounted atop the center pole seemed alive. *Die, lying coward,* its cat spirit

seemed to spit at him. Gloomy clouds gathered behind the tent; the
tension of coming rain was like withheld tears. He saw the lynx
skin that draped the door was ominously dropped in place—
always the entrance to this tent was left open, a symbol of
Baldemar's readiness to hold council with any man of his
Companions who came forward.

About the tent nine honor guards were posted, huge fists
clutching upright spears, wolfskins draped carelessly over their
shoulders so they appeared half man, half beast. Witgern greeted
them with a raised hand. He took one more moment to steady his
mind, then he pulled the lynx skin aside and entered.

At first he saw only darkness and the light of two smoking
torches.

Then, between them, he discerned the darker form of a man.
The twin flames seemed to cringe and grow small before the
massive silence of the shadowy man sitting there.

A hand rose up from the smoke and motioned him closer.

He moved forward warily. Baldemar was to him a weathered
mountain, stubborn and monumental, a fortress that crowned his
horizon all his life. If that fortress was broken by sorrowing, he
was not sure he wanted to see it.

Gradually Witgern saw the outline of a kingly tangled mane of
hair, and a chieftain's cloak draped with casual majesty over the
high seat. Then he saw those predatory eyes, steady as stars on a
calm night, shining not with malice but with acute sight. At
Baldemar's side could just be seen the firelit gems on the hilt of
his sword, a weapon as celebrated as the man. Baldemar was
dressed and armed as always for receiving emissaries. Behind him,
hanging from a tentpole, gleamed the great rectangular shield of a
primus pilus, or First Centurion, the highest-ranking Roman he
had taken in battle—it hung there wherever he raised his tent
because it amused Baldemar to irritate Roman messengers with
the sight of it.

Witgern's courage drained away.

*Even if you let me live, my life is stillborn. I am a ghost in the
flesh, killed by my own foolishness. Break the silence, I beg you,
and condemn me!*

But Baldemar examined him unhurriedly, and Witgern felt those
bright, acute eyes plucking at him, stripping him naked not only of
clothes but of all words that cloaked, and even of bone and skin.
His most deeply buried thought, he was certain, wriggled ugly and
alive on the ground beneath those scouring eyes.

Finally Baldemar spoke. "Witgern, my boy, that grim look would take the grin off a skull!" The voice as always was lusty with aggressive humor, a rough, exploring voice that invited challenge.

Witgern then spoke his prepared words, hoping humility would save his life. "Baldemar, I greet you. You see how I am maimed. I cannot live on alms. And I cannot live away from battle. I came too late upon . . . the disaster. My life is cursed. I will die now, if you give me leave."

As he spoke, something in Baldemar's look made the words sound thin and shallow, made him feel another had put them in his mouth. *Who? Why? Am I not speaking properly?* What is it about Baldemar that makes a man question all those things that otherwise he never thinks to question?

Baldemar laughed as at a good joke at a feast and slapped a knee. "At last! I've finally found a failing in Witgern the Good!" Witgern took a step backward, disoriented and bewildered.

"Greed!" Baldemar continued. "He gobbles up all the blame and shame. Save some for your fellows. You will die *now,* you say? At *my* order? You insult me. Wido is out *there,* not in here."

"I—I mean no insult. None! And, happily, you have brought up Wido. I beg you, for the sake of all of us, go and put him in his place! As we speak, he is making off with the army, leading off the expedition rightfully yours!"

To Witgern's surprise this caused not even the barest ripple on the surface of Baldemar's calm. Perhaps, Witgern thought, he's just gone quietly mad, and I am first witness of its visible effects.

"Is he? Wido is a noisy man of small deeds, and he does not interest me now. You interest me more." Baldemar leaned forward, squinted, then frowned. He took up one of the torches and held it close to Witgern as if to better see him.

"Shadow," Baldemar said at last, looking perplexed.

"I . . . I do not understand . . ."

The dark gemstones set in the eagle brooch that fastened Baldemar's cloak flashed warningly. "Shadow," he repeated. "That's his markings, I'd know them anywhere, I never saw a dog similarly marked, brown and white speckles with a black toe."

Witgern felt his whole body seize up like a tightened fist. He prayed he would not disgrace himself and faint. That cursed amulet they'd coaxed him to make from the paw of that cursed dog! He'd gone along with it to make it all look more natural. He had utterly forgotten he still wore it about his neck.

"Shadow was my hound, Witgern. And he didn't bite. Witgern, you killed my dog."

Sweat rolled down Witgern's chest. His throat froze; his whole body slowly became numb.

Curses on Helle. I killed his pet hound. What next? Did ever any man look more the utter fool?

"You clever rascal, you weren't bitten at all, were you?" To Witgern's immense relief he saw a flicker of humor in Baldemar's eye.

Witgern smiled sheepishly. "Where one man sees but a paw, Baldemar sees the whole dog."

"All those qualities and wit too! It's incredible. And it is fortunate for you I care more for men than for dogs. Now tell me what really happened. Out with it, quickly!"

"Your daughter refuses to marry me. I . . . thought the dog was wild and tried to make it look as if—"

"Stop there, I've caught your meaning. I *know,* Witgern. I have messages from Auriane and her mother every day. You should have trusted *me* to save the honor of your name. Then poor Shadow could have lived to a venerable old age. Think no more on it—this secret shall remain yours and mine."

"You mean not to cast me off then?"

"For the eye? I think not. Your soul still sees with two eyes. Just keep a good grip on the one you have left."

"You are most nobly generous."

"Witgern, you returned by much the same route the raiders used. Did any of your men see traces of revelry and rejoicing—I mean abandoned campsites where they may have drunk and partaken of some of their booty?"

The noise outside became so great Witgern was forced to wait before he replied. The chant *"Wido, son of Wodan! Live forever!"* rose over all other cries.

Witgern stifled a second plea. Baldemar did not care. This was like watching a man who does not cry out when a torch is held to his face.

"They left less trace than a fleeing hawk."

Baldemar nodded slowly and sat back, eyes intent, his expression showing this confirmed a thing he suspected.

"The Hermundures on the scent of booty are like flies around honey," Baldemar continued. "You can get them all at one swat. How come our people felled so few of them?"

Witgern had no answer.

"And is it not strange," Baldemar continued, "that this raid which so conveniently impoverishes me comes at the very time when Wido and the Roman governor are pressing for that odious marriage—which among other things would also restore me to wealth?"

"She said the same! Thorgild said Auriane spoke the very same thought when they helped her to the village."

"Did she!" Baldemar's eye was fired with pride. "That alerts me the question's a good one!" Witgern started, missing the next few words, for in that instant it almost seemed Auriane looked through Baldemar's eyes, and he reflected that it often seemed they had one soul: he was its gnarled roots, firmly gripping the earth, and she, the questing green shoots, supple, quick growing.

". . . that Wido's cattle were not driven off, nor was his hall burned, though it lay more directly in their path. They came for *me*, Witgern."

"It's utterly impossible that Wido could be in league with the Hermundures. Serpent that he is, still he has Chattian blood in his veins."

"Hasty words are as deadly as any blade, Witgern. Be careful, nothing here is as it seems." He looked away. *"They came for me,"* he repeated softly, his eyes brilliant and dangerous in the torchlight. But broad good cheer returned with startling speed. Baldemar's grin was a rough embrace. "My boy, do not get settled here! You're the best man for it, so I mean for you to leave at once at the head of a company of twenty-five men I've chosen from the Companions. First they will rebuild my hall—I wish all to think that their true purpose. But afterward you will fetch my daughter from the lodge where Thrusnelda has her hidden and take her to the place of the Midsummer Assembly. The danger is great—if Wido learns the route of her journey, I have no doubt he would lay an ambush for her. Never has he wanted anything so much as he wants her to be bound to one of his sons. Witgern, if you get her to the Assembly healthy and whole for the day she meets her groom, there is no favor I will not grant you."

"What?!" Blood rushed to his face. "Marriage, for her? But she refuses! Who then will she marry? Sigwulf?"

"Sigwulf! Ha! Is that what you think! I'd never see her married to a man with such a rabid aversion to water. If a dog shakes itself dry near Sigwulf, he counts it a bath!"

"Not Sigwulf. Who then? A better man than I?" Witgern felt the helpless anger of a declawed beast.

"Yes, I would say so. A better man than us all."

"I am not good with riddles."

"Jealousy certainly dulls your blade. She named him herself, she is to be the bride of Wodan. By Helle, who else would she marry on the night of the Assembly? I am not immortal, my boy. You know she must be pledged to god or man before battle takes me."

"So you and she decided a *god* it should be. . . . I understand, and yet I do not."

"Noble Witgern. You've too much respect to name the source of your confusion, so I'll name it. You've no doubt heard the gossip that Athelinda will ever be unable to bear more children. How can he willingly deprive the family of further issue, you wonder. It is the greatest sacrifice I can give, is it not? *That* is indeed my aim. I will give the god a greater thing than what he took from me! He took my son. So I give to him all hope of heirs. That should satisfy heaven and earth, should it not?"

Now Witgern did see signs of sorrowing in Baldemar's face. His eyes seemed to look fixedly, imploringly, on the dead, and he sat too solemnly still, as if he were before some altar in a sacred grove.

"And as for her prodigal deed in the Ash Grove—Witgern, it is a sign of battle luck so rare the She-Wolf had not yet suckled Rome when last it happened among us. So you see, the god cast a lustful eye on her already, before I ever conceived of this divine marriage."

Witgern listened in sad, bewildered agreement, thinking: Baldemar commands even the Fates, for they have so neatly worked his will. The old fox. The clever beneficent fox. They are alike. Now they'll hunt together forever, Romans instead of hares and deer. Always he has wanted her near, daring what he dares, living as he lives. That is the sort of immortality that pleases him, not the fleshly sort. He would see his spirit gallop on, head up in the wind. Yes, there is the same wild horse spirit in them both.

"Battling Rome is like carrying water in a sieve," Baldemar went on. "Perhaps *she* will be the one to arrest the plague. Sometimes I think her spirit is mine, purified. What I do with might, she does with innocence. And she has no notion of it, none whatever, no more than the doe of the field. She might slay a dragon with innocence. . . ."

The cry of a battle horn rose up like a high wind.

"Wido!" Witgern whispered, half turning round. "Do you not

hear him? Did I not tell you? Baldemar, I beg you listen! They are leaving!"

"Why yes, I do hear it. You are right. Wido is indeed leaving."

"I do not understand you! Your Companions are leaving, too! Did you know twenty more deserted you just this morning?"

"Twenty-three, to be precise," Baldemar replied. "When a tree's given a light shake, the rottenest fruit always falls first."

"I can abide this no longer! Every moment we delay punishing the Hermundures shames us!" At these words Witgern felt his face redden. He had not meant to say this; it was too close to direct criticism. And had he not earlier heard Wido speak nearly the same words?

But to his surprise Baldemar was not angry; his eye grew reflective. "A more intriguing question is one you did not ask—where is Wido's wealth coming from? All those new Companions gathered so quickly, all those fresh foreign faces. How does he provide them all with longswords when he scarcely leads a raid?"

"Curses, I do not know. The hoard, I suppose, the hoard that he always claims he found buried. . . . I beg you! Stop him! Why do you not fight for yourself! If you will not, then I will!" Witgern wheeled around and began to stride off, his sword drawn.

"Halt!" His voice rang out like iron striking iron. Witgern halted in mid-step. "You're an overeager pup that needs a tight leash," Baldemar said sharply. "Turn round."

Witgern slowly obeyed. "Precisely," Baldemar continued, his tone casual and expansive once more. "A hoard. A *generations*-old hoard, he claims! Well, I've had some of it brought to me. Those coins have images of Nero on them, *Nero,* by all the gods! What does Wido take me for? It's a fool that assumes others are fools."

"You are too quick for me on these matters, Baldemar, but I know my enemy!"

"Do you really? Witgern, we were *not* attacked by Hermundures."

"What? *What?*" Witgern stared at him blankly, numbed and senseless as if thrown from a horse. "Not attacked by—but—but with all respect, they were seen! They were seen by many!"

"And what is even *more* interesting is that Wido, that scoundrel, *knows* it."

"This is beyond belief."

"If Wido goes anywhere, he's leading his men in the wrong direction. But don't worry over Wido sneaking off with the army.

Romilda won't follow him. If he goes anywhere, he fights without food. Wido won't fight without food."

"But already she has drawn up her carts! All twenty of them!"

"Of course. I asked her to do that. Watch what happens if they try to go past her. You must have more faith in our people. There are enough of us left yet who will not be slaves. You may leave me now."

Once more out in the thin morning light, Witgern saw a dismaying scene in the valley below: The mass of the army was sluggishly making its way through the high sedgegrass to the valley's narrow opening, where Romilda waited at the head of her winding train of provisions carts. The tribesmen's rage at the enemy was a dark, musky scent on the air. Several hundred lagged behind, still not ready to give up on Baldemar; their hoarse cries, "Baldemar! Lead us out!" had taken on the sound of a captive begging for his life.

Witgern felt joy and hope drain out all at once, like mead from a tipped horn. This, then, was the end.

Witgern gave Sigwulf a terse account of the meeting with Baldemar. "Either his mind's going," Sigwulf said, "or his vision has become as acute as the gods'. Not Hermundures, indeed. What were they then? Wood sprites?"

As they watched, Wido's mount burst into a canter, carrying him to the front of the line. Only Wido, his two sons, and a picked force of five Companions who served as his bodyguards were on horseback; the common warriors, as always, moved and fought on foot. Wido sat rigidly upright on his horse, his hands high on the reins, his narrow chin thrust forward, determined all should see him in his moment of hard-won glory.

"A lot of good you did," Sigwulf muttered. Witgern ignored him.

Suddenly scattered cries of "What goes? What has happened?" came from the warriors who trailed the march. Witgern saw only that those in front of the march were coming to a clumsy halt. Wido's horse reared, nearly pitching him off. Those behind crowded into those ahead as if the river of men had been dammed. *Had some impassable barrier sprung out of the ground?* Witgern tore off his cloak and climbed partway up a leaning pine. And then he understood it.

"He's got them!" he shouted out gaily. "Hail Baldemar! He's got them!"

Romilda barred their way with the provisions carts.

At a signal from Romilda, all thirty carts came together, those in front speedily backing up, the ones behind moving forward until the gaps between them were closed. It was a quick, precise maneuver that must have been foreplanned. Witgern saw the women in them rise up all at once, holding their spears horizontally across their chests in a gesture that meant "Do not pass!"

The threat was not a physical one—there were but two hundred or so women in the carts, some mere girls, others with infants slung across their backs, and their spears were no more than fire-hardened sticks. What dampened the men's battle frenzy was the women's readiness to die where they stood. Each forbidding face promised that should anyone attempt to force a way past, they would have to maim or kill, and this was unthinkable, not only because the blood-price for the murder of a woman was twice that of a man, but because they believed that in women there resided a fearsome holiness, a power over forces dark and light that was a mystery not to be trespassed upon. Nor would they seek a way around this obstruction: The venture would be ill-omened without Romilda's blessing.

Later, Witgern would hear around the campfires what Wido shouted at the implacable Romilda while she met his eyes fearlessly: "Lovers of the Hermundures! I trust you like their foul embraces as well as your husbands'! What favors has Baldemar given you for this! Traitors! Nidings! Hags from Helle!"

Wido then galloped up the rise to Baldemar's tent, flanked by his two sons and five Companions. He pulled his mount to a rearing halt and with casual grace unsheathed his sword.

Wido is a sight to terrify the steadiest heart, Witgern thought.

Wido had removed his boar-tusk helmet, and his hair, matted to his skull with bear's fat, had been loosened by the wind so that it hung free in coiled clumps that made it seem serpents wriggled from his head. His eyes were wild and cruel. Sharp, straight teeth showed beneath a scraggly untrimmed mustache. A bloody bandage on his right arm where a sword wound had been dressed came half unwound and flapped free. Wido himself had the look of small vicious rodents active at night: prominent nose, negligible mouth, gleaming black eyes. He was not massive in size but flexible and strong. His colorless skin and sunken eyes gave him a curious drained appearance that Baldemar's Companions liked to attribute to the sexual insatiability of his wife, Grimelda, who was heavier than him by half, had many murders to her credit and was never without her axe.

"Baldemar!" Wido cried out. "Thief of glory! Serpent that crawls by night! Crawl out of there and order that hellhag to let us through!"

The better part of Wido's Companions, some of whom followed at a run, began to collect about him now. Wido's younger son, Ullrik, sat a horse at Wido's left. He was a youth of sixteen; in features and size he favored his father. It was said he bayed at the moon and that his first kill had been carefully arranged for him. But for the eminence of his father, he would have been cast aside as a simpleton. He had a vulnerable face, eyes that had learned not to trust, and was visibly unnerved by the hostility of Baldemar's Companions.

The other son was Odberht, who was nearer twenty, and of him it was said when the Fates formed him, they gathered up all that was most brutish in both parents, blended these traits, then increased them in fivefold measure. In features and body he favored Grimelda: He had his mother's bovine bulk, her coarse, dark blond hair, her crude, rounded shoulders that seemed they could take an ox yoke, and her thick square face in which a cherubic mouth seemed almost lost. The balefire that flickered in Grimelda's eyes was present in Odberht's as well—at feasts they liked to drink together from the gilded skull of a wayfarer who had the poor judgment to take shelter too close to one of Grimelda's prized milch cows and so had become one of the many victims of her axe. While Odberht had gotten a good share of Wido's sensitivity to ridicule, he had received a smaller portion of his father's cunning, and none of his sense of balance. Nothing about Odberht was fine or small; his hands as he guided the horse moved in brutish sweeps; his stout legs seemed ready to squeeze the breath out of his too-small mount. Two seeresses at different times had told him with great confidence, *"You shall not die by the sword."* Odberht took this to mean he would not be slain in battle at all, and this made him recklessly brave: He took his first man at fifteen, and had already begun forming a small retinue of his own, leading secret raids across the borders and harassing the weaker tribes with whom the Chattians had treaties of friendship.

Odberht grinned at Witgern to let him know he approved of his loss of an eye. Wido's older son had perfected a sort of bullying rudeness all his own that threatened to punish you if you took notice of it, while promising to mock you if you did not. Witgern met his gaze with a look that was bold and blank, which irritated Odberht so much he spat loudly on the ground.

Baldemar emerged at once. He stood in solemn silence, regarding Wido; his gaze was a sharp, subtle weapon aimed at a vital place. The sight of him brought relief to his Companions—in the lift of his head, in that proud wariness, there was as ever something of the indomitable wild horse, unaware of its rough beauty while never forgetting its strength. Grief was a fire Baldemar would use to consume his enemies; it would never burn him to ash.

Wido had expected to see a crippled spirit; to cover his unease, he spat noisily on the ground. Witgern smiled, amused, realizing Odberht's spitting was a quirk copied from his father.

"Friends!" Baldemar said. That voice commanded immediate silence. "Every man of us lost treasures in that raid, and mothers and fathers and daughters and sons. How is it Wido lost nothing and no one?" Baldemar allowed himself an overlong pause, letting the people's impatience gather; instinctively he knew how to heighten attention. Then he trumpeted: "It is because he removed all to safety on the day before!"

The words fell like an axe blow on the neck of one who sleeps. The silence was vast and full of terror and awe. When the crowd stirred again, murmurs of amazement traveled through the throng, swift as wind-blown ripples over water. Surely collusion with the enemy was too great an act of treachery even for Wido. But it was just as inconceivable to them that Baldemar would level such a charge without cause.

Wido was a master of concealing feeling; he threw back his head and let out a careless staccato burst of laughter. But the men were quick to notice Odberht's hands shivered visibly on the reins, and Ullrik looked steadily down, as if he believed that if he met no one's eye, then no one would see him.

"Of course, he speaks so!" Wido called out with a grand sweep of his hands. "Nothing would gladden his heart more than my destruction!" Witgern reluctantly admired Wido's calm. "Who will listen to the lies of a bitter, wasted old man, envious because his war luck has fled, a man jealous of me because even his own Companions are wisely deserting him for my camp? Baldemar, if *I* were your dam I, too, would have leapt into the flames—it's a kinder fate than watching you hobble to your end!"

Wido laughed again, but now his laughter seemed to rattle in silence, a lone pebble in an empty pot. Grim faces searched Wido's, then looked inquiringly to Baldemar.

Undaunted, Wido continued. "The property he says was moved," he said, indicating Baldemar, "was moved by *him!* What of those twelve mares, you rogue? You borrowed them, I suppose, and mean to give them back."

Baldemar's look said clearly: The charge is too ridiculous to deny.

Then Baldemar continued serenely as if Wido had not spoken. "Wido, before the Holy Ones and the immortal gods, I charge you with foreknowledge of that raid. And I charge you with detaining me here by design with a false dispute over spoil—so as to lay my family open to attack!"

A sound like a single great groan passed through the throng. It was the heart-stricken sound of people who did not want to see what they beheld, of one who comes upon a whitened skeleton in a moonlit glade and knows it is the missing kinsman.

For Baldemar left Wido no choice but to challenge him to single battle. If Wido did not, the words would stick to him forever like some poisonous mud, and his spirit would slowly sicken and die.

Wido's eyes burned hot as a kiln. "Not only is your fate blighted—not only have you become useless as pot scrapings—you've gone staring mad, Baldemar, moonstruck as a loon!" His voice rose to a modulated shriek. "My blade's long been thirsty for your blood. I beg the gods for a chance to cut that lying throat!"

A strident voice from among Wido's Companions cried out: "Trial by combat!" The cry was quickly taken up by all who loved Wido. Many of the men most recently aligned with him had never seen Baldemar in battle and readily assumed trial by combat would favor Wido, the younger man.

The clamor continued until Geisar, First Priest of Wodan, and Sigreda, who was to succeed him, hurried into their midst and raised their staffs for silence. Geisar standing beside Sigreda was often likened to the dying oak overlooking the young tree in first flower. The old priest's face was the petrified record of some long-spent fit of fury. His body was so warped and wasted by age his neck was thrust forward almost horizontally; wispy white hair fell like a mane. He had milky blue eyes that frightened children—the left eye slewed to the side, as if he strove always to catch a tribal offender unawares. Sigreda was raven-haired and young, with a delicately rounded face polished and smooth as an apple, a mouth that was shapely and cruel, and half-shut eyes that were curtains dropped on mystery. Geisar had great authority because he had lived so long, and Sigreda, because she had once been apprenticed to Ramis—the people chose to forget that after a year Ramis drove her off as unfit. Witgern trusted her no better than Geisar.

Gradually they were obeyed and the crowd grew silent. "What say you to this?" Geisar said in his belligerent whine, looking first at Baldemar.

"If I must fight to prove the truth of my words, I must. I will meet him here, in this place, tomorrow at dawn."

Witgern cast down his eyes in misery. Baldemar was in fine battle form, but surely he could not hope to equal Wido in stamina. It was difficult to imagine the world without Baldemar in it.

"That is satisfactory," Wido replied. "I agree to rid the world of you here, tomorrow at dawn. And when you are dead, you may rest easily in your heavenly abode, knowing your fetching daughter has been taken into my hall. What a pity. Had you given her to me already, we would be kin . . . and your life would be saved." Wido grinned and turned to look at his sons. "Odberht, Ullrik, can you decide between you who shall have the maid without coming to blows over it?"

Sigreda gave Wido a sharp look. "Just say whether or not you agree, Wido." Witgern thought: She is acting a part. She does not want anyone to know how much she, too, wants Wido victorious. But why? What has Wido given them?

"Baldemar!" cried out a man of his own Companions. "Even given your words are true, Wido did not act alone. Why do you not lead us out at once to punish the Hermundures?" This brought a chorus of voices raised in assent.

Baldemar responded by nodding to one of the Companions who stood guard round his tent. The Companions disappeared within, then emerged bearing six native spears bound together with cord. Baldemar took them and held them aloft. "These spears I had brought from six villages where the raiders struck. Any one of you, come forward and look. On not *one* of them is a village mark or a name-sign. One madman among the Hermundures might have forgotten to mark his weapon so he could proclaim his kill—but six, at all different villages? And this is but one of many things they did that Hermundures surely would not."

Everywhere Witgern heard murmurs and saw looks of puzzled

alarm. Then he looked quickly at Wido and was certain he saw in one instant a start of terror in those small bright eyes. What did he know of this? More than any of them, Witgern was quite certain.

"When I learn *who* attacked us, I will lead us out. If you would know it at once, ask him!" Baldemar declared, pointing at Wido. "Perhaps he will consent to share his great knowledge of the enemy with his own people!"

Odberht could no longer keep silence. "Serpent tongue! You prepared those spears yourself. You'll not long outlive this lie!"

Odberht's small bay stallion nervously tossed its head and Baldemar saw for the first time the man mounted behind him among Wido's foremost Companions, a man who seemed somewhat remote from the passions expressed all about. His arms were bare of rings; he had neatly combed straw-colored hair, a russet beard, and tantalizingly familiar faded blue eyes. Baldemar frowned, struggling with a memory.

"You there," Baldemar said. "Come forward. I would have a look at you."

"Stay there!" Wido ordered the Companion. "Trickster! Get off from us!"

But Baldemar ignored Wido and approached the young man until he stood in his shadow. "Your face is known to me, I would swear by my mother's ashes," Baldemar said softly.

"You are mistaken," the young Companion replied, his voice wavering like some top-heavy object ready to fall. He grabbed it by force of will and held it steady. "I am Branhard, a man of the Bructeres, and I left my own land but two full moons ago. I never have set eyes upon you before this day." He spoke a fraction too forcefully for a man innocently responding to a question, and all stared at him.

"Truly? Then why are you frightened of me? The Bructeres, you say? Then you are of my wife's people. You must have recent news of Athelinda's mother. Tell me, has Gandrida recovered from her illness?"

Wido gave Branhard a look that meant: Don't answer him, fool. But the young Companion was too unnerved to notice.

"Yes," he answered. "Yes, she has, and she fares well."

"Gandrida died last year."

The Companion flushed. Sharp shouts erupted among Baldemar's men. *"Who are you? Name your country!"* they cried, crowding closer, a pack of hounds barely restrained from seizing their victim's throat. Had Sigreda and Geisar not ordered them back, they might have murdered the young man right then. Wido's defenders moved close, spears upraised, and formed a protective ring about him, while those too far off to have heard these words continued their dogged chant: *"Trial by combat! Trial by combat!"*

Baldemar chose his question well. Gandrida had been a celebrated and powerful woman of rank, and her death was known well beyond the borders of her people's lands. The Companion's ignorance showed him to be not a man of the tribes at all, but a southerner who must have dwelled all his life in the lands controlled by the Romans.

Odberht whispered something to his father, wildfire in his eye. Wido shook his head angrily at whatever Odberht proposed.

"Lay your traps now, Baldemar, while I tolerate it," Wido shouted over the din. "But beware you're not caught in one of your own snares, you too-clever man." Wido smiled an oily smile and turned his head to nod at his three hundred well-armed Companions, a gesture that meant "I've thrice the fighting force you have and I will use them now if you're fool enough to try to corner me again in all the people's sight."

"Speak no more!" Geisar broke in. "One of you spews untruths and is not fit to walk among us. Tomorrow at dawn, let the spirits determine who shall live on and who shall be punished. Depart now, one and all!"

The crowd began to withdraw. Wido and Branhard turned their horses, and Baldemar strode off toward the lone oak at the crown of the hill to make a sacrifice of a white calf for the welfare of his family. Sigreda, who meant to assist, was a dark spirit moving gracefully at his side. But Witgern noticed with a start of unease that Odberht did not move; he sat rigidly on his horse, his gaze fastened on Baldemar's back.

"Baldemar," Sigreda was saying, watching him with those torpid eyes that concealed swift calculation, "I dreamed I saw your corpse on the ground with a stake driven in, while Wido rode by on a horse caparisoned in silver and gold. It is because you have not sacrificed what we asked. I warn you, you must send us the appeasement gift now, lest you never get a chance to give it."

"That is because I have decided mere cattle and sheep and silver are not enough! I plan to give in addition the most valuable thing a man can give, and I mean to deliver the whole of the gift at once."

"That is your life, Baldemar. The god has not asked for it. We seek not to destroy but to purify. And you cannot give your life twice. What if you die tomorrow?"

"Do the gods preserve the innocent?"

"Of course."

"Then you've little to worry about."

From behind them came a barked war cry and the hammering of hooves. Sigreda spun round and saw a flare of sunlight on an upraised blade. She screamed and flung herself to safety.

The leadline by which Wido restrained his oldest son had finally frayed and broken. Odberht, sword raised, bore down upon Baldemar.

Wido wheeled his horse about. "Odberht! Damnable idiot! *Halt, I command you!*"

To strike an enemy from behind was an act so dishonorable that often the culprit was condemned to death in the bogs or driven from the tribe. Wido's status probably would save Odberht from such a fate, but still it was a stain on the family honor that would never quite wear away. Wido himself had no objections to murder by this means if it were done secretly, but he was horrified his son had the bad judgment to do it openly, before the army and the Holy Ones.

A half dozen voices shouted out a warning to Baldemar. Witgern bolted forward, meaning to push Baldemar to safety, even though Odberht was hopelessly ahead of him.

For a harrowing moment that seemed to last a day, Baldemar made no move to defend himself, striding on confidently, seeming resigned to death.

Odberht galloped alongside Baldemar. The heavy blade slashed down.

Baldemar spun round so swiftly he might have been a ghost on the wind. No one saw him draw his sword, though he must have as he turned, for in the next instant he brought it upward with such force that Odberht felt as if his own blade struck a wall of stone.

There followed a penetrating clang that might have shattered the skull of an ox, and a great shower of sparks. The impact nearly unseated Odberht. The throng of three thousand stood mute, transfixed; none dared interfere.

Odberht was thrown back onto the rump of his mount but quickly righted himself by grasping the horse's mane. Then he resumed the attack with frenzied energy, emboldened by the seeresses' words *"You will not die by the sword"*—which he carried as a sort of shield. He executed a rapid series of savage down-cuts aimed at

Baldemar's head. But Baldemar blocked each stroke with almost careless ease, as a father might contain the tantrum of a child who thrashes out blindly. Soon, to the amazement of the crowd, Baldemar forced both Odberht and the horse back, step by step. Hearty cheers broke out among Baldemar's Companions; it was a sight that would feed many winters' tales.

Then with one neat stroke Baldemar cut the right rein. Odberht's horse wheeled to the left, following the pressure of the remaining rein, and simultaneously Baldemar lunged forward, surprising Odberht on his shield side. He grasped the young man's left leg and pulled him from the horse.

Coarse laughter mingled with moans of despair. Wido covered his eyes and wailed unheard, *"Now I have no son!* One the gods made a simpleton, the other a niding and a fool!"

Odberht fell hard on his side, raising a dust cloud. But rage brought him up at once and he charged like a dazed boar, swaying a bit, sword held low as if to disembowel his foe. Baldemar sprang forward to meet him, and blade crashed against blade; then came the furious erratic rhythm of iron on iron as the tempo of the death dance whipped into ecstatic speed. Odberht's feints and parries were crude and blunt with the clumsiness of youth, and for a short time he held his own. But most eyes were on Baldemar.

Was there ever another like him, Witgern wondered. Love of fighting was evident in his every leap and strike; each move blended artfulness and calm with the animal smoothness of the galloping horse, the darting stag. It was like watching a musician of great skill who gets wondrous effects from the barest touch of the hands upon the strings, set against one who compensates for his awkwardness by striking louder notes.

A dark stain appeared on Odberht's tunic. He was quickly driven to the edge of the crowd, forced to his knees, and then to the ground.

"Baldemar! Greatest of chiefs!" his Companions began to chant. Many of Wido's followers thought in that moment: Age has not slowed Baldemar. Wido is a dead man.

Baldemar pressed the point of his longsword to Odberht's neck.

"Kill him . . . kill him," came a dry, whistling voice behind him, a voice like wind hissing round rocks. At first Baldemar heard only his own heaving breath and thought the words some trick of his mind. Then he realized that Athaleiea, the ancient seeress who followed the army, had scuttled close to him. Her sun-browned face was turned to the sky, her eyes were closed, and she was prophesying. Had she added the words ". . . or die in your turn," or had he imagined them? In coming days those words would prowl the recesses of his mind like ghosts, dread presences threading in and out of consciousness, felt but never quite seen.

Odberht, poised between death and life, watched him, glassy, wide-open eyes begging silently. Were their positions reversed, Baldemar knew, Odberht would have finished *him* without pause. Baldemar had a mind to slay him just to disprove that irritating augury Odberht was always quoting, which had led him into such mischief. But Baldemar found he could not. What stayed his hand was a memory of his own youth—when he was no older than Odberht, he himself had been spared when he foolishly challenged Hrodowulf, a master swordsman.

But I did not strike Hrodowulf from behind, Baldemar thought, as though an Assembly in his mind debated the case. And this is hardly a young man. He is closer to the fox, the wolf, the worm.

But there was a strain of sentiment in Baldemar that showed itself when someone young and unschooled in the harshness of life was utterly at his mercy.

He thought: It is greater punishment to let Odberht live on a while, knowing what he has done. Let him live, shunned by all as a niding.

"Get up," he said softly. Odberht, who counted himself already on his way to the dim valleys of Helle, stared at him, not comprehending.

"Arise!" Baldemar repeated. "I will not foul my blade with your blood."

Odberht seemed to peel himself from the ground. It took a few moments. Finally he gathered the strength to muster a fresh look of contempt.

"I could have killed you! Trickster!"

Baldemar regarded him quietly for a moment. The Odberhts, he thought, are more dangerous than the Romans, because the Romans do not really know us or our country. Honor is such a fragile thing, difficult to nurture even in easy times. Young men like this are bred when a people begin dying.

"Yes," Baldemar said softly. "You may kill us all. Get along with you. You're Wido's problem, thank all the gods, not mine."

The chant, "Baldemar! Lead us out!" was a joyous shout thrown up to the sky.

Wido rode up to his beaten son. Looking down at Odberht, he shouted over the people's cries, "All the world should lament with me for being cursed with such a son. It makes me sick in heart to even look at you. If you touch a well, you will pollute it. Any mead you sip is poisoned by you. Get off from me!"

And Wido caught the rein of Odberht's horse, then cantered off, leaving his son on foot among his enemies. For long, Odberht could not move; the humiliation was so great his joints seemed fused, his muscles rigid as a dead man's. His whole mind was afire. In that moment was born in him a hatred for his father that was vigorous and raw, and more powerful than his loathing of Baldemar, because once he had struggled for his father's love. There stirred in him a lust to plunge his sword into his father's back, a thought that opened a black well of horror—for the killing of parents was a crime so great all believed the Fates would rend such an offender apart before any earthly judge could condemn him.

"Take this bridle—it has two reins!" Witgern called out to Odberht, grinning broadly.

"Ha! He'd do better with *no* reins—a horse has a better sense of where not to tread!" Sigwulf called out gaily.

"Next time you strike a man from behind make sure he's falling drunk and bound in chains! Why take needless chances?" Thorgild joined in, laughing.

Odberht limped past, thinking: One day I will see on a skewer every last man of them.

In the stillest part of the night Baldemar ordered a guard to rouse Witgern and Sigwulf.

Why is he not sleeping? Witgern wondered irritably as he entered the tent. In a short time dawn comes, and he will be fighting for his life.

"I have dreadful tidings," Baldemar began in a low voice when they sat before him. "Tidings that change everything. *I know now who Branhard is.* In a dream I saw him as he was, and when I awakened, I knew the day I saw him last. It has been seven years, you see, and he's done much to change his aspect."

Witgern felt a lurch of nausea, full of a dim foreknowledge of what Baldemar would tell them next. Baldemar paused to gather his words, taking up a bull's hide boot and brushing the caked mud from it, leaving them sitting expectantly, their eyes riveted on him.

He does this on purpose, Sigwulf thought. He likes to let us stew in our impatience.

"I saw him before, friends, in the Governor's fortress, where the

Rhine meets the Main. Branhard stood next to Marcus Arrius Julianus, and he was garbed as a Roman officer.''

The silence that followed was foul and full of night terrors, the sort of silence that falls at the end of a ghost tale as all move closer to the fire for comfort.

"I hear the words you speak, but it cannot be true," Witgern said.

"Sadly, it is." As Baldemar gazed into the dark recesses of the tent, the Governor rose before him like some specter. That day so long ago was the only time he and his great enemy, Marcus Arrius Julianus, Governor of the province of Upper Germania, had ever looked upon one another. Baldemar told them the tale in a few stark measured words, but as he spoke, he relived vividly what had passed on that day.

He felt again the stony chill of the grand Praesidium, the massive hall where the Roman war leader had his enemies brought before him. Seven years, and still he smelled the sickly scent of some spiced water in which the Governor washed himself mingling with the sweet odor of the costly oils in the many lamps, saw vividly the pockets of flesh under the Governor's eyes, the thickness of his girth from letting others fight for him. He had about him that peculiar combination of softness of body and hardness of mind one often found in Romans. In those days they made treaties still—and they had just concluded the one that was to be their last. Baldemar was ready to depart when Julianus motioned him closer. He had sharp little eyes that saw all the vastness of the world not as it was, but as a part of himself, another common feature of Romans.

The treaty was typical. One mile of land was to be left uncultivated between the territories of the tribes and the territory of the Romans. The Chattians were not to cross the Rhine at night. Baldemar could not imagine what else the Governor might have to say to him.

"Baldemar," he said, speaking through a native interpreter. His tone had shifted; he sounded now more like an indulgent father. "I have a better way to solve our differences."

And he remembered the vast silence, broken only by the whine of a fly, the patient scratching of scribes' pens. Among these people the more powerful a man is, the quieter it is about him. Among our people it is the opposite.

"I am offering you a partnership with me. It means a chance to bring stable order to your people and an end to our ceaseless warring. I know well that a mold has eaten your crop, and many of your people are starving," the Governor went on. "I will give you rich seasonal payments in gold so you can barter for food when your fields fail—and I'll see every man obedient to you supplied with a longsword, finely made, and enough cattle to make him strong among you. You will be able to build your miserable little band of Companions into a king's army! Before long, not only your Companions but all your people will be at your bidding.

"And in return," Julianus said, "I require so little of you. All you must do is keep the power in your hands—and your head on your shoulders—while you give me occasional reports of your people's movements and plans. And it shall bring to you wealth and kingly pleasures such as you scarce know exist. Of course, your people, for your own protection, must catch no scent of your cooperation with me."

"So I will be a king, and at the same time, your slave."

"All the peoples of the civilized world are our slaves, as you say. Who are *you* to be proud? Now this man here"—he pointed to a man behind him with sand-colored hair, broad face, morose blue eyes—to Branhard—"will go with you, disguised as one of your Companions. His name is Sextus Curtius, and he is fluent in both languages. We will speak to you through him. As you can see, he is of strapping size—in a season's time, if he does not cut his hair or shave his beard, he will look more Chattian than you do.

"I offer you a chance to be your people's savior. Know this well—if we continue thus, you will one day goad us into annihilating you."

Baldemar still remembered, amused, how his reply soured that avuncular smile.

"You study us and think you know us, clever man. You learn just enough of our ways to know how to best entrap us, but you will never know our hearts. To know that you would need to live with us and starve with us. Give me a brief life of starvation that is free, rather than a long and comfortable one as your pet dog."

Baldemar returned his attention to the two men before him in his tent.

"The offer I spurned," he said quietly, *"Wido could not resist."*

"By all the gods he is the greatest horror that ever has arisen among us," Witgern whispered, shaking his head. "He's sold us to the Governor like so many cattle. I fear the people will not believe it simply because it is so monstrous!"

"And the raiders . . ." Baldemar continued, "*my* guess is that they were Wido's own men, in disguise."

"What will you do?" Sigwulf asked, black eyes ignited.

"Denounce him when he meets me at dawn," Baldemar replied. "It may well be my last chance."

"You will set all the people against all Wido's well-armed Companions."

"They are set against each other now. It might as well be brought out into the full light of the sun."

"You must not!" Sigwulf protested. "Wido's rewarded his men so richly that they just might choose *not* to believe it. And you can be sure Branhard isn't alone—where there's one rat there's usually a nest. Romans have no honor in these matters. They may well murder you at once to silence you. You stood against one Odberht. Can you stand against a hundred?"

"Honor leaves but one way—to denounce him."

"It will tear the tribe in two. It will mean war, our own against our own, kinsmen slaying kinsmen, a bloody battle no one will win."

"Should you find as many reasons as there are stars in the heavens, you will not alter my course. I ask one thing of you—stand with me at dawn."

CHAPTER V

Thrusnelda's oakwood lodge lay among the shadows of oaks below the Village of the Boar. A gentle-featured young novice put a steaming compress of snakeroot and marigold to Athelinda's sword wound while reciting the words of a healing charm. The girl's big hands were clumsier than usual; she was uneasy treating so noble a patient. Auriane looked on, quietly fighting the growing alarm she felt: In the last days her mother's spirit had not healed. Athelinda watched her with stagnant eyes. Her mother had washed herself a dozen times in holy water carried in from the temple's well—a source said to contain Fria's own blood—but still she thought she could smell her attacker's flesh.

In the adjoining room Thrusnelda boiled chamomile in a bronze cauldron; the pungent mellow steam filled all three rooms of the lodge. From the ceiling bundles of dried herbs were hung, creating the look of a curious inverted forest. The novices in their long tunics of undyed wool moved languidly about their tasks, exchanging close, conspiratorial glances and tales that brought frequent laughter. There was a gaiety in the life of the Oak Lodges that carried on, Auriane heard it said, from generation to generation. When these novices learned all Thrusnelda had to teach, they would wear the gray robe of an Oak Priestess. Some ground herbs to powder with a mortar and pestle; others mixed the powder with lard to make ointments or baked moon cakes and braided bread-loaves for the coming midsummer festival. One incised magical markings in the wet clay of an urn to be used to receive the ashes of a smith who had just died in the village. All the while Thrusnelda called out for various plants and roots as she needed them. A dried toad, a charm to repel evil, hung in the connecting doorway; it swung gently to and fro as the novices brushed past it.

"The battle is done," Athelinda was whispering to Auriane. "Others know . . . and I who am his wife do not!" Athelinda wore a necklet made of the delicate spinal bones of a hyena, a potent charm against fever. But not potent enough, Auriane thought, judging from that dazed but intense look in her mother's eye.

"I'm certain the messenger rides without halt," Auriane said with all the authority she could muster. "Baldemar is victor. Wido is dead. How could it be otherwise? Vengeance is the god's own voice."

But Athelinda was not comforted; her eyes filmed with a pain no herb could relieve. "Have the rites been performed for our dead?"

Auriane nodded, her voice pale. "Yes . . . and beautifully."

"And . . . my baby?"

Auriane paused, grappling for the right words. "All the Holy Ones agreed . . . he is happy where he is."

"And yesterday's message? It sounded like nothing good."

"It was about Sisinand." Sisinand was Baldemar's sister. "Armed men came to her gate, demanding *me*. They said they came from Wido. But that was strange, because Sisinand did not know any of them. They tore her cattle shed apart and desecrated her mead house."

"By Helle, Wido's bent on that marriage! Upstarts and nidings! Sisinand will bring a case, of course, before the Assembly."

"Mother, you live in times past. No one has dared bring a case against Wido for many seasons. Witnesses against him never manage to survive to the day of the Assembly."

Athelinda shut her eyes. "Once treachery was a Roman disease. I wish I had not lived so long."

They were silenced by a clatter of hooves from behind the lodge, and laughter and shouts from the children playing in the dirt nearby. The *messenger*, Auriane thought. She peered through a crack between the oak logs. Yes, he was one of Baldemar's—it was young Ganax on his black mare. Whatever he had to tell, he had blurted out already; she saw a somber look on the face of the novice who greeted him. Auriane felt a wintry coldness in her chest. The children—who were the novices' own, the god-begotten fruit of the rites of spring—heard it, too, as they played with knucklebones in the dust, and their chatter carried to her.

". . . and how many will fight for Wido, do you think?" one asked brightly.

Athelinda heard it too. *Will fight for Wido.*

Wido was alive. Then Baldemar must be dead.

The dark stains on Athelinda's bandages began to grow. Her eyes became senseless and wild.

Ganax's shadow fell across the entranceway. In a rapid monotone he recited to Thrusnelda, "Messages for the noble Athelinda, daughter of Gandrida the Wise in Council, daughter of Avenahar the Seeress, out of noble ancestresses back to Embla . . . I ask leave to pass." Auriane felt her whole body prepare for grief.

Ganax was a half-grown boy plastered in mud up to his thighs. He threaded his way through the herb bundles—they hung too low for him—and stood before them with his flushed, eager boy's face. He felt ungainly in their presence and folded his arms in an unconscious effort to make himself smaller. Reverently he inclined his head.

"Say it quickly!" Athelinda whispered.

"Baldemar lives—"

"They *cannot* both be living!" Athelinda retorted.

"—but is gravely hurt," Ganax quickly added. "The medicine women say, though, that he will not die."

"Not die?" Auriane half rose. "What are you telling us?"

"The tale is a strange one . . . but I swear by my ancestors, it's the truth." Thrusnelda brought the boy a bowl of oxtail broth and a horn of mead. He ignored the broth and drank just enough of the mead to wet his throat. All stopped at their tasks and fell into rapt silence.

"Baldemar met Wido at dawn on the plain of Sheepshead Hill, to try the truth of Baldemar's words."

Auriane nodded impatiently.

"All gathered round, Wido's three hundred and more Companions on the right, and on the left, the people by the thousands, along with Baldemar's hundred. Baldemar's *greeting* was his best blow! It knocked the breath out of all who heard.

"'Hail Wido, slave of Marcus Arrius Julianus the Governor, and good servant of Rome!' he calls out. Imagine the tumult! 'Tell me, Wido—or is it *Marcus Arrius Wido* now?—did the Roman Governor tell you he would make you a king?'

"The stupefied look on Wido's face!" Ganax went on. "I thought he would drop his sword. He stood stiff as a wood image, then took a step backward, looking like someone trying to back carefully out of a snake pit without rousing the snakes."

"This cannot be!" Athelinda interrupted, struggling to sit. Auriane was more alerted than shocked, her mind assessing this with great speed, linking it swiftly with what she already knew.

"He did, my lady—ask the others who were there." It was the hurt protestation of a child who mistook Athelinda's words for genuine disbelief. "And then, to the one who calls himself Branhard, who stood by at close hand, Baldemar spoke these words: 'Hail Sextus Annaeus Curtius, Roman spy and Wido's master.' Three names the little wretch carried, my ladies, this wretched Roman rat gnawing at the center beams of all our houses! What perfidy."

Athelinda shook her head, half gasping, half laughing now.

Auriane whispered, "The viper! All this time Wido has been buying Companions with Roman money." She looked suddenly at her mother. "His Companions! Mother, *that* is who the raiders must have been—Wido's own Companions dressed to look like Hermundures! He is thoroughly mad!"

Athelinda nodded faintly, more interested in the story than in Auriane's speculations. Auriane fervently wished Baldemar were here—he would want the speculation as much as the story.

"And Branhard," Ganax continued animatedly, pleased to be telling such a startling tale and punctuating it with frightful grins that showed knocked-out teeth, "—or Sextus Curtius, I should say—now there was a fool's fool! He turned white as the hair on old Geisar's head. He was so terror-stricken he lost all his mother wit and approached Baldemar, babbling to him the likes of 'Come with us, it is not too late for you, it is a better life, I'll see the Governor honors you,' and so forth, incriminating himself, and hopelessly so, before them all! If there was doubt among any of the people, *that* trounced it.

"The people began to grumble and shout. Some started to draw weapons. Wido made one bold attempt to take the situation in hand. 'I am through with children's games,' he shouted at Baldemar. 'You are now my prisoner, Baldemar. You'll be freed unharmed when you yield up Auriane for one of my sons.'"

"My *prisoner*!" Auriane interrupted. "He speaks like a Roman slave dealer! What did the people do?"

"The bravest among them raised shouts of outrage. Wido called out for his Companions to fall on them with their longswords. They killed like Romans, not sparing the old, the feeble, or the young. It was Baldemar who turned the tide. Someone brought him his horse. When the people saw him mounted, braving all those spears and wearing his fury like a shield, they found their courage. With the whole of the people at his back, Baldemar rushed at Wido's men. They fear nothing when he leads them. Even the artisans and tale-singers and mothers with children charged after. Wido's mercenaries shrank back before their fury.

"Branhard tried to escape on horseback, but someone killed the horse beneath him and the people were all over him like wasps. There was blood, horse's blood, all over him, and then I couldn't see the rest. But I know they tore him apart. I have his right hand with me, here in my sack—Thorgild took it actually, but I won it from him at dice." He moved to take out the gruesome token and show it to them, but Athelinda stopped him with a curt gesture.

"Hurry on with the tale," Athelinda commanded. The boy looked briefly hurt, but he continued.

"Wido's men closed round him tight as an eggshell round an egg, and the traitor got away. And Baldemar—if only he'd turned round when he had them on the run! But he kept chasing them and harrying them. Finally someone felled Baldemar's horse with a spear—and the beast fell on his right leg, crushing it."

"I must go and tend to him!"

"Mother, no. If you travel anywhere, it will be your death." Auriane, too, felt a sharp fear for his welfare but dared not show it; Athelinda would only suffer more. "Do you know more than the medicine women? All will be well, I know it."

"She is right; Baldemar will be well in time," Ganax went on, "but this is disaster. The leg is broken in two places. They say he will not fight again before the festival of Maia, three seasons off."

"By that time the Romans will rebuild every fort and signal tower we burned," Auriane said. "By then, they will own the Taunus Mountains."

"At the camp, they mourn," Ganax went on. "A small battle's been exchanged for a far greater one, and without the war-luck of Baldemar, all say we have little chance. The Companions even sent for Ramis to come and heal him, but she sent back one of her riddling replies— *'When the right limb is gone, put forward the left'* or some such thing—plus some mutterings about how it was the will of the gods that she do nothing."

She is as useless as ever, Auriane thought sourly.

"Wido and his Companions," the boy continued, "have burrowed into that earth fortification on the plain built by the Ancient Ones, on the east side of Sheepshead Hill—"

"That is well," Auriane broke in eagerly. She knew the fort: It was ringed by three concentric circles of earth with staggered entrances, a device the Ancient Ones used to hinder an enemy's approach. The fort itself was built of half-rotted wood, its gates in bad repair. "There are many breaches in it. Wido is ever the fool in picking campsites—he'll need twice the men to defend that place as he would have needed if he'd simply climbed the same hill."

The boy paused to look at her, surprised at her knowledge of the terrain. "And now Romans come and go openly from his camp. Wido strengthens himself with each passing day. . . ." Athelinda and the boy both paused to look at Auriane, who, unmindful of them, was using a counting stick to make diagrams on the earth floor.

"What is that?" Athelinda asked.

"This is Wido's fort. Here is Antelope Ridge. *Here* is where the opposing camp should be set, above the plain where Willow Creek runs down, at the very point where Antelope Ridge slopes to the south."

This time the boy was more than surprised; he felt a chill. "That is precisely where Baldemar *did* set the camp," he said softly. Ganax had heard some of the talk of it; Baldemar fought and overrode the opinions of Sigwulf and several others. How could she have guessed it? The decision had been a complex one, involving great knowledge of the features of the land.

Ganax straightened and went on. "Geisar bleeds more men from Baldemar every passing day by screaming about how he is cursed, and his Companions are saying . . . are saying that . . ." The boy slowed, discomfort in his face, fearful he might give offense.

But Auriane calmly finished for him, ". . . that Baldemar is a man with unavenged dead, and as long as this is so, ill-luck will dog the good. No doubt they whisper: Had vengeance been taken at once, Baldemar would still have two good legs."

The boy gave her the faintest nod of appreciation. She is her father's daughter indeed, he thought—clear in thought, bold in speech.

Auriane thought again of Decius—many times in the last days she had tried to find some way to steal off unnoticed to his hut so she could ply him with questions.

He will mock me, but I must go to him. Surely he knows better than all of us how best to battle his own people.

Auriane rose, then went to her mother's strongbox, and took out two silver rings to pay Ganax for his trouble. But before he left, Athelinda gave him a message of her own for Baldemar, a short one full of affectionate words that caused Auriane to feel a jolt of bleak emptiness.

I will never know such a love. The love of the gods will have to be enough for me. My whole life, it seems, will be a preparation for death.

Ganax was quickly gone.

Athelinda said wearily, "Winter will never leave us! And now my last child is to be taken from me because all the Holy Ones are crying. 'Let us have her to marry to the god.' What if even this desperate sacrifice is not enough? After that, we truly will have nothing left to give."

"It *must* be enough. And perhaps a sacrifice of heirs will"— Auriane's voice dropped to a frail whisper—"purify my own evil as well."

"What are you speaking of? Who has said *you* were evil?"

Auriane looked tensely down.

Ask it. Ask it now.

"Hertha has said it. Mother, I've a thing to ask you that I've feared to speak of. . . ." Blood pounded in her temple as she edged close to the subject of Hertha's dying words. Athelinda must convince her they were nonsense, or else they would stalk her like wolves. She fastened her gaze on the gently swinging toad, reaching for the comfort of its modest but beneficent power. "Her last words to me were horrible."

Athelinda averted her eyes. It put Auriane in mind of a small animal running for cover.

"Mother . . . , Hertha died because of me."

Athelinda's eyes showed unspoken denial.

"Yes. Because of *me!* She said it as she walked into the flames. She said *I* brought about the raid. She said the evil has only begun. Were she with us now she would say I caused Father to fall and crush his leg. She said—oh, I cannot speak the words!"

"She was old and sick and bitter," Athelinda said too quickly. "Be sensible now, and put it from your mind. Hertha was . . . a trifle mad toward the last days."

"No, Mother. She spoke with soundness and certainty. She said . . . I fear to even say it aloud! She said—" Her throat felt as if someone tightened a rough noose about it. Athelinda looked away, braced, unwilling to help. The sunlight that broke through cracks between the logs touched her mother's eyes; they were of clearest glass, tinted blue, oracular eyes full of gentle knowing, mysterious as the Holy Ones' crystal orbs. *She knows. Why does she behave as if she does not?*

The words came in a bruised whisper. "Hertha said I would be the bane of my own father. . . . She said that Baldemar would be slain *by me*."

Auriane saw a start of fear in her mother's face, but no true surprise. *She has heard this before.*

Athelinda found Auriane's hand and pressed it to her chest: "Auriane, Hertha was *wrong*. You're not to say it again, while earth is below and sky above. Hertha had her wits about her most times, but on this matter she was addled as a hare at first thaw."

"You *have* heard it then! When? At my birth?"

"Yes."

"It came from Ramis."

"Of course not! Hertha was . . . ill with fever just after you were born. Demons whispered things to her while she slept and convinced her their words were true prophecy from the Holy Ones. Now I command you, put it from your mind!"

Reluctantly Auriane relented. She got up, found her cloak, and told Thrusnelda she was going out to the fields to gather thornapple, remembering as she spoke that this plant's dark green leaves should be harvested in the morning. But Thrusnelda was too distraught by the messenger's news to notice the mistake, and Auriane found herself free at last to seek out Decius.

Auriane wanted so much to believe her mother's assurances that for a time she was successful. Why would Athelinda not tell her the truth?

Perhaps she thinks she speaks the truth but suspects she might be wrong. Perhaps the truth is too fearsome for her to accept.

In the end Auriane got no solace from her mother's reply; Hertha's words clung like river mud. Auriane could never feel a tremor of happiness without it being darkened by a sense of evil worming in, spoiling what was fresh, bringing the murky memories, the smell of rot, the shadow of a coming crime greater than Wido's.

Decius tossed another potful of river water over the thatch of his hut. He was fireproofing it. Last year two thralls burned to death when a band of raiders bearing the boar standard of Wido threw firebrands at the thatched huts of the thralls who worked Hertha's lands, and he did not plan to fall victim to this latest war between the clans, the blurred details of which reached him through the gossip of the field thralls. The milder climate of the months of *Julius* and *Augustus* seemed especially to incite their savagery— but what were names of months in this god-cursed place? Here there was only heat or cold, dry grass or snow.

He could not guess when this latest spasm of violence would end and he looked for no cause. Barbarians were more of nature than of man; they stormed and were calm in elemental rhythm. As a legionary soldier at the fortress at Mogontiacum he had learned to view them as vermin infesting the frontier whose numbers needed periodically to be thinned. "Take no prisoners" was the order given before every campaign. "They're too savage a breed, and they make poor slaves. Spare neither the females nor the young—or in a generation's time they'll replenish themselves and our labor will be undone."

But after two years of enslavement by them his view of them had softened somewhat. Now he saw them as some lower species of man, a child-people capable of a surprising amount of human feeling, brigands and borrowers who nibbled at the edges of civilization, seeming half eager to be let in. Some of their traits amazed him, such as their laws of guest-friendship, which declared that a wayfarer who sought shelter under your roof must be protected even if he was a fleeing murderer, or their profound—and to his mind slightly absurd—reverence for their mothers: The most celebrated and bloody-minded warrior often would not act in war or in peace without first seeking her counsel. Their relationship with their gods was so intimate it called up lost longings in him: Unlike Roman deities, who were the remote partners of emperors, the spirits of the Chattians haunted the humblest hearth fire and hovered over every ripe field; the stalks shivered with their breath. Every act of their daily lives was homage to a deity; even as they harvested their crops, they imagined they relieved their goddess Fria of the heavy fruit of her womb. Their minds seemed innocent of impiety; it would never occur to them to cheat their gods in the way his own people often did.

And they were exceedingly faithful; often he mused what excellent soldiers they might make if that willingness to die in battle for their chief could be transferred to a legionary commander. His final judgment of them was that with patient care and perhaps a generation's time, they might eventually be brought to accept some of the benefits of Roman civilization.

It was a task far too large for himself, however. He wanted only to quit this prison of trees and set eyes on a marketplace again, to hear running water issuing from a fountain and not from untamed earth. The rigorous, sensible routines of the army seemed a sort of ritual prayer torn from his life forever, leaving him adrift in a formless place. He ached to hear the sound of true human speech and not the barbarian barkings that ravaged his nerves every day. He felt shame when he looked at his hands—once they had borne a soldier's calluses—now they were the burnt, roughened hands of a field slave. Most of all he missed the sense of moving *forward* in life, of bettering things. In the army, as in all life, there was always some circumstance to change or improve—whether it was the draining of a swamp to create a healthier climate, the returning of a shipment of poorly made catapult bolts that did not fire straight, or the conditioning of fresh recruits into units that fought as one man. In the old life his restless need for change was always gratified. Barbarians, like all lower creatures, knew nothing of this need; they moved not in a straight line with eyes upon a goal but in endless unknowing circles, prodded by the revolving seasons, blindfolded by their traditions. They never expected conditions to worsen or improve; they feasted, fornicated, farmed and fought without wondering why, and their lives were as fixed as the stars. It deeply mystified him.

Decius' life until his capture had been a succession of minor successes interspersed with moments of amazing good fortune. His first post was as a common legionary soldier in the remote province of Britannia. He came with carpenters' skills and a more sophisticated education that was given most shopkeepers' children in the small Etrurian village of his birth, because a celebrated naturalist had happened to settle there and found a school that took in boys of modest means. Decius' first month of provincial service fell in the year of the great revolt of the Britons. He had scarcely completed his training when some nameless superior decided men with carpenters' skills were needed on the Rhine frontier. An order for his transfer came, and he set sail just one day before the rebels of Queen Boudicca burned his fort, massacred the inhabitants of a neighboring veterans' settlement and slaughtered every man of his cohort. From that day forth every night before he retired he poured a libation to Fortuna and swore to do so until the end of his life.

He was sent then to the great fortress of Mogontiacum and put into a century of the Fourteenth Legion composed mostly of illiterate farmers from lesser villages of Gaul. The ceaseless violence of the Rhine frontier aided his rapid advancement, as it presented many opportunities for acts of reckless courage. After one ambush he was awarded the *corona civica* for saving the life of a fellow soldier. As he was as well the only man of his century who could read, he rose quickly to the rank of Centurion. Though he was a lowly one, his promotion incited comment because he was but twenty-three years old.

Decius was little impressed by this; it seemed but a collection of lucky chances. The accomplishment that most filled him with pride was that he was known throughout the fortress as the only man of his cohort who never paid for love. He had no need to fall back upon the tepid embraces of the camp followers with their flea-ridden blankets and battered tin cups rattling with coins; he had his pick of the shy, doe-eyed maiden daughters of the *canabae,* those settlements of native craftsmen that always sprang up in the vicinity of a legionary fortress. He took them in the open fields where the brisk northern wind burned the skin, and often as not they declared their great love for him and followed him back to camp. That, he maintained, was success in life, but the army stubbornly refused to give decorations for it.

And then came the day that Fortuna abandoned him. He was overseeing a detachment of the Fourteenth engaged in laying logs for the base of a rampart of a fort under construction in the valley of the Wetterau, gateway to the limitless forest northeast of the Rhine. At dusk, when his men were exhausted from heavy labor, a horde of Chattian savages came boiling from the forest; Decius' unit was a tiny craft swamped in a barbarian flood tide. The men not slain at once were dragged off to be nailed to trees as a sacrifice to Wodan, their blood-loving war god. He was never certain why he was spared, but thought it might be because he had a bookroll in his pack. The barbarians northeast of the Rhine seemed to worship the alphabet—or at least, their own distorted form of it which they called runes from their word *runa,* which meant "secret"—and he surmised that his pitiful stained copy of Martius' *Art of Siege Warfare* caused them to take him for some sort of holy man.

He unrolled that book now, letting the all-too-familiar sentences conjure up comfortable memories of the safe sameness of his days in the army, waiting while his boiled calf's head broth heated over a small yew fire. After a moment he sensed he was being watched. He looked up.

There she was again, the daughter of their chief, the fierce little vixen who had bitten him. Auriane. He felt a clutch of excitement. Often she came to stare at him, but never had she crept so close as this. She stood motionless before the crumbled place in the stone wall, a sorrowful figure almost wholly concealed in a gray-brown hooded cloak.

He made a show of ignoring her and returned his gaze to his book. Yet he found himself wishing her closer, trying to draw her with his mind. You *are* lonely, he admonished himself, to want the company of one of their women. Bury your wants—she'll not come any closer.

But when he stole another glance, he saw she had halved the distance between them. He was surprised at the pleasure this brought. This maid was the only one of his captors with whom he felt any kinship whatever, perhaps because she alone exhibited curiosity, a rare quality in a savage. She almost seemed to *study* him in the manner of a Greek naturalist—a curious reversal of common roles, he reflected once—here, nature studies man, instead of the other way about.

Careful, Decius, he cautioned himself. She's food to a starving man. Anyway, their women are notoriously chaste.

Normally he thought of this little, for the Germanic women in general did not interest him—if women they could be called, these she-beasts of the north who preferred torturing prisoners to decking themselves in colored silks. They were mostly sturdy beasts of burden on whose broad faces he could not imagine powder or paint. They provoked a powerful uneasiness in him— perhaps it was the lack of womanly compassion in them, or that every one had the taint of sorcery about her, or that their nature truly was as violent as the men's. Tales abounded of women taking bloody vengeance with a sword when they found their menfolk slow to act. But *this* maid might have passed for a real woman in fact, if someone would teach her a little grace—she walked like a soldier on a forced march—and coax her to comb her hair.

He heard the snap of a branch. Now she was very close, but still animal-silent, approaching with the timid persistence of the red foxes that often crept up to his campsite. Her head was slightly raised; she seemed to be taking his scent like some beast. Her eyes were bold and hurt. And so, he thought, the savagery of her fellow savages has shaken her a bit and reduced our haughty barbarian princess to a little beggar for scraps of—of what? What did she imagine that he, a mere thrall, could give her?

He felt sharply for her in one moment, but tender words would not come out of Decius—life had never taught him to speak them.

Her long silence began to annoy him. "Greetings!" he called out in her tongue. "Do you speak? No?"

She cocked her head slightly, struggling to pick out the words concealed beneath his Latin accent.

"What schemes, I wonder, drive the daughter of Baldemar to lower herself and have dealings with a thrall? Could it be you're drawn by the enticing aroma of boiled calf's head? Or maybe you liked the taste of my flesh so well you'd like to try a bite of my other hand!"

She cast her eyes down, full of hurt-animal wariness.

"I am sorry for the bite," she said at last. Her voice suited her, he thought. It was milky and low, venturesome and vulnerable at once. "It is the god's will you stopped me. I could only have done harm, and I could not have helped . . . anyone." He noticed her curious use of the word *anyone* instead of *my mother* and supposed the unobstructed truth brought too much pain.

Slowly Decius mastered his surprise. He expected anything from her but remorse. Finally he held up his swollen, purplish hand and replied clumsily in her tongue, "Never mind about it, it's healing well, and all is forgotten."

She came forward then and held out a silver arm-ring. "I give you this ring in payment for the bite," she said gravely. "Fria, Wodan, be you witness that I have paid."

Hastily he got to his feet to accept her gift—to hesitate would give greatest insult. He knew at once her gesture was a startling departure from tribal custom. Never in all his time in this country had he seen anyone give a reparation gift for an injury done to a thrall. Thralls were not a part of the human community. This was, he realized after a time, because they were without families, and a person's measure of humanness in this place increased with the greatness and number of his kin. But for reasons known only to her, she chose to treat him as a man of the tribe.

He quickly mustered the polite response. The Chattian words felt knotted and strange in his mouth. "May your family grow strong as the many-branched Oak. May your cattle increase and your fields be blessed, all your long life."

He then brought from his hut the length of rough wool that served him as a blanket and spread it on the ground for her before the fire. She hesitated a moment, then set down her burdens: a basket full of some weeds with white trumpet-shaped flowers—thornapple, he guessed, for some witches' brew—and a mysterious, bulky linen-wrapped bundle. Then she warily settled herself before his fire.

He took out a leather flask of brownish wine acquired with great difficulty, through barter with a fellow Roman slave who dwelled in the village. Then he settled himself beside her and held it out to her. "For *you*, I bring out the best wine in my cellars! Drink in friendship."

Auriane looked guardedly at the flask, then exuberantly seized it with both hands, put it to her lips and began gulping it down as if it were a horn of mead.

Table manners, Decius mused, were another nicety of civilization that stopped abruptly at the Rhine.

Before he could stop her, she drained half the flask. Her face reddened and she spat much of it into the fire. Laughing and shaking his head, he took it from her, while she regarded the flask as if it were a hound that snapped at her.

"It's *unwatered* wine, my feisty princess—did I forget to tell you?"

She frowned, smiling tentatively, only half understanding. Decius lapsed into Latin when he did not know a word in her tongue, and his manner said, "If you don't understand, it's your own problem—do not expect me to explain."

"Like this!" He demonstrated, taking slow, measured sips.

She took it again and imitated him with the barest hint of mockery. Something in that small show of pride she mustered in spite of her sadness reached the rarely touched tenderer parts of him.

The wine seized hold of her with numbing swiftness and she sat suddenly still. He saw the sharp point of sadness in her eyes dissolve somewhat, to be replaced by a softer, more open look. She seemed not so far from him now. One of the unsung properties of wine, he observed, is that it sometimes can cause the chasm between different races of men to seem more like a fissure.

She looked at him. "Decius," she said, slowly pronouncing the syllables of his name as if it were three words. "I have great numbers of questions for you about the magic of your people, and . . . a gift to ask of you, if you will give it. In return, I'll give to you what gifts I can, anything you desire, and if I can't get it myself, perhaps my father can. Please, do not laugh at me."

"I laugh not at *you*, princess, but at the world. Really, I like a bartering spirit! But I hardly see what you can *give* a man like me. I've got a roomy hut large enough to turn around in, and all the stringy half-rotted deer meat I can eat, and field mice for companions at night . . . and fine rags to wear, plus plenty of water through the roof. I want one thing from you, my saucy little maid, and I know you can't give it to me—to get out of this pesthole."

"You are unhappy here."

"Curses. You've found me out! I thought I concealed it well."

Auriane made a quick snatch at his bookroll and examined it closely, turning it round and round.

"Grimy paws off that, you little vixen! That's my *one* book!"

"These are words? Just as we are speaking? Tell me what is spoken here."

"Slow up there, frisky filly. It's about . . . dull and complicated things that little girls and barbarians don't need to know anything about."

She held him fast with that bold gaze; he felt like a snared animal. Something in those eyes, their mixture of lucidity and pain, brought a sudden silence around the heart.

"I am no *girl*. I am a woman full grown, who celebrated three whole years ago the time of her first woman's blood."

He managed to suppress an expression of mild surprise and cover it quickly with a wan smile. Fissure became chasm again. What woman of his own people would speak of such a thing at all, let alone speak of it with pride? There was pride in her voice, and more: It was almost as though she expected him to be intimidated by knowing this.

"*Pleased* to know that, I'm sure, and a million apologies. Now that *that's* settled, I'm—"

"You are mocking me!"

"You've got to learn to ignore it, princess. I don't know any other way of talking. The army's crawling with crude roughened beasts like me. Now let's hear those questions before the wine runs out and our senses return."

"Your people have the most powerful magic on earth. I want you to teach me what words you utter over your weapons . . . what songs you sing before battle. . . ."

"*Magic*, you say? If I had powerful magic, would I be *here*? I'd be flapping out of here on wings. I might stop first, though, to bewitch you into my bed. You're infinitely more appealing than the field mice."

Her dead grandmother would have wanted Decius drowned in the bogs for speaking those words. Another maiden of her age and rank would have at least sprung up and haughtily stalked off. But Auriane was a huntress close to her quarry; she would not be distracted.

"If it pleases you to be rude, I will endure it. You are Roman, after all."

"Rudeness, you say? That's a soldier's flattery, little pet. Forget all this talk of magic; we hardly use it. We invoke our gods, like anyone, but where war is concerned, it's live or die by your wits. We employ just plain, practical good sense."

"Then why do your javelins fly farther than our spears, though your people are no stronger of limb than ours? And why do the javelins sink into our shields so they are useless and we have to throw them down? And what are those terrible bolts that fly at superhuman distance . . . and what are those monsters that tear down cities?"

"I've a mutt fastened to my leg that won't let go!" He laughed softly. "These are all things that men *make*, Auriane, and nothing more. To a man who eats roots and berries, a plow is magic, I suppose. I'm not sure the javelins do fly farther—they've greater penetration, perhaps, because there's a thong attached at the point of balance which causes them to twist and spin as they fly. Why am I telling you this? I must be mad. They sink into your shields because the iron of the barbed point is left in a soft state, not hammered. And if you want an explanation of catapults and siege engines, I've already had too much wine. You'll have to come back tomorrow."

Undeterred, she asked in fast succession how close together legionaries normally fought, if they always attacked all at once, how many men they normally left in reserve, how cavalry was placed, and about the siting of camps. He was stunned by the thoroughness of the questions. He found that answering brought him pleasure and a sense of pride in his homeland, for the questions themselves were a sort of homage. He did not worry much over the possibility that he might be revealing secrets to the enemy, for he counted this girl a precocious oddity—barbarians in general had little interest in foreign ways and weapons, and he believed they would show no inclination to put this knowledge to use.

She asked as well questions about Rome. Was the Emperor truly divine? If so, why did he suffer death? And why was he not reborn? Where were the Roman women? She had never seen one. Why did they not follow the men into battle to bind the wounds, take up fallen spears, and help when a battle hung in the balance, like a normal woman? Had they no love of their country? Romans ate lying down, she was certain of it. Why did he eat sitting up? And was it true they all lived in stone houses grand as small mountains, through which they trained rivers to run?

And as he listened to these tireless questions, without his realizing it, without her intending it, some part of him adopted her. Subtly, surely, his soul was allying itself with hers, pulled close by the earnest eagerness in her voice, the guilelessness of that pride mingled with womanly confidence, the glint of coltish playfulness in her eyes, the way she carefully selected her words, as though the fate of her world rested in getting them right. For too long now he'd had no one to care for but himself. Now he yearned to shield her from the precariousness of life; it drew him from his own misery. More and more he felt a thought not fully voiced: *She might get into trouble without me. I'd best watch her.* It was a tribute as well: He sensed she was capable of getting herself into prodigious amounts of trouble.

Finally she hesitated, then said with great gravity, "Decius . . . I have something to show you." She began opening the linen-wrapped bundle. He guessed she felt she had to test him first and make certain he treated her questioning sincerely before she risked revealing to a man outside the tribe whatever potent treasure was within. When she shook the contents out onto the ground, Decius gazed, puzzled, at an ivory-handled dagger, a roll of papyrus, a heavy leather belt, and the broken-off head of a spear.

"What sort of man was this?" she said, her voice slightly hushed. "He came with the raiding Hermundures—if Hermundures they were. He chased me for a long time and made a great effort to kill me."

Decius was remote in silence for a long time. He first picked up the dagger, looked at it briefly, and tossed it down. Then he unrolled the fragile papyrus. She saw his face contract into a frown of mild disbelief.

"It's a *map*," he said at last. "By the paps of Medusa! What next! The savages will be turning *ballistae* on us. Something's not right in this, I say."

"What is 'map'? Is it something to work a curse on us?"

"No, nothing of the sort. It's just a . . . a picture that tells a man who knows nothing of your territory where to go. A thing no warrior of any of your tribes would need or have because he would know your land like he knows the backside of his plough-ox." He took up the belt with its tall, graceful letters carved into the leather, its heavy silver buckle inlaid with black niello. "By the tail of Cerberus, what's *this*?"

She sensed it had many messages for him but for a frustrating length of time he said nothing. Once she thought she saw a fleeting look of mournful regret cross his face.

"Tell me again. . . . He *chased* you, you say?"

"Why do you look so, as if you know him? He is dead. I killed him with a spear."

"You . . . ?"—his response began as a question and ended as a statement soft with disbelief—"killed him." He looked at her then, and was aware suddenly of the length of her still growing limbs, of the bow casually slung from her side, the hilt of a dagger just visible through the opening in her cloak and those strong hands, well capable of using it, of the implacable soul just visible beneath a veil of shyness, and he shuddered within. What *was* she? Woman or demoness? Had this grim smoking land conjured up Atalanta, the hunting maid of ancient tales?

"Auriane," he said gravely, "had he roughened skin, here, along the jaw, as if from a childhood pox . . . a healthy head of black curly hair . . . and strangely light eyes?"

Slowly she nodded. "Decius, how come you to know a warrior of the tribes? Are these things signed somehow on the belt?"

She watched impatiently as Decius sat in troubled silence.

Abruptly he turned away from her. "Already, Auriane, I have spoken too much. If I speak on, I will be a traitor to my people."

"To *your* people?" The air about her seemed delicately to spark. "What have *your* people to do with this? Anyway, *my* people are your people now. You are a thrall and you belong to us, and it is to *us* you should not be a traitor! You are *vile*—you tell me just enough to goad me to madness, then you fall silent. I'll not be played with so!"

She got drunkenly to her feet, half stumbling, then righting herself with exaggerated dignity.

"Auriane, I beg you, stay. I'll tell you anything else you wish to—"

"Curses on you! Sit on your silence. It is time for me to depart.

I'll behave as if we've never spoken—and I'll never have words with you again!"

With that swift soldier's stride, Auriane began stalking down the path that led through the crumbled place in the wall.

Desolation fell on him. She left a draft of bone-chilling emptiness in her wake. Conflicting feelings jostled in him; rapidly he wrestled to sort them out.

What does it mean anymore, to be a traitor? Can a man truly be called traitor, if his words harm no one?

The word, as he reflected upon it, sounded shrill and empty here, no more than the army's means of compelling obedience from afar from a man who no longer had anything to gain. The legions seemed more remote with each passing season—that cumbersome machinery that functioned quite well without him and seemed evidently to have forgotten him, with its aristocratic commanders who knew nothing of what it was to carry a hundred-pound pack all day or dig a ditch around a fort, working until the blisters bled. . . .

As for my oath to the Emperor, he thought, it no longer seems a living oath—it was based on a sort of comradeship, however distant, but *that* ceased with my capture.

Auriane, on the other hand, was vital and close; that *she* needed him was painfully evident, and, the gods knew, he needed her. She was a brilliant bloom on a plain of ice.

"Auriane!" She did not slow.

"All right, you have it then! Anything! I'll tell you anything. What do I owe the cursed army anyway? They haven't even come looking for me. To Hades with them! You're right. I belong to you. Come back here!"

She stopped and turned. He expected to see a glint of victory in her eyes, but there was only softness and tragedy. She is what we were once, in the days of Romulus, he thought. We Romans fight for pay. She fights for love. I cannot compete with her—not by myself anyway, in this bleak, god-cursed place.

When she settled herself again, he testily tried a fatherly hand on her knee, and for the first time in his memory, he was not certain of his motive with a woman—he could not say whether this was a lame attempt to seduce or a clumsy groping for companionship. She accepted it more as a child than as a woman, a child who badly needed the comforting of an adult.

"First of all, Auriane, he was certainly *not* a warrior of the Hermundures, nor was he a man of Wido's Companions. What I see here, I take as certain proof *none* of them were men of the tribes."

"How can that be?"

He firmly held her gaze. "That raid was a *ruse*, Auriane, a trick to incite your people into war with your neighbors. Those raiders were Romans, disguised as Hermundures. Do you understand? They inflame you into making war on the Hermundures, both tribes suffer great losses, and the native population is effectively pruned back—without shedding a drop of Roman blood. It's a trick old Julianus used to talk of, that, apparently, he finally decided to try. These men were drawn from a Roman cavalry cohort, picked because they closely resembled Hermundures in features and size."

He saw a jump of horror in her eye as if the whole earth cracked open to reveal nothing within but blood and rot.

For Auriane the turmoil and uncertainty all about condensed into one form, a single dark dragon: the Romans. It was they, then, who savaged her mother, who tore them all from the peaceful round of life. It was their coming in disguise that haunted her most. They were shapeshifters who winnowed in, burrowing into sacred places; no spear, no palisade could stop them. Would storms in the sky, would ravaging wolves also prove to be masks of the Romans?

For long moments she sat intent in silence, and Decius knew the course of her life was setting like quicklime.

Finally she said, eyes brilliant with hurt, "We cannot live on this earth with you. We believe ourselves free, but we are your prisoners already, all of us. Your people cannot abide the sight of anyone living in freedom! We do not belong to you, nor will we ever, even if you murder us all!"

Decius thought: They suffer as we do. We are tormenting children, murdering parents. But it has always been so, and a frontier must be maintained. It is my misfortune to view their suffering so close.

"You are right," he said gently. "It's just that the world doesn't particularly care that you're right. The powers on earth listen only to other powerful voices."

He picked up the belt. "In answer to your question," he continued, "I know this man because it was hard not to know him. He was Valerius Sylvanus, prefect of cavalry, a man of equestrian rank—that is, a sort of chief. The words carved here name his cavalry cohort, the First, and here, *Legio XIV*—the Fourteenth

Legion. He was probably the expedition's leader—which makes a certain amount of sense, I suppose—a man of the rank and file would not have broken off to pursue you."

"I killed a . . . a sort of chief?"

"I knew you'd smile again one day. He must count for at least forty or fifty common ordinary soldiers, no?"

"It makes the deed's power greater, if that is what you mean. Decius . . . , when I travel to the Assembly, I would have you accompany us. You must tell all these things to my father."

Decius carefully controlled his delight. He knew how close to the border the place of the Assembly was.

"I will come willingly."

"Too willingly, it appears. I see your thoughts clearly as I see that pot. You plan to desert me once we're there."

"I'll see you get whatever it is you want first. *You* are the one who should not go, lest you blunder into Julianus' net and find yourself joined in marriage to that blustering lummox Wido calls son. Why do you not flee to the north?"

She was silent a moment while she met the gaze of the moon's soft sleepy eye as it nested in the tops of the pines. In one mad instant Decius imagined some swift communication between the moon and Auriane.

"You know me little, Decius. I would never, never leave her."

Decius assumed that *her* referred to Athelinda, but Auriane did not know as she spoke whether she meant her mother or the land—just then they were mingled in her mind.

She then announced with a drunken mockery of queenly calm, "I have not asked you for the gift or spoken of its terms."

"The gift. Right. You should ask for a fast horse. Auriane, my troublesome princess, you're missing a useful element of human nature—good, healthy fear."

"The first part of the gift is this: I want you to teach our armorers precisely how your Roman short swords are made, and the shields of bull's hide, and the far flying javelins. Of course, before you begin, I must persuade my father to convince the Assembly to agree to this. And the second part must reach *no one's* ears, not even those of your fellow thralls. It is this, Decius. I want you to instruct me in the art of the sword, exactly as your legionary soldiers are taught."

As she spoke, her eyes ignited with soft fire. She might have been a maid at a first tryst, catching sight of her lover.

"No more of *this* for you," he said, putting the flask of wine out of her reach.

"Ask me tomorrow, without the wine, and I will speak the same words."

"Well, I've seen all sorts of pitiful madness in my time, the gods know, but this is a novel sort."

"Your churlish jests, Decius, will not sway my mind."

He reached up and took her hand. "You've got it all backwards and inside out, Auriane. Will you let me be a schoolmaster for a moment and give you a very brief lesson in military science and history? Listen, pet. It's not the weapons, they've little or nothing to do with it. You'll not chase the Romans out of your country with a few miserable copies of legionary arms—even if you *could* persuade your people to actually use them in battle instead of stringing them up in trees. *It is our people.* We fight as one. We obey our commanders, even in time of peace, a thing your people call slavery. We're not hobbled by a thicket of sacred laws—we do whatever brings results. It's *discipline*, not weapons. The whole world is with us now and has been for over a century. You might as well go armed to the seashore and do battle with the waves. Give it up. Certain races were ordained by the gods to rule, and others, to be used by them and knocked about, and we poor fools in the middle of it all have little choice but to stand out of the way and make the best of it." He paused and sighed. "I can see clearly I might as well be speaking to a rock, but I've done my best. So much for lessons in military science and history."

"I want you to begin instructing me at once," she went on, eyes intent. "By next spring, Decius, if I am adept, you may have anything you wish of me—anything, that is, that is honorable."

By next spring? he thought. Curses. If I agree, I scuttle my chances of escaping from Baldemar's camp.

He was aware suddenly of how swiftly light drained from the sky, blackening the trees, shrinking the world to the size of the warm bright place around his fire. In one moment he envied her that she belonged in this world—to her the nighttime forest was a womb. To him it was bleak, and malignly alive.

"All right, you have it then. I guess I have less sense than I thought. If I can help one sparrow become a hawk, where is the harm? I'll attempt to turn you into a fair copy of a legionary soldier, as well as I'm able given your certain appealing physical limitations, if that is what you truly want. But here is what I ask, and I'm sure you know it already. I want *out* of this pestilential swamp."

"Decius—you belong to the whole tribe. If I help you escape, it would be like stealing from the whole tribe. It is not done among us."

"Horseballs! I can't believe I'm hearing this. Everything I see you do 'isn't done.' Why draw the line at *me,* you capricious little wench? You boasted before you were a woman full grown. Well then, prove it and act on your own! Do you think I care less for my family than the Chattian warrior who kills himself when he's captured so he can return to his? A thrall's not born a thrall! Restore me to my family, and I'm a thrall no longer!"

"Decius, please, do not speak to me so! I am wounded for you, but I cannot do this thing! We would say, you have the fate and luck of a thrall, so you *were* born a thrall——"

"Then send me back, and you *change* my luck. Admit to it, I won that throw!" He saw doubts collecting in her eyes, so he pressed harder. "*This* is curious. Suddenly, I'm forgetting everything I ever knew about swordsmanship! It's all leaving me. Who's going to instruct this cantankerous Amazon?"

She looked at him challengingly, then turned away, eyes in ferment. He waited tensely. Part of her dwelled with her people, and a part of her dwelled—where?—in an empty place, a land without laws or roads, a world where rivers had no banks. She is a strange creature, he thought, so unlike her fellows. To this void she seemed irresistibly drawn. I pray it draws her now.

"I judge that you are right," she said at last, "and not because of your threat not to teach me, which dishonors you. It is a larger tribe you speak of, but the law is the same. You lost your family. I will try to bring you to them. Decius, I will help you. I will get you a horse and guide, but not before next spring."

"Blessed Fortuna. You had me worried there a moment, little dove. Now how do we prevent you from being carried off by my countrymen? If that happens, I'm still in prison."

"That is in the hands of my family and the gods. Just be ready to travel south with us at cockcrow, on the day after the morrow."

"Curses. You've scarcely given me time to settle my many affairs and pack up all my belongings."

She swiftly rose, and he caught an amused smile as she turned, a smile she did not mean for him to see. He kept his eyes on her, watching her protectively—yes, *protectively*, he realized—until she made her way through the break in the stone wall with that stalking stride and became a fluttering gray ghost that melted into the blackness of the forest.

He realized he was as unsettled by her troubles as he was by his own. He found this utterly bewildering. *How can she, in such a brief time, have made me care for her so much?*

CHAPTER VI

The company of Companions mounted their horses by torch-light before the skeletal frame of Baldemar's unfinished hall. They waited impatiently while Thrusnelda's novices completed their ministrations: Working swiftly, two rubbed nine-herbs ointment onto the horses' legs to ward off injury, while two more wound wolf's hair round the browband of every bridle to protect the party from ambush. There was little talk among the twenty-five Companions; to Auriane their faces looked haunted and gaunt in the cold predawn light. In every eye she saw the question: How long can Baldemar hold the people's love if he is too broken in body to lead them?

Auriane sat a lean, long-limbed bay gelding—a stolen Roman cavalry horse, as were all the mounts of Baldemar's Companions. At the withers the beast was nearly as tall as a man, and Auriane was uneasy with this new, greater distance from the ground. It matched the way she felt about all life in these times: *I am thrust up into the world of women and men before I am ready.*

As they left the yard at a brisk trot, Auriane stole a furtive look at Decius, who rode in the rear among the pack animals, appropriately mounted, she thought, on a mule. Her mind was aflame with his words: *"Those raiders were Romans."* Her mothering forest roused a new wariness in her: Before, it had been a temple demanding difficult worship but giving all in return. Decius, with a word, had transformed it into a lair of monsters.

As they set out, Witgern rode at their head with Maragin, a seasoned Companion whose beard was flecked with gray, and the feast-loving, golden bearded Coniaric, a newly made Companion recognized by all for his formidable feats of strength. Alongside them rode the pathfinder, a man of mixed Batavian and Gallic blood recruited from the *canabae*. In the next rank were the Holy Ones—three swans taking flight in their billowing robes of snowy white. One was Hylda, who came to stand as witness to the Ash Grove slaying; the middle rider was her novice attendant. The third was Auriane in disguise, the hood of her cloak pulled well forward to conceal her face. Witgern looked back from time to time to torment himself with longing glimpses of her, dulling his pain with the thought that Auriane's circumstances were now at least as pitiable as his own—for when next the moon was full, Wido might well call her daughter.

And Auriane from time to time glanced farther back to snatch looks at Decius. The man, his stores of knowledge, and his Romanness were mingled in her mind, enhancing him in her eyes until what began as sharp curiosity became a full-blown seizure of youthful awe. In spite of the fact that he was an initiate into the mysteries of the greatest power on earth, still he was close and real with his world-weary look, that face so like a devilish boy who had missed a night of sleep, that quick, disarming smile coupled with warning eyes that pushed you away. A hundred times she cautioned herself: He is an enemy and a thrall. You cannot allow yourself to care for him, or even worse, desire him. Yes, *desire* him. There, you have thought it. Are you staring mad? He is Roman. Remember what another man of Decius' race did to your mother.

They moved into a loping canter when they came to the grassy avenue that separated her family's field of einkorn wheat from the pine forest. The close, moist pine smells embraced and comforted her. A soft white ground fog lay contentedly on the forest floor; the trunks of the trees were pale, slender stalks rising, smooth and bare, from dreamy mystery. Pools of blackness remained, the lingering tidepools of night. Occasionally she saw the flick of white that she knew was the tail of a doe, and for an instant she fiercely envied all forest creatures. They, too, have destinies that bring them to suffering and death—but it is their good fortune not to know them.

By noon she was miserable and wet—they were forced to avoid the common river-fords because these were places where ambushes were likely to be set; twice they swam their horses across flooded creeks. As they traveled, their ranks became less distinct, and when she could do so without attracting much notice she rode near Decius and besieged him with a fresh volley of questions about warfare. That night they made no fires and dined on rations of dried venison and hard rye bread. She slept with her head pillowed on moss, blanketed by the sky's soft black, cradling a fire-hardened spear at her chest like some child at the breast. She begged Fria to send her sleep without nightmares of Arnwulf's soulless body and Hertha melting in flames.

On the second day of steadily journeying southward, as the sun found midheaven, the pathfinder slowed. Auriane heard Witgern mutter a curse, and understood why—this was no place to pause; the country was too exposed. The pathfinder shaded his eyes, staring bewildered at Fallen Pine Hill. A lightning-struck tree he employed to find his way was gone without a trace. He frowned. Auriane sensed fear and confusion in his jerking movements as he looked from side to side.

Had he turned too soon after the three willows at Red Fox Lake? Or had some witch temporarily thrown the land out of joint?

Witgern and the pathfinder exchanged sharp words; then they led the company into a thick elm wood, down a narrow, twisting path edged with smooth stones.

At once Auriane sensed something disturbing in this wood. It seemed to hum with secret life. It was a place where gnomes might venture out in the light of day, where galls on the trees were watching eyes, where birds peered at you with intelligent interest and you knew an ancestor's soul was imprisoned within. Desolate faces appeared just out of sight, and when you turned, they vanished. Those spiraling branches above—surely they came alive at night and struck like serpents. She heard a Companion behind her mutter, "Pathfinders do not get lost. Wido's had a sorceress bewitch him. There's enchantment about, I say."

The horses seemed to confirm this; Auriane's gelding tightly bowed his neck, fighting the reins with nervous snorts, while his coat darkened with sweat. Then came a rushing of wind that sent the boughs high above into a frenzied swaying dance; it was as if the wood itself erupted with rage at the intrusion. At a turn in the path Auriane saw, half hidden in the trees, a lichen-covered stone tall as a man and carved with rune-signs traced in blood. And as they traveled on, suddenly all about them, hung from every bough, were myriads of bronze chimes shivering with each wind-breath; their thin ghostly chorus filled her with an aching, dreamy sadness.

I remember this place. What am I saying? I've not been here before. Yet somehow . . . it is all familiar as an owl's cry, as a night wind bearing the scent of yew fires. . . .

From somewhere came a desolate screech that could have been human or cat. They passed a divergent path; a short distance down it was a gnarled oakwood gate that hung open as if inviting them in. And beyond the gate, mounted on an elmwood pole, was a richly carved wheel with thirteen spokes, the number of moon-cycles in a year. *The Wheel of the Year,* Auriane realized with alarm. In the dark of night it turns on command and causes the dead to speak prophecies from their graves. It was a certain sign some great prophetess had settled in this wood.

Witgern and the pathfinder lashed their mounts with switches, anxious to get beyond this place, but the terrified beasts managed no more than a nervous, high-headed canter hardly faster than a walk.

Then the horses behind began to collide with those in front; Auriane could not see round the bend in the path but guessed the two lead animals were brought to a halt by some dread thing barring their way. For the first time she felt a fear that was immediate and sharp.

Witgern and Maragin fought to turn their mounts about, but their horses were wedged among the others and soon it was impossible for anyone to move. Maragin, the roughened veteran of a hundred battles, was in a position to see whatever was there. When Auriane saw badly concealed terror in his face, she felt all her muscles tense for flight.

Then a voice called out from beyond the bend in the path; it was strong and supple as vines, masculine and feminine at once.

"Halt and be at peace! Come forward, Auriane."

Auriane was numbed by the sound of her name. All gazes turned to her. She found she could not move.

All at once she recognized that voice. *Ramis.*

It cannot be. So I'm to be taken by Ramis, rather than Wido's men or the Governor's soldiers. *This* is a menace no one counted on. It's hardly better. At least the world of day is one I know; I know nothing of the world of night.

The next voice she heard was Witgern's. "Auriane, stay there!"

There was dark silence. Then Ramis spoke again.

"Choose, child. You cannot obey both of us."

She has many apprentices to serve her—why can't she let me be? Have I not troubles enough? Why is this wretched woman so greedy for *me?* Mother knows her well: She is not to be trusted.

Auriane dropped to the ground, her fire-hardened spear upright in her hand.

I could run. But then she might do harm to us all. Better to threaten to kill her if she does not let us pass. *Kill her?* With this miserable weapon? She probably reads these thoughts as I think them!

Slowly Auriane threaded her way through closely packed horses, coming round the crook in the path; then she halted beside Witgern. At the sight of Ramis, the last of her courage drained out of her. She felt she faced a powerful blast of wind.

Ramis was astride a milky white mare; the beast was turned broadside to them so that she blocked the path. The sorceress regarded her with a look that was faintly amused, cool and intimate at once. The passing years changed her little; the bones of her face asserted themselves more boldly through the flesh, emphasizing the curve of her brow, the commanding arch of her mouth, the cold passion in those eyes, those wells of thought a hundred lives deep. She had the look of some serene androgyne, a creature all mind that preserved just enough flesh to keep alive. The very air about her seemed to ignite and shiver with unseen fire.

That bright, brazen aliveness about her—what is its cause? Auriane wondered. Can one person be more alive than another?

The spear slid from Auriane's hand.

Ramis' mare half reared, snapping at the air; a horse-serpent with snaking neck and lashing tail, fighting the control of expertly held reins. Auriane moved back a step, realizing this was one of the sacred mares of the horse-groves, whose neighs and snorts were used for divination. They were said to be flesh-eaters. Disgraced warriors occasionally mounted one of them as an act of suicide. The hooves of the mares of the grove leave little of a man left to burn, it was said. Yet this one submitted, if barely, to the touch of those strong white fingers on the reins. "If the Mare does not kill you when you venture close," Thrusnelda had once told her, "it is the surest sign you are destined to become one of the Holy Ones, and of high degree."

Witgern seized Auriane's shoulder in a powerful grip.

"No closer!" he said sharply, staying very still so he would not incite the viper to strike. Many of the men shielded their eyes, while others traced in the air the runic sign that gave protection against sorcery.

"Witgern, let her be." Ramis' voice was lilting, yet cold with warning.

"She is mine to protect in the name of Baldemar," Witgern replied.

"To *protect?* Now you amuse me. Can you protect her from misfortune? Or from her inevitable day of death? Stand aside, Witgern, these matters are not of your world."

Still he did not release his grip on Auriane. And Auriane all the while felt her terror ebbing away, while an obscure excitement took its place. Some questing part of her rose up of its own will to sense and taste that cool fire about Ramis. It seemed then that Ramis' very *presence* was a strengthening draught. Do the others feel this? Auriane wondered. Has she bewitched only me?

Ramis took a pinch of some black powder from a leather pouch at her belt. "You know not yourself from another, Witgern," she said. "Nor day from night. How can you know truly who is your enemy?" She flung the powder at Witgern. *"Sleep,"* she called out in a silky whisper.

Auriane felt Witgern's hand ease from her shoulder. Had she cast a sleeping spell on him or merely made him think she had? Witgern slumped forward on his horse as if his bones had become soft, his one good eye glassy and sightless.

Murmurs and moans came from behind. Auriane wondered what Decius thought of this. Did he mock, or was he terrified as well?

Now she will drag me off to the dark caverns where she animates the dead. I will never again set eyes on my mother and father.

"Come," Ramis said to her softly. "You wear your mother's fear, not your own. Now bare your feet, and unbind your hair."

"I will not." It was a feeble protest, the last kick of a dying animal.

"As you delay, a party of Wido's men approaches this place. Do as I command!"

Auriane pulled out the bone pin and a heavy mass of chestnut hair shuddered down. Then she unlaced the leather thongs that bound her calfskin shoes and shook them off. She had a sense that the earth was flesh, that her bare feet stood on the hide of a great beast.

"Never forget the power of hair. It is both a shield and a

birth-string, binding you to earth. Now, my mare has taken a stone. Take it out!" Ramis held out a bronze hoof pick.

Slowly Auriane shook her head. "If you want to murder me, use spells to stop my heart, not that mare. I will not have my mother forced to look upon what is left of me."

Ramis smiled. "Perhaps you will not be so fortunate. The smoothest of lives is still more difficult than death, and yours is set to be anything but smooth." Then her voice rose up like a gale. "In you dwells a spirit old as mine. I command you, *give it voice!*"

Auriane's mind was erratic and wild as a cornered stag.

Bolt into the forest. Pick up that spear. Kill the horse. Kill her.

No, it is no use. She will not let us be until I obey her. Do it. Make yourself walk. Trust that she is not evil enough to make Athelinda a gift of your mangled body.

She moved toward the mare. The beast's head came up sharply, ears flattened.

Then there settled over Auriane a strange luminous calm, a certainty that all that passed and all that had ever passed was, at its core, benign. Fear seemed to gently float out of her, leaving rich emptiness in its wake. Every sense feasted and knew contentment, as she had not thought possible in life; she swayed in an ocean of souls, feeling the close comfort of every being she had ever known, living or dead. The worm in the earth was beautiful as the lily; the weed by the path as necessary as the stalk of wheat. The sense lasted but a moment as she stroked the silken neck and felt the bunched muscles of the mare's shoulders relax at her touch. It encompassed every sort of love. The thought—*the mare is not my enemy*—came to her, and she realized that the word *enemy* had been stripped of meaning—she groped for it but it was not there.

Swiftly she took the pick from Ramis, lifted an enormous hoof, and pried out the stone. The mare's charcoal muzzle grazed her neck and agile horse lips pulled at her hair.

Then the enchantment was gone, leaving her with a fierce, bottomless hunger for its return, a lust deeper than any desire for an earthly lover.

Fears crowded back in. She looked, alarmed, at the stone. She heard several soft voices behind her cry, *"Ganna, Ganna!"* They were calling her an apprentice sorceress.

She looked at Ramis. "Let me *be*. I am *not* one of yours. This is base trickery. You have given the mare some draught!"

"Then why are her eyes so fiery? One of you!" Ramis called out to the company at large. "Come forward and stroke her neck. She is drugged." Not one of them moved.

"Tell me, Auriane, how did you know which hoof?"

Auriane felt a jolt of unease. It was true. Ramis had not said which hoof.

"I . . . I do not know," she said with bewilderment. Her voice hardened. "And I do not care. I'll take my own life before I'll go with you."

"It is time you know it, Auriane: They come of their own will, or I do not want them. I have no use for captives. I want only what the thrall wants when he touches the fire of a living torch to a torch that is cold: to light the hall. I come to cast light upon what you will not know."

"I know it then, and it means nothing to me. I've a choice then? I choose not to be a *ganna*. Am I free, then, to go on my way?"

"*Free* is an unfit word for it. Yes, you are free—to take up your bonds again. Or you can die now, and let me show you life. You have come to one of the times of turning, when a new path may be chosen. I was impelled to ask, though I guessed you would refuse."

Then Ramis seemed to watch Auriane across a gulf of years, and her voice dropped low, becoming woeful music: "Oh, yes . . . , I see you now in a necklace of bones . . . a cloak of human skin . . . and corpses strewn at your feet. At your side a bloody sword hangs—the more it drinks the more it thirsts."

"You flee catastrophe, but you cannot see . . . catastrophe is fertile—it brings forth worlds. You flee sorrow as you feed on sorrow, all the while strewing it in your bloody wake. War will not make you safe, nor will it save your mother. Listen well, little blind one—you strike at your enemy and you strike at yourself."

Her voice rose up powerfully again. "Off with you now, Priestess of Death—go and play in the world! I do not want you, and I sorrow for you. You've stepped into the mirror maze—now you'll trick yourself for years."

Ramis wheeled the horse about. Auriane felt a desperate need of her then that she did not understand.

"Why do you not help Baldemar!" Auriane called out, partly to bring her back.

Ramis pulled the horse to a halt and looked round at Auriane. "An empty question from one who knows not what help is."

"Why did you let Hertha torment me?"

"It was not her torment that gave you sorrow, *but your belief in it.* If there is some shame lying about, how greedily you take it up and say, 'It is mine.'"

"How could you allow Wido's evil?"

"Whom do you take me for? I am a mortal woman, Auriane, not the Fates." Again she started off down the path.

Auriane felt her rage rising dangerously, a thick soup coming to a precarious boil.

"Why do you torment me! You've haunted my whole life! You are a curse in the flesh!"

Ramis pulled the mare to a sharp halt.

"*You* started the tales I am ridden with demon's blood!" Auriane shouted. "You made my grandmother hate me. All that gives human comfort, you call folly. You come and tell me so—and then you abandon me!"

Those behind listened in stunned horror. Ramis would utter a single word of power and all of them would fall asleep for a thousand winters.

The soup flooded over the rim of the pot. "Yes, abandon me, casually as a bitch-dog walking off from her young! You speak of life! Where is Arnwulf's life? How is he helped by your twisted, riddling words? You spew out words of confusion while everywhere we are dying of blows! Go and confuse the Romans! You would do us more good. Teach to others your utterings of no sense!"

Auriane stopped, feeling suddenly deflated, and the stark silence all about awakened her to what she had done. Exhilaration gave way to vertigo, as though she scrambled too high up a pine, then looked at the dizzingly distant ground and knew she could not climb back down.

What have I done? She will call down a bolt of lightning and we will all be cinders.

Gradually, through her fright, she realized Ramis was laughing—yes, laughing—with light clear notes.

The woman is incomprehensible. Perhaps she is simply mad. But no, madness is emptiness, and never was I so *full* as during that enchantment she sent, or awakened, in me.

"This is well," Ramis said, softly as a mother now. "I am pleased with you. When I had about as many years as you, I spoke in that wise to my own teacher. Though I believe I called her a she-ass instead of a bitch-dog, if memory serves. Your spirit is great and you progress well, *but it is not time.* I must leave you. We will meet again at the next turning of the times."

Ramis then galloped off. Auriane for long moments did not trust herself to move — she felt as though the horizon suffered a slight tilt, and feared she might fall. The stone she had pried from the mare's hoof rolled from her hand. Soon she was aware that the men were muttering in low voices while stealing baffled looks at her, regarding her not as if she were a half-grown girl but as though she were some natural phenomenon.

She chastised Ramis and was none the worse for it, as they would later tell the tale. And she was received gently by the Mare.

Witgern came up beside her and put a steadying hand on her shoulder.

"You're well and alive. You've much courage, Auriane." She looked at him gratefully and numbly pulled herself back on her horse.

She saw one of the men dismount. To her dismay, he picked up the stone she had pried from the hoof and kept it, probably to make an amulet. She knew then that no matter how much she tried to deny what occurred on this path, those who witnessed it would keep it alive.

She met Decius' eye before they set out again. He grinned at her — that rogue grin. Decius seemed maddeningly unmoved by it all, as if Auriane had paused to ask directions of a farm wife. Were Romans incapable of any sort of reverence?

She felt a stirring in her loins then, for which she cursed the gods. Why now? And why Decius? Why cannot the passions of the body be controlled? The feast is laid out — and my eye strays to the dish that is poisoned.

Auriane lay awake most of that night, trying on and shrugging off Ramis' words, and through all her fears for the future — or perhaps because of them? — she was sharply aware that somewhere nearby lay Decius. In one moment, her need to crawl through the grass and find him was so powerful it left her shivering. In the next, the pleasurable shudders brought in their wake a stark picture of what happened to her mother. Glimmers of knowledge of the pleasures of the body had come to her, gathered from dreams, from intuition, from dimly sensing the relations between her mother and father. To be joined in passionate embrace was love made flesh, a heart-warmth overflowing into the loins. She had been certain of that before, but now she wondered: Could the same act also be one of hatred, of violence? Was it always a bit of both? Who might she ask? There was unknown danger here, a black shadow cast over desire. It fit well with all else she lately sensed: No place was safe, and nothing was purely the one thing it first seemed to be. *Beware, beware,* she heard in the cry of a low-flying nightjar.

That smile of his—if I possess it once, will it stop tormenting me? Decius, you are a fiend. I will rejoice when you escape.

As night wore on she struggled to quieten her mind but her body remained tense, as if it knew better and expected something.

In the most still time just before dawn she heard the sound of a leather-soled shoe scuffing against stone. At once she sat up.

Their camp was on a grassy treeless rise; the sentry placed nearest the forest was not to be seen. She crouched and quietly moved toward his post. The barest beginnings of dawn lightened the sky to a cold iron gray. She stole past the dark sleeping forms on the ground and at last saw the sentry. He lay asleep in the grass.

Asleep. It was impossible. She felt a twist of sickness in her stomach. She reached out and shook him. He rolled to his back. Embedded deep in his chest was a Roman catapult bolt.

She leapt to her feet. A quick glance about proved the pathfinder was gone.

He led us to this place and deserted us.

She almost stumbled over Witgern. "Arise!" she whispered. "We are betrayed! The pathfinder was our enemy!"

Witgern got to his feet, instantly awake.

Their encampment was well disguised among the long grasses; it would have been difficult for an enemy to find without the pathfinder's aid. Together they swiftly, quietly awakened everyone, ordering them to stay low and make no sound—Auriane feared the sight of their smallest movement might induce any enemy below to attack. Decius was alerted on his own, but at first he kept a respectful distance.

Auriane took Witgern's arm. "Look." Witgern followed her gaze and saw the dawn light reflected off something dully metallic in the furze bushes below. A helmet. No, more than one. At least twenty in that one place. "By now, for certain, we are surrounded," she whispered. Slowly Witgern nodded.

Witgern motioned for them to form a ring, the best defensive position for an attack on all sides. He attempted to put Auriane in the center with Decius and the priestesses, but she pushed roughly past him and took a position in the outer circle, armed with nothing but her fire-hardened ash spear.

"You've no shield," Witgern whispered angrily.

"And a serpent doesn't have wings."

"Auriane—!"

The lift of that chin, that will of bedrock, Witgern thought. What am I to do with it? "Get behind me, I command it! I gave my word to your fa—"

"No one commands me. And if you haven't the mettle, *I'll* answer to Baldemar."

A moment later Decius took a place beside her. She saw that somehow he found a spear, probably purloined during the confusion when all were awakened. Auriane heard Thorgild mutter, "That thrall better pray he's felled—it's kinder than what I'll do to him if we live."

"Leave him be," Witgern whispered to Thorgild. "The Roman swine fought against us—let him fight for us!"

Decius called out in a sharp whisper, addressing them all, "Move closer together—*much* closer—now, shields together! And down on your knees!"

"Decius, what are you doing!" Auriane whispered.

"A speaking thrall!" Thorgild muttered. "Next we'll come upon a talking mule."

But in the next instant Auriane realized: Decius is right. Our bodies are better protected that way.

Auriane then ordered softly, "Shields together!" She repeated all Decius' words—he spoke their language so poorly she was not certain they understood.

Witgern looked at her, offended at this usurpation of his authority. But when Coniaric hesitantly obeyed, followed by Thorgild and then the majority of the others, he reluctantly did likewise.

But Maragin and two elder Companions, whom age made stubborn, remained standing; they could not forget that the command was first spoken by a thrall. For the rest it made no difference from whom the words first came—for Auriane blessed them by speaking them herself. Did not Ramis herself pay heed to her words?

Decius commanded, voice low, "Do not break from this form, even if they attack only from the south side—it could well be a ruse." Again Auriane repeated his words.

From the thickets below rose the dark discordant moans of many war horns. Spears arched up; all at once the sky was full of them. They rained down, a lethal hail thudding hard against upraised shields.

Auriane cried out "*Wait!* Hold your weapons!"

Decius looked at her, amazed—she spoke the very words he meant to say. The spears had been fired from some sort of spring gun; their quarry was still at a distance no mortal arm could hurl a spear. An answering volley would only have divested them of weapons. He wondered: How did Auriane know? I told her of catapults but I did not tell her of anything like this—indeed, I've never seen anything quite like this myself. They have improvised weapons.

Spears struck wood and threw up turf; as their rhythm began to slow, Auriane heard a hoarse cry at her back. Maragin and the two elder Companions dropped, writhing, to the ground.

The thought was common among the survivors: They acted against the words of a ganna—and for it, they died.

Auriane covered the dead men's faces with their cloaks. One high, short blast sounded, and the enemy moved out from their cover, halting just beyond spear-casting range. Auriane and Witgern crawled forward, parted the grasses and looked down.

"Mother of the gods! We are done!" Witgern whispered.

Sunlight gleamed on a small sea of helmets. Upraised spears were thick as marsh grass. The warriors wore the woad-dyed blue tunics of Wido's Companions; one raised high the standard, a bristle-backed boar carved in wood. They were but a detachment of all Wido's Companions, and they numbered three hundred. In the rear were horsemen in scarlet-crested helmets and glittering mail; by the design of their iron-bound oval shields she knew they were men of the Roman native auxiliary cavalry—doubtless many of the same men who took part in the raid.

"Prepare the attack!" Witgern shouted to his own men.

Auriane stared at him in disbelief. "Witgern, no. You see our numbers are pitiful against them!"

"That counts for little in the afterworld. We fight until we die."

"No! We know what they want." She grasped his arm. "They want *me!*"

"I failed Baldemar once, I'll not do it again. I pledged to protect you unto death. We fight them!"

"That is madness! I cannot let everyone die in a doomed effort to save me. I shall surrender to them. You are not giving me up—I go of my own free will."

"No, Auriane. How does it look, me returning fit and unharmed after leaving you behind in that nest of nidings, to be wife to that pig-ox of a son of his?"

"It makes you look like a man who cares for the lives of his men! Better one life of misery than that all of us should die."

"I *cannot!*"

"Curses on your pride! Share my fate then. Follow me into captivity and let the rest go."

From below a coarse jubilant voice bellowed, "My friends! Have you had enough, or do you want more? Send down the daughter of Baldemar and you will suffer no more harm."

She recognized the voice below as Odberht's. Taking Witgern by the shoulders, she said, "If you share my fate, Baldemar will be kind. At least, you did not leave me. You might get free one day. As for me, be certain, whatever they do to me they shall first have a good fight."

Witgern looked restively down, then at the force arrayed below, and then at his own men, who had lost all taste for fighting because Auriane's heart was not with it. All the while he scowled fiercely and adjusted his eye-patch, believing this somehow made him appear less indecisive.

Auriane did not wait for his reply; she approached one of the priestesses and asked for her white cloak. As she passed Decius, she whispered quickly so only he could hear, "Farewell, great and good friend." To her amazement Decius seemed near tears. She thought: Surely it is but dust in his eye.

Then she returned to the edge of the slope, holding the white cloak aloft. White was the color of truce because all that was white belonged to Fria as Weaver of Peace: The doves that were a manifestation of her love, the clouds that were her thoughts, the shining white of the moon that was her raiment.

On the plain below, hundreds of spears were lowered as if by one hand. Auriane looked back at Witgern. After hesitating a moment longer, he walked at her side.

She did not realize the relief and joy of those behind her or the love and pity they felt for her then—she who bought their freedom at the price of her own.

Auriane saw Odberht on a forbidding black stallion that must have been provided by his Roman masters. He grinned at her. The bone handle of his sword was studded with rubies; his mount's bridle was inset with flashing medallions of silver. She kept her aspect calm, but within, her spirit collapsed in despair before the polished hooves of that steed.

I cannot have come to my end. Ramis, is this your curse, after all? Look at Odberht. He is licking his lips like a dog.

She fought panic by taking stock of all about her, measuring with her eye the space between horses, noticing how they were armed, who was alert and who was not. She looked for the contrivances that had shot the bolts and realized they must have been loaded into the wagons that followed the march.

Odberht threw a length of cord to a young Companion. Auriane's and Witgern's hands were bound behind them and they were put on horseback; another Companion secured them by lead-lines. Auriane judged that in two nights' time they would be in Wido's camp; from there, escape would be almost impossible.

Wido retired to his tent within the timber walls of the ancient Celtic fortress. Rain pelted the leather roof, causing his bones to ache. A sentry entered with Cerdic, the thin nervous youth who carried Wido's messages.

"The maid's been taken!" Cerdic announced. He had galloped ahead of Odberht's company to break the great news. "They'll arrive by sunfall, tomorrow."

"She is unhurt?" Wido asked, not allowing himself even a fleeting triumphant smile, too aware of how all good news carried the seeds of the foul. He pulled fretfully at his scraggly mustache, then gradually allowed himself to indulge in a bit of pleasant contemplation.

That is well! Baldemar tricked the people into hating me. When his daughter's one of us, they'll have to eat that hatred. The golden luck Baldemar always hoarded for himself, he'll be forced to share with me.

Grimelda was planted solidly behind Wido, engaged in changing the dressing of a sword wound that had nicked an upper rib; her eyes glimmered with displeasure at this interruption. Her stout red-blond braids were thick as an arm; they stuck out in a way that the messenger might have thought ridiculous, had she not made him so uneasy. When Grimelda was about, a man thought of one thing: Where is her axe? Almost any misstep could fire up that temper, except for one of Wido's—her husband she indulged like a child. In fact, she behaved as if Wido *was* her true child, and her natural children cur-dogs that got in her way.

Grimelda held Wido firmly in place, enveloping him in her fleshy vastness, giving a deep grunt as she pulled hard at the dressing. Wido cursed at the fresh pain, pulling away from her, which caused her to coo a stream of affectionate curses. The boy debated briefly whether that repellent rotted-cheese odor was coming from Grimelda or the wound.

Beneath a breast that put Cerdic in mind of a partially deflated wineskin, he saw the handle of her axe.

"She has some minor wounds that are her own fault," the boy answered, taking a small step back that he prayed would not be noticed. "We felled fifteen of them when they were taken," he lied boldly. "Baldemar's men surrendered like sheep! But later, we lost three of our own. She got loose, somebody untied her bonds and—"

"And I suppose that ox-brain son of mine didn't find out who."

"And she fought like a polecat, they say. She killed them with their own weapons. But they've got her securely now, do not fear."

"That son of mine will be my bane," Wido said, vigorously shaking his head so that his serpent curls lashed Grimelda across the face. "The boy needs a bit more discipline, I say. Cerdic, you will ride back to them at a good clip, with these words. And make sure you say them loudly so all Odberht's Companions hear it—you see to it that boy is *shamed*. Say Odberht is not to be given the maid at all. She goes to Ullrik, yes, to the *idiot* rather than to him."

A sharp voice behind Wido broke in then.

"I forbid it!" It was Claudius Hilarus, who had been quietly listening from a shadowed corner of the tent—he was the Roman emissary who kept a close eye on Wido now that Branhard was dead. "Nor will my lord the Governor allow it. Your warriors would never follow Ullrik into battle."

"Hilarus, one day you'll say, 'I forbid it,' one time too many and end up in Grimelda's stew," Wido said with smooth malice. "Do you think I'd throw away all we've been given? Drown me in the mead cask when I become that much of a mooncalf. Of *course* Odberht still gets her. Your alliance with us shall go on into the times of our children's children, so trim those Roman claws. I just want my son to think otherwise for a while—you know, have a little fun with the boy."

Cerdic intruded uneasily, "My lord, there is one more thing I was charged to tell. Odberht's men caught and tortured one of Baldemar's messengers. Baldemar's daughter, it seems, has made a great kill. She is the slayer of the missing cavalry Prefect, Valerius—"

"*What?*" Hilarus interrupted, rising slowly to his feet. He took

a decisive step forward until he stood beside Wido, the tendons of
his neck standing out prominently, a hot flush beginning to spread
across his stolid face. "What is that, boy?" he said softly.

". . . Sylvanus . . . ," Cerdic said, finishing with the falling
tones of one who realizes he has said too much.

Hilarus turned to Wido. "Sylvanus' murderer! She is a common
butcher! By the brow of Minerva, I am among savages! Wido, if
this be true, *you must hand that maid over to us for execution.*"

Wido required a moment to catch up. Then with oily slowness
he turned, meeting Hilarus' gaze, masking feeling with a tight,
contained smile while his eyes sharpened to steel darts.

"Hilarus, you've a gift for getting in my way when a half-
starved bear has the wit to stay off from me. She is no *murderer.*
She killed a man of the Hermundures who invaded our lands. It's
not her fault he was who he was. She is *mine*, you abominable
pirate, and you'll keep your swinish Roman hands off her!"

"If the victim were of lower rank, I could accede to you, Wido."
Hilarus was a creature of dulled instincts and he unwisely chose to
regard Wido's rage as the temperamental fit of an excitable boy.
"But she murdered a man with family ties to the Emperor himself,
and Rome must be given an accounting."

Only the boy Cerdic noticed Grimelda slowly drawing out her
axe, but his throat clenched closed and he could not speak.

"I say *no* to you, and I will hear no argument," Wido said,
settling back into calm as if that settled the matter.

Cerdic watched, paralyzed, as in one rolling motion Grimelda
and the axe rose up together. The boy tried to cry out a warning but
all that came out of him was a frightened squeak. In her
enthusiasm Grimelda heaved her bulk forward as she brought the
blade down on the back of Hilarus' broad neck. *Thuk.* The boy
fainted.

Wido took a moment to collect himself. Then he bellowed for
his guards. As they crowded in and looked about, stupefied by the
sight of blood everywhere and the still twitching corpse, Wido was
regarding Grimelda with a proud and loving look.

"Better about the place than fifty guard dogs, my dear Grimelda
is! Take him out. And the boy, too. What a mess."

Wido thought swiftly. Bury the Roman slime in the darkest part
of the bogs. We'll make up a tale for them. This one won't be
badly missed—he was of humble birth and held no great rank
among his people.

"And cut the boy's throat," Wido added as an afterthought as the guards were dragging out Hilarus' body by the feet. The boy Cerdic would not be allowed any chance to spread lies about his son's bride. "And send me another messenger for instructions, at once!"

But what if the lie makes its way to the Governor? I will deny it, Wido decided. I'll say Baldemar's men invented it to add much needed grandeur to his crumbling name. Surely Julianus will not be fool enough to sacrifice his influence in the whole of the north for one miserable cavalry Prefect, relative of the Emperor or no.

Auriane shivered beneath a deerhide blanket, her back against the rough bark of a pine. She saw a bent form lurching toward her through the night, bearing a steaming bowl of gruel, and was cheered when she recognized Ullrik's hobble-and-skip. Odberht had doubled her guard since her attempted escape; ten warriors stood about her in a ring. But they paid no mind to Ullrik; all thought him a gibbering fool—the boy might have been a squirrel nosing about the camp.

Ullrik spooned the gruel into her mouth, for her hands were bound behind her back. Something pale and ropelike moved in the wet leaves behind him. She realized Odberht or one of his comrades had tied a string of badger tails to the back of the boy's tunic to torment him.

"Blessings on you, Ullrik," she whispered between gulps. "Once again, they forgot to feed me."

Ullrik leaned close, doe-soft eyes opened wide. "My brother comes now," came his childish whisper in her ear, "to do an evil thing to you."

Auriane felt her stomach tighten. "Ullrik, what are you saying?"

"My brother has just been told you are to be given to *me*, and not to him—and he is very angry."

"Does Wido mean it truly?"

"No. He would never marry you to me." The words spoken without rancor were the more pitiful to her. "But he's made Odberht believe it. He is on his way now to . . . to . . ."

"To have one last chance at what's to be taken from him."

"I am sad for you. I am. . . ." Ullrik put his hands to his head and softly cried.

"Quiet, Ullrik, please, for your sake!" she whispered. The boy sniffled. "Ullrik, that drinking horn you carry—it is of Ubian glass, is it not?"

Ullrik nodded eagerly, the smallest flash of proprietary pride in his eye.

"If you will give it to me, you may have my silver and garnet necklet in exchange."

"Oh, but you cheat yourself. The necklet is worth far more."

"But I fancy it, and I do not care."

"Here, then, I wish you to have it." He tied the glass horn to her belt, then fanned her cloak about her so it was concealed. "I want nothing in exchange."

"Ullrik, no. You have so little. . . ."

"Ullrik gives a gift to his kind sister."

"Ullrik, if I live and Baldemar is victorious, I will send for you. You will be treated with kindness among us, I promise it on my mother's name. You can serve Baldemar as a messenger."

Five lurching torchflames approached to the accompaniment of leather-clad feet tramping in mud and leaves. Ullrik froze where he crouched, tipping the gruel, which slopped onto the ground. Auriane looked up. Lit by torchlight was a thick sweating face with a soft, pursed child's mouth, Grimelda's snout, and eyes that were flint-hard but vague—Odberht.

"Look, Ranulf," he said to one of his Companions. "Did we catch them in time? I believe my wicked little brother was ready to mount the bride before the wedding! And is this young cock to be blamed? Look at her!"

He raised and lowered the torch as if to show off Auriane to his Companions. "Behold the disputed maid—strong, well formed, firm of flesh. This young mare's still half wild, I fear—she needs a better rider than *you* to tame her, little brother. She'll throw you off."

Auriane flattened herself against the tree, feeling the blank fright of the prey-animal cringing before the predator's claw. Odberht hoisted Ullrik to his feet, then, grunting with the effort, heaved him into the brush with a great crash.

"Brothers should share, don't you think?" he called out to Ullrik as he hurriedly unbound Auriane's legs. "You'll have her all the rest of your nights. I promise to return her just as I found her—well, almost! Don't look for her maiden's flower."

Auriane fought to conceal her terror, sensing it would incite him the more. She shut out the picture of what had happened to her mother for fear it would send her into a fit of madness.

Odberht prodded her down the path, her hands still bound behind her back. Ranulf and the others followed at a short distance; Odberht knew every man of them might be needed to restrain her.

The path sloped sharply downward. Soon the air was like the breath of serpents; she guessed they approached a marsh. A high moon, nearly full, was reflected in oily water; they had come to the bank of a reed-filled pond. She sensed no love in Fria's eye; that moon seemed to measure and warn. But she found meager comfort in the water, which by nature takes the form of whatever is about—it is lost, it finds itself again; it is bright, deep, eternal, its water sounds full of whispered assurances to the dead.

But the terror still hugged her close, a simple childish fear of pain. Odberht ordered the others to stand near, but not too near; she heard his gloating words as if from a great distance. Then she stood alone with him in the bleak moonlight, among angelica weeds, shrubs of white willow, and the urgent warning calls of frogs.

Fria, I do not feel you close. You watch, but you do not care. Why has my heavenly mother become a judge?

Odberht examined her, one hand under her chin, savoring her helplessness. She watched him, eyes brilliant, chest heaving with her ragged breaths. His eagerness was bestial and horrible—she felt herself a choice cut of meat ready to be bolted down by a hungry hound.

Fria, give me back the smallest portion of my mother wit, and I promise you a sacrifice of milk and mead richer than any you've yet seen at midsummer.

"If you please me," Odberht said softly, "I won't give you afterwards to *them*." He indicated his fellows with a broad wave of the hand.

"That is well," she managed in a voice free of trembling. "After *you*, they would be disappointing as a bowl of nettle soup after a boar feast."

This was a pleasurable slap that threw him faintly off balance. He looked closely at her. That timorousness—was there not something slyly passionate in it? Was that fear . . . or closely bridled desire?

He tried to shrug the moment off, but was not entirely successful; her words subtly altered her in his sight, and this undermined him even as he refused to acknowledge it. With great contempt, he ripped her cloak from her shoulders and flung it to the ground. He wanted her to suffer the shame he felt on the day

Baldemar treacherously pulled him from his horse. All whom Baldemar loved would pay him well for that crime.

As the cloak fell, Auriane felt Ullrik's horn drop near her foot.

"You think me stupid and coarse," he said loudly, legs planted apart. "You think our whole family stupid and coarse. But no matter. Whatever *we* are, you soon will be also."

"Coarse, perhaps. But can it be entirely laid to your account?" She braced herself for a perilous chance. "How could the child of two guest-murderers be anything but coarse?"

She felt a start of relief. The notion seemed to agree with him; he evidently loathed both parents enough to want to be seen as above—and apart—from them.

"You've a scrap of good sense, considering you yourself are the spawn of a villainous night crawler!" Odberht responded. "It is true . . . *I* slay only my enemies."

He took his dagger, made a cut in her tunic, and began roughly tearing it.

"*That* betrays whose child you are!"

He paused, irritated by the rebuke, but intrigued.

"It is evident no one ever taught you that love can be as a musician's art," she went on quickly, "and that the strings make a finer music when lightly struck."

"Musicians are not men," he replied, assessing her warily. "If you want a blow across the face, liken me to them."

"Tread softly when you mock, Odberht—for it was Ramis who taught the love-arts to me."

His eyes widened. "She does not teach such things." It was as much a question as a statement.

"Oh, but she *does*. She teaches of all of life. Her apprentices must know the ceremonies that give new life to the plants and raise the sap in the trees. Of me, she said I had skill enough to coax a barren patch of waste ground into feeding a village for a year." In his eye she saw a jump of interest. "And it is vexatious when one is schooled, and not given a chance to use one's skill. . . . A warrior in time of peace must know this."

Ranulf called out, prodded by his fear of will-o'-the-wisps: "Odberht! Are you going to bandy words all night? The bold warrior attacks and retreats quickly!" His fellows laughed nervously.

"Ranulf, you couple like a dog. I at least am a man."

"Well spoken!" Auriane said softly. She moved closer until there was but a hand's breadth between their faces. Odberht marveled at the power of those eyes to numb good sense, to make him want to follow, to believe, to drown in them.

"On some other night," she whispered, "I might teach you . . ."

"I despise empty words. You'll show me *now*." As he spoke, he began swiftly shedding clothing, tossing his sword and swordbelt well out of her reach.

"But . . . I cannot."

His hands jumped to her throat, "You *will*, or you'll not draw breath long enough to cross me again!"

"My hands are bound. In love, hands must speak—"

"Slippery wench! As though I were fool enough to unbind your hands!" But she heard a trace of angry regret in his voice.

"Well, no matter, for Ramis has laid a death curse on anyone who reveals it to anyone outside her holy circle. . . ."

From his face she knew curiosity and lust had finally trampled caution.

"*You're* cursed already, you've little to lose," he said, grinning. "And if the curse spreads to your night-crawling family, so much the better! I'll loosen *one* hand," he said as he adjusted the cord so that one hand was bound, and secured the cord's trailing end to a tree. "And if this be some sly trick, your blood will soak the ground!"

Then he cut the rope that secured her riding breeches, and they fell into a heap at her feet. For a moment he stared in wonder at her naked form in the wan moonlight; she was eerily white, an idol in luminous bone. He could scarce believe this lofty nymph was entirely *his*, to use as he pleased. Roughly he dragged her toward him, crushing her breasts against his chest. Then he regarded her expectantly. She fought vainly for calm.

After a moment of hesitation, she snaked her free hand about his neck, moving delicately over skin that felt like bull's hide. She improvised caresses, attempting to touch cleverly, knowingly, making a complicated progress down his back toward his buttocks, that hand a desperate actress playing a role it was never taught. Fighting revulsion, she made a naïve attempt at a lingering seductive kiss, while that fugitive hand made awkward crab-walking progress round to the front of him, ready to make a game and pitiful attempt at caressing his sex. But all at once—she never knew whether it was because he loathed to have her touch him there, or some more obscure cause—it seemed a demon was released in him.

He seized her shoulders, pushed her roughly back, then threw her down onto her cloak. She struck a rock and cried out in pain. Her cry seemed to excite him more than her caresses had; he collapsed on top of her, breathing heavily, pinning her beneath his bulk, attacking her face with fierce, biting kisses that bruised her lips. Once he drew blood and lapped it like a beast. She gave up all attempts to feign knowledge—he lost himself in a rutting haze and no longer seemed to remember she was to teach him the love-arts. She fought desperately to push him off before he cracked her ribs, feeling black bog water close over her head—this then, she thought, is what it is like to drown in mud.

With her free hand she grappled about in the mud and leaves, searching frantically for the glass horn, snaking beneath his leaden weight, evading him as he tried to enter her. Her struggling only fanned his ferocity.

"Too good for us, are you?" he said between heaving breaths. "I will show you what you're good for." He pinned her unbound hand and struck her hard across the face. She saw white light. The hand slipped free, lubricated by the sweat of his palm. This time she found Ullrik's horn.

She struck it hard against the ground, hoping it would strike stone and break, but suddenly there seemed to be no stones anywhere. Then in her struggles her left hand worked free of its noose, and at last both hands were free.

Battering ram knees drove her thighs apart. She lay limp and defenseless; she had exhausted herself with struggling.

Mother, she thought wildly, why should I escape what you suffered? You were the innocent one, and I the one born with the demon's mark.

He moved over her with the top-heavy grace of the bull mounting the cow. Then he forced himself inside her with one brutish thrust, and she felt a flare of pain in her loins that flashed out all through her body; she was afire, burning as Hertha burned, twisting in agony. She stifled a scream.

His movement within her had the manic vigor of beasts. She felt herself not so much a woman as a morsel of food—who considered the feelings of the bread when taking the first hungry bite?

Triumphantly he studied her face. The shame and suffering he saw pleased him greatly.

She was his. He had put out that proud light in her eye. And she would remain his. He would make certain his brother never bedded her at all; the children she bore would be sired by him. All that kept him from perfect ecstasy was that he would be denied the sight of Baldemar's face when he learned of this, because Baldemar would soon be dead.

Auriane summoned a last reserve of strength, and once more struck the horn against the ground. This time she struck stone. The glass cracked and broke, leaving a jagged edge sharp as any dagger.

His whole body shuddered with pleasure; a series of pig grunts came from him.

"At last!" Ranulf called out from his post. "Nature would perish away, were all creatures as slow to couple as Odberht!"

She stabbed the only place she could reach: the side of that bull neck. He did not realize at first that the warm liquid trickling down his neck was his own blood.

Then he felt the pain, dull at first, then terrifying when he realized what she had done.

"*She-viper!*" he breathed, heaving himself up. He clamped his hands onto the wound to staunch the flow of blood. "I'll see you trampled under horses! Ranulf! Ethred! She has not had enough. Come and take her!"

Auriane took swift advantage of the situation, throwing herself into a sitting position, shifting his weight off her so that she was able to fight her way to her feet. Then she sprang forward blindly as a hare in a net, ignoring the white hot pain in her loins; she struck Ranulf and knocked him down. Then she bolted off through the willow thickets.

"Demon woman! Get her!" came Odberht's shout.

"Spawn of a loon! You unbound her!"

The five young men gave chase, following the sound of her crashing through the undergrowth. She burst into an open path and ran quietly for a time, then she startled a doe with two spring fawns. They bounded in three directions, making their own crashing sounds, confusing her pursuers. Unknowingly, Odberht followed one of the fawns. After a short pursuit the fawn stopped in a glade and peered back at him, immobilized with fear. Limpid eyes looked at him piteously.

The other four caught up. They demanded to know what was wrong.

"*Shapeshifter,*" Odberht whispered in spirit-terror, edging away from the fawn. "Foul sorceress! Vile witchery! Look. She transformed herself into a fawn. But those are her eyes. Look!"

Not far off, Auriane slipped quietly into the pond. She swam as long as she could beneath the shallow water, hating the muddy bottom with its treacherous branches like so many slimy fingers struggling to snare her and drag her down. She surfaced amid reeds and rolled onto her back, allowing only her face to break the water.

Terrified of the horrors that lurked by night in a marsh, she imagined herself some water plant that belonged there, drifting gently, her face a night bloom turned to the moon. She heard Odberht and his fellows thrashing around for a time, and then there was silence. She whispered a prayer of thanksgiving to Fria for sending the deer. She did not move until smears of purple and orange above the spruce trees signaled a sad dawn.

As she rocked slowly and the breeze of day began ruffling the water, she cried inside: Give me back the old world! It was more a throbbing in the heart than a thought. Where is my home? It is a fiery furnace. Where is Baldemar? Lying broken somewhere. And who am I? A fouled maiden covered with slime who should have followed Hertha into the flames.

She felt rotted through with shame; it lived in her like a grinning serpent. His violence to her was her own evil made visible. The animal in her wanted never to be touched by a man's hands again, but her reasoning self replied, no, it is not that simple. That was not a man at all, but a large and dangerous child.

But I escaped from him. Is it of importance how?

Only the Assembly mattered now—if she did not reach it before this day's eve came, she would have to wait another year to marry the god and take the warrior's oath. And Baldemar could not wait that long for vengeance.

Gradually a strengthening anger came, buoying her up. Slowly she crept back to the scene of the last night's struggle, wearing nothing but the earth amulet Ramis gave her, listening for signs of human life. She heard none. There were her clothes, and the bloody, broken horn. Only her cloak escaped Odberht's dagger; gratefully she took it and wrapped herself in its warmth.

She found the stream that fed the pond and followed it south, feeling herself more deer than woman.

You are an animal alone. To the world, show only claws.

CHAPTER VII

The full moon of midsummer brimmed with magic. It shed so much light at midnight it might have been an eerie day, a colorless noon of bare hills gently rolling, broken by occasional groves painted in shadow and light.

The Midsummer Assembly was the greatest of the year; all who could ride or walk flocked to its sacred promontory. It lay in the hill country, far in the southern reaches of their lands, close enough to Wido's camp that sentries would have been posted except it was unthinkable that anyone of the tribal blood would violate the sanctity of the holiest full moon of the year.

The hill was chosen because it was crowned by a lone oak of such fearsome magnificence it was commonly said if all the land's oaks formed up in battle this one would be their king. It was a sapling before the Romans came; now it was a gnarled old god, grand enough to shelter hundreds. Bitter roots clenched the earth; a stout trunk split into myriad branches spiraling out into anguished fingers that seemed to scratch at the sky. This oak was thought a bridge between heaven and earth, uniting the spirits underground with the sylphs of the air. When the cold, potent light of the midsummer moon fell on that oak, the people believed no judgment given beneath its branches could be false.

Set about it was a ring of torches; within this ring the twelve High Priestesses and Priests of Wodan stood masked and crowned with oak leaves. The people camped all over the open land, up to the edge of the beech and oak forest where night hovered close. None strayed off alone into the wood—on midsummer night, it was said, the caverns leading to Helle yawned open and multitudes of unholy things with cloven hooves and glittering eyes ventured forth to frolic about, couple, or keep still, quietly watching.

It was the first Assembly in the memory of most that was not overshadowed by the presence of Baldemar—the medicine women insisted he not be moved from his tent in the war camp. His Companions sat in a place of honor in the forepart of the throng, nearest the oak. Baldemar's place was represented by an empty bench on which his sword was placed. Sigwulf and Thorgild sat at the head of his Companions.

On the day before, the Companions who had accompanied Auriane arrived with the news of the ambush and her capture. And so the measure of hope the people gained when Baldemar drove off Wido was lost. This was a blow that surely Baldemar would never survive. The tale of the Ash Grove slaying also spread rapidly, and was known to everyone at the Assembly, but now it only brought looks of puzzlement. "How was an omen fit for a battle-hero given to one with the luck of a thrall?" it was asked.

During the opening ceremonies, Sigreda slaughtered and offered up a white mare and a black stallion. The flesh was passed among the Holy Ones and eaten. The beasts' heads were hung in the low branches of the oak.

Then a gong was struck to summon silence. The tone was soft but long-lived, a dark purplish sound that shivered out until it melted finally into the honey-musk smells of night, leaving a quiet so vast many could hear the blood dripping from the horses' heads onto muddy ground.

Geisar and Sigreda performed the cursing ritual: The priest placed a figure of straw that represented Wido into the sacrificial fire while Sigreda spoke the words that swore the traitor out of the tribe. Then, one by one, judgments were given on various matters: the disputed ownership of a strip of prime farmland, or the possession of thirty head of cattle that wandered from their home pasture, or the occasional case of murder to be settled by payment in rings rather than by blood vengeance.

When the last judgment was given, the priestesses and priests began the mass rite of receiving new warriors into the tribal army. Two dozen wild boars caught for this purpose were ritually slaughtered. A candidate came forward and offered proof he had slain an enemy with an honorable weapon of war—generally the proof was a witness as well as some token taken from the fallen man. If he was accepted by the people, he ate a small portion of boar's heart and took the oath. As night progressed, the tribal army was increased by one hundred thirty-nine men—mostly warriors' sons—and five women, all daughters of the groves. The number was pathetically few, many feared, when they thought of Wido's steady supply of seasoned foreign soldiers.

Well into the night Sigreda's bell-clear voice proclaimed: "Now we summon Wodan to lay a hand on the head of the one who must lead us out to destroy the traitor. Who shall carry the standard?"

Sigwulf leaned close to Thorgild. "Watch well," he whispered. Thorgild nodded. They were certain Geisar and Sigreda were Wido's pawns, and they suspected the priest would try to put forward the name of a man in Wido's pay. Among themselves they planned to call out only Sigwulf's name; if the name of more than one man of Baldemar's Companions was put in, it might cause division among the people and give Geisar the chance to break the stalemate by putting in a name of his own.

There were moments of sad silence and glances at Baldemar's empty seat. Then finally, hesitantly, names were proposed. Thorgild waited through the first ten or twelve; each brought cheers from one section of the people and volleys of gnawed bones and rotten fruit from another. Then he stood and shouted Sigwulf's name. Spears were clashed against shields and a greater noise was made than for any other candidate. This was as they expected.

And then a little known man among the free warriors proposed Thorgild's name. The cheers raised up equaled closely those given Sigwulf.

"Who is that fool? I'll have his head on a spit!" Sigwulf muttered.

"Geisar paid him well, you can be certain," Thorgild said.

What followed did not surprise them. Geisar came forward and humbly announced, "Since we cannot agree, sacred law demands I decide between them, or offer you a third choice. Sigwulf and Thorgild are of equal eminence—it is impossible to choose. Therefore. . . ." Geisar paused.

There was some disturbance at the back of the throng and the sound of determined chanting. Geisar strained to see and hear, but the participants were too distant. He exchanged an anxious look with Sigreda. She gave the barest shrug.

"Therefore," Geisar continued, "I name Unfrith."

"The viper! He has done it!" Sigwulf said in a covered voice.

"Unfrith. I can scarce believe it! He might as well have named one of Wido's sons!"

The man named Unfrith stepped nimbly to the front, a faintly amused smile on his face. His trappings spoke of new wealth: A fine cloak of ermine swept the ground; his swordbelt was of polished new leather, its buckle of heavy gold. That calfskin tunic and those high-laced boots had never seen mud. Had he traveled here in a Roman covered carriage? Sigwulf wondered with contempt.

The response was half-hearted, uncertain. Hasty looks were exchanged to see what others thought of this.

"The fox," Thorgild agreed, slowly nodding while his hand moved unconsciously to feel the hilt of his sword. "And the people have no notion. He named a relation of the father's side. Were it the mother's, he knows well they would tear him apart!"

Where they trusted the priest, they applauded loudest, from piety more than enthusiasm. But there were pockets of silence all through the throng. The common people did not consider Unfrith a close relative of Wido's at all—only those of higher rank counted relations in the Roman fashion, through the paternal line—and so suspected nothing on the face of it. But with the animal sense of crowds they scented something was amiss; Geisar seemed all too pleased to announce this man. And Unfrith was a pathetic replacement for Baldemar.

Sigwulf knew Wido counted Unfrith a close kinsman; privately Wido imitated closely the customs of his Roman masters, even as he belittled them. The traitor's influence would live on. Unfrith would quickly acquire fame if the battle was won, and Baldemar, when he recovered, might never again reclaim the standard.

Geisar was working himself into a fury even so, Sigwulf saw, pacing fitfully while stabbing at the ground with his staff. The response was too tepid for him and he was insulted.

Geisar paused to look once more toward the forest, his hair floating out like ghostly wings. The chanting and the cries from the back were gaining in force. It had a rebellious note that stiffened the priest's spine. From his vantage point he could see a knot of people far down on the slope; the crowd made way for them as slowly they worked their way toward the Midsummer Oak.

Now he could hear what they cried.

"Daughter of the Ash! Lead us out!"

• • •

Earlier in the night while the new warriors were still being made, a muddy urchin clad in a bramble-dotted cloak fastened with thorns emerged from the forest. When she approached the nearest of her countrymen, a black-bearded smith, and asked where Baldemar was, he answered with a scowl and silence. When she told him who she was, he gave a mocking laugh.

"This little mud-hen Baldemar's daughter! A shame no one's told you she's better guarded than a Roman fortress. Off with you!"

She nearly lost heart then, and slipped back into the forest. She had walked all day and most of the night, sleeping for a short time at midday, curled in a hawthorn thicket among beetles and ants and the noise of birds. She was exhausted and dirty. For a moment she could not remember why she ever wanted to take the oath. Perhaps marriage to Witgern . . .

But Witgern was a prisoner. Her brother was dead, slain by the Romans. Neither her mother nor father could walk without help. Her family was dying, and it would live again only if one of its members won a great act of vengeance. The Assembly would disperse at moonset; she must go forth now or not at all.

She approached an old farm woman with the same question; she proved to be Herwig, whose lands lay alongside her family's.

"Auriane, it truly is you! Your father is well enough, but he's not here."

Gradually others turned to look and knew her too. They gathered round to gape.

"It is a prodigy!" someone cried.

"She cannot have escaped, yet she has!"

"The Fates freed her to save us!"

To save us? she thought. I myself am but a few steps away from death; how can I save anyone?

"Daughter of the Ash!" came a triumphant cry. Others liked the sound of those words and quickly took them up.

She struggled to get past them. "Let me pass. I've little time left—I mean to take the oath!"

"Not looking so, you won't," Herwig called out, producing a comb and holding Auriane fast. She tried to drag it through Auriane's hair, but after a short struggle she gave it up as hopeless; the mud had dried in it. A wealthy herder who had several cloaks he meant to sell placed one over Auriane's ragged cloak to conceal it. Quietly she thanked him and moved on.

As she moved forward the scattered cries, "Daughter of the Ash! Lead us out!" became unified and took on a joyous, aggressive rhythm that was irresistible; first dozens, then hundreds joined in.

As more in the throng recognized her, it was as if they caught fire. If Baldemar had appeared among them, they could not have felt more exultant. By the time Geisar brought Unfrith forward, two hundred and more followed her closely—a sort of honor guard drunk on mead and moonlight, conducting her to the oak.

They half dragged Auriane up the hill like some unwilling donkey. The crowd's abandoned wildness was beginning to frighten her; it seemed but a breath away from murderous frenzy.

Gradually she realized they meant for her to take Baldemar's place.

When the twenty-two surviving Companions Baldemar had sent to take her south caught sight of her, it was as though fresh logs were thrown onto a bonfire.

"Ganna! Ganna!" they cried. Already they had spread everywhere the tale that she had saved their lives when she gave up her freedom to Odberht. And the story of the encounter with Ramis was embellished with each retelling, until it became a sort of war of magicians, which they assumed, because Auriane survived, she must have won.

Unfrith scented the crowd's dislike of him and wisely yielded, falling back into the throng. Geisar's shrieks for order went unheard; the people seemed to have forgotten him.

Hylda came forward from among the Holy Ones and took Auriane's hand in a wiry grip. As Hylda braved the thickest part of the throng, leading Auriane, she showed her cursing finger to any who seemed ready to bar the way. Eventually they gained the sacred circle about the oak.

Sigwulf viewed it all with relief and hope—Baldemar's power would not be wrested from him while he lay wounded. But when he saw Auriane, relief became pity. She looked more gaunt than he remembered, and tragically older; in one summer she had passed from wise child to care-burdened young woman. He saw her brave struggle to hide her weariness; she stood solemnly straight, eyes cast down, her tangled hair making her appear some orphaned maid abandoned to the forest. Her only ornament was the chaplet of vervain someone set on her head.

Geisar stopped before her. He seemed some frail thunder god, debating whether to hurl a bolt of fire.

"You are a fount of evil," he said softly, lifting her chin. "You make a mockery of sacred law. Off with you, before I break my staff and condemn you!"

She met his gaze calmly, too weary to feel fear. "It was never in my mind to carry the standard, only to take the oath. And I mean to take it."

"You are the last child of your family. You are needed to produce heirs."

"It is not to be, Geisar. Baldemar charged me to tell you, *I* am the appeasement gift. This is our sacrifice. We offer up all hope of heirs."

She saw a spark of alarm in his eye as he realized her full purpose.

"Never on this earth! I will not allow it."

"He will not allow it!" shouted a man of powerful voice for the benefit of the crowd. This brought an angry groan from the people, followed by another rain of refuse—Geisar was narrowly missed by fishbones, entrails, broken crockery and dung, while Auriane and Hylda shielded themselves as best they could. Those at the front of the throng watched open-mouthed—never had they seen Geisar so abused.

Geisar struggled to maintain a look of outraged dignity, but fright undermined him. The fearful respect he always commanded was so swiftly withdrawn he had not time to fully accept that he was naked of it, and vulnerable. Though he always counted his hold on the people a fragile thing, its means mysterious, he had long lulled himself into thinking of it as unshakable.

From far back in the crowd, someone cast a spear. It bit deep into the earth, striking within a finger's breadth of the priest's foot.

Geisar gave a hoarse shout, eyes blank, face agonized as if his heart had been pierced. He sank to his knees, tearing at his hair, writhing and wailing, certain this was a sign he angered Wodan, god of the spear. Sigreda, terrified too, rushed forward, pulled him up, and had him led off to the deerhide shelters on the far side of the circle. To soften the crowd, she ordered the two sacrificing priests to give Auriane the oath.

When all was in readiness, Auriane was veiled as a bride. She faced Sigreda across the firepit, where precious woods smoked and burned. Sigreda was masked as a cat; to the people she was possessed of the soul of Fria. Beside her was a priest in a boar's mask, an upright spear in his hand. He embodied Wodan. An assisting priestess made her way slowly toward the fire and put a bone flute to her lips; she was clad in a bloodied boar's hide, her face reddened with ocher.

The flute brought a spirit-filled silence to the people as its light note darted about, dipping low, soaring suddenly, then dissolving into ripples as though wind disturbed the surface of a lake, its tone unpredictable as life, first sweet, then sour, always achingly clear. Auriane's eyes glistened with sadness, and she was not certain why—she felt some terrible jest was being played on all creatures living, and she was helpless against it.

A sacrificing priest took a bit of boar's heart from the great bronze bowl atop its tripod, spitted it, then thrust it into the sacred fire.

Then Wodan spoke to Fria: "Tree of life, whose roots go down and down into nether rime, we bless you and praise you. I who am the steed of the dead, I who am war, I who suffered and died to see the secrets of the Well of Urdr, take this woman as bride."

And Fria responded: "I am memory. I am Chaos from Chaos in the time before time. I brought the age of Ice then took it away. I brought forth all that flourishes in the Three Worlds. I create and destroy with one hand. The Sun and almighty Moon are my eyes. God of War, I bid you, raise the veil."

With the point of the spear Wodan lifted the veil from Auriane's face. The act married her to him.

"Now I mark her as my own," the priest who was Wodan intoned. He bared Auriane's left upper arm and, with a bone dagger, carved into her flesh the runic sign of the god of war. Auriane's tears flowed freely from the pain. Then Fria reddened her finger in the boar's blood and drew the same sign on Auriane's forehead.

Next the assisting priest held out to her the roasted heart. It was still dark and bloody. Auriane ate slowly, using all her strength not to vomit.

"This heart gives her the heart of a boar that never falters in the charge," Wodan proclaimed. "Now, draw forth a plait!"

As Auriane obeyed, she felt boar-spirit surging in her. She saw herself with fierce bright eyes and a dark heart pumping angry blood.

Mother, a girl cannot protect you well. But a boar can, the dim words came half formed in her mind.

Auriane then chanted the words of the oath along with the priest who was Wodan:

"I foreswear mead shed, hall, and farm. I foreswear peace while my enemy lives. I foreswear all mortal marriage. Vengeance is my meat, blood is my mead—"

They were interrupted by a furious beating of heavy wings. An owl dropped out of the night, flapped angrily before Auriane, then was off. She heard murmurs of unease all around. The bird was strangely bold; Auriane felt it knew her.

I feel Hertha's spirit is that bird. This ceremony is hateful to her; she wants it to stop. She is certain it leads to some great evil. Hertha, you harried me enough in life! Stay with the dead.

"In your name, Wodan, I redden my spear with enemies' blood. Bringer of victory, I am your own."

"Hail, Day. Hail, Night. Hail, all hail," the masked Sigreda responded softly.

The priest who was Wodan then placed a twisted ring of silver on Auriane's right arm. When she felt the weight of the warrior's ring, she had a sense of welcome emptiness. Now the bridge was crossed and torn down. She found herself alone on a wilder shore, a bleak and dangerous place, but at least it was a place of hope.

Hylda took up iron shears and began cutting off Auriane's hair. A woman's hair was a house of spirits, rendering her too holy to touch weapons of iron. As the heavy tresses fell and collected in the dirt, Auriane for one horrified moment knew them as sentient things, severed and bleeding. She was taunted by Ramis' words, *"Never forget the power in hair."*

But I shall forget it, Auriane decided. *Take your shadow life from me.*

As Hylda swiftly wove the shoulder-length remains into one thick braid, Auriane felt her neck exposed to the chill breath of demons. She felt too light, as if her hair had anchored her down—now she might float off and be swallowed by night.

Hylda burned the cuttings in the fire, lest anyone retrieve them and use them to work magic against Auriane or her family.

"Bring forth the standard!" a voice from the throng cried out, followed by an eruption of cheers and a resumption of the chant: *Daughter of the Ash. Lead us out.*

Sigreda debated briefly, despising the fact she was forced to do the bidding of an unruly crowd, but she was wise enough to know that on this night, the battle was lost and the throng was victorious. She nodded to the assisting priest, who approached with the standard.

The standard of the army was a cat skull mounted on a short pole hewn of hazelwood. As Auriane took it from Sigreda, the throng raised up a mountain of noise that surely was heard, Auriane thought, in Roman Gaul. As the joyful thunder went on and on, Auriane watched the firelight play on Sigreda's silver cat-mask with its great staring eyes, warping it into forbidding shapes. In one moment Auriane saw the living eyes within the holes bored into the black-painted eyes of the mask; Sigreda held her gaze for a time to make certain Auriane was aware of the cold hatred there.

Auriane knew then Sigreda held her to account for the humiliation of Geisar. She knew, too, of Sigreda's vindictiveness, and her long memory.

She will work and plan for as long as is necessary until she finds a way to condemn me to some shameful death.

When the midsummer bonfires died and the Assembly dispersed, Auriane rode with the Companions to Antelope Ridge, where Baldemar was camped. Her arm burned with pain from the god's mark—but never had pain been so welcome. The oath protected her from Wido better than any high palisade; he might murder her, but no power on earth could marry her to one of his sons, for she was married already. In some moments she felt not joy but a great hollowness, and she envied other women their mortal husbands.

The tribal warriors followed at a slower pace; by the second day ten thousand were camped among the beech trees on the ridge. Before Auriane presented herself at Baldemar's tent, she looked long at Wido's encampment on the grassy plain below. It was a busy ant colony atop its gentle mound of earth. Roman order had but a slight effect on barbarian disorder, and the placement of buildings and tents was to Auriane familiar chaos. Roman military wagons moved in both directions through the fort's main gate, which had been rebuilt in the fashion of the drop-gate of a Roman fortress. Some sort of cavalry exercise seemed to be in progress.

The camp was a festering wound on the body of her country. Hopelessness fell on her like a yoke. The numbers of Wido's troops and their supplies were inexhaustible.

The guard of honor before Baldemar's tent let her pass unannounced.

She paused to let her eyes know the dark. The tent's smoke hole was open; Baldemar sat isolated in thought before a small yew fire, birch rod in hand as he drew symbols in the dirt representing land features and men. The leg, heavily bandaged, lay on a pile of hides.

"Father, I am here."

Baldemar did not look up. She smiled, doubting he heard. Then she moved close and began studying his marks in the dirt. Soon she was as absorbed in the battle plans as he.

"The pits and the stakes—so that is how they are set out," she said intently.

"Yes. The thrall you brought with you calls them *lilia*—that is their Roman name. See how they are dug in patterns of five. It explains why Wido waits for us to attack. The Romans see no dishonor in trapping an enemy like a hare."

"They must have crept out to dig them on moonless nights," she said. "If that is how they are dug, when we find the first row, we know the position of the rest. We could crawl on our bellies like snakes and thread our way through. We must attack at night then."

"Yes. I've learned they protect two gates—the Main and the West. My guess is Julianus got impatient and cut off support and money before Wido had a chance to dig them everywhere he wanted them. I know he was not given the material and men to fortify the West Gate as he was the other three. It is there we should break in, of that I have no doubt. But what I do not understand is . . ." And then they were lost in speculation, without even a word of greeting. Neither thought it odd. It had always been that way.

The sun was directly above, sending a shaft of light through the smoke hole, before he looked up and truly saw her. He regarded her for a long, full moment, nodding faintly, a well-pleased look on his face.

"My little hunting cat." He caught her hands and pulled her closer. "You have done us great honor, great honor indeed. The tales that have come of you! I tell you, I do not like to be outdone!" He smiled broadly, but his face saddened her—the sorrowing he felt was written there clearly as the word signs on Decius' book.

A kettle of herbs—a preparation to aid the knitting of bones—boiled over then, making the fire spit and hiss. She moved quickly to take the kettle from the fire before he reached for it, for she knew that moving about caused him much pain, though he would never speak of it. Then she poured it into a clay vessel for him, dropped to the ground and sat next to him, looking at the injured leg with concern.

"It is a small matter, and it quickly heals," he said, following her gaze. But she wondered. Bones did not heal quickly at his age. He smiled. "It pleases me, Auriane, to see the god's gift is a gift to you as well!"

She gave him a quick conspiratorial smile. "Do not the priests always natter on that the willing sacrifice is best?" The smile vanished, and she went on, her voice taut with grief, "But nothing has happened that is good that was not bought with more than we had to give." Tears came, and she did not try to stop them as she would have with her mother.

He put a steadying hand on her shoulder. "I know. I ask it again and again of the gods — why are we tormented so? Why did they not take one of my limbs instead of Arnwulf? Take me, not my child, I would have said . . . but the gods did not ask. I would walk in fire myself, if I thought it would bring an hour's solace to Athelinda. The beast strikes hardest at the vulnerable and the young! Day on day, I try not to think of how we bleed. In the end, fighting's better than grieving, sorrow keeps the wound open. Ah, I praise the gods for your brightness! You are shining proof we've life in us yet!"

She looked into the fire, pushing sorrow away for his sake, her gaze fixed on a wood louse as it scurried to safety from a log that took flame. She felt sharply the agony in his words and thought suddenly: One day he will die. Yes, he will die, and the world will move on, dumb and unknowing. How can it? He is the center beam for the sky itself.

But by my hand? How could Hertha foul the air with those words?

He caught her gaze and held it. "Auriane, tell me, how did you get free?"

She felt a lurch of sickness in her stomach.

Why is it I have no good fortune whatever that is not ridden with maggots?

If Baldemar knew the truth, she was certain some of the horror of it would be released. But the words would not come.

Why heighten his wrath against Wido and his son when he is wounded and cannot fight them? It would be a cruelty.

"I won Ullrik to my cause and he cut my bonds. It was night and there was carousing in the camp. It was not difficult."

He studied her face gravely, with a trace of wonder and pity. She sensed he discerned the lie.

"And . . . that was it. A simple matter, to get free," she added.

"You do not wish to tell me then," he said gently.

She met his gaze once, then fled from it, looking hard at the fire. A storm brewed in her chest. "How foolish of me to think I could hide it," she whispered. "I beg you, don't ask me to tell it, let it die with me. You do not need more horrors to bear in mind. And we have reason enough already for vengeance."

"Then raise your head up, and do not act as if you merited such a fate," he said with gentle sternness. There followed a long pain-filled quiet. "My poor child. You do not suffer alone. What befell you befell all of us. When one part of the body is injured, what is healthy marshals strength to heal it. When vengeance is taken, the memory will not hurt."

Still she looked away.

"Auriane. Why do you not see your own formidable innocence? You must be greatly beloved of the god, or he would not have given you the standard or accepted you as bride." He covered her hand with his heavy one and left it there; gratefully she drank in its strength.

But still she struggled through confusion and shame. And over it all leered the vision of the violence done her mother, which was in a way the more painful memory. Odberht's attack on her was terror-ridden, but it could in the end be contained as some sort of loathsome practical necessity. The memory of the attack on her mother could not be contained—it threatened to unravel the world.

She was aware of him watching her kindly, of the wordless love in his eye.

"Tell me, did Ramis ask you to follow her?" he asked finally.

This, too, made her uncomfortable, but in a way she did not understand. "Yes. She did."

"I thought as much when that strange story was brought to me. You know, she will ask again. She never asks just once. I bid you . . . refuse while your mother lives. She fears that so much."

"While Mother lives? You think truly one day I will be tempted?"

"Yes."

"Never will I! I despise her as much as Mother does."

"So you say now. But the human spirit is of the substance of clouds, always shifting shape."

"Others may change, I will not! You need trouble yourself over that no more. I want vengeance, not white robes, prayers and silence."

They dropped into companionable silence. Then she ventured, while closely watching his face: "The Roman thrall that came with me knows many wondrous things—the arts of constructing Roman javelins and swords, and all their machines of war . . ." She hesitated, then eagerly leapt in. "I have been thinking, he could teach us all that he knows. . . ."

Baldemar said nothing for long moments. She knew at once he was much opposed to the idea, and this startled and saddened her.

"He is useful in understanding the enemy," Baldemar replied, choosing words cautiously, for he disliked dampening her enthusiasm. "But I will not use him in any other way, nor will I attempt to change our rituals of war. You must understand something—some ways are not meant to be altered. A tree grows always with roots in the ground. In this matter you uproot trees. To battle other than as we have is to give insult to our ancestors. We are fighting to preserve our ways. Is the best way to do this by abandoning our ways?"

"But I am not always certain our ways are best. I have heard it said, for one, the swine's head formation was learned from the Romans. And now we use it always. Why is that not unholy?"

"Like all good hunting animals you do not give up! The swine's head was accepted slowly, over several generations, and was blessed by the Holy Ones. The better part of our people hold we received it from Wodan. There's much difference between that and supplying everyone in one journey of the moon with foreign weapons. It is not change I stand against, but how swiftly you wish to bring it about. No one knows our people better than I. New ways must be presented as old, or you get nowhere with them."

"How then have the Romans captured through arms almost the whole of our Middle Earth—"

"Through treachery and trickery! Is that truly what you want? I would choose to fall in battle before I would win that way. Watch and wait. Perhaps years will bring you to sharing my mind."

She concealed her bitter disappointment.

He met her eyes firmly. "We must send the Roman thrall back. His presence here might anger the men."

She nodded. But she knew with sudden certainty she would not obey.

What demon possesses me? Father is right, but I do not care. Has Decius cast some spell on me? Hide him. I'll hide Decius here, and have him teach me what he knows in secret.

• • •

When she took leave of Baldemar, she went to the casting ground.

Until dusk came, she practiced spear-casting among the other newly made warriors while Sigwulf looked on with a sour, critical eye; their target was a swinging grain sack suspended from a bough. The native spear was light and familiar in her hand. It was the universal weapon of the tribal army because it was effective both in the forest and on the plain, for it could either be hurled or used as a lance. The majority of the warriors would never own a longsword and Baldemar never mentioned equipping her with one; she knew he would oppose her taking up a weapon that forced her to get so close to the enemy. She was relieved that the other newly made warriors were easy with her and showed little deference for her rank.

As evening came, Auriane walked alone to the old well that lay outside the camp, by the great north-south trail. She shed sadness into its depths, breathing the fungal smells, listening to the rustlings of ancestresses, letting the earthy vapors hold her. The solace that came was strangely intoxicating; that luminous state in which she pried the stone from the hoof of the mare settled on her briefly, then flitted off. She felt the presence of Ramis so intimately close she shivered and looked restlessly about.

Then she saw that a woman approached on the trail from the north. She felt a start of unease. It was odd for anyone, woman or man, to be traveling alone and on foot in this country. And this twilight apparition seemed made of the stuff of ground mist. Auriane tensed to run, frightened of ghosts. Finally she realized the traveler's spectral appearance was but the effect of the wind pulling at the fine-spun cloth of her gray cloak. She judged the woman was an apprentice, from what grove she could not tell.

The woman approached boldly, and Auriane suspected this stranger had been camped nearby, awaiting a time when she came to the well. She was big-boned and strong; slung over her back was a sack of provisions that would have been a burden to any man. Her face, however, was soft and mild; her great round eyes seemed hungry for sight. The woman's silver ornaments flashed in the last of the light. A crescent moon hung from a thong about her neck revealed her as an apprentice of Ramis.

"I greet you in the name of the High One," she said, slightly inclining her head. Her voice was gentle and direct. "I am Thora. Grace and luck to you."

"What do you wish of me?"

"I am sent to you with a gift from Ramis. She fears for you greatly. She cannot give you warriors or weapons of iron, nor will she speak of the methods of war. But she can give you the favor of the moon. Watch and wait while it completes one cycle. When next it is one day from greatest fullness, at the still time when night is nearly done, the moon will be swallowed by a wolf."

Auriane stood still, mildly stunned, then managed to reply, "The gift is great. Please bear to her my gratitude."

Thora made an avertive sign while reciting words of blessing, then turned round and went north once more, leaving Auriane's mind in a fever.

More than ever she sensed how gravely all was threatened. Why would Ramis tell her of a fearsome prodigy in the sky? She never involved herself in the outcome of battles; that she did so this time was extraordinary.

She must think all that is holy faces extinction—the sacred groves, her centers for apprentices, the holy wells, the fields of grain, the children of the villages.

But why could not Ramis call the wolf sooner? Surely they would be lost if they waited through two cycles of the moon.

On the next day Auriane sent Decius out into the forest to gather kindling for cookfires. Then she crept off herself and met him in the forest behind the well; together they searched and finally found a place to conceal him that was near enough to the camp, but arduous to reach. Here they built him a shelter beneath an outcropping of rock. It could only be reached by an exhausting climb up a steep grade through thickets of scrub pine. She knew she would gain in endurance from this journey when she stole off daily for his teaching.

Decius fashioned two crude wooden swords out of pinewood, making them roughly twice the weight of a legionary sword so when she wielded a real weapon it would feel weightless. She managed to obtain from the camp two round shields of linden-wood. Slipping off from the camp was not difficult; hunting expeditions went out every day, and no one wondered when she was diverted off on her own. Her greater fear was that she and Decius would be seen. She had lied to Baldemar. The thought of the disappointment in his face should he learn it was past bearing. And if Geisar learned somehow that she spent much time alone with a man who was an enemy and a thrall, she scarcely dared guess what might happen. Geisar once condemned a village maid of lying with a foreigner. He had ordered her hair shaved off, then had her whipped naked through her village, and finally drowned beneath hurdles in Wolf's Head Bog.

Auriane was impatient with those early lessons; why, she complained, must they take so long with such tedious things as proper grip, the angle of the wrist, the calculation of striking distance? Barbarians, Decius complained in return. Like all of them, you want no hard work, no planning—just the headlong rush into battle.

Every day before they began, he had her run an ever-increasing distance with a pack stuffed with stones and straw strapped onto her back. In the early days he spoke the lessons, demonstrating a maneuver, then requiring her to copy him. He often emphasized the inferiority of the native sword: Unlike a legionary sword, it could not be used as a stabbing weapon, which rendered it near useless in close quarters. He taught her a bit of anatomy. The lung is *here*, he warned again and again. Always keep your arm low, to prevent a strike to the ribcage, which causes the "sucking wound" and eventually, lung collapse. The abdomen is best for a kill, he insisted repeatedly; do not bother with the region of the thorax— its bony protection is a nuisance. He warned her to shun the long, slashing strokes favored by her tribesmen—such barbarian fool-hardiness, he insisted, exposes the whole side of the body to attack. Then he began to show her the basic cuts used by legionary soldiers, and how to execute them with economy and safety; in the beginning she practiced against a stout post.

In those early days it surprised her that Decius did not simply run off in the night, for the border was temptingly close. He meant to be true to his word, it seemed. She dared think hopefully it might be for devotion to her. But words he spoke one day suggested there might be another reason.

On this morning they sparred together for the first time, fighting a mock battle using the elementary advance and retreat he had just taught her. As usual, she pushed herself to near exhaustion before she would agree to rest. Her wrist and arm ached fiercely. When she finally sank to the ground, he sat beside her, took out a flask of watered wine and asked suddenly, "There is a thing that troubles me, my pet. What happens to the fortunes of this miserable thrall if your people do not win?"

She waited until her breath slowed, her cheeks flushed rose

from exertion. "I will not speak of our defeat in battle—it brings ill luck."

"All right then, I'll speak of it. Wido's wild men will seize me in one of your people's blood orgies and nail me to a tree as a gift to his god. Or perhaps I'll be more fortunate, and my own people will pick me up—and torture me to death for collaborating with the enemy."

"Or perhaps a certain maid will pour a horn of mead over your head for using on purpose words she does not know!"

He explained the meaning of "collaborating" and she gave an inward sigh. He did not stay for her sake, but because he feared his people counted him a traitor.

The days flowed quickly, blending to one. Painfully, slowly, she began to learn the secrets of turning a retreat into an attack, of tricking an enemy into exposing himself to her blade. All went well but for his habit of belittling her efforts, which grew worse as they became more used to each other.

"Now pay close attention while I show you the right diagonal cut," Decius began one day. "I pray all the gods the ghost of my father isn't watching. For the fifteenth time—or is it the sixteenth?—you are not standing right." He took hold of her shoulders and forcefully moved her. "There. Now do as I do. What I will not endure for freedom!"

She imitated his downward cut a little unsteadily at first, then after several repetitions, with smooth sureness.

"A bit better—but not much. Now stand, again, in the balanced position." She obeyed.

Not much better? She could not argue it—she had no one with whom to compare herself.

"That's passable, but just. That expression on your face is not necessary, though! Frighten the enemy with your skill, not that face!"

"Oh, let me be!"

But she knew, too, there was much wisdom in his teaching.

"Now ready yourself," he began on another day. "I am the enemy, I am gaining ground. Now when I think I have mastered you, I want you to strike. Remember, choose the moment when I lift my foot so you'll catch me off balance—then lunge forward into my step."

Without warning he leaped at her and made a powerful downward cut, almost knocking her wooden sword from her hand.

She recovered and met him with strokes that were broad and clumsy but also, he thought, surprisingly aggressive.

"Press on! Advance!" he ordered.

She came at him steadily, doing exuberant imitations of the two basic cuts he taught her; he gave ground. Then he snapped forward, easily evading her defense, and delivered a blow to her stomach with the point of his wooden weapon.

"A strike! You are dead or dying from that one."

But she hardly heeded him; she doubled over for a moment, collected herself, then, gritting her teeth against the pain, redoubled her efforts, once again pushing him back. Then a hand snapped round her wrist and jerked her hard in the direction she was already going. She fell flat onto her stomach.

"That was unfair, treacherous and vile!" she said through gasps for breath. He helped her up, amused and unapologetic.

"All war is treachery. Your enemy does not follow your rules. You assumed wrongly that the sword was the only weapon in that bout. But the enemy also has hands and feet and teeth, not to mention anything he might pick up from the ground. You moved in too close, and you exposed the whole front of your body. And what else?"

"I was off balance and you turned it against me."

"I used your own strength to pull you down. I did very little except stay alert. All that I did came from you. I forgot myself and entered your mind. I felt your blindness and simply moved where you were not."

They shared the water they brought and sat in silence, watching kites circle an unseen carcass below. Then Decius spoke.

"Auriane, what is your father doing?"

"He bargains for arms with Gallic traders to get better weapons for us, he sends out pleas to the villages of other tribes—"

"No, I mean why does he not strike? He knows all he needs to know. The advantage in this battle clearly lies with the force that strikes first."

She was silent a moment, caught between wanting his opinion and wishing him to think well of her father—and wanting to avoid the ridicule her reply might bring. Finally she answered carefully as if she moved through a thicket of thornbushes, "I will tell you then. It is secret knowledge, but I suppose it matters not at all if you know, for you are not one of us. We wait for the moment the moon is swallowed by a wolf."

Decius frowned, thought for a moment, then began softly

laughing, shaking his head. "Forget about it, my pet. A primitive people with no knowledge of the motion of heavenly bodies cannot predict the times of the moon's eclipse—only a very few Chaldean magicians can do it properly. It isn't going to happen. I hope you weren't depending on it too much."

"You arrogant rooster. Ramis always knows when the wolf will come. What is a predict? What is an eclipse?"

"I never guessed a frisky maid's curiosity would be the cause of my death! Auriane, there is no wolf."

She crossed her arms and narrowed her eyes. "There certainly is."

He smiled. "It would have to be a monstrously large wolf. Three centuries ago a clever Greek named Hipparchus calculated the moon's diameter at—"

"Stop that Roman jabbering! Did I say what size wolf?"

"Auriane, the earth is a ball," he said, reaching to pick up three stones. "A sphere, if you will, like the glass spheres you use for divining. This stone is the earth, and—"

"Fool, you haven't said which earth—Lower, Middle, or Upper?"

"By Minerva, I don't know! All of them! The sun is here," he said, lining up the three stones on the ground, "the moon here, and here's the earth—or earths, if you prefer—in the middle, see? This fearsome marvel is nothing but the earth's shadow on the moon."

She looked away, a long-suffering look in her eyes. "You are trying my patience with such nonsense. You are only an ignorant Roman after all."

He laughed easily. "Then why do you ask me so cursed many questions!" He tossed the stones one by one down the rocky slope. "You've been given privileged knowledge of the sages, and you're too benighted to know it." Half to himself he added, "It's a great shame it won't happen—it would frighten the Romans as much as Wido's men, they're such a superstitious lot, soldiers are. And as a rule they tend not to read Hipparchus or Eratosthenes. It might give you some chance at victory. As it is now, you've little or none."

"Decius, be silent, or you curse our luck!"

"That's been done already, I think. I taught you retreat is the first method of defense. It is true in this grander case as well. Your people should retreat into the cover of your forests, that's where your true strength lies. You do not know the size of the world, nor

do you know the size of Rome. She has trifled with you to this day.
You may win a skirmish here and there, but woe unto all of you if
my people turn their full strength upon you. Do you know the Isle
of Britannia?"

She frowned and shook her head.

"Albion?" he tried.

She brightened. "Albion! The land of the White Moon, where
druids are schooled."

"Right. Do you know of its size and the number of its tribes?"

"Many peoples dwell there, yes."

"Well, near all of them revolted against the Empire seven—or
is it eight?—years ago now. I was there at its beginning. In one
season the Britons did more injury to the legions than your tribe
has done in all your battles with us. But within a year the island
was thoroughly put down and chastised. More died miserably for
their foolhardiness than you have warriors in all your tribe. So you
see, if you lose this battle, you lose, and if by some freak of
providence you win, still you lose. You might thrust a nail into the
heel of a giant. You might do him some small injury that seems
large at first to you. But beware the day he turns his full wrath
upon you and destroys you."

"Perhaps you are right," she said thoughtfully. "But it does not
matter. We have cat spirit in us, and the wild cat does not submit
to the cage without a terrible and bloody fight."

When but five days remained before the coming of the Wolf,
Auriane came as usual at dawn, bearing drink and meat for Decius.
On this day when she sparred with him, something was not the
same.

Always before when they practiced she would struggle to
remember his words, then give directions to her limbs, a clumsy
two-step process. But on this day there were moments she had the
curious feeling her movement had a wisdom of its own. Once or
twice it seemed she took flight, soaring above thought, and all
seemed play—but the sense did not last long. It was not too
dissimilar from the odd and brilliant stillness Ramis caused her to
feel. Decius noticed nothing—or at least, she thought, he behaved
as if he had not.

She was almost certain then there was a knowledge steadily
growing in her, far from fully expressed. But not certain enough
that Decius' mocking insults did not cause doubt. She wondered if
her efforts were not the awkward first steps of a foal—a foal that

would one day be a horse plunging into valleys, galloping mightily, flying over a wall. If that was true, why could Decius not have patience with the foal?

But her frustration never lasted long. Curiosity and the animal joy she took in fighting left little room for it.

"Decius," she shouted out once as they parried, "did you ever set eyes on your Great King?"

She thought she saw faint embarrassment in his face.

"The Emperor Nero?" he replied reluctantly. "Well, yes, once. *Stop! Badly* done! Hold it like this! And don't step so far! See, you left yourself open beneath the arm. I was in Rome for the village market day."

"Yes?" she prodded breathlessly. "What did he look like and what was he doing?"

"He was on a stage. . . ."

"Stage?"

"A place where stories are acted out by people pretending to be other people."

"Well then? Why don't you finish? What sort of story was it and what was he doing there?"

He slowed and stopped, heaving for air. Discomfort left his face; now she sensed only Decius' anger at their king. It puzzled her.

"In one play he acted the part . . . the part of a woman in one of our myths, Nemesis take us all, he played the part of a woman in labor, on the stage."

She gave him a spirited glare. "I do not want ever again to hear you say my people are odd."

"You do not understand. It is depravity, not oddness, for him to be on a stage at all—Hades take him! Now, if you are not tired . . ."

"I am not at all tired."

He was tired, and impressed by her endurance, as well. But he would not say it. That enthusiasm was relentless—it was not dampened by bruises, strained limbs or sharp criticism. And was it his own imagining, or did she learn with striking speed?

"Now we will do the third attack. You must be perfectly relaxed as you begin. . . ." And this time as they sparred, he did notice her growing grace; it struck him all of a sudden, like someone who took note of a tree in bud yesterday and today finds it in bloom.

"That is enough. I'm tired if you're not."

"Decius," she ventured cautiously. "I . . . cannot be doing as poorly as you say. Am I?"

"You do not need to know if you are doing well or not," he said irritably. "Praise makes for laziness, especially in the young."

"You might at least tell me perhaps just once when I have done a thing well."

"But I see so much more wrong than right. Praise would only confuse you."

She threw the wooden sword to the ground.

"You goad me to madness! When you escape it's me you're going to have to worry over! I'll tell my father's men which way you've gone and set them after you and laugh when they toss you into the slimiest bog!"

"Ungrateful wench," he said, grinning broadly. As usual, that grin had a strangely powerful way of disarming her. She shut her eyes so she would not see it, but perversely, she saw it with great clarity in her mind.

"Just do not ever let on I was the one who instructed you," Decius continued, "and I'll die in peace."

"I understand you now. You are like a porcupine."

"Not again. That's what all the women I've bedded say to me."

"Oh, silence, and listen! Your mockery is like a porcupine's quills. It is a way of keeping people at bay. And that is all it is. And there is this about you: You want me to do well, but only so well, and only so long as my efforts give praise to you. You are the teacher. If I were the teacher, you would not know what to do with me. If I were the teacher, you would abandon me."

She just caught an off-balance look in his eye that revealed her aim was true. Then his face softened, but only slightly. "Perhaps I am a bit too hard."

"A bit? A very large bit."

"Much too hard then," he amended, smiling amiably. "But it is the way I was taught."

"Your teachers then are in the habit of making a laughingstock of those they teach."

"All right, you have it. I am sorry. You are doing . . . surprisingly well."

But the words sounded like another put them in his mouth. She glared at him in quiet frustration; this was not much better than his insults.

She left her eyes steadily on his, probing without result for whatever it was in him that drew her. Surely it was more than that cursed smile. If that were all, she thought, if he never smiled, then I could forget him.

He looked at her for long moments, trapped like a fly in amber in that gaze. "Auriane, I . . . I am sorry," he tried awkwardly, as if the words would disengage him from those soft, engulfing eyes. *What mad words had she uttered? A porcupine? Perhaps it is true. But doesn't everyone speak words to keep others at bay? Why cannot I say words of affection, an affection that, in fact, I feel?* "It . . . was not my wish to wound you in any way."

She moved closer, not at all certain what she was doing, blindly following sharp curiosity, the pull of that dangerous warmth in the loins. Once she was brought up short by terror and the stark memory of pain. But she defied it and came still closer. *What would lying with him be like, were she free of the trappings of family and tribe, of shame?*

"No," he said finally, backing away. "Do not look at me so. I don't want my hide to end up as a tent for one of your father's men. I know where not to tread."

"If I were a woman of your people, you would want me."

"That is silly, Auriane. I would want you no matter whose people you belonged to." He turned away. "It is difficult enough alone out here with you, day after day. Do not make it impossible."

Then came the day before the dawn of the Wolf. As she took leave of him on this last day, without warning he drew her close and kissed her, a sad, desperate kiss. For long moments she was lulled into surrender, drowsy with pleasure. Then with a jerk like a sleeper awakened, she broke away. Her eyes welled with tears.

"Careful, lest you betray your divine husband," he said, smiling, taking her chin in his hand.

Her smile was shy and young. "My divine husband betrays me every year at the rites of spring."

They looked at each other wordlessly for a moment, and then she was off. Immediately afterward, Decius heard scuffling and the sound of running feet above him on the outcropping of rock. Someone had spied on them and, doubtless, witnessed the embrace.

He scrambled quickly up the steep path, grasping at roots to pull himself up, heart pounding. He reached the rock roof of his shelter just in time to see a fleeing figure in a tunic of woad-dyed blue become enveloped in the forest. He knew of the savage punishments her people sometimes meted out to women who lay with

men outside the tribe. Would a tale of this be taken to that priest
who despised her? Who might then order some barbarous death
for her? Nemesis, he thought miserably. Have I slain her with a
kiss?

Marcus Arrius Julianus, Military Governor of Upper Germania,
looked up restlessly from his array of field maps and out into the
fast-falling night. From the window of his study in the commander's quarters of the fortress of Mogontiacum, he had a broad view
of camp and countryside.

The wind carried the scent of pine fires. A lustrous moon one
day from full was strangely unsettling—its bald eye seemed to
follow his movements with the bright sharp interest of a predator.
The moon had a different character here in the northern wastes; it
was not the calm, complacent beauty it was at home, but a
soul-devouring Fury, its color not silver but deathly white—a
cloud-shrouded thing that summoned ghosts to walk and wolves to
howl. He took comfort in the sight of the orderly rows of soldiers'
barracks, the long colonnade of the camp hospital and beyond, the
parade ground; this fortress was a small, brave island of reason
and light, its shores battered by the wild gloom of the barbarian
sea. Past the fortress's wall crept the sluggish Rhine. It was
sky-colored in the waning light, and comfortably wide, dotted with
long barges carrying grain, horses and supplies to the other Roman
forts along the river. His eyes paused with contempt at the
equestrian statue of Nero just within the arched stone gate of the
Fortress.

There is the cause of my trials, Julianus thought. Because of his
obscene spectacles that drained the treasury dry, leaving nothing
for the defense of the frontier, I am forced to depend on the whims
of a mountebank like Wido to secure a vital piece of land,
necessary for shortening the whole northern line of defense. The
madness of these times.

His Egyptian steward announced Junius Secundus, his Senior
Tribune.

"My lord, I fear I've more foul news," Secundus began after a
brisk polite greeting. Julianus found Secundus irritatingly typical
of aristocratic young men bound for the Senate: All seemed to
have the same lilting way of modulating their words as they
expressed feelings ranging from boredom to mild interest, the
same aloof stance that fell just short of arrogance. "A new petition
was brought in from the war camp—"

"Damn him to Hades, *now* what does Wido want?"

"Fifty Arabian archers."

"That is preposterous! He has no need of them! And that's half the number we have on hand!"

"And he wants them not for the battle itself, but to shoot game, of all things. It seems his men have developed a superstitious fear of that maid, Baldemar's daughter—they think she can assume at will the form of a hind or a raven or any other animal, and enter the camp to work evil magic. He wants all wild creatures shot dead that stray too near his camp."

"He is making fools of us! I've indulged him overmuch already. If the archers are destroyed, the Palace will send no more. Wido should know it—with his tantrums and his games, he is in grave danger of becoming useless to me!"

"But he promises this time on his own blood to provoke Baldemar to attack as soon as the archers arrive."

"Does he? Well then, we shall hold him to that. Give him his archers. Tell him I expect to get them all back, alive. And have him told that if he does not attack Baldemar in three days, I shall order my archers to slay him."

"Done. And he also wants to know—what is he supposed to do with Baldemar when he captures him?"

Julianus shifted a wooden marker on the map, restlessly repositioning a signal tower one mile to the north, then moving it back; there was uncertainty in his eyes now.

"He's not to harm him—he is to secure him and send him to me," he replied at last. "And the maid as well. If she lives, they will rally around her as they do around him, that's clear enough, and she's of no use to us if she cannot marry one of Wido's sons. I've thought much on this, Secundus, and my decision grieves me, for here is a noble enemy, but *there must be no more Baldemars*. He has cost us too much. He—and the maid—must be executed by Rome so the natives understand our authority. A public execution would be most effective, with perhaps a few of their elders made to watch. Do you . . . find that harsh?"

"Begging your pardon, but it is a thing only *you*—so famous for your clemency—would even ask! You speak of human beasts scarce capable of intelligent speech! No Rhine commander has ever shown mercy to this race."

But the governor hardly heard these words; perversely, he saw the reproachful eyes of Marcus, his son. How vile you would think those executions, Julianus thought. You would count them noble

creatures of the wild, not enemies, I know it well. You must kill
Endymion in you, Marcus, and all that generous fellow-feeling for
the lowly, if you would ever have authority over men.

"And that captive brought in today?" Julianus asked then. "Was
anything useful learned?"

"That's the rest of the foul news. The wretch died on us—it's
the fault of those fool questioners—they took him along too
quickly. The man was for certain one of Baldemar's messengers.
But all we learned is that the old fox shows no sign of breaking
camp."

Julianus stared blackly at the river. "Baldemar's forces have for
two months been massing on that ridge. His friends have come to
his aid. Why does he not strike? Did that fall knock out his wits?"

"The fellow did speak one bit of odd nonsense . . . something
about a *great black wolf* that would soon come to Baldemar's aid."

Julianus swung round. "Nonsense? I think not!" he said sharply,
beginning to pace. "Wolf, wolf, what is that? More tribal reinforcements on their way, some clan under a wolf totem, perhaps?"

"Or a lightheaded fantasy conjured up by the undisciplined
barbarian imagination," Secundus countered quickly, offended by
this assumption he had overlooked a vital clue.

"You do not understand these people. Their poetic fancies near
always have some plain and obvious material reality at their core."
Julianus felt a welling of unease. He would have to go through his
natural history texts and field reports, and search out all references
to the northern savages' beliefs concerning wolves. Something
was afoot, he was certain of it.

"If that is all," Julianus waved Secundus off with distracted
impatience, "you may go."

*Baldemar cannot slip through my net now. By the girdle of
Nemesis, this is a battle I dare not lose.*

If he did, he knew for certain he would be recalled. And by
winter, he would be ashes. In Rome a fresh round of persecutions
had begun. Nero, it seemed, had seen a comet, visible three nights
running, and it was common knowledge that comets heralded the
death of great monarchs. But Nero's astrologer, Balbillus, assured
him the dread omen could be diverted onto others' heads if
important members of the nobility were put to death in his stead.
Julianus believed he lived on still only because of his great
distance from home, and his usefulness in performing a task that
brought no glory—a task no one else was qualified for, or wanted.
What was more frightful was that this time Nero was exiling or

poisoning his senatorial victims' children. Julianus had long accepted that his own fate had played itself out. But young Marcus—his difficult, bafflingly brilliant, lost-and-found son, who in the last years had begun to amaze all his tutors—*must live*. Or else his own life's work would have been in vain.

It was for his son's sake that he ordered Secundus back just as the chamber's guard stood crisply aside to let him pass.

"Secundus! An amendment to the order! Give Wido all one hundred of the archers. I want that rascal to have no excuse whatever for defeat."

CHAPTER VIII

On the next morning Wido got his hundred archers. He ordered a boar roasted in celebration and sent a solemn promise to Julianus that on the morrow he would strike at Baldemar.

But it was never to be, for this was the eve of the Wolf.

Midway between dusk and dawn, Baldemar summoned a priest of Wodan to blow the cattle horn and call his forces together. High above a stand of aspen rose an expectant moon, one day from full.

An aurochs was taken from the priests' herds and sacrificed with great secrecy. As the warriors stood grim and silent before Baldemar, Geisar and Sigreda sprinkled the animal's blood on the wind over their heads. If they took offense at being left out of the plans until the last, nothing showed in their faces as they droned the victory incantation.

At the ceremony's end Geisar and Sigreda shared a horn. Baldemar saw to it the mead was strengthened with a draught one of the medicine women prepared for him, a blend of valerian, passionflower and poppy, so they would fall into a heavy sleep. He wanted them kept from mischief until the battle was done.

Then Baldemar came before the assembled warriors to give his encouragement. He could walk now, if painfully, leaning heavily on an oak staff. Only then did he tell them of the coming prodigy in the sky—had they known of it sooner he feared a deserter might have found his way into Wido's camp with the news.

"When you see, do not fear," he told them. "All the Holy Ones agree, the Wolf comes to aid us. He signifies evil only for the traitor and all he shelters in his lair."

He told them next of the arrangement of the pits and stakes. "Move slowly, follow carefully behind those in the vanguard, and these traps cannot harm you. Roman cleverness is despised of the gods. It shall avail them nothing."

To better conceal themselves the warriors were draped in the skins of black-coated animals, and they darkened their faces and arms with lampblack; the open circles left about the eyes gave them the look of owl-eyed demons. Baldemar then brought out the standard, and one of these frightful creatures stepped forward, a warrior with proud carriage, slender limbs, and soft, clear voice. It was only by that voice that she could be distinguished as Auriane. Baldemar placed the tribal standard in her left hand, signifying he transferred his own war-luck to her.

This brought subdued calls of *"Daughter of the Ash!"* He embraced her in a manner that was outwardly stately and formal; only Auriane knew the fierce hope and love in that embrace.

The warriors descended to the plain in twos, the Companions first, then the common warriors of the Chattians, and last their allies from other tribes. All were armed alike with two native spears and round wicker shields slung over their backs, except for Auriane, for whom the standard served as a shield, and Baldemar's senior Companions, who also carried longswords. They fanned out in a wide semicircle into the moon-washed sea of sedgegrass about Wido's fortress, creeping forward on hands and knees through the aromatic grasses, avoiding the northeast side because that was the direction of the night wind. They halted just before the great circle where the grass had been roughly trimmed by Wido's men.

Auriane felt she clung to the earth to make herself smaller. For long after, she would remember the clean grassy fragrance of the sedge mingled with the bitter taste of terror at what was to come. She sensed the standard was potent and alive; cold fire glowed in the bony sockets where once a cat-spirit dwelled.

When the wind was still, they heard laughter drifting out of Wido's camp. It did not, Auriane knew, signify that they were not alert. The Romans especially were never fools. She guessed they touched neither wine nor mead.

She heard Sigwulf curse nearby and looked over questioningly. Snakebite? Fire ants? She could just make out the outline of his wicker shield. She crawled close, and he quietly signaled that nothing was wrong.

They heard a wild thrashing, followed by a dog chorus— several stags had been released as Baldemar had planned and, hopefully, were seen by Wido's sentries. Baldemar's purpose was to cause the camp's dogs to bark so the sentries would not be inclined to question further if later the dogs picked up human scent. This was also the signal to move forward again. They were adders in the sedge, wriggling forward. The grass was shorter here; only the dark concealed them now. As they crawled, they tested the ground with the points of their spears, and then they found it: a place where the earth gave way. Here was the first row of pits, carefully concealed with brush. In them, she knew, were sharpened stakes and upright spears meant to impale the unwary runner. Others found the pits, too; slowly, laboriously, the mass of warriors threaded their way around them. When they passed three rows, there were no more; here they halted to await the aid of the moon.

Auriane turned her face anxiously to the lunar disk. It lay low in the sky, seeming sated, overfull, too drowsy to ascend. She wondered if Baldemar ever feared the Wolf would not come. The matter seemed not to have occurred to him. "As I own the field of battle," he had said once, "so Ramis owns the moon." But Decius hinted at a larger world where a different order prevailed.

Decius, you scoundrel. You put a seed of doubt in me, and it is sprouting. Your impiety will offend the Wolf, and he will not come.

The moon itself seemed to gently mock her with a chill smile that told nothing. Cold clear words formed in her mind that seemed to issue from it: You cannot escape me through far wandering, for my light falls everywhere. I am your teacher. I do not wait for your command or for your obedience. I wait for you to come of age.

Soon the eastern sky would pale to gray. She felt a grip of panic—dawn would reveal them to the arrows and spears of the camp. Now she could see smoke curling above the palisade.

Inside Wido's camp many were arising. The sentries stared placidly out at the plain. One sentry did have a lingering sense something sinister was in the ocean of grass, but it was nothing he could name. He stared hard into the darkness.

And he was jolted to attention. Something descended the ridge from roughly the position of Baldemar's camp—a white shadow that seemed to wrestle with itself, rippling like a shroud just above the grass. Smoothly, steadily, it approached. The sentry shouted for Wido.

Baldemar's forces saw it, too; a thing formed of moonlight moved gently closer.

What comes for us now? Auriane thought. Have not we trials enough?

Gradually she realized it was a line of five or six white-robed figures. *We are done. Geisar and Sigreda have awakened too soon.*

Sigwulf saw and thought the same. "Foul night! They come to betray us!" he whispered to her.

And from the palisade, Wido saw it. Geisar? he wondered, squinting. Can he be fool enough to approach me so openly? What does the cursed idiot think he is doing?

"Ride out there," Wido ordered a young Companion, "and demand of them their purpose!"

"That's nothing human out there! If I go, I want a rowan spear made beneath a waxing moon and fifty good men at my back."

Auriane could see them better now; six Holy Ones walked in file. The lead figure moved with a gentle rocking gait; Auriane guessed this was a woman. Her robe sparked with faint luminescence as though it were embroidered with star matter and gold. She strode with serene confidence, halting when she came within spear-casting distance of the circle of concealed warriors. Then she stood solemnly still. Auriane drew in a breath—it seemed the woman had no face. Gradually she realized this Holy One was masked.

From Wido's camp came shouted questions as many crowded on the palisade.

Then a wild warning trill rose up, not unlike the harsh music of swans. It seemed to arrest all nature. She realized the attendants who followed the masked one lifted flutes and brass horns to their lips; they blew with all their souls, making a chaotic wail that pulled the breath from her body, that tore at time, that cried out in protest at all the grisly terrors of life since the first predator's claw slashed the first warm throat. It was a hymn to bones, calling them to bloody rebirth.

It brought dazed silence to Wido's camp.

And then Auriane knew the lead figure was Ramis. Who else would so defy normal good sense and walk right out onto a battlefield? Those about her began to guess it, too—she heard them softly mutter Ramis' name and knew hands moved in the dark, making the sign against sorcery.

But if it is she, Auriane thought, then she must be calling the Wolf. Yes, it must be. Why did I doubt?

Slowly Ramis raised her arms; they were gently curved like two crescent moons. She seemed to lift the trilling to more urgent pitch; it was evil noise potent enough to pull giants from the earth. Auriane wanted to stop her ears but she was afraid to move. Finally she forced herself to look at the moon.

Softly, slowly, it began to shut its eye.

At first she was seized with childish terror at the sight of the unchanging, ever-changing moon abandoning them on a clear night, leaving a strange bloody shadow where its whiteness had been. Then she allowed herself cautious ecstasy.

Decius, you were a fool to doubt our ancient wisdom.

Cries of terror and howls of despair rose up from Wido's camp. Auriane saw shadows darting on the palisade, colliding with each other; some fell prostrate, others fled for their tents.

The gate to vengeance was flung wide.

Auriane felt she joined the wind. She shot up, the cat-skull raised high. She did not even hesitate to make certain the others followed after, bolting over the grasses in mad free flight, veering sharply right, where the old West Gate lay. Close behind her came the ladder bearers and fifty Companions, all running stealthily as a river underground.

When the main body saw Auriane rise up, torches were lit from fire-sticks and fires bloomed all along their lines. They clashed spears against shields and began making the cries of wild beasts. Then the thousands rose up all at once and sprang straight toward the wall with Sigwulf at their head, their wolf howls, growls and crashing sounds making a frightful noise meant to distract Wido's men from the assault on the West Gate. It was dark still, though dawn was close, and the disappearing moon threw all into greater gloom.

To those on Wido's palisade it seemed demons sprang up from the earth, summoned from Helle's caverns by the shrieking flutes. Most fled in terror; only the Arabian archers managed to keep their wits. They lifted their bows as one and took aim.

Simultaneously Auriane and the ladder bearers closed in on the West Gate. It must be taken swiftly; it would not take Wido's men long to realize they had been diverted.

Quietly the ladder was put to it so two warriors could climb up and unbolt the gate from within.

At the same moment the Arabian archers let arrows fly. The men following Sigwulf died by the dozens. Their startled shrieks encouraged the archers—these monsters, it seemed, could die like mortals. They sent out several more volleys.

When the main part of Baldemar's forces came up to the ditch and wall, hurdling the bodies of the fallen as they charged, they too began to move to the right, making for the West Gate, trusting it to be open when they gained it. They were easy prey for the archers, who ran alongside them and felled them at leisure, as if they shot wild beasts for sport in a hunting theater. The rain of arrows was relentless; Sigwulf, at their head, feared they might bolt off in a panic.

At the West Gate one of Baldemar's warriors quietly mounted the ladder. Two Companions had volunteered for this most dangerous of tasks. Baldemar had rewarded them in advance, giving to each a hundred cattle and a hundred rings. Auriane and the others waited, tensed to charge in.

As the first shadowy skin-clad form came to the top of the gate, his body jerked suddenly as if someone pulled with great force on a rope about his neck. They watched with horror as he lurched back, then dropped heavily to the ground. All thought him pierced by an arrow. The next Companion climbed up gamely, but he, too, was struck just as he cleared the top of the gate. Both lay twitching and dying at their feet.

"We are lost," came a voice in the dark.

"It is the vilest of omens! Helle claims us!"

"The dark moon! It has been turned on us!"

Auriane raced to the first warrior, whose vacant eyes were already turned to the stars. She saw at once that it was not an arrow that pierced his throat, but the bolt of a ballista. Suddenly she knew what must be done.

She gave her spears into the nearest hands, seized the ladder and dragged it to the right while they watched her as if she were mad. Then, carrying only the standard, quickly she began to climb. There was not time to explain what she was doing or why, or give directions to someone else. Their presence at the gate was known within; in the next moment every archer's bow would be trained on this spot.

"You must not, Auriane!" Thorgild caught her leg. "Do not curse us with your death!"

She struggled for a moment and got free of him. Then she climbed on, begging Fria to shield her.

She knew the war-engine called the ballista was one of the more cumbersome Roman war machines; normally, Decius had told her, it was manned by ten soldiers. That it had been correctly aimed must be counted to sheer luck; probably it was aimed always at the center of the gate. If she climbed in a different place, she judged, they would not have time to move it.

If I am wrong, I die.

She swung over the top of the gate, keeping her body low, braced to feel one of the powerful missiles knock her down to her death. But the next bolt tore past her harmlessly in the dark. She guessed rightly. But there was still the gate to be opened.

Now I drop into the open jaws of the beast.

She hung for an instant from the inside of the gate; the distance to the ground was perhaps the height of a man. Now the sentries Sigwulf's men strove to distract knew of this assault on the West Gate; shadow-men darted down the palisade walk toward her. And then they rushed at her from everywhere, hounds closing in on a hare. She dropped hard to the ground and rolled.

As she leaped to her feet, a flurry of arrows missed her narrowly, tearing through her hair, grazing her neck, the flesh of her thigh. The gate seemed to have sprouted quills. As she pulled at the rusty bolt, a javelin tore through the sleeve of her leather tunic, pinning her to the gate until she freed herself by tearing the cloth. And still the bolt refused to move. Terror flooded in; all about her seemed to move with the dreamy swaying of a reed under water.

After all, I am to die. I do not want to go where you are, Hertha. I want to stay with Father . . . and Decius. Fria, Mother of All, lift me up, preserve me!

"Kill him! He opens the gate!" The cries were so close. All her prayers stopped in her throat, lodged there like a stone.

Then the balky bolt came free so quickly she fell sideways. From beyond the gate she heard jubilant cries.

She did not have to pull on the door. A hundred bodies pushed it in. In a short time all Baldemar's forces were streaming into the camp.

They flooded round her, shouting encouragement to her and to each other. A spear was put into her hands and she ran in their midst, charging into dark chaos. She scarcely heard the enemy's shrieks of spirit-terror all about; she was only aware of the exuberant war cries of Baldemar's Companions. As they broke in, they stayed closely packed together, a human spear thrust deep into the fort's heart.

The archers on the palisade sent fresh volleys of arrows into their midst. But Baldemar's warriors with their blackened faces were difficult to see, and now the archers slew Wido's own men by the hundreds. As the archers were not of native birth, this did not matter to them overmuch—a barbarian was a barbarian—and so they went on slaying five of Wido's for every man of Baldemar's, for as long as the fighting remained within arrow shot.

The scattered forces of Wido mounted a desperate and disoriented resistance. Auriane saw only by the torchbearers' uncertain light and so witnessed but fragments of the whole of the struggle. Once a disordered group of legionary soldiers rushed at them; half had not had time to fasten on their armor and were clad only in the woolen tunics soldiers wore beneath. A soldier near her balanced a javelin in hand, ready to fling it into the Chattians' midst. She slowed, took aim without thought, and cast her spear, killing him with fluid ease; then she retrieved a fresh spear from the ground. On either hand, great numbers of Wido's allies bolted like startled herds before them while others dove into their tents to shield themselves from the horror in the sky.

To her amazement all fear had fled; she felt only rage bursting forth in a roaring torrent, bearing her up and sweeping her off, quenching at last the fire of her burning hall, a joyous, rampant wrath that cleansed the blood. Animal cries came from her throat. The boar's heart pumped its dark angry blood. That freedom in the blood was stronger than Roman wine—she lost all belief in defeat, in her own death.

Intoxicated by this festival of vengeance, Baldemar's forces put torches to the rows of soldiers' tents, the storehouses, the animal sheds, chasing down Wido's Companions, who fled from them like geese from slaughter. Bolting horses blind with fright trampled their handlers or galloped in frenzied circles, dragging overturned carts behind them.

As they drove into the camp's center, a heavier resistance was formed; the best of Wido's Companions joined the Roman cavalrymen and a detachment of the Fourteenth Legion in a hastily made version of the rectangular formation commonly used to repel an attack from all sides. Auriane saw the dull gleam on the iron bindings of legionary shields, heard frantic orders barked in their harsh, alien tongue.

Surely, Auriane thought, this is where Wido and Odberht will be.

Using their spears as lances, the Chattians bored into the detachment before its ranks were sufficiently closed and swiftly divided it in two. They then surrounded the shattered formation with their greater numbers.

Auriane never thought she fought singly; she felt herself one part of a great angry beast, lashing out with hundreds of stinging points. And there, in the midst of the enemy—with iron striking iron, and death a breath away, and the underworld yawning open at her feet—paradoxically she felt *safe*. Dark ecstasy flooded her heart until she felt no fleshly bonds. She had bristles and tusks and small glimmering eyes as she struck and killed, impaled and brought down. Her marriage to war was consummated then. Her divine husband bathed her in blood; they lay together and brought forth corpses. Each strike was a blow against helplessness, each wound she inflicted healed a wound. She raised Arnwulf from the dead. She washed clean with blood the vile insult done her mother.

In one night, she thought, we drive the Romans from this land.

Much of what passed was lost in the dark of the moon, and in future days legend overtook truth. The tale-singers claimed Auriane entered the fort as a raven, taking human shape once more to throw the bolt. Some told the tale as if Baldemar had been present, his injury magically healed, his eyes molten iron as he galloped before Wido, demanding single battle—the battle that in life they never fought but that all longed to see. Others claimed to have seen the Choosers of the Slain, those fiery sylphs that hovered over battlefields, as they waited to take up the bravest of the fallen to their starry castles. And there were tales that Grimelda was transformed into a demon with glowing red eyes and multiple arms, shrieking and laughing and hacking off heads with her axe until the warrior-woman Freydis felled her with a spear thrust to the heart.

By the time they gained the camp's center, Wido's forces were broken. Sigwulf looked vainly for Wido and Odberht, his contempt and amazement growing. Their place was with their men. Had they secretly fled?

Few saw the moon return simultaneously with the dawn; weak sallow light fell on a scene of torn bodies strewn as if the wolves had already come. The scent of terror and blood was thick as smoke.

Great numbers of Wido's allies fled on foot and on horseback toward the East Gate. Auriane and Thorgild found the prisoners' cages and began throwing them open with desperate speed, searching for Witgern.

They found him at last. Thorgild pulled Witgern from his wicker cage moments before it caught fire. Auriane gave a cry of delight at the sight of Witgern unharmed.

Witgern knew the camp well enough to make a good guess where Wido might be. He led them in a limping run past the blazing tents of the ranking Romans. When they reached the covered stables where the cavalry horses were kept, they came at last upon Wido and Odberht.

Wido, black eyes afire with rage, was pulling himself onto a wild-eyed skittish mount. His flesh was drained of color, his marten-skin cloak badly askew, baring one bony shoulder as he looked furiously from side to side, shouting sharp staccato orders to his men.

Odberht was more composed, almost surprisingly so; his look was contemptuous and self-satisfied, as if he had played some grand joke and bested them all. The stately stallion he rode, with its disapproving snorts and proudly bowed neck, seemed to echo its rider's contempt.

Both horses broke into a slow canter with Odberht in the lead. Their bridles were plated with silver; their saddlecloths were studded with precious stones that flashed tauntingly in the first light of the sun. Slung over each horse's withers were sacks laden with treasure. Wherever they fled, they did not plan to be poor. Wido's Companions kept close about father and son like a loyal dog pack, protecting them and hampering their progress at the same time. Their destination was the East Gate.

Baldemar's Companions fell in step with them, vying with each other to get close enough to Wido to bring him down. It would be a deed told in song for generations. Wido and Odberht leaned far over the horses' necks while the Companions nearest them held up shields to protect them from the spears of Baldemar's men. Auriane knew if they were not taken before they galloped beneath the gate, the pair would be lost to them forever.

Auriane was close enough now to hear Wido shouting, "I'll see them roasted alive!" She realized he promised grisly deaths to the sentries who had failed him. Spears arced up, aimed at Wido; all were deflected by his Companions' shields.

Auriane realized they were more intent upon Wido than Odberht. Baldemar's warning sounded in her ears: *"If Odberht escapes, Wido will live again, and in monstrous form, for this will be a Wido without shame."*

She sprinted ahead until she was abreast of Odberht. To her surprise he seemed to know her in spite of her blackened face, and he grinned, his look suggesting they shared some shameful secret. That supremely confident grin did not fade even as she took aim with a spear.

She measured her motion against the horse's rhythm and put all her mind on her target. Fatigue was overtaking every muscle. Then she summoned all her strength and flung her weapon.

The throw was skillfully aimed, but it did not have enough power. Her spear arced down too soon and struck not Odberht but a Companion who ran alongside him. As the man fell, she heard a cheer raised by Baldemar's men. She looked back briefly. Before the man sank down she saw a face that was startlingly young—a distressingly familiar face.

Ullrik. It cannot be, let it not be. But it is.

A heavy misery swamped her. How could the Fates let her slay Ullrik, to whom she promised sanctuary?

And why had they not given him a horse? Then she would have known him. To the end, Ullrik was more thrall than son.

Auriane felt quickly gathering despair. The two horses lengthened their strides as they approached the gate; now she could scarcely keep pace. Sigwulf, Thorgild, young Coniaric and the better runners slowly pulled ahead of her.

And then she saw a thing that would haunt memory for years. A length of netting flared up against the sky, the sort of net young warriors used to trap small game. It was impossible to tell who had thrown it, though it seemed to come from one of the warriors who ran alongside Odberht. The net settled over the head of Wido's horse, entangling its forelegs, causing the beast to thrash frantically. Wido slashed at the net with his sword, but it was no use. The horse bucked once, then reared sharply, twisting its body to the side; the saddlecloth slipped and Wido was thrown hard to the ground.

Odberht never looked backward. His mount passed beneath the gate and burst into full gallop, racing out onto the plain. He was free of everything: his father's loathing, the contempt of his tribe, all sacred law. The pine-clad hills were his.

As for Wido, his life was done, and he knew it. Baldemar's men cut their way through the last of his loyal Companions and surged over him. A dozen swords gutted him; so many were Wido's slayers that it was a kill no man could claim. Vengeance was taken, it was said, by the great spirit of the wild mountain cat itself, against whom Wido had so offended.

Many of Wido's men killed themselves with their swords at once, for to survive him would have brought the greatest shame. The ones who did not mind the shame fled after Odberht. They were not pursued—Baldemar's men were too exhausted to care and too jubilant over the slaying of Wido.

None heeded Auriane's hoarse shouts. *"Odberht! He gets away!"*

She picked up a spear from the ground and gave chase, though she was so fatigued her legs could scarcely carry her. She cast the spear at Odberht's fleeing back; it arced bravely but fell short. The horse's gay upraised tail mocked her, fluttering like a victory banner.

She slowed and turned, heavy with defeat.

I know well Odberht will go straight to his Roman masters. They will give him men and gold, and he will raise another army.

She averted her eyes as she moved past Wido's slashed and bloodied body. The net lay nearby in a heap. She heard excited speculation among the warriors grouped about the corpse, and many voices demanding to know who threw that net.

Whoever cast the net, Auriane thought, was the true slayer of Wido.

All supposed it must have been one of Wido's own Companions. But that seemed impossible—why would one of them have committed such an outrage after remaining loyal for so long? Surely men ready to give their lives for him would not have pulled him down to such a humiliating end. It remained a troublesome riddle, and Auriane reflected that rarely did the Fates allow vengeance to be perfect; always they tossed some shadowy ingredient into the cauldron, as if to keep the avenger from becoming too drunk on certainty when he tasted victory's brew.

Auriane threaded her way through the dead and dying, looking for Ullrik's body. She came upon a young Roman soldier dying in slow agony, crying like a babe for his mother; without a thought she stole up behind him and gave him a merciful spear thrust to the heart, sending him to the Mother of All. Behind her came sporadic shouts: *"The traitor is dead! Long live our people! Wodan is great!"* as the Companions cheerfully climbed over bodies to reach the storehouses that had not burned so they could loot them. Only the soul that is part blind could revel in this wretched scene, she thought angrily, then began to worry that perhaps her own soul saw too much. I must hide my revulsion. For surely I am wrong, and the death of enemies is beautiful.

The sun shed a thin sickly light on the field while the moon held on stubbornly. Clouds of flies appeared from nowhere, busy over the dead. Now every stiffened face was a reproach—each of the slain had the features of poor Ullrik. She quivered in every limb. She realized her moon blood had started to come. It was comforting and warm; she shed life onto a field of death. She looked up to meet the eye of that phantom moon before it faded in the full light of day.

Beautiful watcher, merciless and bountiful at once, she thought as she wondered at its awful power to raise and lower the tide of blood in her body. She made no effort to conceal it—there was so much blood everywhere, who would recognize the sacred blood and become afraid?

Finally she found Ullrik, and knelt beside his body. Her spear leaned from his back like some heavy quill. A dozen or so of the Companions gathered round her, their eyes alight with pride in her.

"A fine trophy!" Thorgild said as they looked at her, then nodded among themselves with approving smiles. None noticed her eyes glistened with tears.

"She has the war-luck of the gods!" young Coniaric proclaimed, giving her his flashing smile.

Sigwulf offered grudgingly, "That is good, Auriane, very good! He was not important, of course—but he *is* a son of Wido. A fine kill!"

She looked at him. He was not prepared for the bitter sorrow in her eye, the leaden voice. "Sigwulf, do not speak so. He was my brother."

Baffled silence followed these words. Sigwulf broke it, always ready to tread where others would not.

"Well then, you might as well have married into that family, after all, if you want *him* for a brother. Why, those might even be called traitor's words."

The silence became sharp. Coniaric's smile vanished. Auriane replied without rancor, "Sigwulf, you know only one sort of kinship."

Thorgild looked hard at Sigwulf. "Speak more so, blackguard, and you will die right here on the ground. You've grievously insulted one the gods love. She gave us victory!"

"Thorgild speaks the truth!" came a cry of agreement.

"It's envy, Sigwulf—she shone more brightly than you!"

"Swallow those words, rogue, or fight us all!"

And Sigwulf was silenced beneath an avalanche of abuse. He shrugged and relented, but said nothing to Auriane to make amends.

Then they moved off to resume stripping weapons and treasure from the dead. A number of mead casks were found in the stores, and the warriors progressed from battling to drinking with hardly a pause. Auriane still hugged Ullrik's side.

Ullrik, I made a mockery of my promise. Once again my evil rises up, fulfilling Hertha's words.

And then she thought of a way to give comfort to the dead boy.

I promised you we would take you in, and we shall. I doubt Wido wants you any more now than he did while he lived. Your ghost can come with us.

She smoothed back Ullrik's hair, and using her moon blood, which all the tribes believed had the power to give new life, she traced on his forehead two plain crossed lines, the sign that worked the magic of rebirth. All the while she uttered the ritual words to invite his ghost to inhabit the next child born to a kinswoman.

"Be born among us, be born among us, live again!" she prayed, and felt a stirring behind the membrane that divided the worlds. *"Drink our mead, eat meat from our board,"* she intoned—and she sensed a quickening behind his lids.

She looked up to meet the eyes of a young Companion who paused, amazed, in the midst of stripping a corpse to watch her. She met his eye calmly, refusing to explain.

Then she rose and left Ullrik where he was, consoled by the belief that she would see him again one day, in the body of one not yet born. With the others she wearily worked her way back to Baldemar's camp. Witgern kept close by her side, remorse in his manner as he silently offered renewed friendship. Those too drunken to walk were loaded into the carts with the treasure. The Roman dead and Wido's Companions were left for the ravens.

Baldemar gave the order for a great bonfire to be built on the ridge so the spoil could be dedicated to Wodan. It seemed to Auriane, when she embraced him on her return, that his eyes shone fierce and alive as the eagle's as it falls on prey. She was certain his vital strength had grown greatly in the span of this one night.

Already, she thought, *vengeance has begun its work of healing.*

It was not until she sought an herb woman to treat her

wound—a sword cut that penetrated the collarbone—that she realized the *aurr*, that amulet of earth she had worn all her life, was gone, cut off most likely by the blade that made the wound. She felt a twisting sadness. It could not be. But it was.

I have lost the protection of earth. Surely, it is because I have killed.

Ramis is the great enemy of war, and so she took back her birth-gift to me. *"Never forget the power of hair,"* Ramis warned, and I willingly let mine be shorn.

But I cannot so easily let it go! I'll go tomorrow and search among the corpses until I find it.

No. That would be to no purpose. *She has taken it from me.* She will not let me find it. I must travel on without it. What need has a bride of Wodan for the protection of the earth?

The victory festival was so joyous and abandoned she forgot for a time the amulet's loss. They shouted praise-songs to the god in loud, lusty voices as Roman legionary shields, swords and javelins, horse trappings and leather armor were thrown into the bonfire as thank-offerings. And because the god had a great love of horses, thirty cavalry mounts were sacrificed as well, after one fine black Thessalian stallion was saved out for Baldemar to replace the horse killed beneath him. As the celebrating went on through the night, Auriane managed to conceal two legionary short swords before they were given to the flames, so that she and Decius could practice with them. This was a brazen theft from the god, but a small one, she reasoned hopefully, and her fascination with them was stronger than her fear.

The victory festival went on until the mead and wine ran out. For four days and nights, sword dancers performed their stalking dance round the fire, their blades sparking as they were struck together to the accompaniment of pipers and drummers who played hard to be heard over the flames. The ground was swampy with spilled mead. Horse races were run, and cock fights staged. A whole ox was roasted, and fortunes were told by seeresses who gazed into bowls of blackened silver filled with water from divining springs. Traveling songmakers came into camp with their gaily colored cloaks and battered harps, and sang familiar lays to slowly plucked strings or composed new ones in honor of the battle just won. They sang that the victory was Auriane's, for hers was the hand that opened the gate.

When they had no more spoil to burn, the bonfire was fed with whole trees and Roman wagons. It was such a potent fire, people said, that anyone who came near its gusts of heat would be cured of all manner of ailments, from festering boils to the wasting cough, and that barren women who danced round it would conceive within the year.

This, then, Auriane thought, is the rapture of vengeance. The great cat-spirit that guards our souls smiles and licks its paws. The sun loves us. The moon fills our wombs.

But the taste was so much more pallid than she had expected. She sensed a crouching evil behind the celebrating that the others seemed not to feel. Perhaps it was because Odberht still lived. All was not well—she knew it in the blood.

When four days had gone, they watched from the ridge as a party of Romans returned to the field of battle. They were petty and small in the distance as they methodically collected their dead for the pyres. Auriane heard her people laugh and mock and call them cowards and slaves.

She saw Decius but once before they broke camp. She had arranged for him to go secretly ahead of them with a native thrall for a guide. When she came to take leave of him, he told her of the spy who had witnessed their last embrace. Decius asked what would become of her, were she accused of shameful acts with a foreigner.

"Nothing, while Baldemar lives—no one would dare harm me, not even Geisar. My father has always honored his own law above sacred law. But if . . . if . . ."

"Baldemar dies."

"Yes. Then I am certain Geisar would see me tried and condemned by the Assembly."

"Condemned. That means . . . the bogs?"

"It would be necessary, to keep my evil from infecting the whole tribe."

"The compassion of savages, truly, it tugs at the heart. Well, my little dove, you must tell your father to *stay alive*."

"Please, Decius, do not mock."

On the next day the army dispersed to the tribal farms, hoping to return in time for the harvest. Baldemar could ride if the pace was slow, though not for long, and so began a torturously slow journey home.

They were hardly under way when one of Baldemar's young messengers galloped toward them on the trail, coming from the north. He was shaken and pale from loss of sleep, and he had already ridden one horse to death.

A number of northern farms were being pillaged and burned by raiders of the Cheruscans, he said. There have been massacres at the outlying farms. A stream of refugees traveled toward them now.

Baldemar had feared these ancestral tribal enemies of the far north might take advantage of his long absence in the south. He quickly arranged for Witgern to ride ahead at great speed with a company of five hundred to surprise and punish the brigands.

When the five hundred were ready to depart, they began to clamor for Auriane to ride with them. Baldemar firmly refused.

But the cries of _"Daughter of the Ash! Bringer of victory!"_ only became more determined. She was their living talisman; the men were outraged that Baldemar would deny them her protection.

"This will bring no happiness to Athelinda," Baldemar protested to Auriane. But when the men dismounted, set down their weapons and refused to ride out, Baldemar at last relented.

Auriane privately rejoiced that she was not to return home. Her unsettled soul needed movement in these times, and the newly built hall was not home anyway. The spirits of childhood no longer dwelled there; they had been driven off by the fire. What did dwell there were pitiable ghosts—of Arnwulf, of Hertha. The shifting grasses of the plain were her fields now; all the trees of the Hercynian Forest were the pillars of her house. Most of the time this was as she wanted it. But somewhere within, it caused a dim point of sadness; sometimes it seemed like too much house. If everywhere were home, then nowhere was home.

As they journeyed north, the air became sharply cold, and she sensed a ruinous winter settling in before its time.

ROME

CHAPTER IX

Summer withered into fall. As the wind stripped bare the trees of the northern forest, preparing them for the anguish of winter, in the gentler climate of the capital city of the Empire a different sort of winter closed in upon Marcus Arrius Julianus the Younger, once Endymion the slave. In these, the last blood-washed days of Nero, he who, ten years ago, had gained all, prepared now to lose all: Before him loomed a treason trial, his family's ruin, and a humiliating death.

Young Marcus' earliest days in the mansion on the Esquiline were filled with the ecstasy of the blind man given sight. Endymion had come upon his true country—the lecture halls of the philosophers' schools, the Palace libraries, and the famous and not inconsiderable library in his father's house. He devoured with the relish of the half-starved the principles of geometry and harmonics, the theories of the Chaldean astronomers, the histories of the great nations back to the time of Saturn. He immersed himself in such diverse studies as the laws of architectural symmetry, the art of augury, the science of siting a temple, of laying a forum, of planning the acoustics of a theater. He committed to memory much of the great works of the Greek and Latin poets, while learning the whole of the art of war, from stratagems of the field to the tuning of catapults. As he grew to young manhood, he traveled to the Academy at Athens to hear lectures on the nature of existence given by the great Platonists and Epicureans of the day, and then to the schools of Alexandria to learn human anatomy and the deeper mysteries of the moon and stars. On his return he set himself to the study of civil law, for the profession of advocate was considered necessary for advancement in government, and he attended the city's most celebrated school of rhetoric, where his student orations were so highly praised that teachers of rival schools came to listen. At twenty-one his treatise criticizing the strict materialism of Democritus was read at the Palace before Nero and became a popular text for students of the natural sciences. All his tutors agreed he was possessed of uncommon memory, tenacity and brilliance, and by twenty-five he was as celebrated for his learning as Seneca had been at the same age.

Through much of this time, Marcus Arrius Julianus the Elder was absent at his post as Governor at the fortress of Mogontiacum in Upper Germania, and Diocles, the chief steward of the house, watched over the boy carefully, writing regularly of him to his father. As Marcus grew to young manhood, Diocles' letters became catalogues of dangerous improprieties: Young Marcus held readings of the works of philosophers who had been exiled or banned, attended by "parasites of the lowest classes whom he calls friends." Marcus, Diocles suspected, had assignations with the concubine of one of the most powerful legionary commanders, a freedwoman far older than himself noted for her cleverness and learning rather than her beauty; how could he even *look* at such a vulgar creature, Diocles complained, when he is betrothed to Junilla, chastest bloom of maidenhood in the city? Marcus, Diocles scribbled on, drove from the house his most illustrious tutor, the Greek historian Archias, by arguing that Alexander the Great, who was this teacher's god, was in reality no more than a highly successful murderer and thief. And the boy infuriated Antigonos, his tutor in languages, by putting forth a theory that the rude tongues of the Gauls and the savages of Germania were related in form to Latin.

The elder Julianus' dismay increased when Marcus turned his attention from the respectable philosophies of the day, such as the staid Stoicism popular at court, and began secretly pursuing esoteric disciplines too mystical for the aristocracy's Greek-tutored tastes and too critical of all social order. Once Diocles saw Marcus arise with a lamp in the deep of night and followed him. If his charge went off to an assignation, the steward meant to be certain it was a highborn girl or proper married matron and not some tavern trull or Circus catamite. The boy's father would want to know. But Marcus stole back to the library as if to a lover that would not let him rest. At dawn Diocles found the young man asleep at the reading table; about him were copies of such books as Pythagoras' theory of the transmigration of souls, Isodorus' essays on the evils of any man, be he emperor or king, assuming rulership over others, and Apollonius of Tyana's diatribes against the temple sacrifice of animals—subversive texts with no place in a Roman education. It shocked Diocles as much as commerce with the meanest of prostitutes would have.

And then the improprieties, to his father's horror, became ever more public. In one of young Marcus Julianus' first civil cases as advocate—he spoke the defense of a freedman accused of stealing sacks of grain from the government stores during a severe winter grain shortage—Marcus in his summation speech mentioned the recent arrival of an Alexandrian grain ship, revealing it was loaded not with desperately needed wheat but with sand for Nero's private wrestlers. "The young fool's words touched off a food riot," Diocles wrote to the Governor. "They are starting to say of your son, *'What others scribble on walls at night, Marcus Arrius Julianus shouts in the shadow of the Palace.'*"

But the final outrage, in Diocles' opinion, came when the young man began openly attending the street lectures of Isodorus, a Cynic philosopher who owned nothing but the filthy rags he wore. Diocles convinced Marcus' father his son meant to give away all his possessions, go barefoot and follow this Isodorus, sleeping beneath bridges with him and eating fruit fallen from carts. Diocles wrote to the Governor: "You must return home at once! Unless you are content in the knowledge you pulled that young man out of one gutter just so he could crawl back into another."

The Governor attempted to resign his post in Germania in order to watch his son more closely. But as always Nero's council of military advisors would not allow it while the tribal coalitions led by Baldemar still harried the border. In addition, Nero detested Julianus the Elder and did not want him about, imagining old Julianus reproached him in silence for his abandoned life, as Seneca had.

When the time came for the military service so necessary for a senatorial career—it was customary for the sons of senatorial families to serve two years as a tribune to learn the routines of the army—the younger Marcus requested to be stationed in Egypt. *Of course,* his father thought. *He will see no fighting in peaceful Egypt.* Julianus the Elder could almost hear the lecture on the evils of war. *"There is not a difference,"* Diocles once warned him that Marcus had written in a school essay, *"between the seizure of a neighboring country and the seizure of your neighbor's house."*

So the Governor responded by promptly arranging for his rebellious son to be posted in the North African province of Numidia, a desolate border of the Empire where the fighting with fierce nomadic tribes was almost continuous. For all his loathing of war, Marcus did remarkably well, old Julianus thought—he came home with high praise both from his commander and the men, and was credited with saving the entire garrison of one of the desert forts through his quick action during a surprise attack by moonlight in which he was engaged in hand-to-hand fighting. But the young man returned to civilian life with his heretical beliefs intact. Julianus did not cease worrying over his son's "lust for the impractical and the invisible" until the day he learned from his sister Arria that Marcus had been voted into the lowest office of the Senate, an almost unprecedented honor for a man not yet thirty—though admittedly over the noisy opposition of a small clique on the floor who claimed Marcus was not his father's son at all but Endymion in fact, a spirited urchin of no parentage whom the old man had taken in, cleaned, dressed, and educated.

The Governor wrote back from the fortress at Mogontiacum, "I am overjoyed you at last decided to live a responsible life. A man should live *by* philosophy, not for it."

But his relief was not to last.

On one day early in the month of *Maius*—in the same year that the auxiliary forces of Julianus the Elder, led by Wido, were defeated by Baldemar—Marcus Julianus stood on the steps of the Temple of Minerva with old Lycas, living on still despite a half-dozen afflictions; they listened to one of Isodorus' harangues on the wretched state of the city.

Isodorus spoke before a knot of several hundred or so curious students, idlers, merchants and worshipers bearing gifts to the temple. In the street below flower-vendors' carts overflowed with joyous color; ruddy afternoon sunlight softly ignited the bronze statuary of the roofs of the temples and government buildings all about, melting them to liquid gold. Isodorus' strident shouts rose over the hum of priestesses intoning a dark hymn within the temple and the cries of fishmongers in the street below.

Lycas leaned heavily on a knotted stick, squinting, wheezing and shivering with palsy. He himself had no love of philosophers, but as age shortened his sight and hobbled memory, he closely followed Marcus everywhere, as though all that was familiar and safe resided in him. As for Marcus the Younger, he was now wholly grown into the intricately ordered world of the aristocracy. He had a comeliness that did not seize the eye at once like some master's image of Apollo; it was apparent slowly and came as much from the soul within as from the fine and resolute lines of that haunted face. A linen tunic and gray mantle fell gracefully on a tautly muscled frame; the years in the desert had left him well conditioned. He wore but one ring—the plain gold one given him upon his entry into the Senate. None observing him would guess he had ever lived anywhere but among great libraries and quiet colonnades. But Endymion was visible still in those eyes; as ever, they were ardent and dark, ready to flash to brilliance at the sight of injustice.

Marcus shielded his eyes from the sun—and then he saw it: a glint of steel just visible through the smoke of sacrifice, within the gloom beyond the vast bronze door of the Temple of Minerva, fifty steps or so above Isodorus. He tensed as if for battle.

No one goes armed into a temple. Not unless ordered there by one who counts himself higher than the gods.

"Lycas," Marcus said in a covered voice, "there are Praetorian Guards stationed within the doors."

Quiet terror seized Lycas; he hugged Marcus' side more closely, seeing nothing, while fretfully brushing back a lock of silver hair that fell into his eyes like some horse's forelock.

Isodorus was thundering forth like a dramatic actor in the final scene of a tragedy. "These then are the diseases of cities! Look at the lives of those about you! He who does not languish in a torpid idleness that would shame an oyster in its bed, indulges in excesses of frenzied, unnatural work—dictating during meals, fearing even to sleep at night lest he do less than his neighbor! Look about and you will see ambitions above the gods'! You will see greed that disgraces humanity! A tenement collapses, killing all its inhabitants. It is built again at once, in the same fashion . . . and it kills again!"

"Lycas," Marcus said with urgency, "they've moved into sight. They've come to arrest Isodorus. He must be warned. Stay here . . . if I can pull him into the mob, perhaps they'll lose sight of him."

"*What?* No! You are mad!"

"Perhaps," he replied as he began a smooth, stealthy progress forward, working his way through the crowd.

"Do not leave me!" Lycas said with childish fearfulness, snatching at Marcus' arm to pull him back.

Marcus dragged him up a few steps, then turned and gently seized his shoulders. "Lycas, *stay here*. It is little matter if I am arrested, not so for you!" Lycas, as a freedman, could be subjected to brutal punishments from which the law exempted one of the senatorial class.

When Marcus continued on, Lycas hesitated but a moment; with brisk hobbling walk he set out again, a step or so behind, using his walking stick alternately to gain the next step and push people off.

". . . where, in the Circus, dogs are trained to walk like a man!" Isodorus was crying out, "and, in the Palace, humans are made to crawl! . . . where a rich man is followed by a retinue of one hundred, all choking the streets so none can pass, and their only purpose is to applaud his words!" Isodorus had a small, simian face, bright close-set eyes, a voice as soothing as a rope burn. As Marcus climbed closer, ten Praetorians began moving stiffly, purposefully down the steps, red cloaks whipping in the wind, armor glinting evilly. Most in the crowd were too rapt to notice.

". . . where we keep close track of every hour—all time is to be filled!—and at the end of the day the result is tallied up—did I do more today than yesterday?—as if doing more would bring peace," Isodorus went on, swaying slightly in a sort of grim ecstasy. "Never do we eat grains we harvested ourselves. *How many bodies, how many walls, stand between us and pure, vigorous nature?* And might this not be the cause of cancers like Nero and of the desperate unhappiness on every hand?"

I wonder, Marcus thought, if a Cynic does not *need* a Nero as much as he despises him. But Isodorus speaks his own thoughts, and a man should be able to speak them without losing his head.

"Marcus, no!" Lycas called out. The Guards were too close.

When Marcus was one step below Isodorus, he called up to him, "My good man, look behind! They come for you. Save your life!"

Isodorus looked briefly at Marcus, then that mist returned to his eyes—Marcus knew the philosopher saw him no more. "And *must* some be above, and others below?" Isodorus went on, his voice hushed as if he crept up to something very holy. "But, you say, it has *always* been so. Some must rule. But in the time of Saturn it was *not* so. In those times all ate at one board. Why have we fallen from this? There are yet, in remote places of the earth such as the wastes beyond the North Wind, people who live in

Saturn's state, keeping only what they reap, speaking an honest tongue that has no word for 'slave' or 'king,' and loving the law of moon and stars—"

These were the last public words Isodorus was ever to speak. Marcus leapt up beside him, seized his arm and pulled him down. In the same instant the crowd saw the Praetorians and began to bolt. At ten paces the Guards drew their swords. Marcus tried to drag both Lycas and the philosopher deeper into the crowd, but the Praetorians swiftly caught up to them.

One seized Isodorus and pinned his arms behind his back; a second raised his sword to strike Lycas' head with the flat of the blade. Marcus whipped about, snatched the walking stick away from the old man and brought it up hard against the blade, snapping the walking stick in two, but managing to deflect the blow, giving Lycas just enough time to drop to the steps and evade it. A second Guard kicked Lycas in the stomach while Marcus struck blow after blow on the Guard's steel-armored back, then tried to strike at his eyes with the broken half of the stick, amazing the Praetorians who did not expect such spirited resistance from an unarmed man in the street. A third Guard came from behind and struck Marcus a blow to the face with a length of chain; he sank dazed to the steps. Distantly he was aware that old Lycas was being kicked to his knees and swiftly trussed with cord.

By force of will Marcus fought his way to his feet. He thrust his body between Lycas and the Guard who held him.

"Are you mad?" Marcus called out breathlessly. "This man has naught to do with this! He is here only because I am here. Release him!"

They had had enough of this troublemaker. The first Guard calmly raised his sword for a blow meant to decapitate him.

"Halt!" the second called out with alarm. *"Mind who that is!"*

The first Guard slowly lowered his sword. *Old Julianus' son.* He grunted a cautious obscenity, momentarily horrified his exercise of summary justice nearly got him charged with the murder of a powerful Senator's son. *Why does the young fool always go about so humbly dressed?*

Marcus in his fury scarcely knew he had been recognized; he knew only the blind horror of one who watches his child borne off by wolves.

The Guards contented themselves with pushing him off with great force; Marcus fell hard to the steps and lay there bleeding, looking after them while they swarmed about Lycas and Isodorus, prodding them with javelin butts, herding them like swine.

"Cowards!" Marcus cried out in a voice so harsh and compelling it caused the Guards a moment of unease. "Leave those two old men! Arrest me!"

"Your day will come!" one of the Praetorians jovially called back to him.

Lycas, I have murdered you. You will never survive their stinking prison. Bestial world, traitorous Fates, why did you let him follow me?

After he made his way home, he spent the rest of the day sending swift messages to the Petitions Office, the Praetors, various imperial secretaries and a dozen influential members of the Senate who were his father's friends, even the Emperor himself, begging Lycas' release. He knew well there was little he could do for Isodorus, who had long flirted with the limits of imperial tolerance; doubtless Nero meant to make an example of him. Only old Antoninus Saturninus, his father's close friend and one of the three most influential members of the Senate, sent a reply: "Give it up—they are dead men. All are intended to perish in Nero's Olympic Celebration Games."

In his desperation he even sought the aid of a fellow student from his school of rhetoric, a young man of obscure family and unlimited ambition named Domitian, whom normally he avoided in grave matters because Domitian took too few matters seriously for Marcus' taste. But he was part of Nero's inner circle of friends.

"It is a joke," Domitian explained. "Cynic means *dog* so Nero decided: Dogs to the dogs. And they are desperately short of victims—Nero wanted an even hundred, and in a whole month they only flushed out twenty Cynics. You know what that means. No reprieves, no bothering with petty annoyances like guilt or innocence. Your Lycas struck a Guard. That's guilt enough."

"Help me to petition him in person then!"

"You've not a chance, nor have I. He sees no one—he must pamper the Divine Voice. As we speak, he's resting in his dark chamber with lead plates on his chest while they feed him leek broth till he vomits. Have you forgotten tonight's the first night of his new tragic play? He's the *cantator*, you know."

"He causes a far greater tragedy than any he ever conceived for the stage," Marcus replied, "and he has no more notion of it than an ass would."

The Olympic Celebration Games were to be held in the Field of

Mars, where a makeshift wooden arena had been constructed for a week of contests between men and beasts. The execution of Isodorus and his followers was to be part of the morning show, to whet the crowd's appetite for the bloodier combats to come later. After midnight Marcus set out by torchlight for the Field of Mars. A bribe to a guard got him into the rude holding pens where the next day's victims were kept.

"Lycas!" he called out softly into the vile blackness of a small square cell into which twenty or more prisoners were packed, leaving no room to sit. The stench of offal brought him close to nausea. He spoke into a living crypt, full of muffled crying, moans and whispered prayers. "Lycas, speak if you are here!"

After a time a hand groped through the bars and strongly seized his own.

"Young man," came a familiar, irritating voice.

"Isodorus, it is you."

"Young man, your old companion is dead."

"No," he whispered. "Do not tell me this!" At first Marcus felt nothing; Isodorus' words were empty of meaning. Then slowly a dull heavy coldness crept over him; it seemed the stiffness of death claimed him limb by limb. Then he knew it fully, and he was seized with a furious grief too great for tears; it called for gnashing of teeth and flinging oneself to the earth. He sank against the bars and remained for long moments in stricken stillness.

Companion of my whole life, Endymion's true father, you cannot have left me. My living heart has been torn from my chest. How can I struggle on with life without the interference of those grumbled opinions, those sour objections, that sturdy love that weathered everything? It is like losing the horizon line. It is like losing . . . the house of your birth.

I killed him. I could have prevented him from following me.

"How?" Marcus managed at last. "Which one of those jackals killed him?"

"None of them and all of them," Isodorus replied. "He was not strong enough for such rough treatment. He lies dead in here somewhere; he just quietly slipped off from us. Rejoice—it is a blessing. It is a far better death than that which comes tomorrow."

Marcus felt his whole soul collapse into blackness. "I swear by all that is sacred he who has done this will suffer."

"If you mean Nero, his suffering is assured. As for your old friend, his life was complete; he lived out his time. You must not take death so seriously—it happens all the time. Now, look at me." Isodorus reached a bony hand through the bars and turned Marcus' face toward the feeble light of the torch in the hand of the jailer stationed at the door. "*I know you*. Tell me, was it not once prophesied of you that the fate of the whole country would rest in your hands?"

Marcus was startled out of his misery. Other than his father, who was in distant Germania, all who knew of that prophecy were dead.

"How do you know of such things?"

"I know them. Look to yourself and stay alive. The ancient days stir in you." Isodorus leaned closer; his words were half sung like some baleful lay. "You are of the time of Saturn, not of our times, and you are the bane of rulers. Your destiny is back of the North Wind. Your god is Dionysus, bearer of freedom." Then he said, casually as he might have asked for a bite of an apple, "Will you look after my pupils?"

"Your pupils?" Marcus could scarcely believe Isodorus meant to honor him by entrusting his followers to his care. "I would gladly, but—"

"About thirty of them live on in hiding. They need someone to shelter them and encourage them and keep them from harm."

"But . . . I was not one of your followers. I am a man who does not yet know what he believes."

"Of no importance. The temper and mettle of the man is more important than precisely *what* he believes. They do not know what they believe either." He worked a ring free from his finger. "Already, though you know it not, you have passed from the life of one who is sheltered to that of one who shelters. Take this ring so they will know it was my will."

"One day I'll either curse you or praise you for this." Marcus then took an ivory-handled dagger from his clothes and pressed it into Isodorus' hand. At first the philosopher pushed it away.

"Take it," Marcus insisted. "It's a better death than the dogs."

Finally, with a measure of indifference, Isodorus complied. "You do not understand death," he said, "but I bless you for your kindness anyway."

On the following day at dawn Nero ordered all copies of Isodorus' works seized from the bookstalls and libraries and even had private mansions searched. Then his writings were burned in the Old Forum. At the second hour, when the games commenced, the young nobles of the equestrian and senatorial classes were seated alongside the imperial box so that Nero could view their response to the bloody lesson he gave them; they would learn the fate of those wretches who tried to lead youth astray.

When the huddled victims were dragged out, Marcus saw to his dismay that Isodorus had not used the dagger—though apparently half the captives in the cell with him had, to the great frustration of the guards who discovered their corpses at dawn. Isodorus was naked but for a loincloth, his hands bound behind his back. Marcus made himself watch; not to do so seemed a sort of abandonment. An animal handler, whip in hand, raised a grate and out sprang ten half-starved Molossian dogs.

The image of it never left Marcus' mind: Isodorus so white and thin, the horror and confusion of dogs, the blur of fur, the bloody foam in their mouths, the whiplike motions of their bodies as they swarmed over the frail philosopher.

The next day Marcus recovered Lycas' body from the open pit outside the city where unclaimed dead were taken, and arranged a costly funeral; he insisted Lycas be dressed in finery and carried through the streets on a gilded couch with a full procession of mourners. Then he had Lycas' ashes put in the grand family tomb a half mile from the city along the Via Appia. This deeply embarrassed his father, his aunt Arria, and the greater family—it looked absurd, they protested, to lavish so much honor on a former slave.

But as he watched his lifelong companion's body burn, the sturdy Endymion-soul resurrected itself as it always seemed to when given time enough. *I did not kill Lycas. Blind bestial tyranny killed him.* Tyranny wears a multitude of masks; the mask it wears now is Nero. Tomorrow it will wear another.

And so it was in Lycas' name that he committed the act of rebellion that established his notoriety for all time—and brought about his father's fall.

He owned one book of Isodorus' writings that escaped the purge. He engaged copyists to reproduce it, then employed his father's poorer clients in secretly distributing the copies to the owners of the bookstalls, who wanted them in spite of the danger because the persecution excited the people's interest in Isodorus' sayings. And so he resurrected Isodorus in the only way he knew. Soon after, a copy of one of the works of the banned poet Lucan came into his hands. This, too, he had copied and distributed. *"Your god is Dionysus, bearer of freedom."* Isodorus' words sounded in his mind in ghostly affirmation. Within a short time he had brought a half-dozen damned poets and philosophers back to life. The steady influx of illicit works into the bookstalls baffled and enraged the five Imperial Advisors, who strove constantly to trace the source.

When Diocles wrote to the elder Julianus that he had seen and heard things that caused him to suspect the younger Marcus was the notorious producer and distributor of banned books, the old man could bear his son's indiscretions no longer; against orders, he started for home. His timing was to prove fatal.

In these times, conspiracy followed conspiracy, each more ruthlessly put down than the last—Nero had ruled through murder for too long. The Emperor realized in his more lucid moments he was trailed by wolves, and as instinct warned him they crowded ever closer; he responded in the only way he knew: by planning more murders, on a broader and more efficient scale. When Nero eventually decided all the northern legionary commanders posted in Germania and Gaul, Marcus' father among them, conspired to turn their legions against him and put one of their number on the throne, the Emperor ordered them home with the intent of staging a mass trial and sending them together to their doom. But in an unprecedented act of collective defiance they refused to obey.

Old Julianus, however, had already journeyed half the distance and had no intention of turning back—he meant to bridle his errant son, and he half believed his innocence would somehow shield him. Marcus realized, alarmed, Nero would have only his father upon whom to vent his wrath.

Julianus the Elder was in such a weakened condition the journey home took four months; it was midwinter, past the time of the Feast of Saturnalia, before he returned to the mansion on the Esquiline. He had to be carried into the house in a litter, so ill was he from a malaise ascribed by his physicians to the noxious vapors of the boglands of the north.

Marcus scarcely knew this man with his bleak stare, the flesh of his face loosened from the bone. Anger had burnt itself out in the old man's eyes; they were a place of ashes. That very morning he was notified he was charged with treason; his trial on charges of "criminal ingratitude, treasonable impiety to the genius of our lord, and conspiracy to seize the throne" was to commence on the third day after the Kalends of *Februarius*, a bare month away. As Julianus was carried through the gardens, Marcus stayed beside him, attentive and close.

His father was momentarily shocked from his misery at the

sight of his household. The house was no longer his own: It reflected wholly the mind of his son.

It had become more school then residence: Everywhere teachers and philosophers of various schools mingled familiarly with students. They paced the colonnades with bowed heads, narrowly missing colliding with one another, eyes vacant with thought, then sharp as they pressed home some argument, or they sat by garden fountains, listening to lectures or bent over esoteric texts. They were of every class, of both sexes. Some, Julianus saw with disbelief, were his own household slaves. Next to the great dolphin fountain, which was stilled, and overgrown with scum—his negligent son, he saw, had not bothered to have the servants clean and repair it—he recognized the woman Theophila, the greatest living authority of Epicureanism, thoughtfully sipping his wine with an amiable, aged historian who was supposed to be in exile. As Julianus was carried past the library, the old man saw it had flooded its boundaries and invaded four adjacent rooms; avalanches of bookrolls spilled out of the wall niches and buried the reading couches. His son, it seemed, had acquired no possessions in his absence other than books. This was the abode of a man who found the material world an intrusion.

"This is not my house!" he said gruffly to Marcus as the litterbearers set him down on a hard bed in the gloom of his starkly bare sleeping chamber. "It is a public square! So this is what happens when I am not about! I trust they are not living off alms!"

Moving more swiftly than the servants, Marcus covered his father with a woolen blanket against the chill. "A certain few *have* needed my assistance, though I would hardly call it alms," he replied, "but if I thought it would give you one hour less of misery, I would send all of them away at once."

Julianus heard the succession of emotions in his son's voice: sadness, resignation, and the bearing up; a voice so solemn and sure, so possessed of—what?—a well-tempered strength joined to innocence, an innocence born not of inexperience but of an excess of living, a pain that drags a man close to death yet leaves him alive. And he truly looked at his son for the first time.

Marcus had grown taller than his father, and despite the reflective intellect apparent in those eyes, Julianus had little trouble imagining him fighting the fierce nomadic tribesmen in the deserts of Numidia; a scar from a sword cut perilously near the throat showed how nearly he had been killed. Diocles, he realized, had not written him of this. He sensed in his son's manner an uncanny ability to assume rulership in any circumstance without being overbearing, a natural part he probably assumed without knowing. *It is a pity he will not long survive me—he might have made a fine governor in my place.*

"I am sorry," Marcus went on tentatively, not sure what his father was thinking. "I mean to stay on even terms with you—we have not much time left to us."

"I saw Diocles give you a document." The old man's tone was still unyielding. As always, Marcus thought sadly, he keeps me roughly at a distance.

"*More* foul business. A love note from Veiento." Veiento was the most feared of Nero's senatorial advisors, a ruthless minister who encouraged common informers with rich money gifts. "It seems your trial's to be held in secret, with five of the Imperial Advisors as judges." To Marcus this was the final disaster, to have his father's life snuffed out in some hidden chamber where he could rouse no one's ire, raise no public sympathy for his plight. "Veiento writes on: 'I am not completely unfeeling—your execution will be public, if not your trial.'"

Julianus said nothing, his gaze fixed as a hawk's.

"I mean to fight this, Father. Veiento *must* have some evil secret he does not want aired in an open trial before the Senate. I mean to discover what it is and lay it out before Nero."

"To no purpose! That smooth-tongued eel has sole possession of the imperial ear—all you say will be turned round against us." The ferocity of his father's sullen resignation began to rouse uneasiness in Marcus. Old Julianus looked at him. "Veiento sent a message round just to gloat over that?"

"No, there was more. They . . . added some embellishments to the charge."

"Well?"

"Now they assert your arming of Wido was a long-premeditated act of sedition," Marcus replied, holding out the rolled document to his father. "When the time was right, you planned to unleash Wido and all the barbarian hordes on us."

"What outlandish madness!" His father erupted from his lethargy and tore the letter from Marcus' hand. For long moments he stared at it, hands trembling, not really seeing, then he looked away, in his face the look of one who gazes upon the body of a loved one who died under torture.

When he spoke, his voice was unsettling; it was so empty of anger. "Until this time I thought I dealt with, if not a worthy adversary, at least one that was sane. They might as well bay at the moon and say a cabbage is a herring. Some insults cannot be answered, lest they debase the innocent."

"But they must be answered! They will interpret silence as guilt."

"I no longer care how they interpret silence." His father stared for long at the leaden sky visible through the door, and Marcus saw bitterness ebb out of his face, to be replaced by implacable surrender; the old man seemed to shrug off all the garments of his life—every duty, every belief—until Marcus felt he sat next to a naked child.

When the old man finally spoke it was in a close and gentle voice Marcus had never heard from him before. "You know, Marcus, I might not like what you have done to this house . . . but you have courage and a great heart. You search out truth in places others haven't the wit to search. And that was gallant, what you did for Isodorus. If a man dies for such things, then these times are not worth living in."

Marcus was quietly seized with astonishment. He always believed his father counted him little more than a rebel and a nuisance. He felt a rare pleasure, an immense relief, then a shadowy sadness that would linger, for all those years he felt estranged.

But the words had the quality of a final peacemaking before death.

His father placed a clumsily affectionate hand over his own. "Now, I beg you, my son," he said, "leave me in peace until the tenth hour."

Wariness sharpened to alarm. He started to question the meaning of this, but the old man's eyes forbade it. Reluctantly Marcus left him and retired to the library, setting himself to the grim task of searching through his father's military reports and correspondence, the initial steps of preparing a defense.

At the time of lamplighting, Diocles came in soundlessly and interrupted Marcus' labor. The steward's ancient face was still as a death mask; his morose hound's eyes were red-rimmed. Marcus realized Diocles had actually shed tears. Trembling, he rose to his feet.

"What is this?" Marcus whispered.

"At the ninth hour, your father opened his veins."

Marcus felt stable earth fall in beneath his feet. He dropped into formless darkness.

No. I refuse this. It cannot be! He would not desert me with such cruel suddenness.

He broke into a run, almost knocking Diocles off his feet. The hour now was the tenth. He bolted through the garden to his father's chamber, as if quick action could make a difference, but truly he knew better: Death had already won. In his chest was a hollow agony; he knew no past, no future; there was only a heart pumping blood into water, a great benign presence leaving him to do battle alone.

At the door of the chamber he stopped. He was met by thick humid air, a sickly silence. The walls glistened with the damp. An acrid incense did not completely cover the heavy smell of blood. Old Greek texts claimed that ghosts craved blood—was that this ritual's original purpose? To lure the ancestors' ghosts to a feast? A tub of iron had been put in there and filled with warm water. His father lay in it, his head resting on the rim; Marcus could just see his face, dreadfully still in the dim light; it seemed made not of flesh but clay, as if already he had completed the material cycle, from earth to earth. Marcus was glad of the gloom; he did not want to see the color of that water.

"Father?" He felt like a profane intruder, as if he blundered into the dim inner rooms of a temple and found priests of Libitina laying out a corpse. The old man's eyes opened halfway, and he peered at him through glassy slits. Marcus was horrified by the sound of his breathing—the struggles, the catches, the stops, were so like the last staggering steps of the dying.

"Father . . . , *how can you leave us?"* His voice quivered with effort, as if he thought through the strength of his voice alone he might raise his father up. He edged closer.

"Forgive me." The words did not seem clothed in flesh. "I sent for you when it was too late, lest you try to stop me."

"It is not too late! You are strong still. I'm summoning the surgeon to bind up your wounds!"

"Do not! I command you."

Marcus moved to disobey, then stopped. It was futile; he could not force life on one who did not want it. Nor could he watch his father die. He felt every move, every thought, trapped him deeper in mire; he could scarcely breathe in the dank air. He thought of what the great Stoic teachers had lectured of death, but their words were mocking noise. Grief itself was too deep, elemental and wild. All the letters of consolation written by the philosophers were bloodless words on dry paper; they no more mastered grief than ships tossed about on the surface of the wildest ocean mastered the cold, formless abyss below. He returned to his father's side and knelt down.

Outside it stormed; all the gutters of the house were small roaring rivers. The sound caused his every muscle to tauten with grim urgency. Storm wind somehow found its way into this enclosed place and the flame of the one lamp was whipped into a wild dance; first shadow engulfed the room, then light gained precarious sway. Shadow will win, he thought. The lamp cannot burn forever. Dark need only be patient; it is older, far older than light.

"For what would you preserve me, Marcus?" His father's voice groped for him. "So I can be reviled in a mock trial? So I can be called a criminal by a criminal . . . , then pelted with mud and given to some filthy pig of an executioner? And delight the scum that always gather to watch such things with the sight of my foolish head separated from my body?"

Marcus pressed his father's hand to his forehead. "*This should not be!* You have done no wrong!" The words hung in the silence for a while, pitifully inadequate to aid them.

"They want our death, Marcus. *Our* death. Innocent or not. Nor will Arria or her children thrive long. Treason's a contagion—Nero will assume they've all caught it from us. The Fates are tired of us, my son. A wise man knows the best time to leave the banquet, and he leaves early on. . . . The longer into the night you stay, the more dignity you lose."

In the pause, Marcus tensed, knowing what his father's next words would be.

"*Die with me,* Marcus. You'll be charged, soon as I'm dead. Nero *cannot* let my son live. It's an uncommon ruler that doesn't fear the vengeance of a son, and there's nothing uncommon about Nero except his lust for cruelty. *Come with me.* . . ." His father's damp hand crab-walked along the rim of the tub and seized his own in a feeble grip, giving ghoulish comfort. The old man's whisper became excited. "Posterity will say both father *and* son pushed away the cup of dishonor. The world in these times is a cess trench! Refuse it with me!"

Marcus reflected but an instant on that death, with ancestors' ghosts lauding your courage, arms outstretched to take you in among the blessed shades. Then he vigorously pushed it off.

"I am sorry, Father—I can't die for honor alone. It might be I've too little love of it because of insults to it I suffered as

Endymion." He felt his father's furious disappointment. "But I *am* willing to die seeking out justice. And I cannot do that here in the dark, in a tub. I can only do it in an open trial in the Senate. I *want* those jackals to bring me to trial. I *welcome* it. I will not let your name be vilified without a word said in your defense!"

"Reason is no weapon . . . against the boundless foolishness of youth."

"And Father, there is also Arria. She might be sentenced to deportation and sent off in chains. And there are even darker matters to keep me here. Arria's girl is six; her boy is eight . . . *just the age Nero likes to take them.* I dared not put this in a letter, but when last I attended the morning audience at the Palace, Nero asked to see them. You know for what."

"You believe those tales!"

"And so you must! Awaken to the age we live in!" It was commonly known that noble children, usually girls, had for years been borne off to the Palace over parents' protests to be given "schooling" by dubious tutors selected by Nero, ostensibly in etiquette and the arts—but the reality was a horror speculated of in whispers. Often the children would be returned home after years, listless and half mad, or without sympathies or passion. If so instructed, it was said, they would murder a parent. Tales came of them being kept in darkened cells for years while the Emperor came to them wearing masks and skins of bears or panthers while he took his pleasure of them. Incest fascinated Nero particularly; his greatest amusement was to force brothers and sisters to couple while he watched.

"Let them all go," the old man breathed. "You can do nothing. They are prizes of war. We lost to Chaos . . . and must pass under the yoke."

"*Lost?* I've not yet drawn a weapon!"

"I *command* you, as is my right as your father! Die with me!"

"And I disobey. Have Diocles bring the documents. Disinherit me. I choose to live."

"Curses on you and may you roast in Hades!"

The young man heard then a horrible, impossible snuffling sound; his father cried like a babe. Marcus dared speak no words to acknowledge those pitiful tears for fear of humiliating the old man, but he moved closer and put a hand on his father's to say: Sob if you want, I think no less of you.

When his father collected himself again, he whispered, "I'll wait for you then, on the near side of the Styx."

Marcus felt momentary relief that this battle was won, then fresh grim thoughts crowded in: I am utterly alone, and all rests with me. I have fought in the courts for someone else's life. But to fight for my family's, and my own? It is, I suppose, like learning, as acrobats do, to walk the wire and not look down. I will not have much time to teach myself. *"Already you have passed from the life of one who is sheltered to one who shelters."* Isodorus pronounced those words so calmly, as if this role could be assumed simply as donning a new cloak.

"Marcus . . . , have you that black amulet still?"

In these times he never thought of that dark foreign pouch of earth. "No. I removed it when I became a man."

"Humor a dead man and restore it to your neck. Divine forces are needed in this, if ever in your life. I mean not to dishearten you—"

"But you think my chances of saving us roughly equal that of the novice beast-fighter armed with a stick. I know my chances are poor. I see at once I will have to forge my own weapon. But if all I can do is see that the beasts suffer dearly for their meal, it will be enough."

"The pain . . . ," his father breathed. "Bring in the surgeon for another cut, behind the knees this time, I've borne this long enough."

Marcus shut his eyes, forcing his mind to emptiness to drive out the horror and pity. "I beg you," he said softly. "Take a quick poison!"

"I am stronger than any poison. I have taken the small doses for years. . . ."

Then the old man's head dropped heavily back, and Marcus knew the surgeon would not be needed. He studied avidly every feature of his father's face in the near darkness, struggling to retain a precise memory of it.

But his father managed to speak again, his voice now a child's dulcet pleading. Marcus looked down, scarcely able to bear it. *"My books*. . . . I wrote on sand. They will be burned. . . . All that labor . . . a lifetime of . . . labor. . . . In ten years those that remember my name will spit on it. . . . My great work on Germania lies incomplete. . . . It is like dying while a helpless babe still needs you. . . ."

"Your works will live," Marcus said firmly, dismayed at how completely their roles had turned about: He was the parent who comforted, and his father, the child to be helped to sleep.

"Among the gods, perhaps."

"No. Among men. Father, I will complete those last four books myself, and tell no one. Your works on the customs of the tribes of the North will be the highest authority. They will grace every library from here to Alexandria! The world will think you finished them. It will be my gift to you."

His father turned faintly toward him. "That is well . . . very well . . . ," he began eagerly, then lost his strength all at once.

Marcus doubted his words could have given the old man much comfort, believing as his father did that he himself was doomed as well. But in his weakness Julianus seemed to have forgotten this. "Not die, forever," the old man whispered. "Yes, I will . . . think on that. Marcus, by all the gods you are dear to me. . . . Will you forgive—"

He stopped abruptly as if he softly struck some unseen barrier. A shuddery breath escaped from him.

Juno have mercy, it is too soon—let him finish his words!

The lamp flame did a frightful, twisting dance, as if making way for the passing of his father's shade. Then it died—the oil that fed it had run dry—and Marcus sat in darkness. He did not move, though he knew Diocles and the surgeon waited outside; he was not yet prepared to endure the sounds of the household's wailing.

"Forgive you what?" he spoke aloud to the corpse. "That you mocked my pursuit of learning and thought it excess? Think no more on it, it was your nature, as it is the nature of horses to run. Why is it always those who need no forgiveness who in the end beg it? It is the ones who drove you to this death that I forever refuse to forgive.

"A lifetime of faithfulness, and this is your reward. If I live, I won't serve out of duty, as you did. Perhaps duty, that is where we went off course. If we serve it should be for—for what? For love, love for what might be?"

In one swift moment he had the brutal thought his father was soulless matter, and nothing now existed of him anywhere. The existence of the spirit was a hoax perpetrated by priests to encourage offerings at the temples.

But then he sensed pricked, listening ears, a deft, questing mind, attentive, benevolent as it closed about him in the dark.

"I will give back to you what you gave me: *the world*. That is what you gave me, no less. I will see that it dignifies you and speaks your name with reverence. You want an august memory. I will go and get it for you. And not from duty—that is a mule's harness—but from love." He imagined he felt his father's spirit flinch. "Yes, from love."

Why could he not have clung to life a little longer to hear that? Marcus thought. But then, he realized, *I would not have said it; I needed the dark safe distance of death.*

The corpse was not cold before a detachment of Praetorian Guards was dispatched to the house; two forced their way in to verify that Marcus Julianus the Elder was dead. When the suicide was reported to Nero, he at once charged Marcus Julianus the Younger with treason, claiming he abetted the conspiracy, then tossed in a charge of "filial impiety" as well because Marcus Julianus had not followed his father into death.

At dawn the following day Marcus sent a message to the family of the maid Junilla, offering to release her from the betrothal. Junilla had been promised to him almost a decade ago when she was scarcely out of her mother's arms; he knew even if he survived he would be a poor match for a maiden of such ancient lineage—the pall of disgrace would never be completely dispelled from his family.

And within the hour Marcus received an odd note in reply, written in the Emperor's childish hand and delivered by Nero's newly made wife, the eunuch Sporus: The wedding to Junilla was to be celebrated as planned, and at once; his trial date was to be moved back to make sufficient time for the young bride's preparations. *Why, in the name of Nemesis?* It made sense, Marcus supposed, to a madman. Wedding, trial, execution—what perverse amusement did Nero mean to derive from this mockery of the passages of life?

And I wonder this about a man who set fire to half the city just to watch it burn.

As his father's embalmed body was carried through the city, groups of citizens shouted: "The traitor is dead!" and mocked the elder Julianus' writings, attaching them to poles and dragging them through mud. Marcus as he walked behind the mourners, bearing the family's ancestral masks, looked on in silent wrath as mud struck the pallbearers, the corpse itself. His father had so wanted to be loved by them. *Before the gods, I must speak his defense!*

The imperial government treated Marcus Julianus the Elder as if he had been condemned in fact, in spite of his suicide: The family estates scattered over five provinces were seized; Marcus was left with the great-house and its library. Arria, his aunt, fared less well: She was even stripped of her house because one of Nero's concubines fancied it; she and her terrified children were forced to take refuge with Marcus Julianus in the mansion on the Esquiline.

When mid-month came and the time of the wedding drew close, one day at dawn as Marcus Julianus was conducting the morning audience, a stranger appeared, disguised as one of the family clients—those poor free citizens attached to every great-house who gathered at their patron's door at first light to give a formal salutation and a promise of small services in exchange for money gifts. The interloper, concealed in a hooded, oil-stained cloak, hung back until the last retainer had departed with his small pouch of silver coins.

"Quickly, state your name," Marcus said with weary tolerance. The hooded stranger emerged through the entrance hall with long strides full of the bullying arrogance of youth, then he paused dramatically before the light-well of the atrium, watching Marcus through the shaft of morning sun slanting down in the space between them.

"We are more testy than usual today, are we not?" With a grand gesture he threw back the hood of the cloak.

"Domitian. My wretchedness was not complete. Now it is."

He had not seen Domitian since the young man had come to his house for the last day of the Saturnalia celebrations. Lately Domitian had been elevated to the position of a sort of peasant crown prince, courted by everyone, for if civil war erupted, he had a more than fair chance of becoming an emperor's son. His father, Vespasian, whom Nero had sent out to the province of Judaea to put down the Jewish revolt, had more legions under his control than any other commander—and so was in the best position to take the throne by force. Domitian strained his newfound privileges to the limit, borrowing huge sums of money, seducing women above his station, giving rich banquets, making friends among the Praetorian Guard. That he might *not* one day be within a breath of the highest office on earth rarely occurred to him—he would worry over that one if the time came. Because he was ashamed of his own provincial education and an important man had to affect a command of the arts, he copied Marcus Julianus closely in matters of learning—Domitian's flawless instincts for such things told him the younger Julianus was the man to imitate—studying with the same teachers, attending the same lectures, even echoing Marcus' opinions at dinner-party debates.

"Excuse the disguise, but I knew no other way to see you. Best of friends and old school companion, I—"

"Best of friends! You would make a fine auctioneer. The last time you were here I ordered you out."

"A lapse of taste on your part *I'm* willing to forget. Come, we have a common goal, we *should* be friends."

Marcus could not contain a faint smile at such audacity. "Caesar and Marcus Antonius had a common goal. It did not make them friends."

"What you call cruelty," Domitian said with an impish grin, "I call sport and a good time. Must two men always agree?" Their fight came about when Domitian, between courses, decided to show off his skill in archery to Marcus' guests. He ordered one of his attendant slaves to go into the garden and stand next to a tree with fingers outstretched so he could shoot arrows between them. That the terrified slave got off without injury had not lessened Marcus' anger toward him.

"On some matters, yes, they must." Marcus' tone became gentler. "Well, tell me then—how have I become useful to you?"

Encouraged by this barest sign of relenting on Marcus' part, Domitian approached closer with the sly smile of one preparing to tell an obscene joke in confidence. Domitian's wine-flushed face had a heavy handsomeness bordering on fleshiness; it put Marcus in mind of a sullen Apollo cast too large. The young man managed somehow to look thoroughly world-weary at seventeen. Those eyes were ever watchful, swift to calculate the relative power of others in a given room—dark, lively eyes marred by a morbid look that easily attracted lovers of both sexes. He would struggle a few more years to keep that heavy-boned body conditioned, Marcus surmised, then give it up. There was a blunted, dull solidity about his head, his shoulders; his tall, brooding form gave the sense of a spirit weighted down. He was the sort to retreat to dark places and nurse hurts at leisure, waiting for the moment to rush out and attack while his quarry basks unawares in the sun.

"You have it then. It *was* cruelty. I do not do such things anymore." Domitian was struggling, but with what? Marcus considered. A genuine impulse to control that playful sadism, or with sincerity fallen into long disuse, or the final refinement of his acting ability?

Best for now to treat it as sincere, Marcus decided. It was one of those moments that would linger in memory—the one time he thought he might have seen a childlike openness in Domitian's manner, a youthful suppleness of mind.

"It is past then. Let us speak of it no more." Marcus rose then and embraced his friend, chiding himself for still holding onto a good measure of distrust.

"First I'll cement our rekindled friendship with a gift," Domitian said, smiling, "an offering of choice information. I've learned why Nero seems only in a *moderate* hurry to dispose of you—by rights you should be dead already, you know. You know those tiresome literary competitions Nero bores his guests with when the courses are done? Well, an ode *you* wrote last year somehow got put in with the rest, and the cursed thing—truthfully you've written better—got chosen as victor over Nero's, because the judges got confused over who wrote what and—"

"Nemesis! Why was I not told of this?"

"I wasn't there, nor was anyone loyal to you. Your good friend has razor ears or you wouldn't be hearing it now. They corrected the mistake right away, but it was too late—and now Nero's haunted by ugly suspicions *you* might be better at scribbling odes than he is. He mocks what he's in awe of. One time when he speaks of you, he'd like to pin asses' ears on you. The next, he's begging someone in confidence to tell him if he's ever heard some chance remark of yours praising his poetry, or his music, or *anything* he's done. He won't rest until he contrives some way to hear of you praising him truthfully, when you're not expecting word of it to get back to him. This is excellent, my friend! You've not the knack of taking advantage of men's weaknesses, but it's power in your hands. You are his fixed star today, by which he calculates all else—you should make use of it while you have the chance."

"I want nothing from that ballet-dancing butcher except an open trial."

"He'll *never* relent on that! He's too frightened of that famous mouth. Do you think he's fool enough to unleash it in a public place? Anyway, public or private, a treason trial cannot be won."

"I would not waste effort attempting to win. I mean to speak my father's eulogy and to trick Nero into leaving my family alone."

"There need be no trial at all! Marcus, good friend, I come with . . . encouraging news."

Marcus looked sharply away. "I *know* what it is, and it does not encourage. It turns the heart to stone." Through his own carefully cultivated network of spies, Marcus knew of this month's assassination plot. The conspirators had enlisted the services of a robber condemned to be thrown to the beasts by luring the wretch with an offer of a better death: At a banquet in Nero's Golden House the robber would be concealed above the ceiling behind one of the movable panels just above the Emperor's couch. He would fall upon the Emperor, slay him, then be immediately slain himself— they hoped—by the Guard.

"And it hardly seems well thought out," Marcus went on. "What is to keep your man from being tortured instead of killed outright—and revealing all of your names?"

Domitian stared at him in mute fright. Sometimes, he thought, it seemed Marcus Julianus saw through walls.

"Have no fear," Marcus said quickly. "It's gotten no further than me."

"If that monster in the Palace dies before your trial, you live. I do not understand why you oppose us."

"You speak of deliberately provoking civil war."

"Not I. Others are doing it for us. And so like you, to name worst outcomes."

"I do not know why you are so certain your father will emerge atop that bloody mountain of bodies."

"I wish you would learn to look at life more as a sport."

"It's a sport until the suffering is your own."

"All right, then, whatever you say, but . . . when freedom has been won . . . and if you still walk this earth with us, there is a thing I ask of you, Marcus Julianus: Will you speak my father's cause before the Senate?"

"There are many ready to speak for your father. I do not understand your need of me."

"You truly do not know, do you?" He shook his head slowly in puzzlement. "You are so . . . innocent of the effects of your own presence. I don't know if they're intimidated by your learning or if it's the way you look at them, but the Senators credit your words more than men three times your age. *I* see it if you don't. But I also need you because my forebears, let us speak plainly, were turnip eaters, and that's all we'll ever be, even wearing the purple. We sorely need the endorsement of one who traces his ancestry back to Venus."

Marcus rose and paced. *Curses on him,* Domitian thought, *he has to think about it!*

Finally Marcus halted and turned that direct gaze upon Domitian. "I've nothing whatever against your father. He is a plain and fair man—most likely he *is* the best choice. It's . . . it's *you* I'm uneasy with." Regret showed almost at once in Marcus's face. "I am sorry, but nearness to death makes such things easier to say."

Domitian laughed a thin laugh that did not disguise the flare of anger in his eyes. "I've never seen a man less afraid of losing his head. What must I do for your approval?"

"This is absurd," Marcus answered sadly. "Change your very nature."

"*Done*. Anything else?"

"Do you want other than the truth? Of what use is it? A lie may succor now, it kills later. There is a vein of cruelty and suspicion in you, and it is not a terrible thing in an ordinary man. But if an extraordinary life claims you, what would you be? Reflected a thousand times your size, daily good humor or bad humor makes you god—or monster."

"Very well, you are not needed then," Domitian said with feigned lightness as he spun about to leave. "I have many men around who—"

"As Nero has? Flatterers? To lead him blindfolded and singing to his doom?"

Domitian stopped and turned. In his eye for one instant was the quick frantic look of one pushed off balance. He had never thought of Marcus' cult of truth as a thing that might keep him safe; the idea, once sown, began to take root.

"Perhaps I do not take your youth enough into account," Marcus said then. "I mean not to offend. It might be I jump too easily at the least whiff of tyranny because I have seen so much of it of late. And anyway, it looks more and more as though you are inevitable. I will settle for a promise, then."

Domitian was surprised at the depth of the relief he felt. Why was Marcus Julianus' favor worth so much more to him than that of other men. "Yes?" he said, carefully reining in his delight. "Ask it."

"Vow to me that when the supreme power is yours, you will not persecute men of letters or any school of thought, nor burn their writings, nor the philosophers themselves, for that matter," Marcus said carefully. Domitian found himself transfixed by that sharp, clear gaze. "Give me your word the owners of bookstalls will not be made criminals, nor will anyone who declaims on the street crossings be made a plaything for dogs."

"A simple matter! I *myself* am a poet—now *really*, would I persecute my own kind?" He smiled the quick, mobile smile of a pantomime actor.

"That you call it a simple matter causes me to suspect you mouth the words with as much comprehension as a talking magpie. *Hades take you* if I give you my support, and you turn on us."

"You have my sworn word! Never will I persecute any for their writings, not even the most foul-mouthed of Cynics who beg you to execute them!"

"When the day comes—*if* it comes and I still live—I will speak for your father."

As Domitian took his leave, Marcus called after him. "I've a question for you! Why does the Emperor waste a rare prize such as Junilla on a man he means to destroy?"

Domitian shrugged. "I wouldn't look for a normal human motive behind Nero's acts. Last night at dinner he had all his concubines costumed as fish. By the way, since we are friends again, can I come to the wedding?"

"No," Marcus said with mock annoyance, "you'll snatch the bride."

"I promise to wait at least a month out of common decency."

"Come if you wish. Sad puppet show that it is, I wish *I* had the choice not to come. The air in this city is foul as an animal's den—it's the stench of captivity."

Domitian then added with a reverence so uncharacteristic of him that Marcus first thought the words were meant in jest: "She has a beauty not of this earth." Domitian alone had set eyes on Junilla, who was kept in seclusion by her mother; once he had climbed over her garden wall and, in the instant before her maidservants drove him off with rakes and hoes, managed to steal a glimpse of her as she sat reading. "She was Psyche, she was Selene. You are the most fortunate of men—if you live."

"You love her! Curses, even *you've* got a motive for murdering me now!"

When but two days remained before the hastily arranged marriage to the maid Junilla, Marcus began yet another night of studying his father's military correspondence and records, going through these documents in order of year. Earlier that day he remembered his father's wish concerning the sorceress's black amulet; after retrieving it from the strongbox in the *tabularium*, where the family records were kept, he placed it once again about his neck. He could see no reason not to humor a ghost. The amulet felt right there, as though a tessera taken from a mosaic were returned to it. It brought a rush of memories—of running with bleeding feet on cobblestone streets, of hard moldy rye bread and rough vinegar water, of Grannus' leering grin, of the fiery agony of the lash.

Three times during the night he had to pull the wick of the lamp as he read ever on, struggling against a downward pull into deathlike hopelessness. If his father could not survive in this world, why did he presume he could? Names blurred and became confused. One treaty with Baldemar began to look like the next.

But all he had read so far vindicated his father. It was apparent at once that enlisting Wido was an attempt to get by with very little—rarely was his father granted what he needed to train new recruits.

It was well past midnight when Marcus realized that the years his father was shortest of funds corresponded with the time Veiento acted as minister of the Military Treasury. Suddenly he was sharply awake.

Could Veiento have thieved from the Military Treasury during his time in that office? It must be so. It would explain why he was so intent upon avoiding a public trial.

But how to confirm this? Somehow he must obtain the military records from the Palace and compare the figures to his father's, to see if divergences appeared. He remembered then that one of his poorest clients had a cousin who was a freedman accountant in the military records room and had access to confidential documents. No, he could not ask. The fellow, if caught, would be executed.

But what was the alternative? The world would continue to think his father incompetent and a traitor. Perhaps if the theft were carefully planned, and the fellow royally paid for his risk. . . .

He felt a small jolt of hope. He *must* somehow procure a public trial. But how to get Nero to pay attention to his plea?

He read on, gathering more proof his father had used Wido solely as a means of controlling Baldemar, going through individual journals of soldiers, quaestors' reports, his father's private letters. As the night became ever more still and the hour of spirits approached, the uncanny lands of Germania seemed to hover about, vivid and close, that dark ocean of wild forest where trees trapped the spirits of the dead, magic mists swallowed armies, human sacrifices dangled in groves, and quaking bogs digested generations of dead. Who knew what flourished in such places? Barbarous mysteries bloomed everywhere like flowers in the dark. In one report his father recorded the words of a sorceress called Ramis after one of the treaty meetings, and to Marcus' amazement she spoke words on the rebirth of souls that closely echoed the sayings of the Pythagoreans—yet this was an illiterate tribal woman who cooked over open fires and at night lay down on earth. What could account for this?

And he wondered if he had not found, in this northern waste, humans in the idyllic state, living what many philosophers called the natural life. It seemed they lived in a sort of extended innocence, were cruel only of necessity, and uncorrupted by the worst temptations of power and greed. Was it of these people that Isodorus had spoken when he said, *"In the wastes beyond the North Wind they live still as in the time of Saturn"?*

Again and again through the letters and reports he found references to a mysterious maid who bore arms. She confused him at first; it was not clear if she was a woman of flesh and blood, or a local manifestation of one of their earth goddesses, or possibly some nymph of a spring or well, described elsewhere in his father's writings. She could shift shape; she could shield a warrior from the bite of weapons and outrun a deer. "Her hair is full of spirits, and she is clothed in night" were the words of one Chattian captive.

In one treaty it became clear she was quite mortal—and was, in fact, that same daughter of Baldemar whom his father had sought to see married to Wido's son. Her name appeared, then disappeared, wending its way through the records, taunting, elusive, twisting sinuously through tale after tale like a wild vine: *Auriane.* The name conjured up so clearly the woman—surely it was the lateness of the hour—but there she was unabashedly before him, so clear and close he could see the shadow of a lash, the dew on her hair, a creature who in some archaic way coupled beauty and strength, not unlike the heroines of the oldest tales of the Roman people—Camilla the warrior or Tanaquil the queen. She was the spirit of streams breaking through rock, the numen of primeval places.

Then he came upon a report made by a soldier who had witnessed an incident deep in the interior of Chattian lands. The soldier had a tendency to florid words, but Marcus sensed a core of truth in the tale, and it was the beginning of a haunting that would flourish through the years.

He was a cavalry centurion with the detachment that accompanied the native army of Wido's son, Odberht, and he had witnessed the maid's capture.

"They were surrounded by us and set to fight to the last," the Centurion wrote, *"but she held out the sign of peace and brought a stillness everywhere, and so sacrificed herself to the enemy that her tribesmen could live. Who since the time of the Kings has seen such hallowed devotion? She passed close by me. Such a purity in that eye, and a look of one who walked easily with the powers of Night. And she was full of Magic, for within days she escaped, taking the form of a doe. She again materialized at the final siege, where she assumed raven shape and opened the gate to victory."*

Without knowing why, avidly he searched for more. He came upon another text transcribed from the words of a deserter that made it quite clear she had led the final engagement itself.

Of course. Baldemar was injured. Why was her story so obscure? His father mentioned her hardly at all, perhaps out of embarrassment that his plans were foiled by a half-grown maid. The tale stirred Marcus like some powerful dirge or lay. She demanded to be known. She haunted his thoughts like a god-sent dream. Her image released something in him, a crying out for another world.

Marcus felt an obscure strength gathering in him then, muted and small like a campfire in the distance, but numinous, alive. He no longer felt so keenly the pain of Lycas' death, his father's destruction, of fighting tyranny alone. She was a wild ghost, fighting nearby, and despite the vast space between them and the distance between their customs and ways, he sensed their enemy was the same. It made little sense in the full light of the sun but was triumphantly obvious in dreams.

Near dawn he fell asleep amid the rolls of records.

He dreamed he trod a winding path in a dense elm wood. His way was barred by a solemn crone on a white horse; her face glowed softly like the lunar disk. The wood was littered with bones. She beckoned him to follow, silently sounding the words, *Die now, and let me show you life.*

He awakened, shuddering with cold, thinking he smelled damp pine forest and oak fires. Who was that frightful hag?

It is the amulet. It is sending strange and powerful dreams. No, such thoughts are for men ruled by superstition.

It was as though that pouch of earth bid him look long at the lamp flame. And in one moment he melted into it, shedding resistance naturally as a serpent's sloughing of skin. Then came an earthy and sensuous sense of the rightness of all things; he could not fall or die, and life and death dwelled in him together. Sacredness did not stop at temple doors; it was infused into everything, it lived in mud, in dust. What was this sublime spell? This brilliant sense of things mocked all attempts to seize it with words. He had flown beyond the philosophers; he could see them far off, huddled about their words, poking them, pushing them, prodding them to do what words could not.

The amulet, he thought, tearing his gaze from the fire and looking at it. The cursed thing has worked some witchery.

He fought a powerful urge to fling it into the fire.

CHAPTER X

At midmorning on the wedding day the household was alive with preparations. Servants washed down the walls, garlanded pillars, and strewed green boughs lavishly over polished floors. The kitchen women muttered prayers to Juno as they set the wedding cake of wine-steeped meal on its nest of bay leaves; boy-servants waved feather fans to keep off the flies, while the chief cook shouted orders as he prepared a feast of peacock, pheasant and suckling pig. Diocles worried himself into fits of trembling over the proper order of the guests on the banquet couches. As if it matters now whom we offend, Marcus Julianus observed with dark amusement as he passed the morning drafting another plea for an open trial. It might have been a wedding among the Shades, so grim and silent was the household; he had not needed to overhear a kitchenmaid whisper, "The month of Mars is an evil time for a wedding—it will be fraught with battles," to know what the servants thought of this union. The vast gardens seemed a place of ghosts; the cypresses planted along the gravel walks on the day his father was taken to the pyre swayed faintly in the wind as if moving to the tones of wailing for the dead. Everywhere the fountains were dry; only the dolphin fountain managed a feeble trickle; the water dribbling from that gaped bronze mouth was like softly shed tears that would not stop.

Across the gardens in apartments set aside for her was Junilla, that brilliant mystery he would soon claim as his own. Shrieks of laughter came from those shuttered apartments as she submitted to the elaborate ritual of the dressing of the bride, performed as custom decreed by six noble matrons who had married but once. By age-old tradition they began by parting the bride's hair into six plaits with the head of a spear to dispell evil spirits; when their work was complete, they tied the cord of her wedding tunica with the knot of Hercules, which only the husband could untie. All in the household stayed well away from those chambers; it was unlucky to view the bride before the procession.

Marcus thought: It is a bitter thing to come this close to a life that is not to be lived. Junilla was a child; what would become of her after his early death?

An hour before the guests were to arrive he was interrupted when Arria rushed into the library in flowing undertunica, her hair loose, her face half painted. Arria was a widow of middle years with blunt plain features, burdened eyes, an instinctive distrust of frivolity. For a long moment she stared at him, too numbed by grief to speak. Slowly Marcus rose to his feet.

Then with a savage motion she buried her face in her tunica. "Just now came some cursed gift of wine from the Palace," she cried into the cloth, "and with it an order to give up the children!"

He came forward and caught her shoulders as she collapsed onto the reading couch, her body convulsed with deep, silent sobs; she was like a creature with its back broken, crying for mercy while expecting none. He knelt beside her, steadying her, while several half-formed plans rushed through his mind, all involving much risk.

"If I were merciful," Arria cried, "I would end their lives now, myself, and spare them this!"

"Arria, do not speak so!" He harbored little hope, but he could not bear her grief. "You must trust me to think of some ruse!"

"What can you do? You cannot stop the Guards."

"I'll have *some* plan together before the last hour, Arria, I promise it."

"The gods preserve you, you have troubles enough."

"Do not think of it. Arria, listen to me: *Tonight at the wedding feast you must not look frightened or distraught.* Expect an informer at every table—speak only of things of no consequence. Be calm. Nero plays with his victims. If you act as if there is danger, he will think there *should* be danger."

"What is the use!" She numbly shook her head; tears streaked her cosmetic mask of white lead. "You will be condemned in a hidden chamber and will die horribly! I will be driven naked from the city, and the children will—"

"You must bear up a little longer! As I live, I'll find a way."

At lamplighting the wedding guests began to arrive; they were an odd mix of the aristocratic, the scholarly, the nobly poor. Powerful friends of his father were there, among them old Saturninus, his father's greatest friend, but there also were penniless students in freshly cleaned rags, a collection of tutors and tenement-dwelling philosophers who had become friends, and more distant kinfolk who traveled in from their country estates, as well as his friends from the city academies, among them Domitian. The noble guests, Marcus thought, had the look of hostages—they dared not stay home from such an affair, for Nero nursed dark suspicions about any among the aristocracy who shunned society, but attending was equally dangerous when a single ill-considered word overheard by a friend-turned-informer could result in arrest for treason.

For the ceremony itself the guests gathered in the grand hall, seated on finely worked chairs of walnut wood and ivory, set in a semicircle, facing Marcus Arrius Julianus as he poured a libation of Falernian wine at the altar of the Lares, the old guardian spirits of the house. Bronze candelabra in the form of many-branched trees were set along the walls; their myriad flames were a constellation of modest stars—every surface of the hall was lustrous in their quiet light—the moldings of mother-of-pearl, the glossy paint of the pastoral panoramas seeming to roam over the walls, the slender columns of Phrygian marble that divided the hall from the garden. The rooms were haunted by the music of concealed kithara players, their drowsy tones accumulating like smoke, lulling the guests into a wary contentment.

As Marcus Julianus filled a gem-studded winecup from one of several amphorae bearing the stamp of the Palace cellars, the guests watched with suppressed alarm; all knew the wine was sent by Nero. What a fine, and not improbable, joke it would be for the Emperor to have spiced it with aconite—certainly there were enough guests present that Nero would consider himself well rid of.

When a cup was passed to each guest, Marcus Julianus lifted his own and calmly drank from it. Domitian watched this with mild amazement. He personally would have given it first to one of his slaves. Marcus was an unnecessary fool sometimes.

And Domitian noticed that the company, filled cups in hand, tried discreetly to leave them untouched for a few moments while they waited to see if the host fell dead, some feigning intense interest in the conversation of a companion. Domitian did not judge himself for doing the same as he observed the proceedings with his usual sour curiosity.

Then Marcus Julianus signaled to the augur to bring forth the lamb so the auspices could be taken for the marriage. He would not have animals slaughtered for sacrifice, but this was an augury. Junilla's mother had protested that without it wedded happiness was doomed. Marcus did not know how he had room to pity that frantic creature writhing violently in the augur's strong hands, while Arria's children were huddled in the back rooms faced with a far more savage fate.

The augur held his silver knife to the throat of the lamb.

A resounding crash came from the front part of the house, followed by hammering as if a Herculean fist pounded on the house's heavy outer door. This was followed by curses, scuffling, belligerent laughter. All sat tense and straight in their seats. Had a gang of street bandits forced their way past the doorkeeper?

Marcus Julianus softly cursed and signaled to the augur to lay down his knife. *My family is allowed no dignity in death or in marriage.*

The company watched in taut silence as he strode toward the atrium.

Who would dare demand entry at this time? He felt his house a ship lurching into a gathering storm. Before he gained the entranceway Diocles barred his way, eyes afire with indignation. "My lord," he said, clutching his hands together, "we've been invaded by musicians!"

"Is that such a grave matter? Now, acrobats or pantomimes," Marcus said smiling, trying to tease Diocles out of his terror, "*that* might be cause for alarm, but—"

"You do not understand!" Diocles persisted, following Marcus as he continued on to the entranceway. "These are vile and mettlesome musicians with the manners of asses and sows! I told them we've engaged musicians already, but they would hear none of it! I beg your lenience that I could not stop them—"

Marcus put a reassuring hand on his shoulder to indicate that was not necessary. "Settle your mind, I am certain you did all you could. Wait now while I have words with them."

In the atrium he came upon a macabre ensemble hard to

comprehend at a glance; it was like looking at some mythical beast like a hippogriff, made of mismatched parts. The musicians numbered twenty-five or so; some, garbed in costly robes stained with mud and blood, looked like rowdy youths after a night of mischief; others had the look of the soft eunuch priests of Cybele, while others, surely, were catamites from the Circus stalls, with plucked beards, gold hoops in their ears, and eyes boldly outlined in black paint. A reek of sweat and rancid Oriental perfumes rose from them. One was a tall youth of indeterminate sex with long dirty red tresses; he—or she—carried a scabellum, a raucous instrument consisting of boards fastened to the feet that was played by dancing; its music was more appropriate for accompanying a farce in a brothel than a wedding. Beside him was a woman with orange-dyed hair; the veins of her forehead were outlined in blue, and her damp tunica of white silk clung like a loose skin to her great breasts, revealing gold-tipped nipples. She held a sistrum in her right hand and was rattling it idly. Three slender blond boys, naked but for panther skins about their loins and precious gems braided into their hair, bore antique country panpipes. A small gnomelike man wore a red leather tunic trimmed with bells; slung across his chest was a skin drum that he played with human thigh bones.

"Look at them!" Diocles whispered, unable to stay behind. "What is this monstrous insult? They should be performing beneath a bridge. I hope the lice stay put!"

Marcus signaled to Diocles to be silent. As he approached them, some fine instinct for preservation carried over from his days as Endymion curbed an impulse to anger. Politely he asked how he might assist them.

A heavy-browed brute who held a double flute as though it were a club planted himself in front of Marcus Julianus and put a rolled document in his hand.

"For Marcus Arrius Julianus the Younger, on the day of his wedding," he read, "we send blessings and hope of good fortune. We are the gift of Nero."

Marcus allowed no expression to come to his face. He inclined his head and said in a courtly voice, "How thoughtful and kind." The brutish musician grunted, somewhat irritated by Marcus' calm. Quickly Marcus passed the letter to Diocles so the steward could discreetly inform the guests whose gift this was, so they would show only gratitude.

Marcus then directed the musicians to the banqueting rooms, his mind in ferment: Was Nero merely amusing himself by debasing the sanctity of a wedding? Or was there some more sinister purpose here? As the grotesque company filed past, an ungainly man in their midst caught his eye.

He wore a drape of spotted fawnskin adorned with strips of goat hair over an ungirded tunic of gauzy material patterned with flowers, revealing soft dimpled arms and knees. Marcus realized he was dressed as Dionysus, god of ecstasy. He seemed to stay purposefully in the center of the troupe as if to conceal himself. In one hand, he carried a tambourine; in the other, the god's symbol—the thyrsus, a pinecone atop a fennel stalk. His mask was disturbing and seemed to have an evil life of its own: It was blue-white with leering blood-red lips, prompting Marcus to remember that Dionysus' celebrants in archaic times consumed their sacrifices raw. A long wig of free-flowing black hair had slipped slightly, and Marcus caught sight of the man's own hair beneath—tight blond ringlets, curled patiently with an iron.

Marcus felt a sickening twist in his stomach. *Nero.*

In the next instant such a storm of fury arose in him he feared it might drive him to a blind fit of murder.

Fall on him with your dagger. The cut of one blade across one throat will free thousands.

And that same cut will destroy hundreds of thousands when the deed unleashes civil war.

He steadied himself, fighting dizziness, letting the fury break over him like a wave.

I must not let it carry me off. Too many have need of me.

Before the doorkeeper pulled the oak door closed, Marcus looked briefly into the street and caught a glint of steel, the unfurling of military cloaks. Nero took no chances when he came uninvited to dinner—the house was surrounded by Praetorian Guards.

The musicians took their places at the right of the altar, arranging themselves in no order, some sitting, some standing; they grinned at the guests, or scratched themselves, or idly thrummed their instruments. It was the sort of thing that in most circumstances would be humorous. Marcus saw Domitian was using all his strength to throttle laughter and, except for a few stray facial twitches, was succeeding. But most of the guests were terrified, half expecting the sinister company to fall on them with their instruments. It was just as well, he thought, none seemed to suspect who was behind the mask of Dionysus.

An eerie lowing of flutes floating out from the garden announced the coming of Junilla. The augur made the sign against the evil eye over the marriage cakes. Junilla's torchlit procession wended its way through the garden, then came through the garlanded columns that flanked the entrance to the hall. They were led by four flute blowers, followed by four flaxen-haired girls of noble parentage, chosen for the task because each had both parents living. Each bore a torch of whitethorn meant to propitiate the goddess Diana, who loathed marriage ceremonies and was pleased only when all creatures coupled freely.

Then came Junilla herself, a stately specter in her loose, rippling marriage clothes. Her tunica was of white muslin woven by custom on the upright loom of earlier times. Over this was a striking flame-colored veil secured at the crown with a wreath of marjoram. The company watched with curiosity sharpened to a keen pitch; for too many years they had been teased with rumors of her haunting beauty. At last, that mythic face would be seen.

Poor child, Marcus thought as he awaited her next to the altar. Surely their stares upset you. My difficulties are at least known to me; you are a half-grown girl expected to join a doomed household and give yourself without complaint to a man you have never seen.

As she approached, he noticed an odd unsteadiness in her walk. He did not know what to make of it. He flushed with anger when he caught the too-loud whisper of one of the guests among the students, "Either the bride's sandals are too tightly laced . . . or she's in her cups!" Marcus stole a look at Domitian and saw the young man look a little embarrassed, sorry perhaps he had told everyone he loved her, as though Junilla somehow deliberately shamed him.

Then his bride stood beside him. The orange-red silk fluttered faintly with her breathing. In that red-gold shadow he imagined he saw the bare glint of a glorious eye. She hoarded her mysteries as long as possible, he noticed; she would not even give him her hand when he reached for it to offer comfort.

The augur seized the lamb. With capable and oddly gentle hands he slit its throat and opened its belly to view the entrails; from long training he managed this while spilling scarcely a drop of blood.

Marcus just caught the look of horror on the face of the augur's assistant before the man moved round so no one else could see. *What was there? A nest of maggots?* But the custom of these times was: No ill omens at a wedding. The augur straightened and managed a professional smile.

"Many happy years to you both!" he called out musically. "The omens are of the best. Now lift the veil!"

The player of the scabellum beat an obnoxious rhythm on the floor. The man with the double flute shrieked an alien note that veered off on its own. The lyre player played an instrument so badly out of tune that the notes sounded like a drunken walk. Behind them the woman in white silk danced heavily to the disjointed beat. It was the perfect sound accompaniment, Marcus thought, for the madness of the times.

Then the room was so still Marcus could hear Nero's rasping breaths beneath the mask of Dionysus.

Junilla turned to face him. He sensed the company leaning closer: *Let her be seen!* The musicians too seemed to lean forward in a body; there was something akin to hungry hounds in their eagerness to feast their eyes on the bride. No new masterpiece by Praxiteles could have been awaited with greater expectation.

He gathered the cloth of the veil and threw it back.

Arria shrieked. From all about came small cries—he heard every god and goddess in the Pantheon invoked for protection against evil. But most sat starkly still, open-mouthed in horror.

Before him was a hag of over a hundred winters. Her head was thrust forward on a neck like a vulture's; protruding eyes brought to mind a carp several hours dead. A few feeble strands of hair sprouted from her skull. She grinned impishly, proudly revealing one blackened tooth, looking slowly from side to side to gather the effect. She reeked of the dank heavy essences used at funerals.

The musicians beat, blew, plucked, or stamped their feet, raising a raucous noise that was not so much music as loud, rude laughter.

Marcus felt first a terrible sadness, for the old woman, mocked so and not knowing it, and for them all; then came a rush of rage at being prodded about like a Circus beast. He was sharply aware of Dionysus, who was performing an ungainly pirouette.

Nero, you will pirouette in Hades.

When the musicians were silent, the only sound was Arria's muffled crying, and he could feel the collective thought: What a prodigy of evil. We live in a tomb.

Where was Junilla? he wondered angrily. Somehow Nero's agents broke into her apartments and dressed this poor creature in her clothes.

I dare not show affront—it could be the undoing of us all.

Facing the guests, he forced himself to say calmly, "A clever jest, was it not? Yes, a more inspired jest than I have ever seen at a wedding!"

Before he could say more, the old woman, while gently nodding her head, began reciting lines from an epic poem in uncertain voice, dribbling out her words, faint delirium in her eyes. She has been chewing the leaves of cherry laurel, Marcus thought, or else she is more than half mad.

The guests exchanged looks of bewildered revulsion, each expecting their neighbor to have some explanation for this sad show; a few glared at Marcus Julianus, uncertain if he was victim or perpetrator. But Marcus remained alert, listening carefully to the old woman's words; the lines, some passably deft, some painfully grandiose, were familiar. Suddenly he remembered hearing Nero recite them—was it one or perhaps two state banquets ago? He silently thanked the Muse of Memory. They were Nero's own—or at least, Nero thought they were; in fact, the lines so closely followed a passage of Virgil they might be regarded as stolen outright, with a few clumsy embellishments put in to cover the theft.

He means to startle me into a candid response to his poetry.

Marcus Julianus was not surprised when the musician dressed as Pan, in hairy tunic and goat beard, danced toward him and did a tight bow. "Tell me, what think you of these lines, my lord? First, who wrote them?"

He was too irritated to flatter, even if it meant his head. "Virgil wrote them."

Pan paused, feigning deep consideration of the reply. "Well spoken! You have given the highest praise to the Emperor."

"I praised no one; I simply stated a fact."

"Nero wrote the lines."

"If he did so, he wrote them with help—too much help—from Virgil."

Domitian looked at Marcus Julianus with anxious fright. Surely he knew the room was thick with spies?

Then to Domitian's dismay Pan came straight toward him with that mincing walk and nearly alighted in his lap.

"And what think *you* of the lines, my young prince?"

"My young prince?" Domitian thought frantically, feeling death creep slowly over him. How dare anyone address me so, publicly?

Too stunned to feel foolish, Domitian managed in a stiff

monotone, "The lines were elegantly put together. Marcus Julianus is mistaken. They are . . . *better* than Virgil."

Pan grinned with evil relish, nodding first to Marcus Julianus, then at Domitian. "This one does not flatter, this one does. Which tells the truth, which lies? Which should live—and which should die?"

The guests sat rigidly, most perspiring with fright; some bolted their wine in one or two gulps while others let their cups tip in numb hands, spilling the contents onto the floor. This was a trial in Hades—the court could materialize anywhere, and judge and jury were madmen.

Pan spun about, put his arm round the ancient woman, then led her to a place in the rear of the ensemble and supplied her with a harp; there she sat in her wedding clothes, still silently mouthing lines. Then he went on in his lyrical voice, nodding significantly at Domitian:

"*Your* friends stole Junilla, my princeling, to give her to you as a gift! Then after you've murdered Nero and seized the throne, they will have won your favor eternally."

Marcus thought: *He is a dead man. I must do something to save him.*

Marcus fought for steadiness. *How long can I keep the beast at bay?* He prayed he guessed correctly: that Pan was instructed to say these words more to test everyone's response to them than because Nero had real evidence against Domitian.

"An unsophisticated theory," Marcus Julianus broke in, gesturing broadly with an easy smile, "from one who speaks before he knows. In the first place, Domitian's friends are such rogues that if they snatched Junilla they would keep her for themselves." He felt Nero lusting for every word. "And anyway, she should have a husband of her own rank."

Domitian was too numb to follow this well, but understood he was being helped.

"Her own rank? What nonsense is this?" was Pan's mocking reply.

"Domitian means not even to stand for the Senate—how could he possibly have ambitions for the throne? That is the key word, *stand*. He would have to shy away from the grape for two days running. And anyway he means to have a hand in business enterprises of a sordid nature, such as disqualify a man from the Senate. And look at him. That dithering pup could not rally a cohort of Vigiles behind him. Really, an informer should be better informed lest he lose his good reputation—who then would pay you for your murderous gossip?"

Pan recoiled faintly but never lost his cheerfully manic grin. Domitian felt a rush of relief that was quickly soured by anger. Admittedly he drank too much wine but it did not rule him, and a brickmaking factory was not a training school for gladiators; he never meant to disqualify himself from the Senate. Marcus Julianus to his mind seemed to enjoy these lies a bit too much.

Marcus could not tell how successful he had been; Nero was so susceptible to influence that Marcus feared the effect of his words might only last until the Emperor encountered another opinion offered by someone who sounded equally sure of himself.

Pan then looked discreetly at Dionysus, who gave him the barest of nods; Marcus alone noticed the exchange. Then the goat-bearded musician clapped his hands. "Let the games go on! Now for the true bride—that is, if you think you are ready for her."

Domitian felt danger pass on. But he was consumed with ambivalence toward Marcus Julianus, who had saved his life, yes, but by ridiculing him before those he longed most to impress. And so, while hardly aware of it himself, Domitian ascribed a malice to the act that was not there, and stored it away as a hurt to be avenged later.

Junilla had apparently been taken nowhere because within moments the attendants fetched the new bride. This woman was a trifle taller and like her ancient sister wholly concealed beneath a voluminous red-gold veil.

This second bride halted beside Marcus Julianus. He went through the same ritual acts, closed to all feeling: For all he knew, Nero meant to play with them until dawn and have him unveil ten false Junillas. It might be that Nero fancied the poor maid himself, and she was now hidden somewhere in the plush depths of Nero's Golden House, or perhaps he had murdered her and she had been thrown into the pits for unclaimed dead, a discarded victim of some Palace frolic.

And I mean to appeal to this madman for a public trial?

The new bride's shoulders shuddered with excitement or fear. The augur signed to him to lift the veil. He lifted it slowly, with reverence, so as not to frighten her more.

This was Junilla. The whole company dropped into deep silence.

That shyly downturned face was delicate perfection. Despite a pedigree old as the city, it was touched with the exotic. There was a faint Asiatic curve to her cheek, a hint of the Egyptian in the length and slenderness of her neck, her stately bearing. That rose and ivory skin seemed to have been bathed daily in milk. She looked up at him with great, luminous Indian-dark eyes. Her lips, darkened with wine lees, were full and boldly arched; they parted slightly, putting him in mind of the imperceptibly slow opening of a rose. A soft radiance emanated from her dark, shining hair, pulled tightly into six braided locks secured by woolen fillets; pearls beyond counting were woven into the plaits.

He tried to join his gaze with hers but felt he glanced off the onyx surface of those eyes; they were polished shields that let nothing in. Of course, he thought, the child is frightened.

They joined hands. He felt such awe and pity and desire to shelter her that in that moment he could believe nothing evil of her; surely there was a perfection of soul to match that face. He must find some way to survive. This was Nero's cruelest jest—to show him this creature with whom he would have lived his life.

Her voice was soft and muted as doves as she spoke the ancient ritual words by which she declared herself his wife, *"Where you are Gaius, I am Gaia,"* which meant, "Now I belong to your clan." As they shared the spelt cake those brilliant eyes continued to watch him. *Was* that fear there? Or was she somehow taking his measure? He considered that what he saw in those eyes might not be shyness but stealth.

And then he had the marriage tablets brought. Guests exchanged discreet perplexed looks; normally at this time a pig would be sacrificed; to omit this was unaccountable. A few remembered Marcus Julianus' peculiar reluctance to see animals slaughtered, and whispered of this to the others.

Then with ten guests standing as witnesses he and Junilla signed the tablets, which gave the terms of the dowry. This was followed by applause, during which a number of the guests came up to embrace him. One wealthy young matron of sultry manner pressed a note into Marcus Julianus' hand that he knew was an invitation to a tryst; her lovers must indeed have become scarce, he thought, smiling to himself in mild amazement, if she stalks the groom at a wedding.

As they walked to the twelve banqueting tables, followed by the hundred guests, he spoke to Junilla, careful that none should hear, "Take heart, dearest, we are captives—but it will not always be so, I promise it. You'll not be mocked like this again."

She gave him a look strangely empty of emotion; he had the unpleasant feeling he had spoken in a foreign tongue. "No one mocks me," she said with delicate irritation. "And in any case, everyone is a captive, except for His Divinity—but that is as it should be." She lowered her voice; the exquisite eyes ignited with mischievous fire. "And who admitted those clever-looking plebeians in overwashed rags to my wedding? Do you not fear they will steal the silver plate?"

She is a child, mouthing what she has been taught, he told himself. But a small knot of disappointment started to form. Part of him knew she would always think so.

"They are my friends from the academies, and I wish them to be treated with respect," he answered coolly.

The dining tables were strewn with parsley and early wildflowers. Arranged in a semicircle about the tables were three couches, each accommodating three diners to make a total of nine; the bridal table was at the room's center, beneath a multitiered chandelier in the form of a Babylonian temple sculpted in fire and cut glass. Marcus Julianus settled in the host's place on the third couch, but the position of highest honor, the third place on the middle couch, was left empty in honor of his father. Domitian, without asking, speedily usurped the place on the couch opposite Marcus Julianus, taking advantage of the fact that the former consul assigned that position never arrived. Marcus knew Diocles, who observed this clumsy breach of propriety from his place by the wall, was wishing he could set the doorkeeper's dogs on the young man.

The wind whipped the torches set in the garden; to Marcus they were bright warning spirits urgently trying to get his attention.

Junilla, reclining at his left, observed him closely with those luminous eyes while she answered the polite queries of those about her with short, simple responses that invited no conversation. She knew the power of her beauty, he observed; she portioned it out like sacks of gold to those she thought worthy. Her gaze lingered long over Saturninus; a smokiness came into her eyes. The students, on the other hand, might well have been dogs; she simply did not see them. Occasionally her gaze slipped over to Domitian, and with him, too, she seemed to consider, to measure; Marcus had a momentary feeling she might have forgotten which was her husband. It struck him her nature was far closer to Domitian's than to his own; both seemed to attune their senses to reading the weaknesses of those about them. He doubted her curiosity ever strayed to questions of nature and being—she concerned herself only with who held power, and who was ready to lose it.

Nero's musicians followed the whole company and hastily reassembled themselves around the bridal table. They played softly now, but also they listened; Marcus felt he dined next to unfed hounds. As the iced platters of cultured Lucrine oysters were being set on the tables, Marcus tensed, remembering Nero had a passion for them. How long would he be able to restrain himself? Marcus had no wish to dine with him openly, when one question not skillfully answered could mean death.

And sure enough, moments later as Domitian was insisting drunkenly to a doubtful Junilla he had cured a toothache by rubbing the tooth with the ashes of a weasel and a black chameleon, Dionysus began edging closer as if to better hear the recipe. Then he flopped down heavily on the couch of honor next to Marcus Julianus.

The guests watched this with outraged astonishment as if they had seen a worshiper in the Temple of Juno lift his tunic and relieve himself on the sacred image.

"Allow me to remove my mask," said Dionysus in that familiar, ringing girl's voice tinged with hurt. "It is most difficult to eat with it."

"You are a most impertinent musician," Marcus Julianus replied, his tone cautiously playful.

"Yes, and an overly indulgent Emperor," Dionysus responded, disengaging himself from the heavy mask.

Marcus found himself looking into the broad, sweating face of Nero.

Knowledge of his presence pervaded the room slowly, like the scent of death.

Nero's puckered too-small mouth was set in the pout of the deadly child who needs to be continuously petted and praised. Damp ringlets were matted to his wide heavy forehead; his eyes were an empty, faded blue. His nature had begun already to assert itself in his face: Those cheeks, Marcus thought, seemed swollen and mottled with poison, as though he were drugged with the pleasure of cruelty, with the lies his flatterers dosed him with daily. His frequent nightmares seemed to have taken their toll as well; those eyes protruded slightly as if permanently frozen in fright. He had a gaze that seemed to stalk and trap every movement about him as a cat its prey; his gaze was oddly agile, considering that indolent body with its settled layers of flesh. A fleecy beard covered a chin that went smoothly down to a bloated neck that seemed ready to inflate like a bullfrog's. But it was that mouth that was always most disturbing to Marcus—its babyishness coupled with its deadliness—a soft, sucking mouth that drained not milk but blood.

Nero motioned with one plump hand for a washing basin; the flesh between his multiple rings was pinched like dough. One of the servants stationed behind the table, a frightened boy, came forward unsteadily with towel and silver bowl. Nero sloppily washed his hands in the warm flower-scented water, then, ignoring the towel, with bored deliberation dried his hands in the boy's fluffy blond hair.

When all the company realized who was among them, there followed a stifling moment in which no one knew what to do. Should they arise, and prostrate themselves? Should they call out a greeting?

Marcus Julianus solved the problem by rising quickly and giving a slight bow.

"This house has never been so honored, Divinity. I greatly regret we did not know; the fare is far too modest."

"Ah, what's missing in the fare is *more* than made up for by the amusements to be found here. And you *knew* me, you sly conniver! You are not surprised enough. How did you know?"

Marcus paused, tension accumulating as he rapidly thought.

I recognized your silly curls. I would know that ungainly body from a hundred others. What can I say that will not get us all damned to Hades?

"It was the old woman," he said at last. "She was . . . your own touch, such a clever act of . . . the use and transformation of ordinary lives and events into a dramatic play of your own devising. You made a play of life! I did not think you would be absent and miss its effect."

Domitian thought: Thank all the gods for that gift of spewing intelligent rubbish with no preparation. He felt such gratefulness to Marcus that he almost forgave him the insults.

Nero brightened like the child who finally elicits the praise he craves from an elder. "Tell me, do you think it will become fashionable as a form of drama?"

"Well, no, I think not."

Nero's scowl was like a terrible shift of the weather.

Marcus, be an idiot with your own life, Domitian thought. Leave us out of it!

"And why is that?" Had he not a hundred sharpened swords at his back to redress that hurt, the scowl would have been simply ludicrous.

"Because it is a game only emperors can play. If I, for instance, did such a thing—I would be charged with a crime."

Nero nodded meditatively. Domitian knew then what a wise answer this was; Nero took great pride in being able to do deeds not allowed to ordinary mortals. "Well spoken, Marcus Julianus. And I judge you were right earlier: Virgil wrote those lines. Though it hurts, mind you. But great artists have great hearts. Now, what do you think of the bride?"

"What anyone would think—she would make the Graces weep."

"Ha! Well, I hope you enjoy her. I know *I* did," Nero said idly, suddenly inspecting a gold-painted fingernail. Marcus Julianus refused to react to this. He stole one glance at Junilla, but in her look was only blankness, as if those lustrous eyes were blind. Had someone drawn out her soul as a spider sucks juice out of a fly?

"Tell me, my good man, why was no pig sacrificed?" Nero leaned close so that Marcus could smell the sweet stink of nardus oil in his hair. "What makes you so certain the gods do not want blood?"

"I am certain of nothing, my lord. But once all nations believed the gods required the blood of men. When the practice was stopped, did the Heavens raise an outcry? They did not, and now we believe it a cruelty, for nothing. The passing times better us, and who can say but that one day we will think animal sacrifice, too, a cruelty for nothing."

"Oh, silence, now you remind me of someone I didn't like." Marcus supposed he meant Seneca. "Were the hundred filleted white bullocks sacrificed on the occasion of my Olympic victories then slaughtered in vain?"

"I say yes, I am damned. I say no, and I lie," Marcus Julianus replied. "Which do you prefer for a dinner partner, a liar or a dead man?"

Domitian put his head in his hands.

But Nero only laughed a heaving laugh. "The dread honesty of the condemned! I should sentence all my Council to death, then maybe I would entice honest sentiments from them!" Without warning Nero turned on Domitian.

"Now, *someone* has eaten every oyster," Nero said sulkily, "and left not a *one* for anyone else at this table. Domitian?"

Domitian looked at him with a jerk of his head, then turned away, flushing deeply. "I apologize, my Divine Lord. I didn't realize . . ."

"Nervous men eat without realizing it. What are you nervous about?"

Domitian suddenly felt he could not move; he was pinned beneath the tyranny of those yellowed eyes. "I beg your indulgence, but I am—I am not—"

Nero smoothly drained his wine cup, then set it down so forcefully wine splattered everywhere; his tunic seemed flecked with blood. His voice fell to a gurgling whisper as if his throat had gone too slack to swallow the wine. "I will tell you what you are nervous about, since you seem a little shy. You've a lot of friends, important friends, with complicated plans for my demise. I imagine that weighs heavy with the victim right here, and oysters make a distraction if an inadequate one. Tell them not to bother sawing through the axle of my racing chariot. You know, it doesn't work very well, I've tried it on others. It tends to leave them mangled but alive. You, there," he called to a passing servant, "bring some more of those enticing little sea creatures for the rest of us and keep them out of *his* reach this time."

Domitian opened his mouth to speak, but his breath was gone. He felt he was made of stone, sinking heavily into the cushions; he couldn't breathe; the cushions would smother him. And he found himself wishing desperately he were just that, a stone image, not a man of flesh and blood with a living throat to be cut, a body to be put to torture.

"Now we will play a little game," Nero said, his sleepy, lethal eyes fixed mildly on Domitian, regarding him as prey that must be calmed before it could be killed.

"I have no plotting friends!" Domitian managed hoarsely. *"I am your most loyal of servants!"*

"Really? I will prove to you in a moment that you do."

Domitian started to take up his wine cup and three servants rushed forward to aid him. Humiliated that the trembling of his hands was so obvious, he set it back down, deciding he wanted no wine after all.

"Ah, you're a man to make me feel like Jupiter himself!" Nero went on, "a man of clay, to be formed into any shape I wish! Well, my young cock, so puffed up with your certainty you are more morally fit and firmer of purpose than me—I will demonstrate to you that your Cappadocian footmen are more fit to rule than you."

Nero wriggled into a more comfortable position on the couch, languishing in the pleasure of the moment, settling into his layers of flesh long enough to raise a wild hope in Domitian that he might fall into a drunken stupor. But after a short time those eyes returned to bright, malicious life.

"I will do the difficult part. I will name the names, you won't have to dredge them out of that wine-pickled memory." Nero chose a name at random from the rolls of the Senate. "Servianus, does he plot against me?"

Domitian's voice was a frantic whisper. "I am no informer, my family has always hated informers, do you think me capable of—"

"I think you capable of *anything*, if it gets you what you want. A simple yes or no!"

"I will say nothing!"

Everyone averted their gaze, too polite to increase Domitian's torment by looking at him. All except Junilla. She smoothly licked her lips and smiled. This was more delicious than any banquet fare.

"I think you *will* say something! Your loyalty is worth mud. Speak, or . . . or . . ." Nero paused, face contorted in a caricature of deep thought. "Ha!" he cried as if he had just thought of it, "I will draft an edict on the morrow making it a crime to harbor eunuchs in the city."

Quickly Domitian looked at him. "This is for certain?" He felt ridiculous asking, but the question burst out of its own accord.

"Do you think I play children's games! For doubting me I should do it whether you yield or not!"

How did Nero know? Domitian wondered frantically. Nero seemed to have second sight when it came to flushing out the secret passions of others that they counted shameful.

"Do you think I would destroy my friends to keep my eunuchs!" Domitian's forehead gleamed with perspiration.

"The likelihood frightens me. But *that's* only the appetizer," Nero went on merrily. "Here comes the main course: If you do not give me names . . . , I will recall your father from Judaea."

Domitian felt as if a blow landed in his stomach. Nausea and fright gripped him.

I cannot let him block my one near-certain route to becoming emperor. He suspects the whole of the Senate anyway, Domitian rationalized; it means little if *I* give names. It means little. . . .

Numbly he nodded a yes.

"Out loud, my boy," said Nero, grinning. "So all can hear!"

"Yes!" Domitian said in a taut whisper. A sound like a sob came from him.

Nero then followed with name after senatorial name; as Domitian spoke the last yes, he felt his tongue was covered with slime.

Marcus Julianus thought: Once again the streets will run with blood. Is there no end to this?

"Now, let us confirm all this with our dear host, Marcus Arrius Julianus," Nero went on. "He, too, knows everything about everyone, though from quite different motives. Tell me, Marcus Julianus, does Servianus plot against me?"

"I will spare your voice, my lord," Marcus Julianus replied, his tone clear and hard. "All are innocent—you need not go again through that list of names."

"All? How odd. For some reason I do not believe you. The Senate has two kinds of men, you know—wolves and sheep. And the sheep have long since been eaten. Now answer, name by name! Servianus!"

"At the risk of boring you with another's lines," Marcus said quietly, "I am no informer."

"And bore me you have! Or perhaps you flatter my imitation: I pilfered from Virgil, as you have kindly pointed out to me, and so you filch a line from our lusty young cock here who'd rather see his compatriots die miserably than be deprived of his base pleasures. How then shall I bring *you* to heel?"

Nero creased his brow in thought. "Domitian lives for his lusts and for his criminal ambitions," he went on, "and *you*—you live for learning, or you *seem* to at least, unless you've got some fascinating secret fetish you've managed to conceal from me. . . . Let us see. . . . If you do not answer I will . . . I will set fire to this house of your ancestors, beginning with your library and all its rare books. There! A clever equivalent of the test I gave him, is it not? Am I not a wise player on the instrument of human feeling?"

The fleshy hand clamped about Marcus's arm, and he leaned close. There was a smell about him of rotted meat. "*Yes or no, Julianus.*"

Marcus Julianus shut his eyes briefly, feeling he drew all his life about him. *Nothing in this world can be protected.* I know that.

Why, then, the horror? This house is a temple of family ghosts. I would prefer he burned my own flesh. I would throw my body over those books as if they were a living child.

He looked off once in the direction of the library, as if the act of looking could somehow protect it. Every gaze was drawn to him. Junilla watched him doubtfully.

Domitian watched him most intently of all. *Speak up, curses on you! Come with me! You are no better than I and no more loyal!*

For Marcus Julianus the need to save all in the house was pulsing, alive. The names are damned already, he reasoned. The plot was crushed anyway. Humor the tyrant. He only wants one simple word. *Save the books.*

But then a bright stillness settled over him, and a resolution rose up higher than temple doors. The wanted words would not come. What were the books if nothing human was left to read them?

Marcus Julianus replied softly, "Raze the house."

Nero jerked back slightly in surprise; then slowly he collected himself. "You refuse then to answer your Emperor and God," he said coldly.

Nero nodded to Pan, who lit a torch from a wall sconce. The Emperor then gestured toward the library. Pan ran lightly, threading his way through dining tables; he was still in sight of the guests as he paused in the ornate doorway of the first room of the library. He tossed in the torch.

The bookrolls lay in convenient heaps; they might have been set out purposefully as tinder.

The flames were timid at first, then they found their strength, crackling, accumulating, licking round the bookrolls' cylindrical parchment cases, stretching to the ceiling. There came the smell of burning cedar, growing stronger. The guests watched wonderingly for a moment, as if it were not real.

Marcus closed his eyes and looked down. He felt his insides crushed between two stones. Burning were a volume of Zeno said to be written in the philosopher's own hand, a work of Anaxagoras' astronomy that existed nowhere else, poetry in his father's hand, which he had written as a boy . . . all sacrificed to Chaos. *That life offends. Pluck it out.* And a child's tantrum immolates it. Who will restrain the child from destroying worlds he will never even know?

But Marcus could not acquiesce. If he held firm he might bring the Emperor to doubt Domitian's denunciations, given Nero's changeable nature.

As the flames began to spread more rapidly, the guests rose up all at once like some frightened flock of birds; they began overturning couches in their haste to get to the doors. Marcus did not move and he saw that Junilla, too, remained in her place; he had the disturbing sense that this was because to Junilla, Nero's divinity was fact, and she believed his presence could somehow shield her from fire.

"*Halt!*" Nero shouted. "Headless chickens have more dignity! Do you think I will sit here and be burned alive while you vagabonds scurry off to safety?" He turned to his own servants. "Let the flames feed for a time and get their fill of rare words. Then, put them out."

Nero leaned close to Marcus Julianus, staring at him with mock bewilderment; then he smiled at Domitian, who had collapsed into the cushions as if his bones had turned to pudding.

"Look well, young man!" Nero said patiently to Domitian like a teacher with a slow-witted pupil. "*This* is what steadfastness is! I demonstrate because you might not ever see it again, and like comets and other such prodigies, when these things occur we should examine them. Nature is perverse, is she not? You, with your vaulting, pathetic ambition, are of the stuff of which knaves are made, and he, who has no ambition to rule and won't live out the next month, would make a fine ruler indeed!"

Nero leaned toward Domitian and patted the young man's hand. Domitian jerked back from him, feeling like a flayed animal prodded with a sharp stick. Domitian found himself despising Marcus Julianus as much as Nero, as if his good friend had planned it all. From that moment Marcus Arrius Julianus became not just a friend whom he admired and envied, but something more—a potent mix of father, teacher, and judge. Marcus Julianus was the embodiment of all he could never be. Domitian saw swiftly how this could sour even gaining the supreme power: Marcus Julianus would manage to be above him, even then. In one moment, Domitian felt relief that Julianus would soon be tried and executed; in the next, this thought made him greatly ashamed.

Nero then ordered his musicians to put out the fire. They gathered up the empty amphorae in which the wine had been brought, and ran to the nearest garden fountain—but it was dry.

They were forced, finally, to run out to the street fountain. A number of the Praetorians were pressed into service as well. Nero ordered the drummer and the boy with the scabellum to play an accompaniment to this chaotic firefighting, covering noise with worse noise. The smoke was dark and dense; it drove everyone from the north part of the house.

During all this, Marcus Julianus saw a way that some great good might come out of this vicious farce. He fought briefly with himself, considering the risk. Then he motioned to Diocles and whispered rapid instructions to him; the pandemonium all about ensured that Nero, who was ignoring everyone and lustily finishing off the oysters, did not hear his words.

After a good half hour of shouting, running, and sloshing of water, the blaze was finally doused. The fire had been contained by surrounding stonework to two of the four library rooms, but to Marcus the house's heart was gone. Then all was still once more; everywhere was standing water, the stench of burnt brocade, the mess of ashes, muddy footprints, and overturned tables.

"I made another play out of life, did I not?" Nero said, his musical alto jarring in the fresh silence. "Tell me, Marcus Julianus, why are your fountains dry?"

Marcus Julianus knew well that Veiento was responsible for this; to harass him, Veiento ordered the commissioner of the water supply to replace the main pipe that supplied his house from the city reservoir with a much smaller one that barely sufficed—lack of water pressure was often a telling sign of loss of favor.

Can it be the gods have handed me a chance to provoke this monster into giving me a public trial?

"It seems, my lord, I displeased the wrong person, a powerful and subtle man—Veiento," Marcus replied, choosing words as the painter chooses colors, for precise effect. "I petitioned him to let me defend my father's name before the Senate. It was odd. Not only did he refuse, the request seemed to anger him—and you know an angry man is often a frightened man. I wonder sometimes what he was frightened of. In any case, by his order—it *must* have been by his order, you know how all jump at his command—the water commissioner turned on me and reduced my water supply to a trickle."

Marcus saw a sharp light of interest in Nero's eyes, followed by a dark, turbid look. Once he made a sound like a dog's growl while looking at Domitian, who was staring significantly at his wine cup as if he wanted to drown himself in it.

Finally Nero turned to Marcus Julianus and put a cushioned hand on his shoulder. "I take amusement from your arguments, Marcus Julianus. It is like watching a good beast fight. What a show it will make: you, pitted against my good and faithful serpent—I mean *servant*—Veiento. You shall have your public trial."

Marcus Julianus carefully concealed his elation. So Nero *was* suspicious of his Chief Councillor. He looked once at Junilla; to his surprise she appeared greatly alarmed by this turn of events.

"My gratitude is beyond expressing," he said quietly to Nero.

Roasted pheasants stuffed with herbs and minced quails' eggs were then swiftly set down on each table. Nero scooped out a good measure of the stuffing and put it on a dish. As he ate greedily, he looked at Marcus Julianus, stuffing dribbling from his mouth as he spoke.

"I'm not granting you *life,* mind you, only a Senate trial. Your father was a traitor, and most likely you are too—like insanity, it's passed on in the blood from father to son, you know. Fine pheasant, by the way. My own cooks cannot do better, and I've brought them from every part of the world."

Just then a soft wailing was heard from the remote parts of the house. All paid it no mind at first. But it persisted and finally got Nero's attention. Marcus sent for Diocles for an explanation. The steward appeared, his face and clothes smeared with ash. Behind him were two housemaids, their hair disheveled, faces swollen from tears. Diocles spoke confidentially to Marcus Julianus.

Marcus then turned to Nero to explain. "My Lord, there have been deaths from the fire," he said quietly. "If you will excuse me, my steward needs a word with myself . . . and Arria alone." Arria heard her name and let out a raw cry; she knew already what they would tell her. She rose up, then fell into a faint before Marcus could catch her. Diocles helped him carry her out.

Nero looked on with impatient bewilderment. When after long moments Marcus Julianus resumed his place on the couch, Nero demanded, *"Well?* So you've lost a housemaid or two? I suppose you want me to pay you!"

"That will not be necessary," Marcus Julianus replied. "Three housemaids died from the smoke, as did Arria's children, who were sleeping in the bedchamber next to the library."

Nero's yellowed eyes were at first stupefied and blank; gradually his face contracted in petty fury. He threw down his oyster spoon with a loud clatter and staggered up, meaning to leave. Five of the musicians hastily set down their instruments and rushed to help.

"You are a wretched host," Nero sputtered. "The pheasant is vile. I wanted those children. You've quite ruined my evening. You know, now I do not want dessert. I want two more children, like those." He considered ordering Marcus Julianus' death at once, but he disciplined himself: He wanted to savor the coming duel between Julianus and Veiento.

Marcus Julianus rose and uttered a stream of formal apologies.

Would Nero ask to see the bodies for proof? He was ready for that if necessary. He wondered if Arria, when she came to consciousness and found her children well and alive, would ever forgive him this bit of desperate playacting. Had he warned her of the ruse in advance her reaction would not have been so genuine; Nero might not have believed it so readily.

And the children were safe but for the moment. They could not be hidden from sight forever. The city must be delivered from Nero.

The guests escaped quietly and quickly when the entourage of Nero was gone.

When Marcus pulled aside the brocade curtain of the bridal chamber for the ceremony's final rite, the house was filled with the oppressive quiet of muted fear. Somewhere beyond the curtains a single kithara player still plucked at his instrument, his music closer to the elements than to art as he struck the same three strings in a dully repetitive melody, as if he had fallen under a spell.

What meaning can there be in such a union? We are captives. And her interests lie not with me but with others.

Junilla started as he entered; he had a sense this was an unwanted intrusion. Quickly she turned to him. Her tunica, a vapor of white, was set in motion about her, settling softly like calming feathers. At her back was a rosewood table on which was a forest of cosmetics jars—rouge in terra cotta pots, jars of antimony with griffins' head handles; he was certain she moved to cover them from his sight.

Then she watched him with those great silent eyes.

How like the old mountain rites of Bacchus this is, he thought, to take a stranger in passionate embrace.

The bridal room had been carefully prepared ahead of time. Lamps filled with cinnamon and hyacinth oil were placed in the wall niches. A low table supported by wooden acanthus leaves held crystal ewers of water and hundred-year-old wine, a gilded bowl of figs and dates. An altar to Juno was set against one wall, her stern matronly face veiled then unveiled by the smoke of the incense that burned at her feet. A wedding scene was painted on the wall above the bridal bed, the whole bordered with an encaustic rendering of birds and flowers; it showed a reluctant bride—a ghostly figure seeming to float in her gauzy garments—being led to the groom, her downcast eyes terrified as she was coaxed by her mother, on one hand, and the god Hymen, patron of marriages, on the other.

Junilla seemed to have shed that imperious confidence he had seen at the banquet table; those beseeching eyes, that awkward stance made him think of a startled foal. So many unpleasant mysteries stirred in those eyes.

Softly he said her name, trying to reach across the gulf of darkness between them, to touch her with his voice.

"Junilla, what is wrong?"

She looked away and shook out her hair, seeming more half-tamed creature than woman—as likely to reply with a gesture or movement as with a word. She loosened the pearls that dotted that dark, rumpled mane; with quick, tapping sounds they struck the mosaic floor. She made no move to retrieve them; they might have been cast pebbles. It made him sharply aware of the difference in their attitude to wealth. For him, it was to be put to use to gain knowledge. To her, it was water from a crossroads fountain—there would always be more.

"Utterly *nothing* is wrong," she said finally, her voice too eager and light. "I am a fortunate woman. I believe I already feel love for you."

"If that were said with any less conviction, I would send for a physician to make certain you had not died. Truly, we know nothing of each other."

She laughed low in her throat, then approached him with a walk meant to be smooth and seductive. With a quick clumsy movement of one shoulder she let the tunica slip, baring most of one creamy breast; it was done casually as a girl pulling out her long tresses to have them admired. It was arousing but also amusing, like watching the young daughter of a prostitute unwittingly imitating her mother.

He drew her close and gently lifted her chin. "You seem to know your way about a bridal chamber. One would almost think it's the third time you've been married this year."

"You are so very *amusing,*" she said silkily, a fevered emptiness in her eyes.

He tugged at the knot of Hercules, loosening it, letting the filmy tunic fall free to its full length. Now he was aware of the comfortable roundness of her body just visible through its white mist, of the shadow in the cleft between overfull breasts barely contained in the breastband. Desire, he thought, struggles up in the most inhospitable of circumstances. That mysterious body—would it be like her face? Pearly satin, pliant ivory, a rose-flushed garden of delicate mysteries?

She moved for him swiftly, seizing his mouth with hers, all the while wriggling free of the loosened tunica. Then all her boundless softness was pressed against him; languidly she arched her back, moving against him in a practiced way. As he guided her toward the marriage bed, she remembered to struggle half-heartedly—every girl was taught this was expected of a bride. He felt he wrestled with cushions. Then with the smooth confidence of a dancer she melted back onto the bed, pulling him atop her. *Something is sadly wrong here,* a warning sounded in the outer reaches of his consciousness, but he felt a pull toward her that bypassed the mind. There was nothing in life but her firm but giving flesh, glowing amber in the ruddy light of the lamp, the fine, silken skin of her inner thighs, her quick strong hands roving with a child's eager impatience; and those luminous eyes, whose look—first restless, then calm—recalled bright, darting snakes, signaling danger without direction or purpose.

Finally he pushed her back to arm's length and held her still, saying with more weary surprise than anger, "I have known seasoned concubines less accomplished than you. Did your mother hire you out to a brothel? Junilla, *what was done to you?*"

She glared at him, feigning great offense, that gaze a delicately thrown dart. Her rampant hair fanned out on the bed, giving her a look that was intimidatingly womanly. But she was too young to have the resolution to maintain the look; it dissolved quickly to anxious despair.

"You do not like me," she whispered, looking away.

She looked so pitiable then that he took her up and held her close. "I know I do not like these masks you put on. Look at me, Junilla, and show yourself truly."

She hesitated, approached him cautiously and gave him a child's chaste kiss; then with exaggerated passivity, she fell back and lay still. He had a sense she merely exchanged one mask for another, thinking he would like this one better.

He felt a catch of sadness. Behind these masks was a mangled spirit that would always seek the dark.

After a time he resumed caressing her, and the breastband came loose all at once, releasing those heavy breasts. She gave a small gasp and shot up, twisting away from him, struggling to draw the coverlet over her breasts.

Then he saw it—twin stains on the breastband.

Milk.

His first thought was that this was one more grotesque jest of the night. But swiftly he scented some tragedy here. "Junilla, *who in the name of the gods—"*

"Let me be! Leave me!"

She writhed violently, raw terror in her eyes as he tried to pull her close; her hair lashed his face. Finally he grasped her securely by the shoulders and held her down.

"Stop this at once! Now, you will tell me who has done this!"

She broke into deep, bitter crying, as if vomiting up all the evil humors of the mind, all the poisoned memories she held within her.

"Whose child did you bear?"

She gasped for breath, started to reply, then her courage failed her. She stared at the wall as though she saw something hideous there, invisible to him.

"Answer! I must know who has insulted us so. Junilla, I will not harm you. Tell me!" he said softly, releasing her and gently smoothing her hair from her forehead.

"It's a wrong you'll never redress," she said finally. "He whose child I bore . . . can defile temples."

"Oh, curses on Nemesis! Nero."

"He made me expose it . . . last night. . . . I did not want to. 'You cannot drag a babe along to your first wedding,' he said, 'the second perhaps, not the first.' I did not want . . ."

"You were one of the victims . . . taken to the Palace."

"Yes," she said without emotion. "I have been his concubine since I was nine."

He felt a lurch of nausea. Was there anywhere those sucking tentacles did not reach?

"My mother took me there . . . so he could have me when he wished. Always he was masked. Sometimes before the Guards . . ." He sensed that on the surface she felt the horror of it, but beneath was a desert of indifference.

"Why do the gods allow such a monster to thrive, and when will the world be rid of him!" Marcus said softly.

"Now you despise me. I am defiled—a broodmare, a worn-out sack, ugly and used. What will you do with me!"

For a moment he thought he saw her unmasked. She gave him a look that begged help, and now it did seem those eyes let him in.

"It is no more just for me to despise you than to despise the beaten slave forced to thieve. And you are still my wife, no matter what that bloated viper did to you."

He then pulled her close, held her a moment, and mumbled in her hair, "You are safe, for a time, I will see you safe."

The comforting embrace warmed slowly to a sort of shy passion. What began as ritual lovemaking, necessary to seal a ceremony, flooded its bounds, and soon he was enveloped in plush, rose-scented flesh, drunk on the grassy smell of her hair. Then he was lost in that taking that is also surrender; despite her knowledge of love, he took great care, as if with a virgin bride.

The light in the chamber grew dim during their lovemaking; he was only half aware of her turning once and reaching swiftly, delicately into the array of cosmetic pots.

Soon after, her pleasure came and she cried out, catching him by surprise, whipping about like some fighting cat. She was seized with a Bacchic frenzy, with a madness that did not know him. Cat claws raked down his back, drawing blood.

His own rush of pleasure obscured the pain. But even through the red-gold haze something alerted him; there was something not quite right in the way she scratched him—it was too deliberate.

Within moments, as he lay atop her, spent, an odd, dreamlike sense came to him. The flame of the one lamp still burning seemed to ripple and flow as if it were reflected in moving water. It seemed he knew the true nature of all things—and their nature was horror. Junilla was an undine, rippling beneath him, a monstrous spectral child, those lustrous eyes empty pits, her mouth full of fine, sharp teeth. The pattern of intertwined vines on the coverlet was alive; it was no pattern but crawling scorpions. Horror swarmed over him.

She had poisoned him.

He struggled from the bed and nearly fell. The mosaic floor heaved like a sea. Distantly he was aware of Junilla, upright on the bed, watching him expectantly. He found the lamp and held it close to the cosmetics jars to illumine them, all the while feeling he clung desperately to the regular world he knew.

"Madwoman! What have you done!" he breathed. One clay pot held a thick vile liquid; droplets of it had been dribbled onto the table. He guessed it was adder's venom.

Enough to kill? He seized her right hand. Flesh and venom were still beneath the nails. He flung it down. Roughly he pulled her to her feet. Even through his delirium he was certain there was no remorse in those bold eyes.

"Have you loyalty to no one and nothing!" he said, shouting now, grasping her shoulders and shaking her. "You lay in ambush for me, even after we made peace!"

"I am no madwoman," she said calmly. "I am His Divinity's most perfect creation. Look at me!" Her eyes ignited. "I was *his* for so many years . . . my flesh is his flesh. My acts are divine!" Dawn light filtered into the bridal chamber. In his confused state she was an apparition of unholy light, a sweet demon-child with blood running from her lips.

He pushed her out of his way and sought the bellpull to summon Diocles and a physician. Then he sat heavily on the bed, his head in his hands.

"You have done this because Nero granted me an open trial."

"You know nothing! You are no one!"

"You are the slave of Veiento. You judge he is the next safe port, after the ship you're aboard sinks."

"Traitor, traitor, traitor!" she cried out in a sort of ecstatic delight. "You will fail in all you do, and die! You are mud. You are no one. You would not even sacrifice a pig for me. I despise you!"

As he sank back, eyes glazed but still open, Junilla realized suddenly he was not dying quickly enough. The mixture she purchased from the old Etruscan prisoner was reputedly swift. Marcus Julianus might survive. Nero would protect her from prosecution if Marcus died, but if he *lived*—she would live in fear of him for as long as they both walked the earth.

Terrified, she edged toward him, steeling herself to suffocate him with a pillow, but Diocles came then.

Diocles stared at them, openmouthed.

"Bring Thales and his store of antidotes at once," Marcus Julianus managed hoarsely. "Conduct Junilla to her own apartments and keep her under strict guard—*and say nothing of this to anyone.*"

He sensed the poison might have stabilized, but he was not certain. He thought: It must indeed have been a nest of maggots the augur shielded from view.

With the aid of the burly doorkeeper Diocles dragged Junilla out, and when Marcus was alone there came to him, perversely, a taunting vision of what Junilla was not. It might have been his closeness to death, or it might have been that the poison worked like a mirror, reflecting Junilla reversed. But he saw then a different sort of woman: a shivering daimon rising out of the wreckage of that marriage bed, a maid untouched by all the foulness of cities, innocent and fierce as wild things, bold and curious about the world; a maid with a questing, daring philosopher's soul. The vision fused with the maid of his father's records, that wondrous creature born from a few written lines. *Who since the time of the Kings has seen such hallowed devotion. . . .*

With a wrenching bitterness he knew then how much he *had* wanted a companion of his own heart. Vigorously he shook the vision off. There was no time for such dreams while Nero lived, while he had not yet righted the injustice done his father.

CHAPTER XI

Nero's temper was so changeable Marcus Julianus dared not send Junilla off; he judged it wisest to confine her to a guarded chamber so she could not make any further attempts on his life. In the light of morning she seemed more pathetic than evil, and he wished her no harm—he wanted only to be well rid of her. He believed part of Nero's purpose was to introduce a fanatically devoted spy into the household; Junilla was to listen and report his true opinions of the Emperor's poetic works, of his competence to rule—for Nero literally believed the condemned divinely driven to speak the truth.

But afterward Nero seemed to lose interest in the whole affair; he had much to distract him. The state of his Empire daily grew more precarious; everywhere his hold on the army loosened. As the legions of Hispania proclaimed their Commander, Galba, as Emperor and began their slow march on the capital city to wrest it from Nero, he began the sharp descent into final madness. He would call emergency meetings of the Senate, then instead of giving his prepared address, he would demonstrate a new sort of water organ he had helped design. On other days he would begin preparations to go on campaign and fight for his throne. But he planned to bring his stage equipment so he could perform his tragedies for the soldiers, and he meant to march with a bodyguard composed of his concubines dressed as Amazons armed with axes; once he went so far as ordering them to be given men's haircuts before he abandoned the plan, managing to convince himself once more that all was well.

The trial of Marcus Julianus the Younger was set for a day late in the month of *Maius*. It was but one in a dreary succession of treason trials in which the captive Senators were prodded to condemn one of their own for Nero's pleasure; none who set out at dawn that day for the Senate House had good reason to believe this trial would end differently.

Ten Praetorians in gilded armor came to conduct Marcus Julianus to the Curia where the Senate was housed. The walk was short but the low places were flooded with rain; it seemed to Marcus the city pelted him with mud to humble him. He felt strangely alive, lucidly aware of ordinary things: the red tile roofs sturdily climbing the hillsides like a grand flight of steps to the sky, the feeble dawn touching the glistening cobbles underfoot, transforming them into dark mysterious gems, a crossroads shrine with its pitiful offering of scattered flowers, the hopeful knots of citizens crowded around the bakeries from which drifted the comforting aroma of bread. Already he felt detached from this city that was so like a goddess-mother, nourishing, punishing, all-pervading—this savage, luxurious city that enslaved him, freed him and now set him an impossible task, like some labor of Hercules cruelly laid on a mortal man. *Here it ends, Endymion. Whether I perform it well or fail miserably, either way I am bound for the sacrificial pit.*

As his entourage came to the Sacred Way, the street was thick with crowds; by the time Marcus Julianus reached the Old Forum, their numbers had multiplied so that a cohort of Praetorians was needed to contain them. Shopkeepers, freedmen, aristocrats and beggars stood shoulder to shoulder; they were remarkably silent, he thought, for their numbers. Only gradually did he realize they came to show love for him and wish him well. He knew the tale of the wedding had been retold so often it was transformed into legend with himself cast as hero; his denials had actually won stays of execution for several of the conspirators Domitian named that night; that his steadfastness actually slowed Nero's murderous rampage was counted a near-miraculous thing. But he had not known the tale had moved all classes to such devotion, nor had he realized they were this close to demonstrating defiance of Nero's rule.

With his Guards flanking him, Marcus Julianus ascended the steps of the Senate House; the outer walls of this venerable old monolith were blackened still from Nero's fire. The Curia dwarfed the ceaselessly swarming human life below: the bankers and accountants going to their places of business, the hawkers, the wide-eyed foreigners. Though temples and government buildings of equal arrogance crowded closely about it, still the Curia stood apart with a sort of grim purity; its austere columns looked down on him in stern judgment. As always, here he felt the eyes of the dead—for so long this site had been holy ground. In the archaic earth beneath the foundation the blood of aeons of sacrifices turned to dust, mingling with the powdered bones of mythical kings. Many bold enough to linger about these steps past midnight claimed to have heard the voice of the long-dead Cicero or other great ghosts floating out from the Stygian dark.

As Marcus Julianus passed through towering bronze doors, he felt the sweep of many gazes moving toward him. *The day's victim has come.* He knew their only security lay in the fact that on this day they were safe—someone else was to be immolated.

The Senators formed a small island of white almost lost in the vast gloom of the mammoth chamber. Entering this place even as a prisoner was faintly intoxicating, like being drawn up suddenly among the gods of Mount Olympus—for so many generations the fates of nations had been determined here. The stark light-and-dark pattern of the floor, made of precious marbles laid out in a bold geometric pattern, suggested some gameboard to be played on by gods.

The four hundred Senators who were present sat in a semicircle of ornately carved benches set in tiers; the lowest seats were reserved for the members of greatest eminence. Facing the Senators was a dais; here sat the presiding Consul, Messalinus, as well as Veiento, acting as chief prosecutor, and his three assistant prosecutors. Behind them was a loftier dais and atop it was the imperial seat. Here Nero displayed himself in splendor, his gold-bordered toga spilling over the throne's lion-headed, ivory armrests. He was a sulky god propped precariously on a high, narrow throne, his swollen body all but overflowing the space; Marcus Julianus thought of a potato sack carelessly swathed in the imperial purple. The weighty, gem-studded diadem he wore seemed to press his head down into his neck. Those jowls were comfortably settled, and he sat unmoving. Only his eyes were restless, malign, as they scavenged the hall, gathering information from every face, desiring to learn what could not be learned from a recorder's report, such as who spoke his praises with a faint look of distaste, who looked down to cover an inappropriate smile.

Marcus Arrius Julianus took one of the seats in the rear reserved for the accused. He saw he got the barest of nods even from men he counted allies—few dared do otherwise with Nero examining their faces and occasionally writing notations on a tablet. Two men looked on him with friendliness: One was Saturninus, his father's long-time friend, the sort of man who always turned round and ran against the herd; he risked much with the look. Why, Marcus wondered, does nature produce so few men like him?

The other was Domitian, high in the visitors' gallery, who risked little by his nod and smile of support—Nero held him to be of small account, and in any case the Emperor was so short of sight Domitian was too far off for him to see, even with the aid of the outsized emerald Nero used to improve his vision. Domitian made quite a show of getting his attention, and Marcus understood at once: Now that he was something of a popular hero, Domitian wanted it publicly well established that Marcus Arrius Julianus was his friend.

The Chief Augur, armed with crooked, spiral-headed staff, was taking the auspices. First he set down the wooden cage in which the sacred chickens were kept; then he muttered a prayer and threw them a measure of grain. Of course, they gave the best of auguries, pecking furiously at the feed; as a child Marcus stopped wondering why no one ever objected that the chickens had been carefully starved beforehand. Tradition in this place, he reflected, was the great blindfold. The Senate as a body he thought of as a rigid, remote grandfather walking stiffly through his last days, haughty to the end, affecting not to know he is consulted only for form. Collectively the mind of the Senate was so brittle and unchanging that he accepted his duties here as a heavy price of rank. He had experienced boredom here in great measure, while interminable arguments raged over petty issues—the settling of grander issues the Emperor reserved for himself—and so it was an odd sensation to experience dread, to know those who had bored him meant now to kill him.

The Consul Messalinus rose and with a grand flourish cast incense onto the altar beneath the gilded image of Victory with outstretched wings. A cloud of dark fragrant smoke billowed up.

The Consul then convened the assembly, and minor matters were attended to: There was a short debate over which of two cities in Gaul would be granted the right to erect a new temple to

Nero's divinity; then came the case of a city in Syria that begged one year's remission of taxes because they suffered a pestilence. When the votes had been taken, the Consul rose and announced with an ominous tremor, "Marcus Arrius Julianus, come forward, that we might examine your case."

Marcus Julianus rose in his gray mourning cloak. A sudden thought of his father caused him to touch the black amulet at his throat—and for a heartbeat he was aware of the earth below and felt a bright calm, as after a bell has ceased ringing in a temple. The sense was quickly gone, but its nectar lingered.

As he came forward to stand before the Consul and the throne, the vast space was silent but for the sound of his steps echoing off stone. All saw at once this was no cringing victim. Marcus Julianus inclined his head to acknowledge the presence of the Emperor, then turned to face the senatorial body. As he examined them steadfastly, fearlessly, with eyes that seemed able to expertly turn a soul inside out, the Senators for a fleeting moment had the sense they themselves were on trial. *This was a man who could not betray,* all knew with certainty before he uttered a word.

Domitian was seized with envy; he realized then that part of him hoped this trial would humble his friend as the wedding party had not. Was that faint amusement he saw in Marcus' face? The fool seemed not to know he was ready to be ferried across the Styx.

Veiento rose and prepared to speak. That gaunt, narrow face was severe as a woodcut; soulless eyes looked out blandly from hollow sockets. There was a look of barrenness about him—cadaverous skin was stretched over jutting bones, a smooth skull, a knife-thin nose. His mouth was set in a curt line, revealing nothing of the rich pleasure he took in his role; long ago he learned to keep desire concealed lest an enemy learn too much. He was a creature admirably adapted to this world, Marcus reflected: His single loyalty was to the source of power—its good or evil was of no concern—and for it he struck and killed with the passionless efficiency of a shark.

Veiento did not consider this the beginning of a trial but rather the end of one. He had already won; this was the victory celebration. Treason trials were for form alone; the Senators never dared defy the guilty verdict they knew the Emperor expected. The questioning, too, was for show: A board of judges had already reviewed the evidence and advised Nero of the defendant's guilt. The one difficulty in Veiento's mind lay in making certain the vote was called for before too many embarrassing questions were raised about his own dealings.

Of the three examiners with him, two were senior senatorial advisors, and one, a young Senator named Montanus who had held few offices. Nero himself had chosen Montanus for this honor because he had bested everyone in an eating-and-drinking contest held this year aboard Nero's pleasure barge during the Feast of Mars, consuming wine enough to down ten men and a whole suckling pig—and such heroic voracity, as Nero put it, called for a prize.

Through one turn of the water clock Veiento began to enumerate the many crimes of Marcus Arrius Julianus, father and son. Veiento's voice was not so colorless as the rest of him; it was florid and full as it arrogantly took possession of the hall. Julianus the Elder had used every means, natural and supernatural, to bring about Nero's death, he claimed, and at the last he cried out compellingly that Julianus meant to put his son, standing before them, on the throne. By the end of the speech Nero was convinced all over again of the younger Julianus' guilt; he sat forward, his fleshy face become rigid, his dimpled hands squeezed tight in rage.

When the opening speech was done, Veiento launched into the questioning. "Son of the traitor, did not your father, Marcus Arrius Julianus the Elder, divulge all his plans to you? And did he not give you first place in them?"

"The word *traitor* in your mouth, my lord," Marcus Julianus replied, his voice austere after Veiento's, "is little more than a weapon of murder. Do you not fear such a capriciously wielded weapon will one day be used against yourself? And how smoothly and easily it comes off your tongue, when you've no real evidence—even the witnesses you bribed refuse to speak against us."

This brought sharp silence. Few could believe Marcus Julianus dared accuse one so senior to him of bribery.

Veiento controlled a pitying smile. The fool actually seemed to think this *was* a trial. *Good. Let him enliven my victory celebration.* Veiento stole a look at Nero, who seemed to have lapsed back into a nap.

"Time, perhaps, is more precious to us than to you," Veiento said softly. "Your guilt is established. Had not your father's arrest been ordered?"

"Arrest then is proof of guilt? Well, then, you save us all much time. We can retire from the courts. We do not need law, only soldiers."

This brought cautious smiles. Nero opened his eyes halfway, unpleasantly awake as if after a best-forgotten night of debauch. It was impossible to tell if he was angered or amused.

Veiento broke into one of his controlled furies. The words were fired off in a well-tempered shriek that echoed dramatically off stone.

"The Emperor ordered him arrested! He then does not know the law?" This awakened Nero completely. He looked at Marcus Julianus with great affront.

"His knowledge is not on trial," Marcus Julianus said mildly. "The Emperor ordered him arrested on advice given by yourself. An emperor can be failed by those who give him information. A pity, but it occurs. This contest is more between you and me, not between myself and the state."

"I assure you your situation is too dire for sophistry."

"Yes, you've made certain it is."

"Does each generation of your family double in impertinence? Your children will piss on the throne itself."

"The throne can withstand that far better than justice can withstand your assault."

This brought cautious laughter and curious glances at Nero, who now watched Marcus Julianus with growing interest, as he might an untried gladiator who gained a sudden advantage over a seasoned opponent. Veiento seemed visibly to withdraw, but not in defeat, more as the predator that collects itself before it unleashes the next attack.

Veiento then said, "Conspirators meet openly at your house every ninth day." The last words were a shriek. *"Deny that!"*

"Yes. Our tyrant is ignorance. Our talk is of nature and the spirit, not of government."

"Philosopher and trickster, your philosophy is in *itself* traitorous. Your Zeno teaches the wise must rule—and for certain, wise you count yourself. They have spoken *thus* at your meetings. . . ." He paused to snatch up one of the tablets Montanus dutifully kept ready for him, then held it out theatrically and read, " 'Gentleness is the ruler's best proof against assassination. When a ruler loses himself to his passions and lives by revenge, it is the duty of the wise man to destroy the tyrant.' "

"We live in the world, my lord, not in a maze of words. I hardly

see what those words have to do with this day and time . . .
unless you count Nero a tyrant."

At this a small cold smile of amusement came to Nero's face.

"You talking snake!" Veiento shouted. "Your father counted our
Divine Lord a tyrant, and you know it well! Everyone knows it.
He felt himself a better man, better educated, more fit to rule. He
counted the hours he spent in study and measured them against
the hours our Divinity spent at the games. And finally when he
thought the Emperor's position weakened enough, he invited his
barbarian allies to come south and help him and his fellow rebels
launch an attack on Gaul. His plan would have succeeded had not
even *more* savage barbarians attacked his own forces. And now,
enough of this!"

Veiento looked meaningfully at the Consul, hoping desperately
he would call for the vote. But Messalinus took his cue from Nero,
and the Emperor seemed to be enjoying himself.

Marcus Julianus counted it a victory that he remained calm
through that gale of words; they seemed not words at all but
shrieking wind. His reply was not meant for Veiento or the
Senators—but for his father's ghost. He looked toward the seat
that would have been his father's as he spoke.

"My father, Marcus Julianus, was perhaps the only man among
you who never had such thoughts. He was old-fashioned enough
not to judge those who ranked above—he thought it right to leave
that to the Fates. He was of the ancient sort for whom duty was
god. He gave his life defending the frontier—and a humiliating
death was his reward! I will now prove to you his recruitment of
Wido was desperation—"

Veiento slammed down a tablet. "Enough of this criminal's
rantings!"

But Nero, with the smallest gesture of his hand, motioned for
Marcus Julianus to continue on.

Marcus Julianus brought out two rolled documents he had
concealed in his tunic. "I mean to submit as evidence these
records, taken from the Military Treasury, that begin with the date
of the outset of our lord the Prosecutor's time as minister—"

Veiento tore them from his hand. "This evidence was not shown
to the board of judges!"

But Nero was intrigued by Veiento's displeasure, and he
scratched a quick note for the Consul.

"The court decides this may be used, even though the board of
judges did not know," Messalinus read out.

Marcus Julianus felt a rush of joy. "And there too are my father's records of what he received in the same years so the court can make a comparison."

"These documents are forgeries made by our enemies!" Veiento shouted.

Marcus Julianus gave him a look that a parent might give a child caught lying. Nero's smile was smug and murderous.

"I think not," Marcus Julianus replied smoothly. "As the court will see, there is a great difference between what my father recorded and what the Palace records say he received. This discrepancy curiously disappears during Veiento's year of absence from the Military Treasury and resumes the year he took the office back."

Veiento for a moment let fright show in his eye. How had Julianus gotten that? He must have stolen into the military records room like a thief in the night.

"Forgeries! All forgeries!"

Nero sleepily whispered an instruction to the Guard posted next to him. Then he turned vengeful eyes on Veiento. Embezzlement in itself he counted a rather dull crime to which he was not really opposed in principle; good embezzlers could even be useful for some things, such as milking the provinces. But Veiento had sworn before him and by all the gods he had no shameful secrets for Marcus Julianus to uncover. And this meant that Marcus Julianus the Elder had spoken the truth when he protested the charges, making *him* look the fool as well as Veiento.

The Guards took both sets of documents and gave them to the imperial procurator for examination. The Senators regarded Marcus Julianus with growing amazement. No one had ever successfully attacked Veiento's character before his peers. Veiento sensed the power balance subtly shifting, and he hated more than death this feeling of being on the pitched bow of a ship that was slowly sinking.

Marcus Julianus still felt death's shadow hovering close. It was true he sensed the Senators allying themselves with him—they loved shows of filial fidelity, particularly when done at great risk. But in spite of the grave embarrassments he had inflicted on Veiento, still he had given Nero no good reason to spare him, no reason not to persecute his family.

Veiento rose and paced, eyes afire, lips pale. How could it have come to this? he wondered. In a mere quarter hour all had turned on him, and his own fate had become dire as that of Julianus. Vigorously he began a fresh attack.

"This does not change the truth! Had there not been internal dissension within that tribe—the Cats—" An assistant motioned to him and whispered the correct pronunciation in his ear. —"the *Chattians,*" he continued, "your father would have unleashed these blood-drinking savages on us and succeeded in seizing all Gaul!"

"The dissension in the tribe, gentlemen," Marcus Julianus replied, "was over *us*. None here doubt the hostility of Baldemar. My lord, tell the court his motive for striking at Wido."

"I am not the one being questioned here!"

"The answer has great bearing on my father's guilt or innocence—and on the truth."

Nero nodded at Veiento, demanding an answer.

"Revenge for the theft of his daughter," Veiento replied reluctantly.

"No. Baldemar had with him men of many neighboring tribes. You know well, or should know, that the Germanic tribes band together *only when their common enemy is Rome*. If Wido had been a weapon aimed at *us*, never on this earth would Baldemar have struck at him. Indeed, Baldemar would have *joined* him. No. This barbarian chief called Wido was to be used as a weapon *against his own people*.

"My father was an innocent man, and he has died because of your greed!" Julianus' voice rose to a ringing shout. "You created that tale to destroy my father so your own crimes would never be uncovered!"

The last echoes of his voice died into a powerful silence in which many of the members found some of their terror of Nero ebbing away. Marcus Julianus' audacity was contagious—it taunted them with the possibility of freedom from living daily in fear.

Veiento quickly shifted the direction of his attack. "Your father used witchcraft to undermine the state! It is well documented he consulted a barbarian seeress called Ramis and tried to learn the day of Nero's death."

With this charge Marcus Julianus felt hope vault upward. Veiento had at last fallen into one of several traps he had set. This charge had actually been inserted by Marcus Julianus himself, through "witnesses" in his own pay whom he had sent to Veiento when the Councillor was gathering evidence—for he wished for Nero to hear his reply.

"That is true, in part. But my father had no interest in the day of the Emperor's death. His purpose was to learn the means of quelling night-terrors, to which he was prone in those days, possibly as a premonition of his own death. She knew the means, and told him the prayers and the herbal remedies required, and my father carefully recorded it all. By the way, he wrote to me that it was marvelously effective."

Marcus knew Nero was so tormented by nightmares since he had murdered his mother that in an attempt to elude the Furies, he never slept twice in the same bedchamber of his Golden House. The Emperor had sent as far away as India for concoctions to relieve himself of them. The ruse worked; he felt Nero's interest sharply increase.

Once again, Veiento thought in fury, I grasped the snake by the tail.

Nero wrote out a question and had it brought to the prosecutors—rarely did he speak publicly, in order to preserve his voice for singing. Montanus read it to Marcus Julianus. "Where are these formulae at present?"

"Burned, my lord, in the unfortunate fire recently sustained in my house. I read them through once, however, and I believe that with practice and experimenting, I could rediscover what was lost."

Veiento cursed silently. Julianus had given Nero a powerful reason for leaving him alive—at least temporarily. But I've one arrow left in my quiver, Veiento thought, and this one is tipped with poison.

He readied himself for the death-dealing shot, motioning with a withered hand to Montanus, who, with a smug smile of importance, rose and gave to him what appeared to be a small packet of letters. Then Veiento held them aloft so all could see.

"Marcus Arrius Julianus, these are philosophical essays written by your father, taken from his personal effects—and here is a veritable catalogue of villainies!"

"How did you obtain those?" Marcus Julianus asked sharply.

"It is not relevant; let us just say they were a—gift to the court."

Marcus Julianus said with great resignation, "My father carried those essays with him everywhere, but he did not write them. And truly, I *do* hold with all therein."

"Fine and good! No matter if he wrote them then, if you admit to belief in them! Let us take a passage at random. Here's a likely one—it's a brazen attack on our Divine Ruler's love of the Games: 'The entertainments of the amphitheater are base and cruel; indeed, they corrupt those who watch, for the immoderate letting of blood incites unnatural passions and awakens the savagery asleep in all of us—'"

"I hardly see—"

"Silence, you slithering serpent!"

Nero spoke for the first time. "Let him speak!"

That pale, unused voice made everyone uneasy. Nero seemed acutely interested in this, sitting forward in his throne, an enigmatic smile on those puckered lips.

"And listen well to *this!*" Veiento continued, pleased that he seemed to be gaining an advantage. "This is no less than an attack—albeit a clumsy one—upon the Emperor's competence to rule alone. These passages have been underscored in red. 'Those who have the power to do all are in truth the servant of all.' I am surprised at you, Julianus, I myself found these thoughts quite stale. . . . Shall I continue?"

"Please," Marcus Julianus replied. "To me it is euphonious to the ear."

"As you say. 'Even Jupiter cannot hurl a lightning bolt without first listening to the counsel of the hosts of heaven. If Jupiter does not consider his judgment sufficient, how then can a man? A ruler not subject to his people's will should relinquish his throne.' Stinking treason, I say! You believe the Emperor is wrong when he rejects our advice. It seems, Marcus Arrius Julianus, you've been caught with your hands on the silver plate."

Marcus Julianus said quietly, "Perhaps you should order the arrest of the author."

And then Veiento knew. His thoughts seemed to halt in air and hang precariously like a bird stopped in flight. What he had said could not be unsaid. The predator had dropped neatly into the trap fashioned by his prey.

"Those words," Marcus Julianus replied to the assembled Senators, "my father copied some years ago from an exercise Seneca gave to a favorite pupil, and he carried them with him always because he greatly admired their style and sentiment. The pupil was Nero. Evidently my father had a higher opinion of the young prince's style than you, my lord. A pity. If you think *his* words treasonable, of what worth is your judgment of me?"

There came the silence that follows shattered glass. Then the whole of the hall erupted to life with excited mutterings.

Loud talk nearly overwhelmed Veiento's shouted protestations: "You put it there so it would be found! I know the Emperor's student writings, and this is not among them! This court will not be mocked by a criminal!"

Nero was glaring at Veiento with the primitive fury of the wronged child.

This was a trap Marcus Julianus had set long ago, a suggestion he had written to his father when he was still Governor of Upper Germania, and both caught wind of a coming treason charge. *Nothing will keep you safer,* Marcus had written him, *than carrying around as a sort of fetish some of Nero's writings.* Julianus the Elder had not thought much of the idea at the time, but complied anyway. The essays were with Julianus' corpse when it was publicly laid out—and not closely tended—on the morning it was taken to the pyre. Marcus had rejoiced when he discovered them stolen.

Nero wrote an order and gave it to a Centurion of the Guard, who turned and signaled to Veiento to follow him. There was a stifling silence in which Veiento stared at him, unmoving, all shriveling malice, a great spider slowly contracting as its senses gradually accepted that it truly *was* caught in its own web.

With slow, deliberate movements Veiento set his tablets down. He met Marcus Julianus' eye with a look that promised: *For this you will die a miserable death and crows will pluck out your eyes, if ever the gods grant me the least chance to avenge this.*

Veiento was then taken from the dais, escorted by ten Guards. For the men of the Senate this was a fresh horror: Never had one of their number been arrested before their eyes, within these sacred walls. They speculated in tense whispers over whether Veiento would suffer exile or execution.

The Consul Messalinus then arose and called out, a tightly controlled tremor in his voice, "All who favor acquittal, go right!"

For an unnerving length of time no one moved: Nero's will was difficult to determine in this case. There was no doubt that at the day's beginning he wanted Marcus Arrius Julianus ruined. He had never liked the family, and he was in desperate need of their ancestral estates. But it was apparent now that young Julianus had taken the Emperor's passions hostage.

In Nero's eye was a vacant, vulnerable look, a private expression not meant for subordinates to see; his honor guard stood a little more stiffly than usual, looking faintly away, embarrassed for him. Marcus Julianus knew how to banish nightmares. And old Julianus had actually carried his student writings about—he took such great pleasure in knowing this that he was reluctant to dull it by destroying Julianus' son.

Then Saturninus got up and decisively moved to the right. Several of the bolder members followed, deciding to take the chance Nero wanted Julianus' life preserved. Then, more hesitantly, the rest followed. The vote was unanimous.

The Consul called out in rising crescendo, "The court judges Marcus Arrius Julianus innocent of treason."

The mob pressed about the doors of the Curia raised a joyous clamor of approval.

He has done it, Domitian thought, quietly stunned. He has turned round a charge of treason, and this does not happen on earth. Surely he called down some powerful magical protection. His very presence seems a charm against destruction.

Marcus Julianus felt a great relief like an outrushing tide. His father had his eulogy at last. But relief did not last: He saw his own circumstances were still grave.

The verdict at once began to bring about a change in Nero. Marcus could almost see the shadow pass over his face, and he guessed the sort of anxieties at work in the Emperor's mind.

Marcus knew then neither verdict would have satisfied Nero. Had the Senate found him guilty, Nero would have counted them insensitive to his needs as an artist. But the acquittal inverted Nero's suspicions; he forgot his own part in influencing the verdict and was greatly affronted, wondering: Why have they acquitted this Stoic troublemaker so readily?

Nero motioned irritably to the court scribe. He spoke rapidly while the man copied his words on a wax tablet and marked off names on the Senate roster. This required some time and many tablets. Then tablets and roster were brought to the Consul, who caught his breath when he read what was there; for a moment he could not speak.

Finally Messalinus steadied himself enough to read Nero's words.

"The verdict will stand, for I honor the Senate and I refuse to interfere with the will of this court. But you must know you have incurred my extreme displeasure in acquitting a man who has insulted me time and again, and with relish. Even at his own wedding, an occasion of joy, he stooped to accuse me of plagiarism. This trial was a test of loyalty, and you failed miserably. Let it be known that beginning on the Kalends of the month of *Junius,* the following members will be tried for treason: Gaius Saturninus . . . ," and so followed a list of over a hundred names. A quarter of the Senate would stand trial for their lives.

Angry murmurs rose to a restrained roar. The whipped hounds, Marcus saw, were turning on their master. Does Nero truly expect all of us to bare our necks to the blade? *One torch lit now might set off a conflagration. Nero, we will show you another Great Fire.* But I cannot be the one to light it. I am so close to freedom! But that is foolish. There is no freedom while Nero lives.

I must do it, even if I forfeit my life.

When the hall had fallen into fitful silence, Marcus Julianus turned to Nero. "I beg your indulgence, my lord. I was acquitted too quickly. I had a few more words to say. Might I say them?"

Nero stared at him a moment, protruding eyes opened wide in surprise. *The wretch escaped death today. Doesn't he know he is better off keeping grateful silence?* But curiosity overcame him, and he gave Marcus Julianus the barest nod.

Before he spoke there came, unaccountably, a vision of the maid of his father's records; she watched him expectantly, a gentle lioness afire with natural life. *Who are you . . . patroness of those who offer themselves as a willing sacrifice? A great soul you must have, to touch this hall over such a flight of miles.*

He addressed not the Senators, but Nero. "I do not wish to be absolved by this court. Nor do I wish, Lucius Domitius, to be absolved by you."

A sickened silence fell, full of averted eyes, held breath. He had addressed Nero by his childhood name, bare of titles and honors. "I have what I wanted—I cleared my father's name," he went on, voice gathering in strength. "Your justice I do not want. By Minerva, justice here is capricious as the weather!"

What madness is this? was the question in every eye. Why would one who had so cleverly saved himself turn round and leap onto the blade?

"You now will truly call me a traitor . . . but somewhere within, you must know *I am your only ally.* You have surrounded yourself with men who will not speak the truth. They are flattering you to a bloody end!"

Domitian watched in a fearful rapture. The words unspoken for so long were spoken; it was as if Julianus' words were a blaze of

light that illumined a cavern. All the vermin scurried out, all that
was foul was burned away.

Nero seemed numbed by a poison dart; he did not seem to be
breathing.

"Since what people write on the walls is carefully washed off
before you ever see it," Marcus Julianus went on, "here then is the
truth. The army makes sport with your name, and nothing you can
do will regain their confidence. The whole of the city reviles your
name. You should have lived by your student essay on gentleness—you've murdered too many of us, and you'll never be safe
here. Some in outlying lands love you still because they know you
only by your largesse—but of what use are they without the
army? The thing of which you wrongly accused my father is what
you yourself bring about—endangerment of the frontier. For
when competing armies do battle to the death because you refuse
to name an heir, do you think our barbarian enemies will stay on
the side and watch? No, they will come down and ravage us with
abandon. Preserve your memory, the Empire, and your own life in
the only way possible. If you've any love of good left in you, step
down before you are dragged down with a blade at your throat!
And name an heir!"

The last words rose to passionate pitch. Then there was black
silence. Nero's spirit seemed to have fled his body; he was
propped up stiffly on the throne like some wooden effigy.

Finally life came to Nero's right hand. He crooked a finger,
summoning a Centurion of the Guard. Indicating Marcus Julianus,
he whispered, "Drag this monstrosity from my sight."

Marcus Julianus did not wait for the Guards to seize him; he
inclined his head once in farewell to his colleagues, then stepped
down from the dais, walking swiftly to the door, a stride ahead of
the Praetorians.

Nero cried hoarsely after him, "You'll have all eternity to bore
the hosts of Hades with your noxious moral lectures! Marcus
Arrius Julianus, I condemn you to the dogs! You'll make an
insulting meal for my faithful Molossians, but make a meal you
shall! *To the dogs. . . . Do you hear me, fiend?*"

Marcus fought for that brilliant calm he had felt fleetingly at the
trial's beginning—but it was gone, driven off by the memory of
Isodorus' pitifully thin torso sinking beneath a blur of whipping
gray bodies and blood-flecked fur.

In his wake the Senators exchanged wondering looks as if
mildly surprised they still lived. Marcus knew they trembled on

the brink of freedom—the long-beaten beast had spied the unlatched gate.

In the visitors' gallery Domitian rose to his feet, watching Marcus Julianus until he could see him no more, cursing at the men and women about him who jostled him and blocked his view. He was seized with a kind of wild heartache, a sharp, filial love. All the jealousy he felt earlier was burned away by the thought of the hideous death his friend faced.

By all the gods, that man must live! he thought. There is not another like him alive in these times. I will have great need of him when I rule.

Never will I do what Nero has done, swimming in delusion until the pond is drained and I'm left there to die, stupid and gasping. I will not have a flock of flatterers to blur my sight till I am blind as he is. Men who tell the truth to a ruler are worth the provinces of Egypt and Asia together.

News of the arrest of Marcus Julianus set the mob in dangerous motion; they began to range through the city, hurling bricks, breaking up shops. Fearing the crowds might free Julianus on his way to the Mamertine Prison, Nero hastily wrote another order, commanding eighty of the Guards stationed before the Curia to accompany the prisoner.

But only twenty obeyed him.

It was deliberate defiance. From this time forward they would take orders from their Prefect, not from Nero.

Nero knew then how dire his circumstances were.

But he ordered the Consul to continue on with the day's business, desperate to affect an air of unconcern. Before the day was done, the crowd had begun a dirgelike chant, "*Die, tyrant, die,*" and Nero began to feel all the demons of the sulfurous depths were ringed about him, ready to pull him down. Finally he called for his litter so he could be borne back to the safety of his Golden House.

All was confusion as Guards rushed to close the bronze doors before the mob streamed in. Domitian watched with terror laden with contempt as Nero, all dignity gone, scuttled backward down the short flight of steps leading to his throne, shifting his bulk with a sort of manic agility. A soldier of the Guard caught and steadied him or he would have fallen. A plain litter was brought up, and Nero swiftly disappeared within, ordering the bearers to take him out through his private door.

Marcus Julianus was brought to the lowest cells of the Mamertine Prison, a pit dug out of stone and earth with water puddled on its floor. Hourly he awaited the footfall of the executioner, making desperate guesses as to what passed above. Were enough of the Guard still loyal that Nero could perpetrate one more massacre and maintain his seat? Or had the world cracked open? If it had, he did not credit himself overmuch; he had opened a sluice-gate that would have burst open on its own shortly thereafter.

The throng about the Curia hourly grew more hostile; the Senators passed a desperate sleepless night imprisoned in the Senate House. The next day was ill-omened on the calendar, and they dared conduct no business. The Guard saw them supplied with food. On the third day, dazed by lack of sleep, they began a new session. The augur called it a day of great good omen. In the first hour they seized their freedom: They passed a resolution declaring Nero an Enemy of the People. This meant they condemned him to punishment "in the ancient manner": The victim was stripped naked, his head thrust into a wooden fork, and he was flogged to death with iron rods.

Nero retreated to his audience room and passed three days in frantic indecisiveness, issuing terrifying edicts, then canceling them; he was stunned at how quickly his loyal protectors were fleeing his side. He ordered Locusta, his poisoner, to prepare him a mixture that worked swiftly, and carried it about with him in a golden box. Then he hatched a vague plan to flee somewhere beyond the borders of the Empire, Parthia perhaps, where he might live as a private citizen and support himself by acting and singing. Desperately he tried to persuade some of the officers of the Guard to escape with him, but the Guard shunned him. That night he retired to his bedchamber with a dozen concubines, leaving a strong guard outside the door. When he awakened the next morning, his concubines, chamberlains and valets had fled in the night, and many costly things were missing, including his golden box of poison.

Nero then sent a frantic message to the Senate, promising to win back their love by singing so beautifully for them that they would understand how exquisitely he suffered and forgive him.

When the report was brought to him that the Senate had declared him an Enemy of the People, Nero panicked, got a horse and fled the Palace, attended only by his eunuch-bride Sporus and a single scribe; the three, disguised in rags, took a pathless route to the villa of Phaon, one of Nero's wealthy freedmen, four miles from the city walls. The scribe later reported Nero wept along the way, repeatedly exclaiming, "How ugly and vulgar my life has become!" At dawn Nero was betrayed by a member of Phaon's household, and when he heard the clatter of hooves in the carriageway, he knew it was a troop of cavalry sent by the Senate to carry out the grisly sentence.

He took a dagger in his hands, meaning to plunge it into his throat. But his courage failed; the terrified scribe was forced to seize the Emperor's hand and guide the blade. The deed was done; Nero's blood ran out. A cavalry officer rushed in to find Nero dying. His final words, *"What a great artist the world loses by my death,"* were dutifully recorded by the scribe and passed on to the historians.

CHAPTER XII

Marcus Julianus lay still in abyssal darkness, awaiting the return of the soldiers, the binding of hands, the short journey to the arena, the dogs.

In a delirium of fear he saw Isodorus beckoning with a bloody hand. *"How dare you expect more than this?"* came the familiar caustic voice. *"You completed the cycle of life: you tracked knowledge until you knew too much, you erupted with the truth, now you die for it. You did well! Come! I did not feel the tearing teeth."*

The torch borne by the slave who brought the gruel was his sun; when the slave left, day was gone. He tried to mark time but could not, and was surprised at how disconcerting this was; he felt cut from the moorings of earth, left to settle into subterranean night. He was a worm cursed with intelligence and memory, a shade in Tartarus craving rebirth, lusting to feel again the beat of blood in the body, of rain on the face. Often he dreamed of fire: The mind needs light, he realized, and works to create it where it is not.

When after numberless servings of gruel and muddy water still no executioner came, he began to suspect some imperial caprice saved his life—or perhaps Nero himself had died.

But he was given no news of what passed above. Dark and silence gradually began to tug at all he believed to be true, stripping away skin, leaving him a naked ghost in blackness, ready to believe even daily fear and desperate longing were but clothing that could be shed. Nothing of the world any longer made sense: the mask of courage all were expected to wear, the passion to be remembered, to appear dignified, to pass on a name. Once he dreamed he was Dionysus, leading bands of revelers away from the cities, turning kingdoms upside down, loosing slaves, turning water to wine. Seasons, years, centuries wheeled by—or it might have been a month—only his untrimmed growth of hair and beard kept him, if vaguely, to a true assessment of time. When he judged he must resemble a wild man of the forest, he guessed: *Nine months. A year.*

Once when he was taken to a drier cell and given rank mutton, lentils and vinegar water along with the gruel, he wondered if this might be some small indicator of vast political upheaval above— civil war, perhaps, with a powerful contender friendly to himself gaining gradual sway?

After a span of time like the distance between stars, there came a day when he heard a voice softly calling his name, becoming stronger, then fainter, as whoever it was worked his way through the warren of earthen tunnels.

"He's dead, I say, as I told you yesterday and the day before. He's dead, dead."

Now the voice was close; lantern light teased his sight, appearing faintly, flashing away.

"Here." He could speak no louder than a dry whisper. "I am here." Footsteps stopped near the iron-barred door; slowly it was pulled open, and the lantern was thrust into his face.

"It's him, it's truly him!"

"Ha, there's gifts in this for all of us, and our lord will be grateful."

Behind them came a voice of more authority, "Be thankful if you're not flogged to the bone for losing him!"

The light seared his eyes. Three prison slaves laboriously lifted him to his feet. Behind them was Marcellus, a Centurion of the Guard who was known to him; from the shocked pity in the young Guard's face Marcus Julianus read his own condition.

"Marcus Arrius Julianus, hail," Marcellus greeted him, youthful enthusiasm barely contained behind a brisk, disciplined demeanor. "I am here to tell you—you were falsely imprisoned by Nero. The property confiscated from your family will be returned to you, and you are hereby restored to your former rank—"

"*Slowly!*" he whispered. "How long have I—"

"Eighteen months." Marcellus leaned closer. "It's not the same world up there, I warn you. We've had a war from which we'll never recover. The Temple of Jupiter was razed. There is lamenting all over the world—"

"Civil war."

"Yes, and with it, horrors beyond any the world has seen. The legions soaked the ground with the blood of brothers. You spoke true prophecy at your trial. The northern savages did take swift advantage. They swept down and turned Gaul into a slaughter-house. The Empire was nearly lost."

A crude litter of the sort they used for carrying out corpses was brought up for him. He waved it off; he would attempt to walk. He began moving forward with struggling steps, leaning heavily on one of the prison slaves, sorely conscious of his filthiness and the fleas.

"What became of Nero?"

"Long dead," came the sturdy voice in the dark behind him. "In one year we suffered through three emperors—two were justly murdered, and one committed suicide. None were of a nature to let a man of your . . . notorious outspokenness go free."

"What of my family—my aunt and her children. Have you news of them?"

"They all fare well, and your wife"—Marcellus broke off suddenly, covering embarrassment by fidgeting with the lock on the door leading into the prison's main chamber; then he finished lamely—"she is also well."

"But I was condemned. *Why do I still live?*"

"The tale goes, two times Nero ordered a stay, then once more ordered your death. We know soldiers were dispatched to your house to look for those formulae for quelling night-terrors. Most likely it was *that* bit of clever nonsense that saved you."

Marcus Julianus stepped first into the chamber; the draft of air that touched him, though fetid, was a welcome breath of life. He turned round and seized Marcellus by the shoulders.

"But then, *who rules?*"

"Our lord Vespasian," Marcellus replied with a pride that indicated to Marcus this outcome was universally loved, "aided by his sons, Titus and Domitian."

Domitian. So, old friend, you got your wish.

It is an awesome thing to learn that one with whom you sported, dined and often fought has been elevated among the gods.

Why do I hear it with dread, like the first drop on the ship's bow that heralds the cataclysmic storm at sea? Domitian. It is not as if Nero were to be resurrected.

I am not fair to him; he has showed me only kindness. I worry without need. And anyhow his father will have long life, and there is Titus, his gentle-tempered elder brother, with first claim to the throne. Domitian still may never rule.

Domitian's greeting when they reunited was long and warm, but Marcus Julianus saw his young friend had taken quite a few steps already up the path to Olympus. They met in the physicians' rooms of the old Augustan Palace—Domitian had insisted Marcus Julianus be taken here to be attended by the imperial physicians while he recovered. Domitian came garbed in a purple-bordered toga more suited for greeting a foreign ambassador than an old friend, drenched in Oriental perfumes that would have cost him his yearly allowance as a student. There was a shuttered look about his eyes, a studied gravity to his movements. Close at his side were white-liveried servants bearing tablets and writing implements, in case the young prince was seized with some resonant thought for the ages that he wished to commit to writing.

Marcus Julianus inquired almost at once, "How did Nero punish Veiento?"

"Exile."

"Nemesis! He'll find his way back. Like any viper he'll sleep out the cold—but the earth will warm for him one day, I know it."

"Don't fret over it, he'll expire of boredom first. That pesthole on the Black Sea they packed him off to hasn't a book or a theater or a beautifully bred boy within a thousand miles. Unfortunately you can count on the fact that he won't freeze to death—the wretched village exports *hides*—it's their only industry." Domitian added with obvious relish, "You know, Veiento never stopped calling down a death curse on your name as his wagons rolled out of the city. You've a dangerous enemy there. Enjoy it, old friend! You cannot be a great man without great enemies!"

Later in the meeting Domitian announced with a conspiratorial smile, "I spoke for you for a Treasury post."

"I am inexpressibly grateful, *but I do not want it.* I've my father's works on the northern tribes to complete, and I mean to found an academy of philosophy and natural sciences, one open to all classes."

"If the gods meant for the humble laboring classes to be scholars, they would have given them healthy *purses* instead of strapping bodies! So, you're snubbing us! I tell you, old friend, I'm not pleased with this willful, unmanageable side of you." He dropped his voice. "Come now. My father *needs* you. You know this will be seen as a withdrawal of support from my family's cause—"

"Utter nonsense. My alliances are better known about the city than the latest tales about Junilla."

"A telling point, but, curses on you, *I* made certain you got back all you lost in the war—you're a bit of an ingrate, don't you think?" Domitian smiled pleasantly, but there was iron beneath.

"My apologies but my answer must be *no*—that is, if I have a right to say no."

"Well, *that* hurt. Your victory then—for *now*. By the way"—he watched Marcus Julianus' face with great attention—"those poisoned darts you aimed at Nero at your trial made you quite the hero among the Guard."

Marcus was swiftly alerted to danger. There was awe in Domitian's statement, but also a strong undercurrent of complaint.

"That was certainly not my purpose," he said carefully, knowing as he spoke that this made no difference to Domitian. Purpose or no, he had been given something the young prince wanted for himself. That small distance between them was measurably widened; he knew for certain now it would never be closed.

The vilest part of his return to his former life was the task of reclaiming his house from Junilla.

By common report Junilla enjoyed herself during the war. She sold off the house's furnishings piece by piece to pay for nightly banquets that ended at dawn, counting the night a failure if her guests returned home in their own clothes. Fashionable young men fought for invitations to these frolics; it was said they were fed, oiled and massaged by young slaves naked but for satyr-masks, and that neither girl nor boy nor beast on the premises was safe from debauchery. Her fountains ran red with wine while the streets of the city ran with blood. Gossip reported she purchased a troupe of male Egyptian dancers solely to sate her appetites, and that she accompanied the city prostitutes when they were admitted to the gladiatorial schools, painting her face so she would not be recognized, for she had developed a passion for heavy-armed Samnite swordfighters.

The banquets ceased abruptly when she learned that Marcus Arrius Julianus was alive.

He found her in the warm room of the great-house's baths, stretched out drowsily in the steam as she submitted to the ministrations of her aged Greek masseuse. She was naked but for an emerald necklace. The costly bauble was the gift of an octogenarian Senator who had tried strenuously to marry her, worn to remind Julianus that she was desired by powerful men. She focused on him through hazed slits, as though unwilling to expend the effort required to fully open her eyes. But he was not fooled; he sensed her bracing to fight.

"Junilla! I trust you fare well." He kept a formal distance between them; to come closer, he knew, would be to put power into her hands, and he did not want to feel again that ambivalent desire muddied with futile pity. She smiled languidly, feeling secure in her place. A year of maturing had only heightened the startling perfection of that face.

She said silkily, "Ah, you are still beautiful, my husband, though too thin. Come close"—she gestured delicately—"I don't have lice."

He stayed where he was. She shrugged as if it were no matter, then eased her eyes shut as if even using her sight cost her too much effort. "I trust you've not listened to the ugly stories spread about by those who are jealous of me. You know, I scarcely slept while you were imprisoned—"

"Yes, so I have heard," he said quietly. "Save those loving words for more credulous ears." In spite of the fact that her whole nature caused him to shudder, that opulently cushioned body was undermining him—she was all animal's underbelly, tender and exposed, begging protection, all rosy flesh glistening from sweat and steam. He had to sharply remind himself it was illusion—let any who try and protect her beware.

He tossed her the silken tunica that lay folded next to her.

"Arise and dress," he said firmly. "There is no reason for this absurd marriage to continue for another day. We must divorce."

Her eyes flashed open. "Surely you are too *sophisticated* to believe those lies!"

"I fear your weapons have fallen behind the times," he said without rancor, realizing one benefit of his ordeal was that he had shed the last of a lingering concern that despite any amount of education, he would never be sophisticated enough for this world. "I do not know how much of the tales are true, and it is not at issue. My procurator has prepared the documents; you shall be richly provided for."

Her look suddenly became soft, diffuse. She gave an elaborate cat-stretch that seemed to call every muscle of her body into play, then sat up with shifting, undulating movements as if she were underwater, making certain he had a chance to look long at her abundant breasts before she let the masseuse help her wriggle into a tunica. It hardly concealed her; a flush of pink was visible where her breasts strained against the thin cloth. Slowly she ran her tongue over her lower lip as if she licked honey from it, then pulled free one of her silver hairpins so that coiled locks of black hair sprang free and fell to her shoulders. She was a sleek and lovely Medusa.

"You cannot mean this," she said, shaking her head with a teasing sulkiness that also mocked him. "Not *now*."

"Now?"

Those eyes were two beautiful wounds. "I . . . I just got you back."

"You mean, you just learned you have a husband who not only is alive but—great good fortune!—very much in favor with the Emperor's son. You see me not at all. You see a poor investment that has turned round and become a good one. You see high office and honors and how the city will envy you. When I was *not* in favor, you tried to murder me—*that* is what your devotion is worth."

She drew back a little, eyes delicately registering affront.

"So now you accuse me of attempted murder! Perhaps you would like to accuse me before Domitian."

"I do not care to see what you can manage to get Domitian to believe. I know the truth," he countered sharply, then turned away, silent a moment before he went on in weary exasperation, "Junilla, I did not come here to judge you, that is for the gods. I want only to be quit of you and continue my life. That wedding was a mockery forced on us both—"

"Nero gave you to me. Nero gave me this house. *It is mine and you shall not thieve it from me!*"

"Madness! Junilla, there is no need to see this as a great blow to your pride. This is not an act of war, and I do not despise you. I intend to provide you with a fine house of your own and all the servants you need. You shall want for nothing. And never mind that under the circumstances the law allows me to keep the whole of your dowry—I shall return to you the whole of it."

"The truth is you think yourself too good for me, *Endymion*, you rat that wallowed in slime!" His generosity in the matter of the dowry was puzzling; not knowing what to make of it, she read it as weakness, and this redoubled her contempt for him. "*You* presume to put *me* aside? Never! Go back to the festering sink you crawled out of! Go tread clothes in a vat of piss and drown in it!"

"I will listen to no more of this! You will be out in three days." He swiftly turned about to go.

"You are in love with the Emperor's concubine, Caenis—that hag that keeps the civil accounts and robs people. You've had her many times, don't deny it! Put me aside, and you can be certain everyone at the Palace learns of it."

"Threaten all you want if it pleases you. Diocles will oversee the organizing of your possessions."

"Diocles is gone."

"*What?*" he whispered, turning round and slowly coming back until he stood over her. "*What are you saying?*"

"Yes!" she whispered, a flare of triumph in her eye. "He was worth more than I got for him but—" She was stopped abruptly by the look in his face—she saw she was pouring pitch on a fire already hotly blazing. This was a part of his nature she had not seen—the avenging passion in those eyes was an elemental force not to be opposed. Swiftly she revised the opinion that his returning the whole of the dowry signified weakness. She had no notion *what* it signified, other than extreme eccentricity.

"Where is he? Tell me at once!" he said quietly.

In that voice she sensed power of unknown strength held in abeyance, and slowly she arose, edging away from him. A part of her rejoiced that she had hurt him, but she had erred in determining the dose—it had somehow reached dangerous levels. This man was incomprehensible to her. He behaved as if she had murdered his son.

"Only at Aurelia's. How can you be so upset about a servant? Really." Unconsciously she protectively pulled a drying cloth about her to conceal her breasts. His great contempt roused in her a normally dormant loathing of her body.

"You will leave *now*. Or I will have you forcibly removed." His voice, though still soft, had the finality of the executioner's stroke.

To Junilla it seemed a hero of ancient tales took possession of him then. Now that Marcus seemed so thoroughly to detest her, love for him washed over her in a flood. It was a poisoned love that festered and burned, but love enough to cause her to stand mute and still, transfixed by him as she saw him anew. He was

Hector, he was Achilles, and she, a trembling prize of war awaiting his will.

"I love you. Truly, and desperately. *Monster!*"

She flung herself at him. He caught her and held her fast as she kicked and bit, and tried to pummel him with her fists; all the while he called out loudly for her litter. When it arrived, she abruptly ceased struggling, though still simmering with her need to have and hurt; she was amazed herself at how completely her feelings for him had been turned about. She despised him still, but now for his cruelty in denying himself to her. There he stood, so beautiful in his fine fury, so maddeningly independent of her that she could not bear it. She must wound what she could not have, to leave her mark of proprietorship upon him for others to see.

"Marcus, my husband," she said as she settled herself in the litter, her voice now coquettish and sweet. "My first act after this outrage will be to see Veiento recalled from exile. And when he returns, he will kill you."

"As you wish," he said with cool indifference. "Your effects will be sent after you tomorrow." But within he felt a small twist of fear. Had Junilla *that* much influence? She had. With Domitian she had a sort of incestuous father-daughter relationship, and though Domitian criticized her, when actually in her presence he could deny her nothing.

Smoothly the bearers lifted her aloft. Her whole mind was in ferment. Her soul was divine; had not Nero assured her of it? And this house was her palace, as the Golden House had been Nero's. Marcus would be punished horribly for this. Her divinity demanded it. She would have him and chastise him. *He wins this bout, but there will be others, yes, many others.*

She drew back the litter's silken curtains and leaned out, eyes innocently wide. "Go and look at your library, Marcus. It was a cold spring and I was short of money. I hope you don't mind too much—I burned the last of those useless books for fuel."

Junilla left him in peace for a time, and there was no sign of ill on the wind until the spring of the third year of Vespasian's reign, when an urgent summons came from the Emperor, commanding Marcus Julianus to come to a private audience. Vespasian's purpose was mysterious; as Marcus Julianus readied himself, he swiftly considered what this might be about.

Had Veiento worked some mischief against him? For Veiento had indeed been recalled from exile, in the previous autumn. On the day he returned, Marcus Julianus encountered Junilla in the street as she was bound for her seaside villa with an entourage that halted foot traffic for an hour; she leaned from her litter and gave him a knowing nod and a smug smile, then drew a hand across her throat, to let him know Veiento's recall was her doing.

Or was this to be some sort of imperial reprimand? For he had stood for no offices in the Senate and turned down every post offered to him; the organization of his Academy had become the whole occupation of his spirit. Or perhaps Vespasian merely meant to offer condolences for the death of his wife. After putting Junilla aside, Marcus Julianus had married again, knowing his father's ghost wanted children and immortality. He lived with Claudia Valeria for one year—a union marked with kindness and haunting sadness but not much passion. She died in childbed, their infant girl soon after, and it was rumored Junilla had murdered Claudia Valeria by sending a midwife who tended her with cloths taken from the corpse wrappings of fever victims. But by that time all manner of evil things were said of Junilla, and he did not credit half of them.

The mystery of the summons intensified when the Chief Palace Chamberlain conducted him not to the regular audience chamber but to a humble workroom adjacent to the rooms of the imperial architect-engineers, where the Emperor spent much time overseeing the numerous building projects he initiated. The room was windowless, unpainted and small, furnished with rough benches and a great cluttered worktable covered over with inkpots, rules, architectural plans and maps.

For long moments after Marcus Arrius Julianus was announced, the Emperor Vespasian was oblivious to him, lost in a plan and elevation drawing set apart from the rest, making notations, frowning deeply, comparing it to a cost report. The Emperor was humbly attired in a tunic of rough, undyed wool; he had the look of the sturdy peasant he proudly proclaimed he was. His face had a pleasantly battered look; it was like some rough model in clay with the refinements not yet smoothed in. Those hands, bare of rings, were farmer's hands that might have fertile earth still clinging to them. He was hardy and stubborn as the roots of an old oak, but it was a good-natured stubbornness. For a ruler he was remarkably slow to take offense: Once as he was carried through a crowd, a barefoot philosopher shouted obscenities at him that might have made a mule driver blush, and Vespasian's only punishment was to shout worse obscenities back.

"Julianus. Good!" It was a voice that held the promise of humor even in his soberest moments. Marcus Julianus bowed low and greeted him with all his titles, while Vespasian nodded quickly as if he did not care what his titles were, and resumed studying the plan while motioning for Marcus Julianus to come close.

"I'm forced to divulge to you a family matter of a rather humiliating nature," Vespasian announced jovially, "so before I spill my tawdry family secret and you think less of me, first come look at my masterwork! 'He could not control his sons,' I hear the talebearers prattling, 'but he *could* build for the ages.'"

Marcus Julianus smiled amicably as he obeyed, and was immediately caught up in the architects' rendering before him, deciphering with trained skill the delicate multicolored webbing of lines, swiftly decoding the triangles that represented staircases, the mazes of vaulted passageways, the great clear space upon which this ordered universe of lines converged—an elliptical arena. He knew at once what it was: Vespasian's most beloved project, one he was obsessed with seeing completed before his death—the city's first permanent stone amphitheater. Construction had already begun on the site where Nero had created a private lake for his pleasure barges. The amphitheater would eventually be called the Colosseum, after the colossal image of Nero left standing nearby after the new rulers leveled Nero's sprawling Golden House. Marcus Julianus was seized with a disturbing vision of how it would look when complete: a brooding, malign mass, determinedly eternal—and he shuddered as if at the not-too-distant cry of a wolf. Vespasian's most loved child would swallow nations whole, gulp down rivers of human blood. For a moment quick as the burst of a freshly lit flame, he had the sense of being the one sighted man in a city of the blind.

For certain this thing cast some baleful shadow over the future.

"My palace for the people!" the Emperor said with the mellow smile of a parent pleased with his progeny. "But I did not call you here to boast of this!" He signaled for his Egyptian secretary to depart so they would be left in privacy.

"I called you here to aid me in staving off catastrophe—the fruit of Domitian's latest spree of high-spirited villainy, which, Hades take that young hellion, will be his *last*." Vespasian reached among the clutter of military dispatches on an adjacent worktable and smoothed out a parchment map depicting the lands of Upper Germania and northern Gaul. Then he added with a casualness that made the words the more startling: "I have removed Domitian from public life."

Marcus Julianus carefully refrained from registering approval; to do so seemed a breach of manners, and he had no reason to give offense to this man.

"Ah, polite silence is what *I* get!" Vespasian remarked, smiling. "A signal honor, coming from the Bane of Rulers himself, who had the temerity to hang Nero by his heels in front of the whole Senate. By the way, you alone outside the family know of this, and I expect my confidences strictly kept."

"Of course."

"There's no need for the common populace to know of this. One day Domitian must rule, and Minerva knows it becomes daily more difficult not to have him made into a laughingstock. You are the most knowledgeable man living concerning the ways and customs of the savage Germanic tribes. I need counsel on ways to blunt the effects of this latest act of mischief on Domitian's part."

"He's overstepped himself in the north."

"To put it gently."

Marcus Julianus knew Domitian had been using his newly acquired influence in civil and military matters to provoke the Chattians across the frontier, using threats and bribes to encourage the Governors posted in Germania to launch punitive attacks against native villages, in order to incite the barbarians into retaliation so that a major campaign against them would seem necessary—a campaign Domitian intended to lead himself. For Domitian was intensely—murderously, some said—jealous of the attention given his elder brother, Titus, after his victory in the Jewish war.

"We know these five Chattian villages were razed, and all their inhabitants slaughtered like sheep . . . here, right in a line, northwest of the Taunus Mount. We cannot afford a *skirmish*, mind you, much less to finish what my fool son started, thanks to those extortionists at the marble quarries," Vespasian went on with a brief nod toward the elevation drawing of the Colosseum, the greatest drain on the imperial treasury at the moment. Marcus Julianus thought it ironic that this theater of blood was actually, for a time at least, preventing violence. *That* will not last, he mused; once it's built and paid for, a war will be needed in order to provide victims.

". . . and I know of no better man to advise me on ways of disarming these savages through clever diplomacy."

"I guarantee nothing," Marcus Julianus replied quietly. "To these people, blood vengeance is the most sacred of all rites. But there *are* measures that could be taken that would weaken or remove centers of influence, and perhaps undermine their hostility."

"Excellent!" The Emperor struck a bell to summon a scribe to take down Julianus' replies; then he began asking swift, precise questions about tribal alliances, the methods of supply used by the barbarian armies, the shifting relative importance of various chiefs. When once he paused to order water and wine, Marcus Julianus smiled at the dented, tarnished silver wine cups that were brought—they came no doubt from Vespasian's rural family estate. Marcus Julianus often entirely forgot he advised an emperor, so familiar and forthright in speech, so devoid of all pompousness, was this man; once a map fell to the floor, and moving more swiftly than the scribe, Vespasian actually retrieved it himself.

They talked on, and as the hours passed, Marcus Julianus found he disliked this task more and more—from his long study of them the Chattians had acquired a share of divine essence, even a shadowy, disarming face—that of the gallant maid of his father's records; he began to feel like an accomplice in some obscure betrayal. "Here then is my final determination," he was saying as ruddy late-afternoon light ebbed from the room. "I would begin by paying reparation money directly to their elders, to be distributed among the kinspeople of the families Domitian caused to be slaughtered in the villages—"

"Why do you not just take all the funds I fought so hard to raise and dump them in the Tiber!"

"You scoff, but this is not so costly as war. There is a better than even chance they will accept this wergild for the deaths of clan members and forgo blood vengeance. In addition, I would return the Chattian hostages we're holding."

"We have hostages?"

"Yes, they're at the fortress of Argentoratum. My father long ago secured the three elder daughters of Baldemar's sister, as well as the infant nieces of two lesser chiefs."

"It seems a curious choice of hostages."

"That is the way to get the firmest hold on these people—they calculate lineage through the female line. My father's purpose was to instigate small land wars through removing rightful heirs. And when that is done, I would make a new pact with Baldemar: The

Rhine is only to be crossed at points where Roman troops are present, and our signal towers will extend no farther into the territory of the Wetterau. Halt the policy of forcing their young men into the army, and *make certain this is enforced*. Lastly, I would send a force to the sanctuary on the River Lippe—this is deep within hostile territory, I would dispatch no fewer than two legions—and have them seize that tower-dwelling prophetess called the Veleda and bring her as hostage to Rome. By this, you might avoid war."

"Well enough then . . . but never mind the pact with Baldemar. We've other plans for *him*," Vespasian said meditatively, and Marcus Julianus at first did not pay these words much mind. So many had tried and failed to entrap Baldemar that he dismissed this as mere wishful thinking. "You truly think the removal of this Veleda creature will have such marvelous effect?"

"Yes—to the tribes she is a living goddess. She has for years been telling them the lands of Gaul are theirs by divine right, and exhorting them to follow Baldemar. Unfortunately, 'Veleda' is not her name but a title of her holy office, a word related to the Gaulish word meaning 'to see.' She is the One Who Sees the true nature of material life—but I won't bother you with that. What I mean to say is that when she is taken, a new candidate will at once be chosen to fill her place."

"A risk worth taking—the replacement might not be so charismatic. And once spring is come and Baldemar is gone—"

"Begging your pardon, but I cannot help but question your easy certainty that a man my father could not catch in ten years will suddenly fall *now* into one of our traps."

"Ah, I neglected to tell you—a traitor has come forward, a man Baldemar ill-used in the past, apparently. He claims he is the son of Wido—a claim made by many—and he has some savage name I cannot pronounce. Odb-Od something—"

"Odberht, and he *is* truly Wido's son. And we never had reports of his death." Marcus Julianus felt a touch of cold. The Emperor speaks truthfully, he thought—this time *is* different; in days past, no one had been willing to betray Baldemar openly.

"Good, then," Vespasian continued. "Doubtless you know the tale your father first reported that Baldemar goes unarmed and alone each year to a hidden grove to make his own sacrifice during their great drunken spring orgy called"—he held a military report close to the lamp and squinted—"Ast . . . Est . . ."

"*Astura,* some of the tribes call it—others, *Eostre* or *Eastre*. It's the native dawn festival, the holiest day of their year, oddly similar in some respects to our own rites of Hilaria. My father despaired of ever discovering its location."

"Well, this son of Wido learned of it somehow and made haste to the fortress at Mogontiacum to tell our new Governor there. Baldemar will not be alone when he sacrifices this year—a cohort of cavalry will celebrate with him!"

Why does this so transfix me with sadness? Marcus Julianus wondered then. Has this amulet undermined me, infusing me with their blood and breath?

"I do not like this," Marcus Julianus said suddenly, with more forcefulness than he intended. "Baldemar is a good and fair enemy who always kept to his treaties, who returned many prisoners unharmed, and who fought only to keep his people's lands. He deserves a nobler end than to be dragged off to die slowly in captivity."

For an unsettling moment the Emperor imagined his own soul was being weighed before the gods. Something in Julianus' cold, clear eyes stripped away every trapping of society; they were not Emperor and subject but simply two men equal before the Fates in every way but one: Julianus had the more impassioned will. "This is a foul plan, hateful to Nemesis, and utterly beneath our dignity," Marcus Julianus said with soft finality. "Undo this, and let him live on in freedom."

Marcus Julianus noticed the jolt of affront in the Emperor's eyes, and it broke the spell.

I am a reckless fool. But Endymion will be silenced when he is laid out on the pyre.

For a long uncomfortable moment Vespasian met his eye in a sort of smoking silence; then the Emperor broke suddenly into an affable grin, deciding to treat this as good-natured contentiousness. "If I could afford it, I *would* grant him death in battle," he said at last, but the words were spoken with too much deliberation, as if to say, "I will let you take such liberties just this once."

Slowly Vespasian poured wine, then water into the battered silver cup, then continued on.

"There is another matter, something more than odd, that I omitted to mention before." The Emperor seemed to have entirely forgotten the brief moment of tension. "This month's report from the fortress at Vetera describes a band of Chattian savages, an offshoot of Baldemar's Companions, led by a *ganna*—some sort of holy woman—but unlike most of these prophetesses, this one carries arms. They have been burning every fort and signal tower along the River Main—the forts do not last a season. Even in winter they strike. What is particularly disturbing is that they seized three small catapults, the ones called scorpions. And we have not recovered them from the holy groves."

"Then they must search further. What you imply is unthinkable. Our weapons are tainted and unholy to them. Never would they actually employ them in battle."

"We've also evidence from spies that a captured legionary soldier has turned the worst sort of traitor and is versing them in our tactics and weaponry. What is to stop this wretch from instructing them in the use of those catapults?"

"They've changed their very nature, then . . . or this *ganna* is a singular madwoman."

"As you've noted before, their fanaticism is greater, not less, when led by a woman—and this one's extraordinarily effective because the men of the Fourteenth take her for a witch. This dispatch claims the men will not enter a part of the forest where they think she's likely been. They say she has the power to transform herself at will to a raven, a doe. . . ."

This jolted him to attention. *A raven, a doe?* She must be the very maid he read of in his father's records, whose name brought to mind the tangle of the wild vine. *Auriane.* She still lived.

Who *are* you, wild and brazen spirit not even fearful of your own gods? How came you to have the mettle to take up our weapons against us when none of your people have ever done so?

He realized then he was not going to reveal that this was Baldemar's daughter, that he was withholding information from the Emperor in order to protect her.

Have I taken leave of my senses? That is treason.

"My advice is to leave the matter strictly alone," he replied emphatically. "The 'scorpions,' doubtless, have been sunk into the deepest bog as an offering to their god Wodan. We'll never recover them. And the maid's power resides in her people's grief—once these other measures are carried out, it will cool her fire."

"Well enough then, all this gives us some place to begin." Vespasian then added in an offhand tone that obviously masked a grave concern: "Oh, yes, there is *one* last little matter, before I dismiss you." He pulled a bookroll from a wall niche.

"*This* was published under your name."

Marcus Julianus took the bookroll by its gilded *umbilicus*, saw the imprint of Tryphon's bookshop on its parchment label and himself listed as author, then unrolled it just enough to read its opening columns. It was a clumsily vicious, mocking diatribe against the imperial government that mentioned Vespasian by name.

"I did not write this, nor did anyone under my instruction, I swear to you by my father's ghost. Were I to attack you, which I would not, for truly I hold you the wisest ruler since the god Augustus, I would not do it with such . . . crudeness and lack of all common wit." He felt a sickness within.

This was no less than an attempt at murder.

Veiento. This is his work. His vengeance has begun already.

"Such is your nature, Julianus, that I believe you," Vespasian replied. "You've got a determined enemy out there. I would watch him closely."

GERMANIA

CHAPTER XIII

In these times no one remembered peace.

The Emperor Vespasian's offer of payment in gold was brought by Roman emissaries from the fortress at Mogontiacum to the Assembly of the New Moon on a bitterly cold night in early spring. The people gathered at the Assembly were bewildered by this unaccustomed show of remorsefulness. Some seemed inclined to accept the wergild, among them Geisar—for the Roman Governor meant to hand the moneys over to him for distribution among the people, which would strengthen the First Priest's power over the chiefs and give him an opportunity to hold back a portion of the gold for himself.

But for most, anger was not assuaged. Many had seen the blackened dead of the five villages, where babes in arms and armed warriors were slaughtered alike. And the Roman emissaries, even as they made this concession, managed to sound like princes chastising subjects. When Baldemar rose to answer the Roman delegation, the people began to cheer him before he spoke.

As so often before, his words breathed one soul into them. "Nidings and knaves take gold in payment for their dead!" came his proud cry in sonorous voice. "Who among you does not know it is the highest dishonor to carry a slain kinsman in your pocket? Go back to your master, Roman slaves, and tell him we refuse. *We* will determine the price—and it will not be in the coin of your slave-run mines—but in the coin of your blood!"

The last words hung in every mind season after season, like some immortal tone struck on a god-forged bell; they outlived the man who spoke them. The Roman emissaries barely escaped with their lives that night. The battle chieftains set their Companions even at peaceful settlements now, and nightly in the raiding months Chattian warriors swarmed into Roman-held Gaul.

It was the still time just before dawn, on the first day of the waxing of the Fourth Moon. Auriane shivered in the dark. The waters of the Rhine were harshly cold at night; the bear's fat she and her fellow tribesmen smeared over their bodies before they ferried themselves across the river on their shields kept them alive, but did not keep them warm. Her wet leather tunic was like ice pressed to her flesh.

There came to her the familiar dark excitement at being on the wrong side of the Rhine. The second of the nightly Roman naval patrols passed upstream just before they set out; the third was not due until well past dawn. They secured on the bank the two coracles they had brought for transporting the spoil, and laid down their sodden shields. Then Auriane and the thirty young warriors—all drawn from Baldemar's Companions—crept up the bank and paused at the edge of a vineyard. Before them was the villa of the slave dealer Feronius, notorious among all the tribes, a wealthy Gallo-Roman trader who dealt in children.

As the sky lightened to iron gray, the evil place could dimly be seen—a huddled group of bleached-white buildings with their complex jumble of many-leveled, red-tile roofs, the whole stocked with untold riches, all bought with kinsmen's blood.

Softly she uttered the cry: *"Vengeance!"*

The small band sprang up as one, eager as hounds released on fleeing game. She prayed they remembered her instructions: "Do not strike at the old, the very young, the enslaved. We want only Feronius and whoever protects him, and to purify the villa with fire."

". . . in the coin of your blood." Baldemar's words tolled in her mind. Today we take one more payment.

She felt a rush of joyous animal strength. They were nature's fury: a breaking storm, an angry river flooding its banks.

But as always a small sharp knife-blade of fear pierced her heart.

I have seen my twenty-first summer and still I am gripped with visions of the caverns of Helle at a battle's beginning. I thought age and greater knowledge would lessen the fear. It does not.

She had raided with this band of thirty-one since the dark of the year's second moon, constantly shifting the location of their encampment. Thus far this year they had followed Baldemar's advance, striking at smaller targets such as isolated signal towers or poorly protected work details from the legions as the Romans cleared paths and surveyed the land of the Wetterau for sites for forts, catching them off guard when they thought Baldemar had done with them. Twenty-eight were young men just initiated into arms, and two were maiden daughters of priestesses of the groves, children of the spring rites who, like herself, were consecrated to the god of war. She discovered she took great pleasure in laying war plans and seeing them carried out. In these times Baldemar heaped praise on her deeds of valor at every feast. This raid was the last before they returned to the Village of the Boar for the most beloved festival of the year, the great dawn celebration in honor of the goddess Eastre, a time when weapons of iron must be laid down.

They vaulted a vine-laced stone wall and surged on, shifting spears into battle position. Then they flooded into a graveled carriage-way, meaning to enter through the slaves' quarters.

There came a cacophony of barking, and a dozen mastiffs rushed at them. They were prepared for this. Auriane cried: "Wulfstan! *Now!*" Wulfstan was a warrior son of Geisar by one of Wodan's priestesses—a ponderous, evil-tempered giant who resembled neither parent. He cast a hunter's net over the dogs, entangling them in one boiling mass of snapping and growling, making them easier to dispatch. The company used their spears as lances; soon all lay dead but one who was not caught in the net. The beast fastened powerful jaws on the hand of Fastila, younger of the two shield maids. Fastila shrieked, fell to the ground and rolled, the mastiff still attached. Auriane fell on the dog from behind and cut its throat with her dagger.

Fastila clung tightly to Auriane while sputtering curses at Wulfstan for failing to net all the dogs. Fastila was small and strong, with a deer's grace, her hair glossy black like a crow's wing—a child still, who was fiercely devoted to Auriane and subject to small eruptions of temper that put Auriane in mind of a furiously pecking bird. Fastila had followed them in concealment until it was too late to send her back to the main camp alone. She should not be with us, Auriane thought—she is too young and untried, and if she is killed, I will be responsible before Baldemar.

Auriane hastily wrapped Fastila's torn hand in a length of linen and helped her rise. Then they swiftly rejoined the others. In the gloom of the whitewashed wall a dozen shadowy human forms came forth; Auriane knew at once from their timidness and disorganization they were not war-trained guards.

"Hold back!" she called out sharply. Half obeyed, half did not. Wulfstan cast a spear and brought one of them down; then he hesitated, realizing too late what sort of resistance this was. The remainder of this timid crew dropped the sticks and clubs they carried and bolted for the fields.

"Halt!" Auriane cried. "Do not pursue—they are slaves!"

Auriane paused briefly by the body of the man Wulfstan had felled. She recognized him as a captive from one of the tribes dwelling near the Amber Sea; his forehead was disfigured with the red-brown scar of a brand. "Curses on Feronius' name!" she said with soft contempt. "The coward was warned! Feronius has fled—and left his dogs and his slaves behind to defend his lair!"

"Niding's slaves—we should destroy them all," Wulfstan retorted, needing to justify his haste. He was the one man of the band she disliked; he put her in mind of an evil-natured guard dog that snapped and bit at all that moved, not seeming to know enemy from friend. She supposed it was the blood of Geisar in him.

Auriane ignored this and moved away from Wulfstan, gliding into the shadows pooled about the villa, the rest of the band close about her. Wulfstan followed eventually, with sullen reluctance. The company slowed, stalking rather than running now, moving through a block of slaves' cells, then into a peristyled garden, and on into the dark chambers of the villa itself.

They had penetrated a number of forts and encampments, but never had any of them entered the private dwelling of a wealthy Roman citizen. Curiosity dazed them as they regarded the bewildering spaces, the confusion of the textures of floors and walls, the baffling array of finely wrought things. Gradually Auriane grew certain that the villa was indeed deserted. It appeared the household's departure was recent and hasty: Oil lamps still burned in several rooms, spilled wine had not dried, and in the kitchens some evil-smelling stew still boiled in an iron pot. The place was theirs for the taking. This is the luck of the Fourth Moon, she thought, a blessing of Eastre.

They separated then and began to loot and destroy. In adjacent rooms she heard her fellows hurling statuary to the ground, cracking fragile vases on stone. She felt the heat as they set fire to carpets and brocades, feeding the flames by dousing them with amphorae of oil. Several moments passed before she consciously realized she was not doing her part. A bewitchment settled over her; she could only stare at the marvels about her, like some child at a first festival.

As dawn poured more light into this labyrinth, the wonders multiplied; now they did more than stun the senses; they began subtly to reshape the soul.

It was one thing to hear Decius tell of the things his people made, but quite another to know them with her own senses.

One room was filled with human images of stone. Some were in graceful poses, half clad; others manifested only the head and shoulders; as she walked among them she almost expected them to reach out and beg her to release them from an evil spell—she was near certain they were once alive, frozen in place by the magic of Roman sorcerers. On the walls of the next chamber were vibrant renderings in paint, brilliant as Athelinda's unmixed dyes; they depicted fantastic dwelling places stacked atop one another, regal goddesses, their pink flesh flushed with life, and beasts—misshapen behemoths such as never walked the earth by light of day. One bore a tiny human rider and had a curled serpent growing from its head. In the next room the floor was strangely warm, as if it were alive; she dropped to her hands and knees to touch it. It was as if some dragon slept beneath the floor. And in a great stone entranceway with a hole in its roof was a pool of tamed water captured and put into a square bed of stone—not nature's water such as ran wild in rivers. Decius told her his people possessed the magic of calling water and making it do their bidding, but she did not know it could spout in a silvery stream from the mouth of a fish-man holding a three-pronged spear aloft, arcing with magic grace into a pool.

She came to a table laden with slender vessels of pale-colored glass, meaning to topple them, but she hesitated, feeling an odd paralysis overtake her limbs.

These marvels should be *known*, not destroyed. Decius' people do great evil, but they are cleverer than the most god-inspired smith, and they bring forth things of startling beauty. Surely these wonders could not exist without the blessing of Fria, the great source of all souls. There is a majesty in all this, a mystery profound as fathomless black pools. What if destroying these things is a desecration?

But that is dangerous madness, she cautioned herself. These are the works of the spawn of Lower Earth, the great nidings of the South who were suckled by a she-wolf and raised up on our blood.

The two beliefs warred in her. A part of her wished she had not set eyes upon these things.

She felt a hard gaze on her back and turned to see Wulfstan watching her with contemptuous curiosity. He dared speak no chastising words, but she read clearly in the look: Why do you not break and burn? Auriane felt a momentary twist of alarm, knowing Wulfstan would go to Geisar with the tale of her strange reluctance; it would be one more deed counted against her on that inevitable day when Geisar felt the time right to denounce her before the Assembly.

Fastila came around Wulfstan. "The fire burns too swiftly," the girl said anxiously to Auriane. "It's time to flee." Auriane guessed from the bright angry light in Fastila's eyes that the girl just spoke sharp words to Wulfstan in her defense. Fastila's loyalty had such strong roots, Auriane reflected, she might have been a child of the same mother.

They gathered up all the treasure they could fit into the two coracles—silver bowls and plates beautifully wrought, amphorae of the pale golden wine of the region, finely worked jewelry of topaz and silver, lapis and jet, abandoned by the women of the house.

As they fled, they passed through a room with honeycombed walls—here were hundreds of niches, many filled with rolls of that thin bark covered over with Roman signs that Decius could read. She gathered up as many as she could carry, remembering how bitterly Decius complained he had only one book, and stuffed them into one of the sacks of silver and precious things. Wulfstan glanced back and scowled. *They are worthless and unholy; why do you want them?* But Fastila halted and came back to help; hastily she, too, gathered up armfuls of bookrolls.

No sooner had Auriane and Fastila rejoined the company in the courtyard than the fire found its strength, this dragon they set free, and suddenly it was beyond all human control, raging, voraciously feeding, engulfing roof after roof, its searing breath driving them back to the safety of the open vineyard.

When they finally reached the riverbank with their sacks of

treasure, panting and coated in mud and ash, Fastila laughed softly. "All is well, very well! None opposed us!"

Each took a swallow of the villa's wine, then Auriane poured some of it into the Rhine as an offering to the river nymphs and sprinkled some on the air as an offering to Wodan.

They then launched the treasure-laden boats; two would row, the rest would paddle across on their shields. They would have to hurry; the smoke of the fire was easily visible from the fortress at Mogontiacum; at any time cavalry might be dispatched to investigate.

Before immersing herself in the water Auriane looked back once to view their handiwork and gave a small cry of dismay. Others turned to look.

The villa was spewing bats—first the smoke was speckled with them, then blackened by their numbers; they spiraled out, maddened by the heat. She realized those loathsome night creatures animated by spirits of the unholy dead must have long colonized the crevices beneath the roofs.

Fastila turned away, shielding her eyes. Wulfstan's surliness dissolved into terror, and he fell to his knees in the water, making the sign against sorcery. Auriane watched with a throb of hopelessness; the old specter of her coming doom embraced her with dark arms.

It must be close, she thought, for such a dread omen to appear. A multiplication of evil, as many sorrows as there were of those leathery demons, would be released upon them in the coming year. And as it was she who set them on the villa, she would be its cause.

There was little talk as the company of thirty-one traveled at their best speed to the Village of the Boar, hoping to be home in time for the hallowing of the ground. The sight of the bats caused a gloom to settle over them. Rains and mud and swollen rivers slowed them; fifteen days had elapsed and they had lost half their treasure at river fords, when at last they came to the River Fulda and began following it downstream to the River Weser.

Auriane rode her bay mare, the mount of a Roman cavalryman felled in an attack on a river patrol; Decius rode beside her as always. Her people generally believed the Roman slave accompanied the band to see to the horses and do thrall's chores such as foraging for firewood, skinning game and raising the tents. Her band saw she spent as much time in Decius' company as in their own and knew she asked his advice in matters of strategy—but with the exception of Wulfstan, they did not question. She was a bringer of victory, and her acts were blessed. But because of Wulfstan she was careful, always staying within the Companions' sight when she spoke to Decius.

On the last day of the journey Auriane watched with pleasure as Fria revealed her Eastre face: Flowers spilled over every steep hillside; the softly rolling earth, far as they could see, was fully clad in all shades of green, from pale soft yellow tones to the near-black of the yew groves. She was aware of how the forest pulsed and teemed with life, from the scuttling beetles in the earth to the naked white fungi, deathly pale but so very swift-growing and alive, to the furry, sharp-toothed creatures stirring in violent faun-filled shadows, to the winged ones flitting through the canopy of trees, to the leaf caterpillars, some gaudy, some plain, to the squirrels rippling up pines, skimming their surface, seeming not to touch the tree as they ascended. All were sheltered by the solemn trees themselves, with their muted consciousness, their lofty serenity, those pillars of life that made the whole of the land a temple.

The greater part of the band rode ahead of them with Wulfstan in the lead. Fastila rode closest, and was just out of hearing. The air was penetratingly cold; Auriane was wrapped in a voluminous gray wool cloak that draped to the horse's belly; to Decius she looked like some forest creature with bold, curious eyes, not quite certain it was ready to emerge from its burrow.

"You're passing by ripe fruit ready to fall!" Decius said with weary annoyance, unmoved by the beauty all about. "The fort at Mogon will be without a commander for at least ten more days, and they drew heavily from it to defend the south. If we do not quickly follow up what we've done, when that festival's done, they'll have regrouped."

"You are a magpie, making the same ugly noise over and over. *No,* and no again! You've no understanding of sacred things."

"This cursed festival comes every year, and it is always the same."

"You foreign spawn of a wolf! You've the soul of an ogre to have no reverence for Eastre."

He grinned. In that moment she looked so queenly and so dear, with that stubbornly raised head, those clear gray eyes critically examining him. The spring sunlight burnished her chestnut hair to gold. So vulnerable did she appear then—she who worked so hard to make herself invulnerable—that he felt a jolt of love for her painful in its intensity. But he could not tell her of it; when he tried, he became speechless as a dumb beast.

"Eastre's great gift for me is that another year passes, and I escape being offered in sacrifice. Who is the lucky wretch this year?"

"Our sacrifices are *willing,* at least," Auriane replied. "*Yours* are not."

"I have told you, we do not offer men in sacrifice."

"That is not true. Your people set men to fight to the death. Your sacrifices are to a lesser god, that is the one difference."

He shook his head with a patient, indulgent smile as if any attempt to explain her error would be beyond her capacity to understand.

"The gods want us back. I will hear no more words from you!"

He was quiet for a time, lapsing into thoughtfulness. Then he said, "Auriane, do you believe in the gods? All the time, I mean?"

She frowned, truly surprised. "You might well ask if I believe in the earth. Of course."

"Some men do not, you know, where I come from. It is not a silly question."

"But . . . I *see* them. They are quite noisy and noticeable. Look there!"

"It's just a stand of ash, in flower and quite beautiful, granted, but—"

"What is *'just'?* Do you not see their magic? The trees are Fria's face, and the wind through them is her breath. She is content and pleased today, to show us that face."

"I suppose there are moments when I could believe that. But you'd never catch *me* taking a child leading a procession in a hare's costume for a divine being. For me it takes more than donning a mask to make a god."

"You understand nothing. The child who leads the Eastre procession is only *possessed* with the great Hare spirit, and for a short time. All peoples worship the Hare. It is a mild and modest animal, with powerful birth magic, and it will die for you. If you are starving, a hare will come to you and ask you to cook it and eat it. Decius, you'd better be smiling because you're glad to learn this, and not because you're laughing at me."

"By Minerva, you should be used to it by now, my pet."

"I should not tell you," she went on defensively, warily, "you don't deserve to know . . . but a chosen few of those who follow the Hare through the forest have a chance to . . . to leave sickness and sorrow behind, and walk on through the rest of their days in holy peace. On Eastre's final day, when the Blessed One rises . . ."

"You mean the poor wretch they killed."

"He is a fortunate man, and he does not die!"

Auriane was frustrated but still hopeful of making him understand. "Do you not see the flowers that open in the places where death ruled in winter? It is the same. He lives again because Fria raises him up from the winter underground. Does not the moon die at its cycle's end, only to be raised up again on the third day? So it is with the Blessed One, and so it is with *all the earth* when Fria comes as Eastre. It is the one time of the year that *any* of us, no matter how bitter or old, can come upon the Place of No Sorrowing. That is why the people call her Darling and Dearest Beloved and go up to the high places to couple freely in her name. Many have *seen* her, Decius. She is made entirely of flowers, and she rides round the fields in a silver cart drawn by white cats, and she sheds a soft spirit-light that heals suffering souls, for which they call her Light Bearer. The hares, because of their holiness, herald her and help her carry all that godly light. If that light touches you, then you will find the way you will be at death—it is a bright peace, the Holy Ones all say, and a firm knowing that all are one creature, that all are cherished, even the rats and worms. *I* knew it once, for an instant, so I know it is true."

Desolation came briefly to her face as she remembered the state Ramis had shown her, then snatched away. Decius noticed her sudden sadness, and his mocking smile softened.

"Charming. It sounds to me like a primitive form of the Eleusinian mysteries. I always *wished* I could believe such things." But then Decius shrugged, and all too quickly she thought, put it out of mind. Auriane felt a strange new gulf between them, and she disliked the feeling. Was it that she realized that, though outwardly his world might be larger than hers, in spirit matters it was not, and might even be smaller? That for all his seeming vitality, in some ways his soul was shriveled like dried fruit?

"Auriane, Sigwulf's young son, the one taken captive, was he called Eadgyth?"

"Yes, it was Eadgyth. Why do you ask?"

"His name is in the books you brought me, or I think it is.

Barbarous names have barbarous spellings, and it is hard to tell. I'll have to take another look."

"What is in those books, Decius? Secret spells? Hero tales? Stories of monsters?"

"They are fascinating, my little sparrow. You brought me fifty books of records of slave sales. I shall cherish them always."

"You are never happy with what I bring you."

"If you would let me teach you our alphabet, at least, and perhaps a few words—"

"Never! Words do not belong on paper—they die like captured birds."

After a long silence her spiritedness gave way to a clouded look. "I have a whole crop of enemies now, Decius. It weighs upon me. Wulfstan, when he saw me take those books, looked at me as if I were a Roman spy. There are those who say I have fallen under your influence and that I like foreign ways better than our own. I know we have been seen practicing, and still I do not know by whom. Geisar watches me like a starved vulture. Only so long as my father lives am I safe."

"Well, you know my answer to *that*. Let us be quit of this damp, rotting pesthole. We could found a farm in Gaul. How I despise this country!" Twice now, she had helped him escape. On the first try, her tribespeople recaptured him and brought him back; on the second, one of the senior officers at the fort of Mattiacorum recognized him as "Decius the traitor" and he had fled for his life back into the dark pine forests. ". . . a farm, yes, and then we could properly marry—"

Her troubled look gave way to one of sharp sorrow. He knew the idea was not wholly unattractive to her. At last she steeled herself and said with forced severity, "Are your laws more binding than ours? How many times must I tell you, I am married already!"

"Perhaps if I made the acquaintance of your husband, it would help."

"If you make the acquaintance of my husband, you will need help! Silence with your sacrilege!" Their mounts sailed over a crumbling stone wall covered over with playful, climbing vetch-plants studded with violet blooms.

They rode in silence. Once Auriane jerked her horse to a halt, eyes intent on the ground. The rest of the band traveled on at a trot; only Decius and the ever-solicitous Fastila slowed their horses.

"Look. Sorcerer's mushrooms," Auriane exclaimed, dropping

lightly from the bay mare to the mossy path. "Can you wait? I promised Thrusnelda . . . ," she said breathlessly, rapidly picking mushrooms. "I would gather these for her if I saw them. You know, they say that when you eat these, the things that Ramis says make sense."

"Give *me* some—maybe *you* will make sense!" he said, smiling through his impatience as she dropped handfuls of mushrooms into her provisions sack. She tossed one of the mushrooms at him, striking him in the face, and vaulted back onto her mare. He smiled at her teasingly until, grudgingly, she returned the smile.

"I've some questions for you before we are home, and I can't have words with you any more," Auriane said after a time. "First tell me, do you know why your people abducted our greatest Holy One? Was it to learn her secrets of giving oracles?"

Immediately after they broke camp, one of Baldemar's messengers overtook them and related the tale of a strange act of aggression: Two Roman legions had marched far into the county of the Bructeres, their neighbor tribe to the east, and surrounded the tower of the Veleda on the River Lippe, seizing the great prophetess with the intent of taking her as hostage to Rome. To the tribes it was a terrifying and incomprehensible act.

"Nothing like that, I would wager," Decius replied. "My guess is that it was because she never stopped exhorting your people to go to war, and she made vicious enemies out of even the most peaceful tribes. I would call it a brilliant tactic—one simple abduction, one holy woman removed—and all the northern hordes are disarmed and left in confusion, without shedding a drop of blood, Roman *or* barbarian. And then that council of sorceresses chose this woman called Ramis to fill her place, who inveighs relentlessly against war. I wonder if the Romans knew *her* nature as well? If the government had shown as much wisdom in *my* day, that great massacre in Britannia might have been avoided."

"It is disaster, and you act as if it were a fine thing! *My* people will not stop fighting, Decius. All it means for *us* is that now we battle Rome alone. And Ramis is no good to anyone, with her riddling advice. Now, you never told me why your people offered that payment for the villagers. It's not your people's nature to show regret after they murder."

"You are right—my people are not in the habit of admitting to a great mistake. It is yet another sign of uncommon wisdom in this Emperor, or in whoever advises him. You see, this Vespasian has a churlish son called Domitian, a jealous prince who hates peace. *He* ordered the sacking of those villages in an attempt to provoke war so he would be sent to war, but his father, the Emperor, disowns the deed and has soundly chastised him. It would have been far, far better, Auriane, for your people to have accepted the payment."

"How dare you say my father is wrong!"

"I do not judge his acts. I speak only of the path of coming events. You are now set on an endless course of strike and counterstrike—"

"But they keep us from new croplands! Are we to lie down and starve?"

"You'll have to learn to make the land yield better or migrate anywhere but south. You have no true notion of the full size and might of your foe. I have grim forebodings of the days ahead— *this cannot end mildly*. It does not matter *which* side pushes the stone that starts the avalanche, once it is on its way. The wise man does not do battle with an avalanche. He gets out of its path."

As they came within a day's ride of the hall of Baldemar, they began to see great banners of red, white and black fluttering from the gates of every homestead; these were the colors sacred to the moon and to Eastre, who, the priests claimed, was mothered by the moon. They passed villagers who sang Eastre songs as they gathered fuel for the bonfires that would crown every hill and cleared paths for the processions and dances. Auriane became intoxicated with potent childhood memories: of going through the forest with other half-grown maids, laying lilies on standing stones, plucking mugwort and vervain to be braided into chaplets, of watching the young men as they netted hares for sacrifice, of helping Athelinda bake the crescent-moon cakes, which her mother then left by the wells as an offering to Eastre. Athelinda by now would have readied her dyes, her arms stained red and blue up to her elbows as she colored the sacred eggs of eternal life so they could be hidden in the forest for the children to find. Auriane felt an upwelling of old well-worn joy, heightened by the pooled memories of all the festivals past. She remembered Thrusnelda saying to her when she was still small enough for Athelinda to carry her, "Joy is *meant* to rule—these are the words trumpeted by the lilies."

The shouts of feasters could be heard across three fields as they neared the hall of Baldemar. It was late afternoon, one day before the Day of Sacrifice, when they rode wearily beneath the cat-skull gate and into the mist of high celebration.

The people came from five villages; they filled the yard and much of the barley field in back of the cattle sheds. Wood benches and long oaken tables were set before the hall; they were heavily laden with bread and meat. A line of villagers, arms linked, danced to a skin drum, occasionally colliding with the feasters. Minstrels sang, playing harps with dramatic, graceful strokes as they moved through the throng, telling tales of great warriors, bold maids, testy trolls, evil elves, and wyrms guarding grave-fields. Near the mead shed an eager crowd gathered round a flaming cart, while Amgath, who claimed to be the strongest man of Baldemar's Companions, prepared to clear it with one leap. Everywhere chickens fluttered, leaving trails of arcing feathers, children shrieked, chasing one another in games of tag, and skinny pigs darted between people's legs. Atop one of the tables Sigwulf did a weaving dance, holding an aurochs horn aloft as he wailed a victory song that set Baldemar's hounds howling.

Sigwulf saw Auriane first and called out to her. Then a good part of the throng rushed at the newly returned warriors, urging them to display their spoils. Her Companions were silent about the evil foretold by the bats; no one wanted to hear such things at a festival. During this reunion Decius unobtrusively left them, for his safety and hers, and resumed the role of humble thrall.

She slowly worked her way to the door of the hall, where she thought her mother would be, greeting everyone as she went. Sisinand's daughters stopped her to show her their newborn babes, and she looked carefully into the eyes of her cousins' children to see if poor Ullrik, the boy she had killed accidentally, had been reborn into the clan. But she did not recognize him in either child's face. And then she saw Witgern.

He ran to her and lifted her up as they embraced. All bitterness between them had long since vanished; their friendship felt to her old and comfortable as smooth river-washed stones. His love had mellowed to a tame affection that asked little but close companionship, though once she had seen a flare of hurt in Witgern's eyes when he accidentally came upon her speaking to Decius. With a lover's acute knowledge of the beloved, he knew the Roman thrall roused her affections more than he ever would.

Witgern's boy clung to his leg; the child was old enough to shout her name, and she lifted him up. This child was living proof Geisar's oracles were not god-inspired, she thought—the priest had insisted Witgern's child would be born blind in one eye as Witgern was, and he had refused to perform the boar-sacrifice at the wedding. The child was exceptionally healthy and whole, as if to spite the bitter old priest. Behind Witgern was his wife, Thurid, the freed thrall-woman the Holy Ones had permitted him to marry in spite of his affliction; she smiled with simple pleasure, looking placid and pleased, her belly swollen with their next child. Auriane felt a momentary tug of longing, thinking: She stands in my place. Auriane envied Thurid the warm comfort of her life, the freedom from wandering. But in the next moment she knew she could not live so: She would be like the horses caught wild who were never easy with confinement, always galloping restlessly along the fence, pining for the open hills.

She gave the boy to Thurid, and Witgern began pulling her purposefully through the crowd, shouting over the din, "Come and speak to your father! He will not heed me, perhaps he'll heed you. Why must he get into these cursed contests!"

Her consciousness of Baldemar's mortality, normally kept carefully submerged, surfaced dangerously.

They threaded their way through drinking bouts and tale-tellers, moving past a long table burdened with roasted pheasants, suckling pigs, haunches of oxen, great tubs of cheese, and flat loaves of festival bread imprinted with crosses, the magical sign of rebirth that aided the land in returning to life. Eager dogs pressed about the feasters, waiting for them to toss down the bones. As they slowly made their way around the hall, Auriane briefly saw Athelinda from too great a distance to call out. Her mother was laughing gaily at some warrior's jest as she handed round a horn of her best mead, dispensing it like some elixir of life as she offered her always eagerly sought advice: This horse should be bred to that, that field should be burned and replanted. Her ornaments caught the sun as she gestured gracefully. She is like a dancer among them, Auriane thought—artful, balanced, and quick; at festivals she is at the center of life, where she belongs, doling out hope and blessings as if she were Eastre herself.

Witgern brought her to a strip of ground marked off by ropes; Auriane saw a spear-casting competition was in progress. She squinted into the sun, and at the far end of the partitioned-off strip she saw the majestic form of Baldemar, his lion's mane of hair stirred faintly by the wind. He stood unnaturally still, poised to launch a spear; the world about seemed stopped with him. His opponent, Gundobad, leader of a lesser group of Companions, a man with crudely rounded bear's shoulders, a shock of red beard, broad pockmarked face and mead-reddened nose, had just completed a throw that sank deep into the oak post they used as a target.

"It is begun. We are too late," Auriane said softly, moving back a step so Baldemar would not see her, lest her presence distract him. The distance, she noted with alarm, was already a pace or two beyond what she knew was Baldemar's best throw.

Why must he subject himself to these needless tests of skill and valor? The people do not ask it. And the risk is great. Loss of strength will be read as loss of battle-luck and holiness.

She caught sight of Thorgild, watching him from a place much nearer to the contestants. His face was grim and closed, but Auriane sensed he, too, felt growing alarm.

"I would wager a year's produce of this farm," she said in a low voice to Witgern, "that Geisar's behind this. Gundobad wouldn't have challenged Father on his own."

Witgern's look darkened as he considered this, then slowly he nodded. Baldemar was all that restrained Geisar from lapsing back into Wido's slavish obedience to the Romans. Were Baldemar not in his way, Geisar would be free to do whatever brought him wealth, from goading the chiefs to attack the villages of allies to partaking in the lucrative intertribal slave trade.

She held her breath as Baldemar began a quick nimble run, shifting and balancing the weight of the spear, summoning strength to aging muscles.

No mortal man remains strong to the end of his life—*why must he do this?* He should not be seen humbled before those who take strength from his victories!

Gundobad smiled a wolfish smile, crossing arms massive with muscle and fat.

Baldemar's spear arced out, twisting slightly in flight. It bit deep into the post alongside Gundobad's. She embraced Witgern, near to tears with relief.

It is even! Now, hopefully, Baldemar will remember his age and retire from these contests while they hold in mind the memory of his strength.

But she realized with horror Gundobad was measuring out an even greater distance and drawing a fresh line ten paces farther back.

"Son of a black boar!" Witgern muttered. Auriane used all her strength to hold herself back; she wanted to run to them and implore them, in the name of all Baldemar's past deeds, to stop this folly.

A thrall's boy pulled the spears from the post and ran the length of the roped-in enclosure to return them to the two contestants.

"Witgern, never tell him I was here," Auriane said softly. Grimly Witgern nodded.

Gundobad took his turn first. The arc of his spear was brave at first, then it seemed to lose power. It nearly died in flight, striking very low on the post and hanging there precariously, shuddering with the effort of reaching the mark—but the target was struck. Gundobad's Companions cheered, reminding her of a brace of barking hounds.

Baldemar readied his spear. Auriane knew from his face—she knew him so well—that he expected to fail.

She realized she was trembling. "It is not right!" she said so only Witgern could hear. He took her hand and gripped it tightly.

She felt Baldemar gathering himself for the greatest effort of his life. He burst from stillness into furious motion.

Has he not always done what all said was not possible, through sheer greatness of spirit? But this, surely, is asking too much of the gods.

She saw a number of Baldemar's Companions averted their eyes, unwilling to watch. Auriane forced herself to look and was glad of it afterward. She saw the moment doubt cleared from Baldemar's face, that soul transcended flesh.

Aged or no, he will not be defeated in life.

The spear shot forth in a straight, brutal path; it flew as if Wodan's winds propelled it. It struck with violence, well above Gundobad's on the post.

His Companions raised a lusty roar, as if they expected it as one more gallant feat of their chief. But she saw from Baldemar's face he was as amazed as she was; Baldemar knew this victory should not have been.

He knows this is the end, she thought with dread. He knows he must never enter such contests again, but he does not know how *not* to enter them. Next year Gundobad will humiliate him for certain.

Gundobad laughed as if it were all no matter. And why not? Auriane thought. Time is with him. "Next year!" he cried out at Baldemar in his brazen trumpet-voice, "we do it again!" He started to give Baldemar a genial slap on the shoulder, but the hand was arrested in mid-air when he saw the look on Baldemar's face.

Gundobad shrugged as if the contest had been nothing but a joke in poor taste, then turned and disappeared among his men.

Auriane found herself thinking for the briefest moment: *It would be better if he died.* Let no one see his glory gone! Then she brought herself up short with a sickening lurch as if she stopped just in time and found herself leaning over a bottomless chasm.

No, that thought was not mine! But it was, it *was*—those who are cursed by the gods manifest such thoughts.

And she was taunted again by the memory of the bats.

As evening descended, a grave sadness took Auriane, and she could abide the celebrating no more. She got her mare from the horse sheds and galloped to the rise behind the Village of the Boar, a bleak place where only scrub pines grew; it afforded a vast overview of the countryside—from here she could watch as Eastre's bonfires were lit. She discovered, not greatly surprised, that Baldemar had done the same.

His black stallion capered sideways at the scent of her mare. She rode up beside him without a word, sitting in a somber silence that was not really silence, for she sensed a complex and comforting communication between them. The first bonfire, atop Axhead Hill, was lit while they watched; the fuel was mostly birch and holly dipped in pitch and it flared up quickly, rapidly swelling, stretching for the sky. Soon it was a triumphant torch crowning the hill.

Then a second bonfire materialized on the hill to the south, seemingly touched off by the first. And within moments the high places as far as the eye could see bloomed with the bonfires of Eastre, the most resplendent of all the flowers of spring. As the darkness deepened, it seemed a constellation of warm, beckoning stars had sunk to earth, a meadowland of blooming light. Joy surged through Auriane at the sight. *Fria sees all those fires and knows our devotion, and out of love she brings the dawn.*

Finally Baldemar spoke. "That victory was not mine, Auriane. Gundobad is the stronger. Wodan permitted me one last indulgence. I must not try the god's patience again."

"Gundobad has a small, mean soul and can rally few behind him. You've nothing to fear from him."

"Thus it is so, but he is a signpost." Baldemar's temper shifted suddenly, and he looked at her, smiling with pride. "Tell me, how did you know that fort by the Main was set out as a trap? What a tale! I've heard at least five different tellings."

"They put it in a place they knew would rouse our ire—that's when my suspicions were first roused. They are not fools enough to accidentally bar our route to the salt springs. And they left it so poorly manned, when the gates were not even complete—Romans are never that careless, not without willing it. I looked closer and I could even see the straw covering the ditch where they'd concealed their soldiers. But Sigwulf would not listen."

He laughed and put a hand on her shoulder. "You've the sight of an eagle, the persistence of a wolf. I am well pleased." He studied her face too long, as if to hold it in memory.

"I have things to tell you that I have long held in mind," he then continued, "and you must know them now, so you will be prepared for what comes. First know this: You need not worry over my fading."

She shut her eyes and felt a jolt of sickness in her stomach.

"This morning an owl fluttered close as if it wanted speech with me, then flitted off and landed on the hall's roof," he continued. "I could almost hear Helle singing with delight in the wind, *'He comes, he comes.'*"

"The owl means only that someone in our hall will die. Many abide there."

"Do not look away from this, my beloved child. The abyss brings sadness only for those who fight it. In other matters you fight, not in this. For the abyss is a kinswoman, you know . . . one hoary with age when the Three Worlds were made."

"You are young," she tried to say with strength, but her effort seemed to work against her, and her voice was tremulous, "and strong, without the least sign of . . ." She felt she danced on fire.

"And you are a blind daughter. Even my sight is no longer good—not for the hare at a hundred paces anyway. However, it's *excellent* for things to come."

Her silence and roughened breathing were the only signs that she forced back tears. She braced herself, sensing doors were now to be flung open that had been closed for years.

"I know the Roman thrall teaches you. I have known it for long."

She felt she struck a wall. Her whole soul seized up.

I should have known I could not conceal such a thing from him.

"I do not bless it," he said quietly, "and it saddens me. Perhaps the gods have some purpose in this, though it is obscure to me. You should have concealed it better. When I am gone, you know, nothing stands between you and Geisar."

"I've no shame over it, Father. It is a god-inspired thing, I think, and I could not have done otherwise."

"Have I asked for shame? Shame is for knaves. Perhaps you have been led to the sword down a humble path in back of the hall. I accept what is, as I accept *this*." He slapped a hand against the leg that had never properly healed. "Your whole life, you see, is a god's sign."

He shifted his gaze to the valley between two distant hills into which the sun had died. Its shape oddly resembled a yawning mouth, and Auriane imagined the Great Wolf swallowed the sun as he would at World's End.

"Listen well," he said. "When I am gone, there will be a terrible bloody fight for my sword."

She nodded. The sword of Baldemar was the greatest of all family treasures, a living thing that must not pass out of the clan, for Baldemar's spirit would live on in the blade. Whoever wielded it would have more than human luck in battle, for Baldemar's powerful ghost as well as the spirits of his ancestors would be fighting with him. "Sigwulf and Witgern will await my will," he went on, "and will not murder over it. But Gundobad and others have plans to seize it. When I am gone, I have instructed Athelinda · to bury it five paces behind the mead shed, aligned with the willow by the well."

"Sisinand has sons," Auriane said carefully, feeling she reached out to explore a dangerous place in the dark. "What need have *I* to know where the sword is to be kept?"

"She has sons, indeed, and two of them at least are fair and bold in battle. But none are great-souled, with a *ganna*'s sight and the fierce heart of the lioness who fights for her cubs, nor were any great holy signs given to them that they were to protect the land. The next to carry that sword will be you."

Some part of her must have known, but still it numbed every sense, as if she flew into the sun and all were a blinding blank. She felt a long shiver down her spine. "*I* . . . *?* But I thought you thought . . ."

Then she saw at least one thing clearly. "You planned it this way from the first!" she said, turning to him slowly with a look of cautious triumph. "You allowed the secret practice to go on because you did not want Geisar and Sigreda to know you prepared me to take it up."

He smiled faintly but did not answer. "Now listen well. Geisar has had you watched for years. He knows of the influence the

Roman thrall has on you. He knows you listen to his judgments on matters of strategy, and this is exceedingly dangerous for you. He knows, too, of those war engines you seized, against all our laws."

She felt stripped naked. She cast her eyes down, fighting shame. Did he even know of her feelings of love for the thrall? She prayed fervently he did not.

"And when Geisar can no longer harm me, he will reach me through you. For your own protection, my Companions must stay together after my death. I have charged Witgern and Sigwulf to protect you from him with all their strength."

"I do not need their protection." Her voice betrayed hurt and confusion.

"Proud words, nobly spoken! Auriane, you must take care of Athelinda. Never leave her!"

"Yes."

"And to the end of your days, exact vengeance on the Wolf-Spawn of the south. *Blood alone pays for blood.* Do not ever forget this."

"Yes," she answered firmly, but he discerned the faintest uncertainty in her tone.

"You have doubts. You cannot have doubts about such a thing."

"Decius"—she ventured once more into treacherous country—"makes it all appear differently." Baldemar scowled at the name, but she continued undaunted. "Among their people, as among ours, some are evil, some are blessed, and, as among ours, one should not be held to account for the family deeds of another."

Why do I speak for them? she thought. Has the sight of the wonders in the house of the slave-dealer infused me with a measure of their soul?

His first impulse was to anger. But he honored her too much to dismiss any thought of hers without deep consideration. "The thrall is not wrong," Baldemar said at last, "he speaks his own truth. And your great soul lets you see . . . multiple truths, not just the truths of our people. But you must stop your ears to it because you have taken an oath, and this is a barrier wider than any sea, a thing that cannot be crossed or compromised, a pact made directly with the gods."

She nodded slowly in assent, full of the peculiar feeling he was both utterly right and wrong at once. How could it be possible?

"When you take up that sword, you will never be alone. I will be with you."

• • •

The Fourth Moon continued its waning. The Day of Sacrifice came; on this day a willing victim of noble birth atoned for all the sacrileges committed by the people throughout the year, taking their evils on his own head. The multitudes traveled to Wolf's Head Bog. They were so silent that geese and cattle could be heard in the far fields. At the precise moment the sun dropped beneath the western pines, leaving all washed in wan light, Ramis came forth from the forest, a solitary figure robed in black, that dread face heavily veiled. She moved at a stately pace down an avenue of wind-whipped torches held by Holy Ones from many groves. Eyes were cast down as she came close. Dangling from one of Ramis' slender hands was a short length of rope. Fria's necklace, Auriane thought, with which she takes men back into her body so they might be reborn.

The man who freely gave his life sat at the edge of Raven Pond, on an oakwood throne garlanded with lilies. His eyes were fixed on the sky that was his destination; he did not look at Ramis as she came up behind him, silent as the descending hawk.

She strangled him swiftly and mercifully.

Auriane had been taught to think only of the encompassing love in the sacrificial act—he died so they could live, as an appeasement gift for the whole tribe. As attendant priests took his lifeless body into the lake and weighted it down with hurdles, all felt his spirit in the wind as he was raised up to the place of greatest honor in the Sky Hall. He had not died. And he would return. She, with others, looked on with tears of gratitude.

Land and people waited three days. Then came Eastre's day, when death's victory was overturned by the triumph of life. The man who gave his life, now called the Blessed One, would on this day be resurrected like the moon. At dawn, Auriane sat before the hearthfire, Athelinda beside her, while Mudrin stood by the black pot that hung over the fire, adding honey and goat's milk to a gruel of spelt, rye, knotweed, and vetch.

As Fredemund served them steaming bowls, Auriane listened for the first sounds of the bands of roving children. At dawn on Eastre's day, girls and boys gathered together at the villages and then went journeying, laying catkins at every door they passed— the catkin, because it carried the new life of the tree, was potent with the magic of rebirth. When one of these companies of children, a mix of all ages, finally arrived laughing at their door and dropped their magical catkins on the threshold, Athelinda hurried out, bantered gaily with them, then gave each a colored egg and sent them on their way. Egg magic was exceedingly powerful; wherever the children passed with their baskets laden with eggs, animals' wombs would be filled and fruit trees would bear abundantly.

Athelinda, Auriane and the thralls then readied themselves to go to the bonfires, which had been carefully fed for four days. Baldemar was in the yard, assisting the groom who prepared his horse. The house thralls got in one another's way as they tended the mutton and venison smoking over the fire, or hurried with leeks, herbs, peas, barley, and sacrificial meats for the cauldron, or herded geese out the skin-draped door. At the west end of the hall were the shadowy forms of those of Baldemar's Companions who sheltered here for the night; some were asleep in arms beneath the mead benches, shields of linden covering their faces; others lazily played dice and drank mead as they awaited the festivities about the bonfires.

Baldemar by long custom would not go with them; he held his own ceremony in a place known only to the women of the family. Across Marten River was a lonely summit difficult to reach because the hill was dense with scrub pine—one path, barely visible, wended its way to the top. At the summit was an oddly shaped outcropping of rock hollowed out by nature, resembling the impression of a scallop shell in the earth. As a young man, Baldemar had sacrificed there after his first successful raid, while returning home for this very festival, and he had seen a vision of a mountain cat destroying a wolf. Wodan's priests declared this meant that if Baldemar worshipped here every year on the final day of the Eastre festival, one day his people would defeat Rome, for the mountain cat was the spirit-animal on the Chattians and the wolf was Rome. And so, annually he climbed the summit with nine Ash Priestesses and sacrificed a stag, letting its blood run into the natural vessel.

As years passed, the women thralls knew of the place, too—at first only Mudrin and Fredemund, then eventually all the women who worked the looms: Where so many labor so close together, secrets are nearly impossible to keep.

Auriane stopped Baldemar at the door as he prepared to depart. "Still there is no news of Hallgerd," she said softly so Athelinda would not hear, "and it haunts me. I sense something sinister in this matter." The thrall called Hallgerd had disappeared at the dark of the first moon of this year—and she was among those who had knowledge of the place.

Baldemar smiled reassuringly. "As we speak, she is in some distant village, lying with some beloved she deserted us to join."

"Father, she disappeared in the deepest part of winter."

"She died in the drifts, then, poor, unfortunate woman."

"Or she died at the hands of some Roman torturer, after revealing the location of your ceremony. Had she died in the drifts someone would have uncovered her bones."

He lifted her chin, smiling. "Your mind is in a fevered state this day! I suggest you begin at once with the mead—it's the best medicine for that."

She tried to smile and managed barely. It was the first time in memory that his thoughts did not dart down the same path as hers. For some reason, she thought uneasily, in this matter his acute sight is dimmed.

When Baldemar stood ready to mount his great black stallion, Athelinda went out and embraced him. From the door Auriane watched, not meaning to, but getting caught up in it in spite of herself, in awe of the size of that love, its magnificence, its tenderness. For her it ended with a sharp ache, and she turned away: Never will I know such a love. The god of war is all comfortless spirit, and Decius' comfort is fraught with thorns.

As Baldemar vaulted onto the stallion and cantered out of the yard, she gripped the doorpost until her knuckles were white, so intense was her need to run after him and beg him not to go.

When the sun reached midheaven and the children had delivered all their catkins, they came together at the Village of the Boar and readied themselves for the grand procession which would be led by the Moon Hare. They chose by lot a maid of ten summers to lead the procession; she wore a hare costume consisting of a gray woolen headdress with long cloth ears attached; it covered the shoulders and was open in front to expose the face. The children's laughter floated like the tinkle of temple bells across the fields as they spilled down from the village, following the lead of the Hare, the ears of her costume nodding with her dancing walk. The long chain of children, with joined hands and lilies in their hair, followed no path; Auriane watched them pass along the edge of the flax field while newcomers ran up and joined as they went on their way. If anyone asked where they were going, they would say they journeyed to the moon, but the closest they came, she knew, was the peak above Marten River. She heard far-off shouts and knew they cried, "The Blessed One is risen! The light has come!" From nearer at hand she heard, "She brings the light! Life everlasting is on our heads!"

It was time to travel to the bonfires. Athelinda was directing the loading of the mead cask onto the cart. From across the yard Auriane heard furious scolding and came out to investigate. The angry shouts were Fredemund's.

"Witless, worthless whelp, I don't know why your mother feeds you! She should sell you into thralldom!"

The thrall-woman whirled around to Auriane, small black eyes glowing fiercely, plump hands balled into fists. "This mooncalf let the cart-horse stray! How will we get our drink and meat up the hill? Athelinda should have her whipped!"

Auriane saw that it was Sunia, daughter of one of Romilda's provisions women, a thin, withdrawn girl not yet sixteen whose mother often beat her. Her shoulders were drawn in; she looked down, breathing shallowly as if she thought she did not deserve her share of air. Fredemund had Sunia tightly by the arm; tears left tracks on a dirty face and clumps of hair fell across her eyes. When the girl looked up and saw Auriane, her expression became wild-eyed and lost, a look that said she expected no mercy; Baldemar's daughter was more than mortal to her.

Terror and shame. Does it not make us sisters?

Auriane approached slowly, so as not to frighten the girl, scarcely listening as Fredemund complained that the girl had not properly tied the horse, the one Sunia had borrowed for her mother, and the beast had slipped off while grazing.

"Fredemund, leave her be."

"You cannot mean that! She's low bred and of no account, what do *you* care?"

"I do not care what you think of her birth. Release her!"

Fredemund stared, mouth agape. Kindheartedness was wasted on a girl like this. She tried again. "The pony's gone, do you understand, gone, taken to the deep forests for certain!"

"Go to my own pens and take one of mine, I've got two Plains ponies there with the same coloring and markings. Athelinda will not hear of this, ever. And if you do not tell her, she won't notice." Fredemund pouted, her lower lip protruding as it always did when she made a stubborn stand, and made a calculated guttural sound that meant, "Anyone can see you've lost your wits, but as I am a thrall and you are free, what can I do about it?"

"Nor will Sunia's mother be told," Auriane added. Fredemund

stood still, suspended in frustrated silence. "Fredemund, I command it."

Regretfully Fredemund released Sunia's arm.

Sunia regarded Auriane first with happy amazement, then relief, and finally, simple love. The girl's face was like clear water; all that lay beneath was easy to see. Auriane knew she did not want to go home to her mother at all; she would stay here if she could. Auriane was angered to see the wool of the girl's brown plaid dress was eaten by moths in places—her mother was rich enough in land and could have provided better for her daughter.

Sunia touched her hand, inclined her head slightly, and whispered, "You are great and kind." She started to go, then looked about once more, and said silently, eloquently, with those round, pleading eyes, "I shall not forget this, ever."

"Sunia . . ." Auriane hesitated, unsure how to say what she meant to say. "If ever you are in a . . . a dire situation and dare not speak of it to anyone, you come to me."

The girl stood startled and wide-eyed a moment, considering this; then her eyes began to glisten and she spun round and darted off up the path to the village, stumbling a bit in her ill-fitting shoes.

The Eastre fire on Axhead Hill had drawn hundreds of worshipers by the time Auriane and Athelinda arrived with their household. The multitudes were arrayed about the hilltop, awaiting the arrival of Thrusnelda and her priestesses, and the opening ceremonies. Auriane and Athelinda had a place of honor near the fire; near them were Sisinand and her children and the family of Witgern. The drowsy contentment Auriane felt among kinspeople and friends settled over her as always, but some inner part of her stood straight as a sentinel, alert to something ominous gathering strength just beyond her sight.

Out of silence the sacred drummers began pounding the skins of their long drums. They climbed the hillside in a file, wearing brilliantly dyed cloaks of red, the color of life; they were a scarlet serpent wending their way through the throng. When they reached the summit, they formed a ring about the fire, never interrupting their dark, slow beat, a ponderous cadence that set every heart to its rhythm—it might have been the resonant footfalls of a distant regiment of giants. The beats were eerily echoed by the drummers about the bonfires on neighboring hills; it was as if the land lived and beneath its furry hide was a great booming heart. This was the throb of all life, the kick of the fawn emerging from the womb, the rhythmic motion of serpents, the lapping of waves, the hard hammering of rain. *Death is life, death is life,* the drums seemed to insist. It is difficult for us to understand, Athelinda had explained to Auriane when she was a child, so we must be shown it again and again.

A group of maids linked hands and began dancing round the fire; they dispersed when they saw Thrusnelda and her priestesses approach.

Thrusnelda and her women moved with the drums; it was as if an invisible rope connected them and each beat drew them forward another step. Thrusnelda's gentle round face was closed, remote; Eastre dwelled in her then. In her right hand she carried an upraised torch—this identified her as She-who-brings-fire-into-Darkness, or Fria as Light Bearer. She was clad in a white robe that shimmered with silver; it was embroidered with the symbols of rebirth: an egg overlaid by a cross, and above this, a leaping hare. On her forehead hung a great silver disk representing the full moon.

Thrusnelda walked closely enough to the fire that its gusts of heated air unfurled her cloak. She lifted her arms; then to the music of fire and drum she cried out, throwing her voice to the sky: "You are the Blessed One who rises in spring! Arise on this, the third day, and show us life manifest. They claim your mortal body broken and gone, a feast for ravens, a dwelling place for worms. But the light cannot be extinguished. Show us your living face!" She tossed her torch into the blaze.

"Arise now, O Blessed One, on the day of your resurrection!"

Behind Thrusnelda came a priest carrying a live hare thrashing in a sack. He gave her the hare; she dispatched it with a silver knife and then flung it into the fire. A moment later a dove fluttered in delicate confusion, seeming to emerge from the fire; swiftly it ascended with the smoke. From all about came cries of amazement: The Blessed One himself was incarnate in that bird. Auriane had known since she was ten that the dove was concealed in one of the drummer's cloaks, but still she did not think it an entirely ordinary bird, as she knew Decius would; it was infused with god-substance, and she was certain it knew and loved its worshipers below.

The young men then marked out a portion of the ground for the sword dance. And then the people formed into a long file, readying themselves to stand before the fire and see the Blessed One for

themselves in the blaze. Witgern took a place immediately ahead
of Auriane in the queue; she saw a gravely troubled look in his
face. He was bare of all arms, and their absence made him appear
an unblooded youth full of boyish innocence and increased her
desire to give comfort to him. When Witgern took his turn before
the fire, part of his prayer carried to her.

"Preserve him for another nine years! Take my life before his!"

She knew it was Baldemar for whom he offered to die. She
imagined most of the Companions would make a similar prayer.
What would they do when the inevitable occurred? The world
would swiftly pull apart, then order itself around a new axis.

Auriane approached the fire. She stood before the hot pulsing
spirit of spring, looking long into the molten center of the blaze,
hoping fervently to see the Blessed One's face. Finally she gave it
up with a small shrug of despair. And no sooner had she accepted
failure than there came a long, sensuous honeyed moment in
which the world seemed to smooth out and sorrowing did not seem
possible. She recognized this as the same sense that had overtaken
her when she pried the stone from the hoof of Ramis' white mare.
She clung to the feeling, but all too soon it passed on. The
experience left her with a feeling of urgency, a sense that some sad
circumstance demanded her attention, a feeling of abandonment
followed by aching longing. The memory of the mare shadowed
her always; but for it she might have been able to lay aside entirely
all thought of that long-ago encounter with Ramis.

She tossed in her pouch of herbs, praying for long life for all her
family, dutifully naming every nephew and niece. Then she
paused. She was almost certain she heard the thin wail of a horn,
the warning cry for a raid, but it was obscured by a sudden noise
of geese in the meadow below. She listened sharply, but a second
horn cry never came.

First she sought Witgern, but he was laughing at something one
of Romilda's women was telling him and she knew he probably
had not heard the horn. Then she found Athelinda, who waited her
turn to approach the Eastre fire.

"Mother, did you hear it?"

"A horn? Yes. Someone is hunting or playing. Were it a raid we
would hear it again."

"I'm going to ride back to the hall to be certain all is well."

"If you'd gotten properly drunk in the first place, you wouldn't
mull over such things as hunters calling one another with horns.
Now sit there and—"

"Mother, I have a sense something is very wrong."

Athelinda straightened and sighed heavily, accepting the fact that Auriane could not be dissuaded. "You should not go alone! Darkness comes—"

"I know how to ride through darkness. I will return before moonrise, I promise it."

CHAPTER XIV

Auriane set her mare at a flying gallop for the hall of Baldemar,
meaning to arm herself, then ride to the knoll where Baldemar
sacrificed alone. As she pulled her mount to a halt in the yard, she
felt ever more strongly that something was fatally wrong.

She heard a disturbance in the horse sheds. Thieves, or wolves?
Or elves, lured close by the silence?

Cautiously she approached, as if to a chasm's edge. It was an
evil dusk, seeming full of voices whispering warning. A malign
wind, the exhalation of ghosts, blew dry straw across the empty
yard with a sound like hissing serpents. She heard a flurry of
alarmed neighs followed by a furious battering of hooves. *Had a
wild horse broken into the yard?*

A tall stallion shot out into view from behind the stock sheds; it
circled erratically in a loose, powerful gallop, tossing and shaking
its bridled head, the long reins flapping free.

It was Baldemar's black stallion, and it was riderless.

With a spasm of despair she urged her mare forward and came
round the horse sheds for a better look. The sight stopped heart
and mind in place.

The stallion's reins were knotted at the withers. This meant the
beast had not just escaped and galloped home after being tied to
some post or tree. Baldemar had fallen—or been taken from the
stallion's back.

She did not consider summoning help; the others were too far off, and night came swiftly. She galloped back to the hall, dropped to the ground before the mare came to a halt, and bolted inside. From the weapons mounts on the wall she took three ash spears.

She leapt onto the bay once more and lashed the ends of the reins across the mare's hindquarters, urging the beast to racing speed, not heeding rough ground or pathless places, knowing she must outrun the dark.

He was betrayed. Some enemy learned the secret of the grove.

She shot into a birch forest and was devoured by night. Glittering eyes appeared, then flashed away; all about were the fast furtive rustlings of beasts not accustomed to being disturbed.

Still she could hear the driving pulse of the Eastre drums, pounding, pounding, and now they seemed to throb fearfully like a racing heart, hurrying her on; she held fast to that steady, insistent beat to keep from falling into madness. Then she did not know it from the hammering in her temples. The mare's back pitched steeply as she clambered up the last barren stretch of slope; her horse's coat was sleek as an otter, and Auriane clutched the silky mane, fighting to stay on that broad back.

Suddenly the mare shied, scenting the presence of other horses in this place where there should be no horses. Ahead she saw the fires of many torches, appearing, disappearing through the trees. She slid off the mare's back and tied her in a hawthorn thicket. Then she approached the altar stone at a stealthy run, bent low, spears pressed close to her chest.

As she approached the stone of sacrifice and the ring of pines, she stepped on a broken horn—the one she had heard blown once to signal a raid? Then the waning light revealed, where the pines petered out to rock, a ghostly line of horsemen, and she sensed the presence of many more. She edged closer, careful to stay concealed.

Now she could see much of the sacred place. It was a scene of desecration difficult to comprehend at once: Her father's private sanctum teemed with hostile life. It was like flinging open the door to the stores on which life depended and finding them alive with worms. Everywhere horsemen were carrying out some infernal task in orderly fashion, fearsomely uniform with their segmented armor, the gleaming metal of their polished helmets, the bindings of their shields, appearing to her like so many hominid beetles animated by a single blind, nonhuman mind.

The heads of their javelins were silhouetted against the deep violet sky. Torchlight moved evilly along the blades of drawn swords. From the tall oval shields they carried, she knew these were not native auxiliaries but regular Roman legionary cavalry-men from the fortress of Mogontiacum.

Now they come *without* disguise, she thought, so careless are they in their certainty of their power. The whole of the world is their private slave-pen.

With the nonchalance of swineherds they prodded the priest-esses into prisoners' carts, where they were then bound hand and foot. Auriane looked swiftly about for Baldemar, but at first he was nowhere to be seen.

She looked toward the lichen-covered altar stone. Rainwater pooled in its bowl; there was just light enough to see the water was bloody and dark. She realized the shadowed shape draped over the side was the twisted body of one of the Holy Ones, her white robe fanned out like some broken wing.

A moment later she saw the solitary silhouette of a man with a noble, bearded head, seated on a horse. His shoulders were drawn forward unnaturally as though his hands were bound before him. The horse's reins were in the hands of one of the cavalrymen. She stifled a cry. The captive was Baldemar.

Her whole mind burst into flame. How dared they subject him to this indignity! She became a maddened Fury, too numbed with anguish to care if she gave away her presence. With all her strength she hurled a spear at the featureless face of the cavalry-man who held the reins of Baldemar's mount.

It glanced harmlessly off a skillfully maneuvered shield. A second cavalryman wheeled his horse in her direction and kicked his mount with his heels.

But a ringing voice ordered him back. A lone assailant might mean a deliberate provocation, a means of luring men into a trap. To Auriane's surprise, the order was obeyed.

Their soldiers are closer to hounds than men, so alert they are to their master's command, she thought as she moved sideways about the circle of the natural temple. Finally she came up behind Baldemar.

She sprang into the torchlight amid a volley of curses and shouts, and hurled a second spear at the cavalryman who secured Baldemar's horse. But the soldier's mount reared up sharply as she threw; her spear struck the horse, and not the man. The beast lumbered to its knees, throwing the cavalryman to the ground.

Baldemar turned then and saw her.

She saw: *No! Not you!* in his eyes, followed by a look of swift resignation.

Then they looked at one another for what seemed the span of a night, and all the days of a lifetime were in that ardent farewell—the harsh tearing regrets they shared, his pride in her victories, the fierce love. There was as well in his look a last stern command that she accept what she could not stop.

The cavalrymen concluded this was the attack of a lone madwoman. Two sharp blasts on a trumpet called them to order. All stopped in place—three hundred soldiers looked on as she froze in plain sight, armed with a single ash spear. She was aware of the men's scattered laughter: They regarded her with amazed curiosity, as if some rare wild animal, contrary to all its habits, had dashed confusedly into their midst.

One called out to her with the soft, stern patience he might use with a dumb beast, and she guessed, but was not certain—they used none of the phrases Decius had taught her—they ordered her to lay down her weapon. Another quietly dismounted and approached her from behind, meaning to disarm her by force.

She started to run toward Baldemar, with some half-formed idea of leaping astride the horse with him and making a desperate attempt to escape, not heeding that the cavalrymen were by now formed about them in a tight ring.

Baldemar vigorously shook his head, stilling her with his eyes. It was as if his gaze had a muscular strength greater than her own. She halted.

The next moment seemed longer than a cycle of the moon, though in fact it took not much more time than it takes to drive a sword into a man's chest.

Baldemar nodded meaningfully at her once, indicating her spear; that look was a silent command that could not be disobeyed. In his eye was the maddened ecstasy of the condemned man who sees one last chance to escape.

She resisted knowing his wishes for a fraction of an instant, then collapsed within. They had known one another's thoughts ahead of speech all their lives; she understood precisely what he ordered her to do. Horror was a poison flushed into the blood.

He commanded her to kill him.

To be taken alive by the Romans would mean a living death, a niding's end, so shame-ridden and ignoble he would not be admitted to the Sky Hall at death. There was no life outside the clan; he would waste away piteously in barren darkness. But were he to die now, he would preserve the heaped treasure of a lifetime of deeds of valor. His spirit would abide forever with the tribe; on this night he would fly back to his own hall and sit among them, his hand round Athelinda's.

She lifted the last spear, shivering like a trembling dog, while the Romans watched in a kind of trance, not believing she prepared to do what it seemed she meant to—until it was too late.

The spear felt heavy as a man. Her muscles locked in place. She could not stop the heart that started her own.

How can I fail him in this? How many spears have I thrown? Throw one more. Of what matter is it? Both our lives are done.

He held his gaze firmly, insistently, to hers, willing her strength. *Do it, beloved child.*

The Eastre drums throbbed, sounding malignant, unearthly. There was a small trip in their rhythm now so they seemed to say: *You must kill, you must kill. This, this is the sacrifice we want.*

Her spear-arm shot forward. Distantly she heard shouts of outrage—of course!—the thought flashed in her mind. I steal the Roman wolves' quarry from their trap, right before their eyes.

The spear struck high in Baldemar's chest, toppling him from the horse.

She sank to her knees as if her soul could not support her body, herself a sacrifice, a creature with its still-beating heart torn out.

You are victorious, darkness. Horror claims all. Your will is done, Hertha. Ramis, you must be rejoicing.

Take me, hosts of Helle. Why was I cursed to rip the greatest of souls from its earthly housing, to stop my own blood.

"Accursed one!" she heard Hertha shriek over the flames that consumed her. "You shall commit a crime so great, there is no punishment for it!"

She fell unconscious onto stone.

The soldiers rushed toward Baldemar, then slowed, discipline faltering in the face of the ghastly scene, suddenly uncomfortably aware this land was not theirs, nor were its spirits friendly to them.

Life left Baldemar quickly; soon that slack face was only the soul's shadow. And then a stern peace settled over it. The Centurion, a man named Licinius Paulinus, rode close and dismounted.

So ends the life of the bane of the border for decades, Paulinus thought, the man who was the fortress of his people.

He then turned Auriane's body over to get a closer look. She felt like no woman he had ever touched: lean, smoothly muscled, flexible as a limp cat. In the starlight her face was that of Artemis.

"It is the maid, his daughter," Paulinus said softly to the men at large. "How could she do this thing?"

"What's to be done with her?" inquired the unit's flag-bearer as he dropped from his horse beside Paulinus. Both regarded her as a poisonous thing. Paulinus knew the maid must somehow be disposed of, but he was reluctant to have her destroyed here, before his men's eyes—they would worry over her curse.

Paulinus came to a swift decision. "Let her blood be on the hands of her tribesmen. Bring forward the barbarian, and quickly!"

The barbarian was Odberht, who had served as pathfinder to this remote place. He approached with a majestic swagger, chin lifted in an almost farcical show of pride, his red-blond hair, greasy with bear's fat, swept dramatically back from a brutish forehead. He was careful not to move too quickly, lest they think him their lackey instead of what he was: the leader of an intertribal retinue of four hundred warriors, a free chieftain who inscribed his own law in blood, who surpassed his father Wido in wealth and deeds. His belt and scabbard glowed with gold; his cloak was secured with the royal raven's head brooch of the king of the Cheruscans, the Chattians' ancestral enemies to the north, awarded to him instead of the king's wastrel son. Odberht expected one day to be named the king's heir.

Odberht's smugly triumphant smile died when he saw the corpse of Baldemar. He stood still a moment, stout leather-clad legs planted apart, staring stupidly, as if Baldemar, not living, were a thing that could not be. In uncouthly accented Latin he declared, "He is dead!"

"Well, good, we see these northern beasts *do* know the living from the dead!" Paulinus retorted.

Odberht took a cautious step closer. "You did not say you would kill him!" He contemplated with dread the implications of a blood-debt with Baldemar. No one must know his hand was in this!

"We've no account to give to *you*, son of Wido," Paulinus retorted. "Speak only when questioned!"

Odberht then saw that Baldemar had been felled with his own spear—yes, there was no mistaking the red-outlined runic marking on the shaft.

Then he saw Auriane, lying as if dead nearby. Slowly he began to comprehend the whole truth.

"Quickly, answer me!" Paulinus said, nodding crisply at Auriane. "What is the meaning of this? She slew him. What will your people do with her?"

"She—she is a murderer of kin," Odberht said at once, suddenly greatly relieved. He thought: The people will be so confused by the horror of what Auriane has done, they will explore the deed no further and never uncover my own role. "Hand her over to the high priest of Wodan called Geisar—it is *his* place to try her. You can be assured the Assembly of the Moon will condemn her to death."

Paulinus nodded and rose to his feet. Meditatively he asked, "Can you say why she did this?"

Odberht knew quite well why. But he indicated Auriane with a gesture of dismissal and replied, "For no reason, other than that from birth she was inclined to evil."

The Centurion hesitated a moment more, then declared, "Well, then, so it shall be. Odberht, you will remain with us. Detail four of your men to take her to her father's village. Make them a gift of Baldemar as well, we've no use for him now."

Decius fought gamely to remain conscious. The dawn that followed the night of Baldemar's death found him bound to an oak within the great open-air temple to Wodan that lay one Roman mile southeast of the Village of the Boar; here Geisar carried out sacrifices. Decius did not know how much longer he could save himself from the rope and the spear. The bodies of eighteen of his fellow thralls hung like bundles of pitiful rags from neighboring trees. They had been slain in the manner of Wodan when the god submitted to death in order to know Fria's wisdom: First they were hanged, then speared in the side. The ground reeked of sacrificial blood. Decius' wrists were swollen and bleeding; the bonds cut like knives.

The first news of the disaster was brought to the people by Asa, an Ash Priestess who survived the ambush. Geisar retaliated at once by giving the order that all Roman thralls held at the Village of the Boar were to be sacrificed to propitiate Wodan for the Holy Ones slain by the soldiers.

As the whole of the village was roused by Asa's tale, Decius was sleeping in his little thrall's hut alongside Athelinda's barley field. He was awakened by a piercing wail that he thought would crack open the earth and rend the sky, a cry so desolate it brought him shivering out into the night. Later he learned it was Athelinda's cry. Further into the night, rival warriors, not men of Baldemar's Companions, began ransacking the hall of Baldemar and all the grounds about it.

At first Decius did not understand, but Athelinda did. They came to search for the sword of Baldemar—a thing they would dare do only if Baldemar were dead. They found no sword, but they did find Decius, a despised Roman, and dragged him off to Geisar.

Decius thus far had saved himself by his wits. Geisar's priests promptly carried out their grisly task, sparing only Decius—for he had managed to convince them he knew how to find Sigwulf's missing son.

Decius listened closely to the priests' talk during that ghastly night, struggling to learn the fate of Auriane. He inferred that at dawn a cart bearing the body of Baldemar, abandoned by its driver, was found just outside the gate of the Village of the Boar. And shortly after, Auriane was delivered, bound, to Geisar. But he heard nothing more of her other than one tale too bizarre to credit: The Oak Priest called Grunig claimed Baldemar had been murdered by Auriane. Surely, Decius thought, this was a trick of his own delirium.

When Decius heard twice more from fresh messengers the same preposterous tale, he paid it more attention and felt the first throb of fear for her. Why was this monstrous thing being said? Some sinister plot was being hatched; surely this was Geisar's attempt to destroy her. He knew now that even if he succeeded in escaping, he could not leave her to this vile accusation and her tribespeople's barbarous punishments.

At midmorning, through closed eyes, Decius heard a fresh and welcome voice.

"Butcher that sack of swine droppings along with the rest of them! I speak with men, not lying Roman wolves!"

Sigwulf. At last. Decius forced open heavy lids and felt lightning bolts of pain flash through his arms. Nevertheless, hope struggled up. The first rays of the sallow sun were small, sharp nails driven into his sleep-starved eyes.

Perhaps the ruse that had spared him would now set him free.

"But the thrall speaks of your first son, Eadgyth," the priest called Grunig protested in his hissing voice, making practiced appeasing gestures with blood-caked hands.

Sigwulf's grunt betrayed frustrated anger mingled with sharp interest. His second son had been born with no strength; the medicine-woman claimed the babe had fewer breaths left in him than white calves born in spring. Had he hope of finding his firstborn, whom for four moons he had counted lost to slavery?

"If this be a ruse to busy me while Gundobad ferrets out that sword," Sigwulf retorted, "I will paint that altar with your blood!"

"*Never,* valorous and celebrated son of Wodan!" Grunig responded. "We do not favor one man over another!" Sigwulf's volatile nature terrified Grunig; he treated him like a dangerous horse to be petted and calmed.

"I believe *that* like I believe maggots shun rotted meat." Sigwulf wheeled his horse about and rode past the corpses in the trees, feasting on the sight of Roman dead; vengeance was the only mead he wanted now. He refused to dwell even a moment on how desolate he felt, passing this first morning of his life without Baldemar; with Sigwulf, despair habitually became rage. He came to Decius' tree and put the point of his sword beneath the thrall's chin, slowly lifting it. Decius' long hair was matted to his forehead with sweat and blood. His eyes were muddy pools, stagnant with fatigue.

How small and weak are these Roman swine, Sigwulf thought. How could this miserable race, nothing in themselves, be steadily destroying our people?

"Speak, thrall. What is the hold you have on these Holy Ones that they refuse to give your stinking body to the god?"

"You are Sigwulf?" Decius' voice was a dry rattle.

Sigwulf gave an affirmative grunt. Even half dead and slung from an oak, the Roman vermin managed to sound insolent.

"I have records taken from the villa of the slave-dealer Feronius. The name of your son Eadgyth is there." Sigwulf flinched at the name. "Take me to the first fort south of Mogon Spring . . ." Decius struggled on, his frail voice scarcely audible.

"Set free this meat for flies! Never!"

"You will arm me with lance and sword—" Decius continued as if he had not heard.

"Arrogant wretch! Half our own people do not possess swords!" But fierce hope for his son kept undermining Sigwulf's rage.

". . . and I will read to you the name of the farmholder who bought your son and the name of his village and estate," Decius finished.

Sigwulf looked doubtfully at Grunig. The priest held out a soiled roll of papyrus for Sigwulf's inspection. "It is written here, Sigwulf, or so he *says*," Grunig explained, apology in his voice.

"Auriane brought it with the spoil from the villa. Truly, these could well be the words of the slave-dealer. I would pay heed, Sigwulf."

Decius thought wearily: Auriane, your irrepressible curiosity may have saved my life. Can I now save yours?

"Why should we do this thing," Sigwulf said, looking to Grunig, "when we can torture him with fire until he interprets these signs for us here and now?"

"It's called *reading*, Sigwulf, and I'm the only one you bastards left alive who can do it." Vaulting hope lent strength to Decius' voice.

Sigwulf whipped about to face Decius, eyes simmering dangerously, not catching Decius' whole meaning—for his speech as always was sprinkled with Latin—but certain it was not respectful.

"If you torture me," Decius continued, meeting Sigwulf's eye in his goading way, "certainly you'll get me to say *something*, but how will you be able to prove I've spoken the truth? You've killed any others who could attest to it. And your son's freedom is at stake. You are somewhat dependent on my honor in this matter. If you do as I say, still you will not be certain I am telling the truth . . . but I will say to you, torture *does* tend to put me in a foul temper, and in such a state my natural sense of honor is not so much in evidence."

"What is this long-winded wretch saying?"

"The thrall is a liar," Grunig attempted to interpret for him, nodding placatingly and smiling. "But he will be slightly less likely to lie about your son if you set him free."

Sigwulf hurled his spear to the ground in fury. It might be some time before they could capture another slave who could read, and in the meantime his son might be sold again, and all trace of him lost. And he still could not dispell the thought that this was all Geisar's plot to get him out of the way during the ongoing race to find the sword of Baldemar—for Geisar fervently wanted Gundobad to have it, because the red-bearded giant was the sort of man Geisar could easily bring to heel.

"Tell this sack of dog-dung he has his wish," Sigwulf said at last. "Feed him and strengthen him, then we set out at once."

Decius' joy was marred with bitterness. This was the best chance at freedom he had yet been given, and he had waited long for it. But once free, he would have to return. He could not abandon Auriane.

• • •

Auriane awakened to find herself in a small, darkened pen; from the smell she knew it was a place in which goats were kept. At first there was only smooth blackness in her mind. Then with brutal swiftness the memory came. *Baldemar's face, stiff with agony. His bound hands. His eyes, emptied of life.* A small moan escaped her lips.

She grasped her right hand, wanting to cut it from her body.

Hertha's will should have been carried out at my birth! Mother, you should have let her drown me! And of you, Mother, I cannot bear to think. Were I to come before you now, would you spit on the child you once held to your breast?

From snatches of talk she realized she was in Geisar's hands and that this boarded over goat shed lay somewhere within the Village of the Boar. She learned also of the sacrifice of the Roman prisoners and presumed Decius hung dead from one of the Sacred Oaks.

But in the next moment she was curiously devoid of sorrowing and scarcely felt the horror—her senses had been flooded with too much of it in the last day. It was as if she no longer had a heart; where it had been was a black gaping wound, a numbed nothingness. Her spirit had shrunk to that of a niding, wretched, cowering, caring about little. She thought not at all of escape, for as she saw it in that moment, her enemy was not Geisar. The old priest was only the instrument of her true tormentor, who lived within herself: her own god-cursed soul.

A special meeting of the Assembly was called to unravel the disturbing circumstances of Baldemar's death. In living memory no case such as this had ever come before any assembly or sacred council. Auriane had killed a kinsman, and by ancient law, *intent* was irrelevant, for such an act was held to taint the doer. It was the gods' will that *her* hand was on the fatal spear, so the deed was accounted one with her nature and fate. Since Baldemar's kin could exact no blood-price in payment for the slaying—for kinspeople could not avenge themselves upon their own—this was the most devastating of crimes, causing a rupture in the family spirit that could not heal.

But clearly Auriane had obeyed Baldemar's wish and saved him from the foulest fate that could befall a celebrated warrior—life in captivity.

Was she kinslayer or deliverer? One belief that was absolute was set firmly against another.

Because the case was so baffling, the people raised an outcry when Geisar claimed the right to try her; this matter, they held, was simply beyond his powers. The Assembly demanded that she be tried by Ramis.

Auriane hardly had a chance to be relieved by this decision when word came by messenger that Ramis refused to act as judge in the case. No reason was offered.

Wretched hag of Helle, Auriane thought. You do not miss one chance to put terrifying obstacles in my path and make my misery worse.

So she was thrown once more on Geisar's mercy. Geisar would have taken pleasure in condemning her to be drowned under hurdles in the bogs, but he knew from the temper of the people he would not get off with a summary execution. He must make some effort to convince them of her guilt, a thing far from established in most people's minds. Confusion prevailed even among Baldemar's Companions, who felt they could not champion the daughter without betraying the father.

And so Geisar turned the matter over to the god he served: Auriane would face a trial by ordeal, and let Wodan be judge. The method he chose was the stallion fight. One stallion would be invested with all the evils that lay outside the tribe: the souls of nidings, wizards, murderers and the scaly things of the bogs. And the other stallion, selected by Auriane herself, would be invested with her spirit. If Auriane's stallion was killed by the forces of dark embodied in the other horse, she was guilty and would suffer death by drowning. Reluctantly the Assembly approved this.

At the same Assembly, Geisar ordered Athelinda to turn over the sword of Baldemar to Gundobad. Athelinda, who had sequestered herself in the hall, sent Fredemund with her refusal.

"The great lady," Fredemund reported, "holds that the lowliest thrall would not pollute that sword as much as would the touch of Gundobad."

Geisar swore silently to find a way to bring Athelinda to her knees.

On the day of Baldemar's funeral, Auriane, her hands bound with cord, was taken to the west wall of the village, which overlooked the cremation grounds. By sacred law she could not be prevented from attending the final rites for her father.

Baldemar's body was prepared for the pyre by the order of cremation priestesses called the Daughters of Helle, whose duty it was to conduct the dead through the stages of the spirit journey. Auriane watched from the palisade as the people came from the remotest villages; by midday their numbers darkened the gray-green plain below as they arranged themselves about the carefully stacked bed of wood where Baldemar's spirit would be released to the sky. A few shouted *"Kinslayer!"* at her while making the sign of cursing. Most, however, simply milled about in numbed quiet. It was as though they had been orphaned.

At midmorning the Daughters of Helle emerged from the pine forest clad in vulture-feather cloaks, moving in one file onto the rise of ground set aside for cremations. Their first priestess was called the Vulture Mother; she walked at their head, her face colored bone-white with chalk. As she ascended the rise, the Vulture Mother wailed a piercing, somber song that told of disasters sure to come: The land would never again be green, the barley would wither, the people would die by the sword, now that the Great Protector of the Land was dead.

Behind her, eight priestesses bore Baldemar's body on a ceremonial shield. The pyre was built of woods potent with magic: apple-wood for life everlasting, pine for rebirth, rowan for protection against sorcery. When all fifty-two priestesses ringed the pyre, they laid Baldemar's body on this grim bed.

Auriane refused to cast her eyes down; she knew many were observing her to see if she had the courage to watch. She did not allow herself to cry; she was a woman of stone, like the eerie images she had seen in the villa of the slave-dealer.

I believe none of the lies of Eastre now. Life is made of death. We stand on corpses. The dead outnumber us so, why should death not rule? Eastre's face is gory with blood. Where is my father's resurrection? All are born only to die.

Decius, my father wrung all the sadness out of me and I've not had a proper amount left for you. You are certainly dead, and I've said no farewell. But I do not suppose we will be separated long; Geisar will find a way to arrange my murder and you will be irritating me in the afterworld, if the shades of Romans are allowed to mingle with the shades of my people.

The Daughters of Helle sacrificed Baldemar's black stallion and poured its blood all around the pyre. Then Baldemar's Companions came forward one by one, bearing helmets and shields of linden, and laid them all about the place of burning. Auriane looked for Witgern and found him with difficulty, for all had smeared their faces and hair with charcoal.

How Witgern must loathe me. Will I ever have words with him again?

Then the people began to come forward with their personal treasures as offerings—torques of gold, horns of silver—and these, too, were laid about the stacked wood of the pyre.

What happened next was common at great funerals, yet still she felt a twist of horror in her stomach and wanted to push the sight of it away. First five, six, then seven of the Companions got down from their horses. Solemnly they drew swords and slew one another; the last man living then took his own life. She prayed Witgern was not among them, but at this distance she could not be certain.

The men who chose to die with their chief were then laid on the pyre. By this, they regained lost honor. The Companions who went on living would do so under an evil shadow: No retinue leader would want men sworn to a chieftain whose death could not be avenged. Auriane's spirit shrank at the sight of this immense and awful result of the snap of her arm, the path of one spear.

Then the Vulture Mother approached the pyre holding a torch aloft, still singing her heart-shredding lament, a song that brought to mind withered wastes where no hearthfire ever burned, a black sun, and gaped caverns beneath the earth; the tune's path staggered downward, trickling, falling like a tear. And then she was suddenly silent. She touched her torch to the wood.

Now all the Daughters of Helle joined in an upsurging hymn of praise that gathered in intensity with the swiftly spreading flames. The surviving Companions began to ride their horses slowly, in sunwise direction, about the pyre.

The burning required much of the day. When dusk approached, two Daughters of Helle came forward with the urn that would hold Baldemar's ashes, a red clay vessel incised with eggs and serpents, fashioned by hand, not on a wheel. For some reason the sight of the burial urn broke Auriane's strength and now she freely cried.

I should have disobeyed him! Perhaps he might have later escaped or been rescued. What good can ever come to pass in these times?

On the next morning Grunig came to the hut where Auriane was imprisoned, a slightly apologetic look on his face as he brought her a steaming gruel made of linseed, bindweed, green bristle and yarrow. This was a ceremonial meal intended to make her visible to the gods during the horse test.

He then led her out, and Sidgreda accompanied her to the stallion pens.

Before her in their separate pens were twelve bony, half-starved stallions.

So this is how Geisar plans to murder me. He must have gathered up from neighboring farms every weak and sickly animal he could find.

Escape. Now. I am not that well guarded. If I seized Sigreda's staff I would have a weapon. . . .

But I would be dishonoring myself, and to gain nothing. Baldemar thought it right to trust the gods, and will they not know and see my innocence . . . if I *am* innocent?

Auriane studied with growing alarm the line of angular bodies with their jutting hipbones, lowered heads, dulled eyes, ribs that cast shadows. One had a festering sore near the fetlock; one wheezed, sides fluttering pitiably; another nervously looked about at his flanks, an early sign of colic. Their tails lashed at flies.

Fria, see me and protect me.

Then she noticed the stallion in the last pen. Of all of them, he was the smallest in stature, his gauntness exaggerating further his diminutive size, and like the others, he was listless from neglect. But something about him caused her to catch her breath; there was such a wise look in his eyes and a spirited lift to his head in spite of maltreatment. He was a dapple-gray with near-black tail and mane, and he had an odd conformation: His neck, though thin, was arched like a well-pulled bow; a refined head tapered to a charcoal gray muzzle small enough to fit into her palm. His tail was held proudly and fanned like a banner. His was a graceful shape, if small; she guessed this was once an exquisite animal.

She approached him, studying the line of neck and back. The beast threw up his head inquiringly and snorted; the look was so like a greeting she half smiled. She guessed this horse was from the distant waterless places of the south, a strain not often seen; most likely he was the captured mount of one of the Arabian archers stationed at the fortress at Mogontiacum. She struggled to remember all she had learned of horses from listening to Baldemar's stable thralls, not knowing where she got the strength to think, to decide, when all she wished to do was sink to the earth and mourn. Were not the desert horses called remarkable for their

endurance, intelligence, and speed, and for their ability to withstand harsh conditions?

She held out her hand to the dappled stallion. He stretched his
neck and licked her palm with a rough tongue.

"This one is mine," Auriane said at last.

"*That* one?" Sigreda said with a frown. "A runt and a weakling?
You are certain?" She shrugged as if to say, If you want to give
your life away, no matter. The two grooms exchanged pitying
looks. She could hear the unspoken words: The daughter of
Baldemar does not know horses.

Sigreda held a torch before the dappled stallion to purify the air
and softly intoned: *"Giver of souls! Let the spirit of this woman
inhabit the horse. Almighty bringer of the winds! Breathe the soul
of this maid into this stallion. . . ."*

The Village of the Boar was laid out in circular plan. Wooden
walks radiated out to palisaded walls; these walkways were raised
slightly from the ground so that the villagers would not step in
animal dung. Craftworkers plied their trades here—the workers in
leather, iron, and bronze; here itinerant traders came to sell their
wheel-made pots. The village had one small wood temple to
Wodan, large enough for one priest to sacrifice alone; this was not
a main center of the cult. The village was best known for its
ancient covered well, celebrated about the countryside for its
mysterious waters, said to cure everything from gout to heartsick-
ness. It was also famous for a curious standing stone near the
entrance gate, shaped like a woman bent in mourning. A wizard
was said to be buried beneath it; his ghost, which protected the
village at night, was not overly demanding—once a year he
required the sacrifice of a dog.

At the village's center where the wooden walks converged, the
stallion pit lay; it was a sunken arena covered over with straw,
fortified with a wooden rail. Between the covered well and the
smith's workshops, a quiet crowd of villagers and farmers gathered. Across from them the priests of Wodan assembled, Auriane
in their midst. She was dressed humbly in a thrall's sleeveless
sheath of undyed wool, secured with a rope. The priests had taken
her ornaments, but they dared not remove her warrior's ring until
they heard the judgment of Wodan on this, his bride. By the
village's palisaded gate was the cart that would take her to the
bogs if she were judged guilty.

Auriane found her mother across from her, seated in front of

Baldemar's Companions. With her face invisible and hauntingly mysterious behind a many-layered black veil, Athelinda was a gloomy giantess frozen in mourning shape. Auriane sensed about her mother a towering misery no one could approach. She wanted in one moment to run to her and tear off that veil, and in the next did not know if she had the courage.

Several of the Companions wept openly or simply looked vacant and lost, while others examined her with hostile curiosity. Sigwulf stared fiercely ahead, all feeling well masked. She found Witgern and was greatly relieved; he had not followed his chieftain into death. But his face was inexpressive as a corpse. He never looked in her direction. Witgern, who so loved her—could he so thoroughly have turned from her?

It is possible. After all, my fate has destroyed his. Such things do not kindle affection.

Then she looked to Gundobad's men, who were watching as her small dappled-gray stallion was led into the pen and nodding with satisfaction. Finally she turned her gaze to Romilda's women. Only among the provisions-women did she find an unambivalently sympathetic face: The girl Sunia had pushed her way to the front, and was examining her with a sort of unjudging animal affection, tears in her eyes.

Her gray stallion was released into the pit. He leapt down the short drop to the straw and trotted about, snorting.

Then six Oak Priests led forth the rival stallion.

Moans of dismay were scattered through the throng.

This was a horse gone mad as some men go mad, one of those stallions caught occasionally that must be either killed or let go. He required all six handlers to restrain him. He was a thick and bluntly made beast with heavily muscled shoulders and a short neck that supported a head like a mallet. His coat was the color of yellow river mud. A dark brown stripe ran down his spine to a scraggly tail; his mane was bristly and upright. He frog-jumped sideways, kicking out hard while snapping at the air, eager for something to bite, pulling one of the priests off his feet.

Auriane thought: Today I will know what it is to die.

He is sleek and strong. And no one knows I was forced to choose among sickly stallions. Once more Geisar commits an act of treachery, and none can call him to account.

As the dun stallion was led into the pit, Auriane's dappled horse shook his head vigorously and capered sideways with rapid, liquid strides, lifting each hoof with the art of a dancer; he was a creature of almost feminine grace.

An Oak Priestess approached the pit, leading a mare in season; at the sight of her the ugly dun beast kicked out violently and emitted a nearly human scream of rage. The dappled stallion merely snorted and drew his neck into a tighter arch.

He almost seems to reason, Auriane thought; he knows he must conserve his remaining strength.

The dun was released into the pit. He hurtled forward, ears flattened, charging erratically like a maddened boar. The gray moved lightly around him in a high-stepping trot, thin sides heaving rapidly, eyes bright with annoyance.

Auriane found herself half-shutting her eyes, banishing stray thoughts, and using all her mind to will strength into the gray. She was vividly envisioning his victory, realizing as she did so that this ritual felt obscurely familiar—a falling onto a well-worn path— though she had no memory of having performed it before.

Without warning the dun heaved himself into the gray's shoulder, using that heavy head as a ram. The gray was knocked to his knees. Long yellow teeth sank into the dappled shoulder. The gray stallion kicked frantically, rolled and sprang to his feet; thin streaks of blood ran down to his belly. He cantered around the pit, angrily shaking his head, hind legs snapping out in random kicks of annoyance.

He is too weak to have an appetite for fighting, Auriane thought. Struggling against despair, she renewed her effort to will strength into the gray's limbs.

The dun fell in behind her horse, nipping at the gray's flanks. Then suddenly he lurched clumsily onto the weaker stallion's back, bringing him hard to the straw.

Cries of desolation rose up from the Companions. Only then did she realize that many among them wished her to live.

The dappled stallion's belly was exposed as he rolled from side to side, dark legs striking blindly at air. The dun pummeled him with iron forehooves, then delivered an adder-quick series of kicks to the gray's flanks.

The gray staggered to his feet and sped away from the dun, who chased him with lowered head and pinned-back ears, and then they reared, entangled in each other's legs, necks whipping about like vipers as tearing teeth sought each other's flesh. Bloody foam came from the mouth of the dun and his eyes seemed full of battle-smoke. Finally the crude weight of the dun pushed the gray

over backward. He battered the weaker stallion relentlessly with
outsized hooves, grunting darkly like a bull. The horrible hammer-
head struck again and again; the belly of the dappled stallion was
crisscrossed with bands of blood. Her horse's dark eyes were
luminous with pain.

Auriane felt she lived within that thrashing, bruised and
bleeding body, contracting with each fresh blow. Then all at once
the world about softened, and her focus flashed inward. She saw
her own life as if from a long distance, all brightly laid out. This
struggle between horses was the sum of her days. The dun was
the Three Fates, goring her, trampling her, harrying her through all
the years, incarnate in Hertha, in Baldemar's death, in Rome, until
she learned—what? Words of Ramis' from their last encounter,
dormant in her until this moment, voiced themselves with clarity:
*"If there is some shame lying about, how quickly you take it up
and say, 'This is mine.'"* With grim amusement Auriane realized
even her affinity for shame made her ashamed. Suddenly she felt
Ramis' presence, definite as a gust of wind from a great wing, and
for one vaulting moment she was loosed from all the bonds of life,
a creature that fed on joy, not shame.

She had the uncanny sense the dappled stallion felt her shift of
mind. It seemed that within the beast's eye, an ember burst into
flame. Simultaneously, a wind sprang up in a day that was utterly
still—an insistent, purposeful wind from the north. It animated
hair, lifted robes. Its low whistling seemed faintly to carry the wail
of horns.

The wind filled the gray's distended nostrils, seeming to give
him nourishment. She felt a prickling on her skin, knowing whose
wind that was—she who was older than the mountains, she who
was the keeper of souls.

Vigorously the gray scrambled to his feet; the wind blew his
silken mane upward so that he seemed to wear a frightful crest. He
moved deftly about the dun in a gliding walk, then lashed out
unexpectedly with a sideways kick so swift the throng saw only a
blur of black and gray—and a great gash appeared on the yellow
stallion's shoulder.

The gray seemed to float on the wind as he pranced toward the
dun. Again and again the lighter stallion struck, as if dancing to
some precise but fevered music only he could hear; first his small
dark muzzle shot out, then his hind legs as he erupted in a blinding
flurry of bites and kicks. The dun's evasive movements were
ungainly, out of step with this furious music; he neighed in rage

and started circling backward, becoming dizzy and disoriented. Finally the gray stallion made a bold head-on lunge at the dun—one forehoof raked down his neck, the other struck a stunning blow above his eye. The dun stallion lurched down, then crashed to his side. The gray rose up over him, eyes alight, and with steely hooves rained blows on the head of the fallen dun, splintering bone, crushing his windpipe.

The wind raised veils of dust about them so they were obscured. It trilled, a shrieking voice from the northern wastes where the oldest beings were bedded down, where ice sealed over the great well of the oldest kinswoman, the Abyss.

When the dust was blown off, the gray stallion was still, head lowered as if in awe or regret, brushing his dark muzzle inquisitively over the motionless form of the heavier stallion. The dun was dead.

Then with nimble grace the gray threw up his head and trotted lightly to the fence, bleeding, but with tail high, neighing loudly for the mare he had rightfully won.

For a long moment there was stillness, the only sound the low keening of the wind.

Auriane was aware of many eyes examining her closely. Who but a woman with sorceress's powers would have known such an unlikely beast would have so much battle-spirit?

The soft cries—*"Ganna, ganna!"* and "She is innocent!"— rose up all around. The soul of her family was powerful still, they judged; it had overcome the most loathsome of deeds. Her spirits still protected her from harm, she who faced down Ramis, she who at Antelope Ridge opened the gate.

Geisar stood rigid with rage and disbelief. Her horse's victory was impossible. He had heard odd tales of her for years, but it was far more disturbing to witness such things at first hand. A mortal woman could be threatened, but not a creature with ichor in her veins. Baldemar had been indifferent to his threats and caused him much trouble—but the battlefield alone was Baldemar's terrain, not the unseen world. This maid was far more troublesome, for she was at home in both worlds.

Auriane felt as if her blood had run out. The sense of Ramis' presence had fled, and the throng's words— *"She is innocent"* — echoed on in her mind, sounding first like a taunt, then like an entreaty. She saw Athelinda's shoulders shudder faintly and guessed her mother sobbed. *Does she cry because she is happy and relieved, or because now she must take me back into the family and she cannot bear to live with the slayer of her husband?*

Geisar raised thin arms for silence.

"The horse has given a verdict—and you see how close a judgment it is! Even the god is not certain what to do with her!" He spoke in brutal, measured thrusts that reminded her of someone skinning and gutting an animal. "It is because her soul is weak, and much evil has flowed in! I therefore propose we use a better test, the ordeal by water!"

"No! Release her! You have seen her innocence!" It was Witgern who shouted. His words spurred a chorus of assent. When Geisar managed to quieten them again, Auriane stole his silence.

"Geisar! Look at me!" Auriane scarcely recognized this commanding voice as her own. The throng was abruptly quiet. Geisar slowly turned to her, a look of exaggerated affront in that withered troll's face, as if a thrall had corrected him publicly.

"Geisar, I accuse you of trying to murder me!"

"Blasphemy," he said calmly, a tight smile on his lips. "All can see—"

"You gave me my choice of sick and weakened stallions, and you have made a mockery of the sacred horse test!" she broke in, forcing him to give ground as if words were sword-strokes. "The gods know the truth of it, and they will dry your blood and melt your bones!"

Hundreds of doubtful looks turned to Geisar. Her words roused a deeply buried hostility to the old priest most feared to openly express—and her judgments carried far more weight now that she was shown to be innocent.

Witgern shouted out: "Geisar, answer her. Is this true?"

"Witgern, come forward—you, too, shall be tried!"

Witgern did not move. But Auriane could see the effort it cost him; he visibly trembled with spirit-terror. In that moment she saw Geisar with merciless clarity: Here was a soul calcified, a sealed dry fountain, a man of small magic who understood little. He had no gods behind him and he was loyal to no one, not even to Sigreda who worshiped him.

"Perhaps you did not think the god competent to decide the matter," Auriane pressed on, "so you thought you must help! *Curse us all,* Geisar, and begin with me! I fear it no more than I fear a dog's bark."

"Scourge! Demon-woman!" Geisar seemed to spew brimstone. "You will choke on your insolence! Gundobad! Take her!" Ten of

Gundobad's Companions started forward, though not without a measure of hesitation in their step—they sensed the temper of the crowd was dangerously unstable.

"Do not come near me!" Auriane's voice transfixed them like a spear. Gundobad's men stopped in place.

The moment was a stunning rebuke to Geisar; it showed clearly they feared her more than him. It chased out the last doubt in the old priest's mind: She must be exterminated, by whatever means.

"You who trade oracles for silver," Auriane said grimly, "and call them true, have no cause to judge me. Evil I may be, but I pay my debts. When, priest, will you pay yours?"

With this she turned and walked rapidly toward the open gate. Baldemar's Companions watched her with accumulating alarm. She would never get off with this; she had raised Geisar's ire dangerously. Geisar must somehow be allowed to save face, or she would not survive a day—the priest would send his own men to track her down and slay her in secret.

"Hear me! I would speak!" This voice was Athelinda's. Auriane halted as if her mother's voice were a rope pulling her up short. She heard the sickness and desolation there. Auriane came back, slowly, until only the stallion pit separated her from her mother.

"There is no need to punish her for her blasphemies," Athelinda said. "If she is sworn out of the family, your vengeance is not necessary, Geisar, for what is more fearsome and terrible than being among the lost souls outside the tribe? I say, let her be driven out without food or weapons or water, and sworn out of the clan."

Geisar considered this. Here was a way to be rid of her, and at the same time avoid dirtying his hands with the blood of a sorceress. It seemed an excellent solution. And it was well Athelinda spoke the words—all accepted her as formidably wise. Almost imperceptibly, he nodded.

Athelinda pointed her cursing finger at Auriane. "I declare now that I swear you out. I have no living daughter! Fria, be witness. Let all who give her fire or water be accursed!"

Auriane drew a breath, scarcely believing the words came from her own mother, struggling to discern Athelinda's features beneath the veil of mourning. So *that*, then, was what her mother wished. The veil was lifted. She guessed rightly; her mother could not bear to look upon her.

Geisar had his vengeance when he saw the look in Auriane's face. That which supported her life had been pulled from beneath her. Her lips were white, her eyes, beyond pleading; she looked small and alone and young. And he was pleased, for Auriane had stolen something from him that could not be replaced. Now his oracles would ever after be questioned. She fouled the water in which he swam. Let her die slowly, outside the life of the clan.

Auriane said no more; what could she say if her own mother declared her dead?

Hardly aware of what she was doing—she supposed she simply sought a living companion—Auriane pulled open the gate to the stallion pit. The dappled gray leaped out and nuzzled her familiarly. Holding him by the cheekpiece of his halter, she turned and led him off. The horse had her spirit—who could deny him to her? Sigreda moved to protest, then decided: *The beast is sickly and injured*—let her have him.

All about was uncomfortable quiet; no one was pleased with this end.

Auriane led the gray into the pine forest, feeling she left her old life behind piece by piece like layers of clothing shed and strewn in her path. She was naked and bereft. When she had traveled past Marten Ridge and was starting into the deep forest, she heard crackling branches and light, furtive footfalls not far behind. She stopped and pulled the dagger from her belt. Had Geisar sent someone to murder her in secret after all?

Then she saw it was Sunia. Shyly the girl crept close, breathless and dirt-streaked from tracking, then stood quietly still. She was all round, sorrowful eyes, thin, awkwardly angled limbs; in her face was the bright, unquestioning affection of a puppy.

Auriane knew then this girl's misery was perhaps greater than her own, for her mother had enslaved her spirit. Sunia approached with a cloth-wrapped bundle.

"Sunia. This is madness! You're in grave danger if you give me aid. Go back."

"I have been accursed all my life. I would not know the difference."

Auriane took the gift and partly unwound the cloth. Within was a child's bow with several arrows—hardly much of a weapon, but with it she could take small game. There, too, was a loaf of coarse millet-bread. Auriane stared at these things for a time, tears forming in her eyes. Then she drew Sunia close and embraced her wordlessly, not trusting her voice.

"Go," Auriane said at last. "Do not follow me again."

CHAPTER XV

Auriane wandered for a day, meandering west into the unin-habited hill country, leading the dappled stallion, paying little attention to her direction. She found herself at the Divining Spring shortly after dawn the next day. She paused, feeling she had been led to this place.

To be without family is to be without skin. To be cursed by a mother is to be stripped of all humanity.

She could bear no more the memory of the shock of agony in Baldemar's face the moment her spear struck.

I cannot live on this way. I'll join the watery spirits of the spring and know peace for a while, and hope for rebirth in a better time.

Beside her was a sacred alder tree, said to bleed if nicked with an axe; in it lived a spirit that comforted the ghosts of the drowned. So many strips of white cloth were tied onto its branches that it seemed in bloom—these tokens marked the visits of villagers who came here to beg favors of the nymph of the spring. *They are hopeful flowers,* Auriane thought, *each, no doubt, representing a bitter disappointment.*

She crouched, studying the place where the spring throbbed like a heart, watching how it glistened like some animal flayed alive.

I ask no favors and expect nothing, Nymph. Just take me into the well of souls.

She removed the dappled stallion's halter and released him. Yesterday she had treated his wounds with poultices made from

cloth she tore from her own clothing and soaked in terebinth resin.
As she doctored him, she decided to call him Berinhard, which
meant "brave as a bear." She realized now she should not have
named him—a name would bind him to her.

And sure enough he showed no inclination to leave her; he
stood still, thin sides heaving, finely molded head proudly high as
he watched her, large liquid eyes bright with concern.

"Berinhard, *go!*" But the horse stepped closer, a tender, willing
presence unable to desert her.

"Go!" she cried again with less assuredness, thinking: That poor
beast truly *is* mine. The perverse humor of the Fates—my one
friend at the last is a horse.

She turned her back on him then and waded in, ignoring a flash
of movement behind the alder tree and Berinhard's sudden
nervous snorting.

Let the Nymph watch. What does it matter?

She tripped on a root, splashing noisily to her hands and knees.
Embarrassed, she looked up at the alder tree.

Spring Nymph, you mock me.

Wind rattled the leaves, and she blushed at what surely was the
Nymph's soft laughter.

I will crawl to my death so you cannot do that again.

She sank beneath the surface, and water invaded her nose,
insulted her lungs, shifting from ice to fire in her chest. The
bottom fell away; with a great effort she tried to force herself
down. She opened her mouth, trying to drown more quickly. Her
foot became entangled in grasses, holding her to the slimy bottom,
and a bolt of panic passed through her. Endless caverns of horror
opened in her mind. Body and lungs shrieked for air. Then all
faded into soft, seductive peace and blackness.

Auriane felt a patient hand cleaning mud from her face. Human
or divine?

If this is death, she thought, it is remarkably close to life. I smell
a pine fire and horse droppings, and I feel the sharp ache in the
stomach that comes after vomiting. Surely ghosts know nothing of
such things.

She opened her eyes barely and looked into eyes that regarded
her with a familiar, irritating blend of mockery and affection.

Surely there would be no Decius in the afterworld. Wretched
life still has me in its grip.

Decius! she thought, jolted into greater wakefulness. *He lived!*

She felt a dreamy, diffuse joy as she basked in that comfortably familiar presence, still too weak to fully open her eyes. He was her family now and all her kin.

For long moments Auriane watched him through slitted eyes while he thought she still slept, feeling as if she were awash in pleasantly warm water. For some perverse reason her skin felt acutely sensitive, and that longing to taste with the whole body—that powerful impulse to press her body to his, always before stifled by fear—almost overwhelmed her then. She quivered like a dove held in his palm. This was a new sort of adventure altogether—the possibilities of the pleasures of the flesh, stripped of shame. And now that she was mother-cursed, who would judge her more?

And what are these mad thoughts? I came here to die, not to violate one more sacred law.

Decius realized she was watching him; gently he turned her face to his. "What is the matter with you?" he said softly, smiling. "I was taught all barbarians could swim like rats in a wine-vat. Lucky for you *I* can swim."

"I thought you were the Nymph."

"Now don't try to flatter me. It won't work."

"You followed me. You spied on me!"

"You seemed to need it, wandering about without any weapons and leading a half-dead horse around . . . and then taking a notion to go for a swim on a day when sane people would huddle round a fire."

"I was not swimming, Decius."

"I know that. *Why*, Auriane? You've utterly no reason to die—you've wild young blood in your veins yet. Would you have preferred your father taken by some wasting illness?"

She shut her eyes for a long time while tears escaped from beneath her lids.

"I am sorry, that was roughly said," he amended, putting a too tentative hand on her forehead, painfully aware he had little idea how to give comfort. This felt as awkward as trying to wield a sword with the left hand.

"Decius," she said finally, "how did you save yourself from sacrifice?"

Briefly he related the tale.

"Ah, my books! They were not so worthless after all, were they? Apologize for what you said! Did Sigwulf find his son?"

"I'll never know. Thank all the gods your people are ignorant of our tongue! I take them near the fort and the sentries cry, 'Behold the traitor! Quick, catch him!' and your warriors think it's a warm greeting. It did not go well, I'll tell you. I kept my promise, though. I read to Sigwulf from the book of slave sales—moments before the cavalry came out. And then, Jove be thanked, your people ran in every direction and got in their way while I wheeled my horse about and galloped into the thickest part of the forest. How humorous it would have been if it were happening to someone else. Another gift of Fortuna for your old friend who survives every disaster! I did not realize how notorious I've become!"

He reached past her to turn a spitted hare he was roasting over the fire. "Now I know I can *never* go back," he went on, "I'm here for all the days of my life! My story's gotten worse and worse in the telling. They think I've trained a whole regiment of barbarians in the use of Roman arms."

"Then you are an outcast like me."

"Why should *you* be cast out? Auriane, you *must* tell me why you did this."

She shut her eyes and swiftly told him—it was easier than she expected, for she realized at once from his look he was not judging her as her own people would. Afterward she felt she had been released from tight bonds; she did not mind that, at the end of her tale, her words made him angry.

"I knew you could be a fool sometimes, I never knew how much. First, let us go back to those five villages. Their destruction had nothing whatever to do with you or your evil, whatever *that* is. I told you before, the Emperor Vespasian's son, Domitian—"

"I remember. It does not matter. If this Dim . . . Damation had not been the agent of my evil, something else would have, so don't spew confusing words at me, it does not help!"

"This is ridiculous. Auriane, why can you not see a case can be made for yourself! Listen to me! You did not murder your father. Murder lies in *intent*."

"Intent?"

He frowned in concentration. "How to explain? Listen. Take the case of a man who has been robbed recently. He is still in an agitated state and so he . . . he kills a thief in the night, someone who has entered his sleeping chamber. But the dead man turns out to be his own brother, who entered in haste before servants could announce him. That man is *innocent* before the gods—he killed a thief, not his brother."

"No. He killed his brother."

"But he did not *mean* to. Would you make him as guilty as a man who hunts his brother down?"

"Yes. The gods see that his brother is dead. And they made his life unholy by making him the cause."

"You are beyond the reach of reason. You're of nature, not of man. Anyone with a thimbleful of sense could see that *Odberht* killed your father, not you."

Auriane turned to him, her breathing halted, her whole life seeming stopped in place. *"What are you saying?"* she whispered.

"Odberht. Your old enemy. Are you truly surprised? He as much as *lives* at Mogontiacum. The traders who came back with me could talk of little else—Odberht sold your father's secret for five hundred longswords for his fancy foreign retinue, and a hundred Thessalian horses. At a feast he got sloppily drunk and announced to everyone: 'Only a hero can slay a hero' or some such nonsense, and told them they were fortunate enough to be looking upon the 'true slayer of Baldemar.' Now he's gotten over his shyness about the whole thing and brags freely of it everywhere."

"I've been away from the tale-bearers these last days," she said with such tight restraint it made him uneasy. Decius saw swift changes come into her eyes. In them was that cold, potent rage, peculiarly Germanic, that was low burning but could thrive through years, even generations—a rage that could be quenched only by fatal violence. He cursed himself silently, sensing he had somehow doomed her.

Though I'm not to be blamed when all is said and done, he reasoned; surely she would have learned of it soon enough.

He ventured, "You'll have to help me with this, my little dove, I've a bit of trouble thinking like a savage. Does this mean Baldemar has *two* murderers now, you *and* him? Or are we going to be sensible now and say the courts have let you off, right and proper, and you can go on living, and now your people can go and chase down the true culprit?"

"Sometimes your understanding is as a child's. You know nothing. My own *father* lies unquiet. You did not grow up in the shadow of the Lightning Oak."

"Undeniably, but I'll try and overcome it, if you'll try a little harder to make sense."

"Decius, should I decide to live on, *nothing matters but vengeance.* And it must be won by one of Baldemar's nearest kin—or our life runs out. Theudobald is aged. I do not know if any of Sisinand's sons have the mettle to do it. Mother does not fight, nor can she bear a child to raise to do the deed. Only I am left. I must find Odberht and kill him by light of day with an honorable weapon of war, or all of us will be damned."

"Good. Since that's impossible, we can go now to what isn't, like finding a warm dry place to sleep tonight—"

"You've as much human feeling as a dead ox! Go back and join your fellow slaves marching all together!"

"You've not answered me—are *you* now innocent?"

She seemed to have come to a place shrouded in fog, and she squinted as if struggling to discern solid shapes there. "I am innocent," she pronounced at last with gallant confidence, but her eyes clearly said otherwise; the shame was too old and had too many roots—Hertha's seedling had become a mighty oak. She realized this was so and added, frowning, "But I do not *feel* innocent."

"That artless honesty!" He bent down and gave her a lingering kiss. "I think *that* is what makes me your slave."

Slowly, gently, he began unwinding the blanket, mumbling something about her clothes being dry now. She knew what his true purpose was, but she found herself pleasantly paralyzed, unwilling to stop him, caught up in this novel madness of following desire to its end without fear of condemnation.

When at last he freed her from the blanket, he looked most gently at her naked body. Her eyes brimmed with tears.

"As beautiful as I always thought," he whispered with solemnity; yet even now the barest trace of mocking humor flickered in his eye. "This divine form I've dreamt of, knowing taking it would be much akin to having the Chief Vestal beneath the eyes of the Emperor. You are mine. I know you want it so, am I not right?"

She shut her eyes and partly covered herself again, as if this were all too much to bear, and dreams shifted too quickly into reality. But she whispered "Yes," rasping slightly as if the word hurt her throat. "I have known it done in hatred. I don't want to die not knowing what it is to do it in . . . love."

A hundred fears advanced on her but the warm madness pushed them back. "I've no tribe and no law, so what does it matter?"

But still, Decius saw, she kept the blanket over her.

"When you are ready, then," he said, caressing her cheek. He started to withdraw his hand but she caught it and held it.

Slowly she sat up; the blanket fell away. She was unnerved by her nakedness; inevitably it reminded her of the last time a man saw her unclad. Shivering a little in the cold, she drew him close. "But you know, there is a far, far older law . . . ," she said into his ear as she clung to him.

"Yes . . . ," he mumbled while heatedly kissing her neck, "there is always an older law."

". . . the law of Fria, ancient even when Giants roamed the earth. . . . Fria is sometimes called the Great Lover, you know—she boasts of it even—and she decrees the coupling of a man and a woman is *always* holy, provided both do it willingly and joyfully." She gave him a fast, shy kiss, then drew away. "It is confusing . . . trying to know what is evil and what is not"—she pressed her lips harder to his, feeling she ventured a little further into deep water before she drew away—"so I'll leave off trying because it does not matter anyhow, since in the eyes of Geisar I am dead."

"You look alive enough to me!" he said softly, laying her back down and bending over her. He gazed wonderingly on her body, from her hunting-animal's legs to the fine-skinned dove-softness of her white breasts, those mysteries so long concealed. It amazed him a creature could be so taut and lean and still be so vulnerable in places, and it brought out a new protectiveness in him.

"Poor, starved child!" he said, grinning now. "You should have come to me sooner!"

At this, she took up a small stone and playfully tossed it at him.

She pulled the leather thong that secured his tunic. He kissed her eyes, her neck, her shoulders, savoring each as if it were a rare dish at a banquet, getting in her way as she struggled to pull his tunic over his head.

Then Decius felt agile horse lips on the back of his neck. He threw the newly freed tunic at Berinhard. "Go away!"

Berinhard snorted and shook his head, rippling the mane along his neck, but moved only one step away.

"That beast is staring at us. I don't like it."

"He's protecting me from the Roman scourge."

"He'll have to learn some manners! Away, beast. Go graze somewhere."

Decius pulled the wool coverlet over them to conceal them. Auriane ran an unsure exploring hand down his naked back, relishing its smooth, muscular feel, worried for a moment that he judged her now as he did when they practiced at swordfighting; she even imagined taunting echoes of his criticisms: "*Clumsily*

done! Don't tell anyone *I* taught you this! Now try it once more,
my patience is at an end. No! Hold it like this!"

But to her relief in the next moments the last of his mocking
manner dissolved away. It was a changed Decius, one she did not
know, who caressed and kissed her breasts, her stomach, with
passionate reverence as though her body were a shrine. She felt
one last bolt of fear and a struggling up of resistance, born partly
of the memory of the last time, but it was settled again by his
steady onslaught of tenderness.

They accustomed themselves to each other for a long time,
touching, talking, encouraging. When the fast-falling spring night
brought the calling of owls, they finally joined together in love.

She felt sharp pleasure akin to pain as she was thoroughly
invaded by that warmth; it seemed they feverishly consumed each
other. There was something baffling in the reality of this moment:
She had wanted him for so long this seemed but one more waking
dream; then all the dreams of him crowded in, getting in the way
as she clung to him, eyes intent on the wheel of stars, her body
intent on knowing.

And then there was a time when he seemed to fall away from
her; she whispered his name, and once he cried hers, but as he
grew more intent upon pleasure, she felt a shift, and once more he
kept a distance between them, as always. She could not have said
how it was done, except that now his enjoyment shut her out, as
if he feared to share it, and a stone door closed in her face, quietly
and with finality, protecting some inner chamber she would never
be allowed to enter. *"You must always be the teacher,"* she had
said to him once. Teacher and pupil do not look out of one pair of
eyes. As he was suddenly weak with pleasure, she held to him
more tightly, as if the closer she held him the more she would
know what he knew then. But at the last she felt she groped hard
in the dark and did not find what she sought.

Then she lay still with a sense of pleasant, exhilarated frustration, half waiting for a round of criticism.

He turned her face to his in the firelight. "Well?" he asked,
smiling.

"You are better at this than I am. I fear I did it all wrong."

"No. You did it all right."

"I thought I would have to truss you up and hold a dagger at
your throat to ever hear you say words such as those!" She kissed
him, then looked away. The bright gauzy dream was growing

fainter; remorse was falling like night. *Evil woman!* A cracked dry voice in her mind cried out. Your body is polluted by a foreigner.

But she concealed these thoughts from him, not wanting to lose this sense of close companionship. She took his hand and held it on her breast. In the growing silence her thoughts begged to be expressed.

"You know, it is both less and more than I expected."

"You know how to make a man feel like a king!" he said good-humoredly. "How was it less?"

"I expected to be . . . borne off to the lands of the gods, to feel . . . possessed by the nymph. You know how it is that people talk of such things. I was transported halfway there, perhaps. But I remained myself, and you remained you. The hard ground did not go away, nor did the ants. Love is pleasant, yes, but much overpraised."

She was surprised at how hard he began laughing.

"The barbarian philosopher's judgment upon Eros! Perhaps in coming days you will learn to like it better. It is common for a young maid not to like it at first—"

"You're quite sure *you* did it right," she said, fighting back a smile.

"Better than you'll get anywhere else."

On the next day they traveled east, into the mixed forest of oak, fir, and beech that lay just south of Athelinda's farthermost fields. Here Decius had built a lean-to of interlaced willow branches that did little more than keep out the rain. It was positioned away from the well-traveled tribal pathways, but they did not need to walk far to overlook two systems of fields of rye and einkorn wheat that were worked by Romilda's provisions-women. Auriane's presence here was not secret; the field thralls saw Berinhard grazing in the common meadow and the smoke of her fires. It was Decius who must be kept hidden, for Sigwulf doubtless believed the Roman thrall had tricked him in the matter of his stolen son. They were situated so that she felt herself among her people still, but Decius could escape if necessary by galloping off on his black gelding into the uninhabited hill country.

Auriane traveled every day to the Lightning Oak to entreat Wodan for vengeance, chanting charms before the tortured form of that sky-burnt tree. Need of vengeance was a life-giving draught, all that kept her from sinking into a miasma of mourning. Would her soul join those other damned ones imprisoned in that corpse of a tree? She hoped fervently her mother had heard by now of Odberht's part in Baldemar's death—for knowing that vengeance was possible would give her strength.

Gradually she was aware Athelinda's house thralls watched her from a distance while she prayed; once she recognized Mudrin's ill-fitting red plaid dress.

She knew she had somehow to seize the sword of Baldemar— for with it lay her best chance of stalking and slaying Odberht— the very weapon itself, she believed, must thirst for his blood. But she dared not venture so close to Baldemar's hall. She wondered if Athelinda knew Baldemar had charged her with the sword's care, and decided she must. Baldemar kept nothing from her; surely he had not failed to tell Athelinda something as gravely important as that. Would her mother move to prevent her from taking it up? That, too, was impossible to imagine, even given her curse—surely she would count Baldemar's last wishes sacred.

Auriane and Decius survived by fishing in the brook that ran alongside Romilda's fields; Decius encountered an abandoned homestead on his return and recovered from it, among other useful things, a fisher's net and several hooks and lines. They hunted pheasants, squirrels and rabbits. They were aided as well by the Rule of Three: Sacred law, Auriane explained to Decius, declared that "three are free"—any wayfarer could take three fruits from a householder's tree or three fish from a farmer's pond. Thrusnelda had told Auriane when she was a child that this custom was honored in memory of the remote times of peace and wandering when Fria reigned alone, Wodan was an obedient son, war was unknown and all fruits of the earth were owned in common. It did not, Auriane warned Decius, apply to animals that were bred and daily fed—that would be theft.

A moon had waxed and waned since Baldemar's death. Sunia learned through the provisions-women that Auriane haunted the Lightning Oak, and the girl followed Auriane back to the camp one day. After discovering their lair, Sunia came often with bread, mead and news.

The Companions' lives had become pitiable, Sunia told them. Witgern and Thorgild withdrew into their halls and took scarcely enough food to stay alive.

Apparently, Auriane realized, the tale of Odberht's treachery had *not* reached them, for they lived without hope. She could not have Sunia tell them; she was not sure the girl would be believed, and Sunia would be punished if her mother guessed she sought

Auriane out. Sigwulf alone, Sunia related, seemed ready to bury the past without ceremony; he had begun already to form his own smaller group of Companions. That did not surprise Auriane—of all the Companions, Sigwulf, though utterly loyal while Baldemar lived, seemed to have the least sentiment about his chieftain.

Sunia said too that men crept by night onto Athelinda's land, searching and digging in likely places, desperate to find Baldemar's sword. Athelinda dared not loose the hounds on them because she suspected that among them were men of Baldemar's Companions.

But the most alarming thing Sunia had to tell was that Gundobad was pressing relentlessly for Athelinda's hand. Gundobad's men were counted little more than a band of rogues by the people at large, and he craved acceptance and prestige; the one sure way to obtain it was have Athelinda as wife. The people continued to hold Athelinda in great reverence in spite of Baldemar's unavenged death; always she was herself considered a source, a fount of sacred blood, a sort of magic well from which Baldemar had drawn power.

One day Auriane found at the base of the Lightning Oak one of Athelinda's silver rings, wrapped in wolf's hair. The sight stopped her heart. For long moments she could not touch it. Then she took it up swiftly, as if fearful it was not real.

One of Athelinda's beekeepers had followed her today. She guessed the old thrall put it here just before her arrival and probably waited in concealment to make certain she saw it.

She hurried back to Decius, her excitement causing her to forget her prayers for vengeance, her mind in ferment with possible meanings.

"Why wolf's hair?" Decius asked.

"Wolf's hair signifies a spy or intruder is in the house. But *who?* Gundobad maybe, or a man of his? And why would she want me to know? She must be in grave danger—there's no doubt that this is a cry for help." Auriane was silent a moment, her anxiety gathering. "Decius, I fear Gundobad plans to marry her by force. And I can do nothing!"

"What of Baldemar's Companions? Why do they not protect her?"

"It sounds as if only Sigwulf has any spirit left in him, and Sunia said he's ridden south to drive back the Hermundures— they're encroaching on our salt springs again. Mother is alone."

"Have Witgern and the others no shame? Why do they not help her?"

"Decius, you do not understand us, and I think you never will. Witgern and Thorgild and the others are behaving in the normal way of those who have lost honor. They know that if they fight, they will fail. Their battle-luck is gone. They would harm her more than help her. It is Sigwulf's behavior that is unaccountable—he lives as if the past never were."

"He sounds like the only man of sense to me."

"That is because everything you think is inside out, because you are Roman."

"My thanks to you for clarifying that."

Auriane began secretly watching Baldemar's hall, feeling like a ghost peering back on her earthly life. And she saw much that was alarming.

It appeared men of Gundobad's retinue had taken up residence in the yard, almost in the shadow of the hall. She could see the thralls were frightened of his men and stayed well away from them. She saw too that delegations of warriors and Holy Ones came daily. From their demeanor Auriane guessed that some came for Athelinda's counsel in important matters; Sunia had told her Athelinda in these uncertain times had taken on a status near divine. But she guessed others came on behalf of chieftains who wished to marry Athelinda or trick out of her the location of the sword of Baldemar.

On the days when no petitioners came, sometimes her mother was a stark figure in hooded cloak, haunting the edge of the flax field, a specter clothed in flesh. Even from a distance Auriane recognized the wild, desperate, roaming look in her mother's eye—the look of one slowly poisoned by an unavenged death. At other times Auriane saw her mother staggering with milk-pails, frenziedly pulling weeds from the gardens, or cutting fodder for the cattle—again Sunia had spoken truly: Athelinda's madness had taken a peculiar course, one that drove her to feverishly busy herself with thralls' tasks.

The next day when Auriane traveled to the Lightning Oak, she found another token. This one was a length of bone—from the thigh of a dog, she guessed. Tied beneath it was a miniature silver sword of the sort priests of Wodan wore from a chain about their necks.

This sign she found far easier to interpret. The bone symbolized either winter or the burial ground. Certainly, she thought, Athe-linda meant to indicate Baldemar's barrow. And the small silver sword must signify the sword of Baldemar.

The sword of Baldemar has been taken to his barrow. This interpretation made sense; it was a place Athelinda would consider safe—no one who was not close kin to Baldemar would dare linger near such a place, particularly at night.

As she realized the most sacred and powerful of weapons might be within her grasp, a crowd of new doubts arose. *Will not I foul it with my touch?*

I must not indulge myself so. What had Hylda said in the Ash Grove so long ago? *"Your lot is to protect your people with your own body . . . to be a living shield. . . ."*

She waited for the first moonless night. Then, with Decius, she set out at dusk for the urnfields.

Their horses trotted down night-filled pathways, hooves sinking into the mossy forest floor. The forest's dark perfumes were stronger at night, Decius noticed, or perhaps his sense of smell was more acute because sight was frustrated by the gloom.

"Do we have to dig him up?" he asked once.

"Of course not! The sword and all the treasures will be buried at the head of the barrow."

"It's really quite barbarous, you know, the magical properties your people ascribe to particular swords."

"Decius, some day when you're sleeping, I'm going to sew up your mouth. I tire of you plastering that word all over me like mud. Whenever *we* do a thing and your people do not, it is barbarous."

In the darkness she heard his muffled laughter.

When she judged it was roughly midnight, she saw, barely visible in the starlight, the standing stone that marked one entranceway to the urnfields. Decius jerked his horse to a halt.

"Stop! Someone's there, and it's no ghost."

"It's Andar, the thrall who guards the barrow," she whispered. "Wait. I'll frighten him off."

She dropped soundlessly from Berinhard's back. As he watched, amused, she crept forward and imitated a call of an owl.

"A passing good owl," Decius whispered admiringly.

She moved closer two more times, each time repeating the same call. When the thrall had heard three times the cry of an owl, he straightened, took several stumbling steps backward, then turned and fled in a jerking run, nearly crashing into a tree in his haste to get away.

"I made him think death approached," she whispered. Decius nodded.

In the starlight they found the grim low shape of the freshly made barrow. Quietly they began digging, using pottery sherds. They brought up golden torques, Gallic bowls, gem-encrusted brooches, bronze fibulae and gilded horns, but no sword. Auriane stopped once to look at her bleeding hands.

"We are mocked. I do not understand. I *know* Mother put it here."

"You do not usually give in so easily."

They resumed digging. Ground fog gathered and thickened as morning approached. Their limbs were stiff with cold. Once, while clawing at the soil, she felt an oddly familiar warmth wrapped about her softly as the fog, as if someone well-known and loved pressed close, then passed on. Her eyes blurred with tears.

When she struck cold steel, she stopped breathing. Hastily she cleared away dirt. "Decius! It is a sword. But is it *the* sword?"

Together they dug furiously. At last she grasped a pommel, and pulled it out. In the starlight a snakelike reflection played along a long blade.

"Is that *it?*" Decius asked, running a testing finger along the blade.

But Auriane was wrapped in deep silence, rushed off to old dreams, and she trembled, knowing life had caught and engulfed her visions. That which was to be, unfolded now.

Decius, however, continued to examine the weapon dispassionately. The hilt was of bone, and behind, it was set with a ring of precious stones. Each, he guessed, had separate magical powers: protection from wounds, from curses, from treachery. The runic sign of Tiwaz, god of war, was deeply etched into the base of the blade.

"By Minerva, the cursed blade is pattern-welded—I did not know your people even *knew* that process. I ask again, is this the one we seek?"

"Yes," she whispered a little hoarsely. She inclined her head and softly touched her lips to the blade.

"A beautiful and terrible thing, is it not?" he said softly.

She nodded. "We must put these treasures back and make the barrow look as if it were undisturbed—or Andar will be punished with death for leaving the grave open to robbers."

Then she was suddenly alert, head up, reminding him of the elk scenting the wolf. He saw the tracks of tears and put an arm about her to comfort her.

"I *hear* him," she whispered. "I hear Baldemar in the trees. *'Do my will with it,'* he is saying, *'and your own.'*"

For one course of the moon Auriane sparred with Decius using the sword of Baldemar, accustoming herself to its weight and balance. It was actually lighter than the legionary swords with which she was familiar, though, like most Germanic swords, it was longer than the Roman *gladius*.

She was careful at first, acutely aware of the power of the sword, tightly holding herself back, fearing she might do injury to Decius. Then one day, near the end of a long practice, he came at her with such suddenness he surprised her; she gave ground, backing into a pine. There was a quick moment when she was jolted into instinctive response—she forgot place and circumstance. There existed only the wind and the chaotic rhythm of clashing blades. In one whiplike motion she dropped down, rolled against his back, came round and began rapidly cutting off his strokes before he began them. He felt himself struck by a series of lightning flashes of steel, coming from impossible directions faster than a mind could plan—it felt akin to being on a fast horse that bolted before he was ready. He was two, then three beats behind when she executed a long, sliding upward cut he never taught her; it nearly ripped the sword from his hand.

The downstroke touched his upper arm before it whistled off into air, causing a flesh wound painful enough that he winced in spite of himself.

She froze in place, gave a small cry, and dropped the sword. Quickly she brought a strip of clean linen to bind it, winding it tightly about his arm in worried silence, watching the bright red stain rapidly grow.

After a time Decius said, "It is enough, Auriane. For all time."

She looked at him, even more alarmed. "For all time? What are you saying?"

"I am saying, I have done all for you that I can. Auriane . . . , you have become so skilled . . . I do not even know where it comes from."

"Well, of course. I've a weapon possessed of magic that increases my strength threefold, some say ninefold."

He shook his head. "I put no store in magic. You may call it what you will. I know only I have never seen such . . . grace, such . . . such swift intelligence. By Minerva, you are part cat, part deer, part hawk!"

"Nonsense. And so like you! You will goad me to madness! At last I get words of high praise from you, when *I* am not the cause, but the weapon!"

"You *are* the cause, you little fool."

Vigorously she shook her head. "And you are wrong. The wisdom of all my father's life is in this sword. Look at the blade. Do you not see the fire in it? *That* is where your 'swift intelligence' lives."

He shook his head sadly and shrugged. "Believe what you will. But you do not need me anymore, my little dove. You've flown beyond your teacher."

She sensed the widening gulf between them more acutely than ever before, and a painful chill settled on her chest. If he could not be her teacher, what could he be? Already she felt he loved her less. It was as though she had cut her own flesh with the blade, and not his.

"Decius . . . ," she started softly, and stopped, feeling uneasy. Then she slowly leaned forward and tentatively kissed him. He did not move toward her until the last moment. *For appearances,* she thought miserably. She kissed him with purposeful passion, and he responded barely.

What have I done? she thought. I have only followed the will of the gods. What have I done?

CHAPTER XVI

Athelinda knew at dawn that this day would be fraught with evil. She arose spiritlessly; the three spoonfuls she ate of the honeyed gruel Mudrin brought her had no taste. It was late summer, the day she and Mudrin must go to the garden where her cultivated hops plants grew on poles, to harvest the conelike catkins; when added to mead, they gave it the desired bitter taste and helped to preserve it. Then they would put the new mead into casks. Her mind was an airless room with locked doors on every hand; she allowed herself to think of nothing but mead: Would it be the proper shade of deep bronzed red? Would it foam vigorously with health and life when poured? Had she used enough yeast, enough bog myrtle and ginger, the right measure of honey? Numbly she rolled her hide bedding and adjusted the sacks of seed corn that hung from the roof beams so that mice could not get to them; then she walked among the thralls at the looms to see how the wool cloth progressed, and chided the girl at the stone gristmill for allowing dirt to mingle with the grains. Finally she crossed the threshing floor, Mudrin and Fredemund close behind, and pulled back the doorskin.

"No! *Let me die!*" Athelinda softly exclaimed.

Mudrin came up beside her to see what fresh catastrophe had come.

There, in the yard, Gundobad's men were setting up a marriage tent. The square of white linen supported by four polished rowan poles transfixed her for a moment: It was a banner of white, death's color, the color of winter, of weathered bone, signaling her end.

Four moons had passed since the death of Baldemar and full summer had gone, but the raiding season was far from done—all who could best protect her were still campaigning in the south.

Athelinda sent Mudrin to bring Thrusnelda, hoping the pleas of one of the Holy Ones would move Gundobad to think better of this. At the same time she sent Fredemund to fetch Witgern, though she doubted he would come. As she waited, the preparations proceeded without a word of greeting to the lady of the hall. Athelinda watched them bring an oak table and set it beneath the tent; on it they laid the ceremonial marriage sword. Then they set shields painted with signs to avert evil at the four corners of the tent. A cart had come, laden with gifts; Gundobad's men began unloading them and laying them by her door: a Celtic silver bowl studded with amethysts and carbuncles, an ancient loom, a gameboard with silver and ivory pieces, finches in a cage, bolts of fine embroidered cloth. Greater gifts came as well: Five of Gundobad's men passed beneath the Cat-Skull Gate leading a pure white ox, a Thessalian stallion and three Plains mares, all beautifully decked out for riding. Alongside them came an ox-drawn cart bearing a young harpist, two pipe players and a grim, gray-robed marriage priestess with many amulets hanging from her belt. Tied to this cart was a fattened sow garlanded for sacrifice.

Athelinda scarcely breathed, her mind as frantic as the finches flitting about in their bronze cage. A marriage oath could not be unsaid or undone.

Mudrin returned first. Thrusnelda was a prisoner in her lodge, Mudrin reported; the old priestess was guarded by ten of Gundobad's men. She could do nothing to help but withdraw into her herb-rooms to work spells against the intruder.

When the sun rose halfway to midheaven, Fredemund returned. Witgern was coming, she told Athelinda, and with him, Thorgild and Coniaric, but they were in a weakened state and could not make haste.

What good can they do? Athelinda thought, her whole body contracted in fury. There are twenty-five, twenty-six of Gundobad's men here, and doubtless even more lurk just out of sight.

Gundobad's Companions formed into two files, holding their gaudily marked shields of linden before them, forming an avenue down which the bride would walk. Among them, Athelinda saw, were four who had once been men of Baldemar's. The wretches! she thought, but she understood: She guessed their allegiance to Gundobad was tepid at best, doubtless motivated more by their fear of being shunned and not heard at councils—the fate of Witgern and Thorgild—than by any love of Gundobad.

Finally Gundobad made his entry, approaching the Cat-Skull Gate on a black Asturian stallion, chosen, Athelinda surmised, for its resemblance to Baldemar's steed. He was clad in a saffron cloak trimmed in marten fur, secured with a chieftain's raven brooch, and a bronze helmet to which boar's tusks had been affixed. He carried a small round shield with a binding of gold. His high-laced boots of gleaming red leather Athelinda knew were not obtained anywhere within Chattian territories; they must have been purchased dearly from some trader who imported leather goods from one of the fabled towns of Gaul.

Athelinda might have laughed at the sight of her would-be groom, had she not been so stricken with dread, for his fine raiment only made more apparent how unrefined he was. It was as if a brigand had stolen the clothes of an effete prince. Gundobad looked as she thought elves must look: bristling red beard, protruding stomach, spindling legs, a glimmer of malicious playfulness firing the eye. Even his horse did not seem to like him—the beast snorted and picked up his feet with distaste, seeming to contemplate throwing his rider. Gundobad clutched the reins as if he had a dangerous dog on a leash. His pastry-flour skin was blotched with red from bouts of mead-drinking that lasted a night and a day; all knew him as a man whose appetites were stronger than his will.

"My lady Athelinda, greetings to you!" he called out to her. "It's time you're wedded, and none make a more suitable husband than me. So prepare yourself, and dress in fine clothes. My patience is at an end!"

"You are a pitiable fool to think you can walk where Baldemar walked!" Athelinda's voice was harsh and raw. "It will be the hand of a dead woman you'll take!"

Gundobad ignored this and dismounted near the marriage tent, brushing the dust of the journey off his cloak. He ordered the harpist to play. The fluttery notes, so regal and poised, were so absurdly out of place Athelinda wondered if she *had* taken that last short step to madness. She felt all the venomous sadness fermenting in her boiling up in a violent eruption.

"You bed down here, and you sleep in a nest of hornets!" Athelinda shouted from the doorway. "You lie where Baldemar lay, and the coverlets will burst into flame! Taste my mead, and it will turn your vitals to serpents! I curse you, Gundobad—may you awake tomorrow to find your bowels crawling with maggots!"

This brought uncomfortable quiet to the company; there was something darkly menacing and wrong in the sight of this handsome and imperious woman, the noblest among them, reduced to helpless rage. Surely the powers of night would descend to vindicate her.

After an awkward length of time Gundobad proclaimed with thin gaiety, while grinning and nodding, "I like her spirit!" He was determined to fight the unease settling about the yard in an evil cloud. He ordered a cask of his own mead opened—an unrealized deference to Athelinda's threat. Gundobad himself planned to touch none of it—he seemed to sense he would need his wits about him to claim this difficult bride.

Athelinda regarded Gundobad with empty eyes, a look he misread as defeat. Then she withdrew abruptly into the gloom of the hall.

"Mudrin," Athelinda whispered, "bring out my marriage dress." Mudrin fled past her and opened the oak chest by the hearth and, with trembling hands, brought out a girdle of silver and a voluminous white woolen shift, its square neckline and hem embroidered with entwined serpents in crimson and forest green. Athelinda had worn it when she was married to Baldemar. Mudrin looked at Athelinda, her eyes blurred with hopelessness. "Dare we desecrate this!"

"It is fitting I should die in it. Understand, Mudrin, I go to my death. I mean to slay him before I take the vow, and then end my own life."

Mudrin collapsed into the mead bench and broke into bitter, desolate sobs. Fredemund held her temple while slowly shaking her head, muttering, "Lady of Night, have mercy! Fria, how can you allow it!" Athelinda took a battered Roman short sword from the wall, a relic from the battle with Wido. When she had put on the flowing white garment, she instructed Mudrin to conceal the weapon beneath its folds, and had her cut a small opening in the shift so the sword could be drawn out.

"And bring in the pendant of garnet and the doeskin shoes.

Today I will greet Baldemar in the Sky Hall arrayed exactly as on our marriage day."

Carefully Fredemund arranged the cloth to disguise the sword. Then she put a silver circle on her lady's head and fastened the gem-studded iron clasps at her sleeves. Over this she put a cloak dyed in delicately tinted squares of red and blue, fastening it at the shoulder with an intricate gold fibula in the shape of a boar with a carnelian eye.

"Quickly, the hearthfire, or he will suspect!" Athelinda said to Mudrin. The thrall woman got up heavily as if drunken with tears, found a jug of water, and poured it down the hearthfire's length, extinguishing it. At a wedding the hearthfire must be lit anew. At the last moment Athelinda felt a spasm of faintheartedness, and she turned away from the door.

"I have never used a sword," she whispered. "I cannot!"

Fredemund leaned close, her lower lip protruding slightly as it did when she set her mind on a thing. "You've gutted a hog, haven't you?" she said in her rough, sweet whisper, gripping Athelinda's shoulder with a doughy hand. "Rest your fears, my lady. Wodan will guide your hand."

In answer Athelinda stiffened her spine, nodded slightly, then went out into the sunlight in her finery, forcing herself not to think of the sword, hoping this would prevent Gundobad from noticing its outline against the cloth.

She saw that while she was preparing herself, Witgern and his party had arrived. As she suspected, they were pitifully few—they were a disheartening sight with the hollows round their eyes, the stench of hopelessness about them. Among them were Amgath, who once leapt a flaming cart, and tall golden-haired Coniaric, never defeated in a footrace. Neither looked strong enough to sit a horse. They collected by the gate, quietly watching.

I should not have sent for them, Athelinda thought. I only summoned more witnesses to this loathsome ceremony.

The marriage priestess, a sturdy, bland-faced woman of middle years, called Alruna, stood in the shadow of the tent, her head bowed. In one hand, she held a torch to relight the hearthfire; in the other, a gilt horn of mead for the wedded couple to share.

Gundobad was surprised at Athelinda's sudden docile calm, but he thought: Ah, she admires my boldness—and she is, after all, a reasonable woman.

As Athelinda walked down the avenue of shields and moved into the shade of the tent, she walked a little stiffly but maintained a look of serenity, looking neither right nor left. The blade of the sword was like ice against her thigh. She halted beneath the marriage tent alongside her groom. Discreetly her right hand moved closer to the opening Mudrin had cut in the cloth of her gown. Gundobad stood next to her, smiling smugly, his thrust-forward stomach reminding her of a rooster's chest, his heavy, rasping breaths making him seem greedy even for air. She thought: An ox would have more sensitivity to what passes here.

Do they not see how violently I tremble? What madness! Baldemar, come close and lend me strength.

"I call down Fria to witness," Alruna drawled in settled contentment. Athelinda despised her; how could she take part in this sanctified rape? Athelinda knew then how great Geisar's influence still was among the Holy Ones; no priest of Wodan before him had ever succeeded in corrupting a marriage priestess. These were evil times, a good time to die.

". . . this sacred joining of woman to man . . . ," Alruna droned on. Athelinda paid little attention until she heard the words, ". . . You will now cross hands, left to left, right to right."

Athelinda tensed. *The handfasting.* This was the part of the ceremony that would bind her forever to Gundobad. His hands were already extended. She forced herself to meet his eyes. Slowly she brought her own hands up; her palms grew wet with perspiration.

Now. The sword. Now.

The silence was sundered by a noisy clattering of hooves.

A single rider galloped at great speed beneath the Cat-Skull Gate, then halted abruptly where the flax field gave way to the yard. Athelinda recognized the horse first: It was the dappled stallion from the horse test. She looked more carefully.

She drew in a breath and took a quick step forward to better see, almost toppling the priestesses' oakwood table.

Auriane.

She wanted to cry out a warning. *My child, why do you come alone? They will murder you.*

But Athelinda's throat was frozen. Too late she realized her quick movements exposed the sword's pommel through the opening in the marriage dress.

Gundobad saw. He seized Athelinda's sword, roughly drew it out, then angrily threw it onto the ground in front of his men.

"Behold her! Treacherous harpie!" He grasped Athelinda's arm in one huge fist, twisted it painfully, then forced her to her knees. She uttered a small cry of pain.

Gundobad's men stiffened uncomfortably, their feelings ranging from embarrassment to outrage on Athelinda's behalf. Mudrin ran to her mistress, all reason gone, crying out, "You *swine!* How dare you!" When Mudrin was close enough, Gundobad struck the thrall-woman so hard across the mouth a thread of blood streaked down her chin. Mudrin sank to the ground.

"Gundobad," one of his men said quietly. *"Look behind you."*

Gundobad turned. Auriane had dismounted and was walking toward him. Gundobad shrugged and said with nonchalance, "There is nothing behind me but the ghost of a niding who dares skulk about amongst the living."

"Get up!" he then commanded Athelinda, attempting to drag her to her feet. But Athelinda wrest her arm from his grip and fell back to her knees in the dust. Then she sat motionless, eyes fixed on the sky as she rapidly intoned the words of a curse.

Auriane halted when she was but a horse length from the marriage tent. A taut silence descended as the company shifted its attention to her. Athelinda joined them, slowly dropping her gaze to look at Auriane.

Athelinda was jarred by the sight of her: She did not know this woman who was her daughter. Auriane's hair was drawn sleekly back into a Suebian knot; it gave her a look that was steely, refined. Those gray eyes were remote as she stood alert and still in a warrior's stance, concentrating fiercely upon Gundobad alone. Athelinda felt fear for her and pride in her, standing there so straight and young in a fawnskin tunic; she looked womanish and boyish at once, while calling up something else that was neither, just pure human spirit that was flexible and strong, a creature blending her father's will of adamantine with her own pure and solemn passion.

There was something of ancient songs in the scene. This spear maid returned from the dead to aid the living seemed to have sprung from the imagination of some bard.

Athelinda then recognized the hilt of Auriane's sheathed sword. *She has found it. But what does she think she is doing? Surely she does not mean to engage Gundobad in single battle.*

Impossible fool! Athelinda thought. The use of the sword in single battle requires time and schooling. Even with a powerful weapon such as that, a valiant heart is not enough. Now your blood will soak the ground.

"Leave at once, Gundobad," Auriane said. That voice stilled hearts as if a temple bell had been struck; it was sharp, clear, resonant, yet with a trace of sweetness. Only Athelinda noticed it faintly trembled. "And I will let you live."

"The closeness of marital happiness must have addled my wits!" Gundobad's red lips stretched into a broad grin. "I thought I heard you say—"

"You know well what I said!" With a light swift motion Auriane drew the sword. Athelinda shut her eyes and silently spoke the word *No*.

"Alruna! Commence!" Gundobad commanded. "Pay her no mind!" But Alruna was staring at the sword in Auriane's hand, a look of slow recognition and amazement coming into her face. Witgern, Thorgild, and the former Companions edged close, and they, too, began to regard Auriane's sword with sharp interest. Gundobad did not have time to wonder why.

For Auriane erupted from stillness to frenzy. The crude instinct of a beast of prey was all that saved Gundobad's life, for he drew his own sword just in time to deflect a strike that would have decapitated him.

The soul-shattering clang of blade on blade shocked him awake, and Gundobad realized how close he had come to death. *What was this? A wizard? A madwoman?* So quickly was he spun into the narrow world of life and death he had no time to be amazed at her fury, her art, as that swordblade flashed out with fearful speed and assurance. She was all about him like shifting gusts of wind— surviving this storm was his single thought.

The warriors watched in baffled quiet; in one moment a wedding proceeded, then *this*. They had seen dogfights easier to follow.

When Gundobad recovered from surprise, he collected himself and began to bear down on her, driving hard with coarse, sweeping strokes, striving to push her back through brute power. But Auriane was fluid as water flowing around stones; she performed a seamless dance of whiplike cross-strokes, each executed with raw exuberance as if this were play. Lightly, deftly, she teased him forward.

Athelinda felt a chill as if a spirit crossed her threshold. There was a power here above her understanding, greater than that startling skill, that bewildering speed, that towering confidence— and, of course, it must be the sword.

This is the Fates' deliverance. I am not abandoned.

Gundobad slowly took ground, using his sword like a scythe cutting invisible grain. He was not a subtle man and he knew no cunning tactics, but he had never needed them: In a world where strength was always pitted against strength, he was stronger than most men; he was more than twice her weight and had their blades contacted directly he could have thrown her to the ground with enough force to knock the breath out of her. His victory, he knew, was a matter of time.

But her endurance began to annoy him. And her cunning was maddening. Was she just managing to avoid the full force of his blows—or was he losing his wits? His rage increased as he began to sense he was losing the respect of his men. Destroying her was taking too long. He began to feel as ridiculous as some buffoon swatting and missing a fly, again and again.

He let out a growling roar, his face reddening dangerously. He began to sweat heavily and grow clumsier. He knew he was tiring.

Auriane felt herself but a concentration of energy and force. She had come here ready to die, but to her amazement found herself more triumphantly alive than she had ever felt. She was suspended between earth and sky, lifted high over grief. She felt clean and newborn, unbounded by the limits of the body; she might have been drums and flutes, or a hundred dancers, or some celestial instrument tuned to the stars, drawing beauty from silence. Where was her evil? It could not catch her.

All who watched felt themselves in a holy place, witnessing the gods working their will through this violent eruption of clashing blades. Witgern felt the spirit of Baldemar all around and thought: He dwells among us still. How could I have ever doubted?

Auriane imagined herself a cat in a waking sleep as she continued to lure Gundobad forward, awaiting his first moment of inattention.

Suddenly Gundobad caught one of the tentpoles and tore it free; the white canopy drifted down. Now he had two weapons, the sword in his right hand, the pole in his left.

This brought a volley of objections—from Gundobad's men as well as Baldemar's former Companions.

"Treachery! Dishonor!" Sacred law governed every aspect of single battle, and the code limited each combatant to one weapon.

But Gundobad's rage obliterated all concern with proprieties. He brought up the tentpole and delivered a cracking blow to Auriane's right shoulder; she sank to one knee, pain evident in her face. But she quickly recovered herself, staggered up, and delivered a hard two-hand blow to the pole, snapping it in two. Immediately she knew she had only improved his weapon; it now had a sharp jagged point, and was shorter, rendering it better for maneuvering at close range. And fear knifed in, for the first time.

Gundobad lunged, holding the pole low, aiming the point at her stomach. She found herself melting into step with him, gliding backward, a hand's breadth out of range. Then she grasped the pole's end in her free hand and pulled hard, choosing the precise moment he began a step forward and was most off balance, jerking him in the direction he was moving. Gundobad fell toward her, and she wrenched the broken pole from him as he opened his hands to break his fall.

"Well done! Well done!" cried warriors of both sides. Now Gundobad had utterly lost his own men. He recovered his sword while Auriane tossed the broken pole out of his reach. Then Gundobad lurched for her once more, before he was fully on his feet. Auriane stopped a low cut that would have severed the tendons of her leg; the impact knocked her sideways. When she recovered her balance, she made an answering downstroke, then paused in place, as if uncertain what move to make next.

He thrust energetically at her unguarded left side, not detecting this as a ruse. But she did not complete her cut with a defensive backhand stroke, which he would have naturally expected. Instead, she whipped about.

Gundobad's sword gutted the air. In one continuous motion Auriane spun round to face him once more, moving so swiftly that Gundobad's arm was still extended—and he was still wondering why she was not where she was supposed to be—when her blade struck him a powerful blow in the side.

Frenzied motion dropped into stillness. Gundobad bent forward, clutching at the deep gash between his ribs, trying to staunch the bleeding, fixing her with his battle-glare.

One of Gundobad's men muttered in a low voice. "That truly is it—the sword of Baldemar!"

Gundobad heard, and his whole body seized up. He regarded her sword as if it were some viper with a will of its own. All her skill in swordsmanship he attributed now to the marvelous properties of the weapon.

Auriane sprang for him then; with a double hold she struck the sword from his hand.

Gundobad fell ponderously to his knees. Her blade whipped up, poised at his thick bearded throat.

The company's dread-filled silence gave way to the first cautious stirrings of ecstasy. She had reclaimed her place, and Athelinda's, and set to right what had been wrong since the death of Baldemar. She was blessed, or never would the gods have allowed her to unearth that sword. No one doubted in that moment the power and presence of the Three Fates, those gloomy weavers-of-life who handed out their judgments beneath the World Ash; their primeval spirits looked out of Auriane's eyes. Had not Ramis named her for the *aurr*, the sacred earth on which the three dark sisters stood?

"Victory is ours!" one of Gundobad's men called out gaily.

"Baldemar strikes down his enemy from beyond the grave!" Witgern exclaimed, laughing. Athelinda noticed a blush of life in Witgern's face not there when he rode into the yard. It did not seem odd to any of them that their enmity was gone, and they had melted into one band. All accepted it as the natural result of the presence of Baldemar's ghost.

Auriane was mildly dazed as she stood over her humbled, panting enemy. What *was* that which possessed her while she fought? She had had only a glimmer of it while practicing with Decius; today it nearly shook her soul from her body—that glorious exuberance that heated the blood must be what sword dancers felt at festivals when they danced to near exhaustion. Why had no one told her that swordfighting was like taking a draught of the mead of the gods?

She feared for Decius, now that she revealed her secret to all—but she was fairly confident no one would suspect he had instructed her in secret. If good fortune held, all would attribute her skill to the sword and look no farther.

"I should not let you live," she said to Gundobad between heaving breaths, "for you have gravely insulted my mother."

Gundobad was pitiably childlike without his shield of arrogance. "Let me live and I will serve you all my days," he said in a voice that put her in mind of a dog's whine, ". . . and more loyally than any thrall. I can be of use to you. I will dedicate my band to your service. Think on it!"

Auriane disliked this role of judge, for there were too many unknowns. Who *was* this man, truly? Was there some good lurking in him at all? Forcing Athelinda was monstrous. But what if some demon possessed him then that now was exorcised? He did not appear monstrous now.

But he had fought treacherously, a decidedly evil thing. Finish him then, for the safety of the people. But then, he had been surprised and attacked suddenly. Anyone might have. . . .

She stopped herself abruptly, realizing she was thinking as Decius would, considering not only the act but the circumstances clustered about it. Sacred law was no longer an impenetrable wall; the wall crumbled in places, and she could see beyond.

Athelinda regarded them with a hard, ungiving stare. She knew her mother wanted her to kill him.

Then Auriane knew she could not, and it was not entirely the doing of Decius. The stark memory of her father's face distorted in agony somehow increased her sympathy for all the living, no matter what their station or condition; she saw Baldemar in every death. It seemed mad and unsupportable, for Baldemar and Gundobad were as far separated in honor as men could be. Perhaps, she thought, it is just some weakness in myself.

"I will let you live," Auriane replied, "if you repay my mother well for the injury done her. All these marriage gifts she will keep. Above that, you will pay to her a third of the produce of your family farms for three years."

Athelinda was outraged at first that Auriane was releasing her tormentor, but the size of the payment pleased her greatly, more because she knew it would impoverish Gundobad than because of her desire for these things, and she faintly smiled.

"Yes. It shall be done," Gundobad replied eagerly.

"And you must give oath to aid me in bringing my father's murderer to me."

Gundobad gave a manic nod of assent, too relieved to think closely about the implication of those words. But the others did, and they exchanged baffled looks.

"And you will humble yourself before Athelinda now," Auriane continued, "and beg her lenience." Feverishly Gundobad nodded again. Auriane motioned for him to rise. Gundobad got up unsteadily and prostrated himself before Athelinda.

Only then did full knowledge of what she had done fall hard on Auriane's shoulders. Death had closed so tightly about her she could scarcely breathe, held her for a time, then passed on. *Now* she felt fully the terror of the battle—fury could carry her for only so long, then it dropped her, weak and shivering, back to earth.

She stood very still, her gaze on Gundobad, still not daring to meet Athelinda's eyes, not knowing if the sight of her was loathsome to her mother. Athelinda let Gundobad stay in that humble posture for a while, then she whispered, "Get up, niding's accomplice that you are! Never come near this farm, and I will ask no further punishment for you."

Two of Gundobad's men helped him to Thrusnelda's lodge so she could tend to his wound. Witgern then approached Auriane, who still faced away from her mother. "Auriane," he asked carefully, "what did you mean when you said, 'my father's murderer'?"

Auriane caught her breath when she looked at Witgern; he was so emaciated it seemed a good gust of wind could take him off. "I learned from . . . from a Roman thrall a thing that is commonly known among our enemies." Without emotion, she retold Decius' tale. She shut her ears to the sound of Athelinda's muffled tears, fearful she would go mad.

A slow smile came over Witgern's face. "That is wondrous! Then vengeance can be won!" he whispered. "We are saved!"

From behind them came cautious shouts of joy. It would take time for Baldemar's old Companions to fully appreciate that freedom had come. Auriane could not take any pleasure in their rejoicing at this moment; grief still owned her completely. "Auriane, then you must . . . ," Witgern began, and broke off awkwardly. He meant to say, "return to us," until he remembered Athelinda's curse.

"Go now," Athelinda broke in curtly. "Leave me in peace, all of you!"

Auriane gave Witgern a look of pity and understanding, then embraced him. Gradually all did as Athelinda bid, leaving by twos and threes for the village.

When they were gone, Auriane turned to find Berinhard, who was grazing among the apple trees. She meant to return to the forest.

"But not *you,* Daughter. Stay."

Auriane stopped abruptly. They stood alone in what seemed a wasteland. The wind kicked up eddies of dust; it reminded her of that barren twilight when she came here to find Baldemar's horse, riderless.

Finally the silence pressed too heavily on her chest. "You cannot want me here, Mother. I will go now."

Athelinda said to her back, "I do not say what I do not mean."

Auriane fought hard to say no more; then the words were torn from her: "I do not know how you could have cursed your own flesh and blood!"

Athelinda was surprised to silence. "Auriane," she said at last, her voice now a firm, gentle hand pulling her close, "I thought you *knew*. You must have known. I cursed you to keep you *alive*. Geisar would have killed you after you so boldly named his crime before the throng! I am a mother. Any mother would rather have her child cursed than slain horribly. Grief must have taken your wits—in days before, you would have understood at once."

"Do you count me his murderer?" She winced as she spoke, as if her throat were a wound, and the words, stinging salt.

"Never! Never did I."

"Why would you not look at me on the funeral day?"

"I looked at no one. Grief blinded—I saw nothing."

"Hertha's vile words were true!"

"No. Hers was a loathly and bitter spirit. She saw evil in everything. Should Wodan come to me in face and say it, I would not believe my daughter a murderer of kin."

"You . . . you will undo your curse then?" Slowly Auriane turned round and forced herself to meet her mother's eyes. There was no hatred there, only the look of a creature lost.

"It was undone at once, that very night, in a secret ceremony with Thrusnelda."

Auriane rushed to her then, and her mother held to her tightly; neither spoke for long moments. Stroking her hair, Athelinda continued, "My poor child! *Now* it will be no secret. You have returned, which is to Geisar as if Baldemar returned, or worse, for you so openly thwarted his authority. I want you *here,* understand. But listen to me! It would almost be better if you stayed in the forest, for it will only be a matter of time before Geisar finds an acceptable way of murdering you."

She disengaged herself from her mother's arms. "I must stay here. . . . I am certain it is what Father wanted. What is done is done." She turned to the south, the direction of the advancing Roman plague. "Geisar is a horsefly compared to what menaces us from the south. I cannot abandon our people."

Athelinda embraced her tightly again. After long silence she held Auriane at arm's length and said, "Baldemar's spirit is great, but still you could not have done what you did without *some* tutelage. Who in the name of all the gods taught you the art of the sword?"

Auriane was not surprised her mother had not been fooled. She hesitated, knowing Athelinda would not like the truth any better than Baldemar had, equally certain her mother would know if she held part of it back. "The Roman thrall," she said at last. "The same one that gave me the tidings about Odberht."

Athelinda's eyes darkened. "You have been alone with a man who is a foreigner? That is reckless and mad. What would cause you to even think of it?"

Auriane had no answer. Then from some shadowed place words came unbidden: "'The Fates handed us our holy traditions . . . , but when cycles end, they choose some wise fool to break them.'"

"And for a reply, I get words from Ramis! I thought you despised her."

Auriane started; she had not thought whose words those were. Uneasiness swarmed in then. Was Ramis creeping into her thoughts while she slept—a slow insidious invasion that would leech away her outrage, all her willingness to fight?

"I . . . I do. But, Mother, we are near to destruction! No one bleeds and dies if I am alone with a foreigner. But if I can learn their magic, I might keep us alive longer."

"Like your father, you've a ready answer to allow the uncommon!" Athelinda said, smiling and shaking her head. "This day is the gift of Fria. Swear on a plait, you'll not leave me again except through death."

On the next day Witgern saw that a solemn feast was prepared for Auriane. Coniaric, who of all the old Companions of Baldemar was wealthiest in cattle, provided three oxen to be sacrificed to Wodan for her well-being and roasted for the feast. Horns were blown, summoning those who dwelled in the countryside to the Village of the Boar. This was the first day of gladness since the death of Baldemar; through her holiness, Auriane had driven off the evil that struck at the tribe's sacred center. None near her home village ever again whispered that she was a slayer of kin.

When the mead-horn had gone round many times, Witgern and Thorgild rose together, commanded silence, then entreated her to lead them as Baldemar had. She did not protest—she knew better now—for the current that bore her forward all her life was now swift and irresistible, carrying her midstream. A hundred and ten drank and gave oath to fight and die for her—most were former Companions of Baldemar, but there were also twenty of Gundobad's, a varied collection of unallied young men, and a half dozen young women born temple-children, the issue of Ash Priestesses, who joined partly to thwart Geisar, who had been ever more brazenly robbing their shrines. Auriane suspected that Thrusnelda disapproved of all this, in spite of the smile of practiced benignity on her round face—she believed, Auriane knew, that a woman was debased by handling a sword, that the spirits that swarmed about a woman despised the touch of iron. Most others viewed the situation in reverse: Auriane would not be debased; rather, the battlefield would be sanctified through a woman's greater holiness, and the killings would be transformed into sacred offerings. This uncommon case of a woman crossing from the world of the spirits to the world of war was counted a great good omen by most. But Thrusnelda, as she blessed the fire by sprinkling it with the blood of the ox, looked at Auriane as if she had abandoned her true home.

Auriane spoke to no one of her certainty that even now she was not innocent, of her sense that her evil followed her persistently as night follows day. They might think her mad.

Thrusnelda prepared a fire of ash logs so those who wished could swear vengeance against Odberht. Then she stood before it, bearing Baldemar's sword on a white linen cloth.

Auriane was first to swear; with one hand on a plait of hair, the other on the blade of the sword, she spoke the words of the oath:

"Before Wodan I declare I will not rest, nor will I cut my hair, until Odberht is destroyed by my hand. I will call him to judgment, whether he cross the sea or fly beyond the sky-reaching mountains. Know, Baldemar, you will not lie unquiet. She who stands before you will raise you up through the blood of your bane, Odberht."

She took a horn of mead, drank it down, refilled it, and gave it to Witgern as witness. He took the same oath, drank, then passed it to Thorgild, who grinned at her, a look of comradely encouragement.

They feasted far into the night. The tale-singers began to play but retreated jealously into the background when Witgern brought out his lyre. None had a voice to match his rich, silken tones—strong, dark honey, Athelinda had called it once. He gave them one of their favorite songs—a gruesome tale of a monster from the bogs who attacks the hall of a great chief, nightly seizing ten or twelve of the chief's companions for his dinner, then sharing the meal with his ogress mother. The battle-chief summons a greater chief from afar—here, to flatter Auriane, Witgern substituted Baldemar's name for that of the usual hero—and the great chief comes in glory and slays the beast, tearing it limb from limb. Half of the villagers listened, and half fell into a drunken sleep, for they had heard versions of the tale so many times.

When Witgern and Auriane were among the few still wakeful, he said to her in an offhand way, "Did you know Sigwulf is searching everywhere for that Roman thrall called Decius?"

Auriane was sharply alert. She fought for calm. "Is he?"

"He's even offered a rich reward. When he returns from the south—"

"Witgern . . . , what does he mean to do when he finds him? Is it honorable to put so much effort into punishing one lowly thrall?"

"*Punish?* He wants to raise him up and shower him with gifts. Auriane, that thrall led him to his son."

"What? No!"

"The words the thrall read from the book were true. Sigwulf found a smith at the native settlement outside Mattiacorum who knew the farm this Decius named. Sigwulf's son Eadgyth was a chained laborer in the field—and the boy but a child of nine! They have no shame or pity. Through two separate traders Sigwulf arranged to buy him back, for a sum large enough to make even Geisar smile."

"So there was one happy outcome of that day," Auriane said, carefully keeping her voice flat. She realized with a private surge of joy that Decius need not hide from anyone now.

"You are happier than you show, Auriane."

She looked at him, realizing then his whole purpose in speaking of the matter was to probe her feelings. "Yes," she said, looking at him sadly, then looking down. "You have a sharp eye, Witgern . . . , or else I no longer know myself and have become as unsubtle as Gundobad." She paused, wanting and not wanting to explain. "I do not know if you would understand it."

"Oh, I understand *well* love that cannot be fulfilled!" He took her hand and held it in the dark. "Better than any man of them here." She felt sharp loneliness, as if all the world were empty of comfort, and realized she was knowing *his* loneliness, as if his touch had infused it into her blood.

She grasped his hand with both of hers. "Love is a willful creature that cannot be harnessed, penned or leashed—it bolts and pulls us after it, into a pit for all it cares. We agree upon that, then! My secret will be closely kept?"

"Of course. But it is so dangerous, Auriane. That is my only discouraging thought on the matter. Especially now. When Geisar learns you've returned and that we've formed something resembling Baldemar's Companions, he will declare war on you. How he would delight to know you dream of bedding a foreigner. He would even be evil enough to accuse you of lying with him, you know."

She realized with sharp alarm Witgern accepted most of the truth—but was incapable of grasping all of it.

The next day Auriane rode out to bring Decius back to the hall.

"Does this mean all will be as before?" Decius asked as they galloped together over a meadow scattered with rose-tinted flowers of fragrant marjoram. "I can take up life in my miserable but homey hut with its fondly familiar leaks, and your fellow tribesmen won't try to use my hide as a tent?"

"Better than that," she shouted into the wind. "Sigwulf is insisting you be freed! Thralls are almost never freed."

"*Freed!* What milk and honey that would have been to my ears two years ago! Decius, you're free. Just do not try to travel anywhere in the known world."

"Known world?"

"The part of the world with books and baths and forums and real roads, real food, and steam heat. Tell Sigwulf I am grateful, but it isn't going to make an appreciable difference in my condition."

"Because we are barbarians."

"I was not going to say it."

"Idiot. I hear you thinking it."

As usual, Decius was maddeningly impervious to her anger, grinning as if it were amusing as a child's fit of temper. She released Berinhard, and he shot ahead of Decius' horse—she was amazed at this horse's speed; it seemed there was no steed Berinhard could not catch and pass—but soon her anger abated, and she decided she had made Decius look long enough at her horse's hindquarters. She slowed and let him come alongside her again.

Smoothly he shifted back to the manner of a beloved. "Soon it will be difficult for us to . . . to lie together. *That* is a loss greater than any gain this questionable freedom may bring."

"We will find a way. Let us not speak of it." She was silent for a moment. "Decius, all of this should make me more joyous than it does. I am home. Gundobad is routed. Mother does not despise me. But the hearthfire smokes with poisons and the mead has no taste and there is something great and large missing from the house. And the tasks ahead are near impossible. I do not even know how to *find* Odberht. He is a coward—he will not come at my summoning. What am I to do?"

"I suppose you would not consider putting all that in back of you and thinking on it no more."

"What nonsense! How can I? It is *before* me every day. Could you bear it if it were your own father?"

"I've no answer to that—there was no love between my father and me. It is a shame, that is all, because I see far *greater* problems stalking you. Every time your people cross the river and go looting and killing you bring closer the day that there will be war with Rome, a *real* war, not the skirmishes you've known in your lifetime. I have said it before—you do not know what that means."

Auriane at once sent a messenger north to the king of the Cheruscans, in whose service Odberht was reported to be. As it happened, she knew her challenge was received; the messenger reported on his return that Odberht heard it personally in King Chariomerus' hall. As she feared, the reply was silence.

Then in late autumn of the following year, Auriane saw him.

At summer's end a sacred horse race was held annually on the strip of wild country between the lands claimed by her people and the territories of the Cheruscans; it was part of the autumn festivities celebrated by all the tribes, a rite to give energy to the earth and ensure its revival after winter's death-sleep. This year the prize of the race was particularly rich: enough weapons of iron to equip a king's retinue. It happened that a Gallic trader fished fifteen wagonloads of native spears and longswords from a stream where they had been deposited as an offering to Wodan, then sold them to King Chariomerus. When Chariomerus learned that the weapons had been impiously snatched from the most feared of the gods, he gave them up as a prize of the race in hopes that Wodan would spare his life.

Auriane knew her people had an urgent need of the prize—in the southern reaches of their lands the Romans had begun systematically stripping whole villages of weapons, knowing that weapons production was so slow among her people that years would pass before they could fully replace them. As she judged Berinhard's chances better than most—in village contests he regularly outran the fleetest of the captured Roman cavalry horses—Auriane made the nine days' journey north to take part in the race.

And so she sat astride her fretting dappled stallion, waiting with a field of fifty-nine riders for the starting rope to drop. On the plain alongside the first leg of the course, men and women of all tribes had erected a village of tents; here horse traders gathered and peddlers cried their wares: wheel-made pots, ornaments of amber, fine glass vessels, salted haunches of beef, linen cloth dyed every hue. Arrayed in a line before the impatient contestants were twelve priestesses and priests clad in ocher-stained hides and horse-skull headdresses; they hummed a dark invocation to Erda, goddess of the deep forces of the earth, who was Fria in her most blind and primal form. Among the riders of the race, Auriane saw the brown-red tunics of their enemies, the Hermundures, the sunburnt faces of the wiry horsemen of the Tencteres who were taught to ride before they could walk, and a number of tall, fair riders from the Bructeres, her mother's people. There were as well three sinewy maids of fierce aspect from the tribe of sorcerers who dwelled by the Amber Sea, called the Sitones, or Queen-People, because their chief was always a woman, and two brash Cheruscan youths who laughed loudly at each other's jests while watching her with looks of playful lust from atop rangy Roman cavalry mounts.

It was not until the horses burst forth and Auriane was lost in their jostling, thundering midst that she realized Odberht was among the riders.

He was positioned perhaps twenty horses away, and to her mind, poorly mounted, which was odd, considering his wealth. The sight of that face with those spoiled lips, those pale eyes so strangely empty of feeling, that look of a man who would mutilate the body of an enemy after he was dead, caused her to contract with coldness and nausea. Whenever she stole a look at him, she found him watching her calmly, assessing her as a warrior might one he stalks, weighing agility, quickness, strength of bone.

All at once her first concern was no longer winning the race but staying alive.

The line of horses broke up slowly as each sought its own pace; soon their order was random as scattered seeds. She held Berinhard back to save his strength for the finish, and was momentarily relieved when Odberht was nowhere to be seen; she assumed he had surged into the lead.

The course itself was laid out in a great circle; most if it lay beyond the sight of the throng. At the extreme western end was a treacherous rockslide, terminating in a jumble of boulders far below; beyond that was the shifting, blue-green ocean of the Hercynian Forest, rolling to a horizon that melted into creamy mist. The track was narrow along the rockslide, and there was not room for more than five horses running abreast; occasionally a horse and rider fell to their death, driven over the edge when too many tried to take the pass at once.

Auriane reached the rockslide with three other riders; two buffered her from the frightful slide. Then as if at a signal these two held their mounts back—she was sharply uneasy when she realized both wore the blue cloaks of the Cheruscans, Odberht's adopted tribe. Simultaneously a horseman ahead of her abruptly lost ground and found his pace again when he was alongside her, occupying the inside position—while she now galloped alongside the edge of the slide.

The horseman was Odberht. Berinhard's hooves were spitting stones, sending them rattling down the near-vertical slope. The son of Wido grinned at her—a look full of malign sensuality that assumed her complicity in some great, unnamed crime. She smelled again the rot of the bogs, felt that bullish strength, remembered her terror, on that night he had savaged her in the swamp grasses.

She scarcely had time to recognize him before he pulled out a length of leather he used as a riding whip, shouted words lost in the rushing wind, then abruptly reined his horse into hers, ramming Berinhard like a ship at war. The dappled stallion was badly jolted. Auriane lurched forward, grasping the silken neck to keep her seat. The slide with its tearing teeth was so close she felt she galloped over it rather than just at its edge.

"Outcast! Swine!" she cried out hoarsely. "Fight me honorably, you son of a flea-ridden wolf!"

He grinned in answer and swung his mount into hers a second time. His horse was a solid beast, seeming heavier than Berinhard by half, less suited to racing, more suited to pulling great loads. Had he chosen this beast solely with murdering her in mind?

His horse's shoulder slammed into her leg, numbing it. At the same time Odberht lashed at Berinhard's face with the length of leather. She felt her stallion's forelegs fumble; now Berinhard's forehooves were on solid ground while his hind legs grappled desperately with the slide. Auriane cried out in terror.

The leather strap fell again, striking her face. Blood blurred her vision. But she was so panicked she did not feel the pain. She strove frantically to help her horse by throwing her weight on the side of safety.

Just as Berinhard managed to scramble onto level ground, Odberht came for her once again. This time she heard him over the wind.

"Die, wicked kin-killing spawn of Baldemar!"

The words burned more painfully than any lash. An ungovernable fury took her then. She seized the long ends of her reins and used them as a whip, laying them across Odberht's back, his horse's neck, drawing blood. Once again he strove to pull his horse into hers, but now his mount was terrified of her; the beast skittered away, white showing in its eyes, refusing to obey the rein.

She withdrew the dagger from her belt. The two trailing riders gradually pulled ahead of them; now she and Odberht were alone. They left the slide behind; their horses moved at a jolting canter through a wide meadow bordered with brambles. Berinhard twisted sideways as she struggled to pull him into Odberht's horse.

"Niding! Murderer!" she shouted as she struck at him with the dagger, tearing at air. He guided his horse in a serpentine path to elude her, taunting her with the vengeance he would not let her take.

"Fight me!" Her throat felt inflamed and raw.

Abruptly he pulled his horse around so that he was broadside to her, forcing her to halt to avoid crashing into him and injuring her horse.

"You are not worthy, killer of kin!" he called out teasingly. "Come, follow me down the off-trail and I'll show you what you're worthy of, you maddened bitch-dog!"

"I shall have you! Death will not take me before I avenge! I shall have you if I have to follow you down into the valleys of Helle!"

But already he was turning his horse, and he galloped off onto a half-hidden path that led north into the country of the Cheruscans, leaving the race, forcing her to make a desperate decision.

Should she abandon the race to pursue him? When Berinhard, swift as he was, still might catch and pass the field before the finish? Perhaps his whole purpose was this: to make an attempt on her life, and failing that, to ensure that she did not win the prize for her people. He would not dare come near the finish where Witgern waited, and so many others who had sworn vengeance against him.

With scarcely a pause, Auriane chose the race. He would not face her honorably in accordance with the laws of single battle, so what was the use of pursuit?

Once more he had his will with her, then went off satisfied on his way.

Berinhard bolted joyfully after the scattered horses as they disappeared into a birch forest, his strides lengthening rapidly; he was as eager to catch them as she was. She felt herself flung from a catapult. She no longer sat a horse; she was in the grip of some force of nature, as when the earth moved or the gods hurled bolts of fire from the sky. She watched the lead horses, still far ahead, as they sailed with deer's grace over a stone wall. Steadily they grew larger in the distance.

We will win, Auriane thought with a silent shout of joy. The finish was still far enough off, and Berinhard was tireless as well as swift. He had time to regain the lead. Powerfully, steadily, Berinhard pulled abreast of the riders in the rear. They caught and passed horse after horse.

When at last the racing horses were visible from the finish and the throng saw her coming fast from behind, they knew this was a prodigious effort, and no matter what their tribe, they roared with one voice, urging her on. Berinhard was rippling gray fire, head and belly low to the ground, his dark tail raised like a victory banner, Auriane almost invisible on his back.

Only a single horseman of the Tencteres galloped ahead of her now, and Berinhard was bravely closing the distance.

But the finish rope flew at them too soon. The warrior of the Tencteres crossed it half a horse-length ahead of her. A bitter unvoiced cry caught in her throat.

Odberht had his victory. Were it not for him, the prize certainly would have been hers—and her people's. As she galloped past the crowds, she could not look at Witgern or Athelinda, shutting her ears to her tribespeople's shouted protests to the Fates. Odberht was a human manifestation of her ever-living shame, appearing suddenly as if in a magic mist, snatching her peace, then departing.

She despaired of ever having the chance to set things to right.

ROME

CHAPTER XVII

They will never prove it was murder.

Though they will try, Domitian thought as he stood at the bedside of his brother, the Emperor Titus, who lay dying at Vespasian's family villa in the small Italian village of Reate.

The deathbed had been carried to the atrium so that the imperial ministers and an historian could be witness to Titus' last words. The stale fruity perfume of freshly pressed grapes from the autumn harvest was heavy on the air. A bee drifted in on the shaft of red-gold sunlight slanting from the lightwell, its determined ellipses seeming to beckon to the soul of the dying man, its buzzing insistent in the formal silence.

After Vespasian's natural death Titus ruled but two years and two months when he was stricken with a mild summer malaise. The Palace physicians ordered him to his country estate to rest. The physicians of the estate reported to the Senate that he would soon recover. But yesterday evening, to everyone's astonishment, Titus' condition grew markedly worse.

I have to take solace in my cleverness, Domitian thought. I do not have the good fortune to be loved, as you are, Titus, curses on your name. It falls to my lot to do what is necessary, and be despised for it. You chose lenience and love over discipline and fear. As always, you leave the ugly tasks for me.

Domitian looked briefly at Marcus Arrius Julianus, now a senior magistrate of the courts, who stood across from him among the ministers. There was something active, troubled, in those solemn, clear eyes; they held a hint of sad resignation, as of one who against his wishes readies himself for war.

He cannot suspect me—he's got no evidence. And my ascension to the throne is the greatest good fortune that could befall him, because he knows I intend to raise him up and give him every honor. He must actually be *mourning* my brother. I thought he had better taste.

Marcus Arrius Julianus, never have I needed you more than now! You shall make the first speech introducing me to the Senate when they confirm me in my office. Your gift of being loved is even more remarkable than my brother's, for he gained it late in life with the help of supreme power. *Yours* issues wholly from your own nature. It shall be put into my service.

Titus' right hand struggled up. Domitian tautened in terror.

Now he will point me out and accuse me.

But that hand only groped at emptiness, as though making a last feeble grasp at the awesome power it held.

Domitian had waited many years for this opportunity to claim his rightful place. Titus had for long kept him in enforced idleness, allowing him no hand in governing, while he himself accepted the highest posts and eventually stole the imperial seat itself. Domitian was certain that when their father, the Emperor Vespasian, died, Titus had tampered with Vespasian's will to ensure he and not Domitian became the next Emperor. Was his brother not always boasting of his ability to forge names?

Titus' hand dropped as if his spirit flew out in a rush. Cleomenes the physician pushed past Domitian with his silver tray of aromatic decoctions and sponges, feeling for pulses, for breath.

"He is gone," Cleomenes said, the last word living on in their minds like the stern toll of a bell. From an inner room came the sound of a woman crying.

Domitian closed his brother's eyes. All heard the staccato of galloping hooves in the carriageway as a messenger sped to the Senate in Rome with the grim tidings. About the villa the servants began planting cypress trees, the tree of death.

Only then did Domitian allow himself a dark shiver of ecstasy. It was difficult to comprehend all that now lay at his feet: the city of Rome, from the sewers and teeming tenements to the gilded basilicas, the aristocratic mansions, the holy House of the Vestals. The Senate that scorned him, the haughty Palace servants who played cruel tricks on him. His mind drifted to the thriving cities of the provinces flung out over the earth like so many precious gems, whose inhabitants would live their lives and go about their business in the shadow of his golden statues. The Mediterranean Sea was his own private lake. Legions stationed in lands he would never see were poised to do his bidding. Barbarians beyond the frontier would live by his sufferance. The fates of people from Britannia to Asia to Africa could be altered with a stroke of his pen.

But for some reason he could not fully name, the thought that the Colosseum was now wholly his own brought the sharpest pleasure of all—that family shrine his father began and his brother christened in blood—that greatest of all monumental works to which he would now add the final tier. Perhaps it was because that grand amphitheater was the world he ruled in microcosm—with its well-defined place for every rank of society, from Senators to freedmen and slaves, its ambassadors from subject nations who would look to him with reverence, its life-and-death battles on the sand that would be orchestrated by himself, its exotic beasts representing the far-flung lands at his feet, and its always hungry mob looking to him for largesse. Domitian knew that in the Colosseum's Imperial Box more than anywhere else he would feel most keenly the breadth of his power.

Domitian stole another discreet look at Marcus Julianus, searching that austere face, and thought: He senses the vague shape of these thoughts as I think them, and he does not approve.

Titus' First Secretary slid the imperial ring from the dead man's hand. Domitian took it without thinking and quickly put it on his own finger, as if fearful another might snatch it if he did not hurry. He caught a subtle flicker of surprise in Marcus Julianus' eyes.

And Domitian felt a cold hand grip his heart.

I am done. I am the fool who brings down the world with one hasty act! I should have waited and put on the cursed ring in private. Marcus Julianus is the one man who *knows* I should not be able to get it on my finger. I said an offhand word about this years ago, some lame joke or other about my hand being greater than Titus' and the ring needing to be enlarged to fit—a joke anyone *else* would have forgotten. But Marcus Julianus, as usual, forgets nothing.

That look proves it.

He's deduced, surely, I took the ring to the goldsmith beforehand to be enlarged, that I knew *yesterday*—when all the doctors said Titus would recover—that today the Emperor would die.

Domitian's hands quivered almost imperceptibly; he felt they were pierced by Julianus' keen, knowing gaze, struggling to get free. He saw with disturbing clarity a grim line of faces, the senior officers of the Praetorian Guard, who loved Titus as they loved no other—men who would cheerfully see him roasted on a spit if they knew he was the cause of their friend and benefactor's death. And he saw the faces of the most powerful Senators—Saturninus, Senecio, and Gallus, and Marcus Julianus himself, who would give fine speeches before the Senate, replete with literary allusions and all the trappings of the expensively educated rhetor's art, condemning him for that most heinous of crimes, *parricidium*, the murder of a parent or close relation, and demanding some barbarous punishment.

What is to be done? Marcus Julianus must die, along with all the servants who aided me.

But a tide of shame welled up in him that swept these thoughts off.

Already I plan a Senator's death and I have not reigned a full hour. My father executed one man in all the years of his reign; am I not destined to be a far better ruler than he?

Perhaps Marcus Julianus will be wise and forget what he saw.

In that moment Domitian understood with bright, painful clarity the cruelty of rulers: it stemmed from fear.

When those about the deathbed saw the imperial ring in place, they responded in soft, solemn voices not quite in unison, *"Ave, Caesar, Imperator . . ."* A moment elapsed before Domitian realized they addressed not his brother, not his father, but *him*.

But where was the rich pleasure he had always expected from hearing those words? He felt like an awkward actor forced to play the most demanding of roles before an audience ready to rip out his throat if he misspoke one line.

When the court returned to Rome, they found the rumor that Domitian murdered his brother had flown before them. Lyrics laying the crime at Domitian's door were scrawled everywhere on the city's walls—as usual, lack of evidence did nothing to slow a good tale. It grew spontaneously because of the people's love of Titus and great dislike of Domitian, its rapid growth fertilized by Domitian's gloomy and secretive nature.

On the day of the court's return an imperial messenger came to Marcus Arrius Julianus' great-house with a letter from Domitian, praising his great knowledge of the law and inviting him to be

First Advisor on the Emperor's High Council. Marcus Julianus was that night to attend a banquet in his honor. Marcus judged Domitian's purpose was either to silence him with kindness or to show the world just how undying and great their friendship was—so no hand would be raised to accuse the new Emperor when Domitian arranged *his* murder.

That same day one of Marcus Julianus' freedman clients employed as a scribe in the Petitions Office managed to spirit off to him, in advance of its public posting, a list of proscribed books. Among them were his father's twenty volumes on the customs of the tribes of Germania. He could not have been seized with greater outrage if Domitian had desecrated his father's tomb before his eyes.

He waits not even a month to flout that solemn promise he made in the last days of Nero. Does he think I will be silent? My father's dying torments were eased only because I promised to keep his works alive.

But Marcus Julianus knew his circumstances were already precarious; confronting Domitian on this matter might prove as ill-advised as leaping into a bear-pit armed with a stick. He called his father's old friend, Saturninus, for a meeting, with the intention of informing the aged Senator of what he learned, so that in the event of his own death Saturninus would be better armed against Domitian.

For privacy they walked the labyrinthine graveled walkways of his vast gardens. Briefly Marcus Julianus related the tale of the ring.

"The clever monster! I *knew* he sent his brother off himself! The question is *how?*" Saturninus' frown was deeply inscribed in his face; he looked like old Cronus, set to destroy a whole host of upstart younger gods. He was a gnarled, stoutly-made man with an obdurate spirit that put Marcus Julianus in mind of the bedrock that crops up in fields, breaking plows. Though his features were softly eroding with age—the birthday he had celebrated recently at Julianus' great-house was his seventieth—those eyes still flickered with energy and fire, and when he held forth in full voice, his sonorous rumble could still carry to the highest galleries of the basilica.

"Exactly. How did he manage it? We've a body with no marks of poison on it, and no signs of foul play. It's enough to make one believe in the efficacy of magic spells. By my father's ghost, I mean to learn how he managed that murder, no matter what time and effort it takes," Marcus Julianus said with carefully contained passion. "Two of the three attending doctors died mysteriously the next morning. The third is still alive—a man named Cleomenes, who I learned is a native of the Isle of Rhodes. He got to one of the ports and took to ship. *There* may lie our only hope of ever knowing. I mean to find that man before Domitian does."

"I doubt you'll survive long enough to find him." Saturninus paused dramatically and clamped an urgent hand on Marcus Julianus' shoulder. "Listen to me!" His voice dropped to a warbling whisper. "You should strike *before* he strikes. Accuse him *now*—and the Guard will believe *you* and not him. *Do not give him time to replace them with his own men.*"

Marcus Julianus wearily turned away. "The result would be too unpredictable," he replied quietly after a time. "And we need better proof. At best, I would be burning down a house to catch one rat. Removing Domitian suddenly would touch off civil war surely as Nero's death did. I would not do such a thing unless a successor were named. Unfortunately, Domitian *knows* I think this way and even counts on it. The sly fox will never name a successor now, I'll wager—in order to keep my hands bound."

"Well, you cannot seriously be thinking of accepting that post. Do not be a fool! He knows you *know*. Do you think he'll be easy with an advisor who sees his true nature? Retreat to your farthermost estate and quietly wait out his reign. He murdered his brother who was kind and good to him. He would scarcely think *twice* before murdering you."

Marcus Julianus briefly shut his eyes. "I cannot."

How this man tries to carry the weight of everyone, the living and the dead, Saturninus thought. But this time he takes on too much even for him.

"It's that cursed school, isn't it? And everyone you shelter there?"

"Yes, that's a good measure of it." Marcus Julianus had for seven years nurtured his school of philosophy and natural sciences like some beloved child, providing it with a library celebrated all over the world for its collection of rare and original manuscripts, and luring from the ten Academies of Athens—with a promise of a generous yearly dole—so many of their celebrated teachers that the citizens of Athens brought a formal complaint to the government in Rome. The school was a haven for those too poor or too despised to be tolerated anywhere else. The ragged followers of the martyred Isodorus lived there under Julianus' protection, as well as the humbler slaves of aristocratic households who had no other chance to acquire learning. In spite of the fact that Marcus Julianus did nothing to please the noble classes at Rome—the school was lodged in dilapidated buildings much too near the fish markets, and aristocratic students were treated no better than the rest—his school was fashionable, nevertheless, and they actually began sending Senate-bound sons to him who ordinarily would have finished their educations in Alexandria or Athens. The school kept alive his reputation for eccentricity—for it lost great sums of money since he welcomed any who earnestly desired to come, from poulterer's daughter to matchseller's son, charging only what students could pay.

"And there is this," Julianus went on, his look sad, intent, "I am haunted by the notion I might be the *only* man about Domitian able to keep him in check. You must know, old friend, my relationship to Domitian is . . . peculiar. I do not completely understand it myself. Domitian admires me more than he loves me—and counts me his greatest friend, though I would never count him as such."

"Yes. I have seen that."

"Understand I say this without pride. Another could have played this role, had he been in the right place at the right time in Domitian's youth. Sometimes a man, when young, encounters someone, frequently older, who, rightly or wrongly, he feels he can never equal. The power the older man has over him lingers like some persistent ghost, and that man's opinions carry greater weight all his life. I have become, half by chance, that man for Domitian—"

"Through your defense of your father. You are too modest. Many others besides Domitian praise you for that brilliantly mad act of devotion, my friend."

"What's important now is the effect it's had on *him*. That great need of his to curry my favor *must* be employed to our advantage. I cannot walk away from this. It's a delicate and dangerous balance, admittedly. If I do not love him, it worries him. But my independence is necessary as well, or he ceases to trust my judgment—"

"It is almost as though . . . he is confused and imagines you a parent rather than a friend."

"Precisely. And so you see, if I run to safety, there will not be an act he commits that I will not wonder—could I have averted it or softened it? I'm trapped at his side. How the Fates taunt us when we are grown with a silly shadow of what we wanted when

we were young! Once I had some notion of advising an emperor—
as a proud and noble use of philosophy. Grim reality reduces me
to a trickster who must outmaneuver a monster.''

"I should be well used to your easy assumptions that you can
master a situation most men would shun to approach. But I'm not,
and I grieve for you.''

"Grieve when the battle's lost, not while strategy is still being
laid! But know this, lest I misstep in the next few days."

He lowered his voice, though none were about to overhear but
a curious fawn stealthily approaching them through the oleander
bushes. "Titus documented every attempt of Domitian's to murder
him, in his letters to Vespasian's mistress, Caenis. They greatly
strengthen our case, should we one day be ready to tell what we
know to the Guard. They may even reveal the method of murder
that eventually succeeded. I *know* those letters are locked in some
nether storage room of the Palace—they will require patience to
locate. Domitian suspects they exist but is not certain. We must
cultivate the rumor that they exist in fact—and we must never
stop looking for them."

At the tenth hour Marcus Arrius Julianus reclined at the
imperial table in the dining hall of the Palace of Augustus, on
Domitian's right hand. Seven hundred banqueters gathered in a
vast space that froze the senses with its humbling brilliance—
from the domed ceiling remote as the heavens, to the massive
columns of red granite gleaming in the light of crystal lamps, to
the three central fountains crowded with nymphs jetting water
into opalescent pools, to the pilastered walls of crimson-veined
Numidian marble polished to the sheen of mirrors, the heroic
images of Mercury and Apollo in adamantine basalt set in niches
about the chamber. Everywhere was a blaze of flowers and silks;
silvery music played lightly over the steady, joyous rush of water.
A wealth in gemstones flashed in women's hair, at their breasts.
But all this luminous grandeur did nothing to dispel the warning
darkness that lay over this hall, heavy as the scent of blood on a
battlefield. Domitian's grim shadow fell everywhere; it was
impossible to put out of mind the great crime rumored to be at the
beginning of this reign.

Domitian had selected the eight guests at the imperial table with
an eye to making himself seem a cultured man. Marcus Arrius
Julianus felt not so much honored on this night as used as a sort
of stage-prop to make the new Emperor appear the companion of

philosophers. Saturninus' place was assured because he numbered an esteemed playwright among his clients; from time to time Saturninus gave Marcus Julianus a distracted, worried look, as if alert for the first signs of rebellious behavior. Next to Saturninus was Licinius Gallus, who earned his place because he was a famed gourmand—it was said he could taste an oyster and name the bay from which it was taken. Junilla was banished to a lower table for the evening—no doubt, Marcus Julianus mused, because her single serious flirtation with the arts was that much-talked-of occasion at one of Domitian's private parties when she rolled off her couch onto the esteemed poet and essayist Milo, and, beneath the eyes of Domitian's disbelieving but delighted friends, began idly coupling with him as though she thought in her wine-soaked stupor that he was the dessert course. On Domitian's left hand was his sixteen-year-old niece, Julia, daughter of Titus, his murdered brother, upon whom the Emperor had been lavishing more than avuncular attention since his brother's death. Julia was a frail, tentative presence who at least had the scent of learning about her; unlike Junilla's, the suffering in Julia's eyes had an artistic and thoughtful cast. With her aristocratically arched brows, bewilderingly complex coiffure, and rose-stem neck, she was some icy bloom, seeming pulled back from the world—not surprising since she had been thrust so young into the world of the court.

The next course was held back while Domitian explained the sauces arrayed before them in silver bowls, lost in a display of his knowledge of fine cookery, ignoring the fact that only the diners at the imperial table could hear him—and these were long weary of him and hungry. His white-liveried servants were poised by the serving carts in the crimson-curtained entranceway, awaiting the Emperor's signal. As Marcus Julianus watched Domitian gesturing with almost comic majesty, as if each sweep of his hand created a kingdom or scattered bread to the starving, he reflected: How quickly he is comfortable with the trappings of supreme power. He needed no time to adapt. Perhaps it is because he's always set himself apart from his peers; from youth, he's had that tendency to treat friends as good or bad servants. The imperial purple did not look so immediately right on either his father, his brother, or Nero.

"But the tartest sauce," Domitian was saying, "is *this* one." He leaned across his couch and, to everyone's embarrassment, seized one of Julia's too-thin arms, moved ponderously over her, and before the eyes of the seven hundred banqueters, inflicted on her a devouring kiss from which she could not escape. One clumsy, blunt-fingered hand moved determinedly down her back, boldly claiming territory as it went.

The dinner guests looked away in a sort of polite, muted shock. Julia writhed—the instinctive motion of a trapped animal—but dared not break the embrace. Marcus Julianus knew Domitian intended this act as a slap at his brother's memory, an assertion of his own authority. He is saying to the people: "I will do what I like with my brother's daughter. You will not rule me with rumors and tales. Believe I murdered Titus if you want—even say that I did it so I could enjoy his daughter openly—I do not care!"

I must stop this. Before Julia suffocates. Or her heart stops.

Marcus Julianus signaled to the servants to come forth with the silver carts, then quietly ordered them to begin serving.

He hoped to distract Domitian so he would release his victim, and he was successful. When the heavy gold platter bearing a grilled whole mullet stuffed with minced pheasant brains and glazed with rue-berry honey was set grandly before Domitian, the Emperor looked at it irritably, then heaved himself away from Julia, leaving the imprint of his thick fingers on her arm. Julia's face was ashen. She understood what Marcus Julianus had done, and she met his eye with a fleeting appreciative look that held a trace of a cry for help.

An instant later Domitian realized whose interference this was. He turned to Marcus Julianus with a look that was steely and remote.

"Perhaps you'd like to take a turn on the throne at tomorrow's morning audience."

This was a voice Marcus Julianus had never heard from him—it spoke not to him as an individual but to a collective presence—a whole room full of wayward servants. A sharp chill seized him. But he fought it and managed an amiable smile, as if at an amusing misunderstanding between two cultured men. He leaned close and said in a conspiratorial voice, "Fine words for a man who saved you from disgrace! This dish is ruined, you know, if it's even a *trifle* overcooked."

Domitian hesitated. *Overcooked?* Then he remembered the heating flames on the serving carts. He had forgotten them. His withering look softened a bit, sabotaged because he truly *was* grateful. Did Julianus catch his blunder in time? Domitian stole a furtive glance at Licinius Gallus. Was the gourmand thinking: Our rude, countrified Emperor is too ignorant to know this dish is ruined?

"You're going to wring your own neck some day with this habit of yours of taking matters into your own hands, old friend. Fortunately for you, the wine has rendered me affable."

"Ah, a good servant isn't motivated by desire for words of praise, so I'll let this stinging moment pass," Marcus Julianus replied, smiling.

Domitian looked intently at him, probing for mockery and finally decided it wisest to behave as if none were intended. He then nodded to the flaxen-haired eunuch Carinus, his cupbearer and current favorite in the bedchamber, who stood at attention behind him, indicating the one sauce bowl that was covered. Carinus placed this bowl beside Domitian's plate, uncovered it, then discreetly spooned it out for him. Marcus Julianus caught the stink of putrefaction and knew it was the cheap fish sauce called *garum*, so popular in the streets. Domitian ordered the boy to put it on everything—the fish, the cultivated asparagus, the flat bread—while he cast an occasional defensive glance about the room and shifted his body slightly on the couch so Julia could not see. After the learned discourse on sauces he did not want her to know this plebeian fish sauce was to his taste.

After a few bites Domitian forgot Julianus' small insurrection and seemed to remember why he was here. The Emperor put a proprietary hand on his shoulder, lavishing on him a look that was proud and paternal, his eyes softly focused as if they were beginning to dissolve in the wine.

"Friends!" Domitian called out in his rhetorical voice, commanding the attention of the greater part of the hall. The imperial table was raised on a low platform so that all could view him if not perfectly hear him. "Let us lift a cup to this man in whose honor we are assembled on this night."

A tribute, Marcus Julianus realized with dismay.

Obediently his guests stopped picking delicately at their fish and turned to the Emperor. "I want you to know this man is first among my friends, and I will be leaning heavily on his wisdom." Here and there Domitian inserted a phrase of Greek, meant to prove he was no boorish ruffian. Marcus Julianus and Saturninus made an effort not to wince as he ever so slightly mispronounced them, ending up proving the opposite: that he had not acquired a tutor in Greek until embarrassingly late in life.

"He will not let me honor him in the traditional ways, so I can only give this tribute. Not only is he a man of prodigious learning, he is one of those exceedingly rare men who will speak his mind to a ruler."

Marcus Julianus cast a quick glance about to observe the reaction of his fellow members of the Imperial Council, most of whom reclined at the second table just beneath them on their right. Among them were his old enemy Veiento, in whose eyes Marcus Julianus saw a muted flash of hatred, and Veiento's pawn the Senator Montanus, who met his gaze with vacant eyes, porcine cheeks greasy from overeager feeding, a gnawed quail leg, a remnant of the last course, dangling idly in one hand.

"He will not let me make him Consul," Domitian continued liltingly, grandly, glancing once at Julianus, who read clearly in the look: *Accept my gifts and behave, you too-clever man, and all will be right between us.* "Nevertheless, he has consented to be part of my High Council—and I want it known he will be first among them. Let us drink to the well-being of my great and good friend, Marcus Arrius Julianus."

All cheerfully drank, except for Veiento, who now had a murderous look lurking just behind that mask of blandness as he pointedly made no move for his wine. Marcus Julianus guessed the reason: Veiento had been led to believe he himself would be named First Advisor. His minion Montanus started to reach for his wine cup, but Veiento stopped him with a glance that was a dagger at the throat. Domitian chose to ignore this.

Junilla did drink, allowing a drop of the dark wine to escape her lips so it looked as though she was bleeding from the mouth. Without moving to wipe it, she gazed meaningfully at Marcus Julianus, a bare smile on her lips, recalling some sleekly beautiful beast that had just consumed something bloody and raw. The look convinced him Junilla plotted some fresh vengeful act. With every honor accorded him, her resentment grew—for she counted that honor by rights hers, as *he* was by rights hers. He had noted long ago a contradiction at the core of her strategy: If she did succeed in ruining him as her nature demanded, she rendered the remarriage she so ardently desired pointless.

When the hum of conversation began again, Domitian said companionably to Marcus Julianus, "Ah, here we are, victorious! Remember how we wanted the world to be when we were at the academies together? Now it is ours to shape! Light and knowledge have won! Tell me frankly, Marcus, you did not believe it, did you?" He pointed playfully with his spoon. "I insist you speak to me as friend, not as subject!"

Marcus Julianus smiled, then said with careful firmness, "My lord, I fear light and knowledge still have *not quite won*."

Uncertainty flitted across Domitian's broad, flushed Apollo's face. But he mastered it and returned to effusiveness. "So . . . a cloud appears over the happy kingdom! *Now* what have I done?"

Marcus Julianus discerned a measure of genuine concern. *Thank all the gods he does still require my blessings on his acts.*

But before he could reply Domitian spoke on: "I know you hesitated, old friend, before agreeing to come along with me. That grieves me, you know."

"There was . . . much to contemplate."

Battle readiness leapt into Domitian's eyes. "Many things—or *one* thing?" He studied Marcus Julianus' face intently as if it were a cryptogram. Marcus knew Domitian probed for his conclusions in the matter of the imperial ring that should not have fit. Domitian edged perilously close to uttering the words of that fatal question, the need to ask growing large and painful within him, but in the end he drew back, well aware that one question was all that stood between his friend and death. If Marcus Julianus openly accused him, Domitian would be compelled to charge him with treason.

"One thing did rear its head above others."

"*What* one thing?"

Saturninus looked on with growing alarm.

"Long ago you made a promise to me that you would not persecute philosophers, historians, and men of letters."

Julia's eyes widened at this audacity.

At the lower table Junilla's gaze whipped about; she scented Marcus Julianus' peril and watched him through slitted cat's eyes that slowly focused into a look of crude pleasure.

The relief Domitian felt when he realized Marcus Julianus was not referring to the ring shifted to extravagant annoyance.

"You've a damnably acute memory, my friend. It might get you into a battle you cannot win one day. Sometimes one wishes it were possible to kill memories without killing the whole man." Domitian's smile was unpleasant. "And do you not know it's terrible manners to remind a ruler of promises made long ago?"

"But you asked me to speak as a friend, not as a subject."

"By Minerva, you know how to irritate a man!" Domitian said with easy tolerance, but as he spoke, he slashed at the mullet with his small, sharp dinner knife.

"This morning I received an order to cease publication of my father's volumes on the tribes of Germania," Marcus Julianus pressed on. "What could offend you in these books that treat only of the habits and beliefs of rude barbarians?"

This brought the whole table to uncomfortable silence. Julia's great gray eyes had a look of tragic sadness, as if she watched her only ally committing suicide. Saturninus' expression would have looked well on the chief mourner in a funeral procession.

"They are . . . imitative of my own style," Domitian said a little stiffly, his look evasive, full of playful warning. Marcus Julianus ignored it.

"Come. Those books were begun when you were at your mother's breast. Give me another reason."

The stifling quiet encompassed several tables now. Emperor and guest of honor were actors on a stage in a tragic drama that was careening out of control.

"We *are* having a good time pressing the advantage of old friendship, are we not?" Domitian retorted. The flush on his cheeks began to spread. "*Another* reason. Well then. Those books portray my deified father in a poor light, for they draw attention to the tribes of Germania . . . and the fact that he never properly put them down."

"It is odd, then, that in all his years on the throne *he* never thought so."

"I declare this conversation at an end."

"You cannot mean that. This is the age of wisdom and light, not the age of Nero."

The silence was like that which follows the crack of a whip. Saturninus put his head in his hands. Earlier he had prayed some of Marcus Julianus' audacity had faded with age. It had not. But some part of him could not help but feel admiration tinged with amazement at Julianus' readiness to relentlessly, gracefully pursue his ends so far into the mouth of the dragon.

In Domitian's face was genuine hurt—but Marcus saw something dark and primitive churning beneath the surface and knew for certain the day would come when he would no longer be able to reach Domitian by appeals to conscience.

"My father deserves to have his works *known*," Marcus Julianus went on quietly. "It is as if you erased all trace of his life. You must allow me to continue producing his works."

Julia was still as a frightened bird.

"I say *no*." Perspiration gleamed on Domitian's forehead, though the dining hall was cool.

Marcus Julianus felt he had come to an impassable wall.

Then all at once he understood the ban. The solution to this puzzle was obvious—he did not know why he had not guessed it at once. He paused, remaining silent long enough so that conversation would start again and they would not be overheard. "Well then, I will make you a compromise," he said in a low voice. "I will cease publishing my father's works—until after your victory over the Chattians."

Something jumped in Domitian's eyes. The campaign had not been announced. He disliked being so perfectly understood. His look quickly became veiled, in an attempt to discourage this spy who penetrated to his innermost mind. Marcus Julianus knew then he had deduced correctly: The ban made sense only if Domitian planned a campaign against the tribes of whom his father wrote, and the warlike Chattians were the most likely target. His father's books would belittle Domitian's grand war, for they told the inglorious truth—that the barbarians were poor in goods and arms, that one man in ten owned a sword, that they were not nearly as well organized as commonly believed, that they were hungry not for booty but for land, because their methods of farming exhausted the soil after ten years. *That* was what was incendiary in his father's books.

"Tell me the informant's name."

"There was no informant, my lord."

"All right then, my too-clever magician," Domitian said, looking elaborately bored. "I cannot battle you anymore." Domitian's smile was cold, disturbing. "I relent. It shall be as you say."

Marcus Julianus felt a twist of sickness. Not only had Domitian not relented; Marcus now believed him incapable of it.

Domitian returned to the fish as if the conversation had not occurred. The boy Carinus darted forward to refill his master's wine cup. Carinus' tunic slipped, and Marcus Julianus noticed raised welts from a leather strap on the exposed upper part of the boy's back. They looked painful, fresh. There came memories of Endymion, the stench of urine, Grannus' grin, the reek of pain and death. Underneath this world of gentle pleasures, Marcus Julianus thought, is a substratum of continuous suffering a free man never knows. Why are the voices of the Stoics not heard? They speak loudly enough but society has stopped its ears. Slavery is no more a natural estate than death by an assassin's knife is a natural death.

Domitian caught Carinus' arm and whispered rapid instructions. Marcus Julianus was alert to some obscure danger.

"You know, our poor Junilla over there," Domitian went on in a wine-soaked drawl, returning malevolent attention to Marcus Julianus, "loves me beyond reason. But she'll settle for you. As a matter of fact, she asks *ceaselessly* for me to order you to remarry her. Perhaps that would be the one thing that would make her content."

"Are you threatening me with that spitting cobra as a ruler or as a friend?"

Julia put a hand to her mouth to stop herself from laughing aloud.

"You *do* enjoy thrusting a stick at a tiger," Domitian said easily. "Now, silence! My troupe of Egyptian dancers are ready."

A soft gong brought the hall's attention to a makeshift stage in back of the imperial table. There came a flurry of flutes, then drums that played with an odd stumbling beat. Attendants dressed as Anubis, the Egyptian jackal-god, drew onto the stage a great pyramid of wood painted to look like stone; it was high as a house's second story. All at once the four sides fell away and a hundred dancers spilled out, to the delighted cries of the guests. They took up torches and commenced what Domitian, leaning close, informed Marcus Julianus was the serpent dance. The dancers, bronze-skinned maidens with spectral eyes outlined with glistening black paint, were clad in nothing but feathered head-dresses and snakeskin girdles; their gilded nipples glittered in the torchlight. They wended their way between the tables, whirling, vaulting, scarcely seeming to touch the marble floor, while the flutes screamed, the drums thundered.

Carinus reappeared, his errand complete, and handed the Emperor a rolled document. Over the noise, Domitian half shouted to Marcus Julianus, "I am drafting edicts reestablishing the proper handling of freedmen and slaves and would like you to read a rough writing of my thoughts on the matter."

Why now? Marcus Julianus thought as he took the document and began reading. Domitian indicated one of the dancers. "That one there! See her . . . the one that wriggles like an eel in oil? I mean to take her tonight. And watch—my pettish Carinus will pout for a month!"

Carinus will rejoice, Marcus Julianus thought as he swiftly read. Most of what was written there was predictable; it represented a return to the older order, reestablishing the duties freedmen owed their patrons, denying them certain government posts, although he noted an irony or two: Included were harsh penalties for the importation of eunuchs, while Domitian himself kept a half dozen. When Marcus Julianus had nearly finished and was wondering what Domitian's purpose was, he saw it: Under a subheading directed at preventing "the leading of slaves into rebellion" was a prohibition against slaves attending philosophic lectures without the knowledge of their masters.

A good half of those coming to his school were slaves. Their right to be there was never questioned—whether they stole off or came with the household knowing, he never cared or asked. They were the heart of the school. Admitting them was his symbolic gift to Endymion, the wretched boy who wanted to be human, and all those others who were his heirs.

He knew at once the hand of Junilla was in this. Without her advice, Domitian never would have known this prohibition was such an effective way to strike at him.

Domitian watched him, something eager, predatory, in the look.

"My brother Titus was a softhearted fool and did not attend to many things," Domitian said by way of explanation. "So we see everywhere slaves raised above their station, upstart freedmen in Palace posts that should go to the equestrian nobility, immorality tolerated in the highest places, even among the sacred Vestals. I mean to change this and reinstitute the rule of law. And those who serve me must set an example."

Marcus Julianus put the document down and said quietly, "I wish to resign from the position on your Council."

Because of the noise of the music, only Domitian heard. He was pulled up short, the muscles of his face drawn taut. This had gone awry. Domitian expected him merely to take this as a severe warning against impertinence.

"You're passionate about strange things, my man," Domitian said, carefully composing himself. "You *cannot* resign. Your position, like mine, is for life. Did I not tell you? Wise men have certain duties, a certain . . . obligation to the state. Our fates are interlocked, my friend."

"You crushed the life out of my school."

"Order and justice rectified your school."

"Know then I have resigned in heart. You do not have me willingly—you have me enslaved."

Domitian was transfixed by Marcus Julianus' look. The moment was acutely unsettling—he saw in the clarity of Marcus Julianus' eyes a vision of himself as some demonic boy, looking ludicrous and lost in ill-fitting men's attire, smashing what did not bend to his will. He shook the vision off.

"I didn't realize I had a choice," Domitian said with an easy smile. "*Enslaved* suits me as well, if it muzzles that unpredictable mouth."

Marcus Julianus realized, amazed, Domitian was trying to charm. The successful exercising of authority always seemed to reanimate Domitian's desire to cajole approval from him.

"Did I tell you I sent scribes to the Library at Alexandria to recopy the books our state libraries lost in the great fire?" Domitian asked.

"Twice."

"And that from this day forward all professional informers will be severely punished?"

Marcus Julianus was eloquently silent. Domitian remembered then he had just raised Veiento, the most ruthless of informers, to the Imperial Council. "Oh, *him.* He is the exception. Veiento performed some . . . sensitive services for me at the time of my accession and I needed to repay him. And he's a very able man."

Marcus Julianus briefly met the gaze of Saturninus and knew they had the same thought: *What services? Arranging the murders of Titus' physicians to ensure their silence, for one?*

"My lord, would you indulge me in something?"

"Stop the 'my lord.' Anything my First Advisor might ask! Speak."

"I would like to accompany you on that campaign against the Chattians."

His purpose was the preservation of his friends: Marcus Julianus feared that if he remained in Rome, Domitian's morbid imagination would lead him to believe that he, along with Saturninus and others of the more independent members of the Senate, were hatching plots against the throne.

"A fine idea!" Domitian responded affably. "Though I did want you here to watch over my ministers and accountants—I know they'll start selling offices and extorting money from petitioners soon as my back is turned—but I'll find another watchdog. I'll be holding assizes as we travel, I'll need you for that, and you *do* have a broad knowledge of the ways of these savages. Yes, a fine idea! You'll break the boredom. War can get dull—all that waiting to draw the enemy out. I hope to have them exterminated in six months, but unforeseen delays dog every campaign."

A sense of doom accumulated in the room like the noxious vapor of rot. The word *exterminated* struck Marcus Julianus with a peculiar horror. As did the lash marks on Carinus' back, the sinister mystery of Titus' mode of death, Domitian's petty act of revenge against his school, and the knowledge that Veiento, master of judicial murder, was part of the Emperor's inner circle. He feared Saturninus was correct: He had entered a contest that could not be won—and now it was too late to withdraw. But he vigorously drove these thoughts back, not yet ready to believe there was nothing he could do to relieve the madness of times to come.

GERMANIA

CHAPTER XVIII

The news of Titus' death was sent by bonfire signal to the Roman legionary fortresses on the Rhine. The imperial post followed much later with a fuller report of Domitian's accession; the suspicion of murder came with the news like an ineradicable scent. For the most part the soldiers of the Rhine fortresses from Argentoratum to Vetera grudgingly accepted Domitian, but at Mogontiacum the men of the First and Fourteenth legions broke into open revolt and refused to hail him Emperor.

With the official report of Domitian's ascension to the throne came orders from each of the Legates of the northern fortresses to provide a hundred victims for the Colosseum, to do battle during the month of games planned in honor of Domitian's accession. Lucius Antonius, successor to Marcus Arrius Julianus the Elder as Military Governor at Mogontiacum, delayed this transfer of prisoners as long as he dared because he feared the Chattian savages would make a rescue attempt—for the better part of the captives he presently held were Chattian, and among them was Theudobald, the brother of Baldemar.

The Governor sat on his tribunal in the *Principia*, the fortress' headquarters, before the stone screen that protected the sacred standards of the two legions quartered there. He heard a report from his First Centurion, Rufinus, a steady, methodical man who, with his woeful brown eyes, beginnings of jowls, and simple loyalty, put Antonius in mind of a melancholy hound. Rufinus was uncomfortable before his Legate; he preferred the company of his own rough-hewn, farm-bred soldiers.

"There is no change in the men's mood in the last hour, my lord," Rufinus was saying. "We can only hope they'll accept the inevitable when they see the statues are in place."

Their voices resonated in the vault of stone. Gray light filtered weakly from clerestory windows. From the parade ground came intermittent shouts as the mutinous soldiers milled restlessly, crying out for Domitian's punishment.

"What! They are *still* not in place?"

"There was some trouble getting the heads to fit." Work crews, protected by the two centuries that remained loyal, had attempted to erect three statues of Domitian: one in the native settlement, one within the camp, and one at the first milestone on the road leading south from the fortress.

"Damn them to Hades!" Lucius Antonius was surprised at his own ferocity. It is this country, he thought. It provokes outbreaks of unbridled superstition in even the most rational of men.

He found himself wondering fleetingly if the Chattians had put some curse on his camp. At the fortress at Novaesium the men took the oath at once—if not joyfully, at least without incident. "Those superstitious children will interpret this to mean the state is headless! And the increase in pay? Did you announce it?"

Rufinus nodded curtly. "They were in too fine and mettlesome a mood. 'We will not be bought by a murderer' was the reply." They had said more, actually, likening Lucius Antonius to the hind parts of a certain domestic animal, but Rufinus had learned early in life not to report everything he heard and saw.

"I could enrich the donative from my own purse," Antonius said meditatively. "No. I'll not toss a bribe to a gang of mutinous wretches. Nemesis take them! Those prisoners go out *tonight,* whether the men come to reason or not." Were the transfer delayed longer, given the hazards of the two-month-long journey to Rome, the captives might not arrive until after Domitian's celebratory games. Antonius did not want this post to be the last of his career.

"I'll see to it. I know we took every precaution, but I cannot rid myself of the feeling that wild she-wolf's caught our scent again."

"*This* time, I think not. Only Bassus, you and I know tonight's the night. Anyhow the *ganna* has not been heard from since the raid on Mogon. My guess is she's living well on the wine and loot." Antonius leaned forward with a frown of distaste. "Rufinus, what is that about your neck?"

Rufinus looked down and tucked the silver talisman into his tunic, angry with himself for forgetting and leaving it visible. On it was depicted an upraised hand beneath a horned moon. He knew all his men would be wearing them tonight as a charm against the evil magic of that she-creature prowling the forests, the demon woman called Aurinia who spurred those who followed her to mad feats of valor.

"You set a poor example, my man," the Governor said irritably. "You told me once you believe in only what you touch and see. She's just a woman, Rufinus. She eats, she sleeps, she bleeds, and if she misbehaves tonight, she dies. We've seen warrior women out there before. What is the peculiar power of *this* one that she converts even you into a superstitious old scullery maid?"

Rufinus flushed, sharply reining in his anger. "By your leave, my men *expect* me to wear this," he said with forced evenness. "And come, you *must* admit she's had more than human luck. We think we have her trapped, and a storm comes up, or the ballista specialists go berserk and start firing on our own men, or she just escapes from a place from which there is no escape. Is it prudent to have the men frightened out of their wits before the night has even begun? Why *not* employ every advantage?"

Antonius thought he had a rational explanation for at least one incident Rufinus mentioned. It was his theory that ballista fire turned against the Romans on that day had come from the *savages,* bizarre as that seemed. In the confusion of battle such things were difficult to determine, but he believed his men when they insisted they had not fired. He had seen one of the bolts the camp physician recovered from the skull of a slain man and it was from a small catapult called a *scorpion,* an older type they had not used in the field that day. But Antonius had never dared put this notion forth to anyone, for fear he would be taken for a madman. The thought that the barbarians might turn the weapons of civilization on him frightened him more than the supernatural.

Antonius made an elegant dismissive gesture. "Do what you must then, Rufinus. But get those cursed prisoners out of here *tonight.*"

Rufinus' two centuries set out as the midnight bell was struck in the moon-washed gloom of the parade ground. The one hundred Chattian prisoners, Theudobald among them, were bound with cord and placed in ten mule-drawn carts. Rufinus ordered Bassus, a junior Centurion, to ride at the head of this company of one hundred and sixty soldiers; he posted himself at the rear. Savages preferred to strike from behind—and being savages, Rufinus observed, they never seemed to realize their enemies detected this habit. Rufinus' and Bassus' men were to take the captives as far as Argentoratum, a more southerly fortress on the Rhine, where a fresh escort would take them on the next leg of their journey.

None spoke; all were attuned to the rustlings of the brooding pines at the roadside. The deep forest teemed with malign life. Frogs made their anxious music, joined at odd intervals by hollow owl cries floating out onto the night. Unseen wings flapped; secret cloven hooves crackled leaves. Pungent smells and rotting smells rose up from the earth. The full moon traveling briskly through a troubled, cloud-ridden sky was no friend to them; it was the bald eye of ravening nature, tracking them, illuminating them for their enemies. This land was not theirs, no matter how successfully they seemed to have stemmed the barbarian tide; every man of them sensed the spirits of this place detested them.

For long the only sound among the men was the occasional muted clink of steel on steel, the patient tramp of heavy booted feet. To Rufinus the forms of the men in the semidark were grotesque, unhuman—with their cumbersome shields they appeared to be a line of outsized beetles reared ridiculously on hind legs. When they covered a half mile, a soldier alongside the first cart suddenly fell out of step; he had caught sight of what he thought a hoofprint, unnaturally large, in the mud at the roadside.

"The witch-woman," he said in a covered voice. "She was here."

"*Ganna!*" the men repeated softly up the line, touching the talismans at their throats. "*Ganna! Aurinia!*"

Rufinus shouted out in his harshest voice, "The next man to fall out of line will feel the vine-stick!" The words carried easily on the chill, clear night air.

Theudobald languished in the lead wagon, his muscles slack from age and long confinement, his mind on little; he felt his soul shriveled to that of a creeping thing. He had been taken captive the summer after the death of Baldemar, and had no news of his clan for four years. Lassitude and madness took him alternately; often he dreamed vividly of Baldemar's ghost, begging him to join him. But the sight and smell of the forest was awakening painfully a renewed desire to live. The moon, unseen for so long, was to him a sorrowing mother shedding cool, honeyed light in a vain attempt to comfort. Would the moon still live above in the place they were taking him?

Rufinus increased the men's pace. By dawn, he judged, they would be out of danger.

They approached the first milestone and the statue of Domitian loomed, towering twelve feet high, glowing blue-white in the moonlight. To Rufinus it was ludicrous as it was grand; one of Domitian's arms was paternally extended, indicating nothing. The Emperor seemed a stiff and silly giant standing in blind opposition to all nature.

Here we so clearly do not belong, Rufinus thought. Perhaps the rebels in the camp speak the truth: We've outraged the spirits of this place by setting the image of a brother-killer over her. And the punishments of nature's gods are brutal and swift.

He did not like the way his horse suddenly began to fight the reins in a nervous sweat, its head unnaturally high, cantering at the speed of a walk. He squinted at the towering black mass of trees and saw nothing.

Where were the frogs? Suddenly they were silent.

All at once there came a slow, swishing sound, as if some monstrous serpent threaded its way through the trees. Clouds shrouded the moon, dropping all into greater darkness. Rufinus shouted the order to halt.

But his shout went unheard. It was overwhelmed by an unearthly hum swelling up from the trees, rising into a penetrating ululation that might bore through skulls. It was as if they roused some Olympian nest of hornets.

We are done! Rufinus thought, knowing this was the *barritus,* the ritual cry of Chattian tribesmen rousing their gods of war.

Rufinus signaled to his trumpeter, who blew two piercing blasts. The men swiftly closed ranks and locked their shields together. Rufinus leapt from his mount and took a place at the extreme end of the first rank; he believed a centurion should fight closely beside his men.

From the cavernous dark beneath the trees, a single blotch of flame appeared. It flared, then separated into many, scattered like a string of stars across the somber void, as others lit their torches from the first.

Then came a crackling, tearing sound. Hundreds of warriors broke through the brush, and this dark horror surged toward them. It was as if a sluice-gate had opened. They spilled down the short slope in a rude wedge formation, its apex aimed at the center of the legionaries' line.

The legionaries drew back their heavy javelins with perfect precision, as if every arm were controlled by one mind. The powerfully thrown missiles tore into the horde, toppling many, but those behind vaulted over the fallen and surged on unchecked. The second round of javelins did greater damage, some passing through more than one body, or pinning the attackers to trees. The warriors collided with one another and fell; some were trampled to death, while others were forced to throw down their shields and rush naked of protection onto the Roman swords, for the legionaries' javelins could not be wrenched out. There was one triumphant moment when Rufinus thought disaster averted.

But then came the unaccountable, the horrible. Another shrill, rattling war-hum was raised—from the opposite side of the road. Rufinus was astonished. Savages never held men in reserve; they seemed incapable of it. Like excited children, they could not restrain their headlong rush. But even more remarkable was that they waited until *both* javelins each legionary soldier normally carried had been spent before they sent this second wave. Never had he known barbarians to show such intelligence.

He knew for certain then they were attacked by the blood-drinking Fury his men called Aurinia. Her strategies often seemed a crude mimicry of Roman tactics.

He shouted out the command for the diamond formation, which he judged best for repelling an attack from all sides. But the first battle-horde struck hard, badly disorganizing his front line. Now he felt the chill hand of death closing round his throat. Not only their numbers but also the night was on the barbarians' side. The Chattian warriors—with the whites of their eyes gleaming in the moonlight, skins flapping from their shoulders, axes raised, the heads of freshly killed mountain cats on their belts—were themselves a spawn of darkness; it masked them in demonic mystery, paralyzing his men with fright.

The Roman lines were cleaved in half.

Rufinus felt a blow like the kick of a horse, and a hot burst of pain in his shoulder. He was knocked back, then he sank to his knees, a native spear embedded deep in his flesh. Bassus saw him fall and moved to cover him.

Rufinus could do little now but watch from the ground. Bassus felled one warrior, then two, gutting them with the stabbing point of his sword. But elsewhere all was not going well; the horde numbered over a thousand, Rufinus guessed, and more kept coming from the forest as if nature in her fury vomited them up. It was as if a roaring river swept his soldiers off. To his shame, Rufinus realized that here and there his men were beginning to break and run. But the majority stood their ground, knowing they faced certain slaughter.

And then he saw her—the *ganna* who bore arms.

She rode the familiar deathly pale stallion. With her unbound hair streaming down, she was a barbarous sight that caused fresh moans of dismay from his men. She galloped round the front of the line, her horse nearly striking him with a forehoof as he lay immobilized beside the still gamely struggling Bassus. Then she pulled the gray stallion to a halt, sheathed her sword, and took up a coiled length of rope. He cried out unheard as he realized what she was doing.

She flung the looped end of the hemp rope round the statue of Domitian. It fell to the statue's shoulders, stopped by the unraised right arm; with a tug she drew it tight. Then she wheeled the horse about and urged it to a gallop. The phantom horse struck at air with its forelegs; they were a single wild creature as the beast bolted forward, neck tightly bowed. The rope pulled taut.

The statue's ill-fitting head toppled first, raising thunder in the earth. Slowly at first, then with a whistling rush, the headless stone body crashed down. The statue splintered one of the wagons, emptied already of its prisoners. Then came an instant of utter silence as everyone stared in numb surprise.

To the Romans it seemed abandoned nature passed sentence on Domitian, their posturing god-on-earth. The sight of the dread *ganna* galloping into their disintegrating line took the last of the legionaries' courage. Rufinus thought he watched Death as a maiden; there was something fatal and sweet in her aspect—she was an avenging dove emanating a potent innocence, a raging nymph with blood-matted hair. She might have been a Fate in youthful incarnation, cutting threads of lives with that rising and falling sword.

Then all was a confusion of moon-shadows and eerie light darting down upraised blades. The legionaries who had made a stand broke and fled or were cut down. Then Bassus was struck fatally and could cover him no more.

The spear that pierced Rufinus' side entered painlessly—but he knew at once this blow was mortal. Pain and fear floated off; they were of no service to him now. As life left him, he saw Aurinia again—or was it a dying vision? Her face was now transformed into Fate as Destroyer, a hag with green flesh, lolling tongue and snakes for hair, dragging him down to her sunless caverns.

The sight of the Roman legionaries terrified and running was a powerful elixir in the blood. Auriane longed to pursue. A wealth in vengeance was before her for the taking. Berinhard felt her excitement and strained against the reins. But she knew it was unwise—the task of getting the captives off the road and safely into the deep forest would be slow and difficult, and she had no doubt the enemy would return at once with reinforcements.

But all were not of the same mind. Sigwulf, who aided her with his own Companions—it was he who led the attack from the opposite side of the road—took one of the horses they had brought for the prisoners and gave chase, with a hundred or more of his men bolting after him on foot. Using his spear as a lance, he might have been harpooning fish as he finished the stragglers. She cried out his name and begged him to come back, but he paid no heed. He was a runaway horse, impetuous and blind; he would stop when he tired.

Working swiftly in the moon-bright night, the warriors stripped the Roman dead of their short swords, helmets, cuirasses and daggers, and collected javelins from the ground. Others unbound the prisoners and helped them onto the sturdy ponies brought to convey those too weakened to travel. They worked silently. Most of the trembling captives did not seem to know they were free.

Auriane inspected their moon-washed faces. Most were known to her from the Assembly, but none were kin or close in heart. She began to fear Theudobald was not among them. He must have died and been thrown into some charnel pit.

Then she saw him and realized she had passed him by once, he was so greatly changed. His fine mane of hair was thinned to wisps; those deep-set eyes, once full of brash certainty, now gazed on emptiness. Words came to his lips meant for people who were not here. Gradually she realized he spoke names of his children, all slain in battles past. *"The pine that stands alone soon withers,"* Auriane always heard it said of those torn from the tribe, and here was proof. With the aid of young Fastila, she pulled him onto Berinhard's back—a kinsman should have the best horse. But still Theudobald did not know her.

"Theudobald, I am your kinswoman," she said urgently.

"Auriane?" came his shuddery voice. A hand wandered out and tentatively touched her face.

"Can it be the daughter of my brother?" Theudobald leaned forward, squinting. She realized he was near blind. "Dear you must be in the eyes of Wodan!" he whispered, then strength left him suddenly; he slumped forward onto Berinhard's neck. She saw then the ulcerous sores on his body.

She put a hand on his. "Your life shall be as before," she said with firm assurance as she began slowly walking the horse. "I have kept safe all that was yours, Theudobald. Your herds are together and away from harm. We are hallowed again."

After a long silence Theudobald gathered strength again and said, "Pride makes me twice as strong when I look at you, blessed daughter. But tell me . . . have we taken vengeance for Baldemar?"

Every time anyone spoke this, it was as if a small wicked knife sliced out another piece of her heart. She knew she should have expected Theudobald would want to know this at once. She looked off, not wanting to see his bitter disappointment. "No," she said. "The beast still roams. Odberht lives."

And now she could not stop the inevitable thought: All these years passed, yet Theudobald survived in this place to be rescued. *Could not Baldemar have done the same?* Had she not slain him, Baldemar might have lived to be set free on this day.

But he *chose* death.

But I could have disobeyed. He would be alive.

As the soldiers who had been ambushed streamed wounded and bleeding into the fortress, they related with wonder how nature in the guise of the prophetess Aurinia sent the clearest omen for which anyone could ask. They had been right not to hail Domitian; his reign would be evil. The camp erupted into violent revolt. The legionaries pulled down the image of Domitian erected before the *Principia.* By dawn they set their barracks alight; then the tribunes' quarters and the granaries caught fire while the soldiers held their officers hostage in the *Praetorium*, the private quarters of the Governor.

Lucius Antonius sent out a frantic letter by the last post-rider who managed to leave the camp, specifying it be delivered directly into the hands of the Emperor. The camp was docile, he insisted, and submitting to the new Emperor's rule. But then the savage *ganna* called Aurinia, the principal pest along the frontier at the moment, whipped the men of the First and the Fourteenth into a superstitious frenzy by pulling down his Divine image, and incited the soldiers to mutiny. And so he eased his fears Domitian might doubt his own loyalty by laying the causes of the rebellion at the door of the turbulent forces of nature.

In the afternoon of the same autumn day the band of two thousand Chattian warriors retreated to a thickly forested rise of ground on the river's east side; stretched out lazily below was the broad, stately avenue of the Rhine. Winter pressed close; the whole of the land was dulled to one shade of grim gray-green. Stands of skeletal aspen and oak anxiously rattled the last of their leaves, a desolate death-filled sound. Dense accumulations of clouds clotted a clear autumn sky. Distantly they saw the Mogontiacum fortress on its smooth hill, the flaming barracks buildings glowing molten like some god's forge; this was the only spot of warmth in a hard land bracing for winter.

Auriane remained apart from the others, standing in a drift of ocher and vermilion leaves, watching Mogontiacum burn. Decius sat near her, hungrily devouring leek-and-squirrel stew. He had stayed in the camp with Romilda's women but had not slept, spending the night restlessly retracing Auriane's battle plan to which he had contributed advice, certain they had neglected some small point. The greater part of the Companions slept, fatigued from the night's work. Only Witgern and Thorgild were still wakeful, groggily tossing dice and drinking mead.

Decius was tired and content. In these days he might have been one of them, Auriane often thought—his disguise was near perfect. He had lightened his hair to a Chattian red-blond with a mixture of herbal ashes; it fell in uncivilized tangles to his shoulders. He wore a beard that was wild and untrimmed. When he scowled fiercely, Auriane thought he somewhat resembled Thorgild, though more refined in feature. The deception held until Decius spoke; then his odd mixture of broken Chattian and rapid Latin—which only she could follow—gave him away at once. But to a close observer Decius' eyes gave him away still, Auriane thought. They had a stubbornly Roman way of looking at the world. If a tree fell in his path, he would order it hewn and moved. Her own people would leave the tree where it fell, build a shrine there, then find a path around it. They were the eyes of a man who looked upon nature as a tool or as a beast to be broken, eyes that suggested nature had better get out of his way.

"The hospital buildings are going up now," Decius said to her. "And if I'm not mistaken, the armory. A good piece of work! Alight beside me here, my feisty pet. You look as though you're ready to take flight back there and do battle all over again."

This did nothing to warm the bleak look in her eye. "We lost four," she said with a dark resignation, as if she admitted to a crime.

"And you rescued ninety-six. It was remarkable! Why do you think only of what is lost? All came out exceedingly well, I would say, and it was a fine end to this warring season! In one summer we freed that cursed salt spring—for the third time. We reclaimed all the rich farmlands in the valley of the Wetterau. And Baldemar's brother now will die on his own soil. Cannot you snatch *one* moment of pleasure from all this?"

Decius came up beside her. Had they been alone he would have put an arm about her shoulders, but with the Companions so near he dared not; he contented himself with offering a warm, protective presence. "And you! You are becoming legend, as your father was."

Auriane's dark look remained. "Had I persuaded more warriors to join us, those four might have lived," she said, eyes bright with tangled misery. "The gods help us if we failed to frighten their soldiers out of accepting this new emperor! You are *certain* this Domitian will turn all his fury on us and make war?"

"I would wager my last piece of this boot-leather you call meat," Decius replied, brandishing a strip of dried venison in her face, "that he cannot restrain himself! For too many years he's been lusting for battle like a half-starved hound lusts for a fat hen. And here *we* are, the perfect target—troublesome, defiant, and primitive enough that a good, solid victory is assured. You are baiting a bull and have been for years. If they *do* accept him, you can be certain we'll be a sacrificial gift to Domitian on his accession. But *this*"—he gestured toward the fortress below—"is just one camp. I've little notion what's happening at Argentoratum or at Vetera, or among the legions in the East—or for that matter, at this moment in Rome."

Auriane was quiet but he sensed an active silence, in which she never ceased considering, planning.

After a time she spoke. "I did not tell you what I learned from the last meeting with our spies." She had long cultivated informants among the market women of the native settlement that served the fortress. "The mountain cats are not being taken to work magic against us. Geisar is wrong." The Romans had been observed trapping mountain cats in pits baited with lambs, and carrying the creatures off, writhing and hissing, in wooden cages; her people had been greatly disturbed by this of late.

"Of course not. But *you* tell it," Decius said with an amused smile. She knew he found it entertaining to hear her mangle explanations of his people's customs, but she tried to maintain dignity nevertheless.

"They have built a vast stone temple in Rome, larger than any built before, raised up to the sky by a powerful sorcerer. It is called the Col . . . Colo . . ."

"Colosseum."

"On its altar, men fight men to feed their blood to the sun god, and sometimes men fight and are eaten by animals. The mountain cats are for *that*. The Romans care not at all that they are our sacred animal. Soon there will be—is this right? Decius, what is wrong?" His irksomely self-assured smile had vanished; in its place was a look that was distant, haunted.

"Pretty close. You found better sources this time. Auriane, promise me one thing. That if ever you are captured by my people and you are certain that escape is impossible—*you will find a way to end your life.*"

She turned to look at him, baffled by the grim passion in his voice. "Why do you say that?"

"I just had a nightmare vision of *you* in that place."

This struck her as odd, for although Decius had an overabundance of opinions about events to come, based on acquired knowledge, he was not normally given to premonitions.

"You've no need to make me promise, Decius. I would rather be sold into thralldom to the poorest farmer of the north than be taken alive by your people." But even as she said it, she realized she did not believe in the possibility of her capture.

Thorgild, who despised Decius and still treated him as a thrall, was listening intently to this and growing more and more irritated because he understood less than half of what Decius was saying. Normally he would not even address Decius, but Romilda's mead was strong and they had drunk many toasts.

"Thrall, tell me," Thorgild broke in with a drunken sweep of his hand, "your people are slaves—how is it that they have the mettle to refuse this new king?"

Decius felt a flash of anger. All benefited from his knowledge of war, but few, other than Sigwulf or Auriane, ever showed him gratitude. He forced himself to answer evenly: "There have always been transgressions our army will not forgive. Parricide—the murder of a near relation—is one of these." Decius enjoyed the fact that Thorgild did not catch the meaning of every word and was too proud to say so. "And anyway, it is not *slavery* to give strict obedience to your commanders," Decius went on in pointed tones, as if showing patience with a child slow to learn, "—but wisdom."

Thorgild shrugged—the explanation did not interest him—and continued to watch Decius with hostility.

Decius ignored him and said to Auriane, "Sigwulf should not have given chase. If the camp at Vetera sends reinforcements, he's leading your people to certain slaughter. In a day he'll lose the weapons of iron it took us a *year* to acquire."

"Decius!" Auriane said in a low warning voice. A former thrall should not criticize the acts of a free-born warrior.

But Thorgild had heard. He threw the leather dice cup hard to the ground.

"Do you not have some pig dung to shovel, thrall? Auriane, why do you allow this insolent donkey to prance among us!"

Auriane whipped about, low fire in her eye. "Because he often speaks truth, Thorgild. I count it foolish to muddle over *where* truth comes from, if it serves us well."

Thorgild was chastened somewhat by the force of that gaze. But as he retrieved the dice cup he muttered to Witgern in a covered voice, "The counsel of that thrall! It will be our downfall."

He did not realize Auriane overheard. Thorgild looked up uneasily to find her standing over him. "*His* counsel is also my counsel. Or do you also dispute *mine?*"

Several Companions awakened at that moment and stared at Thorgild. The red-bearded Companion's mind was like some heavy-footed, lumbering animal that once set upon a course can manage no subtle shifts; he could not stop himself now.

"Never would I." Thorgild gave her an inebriated smile, and nodded at Decius. "Unless, of course, the thrall is playing the part of husband with you when no one's about."

Before Auriane could recover from amazement, Witgern leapt to his feet and pulled Thorgild up after him. Then he struck Thorgild a blow near the ear that knocked him to his knees.

Witgern stood over the dazed Companion, legs planted apart. Thorgild looked up at him with hurt surprise. "You are not fit to speak her name," Witgern said calmly. "You're fortunate that is *all* you'll pay for that, Thorgild."

Auriane felt a slight sickness in her stomach. Witgern's trust was so open and pure. *What would they do to her—and to Decius—if they knew?* She seemed to attract secret evils like a carcass draws flies.

Auriane caught an abashed look in the faces of the Companions who overheard, and guessed they had secretly shared Thorgild's thought.

She decided after this incident that she would lie no more with Decius. The decision was a practical one, not one that came from the soul: They trust in my holiness, she reasoned, and I must not snatch that away from them. Now that she no longer counted herself among the dead, was it not proper to follow her people's ways once more? She decided it was, though she was not certain on this point; it was as though tribal law were a garment that was ill-fitting now.

Little did she realize when this decision was made that already it was too late.

When Auriane offered only a token number of the captured legionary swords to Geisar to be dedicated to Wodan in the groves, and handed the rest to warriors of poor means who had none, Geisar formally cursed her before all the priests and priestesses of Wodan's cult. Because of Geisar's resolve to destroy her, she now dared go nowhere without a guard of twenty Companions.

As the first feathery snow fell and fragile ice sheets formed on ponds, word came to them that the new Emperor was accepted all over the world. And shortly afterward, a member of the Holy Nine came to Geisar following one of her ambassadorial visits to the Mogontiacum fortress; in her hand was an edict from the new Emperor Domitian. No imperial edicts had been handed down for a generation; its arrival brought confusion and outrage to the people. This list of laws was to be read before the next Assembly.

On the morning of the Assembly of the New Moon, Decius traveled from the small plot of land Sigwulf had given him to the hall of Baldemar to help Athelinda and the thralls load the wagons for the four-mile journey to the Sacred Oak. Decius was surprised when Athelinda told him as he rode into the yard that Auriane was still asleep, for the sun was well up. Athelinda explained that Auriane had been ill in the night.

Decius found her in the sleeping-enclosure behind the willow-withy screen at the north end of the hall; she was sunk in exhausted sleep beneath a mound of sheepskins. For a moment he lingered to enjoy the sight of her face, dimly visible in the chinks of light that came through the thatch; peace and innocence lay over her like an extra blanket. This creature, he marveled, appeared anything but fierce; it was difficult to believe she was drawn to the sword as other women were to silks and lovers.

"Auriane," he said, grasping what should have been a leg and shaking it. She stirred, mumbled some protest, then was up at once, clinging to him, face pressed hard to his chest.

"Let me be," she mumbled half-coherently, more asleep than awake. "I did not kill him. . . . None say it anymore!"

"Stop that!" Decius whispered. He shook her gently. "Wake up. Of course you did not kill him. Wake up!" It was a well-worn ritual of reassurance that began in the days when they lived together in the forest.

At first Auriane's look was lost; then steadiness and womanly confidence gradually filled her eyes as if she relived in awakening her own growing up.

Briskly she rose to her feet. "This is a gravely important Assembly," she said as she strode about purposefully, readying herself, pausing by a great bronze bowl to splash chilled water on her face, then throwing open an oaken clothes-chest and searching impatiently through its neatly stored contents for her white woolen Assembly shift and gray plaid mantle. "We must hurry."

"Auriane, wait," Decius said softly. She never paused. *"Look at me."* He caught her hand. "Athelinda said you were ill all night. What is wrong?"

She met his gaze, her eyes wells of sadness, then abruptly looked away. "There is not time—"

"There *is* time."

She shook her head vigorously, but Decius would not let her go. He pulled her back until she sat beside him on the sheepskins.

"Moss and mistletoe may grow on me, Auriane, but I go *nowhere* until you tell me."

She looked down, then whispered it quickly, as if delivering a death-stroke that would be more merciful if swift. "Hear it then, Decius. I am with child."

Decius jumped to attention, then looked quickly all about to make certain no one overheard, but only Mudrin was close at hand, idly stirring the hearth-pot, and she could be trusted.

"Nemesis!" Decius whispered. "A death sentence!" He put his head in his hands and was silent for long moments.

"Decius, you must not fear for me. I am in the hands of Fria."

"It's Geisar's hands you're in, you little fool. Gods above and below, why now!" He looked at her. "You *cannot* have a child by a foreign father!" he whispered fervently. Gingerly he took her hand as if it were fragile as a newborn lamb. "If only this had happened *somewhere else,* I would have welcomed it! But here! Even Athelinda and all your kin will condemn you! The only one who will rejoice will be that flea-ridden priest! Now you are his—how gleefully he will order your death! You must go to Sigdrifa and have her rid you of it!"

"No. I will have it."

Decius slowly shook his head. He realized from Mudrin's attentive but incurious look that the thrall-woman already knew.

Who else knew?

"I know this babe will have no kin-fire," Auriane said feveredly, close to tears, "and that the babe will not know its own grandmother. No family ghost can enter this child, and it will be cursed by the Holy Ones. But Decius, life has become so barren, so vile, since Baldemar's . . . death, I would rather have a child of split soul than die without any issue at all."

Her look disturbed him. Usually when her eyes were troubled, they looked as though playfulness were still their natural state; he could always sense it poised to return. The misery he saw there now had no bottom.

"You'll die without issue anyway because you'll not survive long enough to give this child birth!"

"Not if I go away in the last months and hide among Ramis' apprentices."

"I did not think you and Ramis parted on particularly amicable terms. As I recall, a bitch-dog was one of the more complimentary things you called her."

Auriane realized this was true but had no reply. She knew then that she *expected* Ramis to look after her, and was startled by this.

By rights, the woman *should* want to punish me. Why do I assume she will not? Why am I so certain the words I hurled at Ramis on that day long ago were but a storm on the surface of a lake, unknown to the deeps below?

"Decius, I know no one else to whom . . . a babe is a babe, no matter who fathered it. Like the hills and groves, Ramis does not judge. And there too is this . . ."

He only half listened, still in a shock of misery.

"This child was conceived amidst victories, Decius. Sometime between the time of the battle of the Rhine, when we slew a hundred, and the ambush of that foraging party in the valley of the Wetterau, we lay together and made this child. This is my time of strength. It means she—or he—will be potent with the magic of victory. If I die as Baldemar did, without ever driving the invaders from our land, perhaps this child will see it through. So you see, it is a sort of gift to Baldemar as well."

Suddenly there was an eruption of barking dogs, shouting stable thralls, and finally the sound of furiously galloping hooves. Auriane shot up and put a cloak over her nightclothes. Mudrin was closer to the door and darted outside before Auriane passed the hearthfire.

There came the sound of a second horse, as if someone took up pursuit.

When Auriane reached the horse sheds, the field thrall Garn explained to her a horse thief had gotten off with one of the swiftest mounts. Auriane did not believe for an instant this was a common thief—who would dare creep so near this great hall with mischief in mind, unless they were led to believe they had powerful protection?

When she realized the stolen beast had been quartered in the stall closest to the north part of the hall where she had spoken with Decius, cold terror closed round her heart.

The theft of the horse was a spy's cover, she was certain of it. Whoever it was came from Geisar, and she had no doubt he had had an ear to the wall as they spoke.

From the look in Decius' face she knew the same thought seized him.

She tensed, thinking rapidly. The thrall who had taken off after the thief would never catch him. Berinhard was swift enough to catch that horse, but the dappled stallion was grazing in the western meadow, not close at hand.

We are done. I should not risk attending this Assembly.

But I must. My counsel will be much needed, for that vile edict is to be read.

CHAPTER XIX

Auriane sat between Sigwulf and Witgern in the Assembly's
inner circle. She had taken no food that day because of the
sickness brought by the child, though she sipped at Athelinda's
mead. This night was already counted evil; during the opening
sacrifice the boar escaped, goring one of the assisting priestesses
before it darted into the forest. Geisar and Sigreda strove to keep
this foul omen secret, but news of it seemed to be carried on the
wind.

Geisar stood before them, holding aloft a thing exotic to most
eyes—a roll of papyrus on which was written the imperial edict.
The ambassador from the Holy Nine who carried it to him was
accompanied by a literate Roman courier who was to read it before
the Assembly, but Geisar sent the courier off and arranged to have
Decius read the edict instead, because the old priest feared he might
be forced to relinquish the document afterward. This paper that
had been touched by Roman hands and covered over with words
in their wolf-tongue could be used to work magic against them, in
much the same way that magic could be worked with an enemy's
fingernail clippings or a lock of hair.

Geisar raised his staff for silence. The torchlight illumined the
fierce furrows of his brow, a lean-lipped, downturned mouth, and
left his eyes in pits of blackness—it was as if the sockets of a skull
shrank, then grew large and bold, flickering with lively malice.
Sigreda stood next to him with a smile cold as the sliver of moon

436

above, her heavy lids eased half shut; the clouded detachment in her eyes made her appear to have taken a draught. But that swift gaze missed nothing. She was a sleek black carrion bird perched on Geisar's shoulder, hungering for his death while she studied him, yearning to draw the strength of that powerful venomous spirit into herself.

"I relate to you now," Geisar cried out in his piercing whine that carried like an arrow on the wind, "the law of the Emperor Domitian, God-King of the Romans, handed down to us free Chattians as if we were his slaves. His titles exceed the numbers of burrs in your horses' tails. I ask your lenience to allow the foreigner called Decius into this holy circle, due to the mischance that he reads their tongue. Decius, come forward."

Auriane felt a pulse of alarm. No one had warned her Decius was to be called into their midst. Was it some trap? If anyone *did* denounce them, now Decius could be surrounded and might never escape alive.

Decius came through the ragged pathway left by the seated warriors. Auriane at first recognized only that confident stride in the gloom. Then he came into the light of Geisar's agitated torch. Decius looked dear to her then and so out of place. There was a mildly overwhelmed look in his face, discernible only by one who knew him well—a look of one who ventured too far, thinking a thing safe, then too late changed his mind.

She had secured Berinhard to a birch tree that could be reached by moving through the part of the crowd most loyal to her. Beyond was deep forest. It had seemed a perhaps unnecessary precaution earlier in the evening; now she wondered if it were enough to save her life.

Decius unrolled the papyrus and began reading; earlier, he had practiced with the edict lest he mistranslate, so he had had leisure to become fearful over its contents. He moved quickly over Domitian's many titles and the opening salutations, which would mean nothing to them.

"Here now, the words of your Lord and God," he began. Decius' voice was naturally soft, so Geisar screeched each line after him. After Decius, Geisar sounded like a maddened magpie, and the whole effect was as if Decius was producing an outlandish echo.

"In spite of your rebelliousness, your raiding, your pillage and murder, and your many impious misdeeds, we are yet prepared to show clemency if the following commands are obeyed.

"First, you shall not cross the Rhine by day or by night, even at those places formerly designated lawful for trading." Here Decius was forced to pause; the throng began to simmer with angry mutterings. Geisar shouted for silence.

"Secondly, you must leave thirty miles of land uncultivated on the east bank of the Rhine. All villages along this line of cultivation must yield up their arms. Soldiers will be sent to receive them on the Kalends of November. Thirdly, you will not molest the lands and property of the Hermundures, who are under our protection. And you will cede the salt springs to the Hermundures, who shall be granted sole rights to them because of their greater loyalty and service to us."

This brought the simmering to a boil; Decius was forced to silence for long moments.

Did the Romans truly believe they would quietly lay down their weapons while their ancestral enemies poisoned their wells, spirited off prize horses, and kept the precious salt springs—their only means of preserving meat—for themselves?

"And fourth, for her long record of criminal acts, and her abuse and degradation of the Divine Image, you will deliver up for punishment the woman called Aurinia."

Auriane was hardly surprised at this; yet still blood hammered in her temples and she felt the terror of a cornered hare.

"Tell the swine we'll turn in our own mothers first!"

The shout was Witgern's. It was greeted with a rousing thunder of approval punctuated with the nerve-jangling music of weapons crashed against shields. She was their Daughter of the Ash, a living shrine. The passionate energy of this response surprised her and moved her heart; she felt the beginnings of tears.

But then she noticed a thing that caused her powerful unease. A great group of warriors near the oak, close on her right hand, remained noticeably silent. Among them were men of Gundobad's, who chafed still at the impoverishment Auriane caused him after his attempt to marry Athelinda; and her old enemy Wulfstan, son of Geisar, who at Baldemar's death had started a band of his own, and men of Wido's old ally, Unfrith, who after all the years still held her family accountable for Wido's death. She saw Geisar's gaze rest meaningfully on this sector of the throng and was seized with a sense some trap was being sprung. She had always known she had enemies, but why were they seated all together—and so near to her?

When the tumult died, Decius continued. *"You will not gather*

*more than once a month in your Assemblies. At each Assembly
after this night, Imperial Representatives will be present to record
all that passes among you. We wish for peace, but its continuance
rests in your hands."*

Wulfstan came forward and ripped the edict out of Decius'
hand. He bellowed, waving it aloft, "What do they propose to
shackle us with? *This?*"

Raucous laughter arose all around. Sigwulf strode forward and
snatched the edict from Wulfstan. "Season after season we defeat
them!" he shouted. "And now they tell us where we may go, like
a mother to a suckling! *Are we thralls?* Shall we meekly lower our
heads for their yoke?"

A mountainous clamor of approval arose, punctuated by shouts
of "No! Never!" and the clanging of spears against shields.
Wulfstan took the edict from Sigwulf and ground it under his heel.
When he held it up to view, mutilated and muddy, the shouts
became one unified upsurge of rebellious noise.

Fools. Do you not see how the world has turned? Auriane
thought. This is not the time to mock—this is the time to know
fear.

Auriane started to rise, but Witgern pulled her back. "Not now,"
he begged. "Wait until they've settled back into an even temper!"

When the throng quieted, Sigwulf shouted, "This is *my*
answer to the wolf-spawn. I say burn the edict. Let us swarm over
them like hornets. We will flood over them as sea-foam rushes
over sand!" Through the next round of cheers Auriane watched
Decius; he struggled to conceal an expression of amazed contempt.

Sigreda struck a bronze gong for silence. "Do any here mean to
speak *against* this course? Do any oppose the common will?" She
had long heard mutterings that Auriane had odd ideas on the
subject.

Geisar met Sigreda's eye approvingly, then his gaze made a
token journey about the throng, stopping abruptly at Auriane.
"Speak, Auriane, it's plain to see you're of a different mind."
Speak, Geisar thought, and make yourself despised before I see
you destroyed.

Auriane rose slowly, as if bearing all the weight of her sorrow
and dread. Turning their minds now would be like slowing a
bolting horse. The nausea she had felt earlier came strongly once,
then mercifully subsided. As she walked to the place beneath the
oak, she was aware of the rough wool of her sheath moving over

her invisibly changing body. How many eyes took note of how loosely the rope about her waist was tied? She felt Geisar's malevolent eyes upon her, probing beneath her clothes, feeling her body as he might a mare's to discover if she was in foal.

I must drive away such thoughts. I am bound to say what I came to say.

In the gloom, most saw only the firelit outline of her unbound hair, the thin, brave spear upright in her hand. Geisar noticed with displeasure that somehow she seemed greater in stature than Sigwulf and Wulfstan together; her very presence brought an intrigued quiet, a sense of peace and comfort.

Witgern thought: She does not know her own courage or her ability to encourage others. She is like the hand of Fria softly laid over us.

Auriane began quietly, with a hesitant catch in her voice. "It is hard to speak against the will of the people, but I must accept the lot that has fallen to me.

"I believe Sigwulf is wrong. We are *not* invincible, despite our many victories of the last years, despite our wagonloads of longswords." As she spoke on, her voice gradually became supple and strong. "I, as you, until recently believed we had warred them down. But what I have come to see is this: In all these years, never have they retaliated with all their strength."

The words struck everyone like an unpleasant jolt from peaceful sleep. Yet who listening to her, Witgern thought, could believe she meant to do other than fight for them with all her spirit?

"I do not think you understand the size and might of the enemy—for you have seen so little of him. I have seen their drawings of the world. It is vast beyond your imagining and most of it belongs to Rome. I have seen where their soldiers are quartered. Some are set in places so distant that were you to travel there, three moons would come to fullness before you reached them. Some are arrayed beyond the sea.

"Among the Gallic traders who live in the shadow of Mogontiacum, all speak of a mysterious calling of great numbers of their soldiers from the Island of Albion. They say this signifies a great war is planned, next to which all we have suffered so far is a mere skirmish. None are *certain* what nation will fall victim to this attack. We know only that the plans progress day by day.

"But it is the character of this new Emperor that should cause you to see how grave our circumstances are," she went on, her voice coming now to full strength, gently binding their spirits together in solemn silence. "He is for certain no god, despite his demands for worship—we would not even call him a man. He is unblooded in battle because even his own father thought him unworthy and kept him home. 'So, that is well, we will defeat him all the more easily,' you might say to me. And you would make a foolish and fatal mistake, for their people are not like ours. The strength of their magic comes not from the power and holiness of their chieftains but from their curious habits of obedience and of fighting as one. If their Emperor orders every last man of their soldiers sent out against us, they will come."

Again she paused, allowing time for the words to settle like a garment and fall in place in their minds.

"Remember that this new Emperor searches for a war desperately as a niding searches for honor," she continued. "Wherever in the world he scents spirited disobedience, there he will strike. If we are quiet *now*, perhaps he will turn to other prey. For this reason I tell you we should *feign* obedience to the edict for a time, and war upon no one, and allow their spies to observe our assemblies, and tell them you intend to yield me up. Should the day come when I must be sacrificed to save us, I must be willing. I cannot refuse, if it saves so many."

A soft chorus of "No! Never!" rose up. She waited appreciatively until they quietened. She hoped fervently that if she must be delivered up to the enemy, her surrender could be somehow delayed until after the child was born.

"There is no dishonor in all this," she went on. "One man need not be shamed that he could be felled by one hundred. Our strength lies in not allowing ourselves to be goaded into wrath. This is the time for the wise retreat. I beg you consider these words, in the name of almighty Fria."

She inclined her head, suddenly emptied of words. The calm of first awakening, when all appears blurred, benevolent, settled over the throng. One of Sigwulf's Companions said loudly, "She speaks truly."

Another broke the silence with, "She speaks the words of Baldemar."

"Well done! The Veleda speaks through her!" came the voice of one of Romilda's women.

Geisar was astounded at how quickly Auriane had neutralized the people's battle frenzy. He knew even one season of peace would seriously weaken his hold over the people. The money he paid out in bribes to the chiefs who did his bidding, attacking targets chosen for the plunder they would yield, he reclaimed threefold in the rich sacrifices these same chiefs made to him for victory in battle. Without war, the system collapsed.

This battle, by all the gods, she shall not win.

Geisar nodded to Sigwulf, who longed to speak, his eyes bright with discontent. Sigwulf liked this turn of sentiment no better than Geisar, but for the sole reason that by nature he hated peace.

But at the last Sigwulf thought better of it; he felt too great an allegiance to Auriane to speak out against her himself. So he nodded to Wulfstan, who was more than eager to speak for her. If Sigwulf had known, however, the exact words Wulfstan planned to say, he would never have allowed it.

Wulfstan got slowly to his feet. He was the tallest of men, though he did not appear so because he stooped; he had a long, narrow face, a drooping mustache, a sour twist to his mouth, and a complexion that was pale and blotched. Auriane thought he looked like a man who had been poisoned. Tangled black hair fell into staring eyes that appeared not entirely sane.

He pointed a thick finger at Auriane and bellowed out: "This is one who has come to rule over you as a queen! Where there is no war, there is no life and no honor! She has always loved Roman ways better than our own. She looks with reverence upon the artifacts these Wolf-Men make. I have seen it with my own eyes! And I will tell you why. It is because she has fallen prey to the evil magic of this foreigner called Decius!"

Wulfstan took a step forward and his voice rose to a crescendo. "Witness how she counsels us to spare our enemy! *It is because she lies with him!* Will you be bewitched by the twisting lies of one who beds down with a foreign dog?"

For long moments there was only stifling silence, as if the indrawn breath of a god sucked away all the air. Witgern, Fastila and a half dozen of Auriane's Companions stirred to life first; they got slowly to their feet and began to ring themselves about Wulfstan, readying their spears.

The first sound came from Geisar. A moment passed before people realized he was laughing—it was a muffled, snuffling sound somewhat like a dog on the trail of game. Auriane stood absolutely still, feeling nothing yet, mind and spirit braced to fight to the end. Decius was well-schooled in life-and-death situations; he displayed no fear, though his every muscle tautened and his right hand moved imperceptibly closer to his dagger.

Then began murmurs of disbelief. What Wulfstan charged many

had long suspected, but always steadfastly refused to credit. He pressed them to ferret out a truth they preferred to leave hidden. Geisar shook his staff at Witgern and the Companions who stood with spears poised at Wulfstan. "To your places! If Wulfstan lies, he will be punished, and more severely than any of *you* can manage. Go, or I curse you!"

Witgern and Auriane's Companions did not move.

Geisar looked hard at Auriane. "Deny it, Auriane," he said. "And we will believe you."

Geisar knew that as daughter of a line of noble ancestresses from Athelinda back to Embla, Auriane could not speak an untruth. To do so would be to poison the soul all her kinspeople shared, and she was not of a nature to harm her people in order to spare herself.

Auriane longed to be free to speak falsely, so life would go on as always and she could protect the life of her child. But her tongue was made of stone; it was held in the spell of the ancient ways if her mind was not.

I have done evil! My punishment is just.

Time slowed; she felt too light, as if some liquid medium bore her up. A mallet pounded in her head.

"The charge is true," she responded at last. Her voice was clear and without shame.

The words sounded out of place, spoken by that god-infused voice so long trusted. Geisar sensed with acute irritation that many *still* did not believe, so great was their need of her, so powerful their affection. Many looked about with sad, desperate confusion, as if a beloved mother had turned on them.

But Geisar was prepared for this. With the barest of nods, invisible to the throng, he gave a signal.

And they heard the croaking voice of Ulfina, a kinswoman of Gundobad's.

"She is with child!"

Auriane said nothing, looking bravely, evenly, ahead as she struggled to control her trembling.

Ulfina, for her betrayal, earned fifty sturdy cattle from Geisar. Many were so disturbed by her words they began to strike at her and shout curses; she was forced to scurry off and take shelter among her kin. The old woman realized Geisar made her a bad bargain; it was not worth the fifty cattle to be forever despised.

Auriane saw sympathy melt quickly from the faces of those nearest; many averted their eyes. It was Witgern's reaction that seared like fire: He frowned and faintly withdrew from her while lowering his spear. His response might *not* have been utter revulsion, but it seemed so to her then.

"Try her!" came a shout from the part of the crowd thickest with her enemies. "She poisons us all!"

"Geisar! Give us a judgment!" Wulfstan shouted. Even now the majority of the people, though terrified by the implications of such a transgression, wished fervently to be shown a way to allow her to escape. But those most loyal to her were disheartened and disoriented, and her enemies were, as Geisar planned, loudly and energetically crying out with one voice.

Auriane felt her spiritedness start to rise.

Geisar is not fit to judge me. I accept only the judgment of the ancient Fates, and so far they are silent.

"She is judged!" shouted Geisar, eyes glittering like a fox's near a fire. He cracked his knotted staff in two, symbolizing condemnation to death, and held the broken ends aloft. "Wulfstan! Unfrith!" he commanded. "Seize her and take her to the priests' house!"

Her enemies rose up all at once, meaning to surround her; the maneuver was obviously timed and planned. Her Companions shot up to meet them.

Auriane and Decius sprang forward at the same instant, as if they knew each other's thoughts. Decius knocked Geisar to one side and wrested one half of the oak staff from him, to the horror of the attendant priests. Who but a madman would dare lay a hand on such a holy thing? Geisar was too stunned to protest.

A dozen or more of Gundobad's men rushed at Auriane. Decius struck one of them in the face with the staff's broken end, bloodying him and blinding him. Auriane whipped about to face Gundobad himself, who lunged at her from behind, brandishing an ax. She charged him with her spear, using it as a lance, and drove it deep into his chest.

Even with the madness all about, a moment of sickness seized her; she thought she felt Gundobad's heart jump like a harpooned fish. He sank slowly down. She abandoned the spear—there was no time to disengage it from Gundobad's body—and unsheathed the sword of Baldemar.

Now the whole of the Assembly was in furious motion like a lake surface agitated by storm winds. Her enemies, hundreds strong, turned en masse on her Companions—from everywhere came battle shouts and the angry staccato of spears cracking together. A few drew swords and added the ring of iron on iron to the din. Soon everyone was either actively battling or caught perilously in between; the priests' shrieks for order went unheard.

As Decius dropped to the ground to recover the axe from Gundobad's clenched fist, Auriane deflected a club-blow that would have finished him. Friend and foe swarmed so closely about she feared she might strike down one of her own Companions. Her horse—and safety—seemed half a world away. She began fighting her way in that direction; in such close quarters her sword was more effective than the spears most carried, and she made good progress—until an iron hand seized her arm.

She was in the grip of a burly kinsman of Gundobad's, who meant to drag her to death. Slowly, steadily, he began pulling her in the wrong direction; she was caught in a deadly current drawing her into the maelstrom. Her screams were unheard.

Gradually she realized Decius struggled to follow her, though she did not know what he thought he could do to aid her. The axe was gone; he now had a spear.

Then she saw Decius drop to his knees, falling beneath the melee. He thrust the spear's point between the legs of one battling warrior and into the thigh of Auriane's captor. The kinsman of Gundobad screamed a curse and released her. Suddenly free, she was flung backward, but Decius broke her fall on one side, Witgern on the other. She realized she was among a knot of her own Companions. She did not have time to worry if they were still willing to protect her. They did.

She had room to maneuver now; fighting abreast with Witgern, Decius, Fastila, and a half dozen Companions, slowly, step by step, she cut her way through to her horse. Once when the fighting slowed because all were packed too closely together, she met Witgern's gaze—and he averted his eye. In his face was the look of one who counted himself ruthlessly betrayed. That single damning eye called to mind Wodan himself, the One-Eyed God, her own wronged husband, whose wrath surely was upon her now.

But at least Witgern was not ready to hand her over to her enemies. That he helped her while he thought her crime despicable made his judgment all the more painful.

One by one, torches were toppled and snuffed out in the mud; soon the ghastly scene was lit only by wan starlight; no one could tell friend from foe—and inevitably kinsman struck down kinsman. The Assembly of the New Moon fell into chaos.

Gradually Auriane gained ground; now she dimly saw Berinhard ahead in the gloom.

But one horse would not be enough. Witgern seemed to think of this at the same time. "Auriane!" he shouted. "Take *that* one too. Behind your horse—the little mare. It's Romilda's. I'll settle with her."

Then Decius slipped in mud and blood, landing hard on his back. One of Gundobad's men was poised over him with his spear, readying the death blow.

An animal scream was torn from Auriane's throat, and she flung herself forward, sword raised, feeling her whole soul lived in her blade. With a two-hand hold she struck down diagonally, catching the spear in a glancing blow, deflecting it so that it pierced the foot of Decius' attacker. All the man's force was behind it; he shrieked as he realized he was pinned to the ground with his own spear. Hurriedly she pulled Decius to his feet.

When they had nearly battled their way to her horse, she saw a Companion of Wulfstan's gliding toward Berinhard in a crouching run.

He means to hamstring my horse.

Decius saw, too, and gave chase; he sprang onto the warrior's back. The man buckled beneath him, contracting in agony; Decius' weight, flung onto him with such force, caused his ankle to give way and break. Decius fell with him and rolled. Auriane sprinted past them, covering the last of the distance. While Decius dispatched the warrior with his dagger, Auriane cut both horses' reins so she would not have to fumble with the knots.

The Companions then broke through the last of the resistance and swarmed protectively about Auriane and Decius.

"Take Berinhard!" Auriane shouted to Decius. "He is faster. I know the terrain better—they won't catch me." She started to pull herself onto the back of the small black mare, but Decius dragged her back down.

"No! You take the good horse. You are with child. I insist upon it. If one of us lives, it must be you!" Decius gripped the mare's mane and sprang lightly onto her back. "Though I don't personally plan on getting caught, either," he added, grinning.

She vaulted onto Berinhard's back. "Head down!" Decius shouted at her. A stone from a sling passed overhead with a lethal rush. Then Witgern was at her side, holding her horse by the bit, using the weight of his body to prevent Berinhard from rearing and exposing her to missiles, leading her toward the unbounded forest.

Moments later Fastila came up on her other side, helping Witgern hold her terrified horse.

"Auriane, where will you go?" Witgern shouted up at her. She felt a grab of hope in her heart. He must not despise her completely if he wanted to know where she could be found.

"To Ramis," she shouted down to him, feeling awkward, "at her lodge in Alder Lake." She wanted to add, *Witgern, I was dead, for so long I was dead—do you understand at all?* But a rush of pride prevented her. The full realization of what he must think of her collected behind some closed door in her mind, awaiting a time of peace when it would burst out and cause great torment.

As they came to the towering darkness of the pine forest, Witgern said solemnly, "Your luck and your fate go with you, Auriane."

He took her hand, but to Auriane's mind he did it ceremonially, to maintain an illusion of friendship.

Then Fastila cried up at her, "Auriane, I will come to you there when the way is passable, I vow it! We have not deserted you!"

"You must not! You'll be cursed!"

Fastila could hardly hear these words in the din. She shouted again, her voice growing hoarse, "I will come!"

Then Witgern released Berinhard, who snorted, half reared, then galloped free down the wide, grassy lane between the pines. Decius' mount burst into an ungainly gallop that seemed to skip a beat. This was not an animal possessed of natural grace, and Auriane held her breath while she watched Decius struggle for his seat. He must not fall off. In moments it would be known by everyone that they fled on horseback; some surely would pursue. Auriane had to hold Berinhard in or his smooth powerful strides would have pulled her steadily ahead.

And soon there was muffled thunder in back of them. It sounded as though three, perhaps four, gave chase.

"We must separate!" she shouted to Decius, "and pray they come after me." She surmised they would have little trouble overtaking Decius' horse. "Just before the creek, you go north!"

"Right!" Decius shouted back. She hoped they would hear Berinhard noisily splashing in the creek and follow her—and hopefully not hear a lone horse's hooves going north.

He called out, "You saved my life! You are quick and steady—a lioness! The oak-leaf crown should be yours!" He referred to the *corona civica,* the honorarium given a Roman soldier who saved the life of one of his fellows in battle.

She felt a stirring of pleasure at these words, savoring his approving smile, so seldom seen. But even then it seemed there was a certain restraint in his praise, and suddenly she realized his reluctance to praise her stemmed from his fear that the fragile bond between them might be broken, that she would think so well of herself, she would no longer need him. It was not stubborn pride that held him in check, but fear she would desert him. It made little sense to her, but somehow she was certain then that this assessment was true. She felt a rush of pity for him, and a burst of love that was more close and familial than what she had felt before.

They galloped close and clasped hands for a brief moment in farewell.

"Decius!" she cried out, not certain what she meant to say, just wanting to hold to him a moment longer by speaking his name, seized suddenly with the thought she might never see him again. He clasped her hand tightly—a quick, sad last embrace—then released it. Her hand felt cold and empty.

He wheeled his mount north, following the creek. Immediately afterward, Berinhard splashed noisily into the shallow water; fortunately the season had been dry or they would have had to swim across. When she emerged on the opposite bank, she released Berinhard into the wide meadow beyond. Joyfully he bolted; all that power and grace were unleashed, and she felt herself hurled into the night as the stallion's strides grew steadily longer. The dark mane lashed her face as she leaned far over his neck.

Distantly behind her she heard several horses splashing into the creek. That was well: they were following *her*. She knew they would never catch her now—unless Berinhard fell.

How can I ever return? This time the gate is barred forever.

Ramis, you have your wish. I am separated from battle, severed from kin. Rejoice, you sister of Helle! You have me *and* my child.

The brawling beneath the Sacred Oak gradually wore itself down; no one had a taste for fighting in the unhallowed dark, especially now that the cause of it all had fled. As the injuries and deaths were tallied up so blood-debts could be paid, Sigwulf found the tattered remains of the imperial document. He held a torch to it; then to rousing cheers he burned the edict of Domitian, God-King of the Romans.

• • •

Auriane journeyed steadily west, into the desolate fir-clad hill country. She made no fires and stayed well away from the trails itinerant traders used. Often she paused on high ground to climb a tree and carefully study the dusky purple shadows of the deeply folded hills behind her to make certain she was not pursued—she sensed the presence of elves and ghosts rustling in those melancholy deeps, but no human enemy was to be seen—though at times her loneliness was so vast she almost wished for one.

The cold was cruel and penetrating. For shelter the first night she found a shallow cave; on the next she fashioned a crude lean-to of pine branches, meadow grasses, and Berinhard's saddle blanket. For two days she had no food but a portion of a loaf of oat-millet bread and goat cheese she had brought to the Assembly. As she passed distant homesteads, the air was filled with the rank smell of slaughtering. This was the time of year known as the Days of Blood, when the stock animals that could not survive the food shortages of winter were sacrificed to Fria. The people feasted on the meat and salted the rest to sustain them through the snows. Occasionally she passed far-off wisps of smoke and heard joyous shouts.

In all that passed in the last days, hardest for her to bear was the shame she knew she caused Athelinda.

For the second time in my life, I try my poor mother past the limits any mortal should have to bear. And when the great war comes, she will be in misery and alone.

As she came to lands where she was less likely to be known, she was not so careful about concealing herself and she passed close to some of the village celebrations. She was treated kindly and offered meat and mead. Her warrior's ring drew curious looks. Once she was asked if she was the Maid of the Chattians who had done fabled deeds. She denied it because she wanted no talk of her to linger in these places, but she was amazed she was known this far from her own country.

On the fourth day, snow laid a dusty coverlet of white over the hills. She felt she, too, drifted into the deathlike sleep of winter, but with no promise of reawakening in the spring.

She was crossing the outskirts of the lands of the horse-loving Tencteres when she halted at a lonely homestead, meaning to seek further directions to the winter dwelling place of Ramis. An ancient farm-wife emerged with waddling gait from her round hut, meaning to assist the lone traveler. She wore a long, swaying necklace of lynx's teeth for protection against ghosts. Her eyes were slits, almost invisible in folds of fat; she seemed a storehouse of unpleasant secrets. The old woman pointed north, toward twin barren hills so smooth and even they might have been giant's barrows, and told Auriane that if she passed straight between them, then rode on for half a day at a brisk trot, she could not miss Alder Lake, where the greatest of Holy Ones dwelled but was seldom seen.

A little village has grown up about the place, she explained, peopled with those who await her favor. "But mostly," she added, "our lady disappoints them."

Auriane thought grimly: This old woman knows of whom I speak. Ramis makes a lifelong habit of sowing disappointment.

The farm-woman assured her the pilgrims marked the path well with small shrines: piles of smooth stones, sticks of yarrow bundled together, or collections of hares' skulls. Then she finished with a warning: "If you've any mother wit, you'll turn that horse round and go home. You're comely and young and strong—she'll want you for a slave, my pretty. She'll change you into a frog to make music for her at night. That one's got the demons of Helle at her beck and call, all tame as fat geese feeding from her hand."

Auriane thanked her and moved on. Beyond the two hills she came to an avenue of hard-packed earth that parted a sea of snow-feathered sedge and broom; here she urged Berinhard to a gallop. As the stallion began to tire, they surmounted a rise thick with hardy rowan shrubs; she knew from their even rows that they were planted deliberately—for the rowan tree offered powerful protection against harmful magic. She tautened with excitement; her destination must be close. Then suddenly, below her, was Alder Lake, black, shrouded and still; the vapor issuing from it made it appear to exhale ghosts. She realized the lake must be fed by a warm spring. She looked on the scene for long moments, feeling wrapped in an old, familiar peace, as though she nested in the palm of Fria. At the center of the lake was a grassy island roughly as large as a thrall's field, or what one ox could plow in a day. Three pinewood lodges occupied it; the central and grandest one had a red-stained stag's skull affixed above the door. A thin thread of smoke issued from a fire before the door.

That central lodge, she surmised, must be the holiest of holy places in all the northern lands, the dwelling place of the Veleda, she who is the One Who Sees. It was a house that expressed Ramis' soul: austere, remote, but accessible—if one had patience and was willing to travel over dark water to reach her. Unlike her predecessor in the office—a fearful old woman who sequestered herself in a high tower, was never seen unveiled, and spoke to the people only through intermediaries—Ramis walked openly among the villagers, allowing petitioners to speak to her face to face, while actively discouraging those who tried to worship her as a goddess on earth. Auriane had heard a tale of two Batavian tribesmen who traveled here, dragging with them a captured Roman legionary soldier whom they proudly offered to Ramis as a human sacrifice. But Ramis was greatly offended. She ordered the victim set free and even gifted the Roman captive with a small chest filled with silver coins. The Batavians she drove from her presence. Most who heard the tale were utterly baffled—how could the Veleda have refused such a royal gift?

The temporary village, a motley collection of dwellings made of turf and hides and broken carts, was strewn randomly about the lake. The people who traveled here to await an audience with Ramis thrived off the food and gifts brought to the Veleda by wealthy chiefs who came to beg her for oracles; Ramis took what little she needed to live and distributed the rest among the petitioners.

Auriane stopped when she came to the bolted gate in the low fence of staves that ran about the precinct; clearly strangers were not to pass until admitted.

There was a festival atmosphere in this odd place where people came not to live but to wait. She heard the gallop of many drums and saw through the tents the flash of brightly robed dancers. Here were women and men from diverse tribes; she saw a warrior of the Suebians with his black hair coiled into a tight knot over one ear, shepherding a child with some crippling ailment. Two snowy-skinned, black-haired women of the tribe of the Sitones, wearing peaked caps and cowrie-shell necklaces, looked up at her from a board game, their eyes glimmering with magic. An aristocratic Gallic woman with knotted hair held in place with golden netting and a rich checkered robe that brushed the ground was carrying a lapdog while she walked with her two maids. She even saw men of Decius' smaller stature, who must have been of the Roman lands of the far south. Everywhere cattle, goats and geese wandered about unmolested, for none here ate the flesh of beasts.

Auriane pulled the rope of a bronze bell attached to the sagging gate.

A woman stirred within one of the tents, then strode purposefully toward her. There was a look of silence about her, as if she had long ago decided to commune as little as possible with fellow human creatures. Her coloring was that of a woodland creature, from her great, round, mourning eyes speckled with many colors, to the red-brown freckles on her nose, her sienna-and-gray mottled robe, the fox fur thrown over it for warmth. Hers was a big-boned and homely face with an oddly contrasting sensuous mouth, yet Auriane guessed no husband or lover had ever known that thin, hard body; about her was the air of the harsh celibacy of priestly service. She identified herself as Helgrune, Ramis' servant.

"The granddaughter of Gandrida has come, blessed is the day!" Helgrune said it joylessly, as a flat statement of fact.

"Blessings and luck to you," Auriane said, inclining her head, trying not to sound too wary. "But how do you know me?"

"I do not. It is *she* who knows you." Helgrune nodded faintly in the direction of the island in the lake. Auriane guessed from this obstinately brief explanation that her coming on this day had been prophesied.

Helgrune began unfastening the gate, then stopped, looking darkly at Auriane's sword. "Iron belongs in the earth. You must put it back."

Auriane protested and told her whose sword it was.

"Baldemar was beloved of us. Still, it is a sword and must stay outside. Wrap it carefully in linen and bury it just outside the enclosure. It will come to no harm."

Reluctantly, Auriane obeyed. Then she rubbed Berinhard's coat with charcoal to darken it so the horse would not be recognized by anyone stalking her, and put him into the rude stables.

She then began what Helgrune told her was a purification period. Not only had she been polluted with iron, she was polluted with blood. Auriane was tempted to object that it was enemy's blood, but she sensed that would not matter here. She was secluded in a lodge constructed of rowan branches and given only ritual grains to eat. She drank springwater in which sacred gemstones had been placed—each gemstone, Helgrune explained, healed a different quality of the spirit. Daily she bathed in the holy waters of the lake. As one day, then another passed, her unease intensified. Why should Ramis concern herself with the troubles of a woman who long ago had scorned her?

Once a day a petitioner would be rowed to the island and taken before Ramis. From the talk about her she realized there was no readily determined pattern by which they were called; often a newer arrival would be taken before those who languished here as long as four moons. It was said Ramis made the wealthy travelers wait longer. But Auriane thought Ramis' reasonings more obscure than that; she saw a British chieftain, his hair matted with lime paste, his neck and arms heavily laden with gold—a man possessed of a solemn, quiet intensity—be admitted after only fourteen days.

When Auriane had been in this place but five days, Helgrune roused her from her bed of rushes at midnight. Startled awake and blinded by the torch thrust into her face, she forgot where she was.

Where is Decius? Tears sprang to her eyes as she remembered.

Helgrune said only, "It is time." She nodded toward the island.

"Now?" Auriane whispered. "In the grimmest part of night?"

Helgrune would not answer; her manner suggested Auriane purposefully feigned ignorance. Brusquely she gave Auriane a long dress of white linen weighted at the hem with stones of amber, and told her to take off her shoes, though the ground was cold. Then, moving with ceremonial care, she laid a white cat-skin over Auriane's shoulders.

Auriane and Helgrune then walked to the lake, flanked by two torch-bearing apprentices; two more stood ready by a coracle tied at the bank. What was the meaning of this? Night journeys were evil, fraught with unholy things.

Her terror would have grown unmanageable except that she sensed the others awakening about her counted this some unusual honor. Those who were roused to investigate this nighttime procession excitedly awakened others.

"She has been here only five days," Auriane heard them exclaim in furtive whispers. But what seemed to intrigue them far more was that she was brought at *night*. Apparently this had not happened in anyone's memory. And why the white cat-skin cloak, the holiest of garments? Who *was* this war-loving daughter of a distant chief who was allowed to see the great Holy One after a wait of but five days?

Nearly the whole population was now awake and clustered about, watching with great curiosity. Several came forward, shouting or stammering their cases to Auriane in tongues she half understood, thinking she could intercede so they would be heard more quickly. Helgrune drove them off.

The coracle's prow was carved into the shape of a dragon's head; a lamp was concealed in the hollow head so that its eyes glowed and smoked; an ancient consciousness, terrifying but benign, seemed to dwell there. As Auriane stepped unsteadily into the small craft, the smoking head dipped and rose with her weight. She was followed by the two torch-bearers who took their places at bow and stern. A single oarsman bore them off with sweeping strokes. The twin fires of the torches were reflected on the perfectly still waters as if in a mirror of moonstone. Rising like vapor from the dark island came the sound of panpipes playing for a dance of ghosts. The sound of the gentle dipping of oars into water added a slightly askew percussion accompaniment to the wild roaming of the pipes. Auriane was in one moment faint at the strangeness of it all and in the next roused to sharp attention, in spite of the fact that they appeared to honor her. Who truly knew Ramis' mind?

She is dark and unpredictable, and she knows I despise her.

The coracle bumped softly against the bank of the island. Helgrune and the two torchbearers led her up a flight of stone steps. Many tame serpents lived here with Ramis; their patterned backs caught Auriane's eye as they rippled like running water just beyond the circle of torchlight.

They walked beneath a stone arch on which was mounted a hexagonal shield; it symbolized the protective powers of the Veleda, preserver of all the tribes in battle. Just beyond was a wood image of Fria, a plain, polished staff of oak not worked by human hands; its voluptuous curves were nature's work alone. Helgrune halted, and Auriane knew she was meant to kiss the image. Briefly she knelt and did so—and started, near certain she felt living flesh quiver beneath her lips.

The small procession moved toward the central lodge called the temple-house, with its ritual fire never allowed to go out.

As they moved closer to the fire, Auriane saw the solemn form of a woman seated before it with her back to them, proud and erect in regal silence. She seemed vastly solitary, as if she were the first-created of all human creatures. The night was oppressive and heavy about her, but she seemed to hold it at bay as she gently emanated dark power. Masses of silver and gold hair fanned about her; firelight played on it as if it were a mantle of silk. The island's serpents knew this woman was their mistress; here they swarmed thickly as if drawn to her, testing tongues flicking out at the night.

Helgrune stopped and spoke the ritual words meant to calm a petitioner's fears: "She is a mortal woman." Then the haughty serving-woman and the torchbearers departed into the night, leaving Auriane alone with the Veleda.

For long moments that formidable figure froze Auriane in place.

She saw that Ramis sat within a circle of skulls dyed red with ocher. A bolt of primitive fear flashed through her.

It is a trap. Those skulls belong to the poor fools she lured here at night.

But it seemed long, tangled roots held her to the earth; she could no more run off than could the alder trees about the lake. The image persisted, as if Ramis imposed it on her mind: Her arms were spreading leafy branches, sheltering her people, nourishing them, even now in exile. If she fled, they would be exposed, unprotected.

But if she could not flee, neither could she go forward. She knew then that since last they met, her fears had altered, matured. Gone was that childhood terror of being spirited off and forced to live in darkness. Now she just did not want Ramis probing at the torn, broken quivering mass that was her soul. Living was painful enough without that oversharp vision skewering all her hopes.

Then pride lent her strength, and Auriane moved about the fire, uncertain why she felt she had to prove her courage to Ramis if she so despised her. Now she saw the old sorceress in profile, that noble face stark, eternal as an outcropping of rock. Ramis seemed to command the fire; Auriane was certain it swelled and receded with her thoughts. Ramis' lids were half-closed; those eyes seemed possessed of a potent emptiness. Her soul did not seem resident in her body.

Is she roaming the forest as a wolf?

Ramis' words of long ago, "You wear your mother's fear, not your own," came to her then, and in that moment Auriane knew it was true. Athelinda had so feared for Baldemar that reason failed where Ramis was concerned, and her mother saw only the sorceress's threatening aspect. Now it was too late to fear for Baldemar.

Fear caught us and consumed us, did it not? And yet still we live. Mother, now I can see this dread creature with my own eyes.

She knew Ramis wanted her to enter the circle of skulls and sit opposite her.

Hardly breathing, Auriane stepped over the skulls, strung like some frightful beaded necklace round the fire, and settled herself on the ground facing the Veleda.

The face of the greatest of the Holy Nine was like a low moon poised just above the flames; her forehead shone from the heat. How taut that skin was over the severe beauty of her bones, Auriane thought; despite the fact that she was well into the age of grandmothers. Ramis' face brought to mind the smooth stones polished by rivers, softly rounded into the shape of the eternal.

The hooded eyes focused on Auriane, flashing with a restless but disciplined intelligence. They were eyes that knew lake bottoms and the deeps of the night sky, that knew what stirred beneath the barrow, that illumined all shadowed places with their wan light. Auriane shivered, feeling stripped of clothes, of flesh.

When Ramis spoke, it was in an intimate voice that took no notice of the gulf of years separating this encounter from the last.

"Tell me, child, why is there an egg within each skull?"

Auriane looked carefully at the red skulls and saw that within each pair of gaped eyes was indeed an egg, most probably that of a goose. She held in a breath. The eggs seemed to pulse, as if something living within struggled to burst out.

"Because . . . death holds always the seed of new life." She was pleased she had a reasonable-sounding answer and waited expectantly for approval. But she got none.

Ramis' retort was like the precise thrust of a weapon at a vital point. "Why, then, do you grieve?"

Auriane was startled by this shift in mood. "Because . . . because of love. Perhaps I love too much." She thought of Baldemar.

"No. You love not nearly enough. If you did, you would not grieve."

Auriane said nothing, puzzled by this.

"You do not understand because you know only one kind of love, a sad, sickly one that ends in your abandonment. Truly, you are a miser with love. There are a hundred kinds. Love of this moment in time, for one. Do you remember when you were a girl of three summers, perhaps four? *Then* you knew love of this moment in time. That can be regained."

"That . . . but that is for children."

"But you felt something akin to it once, as a woman."

Auriane knew she spoke of the luminous state that had come over her when she pried the stone from the hoof of the mare.

"But that was *your* magic."

"No. It was yours. And it is the natural state of those who are not lost. Auriane, it is time for you to learn the Ritual of Fire."

"I will learn no sorcerer's rituals!"

"Good, because I do not know any. *Sorcery* is the word spewed out by the ignorant when their distorted vision is faced unavoidably with the divine. The fire ritual is a sort of nourishment, necessary if you are to survive the years in store for you, which I must tell you are going to be wretched, but glorious."

"Glorious? I will have fame?"

"I would say . . . *you will be a queen in death.* Now, silence! I will explain no further."

"Will this ritual bring me home?"

"You *are* home. Silence!"

This time Auriane obeyed, sensing that a heavy door dropped in place.

"Now narrow your vision until you see only the fire, yes, and know that this is *all* fires, for all have one united spirit—greedy, devouring, but trustworthy if tamed. Shed your skin, your heart; you are grasping flames, reaching ever upward, ever frustrated, wanting to flow up into the sky but unable."

Auriane's fingers were licking flames, her heart, molten yellow. She panicked and her spirit pulled away.

"Do not do that! It cannot harm you."

Some wiser instinct prevailed, and Auriane let the fire tug at her soul until she felt herself steadying, flickering, floating just above the ground.

"Now turn your mind upon the world before the time of the Giants, when all was frost and rime and fertile sea." Ramis' voice was lilting, low, and strangely seductive; Auriane felt herself enticed inward, step by step, edging dangerously toward what felt like nonexistence. A sweat born of terror moistened her brow.

"And now, before you is the Yawning Gap. The gods are not; they have not yet been created. All is pregnant emptiness. The Abyss is ready to bring forth."

The world snapped into new shape. With a leap of joy Auriane realized it was a shape she knew, from that day long ago when Ramis halted her on the road. She was borne up on warm, nurturing water. All memories were washed and transformed— they were as they had been but with their coating of misery dissolved away so that they were harmonious, brilliant. As before, she recognized the world was made a little differently from what she had supposed; it was one great seamless interweaving, and the weaver was infinitely benign. The crackle of flames was some natural instrument playing along with the rustle of branches above; the water all about was silk, her body a supple and stable form, fluidly balanced. Her attention to the fire was a solemn, rhythm-less dance. She sensed tender light reaching into the grimmest parts of her soul, illumining everything evenly; there was no act of hers she thought it necessary to hide. There was, too, a peculiar sense that everyone she had known, the living and the dead, were *present*. Present and . . . not entirely separate beings.

She was distinctly aware that Ramis chanted words, that rich dark voice the beating heart of all this, and she felt a flash of despair: *I want to be able to come here on my own—I do not want to need her.*

And then, in one moment, she felt a third presence drawing very close, sensing its effect if not its form, like the disturbance on a lake when a large creature comes near to the surface, then dives. The ripples were all about.

"My lady," Auriane said as if speaking in her sleep, "we are not alone."

She realized Ramis perceived this already; the old woman was very still, feeling, listening.

Finally Ramis spoke. "Yes . . . another mind is drawn close. . . . Vast space separates us . . . but your soul touches his . . ." Her voice drifted, as if carried on the smoke of the fire, and Auriane had to grope for it; she was not certain she rightly heard the next words. ". . . because he wears the Sacred Mold."

The sense persisted; the presence was a spirit so like her own she found herself playing with it, twining round it.

Ramis had said "he." In some far country a man wore the *aurr*. Who was it?

But then Ramis broke the enchantment. "Away from the fire now. Away, and look at me."

Auriane felt she had outstretched wings that softly lowered her to earth. She felt the bite of cold air. Her hand went to her throat—she expected that pouch of earth Ramis had put round her neck as a babe to be there and was desolate when it was not. She frowned, not quite remembering what had happened.

"Do not neglect this ritual, Auriane," Ramis was saying, pointing with a forefinger to emphasize the words; her eyes shone with a gentle protectiveness Auriane had not thought part of her nature. "Let it be your ship over black water. It may well be what enables you, in coming days, to keep that mortal body long enough to come into your fate. If you are in a place where you can build no fire, make fire in your mind." Auriane could scarce believe this was the same Ramis of her childhood. Gone was the baffling demigoddess of their last meeting, who hurled down her harsh teachings like a rain of spears; this Ramis was an amicable companion riding the same path to a village, offering advice because she had come this way before.

Ramis answered the unspoken thought. "It is not *I* who has changed, but you. Your spirit is readied for things now that before it was not. It sorrows me, though, that you came here not for yourself, but for the child."

Auriane felt a quiet jolt. She had told no one in this place she was with child. A hand went protectively to her faintly swelling belly.

Necessity pressed in then, and she remembered the question she came to ask.

"My lady, will you . . . protect me here until my lying-in?"

"The gods cannot do that! Of course, you may stay, but I desire a gift of you." Ramis lifted her head and narrowed her eyes as if focusing on some future day; a measure of the old sternness returned. "The child you carry is a girl. I want her."

"I—my child is mine! You cannot have her!"

"If you want that babe to live, Auriane, you *must* give her to me. You are destined to be led into places where no child can survive."

Auriane felt her heart pause. Auguries of late *had* said she would not live long. And had not Ramis herself just made the bewildering—but decidedly sinister—prediction that she would be "a queen in death"?

This child would be damned among her own people. But with Ramis she would learn strength and wisdom and have status, though of a different sort. Decius might be captured or dead—she could not depend on his help. This island *did* seem a tranquil place in a world of raging storms.

"The child is half-foreign."

"To me, none are foreign."

Auriane felt desperate, sad, and trapped.

"No. I cannot give up my child."

"As you say," Ramis said gently. Auriane knew Ramis had not given up the fight; this was a tactical retreat. The old woman would bide her time, then try again.

"Can you tell me . . . is Decius safe?"

"Safe, but not content. But then he is content to be not content."

"Will I . . . will I see him again?"

Ramis smiled and shook her head, like a mother with a precocious child who tries a trick to get something she cannot have. "Some fates are not set and cannot be known."

"Why did you summon me at *night*?"

"Ah. If you knew the answer to *that,* you might dash your head against that rock! You're not *near* ready to hear it. Later, much later, you will hear it and welcome the news." Ramis paused; with a long, delicate forefinger she stroked the head of an adder that regarded her with needle-sharp eyes. Auriane knew that variety to be highly poisonous. *Has she enchanted it, or does she consider death of so little account?*

The next question welled up in her against her will, like sickness. "I must know it. . . ." The words were barely audible. "I beg you . . . tell me . . . why was I led to do the most horrible of crimes?"

Ramis regarded her in compassionate silence for a time. Then she deliberately teased the snake. After a moment the evil head flashed out, and the adder bit her. Bright droplets of blood appeared on the fleshy part of her palm.

Aghast, Auriane started to struggle to her feet. "You let it strike you! Why! Do you wish to die?"

"I will not die," Ramis said calmly.

She is inhuman. She did not even wince in pain.

"That same measure of venom in your body would have you writhing on the ground, for you have so much venom in you already, poor child. You poison yourself day by day—without the aid of a viper. You poison yourself with the venom of shame. My body is too intimately acquainted with death. It moves with it, it does not fight it. I am death's bride. I bed down with it every night." She resumed affectionately stroking the snake.

"The horse test showed you your innocence," Ramis went on. "Yet still you speak of your 'crime.' I thought if I refused to give a judgment in that case and left it to the horses, it might help you believe. Evidently it has not. Why?"

Auriane felt hot tears collecting, filling her eyes.

"I, too, once caused a death," Ramis said softly. "She was my own daughter."

Auriane felt slow shock spreading through her limbs, astonished Ramis trusted her with this secret. It was as though she were shown a thing no living person was meant to see, like the dread, secret image of Fria that each spring the priest veiled in red, put into a cart, and drove over the fields to give them new life.

"In the sacred precinct of Seven Alders, where, as you know, I served long ago as apprentice to the great teacher and prophetess called Matabrune," Ramis continued, the barest hoarseness in her voice indicating the hurt was not completely healed, "we were required to be adept with one weapon. I was accomplished with a bow. One night a band of Hermundures attacked, and in the confusion and darkness . . . I shot her and killed her . . . my own heart's blood. . . . Freawaru was her name. The arrowhead was smeared with hellebore—she died painfully, but at once. I was younger than you then, and like you, I poisoned myself for years. My grief was larger than the Three Worlds. I sorrow still, yes, but now my blood is cleansed." Auriane was even more astonished to see a single tear travel down that smooth cheek. "As I was cleansed, so too can you be, Auriane."

Auriane could scarcely breathe.

"Life is never, *never* what it seems," Ramis continued gently. "That stone, which is so hard against the flesh, truly is emptiness. Baldemar *lives*. Your suffering pains him. I will try to show you, while you are here, your true enemy. It is *not*, as you suppose, death."

"Will I ever be able to return to my people?"

"*There* is your true enemy."

"What? Wanting to return to my people?"

"No. Not questioning that which you desire. Your desires are idols, worshiped blindly. But returning to your people is not even your greatest idol. Greatest for you is *vengeance*."

Auriane felt her body tauten; a vast distance seemed to spring up between her and Ramis. This could not be discussed. Of course, she would avenge Baldemar's death, as spring follows winter. Of course, she would one day challenge Odberht, and kill him. What proud person of noble parents would not? It was sacred law, and all peoples followed it—all except the followers of Ramis, known everywhere for their strangeness.

"Well, we've come to a barrier high as the clouds, and it's a fine place to stop," Ramis said easily, arising. Auriane rose with her. Before quitting the circle, Ramis inclined her head, took Auriane's hand, and shut her eyes. Facing the fire, she began to chant a familiar prayer to Fria:

"You who are pure light shed from the moon . . . you who are the radiant one, whose raiment is the sun . . . you who generate all things and bring forth ever anew the sun that you have given to the nations . . . victory is your divine name . . ."

Auriane spoke it with her; it was a prayer every child knew. When it was done Ramis cast a bundle of dried vervain into the flames as a token-gift to Fria. Then she took up a torch and lit it from the fire. Walking in silence, she led Auriane to one of the small lodges.

She means for me to stay here on the island.

Auriane felt weak and emptied, so great was her relief. There was no safer place—no emissary of Geisar would dare cross this water.

The lodge was spare and simple; on a crude pine table was a jar of water, a hollowed gourd and a bird-bone flute; on the floor was a comfortable bed of straw.

She fell at once into sleep and dreamed vividly of Ramis. The sorceress was conversing with frightful spirits that possessed animal heads. Of all the words she spoke, Auriane heard clearly only one line.

"Yes . . . she is the one."

CHAPTER XX

Midwinter and the days of Yule approached, and the mud began to freeze. At dawn Ramis often walked round the island with Auriane, her stream of talk smoothly weaving the visible world with the realm of spirits; she might begin by speaking of the habits of waterbirds, of which she had made a study, then shift to the nature of death and why so many peoples represent it by the flight of a bird. Once when Auriane spoke of her sense of foreboding about the coming spring, Ramis paused and looked out on the smoking water as if considering carefully what to say. Then she answered, "Remember this, Auriane: That very turn of fate which, in its day, you find most relentlessly cruel—one day you will turn round and know it as your *deliverer*."

Auriane carefully considered this, but it made her feel no more secure. She scented gathering war as beasts scent a storm.

In late morning Auriane would row herself ashore and take Berinhard out to let him run riderless over the bare grassy hills; often she practiced with a spear on these journeys to keep herself conditioned for battle, ever hopeful she would be called back. As the child grew within her, she felt a new sort of love: a warm, diffuse tenderness for the unknown being within. She felt an ardent curiosity about this new creature. Who are you? she wondered a hundred times a day, her hand on her rapidly growing belly. Will you have Decius' nature or mine? Or will you be hideous because of Geisar's curse—and have a calf's head and the body of a black dog?

At the same time she despised this new ungainliness that made it increasingly difficult to get easily about. And then grim thoughts would come: The old must give way to the new. My body will swell and burst, and I will die so new life can arise. The mare is not so encumbered, nor is the doe. Why does nature descend so heavily on the human mother, leaving her staggering about and prey to the wolf?

While Auriane was off the island, Ramis saw the petitioners. Most wanted an oracle or advice in matters of sacred law, land disputes, marriage, or war, and Auriane trusted this greatest of Holy Ones even more when she saw how joyful the petitioners often were when they left her presence. At times Ramis was absent for days, leading delegations to the legionary fortresses to take complaints to the tribes' common enemy, the Romans, or if it was the time of the new moon, traveling to the nighttime gatherings of the Holy Nine in their sacred Elm Grove a half day's ride to the east. Frightful rites were performed there, it was said, that maintained the harmony between the old and new gods and the balance among the Three Worlds. Once she was called to a Law-Assembly by the neighboring Tencteres to settle the case of a battle chief who had broken the sacred law of vengeance, striking at the offending clan by slaying an unblooded, half-grown boy. And so Auriane was often alone with the dour, distant Helgrune.

As the year's shortest days approached, evergreen boughs were nailed above the doors in the little community about the lake—charms to ensure the return of the green in the spring. On Midwinter Day the lake community set Yule logs alight to ensure that the light of the world would not go out entirely in winter. The mead they drank was sent by noblewomen of the Tencteres. The Boar Feast consisted of barley cakes shaped in the image of boars, because they did not eat flesh in this place. Auriane went ashore for the Yule Feast and sat before Helgrune's glowing oak log in bitter loneliness, fearful for her mother and for Decius. Often in years past she had gotten a dim sense of events of the coming year by divining from the flight of the Yule log's fiery embers, and what she saw for the new year she could scarcely bear to look upon—something dark and catastrophic loomed; she could not make out its precise shape.

Two days later, snow came in earnest, first laying a light shroud over the withered ground, then a solid blanket; it weighed down the boughs of the evergreens until the branches drooped low. Like me, she thought, those boughs sag under a cumbersome burden, and like me, they will not be relieved of it until spring. The snowfall sealed the great pathways through the forest, shutting out all but the most determined travelers. This year she despised the winter—it heightened her sense of isolation from her people.

Through the winter the lake remained black and still, strangely free of ice because of its magical warmth. When at last the snowstorms relented and many of the trails first became passable, just when Auriane was near maddened with need of news, Fastila did come, riding with a party of six novices from the Ash Grove temple in which she had been raised. This was nine days into the third moon of the new year; Auriane was so heavy with child she ventured nowhere now, contenting herself with struggling about the island. Fastila came on a day the sanctuary was deserted but for Auriane; Ramis had gone to give a judgment in the case of a man of the Bructeres accused of setting a temple afire.

Helgrune rowed Fastila across the lake. Auriane was astonished to see her in the gray robes and silver torque of an Ash Priestess. As Fastila embraced Auriane, she explained that she had wanted no more to do with the Companions after Auriane was so shamefully driven off, and she returned to the slow, predictable life of her mother's temple.

Auriane saw much of the playfulness was gone from Fastila's black eyes. No longer did she stumble excitedly over her words; now her speech was careful and considered, as if she measured out pinches of herbs for a potion, and an elder-woman's heaviness of mind had settled into her face.

Fastila settled herself on the bearskin by the fire before Auriane's lodge. Auriane waited until the younger woman pulled off her hairy calfskin boots, wrapped her cold-numbed feet in a blanket and took a long, appreciative draught of mead before she demanded to know the news.

"Athelinda is well protected—have no fears for her," Fastila answered to Auriane's first question. "Geisar tried to claim two hundred cattle from her in payment for your 'crime,' but the Companions prevented it. Now they sleep in arms at the Hall. A hundred of her cattle froze to death anyway—spring will see a forest of bleached bones. As if it were not enough, Geisar cursed her crop. There's no end to his vileness and his hatred of your family."

"Take a good measure of our Yule ashes when you go—Ramis will let me have them if I ask," Auriane replied, eyes bright with concern. Yule ashes sprinkled on the fields were held to ensure the land's fertility after a hard winter, and the presence of Ramis would render ashes from this place particularly potent.

"Athelinda will bless you. She steadfastly maintains your innocence, Auriane. You have a noble and loyal mother. 'No daughter of Baldemar would lie with a foreigner,' she insists. 'If you are with child, it is fathered by Wodan or some other great spirit of the wood. She will not believe ill of you."

Auriane dropped her head into her hands and made no effort to stop a quiet upwelling of tears. "She makes it powerfully difficult to tell her the truth! My poor mother. I should let her believe what she will. Fastila, I am ashamed of *some* things, but of this I am not ashamed. I just do not want her to suffer."

"Well, of course," Fastila responded amiably. "I've always held with the older law. The Fates guide all you do, Auriane. Does great Fria know shame when she parts from her lovers? Of course not—her love-acts bless all nature! You *cannot* be befouled by evil."

"If *I* could believe that!" Auriane said, smiling at Fastila's appealingly uncomplicated way of looking at matters. "What word have you of Decius?"

"*This* was sent to your mother." Fastila pulled a damp, grimy roll of papyrus from the leather pouch that hung from the belt of her robe; it had been torn from Decius' book, *The Art of Siege Warfare.* Auriane recognized it and seized it out of Fastila's hands; her breath caught in her throat. It appeared Decius had washed the original writing from the beginning of the roll and added letters of his own, penned with some mixture of dyes.

"He lives!" She pressed the curled paper to her cheek, then held it at a distance and spent a long time studying it, as if by examining it long enough, she might make some sense of what was written there. "I wonder if he is safe where he is."

"You will not learn it from *him*," Fastila retorted. "He could be pinned beneath hurdles with a thousand aurochs bearing down on him, and he would say only, 'Now *this* is an annoying circumstance.'" She paused. "Will you go to him?"

Auriane was quiet for a time, considering in gloomy silence. Finally she said, "No. No matter what is written here, or what he says to lure me, I could not. It is not that I do not love him enough. I'm bound by my oaths, and I'm bound by blood. I know no other way to live. Fastila, I haven't abandoned hope they'll call me back."

Fastila's look betrayed she had no such hope, but she nodded firmly and said, "Of course, they will." From this, Auriane guessed the answer to the next question.

"What is being said at the Assembly?"

"The Fates have not softened. I am sorry. It is hard for me to witness at times. Most will not speak your name, but I know well you are in every heart. . . ."

To Auriane the very air now had a bitter taste. Why, she wondered, was it her fate to never have what all other women accepted as their natural due? A husband who was human and not divine. Rich-yielding land handed down from her mother's mothers. A child of her own family's blood. A great clan all about, and the smallest measure of peace.

Then abruptly she stopped these thoughts. Dimly she knew she would not be content even then.

"Athelinda speaks for you most bravely, as does Theudobald. Every Assembly rings with their entreaties."

"Mother might sway them. But no one listens to an old man who has to be carried in. What of Witgern and Sigwulf?"

"Sigwulf says nothing for or against you. You know how he is. Loyal when he has to be, but not so much that it interferes with his plans. He wants a great retinue, and now Geisar—black curses on his name—controls who is consecrated as a warrior and who is not. But Witgern speaks for you."

"Does he truly? I . . . I am surprised. I thought he despised me now."

"He means much to you." Fastila's voice was suddenly taut; she was carefully examining Auriane's face.

"Of course," Auriane answered, alert to the pinch of jealousy in the younger woman's voice. "But not in the way you imply." Auriane took Fastila's hand and regarded her with gently knowing eyes. "Fastila, you . . . and Witgern . . . ?"

Fastila looked down, flushing deeply; Auriane was the first to ferret out her secret. "Yes. Once. At the spring rites. I love him more than life. But he does not look at me now. If I flung myself naked before him on the trail, he would throw me down a cloak and ride on!"

"Fastila, take care none see you giving him loving looks!"

"Why? Thurid was a thrall-woman when she and Witgern were joined—she has no kin to take vengeance on me!"

"Geisar performed the marriage—have you forgotten? He will act for her."

Fastila laughed with constrained gaiety. "I may be ever the fool in choosing lovers but I am not a fool when it comes to outwitting cutthroat priests. Do not worry over me!"

On the next day, among the people camped about the lake, Auriane found a young man who was a house-slave escaped from a Gallic estate; he had been his master's reader. In exchange for the silver *denarius* she wore about her neck, he read Decius' letter for her.

" 'I am a prisoner of the Cheruscan king, although he calls me guest,' " the young Gallic fugitive read. " 'I suffered capture after two days' riding. I live because of your courage, Auriane. I loved you before and love you still—why could I not ever tell you? I beg you, stay where you are. I am more certain than ever a terrible war is coming. Enclosed is a measure of the king's gold. I pray it is not stolen . . .' "

Of course, it has been, Auriane saw, looking at the flaccid pouch that came with the letter.

The reader continued, " '. . . a gift for the child, who I hope has no taste for war. May the poor babe know more peace than we have known! I am tired of the world. I will send messages when I can.' "

It made her feel jolted and bruised inside. This did not sound like Decius, but a worn and humbled man, and for a brief moment she even wondered if Decius wrote it. She was amazed that the words he could not speak—that he loved her—he managed to *write* on this paper. So people will write what they dare not speak, when there is not the heat of the other's gaze upon them. Perhaps there *was* some good in this odd habit of the Romans.

She judged that Decius most likely saved himself by affecting a great knowledge of warfare—preserving his life, if not his freedom. Surely, she thought hopefully, he will devise a way to escape.

Suddenly Decius seemed unbearably pitiable to her, he who would never beg another's protection. How ironic, she thought, that he who seems so little to need protection arouses in me a desire to give it. All I know of the outer world he taught me, and it seems I did not give much in return.

• • •

It was not until the following day that Fastila told her the thing that was to haunt her sleep and possess her with terror in the days to come. For Fastila thought it news of little account and almost did not say it at all.

"One of Witgern's sources in the village of the fortress," she said idly, toying with the fire, "reports that the Emperor Domitian has left Rome and travels to Gaul for a *census.* What is that?"

Auriane felt every sense tauten.

"They like to count their people from time to time. It is usual for them," she said, watching Fastila with growing concern.

"They say he has with him a great army, and they mean to camp in the country of the Treveres in northern Gaul — Auriane, what is wrong? Is it the child? Are you well?"

Auriane slowly rose to her feet. "Yes, I am well," she whispered, pacing with heavy steps, hands clenched over her swollen stomach. "Fastila, we are done!" she whispered. "Why did you not tell me this at once?"

Fastila shrugged and struggled up after her. "But . . . why would I? I didn't . . . What is so terrible in their counting their people?"

"That is not what they are doing, Fastila! It is a ruse! They used such a stratagem once before, in the time of our grandfathers. What fools they must think us!" She paused and met Fastila's eye. "They do not send Emperors for a census, nor do they send out great armies. They come for *us.* In the spring they mean to catch us unprepared — then they will strike with all their strength!" Auriane looked away, a restless melancholy in her eye. "Fastila, can you bring my mother to me?"

"I . . . I have no influence with Athelinda! . . . Yes, I will try."

"What preparations for war are being made?"

"None. Except against Odberht. That wretched spawn of Wido has enlisted the good will of the Cheruscan king. His companions have swelled to a mighty army, and they're nothing but murderers and thieves. He plans to attack the north ranges in spring — he as much as said so. Everyone who is celebrated means to go north and fight him. He should be easy to put down."

"Curses on Helle! Are they blind fools? *He is in league with them!"*

"I do not understand."

"Do you not see? Odberht means to divert our attention from the south! The Romans have given Odberht a rich bribe, I would wager all I own. When our warriors are drawn north to fight him, we will be vulnerable in the south. Then the Emperor will launch an attack. This is Odberht's final vengeance upon us!"

"But . . . that is too evil even for him! He has a rogue's nature for certain but, Auriane, that is madness—*he was born one of us!*"

"You are wrong. My father once said Odberht would do what even Wido would not, and I know Baldemar spoke the truth. Odberht lusts for renown, and the greater evil he commits, the more tales the people will tell of him. And anyway, he knows he has no chance against us in an even fight. He would not have the mettle to do such a thing without the assistance of the Cheruscan king. In the spring when we're weary of war with Odberht and straggling home, the Romans will strike with greater force than ever in our lifetimes."

Fastila was quiet for a moment, fighting the idea. Then at last she gave up and said with gloomy finality, "You are right."

Another disturbing thought came to Auriane. Decius was a captive of the Cheruscan king. He might be forced to give tactical advice to the Cheruscans in this war with her own people. Would Decius be a traitor to her? He might, if the only alternative was to take his own life. He was already a traitor once—to his own people. Perhaps it would not be so difficult for him to be a traitor once again. The Fates seemed to delight in these cruel tricks.

Surely he will not turn on us. I know him as honorable.

But what is "honorable"? Its meaning must be confusing to a man who lost his people twice.

"Fastila," she said softly, firmly, "you must say all these things at the next Assembly. *Odberht's challenge must be ignored.*"

A look of sharp discomfort came to Fastila's face. "I wish to go on living, Auriane! Geisar wants this northern war. And he has the support of everyone who's important. It's easy vengeance and easy plunder. You cannot stop such a thing as this!"

Baldemar would have stopped it, Auriane thought in a moment of frantic misery. Do you watch us now? How could you leave us to this?

"Here is what you must try, then," Auriane replied. "Explain what I have said to Thrusnelda, and make certain she knows it comes from me. Then have her deliver it up as an oracle."

"That is good! They dare not lay a hand on her, though they'll want to!"

"It probably will not stop them. But it will set their minds to thinking of the folly of going north . . . and hopefully, it will start disputes that might slow their haste."

At dawn the next day Auriane said a somber farewell to Fastila.

At the waxing of the fourth moon, the time of the Festival of Loaves when the people baked barley-cakes for burial in the first furrow of the fields, Auriane was milking one of the goats that roamed the island while looking restlessly in the direction of the two even hills between which far travelers came. Surely war had not begun, she thought; she would have seen streams of people driven from their homes with crying children in tow and household possessions tied onto their backs.

Then came a low bolt of pain that flashed out through her whole body and brought her gasping to her knees. She cried out for Helgrune, who was using a flint axe to crack open the ice that had formed over the watering trough, so the animals could drink.

Helgrune helped Auriane stagger to her hut. Then the serving-woman sent a messenger off to Ramis, who had departed at noon for a midnight gathering of the Holy Nine.

"She will not come," Auriane protested, feeling pitiful and small. Why would Ramis return for a mere birthing when she goes to lead a ceremony that will bring mild weather and good fortune to all the tribes of the north?

"She may not," Helgrune agreed laconically as she steadied Auriane with hard hands, guiding her onto the bed of straw. "She either comes, or she doesn't."

Auriane despised Helgrune then. The woman was comforting as a bed of brambles. The pain struck again—a clutch of excruciating torment, a nightmare in her body that held her hostage for a harrowing length of time before it let her go. A wild madness seized her. *Surely this is Wodan's punishment for lying with a foreigner.*

Helgrune moved fretfully about the hut, first planting a torch in the earthen floor, then marching off to the drying-shed, to return with a cat's skull, which she placed in the doorway to protect the child's spirit from demons, and a snakeskin girdle. Snakeskin was thought to ease birth pangs and speed delivery. Hastily Helgrune fastened it round Auriane's stomach, not meeting Auriane's eyes, seeming loath to touch her. More good fortune! Auriane thought miserably. Helgrune despises this task. I am trapped here with a woman who would rather bed down on a glowing hearth than assist at a birthing.

Auriane recalled vividly tales of lying-ins that stretched for half a cycle of the moon, or ended wretchedly, the babe dead, the mother drained of all her lifeblood. She struggled to do the fire ritual, but it was too new to her; each time her body was gripped with fresh agony she clawed at the straw, a tormented animal that did not know fire from air or water. When the tide of pain subsided, she doggedly fixed her gaze on the flame of the torch, imagining it struggled to give birth to itself.

Evening came; shadows lengthened and gradually overtook the island. Helgrune announced irritably that Ramis was not coming, and she sent out to the nearest village for a midwife. Then Auriane lay alone; Helgrune busied herself somewhere out of sight. Through the door of her hut Auriane watched the sun die and leave a bloody wake; the sky was pearly nacre streaked with blood, lurid and full of evil omen. Desolation gripped her. She realized she had allowed herself to believe that Ramis *would* come.

Wolves began to howl. She tried to read meaning in their rising and falling cries. Were they greeting the child's descending spirit or heralding her death?

She tasted her own salt sweat. The hut seemed stiflingly hot. Her fear was thick in the air; she could scarcely breathe. From time to time she tentatively put her hands on her swollen belly, probing gingerly, striving instinctively to push out the child and rid herself of this grievous burden. Gradually she realized something was wrong. The babe's head was too high. Yes, she thought as she probed again, that was the child's head, near her navel. From the birth-talk she heard all her life she knew that the child should have turned round. By now, the head should have dropped and be pressing hard for release.

Mother of the gods, preserve me! It is a breech. I will suffer long and die, and the child will be strangled by the birth-string.

Each pang brought increasing terror, until she was in the throes of a fright greater than any she ever experienced in battle. *I thought I had more courage than this!* she thought despairingly. *It is because I can do nothing . . . but endure.* Agony owns me. My own body is my foe. As long as it pleases, it can put me to the torture.

Her whole spirit shrieked for the steadying arms of her mother.

Why am I alone? All your kin should gather round at the birth of a child.

The wolves sounded closer.

She heard fast-approaching steps.

"Helgrune," Auriane called out, not really wanting Helgrune, thinking there was something decidedly reptilian about the woman, but desperately wanting a human presence. She struggled up and turned to the doorway. Helgrune was nowhere about.

"Helgrune?" she said again, feeling increasingly uneasy. There was no answer but the wolves, and those swift, sure steps, rapidly coming closer.

What stalking demons of the night might this be?

A tall, hooded figure filled the doorway. *It is some minion of Geisar's, come to drag me to death. It is Helle herself.* Weakly Auriane struggled in the direction of the water jug, with some dim plan of using it as a weapon.

An instant later she recognized Ramis.

She has come! Auriane collapsed back onto the straw and wept openly with relief.

Ramis strode in and dropped down beside Auriane. The old woman cradled her head in her arms as if Auriane were her own child. "Cry out all you wish!" she said soothingly. "It does not shame you. It is far better, and it relieves the pain." Ramis held her tightly through the next grip of agony.

As Auriane clung to her, she could not remember why she ever thought Ramis august and forbidding; the old priestess was gentle and human as her own mother. Auriane understood then Ramis loved her greatly and without reserve—and had always.

"The babe," Auriane whispered feebly. "It is turned round."

But already Ramis had her hands on Auriane's stomach and was lightly, vigorously kneading; gradually, surely, those strong hands shifted the child into the position of readiness. "It is no matter," she said gently as she worked. "Close your eyes, breathe evenly, and think on the flame."

When after long moments this was done, Ramis rose and moved swiftly about, putting things the way she wanted them, bringing an extra torch for more light, laying white linen on the straw. She gave fast, precise orders to Helgrune, directing her to set a cauldron on the fire before the hut, then rapidly naming off the herbs she wanted brought from the drying-shed. As the water began to boil, Ramis added the herbs, each at its proper time. Then she brought Auriane a clay cup brimming with a mysterious, pungent drink. Ramis' birthing herbs were among her close-kept secrets. Auriane guessed there was ergot from rye to stimulate the contractions, as well as motherwort, shepherd's purse, parsley, and rue. To ease the torment, she supposed there were henbane and hops and a measure of balm and celandine. Whatever it was, it was strong and gentle. Within moments the dark drink took merciful hold of her, and a soothing mist blotted out fear, muted the pain. Ramis directed Helgrune to sponge Auriane's stomach and thighs with the same steaming mixture; the bouquet of medicinal vapors brought a hazy tranquillity to them all. Auriane's deep, troubled breathing filled the small room.

Dimly Auriane was aware that as night progressed and the stars made their passage across the black sky, Ramis never let her go; the old priestess spoke to her ceaselessly, and Auriane was strengthened and steadied by that voice that sometimes chanted, sometimes spoke poetry, sometimes gave homely advice or told old tales; it gave her something to cling to outside the pain. She later remembered little of this constant talk, except for a few words Ramis spoke near dawn:

". . . and this, too, is an initiation, you see, as much as first blood or first battle . . . for a birth tests the soul in every way, calling for love to the limit, courage beyond day-to-day imagining, and the strength of aurochs. . . . At the same time it washes you clean and makes your spirit anew . . . for *you* are reborn with the babe. . . . Know that you cannot come into your full human power until you know this divine power of giving life to a child."

Auriane realized then she had always thought of birth as a woman's sacrifice for her child; she had never thought it might also be a part of the mother's own path to knowing.

As the first ghost-pale light formed a halo over the eastward hills, Ramis turned her attention from Auriane to the child.

"The difficulty now is with the babe," Auriane heard Ramis whisper to Helgrune. "The child fears to emerge . . . for the little one senses, through her mother, that the world is all terror and tragedy."

With her hands on Auriane's stomach, Ramis began speaking fervent encouragements to the child, to allay her fears of coming into the world. Then Ramis directed Helgrune, who was unusually strong, to pull Auriane up into a squatting position.

The pain that struck Auriane then obliterated thought. She forgot even her humanity—she was some hapless beast, being slowly, relentlessly, rent in two. She cried out to Ramis to take her back to Chattian lands so she could be laid in her own earth at death.

I cannot die this way! all her mind screamed. The birth seemed some impossible hurdle raised up higher than nature permits a creature to leap. Yet leap it must, if it is to live. To nature there is no appeal.

Outside a dawn wind sprang up; it lashed the branches of the alder tree against the roof. Auriane felt all her viscera were being drawn out through her womb. Then suddenly the mountain of agony was released. A great ocean-tide rushed out of her.

She felt vastly empty. All was small, quiet and still.

Gently they laid her back on the straw. She felt light as a ghost, fearful she might float off like a cinder and be lost. She lay there trembling between heaven and earth, reduced to pure spirit, hovering peacefully above the beaten body she left behind.

Then she heard the rapid spilling notes of a pipe, a sound glittering with life-love and light. She struggled up far enough to see Helgrune playing an alder-pipe and Ramis cradling an impossibly small, red creature that steamed in the frigid air. Distantly Auriane heard the child's fragile, gasping cries—the plaint of a gentle seagoing creature rudely thrust into the harsh world, forced to take in chill air, to battle hunger and lifelong uncertainty.

Some are strong enough, some are not. Ramis, give this child more strength than I had.

Ramis swiftly ascertained what she already knew—the babe was a girl. She cut the birth-string with a bronze knife, then laid the little creature on her mother's belly. The child had fleecy black hair, a color Auriane had never seen on a newborn—the banner of her foreignness. Auriane met the babe's glassy orbs steadily, while tears of amazement blurred her eyes. She was fascinated by what she saw there. Those squirrel-bright eyes seemed full of tales of the other world.

"Who are you?" Auriane whispered to the girl while Ramis looked on, smiling. "Someone from remote times, I think! You seem surprised to find the world this way!" Someone from the time of peace and wandering, she thought, from before the coming of iron. But Auriane saw a glint of Baldemar there, and a flash of Gandrida; poor Arnwulf, too, peered out of those eyes.

You are a living record of great spirits . . . that somehow married themselves to Decius and his black-headed kin, dedicated to our destruction. A strange mismatch of souls . . . yet all exist so harmoniously in those eyes. Ramis once said, "To me, none are foreign," and only now do I know fully the wisdom of this. The two rivers flow together in you, mingling without a thought.

Helgrune gave Ramis a slender phial filled with waters from the sacred lake. Auriane looked questioningly at Ramis. Before the water-blessing could be performed, the child must have a name.

Ramis knelt down and looked closely into the child's eyes, struggling to read the shadowy soul-shape within. Meditatively she nodded. "There is a strong and definite presence here, dominating the others. . . . " Ramis considered a moment longer, then declared with finality: "She is Avenahar."

Avenahar was the mother of Gandrida, known to Auriane from Athelinda's tales. Like Gandrida, she too was called the Wise in Council; Athelinda said she could stun a deer with her eyes.

"Avenahar," Auriane said, testing the sound of it. She reached out with a fragile hand and grasped Ramis', a mute gesture of overwhelming gratitude for all she had done.

Ramis then began the ritual. First she took a fir bough and set it aflame, then passed it quickly three times around the child's head to clear the air of polluting influences. The spirit of the fir tree was said to love all newborn children. Next she took a drop of water from the phial and daubed it on the child's forehead. "Let the water cleanse!" her voice rang out with a slight tremble. She smeared a second droplet on the child's chest. "Sorrows of past ages, begone! Let all wickedness that afflicted you in lifetimes past be banished by water! Evil beings, hurtful things, leave this child forever, in the name of all-merciful Fria!" She sprinkled droplets of the remaining water over the babe's head. "You are Avenahar, come again. You are Avenahar, shining and new."

Then she helped the girl find Auriane's breast. The moment was unending, all-sustaining. Draw in the soul-milk that makes you our own, Auriane thought. Drink in my love.

"I bless you with milk," Auriane said weakly, finishing the ritual naming-words. She put a droplet of her milk on the girl's forehead. "My blood is your blood. My clan is your clan. None can deny you fire and water. I name you Avenahar."

And I will be with you forever, she added in her mind. Let none say otherwise. If you are severed from me, Avenahar, I will bleed all my life's blood and die.

Before exhaustion overcame Auriane and she fell into sleep, she made a last entreaty to Ramis. "When you read her future, my lady, I beg you, whatever it is, keep it from me."

Then came the days of flowers and milk overflowing; Auriane often went ashore with Avenahar on her back, walking the grassy meadows. The valleys and meadowlands seemed intoxicated with color; everywhere were the nodding checkered flowers of snakes-head, the pink flush of woodland anemones. On those days Auriane would hurl a spear at a tree until exhaustion came, with Avenahar nearby in her wicker cradle, watching with huge, uncritical eyes. Or she would restlessly walk the island, nursing the child; it relieved her grieving to feel the tiny mouth drawing her milk.

Once again the garments of Eastre brushed past, her sunny hair streaming down as she moved through the season, unmindful of how her coming resurrected the pain of Baldemar's death.

Summer came in earnest, laying vivid veils of green, bringing ever more color: the violet of hyssop flowers, the yellow of cowslips, the salmon shades of fragrant meadowsweet. Waterbugs streaked over glassy pools; clouds of bees hummed hymns to the sun.

One morning when Avenahar had lived through three moons, Auriane and Helgrune were busy in the drying-shed, laying out freshly gathered coltsfoot. Ramis had journeyed off to some distant chief to give counsel concerning a marriage. Auriane had not wanted her to go, sensing she might need her that day.

They heard an unaccustomed sound; steadily it grew louder. When Auriane realized it was the drumming of many horses' hooves, she whisked Avenahar from the wicker cradle and held the child tightly to her breast.

Then came the villagers' shouts and dogs' barks; now the battering of hooves was very near. As yet they could see nothing; the riders were concealed by a stand of alder.

The party seemed to have halted by the horse sheds; Auriane heard welcoming neighs and men's shouted questions. Then the thunder began again. And a party of thirty and more horsemen emerged from behind the alders, approaching the lakeside on its marshy deserted shore.

They halted just across the water.

Helgrune seized Auriane's arm, meaning to drag her into the shadows of the shed. "Quickly! Hide yourself!" she whispered. "Who are those bold ruffians! How dare they ride so close!"

"Helgrune, let me go," Auriane said, as she fought her way free. "Do you think they do not know I am here?"

Auriane moved closer to the island's bank, showing herself to the shaggy band draped in bearskin cloaks; Helgrune followed, a step behind. The party's many upright spears formed a dense thicket. Dully gleaming warrior's rings of beaten gold girded their upper arms. The band's leader held aloft a cat skull stained with ocher, mounted on a yew pole.

"They are my own people, Helgrune. You must not fear. They've come for me." Auriane struggled with a confused mix of feelings of joy and fright, unsure what this party's intention was. She stood utterly still, Avenahar in her arms, a wary animal poised to protect its young.

She realized they had found and brought Berinhard; that was why they tarried at the sheds. His coat was brushed clean of charcoal; he stood bridled and ready.

They have me. I will be dragged back to Geisar and condemned.

She squinted, desperate to see if they were friend or foe, but she could not discern individual faces. Avenahar felt her gathering tension and began to wail.

Then one of the warriors raised a horn to his lips and sounded a long alto tone.

" 'We come in peace to talk,' " Auriane said, interpreting the meaning of the horn sign for Helgrune. It did not still her heart. *What if they had some evil plan in mind for the child?*

Helgrune said with all her gloomy authority, "You must not cross that water."

"Helgrune, I must." She would not shame herself by begging mercy or attempting escape. She turned about and strode to her hut to find better clothes in which to greet them. Helgrune trailed worriedly after.

Her one fine garment was a long, sand-hued tunic of linen, finely embroidered at the hem with a pattern of green foliage; she girded it with a belt of links of silver embossed with garnet-eyed ravens. Both were gifts from Ramis. Then she loosened her hair from its knot; she had not cut it since vowing vengeance on Odberht, and it dropped in a heavy silken mass, rippling down to her waist. Helgrune helped her brush it out while Auriane opened the side of the tunic and gave the child her breast. Watching Avenahar take her milk, Auriane felt a sharp physical pain at the thought that she might be separated from her daughter. Her need of that small creature was deep, mysterious, subtly overwhelming. Before she had a child of her own, Auriane could not have imagined its intensity.

My whole body will ache without her. I will be a house without a hearth. My arms will know a barrenness that can never be filled.

Helgrune saw the tear that formed in spite of Auriane's best efforts; a disapproving frown darkened the serving woman's face.

To Helgrune, Auriane's unbounded love of her child was weakness. Submitting wholly to love in Helgrune's mind was like tolerating a room left unswept and dirty—a thing that clutters life and renders it distressingly chaotic.

Auriane pulled on calfskin riding breeches. Her only ornament was the warrior's ring circling her right arm. Since it would be unseemly for a consecrated warrior to face any delegation weaponless, she took a ceremonial wooden spear from the temple house. Finally she concealed a flint dagger in her belt—she would take her life with it, if indeed this *was* a trap and they meant to drag her to punishment. She would not die an ignoble death that would shame Avenahar and force the girl to seek vengeance for her mother when she grew to womanhood.

Auriane descended to the coracle, Helgrune walking behind. Helgrune rowed; Auriane stood straight and solemn in the small vessel as it glided over the black water. In one arm she cradled Avenahar; in the other she held the wooden spear, upright like some slender sentinel.

Something startlingly white caught Auriane's attention—a family of swans, idols made of snow, drifted smoothly as clouds over the black waters, moving abreast of them for a time. The lead swan raised its wings as if in salute, then settled them again.

Why have I not seen them before? Perhaps they are the dawn maidens that haunt the deep forest in swan form.

Then she had the disquietening sense the lead swan was Ramis herself, keeping watch on her.

As Auriane came closer to the shore, she recognized one warrior, then another, as men of Sigwulf's retinue. She saw as well two of her own and several who were emissaries of Geisar and behind them one of Romilda's women. It was as though an effort were made to send representatives of every faction of the tribe. She held the baby closer, unconsciously covering Avenahar's fleecy black hair with her hand to shield it from their probing gazes. *Foreign curse!* she imagined she read in their eyes.

Then she saw that Berinhard's mane and tail had been braided with white marguerite from the nearby meadow; sprigs of vervain were woven into his forelock. He was being honored as if he were something holy.

When the coracle touched the bank, Auriane alighted and walked toward them, her manner cautious but proud; she would not let them think she was ashamed of the child. Helgrune walked warily behind.

It was Coniaric who called out gaily, "Long life and health to you, daughter of Athelinda and Baldemar!" Apparently Coniaric, now second among Sigwulf's Companions, had been chosen to speak for them. His dark gold hair shone like amber in the sun. His faded blue eyes seemed not quite focused on her as he spoke.

"We have come from the Warriors' Council," Coniaric went on in his practiced Assembly voice. He smiled broadly, showing strong, perfect teeth. "We bid you return with us and walk once more with your ancestors." She understood why they chose Coniaric to speak for them—he could humble himself without embarrassment, for he had the gift of speaking words convincingly, effusively, without truly feeling the meaning of what he spoke. "Geisar and Sigwulf send locks of hair—they are friends," Coniaric continued, holding out a leather pouch tied to his belt.

She felt the first throb of alarm. A great and terrible thing must have occurred to reduce Geisar to even a moderate show of humility; she sensed the weight of it, saw the size of it in every eye. She began slowly bracing herself for something that would rupture the soul.

"Geisar asks only that you purify yourself of your . . . uncleanness before you enter our lands," Coniaric went on with smooth joviality. "Your clan is in dire need of your strength and luck. You will be treated with all honor, Auriane. Wodan, witness my words."

At the word *uncleanness* Auriane's eyes smoldered. There followed an awkward quiet. They had not supposed she would need much convincing; most assumed she would leap eagerly at the chance to return. None knew what to say next.

"Tell Geisar he must first purify his viper's soul," Auriane replied with soft precision, a flare of fire in her eyes. "All this winter he reduced me to hopelessness while he joyed in my humiliation. And now I am to come quickly because he needs me! How *dare* he! How dare you all!"

She wheeled about, Avenahar pressed close to her chest, and strode back to the coracle with a queenly gait. That passionate pride was so much the image of Baldemar's that the sight of it pained many of them with vivid, sad memories.

This is mad, Auriane thought as she walked away. I know I cannot desert them. But I cannot help it—they drive me to fury.

Then a familiar and loved voice called out: "Auriane! Wait!"

She halted and slowly turned about. "Witgern?" She came closer, barely disguised pleasure in her face. "Witgern!" He had been concealed at the back of the company. When she was close enough to see him well, she suppressed a look of alarm at the change in him. Witgern had in one season made the small but critical journey from the final years of youth to the first years of old age. Features that had once appeared sensitive and refined now seemed closer to fragility; the hopelessness in that one melancholy eye no longer seemed youthful moodiness—now it was brittle and deep-set. His red-gold hair hung straight to his shoulders—she realized he must have taken some vow, for no shears had touched it since last she saw him. "Why did you not show yourself at once?" she asked.

"For . . . for shame. I did not do as much for you as I could. I beg you, let us have no hard words—I've missed you sorely." He dropped from his horse, and they held tightly to one another for a moment; it felt like going home, so well-worn and comfortable was his embrace. Then he drew her away several paces so they could speak privately. They stood facing the smoking waters of the lake.

"Auriane!" he said softly, "listen to me. Many spoke against you but you must not forget those who spoke *for* you. Half of them do not even believe that . . . that you—"

"Witgern, it is *true*. I am ashamed of nothing. I cannot abide this pretense! This is not Wodan's child—Decius is her father and none other! Were you one of those who did not believe it?"

Witgern looked down, acutely uncomfortable. "No. But I suppose I have come not to mind it. Geisar is proclaiming loudly everywhere that all you do is holy. Maybe for *once* the old curmudgeon has spoken the truth, though not for the right motives. But listen to me, I beg you, in the name of our love for each other. Auriane, catastrophe has come."

"Curses on Helle, Witgern, I know already what you are going to say."

Two robins pecked furiously at one another in a mulberry tree, their chatter absurdly cheerful in contrast to Witgern's face.

"Your warnings were true," he continued in a low voice. "Now they call you a god-sent seer. A mighty force is assembled at Mogontiacum. There are soldiers drawn from faraway Albion, along with the legions of the fortresses at Argentoratum and Vindonissa, as well as troops from their elite Palace Guard at Rome. Five legions are poised to strike at us, all under the command of Domitian himself."

She shut her eyes.

"They came with unnatural speed," Witgern continued. "Sigwulf chose to believe when they came to Gaul that it was indeed for a census. Fastila spoke your words in the Assembly and barely got off with her life."

"Fastila! She did it. She is bolder than she knows."

"The last of our allies have deserted us in terror," Witgern continued. "Even the Usipes who have never refused us help are now the Romans' pet dogs. All of them—Sigwulf, even Geisar—say only the Daughter of the Ash can deliver us now. They've revived the old tale that none who follow you die."

Her heart stilled; her mind raced. "Incredible that they say that," she said numbly. "The ones who repeat *that* tale were never with me."

"Let them believe what they must. Terror has humbled them, Auriane. Have pity on them! You are favored of Wodan. You are the Opener of the Gate, Protector of the Host, she who chastised Ramis and lived. They want you—and the sword of Baldemar—on the front line of the charge."

"There is about this the madness of dreams," Auriane whispered. "Why does the enemy come with so great a force? They come not to do battle but . . . to annihilate." She remembered Decius explaining once that his people went into battle with a minimum number of men. A Roman army thought nothing of facing barbarian forces that outnumbered them ten times, so confident were they in the superiority of their tactics and weaponry. Feeling a chill creeping into her limbs, she wondered what Decius would say of *this*.

Miserably she looked at Avenahar, dressed in the bearskin clothes Helgrune had made for her. Then she looked at the taut, hopeful faces of the delegation, awaiting her will.

This was the decision she so dreaded, this decision that was already made. She felt she carried the weight of an ox on her chest.

I am just one woman with a child! Let me be!

Why have the Fates so arranged it that in order to do what I must, I have to give up this creature I cannot live without?

"This child has weakened me, Witgern. I want fiercely now not to die. Would my ghost be able to visit her as she grows?"

Witgern put a hand on her shoulder. "All who are wise say so, Auriane."

"Ah, but I do not believe it enough to feel at peace."

Where is Ramis? Why is she not here to advise? Surely she foresaw this and absented herself on purpose.

What had Ramis said? *"Make fire in your mind."* Auriane envisioned pale flames over lake and sky, and after a moment the cloak of anguish felt faintly lighter, and the air seemed a living medium that connected all souls, no matter how separated by land and water. There was deep comfort in knowing that, in the mind of Fria, she could not be separated from her child.

She felt a wind shift about, somewhere within; it tugged at her with growing insistence, drawing her in the direction of her people's lands.

So it must be. It is my fate to have my attachments sundered. There is no mercy in this world—why do I keep falling into expecting it?

Witgern saw her mysterious shift from misery to certainty; like Decius, he too had noticed her ability to draw strength suddenly from some unknown place. To Witgern in that moment she was remote and full of magic; he imagined he heard about her the whisper of ancestors. It was odd, Witgern thought, to have known her as a child, a vulnerable creature crying when hurt, then to see her now, clothed in a strength beyond his understanding.

Slowly she moved away from Witgern and stood before the delegation. She had a sense of distance from herself, as if she entered someone else's life, a grander one than her own.

"Here is my answer," she said quietly. "I will return—if these things are done."

She turned Avenahar around so they could see the child's face.

"This is my daughter, Avenahar, of the lineage of Baldemar and Gandrida. She will not be treated by you as an outcast. She will have lands and a husband of this tribe if she wishes, and the respect due to one of noble blood."

"That is well," Coniaric replied, that broad smile returning to his face. "And what else?"

"I want a great effort mounted to see us better armed. To rely on the gods alone is madness," she continued, her voice gradually finding its strength. "Wherever there are stores of iron, whether it be tools of the field or weapons fallen into disuse, I want them taken and forged into iron heads for spears. And I would have the captured Roman swords dedicated in the groves to Wodan be taken out and distributed to those who have no sword."

"Monstrous sacrilege!" came an indignant whisper behind Coniaric.

"A plague and a blight will take us!" said a Companion of Sigwulf's.

"Is it a greater sacrilege than allowing me to return?" she replied, soft gray eyes on them steadily. "Or than accepting Avenahar? These times seem to demand sacrilege. How do we know the gods have not originally given us these things that we might make good use of them in the direst of times?"

"I scent truth in those words!" came a voice at the rear of the company, followed by cautious nods and scattered mutterings of assent.

Witgern marveled as he saw gradual acceptance come into their faces. *She enraptures, she calms, she binds—who else would dare propose such things?*

It is like, yet unlike Baldemar, he realized. Both test limits, but she intrudes on another realm, one he never challenged—the precincts of the gods.

"And I ask as well," Auriane continued, "that we give the war-leaders we select strict obedience, whether in the march, the retreat, or the charge, or in the matter of disposing of spoil. All quests for individual glory must be set aside. The hosts of the Romans act as one, and that is their strength. We must do the same." She paused, looking slowly from one countenance to another. "What say you to all this?"

The wind rose suddenly, lifting the horses' manes, billowing her long tunic.

Coniaric grinned. "Well, it is settled then! Come, and mount your horse."

"How can that be?" she asked. "Do you not have to go to the Assembly with these things?"

"It was said at the last Assembly: 'Do what she wills. But do not return without Auriane.' They cannot go back on those words."

This battle so suddenly won, a chilled emptiness came into her chest.

If I am wrong, let only me be punished, she silently prayed. Baldemar, if you heard these things I proposed, things you would never allow, forgive me and know I do this so we can live.

She turned about and walked past Helgrune, pressing Avenahar's silky cheek to her own. For long moments they stood like this, while the wind mingled their hair. They made one sorrowful silhouette against the water. Witgern turned away, unable to watch. Coniaric's horse clanked its bit impatiently. Avenahar, unconcerned with all this, tried to snatch Auriane's ring, on which the sunlight played with liquid movements. Auriane pulled it off her arm and gave it to the child.

"That is your warrior's ring," Helgrune protested sullenly.

"She must have it—I'll have another made," Auriane replied, not taking her gaze from the girl's bright, inquisitive eyes. Then she added, "The wet nurse must be of noble stock."

"Ramis has chosen her already," Helgrune replied. "She is the daughter of Hrethwith, the Gold-Bedecked, who is daughter of Galiena of the Wide Fields, who is daughter of . . ."

Auriane heard no more of this lineage, satisfied; she was not even startled to learn Ramis seemed to know the wet nurse would be needed, having become accustomed to the Veleda's unerring sense of things to come.

"Will you despise me when you are grown?" she said to Avenahar, feeling forlorn as the night-herons that cried out their loneliness from the marshes. "What will you be? Seeress or wanderer, village priestess or noble wife?"

Auriane squeezed the child once, too hard, and finally gave Avenahar to Helgrune. "Tell her who her mother was," she said hoarsely. "Tell her of her deeds. Let her know it was not her mother's will to leave her and that she thought of her every day until she died."

Then abruptly Auriane turned, fearful her courage would desert her before these men who looked on her with desperate hope. They waited while she retrieved the sword of Baldemar from beneath its bed of moss.

Then she vaulted onto Berinhard's back amidst the stirring of many horses, the approving murmurs of the men. Berinhard capered nervously against the tautening of the reins, petals from the garlands drifting from his tightly bowed neck. They were off at a brisk canter, Auriane in their midst. She was grateful for the wind that blew off her tears.

How do the gods permit it, she thought, that so many from so far dare attack a people who wish only to live unmolested in their own country?

In one moment, she yearned for war as for the embrace of a long-absent lover. In the next, she ached so fiercely for Avenahar that she nearly turned round and galloped back.

No. Leave her where it is safe. I will be back for her soon.

As if to torment her, Ramis' prophecy nudged its way into her thoughts: *"You will be a queen in death."*

CHAPTER XXI

The Emperor Domitian as Supreme Commander of the Army faced the legions gathered at the fortress of Mogontiacum, preparing to take the auspices. His purple-bordered toga stirred faintly in a northern wind that carried a warning chill in spite of the fact that it was midsummer. A crown of ivy rested on his head. Two priests of Mars flanked him on a platform raised high enough so all could view him. Behind Domitian was a newly erected statue of himself in solid gold; it looked with lordly disdain toward the rambling hills of the barbarian lands beyond the river. The colossal image generated subtly in the soldiers' minds a vision of their Emperor as some solar hero of old, manifesting himself on earth to pierce the barbarian darkness with light.

Arrayed about him on the parade ground was a sea of helmeted men. The four legions of Upper Germania were here, strengthened by the legion Domitian had raised for this war, called the First Minervia after the goddess Minerva, his patroness, and detachments from the legions of Britannia. On Domitian's left were the cavalry troops attached to the northern legions—both men and mounts were gaudy and brilliant in full parade dress. On the place of honor at Domitian's right were the two Cohorts of the Praetorian Guard who had marched with him from Rome; they numbered a thousand, their beautifully worked gold breastplates afire in the sun. This was not the whole of the Roman forces. Detachments had set out in advance with the army's engineers to

486

begin the penetration of the disputed valley of the Wetterau and the Taunus Mount. Were all assembled, they would have numbered about forty thousand.

Domitian's journey to Gaul had taken three months, for he traveled in comfort. In addition to his military staff and his advisors, he brought an army of masseurs, the Palace's most skilled chefs, an Etruscan soothsayer, his favorite readers, one for poetry and one for prose, an astrologer and a kithara player whom he claimed could cure melancholy with his music. To entertain him at dinner, he brought selected men of wit and literary pretensions, as well as Bathyllus the pantomime and a troop of comic actors, followed by three carriages full of their costumes and masks. For his amorous needs he brought but two concubines. He would have commanded more to come but their furnishings, chests of rich garments, and supplies of special foods required too much space on the march. That he left his eunuchs at home he counted a brave concession to the asceticism required by military life.

The Emperor nodded to the priests of Mars. One led forth a garlanded goat given drugged feed so it would be docile— Domitian would not risk having the men see anything so ill-omened as a victim attempting to flee. A flute blower sounded a long, wan note so no evil sound would be heard; for many moments that anxious tone with its slight quiver was the only sound. Domitian, feeling he played the part of some pantomime actor, first briskly washed his hands in a silver basin, then sprinkled meal, wine and salt on the victim's head.

Domitian had no fears of what the entrails would reveal. Victory was assured. His strategists and engineers had proved that to him beyond a doubt with their detailed diagrams and maps; they had calculated precisely the minimum number of men needed for success and assured him the Chattians would be crushed in five months. Domitian felt he had left nothing to the caprice of a testy and volatile Mars. But soldiers were a superstitious lot; they needed the calming effect of a good augury.

The sacrificing priest felled the goat with a mallet. The second priest produced a knife and swiftly opened its belly. Gravely, Domitian inspected liver, intestines and gall. *"Exta bona!"* he cried at last. "The entrails are good!"

With a grand flourish he gave the entrails to the altar fire. As the smoke billowed, the soldiers responded with a volley of unified, disciplined, deep-throated shouts of joy, a driving sound like the tramp of thousands of marching feet: *"Ave, Caesar, Imperator . . ."*

The love of soldiers, Domitian observed with sullen detachment, is so easily won. They are like hounds: Their instincts are sharp, and when the disciplinary slap is necessary, their memories are short. They forgive all and slobber with devotion as long as you pet them, feed them, and praise them. The Senate and nobility on the other hand are not hounds but foxes, with silly pretensions of becoming lions. Would that my empire were composed only of soldiers!

And what a magical effect my coming in person has wrought. Who among these men *remembers* I had a brother on this day? Titus is but a name in the annals—while *I* am their living god, and gods are entitled to an occasional murder. I should feel the ecstasy of the Olympians. But I do not.

Domitian gave a short battle speech in which he praised each legion by name. His words did not carry over all the vast assembly; most would learn the text from the copies of the scribes. But it hardly mattered. To the soldiers, merely having their supreme commander speak to them was to have the light of the sun shed on them alone.

Marcus Arrius Julianus observed all this from a viewing stand behind the priests' platform, among a half dozen senatorial dignitaries. The soldiers' cheers to him seemed so much controlled yet frenzied noise. There is something monstrous, he reflected, in the sight of these rows of men regular as furrows in a field, their thousands of blades poised for the bloody harvest. Here is the bestial underside of civilization, the tearing tooth and claw of empire, normally neatly concealed. Can this be the natural order, as it is so easy to believe when so many proclaim it is, or is it vast presumption? Here are thousands wrenched from their home ground, prodded out to this mist-ridden place with its spirits older than ours, its primeval laws, then forged into one creature with a single will: that of one quite ordinary man hoisted by the Fates to supreme power, a man driven chiefly by the lust to outdo the deeds of his father and brother.

We do not need the fertile valley of the Wetterau—we are a rich man with ten carriages who out of pride must murder for the eleventh.

That morning Marcus Julianus had received an ominous letter from Rome, written by his chief steward, Diocles, on behalf of a friend in the Senate, a certain Junius Tertullus. It was a desperate plea for help. This Tertullus was certain he was tracked by Domitian's informers. He was openly followed in the streets. His study chambers had been rifled through and documents were taken, coincidentally with the disappearance of a recently acquired slave secretary.

This letter might not have been so disturbing in itself. But already in the past eighteen months two Senators of the old aristocracy that Domitian despised, Fabianus and Serenus, had met what Marcus Julianus counted suspicious ends. The world thought both men dead of natural causes, but Julianus knew their deaths occurred shortly after Veiento secretly denounced them before Domitian, accusing them of privately ridiculing this war. Could Domitian truly have set upon a course of picking off members of the Senate one by one like an archer shooting beasts in a hunting theater?

Marcus Julianus knew his own influence over the Emperor had not diminished in spite of Veiento's best efforts; it seemed rather to have increased, as though travel in strange lands roused in Domitian some eccentric long-buried insecurity. Domitian lately seemed eager as a schoolboy for his approval, seeking his opinion in every odd emergency that arose, even on matters in which he was not particularly qualified—once when an officer of the Guard became ill and died, Domitian asked him to review a list of candidates and name a replacement.

It is as though he cannot shun my opinion as some men cannot shun wine. But he cannot shun Veiento's opinions as some men cannot shun poison. We are delicately, evenly counterbalanced. Can I halt this coming murder?

Philosophy had never seemed a more useless tool.

In the next days the fortress of Mogontiacum was alive with swift, orderly preparations for war. Through the fortress's massive stone gate poured a steady stream of military wagons laden with supplies to last the winter: For the common soldier came wheat from Egypt, first parched to ensure its preservation, as well as salted beef, venison, vegetables preserved in olive oil, live chickens in crates, several varieties of Italian wine, Gallic beer, and dried pears, figs, apricots, and apples. In separate wagons were expensive delicacies for the Emperor's staff: amphorae of the purest olive oils, bottles of old Chian wine, the finest *garum*, or fish sauce, from Hispania, live thrushes, quail, mullet and eels to be prepared to order by Domitian's chefs, and one precious crate of that most sought-after fruit, the cantaloupe.

Two new granaries had been built to accommodate the incoming supplies. The camp hospital was readied to receive casualties, and military doctors were drawn from neighboring fortresses to aid those stationed here, bringing with them their antiseptic resins, their arsenal of tools for cauterizing wounds, extracting spearheads and removing gangrenous limbs. The common soldiers made wills and deposited them with the clerks at the fortress's headquarters. The staff of clerks was increased to keep records of the payments and deposits in the soldiers' compulsory savings bank and to dispose of the property of men slain in active service.

The war began unremarkably enough; for a month the legions encountered little resistance as they began claiming territory with a webwork of roads on the Taunus Mount. Army surveyors set out in the vanguard, protected by outriding cavalry; they determined the lay of the roads and selected sites for timber forts and fenced watchtowers. Along these roads at intervals of a third of a mile signal towers were constructed; the sentries stationed there used a torch signaling system whose code Domitian took pride in having devised himself. The regular legions, broken into cohorts of four hundred and eighty men each, then began cutting roughly parallel assault roads to gain access to the Chattian hill forts. In the event of an attack upon any work site, bonfire signals would be used to summon reinforcements. To increase their mobility, these reinforcements were positioned on the Rhine fleet so they could be ferried quickly to districts where fighting had erupted. The Chattian lands were vast, and Domitian knew the tribesmen would never march out to meet them in a body—a tactic that would decidedly favor the Romans—and so he saw no harm in spreading his forces out thinly over a hundred miles.

The Chattians had no great wealth or concentrated resources, as had other conquered lands, where wealth was generally hoarded in cities. Their principal resource was the people themselves. And so the order was given to slaughter without pity when the legions came upon the occasional small village where the inhabitants had not fled. It was an order normally repugnant to the average Roman soldier; nowhere in the civilized East could they have exterminated children without remorse. But the Germanic savage roused no such sympathies; many thought them not even capable of human speech. They did seem to show some affection for their children, but does not a bitch lick her pups?

   The first earth-and-timber hill forts they overtook were abandoned. The steep pine-clad Taunus slopes lay in eerie sun-dappled silence. The Romans systematically disabled them by forcing the gates by burning, draining the wells and pulling down sections of the timber walls. The whole of this vast engineering effort drew praise from Domitian's military staff, if not from his critics at home; it was said of the Emperor he proved himself worthy of his patroness, Minerva, goddess of rational warfare, as opposed to Mars, that blind stirrer to battle. This was the one interlude in Domitian's reign when he inspired respect without reserve, and he found the taste tauntingly bittersweet, for with cynical certainty he knew it was not to last.

CHAPTER XXII

While Domitian sacrificed, far to the north the Chattian host gathered in the shadow of the Village of the Boar. Massed on the fields between the cremation grounds and Baldemar's hall were the hide tents of eighty thousand warriors. Those camped in high places could see, far in the south, smudged columns of smoke trailing up into the sky, memorials of the native settlements in the path of the advancing legions where women, children and cattle were slain alike.

In this camp was none of the supreme confidence of the Roman forces. While Domitian with cold formality offered one goat, the Chattians dragged forth their most precious beasts — oxen or fine horses if they had wealth, sheep or fat hens if they were poor — and gave them to Wodan with wrung hands and forced back tears. While the Romans made bargains with their gods as if settling an account with a merchant, the Chattians offered pleas to Wodan more like that of child to parent — full of passionate desperation, dark with injured love. While eminent Roman strategists armed with book-learned theories predicted victory to the day, the Chattian holy women who told the future from the rustling of leaves heard the sacred elms rattle with death.

As dusk came and cookfires were lit, the warriors camped on the rise erupted in joyous yelps and the camp's hounds began to bark. Then the others too heard the growing sound of pounding hooves.

A party of horsemen came from the west. As they thundered down the ragged avenue between the tents at an exuberant gallop, the throng recognized Witgern in the lead, holding a torch aloft. And when they saw a woman in their midst, gray cloak whipping free, loose hair flying, many leapt to their feet and shouted out in exultant relief.

"Daughter of the Ash! Lead us out!"

"Baldemar lives! Lead us to vengeance!"

Most had given up hope, assuming the party that set out to retrieve Auriane must have been ambushed by the enemy. As the thirty riders galloped up to the stone altar round which the Holy Ones were gathered, where the ground was reddened from sacrifice, Auriane's horse slipped in bloody mud and she fell ungracefully onto his neck. She righted herself, feeling a jolt of humiliation, then pulled the dappled stallion to a halt and dropped to the ground. Auriane knew from the people's eyes they did not see the frail humanness in that moment—they saw only a young Fate incarnate in a maid. It caused her to long sharply for Decius and his cold rectifying eye.

Decius! The only man whose touch I know, and you are lost to me forever. One more sight of that mocking grin would be more precious than garnets and gold. At least Avenahar lives, as testimony we were once joined. Without her, I might lie down and die.

Auriane wanted only a washbasin and a quiet place to sleep, but Thrusnelda rushed to her, embraced her energetically, then blessed her, dipping a finger in ox blood and tracing the runic sign of Fria on her forehead. As Thrusnelda aged, her face seemed to shrink away from her eyes, leaving them large and spectral; she had the look of a kindly owl. "Walk among them now," she insisted.

Auriane forced down her reluctance.

How can they be so firm in their belief in my holiness when I can see my shame clinging tightly as a shadow? I am so defiled with blood the sacred mold was taken from me.

But Auriane knew she must do what gave comfort, and so she removed her shoes and set out barefoot among the throng. Gravely the warriors extended their spears across her path so she could place a palm on them and lend them her battle-luck. Once she looked behind her and caught sight of Sigreda among the Holy Ones as the young priestess paused in the midst of a prayer over a goat to observe her with banked, smoldering hatred. Sigreda expected Auriane to seek her death, and Geisar's, for had they not vigorously sought hers?

As Auriane trod through mud, she felt she had no more substance than a shaft of light; she was a husk, filled and moved by the energy of the throng. Only the pinched ache in her breasts reminded her she was a creature of flesh and blood. Avenahar had not been put to them in ten days and she imagined them shriveling and drying like some spider's prey.

Avenahar! You are all beauty. Am I mad to mourn as much for my dried milk as for the massacres in the south? Through you, Avenahar, I shall live this life over. You'll not live with the dread I lived with.

Soon. I will see her soon. She is safe where she is. We'll drive the Romans into the earth in one great ambush, and when the Wolf-Men are devoured with fire, I will go, fetch Avenahar and bring her home. Soon. Perhaps, even before summer is done.

Decius, why do I sense you shaking your head *no*? Fiend. How dare you shatter my peace. My aggravating beloved, will you ever see your child? Avenahar! Your name is a noose, constricting my throat. I must not think of it or I will fill a lake with my tears.

As she moved from cookfire to cookfire, touching an axhead here, a swordblade there, she saw ghosts: that child with bright round eyes held tightly in a warrior's wife's arms was Arnwulf on the day of his death; the leering crone squatting beside her with fire dancing in her eyes was Hertha, hissing *"Accursed One!"* Ten faces beyond was Baldemar's kingly ghost, tears of sorrow for her in his eyes while he commanded her to kill him. The need to avenge has become a roaring river, she realized—even Ramis had no power to subdue its mighty strength.

As she moved farther from the altar, the words of the priests' distant droning chant over the sacrificial animals were distorted by her mind into Ramis' warning of long ago: *"I see you now in a necklace of bones, a cloak of human skin. Go now, Priestess of Death. . . ."*

At midnight a war council was held before Baldemar's hall. The five most celebrated war leaders sat round a bonfire kindled by Sigreda, arguing over the best method of halting the advance of Odberht. Sigwulf paced with swaggering step, huge fists clenched, round shoulders defensively hunched, kicking at a spotted hound that kept getting underfoot. Auriane sat still and alert, intent on the fire, half listening, half lost in flights of strategic calculations. Athelinda observed the council from a regal distance, wrapped in stillness, shrewd eyes keenly focused and patient. How many shifts in the world had she seen? Surely this was the last, and she met it less with terror than with detached curiosity.

Coniaric sat with arms crossed behind his straw-colored head, leaning his long ungainly body against a shield and post, more concerned by the fact that they were bickering than by the truth or folly of the various plans put forth; he was a lover of peace, even if it was a mask. Thorgild lay on his back nearby, entreating answers from a gibbous moon while chewing on a strand of overgrown red mustache. Both had given up trying to dissuade Sigwulf from a plan that involved splitting their forces in half. Witgern alone kept up the fight; he was restlessly on his feet, half the time following Sigwulf, half the time standing still in frustration, arms folded as he glared at the ground. He argued dispiritedly, for both alternatives—that of keeping their forces together and trying to outrun Odberht as they moved south to settle into the Taunus hill forts to lie in wait for the Romans, and that of leaving half their warriors here to meet and destroy Odberht—seemed equally doomed to failure.

Sigwulf halted and spat into the oak fire.

"We *cannot* turn our backs on that god-cursed behemoth. We could leave the supply train behind to gain speed—but all of you say no to that. Your way, Witgern, he catches us in four or five days. It's wiser, I say, to face him on ground of *our* choosing."

Witgern looked impatiently at Auriane, frustrated that she was not helping him. But still she sat in active silence, unmoving as if in a trance while that mind, he knew, ran swiftly as a deer through the dark. Witgern remembered suddenly how Baldemar had done the same at councils. He would withdraw into his thoughts until all were stamping with impatience, then finally speak his mind after they'd given up on him. But invariably he would put forward a plan that made his fellows' schemes look like those of children.

Witgern spoke the words he guessed she was thinking. "What if the force that stays here meets defeat? Odberht moves on over our corpses and catches us after we've been halved." Unconsciously Witgern comforted the young hound Sigwulf had kicked, and the spotted dog appreciatively licked his hand.

Sigwulf spun round. "How dare you speak that word!"

"*Defeat,*" Witgern said, his one good eye glowing with melancholy fire. "Accustom yourself to the sound of it, Sigwulf, I wager you'll hear it spoken again. Do you think Odberht will come without reserves? He'd never risk his hide if he did not think he brought more than enough men to destroy us."

Sigwulf's look of injured honor shifted to one of bleak resignation, a look Witgern had seen there only once before—when word came that Baldemar was dead. For long there was no sound but the fire, and Witgern was conscious of it crackling, patiently devouring what had once been a mighty living oak, leaving humble ash.

"I'm thinking of perishing honorably, then," Sigwulf said finally, with a fierce sadness. "We may as well admit it, we're caught in a raven's claw. But I *will not* make Odberht a prize of the Village of the Boar. By the Fates, it is Baldemar's own village! And I won't be herded like kine into the Roman slaughtering pens!" Belligerence flared again in his black eyes. "That fiend will be stopped *here*. I volunteer *myself* for the task if no one else has the mettle."

Witgern looked at Auriane, surprised this did not provoke her to retort. But still she followed her own thoughts.

"It's not a matter of *mettle*," Witgern replied, becoming increasingly irritated with Auriane for leaving him to battle Sigwulf alone. "This is glory-lust talking!"

"I smell cowardice here," Sigwulf said, his back to Witgern.

"Sigwulf," Sigreda interjected sharply. She rose from her oak chair, the boar mask she had worn when she kindled the fire still in her hand. "Speak no unholy words!"

Sigreda cast vervain on the fire to purify the air.

"I don't need Wodan's servants to tell me how to speak!"

"Sigwulf."

This voice was Auriane's. She looked up at Sigwulf from her place by the fire, eyes alight, face glowing from the heat; she appeared to have just awakened from a light sleep. All dropped into expectant silence.

Sigwulf frowned at her, curious but impatient. Sigreda's eyes glittered like a night creature's—she resented the immediate, attentive respect Auriane was given. Witgern felt a jolt of relief.

"At that long-ago feast where Odberht bragged of slaying Baldemar," Auriane said, "did he not get falling drunk on Gallic wine?"

Sigwulf gave an expressive grunt that meant: Yes, and what of it?

Auriane rose to her feet. Sigwulf was a head taller—next to her he was an aurochs beside a deer—but Witgern thought: Of the two of them there is no question *she* is the one to be reckoned with.

"Sigwulf, you *will* stay behind," Auriane said softly, "but we will lose none of our forces, because you will slay Odberht and all his Companions . . . *to a man.*"

Sigwulf drew black brows together and gave a different grunt, one that expressed cynical curiosity.

"We will pull up camp and make certain it looks as if every last one of us has fled north," Auriane continued. "Odberht has a special hatred for the Village of the Boar. As he sees it, all his enemies were spawned here. Deserted or not, he will seek vengeance on it. But not before he loots it."

She turned to the fire, pulling her cloak tighter about her against the bitter night wind. "We'll leave just enough grain and livestock there to catch his attention. He'll think we were so much in terror of him, we didn't have time to load it all into wagons. I know Romilda can get Gallic wine in two days. We'll need to trade some precious provisions for it, but what must be done must be done. We'll leave enough wineskins stocked in the sheds for two thousand to get more than their fill. Witgern, you are good at such calculations, tell me how much will be needed," she spoke on briskly. "They'll consume it at once, they've not the discipline to wait, and they are unused to such potent drink. Perhaps we should add sleeping draughts—"

"Not honorable," Sigwulf interrupted, eyes afire with interest. "He dies by the sword, not poisons."

"As you wish. Sigwulf, you then will bide just beyond Marten Ridge. They will be in such a stuporous haze you will not need half our forces—your own Companions will be enough. I would go by dark, the dark of the same day. The moon will be one day off full if he comes when we expect him—there will be light enough. It should not be difficult to slay two thousand men lying about in a drunken sleep."

Sigwulf grinned, showing flashing white teeth through his bristling black beard. He particularly liked, Auriane knew, his prominent part in the plan, and the fame the deed would bring him.

"By the Fates!" He clapped Auriane jovially on the back, nearly knocking her into the fire. "The great niding dies this time!"

Auriane managed only a wan smile full of sadness.

They ordered the best mead brought out then, to drink to the plan. Later in the night Witgern said in a low voice to Auriane, not wanting the others to overhear, "I like none of this. The Hall of Baldemar will be burned again."

Auriane looked at the hall, that great benign beast of thatch huddled in the dark, sensing dimly she looked upon it for the last time.

"I am not so bothered, Witgern. When the Romans burned it last time, I never looked at this rebuilt hall without expecting *it* one day to be burned." She stopped herself. "Well, this is not *entirely* true—a part of me will cry out—but a smaller part. 'Change is the sound of Fria's beating heart,' Ramis says, and I wish I lived and breathed the truth of those words, but it frightens me. When we've gotten vengeance on Odberht and we have his body, *then* we'll not mind what they do to Baldemar's Hall."

Witgern nodded. He saw the glittery light in her eyes from swiftly forming tears and put a companionable arm about her as she rested her head on his shoulder. To his dismay the closeness of her, the wildflower scent of her hair, stirred the familiar pain-filled desire. Forcing it down brought tears to his eyes.

The greater part of the Chattian army set out for the south at dawn the following day. Auriane rode at the head of the host, carrying the cat-skull standard. Witgern, Coniaric, Thorgild, and a dozen of Baldemar's venerable former Companions rode beside her. The Holy Ones who bore arms came behind in a gray flock, led by the First Priestesses and Priests of many groves; Sigreda and Grunig rode at their head, and Fastila was among those that followed on foot. Their robes were girded up for ease of movement; fire-hardened spears were their sole weapons. The army came after in ragged ranks, grouped by retinue, or if they were independent, by clan. A good half of the warriors were accompanied by their wives, who came to heal wounds and cry out encouragements on the battlefield. Romilda's provisions wagons trailed the army. In one wagon was Sunia, now a warrior's wife three months gone with child; the cart's jolting made her miserable, and she cursed her lot as a daughter of the provisions women. In another, concealed beneath bearskins, was the catapult seized so long ago. Those too aged or ill to fight, among them Baldemar's brother, Theudobald, his sister Sisinand, and Athelinda and her household, traveled with the army for three days, then split off to journey east to a hill fort on the Taunus called Five Wells, which was counted farthest from the lines of battle.

Two cycles of the moon would pass before they would learn the outcome of Sigwulf's engagement with Odberht. When the army reached the Taunus ridge, they took possession of three hill forts set in a line along its summit. The third of the army that followed Auriane settled into a grim spirit-ridden fort of sagging timbers and lichen-covered stone built by a long-forgotten tribe; it lay directly in the path of the Eighth Augusta, which runners informed them was methodically making its way north, clearing country as it advanced. The war council agreed the encampments of the Twenty-First Rapax and the Fourteenth Gemina Martia Victrix could not be engaged, for these legions came forward on open ground. If their ambush of the Eighth succeeded, they planned to move from hill fort to hill fort along the ridge of the Taunus Mount, staying just ahead of the enemy advance. They would lay new ambushes as they moved, while keeping messengers engaged in bringing reports of the movements of the various Roman camps.

Auriane understood now why the legions came in such force: the soldiers were needed as much for the clearing of roads and the siting of forts as they were for the actual fighting. Their forts sprang up everywhere like poisonous mushrooms after a rain. The most secret parts of the primeval forest were laid open to sharp foreign eyes. The land's wild freedom was insulted with ropes of roads binding it tightly, with rude shouts in a strange tongue. The line of legions seemed an insatiable death machine, a mouth full of tearing teeth as it fed on villages. As she stalked the palisade walk at night, Auriane imagined she could hear the thin wails of children's ghosts carried on the night wind.

During the time of waiting the Chattian host lived on little food, shunning tents and sleeping lightly clothed under the sky to harden themselves to the cold. They passed the mornings hurling spears at posts. Nights were left to gossip and tales to still the fears. Auriane saw that the old catapult was practice-fired, and she sparred daily with Witgern, using weighted wooden poles. She walked about when they gathered for meat, saying calming words to the people.

It was in this place that a smith named Unnan was brought before Auriane, bearing a grim tale. She met him in the stone room built into the north wall of the fort, where she received and sent out messages from runners. Unnan stood uneasily before her, massive arms crossed as he attempted to hide split, blackened nails. Seeing he was unnerved, she had strong mead brought at once.

Unnan told her that at the last quarter-moon, at the spirit-time when all was wanly lit, a lone horseman galloped up to his isolated homestead.

"He called out my name in a voice that raised the hairs on the back of my neck. And I am no cowardly man, my lady."

"You look to be nobly brave."

"He said he wanted his horse shod! At that hour, and with war begun! As I'd yet lit no fire, I determined to let him think the house empty—I dwell in a lonely place and it was the time of day to walk well around the grave mound. But he must have seen me through the walls. He waited long. So I opened the door—and a rush of wind nearly knocked me to my knees. Standing there with his back to me as he stilled his horse was a man taller than any natural man, clad in a black cloak that brushed the ground.

"I saw at once his horse was not mortal. It was huge, with hooves the size of water buckets and eyes that glowed like hunters' lamps through the forest, with a coat darker than caverns at midnight. The stranger . . . wore a broad-brimmed hat."

Auriane felt the breath of a ghost on the back of her neck. "The gods preserve you!" she said softly. She had no doubt the visitor was Wodan in mortal guise.

"He raised a hand and stilled the wind. Then he turned to look at me. I threw my cloak over my head to hide the sight of that dread face, but I was not quick enough. I saw it. There was a countenance that would melt your bones! He had leprous skin . . . and one fierce eye, and one gory, blackened one."

"And," she whispered, "did he speak?"

"He breathed one word in the hollow, windy voice of a dead man: *'Sacrifice.'* That was all. What can that mean?"

"Sacrifice," Auriane repeated softly. Tales of Wodan appearing before a smith at a war's beginning were common—she heard them all her life. But what was troubling and strange was that normally he promised swift, glorious victory.

"Unnan, swear on your spear," she said, fighting to steady the tremor in her voice, "you will speak of this to no one."

When Unnan was gone, she rode out alone, galloping in gloomy silence past puzzled sentries, down the northern trail leading from the fort until she came to a rain-dampened grove of sacred elms. There she collapsed onto her knees and prayed to Fria to help her understand the meaning of the god's word.

What has so upset the balance between the seen and unseen worlds? Have we not sacrificed enough?

But no understanding came, either in waking hours or in dreams, and the word *sacrifice* sounded ceaselessly in her mind, disguised in the rustle of pine boughs, in the desolate calls of nightjars as they wheeled through the sunless sky.

CHAPTER XXIII

As summer passed into fall, the Romans continued to advance almost unopposed. There was no sign of the fabled battle-chiefs of whom they heard tales, or their white-robed sorcerers, or the ghostly witch Aurinia. Domitian began to worry that the intelligence given him was wrong. Where was the spirited resistance he expected? Once or twice they found and destroyed a foraging party, but all in all he was slaughtering far too few of the enemy, and he knew this might later prove acutely embarrassing. Great wars needed hordes of captives and multitudes of dead—or the rabble would laugh at him when he rode into the city in triumph. And the new forts the legions were constructing would not be so effective if the natives were not badly crippled at the same time.

Nightly as he dined, his military staff listened to his litany of sorrows. "Where *are* those cunning wretches? Has some traitor in the camp drugged their mead to make a fool of me?"

Once Marcus Julianus responded with: "Perhaps they are confused. For long you condemned them for warring on us. Now you condemn them for *not* warring on us. Give them some time to sort it out."

The Kalends of September came and passed. The one sign of the enemy's distress was the forest's massive silence—festival times came and passed, and no bonfires bloomed on the gray-green hills.

There began a small stream of desertions from the legions, not an unusual thing ordinarily, but remarkable in this war because it stemmed not from fear of the enemy but from spirit-terror. The occasional deserter who was caught was subjected to the *fustuarium*—a punishment in which the culprit was cudgeled to death by men of his own century. But he would first be questioned closely by the Tribunes, for Domitian was eager to know what inspired such villainy. And more often than not the deserter would claim the hills were alive with ogres and elves. The forest floor at night crackled with the furtive steps of the walking dead raised up for revenge by the Chattian sorceresses. One claimed to have seen, reflected in a pool as he bent to drink, the sweetly demonic face of the woman Aurinia, blood trickling from her lips. A soldier of the Fourteenth reported a headless man approached him at dusk—the head, which the spirit carried under its arm, bore the features of the Fourteenth's commander. Others related a tale of a gray stallion of unnaturally large size with eyes that were molten red—and insisted it was the shapeshifter Aurinia in the guise of a horse, menacing, watching, waiting.

When next Domitian summoned Marcus Arrius Julianus to dine with him alone in the commander's quarters, news had come by imperial post that Junius Tertullus, the Senator who had secretly appealed to Julianus for help, had died by his own hand. Officially it was claimed Tertullus was caught with a speech hidden in his clothes, with which he meant to denounce Domitian before the Senate within the hour. Domitian had sent a letter to Rome, demanding the Senate try him for treason. When it was read in the Curia, Tertullus opened his veins.

Domitian's dining chamber was austere; dour-faced busts of the fortress's former commanders looked out pitilessly from their niches in the walls. The room had a stubborn chill; a charcoal brazier supported by three goat-footed satyrs did little to warm it. The cluster of delicate flames of a candelabrum scarcely penetrated the wells of darkness pooling in the stone corners of the room. To Marcus Julianus the gloom was full of visages of the unquiet dead, causing him to feel a vast separation from all he loved: His father was there, tonight looking sternly disapproving. He does not like what I prepare to do, Julianus thought. Lycas was there as well, his expression piteous and terrified.

He saw too the placid, bestial face of their murderer, Nero.
That tyrant I could not stop. This one, I must.
Servants set down the first course: silver bowls of marinated

asparagus, truffles, cucumbers, capers and olives arranged about two heads of fresh lettuce brought in from the markets of the native settlement. Marcus Julianus waited impatiently while a young Greek reader droned through a number of epigrams Domitian counted treasonably offensive, sent by the Praetorian Prefect in Rome; every day a fresh crop arrived with the imperial post. They had been penned anonymously, then circulated about the city. Listening to these defamatory writings had become a nightly ritual for Domitian; he carefully preserved them in a gilded chest. The ones they heard now were of the type Domitian called "fly tales" because they played on a persistent rumor that the Emperor spent the opening year of his reign brooding alone in a closed chamber, doing nothing but stabbing flies with a stylus.

The young reader braced himself to read the tenth of the fourteen epigrams that arrived with this morning's letters and reports.

"My friends, tell me . . . why does our own Alexander go north?" he intoned, his normally full, flowery voice pinched with tension—this was a duty he despised. *"Are not our southern flies numerous enough and valorous enough?"*

Domitian was stonily quiet, his gaze locked on one spot on the wall. The boy realized with dismay the Emperor still had not heard enough. He cleared his throat and selected another.

"Perhaps, my friends, you have heard we are at war?" he read, perspiration beads forming above girlish lips. *"The tawny savages are not frightened at all . . . but it is said all the flies left Germania and Gaul."*

Domitian gave a dark grunt like a prodded boar. A scarlet flush began to spread across his solid features. "Enough," he said, a soft rattle in his throat. "Now get out!"

The boy spun round to flee.

"Halt!" Domitian commanded. "Leave those!"

The young reader set down the gilded chest, quickly as if it burned his hands. Then he was gone.

Domitian shook one of the offensive bookrolls in Marcus Julianus' face. "Why cannot the authors of these horrible verses be caught? Even were I to punish the man who *started* that wretched fly story, still it would not die. A single petitioner creeps up on me once when I am deep in mourning for my brother . . . and so he *does* see me absentmindedly stab a fly or two. And for it, the wits make me out to be a madman!" He looked hard at Marcus Julianus, demanding commiseration. *"Well?"*

"I reserve judgment until I hear from the flies," Marcus Julianus responded coolly. "Now if you've done with that, I've a grave matter to put before you which—"

"I see you trust I still find your impertinence invigorating!" Domitian broke in as he poured himself a full cup of unwatered wine. With baffling swiftness he shifted to elaborate self-pity. "Here, the enemy is asleep. At home, the enemy attacks! I'll have an end to it, I say!"

"If you want these slanders to end, ignore them. The wits never stopped calling your own father cheap, even to his face. Did he ever punish anyone for it? He was wise enough to laugh at it. Even after he was dead, they said he wanted to be hurled into the Tiber because he was too stingy to pay for his own funeral—"

"True enough but . . . that was not quite the same case."

"And why was it not?"

Domitian paused, a mildly puzzled look on his face. "I simply know there *is* a difference. They insulted my father with antic smiles. They insult me with daggers hidden in their cloaks."

"Here is my opinion on the matter: You are not easy with yourself, and you see it reflected in others' faces as if into a mirror. Your ears are stopped to praise and pricked sharp to ridicule. You hear a symphony of ridicule others do not hear."

Domitian looked at him with groggy befuddlement, as if he had been sleepwalking and struck a wall. "What? Say it all again?"

"I'm saying . . . it is but the mind's illusion. Do you know the theory that all life is the soul's dream, a discourse between man and his shadow, put forth by the Alexandrian school of—oh, curses, never mind, I can see when I've lost you."

"And with all else that plagues me," Domitian muttered bitterly into the humid depths of his wine cup, "my concubines are pushing me to celibacy. One tries to bear a child by me, thinking to supplant the other in my affections. The other cries constantly, wasting away of jealousy, and threatens to drink poison. My physician is secretly administering a draught to the one to keep her from conceiving and poison antidotes to the other. And now it's whispered my plodding-but-still-unpredictable wife at home was surprised in her bedchamber snugly beneath not only her coverlets but also the pantomime actor Paris! Tell me, how do you manage your women? I never hear you complain."

The question brought Marcus Julianus an unexpected jolt of hollow emptiness. His women? There had been a string of them, all of slight account, both freed and noble. Perhaps because confronting Domitian made him feel close to death, it suddenly seemed sad and wrong that none were even near to being of like soul. He pushed the thought away. Never would he speak to Domitian of such things; it would seem a sort of blasphemy.

"I am too unsettled in mind about a certain matter," Marcus Julianus replied evenly, keeping gathering anger under tight control, "to bat about questions that have no true answers." He looked with cold precision into Domitian's eyes. "I spoke of illusion. What is *not* illusory is that Junius Tertullus is dead."

There was a moment of taut, dangerous silence. Domitian looked at him with veiled eyes. "And thank wise Minerva for it," he said softly.

"You *must* know Tertullus was not fool enough to carry such a speech about. It was planted there by an informer."

"Really?" Domitian raised a brow in mock surprise. "Many sharp-minded loyalists think not. Would you style *yourself* a loyalist, Marcus Julianus?"

He refused to be forced into a defensive position. "The man couldn't have opposed an assault of goslings. Tertullus was painfully ill at ease speaking publicly in opposition to *anything*—it was not in his nature."

In reply Domitian took out one of the letters that arrived with the day's post, written personally by the Guard's Prefect. He flattened it on the serpentine tabletop.

"I want *you* to understand, Marcus. I care little if the others do." Somehow the words made Marcus Julianus recoil faintly within. They were spoken with a shade too much emphasis, as if Domitian sought to convince both of them. It might be, Marcus thought, that *he* wants to believe he is more under my influence than he actually is. As if he were not yet used to being under no one's influence . . . , but might test it out soon.

"This is a confidential letter. Read it."

When Marcus Julianus had finished, he said firmly, "I cannot believe this." The letter claimed Tertullus tried to seduce the Guard by approaching one of the Centurions, offering to double the Praetorians' annual pay if they would back his try for supreme power. "Let me guess . . . the Centurion of the Guard he approached happened to be a man connected somehow to Veiento— a relative, an ally, a lover."

From Domitian's expression Marcus Julianus knew he guessed rightly. "No matter if it was. Veiento has no ambition."

"Nonsense. He would unseat you if he could."

"Two fighting cocks, you two."

"Do not insult me. He tried to murder me juridically, and I turned it against him. Our fight was *never* mine. You must stop your ears to him. Veiento deceived you—*and then drove an innocent man to his death.*"

Unexpectedly, Domitian's eye became muddied with a misery that seemed genuine. In that moment he seemed to suffer for his acts as any man of conscience would. Marcus Julianus caught himself believing for one instant this was true remorse; Domitian's playacting was becoming disturbingly subtle. "You believe me wrong," Domitian said in a shame-ridden voice. "That is not easy to live with." Then he gave Marcus Julianus a mock-friendly grin that chilled him.

"Would it please you if I stepped down? And let you rule in my place?"

"Thank all the gods—for a moment I thought you seized with a fit of reasonableness and compassion."

"You'd certainly rule *me* if you could, but you cannot, you and all your ilk who sprinkle yourselves daily with the bathwater Seneca died in. I'll tell you what you *can* do, however, to put my suspicious nature to rest, since *you* seem to be seized with a fit of meddlesome helpfulness. I've a task for you I would not trust to any other."

"Only one of us can put your suspicious nature to rest—and it is not I."

Domitian ignored this. "Tomorrow I would have you ride out to the camp of the Eighth Augusta. Ostensibly your purpose will be to inspect those new ballistae to see if they're properly tuned." Marcus Julianus was known as an authority on these war engines; he had written a manual of engineering, and based upon it, Domitian's engineers had built catapults capable of greater range than any previously constructed.

"But your true purpose," Domitian continued, eyes hard and intent, "is to observe closely the behavior of Regulus. Now there's a commander whose men have made an idol of him—"

Marcus Julianus felt a dull throb of disappointment.

Indeed, nothing has changed. Corner him with reason and he vanishes, only to reappear standing behind you donning a fresh mask. Once again I fail utterly.

"Hold your tongue, I hear your thoughts! This case is different," Domitian went on. "I've had several reliable reports that Regulus is stockpiling weapons in a disabled native fort just above the camp. On top of it he's far too pleased with his wit and his looks, and he's just the sort of slithering snake to turn on me out there. You read a man's soul better than anyone I know. Watch him. I want you to thoroughly inspect that camp and look inside that old fort."

"I warn you, you will not like me in the role of informer."

"Surely you're not frightened the Chattians will attack while you're out there? Not after what I hear you did in north Africa."

"What I fear more is that the truth will bore you. Uncovering a conspiracy is so much more entertaining than finding no conspiracy."

"Risk boring me then. It will not be the first time."

Domitian struck a silver bell to summon one of his personal servants. The unwatered wine all at once struck him a stunning blow and he needed aid in getting up. Lately his solidly made form was becoming comfortably and evenly padded with fat; two servants staggered under his leaden weight.

Marcus Julianus was surprised Domitian forgot his collection of treasonable epigrams; wine had indeed befuddled him. It occurred to Marcus that something might be gained by his looking at them. Someone under his protection might be represented there, and he would need to warn the author.

"My lord," he said casually to Domitian's retreating back as the two servants who guided him nearly collided with a third bearing a silver tray of dried figs stuffed with almonds, "can I take these and look at them at my leisure? . . . they are to literature as hog slop is to cuisine, but I would like to more closely study this villainy."

"Be certain to give them back," Domitian replied, obviously pleased, thinking it would do Marcus Julianus good to see what he endured. "I mean one day to watch their authors *eat* that hog slop."

In his own chambers Marcus Julianus read until far into the night, slowly realizing Domitian had been saving these writings since the time of his accession. He was nearly ready to retire when something odd caught his eye at the beginning of one of the two hundred and more bookrolls.

One of the earlier books was disfigured by deep impressions made either by a reed or quill pen; it looked as though Domitian had written a hasty message or letter over it on some light, poor quality paper and the marks had gone through. There was no doubt in Marcus Julianus' mind who penned it: Domitian's hand was distinctive. Intrigued, he closely studied the blank impressions made by the quill. Domitian had written the words, *"These, for certain,"* followed by a list of six abbreviated names.

When he made out the letters of the third name, *"Tertul"* — and knew it must be Tertullus — he felt a cold hand close round his heart.

He quickly lit extra lamps to better see. Then he rubbed charcoal over the paper to highlight the indentations left by the quill. It meant he would have to destroy the book; he prayed time would elapse before Domitian noticed it was missing, which would reduce the possibility the theft would be connected with him. If not, he would have to contrive some excuse for its fate.

The first two names were those of Fabianus and Serenus, whose deaths he already counted gravely suspicious — and then that of Tertullus.

It seemed far too great a burden for coincidence that the first three men on this list were dead. Nevertheless, for long moments he fought the inevitable conclusion: that this was the impression of a letter directed to some accomplice, possibly Veiento or someone in the Guard, listing men who were to die.

He was suddenly certain not Veiento but Domitian himself had arranged for the incriminating speech to be found on Tertullus. He envisioned some anonymous ruffian enlisted for the task; doubtless the fellow brushed past Tertullus in a thick crowd and slipped the speech into the folds of his toga. A short time later a Guard would have been alerted to stop Tertullus and search him.

The next two names were illegible to him. The last was *"Satur."* Again he felt the touch of an icy hand. *Saturninus.* Who else?

The world seemed to melt in sadness and horror. This was the final betrayal, one that could not be overlooked. His thoughts flashed from Domitian's occasional fits of guilt, seemingly so heartfelt, to this shameless, premeditated murder. It made no sense. How could two such diverse sentiments be contained within one mind?

He must be stopped. He must be stopped violently. We the living must arrange it before our own time comes.

But what a task, one to make kings shy off.

It cannot be done without the aid of my peers — and if I approach the wrong man, my own life is done. It cannot be brought about without the support of the Senate and the Praetorian

Guard. And most importantly it cannot be arranged without first selecting an heir all will agree upon—or the atrocities that followed Nero's fall will be repeated and the world will once again erupt into civil war.

I will need at once to begin enlisting help.

Restlessly he paced, scarcely breathing; once he paused before the marble bust of his father that he brought with him from Rome. On this night that worried, well-meaning face gave no comfort; the old man seemed to mock him for thinking he could bind a tyrant with reason.

The bust was still crowned with a garland of wildflowers, dried now, that he had placed there on his father's birthday. Reverently he removed the garland, taking up the brown petals as they fell. He heard his father saying to him on that long-ago day when they were reunited, *"Learn to bend . . . or perish."*

Forgive me. I knew then I could not, nor would I ever.

His hand went to the amulet of earth at his throat, the sacred mold that had once restored him to his father. At the same time he looked into the twin flames of his lamp. After a few moments he felt a strong and steady upwelling of calm, a clarity of mind.

A year elapsed between the first two deaths, he realized. Apparently Domitian was in no great hurry. He would have time to plan.

Here I am on the border of dark and light, the one check on a rational madman who painstakingly rewrites the laws with one hand while he murders in the dark with the other.

Domitian, tyrant and friend—how could you put this on me? You kept not one promise to me. I thought I could soften your blows. It seems I can, but then you turn about and strike another crueler one soon as I've turned round.

I've never seen a duty more clearly. You leave me no choice but to plan your death. And it shall be done if it takes years—I swear it on my father's tomb.

CHAPTER XXIV

On the following day Marcus Julianus crossed the Rhine
bridge with an escort of ten cavalrymen and galloped northeast
toward the line of battle, following the arrow-straight road cut by
the Eighth Augusta. The drumming of hooves intensified his sense
of urgency and his mind ran ahead of the horses as he considered
whom he should approach first to lay the groundwork for
conspiracy. But after an hour's riding the forest's regal peace
quietly overwhelmed him, undermining rational thought, stirring
old dreams. From the first he had allied himself with this land
against his own people. The country about seemed almost feminine, and it seemed to mourn. The hips of gentle hills veiled
modestly in mist, the sweep of changeable sky, had a proud,
enigmatic beauty. The slender pines reached out piteously, begging help, gently struggling to claim his attention. There rose
again that haunting feeling, elusive as ground mist, that something
or someone here was in need of his protection.

When their mounts were well lathered and began to tire, the
road abruptly widened. A V-shaped trench and low palisade
appeared at his right—part of the rectangular fortifications of the
temporary legionary marching camp. Beyond, he caught sight of
the neat, regular rows of the common soldiers' goat-hide tents and
at the camp's center the grander headquarters tent. On his left
loomed a platform of logs topped with a haycock; here a bonfire
could be lit in time of emergency. Ahead they heard volleys of

sharp shouts, the cracking of axes into trees, the rustling rush of their falling. They passed mule-drawn carts loaded with turf-cutting tools and lines of soldiers carrying baskets of earth. At last the road stopped at a wall of soaring pines. Here two thousand men—approximately one third of the Eighth Legion—were set at various tasks, directed by twenty-four centurions on horseback. Working in full armor, helmets slung across their chests, some felled trees while others stood as sentries or guarded the baggage train; some rested while others dragged brush, stacking it to a man's height at the roadside to act as a protective barrier in case of attack. Parties of cavalrymen attached to the legion moved through the trees, searching out ambushes and determining the lay of the land ahead. From somewhere came the sound of a rushing stream. Work progressed swiftly. Everywhere was a sense of taut expectancy—the very air about seemed ready to send lightning. Marcus Julianus was keenly aware of being at the edge of the world. The Chattians, unseen, were yet a powerful, brooding presence, looming high as the pines, waiting, watching.

Marcus Julianus knew then Domitian had a second, unspoken purpose for sending him here: The Emperor wanted him to view firsthand his success—to see the extent of the ground so swiftly taken, to appreciate the thoroughness of his strategy.

The legion's First Centurion, Valerius Festus, rode to meet him; he was a roughened veteran of silent mien, with the look of one who was well-intentioned but inflexible, a man past middle years whose hair was flecked with iron gray. Valerius Festus was visibly unnerved by this unexpected arrival of so illustrious an emissary from the Emperor. Marcus Julianus swiftly made rounds of the camp, deliberating long over the catapults of various design mounted on their mule-drawn carts. Regulus, the legionary commander of whom Domitian was so suspicious, was not prepared to greet him. Julianus was given some hasty-sounding reason, but he saw wreaths cast on the ground and other evidence of minor celebration—a senior officer's birthday, perhaps—and guessed Regulus was nursing himself back to health in the dark and quiet of his tent. Such petty infractions did not interest him. When he inquired why four cohorts were missing, he was told they were sent to aid the men of the Eleventh Claudia who were clearing a parallel assault road five miles to the west, where their progress had been slowed by a landfall. All seemed to have been carried out with predictable propriety, with permission obtained and documents signed. Generally all looked much as it should, though he knew he would have a difficult time convincing Domitian of this.

At the last he asked to be taken to the native hill fort. Valerius Festus rode with him through a quarter mile of forest and brush, then Marcus Julianus looked upward. The freshly destroyed Chattian hill fort lay in reproachful silence atop the Taunus crest, a blackened structure nearly camouflaged by pines.

He was seized unexpectedly with quiet horror. It was as if the crystal air purified perception and he was sharply aware this was not the lair of some half-human enemy but a place of final refuge, a scene of dark and barbarous tragedy.

"Was it taken without battle?" Marcus Julianus asked, realizing his tone was too hushed, as if he spoke near a tomb.

"Well, it was nothing *I* would call battle," Festus replied, concealing an expression of puzzlement. "A few females and their young had to be rooted out and destroyed, that was all."

Marcus Julianus wheeled his horse about. "I'll be back directly—I mean to have a look at it."

"You mean to go *alone?*" A look of sharp alarm came to Festus' eyes. "That is unwise! There would be no way for me to guarantee your safety."

"I'll have to guarantee my own then."

Before the First Centurion could raise another objection, Marcus Julianus urged his horse to a canter and began climbing the twisting path cut through scrub pine that led to the hill fort's gate. He did not know why he felt so little fear; it was as though he shared some uncanny understanding with the enemy, as if their minds and his were somehow linked. For no reason he could name he touched the amulet of earth through the cloth of his tunic, haunted by an obscure sense it had somehow brought him to this place.

He felt he ascended into another world, a wise old gentle one whose wisdom lay in its millennial patience. He felt the closeness of the *genius loci* itself—the spirit of this place. She was an ancient hag who was yet young, with sad, watery eyes and masses of grassy hair that never knew a comb, a being formed of earth and chill air. The wind was her garments whipping about exultantly, pulling him urgently one way then another, but it was also her ardent soul, animating the surface of waters, pooling in unknown valleys, lifting the swan, carrying the ashes of the dead, hurrying the rain, a wind never held and fouled by cities.

A goshawk shot up from behind the palisade of the fort and

glided toward him silently with an occasional bat of a wing, a sentry of nature's gods come to have a close look at him. He felt the *genius loci* accepted him.

As he came closer, he saw the palisade had half fallen in one place, hanging loose like flayed flesh. The gate had been forced by burning—legionary battering rams were of little use against the hill forts of the northern forests; the native forts' earth-and-timber construction rendered them too resilient to be vulnerable to the heavy blows of a ram. Within, he heard a flapping of multitudes of wings as if in an aviary; the place was alive with many varieties of birds come to peck at the spilled grain streaming from a broken bin by the gate.

As always the dead nourish the living, he thought, filled with the sense he ascended not to a crushed enemy fort but to a temple of the mysteries, one immeasurably old, formed out of earth in some natural eruption, a place of the intersection of death and life. In seeking the mysteries we go underground or to the high places; is it, he wondered, because the vast stillness there leaves loud the rustle of spirits?

He rode through the gate, sensing injured presences crowding the air. He could see straight through the broken fort to the hazed, violet hills beyond. He saw at once no weapons were stockpiled here, and he had expected none. But Domitian had a greater enemy here: Nature itself with its rambling, rebellious growth would ever be troublesome to kings.

With a sure eye he appreciated the hill fort's straightforward design, sadly aware this, to the world, was not architecture at all but the work of beasts, comparable to a bird's nest or a beaver's dam. Near the grain bin was a well, its source drained off by the Eighth Augusta's engineers; about it the earth was packed hard where ring-dances had been performed.

A dark and terrible stench came with a shift in the wind. He looked toward a timber shelter at the back of the fort. In the sun-dappled gloom was a confusion of corpses—three women, a boy and an infant who had died clinging to one another. Nothing could prepare a man for the look of this, the boundless terror frozen in those faces, the mother's stiff white hand still protectively round the child. The blood was black. Their eyes were open. He fought a need to close the eyes of the babe, to protect it from the sight of what it beheld at the last. Their weapons were a cookpot, still in the hand of one of the women, and a barrel stave.

All had been efficiently gutted with the stabbing point of a legionary short sword.

He trembled, fearing the monstrousness of it would bring him to his knees. Nausea gripped him.

Most men would call this faintheartedness. I call it knowledge. It is my curse to *know* what it is to be thought not human, to be thought a thing fit only for work or slaughter.

He had a desire not to leave this place; here he could let life unravel until he found its source. In such a place he could live as human creatures were meant to live, not immured behind wall upon wall with musty books that were copies of copies written by men who never saw the things of which they wrote. Every leaf about him seemed a volume in its niche, every trill of wind the voice of a philosophical teacher.

Suddenly his horse's ears pricked forward.

And he found himself listening to new sounds—fast, furtive rustlings that seemed to draw steadily closer, issuing from the deep pine forest north of the fort.

Multitudes of light, fleet predatory creatures advanced upon the site.

He was jerked from peace into nightmare. The forest was alive with the enemy.

The Chattians had attacked.

He uttered a curse, knowing he was trapped. Then he leapt from his mount, unbridled the beast and struck its haunches, sending it off at a gallop, knowing the horse's Roman trappings would give his presence away. Then he sprinted to the sentry platform and hastily pulled himself onto the walk, his dagger in his teeth. He lay flat atop it, shielded from view by the palisade on one side and by the sagging grain bin on the other. Through gaps in the hewn wood of the palisade he had a good view of the camp site below and of the pine forest to the east.

All at once the air was ravaged by trilling war cries. They began at a low pitch, then rose up to elemental strength, fierce as any gale.

From the nearness of the cries he judged the hordes were crowning the ridge, surging through the trees on a broad front. The broken hill fort lay directly in their path.

Far below in the Roman encampment, he heard the sentries on the tower crying the alarm. Instantly the whole of the camp was in ferment. The haycock was lit. The trumpeters blew a series of short, sharp blasts on their coiled instruments to call the men to arms.

It seemed to Marcus Julianus that time compacted into one interminable, swaying moment. He was caught in the path of an erupting volcano. The forest about was disturbed as turbid water. Through the cleft in the wood, now he glimpsed warriors by the hundreds flashing with gazelles' grace through the trees, then spilling down the slope, their garishly painted shields held aloft. Many streamed through the fort, but most flowed around it as a river round an obstruction. All were great in stature, powerfully muscled, with long hair whipping on the wind like war pennants. Their greatest weapon, he knew, was not the crude spears they bore but their avenging rage. Gamely he fought against falling into terror and madness by forcing himself to observe dispassionately all that passed below.

He heard the hoarse shouts of the centurions, sharp with alarm, as they gave orders to the flagbearers to signal battle positions. At first it looked as if the orderly work of an anthill was disrupted by the strike of a foot. Then rank and file rapidly came together, and the Roman forces formed one dark, compacted mass with javelins poised. He saw the small ballistae wheeled round on their wagons. Already torch signals were being passed rapidly from tower to tower, summoning auxiliary cavalry from the Eleventh Claudia's encampment five miles to the west.

It was then he saw a thing that at first he thought a trick of the mind. A half-dozen men of the legion's first rank toppled to the ground. Some heavy missile had torn into the Roman line.

He raised himself up to better see. What madness was this? The Chattian charge bore down on legionaries swiftly, but none of the warriors had yet hurled a spear.

A second missile ripped into the Roman ranks, knocking five more soldiers to their knees. Now the legionaries were disoriented, breaking formation and getting in one another's way. The mysterious missiles effectively stopped the first flight of Roman javelins.

Then he knew the missiles were catapult bolts fired from the open forest to the north. And so that old tale, close to legend—of a catapult in the hands of the barbarians—proved true after all. He attempted to note its position, its range, still struggling to keep his hold on the rational world. He found himself feeling an errant pride in the Chattians; they had chosen well the place and time to use their long-hoarded weapon.

The barbarian wedge-formation struck the Roman line, and the two forces collided into chaos. He saw the Chattian standards bobbing over the melee, pushing past the Romans battle flags as the masses of men intermingled. The tribesmen broke up the Roman forces, forcing a battle on their own terms, giving the legionaries no choice but to fight as the barbarians fought—as individuals, warrior against warrior.

He then witnessed a second unaccountable sight: At the southern extremity of the fighting, where all were packed closely in a dark knot, a group of legionaries dropped their shields and fled, disgracing themselves right before their centurions' eyes. It appeared they fled in the face of something monstrous. But smoke blotted much of the scene, for there were small fires scattered about where the Chattians set alight the mule-drawn wagons. He peered down into shrouded mystery, wondering what horror could have inspired dozens of men to subject themselves to the army's brutal punishments for cowardice.

All through the fray the Roman trumpets brayed, competing with war cries, shrieks of agony, the fierce bell tones of iron striking iron. He judged this smoking cataclysm raged for less than the time of two water clocks, or under an hour, when there came distantly the cry of answering trumpets, and shortly after, the low thunder of hooves from two directions.

Mounted reinforcements closed in at great speed.

Then came the animal plaint of native cattle horns, summoning the Chattian retreat. The tribesmen knew only too well the dangers of tarrying until reinforcements came. Their one advantage lay in surprise and speed of attack; they must now retreat to the wild country, where they knew the perilous trails and the enemy did not. Gradually the Chattians disengaged, then withdrew like some quick-receding tide, leaving the injured and dead heaped on the ground. The warriors stampeded in a wild herd up the slope from which they had come. The few who were mounted set their horses on the same path Marcus Julianus had taken, which passed directly through the ruined fort.

Now Marcus Julianus saw the grim result of the attack: Nearly a thousand Roman casualties lay in the rutted road, and half as many Chattians. Remarkably, the barbarians had given worse than they got. He wondered if anyone would dare accurately report this to Domitian. Erect spears, their heads buried in the earth, were thick as grass blades on the ground. Even from this distance he could hear the piteous cries of the dying.

And now the Auxiliary Cavalry filled the assault road with a storming of hooves, closely followed by a detachment of one hundred Arabian bowmen.

The first of the Chattian warriors burst into the fort, their shouts full of victory; many brandished Roman short swords and legionary helmets. He was tensed and ready, knowing if they saw him they would gleefully slaughter him where he lay.

It was then that he saw, at the rear of the Chattian retreat, the warrior on the gray horse. By what sense he knew it was a woman he could not say; she was still well off from him, seeming almost reluctant to leave the field of battle. She caught his notice because unlike the others she did not simply flee; she seemed to shepherd the warriors like some flock, going back for stragglers and urging them on, shielding them with her horse, staying behind the fleeing horde as though she counted herself responsible for their safety.

It began to unnerve him. Why did she so tempt the Fates? The Arabian bowmen were closing in rapidly, and from her anxious looks in their direction, he knew she realized it.

Then before his disbelieving eyes she dropped from her horse and disappeared into a mass of the stragglers. Moments later she reappeared, struggling with a badly injured man. With a great effort she somehow maneuvered him onto her horse's back.

The Arabian bowmen now galloped alongside the cleared place around the camp, skirting the trenches, raising an accumulating mountain of dust, bearing down on all those last to retreat. The battle-maid climbed up behind her wounded companion, so she could steady him as she rode. Then she urged the horse to a gallop, but her mount moved slowly under the extra burden and she lagged behind her fellows.

"Nemesis!" he uttered softly. She would be the first caught and killed.

He was amazed at how swiftly he was pulled in to the drama of her life. There was something so guileless, so elemental in that devotion.

The tales of Rome's foundation yield up stories of such deeds, he reflected, but who ever witnessed them in these times?

And in the next instant he realized who she must be—the woman Domitian called *Aurinia*, whose name his father rendered *Auriane*—she lived still and was before him now. That great spirit who long ago lent him strength was as resolute as his father's records represented her. But this was also the blood-drinking harpie, the sorceress who sowed madness on the battlefield. Surely

she was the cause of that hasty desertion he had witnessed earlier.
And yet as she came closer he saw nothing fearful in her aspect,
nothing—and then he felt a start of excitement. Nothing fearful,
but there *was* something remarkable there. What was it . . . ?

As her horse toiled up the slope at a labored canter, Marcus
Julianus realized with horror that Domitian would have his prize.
He knew by the bowmen's excited shouts that they recognized her.
Their mounts galloped low to the ground as the Arabian auxiliaries
raced each other in their eagerness to catch her.

I cannot let so gallant a creature fall into his hands.

She ascended by the same path he had taken, for it was the only
way clear enough for her horse. Switchbacks in the trail obscured
her for a moment. Then she was close enough that he could hear
her crying words of encouragement to her mount. The horse
appeared to respond, lengthening his heavy canter. The wounded
man swayed precariously; his leather tunic was soaked with blood.
The bowmen took the same narrow path two at a time, their strong,
wiry horses gaining on her steadily. At their present speed he
judged they would catch her perhaps two hundred feet past the
gate of the fort.

He leapt to his feet, giving not a thought to the fact that he
risked being seen by the trailing warriors still streaming through
the ruined fort. Hastily he gathered up handfuls of the slingstones
that littered the sentry platform and began tossing them into the
broken grain bin, consumed with a need to save her, forcing down
his fear he would be caught and executed for abetting the enemy.

Her weary mount lumbered through the fort's narrow gate. He
stood braced, ready to throw all his weight against the sagging
grain bin, feeling like a beast-fighter awaiting just the right
moment to thrust at a lion. Fall out of step with the fatal dance, and
die.

When she was not more than a horse's length from him, he
clearly saw her face.

For an instant he forgot entirely what he was about; a collection
of slingstones fell from his slack hands. That face startled him to
reverential quiet. It tore away all memory, leaving only the
question, who are you?

I know. I expected you, even counted on your coming. And what
are these mad words?

It was difficult for him to understand later the witchery worked
by that face, seen in so brief a moment. It was more than its
maidenly bloom, its wise warmth, its look of one who scoured for

meaning behind meaning. Here was the old-young *genius loci* of the wood, the fierce-gentle face of nature herself. Long after he would ponder what it was that so snared him and pulled him so immediately close. It might have been that look of hope vaulting out of charnel hopelessness. It was his own.

She looked gamely toward the wild country, head lifted with a spirited innocence. Her refusal to acknowledge the nearness of destruction, and the fact that she expected no help increased his powerful protective feelings. She galloped past, and still he stood immobilized, aware distantly she uncovered a gaping need in him he scarcely knew existed.

How can the countenance of a doomed woman so intoxicate me with hope?

Her noisy pursuers filled the path, whipping their horses, jostling each other and cursing. He roused himself to action, pushing hard on the grain bin.

At first the half-burnt structure was immovable as a standing stone. Swift panic came.

It must move. Sylvanus, Pan, great Rhea and Diana, I call on all nature's deities—give me strength!

He threw his weight against it, trying to shock it into motion. The wood creaked. Something snapped within. Rotted oak timbers were giving way. Gradually it acquiesced to his will, moving sulkily at first, then in a rush, crashing into the opening of the gate, choking it with splintered wood and a small mountain of grain. The slingstones shot out into the path of the pursuing horses.

The Arabian bowmen's mounts collected swiftly behind the barrier. He heard the scuffling of hooves as the horses stumbled on slingstones. The flurry of foreign curses was like the screaming of jays. He moved to a gap in the palisade and saw a confusion of brightly robed, long-bearded riders angrily gesturing, their sun-baked faces stiff with rage.

One raised his bow and took aim at Auriane. Simultaneously, without thought, Marcus Julianus shot up behind the palisade, grasped his dagger by the blade and prepared to throw, aiming for the bowman's throat.

But their white-bearded commander rode up next to Auriane's would-be slayer and angrily pulled down his arm.

Marcus Julianus knew then that Domitian must have given orders the woman was to be taken alive.

He was amazed that he was prepared to slay that bowman and

reveal himself, had it been necessary to save Auriane's life. He knew then how profoundly she bound him to her.

A barking argument broke out among the bowmen as they quarreled over whether to remove the debris or find a route around the fort. They seemed to settle for removing the debris. He prayed they would think this act of sabotage the work of the fleeing warriors.

As they worked furiously, kicking at slingstones, pushing at the bin, stumbling like drunken men through the grain, Marcus Julianus saw Auriane and her wounded companion disappear through the broken section of the gate at the rear of the fort, and into the uncharted forest that was her domain.

For the moment, he realized, she was free. But he felt little relief. Her land was shrinking as the Cheruscans pressed down from the north and the Romans advanced; with each passing month she would have fewer places to hide.

He crept quickly along the palisade; within moments, the bowmen would gain entry. Only Valerius Festus knew he occupied the fort at the precise time of the attack; he wondered how rich a bribe would be necessary to ensure the First Centurion's silence.

Just as the bowmen got past the obstruction and flooded in, he climbed to the top of a damaged portion of the wall, grasped a low-hanging limb of a pine, and leapt down. After a fall of fifteen feet he hit the hard ground just outside the fort; the bowed limb snapped and broke but it softened his impact.

As he made stealthy progress down the slope, he saw that already, life was returning to the mangled campsite, as blood flows back into a shocked body. Camp physicians were bent over the wounded, ministering to them where they lay, extracting spearheads, binding wounds, giving wine and mandragora for pain. Some survivors wept. Others helped gather up the dead and put them into wagons.

Marcus Julianus made a slow, careful circuit of the campsite to disguise the direction of his return. The noncombatants had taken refuge in scattered places, and he discovered he roused no suspicions, if indeed traitorous activity was suspected at all. He first sought Valerius Festus, who held his life in his hands.

But soon he learned no bribe would be necessary, for Valerius Festus was dead.

As he returned to the fortress with a company of seriously injured men, he was aware he no longer saw through Roman eyes, for this defeat he counted a victory, if a small one.

The ravaged land now had a name. *Auriane*.

A gate was flung open that could not be closed. She could not be kept out as others had been kept out. She swiftly filled his whole mind.

I may not live. Nor may she. But now all I do must take her into account.

He knew he had lost something he valued greatly: the invulnerability that caring greatly for no one had given him. There was peace in not loving, along with a certain emptiness. Now it was possible to lose life not once but twice. Peace was banished forever.

I pray all the gods Domitian never ferrets out my feeling for this woman. He would use it as a tool to slowly pry me apart.

CHAPTER XXV

When news of the attack reached the Emperor, Domitian sequestered himself in his chambers and nursed his rage. He refused to see his senior officers and advisors. Instead, he ordered dragged before him a steady string of captives, soldiers and officers who survived the attack, seeking anyone who might aid him in determining who was at fault. As he plied them with questions, he transfixed his victims with those brooding eyes, disdainful and melancholy at once, adopting the air of a stern *paterfamilias* outraged by the shameful deeds of his children. He would not allow himself to be shaved nor would he have a new tunic brought, consenting only to permit one frightened servant to rearrange the folds of the tunic he wore, to conceal its wine stains. He ordered the same for the camp: Until the cause of the disaster was uncovered, no man was allowed to shave or use the fortress's baths.

Within the first hour he ordered the execution of all the native spies assigned to the territory the Eighth occupied when attacked, as well as twenty provincial citizens who he claimed gave him false information. All the surviving officers of the Eighth he degraded in rank. The officers of the remaining legions were outraged on their behalf, knowing fault could no more lie with the Eighth than if they had been struck by a thunderbolt. The punishing hand of Domitian was everywhere apparent about the fortress; so subdued were the voices from the common soldiers' barracks the clatter of crockery and mess tins could be heard as they were washed following the evening meal. There was a curious absence of women's voices—even the camp followers were banished from the fortress.

At the eighth hour Domitian learned an earlier report had been confirmed: The Chattians had succeeded in taking hostage three of the tribunes of the Eighth, including the tribune of greatest rank, Novius Clarus. Domitian in his fury then gave the order to execute the six Centurions of the cohort that broke and fled at the sight of the *ganna* who bore arms. It sent a shock of horror through every officer of the legions.

Marcus Julianus vowed then to halt these punishments. He was crossing the courtyard to the Commander's private quarters, meaning to force an audience with Domitian, when he encountered the steady and dependable Senator, Licinius Gallus, the famed gourmand, serving now as one of the Emperor's chief strategists. He quietly took Gallus aside and in a few terse words told him of the list of men to die. He wanted one man whom he trusted to know of this, in the event Domitian imprisoned or exiled him after the confrontation.

"Thank all the gods you're going to him!" Gallus declared as they parted. "He listens to you alone!"

"Hold your prayers of thanksgiving—even the most careful of beast-tamers has his luckless day when his charge slips loose and he's gored. Tomorrow—provided I'm still alive and a free man—you must meet me at the tenth hour. I have . . . a question to put to you. I will arrange the place and inform your servant."

Marcus Julianus then secured an audience with Domitian by reporting to the Emperor's First Secretary that he had gotten "a good, close look at the woman." He judged rightly Domitian's inordinate interest in the *ganna;* within the quarter-hour a Guards' Centurion conducted him into the Emperor's presence.

He found Domitian in the *Principia* of the fortress, regally slouched on the tribunal before the standards, his rumpled appearance slightly ludicrous within this vast and solemn temple of the legions. Domitian's eyes appeared bruised from lack of sleep. He might have collapsed there and slept the night in that stone seat; only the gleam of scorn in his eyes established with certainty he was awake. Gloom, petulance and stale smells hung about him thick as fog. Displayed on the floor at Domitian's feet was the battered catapult the Chattians turned on the Eighth Augusta. On the day after the attack it had been recovered in the forest where the barbarians abandoned it, and dragged before the Emperor so he could closely examine it.

Domitian gave him a smile bleak as a winter sun, savoring the sight of his First Advisor forced to remain unshaved and unbathed.

"*Well*, old friend," he said with soft malice, "I hadn't heard of a shipwreck nearby. Were you the only survivor?"

"I congratulate you that you've managed to make a shipwreck sound like a welcome thing—it's a bath of a sort."

"Report quickly—and go."

"As you say," Marcus Julianus replied quietly. "I have this to report: There were no weapons hoarded within that fort."

"About the woman!"

Domitian's shriek reverberated off stone. Marcus Julianus felt he touched a torch to pitch.

"No one who survived saw her," Domitian prodded him. "You are spewing falsehoods at me!"

"Not so." Marcus Julianus smiled tolerantly as if at a child's understandable fit of temper—all the while feeling he trod a perilous path through a viper pit. "I saw her well—and I am still living."

"A temporary condition if your impudence continues." The Emperor gestured sulkily to a white-liveried servant stationed at the wall, demanding the replenishment of his water and wine. Then his gaze flashed back to Marcus Julianus.

"Where did you see her, Julianus? Where were *you?"*

This was the question Marcus Julianus feared. He knew the mute terror of a man on trial for his life, waiting for sentence to be pronounced. He dared not lie—Domitian, if he chose to investigate the matter, would eventually learn the truth. He was acutely conscious of wanting to live. Because Auriane lived, he *must*—if only so he could rear a protective wall about her.

"I was trapped in the ruined fort for the duration of the attack."

Domitian was sharply alert, a hound scenting game.

"Then you witnessed that villainous act of sabotage." He gave Marcus Julianus a malignant smile. The fresh wine and water arrived. Domitian noisily mixed them himself with much clangor of spoons against silver vessels, then took a long draught, offering his First Advisor none of it. Cold fire flashed in his eye. "Was it *enemy* sabotage, Julianus old friend?" he said softly, "Or do you despise me so much you took matters into your hands? Did *you* snatch my prize from me?"

Moral outrage, Marcus Julianus judged, would be his best shield.

"Foul ingratitude!" He trumpeted the words as if he reached the crescendo of a speech in the Curia. "I expose myself to danger to settle your mind about Regulus—and am nearly slaughtered on the spot by a band of marauders who hang behind to do the deed. And not only do I receive *no* thanks for my trouble, or any show of interest for what I risked my life to find, but I am insulted with an accusation worthy of an ignorant tyrant like Nero, not you!"

It was then that Domitian discerned the new remoteness in Marcus Julianus' eyes. Domitian thought: Is it a trick of the mind, or does Julianus have the look of one who does not cast his lot with me anymore? I would swear it, a line has been cut. An indifference is there, irremedial as death.

Domitian dimly sensed its shape, and it made him more powerfully anxious than he was ready to admit. Before, he was quite certain Marcus Julianus *sought* things from him—to encourage him to rule wisely, to have his understanding, and to some degree his friendship. Julianus seemed to seek nothing from him now. Domitian was seized with an urgent need to lure him back.

"So," Domitian said, examining Marcus Julianus' face, wondering if the corpse of a friendship could be brought back to life, "I've one worthy man among these villains that serve me. I applaud you then, are you content? Now tell me of her!"

"She was great in stature—Amazonian, if you will—and spirited, with a . . . a low cunning that burned brightly in her eyes. And she had mud-brown hair that hung in barbarous locks."

"She was not . . . beauteous? Fair of face as the nymph Egeria, with the eyes of Artemis?"

Marcus Julianus prayed the small transformation Auriane had already wrought in him was not visible on his face. He felt his spirit contract, realizing he could not bear the thought of Domitian's soured eyes gazing upon her. He managed an indifferent shrug. "If one cares for that heavy, crude, northern sort of beauty, she was comely enough, I suppose."

"Was she . . . fierce of aspect?"

"Hardly. She was possessed only of an impressive determination."

"What then drove thirty men to disgrace themselves and throw away their lives?"

"Superstition, and no more, I'm certain of it. They've heard enough lurid tales of her to distort beyond reason the actual sight of her. Her eyes were not aflame, nor did she breathe fire."

Domitian leaned forward. In his eyes was the hard gleam of the obsessed. "Did you see her . . . strike out with a sword?"

Marcus Julianus knew of Domitian's fascination with watching women in single battle—it was said he would often order pairs of his concubines to fight with wooden swords. Julianus felt a faint queasiness begin to rise in his throat.

"I did not. She was escaping. She lagged behind the rest from charity—she'd taken on the burden of a badly wounded man." He realized he strove instinctively to make Domitian think well of her—*anything to lessen his wrath, if he caught her.* "She was fleeing for her life," he continued, "and she appeared frightened . . . *chastened.*"

"*Chastened?* Truly?"

Marcus Julianus saw the word pleased Domitian.

"But you must be wrong, my dear Julianus. Only a creature of unusual mettle could have dared pull down my statue."

"Then what mettle she had has been beaten out of her by this war. You underestimate your success so far. I would say you have won, my lord. However . . . that order for the executions of the centurions must be stayed. Or you may never catch her."

A bright, dangerous light flashed in Domitian's eyes. "And how is that?"

"The love of the common soldier was hard won—do not toss it off. You do not see the temper of the individual man as I do—your lofty place does not allow it. Punish those men, and the Eighth, the Eleventh, and the Fourteenth will mutiny. This is a critical time. You'll have difficulty replacing them in time with others experienced in dealing with a northern winter. You'll extend the war into a second year. The Cheruscans can't harry the Chattians in the north that long. They have no supply train and must live off the land. You'll allow the woman ample time to escape." Marcus Julianus added to himself: *You need not know, murderer, Auriane will escape anyway. I will see to it.*

"*That's* what you came here to say. Trickster! Using this Aurinia creature as bait! Have you any more orders for me before I'm dismissed?"

"I wanted to resign. You would not let me. Am I to understand then I *am* to resign?"

"Tricky *and* thin-skinned—what an obnoxious admixture of qualities!"

Domitian then nodded impatiently toward the captured catapult, looking broken and harmless at his feet. "That thing there . . . tell me, he-who-knows-everything, could they have others?"

Marcus Julianus looked at it appraisingly. It was one of the smaller types of spring-gun, but heavy enough to need a mule-drawn cart. He walked around it once, examining the windlass that drew back the bolt, the trigger that released it, the trough down which the bolt traveled before it emerged through an aperture in front of the heavy wood frame. "I think not," he said at last. "For, you see, the taking of this is meant as a curse. All the tribes of Germania believe you can destroy a man if you turn his own weapon against him. This now they have done. Seizing another would not be necessary."

Domitian gave a contented grunt, sedated by Marcus Julianus' certainty, vaguely aware of how naturally he fell back into dependence upon it.

"Note the narrowness of the aperture . . . and the grip of the windlass—both show it to be of antique design—"

"From my brother's reign."

"No. Much older than that. It is of the type used by the First and Fourteenth in the first two years of the reign of your father. This means they've kept it about for a long time, saving it for the critical moment. They must *know* they are finished if they chose to use it openly now."

Domitian frowned, unable to dislodge the logic of this from his mind, though he tried. "That deranged harpie drove them to this," he muttered. "For my father and brother everything was simple and normal—they fought *men*—not war-loving bitch-dogs. This is one more fiendish ploy of the Fates to turn my reign into a farce."

"Consider, too," Marcus Julianus went on, "that these natives would only steal the weapon of an enemy they revered."

The word *revered* brought an approving calm to Domitian's eyes. Marcus Julianus was again conscious of what precise, delicate tools words were—how they could be used to provoke the exact state of mind he wanted in the Emperor.

"I would say, if we deal gently with them from this day forward, they may release the hostages unharmed," Marcus Julianus continued. "And clemency will cause their warriors to be more likely to desert to us."

"I thought they burned captives alive as a matter of course."

"I fear you've been consulting sources woefully out of date. We know far more about their customs and ways than in the days of Caesar's *Commentaries*. I suggest you delve into my father's works on the tribes—"

"Don't test me! Your father's *banned* works on the tribes."

Marcus Julianus suppressed an amused smile, "—in which he explains *this* tribe is in the habit of spearing their prisoners in the side and hanging them from trees, for so died their war god, Wodan. But *my* guess is they're still alive. Surely they know bargaining with us is their only hope."

"Perhaps I accept that . . . perhaps I do not," Domitian responded as he leaned back, affecting a look of cultured boredom. Then without warning those jaded eyes sparked with playful malice.

"I've observed a woeful tendency on your part of late to neglect your personal grooming. Rectify that."

"Only if the ban on the baths is lifted for everyone."

"Let them soak in there like frogs and croak for all I care. Have you had enough pleasure at my expense for one day? Now go from me!"

On the next day at the tenth hour Marcus Julianus awaited Gallus in one of the warm rooms of the fortress's baths, judging a meeting in a public place would rouse fewest suspicions. He knew those he approached afterward would come with him all the more easily with Gallus in his camp. Licinius Gallus was a man who combined few strong political opinions with a pure, naïve loyalty to the Senate, a man who had the gift of rousing no one's ire as he made his way in the world. Even Domitian's suspicious nature was never pricked by him. He was a man who somehow made conspiracy seem tame and proper, almost tasteful.

Gallus found Marcus Julianus in the steamy sky-lit haze of the vaulted chamber, seated on the marble bench with a drying cloth carelessly draped over one shoulder, regarding him with calm directness. Gallus crossed the hollow steam-heated black-and-white mosaic floor and sat close but not that close, so that their presence together would appear accidental. Then he eased his eyes closed, as if resting.

From the adjacent tepid-room came the hollow echoes of many conversations rebounding off stone and the splashing of bathers so amplified by the vaults a whale might have slapped its tail on the water.

"That was well done!" Gallus said in a fervent whisper, smiling to conceal his own nameless fears. "I don't know what you said or did, but it worked a miracle. He's stayed the order for the execution of the centurions—I heard it an hour ago."

"It was but half my doing, half the grace of Fortuna. You're a fool to come here, you know," Marcus Julianus said, smiling easily. "This could well have been entrapment."

Gallus tautened in terror. "But . . . were it anyone else but *you* . . . you're not saying—"

"Calm yourself. What I plan *requires* fools—no one too drearily sane would come along with me on this course I mean to propose to you now."

"Well, I've not *your* recklessness—I mean, your boldness. Curses, you're distressing me—this is about that list, is it not? It seems there's nothing we can do but keep our wills up to date."

"Not so. There's no need to go trussed and bound to our deaths. You see, I too have a list. And *his* name is first and last on it."

There was a moment of taut silence.

"Are you saying what you seem to be saying?"

"I fear I am."

"Madness!"

"No. Madness would be to do nothing."

Gallus looked at him. Steam veiled and unveiled their faces. Gallus was trembling. He had a guileless face rounded by well-fed middle years; his earnest hazel eyes protruded slightly with fright. A bold bead of perspiration traveled from his mat of curling black hair, down his short thick neck, on down the twin hillocks of his chest and belly. His breathing roughened. He seemed a frightened boy snared in an elder's trap.

"Have you found some design in all this monstrousness?" Gallus said finally. "Or perhaps he needs none?"

"All the victims were recipients of Titus' greater acts of generosity," Marcus Julianus replied evenly. Gallus wondered how he remained so composed. "Tertullus, for example, would have been forced from the Senate rolls from poverty through no fault of his own, had not Titus restored to him his fortune. Serenus had hordes of relations from Oplontis and Pompeii who were stripped of all but the clothes on their backs after Vesuvius erupted with fire, and Titus gifted them generously from his own purse and saw them all given farmland."

"I am a dead man! Who does not know I sacrifice to Titus on his birthday? One of the illegible names was probably mine."

"Do not weave demons from the dark. We must consider no one

safe. The whip we hold over Domitian is his great fear of what historians will one day write of him. He's obsessed with the *damnatio memoriae*—the Senate's power to damn his memory after his death—so if Jove is with us, his need to murder in secret will slow him down enough to allow us time to do what we must."

Gallus felt the pricking point of a blade at his chest, so clearly did he hear the word *assassination* dangling unspoken in the air between them.

From somewhere near, a low whistle sounded. "We are out of time," Marcus Julianus said, gracefully arising. Gallus guessed someone loyal to Veiento approached.

"Do you want a token of faith?" Gallus whispered more softly.

"Your word is enough. I want now only to know who is with me."

"If I am not with you, who am I with? *Him?* Of course I am with you."

In the next days, as Marcus Julianus went about his assigned duties, researching precedents for the laws the Emperor meant to propose, Auriane's face rose before him with gentle insistence, a bold sylph brooding over his study, drifting into his dreams.

She is Arachne, weaving, binding, holding my spirit still.

He tried unsuccessfully to control the vision but all that held beauty called her up: the fire of gold, the spirit of a horse, the jeweled surface of the river, the mischievous smile of a camp follower's girl. The vision of her was antic and perverse, flitting off when he looked at it directly, then flashing close, becoming humanly present when he turned his mind away.

This is the most awkward of times to become a lovesick boy. I am too old and burdened with duty for this. Are there any I dare tell of it who would not think me mad?

CHAPTER XXVI

The Chattian host took shelter in a marsh, remaining for a month to bind their wounds. Their victory celebration was muted somewhat because of the dwindling supply of mead. They gathered up the Roman spoil stripped from the dead—bronze helmets with iron skull-plates and horsehair crests, richly worked scabbards and gilded belt-plates inlaid with black niello, embossed cuirasses, heavily military cloaks—and gave them to the marshy lake as an offering to Wodan while Geisar prayed and Sigreda wailed a hymn of praise.

Auriane took no part in the celebration, though all credited the victory to her keen sight; she watched the celebrants from the hide tent that once was Baldemar's while nursing an arrow wound to the neck and shivering from a light fever.

We have pulled a few hairs from a huge unfeeling creature, and still it comes, terrifying in its calm persistence.

She tried to sleep through the night's drunken revelry, but could not, for she heard the whispers of the dead and was certain that Avenahar was crying.

Avenahar, I might not see you by summer's end as I promised. Will you forgive me if I'm kept away until spring, or possibly next summer?

Decius, I miss you like I miss a warm cloak, a fast gallop at dawn over hard terrain, an extra fur on the bed at night. There is love there, painful love. But the moorings were cut and I've drifted. Ever widening black waters separate us now. Distance shows clearly the outline of the shore on which we lived. I know now ours was *not* a love of a great and eternal order, like Athelinda's for Baldemar. That makes me desolate. But why should I mind or even think of it? I am dedicated to the gods.

But I do think of it. What a coarse jest of the Fates my life has become. I want to fight where there is chance of victory. Hylda said I would lead my people to freedom—why have I not yet? I want my child, dearest of dear ones, to have my own milk. And in the dark of night when no one knows, though I be hurled in a pit of serpents, though I hear Hertha's voice, half troll, half frog's croak, proclaiming my evil, I *do* want to know a love such as Athelinda had.

Auriane often watched the three tribunes they had taken hostage. These were the first Romans of high rank she had set eyes upon. They were kept in a wicker cage drawn in a cart, awaiting the next Assembly, which would decide their fate. She saw that Roman arrogance increased greatly with rank—these men made Decius appear humble. They sat still as wooden effigies in their wicker cage, staring out with the fierce, blank look of eagles, their whole manner saying: Gawk at us, you cattle and sheep. We are the shepherds of your shepherds, the masters of your masters. They would not touch the food that was brought to them, and when Auriane attempted to communicate with them through an interpreter—she knew better than to even attempt using the camp Latin she learned from Decius—they faintly turned their heads, their features contracted in mild disgust as if her speech fouled the air. She learned what they normally ate and sent them foods not too dissimilar from their own—flat cakes of einkorn wheat, salted pork and apples, rough Gallic wine. This was as much because she felt it beneath her to harm anyone placed at her mercy as because of her certainty they were the greatest prize of the war. But still they refused to eat and daily they weakened.

At the Assembly hers was the only voice raised for their preservation.

"Sacrifices enough have been given," she protested. "I say they should be treated well, so when the war is done they can be bartered for the return of our people taken captive." But Geisar and Sigreda thought they would make a fine sacrifice, a royal offering that might well bring victory. Auriane's will prevailed but barely.

When the hostages learned she caused them to be spared, two began to pick at the food she brought. But the most important of them, the one interpreters said was called Novius Clarius, still did not. She guessed his was a cold, calculated embrace of death, by which he meant to triumph over his captors.

The warriors often prodded them with the butts of their spears and pelted them with the intestines of sacrificed sheep and pigs. One day she angrily scattered their tormentors and placed by them a guard made up of five of her own Companions, letting it be known to all that the captives were under her protection. The younger tribunes looked at her with barely disguised appreciation; Novius Clarius' steely contempt did not soften. By the next full moon he was dead, and the pitiful skeletal body was dragged out to be burned. Auriane alone thought it a sort of tragedy.

It was in these times that Sigreda was driven off forever, barely escaping with her life. It happened that a severe ague broke out in the camp, causing violent shivering, chills and swift death. First Thrusnelda was called on to build a need-fire. She carried out the task with rigorous attention to the laws of ritual, using nine varieties of wood for tinder and kindling it with the friction of two spinning wheels. When the fire burned hotly, the sick were passed quickly through the healing heat. But in spite of this, over two thousand perished. And so Auriane went round from tent to tent and laid the sword of Baldemar on the sick. When five of these died immediately following her ministrations, Auriane's suspicions were roused, and she called Thrusnelda's medicine women to look at the bodies. They pronounced that the victims had been poisoned. Thrusnelda then forced her way into Sigreda's tent and found great quantities of yew juice and monkshood stolen from the herb-stores. She declared before all the people that Sigreda was a poisoner; the young priestess's actions, Thrusnelda maintained, were a desperate attempt to destroy the people's belief in Auriane's holiness.

A savage cry was raised against Sigreda. Even Geisar dared say no word in defense of his appointed successor. In the end Geisar was forced to break the staff and condemn her himself, although it was obvious he did not wish to. He and Sigreda shared one mind, Auriane often observed, just as she and Baldemar had, only this mind schemed to harness others to its will.

The people set upon Sigreda and would have bludgeoned her to death, but Geisar took her into his own tent, promising them justice on the next day. Then he set a light guard about her, and at midnight she escaped. The following day Geisar too quit the camp, outraged that the people reverenced him so little that they forced him to condemn his successor. And so old Geisar abandoned the host—he who for three generations interpreted the will of Wodan—leaving them with no priest to intercede with the god of war. To compensate for the loss of the favor of Wodan—the people feared the god might punish them for their harsh treatment of his first priestess and priest—Auriane arranged for the sacrifice of a white cat and a white cow to Fria, imploring the Mother of All to serve as protectress of the host.

Before the time of the next quarter-moon, the tale went round that Sigreda had sought refuge at Mogontiacum and revealed to the Romans the location of Five Wells, their fort of final refuge. Some thought this unthinkable, but Auriane believed Sigreda capable of it for there was a darkness in Sigreda whose boundaries were unplumbable as bog-lakes at night. Privately Auriane uttered prayers of thanksgiving that Sigreda and Geisar, her longtime enemies, were put to flight. But she found she sometimes half missed them; troubling as they were, they yet were part of the hearth and bedding of the old life, and their passing seemed one more sign of the coming of the shrieking winds of chaos.

When one moon passed since the attack upon the Eighth Augusta, the main body of the Chattian army abandoned the three hill forts they had occupied since the war's beginning and began to march northeast, for scouts of the legionary cavalry were steadily encroaching on the native strongholds, and Auriane feared they would be besieged. As the army retreated along the Taunus ridge, often they came upon multitudes of black kites with their squealing cries, gliding above heaps of rotting dead—most were refugees from villages, caught and slain by outriding cavalry.

The army took refuge in a more northeasterly fort on the Taunus crest. Auriane began to grow anxious that there was no news of Sigwulf, and prayed the cause was only that his runners could not find them. In these times no one remembered their one small victory. They strove constantly to arrange a second ambush, but conditions were never again right. The legions camped always on high, open ground that favored their methods of fighting, and they stayed well away from thick forests and treacherous marshes that allowed her people the opportunity to steal close under shelter. And the number of native auxiliaries and cavalry that covered the legions' advance was greatly multiplied. Auriane knew with fatal certainty that the legions now owned the Taunus, though she would never say it before others.

The provisions wagons traveled on ahead of them, making torturous progress toward Five Wells, where the supply-women would winter along with the tribespeople who could not fight. The way was treacherous, the trails no more than deer paths, and they could not risk having the provisions carts caught in the snows. The wagons moved forward only by night; by day, Romilda ordered them disguised with brushwood. Though every day put more distance between the wagons and the legions, Auriane worried over them continuously. She knew Roman ways too well: They will do what is efficient, no matter how dishonorable, and if they destroy the provisions wagons, the war will be over.

At the new moon the messenger from Sigwulf came at last. She knew at once Sigwulf lived and was victorious—the boy shouted it out to the whole of the camp as he galloped his dun pony beneath the hill fort's timber gate.

The freckled boy grinned as he gave his report to the leading warriors, flushed with importance at being called to deliver messages to such a legendary personage as the daughter of Baldemar and such illustrious elders of Baldemar's old retinue as Witgern and Thorgild.

"Odberht's brigands overran the Village of the Boar," the messenger related. "They lapped up the wine like thirsty hounds and staggered into the forest to sleep. Sigwulf's men fell on them and slaughtered them *to a man*. Not one escaped. Sigwulf is camped now on the grasslands to the north and will rejoin you before next the moon is full."

This was met with muted murmurs of approval, for everyone's capacity for rejoicing seemed to have worn thin. Auriane regarded the boy critically.

"And what was the name of the warrior who slew Odberht?"

There came into the messenger's eye the quick hesitation of an animal that does not know which way to dart. He decided it was better not to disappoint this audience.

"Sigwulf himself . . . I think." Then he thought better of it. "Well, in truth," he admitted, speaking forcefully to cover his uncertainty, "I was not told. That is all I was given on the matter, like it or not!"

"Who viewed the corpse?" Auriane persisted.

"*Everyone.* I do not know all their names! He must have been seen slain, or I would *not* have been given that message," he replied with growing unease.

Auriane looked at Witgern. "Something is wrong in this."

"I agree," Witgern replied. "Whoever did the deed is the most celebrated warrior of our age. Everyone would know his name— he would make certain of it."

The boy looked perplexed and faintly hurt, as if he had offered them a gift that had been pushed back at him.

When the messenger had spoken all his news, he sought Auriane out privately and said, "There is a message for my lady alone, from the foreigner called Decius, sent to Sigwulf from the Cheruscan camp."

She felt a sickness and a complicated pain, sharp and tearing as broken glass.

Decius must actually be traveling with the raiding Cheruscans.

As the warriors departed, Fastila rose to leave with them.

"Fastila," Auriane objected, "not you. Stay." She caught at Fastila's gray robe. There was a comfort in Fastila's presence that was a mystery to Auriane; it was more than the sum of that unjudging resilience, that swift understanding of her pain, which she might expect from a woman who also lived a life away from family and hearth. The bond was strong in spite of the fact that Fastila was not particularly of like mind—the younger woman was far more of a nature to be content to let things be. Fastila since the war's beginning had attached herself to Auriane as a sort of voluntary bodyguard, though as one of the armed Holy Ones she was expected to pitch her tent with her fellows. She looked at Auriane with concern, then sat on the hollowed log they used as a drum, her battered round shield slung across her back.

The boy spoke Decius' words in the monotone of those who memorize. *"I would give my freedom and all my property to pass a single night with you. . . ."*

Property? she thought. Decius never had anything of worth.

" 'Beloved, we've only one life that I know of. Know this, you are doomed! I beg you, save yourself. Do not come to me—it is too perilous. And do not try to return to Ramis and the child—the enemy expects you, and there are traps set for you there. You must flee to a village called Thurin on the River Elbe, in the territory of the Semnones. There I will meet you when this sorry mess is done.' "

Auriane rose, turned, and looked off at the far pines.

Decius, she thought, you never did understand, even after all my explanations. My people and I are not separate. You might as well tell one of my limbs to remove itself from my body and flee east.

"And two more words only, my lady," the boy went on, " 'Forgive me.' He expects a reply."

Auriane shut her eyes.

Even now, she thought, we are fighting against Decius' tactics. I recognize them. The Cheruscans harry our foraging parties continuously, just as he would advise.

And yet even now, Decius, you work your own aggravating magic. You benefit from the idea you seeded in my mind, that a man is not to be blamed for the circumstances into which the Fates drop him. You do what you must to live. By our law, your crime is near as great as Odberht's. But love is clever and deft; it flies round all that and behaves as if your deeds were not.

I know your heart even if I'll never know your mind. I cannot be the one to break a staff and condemn you.

"Tell him," she began, and stopped.

Tell him what? That love and hate are mixed in me like honey and poison? That I am half starved for the rough feel of his cheek, his firm, gentle hands, but that if he comes through that gate, I would have to give him to the priests to be punished with death as a traitor? . . . He suffers. Life is simpler than that. End that suffering.

"Tell him yes," she whispered hoarsely. "I forgive." She cut a lock of her hair and put it into a white linen purse. "Give him this."

The boy's eyes widened in wonder. A woman's hair was alive with holiness, and Auriane's was holier than his own mother's — yet she gave a lock of it to a foreigner. Reverently the boy took it, bowed, and departed.

On the following morning one of the foremost tribal spies came to Auriane, a woman of the Bructeres called Hwala. She traveled among the camp followers of the Eighth Augusta and dealt in dubious wares, selling aphrodisiacs to the legionary soldiers, while peddling the coveted red Arretine-ware stolen from Roman officers to barbarian chiefs. She was a squat creature almost broader than she was tall, who walked with a turtle's methodically slow waddle. Her hair was snarled as a bramble thicket, her skin strangely mottled, and her eyes wide-set and bulging, giving her the look of some demonic toad. Witgern said of her she was the safest creature abroad in the land, for she scared even the wildcats away. Her sources of information were generally the young, fair native girls of the *canabae* bedded by the Roman officers.

"My lady," Hwala said, bowing lower than was necessary. Her attitude was carefully respectful, but Auriane knew Hwala did not hold her—or anyone—in reverence. "The Romans have declared Odberht officially dead. The commander of the Eleventh was heard to say it himself."

Auriane felt a quick, exhilarating flush of relief. "That is well! Very well." She rose and began to nervously pace, aware relief never lasted long.

Surely, she reasoned with herself, the Romans would know if their ally were dead or alive. "Did they view a body?"

Hwala shook her head quickly with a rapid birdlike motion, indicating she did not know. Auriane felt a small throb of disappointment.

"And . . . of the other matter?" Auriane asked. Hwala knew Auriane wanted to know if any sign had been given that an attack on their provisions wagons was imminent.

"They're either cleverer than we know," Hwala replied, "or they've changed their spots. However, the tribune that Mara serves was heard to say: *'We are one ambush away from going home. We've just got to wait for his cursed birthday.'* "

"Domitian's birthday, doubtless."

Hwala slowly nodded.

"Nine days after their Ides of October," Auriane said to herself. "The ogre! A small gift to himself after the Roman fashion, I suppose." In all likelihood, Auriane supposed, Domitian's augurs had told him this day would be an auspicious one for such a vital maneuver.

Fastila made calculations with her calendar stone that marked both lunar and solar cycles, and reported that Domitian's birthday fell on the morrow. The provisions wagons could not be reached before three days' hard ride, if no raiding parties were met and the weather remained mild.

"If that is what your tribune's words meant, Hwala," Auriane said, "then we are warned too late." The safety of the provisions wagons was left to the Fates and the war-luck of Romilda.

Hwala remained impassive. If this woman ever knew fear or regret, Auriane never saw evidence of it. She gifted Hwala with a gaudily embroidered, amber-studded riding cloth for her mule, then dismissed her.

Auriane tried gamely to convince herself Odberht was indeed dead.

In the next five days Sigwulf's victorious men began to trickle into the camp. A kinsman of Coniaric's, an unkempt beast with odd yellow eyes who was called Walest, proclaimed *he* had slain Odberht. He was brought to Witgern's tent to be closely questioned. Walest answered their eager questions, but Auriane thought his replies suspiciously vague. He claimed to have done the deed with an axe.

Auriane asked, "How did Odberht behave at the last?"

"He died screaming curses on your name and Baldemar's," Walest claimed. "He was running away, as you might expect, but he slunk into an abandoned thrall's hut and I cornered him. By Helle, the man had the unhallowed light of the walking dead in his eye! His horrible black locks were soaked with blood from the cracking blow I gave him to his head." The young man's grin was full of challenge; matted hair and flowing mustache all but concealed his face. In spite of his attempt to present a ferocious demeanor something in his face reminded her of a sheep.

She looked at him sharply. "*Black* locks? Odberht's hair is the color of fouled honey."

She saw a start of fear deep in the sheep-eyes. He mumbled several half-intelligible excuses, protesting he had been *told* the man was Odberht, his words tumbling over each other as he backed slowly out of the tent. He was terrified that Auriane would curse him.

"You've nothing to fear from me," she said softly, eyes alight. "You've Wodan alone to answer to for a false tale. Just stay from my sight from this day forth."

When Sigwulf himself arrived, he agreed Walest was a brazen liar. But he said a body *was* dragged before him that closely resembled Odberht. Truthfully, the face was cleaved with an axe, so identification was not absolute, but Sigwulf swore by Wodan he knew those dirty red-blond locks that hung in heavy clumps, that barrellike girth, those knees like boulders—and this corpse was dressed in chieftain's clothes, though all rings and brooches that might help identify him positively had been stolen by the time he saw him.

"Why could it not have been a nobleman of the Cheruscans?" Auriane asked.

"I cannot answer that. But Odberht and all his men were together, and they died every one. If that was not him, and I think it *was,* then another man in that heap of dead *was* him. What matters it, so long as he is dead?"

"You are right—if indeed he is dead."

Three days later a refugee from a lonely farm in the grasslands a day's ride north came to Auriane with yet a different tale. He claimed he saw Odberht alive, ten days *after* Sigwulf's victory at the Village of the Boar, in one of the grasslands villages. "I know the Scourge's face like I know the face of my own mother," he explained. "I was one of Wido's Companions once, you know." He said he traveled a way with this man, who was confident that when he presented himself at the legionary camp of the Eleventh Claudia, the Romans would welcome him as their ally.

"How then did he survive Sigwulf's slaughter?" Auriane asked.

"He was not with them. Though the hogspawn was close enough to hear the screams. He was panting atop some lusty thrall-wench in a bower safely away from where they camped. Sigwulf missed one man."

She found herself struggling strenuously not to believe it.

"He took one look at the carnage and fled south," her informant continued. "I found him with four others, trembling in a root cellar behind a burned homestead."

Auriane related this new tale to Witgern. "Then," Witgern noted, "when—and if—this man presented himself to the Romans, he did so *after* the Romans declared him officially dead."

"Yes. They might well have taken the true Odberht for some opportunist—a man who resembles him, making the best of it."

"And he was doubtless covered with filth, stripped of his riches and in rags. And who now at the fortress knows Odberht's face? Paulinus is gone. When this man said, 'I am Odberht,' they might well have answered him, 'Of course, you are, and I am Nero.'"

With falling hopes Auriane judged that, in the way of such things, the dullest version of Odberht's story was probably the one that was true.

The curse would continue to curse them. How fiendishly the Fates arranged it so vengeance was impossible. She judged Odberht would most likely be treated like a captive: Either he would be slaughtered so the Emperor could have his quota of dead and his war counted grand enough for a triumphal procession, or he would be sold into the obscurity of slavery and lost to her forever.

She would never know.

Baldemar! Is your spirit even now writhing within the tortured trunk of the Lightning Oak?

She tried to prevent the old farmer's tale from spreading through the camp and sowing discouragement, but her efforts to suppress it seemed only to speed its travels; it was dispersed like spores on the wind. Soon all camps and even the itinerant traders were muttering that Odberht lived.

As autumn waned, the Eleventh Claudia pressed close to the Chattians' new sanctuary and began constructing a fort nearly at their feet, protected by hordes of Batavian auxiliaries. The warriors managed one successful attack on a legionary foraging party, and on another occasion they damaged a section of newly completed road by starting a rockslide that killed a number of soldiers—but these successes were of small significance and hardly slowed the Roman advance.

On the seventh day after Auriane's report from Hwala, a warrior's wife who went at dawn to the well just outside the hill fort's gate claimed she saw the well waters turn to blood. Thrusnelda interpreted this to mean that somewhere on their ancestral lands, the earth had recently been soaked in kinsmen's blood. Then at midmorning, when all had eaten their meal of pork rinds, hard bread dipped in sheep's fat and honey-sweetened gruel, there came strident peals from the gate's bell, sounding like frantic cries for help.

The gatekeeper looked down to see three bloodied, soot-blackened travelers, all women, their limbs crudely bandaged, their clothing torn. Two, near death, were astride one horse, propped against one another for support; the third was just well enough to walk the beast.

"Daughters of doom," the gatekeeper shouted down, "who are you?"

"We are from the provisions," the strongest of the three replied. "Open, in the name of Baldemar."

Auriane and Sigwulf conferred, then told the gatekeeper to open the gate.

Sigwulf helped the two astride the horse onto rush mats, and they were carried off to the medicine tent. The woman who led the horse rushed at Auriane, seized her arm and collapsed into sobs.

"Put out my eyes!" she wailed. "I will see no more!"

"Sunia!" Auriane cried. Sunia's face was so swollen from nettles that Auriane did not know her at first.

"All are dead," she said through heaving gasps.

"What are you saying?" A raging sadness began to boil up in Auriane. The population of the camp pressed close, falling into fretful quiet.

"All who traveled with the grain were slaughtered. Romilda is dead. We alone live. The murdering wolves found us!" Sunia sank to her knees. "Kill me. I should not be alive!"

Auriane caught her and held her. She felt the roof of a hall crash upon her head. We are done, she thought. Our spine is broken. Now we fight without food. What cruelly efficient predators the Romans are.

Auriane supported Sunia as they made their way to the medicine tent, all the while expecting the worst because the skirt of her rough wool dress was drenched in blood. But Thrusnelda soon determined Sunia was not badly injured beyond painful but treatable burns and a disorder of the mind that caused her to babble and cry. Sunia was bloodied from miscarrying her child.

Auriane and Witgern stayed by Sunia through the night. She whimpered like a puppy, holding tightly to Auriane's hand, occasionally falling into nightmare-ridden sleep. One of the provisions women who returned with Sunia died slowly in the night from a sword wound that had punctured the lung. The other survived the night, but Thrusnelda determined she too would not live long after she gave her the onion test: the woman was fed strong onion broth, then Thrusnelda sniffed at the wound—and because she smelled onions, she knew the stomach was torn. Thrusnelda explained to Auriane this always meant death; they could do nothing but ease her pain with mandrake.

By morning the next day Sunia drank a little mead and seemed prepared to speak.

"They found us before dawn," came her labored whisper. "Even the *basest* enemy gives some chance to surrender . . ." Sunia covered her face with her hands. When she was able to continue she spoke in a strangely flat voice, as if she had severed the tie from mind to heart.

"We were alerted first by our hounds' barks. We had no chance of escape. The filthy nidings had ringed themselves about us before the sun came up. A few of us got to spears but most did not—there was not time. It was as though the hand of Wodan snapped out of the sky and pounded us into the earth. Hardly were we awakened before they let fly the heavy javelins—half of us were pinned to the stores where we stood, skewered like meat for roasting. I saw babes thrown into flames. I saw my own mother speared through. Why does Fria allow such monsters to walk the earth?"

Auriane cautiously asked, "And . . . Romilda?" feeling she reverently approached a body, knowing it that of a friend but still desperately hoping it was not.

"She did not die in the first hail of javelins. I remember her shouting over all the din, 'Peace! We go in peace!'" Sunia stopped, closed her eyes, and sobbed. "Romilda fought as if possessed," Sunia continued, "and she killed three or four of them with her spear before they slaughtered her."

"Romilda!" Auriane whispered. "She was great and good. When this war is done, I will see to it myself she has the grandest of funerals. What infamy!"

Sunia went on, "I am a monstrous coward. I'm alive because I ate too many chickens' hearts. I should have tasted once the heart of a boar. I fled to the end of the line and crawled under one of the carts and stayed there through the whole of it, clinging to the underside, watching my people fall gutted to the ground for what seemed a day and a night. Eventually the cart was set afire, which smoked me out. But by then the murdering swine had slunk off and I was among corpses, my family and friends draped like bloody rags over the carts. I am the most loathsome of nidings!"

"You're innocent as a newborn fawn," Auriane gently remonstrated. Sunia's shame made her powerfully uncomfortable; it was a wrenching reminder of her own. "What could you have done? Your mother never even taught you the use of the ash spear."

From outside the tent, they heard the quavering wails of many women, some high-pitched, some deep; their cries set the hounds howling and the whole effect was of an unholy music that might have issued from the smoking ravines of Lower Earth. Despair raged like plague through the camp. Throughout the rest of the day Auriane scarcely noticed its mood; she was busied sending out messages to the villages of those tribes that had always been their friends, attempting to arrange a system for bartering for food. As a weak sun sank quickly to the pines, Witgern came to her tent.

"We've had four thousand and more desertions since midday. You must speak to them!"

"*Desertions!* That is madness! Where do they think they can go?"

"Some to the Romans, some to the hills."

"The cavalry will pick them off one by one."

"Evidently they do not care. They reckon in the meantime at

least they can eat. It's roasted rat and squirrel meat for us—when
we can get it. Sigwulf harangues them, but he's doing more harm
than good. You are their Daughter of the Ash. They listen to you
as they listen to no other. Speak to them!"

Numbly she put on her short, soft deerskin tunic and swordbelt,
then took up a single ash spear. Though she too felt all hope gone,
fighting was a reflex, like the blind thrashing of the drowning.

Speak to them. Witgern should have said: *Lie to them.* But I
cannot. Witgern will not like it, but the hard truth will have to do.

She put her palms on the crude wood image of Fria she had
planted in the earth in the center of her tent. "Great and merciful
mother of us all," she softly prayed, "give me the strength to hold
us together / . . so we can die together."

Then she strode into the center of the restlessly milling camp,
propelled by her fury—at the Romans, not the deserters, whom
she pitied. She saw that Sigwulf, Coniaric and Thrusnelda stood
across the camp gate as if to bar it. Sigwulf bullied those who tried
to pass; his words, like wildly thrown blows, cut through the din.
Coniaric, smiling and showing neat teeth, used his usual honeyed
persuasion—though today, she saw, that mask of bland charm was
askew and a hostile underside was revealed. Thrusnelda, her face
tear-swollen as she wrung her hands at them, was a regal mother
turned into a beggar.

Auriane mounted an overturned watertrough. Warriors stood in
groups, revealing ultimate loyalties—some crowded round kin,
others preferred the company of their warrior companions. The
armed Holy Ones stayed in a flock. Most looked stunned and lost
as prisoners awaiting execution. Some, with upturned faces,
uttered endless prayers to an iron sky. Wan-faced mothers held
tightly to children whose cries could not be stilled. At the camp's
center a group of the warriors' wives chanted round a need-fire;
they had blackened their faces, loosened their hair and torn off all
their jewelry, tossing it into the fire in hopes this small sacrifice
would soften Wodan's wrath. The sight of them disconcerted
Auriane; they seemed so pitifully pale and bare they looked like
ghosts. Surely, she thought, our humanness is more than the
treasure about our necks?

Gradually they saw Auriane in their midst and turned toward
her with curiosity. They found it unsettling to see such wrath in
eyes normally so gentle. A winter wind invaded the camp and tore
through the sheds and tents, whipping cloaks like pennants, setting
trees in ecstatic motion. But about Auriane was a stillness that

seemed to defy the elements. The fine, sharp fury in her eyes was reassuring; surely, many thought, that will alone could halt a legion. Gradually they gathered about her as they might around a bonfire. Behind her an army of hostile winter clouds massed in the northern sky, promising a long siege of darkness.

"My friends!" she cried out, bringing a halt to all talk. "I hear that four thousand have laid down their arms and fled!"

Witgern grinned. He thought: No matter how many evil spirits creep into camp, that voice banishes them. How the gods must love her.

"Four thousand forgot who they were and abandoned our sacred ground. The Romans have in abundance all the rich things of the earth. Because we have no riches they'll have our spirits instead. . . . Shall we so easily yield them up?"

She paused, waiting to feel their minds press still closer.

"You must not flee! It seems we've a choice of one sort of death or another—but truly, one is death in fact, and the other is life. This is a fearsome thing, but you have the hearts of boars—you who of all the free tribes refuse to be herded into the ungiving land of the north, you who live proudly on this last scrap of land the Romans have not thieved. If we die together, we shall not die, for the gods will know us and love us. If we die together, we multiply a hundredfold the strength of our fate and luck."

Witgern's grin abruptly faded. He felt a winter cold on the back of his neck. *What in the name of the gods is she telling them? Die together? She is telling them she too has given up?*

And for the first time he knew fully the urgency of their situation. For one frantic moment he struggled against a nearly overwhelming desire to flee to the hills.

"This is *our* land. The ashes and bones of a hundred generations of ancestors lie in the belly of this earth. We are the Ash; the ancestors are our deep roots, fixing us in this place. They need us to stay together if their spirits are to one day have new life. Do you want to be cast into a pit in some barren soil ridden with foreign gods? If you run off into the hills it means naked death, unholy death, stripped of kinsmen's love and comfort. Those who flee die alone, motherless and in darkness.

"We face not warriors but arrogant bandits who have gotten off unpunished after stealing half the world. These swaggering thieves think we raise children to provide thralls for their army. Your goodness and courage shames them, you with the blood of mountain cats mingled with mother's and father's blood. Do they fight in sunlight, striking at the front like a worthy foe? No. They sneak up behind us and steal our food!"

Spirited shouts of outrage were thrown up to the sky. Witgern thought grimly, only Auriane could restore their faith while telling them they were doomed.

"How shall we answer this? I say, by meeting shamefulness with grace. They have stolen your food, but they cannot steal your love of the gods. I know I will never flee. If it comes to be necessary, I will stay to the last and face them alone."

"No!" came a chorus of shouts, some sheepish, some passionate. "We are with you!"

"Who, then, marches on with me under the mantle of Fria?"

They raised a lusty roar, banging tin pots against staves, frightening the horses and dogs. But, Witgern noted, it *is* a thinner roar than the ones they gave at the war's beginning.

She has done it, he thought. But how long can she bind them, once the starving begins?

The main body of the Chattian army was quickly reduced to forty thousand, though their numbers could not truly be counted for the Warriors' Council lost contact with the scattered bands led by lesser chieftains; the Council did not know if they had taken refuge in the gorges or lay slaughtered somewhere. The Roman forces advancing along the Taunus were once again overtaking them—they could not remain. Marching north was impossible—though Odberht was gone, whether dead or taken alive, he had in effect broken down the gate, and now the whole of the north country was overrun with bands of hostile Cheruscans. Runners reported that every fort that could be securely held had been disabled by the legions.

And so the Warriors' Council agreed there was nowhere to go but the fort of final refuge, Five Wells. The spies who reported to Hwala assured them the Romans had no maps of this territory with its lonely hills of linden, beech and birch. Within a moon-time the Chattian host departed, eluding the Roman cavalry by constantly reversing direction under cover of dark. For greater mobility they split once more into three divisions.

Overnight the hills whitened with snow, a soft, thin blanket broken by delicate black spears of grasses. To Auriane the winter hills did not look the same now that she knew the stores were gone: The cold silver-blue slopes with their complexity of ultramarine shadows were no longer a sight of haunting, solemn beauty; now they were chill and forbidding. The black lacework of branches edged in ice and fired by the sun was an exquisite web of death, which would trap and hold them. Unquiet ghosts rustled brittle branches. None here can stay alive, the skeletal arms of ash and linden proclaimed.

On the eve of midwinter called by the tribes the Night of the Mothers and by the Romans the ninth day after the Ides of December, they came to their destination, the fort called Five Wells. For Auriane the one joy in this was her reunion with Athelinda. They embraced for long moments, Auriane drinking in the scent of sweet woodruff that always lingered in Athelinda's hair. When Mudrin and Fredemund came forward, she half expected to see Decius approach and felt a stabbing ache like a birth-pang.

"Mother," she whispered in Athelinda's hair, "you do not know what this means. You should be saddened to see me. We never intended to be driven back this far. *You* now are on the front line of battle."

"It shall be as it shall be. None can harm me more. If they murder me, they only send me to Baldemar."

The Chattian host celebrated this holiest of nights ringed around a Mother-Fire, chanting prayers to the primal ancestresses from across the gulf of ages who hovered near in the dark. All felt wary lest these hoary spirits come too close—the Mother's Night held terrors as well as comfort. The wombs of the ancient mothers gave strength and life, but they were also graves, and it was said that if you glimpsed their hair, the flash of their eyes, or their girdles as they whirled about in the black night, within a day you would die. So all carefully kept their eyes on the fire.

On the following dawn Auriane took stock of the place. Five Wells was built by a Gaulish tribe and the walls were exceedingly well made, using crossed timbers solidly nailed in an open-box structure that was filled with rubble and soil. The whole was fronted by a thick stone wall, through which the ends of the cross-timbers were visible. It was a sort of wall known to give the Romans much trouble. Unless they were betrayed, they might evade discovery altogether. The fort had a good supply of fuel, and some provisions were stored here—there were bins of millet and rye, as well as barrels of apples, hazelnuts, peas and wild cherries—but she judged this would not last much beyond three cycles of the moon. They would have to supplement it by hunting.

Hopefully the Roman plague would recede in spring, and they could find their way home and begin rebuilding their villages.

And I will return to you, Avenahar. It hardly seems possible that in springtime you will be older than a year, in the time of swift-growing intelligence and first spoken words.

But it is well I did not bring you to this sad place. The separation is the most barbarous of tortures, but it must be, so that you can live.

CHAPTER XXVII

"I want these stinking beasts to know we've *won*," **Domitian** announced to Marcus Julianus one night in the deep of winter as they dined alone. "I mean to flush the last of them out of their holes. *Hole,* I should say. They've all scurried off to one place— an old Gaulish fort at the extreme northeast end of the range— we'll get it in the spring, at first thaw."

"You know that for certain."

The start of concern Domitian saw in Marcus Julianus' face the Emperor misread as skepticism about his conclusions on the matter. "Don't pick at me with your doubts," came the testy reply. "Six—no, it was seven—of this fresh crop of deserters described the same place, while being tortured in separate cells."

Marcus Julianus nodded thoughtfully, feigning reluctant agreement. A faint noxious stench emanated from the preparation Domitian used to preserve his thinning hair: It consisted of oil of myrtle, the ashes of a burnt hare, and not enough nard to overcome the reek of its principal ingredient, the urine of a young ass. Marcus Julianus found knowing the Emperor set on a course of systematic murder altered the way Domitian appeared to him: The discerning light in Domitian's eye seemed now to have a manic edge. The increasing fleshiness of his face, which might have seemed part of the normal progress to middle age, seemed now a sickly symptom, soft and repulsive as the swellings or gatherings from illness.

"And such strapping specimens of barbarian manhood these deserters are!" Domitian went on merrily. "I've ordered the questioners not to break any bones—they'll make fine gladiators. I'm having them sent home at once to be trained. But best of all I've found a way to take that fort without breaking in. This Aurinia has a daughter, a *'child of the god'* as they delicately refer to the babe, which means they don't—or don't want to—know who the father is. We've had it described fairly well where the brat can be found. The unfortunate part is that the babe is in the hands of that prophetess Ramis who so terrifies the natives we cannot find any willing to brave her lair. The Batavian auxiliaries refused me flatly—they say she turns men into hedgehogs. I'm assembling a detachment of our own men, handpicked, who claim they've no belief in sorcery and witchcraft. . . . Not an easy thing, since they know *I myself* have consulted such sorceresses on certain matters!"

Marcus Julianus felt a throb of alarm as he nodded with approval. "All the great strategists from Frontinus back to Xenophon would give you a nod," he replied with just enough coolness to leave a measure of doubt as to whether sarcasm was intended.

She has a child, Marcus Julianus thought with alarm. *Why did my informants not tell me? Curses on Nemesis, what to do now? Perhaps a single, unarmed native emissary bearing a warning might get through to Ramis' sanctuary. . . . There is that frightful old woman of the* canabae *called Hwala who peddles aphrodisiacs, in debt to me since I bought the silence of that smithy ready to report her as a spy . . . I could enlist her to find someone fit for the task.*

"High praise from one so miserly with it! I'm surprised your tongue didn't shrivel!" Domitian returned to the platter of capons stuffed with truffles and lustily finished it off, not noticing Marcus Julianus scarcely touched his own portion. Then he turned to Julianus, suddenly intent, not bothering to wipe his glistening lips.

"My friend, you know the . . . the *problem* I spoke of once, with my concubines, the one I warned you if you spoke of it to anyone I would personally see your tongue cut out?"

Problem? He had to think for a moment. Then he remembered—that inability to "do his duty," as Domitian had put it, with his women. Domitian's physicians disagreed over the cause. Some said it was the wretched climate and the slow progress of the war; others laid it at the door of the concubines themselves, assuring Domitian their constant squabbling would leave the lustiest satyr of the wood unable to perform. Marcus Julianus realized then the amulet about Domitian's neck was one of Hwala's most popular ones for potency—the dried right testicle of a goat dipped seven times in oil.

"Well, I think I have found my tonic!" Domitian went on happily. "What I need is a simple, uncomplicated female, and I know where to find one. She's loping free up in those hills, a little hungrier than before, but as you said a while back, somewhat *chastened*. Yes, this is one barbarian I mean to subjugate personally. She must be firm as a youth, war-trained as she is. What is it, my man? You look as if I stabbed at a quail's egg with a carving knife before the eyes of the Parthian ambassador. You truly are a master of the look of delicate distaste."

Marcus Julianus had never fought so hard to maintain an air of bored neutrality.

"I assume you jest about this maid."

"I know you said she was not particularly comely . . . but beauty I can command whenever I wish. What I want is a woman not schooled in feminine wiles—"

"I refer not to her charms or lack of them," he said evenly, a curtain of darkness falling in his mind to shut out the sight; he felt a tide of sewage rising higher and higher, threatening to choke him. "But to the fact that she hardly deserves you. Remember what she *is*. And who you are. Would you *reward* her infamy by elevating her to your divine bed?"

"Ah, late in life you've conceived a fussy concern over my loss of dignity."

"The common soldier will think she bewitched you. They'll count you a fool." The taste of defeat was acrid in his mouth.

"Well then, no one shall know about her, Julianus, old friend—except you."

CHAPTER XXVIII

Winter wore on in the Chattian camp, and the hunters could not keep apace. As Domitian intended, starvation did his fighting for him now. Hunting parties were sent out every day into the snows, seeking the gray-brown roe deer that foraged in morning or herds of elks with their young; once they caught an aurochs calf abandoned by the herd. They sought smaller creatures as well: the far-leaping red squirrels active just after dawn, the occasional hazel grouse, the mallard ducks in the frozen marshes, or the common brown hares with black-tipped ears that everywhere left their fast signatures across the snow. In spite of the hunters' small successes, by the third moon after Yule the population of Five Wells dared not eat more than once every other day. Wolves were heard to creep close at night. Daily they lost warriors who fled from fear of starvation or of the coming final battle.

Auriane while hunting was glad of the snow—it blanketed the bodies of slaughtered refugees scattered throughout the forest, leaving all innocently white. Never had she been made so conscious of the struggle of all creatures to survive. Flocks of starlings pecked frantically at the snow, desperate for food. The frozen carcasses of deer lay everywhere, the delicate sickle-curve of their white ribs visible where their flesh had been torn open by wolves.

Like the animals, now we too can be massacred by winter.

In the camp there was little talk or spontaneous movement;

many passed whole days playing lethargic games of dice, using as stakes their rations of dried aurochs flesh. Some fell into a sort of human hibernation, crouching silently in their hide tents; others became wild and maddened. Sigwulf was like a nervous stallion confined too long in a stall. He strode about seeking fights, and eventually was avoided by all after he killed a man who accused him in jest of planning to "go over the wall." Coniaric initiated contests to see who could bring in the most game, which he pursued with frenzied zeal and regularly won. Athelinda came forth from the isolation she had imposed on herself since the death of Baldemar and was like a mother with a thousand children, formidably patient as she sat all day with those stricken with illness, telling tales and wrapping wounds. Witgern's placid wife, Thurid, cried constantly and her sixth child was born dead. Witgern himself divided his time between long stretches of sentry duty—he volunteered for more than was necessary to keep away from Fastila, who ever more piteously and aggressively showed her love for him—and concealing himself within his tent, where he composed mournful, meandering love songs to the tinny notes of his battered lyre. The songs were for Auriane, but he scarcely let himself know it.

Auriane was often alone on the palisade, a single sentinel ardently gazing southwest, as if by constant watching, she could keep the enemy at bay. As Athelinda comforted the aged and ill, Auriane gave strength to the warriors. The times enhanced the tales of her, and more than one man imagined as she restlessly paced the palisade on moon-washed nights that this great, somber spirit was kindred to the swift-flying Choosers of the Slain, the ghostly battle-maids of songs who were half warrior, half swan. She lit the way to vengeance. As Athelinda preserved life, Auriane promised death would have meaning. All felt that if there was purpose here, it was hers. Without her, when the Romans came the fort would become simply a slaughtering ground; with her, it was transformed into a temple of sacrifice.

She arose every day well before dawn, alert as if she had not slept at all. Alone in her hide tent, she performed Ramis' ritual of fire and prayed to Fria to comfort and preserve Avenahar. Then she put on her gray cloak, wrapped her feet in hides and tramped through the snows, inspecting the stores, seeing to the reinforcing of the walls, joining those who cast spears on the casting ground. She always seemed to know who was losing heart and she sought that person out, her presence sustaining as mead, comforting as bread. At night she was the last to collapse onto her mat of rushes. Hunger gave her eyes a steady brilliance—and she was hungrier than even Athelinda knew, for in order to keep the two surviving Roman tribunes alive, she secretly fed them from her own ration. She knew no one else would see them fed, and she was determined to see them treated honorably.

She found that for the first time in her life she dreaded the onset of spring. She was certain that this year its promise of eternal life would not be kept, that freedom would melt with the snows.

Spring came swiftly, heralded by the wild warning music of swans. The population of Five Wells ate every third day. The priest called Grunig ordered the empty grain bins torn open so the god could witness their plight. Fastila chewed on bark to assuage her hunger. Auriane put a guard around Berinhard so no one would steal up to him at night and slaughter him for food. The camp dogs disappeared one by one; even the rats seemed to know to stay away. No one dreamed of anything but food; every round stone looked like a loaf of bread; every pool of water brought thoughts of a thick stew. Clothes were so threadbare everyone wore multiple layers of rags against the cold. At night all slept closely packed together for warmth and rank was forgotten; noble wife lay back to back with farm thrall.

One spring morning in the time when the snows were beginning to recede, leaving ugly patches of black mud and brave green shoots, Thrusnelda saw a golden eagle drop a mountain cat cub, torn and bleeding, into the grass outside the fort. The young creature had proved too much for it to carry. The eagle flew off, solemnly flapping, floating, flapping, until it disappeared into the depths of the sky.

"*We* are the mountain cat cub, of course," Thrusnelda explained that night around the central hearth, "and Rome is the eagle. It means we will be seized and borne off. We will be crippled and grievously wounded, but in the end we will still have life, young and vigorous life!"

Few of those who listened showed signs of believing this. Auriane thought: The Romans' coming will be a blessing to many. Slaves at least are regularly fed.

Nightly the Warriors' Council debated the wisdom of sending men out at once to lay ambushes for any Roman cavalrymen who might penetrate this far. They debated whether the trails were clear enough to allow attacking warriors swift escape. Auriane worried their sharply divided councils caused them to delay too long.

Finally, one day well after the fourth moon, before the sun rose above the stand of silver firs guarding the fort's eastern side, fifteen scouts were sent out to determine the Romans' position. They were given orders to return at dusk, whether they were successful or not. Actually *no* success would be true success—it would mean the Roman forces were still camped a comfortable distance away.

When all fifteen scouts failed to return at dusk, Auriane felt a cold ball of iron settle in her stomach. Witgern and Sigwulf and those privy to the plan revealed none of their anxieties to the others, but Thurid guessed it from Witgern's stricken face.

Athelinda too knew something was gravely amiss. To allay her fears, Auriane insisted the men were most likely ambushed by a band of Cheruscans before they got further than Wolverine Valley. But Athelinda knew each scout had taken a different track. Athelinda said nothing; both felt a shadow cast over them that was grimmer than the fast-falling night.

As the sinking sun touched the crowns of the mountain ash trees on the fort's western side, one of the sentries on the palisade gave a desolate wail.

Coniaric then called out, a hush in his voice: "Auriane. *Come.*"

Suddenly all the sentries were shouting, some cursing Wodan for treachery, some imprecating Fria, others crying out the names of kinsmen to come and look.

Auriane dashed to the palisade, not bothering with the ladder, letting the sentries haul her up.

The sight of the Primeval Worm could not have filled her with more horror. Before her, on the broad, gently sloping southern plain, she saw wisps of smoke drifting from myriad points of quivering light. She knew she was seeing a multitude of cookfires set out regularly as planted furrows—the fires of the legions.

They had come, and with baffling swiftness.

Auriane moved past warriors on their knees weeping and shaking their fists at the sky, and warriors unable to move, staring at the sight with mute terror. "It is the will of Fria," she said, fighting for strength, struggling to reassure. "The waiting is done."

She stopped before the faceless wood image of Fria mounted on the palisade, fashioned from a single, polished branch of ash. The sentries were silent for a moment, watching her sun-reddened face as she bowed her head and placed her palms on the wooden idol.

For the flash of one moment several thought she might perform some ritual of magic that would cause the Roman fires to vanish.

But she prayed, and they were at once caught up in the intensity of it; the effect on them was deep-reaching and physical, almost like the act of love.

"You who are pure light shed from the moon," she intoned, starting up unsteadily. *"You who are the dark as well as the light . . . in your all-merciful body, life and death are one."* Her voice gained in power. *"Embrace us now. Comfort us with your red-gold tears. Give us peace, the heavenly peace that . . . comes from knowing that in the beginning and the end of all times, you are benign."*

The gauzy contentment lasted but a moment, then evaporated like groundmist. Below, the whole population of the camp milled, looking numbed, uncomprehending, asking frightened questions for which no one had answers.

"Venison!" Coniaric exclaimed, shaking a fist at the field of fires. "Curses on them, they're cooking venison! And baking bread!" Both smells drifted separately from the legions' marching camp; they had the overwhelming power of dreams.

Athelinda climbed up to look. "With all the peoples of the earth at their feet," she exclaimed, "it's bewildering how eager they are for our empty horns and our nettle soup!"

Auriane shouted down to Thorgild, whom she saw fighting his way toward her through the crowd, "Break up the huts and carts. We raise the walls tonight!"

Thorgild nodded, and all worked feverishly by torchlight. There was nothing to be gained by keeping their fires extinguished; who would be fooled? All who could stand labored far into the night, laying fresh timbers along the walls until exhaustion came. Most fell asleep where they worked, succumbing to dreams of venison and bread.

Deep in the night Auriane found Athelinda still wakeful. They sat together, huddled under one ragged blanket. Auriane's tent was pitched strategically between Berinhard's stall and the hostages' wicker cage so she could watch out for the welfare of both. The hostages' human souls seemed long ago to have fled; some lesser, more bestial spirit animated those listless forms now. If they believed themselves close to freedom, they showed no sign.

There was no moon; Athelinda was just a voice and a snug presence. "You should sleep," her mother said.

"I know. But I must stay awake to have time to say farewell to everything."

"This is a wretched place to die," Athelinda said softly. "Animals will strip our bones. We'll have no funeral songs."

"Let the birds sing them." Auriane rested her head on her mother's shoulder. Her body was so taut and battle-ready Athelinda knew she did not feel as undaunted as she sounded.

"Even though we die tomorrow," Auriane went on, more frailty in her voice now, "I don't think our people will vanish from the earth. . . . Ramis said once . . . in coming ages our blood will mingle with the blood of others—and in nine generations' time, when the wheel turns again, we will overrun and humble *them*."

"Ah, I pray to be reborn in that time!"

"But she would say, Mother, it is as likely you would be reborn one of *them* as one of us."

"What an odd notion."

"Mother, I understand none of this! Just when I think I do, life is unmasked—and beneath is an even more frightful mask. . . . Why must all suffer so? It is my evil!"

"*No!*" Athelinda gripped Auriane's face in her hands and looked hard into her eyes in a way that made Auriane feel her mother's strength. She was the daughter of Gandrida now, tributary of a great river of earth-born power. "Never say it more. I know an innocent heart, and I know an accursed one. First Hertha, then Odberht smeared you with blood-soaked mud, but it did not stick. . . . You live in grace, you die in grace, like the lily, like the swan. Why can you not know it!"

Auriane let sobs surge from her in welcome waves. Her whole body was overtaken with the rhythmic contractions of long-needed release, but she muffled the sound as best she could, lest she terrify the others sleeping nearby. Her mother's hand crept over her own with the light, tentative movements of an autumn leaf; then Athelinda seized her hand with strength. When Auriane's tears were spent and she felt peaceful and empty, she said simply, "Hylda's oracle was false. I cannot save one flea."

"Not so. You *are* a living shield. I tell you your spirit is not the same since your time on Ramis' isle. . . . Godly light burns through your eyes. Do you not see how it heartens the troubled, if it does not literally preserve the flesh?"

They heard the moan of a woman in labor. Auriane thought of the sleek, wet form soon to emerge, a fresh creation to be devoured by this savage world.

Avenahar! Have you been consumed already? And I thought I would see you by last summer's end! I will see you never again in this life.

"No, I do not see it. Sometimes, though, when I stare into the holy fire, I *know* in the beat of my blood that this is just the part of life that shows—that if we saw all of it, we would understand."

There was a forlorn stretch of silence broken only by the churring of a nightjar.

"Auriane . . ." Athelinda ventured forward like someone testing a plank over a chasm. Auriane stiffened, alerted to danger. "I . . . I cannot let myself be taken captive tomorrow and made into a thrall. Tell me you understand! At dawn I mean to ask Thrusnelda for a draught of poison."

"Mother, no! Do not leave me!"

"Daughter, you cannot fool me into believing we've any chance of victory."

"I would not try. But I won't act as the Fates. Let the gods say it!" She pressed her mother's hand to her cheek. "I beg you! All I have loved are gone!"

Athelinda sighed heavily. "For *you*, then, dear child, I'll live on a little longer. But just a *little*. I'll wait until they're pouring over the walls before I take my poison."

Athelinda drew Auriane's hand tightly to her chest, stroking her hair. In that position they fell into fitful sleep. Auriane dreamed of trolls' halls, quaking earth, dancing walls reflecting fire, and groaning voices underground begging for help.

When Auriane awakened, all still lay in predawn darkness. She disengaged herself from her mother without disturbing her and lit a torch from the central hearthfire. Working swiftly, quietly, she began drawing water from the well, meaning to soak the front gate so it would not burn. Witgern and Sigwulf were roused soon after and without speech began working alongside her. Gradually others rose in dozens, men of Sigwulf's Companions and her own. While they labored, magpies and jays started their raucous music as if this dawn heralded a day like any other, to be filled with hunting, feasting or ploughing.

Auriane directed the aged, the children and the women who could not fight to the sheds along the north wall of the fort, where the approach was too steep for an army to attempt entry. Among them she saw Sunia, huddled in the gloom of the sunken floor of one of the huts, round eyes watching her mournfully. Auriane strode toward her and took Sunia's hands in her own.

"Sunia, you have been a great and good friend."

Sunia gave Auriane one of her cautious smiles. "Can I . . . can I have a piece of your cloak?"

Auriane hesitated a moment, then took her dagger, pierced her cloak near the hem, and tore off a strip.

"And wet it with your spittle?" The spittle was said to carry the essence of the soul. Auriane complied. If this pitiful charm made Sunia feel safer, where was the harm?

"We'll not be seated near each other in the Sky Hall," Sunia said, eyes downcast. "I'll be by the thralls, and you, next to Baldemar. So farewell for all time."

"Sunia!" Auriane moved toward her. Sunia clasped thin arms around her.

A sentry's cry shocked all to stillness: *"Look ahead!* They've readied themselves!"

Auriane left Sunia and quickly made her way to the palisade.

Through the rolling ground mist and gauzy dawn light she saw a legion assembled on the gently sloped plain—a dark sinister square of men at a distance of three arrow shots, protected by a gleaming carapace of massive, interlocking shields. Their javelins formed a bed of spikes, all in neat rows. They were a single weapon trained on the fort, one monstrous machine with the power of gods. Cavalry was arrayed on their flanks, and in back of them a second force waited in reserve, almost concealed in the purple-black shadows of the mountain ash trees.

Panic stopped some hearts and caused others to race. Men went for their weapons, some moving with noble calm, some breaking into a frenzied run, stumbling over empty cookpots, loose timbers and picked-clean bones. Children wailed. A number of warriors, expecting to die and caring for nothing, broke into the last of the rations and consumed them all—they at least would not die hungry. Most, though, could not have swallowed the smallest bite of gruel and cared little that their share had been taken from them.

Athelinda gave Auriane some dried millet bread. She took it so Athelinda would think she ate it, but hid it in her cloak.

Auriane then saw that quantities of water and pitch were boiled so they could be relayed to the walls when needed and cast down on the enemy. At the same time Sigwulf ordered the camp's hoard of spears brought out. Then she directed the women who were not war-trained to collect stones of various sizes, which they arranged in piles alongside the palisade. Those stones look like cairns for the dead, Auriane thought. All the while she kept an anxious eye on the sentries, who were to sound a horn if the Romans moved.

She found Sigwulf, and together they selected the men of their Companions who were best with a spear and stationed them on the palisade. The boiling pitch was brought, and she readied the lifts. The main body of the warriors—but four thousand and more, all pitiful skeletons hung with rags—were formed up on the casting ground to act as reserves for the men on the palisade.

Then Auriane mounted Berinhard and rode the circuit of the walls, looking carefully for places where they might be breached. She felt spasms of hollow anguish alternating with strengthening bursts of rage. From time to time all about dissolved into dreams; surely this was all no more than a hearthfire tale. Was that truly a legion out there or some phantom shape, conjured up by a mind overwrought by tragedy?

The palisade was thick with men standing shoulder to shoulder, brown cloaks fluttering solemnly in the first stirrings of breeze. Bowmen stood between the spear bearers, their pitch-smeared arrows ready.

As she rode between the two crumbling wells near the east wall, she was approached by a man she had never before encountered in the camp. He was a musician—under one arm was a well-polished lyre carved with cleverly interlaced snakes and vines. The man grasped Berinhard's rein and regarded her with bold reverence. He would have possessed the angular beauty of some young hero were that face not so elongated and gaunt. His eyes were light and luminous like an owl's, seeming to gaze inward and outward at once.

"Who are you and what are you doing here?" she asked sharply.

"I am Eota, greatest songmaker of all the tribes, lately from the hall of King Chariomerus, whom you so boldly defeated in battle, glorious be your name."

She scarcely felt the praise. It came too glibly and often from foreign travelers. "You chose a poor time to pay us a visit. This is not an honorable enemy who respects the nobility of musicians. You will be enslaved."

"Or killed, perhaps. But I had to come here to see your face, Auriane, before I died."

This shifted her off balance. Rarely was she presented with such clear evidence of the great regard in which she was held among neighboring tribes. Apparently even Sigwulf's victory foreigners ascribed to *her* battle-luck.

She wanted to say: *Look at the bitter beaten mortal before you! Surely the sight of me is the undoing of all your adulation. I die alone today, wrest from my child, after having failed in all I sought.*

He seemed to see only what might have been.

"You do me greater honor than I deserve," she replied, feeling uncomfortable. Then she added, smiling, "If I am to live in your songs, *you* must live. Go now, and hide in the well in back of the midden."

She rode on, but Eota did not move; she felt that spectral gaze clinging to her back. Finally she turned about and said, "Eota! Beware of reverence, it's a trick of the mind. And when you sing, do not forget *them*"—she indicated the pitiful host—"all these who did not run away."

Eota nodded, still staring. Auriane rode past the wicker cage in which the two surviving hostages were kept, and held out to them the millet bread she could not eat. She watched them as they accepted it without any show of gratefulness, divided it, and ate it. She said to them with her eyes, *This is how I treat my enemy.*

One met her gaze. He was wrapped in a horse blanket; only his eyes were visible. There was no human understanding in that look; it was the unblinking stare of a lizard. She knew he counted her feeding him not kindness but prudence: She wanted a good report made of her when she was at his people's mercy.

She then rode before the assembled warriors and dismounted beside Grunig, who had begun the ritual of consecrating the host. After Grunig thrust a ceremonial spear into a cauldron of horse's blood, then raised it up to Wodan and traced the sign for victory in the air, Auriane tore open the leather pouch containing the ashes of the white cow and cat she had sacrificed in autumn. Calling on Fria, she cast them onto the air and let the wind disperse them over the armed multitude.

Sigwulf shouted from the palisade, "A horseman comes!"

Auriane mounted the walk. A single cavalryman had broken away from the legion. As he galloped closer, they recognized Siggo, a distant kinsman of Sigwulf's, captured in a raid four summers ago. Siggo was now part of the auxiliary cavalry of the Eighth Augusta.

Siggo was greeted sulkily by the warriors on the wall as he pulled his horse to a halt below them. She heard Sigwulf mutter loudly about a "strutting cock who traded honor for a richly caparisoned horse."

Siggo wore a helmet of gold with a long yellow plume and a beautifully worked breastplate buckled over a leather jerkin embroidered with scarlet. His horse was resplendent in parade trappings; saddlecloth and bridle glinted with bronze medallions and pendants of brilliantly colored enamel. His mount's head was fitted with a bronze parade frontlet with intricate eyepieces. All stared in fascination, for the horse's armor made the beast appear as much a warrior as its rider.

Siggo removed his helmet, revealing yellow-blond hair cropped short and combed forward in the Roman fashion. But the warriors on the wall noticed foremost how healthy and well-fed he was.

"I would speak to the daughter of Baldemar!" Siggo shouted out importantly.

Auriane called down in a strong, clear voice, "I am here, Siggo."

And now Siggo stared, obviously appalled by the condition of his fellow tribespeople—they looked like wild men who never knew the shelter of roof or hearth. Their sullen, threatening mood unnerved him—he had agreed to this meeting only because he was promised a promotion to officer's rank—and because he believed he would be protected by the power of the kinship bond. But now he was not so certain. Starvation and fear had worn away at the constraints of ancient law and made madmen of them. He wondered if his own brothers would avenge him if these men on the wall struck him down.

"Auriane!" Siggo began, fighting the impulse to wheel his horse about and flee. "It is no use! You must open the gate to them. They found your child!"

Auriane gave a low cry heard only by those near. But she kept her head proudly raised, revealing nothing of her agony to the man below.

"*Avenahar,* that is her name, is it not?" Siggo continued. "A black-haired girl aged just over a year?"

The very air scalded her skin. She felt she had been run through by a sword still glowing from the forge.

"The babe will be spared if you release the hostages now, and throw open the gate. If you make them force their way in, they will show you no mercy. Obey and open the gates, and the babe will live!"

"*Liar!*" dozens of tribesmen shouted at once.

"Look how pretty he is with his sassy plumes!" Sigwulf taunted.

"Go back to your hot baths, Roman slave!" another shouted.

"Wine-swilling dog of a dog!" Coniaric cried. "Show us your tricks! Roll over for us the way you do for them!"

"Siggo eats lying down!"

"And loves standing up!"

"Yes! With tender, half-grown boys in the baths!"

"Silence!" Auriane cried, her voice piercing the din. She wondered if Siggo saw how she trembled. Fastila took her arm.

"It could be a lie," Fastila said in a fevered whisper, trying to will Auriane strength with her eyes, her voice. "It could be a trick! Who would dare seize a child in Ramis' keeping?"

"And it could be true," Auriane replied. "Our last Veleda was taken alive by them." She closed her eyes. "True or no," she whispered, "there is only one answer to give."

Once again the gods leave me no choice. Ramis, can they have wrest the child from you? Or perhaps you gave Avenahar up for some dark, obscure purpose of your own? Avenahar! If this be no trick, my next words condemn you to death.

Siggo could not see that within, her heart had collapsed; he saw only a gaze so brilliant with scorn he felt he might be scorched, and an intimidating mane of hair flared menacingly by a sudden wind.

"Go from us, Siggo," Auriane replied in a low voice. "It shall not be. Do you think I will bargain for the life of only *my* child when children of every clan have been murdered by you or taken into slavery? Do you think I would betray all these valorous ones by opening the gates? You've lived with them too long, Siggo—their ways have poisoned your blood. Leave us!"

Now I should rip out my tongue. I am populating the heavens with loved ones whose deaths I have caused.

Auriane's words brought a fresh cacophony of approving shouts from the warriors on the wall.

"We'll use your guts for lyre strings, spawn of a troll!"

"Heap of dung from a niding's pig!"

"Lice-ridden dog of a guest-murderer!"

Siggo's courage broke. Without bothering to replace his helmet, he yanked his horse about and urged it to a gallop.

One of the warriors on the wall—Auriane never knew who—hurled a spear.

"Do not!" she shouted. "He is an envoy!"

But it was too late. The weapon was well aimed; it struck Siggo in the back of the neck, penetrating through. Siggo toppled from the horse, writhed fitfully for a time, then lay motionless.

The envoy was slain before the legions' eyes.

The riderless horse cantered back toward the Roman lines. All along the palisade a great cheer was raised.

Auriane hurled a spear with all her strength, aiming at the distant legion. *"Murderers!"* she cried out in a savage voice she did not recognize as her own. The wind caught her spear and carried it, extending its flight to an impossible length. But still it landed far short of its mark. Dimly she was aware the flight of that spear was not unlike the course of her life—always she struggled mightily, and it was never enough.

Moments later came the brassy bleat of a Roman trumpet. Auriane saw shifting movement within the dark ranks. The first cohorts of the legion were advancing.

The bowmen on the wall readied their weapons. When the first line of soldiers were within arrow-shot, she dropped her arm.

The fire arrows flew. Most thudded harmlessly against the heavy rectangular shields.

The men of the legion halted at this distance, and there was a pause during which the warriors on the wall saw much mysterious and purposeful movement. It seemed something bulky was being unloaded from carts.

Then a structure that resembled a great shed on wheels was dragged into view. It was made of screens sheeted with iron plates; the whole was about two horse-lengths long and a horse-length wide. Another came behind it, and another. It was apparent they meant to form a corridor with them so they could approach the wall in safety.

"Mantlets," Auriane said in a low voice to Sigwulf. Decius had described them to her. "Under their protection they'll most likely bring up scaling ladders."

"What skulking cowards!" Sigwulf spat the words, his weathered, pockmarked face contracted into a troll-scowl. "And where is their God-Emperor Domitian? Why is he not at their head? They have a chief who does not lead!"

Moments later the bowmen let fly a barrage of arrows at the slowly approaching mantlets, but they clattered off the iron sheeting and dotted the field with shivering tongues of flame.

Auriane shouted at them to cease. Some new and sinister activity at the wings of the Roman formation caught her attention. She felt her body tense, though she saw nothing, for all were momentarily blinded by the rising sun—a disadvantage she was certain the enemy took into account.

"What is it?" Sigwulf asked, frowning, expecting her to know because of her long association with Decius.

There was no time to reply. With a certainty that was part instinct, part rapid deduction, she cried out, *"Down!"*

Most dropped to the floor of the sentry walk in time.

Above them was the rushing sound of air being torn by heavy missiles. Twenty-one men were violently thrown back onto the hard ground ten feet below.

The Romans had been setting up catapults, fifty, perhaps sixty of them. The women stationed in the rear of the assembled warriors raised a cry, dropped their staves and stones and sprinted forward to see if their own husbands were among the fallen. Five found their men dead or dying and collapsed onto their bodies, wailing and tearing at their hair. One took up her husband's sword and stabbed herself through the heart.

Auriane had no choice but to order a party of men to drag them off; this tragedy played out in full view of the army was a sight too demoralizing to be borne. Later she would feel sorrow for them; now she felt herself a being composed solely of fire and iron.

The men on the wall did not dare rise; volley after volley of bolts ripped and slashed the air just above their heads.

"Wodan, preserve your worshipful servants!" she heard one man pray repeatedly in a piteous, quavering voice. Auriane felt doom swiftly gaining ground. A part of her accepted it without struggle. What was left of life?

After a moment of paying close attention, she began to recognize a certain erratic rhythm in the volleys. In an instant she judged to be safe, she stood up quickly, tried to assess what the Romans were doing, and dropped back to her hands and knees.

Fastila and Sigwulf were alarmed by the look in Auriane's face.

"Auriane, what is it?" Fastila whispered.

"They are bringing up some sort of siege tower," she replied. "A small one. Doubtless it's filled with soldiers. They think they've cleared the wall—now they mean to occupy it. The tower will drop a plank and they'll rush out in force."

"We'll have to set it afire," Sigwulf said. Auriane did not think that would succeed; it seemed to be covered with hides, and doubtless they were water-soaked. The men inside were well protected; until the tower put down its plank, the soldiers within would not be exposed to weapons fire.

Sigwulf signaled to the archers.

"Aim high," he ordered. Auriane was glad of his calm; he seemed immovable as a ring-stone. His bristling black beard and wild, tangled hair were near white with fine dust and dirt. She had always seen him as a problem to be gotten round, but in that moment she felt a powerful surge of affection for him.

He withstands this better than anyone, she thought; his habitual lack of reflection on this day serves him well. To be a creature that lives only to act, without wondering why or worrying over what will come of it!

The bowmen set their arrows alight, sprang up, and fired. Seven or eight hit their mark; they landed high on the cumbersome tower's sides. The bowmen fired twice more. Soon it bristled with flaming arrows, but the flames would not spread. The siege tower, primitive and terrifying, continued its ponderous, swaying progress.

Sigwulf said grimly, "It is made of some material that does not burn."

The catapults responded to the assault on the tower with an angry barrage, and it seemed to Auriane their firing was purposefully more irregular now, so that it was impossible to find a safe moment to stand and aim a weapon.

"Retire to the main body," Auriane said to the archers, trying to make the words sound like a command rather than an admission of defeat. "We'll have to destroy them as they try to mount the wall."

Sigwulf leapt to the ground and shouted for the wedge formation, in which every warrior knew his place. Auriane walked through the ranks, comforting as best she could those who seemed near to panic, explaining carefully what was happening, cautioning them against the dangers of bunching too closely together once the battle began. Then she took her place at the front of the wedge, with Witgern and Sigwulf; Fastila was just behind her. She felt they formed a last brave island of humanity, ready to be pulled down into a cold, green-black bottomless sea.

Now they could just see the tower's pitched hide-covered roof above the wall as it lurched with irregularities in the terrain, approaching with patient, bestial determination.

The sun grew hot as they waited. She listened to the sounds that were near so she would not hear the sounds just beyond the wall: the whine of flies, the whispers of the bolts overhead, the rising and falling notes of the women's wails, the weak but insistent cry of a child, the rough guttural prayers men muttered over their weapons. Everywhere was the reek of old sweat and the smell of sickness. From somewhere behind her a man dropped to the ground, prey to the illness that came with constant hunger. She heard rapid scuffling as his kinsmen removed him to relative safety.

But in spite of herself she heard the scraping sounds beyond the wall as scaling ladders were placed against them, and the creak of wheels.

The beast is so close we feel its dank breath.

CHAPTER XXIX

Auriane felt Witgern's gaze on her and turned to meet his eye.
In that look was the sorrow of a hundred last embraces. *We
married after all, did we not?* she imagined he thought. *Our house
was the war camp. We cast our lot together, we fought together,
and do we not love? Close kinsmen, wife and husband, could not
love more.*

She gave him a bare smile, meant as acknowledgment of this
lifetime bond. Yes, Witgern, Auriane replied with her eyes. In
this world where things and people never properly fit, I suppose
this honest understanding between us is close as I will come to a
great love. I understand nothing, and it is time already to die. I do
not even hate the enemy—it is all too overwhelming for hatred.

Fastila saw the look they exchanged, and Auriane felt her
jealousy as heat from a hearthfire. Auriane at once felt regret and
pity for her.

Is there no help for us? Auriane wondered. She would have him,
he would have me, and I would have one who exists nowhere. And
today it all ends with our souls half full, our courses half run—the
prize goes to others.

The tower's bridge crashed resoundingly onto the wall. Before
it could disgorge all its men Sigwulf and Auriane burst forward,
spears aloft, their Companions close behind. And then the sky was
full of spears arcing gracefully into the air. Some must have met

569

their mark—from behind the wall she heard torn-off screams of agony and the thud of falling bodies.

The catapult fire ceased, for the legionaries were now in its path. The sudden silence was horrible as their whistling noise had been. The Chattian band clambered up the ladders onto the palisade walk. Auriane and Sigwulf dropped their spears and charged the tower bridge with swords drawn, followed by as many warriors as could find a place on it. The impetus of the charge drove the Romans back to the opening of the tower. For long the Chattians held them at bay, and the Romans got no farther than the center of their bridge.

Auriane felt a hope-drunken madness seize her then. Though Sigwulf battled next to her and she felt the press of their warriors at her back, she fought alone, taking one opponent at a time, seeking the exposed throat, the unguarded moment, feeling her sword flash out with its own intelligence. Each time it pierced flesh and bone and a soldier toppled to the turf far below, the familiar dark pulse of ecstasy came. She felt herself all ether and fire, boundless and tireless, the one life set between her people and death.

But this rapture was all too brief.

Gradually she realized she had less and less room to maneuver. Too many warriors had crowded onto the bridge. Auriane watched, horrified, as three of their own were pushed off, to be casually gutted by the soldiers below. Auriane and Sigwulf together screamed at the men behind to back up and give them room—but everyone was shouting and no one heeded or heard. Soon the Chattians were hopelessly in each other's way. Many were struck down by the spears of their overeager fellows behind them.

The Romans, by contrast, continued to advance slowly, methodically, four abreast with shields locked. Relentlessly they came, gradually pushing their way beyond the bridge's center. Auriane felt herself being dragged back as if she were caught in the suction of a spent wave.

Elsewhere along the wall, all was going badly. Witgern worked frantically alongside all who could find a place, struggling to push scaling ladders off the wall. Once he managed to tip a bucket of boiling pitch onto a line of legionaries ascending a ladder; as the pitch splashed down and got beneath the soldiers' armor, their screams rose above all other battle sounds. But more ladders were brought by the dozens; soon the warriors on the palisade walk were overwhelmed.

And then all became smoking chaos; no one could have known what happened in every part of the field. But Auriane saw well enough the Romans controlled the bridge. From there they spilled out onto the sentry walk. Within moments the warriors packed about her were pushed or forced to leap down into the yard.

Before Auriane leapt down, she briefly saw what passed elsewhere.

And she knew they were done.

The fort was a ship with a dozen leaks in its hull, ready to go rapidly down. Scaling ladders had been set in countless places. Soldiers streaked up them with an agility and orderliness born of long training, then fanned out along the palisade walk, where they hurled javelins into the melee below. Enough legionaries had broken in to overwhelm the tribesmen defending the gate; slowly, from the inside, the Romans began pulling it open. Soldiers rushed in like a river that had burst its dam.

There is little left to do, she realized, but die nobly.

Auriane and Sigwulf struggled to form the surviving tribesmen into a wedge formation, to face the enemy ranks pouring in through the opened gate. Then this ragged band of four thousand and more, all that was left of the barbarian army, charged at a half run.

But the palisade walk was thick with legionaries now—and they had the advantage that comes with high ground. Their javelins did terrible damage. Then, at a flag signal accompanied by two short trumpet blasts, every second soldier dropped into the yard and these began to form into ranks. The timbers reinforcing the wall caught fire, and a brisk wind blew pine smoke into the yard, mercifully veiling much of the bloody spectacle.

Javelins rained on the Chattians. When the smoke parted, Auriane saw the bodies of her tribespeople lay in mounds. Once she vaulted over two still-living men pinned together by a single, powerful javelin thrust. When the iron wall of Roman shields was close enough so that Auriane could see the thunderbolts embossed on them, the Chattian warriors let fly their spears. But these were no more than small irritants to that advancing wall of steel.

Then the legionaries drew their swords. Frantically, desperately, Auriane struggled to pull injured warriors out of the path of those heavy, tramping feet, trying to put her Companions' wooden shields back into their hands. Through the smoke she saw Witgern doing the same; he was dragging a badly wounded man by the feet, removing him moments before he would have fallen beneath the soldiers' boots. The legionaries were one faceless, pitiless, many-legged beast, their swords a row of spiked tongues thrust from that darkly gleaming shell of shields.

The two forces met. Auriane felt the tension of a sword engaging her own. In the next instant her tribesmen flooded in around her. She was lifted from her feet by the surge of men. A legionary shield-boss badly bruised her side, and knocked her to her knees.

It was as if a great iron hand pushed them back. Beside her, Sigwulf slipped in gore and fell on his back.

"Sigwulf!" she screamed unheard. *"No!"* He fell beneath the line of Roman shields, ready to be consumed by the beast's spiked teeth. She protected him as long as she could, frenziedly deflecting the sword blows aimed at him.

But his end was inevitable. Their eyes met once. Even through his terror she knew he recognized her effort to save him. Then he was trampled underfoot, and a sword came down swiftly, efficiently, on his neck.

Sigwulf was dead.

Sigwulf! she cried with all her mind. All that raw animal courage availed you nothing. You end your life as a scrap of food for a beast that is never filled. The Fates played a cruel jest when they gave you the name *"Victorious Wolf."* So much for the magical protection of names.

Auriane fought defensively, crushed among her tribesmen, her eyes blurred with tears. First singly, then by dozens, her fellow warriors broke and fled. Some sought death by running to the wall, purposefully putting themselves in the path of the javelins. Others leapt into a thatched hut that was aflame, immolating themselves.

Auriane saw numbly that among these was Thrusnelda. The old priestess's robes caught fire first, and she paused, glorious in a corona of flame like some minor deity. Then she shrieked a curse and flew into the inferno. Auriane's capacity to feel horror was dulled by the day's steady assaults on it, and she watched with an odd, mute detachment the death of the old priestess who had patiently explained the world to her as a child.

But the majority of the Chattians ran like stampeding beasts toward the far end of the fort's enclosure; they were a swift-running current of men in which she refused to be caught. She cried out, she imprecated, desperate to rally them once more.

The gods see us. We must die fighting.

But now few cared. The Chattian defense was utterly broken.

Coniaric and a small cluster of warriors caught hold of her cloak and cried, "Auriane! Die with us!" She could scarce comprehend that they still believed in her holiness.

"Leave me be!" she shouted as she struggled away from them. "I am a curse!"

Now she ran against the tide of fleeing men, not even attempting to dodge the hail of javelins, protected somehow by her own madness, meaning first to find Athelinda and wondering if her mother still lived. She passed men trying to conceal themselves behind the heaps of dead; the legionaries found them and cut them down. Slowly she fought her way to the animal pens where Berinhard was tethered.

She meant to perform one last rite.

Long ago Baldemar had offered her in marriage to the god as an appeasement gift, and good fortune followed for many years. What if today she made another appeasement gift, this time ritually offering her life? Perhaps it would soften some of the Fates' anger toward her people. It would have to be done in the proper way, beginning with the prayer of sacrifice. . . .

Somehow Fastila found her and half ran to keep apace. "Auriane!" she cried. "Let me die next to you!"

"If you wish to," Auriane shouted back, "then you shall. Come!" They had not made much progress when Fastila saw Witgern, face down in the dust.

Together Auriane and Fastila pulled him up. Witgern was stunned but without fatal wounds. Life flowed back into his face when he saw Auriane, and he smiled the careless, mischievous smile of a boy who has played a joke that has come off badly—a smile absurdly out of place. He managed to walk, leaning heavily on both of them.

"However you end your life, Auriane, that way I will go too," he said after a time.

"I would be greatly honored, Witgern." She found herself cheered by this offer of company—it seemed less desolate to sacrifice her life with friends. She looked about for Athelinda, wondering if her mother had kept to her promise to take poison. Then at last Auriane saw her, near the entrance to the horse sheds. Athelinda seemed strikingly composed as she looked out upon world's end.

As Auriane made her way toward her mother, she heard the shrieks of children as the Roman soldiers found the warriors' families. She prayed they would consider what a handsome price that hoard of young fair captives would bring in the slave markets, and let them live.

Sunia is among them. And I can do nothing for her—except hope my appeasement gift betters her lot, too.

Auriane was seized by a need to hurry. She sensed there was little time if she would do what she planned. The battle was nearly ended; the slaughter was slowing. The soldiers were more concerned with taking captives now, herding the women and children into groups of ten so they could be chained and put into carts.

When this party of three came to the animal sheds, Athelinda flung herself on Auriane. "Child! You are alive!"

"You did not take it, thank all the gods!"

Athelinda held out the leather pouch that held the dark herbs. "Five and ten times I started, and stopped. I could not leave you."

"Mother, what will become of you!" They locked in a desperate embrace. After a moment, while still holding tightly to her mother, Auriane said to Fastila, "Go, and bring two horses from the stalls, one for you and one for Witgern."

Without questioning her, Fastila darted off to get two horses.

"Auriane, what are the horses for?" Athelinda asked.

Auriane said only, "Mother, you must not watch."

Through the confusion and dust, a lone Roman cavalryman approached them at a gallop. He pulled his mount to a rearing halt before Athelinda and Auriane.

"You are Auriane," he shouted down to her.

Her right hand moved slowly toward the grip of her sword.

"I am," she answered. She looked up into a face that was rough-carved but not unkind. The cavalryman removed his plumed helmet and leaned closer, speaking rapidly, keeping his voice low.

"I have come to release you from your fate, if you would have it so. I am sent by one you will never know, who wants only to see you live free. Come quickly. I have a horse ready for you outside the gate—you must not ride your own. Put on this hooded cloak. The camp is surrounded by cavalry but I have leave to pass. There is a fresh horse waiting at a station thirteen miles to the east. Hurry. I bring you safety and long life."

She stared at him, at first not quite believing what she heard.

"What is this? You would set *me alone* free?"

"Not *I*, actually, but another."

"This lone sample of kindness after you've skewered children and put whole villages to the sword must be amusing to your gods. Are you mad?"

"No, lady, and you must hurry!"

Auriane stepped decisively away from him. "You should have come with a thousand horses. Never would I save myself alone. You insult me."

She saw the barest sign of offense in the cavalryman's eye. She realized he was not an evil man, amazing as that seemed at that moment.

"Tell whoever sent you I am grateful to him," she said in a gentler voice. "I do not hate life. I truly wish it were possible to live. But my answer must be no."

"Auriane, go with him!" Athelinda wailed, shaking her head. "One of us can live!"

"I cannot do it, Mother," Auriane said softly.

"Lady, you are foolish," the cavalryman replied. He wheeled his horse about and galloped off into the smoke.

A distant trumpet sounded a fanfare of shrieking, arrogant notes; it was the signal for the Roman retreat. Now the soldiers gave themselves up entirely to reaping this fine harvest of captives, most of whom were so stunned they hardly needed bonds. As Witgern and Fastila led two bony horses from the sheds, Auriane looked about the fort one last time, that smoking remnant of the world she knew. Everywhere was a too-sudden stillness that was almost awkward. The fruits of conquest—the dead—were strewn everywhere. Thoroughly finished and harmless now, they seemed to mock the ferocity of their conqueror. Silent, gaped mouths cried out: *Is this, then, what you wanted? You have it then. The strong can destroy the weak. Rejoice in that, murderers.*

She turned away from Athelinda, grasped Berinhard's mane and pulled herself with difficulty onto his back, for she was near exhaustion.

Athelinda seized Berinhard's rein. "Auriane, what is this? *What are you doing?*"

Auriane's eyes filled with tears and she could not answer. Instead, she turned her face to the sky and began saying the ritual words of offering.

"Lord of the Sky whose bride I am, receive me on this day. Fria, Mother of All, raise me up to your sky-domain, for I perish in your name. . . ."

Witgern and Fastila understood now what Auriane meant to do. They mounted their horses—Witgern with noble confidence, Fastila with some hesitancy.

Athelinda shouted *"No!"* in a desolate howl that trailed into

silence, shredding Auriane's heart. Berinhard reared in fright.
Auriane tried to wrench the rein away from her—what more could
be said or done?—but Athelinda still held to it tightly. Those fists
were stone.

The three turned their horses toward the open gate, positioning
them so they stood abreast. Auriane and Witgern drew their
swords; Fastila raised her spear. Auriane saw Fastila's fright and
misery—too late the young warrior-priestess discovered that
dying with Witgern did not appeal as much as living with him.

"No!" came Athelinda's cry, weaker now.

"Mother, stand away!" Auriane spoke through streaming tears.
"You will draw their attention to us! I beg you, let me go! By this
day's end, no matter *how* we die, we will be together. If I offer
myself, it might undo the fact that Baldemar lies unavenged!"

Athelinda understood the rightness of this, but at the last mother
love ruled; it was a primeval flood tide that bore off all the flimsy
housings built by the mind, older and wiser than all man-made
laws of vengeance. She kept her fierce grip on the rein.

With her sword Auriane indicated the distant legion in reserve,
visible through the open gate; the soldiers stood at quiet attention,
a dark band of men on the brown earth mottled with old snow, half
hidden in a grove of spruce and linden, their upraised signal flags
whipping in the wind. Grimly Witgern and Fastila nodded.

"There is the enemy. We will die striking them down and give
ourselves back to the earth."

They kicked their heels against their horses' sides. Witgern's
and Fastila's mounts burst into a gallop. Berinhard followed at a
frustrated canter, half dragging Athelinda.

"Mother! Let me go!"

Auriane saw then a party of soldiers within the fort recognized
her. One nodded curtly and an order was barked. Auriane shut her
eyes; this was past enduring.

She raised her sword. "Beloved mother, forgive me."

And she brought it down on the taut rein. It snapped; Athelinda
stumbled forward. Berinhard danced sideways as if surprised by
his sudden freedom, then he shot forward like a bolt from a
catapult.

Auriane guided him with her hands. By the time he streaked
through the open gate, Berinhard hurtled past the slower mounts of
Fastila and Witgern.

"Auriane!" Athelinda's shriek pierced her like an arrow.

• • •

Athelinda dropped to her hands and knees before a muddy pool that bloomed with blood. She scooped up a handful of mud and smeared it over her face, still moaning ceaselessly, *"No . . . no!"* One of Thrusnelda's surviving apprentices caught her shoulders and steadied her.

"My lady, it is her fate," the priestess said urgently. "The great Lady who birthed us all loves her still." But Athelinda was past hearing.

The poison. Take it now, you've lost all reason not to take it. Quickly!

Athelinda struggled to her feet, fumbling for the pouch of poisons at her belt.

It was knocked from her hand with the butt of a javelin. Then hard, swift soldier's hands caught her from behind and dragged her toward a line of chained captives. She did not struggle or scream.

Athelinda accepted it as the Fates' will. She was meant to live.

None in the line of old women with whom she was chained recognized her mud-smeared face, and so did not realize Athelinda herself, daughter of Gandrida, wife of Baldemar, was manacled next to them like the commonest of farmwives.

Auriane, Witgern and Fastila bore down upon the legion, with Berinhard well in the lead. Raw cries were torn from Auriane's throat; she could no more stop them than she could control her horse. He bolted forward in a furious, headlong rush, belly low to the ground, an equine storm with whipping tail and mane.

When the legionaries on the wall were alerted to this breakout, five whirled about and hurled javelins at the flying horses.

Fastila was struck in the back. The heavy missile penetrated through her and pierced her horse's neck. The beast arced into the air, throwing up its head as a spasm of agony twisted its body, then fell heavily onto its side. Fastila died at once.

Witgern looked back in farewell, responding instinctively with the whispered words, *"Fria, be gentle with her soul."* Auriane, far in the lead and intent on her quarry, did not even know. Her face was pressed close to her horse's rhythmically surging neck; her spirit lived in his clamoring hooves. Her upraised blade was an exclamation of outrage at the Fates.

The javelins fell well short of Witgern. But moments afterward, his mount found a rabbit hole and cartwheeled onto its back.

Witgern was thrown free; he lay stunned and motionless on the ground.

Auriane galloped on alone.

The first rank of the legion loomed close. They stood at stony attention, concealing well their alarm at the sight of this flying horse, this frightful vision of womanly thunder bearing down on them. Their commander, calm and dignified on his mount, spoke rapid instructions, and signal flags whipped about, relaying orders to the men.

Auriane knew only that she vaulted into emptiness. Life's garments were torn off by the wind, piece by piece, as she sped from all she was: shame-ridden daughter, sorrowing mother, doubtful apprentice of Ramis, debtor to the Lightning Oak. Her spirit dissolved into solemn, active quiet; the world about became vastly barren. She was naked and wet in a gale, a shivering babe cast down to be reborn on the blasted plains of Helle, she whose cackle was like the crack of ice.

I know now why old Helle's face is blue. It is the cold, the awful eternal cold.

We are all motherless. My life was a cloak rent with a knife—slowly, as the years turned, it all unraveled. I struggled well and mightily, only to hasten the pull on the threads. Ramis is a clever liar—the stuff of everything is *grief*. Of what use were the god-blessed victories? I do not want to play any part, noblewoman or thrall, in a world where gallantry is punished and beasts with tearing teeth are loosed at the last.

The doomed bride rushes into the arms of her cruel bridegroom. I despise you, Wodan, for accepting this shameful sacrifice. I loathe you, Fria, for bringing forth this iron-cold world. Great Wolf, open wide your jaws.

When Auriane was so close the men of the first rank could see the fury in her eyes, one thought sprang into many minds: How I would disgrace the standards if I ran from a single woman!

But *was* that a woman? Or a northern Medusa erupting out of the bogs, come to rend their orderliness with her wildness? She was the earth-born emanation of all they were disciplined to force back into the dark: primeval rage, impetuosity, ecstasy. She came not to judge but to destroy, simply because it was *time*—rational man had ruled too long, and nature was out of patience.

In the final moments Auriane forgot utterly where she was. Sky, earth and forest were stirred in one living cauldron until they blurred into lambent mist. She urged Berinhard on not to death, but to victory in the sacred race. The bristling wall of legionaries was her tribespeople, urging her on.

We have won! The rest are so far back I cannot see them. There is Decius, hailing me and complaining I've done it all wrong. There is Baldemar, standing before the Eastre fire, sword drawn to protect it forever. All is as it should be. I know I fought hard enough, by the mothering moon, the wheeling stars. No one could have fought harder.

She struck the first rank. It gave way a fraction too late; the impact of her horse broke a soldier's shield arm and knocked another under iron hooves. The second rank opened, then the third and fourth in rapid succession.

As Berinhard ploughed through mail-covered men, his hooves sending sparks as they struck the iron bindings of shields, Auriane brought down her sword in a furious rhythm, striking helmets, crossed javelins, laminated iron cuirasses, and occasionally flesh— but no drawn swords. Strong hands reached for her horse's bridle, and javelins were extended across his path, slowing him.

She realized then they were not fighting back. They meant to evade her blows, then pull her from her horse and disarm her.

"Fight! Fight me! I want to die!"

Then Decius' warning flashed into her mind: "Promise me you will *never let my people take you alive.*" No admonition he had ever given her was spoken with such heartfelt urgency.

How pleased Decius would be to know I ended heeding his advice.

She grasped her sword securely in both hands and raised it high, meaning to plunge it into her heart.

Swiftly she brought it down. But her sword struck calfskin-covered wooden planks—one of the legionaries just managed to thrust his shield between the sword's point and her breast. Then powerful hands seized her from behind, dragging her from Berinhard's back. She struggled blindly. After a short struggle they wrenched the sword from her hand.

I am disarmed by the enemy. Vile hands pollute Baldemar's sword. Now, truly, the luck and life of our clan is broken.

Fria, open the earth for me. I will sleep in it as a bed. I will live on in the roots of trees, in ripe wheat; there I will grow and know peace until it is my time to be reborn. Let my people dance on me at festival time.

As they held her pinned to the ground, she was distantly aware they exerted only enough force to subdue her; other than that, they handled her with care.

Beware. They are saving you for some purpose.

And still she somehow managed to tear one hand free. She caught her horse's slender pastern and held it, seeking comfort in the familiar feel of silken fur over bone. It was her last embrace of all she had known. Berinhard seemed to sense something ended as he bent down and brushed his muzzle inquisitively over her hair.

Then her arms were hers no more; they were bound behind her back with strong cord. The bridegroom enveloped her in his pitiless embrace.

Marcus Arrius Julianus had already departed from the fortress of Mogontiacum when Five Wells was stormed and taken. For Domitian decided quite suddenly he could no longer bear his festering suspicions of plots afoot at home; with all the imperial staff he hastily decamped for Rome mere days before the final battle.

On the morning of Auriane's capture the imperial party had journeyed no farther south than the Rhine fortress of Argentoratum. Marcus Julianus was immersed in the tiresome task of reviewing Domitian's correspondence with the Governor of Bithynia, who requested certain revisions in the province's criminal laws, when a trusted secretary, the one other man in his confidence in the matter of Auriane, interrupted him with the news that Auriane had spurned his offer of freedom.

Of course, I should have known you would not be saved while your fellows died.

He quietly put his head into his hands.

Magnificent fool! Has such a creature ever lived? How can you possibly live in captivity? How nearly impossible you make my task now!

ROME

CHAPTER XXX

The sun burned Auriane's swollen eyes. She forced them open.
Before her was a strange landscape divided by bars. Every muscle
was aflame with pain; the air hurt to breathe. Chill iron encircled
her ankles and wrists. She refused to look at her chains but knew
she could not hide them from the eyes of ancestors.

The memories flooded back.

*This is my first morning in the Land of the Dead. They have
taken even my warrior's ring—my arm is naked as a child's.*

She rode in a mule-drawn prison cart, shackled to nine of her
tribesmen. Their chains kept up a monotonous chatter as, one by
one, her companions stirred in painful sleep. To this was added the
jingling of horses' bits—files of cavalrymen rode alongside, their
faces alien and expressionless. Dully she struggled to make sense
of the situation. She guessed the captives and spoil trailed the
march of the main body of the army. She assumed they would be
sacrificed to the Roman god of war. But why had this not been
done already?

The air was heavy with the odor of terebinth resin and blood.
Slowly she realized the man who lay next to her was Vangio, a
middle-ranked warrior of Sigwulf's Companions. His shrieks of
the night before reverberated still in her mind. An army surgeon
had come to remove the head of a javelin from his thigh. The
surgeon worked swiftly and savagely, using a variety of odd iron
implements; to keep the wound from festering he applied the resin.

Vangio lay now in the heavy stupor that comes before death; his eyes, opened barely, had a milky glaze.

Auriane noticed the surgeon had left behind one of his sinister implements—a curved needle-sharp tool of iron. She covered it with one foot and dragged it within reach. The cart jolted to a stop. She dared not move her foot lest it be seen.

The stillness hummed with flies drawn to the feast of wounds. Slaves appeared bearing skins of water and grimy wooden bowls filled with a bland, cooked grain unknown to her. She ate slowly, ashamed of the pleasure she found in the enemy's food.

She saw Vangio had not stirred. He must have water, at least. She nudged him gently, but he only made a sound like the lowing of cattle.

"Vangio!" she whispered. The whole of her lost world resided in this man only slightly known to her. He must not die. She held the water to his lips and was elated to see it course down his throat.

The haze cleared from Vangio's eyes. "Auriane . . . it is you . . . *you!* How do they dare—"

"Vangio! Eat this."

"It is no use. . . ." He breathed like a woman in labor. "The pain . . . it rages like a house afire. . . . Give to me what is under your foot."

He had seen. The nearness of death must have given him sorcerer's sight.

"Vangio, do not leave me."

"A god could not endure this pain. How can a man?"

She knew she should not beg him to live. It would be cruelty to refuse him simply because she could not bear to go into the darkness alone.

"End your pain," she said softly, helping him position the surgeon's tool between his knees, for his hands were manacled behind his back. "Go in peace. Greet my father. Tell him I tried to go to him, but Fria closed the gate. And . . . ask the gods' pity for those of us condemned to live."

She turned her head away as Vangio pressed his body onto the sharp implement. Then she regarded him without tears, thinking only: How efficiently the surgeon's tool kills.

That is good. It is a fine weapon.

She wiped the tool clean of blood and hid it in her battered shoe.

Night came, leaving her to the boundless desolation and terror of the babe exposed on the midden. She drew out the surgeon's tool and felt its point, hungry for death.

Avenahar! Be quiet now, cry no more. Your mother comes to you.

She shook violently, the deadly point poised before her heart.

Then another memory came. A man of the enemy had tried to save her at the last. Why? She might have understood, had he wanted her for a warrior's prize. But it seemed he meant only to set her free. This inexplicable act of kindness haunted her, for it accorded with nothing else she knew of these people.

She knew then it was not her time. She was too full of bitter questions for both men and the gods.

And there was yet hope for vengeance. Not against Odberht, perhaps, but against their Emperor, who had Avenahar's blood on his hands.

Let this surgeon's tool drink other blood than mine.

She had as well a more formless reason for choosing to live: All her life she had felt a gentle current ceaselessly pulling her outward, down the narrow river along which her people dwelled, toward the greater sea with its unimaginable depth, its peoples and ways both wondrous and monstrous. Before she met death, she wanted to look once upon what defeated them, to see the lands and dwellings of that terrible race of men who stood in back of Decius. The cart moved with that steady current, giving her a dim sense she traveled in the right direction.

She sank into sleep, then awakened to the harsh shouts of the cavalrymen, the brutal sun, the curses of the slaves when they discovered Vangio's body. They dragged him out like a dead animal. She was relieved they did not examine the body too closely; Vangio's wounds were so many no one questioned that he died of them. Her weapon was safe.

A short time afterward, two cavalrymen stopped alongside her cart. One pointed her out and gave a terse order; the other crisply nodded. Moments later she was unchained, separated from the others and put into a cart by herself. This better treatment was mystifying. Was it because they realized she was a woman of rank? She was also given a blanket, and what she supposed they believed was better food—wheat, the ration of the common soldier, rather than the unidentifiable mush. The Romans she saw seemed rarely to eat meat. How had a people who subsisted on horsefeed managed to subdue the world?

They traveled a road that was relentlessly straight, no matter what the terrain; such a path, she realized, was made not for animals' hooves but for the feet of marching soldiers. She clung as long as she could to the last of her land's maternal hills, crying softly at times as she held out her hand to them, tracing their outline so she would have a clearer picture of them in memory.

After many days they came to a place where the forest no longer ruled; it submitted quietly to impious settlers who hacked down the gods' groves to make tidy clusters of villages and plant small, brave fields. Rivers here were sturdily bridged. Another road, also arrow straight, intersected the one on which they journeyed. What insult, she thought, to the boundlessly roaming earth. Everywhere cocks crowed and well-fed cattle kept up a constant medley. This was, she knew, the part of the Romans' country called Gaul. The openness of the land made her increasingly uneasy. Trees were Fria's house and dress—how she must despise these people who strip her naked.

Occasionally when they halted, villagers would collect about her cart and gape, sometimes with amazement or hatred in their faces, sometimes with simple bovine docility. Their children, ruddy cheeked and cruel, pointed at her and cried her name. She could scarcely believe they knew it even in this far-off land. To them she was a savage predator who, to their relief, was finally trapped and taken.

When they had traveled for one complete cycle of the moon and seven days into another, she learned from the slaves' talk they were but halfway to Rome.

The country grew harsh and mountainous; here the earth was ruptured and angry. It was cleaved by savage gorges that disappeared into a blue-gray mist, and graced with impossible peaks, nobly high, streaked with long fingers of snow. These frightful heights were laced with narrow paths; it seemed to her they rode through clouds like the gods. Once, the cart in front of her own veered off the track, pulling its mules after; the screams of the captives as they plummeted into the misty abyss sounded in her mind for days. And yet there were times when she fiercely envied them. Their passage through the world was done.

When the land flattened again, it began subtly to change. Soft gray-greens dried to reds and browns, and sometimes rock punctured the earth. The fields became vast as seas. In many she saw the playful coil of grape vines. There was gaiety in the fine gold light, though it was not meant for her. The sun was far bolder here, and its shadows sharp. In the distance walled towns arose; she stared with great curiosity at these fantastic aggregations of human dwellings dominating the hills. Here the forest was defeated utterly—the cypress trees, plane trees and olives scattered about were but a whispered memory of the majestic groves she knew. The road behind was crowded now with merchants and travelers; at every halt laughing camp followers gathered around. She heard no birds' chatter here; instead, there was a constant jangling of donkeys' bells, each with its own distinct voice, their notes alternately clashing and harmonizing. She loathed the look of this land: To her it was not colorful, but garish; without its heavy garment of trees it put her in mind of a pitifully thin body she would have preferred to see clothed.

This is emptiness without end. I cannot feel Vangio's ghost anymore; even the spirits have fled.

Surely they could not travel much farther. They would plunge into the stream of Ocean that girded the whole of Midgard on which all nations dwelled and be swallowed by the Great Wyrm. She saw the cavalrymen were suddenly in better humor, shouting jests at one another, as warriors will when coming near to home. That anyone could call this place home was a wonder. She guessed the army must have taken on provisions, for dried figs and dates were added to her fare, and wretched wine worse than that which Decius used to give her.

Again and again she tried to learn from her sullen servitors where they were and how much farther they had to go, but they laughed at her stumbling Latin and turned away. Finally she got a reply from an amiable boy hauling water buckets for the horses. "Not much farther," he called out to her. "Seven days at best."

"What is this place?"

"That walled town there?"

"No, the whole land."

The boy's eyes widened in amazement, then narrowed with scorn. "It's true then—these Chattian beasts have cabbages for brains! You do not know *Italy*, the land that lies at the center of the world?"

CHAPTER XXXI

The imperial party reached Rome at the time of the Festival of Vinalia, celebrated in honor of the bringing in of the year's first wine. The morbid August air brought fever, and the whole city seemed to grow listless. Domitian remained outside Rome in his rambling villa set into the side of the Alban Mount, for it was the custom that a conquering general not enter the city gates before he did so in the triumphal procession.

Domitian's agents brought him daily reports of what was said in the streets and taverns about his victory over the Chattians. They learned quickly the city seemed not to care that the war was over, or that it had ever begun—the people cared only that the wine was not free at this year's Vinalia Festival, but none dared put this so bluntly to Domitian, who believed the common people saw him as their savior.

Marcus Arrius Julianus on his return spent long days at the Palace undertaking those imperial duties Domitian found distasteful—hearing petitioners from every province in dull cases, or corresponding with provincial governors concerning routine legal questions. At the same time Domitian made use of his First Advisor's knowledge of the art of the architect-engineer, giving to him the task of counseling the magistrates who were preparing a case against three contractors accused of substituting inferior materials for the precious marbles ordered for the construction of the Emperor's new Palace. In this last matter, as far as Marcus

Julianus could see, both sides were guilty. The contractors' deviousness was surpassed only by the government's brazen attempts to underpay the laborers by cleverly miscalculating the number of days worked. Life at the Palace was starting to seem like a daily draught of poison. Whenever he looked into the bitter, avaricious faces of both the magistrates and the accused, or passed some ruined noble who could scarcely afford to feed scraps to his slaves riding to the theater in a hired litter so all would think he still had his wealth, or heard the sharp shouts from a fish market as a fight erupted over the price of an eel or a pike, or paused on the Palace steps to give alms to a starving beggar right after hearing yet another tale of some dissipated gourmand who had squandered half his patrimony on a single dinner party, it seemed to Marcus Julianus the solemn dignity of the northern forest and the warrior-maid it produced were some vision from a fever dream.

Dreaming fool, he thought. Auriane does not exist. This vile world about you is the only world possible.

In these times Domitian's victory over the Chattians emboldened him, and he began to make demands upon the Senate he would not have had the mettle to make before the war, for fear of being charged with impious presumption. First, he pressed them to declare that the month of his birth, October, would henceforth be called *Domitianus*, implicitly challenging the Senators to dare count his reign less magnificent than that of Julius Caesar or Caesar Augustus, each of whom had had a month renamed in his honor. The proposal was made by Veiento, who introduced the matter casually, as if it were open to debate, but all knew Veiento spoke Domitian's ardent wish—and all had seen how a Senator's fortunes had a way of taking a wretched turn once he voted against a measure Veiento put before them. Next, Domitian compelled them to name him to the office of Censor for life, an ancient title the Emperor usually shared with the members of the Senate. This empowered him to degrade at whim any Senator he felt was "morally unfit," and was considered by the Senators to be the gravest step he had yet taken toward autocracy.

Immediately following the close of that day's session, Licinius Gallus and Saturninus sought out Marcus Julianus and demanded a confidential meeting. By this time Saturninus too knew of Domitian's list of men to die—and that his own name was last on it—and he had wholeheartedly joined the conspiracy. They met in the garden of Marcus Julianus' great-house. Old Diocles conducted the two men down the garden's labyrinthine gravel paths. They found Marcus Julianus deep within its recesses, standing calmly with his back to them, lost in contemplation among the garden's pomegranate trees, gazing into a greenish octagonal pool glimmering with golden carp.

Gallus burst out without a proper greeting: "Julianus! Could you not have stopped him!" His voice soared in pitch. "He's a couple of edicts short of having us fall down and kiss his feet like some Persian satrap!"

Marcus Julianus turned swiftly round and smiled. "That is flattering. You must think me a magician. Calm yourself, my dear Gallus." He seemed distracted for an instant, wrestling still with his own plans, then swiftly he moved to a stone bench set by a small cascade in the artificial stream that fed the pool—the rush of water would cover their words well. He invited his two visitors to sit.

"His wanting the title of Censor," Julianus went on, "is actually a last, lingering sign of honor in him—it proves he still strives to preserve the *image* of doing things legally. Though, ultimately, he'll find a way to do what he wants, legal or not."

"October's still *October* for me," Saturninus spat bitterly, looking like a disgruntled Bacchus as he eased himself onto the stone seat. "What vainglory! I'll never use *Domitianus* except when I have to in public. I am so wearied of his veiled threats and his pretensions, I'm ready to *end* this playacting, I tell you, and stretch out my neck for his blade!"

Gallus looked at Saturninus with horror and pity, then at Marcus Julianus. "Well," he said with an attempt at lightness, while nervously knotting the cloth of his tunic between his hands, "we'd best get on with hiring someone to strike him down, no?"

Gallus realized as he spoke how little he knew of the practical steps involved in disposing of an Emperor.

Marcus Julianus regarded them both severely. "That is the *last* thing we do. Would you set the old cycle in motion and let the dice fall where they will, as when Nero died? No. This time we will do it the wise way. First, we agree on a successor. That means the entire Senate—*and* the Guard."

"Impossible. The Guard will never like who we like," Gallus protested. "Anyway, he's paying them off shamelessly. And for another thing—it sounds too *slow*."

"I know what he pays the Guard—we'll offer them more," Marcus Julianus replied. "And remember, there are men among them so loyal to Titus' memory they would turn on Domitian in an instant if they *knew for a fact* he murdered his brother. And proof is coming. I know now where Caenis' letters are to be found— they're concealed within a wall in her shut-up library rooms off the east courtyard of the Old Palace. The difficulty lies in safely *getting* to them without rousing suspicions. I must somehow break in there without alerting the guards. I'm also close to ferreting out that physician who took part in the murder—he bolted once, but my agents found him again. Do not forget how slowly Domitian must move in order not to alert us to his intentions. We'll just have to get to work at once and find the man who offends fewest of us."

Saturninus and Gallus both looked at Marcus Julianus as if seeing him for the first time.

"Do not even *think* it!" Marcus Julianus spoke up quickly, knowing their thoughts. "I cannot imagine anything I'd like less! The only thing that has the kick of life about it for me is philosophy. Anyway, there are able men whose lineage is less distant from the Julio-Claudian line than mine. Nerva, for one. No. We'll draw up a list of names and take them about in secret, man by man."

Marcus Julianus smiled affably. "Do not look so woebegone, both of you! I got him to lower the taxes for those farms in Tuscany and to let us vote on the corn issue. And, Gallus, I'm certain I convinced him to rescind your brother's sentence of banishment. The world has not ended."

Gallus stared at Marcus Julianus, his mouth slack and open like a fish left on a bank. "I do not know how to properly repay you!" he said finally. "My dear Julianus, my brother owes you his life!"

"He's got a greater opinion of living in Rome than I do, then. It's convenient you should broach the subject of repayment, however. I *have* thought of a way."

"Name it!"

Marcus Julianus put a rolled document into Gallus' hand. "Find someone to read this in the Senate as soon as it can be arranged. The man must be someone much your junior—he'll better be able to get away with it. And it must be someone no one will connect with *me*. I want it read at noon."

Gallus swiftly read. An expression of dismay came slowly over his face. It was a speech Marcus Julianus had written the night before—a plea for leniency for the captives and an impassioned defense of Auriane. In it he reminded the Senate of the clemency shown to the native rebel Caratacus, who led a revolt of the

Britons in the time of the Emperor Claudius. When Caratacus was finally apprehended after ten years of struggle, the Senate judged him a noble enemy and spared his life, allowing him to live on in the city on a small pension. Like Caratacus, Marcus Julianus argued, this rebellious woman and her accomplices tortured no prisoners, were never treacherous, and fought only for freedom. And when they had the three tribunes at their mercy, they treated them quite well by barbarian standards; there was evidence that the woman called Aurinia, in particular, argued that their lives be spared. *"We have a long tradition of showing clemency to a gallant enemy,"* the speech concluded. *"Why put it aside in this enlightened age?"*

Marcus Julianus expected this measure would be soundly put down. But he also knew that the mob would, as always, be pressing about the Curia, listening for the results of critical votes, and at noon its doors would be open because of the heat. His purpose was to present her sympathetically to the people— intuitively he was certain the common people's love, if managed properly so it did not rouse Domitian's jealousies, would one day protect her.

"This cannot be a jest," Gallus said, looking politely befuddled. "Your sense of humor generally doesn't run to inducing innocent colleagues into making idiots of themselves. And it cannot be serious. So what is it?"

Marcus Julianus smiled good-humoredly. "I fear I must leave you puzzled, good friend. This one time I'm forced to prevail upon your generosity. Trust me the cause is a good one."

On the next day Diocles interrupted Marcus Julianus in his library with a letter. It was a decoded version of an original that had been handed through a network of men, originating with an aide of the Prefect of cavalry in charge of the captives' transport from Germania.

"It's about that barbarian woman, isn't it?" Diocles demanded to know, full white brows drawn together as he mustered his most formidable look. Then he winced, spoiling its ferocity—nervous excitement always seemed to worsen his gout pains.

Marcus Julianus nodded in assent, his expression suddenly tense, alert, sad. An instant later he saw Diocles' discomfort and rose swiftly to help him settle into a chair, setting the old man's afflicted leg on a footstool. Then he took up the letter and began to read.

Diocles' voice rose up into a petulant whine. "I cannot bear it when you make yourself a laughingstock! You cannot civilize an adult savage. You must capture them as infants. Anyone knows that. This one will be clambering up the trees in the gardens. Why is it *I* always care more for your dignity than you do? Why, your father, if he's watching . . ."

Diocles' protests died in his throat as he saw the haunted desolation coming into his master's face.

After an awkward silence Diocles ventured, "Is she . . . well?" with cautious apology in his tone. In reply Marcus Julianus read from the letter.

" *'She is eating the dried fruits you procured for her, and I am able to see that her food is free of maggots and mold. She seems well enough, though she languishes in a misery pitiful to see. But it has become apparent there is official interest in her at the highest level, for Camillus himself ordered her moved to a better wagon in which she travels alone. . . .'* "

That bit of news chilled Marcus Julianus even as it pleased him. Domitian obviously wanted her to be in good health when he took his pleasure of her, or—how had he put it?— *"used her as a tonic."*

Marcus Julianus read on: " *'They do not molest her, however, and none suspect I watch her. The situation is safe for now, but a new problem has arisen. Now that she is not half starved, she is quite comely to look upon, and she attracts too much attention. But I judge that if grief does not kill her, she will live.'* "

"You did not tell me the Emperor had an eye on the wench!" Diocles exclaimed, jowls shivering as he struggled to his feet.

"You worry so overmuch about everything. I feared it would bring on another heart seizure."

"I *must,* because you do not worry *enough.* The gods help you *and* her if he learns you mean to have what he covets!"

"I know."

"When he's had his fill of her, he'll have her killed in some barbarous way—for the pleasure of watching your face."

"He will not lay a hand on her."

"You must be Jove then."

"No, just a mortal man who knows our august ruler's embarrassing weaknesses."

"He'll have her brought to the Alban Mount, soon as he's seen her fattened and cleaned up. What will you do, storm it with soldiers?"

"I do not yet know. I'll manage something. All I can do now is have her closely watched . . . and wait." He looked off into the garden, studying a stand of wind-ruffled olive trees. "The game becomes maddeningly subtle. Of late, Domitian's senses have become acute as a wolf's. He *knows* I've drawn back from him, though I swear there's no rational way he could know my plans. Now it's as if he's courting me. If I do not come to his pretentious Alban dinner fests, he frets. Of course, I've learned how little good it does us—I've seen how he can court and kill." He sighed, his face composed but somber. "Domitian's lingering need of my good opinion is the only weapon I have left. When *that* is gone, the gods help us both."

CHAPTER XXXII

The captives' journey ended in the twilight underworld of a stone prison within the Praetorian Guard's camp just outside the walls of Rome, where they were to be held while awaiting the triumphal procession. It was September, the time of the *Ludi Romani* or Roman Games—fourteen days given over to revelry and races in the Circus Maximus—but little of the gaiety in the city's streets penetrated this place of stern monumental walls and pitiless reverberating voices.

On the first day male and female captives were herded into separate cells—and Auriane saw at once Athelinda was not with them. She learned many captives had been sent to the great slave markets near Alexandria, and could scarce bear to think of her mother in such a monstrous place. She prayed Fria gave her a gentle death and that she was with Baldemar. The captives numbered about five thousand; she saw no one with them who was sickly or aged past thirty winters—the tribe had been pared down to its young, muscular heart.

She found herself in a cell not much larger than a horse stall; moldering straw littered the floor. Everywhere about the vast chamber that housed the cells lingered the smell of strange, pungent herbs and sweet rot. The whole of this land she found stiflingly hot, but in this place the wind was kept out utterly—she might have been sealed into a great clay oven, left to slowly bake to death. But she at once made a discovery, and it was the greatest good fortune to befall her since her capture.

Among the five women who shared her cell was Sunia.

When first they saw each other, they mutely stared, fearful if they spoke each other's name the vision would vanish. Auriane felt a knot of joyful sadness collecting in her throat as she forced back tears. Sunia was a pale, elfin creature regarding her with solemn orphan's eyes. She was all jutting bones; her rags hung on her like cloth caught on tentpoles. Her mouse-brown hair dangled in ropes. But to Auriane nothing could have been more welcome than the sight of that well-meaning face, that downcast, hesitant, hopeful glance, calculating always, but from fear, not deviousness, and the cautious appearance of that crooked smile.

"Sunia," Auriane said at last, her voice low in her throat. They came swiftly together, clinging to each other with joyous desperation while the four other women in the cell dully looked on.

After a time Sunia said, "Of all the people, kinsmen and friends, who might have followed you here, you get *me.* What a low jest."

Auriane held Sunia at arm's length and gave her a reproving mother's look. "Do not ever speak so again. You are my beloved kinswoman."

A progression of days began that were no more than times of dark and light, punctuated with regular feedings and the resonant barks that announced the precise movements of guard changes. Auriane and Sunia stayed close by one another, telling rambling tales of their lives, weaving a closeness, while by degrees Sunia overcame her fear Auriane would find her company a burden—she could not believe Auriane truly wanted a companion of such humble origins. And Auriane found that being in the presence of someone whose shame was more crippling than her own made her look differently at *all* shame: It seemed less like part of the soul's center and more like an affliction, like boils or ague.

As she thought this, she thought she saw a fleeing vision of Ramis.

One morning Sunia awakened before the others and saw Auriane standing in the hazed needle of sunlight slanting from the narrow window high in the wall. She kept her eyes closed so Auriane would think she slept, and managed to hear part of Auriane's prayer:

"Radiant One, whose garment is the sun, Mother of all Knowledge, you who give all, and at death, take all away—I give praise to you for preserving Sunia. . . ."

Sunia held in a breath with amazement, then felt warm and wanted for the first time in her life. Auriane was actually offering a prayer of thanksgiving for her.

Their cell was separated from its neighbor by iron bars; this adjacent cell was crowded with twenty women captives. In its back wall was a small hole in the mortar; beyond this, in a larger cell, were a hundred or more male captives — among whom, she learned from the women in the next cell, were Coniaric and Thorgild. They too were reasonably fit and healthy. These four quickly formed a makeshift family, communicating through the women in the connecting cell.

Auriane's favored treatment continued: In addition to the prisoners' mush, she was given dates, pears and apples, which secretly she shared with the other women. Army surgeons came to examine her and treat her injuries — fractured ribs, swellings, a festering sore on the ankle. She alone was allowed to wash. It was mystifying and foreboding.

Unsettling to her also was how hurried and impersonal this race of people were. Rarely did she see any of them greet another as a friend or brother, from the arrogant soldiers to the legions of slaves, physicians, armorers, leatherworkers, and grooms. Do people live in families here? she wondered. The slaves who tended them had the faces of every nation — and they too seemed scarcely to know their comrades. The very gods of this place, she thought, must be strangers to one another. Another marvel was how closely they measured time in this place. As the bars of her prison cart had divided the sky, so the Romans' days were divided into even parts, called *hours,* and this seemed to govern all activity. An hour would be called, and the nerve-jarring clamor from the armory would cease, or the measured tramp of soldiers' feet would start on the parade ground, amidst a fanfare of trumpets.

By the seventh day, Auriane was attempting speech with two men of the Guard often stationed before the captives' cells. Because it was a festival time discipline was lax; eventually the pair began to banter with her when their officers were not about. By the ninth day she persuaded these two Guards to play dice with her.

They gave her a few copper coins to start. Before their watch was done, they were cursing her and laughing as she won again and again.

Between throws, Auriane carefully plied them with questions. The other captives drowsed, or watched her with vague amazement, wondering how Auriane had the spirit to extract information from the enemy when they were still paralyzed with sadness.

"Tell me," she probed as she paused, dice cup in hand, pronouncing each Latin word with trepidation, "what is the meaning of this 'procession of triumph'?"

"I'd find that schoolmaster who tutored you in our tongue and sue for my fee back!" the one called Justus replied, grinning. He had an abandoned laugh, sharp, watchful eyes, and a cynicism that seemed to her a poor copy of Decius'.

"A silly, gaudy show to dazzle the rabble into grateful silence is what it is," responded the black-haired Guard, a massively made young man with a gnomish face that gleamed with perspiration, a name she could not pronounce, and breath that reeked of an as-yet-unknown spice these people heaped on all their food. "The cursed procession—and not the land taken—is the *real* purpose of war, if you ask me."

The answer was unsatisfactory, but Auriane sensed they were growing impatient with her queries. She gave the cup several more half-hearted shakes, then tried to insert one more question. "Who then is this man I hear everyone speaking of, night and day—this *Aristos?*"

"Enough talk!" Justus protested with mock annoyance. *"Throw!"*

Auriane released the dice.

"Venus again!" the black-haired Guard exclaimed while he regarded the dice as if they were alive and full of malice. "This northern wench has Fortuna hog-tied!" Sulkily he slid another copper coin beneath the bars. "She's thoroughly shaken out *my* pockets."

"If she wins any more from us, I say it's time for another search," Justus responded. "Your last throw, my barbarian Circe. Have the decency to lose this time."

Auriane drew the cup farther from the bars, tarrying on purpose, transfixing Justus with clear gray eyes, not knowing where she found the strength to say teasingly, "World's end will come and go before I throw these dice, unless I get my answer."

"Persistent as rodents, are they not? She'll chew our arms off if we don't tell her. *Aristos,* then. You know, Justus, they should march *Aristos* in that fool's parade. Word is, the Palace is *pitifully* short of captives."

Auriane frowned in puzzlement.

"He means, Aristos was a captive of *this* war," Justus explained, "right back at its beginning, over a year ago it was, but now that he's celebrated and all—"

"Of *this* war? He is one of *us*?" Auriane asked, sitting forward, eyes intent. "But you speak of him as if he were a prince of your people!" They talked in riddles when they spoke of Aristos. He was condemned to death, but he dined with noblewomen. He was not a soldier, but he won battles.

"Well, he's a prince to us! He's—"

They heard fast, clipped steps on stone.

"Fabatus!" Justus said in a low voice.

Auriane quickly hid the dice cup in the straw. Both guards sprang back to their stations along the wall. But their Centurion was in an affable mood; he strode up to them and put a hand on each of their shoulders.

"Aristos won!" Fabatus said loudly, and slightly drunkenly, Auriane thought. She felt a line had been pulled taut; she stood very still, struggling to catch every word, full of a shadowed sense it was important she understand this.

"He saved us and half the city, praise be to Nemesis and Mars!" Justus responded.

"He's to be formally given his freedom tonight," Fabatus went on, grinning proudly as if he spoke of some great achievement of his own son.

"He's signing *on* again, I hope," the gnomish one asked, true alarm in his voice.

"Of course. Kings don't step down." Their Centurion added in a covered voice, "Torquatus opens the School to the public tonight. There's to be a banquet celebrating Aristos' freedom—a hundred sesterces apiece gives you both leave to go."

After this, they said no more. And so she learned little more from this baffling exchange than what she already knew—that bribery was rampant at all levels of their army.

The next day these two Praetorians were replaced with others, and when their festival time was done, the Guards played dice with her no more.

Auriane recorded the number of days by scratching marks on the wall with a copper coin the Guards forgot. It was on the eleventh day that Sunia threw herself on the straw, convulsed with hard sobs. Auriane went to her and knelt down, taking her shoulders in her hands.

"Sunia, Sunia," she said softly as if to a lost child. "I feel as you do—"

"You! *You* seem quite at home in this place—playing dice with them! I have not your nature—I can only live in one place. Let me die!" Sunia began clawing at the straw, groping for the surgeon's tool, which Auriane had hidden because they were regularly searched.

"*Stop* this! Sunia, you must have patience. Fate always turns! We learned to live in *that* world, we can learn to live in *this* one. When they play dice, they talk, and when they talk, we are given weapons and tools so we can live in this place. Sunia, I need you with me! I'm reaching my mortal limits!"

"*That* is kept well concealed!"

"Then you've no eyes to see! I awaken each morning and I feel my whole soul battered, bruised and broken and left for dead by the roadside. I am nothing but a wretched body with severed limbs—one limb is Decius, one is Avenahar, one is my mother, one is the land. . . . I bleed to death slowly, with no draughts for the monstrous pain. I am close to madness, Sunia. I need *your* strength as much as you need mine."

Sunia sat up slowly, looking faintly bewildered. The notion that anyone, much less Auriane, might need her was a novel one, and it distracted her from her misery. Auriane lifted the last of the watered wine the Guards had stolen for her to Sunia's lips.

As she watched Sunia drink, Auriane thought grimly: I truly *am* starving for lack of hope. If I am not soon given more reason to live, my life is done.

At dawn on the seventeenth day, Auriane started as if a spirit-hand shook her to wakefulness. She sat up, feeling expectant. The sun streamed in as always through the high, narrow window, but this morning it seemed to be the steady golden finger of a divinity, indicating her time. She looked over at Sunia, a comfortable dark mound sunk into the straw in animal contentment.

She does not feel it. Whatever has come, has come for me.

A lukewarm porridge of barley was brought. Then at the morning's first guard change, the cell door was loudly thrown open.

Two ladies' maids entered. They were startlingly brilliant in multicolored garb, and, Auriane thought, haughty enough to serve an empress. One was an Arabian girl in a tunic of saffron, with mysterious smudges of dark beneath great shining eyes. The other was an Ethiopian maid swathed in crimson, with brilliant beads of glass woven into her hair. Both wore great hoops of gold in their ears and smelled of cinnamon and hyacinths. They were followed by four slaves bearing an ornate bronze jewel case, a chest of cedar, a bucket of water and several rolls of linen. The captives watched all this in silence, puzzled and alarmed.

The Arabian girl addressed Auriane in a high, strident voice. "We are ordered to prepare and dress you. If you make it difficult for us, then we'll call the Guards to dress you."

"*Dress* me?" Auriane said in a low voice. "For what purpose?"

The two maids looked at one another, as if uncertain whether they should reply. Then the Ethiopian girl said with a sly smile, "For the pleasure of a god."

Auriane felt a low shock pass through her, followed by dark excitement. They were giving her to someone of importance, and if the Fates were with her, perhaps it was the Emperor himself. She had not expected to be granted so soon a chance to exact vengeance.

As Sunia looked on like some cornered beast, the Ethiopian girl threw open the cedar chest and swiftly began taking out a collection of terra-cotta pots; the multiple gold rings about her upper arms glinted as she worked. With nimble fingers the Arabian girl removed Auriane's prison rags and started scrubbing her with pumice. Then, with sure hands, she massaged her all over with hyacinth oil. The maids chattered happily as they worked, but they mixed their oddly accented Latin with an unknown tongue and Auriane understood little of it.

"Don't look so, they're not torturing me," Auriane said once to Sunia as the maids fastened what they called a breastband about her chest and pulled a tunica of thin, fine white wool over her head. Then the Arabian girl, while humming an eerie amelodic tune, began lightly dusting Auriane's face with powdered white lead. She next brought out a jar of *purpurissum*, with which she rouged Auriane's cheeks. Then she darkened Auriane's brows with antimony and smoothly shaded kohl beneath her eyes to make them appear round and brilliant, her fingers moving with the quick, polished delicacy of an artist. Finally she blotted Auriane's lips with wine lees, making them startling and dark.

The wondering silence of the women captives was broken by Sunia's high nervous laughter.

"Don't laugh at me, Sunia, please," Auriane whispered tensely, beginning to feel uneasy about it all.

They are mocking my face. They are making me grotesque. What sort of cruel game is this?

"Forgive me, it is just that it is . . . *different,*" Sunia said. "No, Auriane . . . it's beautiful."

Next the Ethiopian girl gathered up Auriane's hair and bound it loosely back, securing it with two tortoiseshell combs. Then she divided the free-hanging hair into three plaits. Working together, the two maids wove seed pearls into the plaits, then loosely entwined the tresses and put them into a serpent-coil atop her head. This was secured with silver netting. At the last they sprinkled the whole creation with gold dust.

Sunia drew in a breath, envious now rather than amused. She edged closer, extending a hand to touch Auriane's hair but one of the maids slapped it down. The Ethiopian girl then drew from the cedar chest a garment of shimmering white cloth so fine it seemed to be made of some fiber woven with mist. Auriane shivered as it slid like cool water over her skin.

The Arabian girl said irritably, "Don't tear this, or you will be punished. It's worth more than *you* are—it's silk, and it's sold for its weight in gold."

Sunia had always thought Auriane pleasing to look upon, but *this!* It was still recognizably Auriane, but she glowed softly like the moon. This clever exaggeration of her beauty made it seem some sylph possessed her, gently altering her soul. Or perhaps this *was* her soul all along, and it was only now made shiningly apparent.

While the maids were placing a chaplet of golden vine leaves on Auriane's head, Sunia moved stealthily up to the cosmetic case and purloined several small squat jars, stashing them in the folds of her rough wool dress. Later she would practice this magic on herself.

The maids put gem-encrusted sandals on Auriane's feet, remarking unkindly on how large they were. Then they stood back to admire her.

"She is perfect," said the Ethiopian girl. "A barbarian Aphrodite!"

"No, a wood nymph, that's what she's supposed to be. Wait— the woodland scent!" The Arabian girl reached into the cedar chest and brought out a slender-necked bottle of blue-tinted glass. She moistened a finger and daubed the oil-based pine scent onto Auriane's throat and temples.

Auriane thought miserably, How do I fight in these flimsy shoes, these filmy clothes?

"*Come*, Niobe!" the Arabian girl exclaimed, handing Auriane a bronze mirror. The two maids looked at each other and giggled. "Behold yourself!"

Auriane started at the sight of herself, then felt relief. No, they had not made her ugly. It was just, as Sunia had said, different. She might have been wearing a translucent mask: She could still see herself, yet a strange woman looked back at her.

This, then, is what is pleasing to their men. What an odd people. What is wrong with a woman's face as it is?

When they prepared to take her out, Auriane signaled to Sunia with a furtive glance. Sunia understood. What she must do, she must do now, before everyone's eyes. Slowly Sunia edged toward the back of the cell. One hand fumbled in the straw, seeking and finding the surgeon's tool.

Auriane heard then the angry mutterings of the men in the cell beyond. They could see little, but by now word of this sinister ritual had spread to every cell.

"*Swine!* She is our holy woman, not a present for one of your soft, lazy noblemen!" Auriane heard one voice above the others and recognized it as Coniaric's. She feared they might throw crockery and garbage at the Guards. Swiftly she moved to the bars and spoke rapidly in their own language, knowing the women in the next cell would relay her words to them.

"All of you! Do not fight for me! I beg you. You will only bring grave trouble on yourselves, and you have already endured the sufferings of world's end. If I do not return, then *rejoice*—for it means I have won holy vengeance!"

The women in the next cell watched her sadly. Two softly cried.

Then four Praetorians came to take her off. The one who opened the cell door proved to be the same black-haired Guard with whom she once played dice. He grinned broadly as if this were all a lascivious joke. But he betrayed no sign he had ever seen her before.

Sunia knew she could delay no longer. She rushed at Auriane, crying piteously: "*No! Do not take her!*"

Auriane whirled round to meet her. For a brief moment, her back was to the Guards. As they clung to one another, Sunia brought the surgeon's tool up, slipped it beneath Auriane's tunica, and secured it in the breastband.

"Well done, extremely well done!" Auriane whispered in the Chattian tongue.

"*If they search you again—*"

"They will not."

"Get that she-ass off her before she smears her paint!" barked a Guard.

The maids seized Auriane and jerked her away. Swiftly the Guards manacled her wrists.

She is a strange and heartbreaking sight, Sunia thought. A chained nymph, a fettered goddess.

They led Auriane out into the waiting afternoon.

When Auriane saw the plumed Guards who served as outriders, the bewilderingly ornate carriage into which they put her, the monumental city with its endless ribbon of wall, and the brilliantly garbed footmen shouting at the wheeled traffic, ordering it to make way for them, she felt she floated into a lovely, lurid nightmare.

CHAPTER XXXIII

Domitian's hunting garden, the jewel of his sumptuous villa tucked into the side of the Alban Mount, was stocked this day with ostriches. Domitian stood on the hunting platform overlooking the rambling gardens. A gently fluttering canopy of checkered aquamarine-and-rose sailcloth protected him from the dying sun. Beside him brooded his ascetically thin Councillor, Veiento, concealing boredom and distaste with a cold, courteous smile, and Veiento's partner in informing, the Senator Montanus, who was often cruelly reminded by Domitian of how happily apt his name was, for he was a small mountain of a man who got his bulk about with difficulty. Montanus was propped precariously between two Egyptian slave boys, who served him as crutches.

Veiento sensed Domitian was strangely unnerved on this evening. In the midst of the seventh course of a dinner honoring the return of the Governor of Hispania, the Emperor had risen restlessly, ordering them to follow. Veiento saw the guard about the hunting garden had been doubled. By Minerva, he wondered, what was going on? And what was the meaning of the *satyrion* in white wine the Emperor called for an hour ago between courses? Did he need an aphrodisiac to help him kill an ostrich?

Montanus noticed none of this—he was in mourning for the seventh course, his favorite quince pastries. *Petty overindulged tyrant!* Montanus thought. The ostriches will be here tomorrow. The quince pastries won't.

Leonidas, Master of the Gardens, appeared promptly with quiver and bow. Domitian took them in a manner that was studied and grave, as if even this small act would be recorded and cherished by the historians.

Domitian drew the bow, impatiently scanning the shifting green shadows and rambling undergrowth of the vast garden. It had been planted with an eye to imitating the random work of nature. The confusion of acanthus, myrtle and Mediterranean fan palms, the masses of oleander, stately plane trees and dwarf pines were roped with serpentine paths. The whole abounded in wild and secret places. Playful statuary loomed throughout—here, dancing Satyrs playing pipes with wineskins slung over their shoulders rose unexpectedly among fragile blooms of autumn crocus, artemisia, and lilies of the Nile; there, a bronze dryad fled through yellow cyclamen, an antic Pan strove to mount a she-goat cavorting among the flowering dianthus. A brook had been diverted through the garden; it looped round, pooling in granite basins, trickling beneath stone bridges, rippling down artificial waterfalls. Rosemary, basil, lavender, and other herbs selected for their scent were planted throughout; the garden's perfumed breath enveloped them with each gust of wind.

Quite suddenly an ostrich emerged from behind a rose bush. The creature gave them a befuddled look, then abruptly turned, as if realizing it had made a grave mistake. As the ungainly bird attempted to speed away with long, floating strides, its questing head thrust forward, Domitian aimed and shot. The small head snapped back; huge feathers scudded upward. The creature's neck was broken.

Montanus and Veiento clapped noisily. "Well done!" Veiento exclaimed, the studied modulation of his voice the only sign that such blandishments did not come easily to him. Veiento was not in the habit of using flattery for survival. "And at such a great distance."

"Incredible!" Montanus sputtered. "You should hold a competition open to the whole of the city and enter it in disguise so your majesty would not frighten them off. You would win!" Montanus did employ flattery as a first line of defense, but his taste for it was crude and exaggerated as his taste in food. Domitian gave Montanus a pitying look and ignored Veiento completely.

"Leonidas!" Domitian called out sourly. "How many of these bungling birds are left?"

"Six, my lord. You killed twenty today, I believe."

"Well then, where *are* they? I despise it when creatures get clever. Go and flush them out!"

"*At once,* my lord!"

"Veiento, amuse me now with what those quibbling old women prattled on about today."

Veiento concealed the flash of hatred that filled his eyes. As he drew from his tunic a copy of that day's proceedings of the Senate, he thought: Grandson of a tax collector, son of a muledriver, do you think we do not know your need to make the Senate look like a pack of fools is envy and jealousy?

"They opened with another prayer of thanksgiving for your glorious victory," Veiento reported with his usual dry efficiency. "The very first order of business was to vote you the title *Germanicus.* The whole world now hails you as the conqueror of Germania. The vote was unanimous—and sincere."

"This is where Marcus Arrius Julianus is worth ten palaces, and you are worth dung," Domitian said lightly. "He would have told me every man as he voted had one eye on his neighbor to see how *he* voted. But then, that's not why I keep you. By the way, where *is* that man tonight?" A genuinely wounded look came into Domitian's eye. "This is the third banquet of state he's missed in as many nights."

"He chose at the last moment not to come," Veiento said with silky malice. "He disliked what you were serving tonight."

"It's irritating when someone with no sense of humor tries anyway," Domitian replied, seizing Veiento with dark brooding eyes.

"He will be here," Veiento amended hurriedly, regretting that even for one rare moment he allowed his hatred for Marcus Julianus to show. "He sent word. He was detained at the investigation of evidence in that business of the counterfeit Parian marble. It seems he's the only man in Rome who can tell what quarry it comes from."

"Much better. Show the man a thimbleful of respect. You've a talent for courteously slitting throats, my dear Veiento, but admit it, *he* has all nine Muses on a leash. What is that man not expert in?" Domitian smiled blandly at Veiento. He took great pleasure in keeping the two Councillors at each other's throats. It was a delicate business. Causing Veiento to despise Marcus Julianus was almost too easy. But the reverse required more expertise; Julianus was not naturally inclined to think ill of his fellows.

"And what else?"

"They proposed and passed every measure you wanted."

"How surprising. I do like a well-trained Senate."

"There *was* one unpardonable moment of insanity. Young Lucilius must have been off his head—it's stupidity, not ingratitude, I think—but he proposed that the rebel leaders be pardoned and pensioned off, including even that Amazon. *'Are we to show less clemency in this enlightened age,'* or some such thing, he finished off."

"Are they drinking wine in the Curia now?"

"I think it is more serious than that," Veiento replied, narrowed eyes bright with suppressed rage. "The mob about the doors of the Curia cheered the measure and raised quite an angry shout about it when it was put down. They're oddly disposed to sympathy for those Germanic beasts."

Another ostrich strode confidently into view, blithely oblivious to mortal danger. Domitian raised the bow and squinted, his forehead gleaming with perspiration in the autumn heat. But the muscles of his arms were rigid with frustration. He shot and missed for the first time that day.

"A plague on Nemesis!" His face contorted with disgust. He thrust the bow at Leonidas.

"Of course, mobs swarm round silly futile causes like ants about honey cakes," Veiento continued smoothly with a small, tight smile. *Stew in your anger, you strutting, lowborn tyrant.*

"That was today," Montanus spoke up like an eager schoolboy desperate to join the game, his voice sweet as ripe melons. "Tomorrow they will have forgotten the whole matter, and all that will concern them is if Scorpus the charioteer wins his next race."

Domitian hoped this was true, but he did not want to hear it from Montanus. He turned to him coldly. "Go and change that tunic, *Mountainous*. It looks like it was worn by a blind beggar at Saturnalia."

Montanus sputtered half-coherent apologies, but quickly saw it was useless; Domitian continued to glare at him as he spun about with ponderous agility and scurried back to the banquet, the Egyptian boys hurrying to keep apace.

How did those barbarian animals, Domitian wondered, manage to secure for themselves the very thing that was always maddeningly just out of his reach—the unprompted love of the mob? A polite, muted clap was the best he could ever draw from them. After finally winning the army's adoration and deriving a brief moment of pleasure from it, he learned it did not satisfy. He yearned now for love freely offered, inspired by his person, not by his deeds.

I want this stinking city to sacrifice in secret *to my health, as they did for my cursed brother.*

Leonidas returned unobtrusively as a cat, bowed gracefully, and said with aristocratic humility, "My lord, she is here."

Domitian gave him the comically fierce scowl he reserved for menials. "Well then, you just tell her to pack herself back off to the Palace at once."

Leonidas looked bewildered for an instant. Then he said quickly, "Not your *wife*, my lord."

Domitian's scowl melted away, and a look Veiento had never see there, akin to childlike wonder, came into the Emperor's face. "In the garden? She is here already?"

"By the Serpent Fountain," Leonidas answered smoothly, bowing again to conceal a faintly amused smile.

"Excellent!" Domitian exclaimed, smiling and rubbing huge hands together. "Why are you two hovering about like flies? Leave me!"

Leonidas slunk away with dignity, like a cat. Veiento whipped about and crisply walked off, lost in angry puzzlement.

Domitian set out at once into the garden. The sun illuminated the tops of the fan palms, then sank swiftly behind the garden's walls, suspending all in unearthly blue-gray mystery. Low lamps held aloft by capering bronze fauns were set at intervals along a path no more than a hunter's track; as he advanced, their firefly-lights loomed large, then melted back into numinous gloom. Occasionally he startled a peacock. A wind tugged anxiously at the cypresses, bowing them; he fancied nature herself paid him homage. He was a young Hercules out on his first hunt. A marble Satyr half clad in ivy leered at him, approving heartily of the lusty adventure he set out on now. Though a detachment of Guards was posted so close he barely had to raise his voice to summon them, they were carefully placed out of sight—and Domitian easily imagined himself lost in some remote fastness of nature, trapped in mythic time.

Here I am just a man, coupling with a primeval woman whose mind is not poisoned with the vices of cities. She cannot have learned our women's varied and deft ways of belittling a man. With this wild creature who knows nothing of me but that I rule, I'll prove this cursed infirmity is *their* doing, and no fault of mine.

He found himself conscious of his body in a way he never was with his wife or with poor, frightened Carinus. Would the musculature of his chest and arms, well-formed from his frequent practice of archery, be pleasing to a lover?

Perhaps I *am* wrong to waste myself on this primitive woman who will not fully understand the honor I confer upon her.

He heard the urgent sound of rushing water. Before him was the Serpent Fountain. From the center of an oval basin of black marble rose a great bronze serpent, its muscular body coiled round a tree of bronze; at the height of a man the serpent's body separated into five parts with as many evil-looking heads. Each gaped mouth emitted a thin stream of water into the pool below.

Behind it, half hidden in oleander, was a small temple to Sylvanus, the forest god, carved in soft, white Luna marble so translucent the lamps within caused the whole to glow with gauzy, incandescent warmth in the dusk; it was a fragile wonder promising dreamlike contentment to all who entered. A scent of frankincense drifted from the altar.

A woman stepped from the door and faced him boldly.

Auriane stood still as a deer, her whole body braced as she watched the approaching stranger. She had been abandoned to her wits in this eerie wood that thrived within a house. Small birds taking flight from the scented trees first warned her someone approached. Then she heard the heavy tread of a solidly built man—a step that seemed to combine aggressiveness with hesitation.

The intruder halted when he was little more than a horse's length from her. Who was this richly robed, overproud man? She tried to halt her trembling, but found she could not.

Domitian flushed with rage.

Those imbeciles brought the wrong woman! Some reckless fool just played his last prank.

Before him was a sophisticated young maid with knowing eyes and a bold, delicate beauty that spoke of southern blood; from her shoulders a pale silk stola fell with studied grace. Her hair, styled precisely in accordance with young patrician women's fashions, gave her a look that was polished, serene, unapproachable. It seemed those artfully shadowed eyes observed him with amused doubt.

Was this civilized beauty in on the joke?

Scowling, he took a step closer. She took a measured step back.

Then he knew suddenly this *was* Auriane. No woman of his own nation and class would be so unaware of her own startling beauty. And her stance was less that of a woman, more that of an alert leopard. She looked at all about her as if she stood outside it, facing him as if they were predators of different species. She was possessed as well of a most unwomanly self-confidence.

And she was tall—her gaze met his almost levelly. A brief fear seized him and passed, to be replaced by a deeper, fiercer excitement than he ever felt, even during his first fevered couplings with Carinus. Never had a woman looked at him like that! It was a fearless, exulting, almost masculine look of challenge.

His voice husky with desire, he spoke to her in the soothing singsong voice he might use to quieten a half-broken horse.

"Be calm, pretty creature. That's good! Did those animals that spawned you ever tell you how pretty you were? But then who would know when you were always covered in hides and encrusted in mud? Who would have thought such a pretty, pretty creature would have caused me such endless trouble?"

She edged farther away, head lifted warily while she took in the smells of civilization—a confusion of flower-scented oils, an astringent perfume, breath heavy with garlic and wine. And then she understood.

This was their Emperor.

Of course. He even resembled the crude image on his coins: There was that stubbornly thrust-forward chin, that mouth that just missed being feminine, set in the familiar smug smile.

Auriane's courage fled. The city of Rome, that dwelling place of gods sensed if not seen, and this omnipotent man fused into one. She was sharply aware the jewels on one of his hands were worth more than all her father's herds. This was the mind behind the machines that crushed nations, the will that moved the legions, the divinity set over the string of mighty cities she had passed on her journey. She could not look at him; it was like gazing into the rising sun.

I am but a weed to be trampled beneath his foot.

Then her own words to Eota the musician sounded in her ears: "Beware of reverence—it is a trick of the mind." She strove to sense the earth beneath her feet, stilling her soul so she could look with remorseless clarity at the man.

And she saw before her a quite ordinary man of middle years, whose height rendered him awkward rather than formidable—a man well padded with the cushioning of flesh that was the bane of these city-bound foreigners. Here was a man who had never gone without cover in winter or lived on what he could kill in time of war. However he obtained his kingship, he had not done it with the sword. Even if she had not already known, she would have guessed he was the sort to use his people as a shield against enemy blades. That arrogant stance was oddly at variance with the uncertainty in his eyes—this was a man who could not draw strength from the earth-born gods and so leeched it from fellow men. She did see penetrating shrewdness in that eye—but she sensed it served the purposes of deviousness, not the rigors of truth-seeking.

I see a man who lives to deceive and dazzle others with wonderment, which he never does so well as he deceives himself. How can it be that this all-powerful people who have overrun the earth are ruled by such a faithless, small-spirited man?

With her head slightly lifted—the sensing, testing gesture of a wild creature—and the barest glint of mockery in her eye, she spoke the words of the formal challenge. Her voice surprised Domitian; those alto tones were somehow sensuous and naive at once.

"I challenge you, Emperor of the Romans, to single battle. Wodan, witness my words! Choose a weapon. May victory fall to the one who walks with the sun."

Domitian broke into the light, amused laughter he reserved for children.

"We would have welcomed you at dinner tonight!" he replied. "You're far more amusing than the usual idiotic mimes and the tired old jokes about Circus prostitutes and our old standby, watching Montanus eat. It's a *gift!*" With sensuous slowness he gathered up the silk of the stola and drew her close.

His tone shifted to that of practiced seducer. "I *accept* your offer, my pugnacious little wood nymph—but I alone shall have a weapon, and the combat will take place in the bedchamber."

She transfixed him with soft gray eyes.

"Do you find willing women in such short supply, ruler of the whole world?"

It happened so swiftly Auriane thought one of the bronze snakes might have flashed out and struck her. Domitian lunged, hitting her with either a fist or a shoulder, knocking her backward. She fell onto goosedown cushions; feathers exploded upward.

Then he produced a small riding whip he carried always and struck her hard across the face.

Bright blood sprang to her cheek. The pain brought tears to her eyes. He stood over her, straddling her. Auriane's breath came in deep gasps; her wine-darkened lips trembled. But still she looked at him with bold eyes.

"How *dare* you, you mulish vixen. One more insolent word and I'll see you branded and flogged!"

I was wrong to try gentleness, Domitian thought. *A barbarian respects only naked force.*

"You live on my sufferance. I granted you a chance to atone for your crimes and repair the insult you gave my majesty. And you fling it in my face!"

For a moment their gazes were locked in mortal combat. Then to his surprise the look of challenge gradually melted from her eyes, as though, he thought, she could not withstand the heat of his wrath. Her face softened, and her gaze wandered uncertainly down to his feet. Her arms and legs were splayed awkwardly; she seemed trapped in this humble posture like some small creature caught in a snare. All at once sobs gently shook her shoulders.

For an instant he thought it the work of a well-schooled actress. *But are rude barbarians capable of such deception?*

When she spoke, her voice convinced him she was not playing with him—it was breathless, tortured, frail.

"I beg you do not harm me! Please . . . terror has stolen my wits. I have shamed myself. I have shamed my people."

"Who am I, then?" he prodded sternly, lifting her chin with the coil of the whip. She looked at him with frightened doe-eyes, then quickly dropped her gaze.

"A divine ruler over rulers," she whispered. "A king of kings . . . our Lord and God."

He felt a flush of pleasure that embarrassed him with its intensity.

Lord and God! That sounds well! These Germanic women are all prophetesses. I believe she senses much that others cannot—my importance in history, how near to divine is my reign. And she is the first to proclaim it! From this day forth I shall insist all provincial petitioners address me so.

He watched her for a time, slightly drunk on her fear. He felt all nature cowered at his feet. The pleasure he failed to get on the day he defeated the Chattians he received now in a pure, warm stream. *It is odd,* he thought, *that I feel it more distinctly with this single* specimen of their race than when presented with the sight of thousands of them under the yoke.

In a voice that was a stern caress he ordered her to rise. She struggled up on foal's legs, her face turned shyly from him.

Yes, she is truly broken!

He buried a greedy hand in her fine, soft hair, loosening the strings of seed pearls, taking mischievous pleasure in ruining the stylish coiffure as some boy might in crushing intricate pastries. She cringed slightly but submitted, eyes downcast.

"You must realize I cannot forgive you completely," he breathed. "Smile for me, now! That is better. But if you please me on this night, my pretty thing, I certainly might be moved to lighten the sentence I intend to impose on you."

One huge hand took possession of her shoulder; the stola slipped from it at his touch. Slowly he kneaded the flesh, devouring it with his hand. Then he moved so close she felt his quickened breath on the back of her neck.

"A woman should not develop her muscles like this, you know . . . but on you, somehow it is comely," he mumbled into her hair.

"I am pleased if it pleases you," she said softly. She turned round then and reached for his neck with shy hands. He looked carefully into those clear gray eyes, still probing for deception, but saw only gratitude and a child's adoration.

He smiled intimately. "Do savages kiss?" he whispered when their lips were close. "I'll wager they know nothing of the *art* of it, if they do. I've more than one sort of fine cuisine to show you." Languidly he pressed his lips to hers, slowly applying more pressure, crushing his body against hers until she could scarcely breathe. In a panic she wrest herself away, chest heaving as her breath came in gasps.

"Pretty thing, I hurt you! But there's pain in love, you know. In careful, measured amounts . . . it increases the pleasure." He drew her close again, staining his fine purple and gold-bordered tunic with her blood, then once more he seized her mouth while one hand traveled down her back, getting a bruising grip on her buttocks.

To Auriane the touch of dead flesh could not have been more loathsome than the feel of him, but she pretended she watched from a distance while another woman's mouth yielded to his.

He pulled back slightly, looking down upon the finely molded nose, the delicate bloom of her lips, and was suffused with protective feelings. He kissed her gently. *Poor sparrow,* he thought. *She trembles as if her heart will burst!*

From somewhere quite close, a Guard coughed.

By Nemesis, why did I post them so close? I do not need them at all.

Auriane held in her breath, overcome by the rich scent of myrtle oil, through which penetrated the sharp tang of sweat. She let her body go limp, and they sank together onto the cushions.

He moved his hands down her body, fascinated by how its lean contours were yet silken and soft. His touch was gentle enough on the surface, but she sensed long-stored hunger close to savagery just beneath. Auriane knew the threat of greater force was always there, standing guard like a sentry alert to the barest sign of insurrection.

Then slowly, deliberately, as she lay back on the cushions, he began tearing the silken stola down the front, meaning to save her the trouble of having to rise. He smiled significantly when he saw the faint surprise in her eyes.

Auriane could not help remembering the dressing-maid's warning: "It is worth its weight in gold."

"This is the most extravagant sound your ears will ever hear," he breathed. "A sound my women can hear every day if they wish. Satisfy me and you shall live in golden rooms with a different maid for every task . . . one to wash your pretty feet . . . one to pare your nails . . . another to catch the parings . . . one to tell you the hour, another to announce the quarter-hour . . . and they'll all mop their noses with silk."

The stola fell away, leaving her in the thin undertunica. This, too, he eagerly tore. Then abruptly he stopped. She looked at him, baffled.

After a long silence he said, "I have seen twenty-year veterans with fewer scars." He ran his gaze over the dark crisscrossed lines on her belly, her thighs, the legacy of dozens of close encounters with enemy swords. "A pity. A true pity," he said, shaking his head. "There are some clever physicians who can make these less visible."

He looked at her quickly. "But do not worry—I still find you comely."

His eyes said otherwise, however. For a moment he seemed like a man who had lost his appetite, as if he had been given a dish at a banquet from which a bite had already been taken. Finally he moved to the bronze candelabrum and snuffed out all its flames but one.

Auriane realized he dimmed the light so he could not see her scars. In spite of her contempt for him, still she felt a small, vicious stab of hurt surprise. She concealed it by lifting her chin in defiant pride and moving a fraction farther away from him.

"You incorrigible little nymph—do not pull away from me!" He dragged her by the woolen undertunica, pulling it from her shoulder, exposing a milky swell of breast above the confines of the breastband.

"You *do* please me, and more than any other, and I shall prove it to you." He eased himself on top of her, though still clothed. Already he was moving rhythmically against her with the dumb, probing insistence of an animal. She responded with small, desperate kisses like timid offerings to a god.

Those kisses made him feel he held all existence at bay. *This* was the way he once thought he would feel always, after becoming Emperor—magnanimous, adored, and strong as Atlas.

Auriane feared she would suffocate in damp, solid flesh. A determined hand claimed her thigh, eagerly working its way upward, a predator languorously devouring prey, remorselessly approaching what it wanted most. They rolled over once, toppling a lamp stand. Hot oil spread quickly over the travertine floor. She was pinned beneath his weight and could not move as the consuming hand moved higher. Blunt, bruising fingers suddenly found and rudely intruded upon her sex. He was not gentle now, but powerfully persistent, imagining he tormented his quarry with pleasure. Her moan of pain he heard as a cry of unbearable delight.

He felt his own excitement and readiness. The warm eagerness in his loins fogged his vision, made him certain her desire matched his own.

Yes! he thought, though it was more a blind groping in the dark than a thought. She has done for me what no other woman could! I am a man again. She is worth more than emeralds. Would that *all* were like her—pliant and sweet. She is a wonder.

She shall be kept near me forever.

He brought out a small gilt dagger and began to sever the breastband.

Blind fright tripled Auriane's strength.

The surgeon's tool! With one violent movement she whipped her body about and got free.

The anger in his face was quickly replaced with a look of fuzzy tenderness.

"Poor creature . . . still frightened!" he said softly, stroking her thigh. "You should not be—you are perfect. You put to shame every woman or boy I've ever lain with. I will raise you up to first place among my concubines. You are too ignorant to know what that means, but let me assure you . . . *you will be the envy of all women in the world.*"

Her hopeful, grateful look cautiously crept back.

"Wine, perhaps, will help Amor conquer this fainthearted Psyche."

A silver wine service had been set out on a low cedarwood table. He turned about and took up a heavy wine cup studded with carbuncles and amethysts. First he poured in hundred-year-old Falernian, then hesitated before adding the water. For a moment he deliberated over the ratio. He wanted her in lusty temperament, but he also wanted her to have her wits about her, so she would not for one moment forget who he was.

For some reason he turned to look at her as he poured. It might have just been to enjoy the sight of her looking like some injured nestling at his mercy, or it might have been the ancient fear that always rose in him at dusk when deep shadows reached out with hungry hands. Or perhaps he saw a movement reflected in the bronze serpent's cold glass eye. He heard no sound but the steady rush of the fountain.

Auriane loomed over him, hands aloft, brandishing something viciously sharp that glinted in the last of the light. Her hands and the iron tool were one, a beast's claw eager to rend flesh.

Domitian whirled round and staggered up to his feet. Too surprised to cry out to his Guards, he caught her wrists to stop the blow. In another instant he would have died.

He forced her hands apart, but still she held fast to her weapon; for long moments neither gave ground. He was amazed at her strength. Their breath came in desperate rasps.

"*Viper!*" he breathed between clenched teeth.

A thousand lamps blazed in her eyes. He saw there the concentration of a seasoned fighter who never allowed fear of death to interfere with sensing and measuring an opponent.

This is no woman, but a she-monster, a Scylla, a Gorgon.

In regular circumstances he would have called out for the Guards at once and ordered her executed before his eyes. Domitian was never possessed of great physical courage. But his joy at the return of his abilities in the bedchamber and the fog of passion blotted out fear. He was in a fever to finish what he had begun. A part of him desired desperately to believe this had not happened.

He would subdue her himself—she was, after all, only a woman. Then he would couple with her violently and regain that bewitching, elusive sense of power he had felt moments before.

Slowly he forced her hand down; the weapon's point raked her flesh. He knew she waited for an instant of inattention. He forced down a start of fear.

She is only a woman, yes, but look at the darkness in those eyes. She will kill you not with strength but with barbarous magic.

He backed her through the temple's door and out onto the grass, but still somehow she held her own. Then with swift assuredness she dove under his arm, wrenched her weapon hand free and tripped him as she came up behind him. He fell clumsily onto his side. Before he recovered from surprise, she sprang on top of him.

She raised the surgeon's tool, while rapidly uttering soft, savage words unintelligible to him.

"In the name of Wodan, by Fria's grace, I now claim vengeance for my mother, for my people, for Avenahar—"

"Guards!" It was more a shriek than a spoken word.

From every direction came shouts, the jerking light of torches, the rush of boughs roughly pushed aside.

Domitian had waited too late to cry out. The surgeon's tool flashed down.

But at that instant Auriane caught sight of a blur of white. She turned to look.

An impossible creature bore swiftly down on her. It had tufted eyes, a neck like a snake, a body much too large for it, and long thin bird's legs. It came at her in a rapid glide, a preposterous ghost that seemed determined and confused at once.

What beasts from Lower Earth are loosed in this place at night?

The surgeon's tool bit deep into the earth, narrowly missing the Emperor's neck. The grotesque bird-monster collided with her heavily. Strong leathery legs knocked her aside—and she rolled into the arms of four officers of the Guard.

Confusion and darkness engulfed her as a dozen and more Guards crowded round, torchlight flashing on gold breastplates as they knocked each other aside in their eagerness to seize her. She felt a hot pain in her arm as she was wrenched to her feet and secured in powerful hands. The ostrich turned and fled into darkness, stupidly oblivious to what it had done.

Domitian, on his knees, pulled the surgeon's tool from the earth and dazedly turned it over in his hand. Whoever was detailed to search her would die for this.

Two Praetorians carefully, respectfully, helped him rise. "My lord!" one began excitedly, "your life was saved by—"

"Silence!" Domitian bellowed. All were jerked into awkward stillness. The Guards watched, perplexed, as the Emperor looked steadily at the barbarian woman, the wrath in his eyes entangled with hurt.

Auriane looked harmless and pathetic in the hands of the four massively built Guards. But she glared haughtily at Domitian as though she were some ruined Eastern queen rather than a creature that ranked scarcely above the ostriches. Her hair tumbled into her face; one wild sad eye was visible. The torn undertunic fluttered free from her shoulder, baring one breast.

For Auriane the moment was a bitter one. She had allowed herself to believe she would at least be granted this one victory before her death and now even *this* was wrest from her. Wearily she wondered what would be the manner of her death.

The Guards' bafflement began to shift to disbelief as Domitian approached Auriane, his gaze locked beseechingly to hers. He should order her dragged off to punishment. It was dangerous not to execute an attempted assassin at once—it would only encourage other malcontents to try. Propriety and his position demanded it. He was letting a worthless woman make a fool of him.

And ordinarily Domitian would have been more sensitive to the mood of his Guards. But he needed so much to believe the real Auriane was that hauntingly sweet half-human, half-nymph, that still he held out a small, strong hope. He would bring the true Auriane back.

How she rouses me like no other!

With leisurely slowness he cradled her bared breast in his hand, reestablishing ownership. In spite of his near escape from death, once again he felt a powerful stirring in his loins.

His face close to hers, he whispered, his voice full of pleading, *"Why?* How could you spoil such beauty? How could one so tenderly nursed by Venus be so violently possessed by Mars? I forgave your transgressions. I showered you with grace."

His tone shifted, becoming threatening and low. "I suppose you learned treachery on your mother's knee. Well, you will unlearn it.

This is but your first lesson, my little anemone. You will be broken, like a donkey, like a mule, no matter if it takes months. You will learn to beg for my embrace!"

The Guards' amazement turned to shame. Discreet looks of contempt were exchanged. This moment would not be forgotten.

Auriane realized that she had one weapon left. Words, if well chosen, could tear open a man's heart.

"You are no fit king!" Her voice carried clearly on the night. "Your lowest servant, the men who shovel dung in your garden, would make finer kings! How came an earthworm like you to be raised up over a proud people? Go and couple with pigs, you—"

Her words were cut short as Domitian's hands leapt to her throat. It was as though a quick-acting poison were released in his blood. All the demons lurking in the depths of him rushed up into his hands.

Crush the throat that spoke those words. Drive the viper back into the earth.

That she was an unspoiled barbarian who knew nothing of him—a woman he imagined a moment ago might be a prophetess—made her words the more unbearable.

Auriane writhed violently. The Guards dared do nothing; they watched in tense silence, praying he would kill her quickly so this humiliating farce would end.

Domitian then heard a calm, authoritative voice behind him—a voice that could not be ignored.

"Stop at once, in the name of all you hold dear! She is not worth this!"

Who dared interfere? Domitian dropped Auriane, who slumped, semiconscious, in the arms of the Guards. Behind him was Marcus Arrius Julianus, watching him urgently, quietly.

"Julianus! What in the name of Nemesis do you think you're doing?"

"My apologies," Marcus Julianus replied. "I'm inexcusably late for dinner." The barest smile of amusement crossed his face. "When our good Montanus told me you were taking dessert out in the gardens, I rushed to warn you . . . this dessert is laced with poison."

"Clever. You mean to outthink me even in matters of love. Now what—"

"Love? You are jesting! You walked straight into an ambush."

Domitian's eyes were bright and dangerous. Marcus Julianus' presence always made him sharply aware of how he appeared to others; suddenly he felt his loss of dignity like a freshly opened wound.

"You have tried me to my limits this time! You mock me, you best me, you make me look the country ruffian—I want you banished from my presence forever! *Plautius!*" he addressed the Centurion of the Guard, one of four who had a grip on Auriane. "Arrest him!"

Plautius hesitated, looking acutely uncomfortable.

Domitian was pitched into one of his familiar nightmares, in which he gave orders but no one obeyed. He was once again a small, frightened child, ignored by everyone.

"Arrest him!" That hoarse shout dragged hearts to a stop. His face flushed purplish-scarlet.

Plautius ventured cautiously, "I *will* arrest him if you wish, my lord. But you must know that this man, Marcus Arrius Julianus, just saved your life."

"What are you saying?" He took a step closer to Plautius, regarding him as if he were simpleminded. "Saved my *life*, did he? And how did he do that?"

"That ostrich that came at you," Plautius nodded almost reverentially at Marcus Julianus, "*he* thrust it at her to frighten the woman and deflect her blow. We could not have stopped her in time. We, the city, and indeed the whole of the world are most indebted to the quick thinking of this man."

Domitian stared dumbly at Marcus Julianus. Slowly Plautius' words began to take effect in his mind.

Marcus Julianus had saved his life? He thought: Never would I have laid a heavy wager Marcus would have done such a thing, particularly in a circumstance such as *this,* when he could easily have let me die. Perhaps I am too easily suspicious of him? Perhaps he loves me still? Maybe he truly *is* my greatest friend, and I have been unfair?

Domitian turned to Marcus Julianus. "Then how dare you interrupt my chastising of this woman!"

Marcus Julianus gave the faintest of humble bows. "If I would say more on the matter, we must speak in private."

At that moment Auriane opened her eyes. Darkness was complete; at first she saw only the flame of a torch as it wrestled with the wind. It illumined the face of a man behind the Emperor. From his voice, she realized this was the same man who, moments before, bade Domitian stop. She came to full consciousness with a jolt.

But for him, I would have died.

She watched this man with her whole mind, as earlier she had watched Domitian, sensing his full nature. And she was caught in an updraft of joy that made her feel she had no more flesh and bone than the torch's whipping flame.

My blood and my heart know you, as one knows the kinsman never met.

Here was a man beside whom the other who had hurt her seemed half grown, half formed. There was about that face a fineness of line arresting in itself, but it was the spirit that animated it that alerted her that her years of solitude were coming to a natural end. She sensed a soul that uncannily matched her own, a great benevolent intelligence not bounded by clan, a mind that saw keenly right through city walls. She saw the carefully banked fire in his eyes and knew that, despite his composed expression, this man loathed Domitian.

For a moment she was wrapped in a sacral stillness, aware only of the drag of the night wind, which she knew as the approving sigh of Fria, Mother of all Living. She saw the dying face of the warrior she had felled in the Ash Grove at the last time-of-turning. It means, she thought, once more life is altering forever.

There was a man who *was* a fit king.

Marcus Julianus felt Auriane looking at him with gentle intensity, and he thanked every god for lending him the strength to resist turning to look at her. *Betray nothing!* he commanded himself. How much does she understand? Will she despise me when she realizes I was the one who spoiled her act of vengeance? Will she understand I saved *his* life only because it was necessary to save hers and the lives of others? Who would have guessed, Auriane, you would try a thing no man in this city had the mettle to try? But had you succeeded they would have slaughtered you on the spot, and you would have unleashed on the world a firestorm of civil war. You want what I want, but this is not the way to get it.

Domitian's anger was a boiling liquid that must spill one way or another. Finally it brimmed over onto the men of the Guard.

"Secure her!" he barked. Two Praetorians fitted Auriane with heavy chains. "Now, *get out,* all of you!" Domitian strode among them, making cutting gestures with his hands. "None of this is to be talked about, not to your wives, your boys or your whores, not to *anyone,* and if I hear it whispered of, every man present will be held to account. *Go!* You look foolish standing about staring!"

It seemed to the men of the Guard the Emperor meant to punish his loyal protectors more severely than the murderous barbarian woman. Marcus Julianus noticed with satisfaction this firmly planted seed of disaffection among them.

When they were alone, Domitian turned round to Marcus Julianus. "Now. Tell me why you made me look the fool."

Auriane listened intently, momentarily forgotten by Domitian but not by Marcus Julianus.

"I stopped you from looking *more* the fool. Had you disposed of her *that* way, in a heat of rage, it would have trumpeted to the world you feared her words and believed them the truth."

From the faint shift of uncertainty in the Emperor's eye, Marcus Julianus knew Domitian thought him possibly right. But his wrath was not spent.

"That treacherous harpie boils my blood! Anyone would have done the same!"

"I tried for long to warn you she was far more dangerous than you knew. And treachery is, in truth, not quite the right term for it."

"And what would *you* term it?"

"The natives' code of honor. She is its prisoner—and it demands the blood of the *best man* of the enemy tribe. She could hardly help herself."

Marcus Julianus thought he felt a warmth, as if Auriane smiled at him.

Again Domitian foundered. Marcus Julianus spoke the words he ardently wished to believe. Now he was trapped between a lust to punish and a fervent desire to find some way to leave her alive. He wanted her to taste terror and helplessness at leisure, but he wanted more to change her mind, to rub her face in mud and blood until he forced her to adore him. Perhaps, he thought, this was in truth not an assassination attempt at all. Does not a beast follow its nature? Possibly *this* beast could still be tamed.

He turned round to Auriane, seized the torn strip of her undertunic and ripped it off the rest of the way, baring her back. "Animal predator you may be," he said, "all the more fitting then you should taste the whip. If you are fortunate, I'll stop before you die."

Auriane closed her eyes and bowed her head but uttered no sound.

"I would advise against that!" Marcus Julianus said quickly, struggling with the murderous heat accumulating in his hands.

If he harms her he dies! No! Betray nothing!

Domitian turned to look at him. "You wretched pedant. I'm in no mood for some sleep-inducing lecture on Stoic principles."

"You are short of captives for the procession. Harm her and you'll be much shorter of them, for those captives you hold now in the Guard's camp will rise in revolt and have to be killed. She is their holy woman—they love her and they're ready to die for her. If you want to silence those who mock this war, I would leave her be."

To his relief Marcus Julianus saw a jolt of frustration followed by angry resignation in Domitian's eyes. The silence that followed seemed full of Auriane's soundless laughter.

At last Domitian said with disgust, "I never despise you more than when you make sense, curses on you." His temples felt they were being prodded with knives. "*My head!* Loathsome woman. Ungrateful city. Piggish populace." He turned round to Auriane, regarding her with a malignant smile, running his gaze appraisingly up and down her frame as if noticing its sturdiness for the first time.

"I have it now—the perfect punishment for her, in keeping with her unnatural viciousness and her love of war. And it will be carried out *after* the procession, so we'll lose no captives."

She is done! Marcus Julianus thought. What more can I do? I have come to an impassable wall. But I cannot stop trying.

Domitian looked steadily into Auriane's eyes as he spoke. "Tell me, Marcus, good friend, did you attend any part of the September Games?"

"The races, once," he answered quietly. Marcus Julianus tensed; already he felt horror's first prickling touch.

"A pity you are incapable of appreciating the arena. When we lose sight of the elemental struggle of life against death, we become useless as aging eunuchs. The point of a blade—*that* is the fulcrum of life. I am sorry you missed my re-creation of the siege of Troy. It was *months* in preparation. I had two architect-engineers build me a wonderful model of the walls of Troy, with trapdoors, a higher tower than anyone's ever seen, and collapsing walls. We even made small siege engines. Four hundred died that afternoon—and all fought like heroes. It was *most* inspiring." He turned to Marcus Julianus, smiling with pride, his headache vanished as he delighted in the memory.

"And you know what else we had, my dear Julianus? *Women.* Twenty-nine of them." He ran a finger slowly down the line of

Auriane's throat as he whispered this. To Marcus Julianus there was something horrible in the gesture, as if he imagined slitting it open.

"They were supposed to be the Amazons who attacked the Greeks at Troy. We had Aristos himself garbed as Achilles—can you imagine! He's an ignorant beast who knows no more of history than a baboon, but someone must have filled his head with legends because he slew the Amazon Queen Penthesilea and ravaged her corpse and gouged out her eyes, just like the real Achilles in the tales. *Clever*, no? And all his own idea! The applause he got!

"But Troy—that was *my* creation. I tell you, Marcus, there was not a spectator, plebeian or noble, but who loved it. And the women! It is so *amusing*, watching women fight. There's such a wild, catlike desperation to it, such a low cunning. I tell you, women have a savage survival instinct hitherto underappreciated."

He shrugged and turned back to Marcus Julianus. "Unfortunately, none of those women survived. So I've got to train a new batch."

"You cannot mean this." Now Marcus Julianus made no effort to disguise the horror in his voice. He had not felt such impotent rage, such loathing of all life since the urine-soaked Lucius Grannus seized him to drag him to his death. *With all I have gained since those barren days: wealth beyond any procurator's ability to calculate, influence that is the envy of all, the companionship of philosophers, a school and library that together form a fortress of knowledge—still I can do nothing for her.*

"My sweet viper . . . ," Domitian continued, looking severely at Auriane, "I condemn you to the arena. And since you show such precocity in fighting men, you shall be matched against men. You will fight for your life until all the fight is worn out of you." Terror flickered in Auriane's eyes, though she did not perfectly understand all this. Domitian finished in a whisper: *"I'll see to it you envy the dead!"*

If you live that long, monster, Marcus Julianus thought. You'll want her trained first to make it more amusing. It leaves me ample time to prepare your death.

To Marcus Julianus' dismay, Domitian swung round, content now and smiling expansively, and put a huge, paternal hand on his shoulder. "My great and good friend! You saved my life. I shall not forget this, not ever."

"One ostrich, well aimed. Really, it was nothing."

"Ah!" Domitian clutched his temples dramatically and lowered himself onto a stone bench. "Knives! Knives in my head." Domitian appeared almost physically smaller now, not imperial at all; he might have been any weary, disgruntled shopkeeper.

"Sit, my lord. I will summon the litter so you will not have to walk back to your chambers. I'll relay to the Guard that you want the woman taken at once back to the camp. And I'll order your audiences canceled tomorrow."

"Excellent! I scarcely know what I would do without you. Ah, for the life of a simple artisan!"

Within the temple was a bellpull with which Marcus Julianus summoned litter bearers; in moments a litter borne by eight Bithynian bearers in Domitian's white livery loomed into sight on the torchlit pathway. The litter descended; Domitian climbed in. Swiftly and silently they bore the Emperor off.

Marcus Julianus then sought Plautius at his post along the portico. Plautius had lately been brought into the conspiracy, the first man of the Praetorians with whom Julianus had succeeded. It was Plautius who had alerted him, almost too late, that Auriane was to be brought here tonight—a service for which Marcus Julianus meant to reward him with a hundred silver *denarii*.

"Is it not too *soon?*" Plautius whispered to him. Beneath his gold helmet all Marcus Julianus could see of him was a formidable jawline and eyes that were small, glowing fire-pits. Plautius was still roused by Domitian's affronts to his dignity.

"That was *her* attempt, not mine," Marcus Julianus explained quickly. "She's to be taken back. Have that carriage brought round *slowly*—I mean to look about here for a moment."

Plautius nodded knowingly, not questioning, assuming Marcus Julianus meant to investigate the layout of temple and grounds as a possible site for the deed when the fateful time came.

"Clever of you, discouraging him from destroying the woman," Plautius whispered. "That shredded the last scrap of *my* men's respect for him—you've ripened the fruit for plucking!"

"Don't try my famous modesty by overburdening it with praise. Go. And slowly!"

Plautius gave him a grim smile, turned crisply about, and was gone. Marcus Julianus returned to the small temple of Sylvanus, where Auriane still waited in shackles.

He struggled briefly with a spontaneous fantasy of bearing her off like some hero of old, knowing the notion utter folly even as he thought it—they would never get beyond the first milestone.

These are, after all, he mused, modern times: If she can be saved at all, it will not be through the labors of Hercules but through the more subtle and methodical labors of the mind.

He halted when he was ten or twelve feet distant from her. She watched him warily, putting him in mind of a wild horse that might bolt at his approach.

I must be prepared for it if she never comes to me, if she lives out what remains of her life in bitterness toward all mankind.

A three-quarter moon had risen over the top of the Alban Mount; he had the sense it was the archaic eye of some sky-riding night hag, old when Diana was young, possessively tracking Auriane. A dark wind animated the fan palms, ruffling her mane of tumbled-down hair. It scarcely seemed possible he was at last alone with her, attended only by the five bronze serpents watching with malign eyes.

She shivered faintly in a night that was colder than it should have been in this season. He unfastened his cloak and began walking toward her slowly.

The diminishing distance between them seemed alive. That was not wariness he saw in her eyes, he realized, but wonder. *Those eyes!* They were tremulous pools of distilled intelligence, watching him with the bright silence of a woodland creature.

But still he could not guess her thoughts, and the torment this brought was new to him. He came up beside her, gently drew the cloak around her shoulders and fastened it, careful as he did so not to touch her or look upon her bared breast, lest she despise him and count it one more act of violation in a night of many. Subtle scents of pine and grass drifted from her hair. Her skin sparkled faintly with gold dust. She lifted her head slightly to hold his gaze—he was taller than she, but barely—and the look in those great, round eyes was like a soft, exploring touch. The silence was like wine, fortifying and warm.

He broke it when he saw the cut from the whip. He put a hand to her chin and turned her head gently to better see.

"The *swine!*" he muttered softly.

"That is an insult to swine!" she replied with such sober earnestness that he smiled. That voice put him in mind of the lower notes of a wooden flute.

"I mean to aid you," he said, feeling he extended a tentative hand across a gulf between worlds. "I mean no harm. . . . do you understand? I beg you, do not judge me by the others." More to give comfort than because it was necessary, he reached out and gently straightened the cloak, which was too large for her and began to slip from one shoulder. "I would have you count me a friend . . . but that may not be possible."

With a look she asked the question, *Why?*

He told her his name. She repeated it slowly, taking possession of it. Her eyes darkened with recognition. "The name is known to me. It is that of my father's old enemy, the Governor."

"I am his son. By your custom, I am your enemy. Though for myself, I prefer to select my enemies personally—I do not inherit them."

Those somber, searching eyes studied him intently. "I count you a friend, even as a friend of old, though I cannot account for this."

"I too can account for none of this," he replied, marveling at how she could seem so artless, yet so knowing. Urgently he spoke on. "There is much I must tell you, and I must say it quickly. First, your child is alive—at least there is no reason to believe she is not—"

"Not *truly!*"

"Yes. They lied to you to force you to open the gates. They never found the babe. When our soldiers came to Alder Lake, there was no island—and no Ramis." To Marcus Julianus, this meant some clever native had led the Roman forces to the wrong place.

But Auriane took it to mean Ramis rendered the island invisible through sorcery. Joy came like a sudden flush of drunkenness. Warm strength flooded into her, as if a dead limb on her body were rejuvenated with blood. *"Avenahar!"* she whispered. "Blessed day. She lives!" She looked off, eyes silvery with tears. Then she looked back at him, recognition in her eyes.

"You are the man who tried to save me in my own country."

"Yes."

"And yet, if I had done as you wished," she continued haltingly, painfully conscious of how rude her speech must sound, "you would never have seen me again. You would have gained nothing . . . except the possibility of causing your own ruin."

"It was a choice of your death or your living free. There were no other choices, then."

It seemed her soul edged very close, but still there was a hesitation, a distance. But what truly did I expect? he thought, quietly despairing. It is foolish to think that great love, just because it is felt, will be returned in equal measure. "Come then," he said gently. "I'll take you back."

It was then that she banished all his doubts.

Swiftly she caught up his hand in her own. It was done with such passion and urgency it was intimate as a coming together of bodies; at the same time it was an embrace of spirits, rich with the rapture of unbounded understanding. His joy was almost too great. It closed all wounds. He felt what some philosophers promised for the moment of death: union in brilliant light with all that was ever desired, a moment not merely of feeling love but of becoming love.

She closed her eyes as if overcome. He bent his head, raised that hand to his lips, and softly kissed it.

She came close then, moving her head inquisitively against his chest, nuzzling him like a pony, and then was still, resting against him contentedly. He found her complete and immediate trust in him a surprise and a delight; it was like that of the child who has never known hurt, who has no doubt it will be loved. *Yet, of course, she has known abominable things. How she trusts so well is a mystery.*

Without knowing what prompted him to act, he took the amulet of earth from about his neck. He paused for the briefest moment, thinking: Am I mad? I have worn this all my life. My own father gave it reverence; it is infused with his soul. It brought me out of Hades and led me into the light.

But he placed the amulet about Auriane's neck anyway, certain that was where it belonged.

Auriane held it to the torchlight, regarding it in dread silence as if it were the most sacred of temple relics. Then she looked at him.

"Who *are* you, that you have this?" she whispered.

"I am no more than who you see. As for how I got it, that's a tale for another time."

"How can this be? I had its twin . . . before I bloodied my hands. I . . . I cannot keep it! I lost the right."

"Who has said so?" he said, smiling. "I'll not be content unless you take it."

A long shudder passed through her. She smelled a pine fire and saw a hooded figure in black chanting low, life-bringing words. That I have even *seen* this holy thing, she thought, signifies Ramis opened her eyes to look at me. I bolted off her path. Have I somehow blundered back onto it? Have the gods sent this man as a pathfinder?

From far too near came loud talk and the clink of metal. The carriage was readied. "Plautius!" Marcus Julianus called out loudly, to allay any suspicions that might arise among the rest of the Guard. "Help me with her. She's dead weight here, she lost consciousness!"

Then, holding her tightly, her cheek pressed to his, he whispered, "I mean to get you *out* of this wretched predicament or die trying. Do not worry, I won't let them use you as part of any bloody spectacle! Be patient and do their bidding for now. I cannot let the Emperor know I am aiding you. As I live, I mean to see you free."

He saw blots of light through the oleander, and a torch's reflection on a gold breastplate. "Fall in a faint!" he whispered. She did so, and he caught her. Then Plautius and two of his fellows came up noisily.

Auriane imagined she dropped into warm, nurturing water. All the while she was aware of the close tender presence of the moon, seeming to affirm, *Yes, still I am here. Yes, still I wait.*

And there came then secret, sure, swift-gliding serpent thoughts she knew came from the mind of Fria: *Your fate has turned. All dies to rise again. What you learned in darkness, you will learn again in light.*

CHAPTER XXXIV

On the following day Domitian's spies disguised as fishmongers brought him alarming news from the city's streets. A troupe of actors had presented a play on a makeshift stage before the Temple of Mercury. His informants said they thought he should know the play told the story of a young Parthian prince who fought with his father the king, and was despised by his older brother, the designated successor. The prince gained the army's support through bribes, then provoked a war on the barbarian frontier— but the war brought him only ridicule, and he did not regain his father's favor. The unloved prince was tall, tending to baldness, had an inordinate love of eunuchs, and practiced archery. There could be no doubt as to who was being ridiculed.

"How did it end?" Domitian demanded to know. The young prince, they related, murdered his older brother, but never took the throne himself because he was torn apart by an avenging mob.

This caused the first grave crack in the dam that contained Domitian's rising rage at the populace. To worsen matters, Auriane's words, *"You are no fit king,"* prodded him continuously, seeming in one moment an uncouth woman's simple nonsense, easily ignored, and in the next, a prophetic and profound thrust to the heart.

When the hapless players set up their stage in the same location on the next day, a detachment of the Praetorian Guard arrested the cast and scattered the audience, many of whom were crushed to death when they choked the narrow streets attempting to escape. The actor who played the prince was crucified on the stage. The author of the play attempted to hide, but was hunted down and murdered the next day while bathing in one of the cheaper bathhouses.

It brought a wretched gloom to the city's streets. That play, people exclaimed, had first been performed in the reign of Nero—resemblances must have been accidental, though doubtless made more incriminating by the informers' imaginative exaggerations. Overnight, no more plays were performed before the temples; laughter lessened, whispering increased, and the tanner squinted suspiciously at the fuller, wondering if he was a spy. Not only writers of plays but anyone of education who happened to have an epic poem or ode lying about in his study quietly burned it for fear it might be found by a servant, then turned over to an informer for pay, and duly misinterpreted. Every pen carried a burden of fear. Domitian was mystified and hurt when he was told of the people's temper and accepted no responsibility for it.

In the last days before the triumphal procession, Domitian was heard often to mutter to those about him, *"On that day I give the rabble one last chance to redeem themselves."* Marcus Julianus prayed the people would pay him proper homage so they would suffer no more.

The dawn of the day of Domitian's processional entry into Rome found the city washed clean and gaily dressed—streets were swept, temples garlanded, their doors companionably left open. The smoke of thanksgiving sacrifices rose delicately, wistfully, before the temples' majestic doors. Chaplets of roses were sold in every street. The multitudes of statues of goddesses, gods and men crowding the Forums were wreathed with laurel. All labor, slave and free, was halted for the day.

Before dawn, men of the City Cohorts lined the procession's sacred route. It would begin at the Triumphal Gate. Then it would wend its way about the city, going down the Via Lata, round the course of the Flaminian Circus, then about the Palatine, past the Colosseum and the house of the Vestals, until it came to its destination, the steps of Temple of Jupiter, where Domitian would preside over a great sacrifice of one hundred and twenty white oxen. Everyone, from rag sellers to patricians, rose before first light to battle for space. They thronged the rooftops and the steps of temples; they crowded into the windows of the upper stories of tenements and onto the makeshift tiers of seats erected in the Forum. Those who had rooms with windows and balconies that overlooked the processional way sold their fellow citizens the right to enter their quarters and watch.

As the October sun gilded the city's jumbled red-tiled roofs and began its steady climb, parasols of all colors bloomed throughout the throng. Along the route, vendors set up stands and began their melodious cries, selling melons, figs, sausages, meat pies, hard-boiled eggs, and for drinking, fermented quince juice, vinegar-water and cheap wines sweetened with lead. Others set up shop selling votive statues of the city's patron gods and small commemorative equestrian statues of the Emperor. All the people that fed on crowds—jugglers, acrobats, snake charmers, Etruscan fortune-tellers—appeared spontaneously wherever they could find space. Prostitutes set up flimsy stalls with little more than a blanket hung in the doorway for privacy and settled before them, awaiting customers. So many citizens were arrayed in white in honor of the victory it would have appeared to a hawk above as though northern snow came to the city for a day.

This was a spectacle not witnessed since early in the reign of Vespasian, when Titus entered the city in triumph after the fall of Jerusalem. The excitement was touched with some solemnity, for this was the one time when war, normally so comfortably distant from the capital city, revealed to the populace some small measure of its reality and horror. For all the eight centuries since the founding of Rome, the right to enter the city in triumph had been the highest honor the Senate could confer upon a conquering general. The glory of it hardly lessened in these latter days, in spite of the fact that the game was no longer open to any contender and it could now be awarded only to the Emperor or members of his family. The procession's origins stretched back into the mythic haze of the most ancient days. Some maintained that in those shadowy times this grim parade was the ritual last ride of the god Mars in the guise of a mortal man, journeying to bloody sacrifice in a chariot drawn by four white horses. Even to the present day, by long custom, the triumphant general's face was painted red, a practice learned men could only explain if he were indeed once Mars, the red god, on his way to die for the land. The earliest processions were modest affairs, carried out with an air of melancholy necessity, as sacramental rites meant to propitiate the gods for crimes committed in war. But as Rome conquered vaster territories, as not just neighboring city-states but whole kingdoms fell before it, the processions evolved into theatrical display, in which the captured wealth of nations was flaunted before the world. Rome never completely forgot its beginnings as a small, beleagured city-state constantly threatened with extinction; the sight of hordes of prisoners of war herded before the triumphal chariot offered a primitive reassurance, a promise that now their city could live in safety forever, that Roman rule would never end. It was a time when the humblest baker could feel he sat upon Olympus, gazing down upon a subdued and obedient world.

Silence came to the crowd massed about the Triumphal Gate as the third hour of morning approached. Twenty-four trumpeters arrayed in scarlet and white passed beneath the Gate and halted. Thousands of heads turned to them; the hum of the multitude died as if at a signal. Then the trumpeters assaulted the silence with a fanfare that was at once pompous and barbarous. Many felt their souls seize up in reverential wonder before this brassy assertion of the everlasting power of their state.

The trumpeters then began the march. Directly behind them came the Senators and magistrates, walking with funereal slowness. The crowd stirred and grew restless as all strained to see. Most wanted only to view the captives, the wild Chattian warriors of whom they had heard fantastic tales; they did not expect this procession to have impressive heaps of spoil—this enemy had no wealth to match that shown off after the sack of Jerusalem in Titus' day. Germania was so remote to most as to be a place of fantasy; many had heard tales the captives were of superhuman size, or so frightening in aspect that women would fall in a faint at the sight of them. Everywhere there was excited speculation about them: At what hour would they pass? Would their chains secure them? Would they be seven feet tall and have golden hair flowing to the ground? Several battle-maids were said to be among them, an added curiosity that made them seem more barbarous still. This war had caused blond tresses to be in fashion. Great numbers of the women in the crowd bleached their hair for the occasion, using goat fat and ashes of beechwood, or wore blond wigs fashioned from the tresses of their fair-haired slaves.

On the night before the procession, the Chattian captives had been put in heavy chains, shackled in rows of ten abreast. They were given no food, little water, and allowed no rest to render them more tractable as they were assembled on the Field of Mars.

Of the journey to the Triumphal Gate, Auriane remembered only the brutal glare of the sun, the stifling heat, the nip of dust in the throat, and the weight of ponderous chains. Their feet were left bare; hers were cut and bleeding before the captives even finished this first miserable leg of the journey. A guard rode up and down the line, snapping a whip. She and Sunia were chained together in the rear of the long file of captives; battle-maids were but a small joke for the people. Coniaric, nobly tall, and the massively muscled Thorgild were what they flocked to see; she knew they were chained in the first ranks of this shameful regiment.

They treated her as a beast and, mercifully, she became a beast, allowing herself no reflection, but one fear crept in nevertheless: How much humilation can be borne before the spirit shrivels and no longer supports the body?

Junilla watched the procession from the cool colonnade of the great-house of her sometimes friend, sometimes enemy, the aristocratic Sabina, wife of one of the more loyal and plodding members of the Senate. They reclined among bright silk cushions on couches carved in the shape of swans, inlaid with lapis and mother-of-pearl. Since dawn they had been sipping watered Chian wine cooled with snow. Sabina's house offered a fine view of the Via Lata.

Junilla was saying in a sleepy drawl, ". . . and so I was forced to pay two hundred thousand for a *horse!*" Her eyes, normally dark, glinting jewels, today were hazed and harmless as a well-fed cat's. She turned over with the languid, undulating motion of a ship rolling on a swell in a calm sea and looked irritably at Sabina.

Her friend lay deep in the cushions as if she were weighted by stones, her dark hair matted to a damp forehead, her fleshy arm half concealing a wine-flushed face. Sabina tolerated Junilla because she was the best source of scurrilous gossip in the city. Junilla's bond to Sabina was flexible and somewhat frayed, and always dependent upon circumstance. Lately they were allies because they shared a common enemy, Marcus Arrius Julianus. Sabina loathed him because he was responsible for bringing her husband before the magistrates on a charge of abusing the slaves on one of his estates. And Junilla's malice toward him had, through the years, hardened into avenging passion—all the influence, honor and renown he enjoyed he should be sharing with her. Junilla was drawn to Sabina's perfectly maintained cloak of respectability; publicly at least, Sabina played convincingly the role of upright matron, welcome in any aristocratic house. While this social solidity fascinated Junilla, at the same time it brought out in her an uncontrollable desire to nip away at it.

"Sabina, are you *listening* to me?" She is disgustingly drunk, Junilla thought, reaching out slyly and moving Sabina's wine cup out of her friend's reach. "It's the *very* horse, mind you," Junilla went on, her eyes easing shut, "that belonged to that *Amazon* they brought back with the captives. I did it, my dear, because I found out quite by accident who the other bidder was—an agent of none other than our own dearest Marcus Arrius Julianus, may a dozen Harpies rip out his vitals. And it was quite obvious my curiosity frightened his agent off. Now *why* do you suppose that a man who has as much interest in racing as you do in sleeping with your husband was willing to spend a fortune on one horse?"

"You are amusing as a case of scabies, Junilla," Sabina replied, her face muffled in cushions. "Wake me when those beautiful, barbarous, *bestial* German men come by."

"This is why you never learn anything interesting that passes in this city! If you had a little more *curiosity* that elusive husband of yours would not get away with so much. He'd be about more, and when you got an itch, you wouldn't be forced to couple with those cold stone satyrs in your garden."

"Junilla!"

"Sabina dearest, I'm only trying to keep you awake. Listen to me. I have an amusing suspicion about my former beloved husband, he who has the temerity to count *me* not good enough for *him*. Just what does he intend to *do* with the beast? Tutor it in philosophy? I can't *abide* not knowing. If he tells me what he wants it for, I may even sell the nag to him, for triple what I paid, of course. Sabina, what are you thinking of? It's clear you're not listening."

"Lots of things. Their heaving chests . . . their broad shoulders . . . their muscular legs . . ."

"Sabina, do you have anything *else* on what is left of your mind?"

Sabina narrowed her eyes, a warning to Junilla that she overstepped even the greater bounds she allowed her friend when she was drunk. But Junilla did not notice.

"Imagine poor dear Marcus' anger when he found out who got the horse he wanted so terribly badly. I'm going to chase this mystery down to the end, like hounds at the hunt. It might be just my fancy, but I smell some connection between him and that

Amazon. Things have been so *boring* of late—it's the curse of the times when we're saddled with an Emperor who has no sense of humor. I miss Nero. *Think* of it, Sabina. Our cultured Councillor, paragon of virtuous behavior, legal advisor to the Great Virtuous Bore himself, panting after a she-beast who probably tears animals apart and eats them raw. It could be the most amusing scandal since Vinicius' blushing bride turned out at the end of the ceremony to be a boy."

Sabina, still smarting from Junilla's verbal slaps, raised her head with effort and narrowed her normally soft, tolerant blue eyes. "Or," she retorted, "since the time a certain noblewoman was hauled before the magistrates because the tender young flower of boyhood she plucked off a back street and depetaled slowly in her boudoir, debauching him in every way known to man or animal, turned out to be the unfortunately unattended son of the sitting Consul."

The haze cleared quickly from Junilla's eyes. "Sabina, if you *ever* mention that again, we are no longer friends!" Junilla turned from her and sank into smoking silence.

Below them the procession moved on with the infinite patience of an incoming tide, continuing down the Via Lata. Two dozen sacred fluteblowers followed the parade of magistrates, adding the chill, airy sound of double flutes to the continuous purring roar of the throng. They were followed by public slaves prodding the one hundred and twenty white oxen bound for sacrifice. The tips of their horns were gilded and garlands were laid upon their heads; their red-braided fillets gently swayed. Behind the oxen came the twelve assistant priests who would carry out the sacrifice, bearing poleaxes and knives.

After them came a train of wagons drawn by plumed black Thessalian horses; in them were heaped the spoils of the Chattian war. In the first ten wagons were the captured arms of the warriors slain in the final assault: shields splashed with bright, barbarous color, spears with fire-hardened ends, exotically made swords heavily encrusted with gems. Then came wagons heaped with treasure: fine horse trappings, ceremonial drinking horns, great embossed silver cauldrons and cups, and all manner of ornaments of amber, gold and jet. Some murmured admiringly that they had not known the tribe possessed such wealth. Others insisted the wagons were not actually piled so high as they seemed; blankets were concealed beneath, then covered over with the plunder to make the spoil appear richer. This tale spread slowly near the gate where the crowd was thickest with the veterans of the war, then more quickly as it moved into the inner districts of the city where the poorer people were closely massed. The crowd was bored with the spoil long before it had all passed. How much longer, they muttered, before we are shown the captives?

But next they were given a parade of creatures native to the north. Three aurochs were exhibited, each hobbled and blindfolded within its own wagon and held securely by two public slaves. Then came an elk, also hobbled and secured, an ibex, and a dozen wild Tarpan horses. And finally a caged mountain cat, the creature that was the spirit-animal of the conquered tribe.

This exhibit was followed by twenty red-liveried slaves bearing a great map painted on wood, showing the extent of the territory that had been annexed to Rome. It illustrated the new frontier line—in some places the old frontier was pushed back more than a hundred miles—but few in the throng were impressed. "One hundred miles of wasteland!" a well-known tavern-keeper was heard to proclaim. "With no cities and no wealth! With what we paid for this in taxes, we could have captured India!"

And then from this same tavern keeper's roof where women of the Prostitutes' Guild were gathered, there came the cry, *"They come!"* A wealthy brothel-keeper, a woman of proud bearing called Matidia, was first to catch sight of the captives. "Have you ever seen such human beasts!" she exclaimed. The prostitutes nearly pushed each other off the roof in their eagerness to see.

When all the captives had passed beneath the Triumphal Gate and the last rank came into view, one of Matidia's women cried: *"There she is!* There is the woman!"

"Look at her! So calm and brave—I pity her!" another of Matidia's women exclaimed.

"But she is not blond!" exclaimed a third, as if this were some shameful affliction.

"You're a fool! She's a pretty thing—she's no need to dye her hair to *your* taste!" Matidia remonstrated, squinting beneath her parasol. "If I could just get a lock of it, I could match that bronze hue on my own head."

The whole of the crowd became more alive; all pushed to get a closer look. The cry *"The captives come!"* was quickly carried into the depths of the city.

On the colonnade of her great house, Sabina sat straight up. "What is to be done with them?" she asked Junilla, eyes alight, her breath coming more deeply as she got her first clear view of the regally tall Chattian warriors. "They're not to be destroyed, I hope?"

"Well, after a fashion. For certain they'll fight in the celebration games."

"Junilla, you've an uncanny influence over the Virtuous Bore. Can you get him to sell me one of those fine ones in front, under a false name?"

The captives numbered five thousand; in rank upon rank they came, moving with the fitful steps of prodded animals. After the brilliant colors of the first part of the procession, the prisoners in their gray-brown rags seemed dull as wrens beside peacocks. Most kept their eyes cast down, feeling very much the shame; others looked about them, dazed and unseeing, while still others outstretched their arms in gestures of begging mercy. The captives provoked hostility in some, but to many they brought an obscure relief. The sight of them brought up fears normally submerged— nestled deep in the heart of every citizen was the terror of being in their place.

Auriane, in the last rank, walked with her hair wild and loose, her head held up not in defiance but in an attitude of carefully maintained pride, her gaze levelly ahead. From the first, the sight of her caught at the hearts of the poor and disadvantaged among the throng, and particularly the women. Of all this sorrowful company she appeared the most undaunted.

Sunia kept her gaze locked to the ground. For all she knew or cared, she and Auriane might as well have been alone; about them was some earthly Underworld peopled with a sea of obscenely grinning demons. Sunia had tried in past days to persuade Auriane to tell her what had passed in the garden of the Roman King, but Auriane seemed not ready to speak of it. Sunia had seen a shift in her temperament, however. Before, Auriane had been a weary woman bearing up well, but one whose hopes were nearly played out. And now, that weary part of her had become more like a child, eager but fearful as she faced a new life. Often Sunia found her smiling a smile like that of a woman first given her child after birth. Well, *that* was reasonable, Sunia thought; Auriane *had* told her she had learned Avenahar lived. Sunia stole a look at Auriane as she walked beside her now in chains. That strength was a nagging mystery. She walks to death and degradation, Sunia thought, as if she were a bride going to her groom.

When the line of captives turned from the Via Lata, moving on to the Flaminian Circus, Auriane sensed a shift in the mood of the crowd: It became more derisive and hostile. Once she heard a voice exclaim: "What is this? What does he take us for?" And farther on she heard a man bellow: "Look *there,* in the rear! Is this some jest?" Auriane was perplexed, but certain that the captives were somehow being mocked.

Among the prostitutes on the tavern keeper's rooftop, beyond Auriane's hearing, Matidia cried out: *"I* should know a blond wig when I see one! Look there, at that man in the middle ranks! *Bona Dea,* if that is not a wig, I am the chief Vestal!" Rivulets of laughter and comment moved swiftly through the throng.

Below her in the tavern's shadow, one of the undercooks of the Palace kitchens called out, "That man there, second from the end, in the fifth rank! By Venus, I *know* him! He's apprenticed to one of the Palace bakers. That's no *captive!* Are we to be taken for fools?"

These words flew like grassfire through the crowds. Within the hour the whole of the throng was convinced that Domitian filled out more than half the captives' number with Palace slaves disguised as Chattian warriors.

But then the angry mutterings were momentarily stilled, for the Emperor approached. Domitian's lictors, the footmen who traditionally cleared the way for a great man, moved beneath the gate with solemn step. The number of lictors allowed a magistrate had always been an indication of the extent of his civil power; so august a personage as the City Praetor was preceded by six. But Domitian, to no one's surprise, awarded himself twenty-four. Each bore on his shoulder the *fasces,* bundles of birch rods and axes secured with a leather thong, symbolizing the absolute power held by the man who came after them. Their march was accompanied by the stern, inexorable pounding of a drum, a sound that reprimanded the soul and warned all to walk in time.

Then four milky horses harnessed abreast emerged from the shadows of the gate; they capered sideways, out of step with the drum, fighting their jewel-bedecked reins. From high on the Gate, saffron was tossed into the air. The triumphal chariot bearing Domitian moved into the yellow mist.

A prodigious roar swelled up at the sight of him. Those massed about the Triumphal Gate were mostly veterans, soldiers on leave, and merchants from outlying towns—people who had either benefited from Domitian's rule or not been adversely affected. They were easily swept up in the exciting delusion that the faraway wooden figure standing in that fantastic chariot of ebony, ivory and gold was an earth-bound divinity, the deliverer of them all.

Domitian stared stiffly ahead, rigid and cold as his ever-more-numerous golden statues. The red paint daubed on his face made him appear to wear a bloody mask—a macabre visage somehow fitting since he had commanded the letting of so much blood. A garland of Delphic laurel crowned his head. In his upraised hand was an ivory scepter surmounted by a golden eagle—spirit-bird of this tribe that overswept the world. His tunic was of Tyrian purple stitched with silver palms, the sign of victory. Over it was a majestic purple toga embroidered with stars. Public slaves walking alongside the chariot bore swinging pots of incense; the dense black smoke drifting from them veiled the chariot, obscuring, then revealing the Emperor, suggesting the clouds shrouding Olympus. He was mythic, remote, a terrible yet merciful colossus deigning to let the common people look upon him.

Standing behind Domitian in the chariot was another public slave; to him fell the duty of holding over Domitian's head a gem-studded Etruscan crown. This slave repeated the ritual words *"Look behind you—remember you are mortal,"* a charm intended to protect the triumphant general from the jealous wrath of the gods.

But Domitian heard the words of the charm no more than he heard the buzzing of the pesky fly that determined to follow him the moment he ascended the chariot in the Field of Mars. He was absorbed in studying every nuance of the populace's cheers as critically as a musician listens to a rival's music.

Yes, he thought, those cheers sound well and sincere. But by the bones of Aeneas they were louder and more laden with love for my cursed brother, after Jerusalem.

All the years I fought for this! And it is naught but empty noise. As always, the prize disappears like smoke in the grasping of it. Those masons there by the way, with their callused hands and bent backs, are more content than I.

Next he thought of Marcus Julianus, who first refused to take

his place among the Senators leading the procession, then at the
last even hatched an excuse not to join the dignitaries awaiting him
at the Temple of Jupiter. Domitian suspected his First Advisor
harbored some obscure and unaccountable contempt for all of
this—the war and the people's need of war. How, he wondered,
can the soured view of one man foul what I have lusted for all my
life?

But it does. Domitian realized then, his eyes watering from the
smoke, how vital it was to him that Marcus Arrius Julianus witness
the procession—that he was not here made it almost as if it had
not been.

Madness. Do I love the man that much? I more nearly hate him.
It is impious, of course, to hate a man who saved your life . . .
but it's difficult to love a man who lays ever more skillful traps for
you, determined to show you unworthy.

Behind the Emperor's ceremonial chariot marched the men of
the legions that had fought in the war, in rank upon endless
rank—excepting the detachments left behind to guard Domitian's
new frontier. Their upraised javelins were green with laurel. The
next titanic wave of cheers were for them. The people threw roses,
which caught on their weapons or were crushed on the paving
stones by booted feet.

The procession passed round the Flaminian Circus's course,
then on into the city's heart, its carts of glittering treasure like
some sumptuous barge drifting through a human sea.

Auriane for long had let herself be aware of nothing but the hot
cobbles beneath her feet, her searing thirst, the press of more
humanity than she knew existed in all the Three Worlds, the
strangely disturbing smells of competing perfumes with their oil
bases growing rancid in the heat, the odor of burnt fat from the
vendors' stalls, the smell of death and sickness coming from her
own people, the mercifully blinding sun that blotted from view the
hard, curious faces of the multitudes. But as the procession made
its way through the Circus Maximus and round the Palatine, and
the sun climbed high enough that it did not blind, curiosity
overcame her and she began to look.

All about her she saw amazements to stop the heart, edifices
Decius' paltry descriptions fell miserably short of capturing. She
was long used to wondrous displays of nature; it was new to her
to be humbled by the works of men. Climbing the hills, almost
seeming to rest atop each other were blindingly white dwellings
for giants, at once massive and delicate as they soared up, pushing

back the sky, many so covered in bronze or gold they glowed with liquid fire as if freshly pulled from some colossal forge. She did not know the temples of their gods from the dwelling places of men. She could no more comprehend the complexity of it all than she could have known every leaf upon entering a grove. The columned temples and government buildings were to her eyes groves of stone, with columns in place of trees, bristling with the labyrinthine mysteries of this strange race. Here nature was brought utterly to her knees, and men made themselves magnificent in her place. Everywhere along the way images of goddesses and gods loomed, serene faces frozen in gold; everywhere water rushed with forceful purpose or leapt playfully as salmon, to land noisily in stone beds. And the bestial roaring echoing through these canyons never ceased punishing the ear. She feared the sights and sounds crashing in upon her would drive her mad.

The Sky Hall itself could not be so dizzying or mysterious. These people need go nowhere after death, she thought; they lived like gods already. If the Three Fates themselves had issued forth from the high doors of one of the temples, her astonishment could not have been greater. This was the most fantastic weaving of Fria's magic, the ultimate source of the marvels of which she had glimpsed but scraps in her own country. The villas, the far-shooting missiles, were marvels enough. But now she came upon the nest; here marvels swarmed.

How simple these people must think us! she thought as she felt acutely the throng's probing looks. Why does this enemy bother with us?

She forced herself then to remember the man in the Emperor's garden. *Marcus Arrius Julianus.* The memory of him was a stable place in the midst of brilliant, pulsing chaos. Already it had begun to animate the dead part of her, to rouse what she thought would never sense again, and tantalize her with the possibility of dissolving old, calcified shame.

Great spirit and friend, Auriane invoked him silently, you who bear the name of my father's enemy, spirit that always was— between us is a graceful, unfathomable understanding, bound to take me to the end of my days.

Ramis would say there's not a mystery in all this; it is only that he mirrors me as I truly am. Somehow that disappoints. Can that be all of it? Normally Ramis makes things too obscure; in matters of love it always seemed she made them too simple.

How utterly strange that he possessed the sacred mold—there are, after all, only two in existence. No matter how he *says* he acquired it, it was given by Ramis. And stranger still is that he gave it to me. Perhaps it is the very one I lost on the battlefield?

Baldemar, witness—I understand none of this! Why was I brought here if not to free you? But I cannot, without spilling more blood. But the return of this amulet can only be a stern warning to shun battlefields forever, a reminder that all who stand on Midgard are of one blood.

She knew suddenly the current that had tugged at her all her life, always dragging her outward, meant to pull her *here*. Here the pull slackened, the deep waters pooled. The city seemed a sentient thing, watching her with subtle, glittering eyes. It had waited long.

She heard a sound like a puppy's cry and gradually realized Sunia was speaking in an ululating voice: *"Now they kill us . . . now it comes . . ."*

Auriane turned slightly to look at Sunia, all the while carefully concealing her own feelings of alarm, for she was determined to give her tormentors no satisfaction. Sunia's eyes were glazed and her head lolled forward; she looked like a beast under the yoke.

"Sunia," she said firmly, half shouting to be heard over the din, "I swear by my mother and father, the *oxen* die today, not us."

"How can you know it? Every tribe of the earth gives its prisoners to the gods."

"Not this one. We're to be saved for another purpose—but know that for now at least, we will live."

Sunia seemed to listen intently, but Auriane saw little comprehension in her face.

"I have . . ." Auriane hesitated. "I have the word of a man greater than their Emperor, a man too noble to say an untruth."

It was no use. Sunia's wild, sightless look remained.

As the procession moved past the House of the Vestals, closing in upon its destination, they came to the district where the poorest and bitterest people were massed, those who had felt most keenly the punishing hand of Domitian, in the form of brutally enforced regulations for small shopkeepers, harsh restrictions on the freedoms of freedmen, and most recently the savage suppression of the street play. Here the throng was like turbid, dangerous water—the jeers directed at the captives were more bold. Some made obscene gestures at her tribesmen or chanted mocking words in unison.

"A poor show!" she heard several voices cry from the upper story of a tenement block. She felt her limbs weighted with dismay. Now the eyes of the mob had the evil, empty light of beasts of prey.

For the first time Auriane began to feel broken inside.

Have they not humiliated us enough by parading us as criminals? Fria, give me the strength to keep my head lifted and walk on!

Auriane struggled to do the ritual of fire. She was aware that Sunia's steps slowed; she feared the younger woman would collapse to the ground and be dragged. She found Sunia's hand and grasped it firmly, while a knot of terror began to form in her stomach.

What possessed this monstrous people? She felt flayed alive. Her shame embraced even her people.

We drag thatch to cover ourselves while they build stone mountains. Is it any wonder they find us laughable? How can they take such pleasure in a foot placed upon a helpless neck? Loathsome people of Rome!

If Auriane did not understand what roused the throng's malice, Domitian knew all too well. The hand that held the ivory scepter began to tremble with wrath. His eyes were no longer empty and remote; they flickered with murderous light.

"Go back and fight a real war!" came a shout from so nearby it was an act of defiance shocking in its audacity, but Domitian dared not risk his dignity by turning to look for the offender in the crowd. The taunts were spreading like fire in a wooden tenement. And he could do nothing—he was closely bound as the prisoner readied for torture. He prayed to his patron Minerva that the City Cohorts would quell this rebellion with a minimum of disturbance to the august occasion.

"Where was the enemy—couldn't you find him?" came a bellow from a rooftop. Domitian was glad of the red paint; it concealed his scarlet flush.

The foul ingratitude, Domitian thought bitterly. Five captives, just to thwart me, died in their cells and so I was forced to put in five of my own slaves to make an even row—and the people behave as if this proves the whole war was a hoax! Any reasonable man in my place would have done the same.

So, you mewling herd of miscreants, you have finally shown me your true face! You despise me, and for no cause but your own perversity.

As they moved past the solemn beauty of the Basilica Julia, Auriane found her growing rage lent her strength. She sought out individual faces in the crowd and met them with bold contempt. She knew Sunia was crying.

But Auriane did not know that, all along the route, she roused deep sympathies. Quiet voices continuously pointed her out, and heads nodded in approval. And in this part of the city the feeling for her was even stronger. Fragmented tales of her had come to them over the years, always badly distorted or made fantastic, lately given sharper focus by the speech Marcus Julianus caused to be delivered in the Senate. They knew she once pulled down Domitian's statue and set off a mutiny among the legions at Mogontiacum. These poorer and more wretched people saw something of themselves in her pitiful bravery, her stubborn pride.

As the crowd began to lose control of itself, becoming drunk with the possibility of making Domitian look ridiculous, fruit pits and pottery sherds sailed through the air. It was done teasingly at first; most missiles struck the pavement or the wheels of the wagons. No one dared aim too near the triumphal chariot itself. The culprits were concealed in high windows and felt themselves safe.

Then one daring rebel pitched down a roof tile, meaning for it to fall just short of the polished hooves of Domitian's four white horses. But a companion knocked his arm as he threw, spoiling his aim, and the roof tile struck Auriane.

She fell to one knee, clutching her ankle; the pain was momentarily blinding. Sunia stopped as well, jerking the rank ahead to a halt. *"Vile beasts!"* she heard Sunia shriek. "Who would strike a person bound!"

Auriane could not move; she lost all feeling in her leg. One by one the ranks ahead were reined in, as all were attached by their fetters, and those behind were forced to stop as well. Eventually Domitian's white horses were brought to a nervous halt.

Tradition and piety demanded Domitian not speak or move. He stood in silent, trembling fury.

Who in the history of triumphal processions has been made to put up with being halted like this? Indignities stalk me like buzzards. If one of those filthy animals fell, whip him up, drag him! The Prefect of the City Cohorts will pay for this. The gods in the heavens shall be called to account for this!

In back of Domitian the army halted, vaguely mystified looks on their faces.

It is an omen, Domitian thought. *A disastrous one.* Because it befalls me on such a grand occasion, it can only portend far-reaching catastrophe. It means my *life* will be halted at a moment of glory, and in my prime. I will consult with the augurs tomorrow—but they will prattle on, not meeting my eyes, saying what they think will please me. *I need no augur to tell me this foretells my assassination.*

The crowd about Auriane fell into awkward silence when they saw her injury, as if some ponderous beast was pulled up short and made to feel ashamed of itself. For long moments they watched her on her knees until collective guilt spurred them to act. It was as if each individual in the crowd of poor tradesmen and freedmen felt he had personally struck her down.

Without warning, effectively as if it had been planned and timed, a mass of them charged through the line of soldiers. They were aided by surprise; six men of the City Cohorts were knocked down before they had a chance to draw a sword, and one was trampled to death.

Fifty or more swarmed about Auriane. Numberless hands reached out to her. Carefully they helped her up; the women uttered soft sounds of encouragement. One tore a strip of cloth from the hem of her stola and made a bandage, knotting it about Auriane's ankle with sure hands.

Auriane was as confounded by this mysterious outbreak of kindness as by the magic mountains all about. She got trembling to her feet—she was not, after all, badly hurt. The crowd stayed protectively about her until she showed them she could walk. Sunia, buffeted by this friendly crowd, looked on with a mildly stupefied expression as if she had seen a wolf pounce on a lamb and lick its face instead of devouring it.

The people then fell back to give her room. When the greater part of the crowd saw her recovered, a joyous cheer arose. Auriane was not ashamed of the tears that stung her eyes. Fria led her through barren waste to a deep, hidden spring of humanity and pity. The mob of Rome no longer had one single demon face. The men and women who helped her had suffering hearts, frail hopes, the eyes of kin.

*I am not weaponless. I am not alone. This land has its fertile
places like any other. Ways can be found to carry on.*

The cheers were punctuated now with cries of *"We are not
fools! There was no war!"* Auriane knew suddenly the people had
never been mocking the captives, but rather their Emperor. She felt
even greater kinship with them.

"Auriane," a faceless voice called to her.

"Aurin, Aurin," cawed a toothless old woman. Dozens now
called her name, saying it softly lest it reach the ears of the
Emperor.

Moments later, behind her the crowd let out a great groan, as of
some heavy animal in pain. This was followed by the clatter of
horses' hooves and a series of piercing shrieks. Auriane turned
quickly round, almost pulling Sunia off her feet. Her eyes brilliant
with wrath, she tried to look back at the place where the people
had come to her aid, but the cobbled street had curved round.

*I know what is being done. The Emperor unleashed his soldiers
upon the people who lifted me up. That niding's soul ever craves
petty vengeance.*

She closed her eyes as she walked, trying not to think of bodies
torn and bleeding strewn in the street.

Still people stubbornly called her name, despite their terror at
the sound of the slaughtering. Domitian committed an act of grave
ill-omen, they muttered, in perpetrating an act of savagery on a
day of public celebration. He will bring down a curse on the city.

Auriane looked into the thousands upon thousands of alien but
friendly faces and all at once felt fear for Marcus Julianus. Why
was he not here? Had Domitian learned his true sentiments, and
murdered him as well? She was surprised at the stony chill this
brought to her chest, the wild emptiness weighted with dull terror.
This was more unpleasant than fear of death.

*What has become of me? Never have I loved like this. I did not
truly know it was possible. It is glorious as flight, but terrifying,
for I give up my last scrap of freedom, the mind's freedom. This
too is new country. Fria, preserve me, but first preserve* him. *And
curses on the Fates for entangling me so.*

As the procession started forward once more, Domitian felt his
pride savaged by dogs. Within, he was a mangled thing, a body
without skin, to which the barest touch brought excruciating pain.

I give the people a heartfelt gift, a gift of victory. And they fling it in my face. They show more affection for the enemy than for their conquering general.

Had I fallen, they would have left *me* bleeding on the ground. From this day, I will simply reward their good behavior and punish the bad, as a man does a pet dog. The rabble is my enemy, now and forever.

Diocles momentarily lost sight of Marcus Julianus in the gloom. He stopped breathing and flattened himself against a damp stone wall. This section of the Old Palace made him extremely uneasy. Unlit, low-ceilinged passages led nowhere, footsteps sounded where footsteps had no right to be, and every kitchen slave and chambermaid knew this hall was haunted by the ghost of that reptile-hearted mistress of Domitian's father, the harridan Caenis, whose only redeeming virtue had been that she loathed Domitian and was bold enough to do something about it. How his master could ever have conceived a passion for her was a greater mystery than Titus' death, than the Sphinx's smile.

There it was again. A duet of sharp, determined steps, approaching rapidly.

"Marcus!" he called out softly. "We are done!"

Marcus Julianus appeared suddenly from a wall niche where he had been probing for the hidden entry to Caenis' shut-up chambers. "It's only the third watch and they are right on time," he whispered. "They'll turn before they get this far." He added in gentle remonstration, "You should not have come!"

"Somebody has to keep watch on you. I'm not certain you're in your right mind." Craving the comfort of light, Diocles scurried into a section of the hall illumined by a window with a balcony.

"The door is not here," Marcus Julianus whispered at last. "And we are short of time. By now, they're slaughtering the bullocks. We're going to have to break glass—but we prepared for that. Come."

Diocles came out to the balcony and found Marcus Julianus had climbed into a cracked marble planter formed of satyrs' heads and was standing in dry earth and long-dead hyacinths. He was inspecting a small glazed window. The glass was thick and clouded, far from the finest of the glazier's art, but the chamber within was only a storage room.

"You're a moonstruck madman if you go in that way."

"You always were a comfort at critical moments. Give me the fire poker."

Diocles reluctantly obeyed. Marcus Julianus waited for long moments, choosing a time when the noise of the crowd rose to a mountainous swell. Then he struck hard and shattered it in one blow.

"I beg you one last time, reconsider!"

"We've come this far. When will we have another chance like this one?" It would be a long time before the Palace would be so lightly guarded as today; nearly every man of the city who could legally carry a sword was pressed into the service of controlling the crowd during the procession.

Marcus Julianus pulled himself through the window and into a storage room accessible only from the chambers that had been Caenis' private library. He prayed silently the letters were here. Diocles gripped the sides of the window, meaning to follow him. Marcus wheeled about.

"No. And I mean it. Stay out of sight! But first . . . the jewel case."

Diocles handed up to Marcus Julianus a finely worked bronze case, complaining in his tremulous whine, "You could have given a banquet that would shame Lucullus with what you're tossing away here. Did you have to fill this thing?"

"Yes. It has to look right. If there's no apparent reason for a thief to break in here they'll look for the *real* reason."

Marcus Julianus stepped into the musty gloom. The rooms had been sealed for a decade. A dust cloud arose about him like funereal incense, and he felt closely Caenis' melancholy presence. He thought briefly of their long-ago embraces. He was eighteen, she, thirty-five. Youthful rebellion was *not* the motive, as everyone claimed. It was her uncanny ability to survive that fascinated him. She rose from slavery to become what was, in fact, Vespasian's unofficial minister of finance. She had a prodigious memory, a wit faster than a viper's strike, and no patience with pretension. It was the last that made her fall out so badly with Domitian. He felt vividly for a moment Caenis' wintry presence, the ragged scars on her back from the lash, borne with a strange pride, the bitter caresses of those cool, strong fingers, that lean body that seemed to emit just enough heat to stay alive. How was it that Auriane, dearer than life itself, whose existence had been even more brutal, seemed beside Caenis like a day of full summer when forest and field are flushed with life?

Marcus Julianus let the jewel case drop; its bright contents flew in all directions. Yes. It appeared the thief was frightened off in the act. It was natural enough to expect someone would try to break in on such a day. He prayed Domitian would not question too closely his last-hour message of regret that he was unable to attend the official sacrifice because Arria was suddenly dangerously ill. She *was*, but only with her regular and predictable attacks of asthma.

He turned round to Diocles, who still stood in the window. *"Go!"* he said fervently as a worried father to a favorite son. Were they caught, Diocles, as a slave, could by law be tortured to give evidence against his master. "I would never forgive myself if you were found in here!"

Diocles braced himself, ready to sputter a new stream of protests. But at that moment Marcus Julianus caught sight of a movement in the garden below—the blood red of a woman's stola flashing beneath the myrtle trees.

"Nemesis!" He reached out quickly, caught Diocles' arm and pulled him inside.

Marcus Julianus then went to the wall with its hundreds of niches. Here Caenis kept her private records. She was in the habit of collecting information about all those she thought might be dangerous to Vespasian, but the most intriguing documents she kept, Marcus Julianus knew, could have been dangerous to herself. He quickly probed the panels of the wall, looking for a hidden door. After a quarter-hour he found a panel that gave way. Slowly, carefully, he pushed it in.

"Now the lamp," he whispered to Diocles. His steward produced a sulfur match, ignited a bronze hand lamp and passed it to Marcus.

And Marcus Julianus saw before him, on the floor of a small chamber, a red-and-black-painted Egyptian chest that he guessed was a thousand years old, robbed from some tomb at the time of the conquests of Pompey the Great—Caenis had a passion for things Egyptian. He opened it slowly, reverently, half fearful it might crumble to dust.

Inside were dozens of papyrus rolls tied with linen. Blood beat in his temples. Patiently he pulled out a single letter and unrolled it, willing his hands to remain steady.

Diocles discerned only the fine, sensitive outline of his profile illumined by the lamp as Marcus Julianus' attention was riveted by what he read.

"Are those the ones?" Diocles asked.

"Silence a moment," Marcus Julianus whispered tensely, tossing one down and taking up another. "Yes! Here is an account of the time Domitian tried to poison Titus with aconite in spiced wine. Even better, here is one of Titus' replies in his *own hand*. Anyone with a knowledge of handwriting could authenticate it. And . . . this one tells the tale of the time he tried to arrange a hunting accident. And here—Minerva be praised—an acknowledging reply in *Vespasian's* hand. It is incredible! They *knew,* yet they let him live and carefully covered everything over to preserve the dynasty. Titus' dying words, *'I made but one grave mistake in my life,'* must have referred to his allowing Domitian to live."

Marcus Julianus looked up, gloom and regret glinting in his eye. "Poor Caenis. No love she ever felt was as sincere and complete as the hatred she felt for Domitian. Perhaps now she will lie content."

"And finally, Domitian succeeded," Diocles said, his voice hushed. "I wonder how."

"Look at this one." Marcus Julianus read silently for so long that Diocles became impatient and snatched the letter from him.

"What are you doing? You've no sight for reading!"

"Read it aloud then! Penelope could not wait for you!"

"It appears to be a scheme to . . . to forge a physician's order. Caenis writes Domitian planned to wait until Titus was stricken with a common illness, a cold, a light fever. . . . Then he meant to order a treatment for him in use in those times among fashionable physicians. . . . The patient is packed in a chest of snow. There are no replies to this one. It is dated just before she died herself." Marcus Julianus felt a cold grip of certainty close round him.

"Diocles, I would swear it before all the gods, *that is how he managed it.* Remember the quantities of water found outside Titus' sickroom after midnight . . . as if someone had taken a bath in there and the tub overturned? I would wager my life it was *melted snow.*"

"He murdered him with snow!"

"The clever, clever monster. Now I must find a way to arrange a private reading for certain influential members of the Guard . . . without being betrayed myself. I'll have to feel my way in the dark. One wrong man, and those of us already in on this are dead men. It will take time . . . too much time. Curses on Nemesis."

"Too much time? For what?" Diocles sneezed loudly in the dust.

"To rescue a certain woman from her fate."

"That barbarian woman? Of what importance is *she* next to this? And you need time, anyway, to find a suitable successor."

"She is nobler than all of them, from magistrates to the mob. All my life I've watched tryants destroy what is great and good. *This time it shall not happen.*"

Diocles shook his head sadly. "You *mean* that. There's no madness in your family that I know of—I cannot guess where this comes from. This is not a Clodia or a Berenice or Helen of Troy we are speaking of. This is a female *animal.*"

CHAPTER XXXV

Auriane was taken to the *Ludus Magnus,* **or Great School,** largest of the city's four government-maintained institutions for the training of gladiators. All the demons of Lower Earth, she swore, could not have schemed a sadder, more unholy place than this. She thought it a mocking imitation of their whole society, dreamed by some madman.

None who dwelled within this multistoried hall of bleak gray stone were free, Auriane observed, even those who claimed they were. Rather, all were stacked in importance like neatly piled logs, with the many below bearing the weight of the few above. At the bottom were fresh captives like herself—a huddled collection of frightened chattel abducted from many nations, bewildered to find crude weapons thrust into their hands. By day, they lived between the whip and the brand. At night, they were thrown moldy mush she swore pigs would not eat and herded into windowless cells in a warren of passages that lay in eternal moonless gloom, where the cries from nightmares were predictable and constant as the lowing of cattle at home. This quarter of the school was known as the Third Hall.

The next layer was made up of men who had survived the Third Hall and managed to murder one of their fellows to appease Nemesis and Mars at one of these people's frequent, noisy festivals. These men were, as nearly as she could determine, a sort of slave-mercenary or criminal-turned-warrior. Though subject to savage discipline and kept closely confined, they were given careful care, much as useful draft animals are. The school's physicians examined them frequently; they were fed only foods these doctors prescribed, given daily massage and regular visits from prostitutes—for the act of love was said to cure the *melancholia* endemic in this place. These were housed in a quarter of cells known as the Second Hall.

Set above them were the slave-warriors who murdered their way to fame. These had fiercely loyal followers, as though they were celebrated chieftains. They needed no prostitutes because free women came to them willingly and in baffling numbers. Noblemen gathered to watch when they sparred in the school's central practice ring; the people of the city brought them gifts and scrawled their names over the walls. They were free to visit taverns and move about the city, yet to her amazement they always returned to this ghastly place as if it were a proper dwelling and not one of the tributary caverns of Helle. These were the men of the First Hall.

And over all these grades reigned a sort of king, successor to a long line of temporary kings—the august and terrifying Aristos. From the talk about the school she learned he had risen to this height with remarkable speed. In his first bout he slew the most formidable heavy-armored fighter in the city, Craxus of the rival Claudian School. Within six months there were none left alive to seriously challenge him. She heard him spoken of as if he were a minor deity; crude busts of him were sold in the markets. Among his devotees was Domitian himself, who curiously somehow counted Aristos' victories as his own, as though they shared one soul. She learned to despise Aristos without ever seeing him; he was a pettish, pampered prince. If the men of the lower grades made too great a din at their meals and annoyed him, guards came to silence them. Once when a cook put fish sauce on Aristos' favorite pike—all were expected to know he liked it bare of seasonings—the man was flogged nearly to death, then sold away. If Aristos disliked the weather on the day of the games, he refused to fight. When he stalked the passages of the school preceded by his troupe of ruffians, novices scattered from his path. For he took great pleasure in seizing a novice and handing him over to his brutes, who would then toss their victim high in the air on a cloak stretched between four men, catching him most of the time.

Alongside these slave-warriors the *Ludus Magnus* housed a second group, the men who maintained it; these too were stacked in importance. At the bottom were the wretches who cleaned the gladiators' damp cells, carried out the slops, hauled water, and during the games turned the bloody sand between bouts. Equally without honor were the physicians' masseurs and the swarms of kitchen slaves. Faring better but still not free were the school's skilled armorers, morticians, tailors and leatherworkers. Then there were the physicians, haughty and independent, and the secretaries and accountants, cloaked in the mysteries of writing. Finally there were the trainers of the three Halls, fiercely competitive as the gladiators themselves. All these cowered before a second king, the Prefect of the school, a man called Torquatus. She glimpsed Torquatus once as he was borne by in a sumptuous litter; within the shadowed interior she saw a malevolent Cupid's mouth eased into a contented smile, the soft swell of an extra chin, and restless, rapacious wolf's eyes.

Finally there was the school's regiment of guards, who fiercely protected one another and formed a clan of their own. And all this strange madness existed, as far as she could tell, for the sole purpose of instructing prisoners of war—sane men in their own countries, men with no quarrel with each other—in the art of killing one another with skill and grace. For this was what the Roman people enjoyed, she realized to her astonishment, more than their horse races or theaters, more than the practice of their religion or going to war. Here was firm evidence a whole people could go mad.

Auriane stood in a sandy practice yard with two hundred fellow captives arranged in ragged ranks and files. The yard's dun-colored walls were higher than the tallest pine; they pressed so close her arms felt bound to her sides. Clouds moved briskly, impatiently across the small patch of sky, taunting her with their freedom. Her masters were stingy with the sky—she found herself turning her face to it often, hungry for the sun.

Before them swaggered Corax, an undertrainer of the Third Hall. He seemed to be caught up in a shouting match with himself; his bullying barks ricocheted off stone. Corax was a short, thick, muscular man whose oily movements reminded her of a rat swimming in a river. He shaved not only the hair of his face—a curious Roman habit to which she slowly was becoming accustomed—but the hair of his head as well, a practice she eventually learned was meant to combat lice. With his too-smooth skin, his frequent flushes that turned his nose scarlet, his balled fists and pink, puckered lips, he put her in mind of an outsized babe on the rampage.

"You are filth and dung!" he cried out. "You are night soil, and criminals into the bargain! Today you're worth more as meat for the beasts than you're worth alive. Will you be worth more tomorrow? Some will, most won't. You should give thanks to your barbarous gods that in this city we've a taste for fine sword-play—or else of what *use* would your wretched hides be?"

Auriane found herself assessing his soul more closely than she listened to the meaning of his words. We are indeed filth and dung to him, she determined. But he says it a bit too dispassionately; it means nothing to him, nor does any appetite of his, nor does any other human creature claim much of his attention. This man lusts for one thing: to move up to the next higher post.

Sunia stood at Auriane's right, frowning as she struggled to follow Corax's tenement-bred Latin. Auriane did not know if Sunia and the five other women in this yard were meant to be condemned to the arena from the first, or if the Emperor decided this in the wake of her own condemnation. She did know the women's presence was grumbled about among the undertrainers, as if their Emperor brought great shame down upon the school. All together, sixty of her tribespeople followed her here, Coniaric and Thorgild among them. There were as well two distant kinsmen of Witgern's, a son of old Amgath of Baldemar's retinue, and a dozen or more warriors who survived the final assault of Five Wells. The rest of the Chattian captives, she surmised, were sent off to rival schools.

In addition to her own people were men taken from distant places known only from legend: pale-eyed men from beyond the northern sea, Arab nomads, Sarmatian tribesmen whose faces were fierce and closed, and elegantly tall men with dark, polished skin from the southernmost extreme of the world. Of the women, all were of sturdy frame save one, a native of the isle of Albion who stood in the rank ahead of her. This woman was a finely made creature with hair that was gauzy and golden and small white hands that had never known work rougher than spinning. Auriane found her presence disturbing. Most of the others, if not yet adept with weapons, at least looked as if they *could* be. This woman should have been sold into some noble house as a lady's maid. Again and again it happened that just when she thought she had begun to make sense of this situation, she would be confronted with some odd and sad puzzle like this.

Corax halted and faced them, shifting smoothly to a practiced, confidential tone. "Life's plain and simple here, my friends. Some beasts can be trained, some cannot. But if you heed well my words, a good many of you have a chance of life . . . a few, even a chance at glory."

His voice rose to strident pitch. "So listen well, you crop of villains! Second of your virtues will be *courage*. The faster you acquire it, the fewer scars you'll bear from the brand. You will learn not to flinch when a naked blade is thrust in your face. Life, death—to you, it will be the same. You will learn to strike first and take bold risks—the crowd loathes a man too covetous of his own life. And at the moment of defeat, you'll not shame us more by shrinking from death—you will offer your neck *willingly* to your opponent's blade.

"But *first* of your virtues will be—*obedience*. There is but one will here—ours."

Auriane felt a twist of contempt. At the heart of what seemed most incomprehensible about this race of men was the relish with which all classes extolled obedience: Why would a proud people raise their own to be slaves?

Corax resumed pacing, bobbing as he walked; that round, solid head was set so close on his shoulders it seemed to Auriane some giant had tried to hammer him into the earth but had given up, finding him too tough and gnarled.

"You do not speak to your superiors of the First and Second Halls, nor will you covet their women or their gifts. Never will you raise a hand against a trainer. Tomorrow you will be taken to watch while a novice like yourselves, a wretch who tried to murder an under-trainer of the Second Hall, is fed to an Indian tiger."

Then he shifted once more to a comradely manner, his voice rich with encouragement. "But for those of you who show *merit,* all manner of things are possible! You'll have money gifts one day, for when you are victorious you're allowed to keep part of your prize, amounting to a quarter of your value as a slave. And you'll be given a bit of freedom. A select few might join the immortals. Your name will be uttered with admiration by the great. How many criminals and wastrels can boast of that? One or two of you might even be freed and made into citizens! So you see, you are not without hope.

"Every ninth day, and on important festival days—those dedicated to our own patron deities, Bellona, Nemesis and Mars—you will be granted a day of rest. And even better, now that the Palace has seen fit to give us the money for it, if you get your throats cut, you'll not be thrown into the *carnaria* with the animals. You'll be given as decent a burial as any man—"

"Thank all the gods for *that* at least!" Sunia whispered. Auriane turned faintly toward her and frowned, warning her to be silent.

"—and as you may know, we pool part of what we earn to be put aside for funerals, so you'll even have a small procession, with incense and mourners. Some of you will live long enough to learn a simple truth—that the finest swordsmen in this school are better men in every way than the soft parasites who lap up the sight of your blood and fritter away their useless lives betting on you. *Your* courage will be real, while theirs, mere bluster. Let them think they show manliness in watching you! Why, they would scurry off in terror from what you will learn to endure! And you'll have what you do not have now—the respect of your peers, the most courageous men in this city and in the world. This is our secret—that we strive not to *equal* the soft, effeminate patrician in the crowd whose worthy ancestors left him wealth, *but to surpass him.*"

An aggressive fly orbited Sunia's head. Absentmindedly she raised a hand and waved it off.

"You there!" Corax's gaze flashed to Sunia. He smiled with cruel satisfaction. "I believe I ordered you not to move! *Come forward!"*

Without thought, Auriane moved swiftly to Sunia and seized her shoulders, forcing her to stay where she was.

Corax's eyes met Auriane's. And he felt a sink of dismay. Long experience warned him this was the most troublesome sort of charge. Now there's a mule's spawn, midwifed by a Fury! he thought, silently cursing his luck. They send all the untrainable ones to me.

"Ah, the loyalty of friends!" he called out with mock sweetness. "I think this show of sentiment will set me to bawling. Where will that mother love be, you stubborn she-ass, when we command you to kill her?"

Corax nodded curtly to four slave-assistants with brutish arms and aprons of bloodstained leather. They withdrew glowing iron rods from a brazier and slowly approached Auriane.

Coniaric looked back from his place, struggling to catch Auriane's eye, silently willing her to obey Corax. His right hand clenched as if readying a spear. Thorgild did not look at her, but shut his eyes, trembling with outrage.

Sunia whispered, "Auriane, let me go, it's not worth what they'll do to you!"

But Auriane held tightly to her, as if by doing so she retained some measure of control over her fate. For too long she had been stripped of every weapon but her wits and her patience. Lately her utter dependency on her captors was edging her close to madness. Her whole spirit needed to strike out against the confinement, the waiting. She found herself humiliated even by her dependence upon Marcus Arrius Julianus, for she knew well escape was impossible without his aid. She feared even to catch sight of her reflection in pooled water, lest she see dependency's disfigurement there. By day she concealed her despair from her tribesmen, but in the dark of night on her straw pallet often her courage broke, and she found herself alternately raging at the Fates and praying feverishly to Marcus Julianus as if he were a god.

The trainers' assistants ringed about her, their brands so close she could feel the fierce heat. She heard a whip crack and a torn-off cry of pain and realized Coniaric was attempting to fight his way to her aid.

A brand was thrust at her bare arm. She was struck blind with an agony brutal beyond anything she had ever imagined; it was soul-splitting, devouring. She cried out, not recognizing her shriek as her own voice; then she lost her hold on Sunia and sank to her knees, seizing her arm tightly in an attempt to staunch the raging pain. Two assistants dragged Sunia before Corax while two remained to restrain Auriane.

While the burly assistants held Sunia securely, Corax ordered a third to bring a short sword from the armory. As it was carried through the ranks, the menacing glint of the blade held every eye.

"You'll not handle one of these until your training is near complete," Corax said importantly, holding it aloft. "But it is not too soon for your first lesson in courage. Look how fine the edge—is it not beautiful?"

Sunia writhed like an animal in a trap, eyes glazed, a slack animal-cry issuing from her throat. Corax grasped the sword by its bone grip and paused before her, eyes narrowed in concentration as he sought his striking distance. "Hold her tight, now," he commanded softly.

He was interrupted by a curse and a shout. Auriane had bitten one of the men restraining her.

"Control that frothing bitch-dog or I'll see both of you packed off to work in the morgue!"

He repositioned himself, squinting at Sunia as he expertly flexed his knees, his whole mind on the point of his sword as he prepared to demonstrate a thrust. Sunia shut her eyes tight, twisting away from him.

"Open those eyes, cowardly sow."

Sunia forced them open to slits.

"*Flies* bother you, do they?"

Corax lunged, executing a thrust that was a flash of fluid motion and bright steel. When he was still, there was not a finger's breadth between the sword's stabbing point and Sunia's right eye. Had he not had a precise sense of his striking distance, she would have died.

Sunia sank into a faint. The assistants let her slide through their hands until she lay in a sad heap on the sand. One kicked her in disgust.

"Rouse her and give her ten lashes," Corax said, grimly shaking his head. "Her cowardice reflects badly upon you all."

"*You are the coward, not she!*" Auriane's voice was like the ring of steel on steel.

"By the paps of Medusa, I've had my fill of that one! Bring her up here."

To his surprise Auriane came forward willingly. As she halted before him, a solemn stillness seemed to settle about her like some invisible cloak. On closer look he found the banked fury in her eyes unnerving. He saw this was not mere bad temper, but an avenging wrath of troublesome proportions, the sort that might sweep multitudes along with it. This one is exceedingly dangerous, he thought.

Corax grinned broadly to cover his unease—a demonic babe now, with jagged blackened teeth. "If *you* blink, you'll earn ten lashes not only for yourself but for everyone in the yard."

Two assistants stepped forward to secure her, but she motioned them off.

"Think you've no need to be held, do you? Aren't we full of mulish confidence?"

Auriane watched him with a sort of active calm, looking down from her slightly greater height; Corax saw, perversely, there was sadness in those clear eyes that pierced deeper into his soul than he liked. He scowled, an unconscious act meant to ward her off. He fought a sense that the world, suddenly, was turned inside out; he was not testing her—those bold gray eyes were testing him.

"A pity—I feel I'm not at my best today," he said, smiling

carelessly. "Today's the day I might slip. Every trainer does now and again, you know."

Auriane did not seem to hear; she was too intent upon weighing, sensing him; she knew at once he prepared to execute a cut this time rather than a thrust. Several times Corax saw her shift her distance from him with small, subtle movements like a musician feeling for the right note. Then she stood very still.

And Corax discovered with quiet shock he did not have to move to find his striking distance. She had accurately determined it simply by observing him.

A fortunate guess, he assured himself. *No one is that skilled.*

As he drew back his arm for the stroke, he saw those eyes grow faintly excited—but not with fear. It was more the look of the huntsman who sights the boar.

By all the gods, Corax thought, the woman is possessed.

He executed his stroke. The blade slashed diagonally past her face, missing it by less than a finger's breadth. The yard was silent but for the sinister hiss of rushing air. Auriane did not blink or move. Corax thought she might have stood alone before the altar of her savage gods; he had an uncomfortable sense he did not exist.

This is impossible, he thought. This is a thing that requires months to master. Most never master it. She is a witch. Or is that rabid insolence just greater than her fear?

He executed another stroke, then another, each more frantic than the last as rage rose like water boiling up savagely in a cookpot. On the fourth, Auriane sensed his anger overrode accuracy, and she took one nimble step backward that saved her life.

Corax gave it up then and announced with elaborate indifference: "So, you've a steady nature. It's nothing, I see it all the time."

She should be killed, he thought. She is too fearless to be controlled.

But she is a phenomenon.

"Ten lashes for everyone in the yard, anyway," he went on smoothly—for he was certain they silently laughed at him. "That's just for her insolence. Oh, yes, and a hundred for her."

Auriane made a violent lunge at him. But five assistants held her fast; she might have been a fly struggling in a web.

At that moment Corax's slave Asterion hurriedly approached. He had come earlier with a message for his master, but paused a short distance off while this drama played itself out. Speaking softly into Corax's ear in a dignified voice that disguised his contempt for the undertrainer, Asterion insisted, "A hundred lashes will kill her."

"You're a bright lad, Asterion."

"That courage is prodigal. My poor advice, if you will hear it, is to keep her. Who can say how she might change your fortunes—or fatten your purse? *Remember Meton*." Asterion was ever alert to the fact that his own fortunes could not rise faster than his dull-witted master's.

Corax's mind was heavy and plodding as an ox, but it worked thoroughly, following Asterion's thought to the end.

Meton had been of no account, just another trainer of novices like himself—and then he trained Aristos. Overnight he was elevated to the First Hall. Now he was paid five times what Corax was given, and the school awarded him a rich money gift every time Aristos won. The scoundrel even dined at Torquatus' table. Of course, *this* novice was only a woman, but a recklessly bold woman might be worth something. Corax's mind lumbered ahead, unable to stop: He could leave his stifling single room just beneath his tenement-block's roof and move down into the cool, spacious merchant's apartments on the fashionable first floor, much nearer to the courtyard fountains. He could free his slave Lycisca and marry her. He would ascend, if not to the First Hall, at least to the Second—and his peers in the Third could choke on their bile.

Corax gave Asterion a dismissive pat on the head, then turned to the assistants and said in a covered voice, a spark of avariciousness animating his vacant eyes, "*Ten* lashes, no more—just enough to reprimand her. Then, lock her up in the pit. Five days. No food, only water. We'll starve that meanness out of her."

Auriane found herself buried alive in the moist earthen bowels of the school. She was chained to the floor, her face pressed against wet stone. The cuts from the lash had been doused with salt water so they would not suppurate, and her back felt like a glowing fire-pit. Regularly the guards opened and slammed closed the iron door of the passage leading to the cell, rousing the rats to fits of frenzied scurrying.

Fria, let me die. There is no way to survive in this mother-cursed place. All here is turned on its head. Courage brings the whip, betrayal brings praise, cruelty brings freedom and fame. I want nothing more from the world. Let me sink into black earth, into peace.

Nightmare-ridden sleep took her. After a stretch of time that might have been one day or three, her hunger-sharpened sense of smell detected the rich, sweet odor of boiled fruit. She opened her eyes and saw in the murky light that a wooden bowl, still steaming, had been placed within the bars.

She struggled with a powerful impulse to seize it and gulp it down like a beast. Something was wrong. Why would Corax amend his order and have food brought?

Several paces off a rat reared up, long body erect, its eyes glowing beads as it watched her warily. Auriane pushed the bowl closer to the bold creature and feigned sleep. It scuttled forward, then stopped, pausing to clean its face with a swift rotating motion of fleshy paws. Silently she cursed. After what seemed half a day it started forward again and seized a boiled fig.

With chilling swiftness its agony began. The little body writhed and jerked while Auriane watched in numb fright, imagining how its vitals burned.

This is the work of some unknown enemy. The Emperor would not deign to murder me in secret. And Corax, for some reason, wants me alive. The trainers, after that day in the yard, must have talked of what passed, and my name has reached the ears of someone who wishes me dead.

But who?

CHAPTER XXXVI

When Auriane was released, the days had a numbing same-ness. The sandy yard, the cramped passages and the cavernous room off the kitchens were her country. This is how the plow-ox must feel, she surmised, walking the same path day upon day, looking on the same scraps of the world. At first light the two hundred novices were jarred from sleep by the guards striking iron rods against the bars. The hours of practice, the miserable meals and the doubtful escape of sleep were the spokes of a wheel, marking the turning of the days. She found a strange good came out of it: The very monotony brought her a startling clarity of mind, the sense that her spirit-flame somehow gathered strength, as if she performed ceaselessly the Ritual of Fire. Was it this—or was it the return of the *aurr*—that made the ways of her country begin to look like a thing *apart* from her, not inseparable from her soul? She remembered Ramis often isolated apprentices and assigned them repetitive tasks. Was her purpose to create this odd sense of belonging not merely to one's clan, but to the preserving sun, the ocean of night sky, and all sentient beings?

Have I in some way in this foreign place become an apprentice of Ramis after all? Athelinda, in spite of your efforts, the sorceress claims me at the last. But she will never have me completely—not while I seek to avenge.

The mornings in the yard were passed in maneuvers designed to build the novices' endurance, alertness and speed, as well as the strength of leg so vital in swordfighting. Corax liked to have them run the circuit of the sandy yard with lead weights attached to their ankles while he stationed the assistants in the yard's center, armed with wooden staves. The assistants would hurl the staves without warning, forcing the novices to dodge them. They did not kill when they struck, but they grievously wounded. In the afternoon the novices were given the same staves as weapons and taught to thrust at stout posts, then at straw men. Soon they were sparring with partners.

Using the staves, Corax demonstrated the elementary steps of the advance and retreat. "Surprise is all!" he would bellow as he strode among them. "Vary your retreats! If you crave long life, never let your man detect a pattern!" Auriane heard these words so often they resonated in her mind at night as she dropped into sleep.

As they practiced, Greek physicians watched them with emotionless eyes, to see that muscles developed properly and were not overstrained. Sometimes they ordered massage; at others they adjusted the amount of barley in the novices' diet or prescribed the swallowing of ashes, a regimen thought to aid in building strength. At first her muscles were painfully sore, but gradually they awakened, strengthened and remembered—and she found herself exulting in the feeling of returning skill and power. The clumsy stave was a weapon, if a feeble one, against this loathsome dependency.

During the times of practice Corax kept Coniaric and Thorgild apart from Auriane and Sunia. He sensed the four took too much comfort from each other's presence, and it irritated him. But at meals they stayed close by one another, sometimes eating in silence, at others speaking passionately of home, carefully keeping to memories that brought a bit of amusement rather than tears. They would tell tales of Grimelda and her axe, but they never spoke Odberht's name. Or they would talk of Auriane's humbling of Gundobad, while leaving Athelinda shrouded in darkness. Almost nightly Coniaric proposed some new plan for escape. It filled Auriane with sadness—none of his stratagems showed real understanding of how far they were from home or of the fact that not just the school but the whole country was their prison. She would listen respectfully, accepting it as a thing he must do to preserve his mind.

She spoke of Marcus Arrius Julianus to no one, though she felt he accompanied her always, watching with affection and concern. The memory of that night was sometimes transcendent, sometimes a brooding shadow. Why had he sent no sign? She could not believe he had forgotten her—he had risked much for her already. And she could not accept that she might have been mistaken about what she sensed of his spirit and his love. Occasionally she heard his name spoken when she overheard snatches of the trainers' or physicians' gossip of affairs at the Palace, and so she knew he lived still. She did not miss the reverence in their tone—she quickly realized that of all their ruling men he was the most beloved of the people.

One day in the equipment room an armory boy who was fastening her leather greaves met her eyes briefly, then furtively looked down. Speaking into the din of daily preparations for practice, he said, "You are Auriane."

"Yes," she said, her body tautening, sensing a gate thrown open to peril.

"I have words from the one who gave you that amulet of earth."

The ground seemed to shift sharply beneath her feet. She felt every sense grow luminously alert.

"Caution's necessary, I'm to report," the boy continued, "and delays unavoidable. For safety's sake, do nothing to bring yourself to the attention of those above. Take heart—soon now he comes for you." The boy looked up, smiling carelessly as if he engaged in idle banter, showing teeth that were brilliantly white against a rich brown Syrian complexion.

"Praise to sun and moon! Tell me—" she began and stopped, realizing Corax was watching her. The boy, nimble as a monkey, moved on to his next charge, and to her relief Corax's contemptuous gaze passed on.

She felt raw joy, confusion and wrenching pain.

He lives, and is maddeningly close, but something is wrong, I sense it. I fear I will not see him again in life.

That night in the dark of the cell she shared with six women captives, she attempted for the first time to tell the whole tale to Sunia while the four others slept soundly in the straw.

"Ah," Sunia whispered when Auriane had finished. "I knew *something* uncanny passed on that night. It sounds like a tale of Wodan in mortal guise."

"No, Sunia—there is a great mystery here, for certain, but he seems a master of the powers of day, not of night."

"Well, if *I* attracted looks of love, it stands for certain you would."

"You've something to tell me, then!"

"There is a net fighter of the Second Hall, strapping, tall, beautiful to look upon. . . . He gave me a rose wreath."

"Sunia, no! That means he wants to bed you once. And I doubt he'll survive until Yule—have you not seen the net fighters are first killed?"

In the blackness Auriane heard only a rustling of straw and Sunia's ragged breathing as she fought against sobs. "All of them are killed! We will be killed! What cursed difference does it make?"

"We are going to *live,* Sunia, this is what I am trying to tell you." But Auriane saw Sunia clung to the comforts of her pessimism like an old woman who will no longer venture from the safety of her house. "Listen to me. The man of whom I spoke is the most powerful of their noblemen. He seems to have cast some spell over the Emperor. I've heard it said by many that he is the one man who keeps the Emperor from becoming wholly evil. He's very close to all these mysteries about us—a fearful thing, yet he seems nobly kind and human enough. Sunia, he's promised to help us escape this place. I'm sure he will, he seems able to do anything—"

"Us?" Sunia said skeptically. "He does not know me."

"I'm not leaving without you, he'll have to understand that. And, Sunia, I swear on our grandmothers, he seemed to know me at once and love me . . . and it is a love greater than songs. I truly did not *know*—"

"Love? Do you think these people love as we do? I think not. They're more than half mad, Auriane. There are too many of them, crawling about everywhere. They scarcely speak to each other. They have no families. They have no hearths. They—"

"Enough of that. Go to sleep. Have you forgotten the throng that raised me up?"

At practice Auriane stayed near Sunia, striving to correct her clumsy mistakes before the trainers did so with their whips. Thorgild and Coniaric would give a good account of themselves, she was certain, but she worried continuously that Sunia would never pass to the next stage of training. She would be taken off to be used in the bloody "morning shows" that preceded the exhibitions of gladiators, where criminals were given to the beasts, or put into one of the mass spectacles where the combatants were scarcely prepared and expected only to die.

Days of games came and passed. The school huddled in the

Colosseum's baleful shadow and the clamor of the throng was to Auriane a titanic and bestial war cry that called up images of limitless horror. Surely it was not composed of human voices — it was the primitive roar of the Wyrm at world's end as it gulped blood and splintered bones, demanding ever more.

On the last day of the games held in honor of Vespasian's birthday, the door of the future opened a crack and its horror rushed forth. It happened that two physicians' assistants were hurrying to the hospital rooms with a fatally wounded man, closely pursued by twenty and more noisy spectators, jostling and crowding. The physicians turned down a wrong passage in their haste and collided with the file of novices going to practice. Auriane saw a linen cloth had been hastily thrown over the dying man. Great dark stains spread from terrible unseen wounds. His helmet had been removed; his head seemed to have been anointed in blood. In his eyes was the wild roaming look of one betrayed. As Auriane watched, astonished, the crowd swarmed about the stalled litter. The linen cloth was torn away from him and the people, daggers in hand, fell on the man, in spite of the curses and blows of the physicians. Guards rushed in soon after, but too late.

Later the meaning of this ghastly scene was explained to her by a novice named Celadon, a Gaul by birth, and the only man in this place not of her tribe who spoke to her with friendliness. Celadon had lived here most of his life and knew the customs. They wanted a piece of his liver, Celadon explained. A bit of liver from a fallen gladiator cures epilepsy, dropsy and gout.

In spite of the fact that she had lived on battlefields all her life, Auriane found herself feeling crippled inside with the horror of it and ashamed for this whole god-cursed race of men. *This,* she thought, is evil beyond measure. War has its reasons, and has existed since the time of peace and wandering, but human creatures were not created by the gods to live and die in a slaughterhouse.

Fall never became winter, though enough days passed. Auriane was amused to hear the trainers grumble of the cold and see them don heavy cloaks when the air was scarcely chilled. The snows did not come. She prayed for snow because its absence was unsettling; if Fria did not throw down her white mantle, there could be no merriment of Yule, no warmth of hope, no serene death-sleep so all could be joyously reborn in spring.

All that changed was that their training passed into the next phase. They were given wooden swords of roughly double a standard sword's weight, and heavy round oak shields. Clumsy as this weapon was, it was yet a sword, the first Auriane had held since her capture, and in the moment when she first closed her hand round its grip, memories of freedom flooded in. The high walls seemed less dense and a faint pine scent haunted the air. She imagined stable earth beneath her feet instead of irksome sand. As they repeated the basic cuts, she fought down exultant feelings, for with them came guilt—she knew she felt them alone. Poor Sunia was in greater misery than before. And to Coniaric, Thorgild and the rest of her tribesmen, swordfighting had never been more than grim necessity. To them, this was but one terrifying step closer to the ultimate dance of death. She carefully disguised her joy.

Fria, you are a difficult mother. Why this, now? We seek simplicity, and you are only content to send complications and desires out of place.

As they practiced, Corax moved among them with his whip, alert to the turn of a wrist, the placement of a foot, the expression in an eye. "A bout can be lost with a look!" he admonished ceaselessly. "Reveal nothing with your eyes! You there! You looked, then struck. I'd have blocked with a cross-stroke, then made you into cutlets! Remember, it's the mind's game as well as the body's. You must be an actor. If you feel confident, feign confusion. If you're weakening, make a show of strength. Never let your man know your true mind. You must scarcely know yourself what you will do next, in the attack, the retreat, the stroke."

Often Corax would secretly observe Auriane from a distance, concealing his acute interest in her progress. Never would he say words of encouragement to her, no matter how quickly she demonstrated facility at any new lesson.

Coniaric was one of the few who consistently drew Corax's praise. "There now. . . . Good man! . . . That's right—parry close to the body," she heard him say one day. "Anticipate your man's advance. Good—you moved into it. You must sense your opponent the way an animal scents fear. Finely done there, Coniaricus!" At first Auriane had been amused by these people's tendency to append -*us* to all men's names; now she scarcely noticed it.

After this, Corax turned to Sunia and began reprimanding her as usual. But on this day something in his voice caused Auriane to whip about and look. It was too soft, too coaxing. "Wrong, *hopelessly* wrong," he was saying. "*Straighten* that arm for a thrust. There. You announce your move every time. Let's hope the panthers have a taste for your hide!"

Corax's hand was closed about her wrist as he demonstrated a feint. His free hand was cupped about Sunia's breast.

"Like *this*. Strike deep enough to draw your man into a parry. Keep those knees flexed, now, that's the way." His voice had become a crude caress. Sunia twisted and writhed while Corax held her fast, continuing with his instructions as if all were well. "Now remember, when you move forward, *that's* when you're vulnerable. And don't forget to keep that pretty head still as you advance—"

Auriane dropped her wooden sword and sprang like a mountain cat onto Corax's back. All three of them toppled to the sand.

This time Auriane fared less well. Corax barely restrained himself from ordering her execution—his desire to watch her die was greater than any lust he ever felt. But once again, he remembered Meton. He contented himself with ordering twenty lashes with a weighted whip, and nine days in the pit.

When Auriane was released, she gave Corax looks of such deep and dedicated hatred the uneasiness she inspired in him bloomed into terror. She was a witch and she was insane. He half expected to awaken one morning and find himself dying horribly from her curse, with maggots crawling in his flesh. He would not work near her unless guards were posted close. The guards promptly circulated a tale that Corax was a sniveling coward, fearful even of his women charges.

Auriane no longer knew how long they had been in this place of no seasons. Had the Day of Rekindling Fire slipped past invisibly, without its solemn dances, and brought them, unknowing, into the time of sowing cakes into the first furrow? Without the moon and stars it was impossible to tell. Time did not move forward here; it swirled and pooled, gathering strength to pull them down. But the day came when Corax announced in his most self-important manner: "In four days' time is the test of aptitude. Those judged skilled enough will stay on with me. Most of you know it from gossip, but I'll say it, nevertheless. The School's to provide twenty women and a hundred men for the Games of Ceres on the third day after the Nones of *Aprilis,* and I've got to give my share. Some of you will be kept on to help us defend our honor against the Claudian School. There are no victors in these tests. I mean only to judge your skill and select the ones with spirit and promise—

and prune out the wretches that will dishonor us out there. *Four days!* Prepare yourselves!"

Sunia! Auriane thought with desolation. She has improved but little. What is to be done?

For four days Auriane scarcely slept, listening to the distorted shouts of guard changes issuing from far down the feebly lit stone passages, the stifled sobbing in adjacent cells. Sunia feigned sleep, but Auriane felt her alertness. She seemed too terrified to weep.

CHAPTER XXXVII

"What I plan," Marcus Julianus said to Diocles, "will be a risk for you as well. Should it fail, I've made arrangements for your escape from the city."

"I'm old and useless, you must not worry over me."

"As if I could not worry over you!" His eyes were in ferment with care and sadness. "Before you heap objections on me, remember we're perilously short of time—her training's progressed more than halfway."

They stood alone on a travertine landing at the western extremity of the fastnesses of the great-house's gardens. Marcus Julianus halted between two sculptures along the low wall: Phidias' head of an Amazon atop a herma, and a bust in Parian marble of Zeno, founder of the Stoic school. Diocles was seized with the rightness of it, thinking: If I were a painter I would paint him thus—poised between that mythic barbarian woman of battles, bringer of chaos, and Zeno, great lover of order. I think he must choose, or go mad.

Before them was a dramatic drop down the Esquiline's slope. The city Marcus Julianus loved and loathed was shrouded in a deathless red-gold haze as the sun eased into the unseen sea. The crowded hills shimmered with mystic light; this chimerical scene might have been a vision from the remote days of Rome's foundation when all humbled themselves before the horned temple of Diana, or a dream of Morpheus, or of some future realm of a philosopher-king. You are ill, he silently addressed the city as if it had one soul. Ill, and with imperceptible slowness, dying. You've blundered off too far from your source, which was—how did Isodorus say it?—*"pure, vigorous nature."* The eye of empire drowses into morbid sleep.

"I do not know if *any* of my messages to her got through," Marcus Julianus continued. "For certain she thinks I've abandoned her, and that pains me beyond measure. And now I've lost my last hope of ridding the city of its scourge *before* she is sent to her death."

Diocles nodded in wary acknowledgment. In the last months the Fates rose to oppose the conspirators again and again. Domitian in these days made a great show of ruling mildly, inspired partly by the terror brought by the omen he received during the procession. He increased the days of games and raised the soldiers' pay by one third. He slackened in his attempts to humiliate the Senate, occasionally allowing them to debate issues of relative importance, which lulled the opposition into blind contentment. Marcus Julianus cursed their shortness of memory and knew this temperance could not last—but it could easily outlast Auriane.

Other events as well stayed the conspirators' hands: A serious war threatened on the Danube, with a group of allied tribes who promised to be far more formidable adversaries than the Chattians; Marcus Julianus judged it too perilous a time to attempt a change of government, for this enemy would take swift advantage of instability in the capital city.

"Months have passed," Diocles objected. "I, for one, am not convinced the Emperor has not simply *forgotten* about her."

"He will never forget about her. One sign is how strenuously he strives to get me to believe he *has*. She has become an evil passion with him, one he cloaks even from himself, for it fills him with shame, so much so that he's given no special orders concerning her to the school's Prefect, lest *he* suspect his obsession. Not so, however, with the guards—the ones I've thus far approached have proved strangely unsusceptible to bribes when the message involves her. He is not watching her, yet he *is* watching her."

"Beware the tyrant that blushes at his own lusts!"

Marcus Julianus gave Diocles a nod of agreement. "And there is this, as well—at the Alban Mount he keeps a new concubine who, in *his* mind at least, resembles Auriane. The real Auriane disturbs him too much—he seems satisfied with his imitation, at least for now. Of late all he seems to desire from Auriane herself is the prospect of watching her fight and die. And if you need more proof she's branded upon his soul, I have seen his plans for the games of Ceres, for which he's re-creating the battles of the Chattian war. The native women he's collected will be used to reenact the taking of the Chattian supply train."

"He would glorify a victory over women!"

"It's an excuse to use them in a combat without publicly embarrassing himself more than he already has," Marcus Julianus explained. "What's peculiar is that Auriane's not to be part of that sad spectacle. He's got more specific plans for her. Domitian has personally chosen a man for her, a certain Perseus, for an individual bout. . . . He's selected a fighter who is strong, but not so strong he would destroy her too quickly and spoil his amusement."

"Perseus? *Perseus!*" Diocles exclaimed. "I know of the man. He's a free fighter. He'll be about in the streets. Have him put out of the way!"

"To what purpose? Domitian would simply find another who'd do as well. Anyway I will not murder an innocent man."

Two gardeners approached on the gravel path; they pushed a small cart and carried shears for trimming the box hedges. Diocles angrily waved them off. Marcus Julianus idly countermanded this, waving them forward again, then he moved farther along the low stone wall so they would still be out of all hearing. Diocles followed him, mildly exasperated. Only Marcus Julianus, he thought, would show such consideration for two practically worthless gardeners while discussing matters of grave import.

"But the *most* troubling thing," Marcus Julianus went on quietly, "is that he's somehow scented a connection between Auriane and myself. Last night, while probing me with those bleary prosecutor's eyes, he spoke thus: 'You remind me of someone . . . a woman . . . that barbarian Medusa.' Then he went on to say: 'What did I *do* with her? . . . I've misplaced her. . . . You've got that same quality of *lofty innocence*.'"

"An oblique threat, by Charon's eyes," Diocles observed. "You've been careful. I do not know how he could possibly suspect your interest. It's uncanny."

"I've heard Junilla called many colorful things, never uncanny."

"*Of course.* She knows! She bid for the wench's horse! Doubtless she hissed all she suspects into Domitian's ear. She must be enjoying herself immensely! You are a dead man!"

"Do not look so! The fortunate thing about Junilla is the more she enjoys herself, the sloppier she gets. And the next throw is mine."

Diocles turned sharply away. "I know already what you're going to propose and I want to say in advance—grief has stolen your wits!"

"Why should I *not* make use of the one woman who can aid us, who, I'm certain—if I can get past her fear—will prove to want precisely what we want?"

"I knew it!" Diocles dramatically put his hands to his temples. "Not the Empress!" He stood with legs planted slightly apart, shaking his head vigorously in a way that put Marcus Julianus in mind of a balking mule. "She's utterly unpredictable! She's got feathers for brains. And she's as approachable as an Oriental harem woman!"

But Marcus Julianus scarcely heard. His gaze intent as a hawk's, he saw only the Colosseum among the complexity of red-tiled tenements, the warren of dark streets, the gilded domes and temple roofs; from this distance the amphitheater's mass looked like the stump of a severed column that at full height might have parted the clouds. The dying sun tinted the brutish structure rose, and he imagined it stained by the blood of the impossible multitudes of men and animals that already had perished there. It was malign and alive, seeming to reproach him for having studied and governed and taught alongside its horrors—this carnivorous child of Vespasian's that had torn loose from the bonds of rational thought and grown primitive and strong feasting on human flesh. Its familiar bands of columns were bared teeth, set to devour Auriane.

"Admittedly the Empress is not a . . . *practical* woman," Marcus Julianus said at last. "But I believe she *is* predictable. I'm prepared to stake my life on what I judge she'll do." He clamped a comforting hand on Diocles' bony shoulder. "I'm sorry, Diocles, there's no other course open to me. She's my last hope for saving Auriane—and my first, for what I plan next."

The Empress Domitia Longina sat naked before her polished bronze mirror, appraising her body with a ruthless eye. She approved of its comfortable abundance, of her stable, settled hips, her skin of ivory silk with its delicate rose flush, the pearly sheen of her heavy breasts. She was less pleased by the blur of fear she saw in her eyes, and the first muted signs of age about her mouth. And delighted even less by the thickening about her waist. *The monster managed to put another child in me! But* this one, *by Artemis' black dogs, I'll have out.*

And she was repelled by the sight of her cleanly plucked pubic triangle. She found it dismayingly ugly, but *he* desired it, demanded it, for such things roused him. Domitian had depilated her himself, as he had all his concubines. She counted it as much a sign of her enslavement as she would a scar from a brand.

She was being prepared for a dinner party in her suite of rooms at the Palace. Though her husband was well away at his villa on the Alban Mount, still Domitian watched her through the eyes of every chamberlain, every Guard posted near her quarters. While a maid applied to the Empress's face a foundation made of sweat of sheep's wool, three hairdressers worked on her coiffure. One applied curling tongs, creating in front the effect of an impressive multistoried edifice of ringlets. A second braided the back and twisted the braids into a coil, while a third skillfully wove in false hair, for Domitia Longina's own tresses were too scanty for the lofty hairstyles in fashion in these times.

The eunuch Carinus slipped in quietly, soundlessly. The Guards called him the Empress's lapdog and were long in the habit of paying him no mind. The boy settled at her feet, content to watch his mistress's transformation. Domitia Longina had for long filled the role of Carinus' mother. He had been stolen from his true mother at so tender an age he half believed the auction-block tale he was begotten by the beautiful Ganymede on a swan.

In Carinus' hand was a bookroll; he put it into Domitia Longina's idle hand. She patted his head affectionately. "What is it, my lamb?" she said as she unrolled it slightly and read its title and author.

She felt a soft jolt. It was a long-banned philosophical work, penned by the notorious Cynic philosopher Isodorus. Quickly she scanned it: Apparently it was one of Isodorus' vitriolic essays on the duty of the wise man to destroy the ruler who descends into tyranny.

She gave Carinus a sharp, questioning look. But the boy would not meet her eyes; his petal-thin lids eased shut as he determinedly rubbed his silky head against her thigh, burrowing in like some pup trying to get closer to its mother.

She unrolled it further, keeping her expression impassive so she would not alarm her maids. At the end of the text was written in a different hand: *"What you will, my lady, can be accomplished. I must have an audience with you alone."*

She passed a moment in fearful confusion. *Who sent this?* The name Isodorus called up surely in her mind the name of Marcus Arrius Julianus. Who did not know the tale of his futile fight to save the old man from being thrown to the wild dogs? An instant later she realized this copy of Isodorus' book was freshly produced. Marcus Julianus published banned books in the reign of Nero; everyone knew that. And it was whispered about the bookstalls that he continued to do so today.

By Juno, Queen of Heaven, I hold treason in my hand. *This is one of his books.* The message is from Marcus Julianus.

He desires an audience with me *alone*? It is a notion so mad and reckless I can make nothing of it. What grievance could Julianus have that I alone could put right? His influence in these times is greater than my own. Surely he knows I cannot respond. He must *expect* my refusal. Perhaps this is but preparation for something he plans later, or some sort of warning. I know he does not count me an enemy, for we share a mortal enemy—Veiento—and by the laws of survival in the Palace, this makes us allies, even though we scarce know each other beyond formal greetings.

"Carinus, dear child," she said with forced nonchalance, gently shaking the boy off. *Who had seen him with this?* She felt a prickle of terror. "Fetch the lamp."

Carinus rose, took the terra-cotta lamp from her cosmetics table and held it before her. Tears pooled in her eyes as, with slightly trembling hand, she held the bookroll over the flame. She could not bring herself to burn it.

Such a precious and dangerous book—I want it for my library. I want also to answer yes—but how can I and live? When was I last free? I scarce remember.

More than ten years passed since Domitian had snatched her away from her original husband and made her first his mistress, then his wife. In the beginning he was courtly, overly attentive, flattering a youthful dreaming mind nourished on ancient epics. She imagined herself a Helen, stolen off by an overardent lover. By the time she realized Domitian's true nature she was caught in his snare, *owned* as much as his household slaves, and he was determined she should never escape while he lived. She quickly discovered his solemn silences were times of brooding in which suspicions grew like fungus in a gloomy cellar. He provided a house of walled-off rooms, which instinct told her she would not want to enter. In the early years she told herself this life was not past bearing. I have been given immortality, she thought, in place of mortal love.

But the glory of being known at the ends of the earth sustained her less with each year; eventually she sought solace with Paris, the most popular pantomime actor of the day. She used to steal into his dressing room between performances, disguised in a satyr's mask, loincloth and robe. One day Veiento's agents caught her. Veiento had his own reasons for wanting Domitia Longina put out of the way: He had a niece that he hoped Domitian would marry.

When Veiento with eager malice reported her infidelity to Domitian, she did not take her husband's humiliation seriously enough; she grasped the mythic and fantastic better than brutal daily realities. With alarming swiftness Domitian divorced her, then arranged to have Paris murdered in the street. When mourners came to offer precious oils and flowers on the site where the pantomime actor was slain, Domitian loosed soldiers on them. Domitia Longina passed a month in turmoil, wondering if his wrath was spent. Then Domitian informed her by messenger that he had set a date for her execution.

As the day approached on which she was to be beheaded, Domitian answered none of the frantic entreaties she sent. Then one day remained before the appointed hour. Domitian was presiding at the games, and the throng seemingly spontaneously began to shout her name, urging the Emperor to forgive her. Domitian relented, careful to make it appear he acted in response to the wishes of the mob. He then forgave her publicly and remarried her—and so he found a way to preserve his dignity while doing what she suspected he had planned to do all along, which was to take her back once he satisfied himself he had terrified her nearly to madness.

Domitia Longina never recovered from the months of waiting for execution; she went about in dread of being condemned again. She began to demand poppy juice from her physician to dull the daily terror. Often she walked to the Esquiline to sacrifice at the Temple of Juno Lucina, Mother of Light, begging the torch-bearing image to be allowed to outlive her husband by many years, praying war, accident, or an assassin's knife would carry him off. She despised women like Junilla who lived with the freedom of Cleopatra and squandered it on debauched nights among companions with the souls of crawling things. If she had that precious freedom, she would pen poetry, live among players and the authors of plays, and finish the library she was having built in her gardens.

Surely, she thought, Marcus Arrius Julianus cannot have overheard my prayers at the Temple of Juno?

But fear triumphed, and she touched the bookroll to the flame.

CHAPTER XXXVIII

Auriane and Sunia sat among Corax's two hundred novices,
awaiting the test of aptitude. Before them was the elliptical
practice arena that lay at the heart of the school. Amber light
filtered through the clouded glass of a skylight fifty feet above; it
gave the sand a lurid, sickly glow, as though some sorcerer cursed
the spot and the hungry balefires of Lower Earth shone through.

*We are dragged still closer to the pit of sacrifice. I feel the heat
of the pillar of fire, the chanting voices of Helle's host below. But
for you, Marcus, and Avenahar, I would shed the world and let
myself be pulled down.*

Had she not been in misery, she would have been amused by the
sight of Corax strutting among the milling staff of the school,
shouting with comic ferocity as he gave orders to his five
assistants and making forced jests no one found amusing.

*He is a dwarf rooster who does not realize it is lost among
grander beasts who would as soon step on it as listen to its
crowing.*

While three assistants brought out leather armguards and
greaves, stout round shields and an assortment of wooden swords,
another hastily prepared a list, determining who would be paired
with whom. Two Mauretanian slave boys smoothed the sand,
dragging about the ring a mechanical contrivance that in Auriane's
mind resembled a plow. An additional rank of guards moved into
place behind those always posted along the vaulted passages

681

leading from the two grand entrances; aptitude tests were common times for attempted breakouts. All this activity, Auriane saw, was carried out with the precision and efficiency of before-battle preparations.

There is no enemy here, you strange and silly people—no enemy but your own peculiar madness.

Curious citizens were wandering in. The visitors' seats opposite began to fill with idle young men of noble families, avid to know before their absent companions if some formidable talent were forthcoming so they could win back at the amphitheater what they had lost at the races. They wore the brightly dyed lacernas currently in fashion; as they gracefully gestured, their hands glittered with rings of amethyst, topaz, sardonyx and gold. Sprinkled among them were spies from the Ministry of Finance, sent to make certain Corax did everything properly and wasted no money. And as the city's shops were closed—this was one of the fifty-one days of the year memorializing Rome's worst defeats in battle, and it was ill-omened to conduct business on such days—shopkeepers and their apprentices appeared as well. Coming with them through the guards' lines was a flock of Matidia's prostitutes, swathed in yellow silk. The visiting company brought startling color to this sepulchral place, as though roses were cast down in a festering sink.

The sixty Chattian captives kept together on the stone seats, as if in a vain attempt to preserve identity and prevent it from dissolving in an alien sea. Sunia was pale as one stricken with ague. Corax began to shout names, and by twos novices entered the arena and began sparring. Auriane pointed out their errors to Sunia, trying to keep desperation from her voice. And numbly Sunia feigned paying close attention, praying to Fria her morning meal of miserable gruel would stay in her stomach.

Auriane was quiet suddenly when the slender-boned girl from Albion rose and took her turn. She was paired with a tall, closed-countenanced Sarmatian woman, wiry and nimble as a race-bred mare, with a nippy temperament to match. The pale girl made a game but hopeless effort, causing Auriane to think of a startled bird pecking desperately and uselessly fluttering its feathers. The Sarmatian woman with two clipped, violent strokes struck the wooden sword from her hand, then with a backstroke, knocked her to her knees. Light laughter came from the visitors' seats. Corax ordered the frail creature off with a contemptuous flourish of the hand.

Auriane felt dull horror settling round her heart. *What would they do with her? Auction her off to a brothel? Lower her, bound, into a bear pit?* Auriane seized Sunia's hand and found it slimy with perspiration.

"Thorgildus—Sunia!" Corax cried out. Auriane masked a smile of relief. It was an absurd pairing, but Auriane knew Corax's object was not to match evenly; he meant only to spur his charges into demonstrations of skill. Thorgild would be easy with her, and he was clever enough to make Sunia look skilled.

Then they heard part of a hushed exchange behind them.

"Tonight's the night we avenge ourselves on those villains of the Second Hall!" a Numidian called Massa was saying. "We'll make it look like a suicide. I know we've got the right rogues this time. By the fleas of Cerberus, once they're disposed of, I'll wager a month's wine ration you'll see no more rat dung in our barley."

Rat dung? Auriane thought, battling an upwelling of queasiness. For how many *months* had they been eating fouled food?

For Sunia this final, if minor, bit of vileness proved past bearing. She rose, then bent over retching. Auriane stood up quickly beside her, steadying her, silently cursing the men behind her.

"Nemesis!" Corax shouted to his assistants. "Douse that sickly cow with water and be quick about it!"

Two assistants came up with a bucket of water and sloshed it hard over Sunia as indifferently as if she were a soiled spot on a wall, soaking Auriane and Massa as well. Sunia, shivering and dripping, her long, braided hair matted to her rough wool tunic, climbed down, took up a wooden sword and entered the practice arena, followed closely by Thorgild. Thoroughly unnerved now, Sunia wanted only to throw down the weapon and weep.

Sunia began with a hesitant lunge at Thorgild that brought looks of amused disbelief from the visitors. Auriane, wincing, forced herself to watch as Sunia swung the sword too broadly, giving Thorgild room for a dozen strikes. Silently Auriane prayed: Fria, descend and fill her limbs with wisdom. When she looked up again, she saw Thorgild played his part well, not pressing her too hard, giving her numerous openings to strike.

Then Auriane saw the wisdom for which she prayed was given to Thorgild. He began to bat at Sunia, hitting her several times painfully on the shins and elbows with the flat of the sword, as one might to annoy a short-tempered beast. Thorgild was well acquainted with Sunia's blind fits of frustrated rage. The ploy was successful.

Wrath was a better instructor than Corax. Sunia's movements were not studied now. With a two-hand hold, she launched into Thorgild with a series of wildly aimed vertical cuts; to Auriane she looked less like a novice executing techniques of the school and more like a madwoman attacking a snake with a hoe. She drove him back several steps, then lowered her head and charged, ramming his chest with her shield. Delighted laughter erupted from the spectators. Skill or farce, it made no difference to them.

Corax cried out for them to halt, then deliberated for long moments while absentmindedly pulling at a flabby lip. Auriane watched his face, feeling frenzy accumulating in her blood. *Pass her, you brutish infant.*

"Thorgildus, Sunia—both pass."

This brought murmurs of surprise from the half-dozen veterans who collected to watch—did true skill count for nothing in these times?—and looks of contempt from the agents of the Finance Ministry.

Auriane was exultant with relief. She could only suppose Corax felt hard pressed to provide a certain number of women. As Sunia walked past Corax, her soaked tunic clinging closely to her thin but gracefully formed body, she saw Corax moisten his lips while tracing in the air with his hands the outline of her hips.

Auriane felt a flash of fury. There, then, was another reason he passed her. Auriane knew Corax had forced himself on Sunia at least twice in the secrecy of the storerooms, though Sunia was too filled with shame to speak of it. Evidently he was not finished with her.

Others took their turns; Coniaric when his time came performed with cool competence and passed easily. He was beautifully conditioned and had acquired much grace; when the halt was called, the visitors broke into spontaneous applause, and Auriane saw the veterans exchange knowing nods. Corax grinned and nodded, acknowledging the applause as though it were meant entirely for him.

It was near midday when Corax called out in his shrill, snappish voice: *"Celadon—Auriane!"*

The number of spectators had greatly increased—noontime seemed to draw them out. A dozen upper trainers and seasoned fighters collected about the ring—as the taverns were closed, there was little else to occupy them. Corax started with alarm when he saw Erato, a powerful trainer of the First Hall, moving casually among them, surveying the novices with an unhurried, predatory eye. There was no man Corax despised more. It was insult enough that Erato had used the fortune won in his fighting days to purchase the tenement block in which he, Corax, lived, then promptly doubled the yearly rent. But twice now Erato had stolen promising novices from him, claiming Corax was incompetent to train them. Damn him to the nether depths, Corax thought. And the pirate appears *now*, as Auriane goes in. My pestilential luck!

Auriane rose up eagerly, feeling a rush of animal exuberance, thinking of little else except that Sunia was, for the moment, safe. She felt she readied herself for a rite of celebration. While Celadon accepted the first wooden sword he took up, Auriane did not hurry, testing one after another for balance until she found a weapon that pleased her.

Corax nudged her with the butt of his whip. "What do we think we're about here—plucking posies for a spring festival? Move along, you hot-blooded daughter of a shrew, or taste the whip!"

Two assistants roughly strapped on their greaves and arm guards. As they entered the ring, Celadon glanced once at Corax strutting saucily before the upper trainers, then met Auriane's gaze with a faintly pained look that said: *Have you ever seen a more colossal fool?* It caused her to like him the more. Celadon was not a captive of war, nor was he a criminal under Roman law; he once explained to Auriane his former master sold him to the school because he needed money to stave off creditors who were preparing a ruinous lawsuit. It was Celadon's evil fortune to possess the intimidating bulk and heaviness of bone counted ideal for this trade, and he had fetched a fine price. Celadon's face at first look appeared brutish and closed as an executioner's, but the man himself certainly was not. Auriane found him always in benign temperament; he seemed to her a great, genial, lumbering bear.

They began quietly. At first she was careful, deliberate, consciously testing and drawing him out, all the while holding herself in check, feeling vulnerable before the crowd's stares. She did not want these rude foreigners spying on her while she was lost in an activity that could fill her with the rapture of the Ritual of Fire. This polite, guarded dialogue continued for a time; then, gradually, it became something else. Celadon executed a deep attack that nearly struck her side; she was roused to a counterattack that put her in range—and then they were ignited. Strike and counterstrike came with whip-crack speed, and the wild, random rhythms made her feel she took wing; in spite of herself she was jolted into the old waking dream. The school dissolved to haze. She might have trod earth packed hard by dancers' feet, whirling round a midsummer fire. The loud, hollow clack of wood striking wood was the body's mute poetry. She was aware of Celadon's sword only as an insistent resistance round which she danced; it was firm earth beneath hammering hooves, the air resisting the beat of a wing, the sand encountered by the fanning wave. She began moving round him as if he were a maypole, binding and unbinding him. For a tantalizingly fleeting moment she was joined to all things, far and present, and old words of Ramis', more felt than heard, wove their way into her mind: *"Know, blind one, when you strike at your enemy, you strike at yourself."*

She struggled to shake these words off, for she did not want to understand them, and the effort pitched her back into worldly awareness. Now she knew she rippled through deft strokes off the rhythm, executing attacks with no name, anarchic parries of Fria's devising, not her own. She felt herself a powerful animal running, conscious too of long strides held in check—a small, strong voice cautioned: Do not reveal too much or let these people see the full measure of your joy. She moved through Celadon like wind through trees. From the first he did not know what to do with her, while she detected his patterns at once—her every feint drew a parry. She moved him about the ring as if he were an animal she had leashed.

Finally, drunk on her own exuberance, she began rapidly taking ground with the joyful frenzy of the race horse that finds a ferocious burst of speed at the finish. She backed Celadon into the low barrier; she had forgotten it was there. He toppled over it and fell to the stone floor beyond.

"Halt!"

Corax's shout made her feel she struck a wall. Mundane reality settled round her once more. She felt dazed as a bird jerked from flight. Almost shyly she extended a hand to Celadon to help him rise. In her eyes was faint disappointment that it was over so soon; she was not tired. Celadon panted hard.

It was then that she noticed the odd silence all about. The assistants stood with slack arms, duties forgotten. The spectators on the stone seats sat unnaturally still, as if a specter had manifested itself and then vanished, leaving them to wonder if they had lost their wits. Slowly she realized they were staring at her. Then she saw the collection of veterans and trainers giving her hard, probing looks; some spoke in covered voices, frowning and slowly shaking their heads.

What do they find so strange and surprising? I am not a freak! Stop looking, you unmannerly people!

The light, efficient hands of the assistants scuttled over her, removing her equipment, taking the wooden shield. She saw Celadon was unhurt. Slowly life returned to the room.

Then the stout, florid-faced man she knew as Torquatus' secretary pushed his way to the front of the crowd, moving officiously past Corax. His voice was sweetly boyish, but with a knife-edged underside.

"Celadon and Auriane, both pass. Celadon, return to your place. Auriane, to the trainers' offices."

CHAPTER XXXIX

And now what dread punishment will they inflict? Auriane
wondered as she approached the line of oak and iron doors set
between slender pilasters; here were the chambers that housed the
mysterious activities of the school's upper trainers and procura-
tors. Behind her she heard a violent argument erupt between Corax
and the trainer called Erato. From the tone of Corax's voice she
guessed he had already lost.

"You'll not get off with this, you plundering schemer! You
jackal! *I* found her, *I* trained her!"

"You trained her? Really? When I want comedy, I'll go to the
theater."

"Lay a thieving hand on her, you shameless poacher, and you'll
learn just how foul your fortunes can become! Your tenement's a
firetrap—I'll have you dragged before the aediles! I've dozens of
tales for Torquatus! You take bribes! You thieve privileges for your
men! I'll expose you!"

"Then do it quickly, little man," Erato replied, refusing to raise
his voice, "because you'll not be about much longer when the
Prefect learns of what we witnessed today. Half these men have no
notion of what they're doing, and the women aren't even fit for
battle spectacles. Meting out punishment is not training. You'll
ruin her. Either move out of my way, or I have the guards drag you
off. Choose!"

Then Auriane heard no more, for a school guard opened one of the oak doors for her and ordered her to stand at attention in the small chamber beyond. Before her was a wall like a honeycomb, filled with records, broken only by a niche with a statuette of Nemesis before which the smoke of incense drifted, and a long, rough-carved table heaped with bewildering clutter. All that was recognizable there was an inkwell and quill—Decius had had these things in his pack, though the ink was long dried—and a crude bust of Domitian, looking out on the room with smug bad humor.

Within moments Erato entered and slammed the door so loudly she jumped. Moving nimbly about the table despite a pronounced limp, he sat facing her on the long bench set before the table. Auriane knew this man's history, for everyone knew it: In his youth he had been a slave in a brick factory. Then he murdered an overseer who made amorous advances, and his master condemned him to the arena. His was one of the rare tales of glory: Deftly he escaped slaughter and managed to kill his way to the highest heights; he was, in his day, as celebrated as Aristos. After three years and a hundred brilliant bouts he was pardoned by the Emperor Vespasian and granted the wooden sword of freedom. But the love of fighting was all he knew in this world: He signed on as a free man and continued to win. As a freedman, he was able to earn rich purses, enough to buy property in the city: the six-story tenement block across from the Temple of Concord that housed Corax's one mean room, a lucrative shop that produced votive images, a company that imported fish sauce from Hispania—and, just for the irony of it, the old brick factory where he had been enslaved. Erato's string of victories ended abruptly during a bout with a treacherous Samnite swordsman. The man was down—he had begged mercy of the crowd and gotten it. Then he sprang up when Erato's back was turned and hamstrung him. The school's best surgeon tried to knit the tendon, but only worsened it. Erato took a post as a trainer then, hired at once into the First Hall because of his formidable skill. By common agreement he was the finest trainer of the school.

It was difficult for Auriane to believe this man with the soft, dignified manners of one who originated in the Greek-speaking provinces, the open, amicable face and the faintly mischievous eyes of a man who would prefer to be passing hours telling humorous tales in taverns, was an extraordinarily successful killer of men. The one sign of all those years lived on the border of life and death was that pinpoint of wary light in his eyes—always he seemed poised to whip about and defend his back. Erato had the expansive manner of a genuinely generous man. He was shorter than she but sturdy as a tree stump; he looked as though he could hoist a mule with one hand. A scar like a lightning bolt interrupted one brow. He had a fine head of curling black hair, combed forward; on his massive arms was a latticework of whitened scars. She noticed with a jolt he was missing an ear. She had been taught to fear the human body when it was not whole; to her surprise this man's misfortune roused only pity. Erato was the chief trainer of Thracian gladiators, one of the two most popular styles of fighting; these were the lightly armored swordsmen so despised of Domitian, who preferred the more heavily equipped Samnite swordsmen.

Erato regarded Auriane at leisure, taking her measure, while she looked at him, alert, questioning, unafraid. Her sweat-darkened woolen tunic clung to her chest; her cheeks were flushed rose, her forehead gleamed. She made him vaguely uneasy—it was as if she were too large for this room.

Erato thought: This is a fighting animal . . . a born predator. I'm not certain what *my* chances would have been against her.

"Let us play openly with one another," he began gently but firmly. "Aurin—how is it you say your name?"

Carefully she pronounced it.

"Auri*ane*." He leaned forward; his eyes seemed to sharpen to points. "Where did you learn to do what we saw out there?"

"I . . . my people are surrounded by enemies. I have fought and practiced since my sixteenth summer. I had little choice— your people stole our peace. Why do you ask me this? There is nothing remarkable in it."

Her voice appealed to him—it was soft, yet it commanded silence; it sounded so young and unhurt.

"Corax never taught you to fight like that," Erato pressed, "and I know you did not learn it from your countrymen. Until they're properly taught, they all swing a sword like they're chopping wood. Now I saw you execute a maneuver called the *trap*, followed by a double-vertical feint, and the difficult forward-falling attack—and it was all done so smoothly and quickly even the well-trained eye could scarcely follow. Novices are *not taught those things.*"

"I . . . I did not know I did those things. I did not know they had names."

"Enough of this!" he said irritably, an ominous light flaring in

his eye. "You displayed an art learned from teachers, and good ones. I'm easy enough to get along with when a man or woman is honest with me, but play with me and you'll wish you hadn't! You're trampling on my patience!"

Her eyes afire with affront, Auriane sharply half turned from him, arms crossed decisively over her chest. "You're a foolish man to speak so rudely to me. Leave me! I'll speak to you no more."

Erato grinned. "Ordering me out of my own chambers, are you? I like that! *Calm* those ruffled feathers. It is just that I saw a thing today that cannot be—that is why I prod you," he said more amiably. "This sounds to me like utter madness as I say it, but in my fifteen years of training, I've seen all types—from lucky brutes like Aristos to great masters of training-manual technique— but I've seen *nothing* like this. It is more than mere skill, it is . . . what? . . . something god-touched, like a great musician's or dancer's art, but full of an animal's thoughtless grace. If a *cat* had human genius, it might fight like that. It is a sort of thing a trainer might see once in a lifetime, if even then. And yet, you had no teacher."

"There *was* a captive kept by our tribe who was a man of your people, a soldier," she said with reluctance. Protecting Decius was instinctive, but what use was there in doing so now? And something in this man's nature elicited from her an urge to be truthful. "And he showed me the standard cuts that legionaries are taught."

"Ah. Truth trickles out. I heard once of such a man, a soldier taken by the natives who rose to some importance among them. Was he not called Decius? Decius the Traitor, or some such thing?"

She shrank within, looked down and whispered, *"Yes."* But she realized the pain she felt at the sound of that name had somewhat faded.

"Interesting, yes, but alas, it's still not enough. I know what legionaries are taught, it's quite straightforward, and what you did was far beyond it. The perverse humor or Fortuna—to find such bewildering skill in a woman." He smiled companionably. "You look somewhat baffled by all this."

And truly, she was. Decius' early mockery of her fledgling efforts had done their work. His repeated taunt, "Do not ever let on *I* taught you!" still jangled in her mind. She never supposed her skill to be much beyond the regular competence exhibited by Coniaric or Thorgild. Decius *had* eventually said, "You have flown beyond your teacher," but only after she took up the sword of Baldemar. Today, however, she had used a clumsy sword of wood—and so was forced to concede if there was artistry there, it must have been her own. Suddenly she knew she *had* dimly sensed it; when Decius mocked her progress, some deep part of her always protested. She trembled now at the certainty. *I am extraordinarily skilled.* It is apparent even in this place where they make a cult of skill and see fine points my people did not. Part of her yearned to try that skill to the limit—not to do so brought to mind the fast horse never allowed to race. She thought suddenly of Marcus Julianus, sensing he was no stranger to such feelings, that he would at once understand.

Stop—this is madness. You are leaving this sad and terrible place. But humor this man Erato. He is kinder than most. He need not know you'll never fight—not yet.

"If you say it, I accept it is so."

"So earnest and solemn you are! From this day forth I mean to instruct you myself. It still has to be arranged. For now you'll go on living with the novices, but you'll not go to Corax—you'll come to me in the west yard at the third hour, do you understand?"

She nodded, still wondering at all this. Erato said softly to himself, smiling as if at a fine prank, "No one is going to believe this!" He rose, signifying the audience was near an end. "Is there any favor you wish of me? Ask it."

"A favor?" she said softly.

Yes, came a bitter voice within, *give me back my life, my country, my child.* "A . . . a cell for Sunia and me alone, without rats, and with a window. And . . . protection from whoever is trying to poison me."

"*Poison?* Poison, you say? Nemesis! The lawlessness about this place would make a pirate's camp look like a sheepfold! Yes, yes. Done. I will see to both those things."

"And . . . leave to sit for a time at night in front of the hearth fire in the kitchens, after the day's work there is done."

"For what purpose? Witches' spells?"

"It is for a rite of my religion."

"I thought your people worshiped trees, not fire."

"Trees *are* holy—"

"Never catch *me* prostrating myself before a tree!"

"Trees at least are alive with the soul of Fria, greater than all the gods, including yours. *Your* idol"—she nodded at the bust of Domitian—"has the soul of a weasel."

Erato looked offended for a flash of a moment, then burst into loud, staccato laughter.

"Your strike! I'm down!" he said with pleasure. "Have your hearth fire then, you're worth indulging. Anything else?"

Auriane remembered how Sunia complained of the monotony of their daily fare of beans and barley. "And . . . for my people, something different to eat, occasionally. Normally we thrive on venison and game birds, and we grow less hardy without them."

"I'm sorry, that is not in my hands. They feed you that way because every physician employed here holds that barley and beans build muscle. There *is* a school of thought that claims quantities of meat are better, but our physicians do not subscribe to it. Wait until you've proven yourself—then they'll care less what you eat." He raised his voice to an impersonal bark. *"Guard!"*

The guard opened the door for her.

"Wait," Erato said then. "I've a final bit of advice for you." He rose, came close, and put a hand on her shoulder. His smile was conspiratorial, fatherly. "Never, *never* let on how much pleasure you take in this! The arena's supposed to be *punishment*. There are those that might be irritated by it, you know."

She started at first, alarmed he divined so much, then smiled with amusement. *"You* say that, yet you signed on again after your release!"

"Yes, well, that's *different*; one would *expect* it of me. But *you*—don't take this badly now, it's not meant that way—but it's well, it's a freak of nature."

The guard then conducted her to a chamber on the opposite side of the practice ring where the novices who had passed were being assigned names. No one, she saw, fought under the name of their birth.

"I will keep my birth-name," Auriane said quietly when Corax and the secretary called her forward.

"You'll do nothing of the sort, spawn of the snarling bitches of Hades," Corax said, still smoldering from the aftermath of the battle with Erato. "We'll call you *Achillia*. That's it, put her down as Achillia the Amazon." Corax grinned at her, pleased by the fleeting panic he saw in her eye.

They cannot! I have one name, and a name is a house that contains the spirit. I have lost too much already—to change it would alter my soul and keep me from rejoining my family at death.

"*Aurinia*, then," she said boldly. Surely that would please them as well; did not these people seem to have a fondness for calling her that?

The secretary whispered to Corax, "We've already got an Achillia. Aurinia sounds all right. There was a celebrated barbarian prophetess called that when my grandfather was alive—Aurinia the Sorceress. It suits her. People will recognize it."

"I dislike it," Corax said with an irritated wave of the hand. "But let it be, she's wasted enough of our time. Get that crafty vixen out of my sight."

Auriane felt a small start of relief. At least she saved the part of her name that meant *sacred earth*—she would not lose completely the magical protection of her name.

CHAPTER XL

The novices' dining chamber was a cavernous soot-blackened room that opened directly onto the kitchens. One long table ran the length of this den of beasts; the smoking gloom was lit by two leering Gorgon's-head lamps hung from the low ceiling. Half the smoke from the kitchens' beehive ovens went up the chimneys and half, all agreed, found its way in here. The guards so hated this post the lowest in rank gambled for it and gave it to the loser. As those assigned to it regularly defected from it, going outside for air and reappearing only when a senior officer was in evidence, it happened that at the moment that night's barley ration was brought, the room was left unguarded.

From the distant First Hall came the low din of a banquet of celebration. They heard raucous shrieks, women's singing, and occasionally an outbreak of cheers punctuated with the cry: *"Aristos Rex!"* With it came the maddeningly seductive aroma of whole roast pig. The banquet was given by Aristos, who had that day defeated and killed Xerxes of the rival Claudian School, preserving the first place of the Great School in this year's games and his title as King.

"May they stew in Helle's cauldron," Coniaric said to all those near. His face was tanned to red-brown; there was a new hardness and distance in those eyes that for too long had looked on nothing familiar. "If we're not made into cutlets, we win a quarter of our value. That bloated bull just pulled down four million."

"But the purse was five hundred thousand," Sunia protested dully into her vinegar water. Her eyes were hazed with sleeplessness. The new cell she shared with Auriane was cleaner, but it was located over the entranceway used by the delivery carts, and they delivered at night. Auriane had that day begged Erato to be moved again. "How did he—"

Thorgild elbowed Sunia roughly. "Keep those ears sharpened, Know-Nothing. Some noblewoman gifted him with a villa by the sea worth over two million. On top of it the Emperor sent round a gift of a million, brought by a pretty, golden-haired slave-wench. Aristos got to keep the wench, too." Thorgild shifted his attention across the table to Auriane. "Do you think it's odd we've never set eyes on him? Celadon says *he* crosses Aristos' path from time to time. . . . Auriane, what is wrong?"

A young kitchen slave had begun ladling the cooked barley from an iron pot; it made a rhythmic slapping sound as it plopped into the wooden bowls. Auriane was holding hers close to the smoldering oil lamp, tilting it as she carefully examined the barley.

At last she pronounced in a low voice: "Wait for the beans."

"Rat dung?" said Thorgild, reaching for the bowl. "Cannot they invent some *fresh* torment?"

Looks of resignation were exchanged along the length of the table, followed by a pitiful, despairing silence. Sunia broke it with a piercing plaint.

"I cannot bear it any more! I want to die!"

Sunia rose to her feet, took her own bowl and threw it at the wall with such force that it cracked the wood. Barley oozed slowly down the oily wall. Dozens of bewildered faces turned to Sunia as she pounded the table and began sobbing.

"I want a chicken! A chicken! A common, ordinary chicken!"

Auriane rose up slowly, her expression grim. All the daily indignities of slavery for long had fed her wrath, and the demon confined grew stronger in the dark, biding its time; now it broke its chains. When Coniaric saw the fury in Auriane's face, he felt a start of panic. By Helle, he thought, that's her fight-to-the-death look, I know it only too well.

"Auriane, if you love life, *sit back down*," Coniaric implored with quiet passion.

She met his gaze. "During the war I took food from our mouths to feed the Roman captives at our mercy. In return, these people—the wealthiest in the Three Worlds—throw filth at us and call it food. *Someone must tell them we will not have it!*"

"Auriane, we are not at home! They will kill you!"

Auriane ignored him and said to Sunia, "I'm going to fetch you something you can eat."

The company of novices stared at her, most with mildly stupefied looks, a few with fanatic eagerness, as if she might actually succeed.

From long habit, Auriane first looked swiftly about for anything that might be used as a weapon; finding nothing, she turned toward the low, arched doorway. She knew she struck out wildly and this effort was foolish and doomed, and she remembered Marcus Julianus' warning, but in that moment she felt like an animal suffocating, scrambling for air. She had no thought of outcomes.

Coniaric leapt up and caught at the cloth of her tunic. "This is madness! *Do you know where you are!*"

Auriane tore her tunic free. Tears blurred her eyes, but she strode off confidently.

Coniaric slumped forward, head in his hands. "When will she learn that here she is not Baldemar's daughter?"

Sunia looked at him coldly. "You're the fool, Coniaric. She still *is* Baldemar's daughter."

Auriane passed beneath the door and was quickly immersed in the brown-and-gray gloom of the adjacent chamber's forbidden recesses. In this vaster room, veterans of the second grade were given their meals. The three halls were set in a row, from humblest to highest, and the revelry issuing from the banquet of Aristos was much louder here.

Auriane strode determinedly down one of the long rows, between crowded tables that glistened with spilled oil and wine. She was not dressed much differently from the commoner sort of prostitute who moved among the men, so at first her presence raised no alarm. All about her drunken voices were raised in challenge or quavered in crude song; coins gleamed as bets were paid, huge fists drummed on tables and wooden ladles clattered loudly against great bowls steaming with a mysterious, sinister-looking stew. A girl of no more than seven, naked but for a bejeweled girdle and crown of vine leaves, did a sluggish dance on one of the tables, as though given some draught, while the men nearest clapped a slow rhythm. *Dead souls underground,* she thought as malignant laughter followed her and heavily muscled arms reached for her from evil shadows. *If I tarry they will pull me into their twilight land forever.*

"Come here, little dove," a man called to her. "See what I've got for you. By Priapus' crown you've never seen the like!" Nimbly she dodged him.

At that moment Corax saw her. He was eating at the last table with a collection of trainers of the lowest grade. He shot up from his place and made frenzied gestures to the guards stationed at intervals along the walls. They ignored him.

As she passed him, he seized her arm. "You crazed spawn of a she-ass! Get back to your place! *Guards!*"

"Give us food we can eat and I will," she replied quietly.

A croaking voice from the charnel gloom next to Corax said, "What are you willing to do for it, pretty little bitch?" A half-dozen hands moved in gestures of copulation.

Corax looked like a colicky infant preparing to erupt into a lusty tantrum. "You'll not get out of this one, *Aurinia*," he said, breathing heavily as he caught one of her wrists, pinning it behind her while twisting it painfully. "I'll see you flogged naked, with chains, before all the men of your grade. And don't think that meddling slumlord-and-pirate Erato will save you."

With her free hand Auriane caught the handle of a bronze bowl brimming with a black, fishy-smelling soup and dragged it toward Corax with all her strength, sloshing its scalding contents all over the front of him. He let out a shriek and released her. There came a brutish chorus of laughter. Auriane got free, then streaked off through the connecting door.

"Guards! Murderess! Stop her!" Corax yelped, hopping, holding his dripping tunic away from him; he darted for the small fountain at the room's center, clutching his burned arms and chest. Several of the guards smiled at him blandly, as if not comprehending, while others gaily waved at him as if he summoned them for an assignation. They despised Corax for his repeated attempts to ingratiate himself with Torquatus by reporting their selling of favors. The unruly wench they counted no more than an amusing distraction.

But one of the guards recognized Auriane and realized she was not one of the prostitutes. Swiftly he started after her.

Auriane, however, was well ahead of him. She had no precise plan other than to seek out and shame some man of rank. She was not fully aware of how much this action would outrage custom. Although she was aware of the ruthlessly rigid hierarchy of social grades among these people, it was too unlike what she knew at home for her to understand how deeply it governed their every sentiment and thought. She was like any foreigner who, under duress, reverts to the native tongue—in her country no one was so humble he could not appeal to the most celebrated chief for redress of wrongs.

She darted through a short, barrel-vaulted passage, keeping to the shadows; then she ascended a flight of marble steps flanked by winged Victories decked in laurel. Beyond, the cramped passage opened into a mammoth cave, its vastness pulsing with ruddy light. She saw it all through a bluish haze of incense and lamp smoke. Competing spicy odors made the air seem too rich to breathe. Everywhere were clusters of small flames seeming to float on air; she realized she was among a virtual forest of delicate "trees" of bronze with tiny tongues of flame in place of leaves. Her senses froze at the sight of this nether cauldron teeming with all manner of odd and glittering life. *They do lie down when they eat* was one of her first confused thoughts as she looked on a field of beds, which must be what Decius called couches. On them reclined laughing, shouting noblemen, flushed with drink, and courtesans with arrogantly arched black brows, jaded eyes, blood-colored lips with a cruel beauty, and hair heaped high on their heads like a complexity of scrolls.

This is the banquet of Aristos, she realized, awestruck as the child who witnesses her first sacrifice. She moved forward, meaning to lose herself in the exotic confusion, conscious she was most likely being pursued. Maids in fawnskin flitted in front of her, sprinkling perfumed water into the air. Tall, graceful slaves glided among the tables, bearing great oval platters of food complex as a cityscape. She saw nothing she recognized, but the sight of such abundance rekindled her rage—there was enough on one platter to keep poor Sunia content for a month. From somewhere came the silky, shimmering sound of a kithara— music that seemed much too gentle for a people who were such lovers of cruel sports and dark punishments. The soaring walls were alive with battle scenes painted all over them; the outsize forms of horses, goddesses and heroes were rendered with such hypnotizing reality she imagined that when she turned her gaze from them, they secretly moved. At the hall's center was a monumental fountain. Here a towering Diana the Huntress loomed up, contemplating her bow; she gleamed like new snow in moonlight. About her naked nymphs played; Auriane looked, amazed, at the twin streams of water jetting from their nipples. Every odd thing that could be, she thought, these people have brought forth.

Then she saw, beneath a great shrine to Mars set into a niche in the wall, a table set apart on a low platform. Surely this was the place of honored guests. As she moved resolutely toward it, the banqueters paid her scant attention; she might have been anyone's slave bearing a message for her master.

It was indeed the table of honor, for as she moved closer she recognized the soft, pendulous outline of Torquatus' profile, and his corrupt mouth; those rapacious eyes were gentled somewhat by strong drink. Was there lingering within the man the smallest capacity to feel shame?

Reclining to Torquatus' left was a woman whose countenance was bold and queenly as that of the painted face of the eternal woman adorning the wall. And to his right, turned so that his back was to her, was a massive man whose shoulder-length, red-blond locks were curled at the ends with an iron; he was crowned with a garland of roses.

Auriane stopped at a respectful distance before Torquatus, who was clapping with delight as a serving girl cut into an impossible pastry fashioned to look like a goose and grapes and other unknown fruits tumbled out.

Torquatus then saw Auriane. From his look, she might have been a rat's carcass floating in his bath water.

Auriane inclined her head slightly and said gravely, "I am sorry to intrude upon you, my lord, but I do so with a just complaint. I come on my own—my companions tried to prevent me. We beg you to find us edible food and . . . to punish the men who are fouling it."

Torquatus' guests stared, bewildered by this humbly clad woman with regal bearing. Torquatus knew her at once for what she was—a novice criminally out of place.

His cold, closed expression gave way to the more hesitant look of one who makes rapid calculations. Slowly, evenly, he said, "Of course. You'll get everything you want. Just stay there . . . don't move now. . . . What was it again you said you wanted?" All the while one hand reached for a jeweled dagger, and the other signaled unobtrusively to the guards stationed by the great door that opened onto the practice arena. Six started forward at once, approaching Auriane from behind so as not to alarm the madwoman and frighten her into attacking him. To delay her further,

Torquatus gave her a barren smile. "For now," he said, "why do you not take one of those chickens?"

Auriane knew at once all was wrong and she was doomed.

Across the table a serving girl was setting down a platter of plump hens cooked in lemon and honey. Auriane looked closely. Yes—*real* hens, not pastries fashioned to look like hens. How they would delight Sunia.

I am a dead woman whether I take one or not. Why not present Sunia with a last gift?

Quickly, warily, Auriane took a chicken, dropping it into her tunic; the rope that secured it about her waist held the bird fast. As she did this, she was aware the powerfully built man with the rose garland remained unnaturally still, carefully keeping his face turned from her. Why did he not stare at her as the others did?

The alabaster-faced beauty said teasingly to the shy man, "Does she frighten you, Aristos?"

Aristos. Of course.

At that moment Auriane sensed the approach of the guards. She whirled round and saw them, coming at a trot, twenty paces off. Their swords were drawn.

She could not let them slaughter her like an animal, not with the sign of the god of war carved into her flesh. She must die with weapon in hand or bring shame on the holy groves. Beyond Aristos a kitchen slave patiently sliced a haunch of mutton. She lunged for his carving knife.

But Aristos chose that moment to heave himself up and extend his wine cup to a girl who held out a jug. Auriane struck Aristos in the shoulder and sprawled beside him on the couch.

It was then that she saw his face.

Oh no, oh no. It cannot be. It is not. You are dead, dead, Sigwulf was certain of it. Officially dead.

Monster, crawl back down to Helle. *How can you be in this place?* Great Niding. Fiend of fiends, murderer of Baldemar, bane of us all.

Aristos was Odberht.

She scrambled up, carving knife forgotten, and began darting around tables. A powerful sickness of heart nearly overwhelmed her.

It must not be, but it is. We are doomed. Baldemar and my country lie utterly unavenged.

She realized the scar on Aristos' thick neck was the result of the

wound she gave him with the broken glass horn, on that night so
long ago when he savagely assaulted her in the bog.

*The health of the Scourge is my people's sickness. How he
thrives in this place! It is no wonder my people suffer so.*

In back of her, Auriane heard women's shrieks, a chorus of
yelping guards. The banqueters rose and milled nervously, terrified by the sight of the guards' drawn swords. Auriane ran blindly,
as intent on escaping the specter of Aristos-Odberht as she was her
own death. As a dozen guards closed in upon her, one of the Syrian
snake dancers lost her snake — the testy serpent, longer than a
horse, glided to the floor and for a time followed Auriane. The
guards dropped back to give the creature room, allowing Auriane
a chance to dart behind the fountain of Diana. The floor about it
was marble, and it was wet. She began to slide, colliding with an
overburdened table; silver platters and ewers crashed to the floor.
Lamps were upset and oil streaked everywhere; the flames
greedily followed the oil, and soon there were several small fires
in her wake.

The cry *"Fire!"* brought everyone to their feet; panicked diners
concealed Auriane's flight and greatly hampered the guards. A few
made token attempts to catch her, but most urged her on, laughing
and shouting. A reveler struck a guard who knocked him down,
and fights erupted. Rising over all the din was the wail of the
Syrian snake dancer calling out in her harsh, masculine voice the
name of her beloved snake.

Auriane leapt in one bound down the flight of stairs she had
climbed earlier, ran hard through the passage and was soon lost
among the veterans and prostitutes of the Second Hall. She felt the
walls crashing in upon her. How quickly all of life had gotten
utterly, fatally, out of hand.

At least I die knowing I protested this madness. This place has
unraveled me. The Fates mock us with promises of order, and toss
us into chaos. Once they would not let me die for my people.
Today they let me die for a chicken. How absurd to perish for a
lesson I thought I learned when young — never to allow myself to
be carried off on a tide of wrath.

When Corax saw Auriane running, the guards in close pursuit,
his loathing of her snatched the last remnant of his reason. He
scurried for the skylit central chamber where the practice arena
lay, pushed past the guards and gave several vigorous pulls on the
rope of the bell that gave the alarm for a general breakout.

That crazed vixen cannot possibly escape just punishment this time.

The manic clangor of that bell alerted the Praetorian Guards at the Palace and caused two detachments of the Urban Cohorts to begin advancing upon the school. The sound of it greatly worsened the general panic; tables were overturned as people bolted for the entrances.

The guards were barricading the passages between the chambers, fearful the men of the Second Hall might attempt to rush the doors. Now, surely, they judged they had the wretched woman trapped. But she was proving as tricky to catch as a rat in straw. There she was, darting down a tabletop. Then she leapt down, disappearing beneath the turbulent sea of people.

Auriane bolted through the final door and into the hall of the novices. Sunia, Coniaric and a number of others pulled her into their midst. Moments later a dozen guards flooded in. Whips snapped; they wrenched her free of the protective knot her tribesmen formed about her. Still more poured into the little room, glutting it with armed men until all began to feel slightly foolish when they looked upon their quarry: one miserable, unarmed woman. Gradually an embarrassed quiet fell over them, broken only by the distant echoing whoops of the slave boys putting out the fires and the sound of an oaken table being dragged back into place.

After a moment Torquatus was there, taking over the room; those eyes glittered with a savage edge that subdued the guards; now they were like chastised hounds. Close behind him as if pulled on a chain was Corax, and following Corax, brow furrowed in concern, was Erato.

"Give her to me!" Corax was begging Torquatus, desperate as if he pled for his own life. With a sweep of the arm he indicated the guards. "These scoundrels did nothing when I told them she broke loose—except laugh like drunken catamites! I'll chastise her *properly*, as I know you'll want to chastise these guards!"

"You'll boil alive in your own broth this time, Corax," retorted a guard who was tying Auriane's hands behind her back with hemp rope. Nodding at Corax, he addressed Torquatus: "This donkey in human skin pulled the great alarm. Send *him* out to explain to the Prefect of the Urban Cohorts that he summoned them because one woman stole a chicken!"

"Wolves! Murderers of guests! I did not steal!" Auriane's voice was clear and arresting.

"Silence her!" Torquatus ordered. A guard struck Auriane across the face, but not as hard as he might have; something in her spirited wildness appealed to the guards. To Corax, Torquatus said, "If I catch sight of your lice-ridden hide skulking about this place tomorrow, I'll have you driven off with whips and brands. *Begone!*" Then he turned back to the guards, who had by now secured Auriane.

"And now, as to the fate of this criminal . . . when is the next date for executions?"

"Two days after the Nones," one guard replied.

Erato spoke up with soft insistence. "My lord, please stop and consider. What happened was not entirely her doing—"

"Erato, when a man becomes soft and mellow-hearted as you, it's time to retire to a sheep farm."

Erato leaned closer and said so only Torquatus could hear. "Listen, I beg you! This sounds incredible but you must believe me, *she is valuable beyond price.* I know what you're thinking, it's only a woman. But in truth I have not seen a fighter of such . . . such *intelligence* since your own favorite in the time of Nero, that man called Narcissus."

"Whoever told you I enjoy practical jokes cruelly misinformed you."

"Nemesis! This is not a jest. You must believe! She'll draw crowds like any luminary of the First Hall, maybe even more so, due to the oddity she's a woman—"

"I do not care if she draws crowds or flies," Torquatus interrupted, enunciating carefully, as if Erato were a schoolboy who had become unaccountably slow at his lessons. "We have under this roof over a thousand highly trained killers, who, should they revolt in concert, could slit all our throats in the blink of an eye and then go and wreak havoc in the city. Such scum can only be controlled by fear. And a good number of them witnessed this villainous wench attacking a trainer—even if it *was* only Corax— not to mention her attempts to sack the place. Perhaps you'd like to pay for her damage from your own purse so we don't have to make a report of this debacle to the Ministry?" He smiled with a feigned fatherliness. "Discipline before sentiment, my good man. Now get on to your duties and be silent."

Torquatus turned back to the guards. "Here is my judgment. On the second day after the Nones, at the noon recess of the animal shows, let her be tied to a stake and torn apart by bears, for the greater amusement of the people."

Sunia began to wail. Coniaric let tears flow, not caring who ridiculed him. Thorgild leapt up, eyes filled with a wild, lost rage, and began shouting curses; five guards were needed to subdue him.

Erato wheeled sharply about, panic and desolation rising, his mind full of hasty, half-formed plans. He realized, amazed, he was near tears for the first time since his wife died in the great pestilence during the reign of Titus. She has ensnared me, he thought, and has become, in some manner, my child. It is perhaps a thing only an aging teacher can know when given the most promising charge of his life.

He knew then that she rekindled long-expired hopes. It was as if she were a panel on which he could repaint his life and perfect it. He had hardly begun instructing her and he wanted more than wealth, promotion or imperial favor to see her fight and win.

Erato set out at once for the Palace, hoping to gain the ear of some influential official who might be persuaded to aid his cause. He reached the Office of Petitions just before they shut up for the night, but its secretaries received him with great coldness. It would be two months, he was told, before he could be given an audience with Domitian, and did he really intend to bother the Emperor with a matter so trivial amidst his preparations for the war with Dacia? Erato went next to the office of the City Prefect, whose secretary told him scornfully the Prefect would summon the "humble witnesses" to that riot in his own time, and to go home and wait until he was called upon.

Frantically Erato thought where else he might turn. The Emperor's advisors? They were all wolves who would devour their own children to increase their influence. Except for one, who reportedly would give ear to anyone, no matter how low in station.

And so he repaired to the suite of chambers housing the secretaries and scribes of the First Advisor of the Imperial Council, Marcus Arrius Julianus. Erato had heard Julianus often labored until the sixth hour after sundown, only to retire to his great-house to work far into the night on his own books of philosophy. True to common report, Julianus was still in the Palace and hard at work long after the other ministers of state had departed. Erato was amazed to find himself immediately and courteously conducted into Julianus' presence. And he was further surprised to discover Julianus seemed to already possess a detailed account of the incident and even knew of the sentence imposed on

Auriane. The man's informants, Erato mused, should enter foot-races in the Emperor's next Hellenic Games.

Marcus Arrius Julianus seemed in a state of great alertness and agitation and shot Erato a series of short, direct questions of a puzzling nature, mostly concerning details of Torquatus' business dealings. Erato answered thoroughly as he could; some sure instinct told him this was not the time to be discreet about his superiors. Julianus dismissed him, then called him back at once, asking Erato a question that made him wonder if his ears had begun to fail.

"Erato, if you had to, could you run that school?"

"I've always thought it idle to speculate on things which are not possible."

"Let us not judge *too* hastily what is not possible."

"Well, yes, then—of course I could. I've no birth, but I know every rathole in the place—as well as who's got what on whom. And *I* at least have the wit to know skill in a swordsman, which is more than can be said by that string of preening equestrian epicures who've holidayed there in the last years under the pretense of governing it."

Erato liked Marcus Julianus' smile; it was swift, genial, knowing.

"Good enough. You may go. Do not be alarmed if you receive a rather surprising message in the morning."

CHAPTER XLI

When Erato was gone, Marcus Julianus departed at a half-run to hire a carriage. The Emperor was in residence at the Alban villa, better than an hour's drive through the windy, rain-dampened winter night. While still in the vaulted corridors of the Palace, he realized, dismayed, he was too informally dressed to go before the Emperor—he wore a good tunic and cloak, but Domitian would count it gravest insult were he not clad in a toga. And if he returned to his great-house he might not arrive before Domitian retired. He thought it dangerous to delay until tomorrow. His plan might be put in motion too late.

He happened to pass a freedman of Gallus' whom he knew slightly. Hastily he greeted him, then said, "Polybius, my good man . . . that's a fine, remarkably clean toga."

"So it is," he replied, puzzled.

"I'll buy it from you."

"What sort of game is this?" But the quiet directness in Marcus Julianus' eyes told him it was no game. "But—it's *cold.*"

"Are five thousand sesterces enough to warm you?"

"You're completely mad!" But he began unwinding it slowly; he was not a rich man. "It's been to the fuller's ten times."

"It's beautiful. Here is a note for the money; pick it up from Diocles tomorrow."

Soon Marcus Julianus was speeding through the winter dark in a carriage hired at the Capena gate. Throughout the jolting journey down the Via Latina, he occupied himself with framing charges against Torquatus. It must be something that warranted exile, but not death. He despised the man, but that seemed not sufficient reason to commit judicial murder. To accomplish this, there were three factors to consider: Torquatus' rank, the nature of the offense, and an unknown one—Domitian's mood. He was still not certain what he was going to say as the guard at the villa's gate admitted him without question to a chamber where Domitian sat entranced over what was, in these times, his favorite pleasure reading—his informers' reports of the most influential Senators' conversations at their private dinner parties.

He found Domitian in an affable temper. The Emperor just received word his wife was with child, and a welcome dispatch had arrived from North Africa while he dined, informing him his legion posted there had annihilated an irksome nomadic tribe that had long refused to pay its taxes. This fine humor was enhanced by the fact that Marcus Julianus drove a distance in haste to see him. As always, he hungered for small signs his First Advisor still held him in regard. Julianus feigned having come for another purpose; Domitian's suspicions would be roused if he too suddenly showed a predisposition for the role of informer. He first asked Domitian's advice on a case he was overseeing involving a dozen jurymen accused of taking bribes in the Courts of Inheritance. Then, offhandedly he mentioned he had devised a new move for the Alexandrian board game the Emperor often played with the advisors. As he hoped, Domitian demanded to be shown it immediately. While they played, Marcus Julianus made an enigmatic reference to the great number of comments he heard in the streets during the past year alluding to the "tarnished magnificence" of the games. This disturbed Domitian far more than he would reveal; he considered the arena contests to be the constant visible evidence of the glory of his rule.

Domitian then asked him anxious question after question, which made Marcus Julianus' first hints that Torquatus could not handle money appear most natural. Julianus threw out tantalizing scraps of information, then withdrew them, letting Domitian snap at the bait several times until at last, with great reluctance, he told the entire tale. Torquatus had, he knew, lost a good fraction of the school's revenues for the first half of the year on a ludicrous shipping venture—and he had been trying for some time to recover the money by overestimating costs to the Finance Ministry and by cutting vital expenses. He was acquiring inferior fighters and reducing their rations, so much so that a destructive and expensive food riot had just occurred, the news of which would very soon come to his ears.

Domitian listened in black silence; then, gradually, he began to look wickedly pleased. "I say we let the frozen north chill that ardor for business ventures!" he said at last. "And since you ferreted the bungler out, I'll reward you by letting *you* choose some edifying place to pack the scoundrel off to." With a stylus he indicated a portion of the great map of the world that covered two of the chamber's walls. "Here, on the south coast of the Black Sea, is lovely Bithynia—a grim and nasty place created by the gods so I would have a place to send traitors, Cynics, bad poets and fools. Choose a village, a *small, primitive* village, one that will bore the conniving rascal to utter madness."

Marcus Julianus masked his dismay, thinking: How shamefully easy it is in these times to ruin a man—it takes but a well-placed word.

He encountered more difficulty securing the post for Erato. His early attempts brought only sulky replies and sullen looks.

"Some might say you're playing me for a fool," Domitian complained, "naming a man of such low birth."

"That's in his favor—he'll not regard it as a station along the way while he frets restlessly, waiting for promotion."

"It's an equestrian post. If I give it to a mere *freedman*, the whole order will take offense."

"It might be good for them, considering how poorly they've performed in it of late. They are all soldiers with war records, and not surprisingly, they're running it as if it were the army. Have you ever tallied up what you've lost, just from the continuous revolts against harsh discipline? Erato would run it as a *school*. The man in that post speaks for you as no other. Others merely pass through those doors, but to Erato that school is his life. He'll be so grateful, you'll find him much easier to keep in hand. Do it, or invite the same troubles over again."

Domitian sat for a time in sour silence, eyes doggedly probing Marcus Julianus' for deeper motives. Then he said suddenly, "The woman—what *was* that demented she-beast's name?" His eyes smoldering with repressed interest, he leaned close, alert as a cat waiting for its quarry to run from cover. "I hear your man Erato has taken her under wing."

Marcus Julianus' whole mind braced for disaster. He said with brisk annoyance, "I would not know. I do not follow such things—you know my opinion of the games."

"Oh, come. What have I done to deserve this tiresome prattle? I'll pry a vice out of you yet! Do you mean to tell me she does not intrigue you, even a *little?* Can all your philosophy tell me why your presence persistently brings her to mind? You've not only her *lofty innocence*, you know, you've also got her unfortunate tendency for stupid, futile heroics. . . . Myself, I don't think of her at all, of course. . . . I mention her only because *you* mention Erato."

Marcus Julianus sought frantically for an argument that would lead Domitian to disassociate his choice of Erato from Auriane. "Yes, Erato," he said at last, "who will not only save money but lives—*expensive* lives—for it is well-known that when swordsmen are thoroughly trained and exhibit impressive skill, the crowd's thirst for blood noticeably slackens."

"Ah!" Domitian said with delight, as if he had won the board game with a surprise move. "*That's* it! You had me puzzled for a time. *Now* I feel at rest—I've discerned your motive! Some idiot Pythagorean notion of compassion, I should have *known* it." Domitian wagged a finger at him. "You're tenacious as a burr. You have it, then. Erato has the post. But if he shows the *least* disloyalty or incompetence, I'll not forget who selected him."

Late in the afternoon the next day, a baffled and amazed Erato moved into the Prefect's offices. His first act was to overturn the order for Auriane's execution; his second, to order a close inspection of the rations given the men of the lower grades.

Auriane felt she had been lifted out of darkness by the hand of a god. She had escaped a miserable and ignoble end. Marcus Julianus was well and living and for her sake had banished the beast, Torquatus. She would not have known who her benefactor was but for the fact that Erato named him, uttering the First Advisor's name with a reverence that surprised her, for Erato was naturally inclined to be contemptuous and distrusting of the great. The love she felt for Marcus Julianus alternately exhilarated and terrified her. It was a flood tide too powerful to oppose that might bear her away from all she knew. But it was also a welcome comfort after the harshness of the last years, lulling as a suspension in birth-waters. For so long she was an ash tree standing alone, giving shelter to others. She had forgotten how it was to be sheltered herself. It brought haunting memories of the days before the Hall burned, when last the world seemed a stable place. But in these days she could not forget its illusory side; in the beat of her blood was the warning: *The Hall will ever burn again.* His protection was a well from which she might drink, not a sea in which to immerse herself. Only Fria protects perfectly, she reminded herself when she found herself taking dangerous comfort from his love.

When Auriane was returned to her cell, she abruptly ended Sunia's joy at their reunion when she told her of her grim discovery at the banquet of Aristos. At first Sunia would not believe. Surely Auriane saw a wraith, a spirit-double, or some conjuring of an evil sorcerer.

"Sunia, it *was* Odberht, and he was alive, *alive* as the worms that animate corpses. It requires no sorcery, no ghosts—only that he was sent off to Rome with the earliest captives, which would mean he's been here for a year and a half . . . which is the length of time Aristos has been here. Doubtless he hoped I would be killed before we discovered him." Her eyes sharpened with a realization. "Sunia, *he* was the one who tried to poison me in the prison cell—I'm certain of it."

Sunia lapsed into miserable acceptance, terror accumulating in her eyes. "Every breath he draws poisons our blood! What will we do? We are prisoners. We can do nothing but watch him thrive!"

"Calm yourself. All of us who are here will stand against him. I'm not sure what to do, but the matter's not mine to solve alone. Tonight over our gruel I'll call a council."

Auriane rose restlessly and walked to the small, barred window of the cell door. Across the passage was a vertical window cut into the thick wall; beyond, the ghostly disk of a near-full moon haunted a clear afternoon sky. She seized it with her mind and fervently prayed, but got no strength from it; that moon seemed too weak, too wan, too distant. She felt certainty draining out of her as it always seemed to when an ill-omened thing occurred and the old shame rose up like some evil sap, fouling her heart, flooding her lungs, suffocating her.

I thought my shame more than half conquered. But still it slinks back when I am weak, like the slender gray wolf who creeps out of the snows when he scents death is close.

Barely audibly, she said, "My own curse is everlasting. It follows me in dreams, it follows me across the world. . . ." Her voice was a cruel hand working open an old wound. "Because of *me*, we are battered down, and Odberht thrives. . . . Because of *me*, vengeance is impossible, the tribe is scattered, and we are mocked in this place where men are trained to fight like dogs!"

Sunia caught her breath at the pain in Auriane's voice. Slowly she rose to her feet. "Auriane, none are left alive who still believe in your shame, except you!" She hesitated as if she tread where she should not, then ventured on anyway. "I have no good understanding of such things, but . . . the Fates must have preserved Odberht's life for some purpose we cannot see. As they've not cut *our* threads, they must mean to weave us into one weaving. That man in the Emperor's garden, who, by your own words, loves you, he who sees with the eyes of Wodan—would not *he* have seen your shame and despised you, had it been there to see?"

Auriane turned to look at her, managing a weary smile. "An interesting turn of thought, Sunia." She turned away. "What does *he* know of shame? Kingly innocence lies on him like a cloak."

Sunia tentatively approached Auriane, smiling hopefully. "Perhaps it's not your curse but your great heart that throws us in with Odberht at this time. Perhaps, for you, he is a gateway to another world."

"Another world?" Auriane smiled more warmly. "You've a gift for saying encouraging words. Till now, I did not know it."

Sunia looked faintly embarrassed. "Nor did I."

Auriane took her hand but said nothing.

I struggle mightily and it is never enough, Auriane thought, remembering the spear she cast at the legion when she was told Avenahar would die if they did not open the gates. Perhaps this time the wind will carry the spear and it will fly at the stars . . . and it *will* be enough.

CHAPTER XLII

Domitia Longina was in torment through the winter, desperate for some way to respond to Marcus Julianus' request without risking her life. She felt like a moth fluttering about a small, still flame, caught in troubled suspension, attraction exactly balanced by fear.

Then one night she found herself unavoidably confronted with him. She dined in her suite of rooms in the West Palace among friends with literary pretensions who still enjoyed imperial favor— a dozen modestly talented lyric poets, among them three noble-women, and several authors of plodding epics—men whose work she could no longer bear to read, for it was so distorted with turgid praises of Domitian. Her dining chamber overlooked a circular garden, the site of the small library she was having built to house her rare volumes of early Greek and Latin poetry. Construction stalled indefinitely when Atrides, an architect-engineer employed by the Ministry of Public Works, halted suddenly, claiming the design she had approved could not be built. His reasons were vague. Sometimes, he complained of the too-sandy soil; at others, he protested that the precious marbles she wanted could not be found. She suspected the truth was that he chose to please her husband rather than her. Domitian saw her library as evidence of anarchic tendencies on her part, as though it were a temple into which she could flee from him and couple with the geniuses of the poets. Or perhaps, she surmised, Domitian was jealous of the fact that *her* love of the poets was real, while his own was feigned.

She entered her dining chamber only after all her guests were in place. Two bored Praetorians flanked the door; a half dozen more were placed strategically about the walls—a reminder that Domitian's unblinking eye followed her everywhere.

And there was Marcus Arrius Julianus, boldly present at her own table, reclining on the couch opposite from the one reserved for her, next to young Castor and the aging Lucullus. She found him maddeningly at ease, jesting with her friends with the easy alertness of a hunting animal at rest.

She felt a quiet start of terror. *Who let him in?* But then, who could keep him out? Quickly she realized the Guards, doubtless, assumed the First Advisor was there with her husband's blessings, sent to observe her among her friends—though she knew better; more likely he was there for some inscrutable purpose of his own. She chose to play his game, greeting him as if he were expected, thinking: Curses on him—he knows there is no privacy here. Panic and obscure excitement knotted together in her stomach as she met those knowing, gently mocking eyes. What did he intend to do? Carry her off to some private chamber under the eyes of the Guards?

The others shied away from him at first, but as they drank deeply of her Setinian wine, they lost some of their fear of him. He asked her question after question about her unfinished library, polite but insistent, and she fought vainly for indifference. She understood why even those friends she counted petty tale-bearers called him a man of uncommon grace. She watched him with great pleasure, holding his eyes long as she dared, then dropping her gaze to his hand as, with swift, assured motions, he moved a dish and traced forms and figures on the table to illustrate a point, showing her that Atrides was wrong. *"What you will can be done."* Was *this* all he meant by that message—that her library could be built? She wondered with a flash of panic if those about her guessed how warmed she felt by his tantalizingly brief smiles of understanding. ·

Once she saw a quick look of concern come into his eyes; it happened when he heard an exchange between Castor and Lucullus, whose talk had long since slid down from the matters of the mind to the mores of Junilla.

"How *could* she?" Castor said with relish. "She might as well mate with a bull."

"That was last year, you've not kept up."

"Are they *certain* it was Aristos?"

"Oh, there is no doubt. I know a man who often lifts a cup with the freedman of the very same guard she bribed to be let into his cell," Lucullus went on, aglow with the attention this succulent bit of gossip was netting him. He decided to make the most of it. "He said last time she stumbled out of there looking like a wrung-out rag! Do you imagine, to please her, he softens the hairs on his legs by singeing them with hot walnut shells?" He paused, waiting for the delighted laughter to die. "Think on it . . ." he went on. "Imagine Junilla's pearly arms, white as sea foam, white as . . . as Aphrodite's milk, encircling that grunting, hairy behemoth, that leather-skinned, lice-ridden bull. An exciting subject for an ode, don't you think?"

Domitia Longina gave them a sharp, reproving look, misinterpreting Marcus Julianus' unease as some lingering loyalty to that creature who was once his wife. But Julianus caught her eye and said in a covered voice, "Let them talk on, it does not offend me."

The true reason for his alarm would have been impossible for Domitia Longina to guess. Junilla, he thought, I know what you are doing. You stalk not one man but two. You suspect something, that's been obvious since you outbid me for her horse. Aristos is to your taste, I've no doubt, but linking me with Auriane is even *more* to your taste. And now you've got Aristos as your pawn, with all his thugs and spies infesting that school at your service. You'll be lingering about, watching, perhaps bribing the same guard I must bribe on that night, soon coming, when I *must* get in to see her.

"That tiresome Atrides will still say it's impossible," Domitia Longina went on, a cautiously muted teasing look in her eyes as she returned his attention to her library.

"Nonsense, more excavating will have to be done, that's all, and the foundations redone. It must be set with piles, and they should be of charred alder or olive wood, placed closely together, like bridge piles. And the intervals between them must be filled with charcoal. I myself could work up a plan for the portico you want. Atrides gave up too soon." He paused, then said smoothly, as if the idea had just occurred to him, "There is still a little light." He cast a professional glance in the direction of the colonnade at the rear of the room, which overlooked the library's site. "Perhaps I could show you what Atrides could not, if you were of a mind to step out onto that colonnade." That look, reassuring but with a glint of intrigue, startled her into the realization that *this* was what he had planned from the first.

She suppressed an answering conspiratorial smile.

Clever man, she thought. He found a way to speak to me alone, while remaining within sight of everyone, including the Guards. In sight, but not in hearing. And to those about us, it appears utterly spontaneous. Who, watching this, could suspect us of collusion?

They rose together, causing hardly a pause in their dinner companions' conversations. Those who did take notice thought her eagerness natural, for all knew how frustrated she was by the delays in the construction of her library. As she walked ahead of him, she felt like some adventurer starting out on a narrow bridge, high over a shallow, rock-strewn stream. Though her mind assured her the structure would hold, on looking down, her palms moistened, her knees quivered.

While they were still within hearing of the Guards, he said, "Now stand *here.*" Below them was the great gouge in the earth where Atrides had tried and failed to set the foundation. "What do you see to the west? That would be the vista, if the entrance were placed as I think it should be. The radiant heating could be extended through here, despite what Atrides says. Now step down here and consider the vista from the east. . . ."

He took her hand to help her balance in her sandals, which were fragile as spiderwebs; she took four mincing steps down to the garden's edge. The hand he held quivered like a trapped dove.

Marcus Julianus regarded her critically, worried suddenly she was too delicate to withstand what he meant to do next. Though Domitia Longina was a matron, her face was that of a woman not fully grown; it was too softly modeled, with a child's fullness and light sweetness in its expression; those lips were set permanently in a girl's petulant pout. Her eyes were blue smears of uncertainty, soft, seeking, gelid; he thought of scallops pulled from the shell. That pale hair, wispy and indefinite as her thoughts, was drawn back at the nape of her neck, but most of it escaped to form a gauzy aura about her face. Her skin had a fine translucence; even the caress of her azure silk stola seemed too rough for its overprotected softness. That unformed body, pliant as cushions, defied utterly the notion that somewhere within was muscle and bone. She appears too vulnerable for this world, Marcus Julianus thought uneasily. Yet there *is* a spirited lift to her chin, a capacity for dangerous mischief in those eyes. She generates her own sort of elusiveness. This, I would wager, is at least part of what keeps

Domitian's attentions upon her, for he is at his weakest with women who imply by act and gesture they do not want him.

He released her hand when they were beyond hearing.

"I requested an audience," he said quietly "and, of course, I understand you could not respond."

Domitia Longina felt suddenly the weight of the night on her chest; she could not breathe. "One cannot always control one's life," she whispered, her voice pale. "It relieves me you know it was not done from ill will toward you." She kept her gaze on the site, frowning and nodding, feigning comprehension of an explanation of an architectural point.

"You are gracious and kind," he continued in a low voice. "Have I your permission to introduce the matter I had in mind to approach you with then, now that our purpose is disguised?"

"Yes," she said breathlessly as a young girl repeating the marriage vows. But she managed to maintain a bland expression.

Moving his left hand as though he described an arch, he said, "I mean to inform you then, I intend to murder your husband."

Her body spasmed as if a noose were tightened about her neck. The fright that came into her eyes was senseless, unpredictable, blind. Slowly she brought up a trembling right hand.

He closed his eyes. *Oh, curses on all of life, on love, on all striving, on the infernal gods. I misjudged her. She is summoning the guards. I am a dead man.*

But Domitia Longina uttered no sound. The hand she raised stopped at her throat. This automatic defensive gesture she smoothly transformed into the motions of fidgeting with an errant strand of hair. When he looked at her again, to his amazement her face was composed, although she would not look at him. He sensed this was protective, as if she feared he might see too much of her soul.

I judged her rightly, he thought. *There's a firm core of sensibility beneath all that flightiness and fretting.*

When she spoke, her voice was bare of lilting, womanly intonations—it was the flat, pragmatic voice of a woman in the marketplace. "You are mad to so casually place your life in my hands. Why are you so certain of yourself . . . and of *me?*"

"It is not done casually. It was a carefully made judgment that your love of freedom overbalances your fear. And I'm not so sure of myself as you may suppose—I've made a life of sounding more certain than I am."

"So *that* is honesty. I've heard tales of it." She looked at him briefly, appreciating what seemed a Homeric determination in his eyes, mingled intriguingly with a quality of gentleness. She thought: I am not so easily read. This is a necromancer who reads in eyes what Chaldeans read in the stars.

"You frighten me." It was a fugitive's voice, not an empress's. She thought suddenly the ground was too distant, and earth and air were all one liquid medium, tugging at her, rolling in gentle swells. This could not be happening, but it was.

"That is the last thing I wish. I'm sorry to tell you this way but . . . you are too isolated by your jailers."

"Most people envy me."

"They are blinded by eminence. They do not see the woman beneath."

"I could change my mind tomorrow. Dawn will come and I won't be pleasantly half drunk, and I'll realize you're off your head. Perhaps *then* I'll go to the Prefect of the Guard. I hold a dagger at your throat."

"I wished it so, for how else could I have gained your trust?"

"Of all the plots conceived, how many succeed—and how many end in a series of executions?" Her voice became a soft growl. "You had better not be playing with me!"

He suppressed a smile at the undisguised eagerness in her voice. The fruit had long been ready to fall; the tree needed but one firm shake. He sensed she questioned him now merely to test how he would respond, as a collector of bronzes might continue to turn and handle a vase after he has decided he will buy it.

"It will succeed because of what I learned from the failures of others. The ground will be prepared slowly; the first consideration will be the safety of the conspirators—there are shortly going to be quite a few of them. We will do nothing until we have found a successor loved and respected by everyone. It might take a year and more. And I must tell you, I have Caenis' letters. If it is your wish, I will show them to you."

"How in the name of Venus did you get them!"

"A tale for another time." He knew he must hurry or her companions would begin to feel this discussion oddly prolonged. "If you wish to be a part, we will go no faster than you determine. But I wanted you to know at once—aid is coming to you."

Marcus Julianus smiled casually for the benefit of a Guard who seemed dazed with tedium as he glanced their way while scratching an arm and shifting his grip on his javelin.

"I will tell you then, I loathe the man more than death itself," she whispered, the low flash of fire in her eyes revealing the wrath of Medea beneath that innocuous face. "Slaves in the silver mines—no, the donkeys that turn the millstones—have freer lives than this! If you would give me the greatest gift, then let me be *witness* to the death blow! I want the monster to know, as he dies, I had a hand in it . . . and that *I* go on living! Know this, Marcus Julianus: While the city mourns my miscarriage, I secretly carry thank-offerings to Juno . . . for that was no miscarriage—I rid myself of it with the pine draughts. I risked my life because I refuse to have his loathsome spawn ripening in me! *There,* are you justly satisfied I am committed to your cause?"

"My lady, please, the Guards!" Marcus Julianus said as he took a quick step forward so that he blocked the Guards' view of her angry countenance.

"I can tell you much. I can tell you, through Carinus, what precautions his astrologers advise him to take when he travels by carriage. We can—"

"Enough now! That is good. But you've galloped too far ahead. Now listen carefully. We will communicate through books. It will look most natural—you are building a library and it is generally known I have sources in Alexandria who supply rare and ancient books for me. There is, however, one thing I must ask of you, and it must be done at once."

"I can deny you nothing. You restore me to the living." She was eager to bind him with a favor, for she sensed this was a man who would not forget and would probably return it fivefold.

"If properly done, this should not be dangerous." He set forth quickly his plan for Auriane's escape, telling her only the part that she, Domitia Longina, would play in it.

"Who *is* this poor, wretched creature, who is not, however, so poor and so wretched as to have failed to attract your notice?"

"It is safer if you know nothing."

She frowned. The woman temporarily in residence fled; the resentful girl returned. She regarded him with bland, innocent eyes.

"I will agree to this only if you take me to your bed."

Curses on Nemesis! he thought—she is jealous of Auriane. What has become of her concern for her own safety? Perhaps Diocles was right—*"She's got feathers for brains."*

"My lady, with greatest respect—you are putting me in a cruel position and yourself in an extremely dangerous one."

She gave a gay, abandoned laugh, eyes glittering with mild

contempt. What a fool you are, her manner said, to take seriously a dinner-party joke. But she was disappointed in her effort to embarrass him; he met it with an understanding, almost pitying smile.

That thirst for petty vengeance, Marcus Julianus thought—in the future it may serve us well.

"I only asked to test to see if it was someone you loved," Domitia Longina said in a voice light and insubstantial as decorative bells, "and I thought that you would ask for something for *you*."

"You said before I would be giving you back your life. Do this, and you will be giving me mine."

She caught her breath; in her eyes was a solemnity close to awe. He saw—though his intention had been no more than to tell the truth—this reply greatly appealed to her.

"Perhaps I should add," he said, smiling, "that her safe removal will irritate Domitian beyond measure."

"Will it truly?" The impish light returned to her eye. Together they turned and began to walk back to her guests. "I am your ally in all things," she replied, her voice almost lost in the rustle of her silken garments. "And *yes,* I will help you rescue your love."

CHAPTER XLIII

After the Feast of Saturnalia, Auriane began tracking the days with charcoal marks on her cell's stone walls so her people would know their festival times and could celebrate them with small offerings to the ancestors. It was the last day of Wolf's Moon when, in the still part of the night, she was startled awake by the light of a torch thrust into her face. She looked into the leering, stubbled face of Harpocras, the guard who was Keeper of the Keys.

"*Up* with you now, sleeping princess!" he said in a voice full of sour humor as he hoisted her by her tunic before she was fully conscious. In a moment of confusion Auriane was thrown back to the time when Helgrune roused her at midnight to take her before Ramis.

Where am I going? Who awaits? Why do they take me at night?

Avenahar, you are not yet born, and Ramis waits over the black water. I go to my life, I go to my death. . . . Ramis, you are going to tell me I will be queen. Whatever in the name of Helle's hosts did you mean by that?

With a dull jolt of fear she remembered where she was.

"Walk ahead of me, clumsy cow. *Go!*" Harpocras commanded, spitting through his broken tooth as he spoke. "There's a man who demands to see you."

As she moved through the twisting, tomblike passage, he guided her with his javelin, directing her toward the kitchens. Harpocras followed with shambling gait—he had a shortened leg from an old injury—and it caused his keys to rattle softly in that particular rhythm that always signaled his approach. "This is against every rule," he complained between bouts of coughing brought on by his catarrh, filling the air with the smell of stale raisin wine. "A word of this to anyone and we guards will put it out you attacked one of us. After we've disposed of you, be sure there'll not be enough left of you to make a healthy meal for the beasts."

Harpocras felt uneasy as a fox trapped in a barn. He had agreed to this meeting only because the bribe was more princely than any he had ever received, and because the man who demanded it presented him with a written order bearing the imperial seal. Harpocras was ready to believe the seal counterfeit but not quite ready enough; if this was some game, it could be deadly, one he had best discreetly play. He prayed Nemesis this breach of security came to no one's attention.

He ordered Auriane to halt before a low oak door opening onto the grain storage room. Auriane said nothing; her heart felt like a dancer ready to spring. She feared to hope.

Harpocras slid a long, slender key into the lock. Once she was inside, he planned to lock her in, just to make certain no one blundered in accidentally and found them. The door's hinges complained with a catlike mewling. Auriane saw by the light of one dim lamp a jumble of grain sacks, a cluster of amphorae of olive oil, and the shadowed form of a man concealed beneath the hood of a *paenula,* who even in this dismal place emanated assuredness and grace. She felt a rush of exuberance as though she drained a cup of unwatered wine. She did not need to see his face; she knew it was he, as any creature knows its own kind.

"Get your miserable carcass in there, spawn of a whore and a goat," Harpocras grumbled, coughing in her face as he herded her through the door. He thrust his chin at her and wagged a split-nailed forefinger in her face. *"One hour* by the water clock is all you get. And remember, if you get yourself with child in there, don't think it'll get you out of a single day of training—and you'll see it drowned at birth!"

He slammed the door so hard it raised dust eddies and sent the twin flames of the lamp into a skittish dance.

"Marcus," she said, her voice low and heaving with longing.

With one motion he whirled about and threw back the hood of the cloak. She hesitated for an instant, caught and held by the sight of his face with its brisk, impatient glance, the patient benevolence beneath. Already that face seemed a safe, familiar country. She half ran to him, her last step a jump for which he was not prepared; he staggered backward, laughing as he caught and steadied her.

"And who is this sleek and frisky mountain cat?" he exclaimed, smoothing back her hair. "Living in a den of horrors seems to agree with you!"

With infinite care he lifted her face to his. He spoke her name and she realized she had nearly forgotten the sound of his voice with its solemn quietness, its faint, comforting edge of roughness—a voice that made her feel like a caressed cat. She met his gaze, shivering within, feeling bare and defenseless, wanting to kiss him but unaccountably fearful: *What if I am utterly wrong, and I desire more than I am desired?* But she moved toward him anyway, making a step into darkness, trusting she would be caught.

She was. It was as if Fria kindled the same notion in both their minds. He seized her mouth gently at first; then he was ardent, fierce. She felt every sense flash awake. A bolt of heat shot through her body. As its warmth suffused her, she felt she melted languidly into a pool of sunny comfort. She wanted not to move, forever, to simply stop life, as if one moment held all its store of grace. This, then, she thought, is what it is to kiss a man dearer than life. It is greater than all earthly wealth.

I should offer all I own to the Fates for letting me know this before I die.

A fever took her, born of too many nights of fearing she had dreamed him—and one hand roamed over him of its own accord, reveling in the feel of taut muscles beneath the cloth, while with the other she searched determinedly for the fastenings of his tunic.

When he saw she was prepared to stop at nothing, he gently disengaged from her, caught the adventuring hand and kissed it. "I fear I must interrupt this act of rape," he said, smiling. "We have little time and we must talk."

She looked at him sleepily, caught up short and somewhat abashed. He gathered her close, cradling her against his chest.

"You must have thought I abandoned you."

"No, I did not." She hesitated. "Well once, perhaps, or twice, in the deep of the night. But do not take offense, you're in fine company—I thought also the Fates abandoned me."

He laughed softly and held her more tightly, giving wordless comfort. "It took me that long to find a breach—this place is sealed tighter than a tomb. It drove me close to madness at times to think of you in this charnel house!" He smiled at her affectionately and added, "Though at times it seemed the school was in more danger from you than you from it! Thank Nemesis you've left off trying to destroy the place!"

"I caused you great trouble."

He firmly met her gaze. "You did not. Think of it no more." He took a linen-wrapped packet from his cloak. "In here is a skin of mead and some hard cheese imported from northern Belgica—not quite your own, but close. And a roasted chicken. Your charming friend Harpocras won't rob you of it. He knows I'll know if he does, and he's greedy to do business with me again."

"Sunia will worship you for this!"

"Sunia?"

"My . . . my kinswoman." Auriane thought: Sunia would drop in a faint if she heard that.

"Auriane, I've come with great good news," he went on, pulling her close again. "You are going to be free."

He did not see the start of uneasiness in her eyes.

"Now listen carefully," he went on. "I've managed to win the confidence of the Empress. At the time of the Festival of *Parentalia*—mid-February, that is—she plans to go to her villa near the town of Arretium, as she does every year. She will travel alone—meaning without her husband—but she'll have with her a small escort of Praetorians and ten carriages bearing her maids and hairdressers and personal effects. And you, my little wild creature, will be among them, disguised as one of her wardrobe maids." He paused to stroke her hair, then continued.

"On the eve of her departure the school will be given over to the Heroes' Feast, one of the most abandoned celebrations of the year. The guards will not be so careful that night about who goes in and out. We're going to dress you as one of the prostitutes. Matidia, mistress of their guild, will see you provided with a yellow stola and garish paint. Harpocras if he behaves will have the honor of secreting them into your cell. You'll hide in one of Matidia's private chambers off the First Hall until cockcrow, when you'll be spirited out with the prostitutes after the feast is done."

He felt her tense in his arms as if she braced for a blow, but assumed she feared capture and punishment.

"Rest at ease, it will all be quite safe. You'll be brought to Matidia's house—she dwells on the Via Nomentana just outside the walls. The Empress's entourage will come by that road at dawn and you'll be taken into one of her carriages. Domitian will fly into a fury when you're discovered missing—he'll have you quietly and thoroughly hunted down. Possibly blockades will be set up on the roads. But you must not worry, you will be in the safest possible hands. The Empress is the last person anyone would suspect of abetting your escape. Domitian himself will never think of it—for what has his wife to do with you? And no troops you meet on the way would dare think of halting her to search her carriages. After you reach her villa, you will continue on north, in the company of one of my clients who peddles woolen cloth. You will be far ahead of suspicion. As for me, I've matters to attend to here. But once you're safe, if there is a way for us to be joined, I will find it. Know for now—the blood-drinking Colossus shall be cheated of one victim."

Slowly Auriane began to pull away from him. Her eyes were somber pools with greater darkness churning beneath. She fixed her gaze on the still flames of the lamp, as if to drink in their knowledge of eternity.

"Auriane, what is wrong? You do not look at all pleased."

"I cannot leave," she whispered hoarsely. She felt his disbelieving silence as a pressure on her chest, forcing the breath from her.

"What are you saying?" he said softly, frowning.

She forced herself to look at him. The hurt and incomprehension in his eyes was as painful as the touch of a brand. "A fearsome thing has happened."

"Auriane, what is it?" he pressed more gently. "You look as if you gaze on the walking dead. Whatever it is, let me put it right!"

"Even you cannot put this right."

He seized her shoulders. "Auriane, what could possibly keep you here?"

"Our warriors' council has met—"

"Warriors' council?"

"My tribespeople who are captive in this place. And they called for someone to come forth and ride the black horse."

He frowned in concern, recognizing the tribal expression for the vengeance rite.

"And before them all, I swore on a plait I would not quit this place until I have slain Aristos."

"What are you saying? *Aristos?* Is this some sad and pathetic jest?"

But from the look in her eyes—veiled, intransigent—he realized with horror it was not. A host of ancestors looked out of those eyes—he faced not one woman, but a tribe.

"What is this nonsense? Why *Aristos?* And why *you*?"

"I will try to explain it," she said with care, as if each word were a blow she must try to soften. "Aristos is really Odberht, son of Wido—" she began.

"Auriane, all military reports say that man died. But no matter *who* he is—"

"He is alive! Would I not know the man who savaged me when I was hardly more than a child!"

A look of abhorrence and pity swept over his face; involuntarily he took up her hand and held it securely. "Auriane, no."

The pain so evident in his face undermined her, but she fought the sadness that welled up; she wanted her wits about her so she could bring him to understand.

"Listen to me, I beg you!" she pleaded, dread in her voice. "At the war's beginning Odberht led his men against our back. To us, this is the most monstrous of crimes, far greater than your people's, for Romans are just natural predators, like the wolf from which your race sprung. Odberht came from the heart of the grove. His soul is not separate from ours. When the kin-bond is so savagely desecrated, all our acts bear poison fruit. And indeed, in this last year we learned from tribesmen most recently taken captive that our crops have failed, a murrain has taken our cattle, and fever rages unabated among our people. It is because *he lives,"* she whispered, the gentle mourning in her voice accompanied by a growing intensity in her eyes. The lamp's faltering light softly remodeled her face, obscuring her eyes, leaving occult pits of shadow in their place—and he imagined in one instant she wore a coldly beautiful ceremonial mask. She was Artemis, poised to purify with fire. "Until I purge this poison from our blood, we will know nothing but tears and pestilence!"

"I am sorry, but that is preposterous!" Impatiently he backed away from her and strode off a pace. In spite of a great effort to remain dispassionate, his anger rose, fueled by a growing sense of helplessness: Reason was the weapon he knew best, and he sensed in this battle it was worth little.

"Auriane, you must listen to me. There are many in the world who do not hold your beliefs about vengeance—I among them. Some would say it cruel nonsense to maintain putting one man into the ground can restore others to life. Among my people the wisest hold the law of vengeance does not stem from nature's laws at all but from man's *habit,* issuing from the basest passions of the mind. Is a belief *true,* simply because you've always held it? Even among your own tribesmen of the second generation dwelling here in Rome, they call it magical superstition after they've had a bit of Greek schooling. The world is larger than that. You seal yourself into a tomb!"

She broke away from his gaze. The mask vanished and a woman, frightened and alone, was revealed. She put one hand to the *aurr* as if it were an irritant—and he had the sense that dark amulet of earth was somehow his ally in this matter. The shudder he saw in the flame of her certainty encouraged him.

"It is poisonous nonsense and you must let it go! And I like it not at all that they put *you* forward," he pressed on. "Have you considered they might be using you to their own ends?"

"Using me? We are one body. Can the foot take advantage of the hand?"

"Why then cannot one of the men slay him? Why cannot the man called Coniaricus do it?"

"The life of the people was entrusted by the gods to *me,* not Coniaric, when Odberht betrayed us. They call me their holy woman, full of godly power. I am their living shield, their Daughter of the Ash. They believe with all their hearts, more firmly than I believe it, that if *I* set out to do the deed, it cannot fail."

"How convenient for them!"

"Please do not speak so! The Fates brought me to this place, Marcus. Whatever you think of vengeance, in my homeland we are bound to it still. I do not know if you know it, but this man Odberht, before the gods, is the true slayer of Baldemar. I am Baldemar's closest living kin still fit for battle—the five sons of his sister Sisinand were slain in the war. There is no one *left* to avenge him but me. If I fail, then I leave the task to my daughter, Avenahar. And if she despises weapons when she is grown, then she must raise a son to do it. I will not put that upon her! I will not have her whole life corrupted by seeking vengeance, as mine is!"

"Ah, the perfect snare. You are enmired forever in your people's beliefs! Nemesis!" He strode off and stopped, silent for a time, unable to believe he could not find a breach in her resolve. Then he swung about, his tone harsher now. "What of your people? Are you not abandoning *them?*"

Again he saw a shift of uncertainty in her eyes.

"They love you and are sustained by you," he went on. "The greatest good you can do for them is to preserve your own life!"

"But . . . to save my life that way is to lose it. That is a niding's path. And . . . and there is this, too, Marcus," she said, keen to find a reason that would claim his sympathies. "Odberht is amassing wealth. It is rumored he sends money to the Cheruscan king. When he quits this place, he expects to establish himself in their lands and rule over those people. The money he sends, I've heard from fresh captives, is being used to pay Cheruscan raiders to attack my tribe. My people are being harried again, now that they are sick and bowed down."

"There is a law against sending gold and silver across the frontier, and it is strictly enforced."

"And yet we are near certain this is being done—those who know have sworn by their own mothers, before the gods."

He paused, realizing what Auriane said might well be true in this case. Aristos' gifts to the Cheruscans, particularly if they were used to attack her tribe, would be so much in the interest of the Roman government there was a fair chance Domitian's parsimonious officials might look the other way. They would view it as rather like having someone else pay their bribes for them.

"Auriane, I *cannot* accept this. Can you understand? It is like standing idly by while my mother, my child, is sent off to slaughter. It is monstrous! And how did you imagine you'd do the deed? Have you some plan to fall on him at dinner with a stolen dagger, then be slain at once by the guards?"

"That would not fulfill the requirements of the rite," she replied with weary determination. "First, a declaration must be made, and he must acknowledge it. The battle must take place beneath the sun, preferably on an island in a stream, but any circular enclosure focuses the power of the gods. It must be done with honorable weapons of war. I am a prisoner and he is well guarded. So I see but one way to do it according to sacred law—in the arena."

"Good, that's the end of the matter, then! You've no notion of what you're saying. You—and Aristos—matched together? Has the world been turned upon its head? No sane trainer, no giver of shows would allow it. Erato will forbid it. And even if Erato did allow it, Aristos' faction would rise up in outrage—he would lose status. So you've no choice but to give in to reason!"

To his alarm, she hardly seemed to hear this.

"Your power is greater than any man's. . . . *You* could arrange it."

"Madness!" he exclaimed softly. "Do you truly believe I would arrange your murder?"

"You are certain, then, I will die. You must not believe I am innocent."

"*Innocent?* What has *that* to do with it? Of course I believe you are innocent! If *innocence* is all that is needed to preserve life, why do newborn children commonly die? Do you not see, all about you, blameless people meeting hideous ends? By all the gods, I can listen to no more of this!" he exclaimed with anguished finality. "This is a *man,* Auriane, who is twice your weight, who could cleave you down the middle with one blow. A man who has been over thirty times a victor. Not even the gods would assist such a foolhardy endeavor. And for this *pathetic* madness you toss aside my plans. And do you really think Domitian has had done with you? If you stay here, he'll kill you in some barbarous way, eventually. I've seen him behave this way before. He pretends to be indifferent to your fate, but he plays a part. I offer you freedom. You fling it off and choose slavery and degradation!"

He turned sharply from her, eyes brilliant with wrath; the heavy cloak flared magisterially, then settled about him again. "You will not move, I will not move. There is nothing to be gained by speaking of this more." For long moments he remained in furious silence.

Auriane was very still, numbed with despair.

He despises me. I have lost him.

She felt she fell from a horse and knew the fright of the ground rushing up. She realized, amazed, facing Aristos in the arena caused her less anxiety than being the object of this man's wrath. But she was long used to forcing herself on despite panic and desolation.

"You will not help me," she said, her voice frail. "Then I must find some other way." She edged toward his back. Hesitantly, she took his shoulders in her hands. His body was wooden and without feeling. She said, her voice tentative, like a creature testing the strength of the ice before attempting to cross a frozen stream, "Do not turn from me, Marcus. Please! I cannot do other than what I do."

He turned to face her, and she felt a sickness of heart as she looked upon him. Those eyes, earlier so direct and clear, were muddied with defeat. He seemed a powerful creature tensed to spring, but there was no place for him to go. She felt she committed some unforgivable act—trapping a magnificent animal in a snare or giving it poison—and she looked down, unable to bear the sight of its futile struggles.

"I count you already among the dead," he said with weary pity. "Farewell to you."

"Farewell," she whispered, swallowing hard to contain a rising tide of feeling. She interpreted his words literally. "You are leaving me?" she asked then, watching him intently; in her face was a mix of vulnerability and courage as she waited for the death blow.

Marcus Julianus knew suddenly how futile all argument was. She perceived this not as a battle of beliefs, for she did not separate herself from her beliefs. She saw it as a repudiation of all she was.

"Of course I am not leaving you," he responded with tender urgency, drawing her tightly to him with impassioned desolation. "I forbid you to think it!" He felt the small shudder of relief run through her body and was sorry for his anger.

"Fortune owes you better," he said after a time. "What destiny would you choose for yourself, were you able?"

"What an odd notion, to think anyone can choose! Now that I am old—"

"Come—you cannot be much past twenty and five!"

"I *am* old, to me. I would want . . . safety enough to watch and consider things—*study,* as your people would say—to have time to ferret out why things are as they are."

"Witness the antic humor of the Fates!" he said, smiling sadly at her. "They take a philosopher's soul, better suited, the world would say, to a young aristocrat preening about the porticoes of a school in Alexandria, and give it to a barbarian woman imprisoned in a gladiatorial training school!" He savored the sight of her for long moments, suffused with pride in her. "My curious, eager lamb with claws of steel! Was there ever such a creature?" Then he fell into more somber thoughts.

"You're being devoured by people who want parts of you—and none has the wit to see the whole. To your tribesmen, you're a goddess without a human heart, and they expect you to live and die for them. To Erato, you are a performer—an astonishingly good one, but still, a performer. To Domitian, you're a reminder of his deficiencies and, I suppose, the promise of their cure. To the rest, you are a fleeting amusement. When they've all had done with you, what will be left?"

She realized, sadly, she might have added: *And to Decius, I was but a clever, promising child that had better not shame him—or grow to womanhood and no longer need his teaching.* Auriane understood in that moment one reason why she felt such solemn unity with this man: he alone strove to see all of her. She had not realized what pleasure and contentment lay in being seen whole.

They held each other in silence for long moments, not wanting to speak of matters that would separate them, miserably aware of how little time they had left.

"Marcus," she said after a time. "Everyone in this place writes, not just priestesses and keepers of words of power. . . ."

He looked at her with a puzzled smile.

"Write my name."

"Your *name?* By sound, it can be done," he said, taking a volume of legal formulae from his cloak and looking about for a writing utensil. He settled on a bit of charcoal. "Keep in mind it's foreign, no two people would write it the same way."

Slowly he formed the letters. "That is my name?" she said eagerly. "It takes so many runes to write it?"

"Letters," he corrected.

"Now write yours." When he had done so, she said, "You have used some of the same letters! Our names are intermingled."

"It is not so wondrous a thing, to be truthful . . . it happens commonly. We've not that many letters to start with."

But he could see she was not ready to believe him. She looked for long at the carefully written names, as if they were the most potent of magical charms. "Might I keep it for an amulet?"

"No, I am sorry, the risk is too great. We must burn it, lest anyone find it and see our names linked." He tore off the portion on which he had written; as he touched the bit of papyrus to the flame, they heard Harpocras' key furtively entering the lock.

Tears swiftly formed in Auriane's eyes. "That was not an hour, curses on him!"

"It could mean someone comes." He grasped her shoulders firmly and said in a voice tender on the surface but with a core of iron, "Auriane, I cannot force you to come, and I am not certain I'd want to. But I warn you—I'm not the sort to sit by and watch unnecessary tragedies unfold before my eyes. It will take much more than your belief in your supreme god, vengeance, to keep me from striving to halt this. It's my intention to see you get what you said you want—a safe place, in which you can examine the world in peace."

"Marcus, you must not suffer over this! Our Holy Ones say, all life is one weaving, and the web is beautiful."

"You mean that!" he said with grief. "You poor, orphaned creature. You would see beauty in maggots on meat!"

The door made its cat-cry. The incoming draft animated the lamp flames; light and shadow lurched about in a macabre dance. Harpocras cursed softly when he found them in close embrace.

CHAPTER XLIV

On the following day Marcus Julianus was tormented by a solution that was brutal and obvious: Why not put Aristos out of the way by murder, thus neatly eliminating Auriane's reason for refusing to flee? The life of a man many times a murderer himself, even before fate brought him here, seemed more than a fair trade for Auriane's.

But by day's end he ceased to let grief blur his reason. It was not so simple to murder a man who was an integral part of the vast machinery used to pacify the mob. A dangerous disequilibrium would result. Who could calculate whom Aristos' supporters would blame for the murder, and what damage they would wreak? In Domitian's mind an attack on Aristos would be counted a strike against himself, and his vengeance on parties both guilty and innocent would be swift and cruel. And Aristos was excellently guarded, for the Palace found him useful: Not only did he help distract the people from Domitian's increasing ruthlessness, he saved the government great sums of money as well—for when the crowd was given Aristos, they needed little else. Marcus Julianus had once heard old Musonius Geta, Domitian's miserly Minister of Finance, assert that Aristos was the equal of a year's supply of zebras, ten rare Volga tigers and a hundred Mesopotamian lions. Tasters sampled Aristos' every meal, and a contingent of the school's guards accompanied him whenever he demanded trips to his favorite brothel. His ruffians stayed close about him as hornets round their nest.

By nightfall Marcus Julianus set himself a different course. After all it seemed impossible Auriane would ever succeed in arranging the bout with Aristos, and so he turned his efforts to ensuring her survival until the assassination freed her from her sentence. On that fortunate day he would buy her from the school — Erato dared not refuse him this — and grant Auriane her freedom. For the present he would conspire with Erato to see her undermatched and exceedingly well prepared.

He summoned from the gladiatorial schools of Capua a certain Trebonius, a trainer famed for his skill in teaching swordfighters techniques for overcoming disadvantages of height and weight, and paid a great sum to have him brought to the *Ludus Magnus*. And he bade Erato to go to the Claudian School so he could observe the Thracian called Perseus at practice and study the habits and weaknesses of this man Domitian had chosen for Auriane.

Erato did wonder at Marcus Julianus' interest in the woman. But a sense of dutifulness prevented him from voicing his curiosity to Julianus or anyone else; he owed his unprecedented good fortune to the man, and it would not have occurred to Erato to betray him. It was not wise to question the eccentricities of the powerful; all his life he had heard the adage: *"Guard well their secrets and they will guard you."*

In the matter of the assassination plot all progressed well, if with disheartening slowness. Marcus Julianus was encouraged by the fact that he had enlisted an influential Guards' centurion, who induced five of his subordinates to follow. Caenis' letters were powerfully persuasive, and the more so in his hands. When he took his first sampling of the opinion of the Senate concerning the choice of successor, second after his own name — which they continued to put forth in spite of his firm refusals — came the name of Licinius Gallus. He thought he had much cause to rejoice, until the night he summoned Gallus to tell him of this. And he then knew all that was bestial in Domitian was rising again, growing in strength, straining at fast-fraying bonds.

Gallus refused to come to him in person. His steward came in his place, bearing a frightfully familiar tale. Gallus was followed in the streets. The documents and letters in his records room had been rifled through. Men who appeared to be soldiers in civilian dress skulked about whenever he made a public sacrifice, doubtless seeking to learn if his offerings were dedicated to some disgraced person or treasonable cause. Servants were steadily disappearing. Their purpose was to get well off, Marcus Julianus suspected, before it was discovered they had informed on their master. And Veiento haughtily refused to return Gallus' greetings when they encountered one another at the Emperor's morning audiences, a sure sign Licinius Gallus was a current victim. The tale was so similar to that of Junius Tertullus, the third man on the infamous list, that Marcus Julianus felt he had been shown Gallus' death warrant.

He began a grim battle to keep Gallus alive. The sense of futile struggle called up the desolate days when he fought to protect his father against Nero, and he found himself committing the same sort of desperate acts. He believed he survived these lapses into audacity only because he drew on the last measure of that great store of good will he had won for himself on the night he saved the Emperor's life. In the Senate he gave a speech in praise of Gallus' life and deeds, for which his colleagues thought him a reckless fool since it was normally counted fatal to praise a man Domitian had abandoned. He published and distributed anonymously a small volume of essays that included a work attributed to Gallus; in it Gallus praised Domitian's recent social reforms. And he even laid his suspicions openly before Domitian, implying the harassment of Gallus was the act of some enemy who wished to make Domitian look the tyrant. Domitian seemed to listen, delivering one of his cleverest performances of the part of the faintly wounded, well-meaning ruler befuddled because he does not know how to manage his pesky subjects.

"Never forget," Marcus Julianus warned once, *"the Senate will outlive you.* It would be tragic if you played into the hands of your critics and gave their historians reason to vilify your name."

As he spoke, Domitian examined him with those cold, stale eyes that were not so much organs of perception as voyeurs of the soul, restless to uncover the secret shame of others. Marcus Julianus was not encouraged.

On a chill, clear evening in the month of *Aprilis* the novices learned their fate. All were assembled in the yard. A somber scent drifted indolently over the high wall in the wake of a passing funeral train—an essence thick and sweet as nectar, with an underlayer of rotted musk. It was the melancholy time when mourning shadows gathered at the base of the walls, and Auriane felt the old forlornness rising in her and knew it could only be healed by hugging close to Ramis' hearth with Avenahar at her breast.

Avenahar, why do I see you in the mind's eye as the babe you are no longer? You're a girl now, not a babe, with your own fate. You are old enough to know your mother left you, but not old enough to understand why. Do not despise me!

Acco, the trainer who replaced Corax, approached with a rolled document in hand; a torch-bearing assistant followed close behind. Auriane tensed as if at a warning rustle in high grass.

Acco was as unlike Corax as a graying dray-horse is unlike a disgruntled boar. He was a placid beast who never fretted over the size of his pasture; no one ever saw him in a state of agitation or anger. As he read the document, he masticated his words slowly, showing all the enthusiasm of a grazing animal. "Let it be known that on this day, the third before the Nones, you have been consigned"—Sunia gripped Auriane's hand so tightly she feared the bones would crack—"to appear in the three days of games commemorating the victory of the Emperor Titus Flavius Domitianus over the rebellious Chattians, to commence during the festivities of Ceres . . . , it being thought fitting by Annaeus Verus, Imperial Procurator of the Games, that on these days honoring our Divinity's glorious victory the greater part of the Chattian prisoners should appear."

Auriane saw several of the novices seemed unconcerned. The Sarmatian tribeswoman yawned, and the Numidian called Massa bent over to rub his leg, seeming more bothered by a blister caused by the greaves than the news he was soon to fight to the death. But for most, Acco's words simply meant their date of execution had been announced. It was the end of the frantic hope that somehow this day would not come. For her own part she restlessly cast her gaze down to conceal her eagerness. She felt her fate had caught her and hurled her forward with exhilarating force—odd and unaccountable fate that it was, to be charged by the gods to fulfill a sacred oath of vengeance in a Roman sand-pit with half the world looking on.

Acco stopped reading, turned his sad, equine face to them, and said, "In the next days we'll select ten of you to take part in the grand chariot-procession on the opening day, and these will be fitted out in our colors of vermilion and gold and"—he paused to swat drowsily at a fly, seemed to forget entirely what he had been saying, then plodded on—"I say, these will practice again and again the presentation of arms before the Emperor until they can do it without bringing shame upon this school.''

When Acco dismissed them, Sunia's knees slowly gave way. Auriane caught her up just in time to break her fall, and they sat huddled together on the sand; Auriane held her tightly to her breast. She said nothing, struck mute by unsettling visions of her own past.

The Hall even burns. Mother, you lie so still. I am weaponless, I cannot help you. I spent seasons and ages building round myself a wall of iron. Now the circle's complete—and I find myself weaponless once more.

Thorgild stood over them. "Sunia, you shame our people."

"Get off from us if you have no pity," Auriane replied in a soft, warning tone. Thorgild did not move, keeping his punishing gaze on Sunia.

"I think you hate her, Thorgild," Auriane said then, "only because you see your own terror reflected in her face as in a pool."

Something swiftly, furtively, withdrew from Thorgild's eyes; Auriane saw anger, disavowal, then spirit-fright there. He took a step back, then sullenly spun about and joined the other novices as they moved silently toward the dining chamber.

"Thorgild!" she called after, voice hoarse with pain. He did not turn round. Auriane suddenly had the sense her house broke apart.

Coniaric knelt by them in the dwindling light. "He acts the fool," Coniaric said, nodding after Thorgild. "He'll make amends, do not bother over him." He returned his gaze to Sunia. "What an unholy thing! They cannot be allowed to use her so!"

Their eyes met as they envisioned Sunia's fate: With twenty-two other women novices she would take part in the reenactment of the massacre of the provisions women. The Chattian captives would defend the wagons against novices of the Claudian School, garbed as the men of the legions.

"If we could get her onto one of the morgue carts . . . ," Coniaric said in a low voice, casting a furtive eye about the yard.

It was Sunia who objected. "I would rather die in their stinking sand-pit than wander alone among this demon race!"

"She would not get farther than the gates, Coniaric." Mustering a confident tone, Auriane said to Sunia, "I'll go to Erato once more."

She had no faith in these words as she spoke them. Earlier she had argued Sunia's cause before Erato with no success, and it seemed now he had even less control over their fates. For now they were in the hands of the Imperial Procurator of the Games, the Palace official who arranged the spectacles at Domitian's pleasure. If Sunia were removed, Erato would be obliged to pay into the Treasury an amount equal to her value or immediately replace her—and there was not time enough to train another woman. Erato had the usual anxieties of a man elevated above his station and was eager to prove his merit by doing everything with exaggerated correctness.

A guard snapped his whip. "You there! Move! This lash is thirsty for lazy blood!"

Coniaric hauled Sunia to her feet. Auriane took Sunia's hand and pressed it to the sacred mold. Sunia gripped it tightly, drawing on its nether strength.

"Sunia! Trust in the power of my clan-luck. You will live. I swear by sun and moon, I will find a way."

Further into that same night Auriane was taken to the west yard where Erato waited. The small, sandy expanse was lit with torches affixed to posts set out in the form of an ellipse. The single guard posted outside the door was a lifelong friend of Erato's; he alone knew of these occasions. Erato feared he could not justify to the Finance Ministry all this time and attention lavished upon one novice.

Auriane practiced in Samnite armor modified for her with a lighter shield. Erato judged this equipment most suitable for her—the double-edged short sword the Samnites carried more closely resembled the swords to which she was accustomed than did the Thracian swordsman's long, curved blade. Auriane thought it unaccountable the Romans termed it *armor*, for all that shielded her from an enemy blade were the leather greave on the left leg, the arm guard on the sword arm, a plumed, richly decorated helmet and the oblong Samnite shield fashioned of wooden planks covered with bull's hide. The chest was normally left exposed or covered inadequately by a short calfskin tunic such as Auriane wore. For safety, on this night their blades were fitted with leather guards.

Erato did not greet her; with brusque, angry movements he began to strap on his greaves, as if even these small acts took too much of his time. When he threw down his cloak, a collection of bookrolls fell out onto the sand.

Her eager question burst out before she could contain it. "You carry a library in your cloak! What is written there?"

He looked at her as if she asked the color of the sky. "A list of times for grain deliveries and of prices. Are you content now that you know that?"

"Your people leave nothing to memory! Your minds must be vastly empty."

"*Vastly empty,* is it? Why am I listening to this? Listen to me, Auriane, we've grave matters to discuss. It seems someone at the Palace has a grudge against you. You're to be matched with a man. A certain Perseus. I know him. He's more than passingly good—he won his first bout handily." Erato watched her face to see if she was properly alarmed by this, but she regarded him with soft, bold deer's eyes, quietly waiting for more. It angered him.

"Overconfidence killed more fools than lack of skill!" he said irritably, fumbling angrily with the buckle of the arm guard. "It's past time you learned respect for the dangers you face. Listen or perish!"

"When have I not fought men?" she asked.

"Not the same. I don't care how many raids you led or how many fellow barbarians you slaughtered out in the woods. This is *different.* You've nothing to compare with this. Fighting someone in the forest wilderness and fighting a man who is cornered are unlike as fire and water. There's no one to back you up and cover you if you slip. There is no advantage of terrain to seek, nowhere to retreat to, and nowhere to hide, even if you are badly wounded. There will be only you and a man taller and stronger than you, who's been trained exactly as you have been trained. A woman and a man—and fifty thousand people ready to crush you like a cockroach if you displease them. Now put aside that stubborn overconfidence and wake up before you find your entrails spilling out on the sand!"

She is hopeless or hopelessly mad, Erato thought. You would think I spoke of a contest of knucklebones.

"It is not meant to spite you. What you call overconfidence I call the grace of Fria."

"The only goddess I honor is Victory and so should you. Now let me see your wrist."

She extended her right hand. He took it and lightly felt the wrist. "It's still swollen slightly, but it's better. Be careful with it in the next days. Don't let anything strike it and do not lift anything. Now I'm going to give you a sword with a slightly heavier pommel to lighten the balance." He handed her the weapon encased in its leather guard.

Briskly he went on: "Tonight you'll use a different strategy. I think you'll find this Perseus, when you test him, will favor the first and second parries, and from what I saw of him, I doubt he'll vary them. Now, stand *here*." He was aware of how attentively those soft gray eyes watched him, and he had the uncanny feeling that, in spite of her seeming compliance, she tolerated him only because his instructions happened to coincide with some secret design of her own.

"Good. . . . I will play the part of Perseus. Begin by feigning weakness. My guess is, with this man, it will be the right way to open. He'll draw you out to see what makes you parry. He will be asking what you can do. And you must lie."

He took a position opposite her. "Start by limiting yourself to the first parry and the fundamental advance," he went on, "and then wait. Let his confidence grow. Soon he'll stop watching you so closely. Remember, too, you'll be tiring him out—you'll be facing a Thracian sword, and your man will be committed to broad, sweeping movements. Keep your parries narrow. Conserve your strength. And don't thrust. Make him begin to wonder if you even know your weapon *has* a thrusting point. Save that for later. We'll engage awhile, then I'll cry out a signal. When I do, *come at me as hard as you can.* Spare me nothing. Come to kill. Do you understand?"

Calmly Auriane nodded. Aggravating wench, Erato thought. She almost looks bored by all of this.

What he had not told her was that he planned to teach her a lesson in humility. He meant to come for her at the same time, intending to catch her off guard with a vicious version of the vertical-jump attack that he had perfected himself. It would probably knock her off her feet, and he hoped, awaken her to a healthy respect for the perils she faced.

They started sparring. She followed his instructions precisely. He let long moments pass, engaging her with an even rhythm that lulled them both with its monotony. Once he briefly reconsidered his plan, fearful he might injure her.

No. The lesson is too important.

Finally he shouted, *"Now!"*

From that instant, Erato's plan went awry. He began his own lunge a fraction too late, so startled was he by the change in her face as she hurled herself at him. An exultant light flared in her eyes; in an instant she was transformed from woman to night predator, some remorseless hunter of men that might have risen from her own vaporous bog-lands. He remembered the shock of their shields' impact. But he never did untangle precisely the whip-quick succession of events that followed. Later he realized she used a maneuver Trebonius had taught her, but it was incorporated so smoothly into a series of baffling cross-cuts he could not believe she had been taught it but two days ago. These things demanded practice, and she had had no time. And she was ready for his upward thrust before he began it, forcing his blade down with a stroke so cleverly placed he felt a hammer blow drove it to the sand.

How had she known? She could not have known. He saw his sword intercepted and trapped; then her foot was where he least expected it—and he tripped and went down hard. This too, though, he deduced later; at the time it seemed he leapt at her only to find himself caught, entangled, then thrust downward by a subtly irresistible force. He was next aware of lying on his back, gasping for breath, looking up at a black sky, a ring of torches, and Auriane, who crouched over him.

Then he saw naked steel poised above his heart. Terror surged through him. Somehow she had managed to remove the leather guard.

This is a madwoman. I am done. She planned this well. Only one guard knows I'm here, and I ordered him not to interfere.

Auriane's eyes were hot and liquid; her chest heaved.

"You must release Sunia!"

This cannot be! Erato thought, struggling to mentally regain his feet. It is too horrible and ludicrous at once. "Auriane, you will destroy yourself. Let me up now."

"You can buy her back. Do it!"

"Auriane," he said carefully, as if quietening a dangerous animal, "lay down that sword like a sensible wench now, *and get off of me.*"

She looked at the sword then, and Erato saw a start of surprise in her eyes. He felt immense relief. She had not intentionally removed the guard; it had been knocked off accidentally. Quickly she tossed the sword aside. As his wits returned and his frozen blood began to warm, he realized her eyes were filled not with hatred but fierce sadness. *Of course*, Erato thought. She does not have a treacherous nature, but she *does* have a monumentally stubborn one.

She crawled sideways, giving him room to rise. Disgustedly he brushed sand from his hair and wiped tears from his sand-stung eyes.

"I warn you, don't test me anymore on the matter! You *know* we're short of women. Yesterday one of Aristos' lust-maddened brigands skewered one of them with a spear, right in front of the guards—who looked the other way. And that one, on top of the four we lost to the quartan fever, makes five, *five* I've lost. I am not the Fates, Auriane. I did not bring her here!"

"Nor did she bring herself here! This is monstrous! Slavery is ignoble enough, but at least set her to tasks to which she is fitted! Help her!"

"Enough I say!" He kicked hard at the sand, throwing it high in the air. She whirled away, shielding her eyes. "Remember where you are! Surrender to fate, you little fool, it is all a man or a woman can do. *You will not speak of this again!*"

She accepted then that he would never bend. Though he seemed a king in his kingdom, he was, in the end, the creature of others. She would have to find some other way.

When Erato saw surrender in her eyes, his anger eased away. "Auriane," he said finally, cautious awe creeping into his voice, "a moment ago when you threw me, . . . how did you know in advance what I was going to do?"

"I watched you."

"You *watched* me? What did you watch?"

"Your gestures, your eyes, your hands. I do not know exactly. Even your anger told me many things. And . . . there is something else, for which I do not know the word in your language."

"Try. Sorcery? Witchery? Second sight?"

She frowned. "No. A *knowing*. A knowing that feels certain."

"I don't like this, I tell you."

"But it comes not always—I cannot summon it."

"*Once* is too often! I give no credence to such things," he said, while discreetly making the sign for protection against the evil eye. "What you did was impossible. Therefore, there must be an explanation for it. Now we're going to walk through this, step by step, and you're going to show me exactly what it was you *did*."

Privately he thought: By Charon's eyes, after this night I set no limits on what this strange creature can do.

The next night in the dining chamber Auriane's attention was caught by a certain kitchen slave, visible through the open door as he sat chopping onions. She had seen him before, but now she tensed with interest as she watched him. He was powerfully built, and had suffered some grievous injury to his knee. The man always seemed out of place to her—most of the school's kitchen slaves were slender Syrian youths or maids. She got up from her place and sat beside Celadon.

"What happened to that man?" she asked him. "Do you know anything of him?"

He followed her gaze and laughed softly. "You've Greek blood in your veins, I'll wager! I've never known a barbarian so astir with curiosity. That one there, that's Pylades. That's a lucky fellow there, happy as a mudlark, I would say. He was a novice who got himself too badly cut up his first time out. He'll never walk again, much less fight, so they put him in the kitchens. Now his only tears are over onions."

Auriane was greatly surprised. The guards would have them believe such unfortunates were thrown to the animals, but that made little sense now that she considered it carefully, for these were a practical people—why would they waste a useful pair of hands?

"Auriane," Celadon said, moving protectively close. "You plan some mischief. I pray to good Diana you tread cautiously."

She gave him a bare smile of acknowledgment, then turned to look at Sunia, who sat without eating, her cheeks shadowed, her eyes full of death. Sunia, she wondered, would you be content working in the kitchens?

Fria had at last granted her a way.

The city prepared to embrace the coming Games like some long-absent lover. Most people's first thought upon arising, whether they lived in a stifling tenement room between a brazier and a chamber-pot or in marble halls amid the splash of fountains, was: How many days remain? For too many generations the common people of Rome were allowed no hand in governing, and their state religion had long since mummified into dry rituals that never touched ordinary passions. It was inevitable, proclaimed the dour scholars of the philosophical schools, that the Colosseum would become their chief temple and the fortunes of gladiators would be watched more closely than the rise and fall of nations. In streets and taverns, talk of the war with Dacia rarely brought more than a halfhearted response—it might be amusing if Domitian bungled another war, their shrugs said, so long as the barbarians did not actually swarm over the frontier and sack Roman towns.

But the Emperor's grand blunders, diverting as they were, could never hope to rivet the attention as much as the coming spectacle of Aristos, their own King, and Hyperion of Capua, the Beast of the South, bent on carving out each other's hearts.

And their lover, the Games, teased them unmercifully. Every day the notice-writers made their rounds; wherever they could find space on the walls of public buildings they posted that day's amended list of the gladiators who were to appear. And every day they failed to add the one name all longed to see: Aristos. Wherever the notice-writers set up their ladders, they were surrounded by the ardent crowd. The people cheered when the name of a favorite appeared and shouted abuse when the notice-writers climbed down without writing the name of the favorite of favorites. The appointed day drew maddeningly close—and still, no Aristos. When but nine days remained, a notice-writer plying his trade in the fly-ridden Subura district was murdered by a testy mob clamoring for Aristos. It was well-known Aristos had recovered from the injuries he sustained in his last bout with his archrival Hyperion. With so many noblewomen praying for his recovery, it was often said, he had no choice. For what perverse reason was he withheld?

The mystery fed speculations; rumors raged like an epidemic. Aristos actually had died, it was said, and Domitian did not want it known before he departed for the Dacian war, for fear the general mourning would be ill-omened and bring disaster upon the departing army. That was not the cause, others said; he's actually run off with Junilla, and the happy pair are living contentedly on one of her estates in Gaul, enjoying a good laugh at all this fuss.

When seven days remained, at last the name of Aristos appeared in red-and-black paint at the top of the notices. The city was pitched into a joyful delirium. The notice-writers that day were lavished with wine and gifts. Shopkeepers and artisans decked their stalls with roses as if a public holiday had been declared. To their delight Aristos was matched again with Hyperion the Capuan. Supporters of Hyperion began to trickle in from his native town; when they met devotees of Aristos in the streets, bricks were thrown. At night Aristos' followers painted *Aristos Rex* over the outer walls of the basilicas that housed the law courts and even the temples, to the horror of the city officials responsible for these buildings' preservation. Under cover of darkness they set up crudely sculpted likenesses of Aristos in the Old Forum and crowned them with laurel as if he were a victorious general—an act considered blasphemous by the tradition-bound members of the city's priesthoods. The followers of Hyperion compounded the infamy by pelting the statues with pigs' intestines. Swarms of shopkeepers, freedmen and idlers gathered about the *Ludus Magnus,* desperate for a glimpse of their king; the streets converging on the school were impassable, day and night. From the prostitutes in their stalls in the Circus to the advocates in the law courts, to noblemen scribbling poetry as they were carried in shaded litters, and even to the inhabitants of outlying towns, the people talked of nothing else.

Which was all precisely as Domitian wished it to be. He had purposefully ordered Aristos' name left off till the last. For he was preparing to murder someone important, a man who would be much missed, and he needed a suitable distraction. Once this one man was quietly put out of the way, he was certain the plague of misfortunes that had lately dogged him would end.

In these times it seemed to Domitian all his acts turned on him savagely, like some snapping beast grasped by the tail. First there was that unfortunate matter of his niece, Titus' wanly beautiful daughter Julia. Bedding her might have been impious; however, he was not the first emperor to lie with his own niece. But Julia, had, perversely, gotten herself with child by him, leaving him no choice but to force an abortion on her so there would be no stain on the family name. And then the troublesome woman died of it, showing the poorest possible sense of timing—for he had just revived the old, severe penalties for adultery, all in the interest of enhancing public morals. And as with his every small infraction, of course, the mob learned of it. Julia had made a mockery and a public show of him. And now whenever he gave an audience of state or addressed the Senate, he could feel the contemptuous laughter in the Senators' silences and the murderous loathing of those who loved Julia, who was all they had left of the even more beloved Titus.

And then there was that equally distressing matter of last year's severe shortage of grain, caused by a poor harvest in Italy and abroad. Who would have *not* thought it a sound plan to decree that only wheat, and not vines, be planted in Italy? There was wine in abundance—what harm could such a sensible edict do? A part of him was convinced that had his father passed such a law, all would have gone well. The result was disastrous. The vine growers rioted, all across the land, and defaced his statues in the town squares by night. Some ignored the edict completely, insisting the soil was only fit to support grapes; others simply abandoned their farms. Derisive verses were composed about him and sung in the streets. One that particularly enraged him ended with the line: *"In war, he takes useless land; in peace, he makes good land useless,"* for it was also a slighting reference to the Chattian war. How dared they ridicule his great victory on the eve of his games of celebration?

Through a logic all his own, he laid everything at the door of Licinius Gallus. He had long counted Gallus' love of Titus fanatical. Did the man not have an ostentatious statue of Titus in the *tablinum* of his house, to which, spies reported, he daily made small offerings? Gallus' quiet inoffensiveness was a cover for his true nature. It was Gallus, he was certain, who fanned the tales of his dalliance with Julia and composed the latest round of scurrilous verses. For a year Domitian waited for the right moment to cut this deadly canker out.

On the eve of the day Aristos' name appeared, a disturbing bit of news spread beneath the general rejoicing. Gallus was dead. His passing was felt directly by many, for he had hundreds under his patronage, and many more still were distressed by the death of a man who, along with Marcus Arrius Julianus and a very few others, exercised a softening influence on Domitian. All that was known was that Gallus mysteriously fell dead in the fish market while carrying an enormous mullet he had selected himself for a dinner with close friends. He had no illness—he was in the best of health—and his chief cook, who was with him, reported that nothing occurred to arouse suspicions of foul play. But Domitian's strategy worked well. The worrisome questions raised by Gallus' death were swept away in the raging torrent of emotion roused by Aristos.

"The blind fools!" Marcus Julianus said that night to Diocles. "Those that pause to give it any thought at all are saying Domitian could not have murdered him, except through magic spells. These are truly dangerous times. His cleverness is starting to equal his malice."

Marcus Julianus did not have to wait long before his suspicions were confirmed. That very night a mud-encrusted peddler of love philters appeared at his door; the man had the look of one who hourly expects arrest, torture and death. He promised Marcus Julianus an interesting tale in exchange for safe conduct out of the city. When Julianus agreed to this, guessing what it was all about, the man said he had killed Gallus himself. He managed it by

stealing up close to Gallus under cover of the crowd and pricking
him with a needle smeared with aconite, a quick-acting poison.
When the peddler named the man who had paid him, Marcus
Julianus recognized him as an agent of Veiento's. The order,
beyond all doubt, was given by Domitian. Marcus Julianus was
certain now that at least one of the first three Senators on the list
of men to die, Serenus, had met his end in the same way. For
Serenus too had fallen dead in a crowd, though all at the time had
counted it a heart seizure.

*But for this wretch in fear of his life—perhaps Veiento suspects
him of revealing too much—I never would have learned it! And
the beast would have gone on boasting he never took a man's life
without a trial. For certain, others will die the same way. This
must be exposed, and at once.*

After he safely removed from Rome the man who confessed to
him, Marcus Julianus arranged a meeting with Domitia Longina
through a coded message put into a book of odes she requested of
him. What he planned could be carried out far more efficiently
with her help.

The next day was the last of fourteen days of racing in the
Circus Maximus. Both Marcus Julianus and the Empress selected
the few dozen servants they trusted above all others and distributed them evenly among the ocean of people who thronged into
the Circus that day. Just before the tenth and most important race,
they began quietly disseminating the tale of the needle murders.
Within moments no one could have said for certain where it
originated. Because of the temper of the people and the growing
undercurrent of hatred of Domitian, Marcus Julianus was certain
this rumor would be believed. The tale spread like fire in a
sun-parched field.

And soon the entire throng rose up in a rage, many climbing on
their seats, shouting at the imperial box: *"Bring to us the murderer
of Gallus!"* Domitian felt he had been set in the path of a hundred
elephants, all bellowing as they readied themselves to trample
their victim. The crowd knew better than to cry out directly for the
blood of Domitian—they had a wisdom born of several generations of living in the shadow of capricious tyrants. They instead
called down curses on Veiento, some demanding his exile, others
his execution. Though the crowd offered Domitian a way to
salvage a portion of his dignity, still the message was too strong
for him to bear. He sat rigid in fury, horrified that somehow they

knew. How in the name of Nemesis had it gotten out? How dare this filthy rabble accuse him or anyone appointed by him?

Domitian attempted to silence them by herald. But the imperial heralds could not make themselves heard. It was only when he ordered out a cohort of the Praetorian Guard that at last the throng lapsed into sullen silence.

Then Domitian delivered his punishment. He canceled the bout between Aristos and Hyperion.

The city became a simmering cauldron. Another Nero rules over us, the people muttered openly. Many were fearful of entering the streets, expecting at any moment to feel the prick of a needle. The cancellation of the bout only served to further convince the people the tale was true.

Aristos was enraged; he sulked and refused to eat. For the first time he felt less like an Oriental potentate and more like a piece on the gameboard of another.

The notices put up that day were pelted with the contents of chamber-pots. A few who were less caught up in the savage feelings saw an odd addition before the filth rendered them unreadable. The name *Aurinia* had been added. And her opponent was not a fellow woman-captive of her tribe, as would be expected, or a dwarf—another of Domitian's favorite pairings—but Perseus, a skilled volunteer fighter who had appeared once and won easily. What sort of silliness was this?

"It's for *him,* not for us," one baker muttered to another as they returned home at dawn from a night's work. "And this is what he thinks of us! Aristos is replaced by a herd of unknowns and women. Nero was a disgrace and a mother-killer but he never insulted the people this way. How can a reasonable man place a bet on such a pairing?"

"Cario saw her at practice and said she was startlingly good."

"Cario would believe donkey droppings were the tears of Venus when he's drunk, which I'm sure he was. Did anyone *see* that practice besides a collection of loitering slaves and besotted wastrels spending their lives shaming their fathers' names? We're mocked, I tell you."

CHAPTER XLV

Sunia, I know you will not forgive me this, not ever. But the Fates leave me no other course. I cannot sit by and let Helle claim you. And I can't bear any longer the sight of your terror and grief. Do not despise me! I am giving you life.

It was the second hour of morning; but five days remained until the days of the Games of Ceres. Acco had not yet arrived in the yard. The novices stared dully or talked of small matters, their minds imprisoned in this narrow moment, daring no thoughts of future or past. The more hopeful practiced in pairs, as Auriane did now with Sunia. As Auriane moved at easy pace through the elementary parries and cuts, her eyes blurred and she blinked to clear them. Her throat ached from choking off a cry of anguish. To steady herself, she thought of the new moon she had seen last night, so serene and self-contained as it shed its heatless light, flowing into all creatures, animating them with the mind of Fria. The time of the new moon was most favorable to risky plans.

Slowly she maneuvered Sunia around, stealing an occasional glance at two guards who looked on with glassy stares. Gradually she positioned herself so their view of her was blocked by Sunia's rangy body.

Now. It is time. This thing rests in the gods' hands.

Auriane vaulted at Sunia. With all her strength, she brought down her leather-sheathed short sword on Sunia's unprotected right ankle. As it struck, Auriane shut her eyes and felt a white-hot eruption of pain as if the blow struck her own body. She thought she heard the sound of snapping bone, horribly magnified. Then she saw her own spear tearing into Baldemar's chest, the shock of surprise in her father's face. Who is prepared for such agony, even when it is their will?

Sunia! How could I do it? I am horrible. Hertha, I hear your icy cackle echoing down the years.

Sunia was slammed into stillness. Her eyes were sky-blank, as if her soul shot out of her body. She convulsed violently once, then collapsed onto her side, clutching at her leg as if to tear it off. Then she regarded Auriane, her eyes swollen with pain and incredulity. It was the look of a trusting child whose mild mother suddenly turns savage and hurls it to the ground.

The guards awakened with a jump and regarded the pair with sharp annoyance. Sunia's words came in ragged gasps, as if hands constricted her throat. *"Auriane, why—"*

The guards were approaching at a brisk walk. Auriane dropped down beside Sunia and seized her shoulders. "Sunia, I beg you—*be silent!*"

"Have you gone mad!" Sunia managed between labored breaths, clawing at the sand. "You are monstrous! Now they will kill me!"

"Sunia, *listen* to me. They cannot use you now. That is why I did it. I could not tell you ahead of time or you would have worried over it. Sunia, they'll hear us, do not give it away!"

"Get off from me!"

"*Sunia!* I beg you to understand!"

"I curse you! *I will never understand!*" Roughly Sunia threw Auriane's hand from her shoulder.

Then the guards were upon them both.

One kicked Auriane. The other wrenched Sunia to her feet; she shrieked as she was forced to put weight on her ankle.

"You rude louts! *Do not do that!*" Auriane cried out in her own tongue as she scrambled to her feet and seized the guard who held Sunia. But the second guard threw a trident-fighter's net over her and she fell in a heap to the sand, thrashing like a netted hare. As this guard prepared to beat her senseless with an iron rod, the one who held Sunia shouted: "Stop! Mind what you're about! That's the valuable one!"

"So it is," Auriane's would-be tormentor muttered, reluctantly backing away from her, "but that one *there,*" he said, nodding at Sunia, "dogmeat! Look at that leg!"

Dog meat? They lie! She'll go to the kitchens. They did not see what I did—that's all that matters.

The trainers' assistants came then and dragged Sunia off. It seemed to Auriane that Baldemar and Sunia shared one pair of agonized, accusing eyes.

Erato shot to his feet when Auriane was brought into his chambers. He regarded her with fiercely furrowed brow, eyes glinting, powerful fists clenched at his sides.

"You are a rash and foolish woman! You deceived them. You did not deceive me!" He nodded curtly to the two guards who escorted her, ordering them to depart.

"I did not seek to," she replied in a muted voice. She felt too sad and empty inside to answer with much spiritedness.

"You willfully destroyed her usefulness."

"I willfully saved her life."

"It is not yours to save!"

"It is not yours to destroy."

He pounded his fist on the wooden table; the bust of Domitian frog-jumped sideways and nearly crashed to the floor. "Save your meddling moral philosophy for peacock-fed noblemen with too much time on their hands! It's got no meaning for those of us who work for what we get. *I do not like it when someone forces my hand!*"

Auriane said nothing, sensing any words she spoke would only fuel his wrath. Erato spun away from her, momentarily trapped in his rage, a bull that cannot make up its mind whether to gore its victim or merely terrify him by charging and missing narrowly.

"What you did was *criminal*—do you understand?" He tried to transfix her with a look like a javelin thrust, but to his exasperation she met it with that lofty, queenly look that meant she was at her most intransigent.

"Oh, this is useless!" he said at last. "I suppose you count it as loyalty. I am not an enemy of loyalty, only of disobedience. The thing is done. Which is precisely what you planned. But if ever you do this sort of thing again, you can be certain I'll know it, and you can be sure I'll see you punished. I want *absolute silence* about this—do you think you can obey me in *that*, at least?" His look was still fierce, but now she sensed reluctant warmth lurking beneath.

She nodded. Then she asked, feeling she edged out onto a precarious bridge, "And . . . what will you do with her?"

"You shattered the bone. She'll have to be sent to the kitchens. Again, you won the throw."

"I thank you for that." She felt a heavy stone had been lifted from her chest.

"Do not thank me for what you forced me to do. And, of course, she'll have to be moved from your barracks to the kitchen slaves' cells. Now leave me."

That she had not planned. She sensed this satisfied his need to punish and said nothing to contest it; it was better to wait. Life's patterns shifted always. At least Sunia would live, though her company was lost.

Later that day as Auriane was being conducted to the west yard, she managed to break free of the guards as they took her past the physicians' rooms, and she briefly saw Sunia.

Auriane was dismayed by the small start of fear she saw in Sunia's eyes as the maimed woman recognized her. Then Sunia lapsed into pain-fogged indifference, not judging, but not forgiving either. Auriane's shame became as livid, throbbing and swollen as Sunia's leg.

She is no longer at my side. The animal part of Sunia will fear me always, like the horse that whitens its eyes at a cruel master's approach. I drove her off in order to save her. My shame is a serpent with a hundred heads. Just when I begin to believe my fate is turning round forever, here comes this leering, mocking proof of the viper, and the poison in my blood.

Desperately she thought of Marcus Arrius Julianus as a last resource of love.

But what does he seek in *me*? He cannot love this darkness I hide. Certainly he has no use for the miserable, defeated crawling thing I am now. And how cruel of the gods to drain all my strength right before I will need it in almost superhuman measure.

That night she sat as usual before the arched brick opening of the kitchen's main oven, preparing to perform the Ritual of Fire. The departing kitchen slaves had long since tired of casting curious glances at the solemn woman-novice, favored of Erato, who nightly fell into a trance before their central oven. On this night Auriane was full of a sense that somehow her life was at stake. Occasionally she coughed from the smoke—as a means of economizing, Erato had ordered the charcoal in all the ovens replaced with wood, and the thick, pungent smoke stung her eyes. Such meanness among the richest people on earth baffled her. The kitchen's four hanging lamps had been snuffed; beyond the amiable red-orange glow of the dying fire, all lay in a nether darkness that teemed with the foreign spirits of this place.

She joined her gaze to the fire. Fertile silence fell over her mind; heat and light gusted into receptive emptiness. She was gently borne up, though as ever it was a troublesome ascent. Then she eased into the shadow-world where all humanness dissolved away. She had no thoughts, only qualities; she might have been golden honey spilling from a table or starlight shed on leaves. Like a bird finding a draft of air, she drifted for a while in contentment, dipping and rising with the will of the winds.

After a time she sensed some disturbance in this otherworld. Even the flames seemed agitated—she imagined guardian fire became guard dog, spasming in soundless barks, scenting a far traveler at the gate. Suddenly she was uncomfortably aware of the well of darkness at her back. Then she became alert with a jerk.

Someone was standing behind her. And it was not a being of flesh and bone.

She took a shallow breath, fearful even the subtle movements of her breathing might provoke it. A light sweat sprang to her forehead. She felt earthy dampness pressing close, as if she entered a bog ground.

Fria, Mother of the Gods, what has come for me?

She smelled strongly the autumn herbs sacrificing priestesses gathered to weave crowns for their victims. And she felt warmth behind her as if another fire were kindled at her back. Gradually fear eased away. *Could it be?* She whispered, her voice a cautiously probing hand: *"Ramis?"*

She felt a cool pressure at her temple as if a palm were placed there; then it seemed the sorceress's mind wrapped itself around hers in a motherly embrace. Auriane was still and rapt. And then she discerned words that seemed to be *in* her mind but not *of* it, words not so much spoken as strongly thought.

Auriane, be at rest. I am she who attends your birth. . . .

"Ramis?" Auriane whispered. "What is this witchery!" Vigorously she shook her head, trying to expel that deft, strong voice from her mind.

This is madness. She is sky-traveling. Or else I've taken a dangerous fever.

Witchery, you say? the airy, rustling voice replied. *Really, no more so than the flight of a common sparrow. I know no distance, nor do you. Quell your fears. The Fire Ritual joins us, star to star. . . .*

Auriane realized then she was suffused with that sense of being warm and settled in the world that Ramis' presence always brought. She thought the question: What do you will of me?

I come to help you light the hall.

A sound like wind rattling down a warren of caverns rendered the next words inaudible; Auriane imagined the vast spirit of the Veleda battling stormwinds and mountains until Ramis found her mind once more. And then she heard:

Ah, you are not the same as when last I saw you on this smoking isle. . . . A spirit callused and hard has grown more supple— you've flowered without knowing. The next time of turning has come, and so I am required to ask again. . . . I would have you follow me.

Auriane was unsettled to find herself not strenuously protesting. In fact, the thought of that life exerted a delicate but irresistible pull, like a gently outflowing tide.

Baldemar, Auriane thought, you were wise to warn me she would ask again. At the time I believed a warning unnecessary. Who could guess she would wait so long or strike from so far . . . or trap me at a time such as this when I feel helpless against her—for now, some part of me rejoices.

Auriane answered silently: *I am not one of the Holy Ones. . . . I beg you, go from me!*

Odd. When you say "go" it sounds like "stay."

I am set on a course— she began.

Of vengeance, Ramis' thought-words flooded over her own. *Come. You know I know. You think the world can be scrubbed clean. It's not dirty. You want evil destroyed. Can you show me where evil is? Point it out. I am curious. I've not been able to find it in all these years. You think you are freeing your father from the stain of dishonorable death. But dishonor is empty calamity. It exists only where men capriciously decide it exists. You think to save your people—but vengeance, my poor, wise fool, does not exist!*

"Away from me!" Auriane said aloud, conscious suddenly of her own roughened breathing. "I am not ready, as I love my mother and father, and I cannot abide this!"

You are full of unintended answers today. "Not ready" is not "No." I'll say no more then, except that the mirror-maze wants to be quit of you. Before you are two paths. One slopes down into shadowland where you will await rebirth. The other is the wide avenue to the moon. . . .

Auriane felt a frantic joy spiced with terror. To walk the avenue to the moon meant to be granted the highest gift of Fria—to dwell in Eastre's place-of-no-sorrowing, to be one who brings light down from the mountain, to be as Ramis herself. Was this why, during her time in Ramis' sanctuary, she was summoned at night?

Auriane silently objected: *But I took an oath, long ago, at midsummer.*

Your warrior's oath? came the mute reply. *Do the gods listen when children swear, knowing not what words they speak? I would have you oathed to something far older. You slake your thirst with new mead when you could drink from the Well of Urdr. But you'll not live long enough to know it if you do not at once cast off this notion of your own evil . . . you've no more time. You cannot prevail in single battle with a mortal enemy in your own blood. Do this thing or die in the task you set yourself!*

"You speak as if it were simple as taking off a cloak. I cannot!"

You can. Look at the years. Has not your stubborn shame only brought you more shame? You have performed many dark, difficult and terrifying tasks . . . and yet you say you cannot do this!

"I have no words for you," Auriane whispered. "I beg you . . . let me rest!" For long moments she sensed from Ramis only a compassionate silence.

Then a thought-question burst from her of its own accord. *Tell me of Avenahar.*

Ah, as ever, came the sighing reply, *you fret over what least needs fretting over. She is safe as the pearl in the oyster. The whole world is her nest.*

Does my mother live? Auriane asked eagerly, then tensed, not really ready for the reply.

As you understand it, yes. As I understand it, no. All this concern over who dies! If you knew what death truly was, you would care less. Earthly life, you see, is a multistoried house. The high floor is thought. The cellar is the life of dreams, the well of ancestral yearnings. Death is the walls. Do you think if you lived in all existence, you would fear the walls of your old, worn, outgrown house?

To Auriane's alarm, the words abruptly grew more difficult to discern. Frantically she groped for the great Holy One's voice, forming the question: *Why did you once say I would be a queen in death?*

But now she felt only cool silence. The fire crackled indifferently, a common cookfire once more. Auriane whirled around. Behind her was no evidence of the Veleda's presence, not so much as a telltale crushed leaf. She shivered, even though that hallowed warmth was still wrapped round her like gauze.

She is a remorseless hunter of souls. And now I am confused beyond measure. I've no notion of what path to take. But it might not be necessary to choose, for she's as much as told me I'll be slain—for I can no more shed shame than I can shed my skin.

But as Auriane departed the kitchens accompanied by two guards, she felt as though the night air held her like some nurturing sea. And she realized that in that god-touched moment, the shame *was* gone. The torches set along the drafty passage seemed to whirl and vault with joy. She felt light as a wraith. The thought of Sunia, and of Baldemar, brought only sorrow and pity, both for them and for herself. The sense did not last long; the next day all seemed much as usual. She cursed its elusiveness; it was a glint of light on a river, flashing, then gone. But she remembered the distinct taste of it. This, then, is what comes, she thought, if I can summon the mettle to claim it as my own.

On the eve of the games all who were to do battle, no matter how humble, were given a banquet of roast pig and lamb. The doors of the school were thrown open so the curious public could wander in and watch. Auriane sat among her tribesmen at a row of rough tables set up in the First Hall.

"And look at this!" Thorgild was exclaiming to the table at large, eyes alight with manic joviality. "All kinds of regular food, heaps and heaps of it, handed round just when no one has any appetite for it! True, you must die for these people to bring out their hospitality, but they do manage decently at the last, do they not?" Disgustedly he pushed away a joint of lamb and drained his wine cup in one greedy gulp. Coniaric knocked it out of his hand.

"Fool. Don't get drunk! Do you see those veterans over there lifting a cup? Do you want to be devoured tomorrow by a mob that hates you already just because you're not Aristos?"

Thorgild shoved Coniaric in reply, then retrieved the wine cup and refilled it. "Leave me be. They don't need drink, they're drunk on their own madness. Look at those mooncalves! Playing dice! They won't live to collect their winnings!"

This time Auriane seized Thorgild's cup and tilted it so that its contents spilled on the stone floor.

"Thorgild, let us see we live to collect *our* debts."

Thorgild regarded her with wounded surprise, then gave a short, gleeful laugh not his own. But this time he slammed down the cup and did not refill it.

Coniaric and Thorgild were to take part in one of the mass spectacles—a re-creation of the Chattian war's final battle, the taking of Five Wells. They would do battle with novices from the Claudian School, who would reenact the Roman assault; for this show the Great School's architect-engineers had constructed a fort with walls twelve feet high, which would be assembled in the center of the arena. From what Auriane managed to learn of such things, the mob's thirst for blood would not be slaked unless at least half the combatants fell to an "enemy" sword. She judged Coniaric and Thorgild had a fair chance of survival if they did not slip in blood or fall to treachery.

"How is Sunia?" Coniaric asked Auriane.

"Complaining of everything; which is to say, well."

"That took great courage, Auriane."

She looked swiftly away, eyes somber, saying nothing.

"Auriane, if I live, I'll be in a single bout next time, as Celadon is."

She started, saddened by the hopeful tone in Coniaric's voice, thinking: How quickly he embraces what these people honor. But she only replied, "You will live, Coniaric."

"The people of this city will know my name, everyone says it. I'll rise to the Second Hall. It heats the blood to think of it!"

"You have already made a good name for yourself, Coniaric. At home you are celebrated." But Coniaric did not hear her.

Just then Auriane caught sight of a flaxen-haired youth who seemed too well cared for to belong to this place. He threaded his way through the milling spectators, approaching her with the arrogant step of one who serves a man highly placed. Then he halted behind her and announced in a tone of challenge: "Harpocras bids you come!"

"Harpocras?" she whispered. He had no reason to see her, unless he acted on some order from Marcus Julianus. She rose up, fearful, expectant.

"Go quickly, and follow the passage that leads past the *latrina*," the boy said crisply. "When you can see the line of guards across the entranceway, halt there. Harpocras will be among them, standing even with the equestrian statue of Domitian. Wait in the shadows opposite the armory door and keep an eye on him. If you see him make this sign"—he rubbed an ear with two fingers of his left hand—"return to your place *at once*."

The boy wheeled about, vanishing among a rank of swift-striding slaves bearing platters of spicy pork sausages and lamb shanks roasted in honey.

"If Acco sees I'm gone," Auriane said to Coniaric, "tell him I got sick from this fool's feast and ran to the *latrina.*"

As Auriane crossed the flower-decked hall, she was scarcely aware of the odd juxtapositions of celebration and anguish on every hand. At one table a net-fighter and a veteran Samnite swordsman toasted each other with loud, comradely belligerence; at the same board was a novice stricken with grief, surrounded by a tearful family come to bid him farewell. She passed a man laboring over a hasty will, anxious that a relative or friend should retrieve his meager possessions after he met his fate. At his feet was a man entwined with one of the prostitutes, their cursory lovemaking covered only by the darkness. Then she entered the vaulted passage that ran round the whole square of the massive school, and halted when she smelled the insistent stench of the *latrina*. There she saw Harpocras with the guards, fifty paces off; he gave her the barest nod. Visiting citizens were streaming in between the double cordon of guards; beyond was the soaring side of the Colosseum and a small patch of ultramarine sky. Carters' curses echoed down the Stygian canyons that were the city's streets. From everywhere came the creak of relentlessly turning wheels as carts crawled into the city with foodstuffs and supplies. This strange city was more alive by night than by day, she observed; in darkness it replenished itself. She moved into the well of shadow opposite the armory door, feeling hollow and cold before the vast indifference of this world.

Two sure hands seized her from behind and turned her around.

"Marcus?" she whispered, facing a tall man in a hooded cloak. Within, she saw eyes that burned too brightly, revealing feelings ruthlessly reined in.

"Yes, it is I," came a reassuring voice.

She held to him for long moments, languishing in rich, warm silence. The comfort she took from him dismayed her, for it was a reminder of how comfortless she was at most times, and she did not want to know it.

"Listen to me," he said, his cheek still fervently pressed to hers. "It's madness for me to be here, but I've been given more vile news. Auriane, you must give this up! They conspire against you. You cannot win!"

She listened tensely, body braced to object. He looked swiftly round once to see if they were watched, then went on.

"I have here a poison compound. It induces vomiting and will make you ill for a day and a half—long enough for you to escape the morrow. No physician will be certain of the cause of your sudden sickness. Take it now, with this meal, and if fortune is with us, the school's physicians will conclude it's the food." He pressed a terra-cotta pot into her hand. "Take it and live!"

"Marcus, no! I still am bound—"

"You must! Aristos' ruffians mean to tamper with your equipment. They'll see you dead before you ever get near him. Erato cannot control them very well—Aristos has too many confederates among Palace officials. Do this for now, and I'll have another escape plan readied before you're made to fight again."

Auriane broke her gaze away once to look at Harpocras. He still stood unmoving.

"Marcus, I cannot be saved. You must let the Fates have their will of me, and trust this thing to my wits. Be at rest! There is nothing god or man can do." She put the poison back into his hand and said hoarsely, "Do not think I am not grateful!" She looked away, eyes moist with suffering.

He caught up her hand and cradled it in his own. "It is fiendish how clever the gods are at putting us into the very circumstances most impossible for us! You confound me! I do not know what to *do* with a person who spurns all aid. You've managed to render me more helpless than I've ever felt!"

He turned her face to his and said with resignation, "If you will not do this thing, then guard well your life. Erato means to let you select your own sword right before your time. You'll go into the armory yourself. After that, *do not take your eyes off your sword*, not even for a moment. The bearers will be walking before you as you enter, so this should not be difficult. Not even for the time it takes to take a breath, do you understand? Exchanging a sword is an old, tried trick, and they are very good at it. And I do not have to tell you that if your sword breaks in your hand, that's just your foul luck. You'll get no pity from the crowd, and you'll be given no quarter by your opponent."

Numbly she nodded, ensnared in his look—so like her own—
of a proud creature determined not to be too hurt by the world. In
spite of his words she felt slightly drugged by the sound of his
voice; it gathered her up and securely held her.

"Erato claims you're astonishingly skilled. I am not much
surprised, you are ever a source of wonderment. You've a good
chance, I believe, if you're kept safe from treachery. Now, when
you stand before the Emperor's box, do not look at me, and I must
not look at you. Domitian is strangely jealous of all that I love.
And do not look at the Emperor—don't provoke him in any way.
Try to look overwhelmed and . . . *chastened*, if you have it in
you." He smiled, softly stroking her cheek. "I have trouble
imagining that look on your face. But you must do it."

"I know his nature well. Have no fear, I will not provoke him."

"Auriane! This could be the last time we look upon one
another!"

"I will not die, Marcus."

"It is uncanny. . . . When you speak those words, I believe
them! I wish I could hold to this. But for me, belief is such a
fragile thing. . . . It does not survive dusk, much less the long
night."

"It is because your people keep your gods locked up in stone
houses," she said, with the beginnings of a mischievous smile. "If
you allowed them out among the people once in a while—"

But he drew her to him and cut her words short with a
disconsolate kiss, finding himself suddenly overcome; as he held
her, he marveled that her body had that same curious mixture of
vulnerability and strength, of softness and firmness, as did her
whole nature.

Auriane was sharply aware of how the swell of her breasts was
flattened against his chest, of the fact that but two thin pieces of
cloth separated their bodies. This is cruel past bearing, she thought
miserably. A part of me wants to turn my back on all my labors,
to steal off from this place and lie with him tonight.

He seemed to hear these thoughts, for he lifted her chin, held her
gaze firmly, and said, "I will find a way, some day soon, that we
may pass at least one night together. . . . *I promise it.*"

She shivered, feeling pleasantly vulnerable, gently paralyzed by
the desire so evident in his eyes. Misery and joy surged up in her
throat and choked off all words.

"All you have to do is stay alive," he said with a playful smile that concealed a savage sadness beneath. "A small thing to ask, I think!"

He then saw Harpocras give the signal. "*Nemesis!* Go quickly!"

She held to his gaze long as she dared; leaving him felt like tearing off a limb. "Forgive me what I do to you!" she whispered, then she turned and fled down the passage.

CHAPTER XLVI

Auriane was roused before dawn by the remorseless pounding of a drum. Still half in dreams, she thought it the festival drums of Eastre.

It is the morning of the Blessed One's rising. Baldemar awaits on Marten Ridge—I need to hurry if we're to watch together the lighting of the bonfires. Soon now, Thrusnelda will be climbing the hill of sacrifice with a live hare in a sack. . . .

She saw a line of dancing children following a high wind ruffling the pines; it was Fria herself as Light Bearer, her fiery raiment creating the dawn as she led first the young children, then all her people to the place-of-no-sorrowing. The earth-quickening pulse of that drum was her great, compassionate heart.

Then Auriane was awake. With a lurch of terror, she remembered.

That drum meant death, not life. It accompanied the raising of the *velarium*, the vast awning of sailcloth that would shield the spectators of the Colosseum from the midday sun. To the beat of that drum, a thousand sailors drawn from the Roman fleet at Misenum turned engines that unrolled great strips of canvas onto the network of ropes that stretched over the seats of the amphitheater. The crowds who came to watch her people die would not be forced to squint in the sun.

As she arose and splashed her face with water from the wooden trough at the back of the cell, each throb of that drum seemed a blow from a hammer in the hands of their savage sun-god, pounding her into bloody mud, driving her down into the caverns of Helle.

She stopped her ears.

Sunia! Do you hear? Do you know I saved you from that drum, or do you despise me still?

She moved to the narrow window so she could see a square of sky, and placed a hand over the sign of Tiwaz that scarred her arm, while struggling to feel the fiery spirit of the war-god. But the sky was barren today. She fought against the first small pricklings of panic.

A guard loudly flung open the cell door. Motioning with his javelin, he ordered her to follow him. On this day the whole of the passage was lined with guards, most of whom were unfamiliar. She was taken to a vast holding cell by the school's entrance and put in with two hundred and more novices. None spoke; all were locked into their private prisons of fear. After a few moments she found Coniaric and Thorgild in the murky light; they seemed distant, as if they still dreamed. When she saw Celadon, he refused to meet her eye. Though yesterday he had seemed settled and confident, on this morning terror owned him, and it filled him with shame.

A dozen guards briskly searched them for sharp implements—a brooch, a stylus, or paring knife—to forestall the inconvenience of last-minute suicides.

As morning progressed, the whole of the *Ludus Magnus* began to awaken to life; Auriane observed it all from the holding cell's barred window. Armory workers and assistants hurried past at a half run, carrying weapons and equipment. Shouts reverberated off stone as disputes erupted between trainers and physicians. Ceremonial chariots were drawn up and readied for the grand entrance of the highest-ranking men of the First Hall, who appeared shortly after, decked in purple robes and finely embossed helmets of gold affixed with peacock plumes. As the hours crept on, her tribesmen began to approach her singly or in twos, to put a hand on the amulet of sacred earth—all they had left of their home ground— while begging her to pray for them. Auriane stayed near Celadon, plying him with questions about all that passed, hoping to pull him out of the miasma that had settled over him. Thorgild seemed to find a store of strength at the last. But Celadon did not, for, as she learned, he believed he was matched with a better man.

The cell's only sounds were murmurs, whimpers and prayers.

•   •   •

As dawn passed into hazy morning, the common people massed into the wide way that separated the *Ludus Magnus* from the Colosseum. Ruffians from the Subura pressed against perfumed nobles, Palace freedmen, cobblers and fishmongers, cabbage farmers from the country about Rome, workers in marble, keepers of shops, and travelers from places distant as Rhodes, Anatolia, or the banks of the Euphrates. Above this human sea swayed the occasional senatorial litter, seeming to float on it like some ivory and gold pleasure boat. Slaves were prohibited entry to the arena contests, but not a few infiltrated the throng anyway, hoping to steal in undetected and take a place in the top tier, where standing room could be purchased for two coppers.

Most made their way at once to the ticket stalls, where they secured tickets of flat round bone, on which was inscribed their seat and row. From here they crowded into the marble stairways located under every fourth arch. Once inside the amphitheater they were taken in hand by efficient attendants, who quickly seated them in the section reserved for their rank. Some paused by the stands built against the wooden barricade set up round the base of the Colosseum to help control the crowd; here they bought programs, rented cushions to soften the marble seats, or purchased sausages, meat pastries, boiled eggs and spiced wine so they could have their midday meal inside and miss none of the show. A knot of people pressed about the betting stalls, arguing the merits of the favorites as they placed their wagers. By the second hour, seventy thousand citizens had crowded into the Colosseum, for in spite of the fact that they were denied Aristos, much interest was excited by the promised reenactment of the battles of the Chattian war. "*What* battles?" the frequent objection was heard around the betting stalls. But others replied it was worth the price of admission just to witness the droll spectacle of Domitian attempting to transform a few pathetic skirmishes in the woods into the battle of Actium or the siege of Troy.

When the Emperor and his entourage were settled in the imperial box, a fanfare and a crash of cymbals commanded silence, and the day of games began. As was the custom, the morning was given over to animal-baiting. The people were first given a contest between two elephants. The beasts were goaded with fire-darts until they attacked one another; their regal trumpeting could be heard beyond the city gates. The victorious elephant then kneeled before the imperial box as it had been carefully trained to do. This was followed by a pairing of a rhinoceros and a white bull with spikes affixed to its horns, then a battle of bears, tied together to make them more vicious. After this came an exhibition of mounted Thessalian bullfighters: Thirty bulls were released into the arena, followed closely by a troop of horsemen, who galloped alongside the bulls, grasped their horns, then twisted their necks, bringing the beasts to the ground. The pace was never allowed to flag; before the last bull was brought down, two dozen giraffes were driven in, to the delighted murmurs of the crowd. Then skilled archers entered the arena, and a swift slaughter began. Finally the officials of the games had to call a recess so Numidian slave boys could drag off the accumulating carcasses with iron hooks and ropes. When this uninspiring sight began to draw hisses and catcalls, a Mesopotamian lion was released to mollify the crowd, which grew quiet as the animal was slain by a brightly garbed Ethiopian woman armed only with a hunting spear.

By mid-morning the crowd became impatient with this endless parade of beasts. But Domitian's director of shows had not exhausted his supply: Next came a mock chariot race—the charioteers were monkeys, driving miniature cars. Then, to whet the appetite for what was to come, the people were given an exhibition of monkeys battling with small javelins. The crowd's laughter was halfhearted. A low, cautious warning chant began to issue from the plebeian seats: *"Give us Aristos! Aristos now!"*

At the fourth hour, in the twilight of the holding cell the captives were brought bowls of barley gruel, which they ate listlessly under the guards' probing stares. Auriane wondered: Do they think we will try to choke ourselves with the spoons?

At midday a brassy braying of trumpets signaled the time had come for the contests between men. The guards returned and began taking the novices off in tens. Celadon explained to Auriane they would open with several unimportant individual bouts; then the first "stage set" battle would take place. All afternoon the single bouts would alternate with simulations of the battles of the war, to allow the architect-engineers' assistants time to ready the scenery for the battle spectacles. Of the many facts Celadon related that day, one remained peversely illumined in Auriane's mind: There were men settled outside this city whose sole task in life was to *grow the trees* for the scenery used in these mock battles. She was astonished anew at the odd habits of this race of men.

When the first bout began, she noticed at once how the sight of human blood transformed the crowd's voice. During the animal-baitings their cries were softer and more scattered. Now they gave single, surging cries with a much harder edge—deep, hungry roars from the belly that seemed to issue from a single throat, punctuated by shrieks alive with eager malignity.

Time stalled; the throng's cries became increasingly laden with dark discontent. When Coniaric and Thorgild were taken, their departure was so swift and matter-of-fact, so empty of the glory she always associated with battle that they might have been setting out to drive cattle in from pasture. Auriane struggled to perform in her mind the Ritual of Fire, but the crowd's growing agitation kept breaking into her silence. She knew well the sounds of a throng ready to riot; she had attempted to calm many such a crowd in her own country. It was alarming because she knew how unpredictable such a mob could be.

She listened to the guards' talk, struggling to learn the fate of Coniaric and Thorgild. But she discovered only that the first exhibition of women—a dozen pairs of Sarmatians from the Claudian School who fought with javelins—had been greeted with a shower of rotted turnips.

When Celadon was taken off for his single bout, he surprised Auriane by embracing her with fierce warmth, lifting her off her feet. "If I don't return, Auriane," he said at the last, "go to Bargates when curiosity goads you. He was a fugitive from the kitchens of a great-house, and he knows this city like fleas know a dog's back. He's of sanguine temperament and won't be maddened by your constant questions."

"Celadon . . . , *live!*" she said miserably as the guards prodded him off.

A quarter-hour passed. The guards returned and selected nine men—and Auriane.

She felt suddenly like a skittish horse.

I am not ready! That throng is a ravening beast. They're murderous today, they'll spare no one. And what if I am victor and the crowd demands I kill? Celadon heard a tale that this man Perseus sold himself to the school to keep his family from starvation. I cannot slay an innocent man. I see no possible good end for this day.

They were brought to the equipment rooms alongside the armory. Two fierce-faced old women began to prepare her. One had watery eyes and hands pebbled with warts, the other, a mobile, toothless mouth; their dry hands scuttled over her body like crabs as they fastened the greave to her left leg, the arm guard to her right arm. One drew Auriane's hair tightly back at the nape of her neck and twisted it into the smallest knot she could fashion. The hair must be kept well out of the way—should a stray strand be caught by the point of a sword, she could be scalped. Together they fastened onto her a tunic of layered leather. Then they placed on her shoulders a heavy wool cloak dyed a deep garnet red.

Behind her, assistants hurried in with carts bearing bloodied equipment plucked from the dead, but she scarcely heard the activity all about—the world of the living seemed to recede and grow small, and she felt faint and light, as if her soul had begun already to seek the sky.

Erato came in then, followed by a secretary and a scribe. At the sight of her he was struck to stillness. That severely drawn back hair gave her a stark, bold look; she seemed all determination and searching eyes. He reflected uneasily on the night when she knocked him down, and once again he had the unsettling sense this was no subject woman, but some mortal emissary of the Fates, who would work their will and then vanish when her task was done. Impatiently he shook the feeling off—the spirit-realms were for the credulous rabble; he believed only in speed, courage and accuracy.

"Let me see your wrists," he said with brisk impatience. "Good! Now, then, what is the meaning of this sign?" Quickly he went twice through the hand signals they had devised. Then he ordered his secretary and scribe to leave him. She sensed some faint awkwardness in his manner, as though he had done a thing of which he was ashamed.

He came close and said in a low voice, "Auriane, there are people who think I'm a madman for the claims I've made for you." He shrugged, then gave her a cautious, sheepish smile. "But some of them in important places have decided to believe me . . . and they've placed some rather extravagant bets on you, solely upon my word. My position and reputation are at stake today. Well, I might as well tell you, my *life* is at stake. One of them is that greedy pig of a Finance Minister, Musonius Geta, and he won't hesitate to slit my throat if he loses his lousy million sesterces. Rescue me from this one, Auriane, and when it's over, I'll see that you get any reward it's in my power to give."

She regarded him with amused disbelief. He had succumbed to an obvious temptation—the selling of information. She would only be an unknown once, and the odds had been set against her at nine to one. But what was his purpose in telling her this? Did he not count her own desire to survive motivation enough? Worry is scrambling his wits, she thought.

"*Any* reward?" she said, suppressing a smile. "I pray you live to regret you made that promise."

"Within *reason*, you minx. No hot and cold baths for every one of your tribesmen, or—"

"I know already what I will ask. Leave me now, before I catch your fretfulness like a pox."

"Why are prodigies so irksome?" he said, grinning. "At last look I was still director of this school, my testy princess. Now, march ahead of me to the armory, and watch that cloak, it's too long. . . . None of us can afford it if you stumble and break your neck."

Domitian's box was a sumptuous chamber that offered most of the comforts of his own bedroom. It was set at the center of one of the long sides of the arena's ellipse, right at the barrier. The Colosseum's seating was planned so that a man's view improved with his rank, and the Emperor's view was beyond compare. To ensure that nothing whatever impeded it, one of the mast-poles for the awning had been taken out, and it seemed to Domitian the dramas of life and death were played out for him alone. The imperial box was enclosed for privacy. Two sets of curtains— the inner ones of gauzy silk, the outer ones of heavier silk threaded with gold—shielded him from the probing eyes of the populace, but on this day he ordered them thrown open so the people might be treated to the sight of him—a magnanimous gesture, he thought, given their treasonable churlishness on this day.

Domitian was sunk deeply into his overcushioned chair, a delicate masterwork of cedarwood and ivory fashioned by Egyptian craftsmen. His footstool rested on a floor of gleaming squares of porphyry set in a chequered pattern of sea-green and pale rose. Behind Domitian, Carinus stood guard near silver ewers of snow-cooled water and Falernian wine, watching fearfully for the slightest gesture of the Emperor's heavily ringed hand. A troupe of musicians played panpipes and kithara, trying to imitate with their music the sounds of trickling water. Domitian had lately given up the struggle to maintain the appearance of one who eschews luxury; it no longer troubled him if the people thought him not as fit and battle-ready as his father. In these days he rarely walked if he could be carried, and his body had begun to thicken like an aging stallion set out to pasture. He sat stiffly still with exaggerated dignity, but his gaze was ever restless, roaming like some truculent bull, always alert to signs of independence in the herd.

Curled at Domitian's feet was the simpleminded boy that lately the Emperor kept by his side like some lapdog; the child was born with a too-small head, and was pitiful in rich clothes that were too large for him. Domitian felt more and more separated from his fellow men, and this boy was like a balm: He could be in a vile mood or a mild one and receive the same unquestioning devotion. The child was massaging the Emperor's feet with an expression of intense concentration on his benign face. Domitian paid him no mind—his senses were pricked to the temper of the crowd. Whenever they shouted *"Throw Veiento to the panthers,"* or *"Match Veiento with Hyperion,"* a deep flush sprang to his cheeks and spread to his thick neck, and his eyes became like a bull's horns, casting about for someone to gore. Carinus would stop breathing and stand very still, hoping Domitian would forget he was there.

Below them on the sand a net-and-trident fighter warily circled a Thracian swordsman. Domitian scarcely watched; the next bout, Auriane's, was the one that promised to rouse him from his sour melancholy.

To Domitian's left Montanus slouched in a humbler chair; a collection of petitions rested in the valley between his chest and the swell of his belly. Nervous perspiration beaded Montanus' upper lip as he read from them in his high, immature voice. Veiento was given leave not to attend, for fear that the people, if they saw him, would probably rend him limb from limb, but also because Domitian had set Veiento at another task today: supervising the torture of every one of his agents to discover who had betrayed the truth of Gallus' death.

And to Domitian's right sat the man who had betrayed it, his confidential counselor and First Advisor, Marcus Arrius Julianus.

Marcus Julianus felt sharply separated from all about him. He felt he had but his wit, his hands, and a will of adamant to pit against the coming horror. The evening before, he had lectured the students of his beleaguered school on the words of the esoteric philosophers regarding the futility of sorrow, hoping it would help him bear his own. The students applauded and wept, but it left him feeling ever more strongly that something was gravely missing from all known teachings. And there had come a memory, invisible and emotionally undermining as old, loved music: He saw again that pine-clad hill and the broken fort where he took refuge on the day he first set eyes on Auriane, and he remembered that striking peace.

Our philosophies are brittle houses of words, Marcus thought; they collapse in every gale. The wind-rattled pines speak with an older voice, one afire with nature's gentle omniscience. . . . Could it be the barbarian shamans *do* have the means of healing the wounds of cities, of showing the way to natural life? Did not that vision-ridden madman Isodorus hint at it? Is not Auriane's primal innocence a sort of proof?

I think sorrow is taking my good sense.

If this day does not end in her death, it will certainly end in our exposure—for how can I restrain myself from rushing in to aid her if she seems truly to need it?

Montanus' next words caused Marcus Julianus to become sharply alert. "Here's one from some rascal named Corax," Montanus read. "He says he was unfairly removed from his post after that Torquatus affair. He wants it back, or a better one."

Domitian gave Montanus the combination gesture-and-grunt that meant: Put that one aside so I can study it later.

Nemesis! Marcus Julianus thought. If Corax recounts the events of that night, Domitian might easily guess that I ruined Torquatus to save Auriane. I must act quickly. I'll either have to buy Corax's silence or find him a better post myself. I sail a ship that daily springs more leaks.

In back of them Junilla reclined on a couch, attended by two handmaids chosen for their homeliness so they would not distract Domitian's attention from herself. Normally Domitian would not flaunt Junilla in public, but he did so on this day in order to punish Domitia Longina—for yesterday he had learned the truth of his wife's miscarriage, after questioning her personal physician under torture. He meant to publicly banish Domitia Longina from his side until she came before him of her own will to confess her crime.

Junilla looked about with worldly confidence; every year her far-flung estates brought her increasing wealth. As long as she occasionally yielded to Domitian's restless lusts, he repaid her by not scrutinizing her private life too closely. Her stola of carnelian silk was so finely spun her rouged nipples were visible beneath; its clasps were studded with emeralds. She had smoothed green verdigris around her eyes, giving them a glittering snakelike brightness. Her hair was set in tight, disciplined tiers of curls that had taken her maids half a day to fashion; the result made it look as though she had summoned an architect instead of a hairdresser. Her periods of imperial favor never lasted more than a few days and nights. Always Domitian quickly found that her intimidatingly perfect mouth, those dark barbarous eyes, that beauty so unchanged as year added to year that it seemed embalmed, and her moods, shifting with whip-crack speed from honey to acid—all began to repel as much as they first excited, and he would dismiss her. And Domitian would realize, greatly annoyed, that a good part of the reason he returned to her repeatedly was due to the haunting allure that enveloped her because she had once been Marcus Arrius Julianus' wife.

But Domitian had not dismissed her yet and Marcus Julianus knew she was at her most dangerous at these times—imperial favor lent a reckless quality to her malice. She scented his unease at the mention of Corax; with a cobra's malign calm that beautiful head glided up. He felt those eyes fixed on the back of his neck like claws.

Domitian abruptly lost interest in Montanus and the petitions and turned to Marcus Julianus. "What is *gnawing* at you, my good man?" he said with obstinate good cheer, putting a bullying hand on his First Advisor's shoulder. "You make me uneasy when you ascend to these reveries! Come down from Olympus for one day, and pay us mortals a visit! Sport with us. Place a bet with me. I insist! Not on *this*"—he waved a deprecating hand at the struggle below—"that net-fighter looks ready to drop dead if his opponent so much as sneezes on him. But the next pair. Don't you think he should, Montanus? *Do* you think, *Mountainous?*"

Montanus started from his frightened fog, embarrassed that he had not responded at once. "Magnificent idea, my lord. I've *always* said our dear Julianus should come down here and sit with us mortals." He tensed when Domitian gave him a chilly look, wondering frantically what he had said that was improper.

Marcus Julianus said quietly, "If offense was taken, I meant none." His smile was not quite readable to Domitian; its amused tolerance would have angered him had it not been mingled with a certain earnest innocence. "But you know it is the tradition of my family not to bet on men's lives."

"Bet on a woman's, then. Got you there! That insolent Amazon comes in next, does she not?" He leaned toward Montanus' gold-lettered list of events, feigning a need to consult it. "Put five hundred on her," Domitian persisted. "Come now, everyone has bet against her—she needs your help."

Marcus Julianus heard Junilla eagerly shifting her position on her couch.

He smiled good-humoredly. "And bet on a certain loser? You think sudden impoverishment will put me in a gayer mood?"

Junilla was enraged that Marcus Julianus was not more agitated by this. Her hatred of him was all the more tenacious, tangled as it was with unacknowledged desire, and as she sensed ever more strongly the bond between him and Auriane, it grew into a misshapen, monstrous thing. Her memories remade themselves as her soul required, and in these times she even held Marcus Arrius Julianus to account for the death of her child, because she *could not* believe ill of Nero, who in spite of his cruel use of her was still the most powerful protector of her youth.

Discard me like some Circus trull, will you? How *dare* you be so sure of yourself, *Endymion.*

"My little titmouse," Domitian said, turning round to look at her. "What do *you* think on this matter—or is that delightfully empty mind of yours still stupefied by thoughts of last night?"

One covetous hand moved over the swell of her hip, claiming it with a collector's pride, as if it were the finest of Corinthian bronzes.

She smiled demurely behind her parrot-feather fan, waiting until she sensed that she had everyone's attention.

"Well, I think a man *should* bet on the woman he loves."

She had struck. Montanus was delighted that he had not missed this. He could scarcely wait to scurry back to the Palace to tell Veiento.

Domitian turned slowly round to Marcus Julianus. He put little trust in Junilla's word, but he knew also she could have chosen more direct methods of ruining his First Advisor. Why make such an odd accusation if it were not true? Slowly Domitian's look became brutal. The thought of anyone having Auriane raised a jealous storm, but the thought of Marcus Julianus having her was past bearing. Even the Guards posted in the box stole covert glances at Julianus—the thought of a man like that destroying himself for a woman no better than an animal was as bewildering as it was farcical.

Junilla gave them her *"What, did I say something out of place?"* smile, then looked triumphantly at Marcus Julianus. But his face bitterly disappointed her. In his eyes was only a calm, flexible strength; it was almost as if he had been expecting this today. With difficulty she restrained herself from tossing the contents of her wine cup in his face.

Marcus Julianus then said to Junilla, "Has Aristos tired of you so quickly, my dear? Your malevolence always was at its most unbridled just after your latest lover realizes his mistake."

Domitian was perhaps the only man in Rome who did not know this, for he had been meting out severe punishments to those who libeled the nobility. No one had the courage to tell him, for none were willing to take the risk of not being believed.

Domitian turned to Junilla, something turbid and violent churning in his eyes. "Aristos?" he whispered, his eyes betraying he was in the act of vividly imagining that embrace. *"Aristos?"* Had anyone but Marcus Julianus said it, he would not have believed it so readily.

Junilla's lips parted slightly in shock. She badly miscalculated. Years of imperial protection had caused her to drift gradually into the trap of believing herself invulnerable to ruin. And she had not counted on Marcus Julianus' fierce protectiveness of Auriane. It left her with no doubt that there was some connection between them.

Domitian withdrew from her as if she were a pail of night soil. His face ashen with rage, he mutely waved her off, as though addressing her directly would defile him. Then he commanded the Guards: "Take that *thing* out of my sight."

Junilla shook her head once in disbelief, the tower of elaborate curls shivering, the deep flush of her cheeks visible beneath her foundation of powdered white lead.

"You can't believe him! He despises me!" Her eyes stung like wasps.

Still addressing the guard, Domitian said, "Tell this female animal she is not to tell me what I believe."

Junilla rose an instant before the Guards caught her roughly under the arm. Fear warred with her rage. What will he do to me? she wondered frantically. Exile. I know it will be exile. Unless I can appeal to him later in a better mood and convince him Marcus Julianus is lying. None of them will get away with this. I will find a way to frame a treason charge against Julianus that will be *believed*, or die in the effort! Who has known such humiliation! I know *no one* who was ever thrown out of the imperial box! By tonight they'll be laughing about this at every dinner party in

Rome. I'll see both Marcus Julianus and that beast-woman he loves roasted on the same spit for this.

When Junilla was gone, Domitian said to Marcus Julianus, "What she said is true, is it not?"

Though Marcus Julianus knew this was coming next, still he felt the ground cracked open beneath his feet. Vile woman, you did your work well, he thought. He knew at once denial would be foolish; Domitian was shrewder than most at detecting lies.

He managed an expression of mild anguish and replied, "I can conceal little from you, can I?" He thought rapidly, knowing he would have to steer a careful course. He knew Domitian enjoyed uncovering the secret vices and degradations of those who seemed to be above them. While confessing some regular crime to him was never wise, admitting to some shameful lust could often endear a man to him. "But what would *you* know of such humiliation?" he added.

Domitian paused, frowning, suspended precariously between jealous rage and satisfaction. Marcus Julianus had been humiliated? The notion was intriguing.

"Now, *out* with it, and quickly, whatever it is you can't conceal from me!"

"Can a man determine who or what will carry him off on a tide of lust? I bribed one of the guards of that school and went in there once, well disguised as you might guess, to hide my shame. He brought her to me and helped us to hide. It is better that you know the worst, somehow it relieves my mind."

Domitian frowned threateningly, but his grunt expressed contentment.

"I think the woman is addled in the mind," Marcus Julianus continued. "At first she was . . . *more* than encouraging. I forgot who was seducing whom. But then, all that alluring sweetness turned to venom at the first touch."

Domitian listened intently, nodding slowly, thinking, *By all the gods, that is exactly what happened with me!*

"She was transformed in a heartbeat from nymph-in-heat to frothing bitch-dog," Marcus Julianus went on. "I was fortunate to walk out of there with everything I walked in with. She attacked me with a broken potsherd. The names she called me still haunt me."

"She's got an adder's tongue, that one!" Now Domitian was smiling companionably. He began to shake with conspiratorial laughter. "We should cut it out!"

"Oh, let her keep it. It taught me a lesson."

"Well, she's getting what she deserves today, is she not? *This* should trim her claws. Don't take it to heart—I'll find you something better. I'm sending you a Syrian maiden, thirteen years old if the importer didn't lie, and proportioned like Niobe, with saucy eyes and breasts white as doves. I meant to keep her for myself but I don't have time for her. She's yours, for as long as you want. But you have to let me borrow her if I change my mind."

Not this again, Marcus Julianus thought. "Your generosity awes me."

What will I do with this one? If I send her off with her freedom like the last one, for certain then he'll ask for her.

And now his rage will be all the greater, if he ever learns the full truth of this matter.

CHAPTER XLVII

In the gloom of the armory Auriane stood before the keenly honed instruments of death laid out upon a table. Torchlight snaked on double-edged blades. She tried one short sword, then another until she found one that had weight yet at the same time felt weightless.

This one is mine. I must mark it somehow, so I'll know if it is exchanged.

Erato waited outside the door. The guard who admitted her, whose loyalties were unknown, looked on with a bland expression. She took up two swords at once, feeling the balance of both, feigning indecision. Then she scratched on the bone handle of the sword she chose the runic symbol of Tiwaz, god of the battle-field—one upright line capped with two shorter converging lines. When this was done, she thought she felt a rush of air, as though the god's swift, invisible blade swept through the room. She sensed the ghosts of all her dead crowding near: Sigwulf, Thrusnelda and Baldemar held out arms that protected—and begged help. Relief rushed in.

The spirit of the Ash is in me still. I have powerful, rambling roots underground.

Baldemar, answer! Was I not the god of war's good servant? You've pride in me still, I know it. Forgive me that I take so long! Walk with me now. Do not send me into that pitiless place alone.

• • •

The route from the *Ludus Magnus* to the gladiators' entrance of the Colosseum was closed off by a wooden corridor. As boisterous groups of citizens attempted to climb it, the barricade thundered as if it were butted by elephants. Auriane fought to keep out the sounds of this raging human storm, striving to hear only the crackle of the flames of Ramis' fire.

Two Numidian boys strutted ahead of her, bearing her own sword and Perseus' on crimson silk cushions. And beside her walked Perseus himself, clad in the azure and saffron cloak of the Claudian School. The wall of a fortress might have separated them. Perseus behaved as if she were invisible and inconsequential, keeping his closed, steely gaze rigidly ahead. She had met his eyes once when first she realized who he was, and had resolved not to do so again, for it had been like gazing into a labyrinth full of wrong turns, traps and trickery. At first look she had seen a lightly bearded man who might have been fair of feature except that his hard blue eyes were set in a permanent look of startled affront. She saw at once his too-upright carriage was carefully maintained—this was a man struggling to hold onto a precious dignity that he imagined the whole world waited to snatch from him. She guessed he felt keenly the shame of being matched with a woman. But it was what she sensed beneath this that disturbed her most. He had the look of a spirit lost. No firm purpose brought him here; his presence was the result of bad choices and accidents and others' greed; here was a man slowly realizing he was being ground up on life's millstone. She judged him ready to use any sort of treachery to set things right.

They moved through clouds of flies. The sun was savage. Behind them came four more red-liveried boys, bearing their helmets and shields. These were followed by six guards walking abreast, their javelins held horizontally as a barrier to the curious who tried to follow. Beyond the makeshift wall an aggressive new chant began: *"No more women, no more unknowns. Give us Aristos or we'll rip the place down!"* The thought of facing that crowd seemed humbling as being cast out in a tiny boat onto a tumultuous sea.

The corridor curved and the great, brooding presence of the amphitheater forced her gaze upward. She allowed herself to look for an instant before she dropped her gaze back to her sword, and regretted it at once.

For the sight was utterly dismaying. Never before had she seen the grand amphitheater while it was infested with the thousands who came to watch men die. It teemed with loathsome life, as when a carcass is found to be overrun with maggots. Even death here is monumental, she thought as she looked on that blunt, brutish four-tiered mountain thrusting skyward; it seemed ablaze on top where the brazen shields set in the arches of the sky-tier were inflamed by the sun. The legions of gilded statues of gods and men inhabiting the arches of the middle tiers were leering spirits, welcoming the crowd while mocking the victims. High above, she heard a sound like a god cracking a whip; the many-hued *velarium* snapped angrily in the brisk wind. The Colosseum was an awesome ship of doom in full sail. She felt like some crawling insect as they passed into its vast sweep of shadow.

Auriane and Perseus moved beneath the gladiators' entrance with its flanking Tuscan half-columns; then they were halted in the dim passage that formed a straight chute opening onto the sands of the arena. As they waited, delayed by some unknown cause, she heard a thin, determined voice cry out above the din: *"Auriane!"*

Auriane looked toward three small, barred windows in the wall of the main passage; these were underground rooms with a viewing window just above the level of the sand, where novices were sometimes permitted to watch the combats. She peered into the confusion of the crowded chamber, and there, to her disbelief, was Sunia.

Carefully keeping her gaze on her sword, Auriane moved to the small window. Sunia's hand edged through the grate. She saw the injured woman leaned on a knotted stick; her leg was heavily bandaged to the knee.

"How come you to be here!" Auriane demanded softly.

"They expect the hospital rooms to fill up with more valuable charges today, and so they drove me out. I'm here because kitchen slaves aren't watched that closely. There's a measure of freedom in being next to worthless, it seems. Auriane, they've made you ugly. Make them comb out your hair!"

"I'll just have to shame you with my ugliness, I suppose!" Her brief smile faded. "Sunia, I do not expect you to ever forgive me, but—"

"*Forgive* you? Are you mad? I breathe because of what you did! To even *think* I would hold you to account!"

Auriane felt happy disbelief. Sunia apparently had no memory of cursing her name. "That is well! Sunia, poor innocent victim of my fate!"

"Speak of it no more. Auriane, take heart—Thorgild and Coniaric are alive, as is the son of old Andar. We've lost only six of our people, and none from this school."

"Praise be to the Fates!"

"Thorgild's in here with us, but they took Coniaric off. He had a cut at the first rib, no organs struck, and an arrow wound. He'll be about again if those vile surgeons don't kill him with their butcher knives and poisons. We'll be watching you—but so will Aristos. He's in the next chamber, we saw him go in. Auriane, beware! Those eyes of night will be on you." Sunia pressed Auriane's hand tightly against her cheek. "Your heart is greater than mine. You must not leave us, Auriane."

Auriane pressed Sunia's hand to her own cheek. "May the spirits of our groves keep and comfort you," she whispered. The passage door was thrown open, admitting a gust of fetid wind from the arena. She left Sunia then and returned to her place.

The door opening onto the sand was still barred by a guard's javelin. At that moment two trainers of the Second Hall emerged from a side passage. One stopped as he recognized Auriane.

"Hail, Aurinia, queen of the first barrack block!" he called out merrily. "Your wealth and domains have increased in the last half hour." He threw a bloody cloak at Auriane. She caught it, uncomprehending.

"This was Celadon's," he went on with a jester's sly smile. "He wanted you to have it—he's got no use for it anymore! Take it, it's yours—at least for the *next* half hour. Then, who gets it?" Both laughed loudly.

Celadon! Auriane thought, a voiceless shriek forming in her throat. Slaughtered like an animal, and unmourned.

They turned from her, still speaking of Celadon. "How dare he humiliate Acco like that, getting himself speared by a mere net-fighter! As always, those that don't listen to us get dragged out by the feet!"

A horde of the Numidian boys employed in turning the sand swarmed in then, busy as flies, shouting and laughing, jostling everyone. Auriane was too angry to pay them any mind. She wheeled round and hurled the bloody cloak at the trainers' retreating backs.

"Wolves! Night-crawling vermin! Blood-drinking jackals!" Her voice was nearly lost in the din.

Then suddenly she understood.

She had been tricked. The trainers were purposely distracting her. She looked quickly at her sword—and she was certain it lay at a slightly different angle on its cushion. She saw that one of the running boys carried a linen bundle—and she would have wagered her life that within it was the sword with the mark of Tiwaz. She watched the boy as he ran in a zigzag path; far down the passage he stashed it behind the open door of a guard chamber.

The small procession started forward again. Auriane thought frantically, uncertain what to do. Should she protest now?

No. I will reveal Aristos' treachery before all the people.

The javelin was raised, and the swordbearers descended to the sand. She heard a trumpet's brassy shriek, and was almost overwhelmed by a gust of the arena's humid air, thick with the rank, lingering odors of animal flesh and human sweat and blood. The perfumed water jetting into the air did little to cover these smells; it served somehow only to make them more nauseating.

Auriane and Perseus took the last step down onto the sand.

Erato spoke truly, she thought. *Nothing could prepare you for this.*

She felt she stood at the bottom of an immense funnel formed of the multitudes mounting steeply upward to the awnings and the sky. It seemed the whole world converged upon the arena, that all paths sloped down to this vortex of elemental struggle, this bottomless sand-pit that gulped the blood of strangers. Here was the heart of unholiness, the boiling cauldron of Roman savagery. Decius' words drummed in her ears: *"Never let my people take you alive."* The vast space, nearly enclosed, admitted one shaft of light that slanted down from the circular opening in the *velarium*. Dark and powerful gods have taken possession of this place, she thought, gazing skyward and half expecting a booming god's voice to come shuddering down. But she saw only a cold, misty abyss hung with the sluggish vapors of slaughterhouse scents, gathering and thickening at the high tiers, which were ghostly behind its veil. The weight of every stare was heavy on her shoulders, and she fought a powerful urge to turn round and flee—but the oak door was already securely closed. She could feel, like penetrating needles, the people's sharp curiosity about life and death as they eagerly examined the faces of those who walked into final darkness—as though they expected a voyager setting out on a journey could tell tales of it in advance.

Auriane and Perseus moved past the Gate of Death with its frightful friezes of demons over its arch. Through which Celadon just departed, she thought, refusing to look at it. At a stately pace they moved around the ellipse, approaching the imperial cubicle with its flanking, laurel-entwined columns surmounted by golden eagles in flight, its medallions of the Emperor, its brilliant tapestries that dropped almost to the arena's floor. The colored sailcloth of the *velarium* cast shifting shadows of pale aquamarine, rose and gold onto the sand.

Beneath the imperial box were the four undertrainers who were always present, ready to goad the reluctant with whips and brands. Erato stood at the arena's center, his keen gaze fixed on Auriane; fretfully he shifted his weight from foot to foot. Next to him was Perseus' trainer from the Claudian School. Each combatant normally had his own trainer present, for even the most seasoned fighter occasionally needed instructions cried to him once a bout had begun.

Across from the imperial box was the Consul's seat; beneath it, the musicians were stationed. It did not seem odd to Auriane that the combats were accompanied by music, for she counted them a form of sacrifice, and she knew all her life that the plaints of ritual instruments drew the gods near. The drummer, the flute blowers, and the seated trumpeters were silent; only the haughty Egyptian woman standing at the water organ was energetically attacking her instrument. The lurching, wailing notes of the water organ made Auriane feel she was carried off on a jolting, runaway journey into an underworld peopled with carousing madmen. More than any other, that instrument, with its cruel, gloating sound, dark as the Styx, seemed to be the voice of this place.

Beside the musicians were two wooden caskets.

Distantly she heard the herald cry: *"Perseus. Aurinia."*

Marcus Julianus, on first seeing Auriane, did not know her. Her smoothed-back hair of burnished bronze, glossy as a horse's coat, made her seem some sleek, feral hunting creature. Those eyes were remote; she walked a battlefield. This creature was first a warrior; all else would ever be second. Yet still he saw all the vulnerability beneath. The way she held her head up with a sort of innocent, animal pride caused him to feel a knot of misery in his chest.

Poor orphaned child of the forest! You've more nobility in one hand than all those in the seats of honor who style themselves noble. Drinkers of blood! he thought, looking about him at the half-sated crowd. When will you awaken and begin to scream? Why is our country's greatest monument a human slaughterhouse? Why do so few ask that question?

The throng reacted variously to the tall barbarian woman and the Thracian swordsman. Those in the balcony seats reserved for the Senators looked on this match with disdain, seeing it as firm evidence of the growing effeminacy and perversion of their Emperor, the murderer of their own Licinius Gallus. Such silliness would never have been tolerated in their grandfathers' day, when it was understood the gladiatorial combats were necessary to instill courage and contempt for death in all ranks of society. But they were too dignified to cry out their discontent; they confined their protest to loud mutterings and vigorous shaking of heads.

Those in the seats reserved for the lower ranking nobility, the men of the Equestrian class whose togas formed a wide band of white close to the barricade, looked on with sullen boredom broken by sporadic shouts of *"Set the dogs on them!"* and *"Save us, Aristos!"*

In the next tier of seats, separated from those below by a bright band of mosaic fashioned of precious stones depicting the battle of the Titans, were the merchants, tradesmen and plebeians. Higher still were the freedmen. In these sections, smoldering rage was ready to ignite into flame. From here, occasional showers of rotted turnips rained down; Auriane and Perseus nimbly dodged them. Perseus despised Auriane the more for this fresh humiliation. Even if he dispatched her skillfully and swiftly, he feared after this day he would have no chance of ever regaining his former status.

But scattered among the plebeians were many who looked on Auriane with a pity they had shown to no other that day. This was that same gallant creature who had refused to harm the hostages during the war, the spirited rebel who had pulled down Domitian's statue. She seemed to be some naive force, unconscious as nature, harmless to everyone except Domitian, and this endeared her to them. This sprite, malign only to tyrants, was their own secret representative.

And in the upper gallery farthest from the arena, to which the women were confined, only a few shouted for Aristos. Most wailed loudly for Auriane—a cry of mourning as though she had already died. The women's seats were so distant from the arena that they could scarcely see; women's natures were held to be too delicate to withstand the sight of gore spilled on the sand—though this was not counted sufficient reason to deny good seats to the six Vestal Virgins, who sat in the lowest seats beside the imperial box, or to the women of the imperial family. Many of the women in the upper gallery threw tear-wetted handkerchiefs in the air and cried:

"She suffers enough! Set her free!" The kindliest among them left their seats in protest.

Auriane and Perseus halted beneath the imperial box. Auriane without knowing it was gradually gathering all gazes to herself; most looks were hostile, but still they were captive. As she inclined her head with almost maidenly modesty, all were rapt—it was as though her every movement were a delicate hand on a horse's rein, guiding them without their knowledge. She was like some prodigal beast-tamer who would quieten a dangerous animal with a touch or a look.

Domitian leaned forward slightly to better examine her face. You stubborn spawn of wild men! he thought. She is far from broken. She seems to gaze upon an empty throne.

He signaled a guard with a curt motion of his hand and whispered a command. It was swiftly relayed to the trainers below. He had decided she must fight without a helmet so he could better observe her face. For this was a sort of rape at a distance, and his pleasure would only come when he saw that smug composure replaced by terror and humility.

Marcus Julianus fought silently with accumulating rage. She wore little enough protection for her body as it was—that leather tunic would tear like cloth—and now she was denied even protection for her head.

The dipping, vaulting wails of the water-organ skidded to a graceless halt. In the fresh silence Auriane and Perseus chanted together: *"Salutamus te morituri"*—"We who are about to die salute you." Domitian found himself aroused by the slight roughness in her voice; one hand unconsciously kneaded the shoulder of the simpleminded boy at his feet, who looked up at him, confused.

Then the bearers presented their swords and shields. Perseus took up his Thracian sword, long and curved like a predator's claw. As Auriane closed her hand round the grip of her own weapon she saw at once the symbol of Tiwaz was not there.

She called to Glaucus, the undertrainer nearest her. They exchanged rapid-fire shouts; neither gave ground. The crowd was astir with puzzled murmurs.

Marcus Julianus understood at once. Do not give in! he urged her with all his mind. Glaucus, exasperated, motioned to Erato, who came at good speed in spite of his limp.

But Auriane did not wait for their verdict on the matter. Breaking away from Glaucus, she lifted the sword above her head, then struck it hard against the barrier. The blade snapped easily, just within the hilt. Then she half turned and stared directly at the small window covered over with a grate, where she knew Aristos watched.

That so many thousands could drop into deep silence was a wonder. Auriane halted a ritual they had never before seen interrupted. There was outrage in that hush as well as surprise, for the people regarded weapons-tampering as a hoax perpetrated directly upon themselves.

But Auriane, without realizing it, mocked Domitian. For as was customary, in a public ceremony at dawn the Emperor had inspected for soundness and sharpness all the weapons to be used in the three days of games so the people would know they were not to be cheated of blood. She made him look the fool before a throng that despised him already. A murderous flush came to Domitian's face.

"Have the man taken out," Domitian instructed the guard. "And loose the dogs on her."

Marcus Julianus prayed to his father's ghost for steadiness. Then he said casually to the company at large, "What low animal cunning, unworthy of the love that people give him!"

Domitian turned to him with a look of cold hatred, imagining Marcus Julianus referred to himself. Julianus met his eyes, his expression mild, almost bored. Montanus wondered eagerly: Perhaps it will be two for the dogs?

"*Whose* animal cunning, Marcus?" Domitian said, signaling to the guard to wait.

"Aristos', of course," Marcus Julianus replied.

Domitian's expression did not change. Aristos was his chosen favorite; as far as his own dignity was concerned, he and Aristos were one. Something bestial glittered in the Emperor's eye.

"So *you too* turn against me, in full light of day, and on the occasion of the celebration of my triumph?" The simpleminded boy became frightened and began to softly cry.

Marcus Julianus smiled amiably, tolerantly, as though amused by a clever but silly child. Montanus prayed: Minerva, if you've any power in human affairs, let this be the time that brazen conniver finally steps into the pit!

"I am only trying, in my humble fashion—" Marcus Julianus began.

"Nothing about you is humble."

"—to tell you what, *doubtless,* you already know. The family of this woman, Aurinia, and that of Aristos are mortal enemies, and have been for two generations."

Domitian's eyes narrowed. Where did Julianus obtain these trivial but often crucial scraps of information?

"And this outrage has nothing whatever to do with you, except that Aristos, in exchanging that sword, has forgotten his allegiance to you in his zeal to destroy his old enemy, and has in consequence humiliated you at your own celebration games."

Domitian looked away, frowning. It angered him that anyone else might try to kill Auriane, especially Aristos, who should be loyal and obedient. It made him feel subtly subverted, as though his favorite had stolen into the Palace at night and attempted to remove some valued possession.

"And anyway," Marcus Julianus continued, "if you give her to the dogs, you'll be doing exactly what the most ungovernable portion of this crowd *wants* you to do. They'll count it as weakness. Do you feed a recalcitrant beast when it bites its master's hand? 'If we make enough noise,' they'll say, 'he'll do our bidding.'"

Domitian looked at him blankly; there was nothing he could say to that. It worried him he had not thought of it himself. He turned away and sank sullenly back into his chair. To save his own dignity before the crowd, he ordered the herald to announce that some malefactor had tampered with the sword after its inspection and that the culprit would be caught and punished.

After a moment he turned back to Marcus Julianus.

"That Syrian girl—she's yours alone if she pleases you. I won't ever borrow her."

Marcus Julianus suppressed a smile. He knew it was the closest Domitian would ever come to an apology.

Auriane waited with growing impatience as her original sword was sought. Delays wore at the mind once she was set to begin. When at last it was brought, a great show was made of passing it up to Domitian, to satisfy the crowd that this weapon was sound.

Domitian turned the sword once in his hand; then his body stiffened. A crawling terror wormed its way into his vitals. He saw the symbol of Tiwaz. As he held the sword in his left hand, the runic sign appeared to him in reverse.

This cannot be. This is insidious!

Many years ago in the time of his father, Vespasian, when the great prophetess called the Veleda, Ramis' predecessor, was captured and brought to Rome, Domitian as a young prince had summoned her and bid her explain to him the mysteries of the runes. She cast an oracle for him and warned him that nothing was so ill-omened for him as the sign of Tiwaz, presented wrong side up. He had not, to his relief, drawn it that day. She advised him that if ever he encountered it, beware—for it meant a sword of vengeance would be turned against him.

I have received a second omen of assassination.

He realized, alarmed, that both omens were closely connected with Auriane. Uneasily, he looked down at her. And now her eyes seemed to reflect a baleful light. Who *was* this strange creature who somehow tricked him out of ordering her immediate execution, then seduced him into craving her adoration as much as he wanted her body and her death?

The sword was passed back down, and the bearer returned it to Auriane. The undertrainers then whisked off their cloaks. Perseus put on his ornamented helmet and lowered the visor, disappearing into monstrous, featureless anonymity. Then Auriane and Perseus turned. While the assistants separated them with outstretched arms, they walked to the arena's center.

The undertrainers halted, dropped their arms, and quickly backed away. And Auriane and Perseus were alone, facing each other with but five paces of sand between them.

A honeyed trill seized the stillness, and there came the hobbling throb-and-trip of a drum—the musicians had begun to play. The double flutes pulled the senses to bowstring tension.

For Auriane, the throng vanished. She stood among tall pines; her feet crushed long grass. The sword of Baldemar was in her hand. Several villagers watched raptly, concealed behind a juniper bush. And somewhere near was Decius, ready to cry instructions, should she need them. A chill northern wind stirred her braided hair; it carried the scent of yew fires. And before her was her old, old enemy, not Odberht, not Wido, but that which first drove her to spurn settled life: the dark, armed menace beyond the pines.

Her gods give her strength! Marcus Julianus prayed. *Her life is mine, and mine hers.*

CHAPTER XLVIII

Sunia could see little but the broad, sweating back of Androcles,
a surly four-time victor, planted determinedly in front of her.
Every time she fought her way forward she was roughly shouldered back. She called to Thorgild, who had managed to work his
way closer to the barred window.

"Nothing to see . . . all's quiet still," Thorgild replied irritably. But then he took pity on her and let her crawl onto his back;
she gasped with pain as muscled bodies pressed against her injured
leg. At first she saw only sand; then, some fifty paces off, she
made out the figures of Auriane and Perseus.

"Her head is bare! Where is her helmet?"

"She'd none to start," Thorgild quipped impatiently.

"But why—"

"*Why,* our know-nothing asks!" Thorgild muttered in their own
tongue. "Here we are awash in a sea of cutthroats and madmen,
and you expect what you see to fit tight to your cozy notions of
normal good sense!"

Sunia retreated back into her frantic misery. It is but a practice
bout, she assured herself as she watched Auriane and Perseus
slowly begin to move around each other with the steely poise of
panthers. Auriane can come to no harm.

White light glinted off their blades as they were touched by the
broad stream of sunlight. Auriane's pace quickened. She began
moving smoothly sideways, her head slightly raised like a beast

that scents something evil on the wind. The crowd was so hushed Sunia could hear a hawker somewhere above the second tier crying that he had sausages for sale. Auriane was moving into Perseus' sword side, her eyes just visible over the top of her oblong shield. Thorgild looked to Erato, who stood near the Gate of Death. He saw that Erato was slowly, approvingly nodding his head.

"Look at him," Thorgild whispered, nodding at Erato. "Whatever she's doing, it must be right."

A moment later Erato stopped nodding. Of course, Thorgild thought. The advantage lies with the one who strikes first. Why does she delay?

Then almost simultaneously, both sprang. Auriane was an eye-bat ahead. Thorgild saw that Erato grinned. She had timed it well.

They erupted into a frenzied engagement that called to mind birds fighting in air. Veils of sand were thrown skyward all about them.

The fast, fierce ring of steel on steel battered Sunia awake. *This is not practice.*

Just as suddenly, both withdrew. Sunia felt an ice shard lodged in her throat, so great was the effort of withholding sobs. Squinting through tears, she examined Auriane for some sign of blood. Apparently she had not been struck. Sunia looked at Erato and saw a guarded, pleased smile.

"What did she do?" Sunia asked.

Shaking his head, Thorgild replied, "Too fast for the untrained eye—Erato alone knows for certain. My guess is, she enticed a strike. You know, to find out what draws a parry. Now, hold your tongue and watch!"

The throng reacted to this opening with mild surprise; the woman almost seemed to hold her own—but they were far from convinced. Time would tell. A few who had a better comprehension of the sport looked wonderingly at Auriane, their faces suggesting they had been shown a magician's trick. In the end most of these simply dismissed what they had seen—it was impossible that she was that skilled.

Gracefully Auriane shifted direction; Perseus followed her. They moved together as if attached by a cord. Erato gave Auriane the signal that meant: *No more test encounters, you risk giving yourself away. Move according to plan.*

A change came over Auriane that was not perceptible to the crowd, but Sunia knew her well enough to know when she was not herself. She seemed to falter in midstep; then she moved like a dancer who struggles for the rhythm and cannot find it.

"What is the matter with her?" Sunia whispered to Thorgild.

"I do not know." They both looked at Erato, but his face told them nothing.

Perseus harried her with a flurry of low, rapid feints, while his trainer nodded in bland approval. Then he became impatient and attacked her with a sweeping down-cut; Sunia could hear the vicious hiss of that scimitar blade. Auriane jerked backward and met his blade not with her sword but with her shield. Sparks showered from the iron bindings. She seemed to half collapse under the blow; then, an instant too late, she engaged him. It was as if she were slung around in his wake. Contemptuous laughter came from the upper seats. "What else could be expected from her?" Sunia imagined them saying.

Perseus then directed a series of tight, fast cuts at her unprotected head. She countered by raising her shield, while retreating in a tortured zigzag path. Soon all her movements were defensive, and all those of Perseus were impatient and angry. What a fool they have made of me, matching me with this! Perseus thought as he greedily took more ground.

Auriane continued to melt away from him. He cut his way forward unopposed, using the sweeping strokes for which his sword was designed; all the while she stayed well hidden behind her shield, occasionally inserting a halfhearted thrust with her sword's point. Heads shook slowly in the throng. He was clearly much too strong an opponent for her. Soon he would have her backed against the barrier. Why was their time being wasted with this? The chant: *"Aristos! Save us!"* began anew.

In the seats reserved for Palace officials, the Finance Minister Musonius Geta fixed a murderous gaze on Erato, mentally hatching a plan to have him kidnapped and tortured slowly. This would be the last time that lowborn rapscallion trifled with him.

Sunia shielded her eyes, unable to watch. But Thorgild had put it all together. Erato was just not alarmed enough for this to be what it seemed. "She's playing a part, Sunia," he said in a low voice. "It's all right. Don't you trust her by now to know what she's about? She has him by a tether! She's dragging him right before the imperial box. And Perseus thinks he has her!"

In the imperial enclosure, Marcus Julianus, who knew of the

strategy, sat tensed to leap. She was playing the role almost too well, and it was unnerving. He fought savagely to shut off all feeling; he was but a consciousness, fiercely alert, living in her every movement, willing her to know the right moment to mount her attack.

Domitian sat forward, carried on a current of dark excitement. In his mind *he* wielded the sword that beat her into submission. Much of the dread he felt at the sight of the omen began to ease away. If she possessed terrible powers, why was she not using them now? He considered whether he should grant her life when Perseus had her at his mercy. Taken all together, she had gotten off unpunished with more misdeeds than anyone who ever crossed him. But if he allowed the death blow, then he would not be able to watch her again. And would it not be amusing to have her brought again to him tonight? Now, surely, she knew his glory and would be humble.

Do you understand now, you worthless wench? I am this city. I caused this amphitheater to be raised. I am your Lord and God.

Perseus no longer cared if he exhausted himself; the longer he took to crush her, the more his status would fall. In his frenzied attempts to herd her against the barrier he was taking three or four steps to her one—although she fought passively, he found her strangely elusive. Soon he was breathing heavily from his exertions, while Auriane had scarcely begun to tire.

And then disaster struck.

A half-dozen members of the mob, drunk on spiced wine and thoroughly bored by all this, had long been gleefully searching out some means of sabotage. At last they found it: They surrounded and captured the lottery box. After pushing past the two imperial slaves who stood guard about the ornate iron chest, they threw the lever of the spring-device that released hundreds of wooden lottery balls into the crowd. This was a means of distributing gifts to the people and was done usually at midday, never when a bout was in progress. The small spherical missiles rained down on the spectators and into the arena; each bore the name of a gift to be presented to the man who caught it. Some were commonplace, such as a cloak or an amphora of wine, but others were wonderful—a ship loaded with cargo or a seaside villa with a hundred slaves. Such things could change a man's life forever. The crowd scrambled for them like dogs after marrow bones. These things were familiar to Perseus, but not to Auriane. The air suddenly was full of strange flying objects; several struck her. And the crowd seemed afflicted with the falling sickness.

The arena's guards quickly arrested the merry culprits. But they could not undo what had been done. Auriane was wrenched from the lucid dream; instinctively she raised her shield to protect herself from the lottery balls. And Perseus seized his moment.

He slid his sword beneath hers and beat it upward. Her lower body was undefended. When that same stroke came diagonally down, it slashed across her middle from breastbone to navel. A long gash opened in her tunic; about it the leather swiftly darkened with blood. From the throng came a ravenous roar, bellowing approval.

The shock of it buckled her knees; slowly she sank to the sand. His next blow struck her shield, which, belatedly, she moved to protect her sword-side; she was knocked hard to the sand. Perseus eagerly straddled her, readying himself for a final blow to her neck.

Auriane felt every soul-weakness shaken loose; all the old poisons shot into the blood. Hertha's voice came like the hot sigh of a bellows: *"Accursed one!"*

Accept this death—it is the proper end for one who walks in shame.

Erato came at a hobbling run, hoping to stop the death blow even though he knew he could not reach them in time. Domitian felt a dark, sweet warmth flood into his loins—her fear was the finest aphrodisiac he knew. This was good. *Yes, let her die. It is meant to be.* The world has righted itself. The mocking woman's face was pushed into the mud. He felt he triumphed over all women, so smugly confident in their power to cripple a man's soul with their potent mockery and cast him off like chaff.

Marcus Julianus leapt to his feet and threw himself against the barrier.

But he knew she was done. It all came about with impossible speed. He felt the weight of the Colossus crushing his heart. His right hand found the hilt of his dagger; he tensed to spin round and sink it into the Emperor's neck. Domitian would not long outlive her. He cared not at all in that moment for the awesome consequences of the act. And so it was a dangerous moment for the world as well, brought unknowingly to the edge of civil war.

But in that moment it seemed to Auriane all the dark chambers of her soul flashed to light. The means was mysterious—whether the *aurr* completed its healing or Ramis' long-dormant purposes flowered at last, or Fria released her from some generational curse, she was never certain. With it came a clean-burning rage.

Treacherous man, taking advantage of a ruse. Vile people, laughing at life and death. You shall not have me.

She whipped over once, striking Perseus' shin with her shield, dimly aware she lashed out at her own shame, that she killed Hertha within her, *and would not hear her voice again.* Then she sprang nimbly up and landed in a spray of sand, positioned at the precise distance that was ideal for her short sword—and too close for Perseus' long, curved blade.

Perseus' death stroke sank harmlessly into the sand. A groan of surprise issued from the crowd.

Then she advanced with tightly controlled violence, her anger only increasing her swiftness and accuracy, and began battering her way into his territory. Perseus' movements were at first fitful, hesitant, as he struggled with the shock of surprise. *What possessed her?* A larger soul seemed to inhabit that body now.

Perseus' trainer looked on, stupefied to stillness, arms limp at his sides. The crowd seemed to collectively draw in a breath, as if they watched a racehorse burst from a standstill into an exuberant gallop. Her blade whipped about like some ecstatic dancer; there was something refined yet relentless in that blinding complexity of strokes. Erato followed ten paces off, nodding eagerly, approving her strategy: She crowded him, giving him no room to maneuver his longer blade, pummeling him with a rapid-fire series of savage backstrokes that allowed him no time to recover. When she had numbed him into believing she would carry on in this fashion indefinitely, she lashed out with her sword's stabbing point and struck flesh, a hand's breadth beneath his collarbone.

Now his blood was on her blade. At the sight of it, eager moans rose up from the throng. She never slowed; Perseus found himself consistently a half stroke behind. If he defended against a thrust, she was beginning a cut; if he attempted a cross-stroke, she trapped it before it began. It was like a violent dispute in which one person shouts, forcing the other to listen. He began to take small, crabbed back-steps, his sword flailing ineffectually, his blade a fugitive now, reduced to running and dodging.

Many found themselves slowly lifted to their feet. They witnessed a thing that could not be. The power of that assault was strangely compelling, like a cry of war trumpets or a chariot team surging into the lead on the last round. It appealed to a commonly sensed need to burst free of pain and darkness; they exulted with her, feeling they beat down their own misery. They seemed utterly to have forgotten that moments ago they despised her, so carelessly changeable were they in their affections. Hands that had just pitched rotten turnips were now clenched into fists, urging her on. Mouths that had shouted: *"Set the dogs on her!"* now cried: *"Get him, Aurinia! Kill him! Our darling! You are our own!"* The cries gathered momentum until they became one rebellious roar of approval and delight.

This acted upon Auriane in a way she could never have guessed—she found it unexpectedly intoxicating to know her every movement controlled a thousand throats. The power of every stroke seemed gloriously magnified by the cheers it brought. Waves of applause bore her up and carried her along at racing speed. For a few moments she felt she held the world permanently at bay. There was no room in her for the irony of it all: that here, in this place that was the heart of her lifelong enemy's house, she at last felt triumphantly safe.

Domitian looked on with sharp uneasiness. Each new surge of cheering goaded him to greater gloom. Those baleful spirits of the north had aided her, after all. She was a scourge, a blight, like some dread foreign disease unknowingly brought home from a war that manifests itself later when you count yourself safe at home.

Foretell my death, will you? I shall foretell yours. And cleanse you from our midst.

The surge of love and relief that Marcus Julianus felt was short-lived. He saw Domitian sat as if braced against a mortal enemy; in his eye was that primitive look that always heralded the meting out of gruesome punishments.

Domitian motioned to a guard and issued an order: Marcus Julianus heard only the name Antaeus, but this was enough. He deduced Domitian meant to set Antaeus the net-fighter against her when this bout was done, and doubtless he would continue to send in new opponents until she died either of exhaustion or wounds. He had feared even before this day that Domitian might use her this way, and he had carefully prepared for this turn of events.

Marcus Julianus signaled discreetly to one of his own servants who stood quietly in the shadowy rear of the imperial box. His voice covered by the din, he put an encouraging hand on the man's shoulder and said, "We're going to have to do it, after all. Go up there directly and speak to no one on the way. *Quickly now!*"

Julianus' servant unobtrusively fled the cubicle; all in the box were too engrossed in the drama below to pay him any mind.

Auriane had driven Perseus to the arena's center. Erato still followed her like a dog at heel, frantically signaling to her to slow her pace. He was greatly concerned by her wound. Was the lung pierced, or the stomach? She must conserve herself and end this bout quickly. And he wanted the full extent of her ability kept secret as possible.

Then Perseus slipped and fell hard onto his back. The slaves who turned the sand between the morning and afternoon shows had neglected to remove the shallowly buried intestines of a rhinoceros, disemboweled by a skilled animal-baiter. At this, joyous wolf-yelps arose from the crowd. Perseus was done. It did not matter that he slipped accidentally; once a bout began, no misfortune occasioned pity. Laughter was mingled with the cry, *"Habet!"* — "She has him!" They did not expect Auriane to pause for the vote. Had *he* paused, when she had been at his mercy? Tentative shouts of *"Aurinia, victor!"* rose from the plebeian seats. The women in the high places shouted praises to Juno, protector of women in peril, and tossed silken handkerchiefs by the hundreds; they drifted like butterflies down onto the mortal play far below.

But Auriane halted and lowered her sword. The crowd seemed to deflate like a bellows; cheers were replaced by murmurs of confusion.

Then she took a step backward and paused, standing quietly straight and still, giving Perseus room to rise. Her chest heaved as she struggled for breath; her cheek was ashen from loss of blood. A sweat-darkened strand freed itself from her tightly bound hair and hung wearily down.

"Auriane, no!" Erato screamed, vigorously shaking his head. Gallantry was foolish. It was never returned. The roads into the city were lined with the grave-markers of those who had let another live, only to be killed later by that same man.

In the viewing chamber Sunia heard a voice in the close-packed room mutter, "She's got less wit than an addled hare! She throws away victory!"

And Sunia was amazed to hear herself shout in reply: "That would be no victory! Who do you think she is? One of *you*?"

After a moment Perseus staggered up like a man under a too-heavy load. The halt allowed Auriane time to become conscious of her wound. Her blood felt hot where it matted her tunic to her skin. Nausea gripped her. The floor of the arena seemed to tilt. The pain was like molten needles thrust into her stomach. She struggled for that sense of wild freedom she had felt only moments ago, but all the strength seemed to have drained from her arms. Despair crept up on her from behind; the whole world began to seem grotesque and wrong.

This place is haunted and god-cursed. I want to be quit of it.

Gradually she became aware the throng was raising a more insistent clamor than any she had heard that day.

The always-unpredictable crowd decided to heartily approve her refusal to strike a man who was down. They saw it as a show of supreme confidence, an act of antique gallantry of the sort often praised by the historians. It was just the sort of reckless disregard for survival bound to win their most enduring love. Had she deliberately planned this, she could not have found a surer means of winning the wild devotion of all ranks, even the most doubtful of the Praetorian Guards.

Marcus Julianus thought: By all the gods, it is the most intelligent thing she could have done. She hardly needs my help! She was born knowing how to incite a crowd's love.

Auriane and Perseus crashed together like wearied, battling stags, striking with less force as both lost breath and blood. The spectators in the lower seats, anxious for her safety now, shouted helpful instructions: *"Watch him now, that's the first attack! Backstroke! Now thrust!"* Erato glared at them, motioning for silence, fearful they would confuse her, but Auriane knew nothing but the random staccato of striking blades. Knowing time ran out with her blood, she put her whole mind to sensing an opening for a mortal blow, inhabiting Perseus, feeling his humiliation, his sour hatred, letting his rhythm become her own. And then it was time.

She advanced, keeping her sword and shield too low, intentionally putting herself in distance. As she intended, he aimed a cut at her neck. In rapid succession she sliced upward, hitting his sword at right angles with a resounding clang; then in one fluid motion she slid her blade along his and feigned an attack to his right shoulder, her purpose to induce him to move his shield. It succeeded. He whipped it laterally to stop a blow that never came. For in the same instant she wrenched her body to the left and with one quick, precise movement thrust the point of her short sword into his naked chest. Both knew at once the wound was mortal.

Curses on all the gods. I missed the heart. He will die slowly.

An almost awkward quiet settled over them both. Then she took a step forward and knocked his sword out of his hand with one hard down-stroke, a precaution of long habit. Weaponless, Perseus sank to his knees, then rolled onto his back. She stood over him, feeling vaguely uncomfortable, as if she played a role meant for another.

We had no blood-debt between us! Will I be cursed?

Perseus' twisting body made her think of a dying wasp. Death was ever a stalking mystery, and in spite of her weariness she felt a fearful reverence.

You were a man-creature, no wasp, whoever you were, and so are deserving of some god's grace. You fought well enough. Now die in peace.

Tumult and confusion rushed in. A slave garbed as Mercury, the conductor of souls to Hades, removed the dying man's helmet and pulled back his head, exposing his throat for the finishing stroke. The throng chanted *"Ave Aurinia, victor!"* and *"Long live Aurinia, our dearest, our darling!"* In one moment she was carried off by the strangeness of it all. Who are these people, and who am I? she thought as she fought to stand upright; once again the floor of the arena pitched like some ship at sea. They are the enemy of all my life, the enemy of my mother's mothers, my father's fathers, and yet they praise me in words they might use with a goddess.

Perseus' right hand struggled up, trembling; slowly he raised an index finger. The cursing finger, Auriane thought, confused at first. Then she realized this was the plea for mercy. She turned her face from his death-ridden eyes, fearing that vindictive soul.

Someone in the lower seats shouted down, *"Cut his throat! Kill the cunning wolf that tried to murder our poor Aurinia!"* His words echoed the feelings of others. The crowd looked to Domitian to see his verdict but the Emperor sat woodenly, seeming too contemptuous of it all to want any part of the vote. The people took the initiative then; everywhere, rapidly, thumbs were turning down.

The trainer called Glaucus gave Auriane a hard shove. "Are you moonstruck? Do as they bid! *Finish him!"*

Erato gripped her shoulders, steadying her. "Auriane, do what you must." Auriane looked at the broad, glistening chest streaming with blood, the thick throat struggling for air. She threw down her sword in disgust. Then she bent over and quietly vomited.

"She is beyond help!" muttered Glaucus. Erato, embarrassed for her, opened his cloak and tried to shield her from view, but the crowd saw, and laughed tolerantly. A number of them even started clapping. This crowd has lost its wits, Erato thought. She is sick and they applaud!

Glaucus shouted at her: "Do you know what *this* means, Daughter-of-a-Mule?" He thrust his downturned thumb into her face and forced the sword back into her hand.

Auriane's voice was numbed and indifferent. "A curse unto nine generations upon one who strikes a foe who cannot strike back."

"What'd she say?" shouted Glaucus' assistant, cupping an ear.

"Some barbarian gabble," Glaucus muttered, grasping Auriane's wrist and wrenching her forward until she nearly stumbled over the dying man. "You're not out in the woods with animals anymore and so to Hades with your nine-generations' curses— they don't work here! You're among regular, civilized men, and their thumbs are *down*. Now cut his *throat,* you daughter of flea-ridden baboons!" He kicked her.

Auriane whirled on him. But Erato lunged at her and caught her arm, stopping the blow and pulling her off balance. Auriane fell on top of Glaucus; Erato fell on her. Erato managed to pry the sword from her hand. But then she seized Glaucus by the throat. The crowd responded with delighted laughter; it put them in mind of the antics of a mime troupe.

"Get him, Aurinia!" came the crowd's exuberant cries. *"Our dearest! Kill them, Aurinia! Kill, kill, kill them all!"*

Erato and the assistant pulled on her with all their strength; gradually she released her grip on Glaucus' neck.

"You little fool, you're throwing away all you've gained!" Erato cried out at her. But as soon as he spoke, Erato realized the people did not care.

It is incredible, he thought. I have seen men pelted with garbage for ignoring the demands of the crowd. Instead, she in a moment makes willfulness the fashion. She owns them completely! They will forgive her anything.

Amidst the confusion an undertrainer crept close to Perseus and unobtrusively did what Auriane would not, dispatching him with a quick dagger stroke. Then a boy wearing a grinning mask of Charon, the Etruscan death demon, touched Perseus with a hot brand to be certain he was dead. Four morgue workers rushed forward; unceremoniously they hauled the body up and dropped it into one of the wooden caskets. All the while Erato fought desperately to contain Auriane, pinning her arms behind her back, fearful she might strike out blindly at everyone within reach.

"Bring before me the man who threw the wooden balls!" she was shouting. "Let the miserable niding answer to me now!"

"It is done, and you won! Stop fighting!" Erato pleaded with her. "Get the palm, and quickly! That wound must be tended to!"

Gradually her rage subsided; she felt emptied of all feeling. Glaucus replaced the scarlet cloak about her shoulders. Leaning heavily on Erato, she moved toward the imperial box and stood quivering and still. With one hand she gathered up the cloth of the cloak and held it to the wound to staunch the flow of blood. She noticed, alarmed, that Marcus Arrius Julianus was no longer there. When had he left, and why? She felt the dull loneliness of one who returns from a hunt to find the hall deserted and the hearth fire cold.

One of Domitian's disdainful white-liveried servants approached with mincing step, bearing the victory palm. But as Auriane reached for it, he let it drop to the sand as he had been coached to do. Then the herald announced from the imperial box: "This woman disobeyed the order to kill. Let it be known—she shall not have this victory. Let the record read: Perseus: perished—Aurinia: defeated."

The crowd paused like some great ponderous beast annoyed and perplexed by a barrier in its path. Then they gathered their energy and charged on through.

"Aurinia, victor!" came the raw cries. *"She needs no palm!"*

Erato thought worriedly: Then that scoundrel Musonius Geta neither wins nor loses. But he cannot justly charge *this* to me. Then, when was that man ever fair or just?

The herald continued, "And now we grant her yet another chance to prove her mettle. . . . Enter, Antaeus!"

"What madness?" Erato shouted, turning quickly around. He saw the door of the gladiators' entrance was slowly being pulled open. And there stood Antaeus with net and trident, eager and untired. *"No!"* he cried. "This cannot be!"

As surprise and outrage traveled through the multitudes, the throng's aspect became black and threatening as a swift-gathering storm. And then, high in the plebeian seats, a small, determined group began a new and purposeful chant: *"Aurinia, victor! Ave Imperator Domitianus, Germanicus,* Ruler of All, Lord and God, Conqueror of Germania!"

Domitian was jerked from his sullen fog. He blinked, then sat forward in disbelief. He must not have heard correctly.

But no. There it was again.

Were those villains at last granting him his title? And admitting that his victory was as great as his cursed brother's? Could they finally be repenting of their treasonable rebelliousness?

The cry continued, rising in intensity. *At last. Love, freely offered.* Domitian believed it to be spontaneous praise, a change of heart brought about by his "gift" of Auriane.

But in fact it was anything but spontaneous. All had been carefully planned, and the men in the plebeian seats who began the chant were all in Marcus Julianus' pay. This was his last, desperate plan to save Auriane from Domitian's wrath.

The cry was taken up rapidly and soon it rang out nearly in unison; a mountain of sound rose up, praising the glory of the Chattian war. For as Marcus Julianus hoped, those not party to the ruse quickly saw what a fine game this was. It was as though the same thought occurred simultaneously in seventy thousand minds. They had at last found a way to strike back at the tyrant. How amusing to trap him by giving him what he long craved, for the sake of this woman who was his Nemesis.

Domitian scowled, pinned between rage and satisfaction. The words were like honeyed wine to him; he drank long drafts and soon was thoroughly intoxicated. So great was his need that it dulled his perception—he was not alert to devious intent. What amazed him most was that even the Senators took up the cry. For Auriane's sake, they even forgave him the necessary purging of Gallus. At long last they acknowledged his natural greatness! For the first time he took his rightful place beside his father and brother.

Domitian examined Auriane's face, pale as milk against the blood red of her cloak. *They loved her that much, and him, for providing her?* Not even Aristos brought him this sort of adoration. He felt like a man whose resources have been rapidly dwindling who suddenly finds a rich new source of income. She began to look subtly different to him: more biddable, more vulnerable. Her insolence began to seem the harmless precocity of a child. He marveled at how she seemed possessed of a curious, indefinable mixture of dark and light, of frustration and satisfaction promised at once. *She can keep her wretched life,* he thought, but *she's still not getting that wretched palm.*

He sent an order to the herald, who hastily announced the officials of the games had miscalculated the duration of the events to come, and there was not time for the bout with Antaeus. In response, the throng shouted his name and the title, *"Germanicus"* with such savage energy that he knew he had chosen the wisest course of action.

Auriane departed through the Victory Gate, aided by Erato. Though guards barred every entrance, somehow the crowds always managed to get through, and they swarmed about her, clutching at her and kissing her as Erato tried in vain to fend them off. Some had iron shears in their hands and began cutting pieces from her cloak. Two women attacked her from behind, pulling at her knotted hair, desperate for a lock. _"The hair of a first-time victor wards off the evil eye"_ she remembered Celadon telling her once.

A first-time victor. The beast has swallowed me whole and I am one of them now. I do not want to be in their songs. I do not ever want Avenahar to know what her mother was made to do. And yet I feel I climbed to a high place. I feel a warrior's pride when perhaps I should not. Baldemar, what in the name of Helle would you say if you looked on this grotesque victory?

When Auriane entered the passage that connected the Gate of Victory with the gladiators' entrance, Erato gave her over to two burly Greek physician's assistants, commanding them, "Take her quickly, before the gods do!" The assistants guided her firmly through the passage; one had a walking stick with a sharpened end, which he used to fend off the crowd.

They had not gone far when the mass of people ahead became like some retreating wave, hindering them, then pulling them back a step. Auriane realized the people backed away to clear a path for someone. Talk became muted suddenly; Auriane saw every head turn in one direction. A man tall enough to see down the passage announced: _"Aristos!_ Stand off from him! He's in choleric temper. Yes, he's provoked about something!"

Auriane stiffened, drawing strength from that despised name. Before the physician's assistants realized what she was doing she seized the walking stick and wrest herself free of them. They broke into a stream of curses that made her grateful she knew no Greek. She strode into the space left open for Aristos and stood alone, her body bent slightly against the pain of her wound as she leaned on the walking stick. Her hair, now half pulled from its knot, hung raggedly, with tufts sticking out where her locks had been cut. Her bloody cloak looked like it had suffered a dog attack.

First she saw Aristos' ruffians. Among them were an acrobat escaped from a rich man's troupe, said to be clever at combining somersaults and murder; a boxer with ears and nose battered into baker's dough, who was in the habit of grinning broadly to show off his gold false teeth; a Syrian-born charioteer barred forever from the Circus for poisoning his opponents' horses, and an assortment of cutpurses and graverobbers who had survived their condemnation to the arena. They called out: *"Make way! Make way!"* mimicking the lictors who walked ahead of the great magistrates in the city's streets. Auriane realized every one of them had perfected a strikingly accurate imitation of Aristos' walk. As ever, he draws to himself lost and frightened men anxious to remake themselves in his image.

And then came Aristos himself with ponderous, deliberate steps, so like that of a man pulling his feet out of sticky mud. This party halted ten paces off from Auriane.

Aristos regarded her with legs planted belligerently apart. For a flash of an instant archaic darkness glinted in those eyes and Odberht was revealed, crude, half-formed, a vengeful ghoul that had lost its human face, a soul that was a sink of putrefying resentments bottomless as the bogs. Then deftly he shifted to his present persona—and it was Aristos who nodded knowingly, giving her a slow, cruel smile touched with urbane amusement. A leopardskin was thrown carelessly over his heavy shoulders, further accentuating their breadth; the beast's head, with the upper teeth still attached, hung down and rested against his massive arm. She saw this life's foreign luxuries had thickened him in the middle; he required a longer belt to gird his tunic than when she last encountered him in their own country. His hair had begun its slow retreat, rendering more formidable yet a forehead so heavy of bone it looked as though it could withstand hammer blows. His gray-blond hair hung in matted ropes straight to his shoulders, for he discovered his women followers admired his long locks. Burn scars mottled his thick forearms, the legacy of drunken tests of valor in which he held his arm over a lamp flame to awe his companions. A scent drifted from him not unlike that of a team of horses after completing the Circus' seven rounds. About his neck on a greasy leather thong hung a preserved wolf's muzzle, an amulet to protect him from sorcery.

"Greetings to Auriane!" he said grandly as a herald, "daughter of Baldemar of noblest rank, flower of numerous illustrious kin—numerous, that is, if she has not murdered them all by now!" His flatterers laughed dutifully.

Auriane was surprised to discover this spear thrust had no sting.

Where is the shame of all my life? Perhaps I truly *have* left it behind.

"Is she not beautiful?" Aristos went on, grinning. "I think the ravens of Wodan got tired of pursuing her and decided to nest in her hair!" He broke into his sharp, barking laugh—that laugh was ever a weapon. "And that is a fetching cloak! I think that bloodstains truly become you, Auriane. Except for the ones on your hands, that can't be washed off!"

Furious that she did not respond to his taunts, his rage rose like a rash.

"Daughter of trolls!" he bellowed. *"Get your skulking shadow out of my path before I twist your neck like a chicken's!"*

Many in the crowd visibly shrank back, but Auriane felt her capacity for terror had been drained off with the last of her strength. She held his gaze steadily, evenly. From the crowd came a distinct voice: "A pity. If our poor Aurinia had as much common sense as she has mettle, she might live till the sun sets!"

Finally Auriane spoke, her voice flat with exhaustion. "Odberht, son of Wido, I greet you. Twice now you tried to murder me in the dark—once by poison, and today by trickery. I give you a chance to try in the light, with honorable weapons of war. In the name of our whole tribe whom you betrayed, before Wodan I challenge you to single battle. Choose a day."

"How about today!" the Acrobat called out merrily.

The boxer gave a braying laugh, and all Aristos' companions joined in. Yet their laughter died quickly for lack of support; the crowd stood in taut silence. But most importantly to his entourage, Aristos did not laugh. They were mystified by this. He stood with head lowered like a beast at bay, looking less like a man confronted with a silly woman who was half dead and more like a man who has been ambushed.

Aristos could not cease being a man of his tribe; he had too much fearful respect for the rite of vengeance to simply ignore her declaration. But he knew also that he could not fight her. He might have cheerfully hacked her to pieces in their own country if that was what she really wanted, but he would not do it here. He noticed at once that in this place women were not counted so holy as among his own people; they did not speak the law here or dispense justice, nor was their counsel sought in grave matters. Incredibly, these people even went to war without listening first to the prophetic utterings of the women—and he knew as well these people saw something faintly ridiculous in women carrying a sword. Disposing of her by the light of day would bring him no honor in this country; it would be as though he accepted the challenge of a thrall.

But *he* knew, if these ignorant Romans did not, that all women possessed uncanny powers, and this one in particular had walked with Ramis, whose name was like a chilly hand on the back of his neck. No matter what the customs here, a sorceress was still a sorceress and Auriane was Auriane. He was pinned between the ancient ways, alive in him still, and this glorious present which he dared not risk. It was confusing and terrifying.

This crazed spawn of Baldemar pursues me to the ends of the earth. She and that flea-ridden hag Ramis should be buried alive together, safely out of the sight of men.

He made a sweeping gesture with a hairy hand. "Stand aside! I've no time for silly women."

He started forward, then stopped again, scowling. What was the wretched woman doing now? Walking stick in hand, she was tracing signs in the sand and dirt of the travertine floor.

Vile witch-woman! he thought, his heart clenching like a fist. She was drawing rune signs across the passage—those sinister glyphs that could disorder a man's fate, foretell the future, or throw the natural world out of joint. He recognized the sign for Tiwaz, spirit of battle; the rest was a mystery—the mastery of runes was for sorceresses and priests of Wodan, not honest warriors. He guessed it was a cursing formula, doubtless promising his bones would melt and his blood turn to dust if he did not answer her challenge before the next dark of the moon.

When Auriane had finished, she moved aside, making way for him. Clever demon woman, he thought. She was forcing him to step over the runes.

Aristos' entourage began to cast curious glances at him. Why did he hesitate? Aristos wanted with all his mind not to step over those dread signs; he was certain that if he did, they would be activated and would begin to work their will upon him—or else why had she written them where she had? But now even the crowd seemed puzzled by his hesitation. *Witless fools!* he thought. You know nothing of the terrible powers of runes. When Aristos heard someone whisper loudly, "What is the matter with him?" he gathered up all his courage and swaggered forth, sarcasm in his step. As he passed, Auriane saw that his lips moved in a silent incantation, and his right hand was clamped tightly round the preserved wolf's muzzle.

The crowd gave Aristos ample room to pass. Auriane sank slowly to her knees; the two physician's assistants caught her up just as her eyes became sightless. Two more hospital servants entered the passage with a rude litter and they hastily laid Auriane upon it. Then all four trotted briskly off with her. She was worth considerably more now than she had been this morning, and they would be punished if they lost her.

Already Aristos' flatterers were busy telling tales of this encounter with an eye to pleasing their master. "I was there—I saw it all!" they would proclaim to all who would listen. "You've never seen such low cunning, married to such presumption! This barbarian wench manages to run poor Perseus through because the wretched fellow slips and falls—and then she comes out and barks at Aristos! This morning I saw a small bitch-dog yapping at an elephant—do you suppose it was an omen?" This, among the followers of Aristos, became the accepted version of the bout with Perseus.

Auriane was taken to the school's hospital rooms with their penetrating smells of resins and herbal powders, and laid in one of the chambers reserved for the dressing of wounds. While she was still unconscious, one of the school's first physicians quickly cut away the leather tunic and began applying strips of wool soaked in deer's rennet and vinegar to halt the bleeding. Auriane awakened and cried out when the stinging vinegar was pressed into the wound, for it was more painful than Perseus' blade.

After a short time Erato entered and sent the school's physician from the chamber. Erato then ushered in Anaxagoras of Cos, followed by five of his highly skilled slaves—that same Anaxagoras who was the author of a hundred and more books on the medical arts, whose name had become legendary among physicians after he saved the life of the King of Parthia when all the court physicians had failed. He happened to be in Rome because Domitian had summoned him to minister to a favorite concubine.

"What in the name of Venus is *he* doing here?" one of the school's subordinate physicians muttered to another. "Only emperors and kings can afford his fees."

Erato alone knew Anaxagoras had been hastily sent for by Marcus Arrius Julianus, and he was sworn to strictest silence. It was not a situation likely to arouse too much comment, for everyone knew traveling physicians were drawn to gladiatorial schools after days of games. They came to study anatomy if they were young or to experiment with new techniques of suturing and wound-dressing if they were famous and established, for nowhere but in Alexandria was dissection of the human body permitted.

Anaxagoras first ordered the school's pots of powders and resins removed. He would use nothing from the stores; he brought his own medicines. A physician could never be sure of the purity of his potions and drugs; a good part of the secret of Anaxagoras' effectiveness was the excellence of his suppliers, who, along with his herbal formulae, were close-kept secrets. He allowed no one but his own slaves to come near Auriane.

The two subordinate physicians watched raptly from a safe distance as Anaxagoras took a wound probe from his instrument kit and examined the long cut to make certain no foreign matter had entered. To their surprise Anaxagoras used no prayers or charms; he seemed to rely solely upon his superior knowledge. When he was assured no vital place was struck, he called for iris oil in which he dissolved terebinth resin pure as Attic honey; with this he cleansed the wound. Then he applied to it a sponge soaked in the juice of the poppy to dull the pain, and ordered his slaves to boil bark of elm for a decoction to close the wound. When Anaxagoras began to stitch the wound with human hair, the spying physicians were seen and driven out; they nearly stumbled over Sunia, who stood vigil outside the door.

Sunia tried to steal inside then, but was roughly driven back by Anaxagoras' slaves. All that day and the next, whenever Sunia could evade the sharp eyes of the chief cook, she returned to that door, imagining her spirit somehow enfolded and protected Auriane's. At first she thought with confidence: *Auriane is a chieftain's daughter, and so, of course, she will heal quickly.* But Sunia's hopes began to wane on the second day, when the grim expressions on the faces of Anaxagoras' slaves did not change.

You who protected me so well—for you I can do nothing! You are all our country. You are the sunward slope, the spring stars, the hearth of hearths. Stay with us. If your life is taken, I'll not survive you long. But what god will listen to my prayers? I am of no importance. Still I must pray on and hope some bird or butterfly will carry my words to Fria. Live, great and good friend.

Sunia was greatly pleased when she realized crowds of curious people began to gather outside the main entrance of the school, anxious to know if "their Aurinia" would recover. They were a mix of poor artisans, young aristocratic ladies, Palace officials, and overdressed young men reeking of perfumes. Many silently deposited palm branches at the door, in quiet protest of Domitian's refusal to award her the palm. The young men left rolled love messages, and scattered wildflowers across the entrance. Sunia was not surprised Auriane had become a celebrated woman in this odd country, for to be renowned was no more than her fate—and, of course, her fate could be expected to reassert itself in any new place.

On the third day, when the door was thrown open but a moment, Sunia heard Anaxagoras saying with sharp annoyance, "I ordered this given five times a day."

"For what purpose?" a slave-assistant replied. "You said by evening, she would be gone."

Then Sunia heard no more; she collapsed to the stone floor as consciousness gently left her.

CHAPTER XLIX

Auriane cried out in her own tongue, frightening Anaxagoras' assistants, whom she imagined were Helle's black dogs rending her flesh because she slew a man with whom she had no blood debt. She despised sleep, for she dreamed of a bloody sun at World's End and the jaws of the Great Wolf gaped wide as he swallowed molten rivers in which her people were thrashing and drowning. In her brief moments of wakefulness she realized she had lost forever a thing she never realized she possessed: a pure trust that she could not be grievously wounded.

I can be drawn like kine. I am a pitiful sack of sinew. My body is a membrane precariously full of blood. I am pitiful flesh quivering at the touch of the sacrificial knife. I am not swift—death is swifter. I no longer have the heart for this! The arena is a rogue stallion that threw me to the ground and battered me with iron hooves—all love, all striving cannot make me climb onto that broad back again.

What was more terrifying still was that she wondered if it mattered.

It must matter. To deny Baldemar vengeance is to deny him meat and mead. I owe him Odberht's death or . . . or *what?* she thought as Odberht's form dissolved into a multitude of ills: Storm, plague, famine—he was a force, faceless as nature, a process, not a man, killing randomly, innocently, like winter snow—*and does one challenge the drifts to single battle?*

She felt a surge of anxiety. *These are nidings' thoughts. This must be how they weaken themselves and turn from honor.*

She smelled the steam of Anaxagoras' acrid preparations, heard the soft flow of his assistants' voices, felt ministering hands—and wondered why they struggled to keep her alive, for now she was no one. If she peered into a looking glass, she would find it empty. Certainties were clouds pulling apart and randomly re-forming. What *was* honor? Was it not after all a sort of blindness?

Ramis, look on your victory. . . . You have won! I do question that which I desire. What is becoming of me? I am falling into stars.

It is far simpler to let this wound carry me off than to find the horizon line again. Fria, let me die.

But she dreamed then of her daughter, Avenahar, a woman grown, bent sorrowing over her mother's cairn. Her mother did not lie beneath for she had died in a foreign land. Snow flurries came and Auriane knew her daughter was alone, bereft of kin, and would die of the cold.

Next she saw herself at a venerable age, dressed in the gray robes of the highest Holy Ones, her hair proudly white. In her hand was a knotted staff of hazelwood studded with amber—Ramis' own staff. She moved through the throng to speak the law at the Assembly. Avenahar was there, in the midst of her many children. Proudly Avenahar pointed out her mother to the people.

Auriane knew she was meant to choose.

Her ghost deliberated. Then it shrugged, shouldered the burden once more, and walked toward the gray-robed Holy One.

I will live on a while, then—not for Ramis' riddling reasons, but for one small, urgent one. I want to see the color of Avenahar's eyes.

Simultaneously, Anaxagoras bent over her wound, sniffed it, lightly prodded it, then drew in a breath and exclaimed, "This cannot be!"

When he had examined it at midnight, the suppurations were of the evil sort—thin and malodorous. Had he dreamed it? The wound was of angry appearance still, and beset with ill humors, but now the suppurations were *bona*—healthy and white— signifying that the wound would heal. Certain he had effected one more miraculous cure, Anaxagoras sent a messenger to awaken Erato with the great news.

At the moment of choosing life, Auriane slept soundly, bliss- fully, and in the diffuse blackness, anguish softened to pleasure.

Before her was a silvery temple with columns delicate as snow-laced branches; over it was poised a sickle-moon, in the time of waxing. Beyond lay fields over which hooded figures walked in procession, bearing fertile cakes, preparing for the old rite of the Sacred Marriage, that magic mixing of woman and man that flowered into the firmament, joining the earth to the sun so all life could increase. Kinship overflowed like mead from a cask and embraced even the humblest of animals. One of the spectral hooded figures beckoned her into the temple-house; with dream-knowledge she knew it was Marcus Julianus. *We have come together, then, to lead each other to the gods.*

But I do not deserve to go within. A father's blood stains my hands.

She felt his firm reply: *Not so.* Here I shall remain until you know your own goodness and grace.

She opened her eyes. Within moments, life settled back on her shoulders like a sack of stones; her near-death dreams retreated to pleasant, distant impossibility. She felt for her resolve. It was there. What was gone — cut away by Perseus' blade — was her trust in her body's inviolability. It was no longer whole. It was a wellspring of pain, vulnerable and unlovely.

She looked about and saw the room was full of gifts from lowly admirers — terra-cotta figurines of humbler gods whose powers promoted healing, dried flowers and honey cakes, cups of colored glass, bronze Celtic mirrors, silver necklets, pots of incense, slender-necked bottles of perfume. The richer gifts, she later learned, had been removed, but whether they had been stolen by Anaxagoras' servants or impounded by the financial officers of the school, she never determined.

She quickly learned she had passed from slavery's anonymity to a dubious and precarious renown. Whether they ridiculed her or thought her wondrous, the people knew her name and invoked it to some purpose, most often to slyly express their loathing of Domitian. Women had since the time of Nero been regularly exhibited in the amphitheater, often in a spirit similar to that of the contests of monkeys that fought with javelins — as a mockery of the shows in earnest to follow. She was accorded more honor than this, but still there was no recognized place for her; she was intruder, talisman, prodigy, or emissary of fate, but never a common veteran of the Third Hall. And in the First, she was viewed as no more than a low jest of Erato's, a novelty run amok who had better not overestimate her worth. She had made a place for herself that was uniquely her own.

Her new status brought small comforts—meat and fowl were served in the Third Hall's dining chamber and wine that did not burn the throat. The cell that housed her was twice the size of the former one, and its narrow window was set low enough so that she could even look out on the city. Sunia was brought to it and so lived with her once again, without Auriane having to ask. The pallets had cushions stuffed with feathers instead of straw and there was even a lamp, though no one ever brought oil so it could be put to use. And the rats seemed unwilling to climb this high. Never had either of them since their enslavement known such comfort. And still gifts came steadily: jars of honey, cloaks of softest wool, gaudy birds, and love poems penned on fine vellum.

How odd, Auriane reflected, to be celebrated and a criminal at once. Status in this place was like hollow bangles that glittered and caught every eye—no one believed for a moment that they truly had value. It was so unlike her own country, where status was a thing of sober weight and low luster, like a bar of gold.

In the months to follow she hid her wound from all eyes, even Sunia's; it was her secret horror, a puckered, livid thing that marked her as broken, infirm. Victor or no, its lingering pain made her feel only defeat. Her mangled body made her spirit sense itself as mangled also, as if the one impressed itself upon the other—in the deeps of the mind, she knew the two were tied. And did not the gods determine such misfortunes? The damage *must* also embrace her soul. There began then a slow, festering conviction that Marcus Julianus did not know just how pitifully marred she was—a growing certainty that when he saw, he would not want her.

These new doubts drove her to observe carefully the Roman women who crowded the street beneath her newly acquired window. She began to torment herself with the ways that they differed from her: their plush white arms, dimpled and jeweled. Their boneless hands that never grasped rein, hoe, or spear. Their smaller, more delicate constitutions, coupled with that worldly lift of the chin that caused idlers to make way before them. The lilting gestures, practiced as a dancer's, that accompanied their exuberant speech. Their boundless, mysterious stores of knowledge—of the language of the great-houses, of how to decipher a love message, of how to cleverly drape and wind bright clothing, of all that occurred in this city, and why. *They are his people. They are far more suited to him than I.*

These doubts fed and grew fat in the days that followed, in spite of the fact that Marcus Julianus sent her small gifts—useful things, well made but not too fine, to prevent their being stolen: a well-woven blanket, or fur-lined slippers—so that she would not feel he had forgotten her. For he made no arrangements, as he had promised, to pass a night with her. Before the wound, she might have persuaded herself there was some good reason for this. Now, she could scarcely hear her own assurances.

The news of Auriane's recovery was conveyed to Aristos as he was being massaged in the warm rooms of the school's baths. He rose up in a fury and strode off to a grimy tavern on Tanner's Street frequented by veterans of the First Hall. From a Samnite fighter called the Cyclops he learned the name of a fearsome Etruscan witch, a woman named Haruna, along with uncertain directions to her dwelling in the Subura district. Her services were dear. But she was so effective in laying curses that the Finance Minister Musonius Geta once employed her, as did a certain Senator, whom the Cyclops would not name for fear of being accused of defaming a member of the nobility.

The following day Aristos found Haruna with great difficulty, for she had moved again, as she was forced to do often, because her neighbors drove her out when they tired of the stench of her noxious potions. She was nearly bald and shriveled as a dried fig. Her rags were ready to rot off her body, which he thought unaccountable, for she could have purchased decent garments with the fortune in gold about her arms and throat. The warts on her hands, she told him, were the result of powerful curses that rival witches had tried and failed to lay upon her.

"Of course, I can undo a runic curse," she assured him. "But I will need the leg marrow and brain matter of a red-haired infant. They don't appear often on the middens so one must be stolen. Can you pay for it?"

He dangled in her face a greasy leather pouch heavy with silver *denarii.* As she reached for it greedily, he snatched it away. "First, the infant, foul daughter of night," he said with a serpent smile.

When one was procured, a frightful ceremony was performed. That night a prostitute from the Circus stalls cried out in vain for her red-haired infant, stolen while she slept. Aristos watched it all to make certain he was not cheated. Haruna boiled a potion composed of the human remains, along with the lung of a white sheep and the urine of a black goat; to this she added a pinch of henbane and Thessalian honey. Next she burned a figure of wax modeled to represent Auriane. Then, while muttering in Etruscan and daubing blood on his forehead and hands, she bade him drink part of the horrible mixture. Aristos drank as much as a sparrow might have, then spit it out and gagged. He was relieved to see that she ignored this. When the ceremony of cursing was done, Haruna proclaimed that not only had she nullified the power of the runes; she had as well ensured that Auriane's heart would freeze before the next celebration of Saturnalia.

Six months passed; Saturnalia approached. Aristos hoped that by this time Auriane was at least feeling slightly ill. He wondered if the curse might have partly turned against himself—his hair was falling out in patches, and he had boils that would not go away. And then he saw her, on the festival's eve. She had returned to light practice, and to his dismay she appeared sleek, spirited and healthy.

He sent two of his henchmen to seek out Haruna and strangle her.

For the first time he thought: Maybe I should just *answer* her challenge. It might be the surest and perhaps the only way of getting rid of this scourge.

You think like a half-wit. This city loves you like a god— overnight you'd have them laughing at your back.

Then he began to dream of her. Auriane would beckon with an encouraging smile; she wanted to lie with him. He became aroused in his sleep. But when he moved toward her to take her, her face began to melt and distort, until it was transformed into the rigid, waxen face of Ramis. His muscles became paralyzed, and he collapsed and lay helpless on his back while that Helle-hag reached in and pulled out his heart to boil in a potion. He would awaken panting and bathed in sweat.

He began to drink neat wine to stifle the dreams, and soon, when Meton did not push him to practice, he was lurching drunk by midday. When a wart appeared on his right hand, he knew Haruna must have cursed him in dying. And so after a month of boils and bad dreams he thought once again of disposing of Auriane in the arena, as she begged him to, calling on Wodan to show him a way to do it without inviting the world to heap ridicule on his head.

• • •

Domitian would have counted Aristos' complaints as gnats next to what he faced. The Dacian War got away from him utterly, and the measures that his military council assured him would bring swift victory he dared not even consider. The first of these, that of marching to the Danube and leading the army in person, meant leaving Rome untended for years, and he was now convinced the Senate was infested with men who lusted for his absence, waiting their moment to usurp the throne. The second, that of assembling a sufficient number of legions to efficiently humble the Dacians, was even more unthinkable—for there was no man of the Senatorial class whom he dared trust with such a massive fighting force. What was to prevent his appointed commander from turning his back on Dacia, marching home, and making war on him? And so repeatedly he sent out forces that were too small in number, subjecting the Romans to a series of humilating defeats; in one engagement in the Danubian wilds, the Dacian king surrounded an entire legion and annihilated it with all its cavalry and auxiliaries. The imperial councillors saw with alarm that for the first time Domitian's obsessive distrust of the men about him began to compromise military strategy. Domitian knew the good will of the army, hard won in the Chattian War, was rapidly eroding, and this only served to increase his certainty that half the members of the Senate were courting its favor with bribes, hoping to seduce the legions away from him.

He calmed his nerves by rewriting the laws, curtailing the freedoms of the humble, solidifying the privileges of the great, imagining he resurrected the glorious old order and made his domains a safer place for himself. A freedman who did not pay proper respect to his former master could be re-enslaved. A plebeian who usurped the seats reserved for Equestrians and Senators in the theater or Circus could be scourged and fined. He limited further the number of slaves a man could legally manumit at his death. Prostitutes were prohibited from accepting inheritances.

Gradually his moral sternness slid into the perverse. He accused the Chief Vestal, Cornelia, of taking a lover and had her tried in secret at his Alban villa. Then he horrified the city by ordering her buried alive. This was the ancient punishment for unchastity among the Vestals and had not been employed for two centuries. At the last, however, he became anxious that she might be untouched in fact—in which case the gods might vent their wrath on *him* for persecuting so sacred a personage. And so before

Cornelia was led into the underground chamber and sealed in darkness forever with but a measure of oil and one loaf of bread, he had her brought to him and took her by force, lest some future tribunal of gods charge him with the murder of a virgin.

In these days Marcus Julianus observed a thing that alarmed him greatly: His ability to turn Domitian's mind on a subject seemed strong as ever when he was in the Emperor's presence. But once he took his leave, he lost *all* hold on him; Domitian's suspicions were a wild gale that buffeted him about, and no human voice could be heard above its shrieks. It happened that Domitian ordered the execution of one of his secretaries, a freedman named Epaphroditus, simply because the man had helped Nero to commit suicide more than twenty years before. Domitian by this means meant to terrify his own freedmen in advance, should they contemplate any act of violence against him. Marcus Julianus argued that this act would accomplish the opposite of what he expected. Its cruelty—for the intended victim was ill and aged—and its unreasonableness—for Nero had ordered the deed—would only serve to unite Domitian's own freedmen against him in common cause. Domitian had nodded, and there even came into his eyes that intent look that signaled he agreed. Julianus considered the matter settled, but on the next morning Epaphroditus was dragged off to death. Domitian had him beheaded in the crowded Old Forum rather than on the regular execution ground so the Palace servants could take heed.

Marcus Julianus passed these months in covertly approaching each Senator in turn, employing Domitia Longina's help in arranging meetings ostensibly for other purposes. Patiently he tricked or cajoled from them the name of the most trusted and best loved of their colleagues. Many were openly terrified of him, supposing it some ruse to test their loyalty. When he had polled all save the dozen or so Senators no longer of sound mind, he found he had marked down the name of one man more than any other—that of the aged and amiable Senator Cocceius Nerva.

For a month Senator Nerva avoided him, guessing what was coming. And then one day Marcus Julianus intercepted him just when his quarry thought he outmaneuvered him by leaving the Imperial Baths through a humble, little-used entry that opened onto the cook stalls. With Julianus hard in pursuit, Nerva walked with swift, angry strides, his gaze locked steadily ahead as if he really thought it possible to pretend he did not know him.

"Off with you!" Nerva sputtered breathlessly. "Go annoy

someone younger. And in a better humor. I'll have no words with a man who makes me feel like a bullock prodded to sacrifice!" He brushed his arm with annoyance as if Marcus Julianus were some stinging insect that had settled on him. From behind them came the hollow shuddering of the gong that signaled the closing of the baths. Both men frequently collided with people in the crowd, most of whom either hurried frantically to evening engagements or felt the necessity to pretend they did so.

Marcus Julianus struggled to stay abreast of the surprisingly vigorous old man, while silently wagering that Nerva had not moved this fast in a decade.

"Now *that's* an ungrateful thing to say to someone who is trying to place two-thirds of the known world into your hands," Julianus replied, "not to mention immortal fame, and the peace of mind that comes with knowing you'll always have a seat in the theater even if you're late."

"Your father was a vexatious troublemaker, and you are many times worse!" Nerva gave him the comically exaggerated frown of one who did not have the face for a convincing fierce expression; age softened it into comfortable shapelessness, and a mild, gentle nature gave him a sheepdog's eyes, full of patience and understanding. "I did not ask for this!" He looked at Marcus Julianus accusingly. "What if I decide, after a year, that it's a life I despise? What *then?* Did you think of *that* while you were making plans for me? It's not a post a man can exactly step down from—not with his head on his shoulders!"

"Well then, if after one year you decide you dislike what I got you into, I invite you to seek me out and avenge yourself upon me any way you like."

"I retire to my estates next year! Now I'll never retire. You are too late. You should have come to me thirty years ago."

"I beg you, slow your pace and listen!" A cart stacked with crates of hens blocked Julianus' way and Nerva almost got away from him. He cursed, ran to catch up, then continued on with quiet fervor. "It will be *you* and no one else!" He forced himself to smile blandly so a suspicious eye in the crowd might imagine they discussed the yield of their vineyards in Gaul or the weather in Umbria. "You alone rouse no jealousies. You've held no high military command, and to our colleagues it's a great point in your favor. In you, they see a way to give power and dignity back to the Senate. You may count it ill, but they don't, that you are distantly of the family of Claudius and Nero. Like it or not, you've got the most illustrious lineage of any man living. A lesser man the army would throw off like a testy horse an unfit rider. Three-quarters of your fellows named your name and the reasons to me are obvious. You've a reputation for firmness and for speaking your mind, yet at the same time you've got fewer enemies than any man—how you manage that, you alone know. You know the government better than any of them. And you're as utterly different from *him* in temperament as it is possible to be. All will welcome a man who *lives* by the laws he makes."

Marcus Julianus was encouraged by the fact that Nerva's strides slowed somewhat; then he thought it might only be that the old man was finally becoming winded.

"I cannot believe," Nerva said almost wistfully, "that they truly want such an old man."

"Even *that* they count in your favor. It's an unflattering reality, but one that must be considered. As one man who I'll not name put it: 'He will die before he becomes dangerous.' No one believes any longer in the ability of *any* man to withstand the temptations of absolute power for long. But whatever their reasons, *you* are their choice and you cannot run from this!"

Before Nerva could object, Marcus Julianus pressed on in a grimmer tone. "There are other arguments I could make. Do it, or die in your turn. He's had a dream about you, you know, and it gnaws at him. He dreamt your mother lay a night in the temple of Apollo and a serpent came to her, and so you were conceived— *just as the ignorant said of Augustus.* Take heed! And what if his new astrologer claims you are destined to rule? No man of high birth is safe from his suspicions—if you don't use your birth to your advantage now, it will be your doom later. I don't really see you have a choice."

For a bare instant Nerva's features seemed to settle into weary acceptance. Then he vigorously shook his head. "Curses on you!" he sputtered. Then he turned sharply, narrowly avoiding a procession of dancing matrons in swirling robes who were sprinkling the street with sweet-smelling balsam, doing homage to the goddess Isis amid airy tunes played on pipes and the rhythmic clicks of silver rattles. Both men were blinded for a moment by the bronze mirrors the celebrants held while the women gestured with ivory combs, miming combing the goddess's hair. The procession forced Marcus Julianus to one side of the street and Nerva to the other. This time Nerva escaped.

But on the next day at dusk, Nerva found himself purposely

taking a route from the Curia that was certain to bring him across Marcus Julianus' path as he departed from the Council chambers in the West Palace. Nerva was a skillful enough actor to make the meeting appear entirely accidental. This time he listened attentively to Julianus' arguments, making no attempts to escape. By the time they turned into the Street of Booksellers, Nerva had nearly surrendered.

"But I have no sons," he said in a last weak protest. "Vespasian at least had sons."

"One of whom was Domitian. To my mind, adoption brings better results anyway. But you must do it soon as you take up the purple. Give the people a sense of continuity *at once,* and your position will be that much stronger."

"This has the stink of dreams about it. You are mad, and I've caught it!"

"Steady on, I wager you'll get used to it soon enough. I can think of one or two worse lots in life. Now, you must begin at once rewarding those members of the Guard who are with us. I know exactly what he's giving each of them—you must double it. Don't trouble me with high-minded arguments. It is necessary. I'll match what you give them from my own purse. Others will do the same—"

"What of the two Prefects?" Both men knew it would be disastrous to proceed without the support of both Guards' Prefects—without them the conspirators could never win a sufficient number of Domitian's pampered, well-paid Praetorians to their cause. With the Praetorians' blades lay ultimate power; the consent of the Senate was empty noise without them.

"There's work to be done there, admittedly. Both have been shy of me, but do not worry over it. Mark my words, I will win them. But there is one more matter. We're never going to secure the whole Guard, that's plain to me now. The ones that remain loyal are going to demand the death of the conspirators. *But whatever happens after the deed is done, you must hold your ground.* You will seriously undermine your rule if you give in to them. Do not advance the loyalists. Stand firm against them. And you stand a fair chance of cheating the probabilities and becoming one of the best rulers we have ever had."

Nerva was actively silent for a time. Then he frowned and looked at Marcus Julianus. "You haven't told me something. Why do you risk so much? What prize do you seek for yourself?"

"Only that monster's death." His steps slowed slightly as he permitted himself to reflect. "All my life I've never been able to shake the darkness of Nero. It clings like dye to cloth, like infernal slime. . . . At times I fall into a belief that destroying *this* tyrant might somehow nullify the curse of the one I could not stop." A restrained anguish crept into his voice. "Though I suppose it is, in the end, for my father, as well . . . and for another poor old man who died with him, who was also my father," Julianus added, feeling a need to do some small homage to Lycas. He was silent for several strides, then he firmly met Nerva's gaze. "However, my good friend, here *is* one small gift I desire of you . . . afterward."

"*Ah!* Of course! If we prevail, there is nothing I would deny you." Nerva thought: I know what gift this man wants. It must be so.

Watching Julianus' face intently, Nerva said, "The Asian province. Ask for it, and it is yours. No, *Egypt*. I would even give you Egypt, in the face of all custom!" The governorship of Egypt, the most prestigious post in the Empire, was not normally entrusted to a Senator, for the extraordinary fertility of the Nile Delta made this land crucial to the well-being of the state. It was feared an ambitious Senator might seize bread-producing Egypt, form an independent state, and wreck the economy of the Empire. The post was given usually to a distinguished member of the Equestrian order, a man who was a trusted friend of the Emperor's.

"An impressive offer and a noble one! But you should have come to me ten years ago," Marcus Julianus replied, echoing Nerva's words of the day before. "Power doesn't beckon anymore . . . only understanding beckons. No, what I would ask for is a minor civil post in the province of Upper Germania, something with little to do directly with governing—for example, to be your First Engineer in charge of public works in the province or perhaps legal counsel to the Governor there. And I would ask for a tract of good land on the west bank of the Rhine in Upper Germania, above the confluence of the river Main."

"My hearing comes and goes. I think it just went! You cannot mean this!" When he saw that Marcus Julianus smiled tolerantly but held firm, he went on, "If you really want to be sent into exile, it can be arranged without *my* help! That's an insulting post in a barren waste!"

"It is fertile waste to one who wishes to teach and write of what he has learned and pass time in considering the words of the philosophers. There, I mean to resurrect my beleaguered school, though admittedly it will be difficult to get learned teachers to follow me. Theophila has said she would come, and Galerius—"

"If *all* of them followed you, it is still mad. Even the civil population out there scarcely reads! Out there, they chase down boar with fire-hardened sticks, not the newest theories of the origins of the universe!"

"If a dozen pupils come, it will suffice. I do not need great numbers. A lust for knowing can be born in the forest as well as in the civilized places, I know that now. In that country, it seems the very air purifies and leads us back to nature's first causes—"

"Your father was just a common eccentric," Nerva interrupted, shaking his head. "*You* are perverse. You would trade all the cities' centers of learning, and the company of the philosophers themselves—as well as all the life of cities, not to mention the authority and renown of a post second only to the imperial office itself—for trees and silence! The frontier line comes close there, too close. You might as well leap about a fire in fawnskins and dig yourself into a mud hut! I never judged you to be one ready to turn his back on all humanity. Come to your senses! I need you here."

"If a man takes time to reflect on the mysteries, is he wasted? There are other worlds in this world, my good friend, besides government."

"*You* are a mystery. I will agree to this only if you understand that in time of peril and great need, you stand subject to recall. And you shall advise me by correspondence as an additional duty."

"Well and good then. We'll worry over that in time. There's much unpleasant work to be done as yet."

Soon after Auriane regained enough strength to return to practice, Erato summoned her to his chambers. He was wrapped tightly in a blanket and burning hellebore for a stubborn winter cough; the biting smoke stung her eyes. The generosity and warmth in his smile caught Auriane by surprise.

"I am well pleased with you, well pleased!" he said hoarsely but happily. "Everywhere I go I hear talk of you! I feel I have uncovered a treasure hoard! The mob knows you're at practice again, you know—they'll not wait for you much longer! The patrons of the next three games insist upon having you, and they want you matched with a man. They'll not have it any other way. Don't fret over it, we'll make sure it looks more difficult than it is. I'll ferret out some opponents I know you're more than a match for, and we'll let it out that they were selected by lot. You're going to be celebrated, my little Aurinia—and if you do as I say, wealthy and free!"

Erato hesitated, aware for the first time of a new fragility in those gray eyes. "Your mind is not set against . . . fighting again?" he probed gently.

She met his eyes solemnly. "I welcome it, Erato."

"Ah. I should have guessed that would be your reply! Nothing about you is quite normal. But that is good! It is what makes you so valuable. Scaurus, the Praetor who is arranging the next games, has already told me he wants you to fight an Indian tiger on the first day, but we'll put a day between that event and the day you face your regular opponent so you'll have time to regain strength—"

"A tiger? A *beast?*" she said in quiet puzzlement. "You mock me."

"Not at all! It is an honor! You must do it! It will be wildly popular. In the spring games a woman killed a Mesopotamian lion. The mob loved it. Scaurus wants to outdo that. You'll have a month to train with the animals. Don't fret over it; it will come naturally to you, I'm certain. The stories they tell of you! The ignorant are going about saying you're a daughter of Hercules, begotten on a Nereid. But the best was that you tongue-lashed Aristos right after you won, and challenged him to fight you! Imagine, *Aristos!* People will believe anything, will they not?"

"Erato," she said, bracing herself for an eruption of rage, "that one is true."

Erato's smile vanished. Then it returned, hopefully. "A small jest, Auriane? Lying near death has given you an odd sense of humor."

She looked down, not replying; tension gathered in the room.

Erato's eyes hardened to steel. "Auriane, are you telling me truthfully that you challenged *Aristos?* What in the name of the infernal host *for?*" He stood up violently, loudly upsetting his bench; the blanket dropped from his shoulders and collected at his feet. "You stay well off from him!" He took several clipped steps in her direction.

"There are simpler ways to destroy yourself, if that is your wish. Hear me now! You will not sport with him or mock him or have anything whatever to do with him, I order you!" His huge fists were drawn back, battering rams ready to smash the gate; the blood drained from his lips. Instinctively Auriane prepared to defend herself, planting her legs apart, scanning the room for anything that might be used as a weapon.

"Oh, *stop that!*" he said, relaxing slightly, turning away and running a hand fretfully through his thick black hair. "You look like a cat ready to spring. I'm not going to hit you. But you must understand, there's a limit upon how much I can bring Aristos to heel. Madden him, and he'll have one of his cutthroats all over you soon as one of my guards so much as blinks his eye. Now, what words, exactly, did you say to him?"

She repeated her words, closely as she remembered—she saw little to gain by covering the truth when he could have questioned any number of witnesses.

"Nemesis and Mars, not one of those cursed blood-debts! That's where your people least have their wits about them. Well, I won't have that here! Anyway, your life is not your own to dispose of. I'll hear no more on this."

Her eyes were clear, soft, direct as a hawk's. "Do not stand in the way of my fate, Erato," she said quietly. "Or I will not fight for you again."

"That is wonderful! When the guards come for you, you'll just say, 'I'm in no mood today, off with you now!' Just where do you think you *are,* my little petted princess? Do you remember a war? Do you remember being taken captive? Or perhaps you think your people won?"

"Stop laughing at me. You can have me dragged out there, but you cannot make me perform like your tame animals. It is not my captive body you need, but the way that I fight. You seem to think me a fool. What good am I to you if I decide to use the sword you force into my hands on myself?"

"Enough of this!" he cried, turning his back on her. The truth was, he realized, she could make things perfectly miserable for him by doing as she threatened. Unfortunately, the cunning wench was discovering she was not without powers of her own in this situation. She had brought him a measure of the respect he sought, and helped still the questions concerning his fitness as the school's Prefect. Would his position be as steady and secure without her? It unnerved him to think about it. The thought of losing her raised a superstitious dread. A dim, hidden part of him said: We rose together; we will fall together.

He decided his best course was to let this thing fall of its own weight. Why struggle with that stubborn pride if it could be avoided? There was no danger really—the crowd would not tolerate such a match, and Aristos would never agree to it.

"I do not want to fight with you on this day!" he said affably as his practiced friendliness returned. He approached her then and closed war-weary hands round her shoulders. "I am too old and tired, and you are too high-strung. You may not believe it, but I love you like a daughter when you're not being obnoxious. I owe a great debt to you. You fought well for me. You got that swine Musonius Geta off my trail. I promised you a favor—I'll wager you thought I forgot! I'm *always* good for my promises. What do you wish? Name it."

She tensed, feeling blood beat in her temples. Should she really ask it? She debated furiously, then leapt into the dark.

"I would have you . . . conduct me to a certain house at nightfall, and trust me to return at cockcrow."

He looked blankly at her. "And trust you to return?" He gave a forced laugh. "What is this? You've more surprises than a farce."

"Stop playing with me! You know I must return."

"You are right. You are perhaps the only woman or man I've ever encountered addled enough to return to this place without coercion. Nevertheless, you go nowhere without guards." He frowned. "*Whose* house?"

Auriane hesitated, reluctant to speak that name. But she knew that some sort of relationship existed between Marcus Julianus and Erato similar to that of a battle-chief and his companions, and such loyalties were never betrayed.

"To the house of your patron, Marcus Arrius Julianus."

"*What?*" he said softly, in his eye the flat, stupefied look of a man struck in the stomach. By Charon, Erato thought, how does she even know of him? When he had wondered in the past if Julianus' interest in her might mean he felt love for her, Erato had dismissed it as exceedingly unlikely. There must be another, odder reason to account for it—for what use would a cultured man like that have for a creature who was, in spite of her rude charms, still an illiterate half-beast?

"Do you know what you are saying, you little fool?" Erato's voice was a rough shove. "His position is precarious. He is important to great numbers of people. You are an imperial slave, and to tamper with you is in violation of the law. Did it occur to you that every little misdeed he commits is likely to be used against him by his enemies?" His voice rose to a hoarse shout.

"How *dare* you risk the safety of the only sane man in the government for the sake of your foolish notions!"

"I think he should be allowed to choose for himself what risks he wishes to take! By what *law* do you choose for him?" She spoke these words with more spiritedness than she felt. Something shrill and hurt in her tone made her realize how great was her fear that Erato's assumption was right: This meeting was of great account to her, and of little account to Marcus Julianus.

But her words unleashed just enough doubt in Erato to give him pause. He sat down slowly, still scowling, while he considered whether he dared risk interfering with what might well be, after all, what Julianus wanted.

He stole a covert glance at Auriane then, regarding her in a way he hardly had since first he saw her—simply as a woman rather than as a skilled performer in the arena. Furtively he ran his gaze over the swell of a well-formed breast, the curve of a sturdy hip, then down that intimidating length of leg. He decided at once: No, this one is not made for bed. Oh, I'll give her that face, that is understandable—it would shame a nymph. But the rest of her? Too tall, too tough and sinewy, too scarred. How can a man's passions be roused by a woman capable of knocking him down? A woman should be pliant and soft. In the dark he wouldn't know if he lay with a wench or wrestled with a mountain cat. And she's got a will as unyielding as that body. No. Nature fashioned this one for war, not love.

Auriane knew she had been assessed and found wanting. Erato's gaze was a rough hand feeling fruit to see if it was ripe and rejecting it with a brusque toss.

With a slightly shamefaced smile Erato probed, "And . . . he truly wants this? He wants . . . *you?*"

"You are vile!" She spun round, arms crossed over her breasts, and stood with her back to him. Tears of rage and humiliation blurred her eyes. She felt herself shrivel within. At that moment her wound began to ache deeply, as if just to remind her it was there, so she would not forget its ugliness and the dismaying new sense of vulnerability it brought.

"All right, then," he said soothingly, reminding himself of how obsessively modest barbarian women were. "Don't take it to heart so. I've offended you without meaning to. I mean no insult or harm. You have it, then—that is, if *he* agrees to it."

Perhaps it would even be good for her, he reasoned. Every physician agreed that sexual activity was a sort of tonic, lending strength to the muscles and a sense of well-being; was that not why they regularly sent prostitutes around to the men? Why would it be much different with her?

"I'll send word when I've arranged a day with him," Erato went on. "May your gods help you if this is some moon-struck idea of your own and you make me look the fool before him! And not a word of this to anyone, mind you, not even that woman who lives with you. You'll go to the physicians beforehand, so they can give you whatever they give to prevent you from adding to the population. This city's too overcrowded already, a man can hardly get through the streets! Don't look so woebegone! Aren't you, as usual, getting what you want?"

Auriane said nothing, still mute with humiliation.

He hesitated, then ventured, "Am I forgiven? *No?* Oh, come now! Well, off with you then! You confound me—I know not what else to say."

Once she was returned to her cell, Auriane's anger soured to dull anxiety. Erato's quick dismissal of her as a woman gave flesh to her worst imaginings and real life to the vague doubts she had begun to feel since her recovery. It was a chill reminder that there was much about the attitudes and desires of these people that differed greatly from those of her own. It was quite likely, she considered, that *all* of them thought a woman should look a certain way, and that this expectation might be like some sort of wall, beyond which they could not see. She knew powerful men carefully chose and collected lovers, both women and boys, searching the slave markets for the loveliest, the most perfectly formed. Among these people, perfection was enshrined: They sacrificed only pure, unblemished animals when they wished especially to please their gods; their sculptors chiseled nymphs to delight the eye with bodies smooth and white as an egg, such as nature rarely fashioned. Any person with a deformity, a limp, or a stutter was quickly a laughingstock. And these people painted their faces as painstakingly as they painted their walls, because apparently nature never made a face quite fair enough. In her own country she would have proudly shown to a husband the evidence of her many wounds. But cities bred leisure, and love became a pastime, not a bond that must aid survival. In this place she was a chipped vase, a smeared painting, an unraveled tapestry. A man could not live here all his life and not be touched by its yearning for unmarred beauty. *He, too, will find my battered body ugly—he will not be able to help himself.* The thought, once framed, nudged its way in and stayed. At times she was almost grateful to Erato, for he prepared her in advance for cruel disappointment.

Sunia watched Auriane questioningly while she brooded. Finally Auriane explained herself, haltingly, painfully; when she was finished, she angrily tore off her garments to show Sunia her naked body.

Sunia regarded it with unabashed awe. "Your whole life is writ upon it. So is the life of our people. The Ash in summer is not more beautiful, nor are the lilies. If any man does not see it, you must turn from him."

"Nobly said. But it is a hard truth to live! Love has undermined me, Sunia."

CHAPTER L

The following spring brought more than fevers and rain. The generations living in the milder era to follow would know this time simply as the Terror.

Its cause was the revolt of Antoninus Saturninus, who was at that time serving as Commander over the two Rhine legions quartered at Mogontiacum. Saturninus had long known Domitian meant to kill him, ever since he learned his name was on the rough copy of the list. He grew weary of the cruelly drawn-out game and decided to strike first. In Upper Germania he witnessed firsthand the army's growing animosity toward the Emperor and judged there would never be a better moment to save himself. And so he made his lunge at the greatest power on earth. To make certain the two legions under his command transferred their loyalties to him, he impounded the soldiers' compulsory savings, which were deposited in the military chest at the fortress's headquarters building. The episode bore little resemblance to Marcus Arrius Julianus' well-reasoned, orderly attempt at a change of government; it was more the audacious gamble of panicked prey who rushes in for a surprise kill when he senses his tormentor is wounded.

Domitian knew at once this was the gravest danger he had ever faced. His agents informed him that as many as ten of the legions stationed in the northern provinces might be involved. From hour to hour he waited to hear that they had formed up under Saturninus and were marching on Rome in a body. The legions of the East would probably remain loyal, but they were too distant; if they set out at once they would not arrive in time to save his throne and his life. He could not drive from his mind the knowledge that Nero, confronted with a similar situation, panicked and committed suicide. But Domitian was of a different nature; when cornered, he stowed his fear in an airtight place until the crisis was past—where it grew potent in the dark, preparing to torment him at its leisure. While danger still threatened, he was a creature of cold deliberation, able to strike brutally and hard.

Domitian set out at once for the province of Upper Germania with the Praetorian Guard at his back. As he marched, spies informed him that Saturninus had even invited the recently humbled Chattian savages to cross the Rhine and join his forces. Terror spread through all Gaul at the thought of vengeful barbarians loosed on their settlements.

But fortune favored Domitian when he had made but half the journey. As the Chattians massed along the Rhine's east bank, preparing to join Saturninus, the river thawed in the night and the barbarian warriors were unable to cross over the ice. Then the commander of the legions of Lower Germany, a man named Maximus, marched against Saturninus and defeated him; dutifully he sent Domitian the traitor's linen-wrapped head, preserved in honey.

And Domitian, gazing into his enemy's sunken eyes, wondered if he might truly be touched with divine essence, as was Alexander of Macedon—for it seemed defeat was not part of his fate.

Minerva will always smite my enemies. Saturninus, you must have been insane to challenge my godhead.

But Domitian's exultant humor died when he learned on his arrival at the Rhine fortress that the victorious Maximus had taken it upon himself to burn all of Saturninus' correspondence. Now Domitian would never know for certain who had remained loyal and who had betrayed him. The more he pondered this, the less he liked it. Maximus' act was a courageous attempt to protect as many as possible from Domitian's wrath, but the deed in fact worsened matters. For now Domitian's suspicions were unbounded by facts, and he was free to imagine everyone had taken part. The revolt proved to him what he had long asserted and all about him denied: His empire was overrun with brazen rebels at every rank. He found a certain morbid satisfaction in seeing his worst suspicions proven true. The brooding fear, until this day always astride him but not *of* him, began to settle down into his bones. It would be his only master to the end of his days.

The treason trials began while Domitian was still in Upper Germania, and he continued to conduct them throughout the march home. When questioning soldiers of the ranks, he resorted to the rack, caring nothing for the law forbidding the torturing of Roman citizens for evidence. Tales filtered back to Rome of suspects interrogated by Domitian himself while the army's questioners singed their genitals with hot brands. The heads of executed men arrived daily in Rome, to be displayed on the Oration Platform in the Old Forum. Of all the soldiers of the ranks whom Domitian questioned and executed, it was said only one man saved himself—a young centurion who claimed he had visited Saturninus' quarters not for conspiracy but for an hour of love. Domitian was aroused by a womanly face, a Ganymede's form, and after adjourning his court for the purpose, as he stated it, of "further examining the evidence," he took an afternoon to enjoy the young man's favors himself. Later he announced the defendant had lustily proved his case, and pardoned him.

When Domitian returned to Rome, he turned his full fury on the Senators, whom he believed were ultimately the cause of the souring of his long, happy marriage with the army. The revolt left him with the sense that the legions were like some powerful consort who could never again quite be counted monogamous— and the Senate teemed with her potential seducers. In this "marriage" he had a partner whom he could not rule by terror as he did his wife; this spouse needed to be courted always and treated with deference. If he could not keep this consort faithful by force, he *could* terrorize her would-be seducers. He proceeded to do so, with dedication and violence.

And so he set the Senate to the task of trying and condemning its own. Gone was his earlier reluctance to play the role of tyrant—he had no use now for poisoned needles. Victim and verdict were given to the Senators in advance of each session, and trial after trial proceeded like a grim series of plays with one plot. The charge was always the same, but the evidence was often ridiculous. One Senator perished because he had a map of the world painted on the walls of his bedchamber, which was read as proof he intended to rule the world. The wife of another was condemned because her household servants reported she had undressed before a statue of Domitian set up in her own house— which showed mockery of his divinity. Informing became a profession and a passion. Among the humbler orders it proved the quickest route to wealth; many a sumptuous seaside villa was bought with an innocent person's blood. It was a lucrative game that anyone could play: All a man or woman had to do was arrange to see one of Veiento's secretaries, and in two days' time he might find himself telling his tale to the great minister himself—and afterward he would find enough in his purse to buy a team of race horses or a cook as skilled as Apicius. If guilt over the victims began to trouble him, that could be cured by reading the daily Palace bulletins the notice writers put up in the Old Forum. There he could learn that the man on whom he had informed had taken bribes, was a follower of foreign superstitions, a defiler of temples who committed unnatural acts with women and boys, a profligate beast who had been narrowly stopped from seizing the state.

As the heads of Senators began to decorate the Rostra, a detachment of guards was posted nearby to prevent relatives and retainers from snatching them down. Domitian chose a place where ordinary citizens were obliged to pass while pursuing their daily business, so all moved in the shadow of those blackening heads. Some grinned like Satyrs from Hades through their halos of flies, taunting the living with the remorselessness of death; others seemed to cry out in shapeless agony; none seemed ever to have been human. By dusk the Old Forum was deserted by the superstitious. But by light of day everyone forced themselves to look—a Palace secretary might discover a missing relative or friend; a plebeian might recognize the head of his patron before he had even learned his benefactor was on trial.

Marcus Julianus fought desperately to save as many as he could; once he hid in his house for a month the three children of a condemned Senator—Domitian would have murdered them lest they grow up to avenge their father. Eventually he arranged to have them delivered from the city hidden under the debris of a garden-cart. The children of others he hid within his school, disguised as copyists. He preserved two Senators' lives by implying to Domitian that, unknown to everyone, they were bankrupt. As he hoped, Domitian saw little use in taking the time to prosecute men with no property to confiscate—for with his many donatives to the army, the Emperor was rapidly emptying the treasury. Marcus Julianus worried constantly for the safety of Senator Nerva, but so far the man's affable nature, which Domitian seemed to count as docility bordering on senility, had kept Nerva safe. There was but one remaining difficulty preventing Julianus from setting a day for the assassination: his failure to gain the confidence of both Prefects of the Praetorian Guard, one of whom, Norbanus, seemed ready to give him an ear before the Terror. For Marcus Julianus knew well that, ghastly as these times were, still it was the senatorial class alone that suffered grievously. The Praetorians could provoke a civil war that would cause Rome's gutters to run with blood and whole cities to be laid waste by contending armies.

Erato's request on Auriane's behalf was delivered to Marcus Julianus shortly after the revolt. He had not dared risk having Auriane brought before this time because his house was watched closely by agents of Veiento, who was eager to uncover any evidence of treasonable acts, and, since her disgrace, by spies of Junilla as well. But this evidence of Auriane's discouragement saddened him and caused him to think less of caution. And so he arranged the meeting, though twice, for safety, he was forced to cancel it; finally it was set in spring, at the time of the festival of Flora. On these days there would be drunken gaiety in the streets, lascivious dances, masked revelers scattering lupines on the ground, and hares, goats and other fruitful animals loosed in the streets. He judged Auriane could be more easily disguised amidst this joyous confusion. As a further precaution he decided it must not be at his own house but at the mansion of Violentilla, a wealthy senatorial widow who was one of the conspirators. Erato was relieved, for it seemed Auriane's melancholia grew steadily worse.

Auriane's recovery required seven months; her devotees among the mob waited out this time with rude, noisy impatience. When she returned, she fought and won three times in one month and each time her fame grew greatly. A prankster set up a crude likeness of her in battle regalia before the Temple of Venus; temple authorities were scandalized to learn that more offerings were set before her image than were brought that day to the goddess. Vendors of votive statues made a brisk business of selling locks of hair they claimed were Auriane's, prompting Erato to remark, "A turbot has more intelligence than the people taken as one! They never wonder that you are not bald!"

Auriane killed her Indian tiger with a fluid grace that belied the tedious hours of preparation. She insisted on choosing the beast herself and spent much time with it, studying its habits. On the night before, she made her peace with the tiger, asking its spirit to forgive her its death. When the final moment came, it seemed the beast leapt obligingly onto her sword.

Her first human opponent after her return was a man called Taranis, selected by Erato from a pool of one-time victors. The bout had the rigor and cold beauty of a well-written tragedy; each tempered stroke brought eruptions of applause. Once again she felt herself a bird taken to flight. The end came swiftly. Taranis was unsettled by her from the start, for he believed only sorcery could have brought about her victory over Perseus; he had as well neglected to learn how to block a powerful backstroke. She did not kill him and the crowd voted to spare him, for they remembered the bout with Perseus and knew it was what she wished. He survived to fight again and was eventually released, living on to tell tales of her to his grandchildren.

Never in their history had the people had so many games lavished on them as in these times. The Colosseum was a world apart that preserved the illusion that the state was guided by a benign, capable hand. It was Domitian's one place of refuge as well; here he could silence their growls in an instant and have them licking his hand by tossing them Aristos, or a show of elephants, or the woman Aurinia, and so nourish his fantasy that he ruled perfectly, absolutely.

On the eves of days Auriane was to appear and on the nights of her victories, idlers gathered under her high window and sang bawdy songs to her until the Vigiles drove them off.

"They care for you not at all, really," Sunia observed with lofty impatience following Auriane's eighth victory, as they were kept from sleep by cries of *Carissima Aurinia!* "When they call your name it means no more than 'Death to the Emperor.' To my way of thinking, they *deserve* that Emperor." Sunia hesitated, then looked at Auriane. "Auriane . . . , was *he* there today?"

Auriane's uncomfortable silence made a reply unnecessary. But finally she answered, "No. He was not. But must he be there every time? There are many possible reasons. . . . He could have been kept at some task . . . then, too, he might be . . ." She hesitated, then ventured on bravely over treacherous ground. "Sunia, do you wonder, ever, why he alone of all their great men should be left alive?"

"Auriane, I *cannot* believe he's come to ill, and you must not. Erato would tell you. Men like that do not perish without everyone hearing of it."

The crowd's torches cast a hobbling light on the wall of the cell;

dimly it illumined Auriane's form collapsed on the bedcushion. Sunia put a comforting hand about her shoulder and discovered that the mob's darling was convulsed with quiet, struggling tears that she obviously wished to conceal. Sunia quickly took her hand away.

She loved Decius, Sunia thought, but not like *this*. It alarms me. This man is to her as the draft of air is to the bird. Fria, as you are guardian of lovers, preserve her.

That November, during the Plebeian Games, Aristos was given his greatest fright since his capture. He was matched with Hyperion in a contest that endured nearly an hour; they battled to an exhausted standstill. There was no dishonor in that; he had known he was close-matched. But Hyperion at the last knocked the sword from his hand, forced him to crawl before him on all fours, then placed a conquering foot on his back as if he intended to use him as a mounting block.

Aristos had never been at the crowd's mercy before. The glory of all his victories, layer by layer, were stripped off; he felt himself small, awkward, grotesquely naked as some plucked fowl. The crowd's hot, eager stares melted all life's acquired armor; he was a boy again, tied to a tree and waiting for Wido to beat him. Even though the people readily spared him and loved him no less—indeed, the next day children in the streets reenacted every part of the battle with staves, and in their games Aristos won, for everyone had trouble imagining any other outcome—he was certain his golden fortune was failing because of the runic curse. His fate was like a body that outwardly appeared still vigorous while inwardly, it was secretly being devoured by worms.

And that night when he thrust a torch into his cell, he was met with a sight that brought a child's whimper from him. Slowly he backed out of the cell.

On the back wall the runic sign of the war-god Tiwaz had appeared as if painted by a spectral hand; it was rendered upside down, in blood. *The death curse*. On his sleeping-mat lay his short spear of linden wood, a cult-object in the worship of Wodan, he who was guardian of the sanctity of the runes; it had been broken neatly in two. Between the broken pieces of the spear was placed his small clay figurine of Nihellenia, the name by which many of the tribes called the death goddess, Helle; her blank round eyes regarded him innocently, pitilessly. The meaning was unmistakable—if he did not answer Auriane's challenge, Helle would rend him in two.

If the ghost of Baldemar had appeared before him demanding wergild, he could not have felt greater dread. He knew this whole barrack block was cordoned off always—there was no way Auriane could have stolen in to do these things.

Aristos demanded and got new quarters.

You have your wish, then, you she-demon, you spawn of guest-murderers. I shall cut you up into pieces small enough to feed to Junilla's pet carp.

The following night, over mutton stew, he listened with sharp interest while Meton complained loudly to a fellow trainer about the annual games of August, held to celebrate the birthday of one of their most illustrious heroes, a man he sometimes heard called Octavian, at others Augustus, a warrior of old who won a victory in a great sea battle over a foreign queen called Cleopatra and her scheming lover, Marcus Antonius.

"The first day is utterly wasted," Meton was saying with a world-weary shake of his head. "Those mock naval battles show no skill, they're just a lot of carnage with newcomers. And then there's that foolish business the next day when the fighters are disguised and the people are guess who they are—*who cares?* And they want *volunteers*, volunteers of status! What man who's made a name for himself is going to volunteer not to be recognized? Whoever hatched this notion should be arranging shows in Pannonia."

After asking several careful questions, Aristos learned that all the contestants that day would be masked and robed as celebrated or notorious personages of history; the final exhibition was a pairing of Cleopatra and her ill-fated Marcus Antonius. He learned that a similar show had been staged in the days of Titus, when Cleopatra's costume was worn by a man of slight stature.

Aristos thought: If this plan I've just conceived bears fruit, I wager our new Cleopatra will be of a more appropriate sex. This is the gift of Wodan, given me because I no longer make war upon the runes. If everyone believes our identities are unknown *even to each other*, until the last when we are face to face before the mob and it is too late, how can I lose status by fighting that miserable woman?

And so Aristos volunteered at once to be costumed as Marcus Antonius. The secretary of Plancius, the magistrate responsible for that show, could scarcely believe his luck when he realized what a prize fish had swum into his net. Plancius' games would be remembered forever, and his master would surely give him some rich gift when he learned of this. Aristos threatened the secretary with a slow and unpleasant death if he broke silence about this to any official of the *Ludus Magnus*.

Then Aristos sent round his henchman called the Acrobat with a message for Auriane. As she struggled through the idlers that gathered as she left the practice ring, the Acrobat approached with mincing walk, then inserted himself in front of her in his gaudy tunic, half red, half blue; all the while he juggled balls of colored glass to disguise his purpose. Fish sauce and garlic were heavy on his breath as he leaned close.

"Antonius desires to meet Cleopatra," he said with a false lilt, as if he spoke lines in a drama, "to teach her a lesson she'll not live to remember. That is, if this trembling ewe before me has the mettle to play the part of a queen."

The Acrobat was disconcerted by the look of triumph that slowly came into Auriane's eyes. Aristos is right, he thought; Mars coupled with a Fury to beget this creature.

Auriane replied, her smile amused, "Tell him Cleopatra trembles with gladness that he wishes to see her . . . and she eagerly awaits the day."

That night Sunia and Auriane embraced each other, laughing. "We have won it!" Auriane exclaimed. "The monster has gobbled up the bait!"

"Thank all the gods for that!" Sunia said, falling wearily onto the bedcushion. "Nothing could force me to go back into his stinking cell again. I've got pig's blood under my nails and splinters in my hands from his wooden spear, and one of those stupid guards poked me with his sword. I think he thought I looked a bit too tall to be one of the cleaning boys."

"It was well done, Sunia, and bravely done. I'm relieved he had the wit to volunteer for that contest—that was what troubled me most."

"Fria is with us, who can doubt it!"

"Until Erato finds out. I'm hoping he'll discover it too late. If this Plancius wants it to be, he won't be inclined to let Erato interfere."

"Who is Cleopatra?"

"Some woman-chieftain of a people whose name I cannot

remember who lost a war to them in the time of their great-great-grandfathers."

"Auriane! You should not dress as someone who lost a war—it will bring ill luck!"

"The man whose mask Odberht will wear also lost. We cannot *both* be unlucky. Our freedom comes, Sunia. May Athelinda know it wherever she might be, and the ghosts of our people. On the third day after the Ides, in the month of *Augustus*, I avenge Baldemar and all our dead."

Carinus slunk soundlessly from Domitian's grand octagonal bedchamber, then down a flight of steps gauzily illumined by a light-well. He leapt over the reflecting pool of mosaic glass at the bottom, one hand firmly on the precious prize hidden in his tunic—a stack of thin sheaves of linden wood—and then he darted into a dark passage used only by guards. This was the quick, safe way to Domitia Longina's quarters; better than anyone, he knew his way about this maze of resplendent public and private rooms that was Domitian's newly completed Palace. When he was nearly safe at her door, a gold-helmeted Praetorian reached out with a surprisingly long arm and snared him.

"It's the Imperial Gelding!" He lifted Carinus by his tunic. "Poor thing, someone's hurt his feelings! Come here, Peach-Face, I'll make it better. What are you hiding in there?"

Carinus panicked. *If he sees what I have here, all of us die.* He bit down on the leathery hand that held him. The guard cursed, then tossed him off, laughing, as if at a bad-tempered puppy. The marble-sheathed halls reverberated with aggressive guard-laughter.

Domitia Longina's maid Arsinoë admitted him to the Empress's apartments. Once safely inside, he felt himself a hero, like Prometheus or Hercules—*as long as Domitian did not awaken*. It will be well, he reassured himself. It would take a herald's trumpet in the ear to rouse my lord from that dense sleep he sleeps after he's taken his pleasure of me.

Carinus' panic was eased by the thought of how proud of him Marcus Julianus would be.

"*Carinus!* Dearest dear, come. What have you there?" Domitia Longina's voice, silvery, frayed with anxiety, rang out from her writing room; he heard in it that languor that signaled she had taken her "tonic" already. That was good. She would be less alarmed.

He pulled out the sheaves of linden and laid them before her.

"The list, dear Mother—it exists, just as Marcus Julianus always insisted it did. My lord had it hidden on himself, that's why I've never found it! There it was, tucked into his underclothes, nearer to his privy parts than any *willing* person would choose to be!" Without waiting for her response he wriggled onto her lap and clung to her, nuzzling one ample breast as if seized suddenly by a blissful memory of being a suckling.

"Have you lost all your wits!" Her body heaved; he was a small craft on an unpredictable sea. "Straw-for-brains! Do you know a cabbage from a herring! Why did you take this!"

Carinus was pitched sprawling to the floor. He looked up at her, mute and amazed; Domitia Longina had never spoken a harsh word to him. The hurt began, poignant as if someone dripped lemon juice on a raw wound.

"He said to *read and remember*, not *take* it. You dunce! You lackwit! You're so starved for a pat on the head you've nearly cut the thread by which we're all suspended!" She was silent a moment, brow furrowed, focusing nearsighted eyes on Domitian's spidery scrawl.

"We are done! Nerva's to be prosecuted on the day after the Kalends. Oh, foul life, why are we not asked if we choose to be born! Put it back *at once*. Make certain he's snoring, or don't do it. *Go!*"

Domitia Longina began to pace with heavy, swaying movements. Carinus edged for the door clutching his unwanted prize; tears stung his eyes. He listened for a time as she spoke to herself, while his stomach felt weighted with lead.

"I am a dead woman!" she said to the tapestried walls, the busts of poets on their pedestals. "This is the *second* time he's marked for death the man Marcus Julianus chose as successor. He knows what Julianus is doing, and he's playing with him! One of the conspirators is an informer. Any hour now I'll be arrested. Will it be the block, or will he let me take my own life?"

"My lady, it could be coincidence! He's prosecuting everyone!"

"Charon take you! Why are you still here!" She threw her inkwell at him. He shrieked and ran out, splattered with black.

Domitia Longina sat down, her mind wrestling off the shrouds of opium until she felt it reasonably free of all that fuzzy comfort, and she could think and plan.

How to warn Marcus Julianus? He must be told at once. I dare not send one of my own maids. Who then shall I send? Eumenes, the bookfinder of the Palace library. Yes, he'll do. That Hermetic text from Alexandria I sent Julianus last month—I've got two copies; I'll send him another with my message coded in the middle. The fact that I've already given him that book should at once alert him that something is very wrong.

But perhaps he knows already. Perhaps even now Veiento's agents are torturing him, prying from him all the conspirators' names.

Domitia Longina's warning was brought to Marcus Julianus' great-house in early evening. He sent out messengers at once, intending to call a meeting of the chief conspirators. They collected at staggered times at Violentilla's mansion on the Caelian Hill. While he thought praises of Carinus' courage and Domitia Longina's quick action, at the same time he cursed the betrayal of Venus—for this was the very night Erato was to send Auriane to Violentilla's house.

As he climbed the Caelian, stepping on crushed lupines and dung, dodging troupes of satyrs and nymphs as the people celebrated the festival of Flora, he swiftly deliberated. Of course, she could not now be brought to this place, and good sense told him to give it up altogether and arrange for another night. But how many nights had they left to them? And what if he were arrested before this month was done?

Sensing suddenly he was being watched, he looked to the pendant moon just above his destination. It was nearly full, seeming conspiratorial and wise as it tracked him, marking this night, mocking him for thinking himself an independent being able to move apart from the deep, blind pulse of life. That moon was a she-demon of the fertile damps, mothering, merciless at once, impatient with reason, infinitely patient with the abyss. Its call was silent but wild and disorienting. He knew then he was falling prey to archaic forces beyond frail knowing, and a sudden, errant curiosity caused him to refuse to struggle against them. He thought of the now-moldering earth religion of his people in the time before time and wondered, are the old gods rendered powerless when people cease to believe in them? Auriane then seemed priestess as well as lover, beckoning him to a ritual old as mankind's first sowing of seedlings into the ground—the shadowy rite of the Sacred Marriage, which certain arcane texts asserted was once celebrated by his own people. He thought of old King Numa, proud in his kingdom of mud and thatch, who wedded Egeria, goddess and nymph, so he could learn wisdom, and remembered that Isodorus had taught the bridegroom was later ritually sent to the next world so that he might have life everlasting.

If there is death in her love, death to all this cramped, regimented, soul-dead life, it is a death philosophers praise. To see her is not so much a risk as a prayer, an offering on the grassy altar of natural life. *I will see her.*

By the time he arrived at Violentilla's, he was firm in his choice, and he sent word to Erato that Auriane was to be conducted to his own house instead. All will be well, he assured himself. She will arrive after nightfall, dressed as a reveler in a hairy calfskin cape and goat mask, with guards, also disguised, who will be selected by Harpocras—surely none will pay them any mind.

The conspirators met in one of Violentilla's cellar rooms. In addition to Marcus Julianus and Senator Nerva, there were three Senators of great influence who had held every office, men who had been with him from the first, and a Centurion of the Guard possessed of phenomenal memory, able to recite all the guard postings through the month, as well as Domitian's Chief Chamberlain, Parthenius, who was more familiar than any man with the Emperor's daily habits. Marcus Julianus listened while they argued dispiritedly over various schemes to save Nerva's life, planning to withhold his own offering until last—for it was a desperate measure. Most of the proposals involved carrying out the assassination at once, but none overcame the fact that they still had not won a safe portion of the Guard to their cause, or that Domitian would be cloistered at the Alban villa for the next eight days with the Guard's most fanatic loyalist, a Centurion called Servilius, while they framed charges and shot elk and antelope in the Emperor's hunting gardens. Marcus Julianus became uncomfortably aware of the passage of time; the sun had fallen, and by now that designing moon would have moved far in the sky. Auriane must have arrived at his house. She would be disconcerted and alarmed to learn he was not there.

And so he called to Anacreon, a trusted freedman and for years his most competent spy, a man who had grown rich from Julianus' rewards for his reckless deeds, and sent him with a warning to Auriane that the moon might set before he managed his way back there.

On this night Anacreon's luck was at an end. He was caught climbing a wall as he took a short route to save time, and the Vigiles who intercepted him turned him over to Veiento's men, scenting that there might be money in it since they saw him come from Violentilla's and they knew this noble widow was under suspicion. He was taken to the Palace and tortured on the rack, maintaining bravely to the last that he knew nothing of the secret associations of Violentilla.

When Marcus Julianus finally began to lay his own plan before the six grim-faced men, he did not know the message for Auriane had not been delivered and that his good friend and servant was dead.

"If this is the best we can do," he began, "I fear we are going to have to go forward with a rather extreme measure." His voice brought a shift in the temper of the room and a steadiness came over the company, as when a fractious horse feels a practiced hand on the rein. "Nerva, you must take poison."

Nerva started from his misery. "Curses on you! I thought you conceived some plan to save me!"

"Calm yourself. I speak of shamming mortal illness. Listen to me. In spite of how it looks, you, Nerva, because of your lineage, are one of the few men he *still* would prefer not to prosecute if he can avoid it. You know how he lusts to be worshiped after his death with the same dedication that Augustus is worshiped, with temples and priests in far-flung places. My guess is that he's long been confused about what to do with you. Letting you live shouts to everyone of his magnanimity and in his eyes nullifies the effects of his many murders, yet I suppose he has decided in the end that he cannot risk it. He knows that by blood, you've more of a right to rule than he does. We will let him think he can have it both ways. *Why should he carry out a task himself that he believes nature is ready to carry out for him?*

"We will make him believe you're in the mortal stages of a deadly ague," Marcus Julianus continued. "I have consulted Anaxagoras—he can concoct a draught that will mimic precisely its effects. He claims to have done this successfully at the court of the Parthian king. The draught will make your flesh livid and your hands palsied, but it won't kill you, though you may pray it does. You must be secretive about this illness—it's the best way to attract the attention of the gossips. Tomorrow, I recommend you send a man to retrieve your will from the temple of Vesta. I'll make certain Veiento's agents 'accidentally' discover this, and I'll send round a legacy hunter or two to make it even more convincing—everyone knows they've finer senses than vultures for ferreting out the dying. And you must never walk anywhere—

have yourself carried in a covered litter at all times. You probably won't feel like moving about much anyway."

"Wonderful."

"And have a man discreetly in attendance who looks the part of physician."

"I am too old for this playacting!"

"You for certain will not get any older if you *don't* do a little playacting."

"It is no use. I think he suspects us all."

"We do not really know what he knows. *He* does not know what he knows. It is foolish to roll over and die. We are the ones doing the will of the gods. If we act with vigor and certainty, surely our momentum will not let us fall into the pit." He looked about from one taut face to another; the only movement was the serpent curl of smoke rising from one small lamp. "Come now, be of better cheer! This cannot be the end! He's won every throw for too long. It is his turn to lose. Very soon now, we'll need to set a day."

"Without even *one* Prefect with us?" asked Herennius, a Senator who was five years his junior; he watched Marcus Julianus with the bright pertness of a boy who thinks he has found a flaw in a schoolmaster's logic.

"As of this morning, we've got one Prefect," Marcus Julianus said quietly. "Petronius is with us." This was met with happy astonishment. Nerva recovered himself first. He grinned, looking triumphantly at everyone in turn.

"And all of you doubted him! That is wonderful. And Petronius is the stronger of the two. Well done! Julianus, how in the name of all the gods did you do it?"

"Petronius owes his rank, even his life, to Titus, as you know. I told him the whole sorry tale of brother-murder, made the more compelling because I've since found that physician who carried out Domitian's order—he was operating a wineshop in Baiae, dispensing a wretched beverage by the way. Before I finished presenting my case, I almost had to physically restrain Petronius from going out right then, seizing our Lord and God and packing *him* in a chest of ice. 'Do not trouble yourself,' I said, 'that heart's frozen already, it might have no effect.' Oh yes, that, and one small lie. I said Norbanus is already with us."

"You said *what?*" Nerva said softly. Norbanus was Petronius' colleague in the office of Prefect. "Was *that* wise? What if he asks—"

"He won't. He believed me. Anyway, they are not much in each other's confidence. And in a short time, it will be true. Norbanus is of an irresolute nature and he's intimidated by Petronius. When he hears we've seduced his colleague, he'll not have the courage to hold out for long."

"By the jowls of Cerberus, it sounds *precarious*," Nerva said, vigorously shaking his head. "I hope to Nemesis you know what you're about. I'll play your game, then—have I a choice? Tell Anaxagoras to send round my poison. Tonight I drink to the monster's death!"

CHAPTER LI

Auriane was met in the vestibule of Marcus Arrius Julianus'
house by a bent, befuddled old man who seemed held together by
his disdain. *Diocles,* she heard a young maidservant call him as the
girl stole close to replace Auriane's heavy mud-splattered sandals
with silken slippers.

"I beg you, enter," Diocles said in his musical whine. "This
house is at your disposal." But delicate distaste emanated from this
man like a rancid perfume, and Auriane heard: *Enter, now that
you're here. But you should have come in by the kitchen entrance.*
He coldly refused to meet her eye but stole a caustic look at her the
instant she turned away. *So this is the exotic and peculiar animal
dragged home from the frozen wastes,* that look said, *over whom
my master lost his good sense and his sense of taste.*

Auriane felt a painful knot forming in her chest. *He behaves as
if my very presence here is some grave breach of manners.* But
perhaps this was just one ill-mannered man. She regarded him in
a way that was proud and open, but not arrogant, then inclined her
head slightly and thanked him, saying firmly to herself: *You are
Baldemar's daughter. If he thinks to humiliate you, then* he *is the
fool, not you.*

Diocles said then that his master was not at home, and added
vaguely that some summons had come from the Empress, but he
seemed to feel no greater explanation was necessary. He motioned
to two maidservants who stood at attention behind an oval pool

that was an ominous black mirror in the lamplight, and gave Auriane over to their care.

As they conducted her silently through the atrium, she felt she entered a perilous kingdom with two malign spirits for guides. One walked ahead of her, the other behind, as though to cover her lest she reach out and topple some precious bust or urn. Though the two maidservants were much alike to her in their foreignness—both had luminous Asian eyes alive with sophisticated mischief, teeth like pearls against clear nut-brown skin, small strong hands that moved like darting fish, and arms encircled with heavy bands of silver that caught the light of the myriad of lamps—she saw one clear difference between them. The one she judged the wiser of the two regarded her with a sort of suppressed pity, while the other watched her dubiously, counting her some beast that could never be fully domesticated, like a wolf or ferret.

Auriane wondered: Is this house overrun with ill-mannered people?

But soon she forgot them and surrendered to childlike amazement—she felt she explored the interior world of a man who must be at once sorcerer, demigod, and king. The room beyond the atrium was so grand it might have held a throne. Its walls were lined with lofty sapphire-veined columns that seemed to support the heavens, and indeed there was some sort of high seat at its center where audiences could have been held. Then they passed through a sensuous mass of silken curtains of saffron, sea-blue, and olivine, and on into a series of rooms where wonders quickly became commonplace. She felt rather than saw all about her, for its strangeness and newness overwhelmed her perceptions. Lustrous surfaces were everywhere; every space was alive and crawling with decorative forms. It was as though the gods had taken all the chaos of nature and given it order. Reality oscillated with illusion; here, an extra room was only a wall painted to look like a receding space, and there, a bottomless pool was actually some magically reflective stone. And all was marvelously replicated: Gold-fretted ceilings were reflected in glassy floors; a stand of columns was doubled in a rectangle of water that ran the length of one room, and in another, softly modeled ghostly-white figures of goddesses and gods were multiplied many times in moonstone mirrors. She walked through forests of lamps that rose from the floor or were suspended from the ceiling. Marbles of every hue, cut into squares, triangles, or thin bands, had been cleverly set into the walls, and she realized that marble could be as brilliant and varied in color as paints; indeed whoever created this had painted in marble. In one chamber she sank into carpets as dense and yielding as moss; in another she hesitated before stepping onto a mosaic floor that seemed studded with gems—surely it was not meant to be trodden upon?—but when the maidservants did so with indifference she hesitantly followed after. Tall screens of thin horn and silvery silk broke up the rooms and made their pathway more confusing.

I am traveling into a magic mountain; all the treasures of the gods are heaped here. Now and again a wall would disappear as they walked, to be replaced by lines of columns delicate as deer's legs, and earthy, flowery scents would betray the presence of a darkened garden. Occasionally she would hear the splash of a leaping fish, and once the rush of a waterfall, but mostly the place lay under a spell of lush quiet—a precious possession in itself, in this city with its continuous din. Their route took them through a vast carved-ivory cage alive with captive birds that seemed dripped accidentally with paint, odd little birds whose presence puzzled her, for they were too small for use as food. They crossed a stone bridge over a brook, frightening off a peacock, and beyond was a row of five chambers in which every wall was honeycombed with niches from ceiling to floor. Books, she realized, more than she ever imagined anyone would accumulate in one place. A grove of books, sacred, doubtless, to him, where his gods spoke their oracles through talking paper.

Her soul shrank even more.

How many of the dead live again on these walls? He has spoken with every sage. While I know only the words of Ramis. *Why would he not count me the most ignorant of women?*

But gradually she realized that, in spite of this house's opulence, this was a dwelling quite different from any she had seen in this city. This place alone seemed suffused with a gentle humanness, a peacefulness and harmony. Unlike the villa and garden of Domitian, which was built to overwhelm, this was a place of relief; she imagined all who lived here must feel the contentment of a stable heaped with fresh fodder. She thought it might be simply because his presence was abiding, because he had lived here so long, as Baldemar's had been in his own hall. Or perhaps it was because she noticed after closer looking, signs of wear, indications of a man utterly at ease with and almost unconscious of immense wealth. Here was a claw-foot table that looked as though it had been the plaything of children, and there a tapestry that needed reweaving. And the books too were tattered and used; many spilled carelessly onto the floor. She sensed that wealth was just a useful thing for him, like an ox, meant for work that must be done, and not a means of making himself splendid in the eyes of others.

Her uneasiness began to creep back when she realized she had traveled so far into the labyrinth of rooms that she no longer knew the way out. A warrior's wariness was roused. She would be trapped. Her steps slowed.

The more contemptuous of the two maidservants sighed, grasped Auriane's wrist and jerked her forward as if her arm were a horse's lead.

"Take your hand from me!" Auriane responded with quick indignation, pulling herself free. "How dare you!" Auriane's look was full of questioning as well as hurt. The maidservant withdrew in mock terror, then smiled wickedly at her guest's rudely accented Latin.

Why did they treat her so? Auriane knew a thing then that made her heart feel weighted with stones: The look Diocles gave her in the vestibule was familiar—it was the same look Erato had given her when she asked to be taken here, and it meant: *No. This is not a woman.*

Has *he, too,* decided: *This is not a woman?* Is that the true reason he is not here?

That is nonsense, and I am more than half mad! This house, this city, has cast a despairing spell on me.

And now as they walked, she became sharply aware of what was *not* in this house. No brightly colored warrior's shields were hung on the walls, nor were there spears neatly laid on their racks, nor did loyal retainers lie asleep in arms atop bear pelts and the hides of aurochs that they had hunted and killed themselves; strangely there was no sign whatever that this was the dwelling of a powerful man of a people who were masters of the art of war. This was a temple of leisure and grace, unscarred by the marks of siege and necessity. And so it must be, she imagined, in all the great-houses of this city—none were warrior's halls, yet their great men commanded numbers of warriors without precedent, scattered out all over the world. This was a sort of power to which she was not accustomed, the more unsettling because of its invisibility.

Look about you, she told herself grimly. No one here listens to wolves at night or sleeps with a collection of stones close at hand, fearing a raid at dawn. No one here struggles to pull food from the ground, their hands reddened with the blood of constant sacrifices to the goddesses of earth, beseeching them to give enough to eat this year. Nor have they felt rain leaking through thatch and worried that the roof would not hold for the night, nor had to decide before winter which animals to kill and which to let live because they cannot feed them all. Here they sacrifice doves to Venus, and their dwellings are storehouses of abundant food. The lowest servant in this place lives in greater luxury than the wealthiest clans of my tribe. Where food and a roof are never in doubt, the spirit is free to ascend and reflect on the gods; I am an animal with a bestial soul because I have *lived* like an animal. All I've learned of surviving is absurdly useless here.

The maidservants halted in an open-air room strewn with roses and wildflowers, where a wine service and honey-cakes had been set out; it opened onto a torchlit garden whose dimensions were vast and unknown. Adjacent to this room were the hot and cold chambers of a bath. The more amiable of the two showed her the dressing room, where drying cloths and a fine white linen tunica had been laid out on a black marble bench. Indicating Auriane's hairy calfskin cloak and rough tunica, she said sharply, "You must get rid of those," and Auriane heard: *They should probably be burned.*

Then both maidservants retired, though she knew they were within calling distance, leaving her alone with her accumulating anguish. Neither informed her how long she would have to wait for Marcus Julianus' return, and pride made her determined not to ask. It seemed too close to begging.

Long moments passed and she walked the garden alone, her feet making soft, crunching sounds on the gravel walkways as she moved between close-trimmed box hedges, laurel trees, pomegranates and old pines. Time moved sluggishly as snakes in winter.

I have been abandoned. And did not the man called Diocles say he was called away by the Empress? *No, you are mad to think that way. You poison your own mind.*

To distract herself from her swift-growing humiliation, she busied her mind with determining how this house could best be defended from attack. *Along that wall overlooking that valley, I would place archers, and behind them, atop that tree-covered rise, a catapult. . . .*

When a summer hour had passed, time became a taunting enemy. She passed an unearthly Diana rising among rose bushes, so magically modeled she wanted to touch that stone flesh to see if it was warm. *The body of an empress must look like that,* she thought—luminous, harmonious, unblemished as new-laid snow, with breasts small and firm as ripened plums. In her is, doubtless, the combined beauty of all women. The Empress Domitia Longina. *Who every maidservant and kitchen slave in this city knows is in love with him.* Auriane drew her cloak more tightly about her as if the house had eyes, and she strove to shield herself from its view. Savagely she forced back tears.

The garden's walks were laid out like the spokes of a wheel. At their center she came upon an eight-sided belvedere, nacreous in the chill moonlight, a house so delicately made it might have been a temple to a god of flowers. It seemed a sentient thing, lying in wait, glowing with mystic life. Spirit-terror gripped her heart.

This was the "house" she had seen in her fever dream, rising before the celebrants of the Sacred Marriage. What was it doing in this place? And above it was that stern full moon, poised just as in the dream. She stared numbly for a moment, while clutching the *aurr.* Then, feeling she fled a haunted bog, she bolted over the gravel walk, returning to the better-lit portico, which at least seemed of the realm of flesh and blood creatures.

She settled on the cushions where the silver wine service was laid out, meaning to calm herself with a draught. She felt the maidservants' prickly presence behind layers of diaphanous curtains and occasionally heard their evil-spirit sounds—rustling, whispering. In spite of it, she felt her first small surge of confidence.

At least in the matter of wine-mixing, I know the proper way. One ewer contains wine, the other water. They must be mixed, one to one. Only slave dealers, auctioneers and thieves that live under bridges drink unwatered wine.

She reached for the wine. *Slowly,* she cautioned herself, *as a city-nurtured woman would. Serenity, grace. Hands like darting fish.*

But the ewer crashed onto its side, seemingly an instant before she touched it. A wine lake filled the silver tray. Bloody drops speckled the marble floor. Her garments were soaked; to her dismay the wine was sweetened with honey and it plastered her tunica to her skin.

From behind the curtains came snuffling laughter from more than two maids—others must have gathered for the show. She flushed hotly, wishing she knew the trick of vanishing, imagining herself some unlovely hybrid of camel and ox. From her wound came soft hammer-blows of pain.

What vile people, what petty meanness! she thought. She suspected they knew that ewer was not well balanced and set it out for her on purpose. Why else would they all have collected to watch?

Then the kindlier of the two maidservants appeared and began silently, efficiently mopping up the mess with drying cloths; once she gave Auriane a quick, pitying look. Auriane watched her in dumb misery, almost apologizing, even though she was near certain she was the victim of a cruel trick, just because she was grateful for even this barest show of comradeship. As the concealed maidservants' laughter died, one whisper was audible above the others: "She belongs in a stable, not a house."

Auriane felt her heart smashed like glass.

I cannot live among these people. I am degrading myself and dishonoring my ancestors.

I am humiliating *him.* But then he, too, is humiliating me.

Slowly she rose to her feet, knowing with certainty what she began to suspect from the moment she entered this house: that no matter how the Roman mob might praise her and lavish her with letters of love, it mattered not at all here—in the halls of the nobility she would never be more than a vulgar curiosity. The Emperor, it was said, kept a simpleminded boy at his side and told him important secrets of state. *To the people of this house, that is what I would be for Marcus.*

"I must leave," she said to the maidservant.

"But . . . you cannot!"

Auriane took a step closer, her voice still low. "I *will* leave. You will show me the way out."

To the maidservant Auriane's face was possessed of a savage calm, with unknown violence lurking beneath. She was uncomfortably aware that this woman, Aurinia, was an extraordinarily successful killer of men. She thought: I was not told to keep her a prisoner. I have not been told anything. My lord was supposed to be here.

And so the issue was resolved by Auriane's determination. The maidservant relayed the message to Diocles, who agreed reluctantly. He sent a messenger to the *Ludus Magnus,* requesting that they take Auriane back. And this time the guards who were to escort her were not chosen with caution; six were called for quickly, without regard for their trustworthiness or their alliances.

Auriane meant to go at once to the vestibule, but she hesitated, irritated by the stickiness of her wine-soaked tunica. She knew that when they took her back in, they would not give her leave to wash herself. Then she remembered those luxuriant baths. Yes, she decided. Surely there was time enough.

Her cheeks streaked with tears, she strode into the cold room of the bath with its glistening Pompeian-red walls, its vaulted ceiling painted with marine frescoes—leaping dolphins, octopuses, sea-serpents—that seemed to float and billow in the light of the bronze chandelier suspended over the water. The cold bath was to her taste—it resembled more closely the shocking cold of the streams in which she bathed at home. With several angry movements she tore off her clothes. Then she dove, feeling she broke glass, shattering the mosaic image of Neptune on the pool's bottom.

She surfaced, her wet head sleek as an otter's, and began to swim, attacking the water with powerful strokes, imagining her arms were blades, slicing the surface to ribbons. A part of her was relieved. Now she need never reveal to him her battered body. Her tears mingled with the water.

Yes, this is best. I would have brought shame to Avenahar, who would have grown up to hear men taunt: *Her mother let a man of the enemy make an utter fool of her—and when he was finished with her, he discarded her like some thrall.* Among my own people is the man I will love.

She lost herself in swimming; the violent motion brought relief to her heart. Time coursed on swiftly without her knowing.

Then she heard an echo of a footstep on marble—a man's heavier tread. She slowed to look and suppressed a gasp. Marcus Julianus came from the dark, walking swiftly toward her. She stopped swimming and became very still, all her senses scattered in alarm. In his face she saw only impatience and anger. How visible his loathing was! She wondered that she had ever been foolish enough to believe this man felt great love for her.

She bolted for her clothes, swimming with frenzied strokes. But she stopped short at the bath's edge. Her discarded garments were just out of reach. And nothing would induce her to lift herself out of the water and expose her body to him. She kept herself immersed to her chin, huddled close to the side, feeling miserable and trapped.

"Auriane! What is the meaning of this? They've summoned

guards for you." His voice reverberated through the vault, and its harshness was magnified.

"Get off from me. I want only to leave!" Her body felt hot, as if the whole of it flushed in shame; even the frigid water could not cool it. She edged away from the side, fearful he might try to pull her out. The space that separated her from that heap of clothes looked vast as a continent.

"Do you understand what you have done?" he said sharply, standing directly above her now. She hugged the side again, crab-walking away from him. "Any one of those guards could have been agents of my enemies!"

"Let me leave!" Her voice quavered precariously; she felt close to breaking apart. She added weakly, "Please give me my clothes." *Now I am begging,* she thought, feeling an upwelling of self-loathing.

"Auriane," he said more softly, recognizing suddenly her disorientation. "You must not meddle in such things. You don't know how delicately balanced are the forces about me. What has happened? What is wrong?"

"Nothing," she said haughtily, with narrowed eyes.

"All right, nothing is wrong. But climb out of there before you get a chill. Here are your clothes." He brought not her soiled tunica but the neatly folded white linen one and the drying cloths. "Do not worry, I swear by all my ancestors back to Aeneas not to look at you."

She hesitated, gathering her courage, then eased herself out, never taking her eyes off his back, not trusting him not to look. She dried herself faster than she ever had in her life, then began struggling with the tunica, skipping over some of its fastenings, pricking herself once with the pin of a fibula because she looked at him and not at her hands.

When she had dressed, some of her confidence returned. "Now take me to the entrance chamber. I am lost in here."

"Auriane, you cannot mean this." He turned around. She saw the weariness in his face then, and the long-stored sadness. In the perverse way of such things, because she did not want to see it now, he looked fair as their images of Adonis, and never had he looked so dear. Soothingly he went on, "I had Diocles send those guards off. You must understand I cannot let you venture out there at night. If you weren't attacked by cutthroats and thieves, you'd be struck dead by the garbage they hurl from the upper stories at night. You'll have to stay here." He hesitated, not knowing quite how to put it, then added, "There are . . . guest chambers."

"Let me pass," she said grimly. "You look upon me for the last time." In her agitated state of mind the words "There are guest chambers" sounded like a rebuff—he wanted to make certain it was plainly understood, lest she have other ideas, that he was *not* taking her to his bed—and so words spoken to put her at ease only reinforced her unease. She took a step forward, toward the door; he moved sideways to intercept her.

"I want an explanation of all this," he said gently.

"You'll mock me no more! I despise you! Stand away from me!"

Then with a speed for which he was unprepared she sprinted forward, darting around him on his other side; he reached for her but she was gone, streaking out into the darkened rooms. Cursing, he snatched a torch from a wall sconce—in the last hour the lamps had been extinguished—and took up the chase. Ahead of him she sped through the silent dark.

"Auriane! Stop this at once!" he cried out as he ran. "Have you gone mad? What possesses you? *Halt!*" She fled blindly, hoping to find the vestibule, but she did not know the way and she was making bad guesses. For a moment he lost her; then he heard a heavy table crash to the floor, followed by a cascade of falling glass. He shifted course and sprinted forward once more.

"You're headed for a fish pond! Halt at once!"

He heard a loud splash, a moment of silence, then fast footfalls as she regained solid ground and continued running.

Auriane without knowing it was traveling in a great circle. Now there was gravel beneath her feet and she was enveloped in the humid perfume of earth and herbs.

A garden. But which one? Fria, let it be the one nearest the vestibule.

The garden's lamps had been snuffed as well, and the fate-weaving moon cloaked itself behind clouds; that moon was a hunter, setting traps, laying a black web over the night. She could scarcely see. Pine branches lashed at her. From the sound of his footfalls she knew he was gaining on her. She ran erratically, and terror fed terror till it grew beyond reason. *My fate is my people's, and Baldemar's. If he shames me more, I will poison the common blood.* Then she slowed, some instinct warning her of a barrier ahead. An instant later she crashed against a wall of open latticework. The moon shrugged off its cloak. She was trapped inside that phantom belvedere, haunt of dreams. The thing conspired against her, together with the moon.

A moment later the fast steps behind her stopped and Marcus Julianus stood in the only door, blocking her exit, his torch filling the small garden room with its unsteady light.

The moments were marked by her labored breaths, shuddering with suppressed sobs. She was flattened against the far wall of the octagonal room, eyes bright and wild as a cornered hare. She felt she clung instinctively to the last of her dignity, as if she gripped a high ledge and felt herself slipping. But she managed to lift her head spiritedly and muster a warning look.

Marcus Julianus determined at once to come no closer. She looked as though her heart might collapse if he did. He waited until her breathing slowed, giving her time to trust he would not invade the territory that separated them, not, at least, without invitation.

"Auriane, you must listen." His voice was a steadying hand. "I do not suppose you know what you did. I suppose you could not know—"

"There is no place for me here and you know it well!" Her wrath had a pitiable quality now, like an animal thrashing in a trap. "I cannot blame you for wanting to rid yourself of a woman who is an animal. But I can hold you to account for making a laughing-stock of me. You left me here since dusk. Now leave me forever. However you may try, you shall not thieve the strength and luck of my ancestors. You shall not!"

"You have guessed at what has happened, and you guessed wrong. You learned today what my people's love is worth, outside the school, and you wrongly assumed mine is worth the same. It is mystifying to me how you could think such things of me. Or how you could so easily forget my love for you—"

"It was not done easily!" She was silent abruptly, as if an icicle had been forced into her throat.

"All right, not easily then. But it is there, and you have forgotten it. It is there right now in abundance, though you cannot feel it. Auriane—" She stood very still, her muscles tensed, aware of him with all her senses, listening to him with her whole body. Carefully he took a step forward. She pressed closer to the wall as if to maintain the original distance between them, but in her eyes was a look of being lulled somewhat just by his voice, which worked upon her like a slow massage.

"You were not abandoned, nor were you mocked. And if you

were tormented by anyone in this household, it was done against orders and certainly does not express my own sentiments——"

"I will not live among people who despise me," she said hoarsely. "Why do you pretend? You must know I will *never* be a woman of your people. Stop playing with me."

"It is true, Auriane. The people of this city are cruel to anyone of foreign birth and they probably never would accept you. And I never expected they would. But I do not intend to stay here. It matters not at all to me what my countrymen think of you. Love is beyond race and custom. And as for my absence, there are certain things you must understand at once. You've little idea what you've come into the midst of—and I am not free to tell you. In this one thing I must simply ask you to trust me, I know of no other way. I was away on a grave matter that arose suddenly, and it had nothing whatever to do with you. I expected that you would understand since in the first hour of evening I sent a messenger——"

He saw a small jump of relief in her eye. "No messenger was sent," she said quickly.

"What?" he said softly, then half turned from her, his expression alert and faraway. He paced back and forth once, going out the door as if swiftly contemplating some action; then he stopped, as if thinking suddenly: It is no use. "If no messenger arrived, I fear a man has died tonight," he said with such a depth of sadness that she caught her breath, feeling intimately his love for the man. Then she felt a fresh spurt of shame.

He sent a messenger. I ran like an animal or a child. Children do not know when to trust. What woman of his own people would have behaved so?

"I am in the midst of a ring of wolves," he continued, "and daily they move closer." His resolute look slowly gave way to a proud smile as he considered her. "But now I have more reason than ever to battle my way out. Auriane, you cannot really believe I turned from you, truly, now. It is a cruel deception brought on by all the torments you've endured. You have gravely underestimated my love."

He set his torch into a sconce and walked over to her then, slowly, patiently as a man trying not to frighten a wild bird from its perch. She was still turned away as he came up behind her and put his hands on her shoulders and left them there, letting her absorb their warmth. She tensed at first, fighting against the animal comfort his hands brought, but it was irresistible, like a slow immersion into steamy water on a winter day. He felt her begin to relax in hesitant stages. But if the wall about her had begun to crumble, he could see that sentries were still out. Much of the wild sadness was still in her eyes.

She felt like a person shaken out of a disturbing dream—its ill humors flowed still in her veins; she was not yet ready to believe a gentler reality had replaced it.

"Well then, if you'd no reason to despise me before," she whispered, "I've certainly given you a reason tonight. I acted the fool, in losing faith in you, in summoning those guards." She turned round to face him, a haunted look in her eye. "This is a strange and foul night. Marcus, I have brought about your ruin."

"That is ridiculous." He smiled easily, shaking his head. "You must not think that. There is no situation that cannot be turned round, with diligent effort. You could not, poor creature, have been expected to do otherwise than you did. All these things are new and strange to you. And the chances are, it will come to nothing."

"This *will* come to something. I see it as I see you. I brought about Baldemar's end. And now yours."

"Stop this! It is futile fatalism and I won't listen while you torment yourself so. You take away all the powers of men and give them to gods. Sometimes things just happen or do not happen, as a man is thoughtful or careless. Not everything is predetermined. Think of it no more; I know I shall not, not, at least, before tomorrow."

Then as if moving to slow music, he pushed her damp hair aside, exposing her bare neck; languidly he kissed it. A delicate shudder ran down the length of her body in spite of herself. To her dismay she realized that something at her core that was covetous and nurturing, overflowing and blind, sought him as the sea seeks the shore, wanting to mingle for a time with no thought of what might happen at the change of tides.

He thought her mind settled then. But to his surprise she stiffened and took a decisive step away from him, putting herself out of his reach. Her look was veiled.

"Something else is wrong," he said, reaching out and softly stroking her cheek with the back of his hand. "What is it?"

"Marcus, how do you think—" she began, rushing into a question she could not finish. He guessed she feared it might be improper, or worse, ridiculous.

"If you truly think I would ridicule you for your fears, you do not know me. What is wrong?" But her look was once more evasive, protected.

"Nothing," she said decisively. As if to prove it, she moved toward him, encircled her arms about his neck and began a confident kiss. But when he responded by pulling her closer, moving his hands through the open sides of the tunica and down the curve of her bare back, she wrest herself free and backed quickly away, a shying colt with white showing in its eyes. Then she looked off, misery in her face. He found it intriguing rather than irritating. Something had made her timid about being touched. Had he violated some tribal custom?

"I am sorry," she said tautly. "I am making you angry and disappointing you and . . . I must seem very foolish. Let us end our love now and say farewell to each other, since the ways of my people are so at odds with the ways of yours."

He smiled, shaking his head. "But that is not what the trouble is. No farewells until this mystery is uncovered. Come over here, and sit."

Reluctantly she sat beside him on a stone bench before a low table of polished granite supported by three bronze greyhounds; on it was a shallow terra-cotta bowl heaped with fruits such as she had never seen. She leaned back against the tapestry of grapevines that wove themselves through the latticework. The little room seemed utterly remote from the world, as though they had made a camp in the Hyperborean lands beyond all the settlements of humankind.

"You are disappointing me but not in the way you might think. I am not a boy. I will not sulk if you do not lie with me tonight. I am a man who wants to spend the remainder of his days with you, however few they may be. I doubt we've a whole year left to live, between the two of us—and for that we've each got only ourselves to blame. I'm disappointed that you trust me so little to understand. If a wall is reared up between us now, it might well be there until we die. You must tell me what it is. If it is something you count shameful, I know I will not judge it as harshly as you imagine."

The words she wanted to speak churned in her mind. Finally she steeled herself, shut her eyes, and said quickly, "Marcus, how do you think a woman ought to look, that is, if she were . . . most pleasingly formed?"

"What sort of question is this?" Had there not been such a look of torment on her face he might have laughed in spite of his promise.

"Just answer it please!" she said angrily, sitting very still, her gaze riveted on the fruit, as though unwilling even to move for fear he would ridicule her.

I cannot believe this, he thought. Here is the most courageous being I have ever encountered—the woman who galloped alone into the ranks of the Eighth Legion, fully expecting it to be her last battle on earth—and she is fearful of undressing before me. The philosopher in him observed: It is strange how inconsistently human courage manifests itself. But the human part of him felt only a welling of compassion.

He replied with gentle patience, "For that, you'll have to give me more time. It's a matter I haven't considered seriously since I was a boy of sixteen or thereabouts—nor has any man who has any sense. You silly creature, there *is* no one way a woman ought to look."

"Truly, you think so?" she said, not at all convinced. She turned to the ghostly image of Diana that seemed to hover among the rosebushes, and said solemnly, "I look not at all like that."

He struggled with a smile. "You'd be depressing if you did. She looks sour and smug and like she's had one too many milk baths. Anyway, that sort of perfection can be bought, and quickly becomes dull. A heart cannot be bought."

"You will think me too muscular and too scarred."

"Who has been putting these ideas into your mind? Such concerns were never in your thoughts before."

"Now you think me ridiculous."

"No! I think it sad, not ridiculous. I cannot believe you tortured yourself with that." He then took up one of her hands and pretended to critically examine it. "Take, for example, this hand," he said, mimicking a philosopher presenting an argument. "To me, it is perfect. Why? Because it is such a well-formed hand? Well, in fact it is so, but that alone isn't enough. It is because it is yours. And so it will go with the rest of you, I promise it."

"You say that now."

"Oh, I cannot believe this." He put his hands to his head; he could think of no more reassurances to offer her. She watched him expectantly, her eyes alert and shining in the torchlight, and he sensed she wanted him to keep trying. It was then that he knew he must stop, for it was useless; it was not a thing that could be proven with words, even were they numerous enough to fill a thousand bookrolls. He could only state the truth and let her sense the rest. The words he had already spoken must be given a chance to do their work, like some medicine that needs time to establish itself in the body.

But perhaps the time required will be too long for us, he thought, as he realized with dismay that one thing he told her was no longer true—now he wanted with great urgency to lie with her on this night. He was slowly becoming maddened by the closeness of her, by that neatly formed mouth, those great, grave, lucid eyes, that small frown as she considered his words, her way of drawing in her shoulders when she feared she said something foolish, the inviting swell of a full breast asserting itself through the thin cloth. *Venus be merciful. For how long will I be expected to bear this?*

She began to fill the silence with small questions about his life, which she used to disguise the fact that, slowly as a shadow on a sundial, she was edging closer. He sat very still, feeling he sought to win the confidence of a squirrel, as, with a sort of furtive innocence, she closed the distance between them. After what seemed a day he felt her warm breath on his cheek; then she quickly burrowed her face in the cloth of his tunic and sat contentedly still. He put an experimental arm about her shoulder, struggling to do it casually. This time she did not pull away. A small victory, he thought. But trust so recently won could be swiftly withdrawn.

Gently he stroked her hair, knowing she wanted comfort, not physical love, waiting as he knew he must wait, for otherwise what followed would not be lovemaking but a man overwhelming a frightened woman, and he might lose all hope of winning her complete trust. He thought then of Domitian whose partners were hostages and victims, and of the countless young noblemen loitering about the theaters and baths who imagined when they consummated their love that they invaded and conquered some rebellious province. No, he thought with loathing, if I am to have her, it must be as unlike that as possible.

Her gaze moved to the contents of the terra-cotta bowl. "What *are* those things? Fruit or rocks?" The tone of her voice was silkier now and came from a deeper place; he sensed her temper was changing.

"Pomegranates," he replied, cutting a moon-shaped slice and holding it to her mouth, "or rock-apple, thought by men of old to bring immortal life. It is the seeds that are eaten, not the meat."

She regarded it suspiciously, then began licking and nibbling at the plump seeds.

"That was my finger! Nothing wrong with those teeth." The fruit's thin red juice ran in rivulets down his hand. To his surprise she began slowly, deliberately licking the juice, running her tongue down his hand with a cautious shyness, a fragile touch that made him fear at any moment it might be withdrawn. All too soon the juices were gone. He cut another slice and held it to her lips.

This time he deliberately let the juices run.

She went after them with more boldness this time, following juice and stray seeds down into the soft hairs of his wrist and arm, tasting him as well as the juice, carefully watching him all the while. The moist feel of that questing tongue, brash and tentative as it explored his arm, drove him to a quiet frenzy. It put him in mind not so much of a woman possessed of Eros as a deer at a salt lick—but because it was not done seductively, it was, oddly, the more so. Somehow this curious licking, not quite animal, not quite human, but of a nature entirely her own, aroused him more than the attentions of any woman he had ever known.

He thought: She seems utterly oblivious to the fact that she is torturing me. Or is she?

He drew her to him then, relishing the form of her back, her hips, his hands asking, encouraging, reassuring, but not demanding. He wanted more evidence her unease and doubt were banished.

Then all at once she gave it to him. She took one of his hands in hers, guided it within the opening of the tunica and placed it on one breast. He caught his breath. All life shivered to a rapturous halt. He enclosed the delicate weight of it in his hand, supporting it; when he found his hand could not quite contain its fullness he moved it slowly, cradling the silken softness of that breast with such infinite tenderness it caused a bolt of pleasure to course through her. That touch was too much to bear, and she gave a small cry, feeling bones, flesh, and heart melt toward him.

Her breathing became deep and determined; she was all hot liquid center, weak and watery inside, as she collapsed against him. The dwindling conscious part of her made a last protest: You fall into oblivion—and he will not catch you. But her senses responded: Not now—worry over that one tomorrow. Then she let go and fell wholly into the warm sea; she could no more have thwarted this pull toward him than could a lily decide not to open or a river check itself before overrunning its banks.

Had he been able to reason he would have realized: I need no more assurances of her readiness. But thought dissolved into rampant impulse. It was the triumph of the moon.

With a few swift sure movements he gathered her up, intending to carry her to his apartments, for her feet were cut and bruised from running barefoot over the gravel. As he struggled up with her, staggering for the first two steps, she laughed softly at him, and at herself for being so difficult to carry. As they passed between the lamps that flanked the arched entrance of his apartments, he thought of the torches of whitethorn borne by the revelers in the wedding procession as the bridegroom carries the yellow-veiled bride over the threshold of her new home. With a flash of grief he thought: Perhaps wedding night and all of wedded life will be contained in one night.

Auriane closed her eyes, feeling a blind rush of excitement in being carried, in sensing a strength not her own. She opened them to find he had taken her to a low-ceilinged room that made her feel enclosed and securely held; it was well padded with overlapping tapestries flushed with every shade of red. Vertical strips of polished moonstone set into the wall caused their reflection to flicker in and out of sight as he carried her past the flame-cluster of a hanging lamp; where the fire was caught in the gold of the furnishings, the moldings, it rippled like a mirage. He eased her onto what she guessed was a bed though it was raised up higher than any sleeping couch she had ever seen; it was set into an arched niche and so had a smaller room of its own. She sank into a wool-stuffed mattress, clinging to him as he came up beside her. From somewhere came the cheerful, primeval sound of trickling water, and the scent of some incense that smelled of damp autumn meadows.

They were mysterious to one another in the dim light as she kissed his face, his neck, with a sort of fevered restraint. Then, overcome by the long-awaited unobstructed closeness of him, she began determinedly tearing at his tunic. Unable to find the fastenings in the darkness, she ripped the cloth when it too stubbornly resisted her pawing. The sudden sight of his bare shoulders and chest with their unconscious beauty, their intriguing interplay of smooth skin and solid muscle beneath, was again too much to bear. She launched herself at him while one hand scrambled with some unidentified underclothing about his loins, struggling to loosen it.

She brought herself up short when she realized he was laughing.

He caught up her hands, held them still, then softly pressed them to his lips. Auriane wondered in a contented haze—for less and less was she able to worry over such things—*Now* what have I done that is wrong?

"Slowly!" he said, still laughing. "This is not mortal combat!" Carefully he set her back among the cushions, marveling at the look she gave him then. Those eyes were alight with mischief, signaling she wanted only to play; yet at the same time, they were fogged with carnal passion. While caressing her face, he added, "There *is* one negligible difference, if you've not been told, between a bed and a battlefield."

She frowned with mock puzzlement. "No. Not really."

"What happens on a battlefield hopefully ends quickly. This, pray, not so quickly."

Auriane nipped at the hand that stroked her cheek.

Then, delicately, as though he eased the skin from a peach, he pulled her tunica down, gradually exposing her breasts, her belly. She rose up and pressed hard against him, flattening the milky roundness of her breasts against his chest; sharply she drew in a breath at the feel of the fine friction of his hair against the keenly sensitive silk of her breasts. He held her there for long moments, bare skin to bare skin, as if to establish the reality of the moment; both felt a shock of delight at this latest frontier crossed and were pleasantly stunned that at last there was no barrier to the physical expression of love.

He broke away and they began delicately negotiating each other as they sat close, still half clad, caught up in a loving dueling of moist, exhaustive kisses, with much drawing close and pulling away, as if to renew the sensation of coming together for the first time. She found herself feveredly seeking in him what was most male, biting at a stubbled cheek, devouring a muscled shoulder with her hands. Then with a controlled, purposeful urgency he began kissing her throat, moving down her body with elaborate patience; she snaked against him and sank back onto the cushions, shuddering at each kiss as though it were an excruciating touch directly on the heart. When she felt his mouth on her breast, she recoiled as if touched by ice; slowly she relaxed and gave them over to him entirely, and swiftly they became suffused with a creamy warmth. After timeless moments he moved away from her breasts, kissing her stomach, pushing aside the tunica as it impeded his progress; somewhere nearby was her wound, red and staring, but those wise, insistent kisses worked as a witch's balm upon it, blurring the memory of its pain, making its ugliness a negligible thing. It was entirely a spirit-wound, she realized then. She saw suddenly her humbled country and her body as one— alike defenseless, ravaged, yet still the only possible home—and she had not known how weary she was from being an expatriate from both. Those hands were sorcerers, enticing her home to her body. Slowly he continued to move down, his purposefulness only apparent after a while, for he stopped often to return energetically to her mouth, her neck, her breasts. Once the thought intruded: *I do not deserve such pleasure, not while my people are starving.* But it did not linger long; the movement of those hands, poetic, firm, was an opposing voice saying, *You do.*

And then he was poised above the place of a woman's pleasure and shame, meaning to kiss her there; with a jolt she realized his destination. Objections reared up; her body became rigid; gates dropped closed. The cautions of mothers and grandmothers jangled in her mind. She saw a vision from childhood: the village woman with shaved head driven through the Boar Gate by the priests as she was taken to the bogs to be drowned for lying with a foreign traveler. This was followed by the lightning realization that her lifelong shyness about her body, never before questioned, was born of terror.

If I object, he will think me silly and childish, or ignorant.

But the tight weave of her own culture was already seriously rent, and here, in this place of no clans, no continuity of life, she had been for a long time weaving one of her own. This new order knew nothing but necessity's commands and the rampant love of Fria, who was the genius of love in all its forms. In this world she learned to condense all life into one simpler law: There was only movement away from love or movement toward love.

He sensed her alarm and paused, holding her still, steadying her, caressing her hips while murmuring words of reassurance. Moments later, when he sensed her acceptance, he returned to kissing her. And when she felt his tongue on that most secret of places, she felt all worldly bonds broke—of childhood to womanhood, of woman to tribe, of fear to life, and she was a blissful, blind creature rocked on primal waters, massaged by the currents, feeling the warmth of sunlight through sea, a simple organism nourished by love. Now her only fear was that he might stop.

She writhed among the cushions, feeling gloriously out of control, whipped about by the ravenous emptiness she began to feel within; she began to fight with him, desperate to pull him up beside her. He purposely resisted her, holding her hips securely so she could scarcely move, tormenting her with more pleasure. As that fierce emptiness consumed her, she clawed at him, scarcely conscious of what she was doing, until at last he relented, came forward and lay along her length.

She hugged her flushed face tightly to his, all her nakedness pressed hard against his, goaded by a fresh spasm of desire as she felt the gentle probing insistence of his sex, and a muscular thigh pressed firmly against her own, determinedly parting them. She felt she reached for him with her whole body, desperate to draw him in, shifting between aching anticipation as she sensed the force of his desire for her, and the luxuriant mellowness of her own vulnerability. But he teased her, finding her womanhood, pausing at the gate, then drawing away. In frustration she bit him hard on the shoulder, though not hard enough to draw blood.

He paused, laughing softly, then took her face in his hands and quietly looked at her; it was as if he feared passion separated them too much, and he wanted to know he reached into all of her, not just her body. In a moment too delicate and still for what had gone before, he solemnly said her name and kissed her eyes, her mouth, as if she were some fragile treasure. Then with one firm yet cautious motion, as if he feared hurting her, he entered her body, and she closed about him, lost in a sense of plummeting and ascending; she felt a gate flung open and that first immersion was a caress, the ultimate one, reaching deeply into her most tender, guarded core.

She lay still as the dead while feeling she burst with life; h[er] honey gushed through her limbs. His movement within b[ecame] her own, erasing the boundary between bodies. Once he [...] turn her face to the dim light, enjoying the sight of h[...] her love-soaked delirium. Then, while gently [...] neck, her mouth with a hail of kisses, h[...] ardently within her, but still it was a [...] knew the precise moment when [...] that a whisper could not be [...] wanted. Had a night p[...] Driven now by one [...] into one, they [...] powerfully [...] look of [...]

[overlapping torn page fragments, rotated:]

At [...] memory. [...] weight pressing [...] she lay still, not wanting [...] fuzzy golden haze that was thick [...] memory of the flood of pleasure lay ab[...] looking with wonder at the powerful body gone [...] been, she felt only comfort. She breathed love i[...] joyously interbound, and always had been. Where her wom[an] world's beginning; she floated through a mythical dusk, caressed by the gentle light-play of dawn. All in life was braided together— he drifted over the black and bottomless pool at the place where the floodwaters became slack and still. Here was world's end. eace and contentment rolled over her like some golden smoke. st time, and she moved to hold him there as long as possible. She felt a final throb of his life in her as he drove in deeply one whorns at a mother's breast. sed eyes as they clung to each other with the blind love of r struggle to become one body for a few moments she kissed his shuddered once in her arms, helpless as she was; she kissed his bearing things. They formed one universe, solemn, whole, as a wonder to her; it must have been one universe, solemn, whole, nd then both fell free, at the mercy of the yearning of all ously helpless before a sweet invasion, overrun by love. e drove her to final pleasure; she felt laid bare,

her fuzzy mind-state, feeling contented as a lily pad on a pond. Reverentially he smoothed the hair from her forehead, and kissed it. "Dearest," he said softly once. And that same hand wandered down, seemingly of its own accord, seeking the dove softness of a breast. Once again he felt the tidal pull, dragging his body to hers.

"Yes," she said sleepily. "Again."

Not wanting her to fully awaken, he carefully gathered her up, and this time their lovemaking was less the previous night's ride on a torrent, and more a dream-journey, languorous as smoke, down a glassy river. They did not stop until the sun was well established in the sky, filling the room with a ruddy haze.

Auriane stood hooded and cloaked, ready to depart through the house's kitchen entrance, which opened onto an alley that dropped down into the Subura. Marcus Julianus judged it better to wait until noon, when the thickest crowds clogged the narrow streets. She would leave with two cook's girls setting out for the produce stalls, who would not know the identity of the woman who left with them; they would follow a meandering route; at the Street of Booksellers six guards of the school disguised as Vigiles would escort her the rest of the way. If his enemies' spies saw her and managed to keep apace with her through the crowds, they would see nothing to confirm their suspicions beyond a doubt.

The larger world with all its jagged edges settled about her once more. Marcus Julianus joined her after he concluded his morning audience with his two hundred and more clients and dependents. He looked younger to her now, as if a life's knowledge of tragedy had been dissolved away by the night, and maddeningly appealing, which keenly frustrated her because now nothing could be done about it.

He recognized the now-familiar look in her eyes. "Do not even *think* of ripping this one off, you destructive little minx!" he said, smiling, indicating the tunic he had just put on. Gently he kissed her. She nuzzled his neck, and he held her for long moments in a rich silence broken only by an occasional muffled word of love.

After a time she said, "Marcus . . . , there is a thing I never dared ask anyone for fear of speaking blasphemy. . . ."

"Ask, please! I thrive on blasphemy."

"What is the *sacred* meaning of . . . of the sacrifices of the arena?"

"A painful question! I wish to Venus they had one—it would be less shameful to speak of them. Oh, they had one, once. Long ago, pairs of criminals fought to the death to please the underworld gods at our funeral rites, and the slain swordsman was thought a fitting servant for the dead man in his journey to the other world."

"But *now* . . . we do not fructify crops, or bring you victory over your enemies, or help the dead? We die for no cause?"

"I fear it is so."

"This will curse you, you know, and all your kind."

"Yes. I believe it already has. But a man or woman does not have to be of one mind with his people. . . ."

"I know that well; all my life I have been reviled for being of a different mind than—" Her words broke off when he held her at arm's length and firmly met her eye.

"Well then, could not that laudable independence of mind be applied to the rite of vengeance as well? Does it matter that the great lot of your people count it necessary? Might not vengeance slayings, too, be death for no cause?"

A look of affront came into her eyes, as if a passerby had torn off her garments. But it was swiftly replaced by a look of confused sadness. Knowing he pried at the very place where her certainties were beginning to crack, he went on with determination.

"Auriane, look at me. You must give this up! By the love you bear me, I insist upon it. After last night I can endure it far less. *You must not fight Aristos."*

She looked away, unable to meet the look of love and hurt in his eyes.

I must not tell him that it is too late, that day and hour have been set. I know his mind all too well. He would be like a cornered beast, bound to fight his way out. And might not he be able somehow to undo my arrangement? His power reaches everywhere and into everything. No, I cannot risk it.

But is it not true that *not* telling him is a sort of lying? The night has made him a kinsman—and to deceive a kinsman is a cursed thing. Once again the Fates set one part of me against another. I cannot serve my people and be truthful to him. But my people will always come before all else; we sprang alike from the Well of Urdr and cannot ever be separate. *He must not know.*

"Auriane." He saw the look of ferment in her eye and was encouraged, thinking it to mean his appeal was being considered. "Surely you know that after what has passed between us, we must both live, and live together. Does not the passion of love heal the passion of vengeance?"

For a heartbeat, she thought Ramis looked out of Marcus Julianus' eyes. She responded quickly, "Holy vengeance is not born of hatred. . . . It is the seal of kinsmen's love," realizing her words sounded like the long-memorized, numbly delivered lines of an uninspired actor.

"Or so you have been taught since before you could talk."

She felt a door open, then slam shut. Ramis' words stirred uncomfortably within her: *"Vengeance, my poor wise fool, does not exist. . . . "*

She whispered tensely, "Well, then, I will think upon this thing." *Another untruth. Now I am twice cursed. The earth may open to swallow me up.*

"You've not much longer to think about it, Auriane." He lifted her chin, making her look at him. "If you want to leave with me, you must be ready to do so just after the Ides of August, whether Aristos is alive or dead. Four months. I have grave doubts that you'll manage to get him to fight you before then, indeed, if ever. I must have your word upon what you will do."

"You have my word—I will be ready to leave with you then, whether Aristos is alive . . . or dead." If *these* words turn out to be untruthful, she thought, I won't be alive to worry over it. She paused, then asked in bewilderment, "Where would we go and not be persecuted?"

She knew now she could no longer live wholly among her own people as before, though she would ever be their servant. A creature that has broken out of its shell and grown cannot fit itself back into the shell that nurtured it, even if the broken pieces could be fitted back together. The old world, though still loved, was sad and constricting, like a house lived in during a poor and uncertain childhood. She thought of the cities she had passed on her journey here, of the bookrolls of Marcus Julianus' library—these things, once seen, could not be forgotten. They set the mind alight, and slowly it burned; now she was beset with a need to know the writings of the outer-world sages, and all the secrets of towns. She knew she could only watch both worlds at a small distance, and wonder. She was condemned to the border.

"It's only in this infernal city that nothing is permitted," he replied. "In the wilder provinces of the far north, you would be accepted far more readily. I have been arranging for years to quit this place when my work here is done. And soon I may have to, for safety's sake. I am having a villa constructed in the province of Upper Germania—it is nearly complete. The land is near the great river and is not more than a day's ride from the lands of your people. It is close enough that you could go to join in their festivals, pay homage to your gods or make visits to your kin who are still living. Indeed, your influence among your people might be useful in maintaining peace. We would find your daughter and I would raise her as mine. The post I am taking there is a minor one and a day might come when I will be recalled—but I cannot worry over that now. Auriane, could you live in such a place? But for this, I see no way for us to live as one, and not be persecuted for such a marriage."

"For such a—*what?*"

"A marriage. Auriane, I thought this understood between us. I never thought of anything else."

"Your people would sooner let you marry a pig or a goat!" Her eyes were bitter and bright. "It is against all your laws. Why even speak of such things?"

"There is nothing in this world that cannot be arranged. It is true that when you are freed, your status will be of the humblest. But a decree of an emperor can change that. And so it shall be. I shall request when the time comes that you be given the status of one born free—"

"I *was* born free!"

"Of course you were. It is but a term of the law courts. But you have been enslaved—your actual status at birth means nothing to a magistrate. When released you will have the rank of freed-woman—and as such you would never be permitted to marry into a senatorial family. The stigma of slavery must be removed entirely. It is rarely done, and only by imperial intervention, but my guess is that when the time comes, my request won't be refused." He drew her close. "Why do you insist upon believing I mean to honor you less than I would a beloved from among my own people?"

"You've galloped ahead of me; you must give me time to catch up." Her voice was hoarse; she held to him, her throat paralyzed. Her amazement gave way in stages to a cautious joy. Guardedly she began to feel warm, enclosed. He truly wanted her for life then; he did not mean to discard her when he tired of her. Here was the first budding of a new circle of kin. She shivered, having only a dim sense of what was being offered her. His wealth surely matched that of kings; she could bring rich gifts to her kin and food to the starving. Avenahar would be a wealthy woman; she would be able to find the best of husbands in spite of her mixed blood. She felt she paused at a gateway; behind her was her whole life, seen through a vapor of strange, sweet sadness mingled with yearning. She wished she could somehow reach back, lift up, and hearten the woman she had been throughout a childhood spent facing world's end, and breathe life into friends and kin who had died savagely, not living long enough for wisdom. And ahead of her was either a luminous, limitless unknown—shared wholly or partly with him, with the curse of kin-killing lifted—in which she would live as the gods intended.

Or death in the arena.

"I have saddened you. You were thinking, perhaps, of marrying someone else?"

"I fear you've guessed it. The King of the Parthians asked for my hand. You are too late."

She gave him a puppylike nip on the neck. He laughed and ruffled her hair. "Truly, Marcus, I am honored beyond measure and filled with . . . surprise and joy. But . . . I have no answer for you on this day, for I do not know what comes for me." She was thinking then of the midnight summons to Ramis' island, and the Veleda's disturbing words: ". . . *or you can walk the wide avenue to the moon.*" Fate awarded her a kingdom she might be compelled to spurn.

"You know there are women among us who . . . cannot marry because they are consecrated to the earth, as Ramis is. . . . I do not know why I say this, for I do not *want* to be one of the Holy Ones, but if I become one, it would not be left to my will, and—"

"Stop! You are a vexing labyrinth of worries and doubts! Wait, at least, until a thing happens before you fret over it! Now we must speak of one more thing: What must be done if you survive and I do not."

"That shall not be," she whispered, "for I would then turn my sword upon myself."

"Stop that, you little fool, I don't want you to die because of me. And you're only making what I must do much harder. I won't listen to such talk. Now listen to me. If things do not go well for me, my property will be confiscated. In that case, you must not come near this house, do you understand?"

Numbly, she nodded. He continued. "They will get the estates and anything else they can seize, but I have much that is hidden away. And I want a large share of it to go to *you*, that you might ever after be richly provided for. Now, unless Erato matches you foolishly, you stand a good chance of earning release. Here is what you must do. This matter is in the hands of a freedman of mine who lives at Veii. You will have to travel there—" And so he followed with a list of places and names, which she committed to memory while her eyes began to well with tears.

At last she said softly, "You are in favor still, in spite of all that has happened. Why think of these things?"

"You've no idea how swiftly favor can be turned round. Domitian lapses into a peculiar rational madness all his own. In these days I fear most for those who appear to be in favor."

"You've some plan to rid the world of him, have you not?" she said suddenly, startling herself as much as him; the words seemed to come into her mind from nowhere, and once spoken she knew they were true.

How can she have known? he thought, alarm hammering in his head. There is no way. She has fine sharp senses keyed beyond the human, wondrous as the dog's ability to track, the eagle's sight. I thank Nemesis that Veiento, Montanus and the rest are not as perceptive as she.

"You judge me for challenging one man," she went on, "and yet you have set yourself against the whole of his Guard."

"All right, that is enough," he said gently. "You must put it from your mind. It is ill-omened and ill-advised, and I have oathed not to speak of it to many brave men and women who might lose their lives. These are hideous times."

He put an arm about her shoulders and walked with her to the heavy oak door that led to the steep alleyway. "Auriane," he said, taking her face in his hands, "you must stop sorrowing for me. I count my chances far better than yours against Aristos. Anyway, if I did not have an unusual gift for staying alive, I would not be with you now."

She was not comforted by this. She studied him intently, as though to remember his face in case this were the last time she should look upon it.

"We will meet again—soon," he said. He knew from her eyes that she struggled to believe it and failed.

She sought his mouth suddenly and kissed him hard, as if to impress her soul on him for all time. Then they separated, and he pulled the hood of her cloak well forward, arranging it so that it concealed her face. When this was done, he opened the door.

"Farewell," she said in a tremulous whisper.

"Auriane," he said, stopping her just as she started to step down. "Do you believe now that I love you?"

She nodded, not trusting her voice. She did not want to go out into the streets shaking with tears.

"Try not to forget it this time," he said, smiling casually. In answer she nodded again and gave his hand a forlorn squeeze. Then the two cook's girls were summoned, and all three set off down the alleyway.

CHAPTER LII

"The Lady Junilla," Veiento's blue-liveried servant announced with the shrill arrogance of the young. He was a Cappadocian boy, a sulky Eros grown too tall too quickly, an amusement Veiento neglected to discard when post-pubescent beauty became marred by stooped posture and poor complexion. As Junilla moved past him amid floating silks of iridescent sea-green, the boy gave her a pert look that meant: Life is difficult enough, you harlot, without your coming here to stir up an already boiling pot. Junilla paid him no more mind than she might a growling cur and presented herself haughtily before Veiento, who was hard at work in his rooms in the West Palace, considering an array of written confessions, purloined letters and transcribed conversations, consolidating evidence for the prosecution of Domitian's enemies in the Senate.

Veiento roughly ordered the boy off, along with two elderly scribes. When they were alone, he gave Junilla a tight, cold smile, inclining his head so slightly the gesture was scarcely made at all. His eyes were two bright, sharp points in their owlish hollows. That shark's fin nose was more prominent than Junilla remembered; flesh shrank from bone as if he decayed while still living. Human blood, Junilla mused, must not provide much nourishment.

"Well, to what do I owe this dishonor?" His voice had the smooth grace of a well-handled dagger. "Have the Circus stalls become too cramped? Or have you come to beg me to put in a word for your dear sisters in the streets who've just lost their right to inherit? Or perhaps you've just lost your sense of direction along with your good sense—the training school is *that* way." He jabbed a skeletal finger in the direction of the *Ludus Magnus*.

Her eyes stung like scorpions. "Shut your mouth, you slimy, slithering snake—you've done worse before noon with catamites that make the sewers look clean, and I wouldn't warrant that all *your* lovers had just two legs. I've come with a gift you don't deserve."

"*My*, but being allowed to live on in this city has left you sassy." Veiento smiled. "I've heard the good citizens of Pannonia—that's where the Emperor was going to send you, you know—sent him a letter of gratitude when he changed his mind."

"I don't doubt it—but I'll wager it was climbing into *your* bed—not Aristos'—that inspired them to think their damning thoughts of me. Now do you want to listen, or do you mean to battle me all day? One more uncivil utterance and I leave—and you'll lose *him,* just when, at long last, I've got him cornered for the kill."

"*Whomever* could you be talking about?" Veiento said with mock mystification.

Junilla ignored this. "And it's yours, for the small price of getting our divine ruler to lower the taxes on my farms in Noricum, as is only right since my crop was ruined by frost."

Veiento laughed hollowly. "Am I hearing things, or are you bargaining with me? You *need* me, you silken slut. He won't *have* it from you, whatever you've got. He won't have anything from you."

"My price is rightly calculated. You want this more than I do, if that's possible. You and our dearest Marcus Arrius Julianus haven't exactly been lovers these last ten years."

"Say I agree." He waved a spidery, blue-veined hand that was the more pitiful for its burden of heavy gold rings. "Go on, go on, and quickly."

She stepped closer and dropped her voice to its dart-in-for-the-kill register. "I have the statement of two guards from the school, claiming they were called for at midnight to conduct that . . . that female *beast* who is the toast of the arena from *his* house back to the school. She was *there,* do you understand? Marcus Julianus has conceived some unnatural passion for her. I accused him of this before the Emperor. You know that—that's when that vicious man slandered me. And after I was sent off, Julianus must have lied to Domitian—he *must* have, or he wouldn't be alive now—

and said he'd had nothing to do with her. He's been aggravatingly careful. I *know,* I've had that house watched for months. But for some reason this once he got careless, and those guards betrayed him. Look at this! Read, and weep for joy!"

Carefully she flattened on the table the papyrus rolls on which the guards' statements were written. Veiento's look was almost lustful as he read. In an instant he had no malice left for Junilla; all he possessed was directed at Marcus Arrius Julianus. He and Junilla were allies once more.

"Yes, yes, this is interesting, extremely interesting, but you've got to take the measure of the man you're trying to destroy. A couple of letters from two ambitious guards won't topple a man who's been the Emperor's right arm for so many years. He'll just talk his way out of this one like he does everything else."

"This is but the first part of my plan—there's more. First, you show Domitian these, just to fertilize the ground and start his mind thinking on the matter."

"Is that so, my bold gazelle?" he said, catching hold of the heavy gold medallion of the cult of Isis that hung between her breasts and gently pulling her forward under the pretext of examining it. He frowned at the medallion. "By Venus, you change religions more often than you change lovers," he said, breathing intently; then he patted the space beside him on the wooden bench. "What happened to that dubious love-cult you joined last month? I liked it better. Settle yourself here, Junilla. What is that charming essence on you? It is *Hyacinthus,* is it not?"

"I wouldn't know," she said, stiffening her back and pulling away. "It's some scent that stayed with my clothes. My litter was halted by the funeral procession of a man whose death you caused, and I don't know what they were burning. And I'll stand, if it pleases you."

Veiento shrugged as if it were no matter.

"Now listen to this," Junilla continued. "I have something from Aristos himself that no one, but no one, knows. He'd have murder on his mind if he knew I was revealing this to—"

"You're telling me Aristos talks in his sleep?" Veiento broke in with malevolent merriment. "Or was this secret blurted out during the sweaty culmination of one of your fevered couplings?"

"Mock all you want, Veiento, but I got a choice morsel from that man that eluded all your professional spies. Aristos is going to be matched with that Amazon during the Augustan Games. Mark my words, it's the truth—he even arranged it himself. He's convinced she's laid a curse on him, one that can only be undone if he kills her himself, by the sword and in light of day. They're going to be disguised, that's how they're managing it. What is this to us? I'll tell you. No one knows, not even Julianus. Now if I know anyone on this earth, I know that man and the way his perverse, plotting mind works. When he learns a day has been set for the combat, he will go mad. As I breathe, he will make an attempt upon Aristos' life.

"You must go with all this to Domitian," Junilla continued. "The letters will unsettle him. Who knows but they may be enough by themselves. If not, you and the Emperor can set a trap for our dear Marcus. You'll have no trouble getting Domitian to cooperate— he enjoys this sort of thing. He'll get more pleasure from it than from a month of treason trials. On a set day you'll have a false spy reveal to Marcus Julianus that his beloved beast-woman has set herself on a course of extinction. Then have it arranged so that shortly after, Aristos is publicly invited to the Palace on some pretext, and reduce his guard. Promise Domitian he will see Aristos attacked along the way. Arrest the assassins, who will come for him, surely as winter comes after summer. Under torture they'll reveal who sent them. He's so close to suspecting Julianus of disloyalty now that this will be like giving one last push to a tottering rock."

"Oh, he won't risk Aristos' life, not outside the arena anyway. A waste of a fine, strapping, fighting animal in his prime, he would call it. . . ." But Junilla could see he was rapidly considering her words; she guessed he'd already added much in his mind to the bare plan she had given him.

"If it's properly arranged, there will be little risk to Aristos. We're speaking of a man who has every means in the world at his disposal, and an artful mind. Banish all thought of the risk. Consider the reward."

"Yes. The reward. Pulling that brazen conniver off his perch, permanently. I tell you, he's only survived this long because we two have not worked as one. Come closer, my little titmouse, my little ring-dove—"

The perfect arch of Junilla's upper lip became delicately distorted in distaste. "My litter bearers arouse my passions more than you."

A murderous look came into Veiento's eyes, but he brought it swiftly under control.

She spun about to leave, all shifting, billowing silk, a bright bird with ruffled feathers, then paused to add in a hissing whisper, "If your good sense matches your genius for treachery, you'll not mention *me* to the Emperor."

"Of course not," he responded blandly. "I would not want to turn all this into a low joke. Off with you now, before the fleas settle. The sewers must not be kept waiting. Go make another grunting wrestler or beetle-browed charioteer glad he was born a man."

Summer came with its profusion of flies, its shimmering heat that drove the poor to gather about street fountains to escape their ovenlike tenement rooms, its swampy air laden with the stench of beasts dead in alleyways, and all its sweet rottenness. Flowers and overripe fruit lay crushed on the pavements, while the gutters glistened with stale honey-wine. But even for summer, on most days the streets were unnaturally empty, and only the sporadic roars, rumbling like a distant avalanche, would have alerted a newly arrived traveler to the capital city that most of the populace inhabited the Colosseum or Circus.

Domitian forbade the Senators to leave for their cooler country estates, as was the usual practice, for the trials continued unabated, and he needed them in the city to try and convict their own. The Emperor rarely left the Palace gardens; frequently he avoided the games altogether because he found the noise agonizing to his nerves, though he had detailed reports brought to him of the behavior of the crowds. He was always eager to know what policies and what men they shouted against, and which gladiators brought the greatest cheers. The foolish few who failed to shout the praises of his favorites often found themselves thrown into the arena to face the next contestant themselves.

Once when the Emperor retired for several days to his Alban villa, he ordered Marcus Arrius Julianus to come to him. He was preparing to take his gilded boat out onto the villa's artificial lake; he himself would be towed behind it in a smaller craft, for lately even the sound of dipping oars was like the crashing of cymbals to his tortured nerves. They walked together through the closely pruned geometric garden, to the edge of the black lake with its strikingly clear reflections of reversed columns and statuary hanging in airless silence like some eerie underwater city. A servant held a sunshade for Domitian. The Emperor's posture, Marcus Julianus noted, was of a man desperate to ward off the world. His jaw, grown fleshy of late, was set belligerently as a boxer's, while his head was kept low as if to ram the opposition. Those eyes seemed to register little of his immediate environment—it was as if Domitian judged there were nothing more to be gained by seeing. If the dead walked, Marcus Julianus thought, they would walk with those leaden sleepwalker's steps, too methodical to be animated by a living heart. Domitian sweated, though this day was relatively cool. Marcus Julianus suspected that he himself had not been provided with a sunshade in order to make him feel at a slight disadvantage. Domitian could see his expression well, but the sun prevented him from seeing the Emperor's.

"A fine day, is it not?" Domitian smiled too broadly, showing teeth. "And how speedily fine days can be ruined. I sent you round the charges against Herennius and Nerva. You returned them unedited and unread."

"They are dead men. Does a man need more than one executioner?"

"Ah, you are clever, Julianus. Odd how I never noticed until recently just *how* clever. Some men will try and subvert you soon as you turn your back to them. And some men do it before your face, with sophistry masquerading as frankness. *Most* intriguing. I've a new board game I'd like to play with you. It's imported from Egypt. We'll try that cleverness."

Marcus Julianus felt his body tauten. Was there something sinister in the way Domitian pronounced the word *Egypt?* Had an informant overheard his conversation with Nerva—and this was Domitian's way of letting him know? He carefully kept his expression neutral, knowing those sallow eyes examined his face.

"Ah, yes, I learned a thing about Nerva today that reveals much about *you,*" Domitian said, his voice soft as an adder's hiss.

Marcus Julianus stopped breathing.

"He's precariously ill with the quartan fever," Domitian went on, "and it's most instructing that *you* did not tell me, for you must have known—you know when any one of those silly old women in broad stripes so much as *sneezes.* Clever, *clever* man. You would have had me try a man when it was not necessary! And such a loved one as Nerva!"

"You are unfair. No one knew Nerva was ill."

"Ah, perhaps the temptation to take advantage of my love for you finally proved too much. Would I be a fool to think I was foolish to ever count you a friend? I wonder. Now tell me, why do

I think your temper has changed? What have you done to make me think so? I find you melancholic, furtive, and cold."

Marcus Julianus was angry suddenly at being batted about like some cat's prey; he could abide no more diplomatic lies. He felt his whole existence had become like the blade of a knife, bound to cut away what was not true.

I will not be played with. If he suspects me, I will drive it out of him.

"It is you who have changed, not I." Marcus Julianus slowed his steps and held Domitian's gaze. "You abandoned the throne after Saturninus' revolt, and you rule no more. *Fear* rules."

Because the sun blinded him, Marcus Julianus felt rather than saw the jerk of surprise in Domitian's eyes, and he wondered at his own lack of fear.

"How fortunate I am to have you tell me these things!" Domitian's tone was open and friendly; those eyes, poised javelins. He was an aging carnivore, a beast run to seed, too spent to work up much excitement for the kill. "And what would your divine lordship have me do, to turn this foul situation round?"

"Only what you gave your word to do, so long ago in my father's house."

"Ah, yes, the Age of Gold would come then, wouldn't it!" Domitian said, tightly leashing his anger, eager to find out just how far Marcus Julianus would go, "and all the criminals would run free. A sight to warm your soul! I see packs of barking Cynics overrunning the streets. The mob robbing the temples. The law in a drunken sleep. Vestals and married women selling themselves for a few coppers. And in the hand of every one of your colleagues, a ready dagger for any poor ruler who dared hold firm on any matter. Tell me, are they your friends, these criminals, or is speaking treason just a pastime born of boredom, now that so many of your erstwhile companions have met with well-deserved justice?"

"You're laying traps with words and eagerly awaiting my tumbling in, and it's all the easier for you because, as holder of supreme power, you give words their very definition. If you would play board games, let us keep to the same rules. Now you call 'treason' what you once called 'acts of patriotic courage' and 'speaking freely,' and this was, I recall, always followed with a remark about how blessed you were that this was possible in your reign. *Has ever a ruler in history rendered himself safe through acts of terror?*" Marcus Julianus paused, feeling he pummeled a corpse, expecting Domitian to order him to be silent—but the Emperor watched him with a noncommittal glare, and so he pressed on.

"I remember, if you have forgotten, you used to say often that if Nero had had *one truthteller* about him, he might have kept himself alive. Hear, then, your one truthteller! They call you a despot. High, and low, they say it the moment they can say it safely—and you *cannot* silence them all. But even now this could be turned around, if you stop the prosecutions. Surely you have seen in life that people *want* to adore a ruler. Winning their love should be no more difficult than coaxing water to run downhill. Begin with Herennius. You know he has no ambitions above the most drab of civil posts. No one listens to him or cares what he says. Let him go."

Domitian laughed easily and put a companionable hand on Marcus Julianus' shoulder.

"But they listen to *you* and care what *you* say, do they not, my dearest Marcus? Would it not be a fine joke on me if I've been nursing a viper at my breast all these years? Do not be alarmed, I'm just *speaking freely*. That's fair, isn't it? One might say you've prepared the ground well. Your counsel has made me hated, but the people throw roses at your feet. Interesting, is it not? I know at last why you always natter on at me about what I said as a boy. I was foolish then, and easily ruled, and you mean to keep me so! Once my destiny settled on me, and I became infused with divine essence—yes, *divine essence,* for that is what happens when you stand so close to the gods for so long—then, you could abide it no more. Ah, but perhaps it's your great talent to get a man to trust you with his life, until you've rendered him blind, deaf, and dumb. . . ."

They had come to the dock with its stone dolphins splattered with pidgeon dung. Domitian said gaily, as if it were some trifling joke on himself, "You know what? . . . This is awkward, but I cannot seem to remember why I summoned you! Perhaps you'd best go back." He signaled to the Master of the Gardens and ordered him to fetch the simpleminded boy, meaning to have him take Marcus Julianus' place in the boat.

Marcus Julianus met Domitian's eyes, and the emptiness in them was haunting; it was like looking on a barren patch of ground that was the site of an old, unsolved murder. There was a glancing memory of life in those eyes, but no more.

This, then, was the end. He knew Domitian would not summon

him again, either as an advisor or as a friend. Whatever it was in Domitian that reached for him had finally sickened and died, poisoned by his fear. The hard shell he had been secreting about himself all these years was now closed, complete. The only face Domitian would ever turn to him would be that of this sly trickster, a crude mask that hardly covered all that gaped emptiness beneath.

His position was more perilous than at any time since Domitian's accession, for now his *shield*—Domitian's deep, inchoate yearning for his good opinion, so pervasive it made him both father and final arbiter of truth—was there no more. He stood exposed before all that bestial imperial ill-will. In spite of this, Marcus Julianus departed the Alban villa feeling only the lucid calm of a soldier on the dawn of battle, and a measure of relief from having spoken his mind. Days passed, then a month, and he was not summoned, but neither was he harassed or condemned. He could not account for it; he could only pray all remained so, until the fateful day. The stratagem was successful; Nerva was safe— that was all that mattered.

Two months had elapsed since the night Auriane passed at Marcus Arrius Julianus' great-house. Auriane lay listlessly on her rude cot, her forehead glazed with sweat, the rough wool of her tunica matted to her back. Sunia stood pressed to the bars of their cell's narrow window, never giving up hope a small wind might stir.

"I like this not at all," Sunia was saying as she fanned herself with papyrus sheaves plucked from the kitchen garbage. "You must know marriage does not mean to these people what it means to us—they do not join for life as we do."

"Sunia, give me rest, not this again!"

"Then attend to what I say this time! Erato's been married three times and Acco, four. It is said a king of former days called Nero married a *eunuch* in a royal ceremony before the whole of the city, because he . . . *she* . . . resembled a past wife whom he'd murdered. We know little of these people, and what I *do* know gives me shivers. Living stacked on top of one another does something evil to the mind. They marry girls off at twelve in this place, *twelve*. In a few more years Avenahar will be old enough for him! He might forget about you and start nursing a passion for your daughter!"

"Sunia!"

"Well, *that* finally roused you from that bed!"

"You may call the rest of them whatever you wish, but if I ever hear you speak of him that way again, I swear by my mother and father we will no longer be friends!"

Sunia felt her stomach twist. She had seen Auriane angry at others, but it was deeply unsettling to feel that fine fury turned on herself.

"I am sorry," Sunia whispered. "I should not have said that." She waited a moment, then added tentatively, "Am I forgiven?"

"Of course. I am weary and heartsick and frightened of what comes, and it's hot enough to bake bread in here. Let us forget it."

Sunia turned her attention back to the window. "Come and look. The soldiers scattered the pantomimes, and they left, but now there's a long line of women with torches, frightening everyone away. . . . They're carrying palm branches."

"The prostitutes," Auriane said lethargically. "I heard it somewhere. They've been denied the right to inherit."

"But listen! A good number of them are crying your name. *'Carissima Aurinia.'* They will raise you up to be queen, I swear on my mother, if you are victor one more time!" Sunia looked about. "Auriane, something ails you, I have known it for some days now. I've never seen you lying about so much. Maybe you ate spoiled food. Or it could be the summer sickness. Perhaps the physicians have some potion—"

"No!" Auriane responded more sharply than she meant to. "I am well as ever. *No physicians.*"

Sunia came closer, mystified now. "You *are* ill. I've been watching you. I . . . I heard you last night." Auriane had vomited up her evening barley gruel.

"Leave me be. It is nothing, I say."

"You do not trust me enough, then, to tell me when you are ill!"

"Sunia, it is not that at all." Auriane covered her face with her hands. "Say nothing to Erato! Swear to it on your mother!"

"Auriane!"

"Sunia, I am with child."

"What? *What?* No!" Sunia sank down beside her. "What are you saying? It cannot be!"

"It can be, and it is."

"Auriane, no!" Sunia closed her eyes tightly and slowly shook her head. She got a firm grip on Auriane's arm, as if to restrain her, too late, from what had already been done. "No!" she said again softly, bewilderment collecting in her eyes.

After a time Sunia ventured, "It is . . . *his?*"

"His," Auriane affirmed, shivering as she spoke the word, surprised that such an impersonal word as *his* could feel so intimate, could steal so softly, so deeply inside. "His," she repeated just because she enjoyed the sound of the word.

"But I don't understand. . . . How did it happen? I mean— what I mean is . . . you were given herbs and amulets and that ghastly wash of vinegar water!"

"I did not drink or use what the physician prepared for me. And I tossed the amulets away."

"But *why?*"

"Did you not see the moon on that night? All below was drenched in its holy light. No creature touched by it could have remained barren. It is unwise to thwart the fruitfulness of nature on such a night."

"Let others be fruitful then! How can you possibly—"

"Listen to me! I will tell you my reasons. It was the day of the Festival of the Sacred Marriage. Any child conceived on that night will be a great bringer of good, be it woman or man. And this babe was conceived beneath the *aurr,* and so will have the earth-magic given me by Ramis, as well as powerful Roman magic from its father, whom I fear I will never see again on earth! Do you not see? This child will have clan-luck far greater than mine and will do for our people what I could not. Sunia, my own circle of kin has been pruned back to a stalk . . . it is pitiful. I must let it flower again, or how will my ancestors ever find rebirth? And . . . it is also because of Avenahar. That I have not seen her budding years sorely oppresses me. . . . With this babe it will be different— this one I'll keep by me always."

"Merciful Fria! *Keep by you always?* You're in prison! They do not have children in this place! How can you fight! And what of Aristos? The day is set!"

"Calm yourself, Sunia. I have thought of all of this. This time of sickness does not last—I know, from when I bore Avenahar. On the day that I fight Aristos I will be still strong and lithe in body, and not yet through half my time. Tell no one, Sunia, not even Coniaric and Thorgild. Erato would order the physicians to force abortives on me. Do not look so! It's not the first time I have done battle with a child in me. Now swear on Fria's name to say nothing, and to help me hide it."

"I swear—" Sunia began, then broke into soft tears. "Oh, this is a sad madness! How could the gods ask such a thing of you? Have you not suffered enough?"

"It is all right, Sunia. Now listen to me. . . . To keep those hawk-eyed physicians from finding me out, I'll need a draught for the sickness. There is a plant called clove root—do you know it?"

"I *think* I saw my mother gather it once. . . ."

"It grows in damp places and has brownish-pink flowers. The root smells of cloves. The leaf is shaped like this." Auriane traced the form of the leaf in the grime of the floor. "When next they send you to the vegetable market, you must steal off to the herb stalls and get it for me. Can you do it?"

"Of course. I will find it," Sunia assured her, consoled somewhat by this small mission—it made her feel less buffeted about by fate. "You'll not be found out, I'll see to it." Sunia looked with bewilderment toward the narrow slice of night sky. "What would Witgern have said of this strange turn of events, or Sigwulf, or your own mother? When the month of *Augustus* comes, Aristos, killer of men, born Odberht, bane of us all, will do battle with . . . with a pregnant Cleopatra! I think the Fates are having a joke at your expense, Auriane. I do not like any of this."

"Perhaps they are. I know Baldemar would find it rightly humorous. But he would in deadly earnest expect me to carry it through."

AURINIA REGINA

CHAPTER LIII

The month named in honor of the deified Augustus came, and with it his festivals and games.

Auriane was like the hungry wolf in winter that pursues its quarry day on day, leaving bloody tracks in the snow as it seeks the creature whose death will give it life. Whether Aristos gulped down wine and meat in the First Hall or practiced in the school's central ring, she observed him with the same neutral intensity with which she watched the flames during the Ritual of Fire. As the day drew close, his strengths and weaknesses became the boundaries of her world. Soon she could imitate the ponderous grace of Aristos' leaps when he shifted target with such merciless accuracy that Thorgild broke into laughter when he practiced with her. Her awakening doubts about the holiness of the vengeance rite served only to increase the ferocity of her pursuit, for now she had to shout to cover the sound of whispered questions within.

But if Auriane had doubts, the three hundred Chattian prisoners housed among the city's four training schools did not. When Auriane first spoke the challenge, excitement spread quickly among them. Though they did not know the hour was set, they sensed her new purposefulness and it maddened them with hope. Aristos' greater strength did not discourage them—had not Auriane sprung from a bloodline that regularly produced great enchantresses and heroes who slew monsters? And had she not lived a season with Ramis, whose earth-born powers would lend her sword the speed and accuracy of a hundred serpents? In great numbers they vowed their hair to her victory.

Whenever the Chattian captives caught sight of Auriane, they made the sign of the war-god, and the chant of old would begin: *"Daughter of the Ash, lead us out!"* Soft and uncertain at first, it would gain in momentum until the vaulted corridors of the school resounded like the interior of a great drum. It alarmed the guards, who understood none of it. Once as she was led to practice, she managed to exchange a few hurried, sad words with a fellow tribesman freshly captured, and got scraps of news from home. She learned a shrine of stones had been built on the spot where she was taken captive, and the ground about it was daily sprinkled with the blood of white ewes. Witgern, to her amazement, was alive. It was Witgern who had led the Chattian warriors when they attempted to cross the frozen Rhine to aid Saturninus in his ill-fated war on the Emperor. Her informant added, "The Helleborne ice thawed that night only because the Scourge lives on and lives like a king."

"Soon now, that will be remedied!" she whispered before the guards prodded her on.

Erato noticed the new restlessness of the Chattian prisoners. When he was told they refused to let the school's barbers cut their hair, and that they muttered uncouth incantations whenever they saw Auriane, on the advice of his senior guards he decided to ignore it. These things were harmless enough in themselves, he was told, and his interference might provoke a costly uprising.

As the day of the bout with Aristos drew ever closer, for Auriane the nights worked in gentle but powerful opposition. As she lay in the darkness trying not to hear Sunia's stuttering snores, Marcus Julianus seemed so intimately close that she felt like a loose lyre string shivering after it has been plucked. In the midnight dark the golden haze stole back, pleasure's insistent ghost, lingering round her loins, haunting her with the memory of the heat of his breath on the back of her neck, the caress of his voice as he uttered reassurances. At such times she hardly knew the creature possessed by the need of Aristos' death. But when dawn came, once again ancestors ruled. Each morning she had to force down the memory of him—which she could not do completely—and fire herself anew with the need of vengeance. By day, her resolve was like an image in a still pool—whole and perfect when she paused to examine it. But the memory of him cast in a stone, agitating the surface, disintegrating that clarity, muddling the world.

• • •

Marcus Arrius Julianus was at first given no sign to show how completely the bond between himself and the Emperor had been severed. Then, when two months had elapsed since the afternoon Domitian summoned him to the boat, his permission to use the imperial post was withdrawn without explanation. Within days of this, three men whom he had recommended for various posts were dismissed for frivolous causes. Friends and relations of clients whose court cases he supported began regularly to lose. No banquets of state were given in these days, and Marcus Julianus suspected the cause was that Domitian would not have him at the imperial table, but at the same time was not yet ready for the city to see such visible evidence of the rift. And when he sent round written advice Domitian requested concerning interpretation of the laws, if the Emperor had questions he would not put them to Julianus directly but asked them instead of his magistrates. Marcus Julianus mused once to Diocles, "It is as if I died."

He put his favor to the test, and the evidence became less subtle: He requested a private audience and was told by an imperial secretary he must go to the Office of Petitions and wait his turn like a common citizen.

Rumors of who was in favor and who was not traveled swiftly as panic of fire; when word of this snubbing got about, Marcus Julianus found his clients deserting him in dozens, seeking the shelter of safer patrons. The favor of the Emperor was like rain on crops—nothing flourished without it. But he knew he had lost only the affections of those who used him to climb to the next post, and he found some grim amusement in the sight of them scurrying off. It would not undermine his plans or prevent Domitian's death. For all, at last, was nearly in place.

He had enlisted more than half the Guard, enough to ensure the transition would be relatively bloodless—at least, as far as it was possible to arrange such things through human agency—and he was ready to leave the rest to the gods. The fateful day had been chosen: the second after the Ides of *Augustus*. On that day the twenty most influential Senators, all ready to proclaim Nerva emperor, would be present in the city. And the Senate would be in session against all custom, for Domitian was eager to begin autumn's round of prosecutions.

Through all this, Marcus Julianus was shadowed by a certainty he released Auriane to her doom. It was apparent from the reports of his agents that she stalked Aristos still, and it angered him. He sent a warning message to Erato, ordering him to keep them well apart. Though he reassured himself repeatedly the two would find no way to meet, the deep-knowing part of him knew better: She was in mortal danger.

As he prepared for his eventual flight to the north, sending valued possessions and volumes of his library to the villa and philosophical school he was establishing in the remote province, thoughts of Auriane would come at odd times to rupture his peace. He would see sunlight suffusing a garden pool and remember with striking clarity those eyes, soft and bold as a deer's, clear as a seeress's. Or he would hear, quite suddenly, her voice: the faint roughness of its northern accent, her overprecise way of sounding words. The bed, empty of her, looked tragic. The garden was alive with her; she rippled through it like some teasing wraith, obscure in the foliage, leaves rattling in her wake, always moving away from him while watching him still. He realized then the seeming contradiction in her: She sought an elusive comfort, a dock to put into, so restless curiosities could flower in peace, but at the same time she needed freedom as a condition of life, as rampantly growing things need it. He longed to give her both.

Soon after their night together an itinerant ivory dealer in his pay came to him with startling news: After a year of searching, he had discovered a woman who might well be Auriane's mother. But he needed great sums of money if he were to bring the woman back.

"The woman you seek is employed as a weaver on an estate outside of Corinth," he explained. "She is called Iona. But her last master called her Athelinda, and he got her from a dealer who buys from the legions. The name is not common, and she was certainly a captive of the Chattian war. She looks to be the woman in every other respect. But her present mistress, a woman called Fortunata, refuses to give her up, in spite of the fact that this Iona—or Athelinda—is old and useless; she's become a sort of companion to the lady in her dotage. But if you were to give me two hundred thousand, I might—"

"Bribe the woman to put aside her affectionate feelings? Stop, you're running ahead of me," he interrupted briskly, his smile amused, reserved. He was not certain how far he trusted the ivory dealer. "First you will return with Thersites," he continued, naming an agent he trusted better and who was also this man's enemy. The ivory dealer would not be likely to go in league with him to steal the money. "And if he agrees that this is the woman

I seek, well then, you shall have whatever is needed to have her brought to Rome."

Seven days before the commencement of the Augustan Games, Erato summoned Auriane to his chambers. He had not had private words with her since her return from Marcus Julianus' house.

The various complaints brought against her by trainers and Palace officials had multiplied so that he could not decide which to hurl at her first. When she was brought in, cheeks flushed from practice, gray eyes fixed on him expectantly, he looked, then looked again. Some bare but significant change had come over her, one he did not have the words to name. He was forced to settle for the effect she produced on him: Before, she made him slightly restless; now her presence was like some mildly calming tonic.

"Tell me, Auriane," he began with no word of greeting, eyes bright with irritation, "has that man gotten all he wants of you? That night of love cost me *thousands*, when you figure in the bribes, the guards' extra pay, the this, the that, the other. Do you think that the next time you get an itch you could lower yourself a little and couple with someone around here, my expensive little Siren? Your opponents will straddle anything with two legs, male or female. *Aristos* is less trouble than you. You'll not go there again! And you'll not speak of it again. Is that understood?"

She watched him, feeling for the source of his anger, knowing that worry over money had little to do with it. She recognized it as his own peculiar sort of jealousy. At first she supposed Marcus Julianus' love of her annoyed Erato because he could not comprehend it. She realized now Erato understood it well enough, and that was the trouble. *He* did not want to lie with her, and he did not care if she bedded a kitchen slave. But still, she was *his*—he had discovered her, he had bought her skill to perfection—and Marcus Arrius Julianus was a man over whom he had no control, who might possibly snatch her away.

Erato gave her no time to frame a reply. His second attack was a verbal kick to the shins, meant to knock her off balance. "You haven't killed in your last three bouts. Now what in the name of Nemesis is the matter with you?"

"But—the crowd does not want it."

"That's because you've got them trained. Do you think I'm deaf, dumb, and blind? If you could train animals as well as you train crowds, you'd have elephants doing pantomimes. It's starting to *not look right*. I'm getting complaints—threats is closer to the truth—from Palace officials. Every beggar in the street knows how expensive it is to train one man. Don't you see, it's starting to look like we're trying to save money. Sooner or later the crowd will decide that's what your true purpose is. So stop it. Next time, *kill*, I order you."

Her next bout, if all went as planned, would be with Aristos. She drew forward a plait of hair. "I swear, with Fria as witness, that in my next bout I will kill—or die in the effort. Does that satisfy you?"

"Oh, don't overdo it, Auriane. I don't want *you* killed, just him, so do an old man a favor and run the bastard through when you're done, all right? Now what do you know about why the Chattian prisoners are refusing to let anyone cut their hair?"

"Nothing," she asserted with a combative ring in her voice, eyes brilliant with the warning look that meant she would challenge a maddened elephant, if necessary, to protect her own.

"I asked that only to test your skill in lying. You're passingly good but not *that* good. I know you're after Aristos still—and if I see you come within twenty feet of him, that's how many lashes you'll get."

"You would not *dare* do that to me."

"Don't test it, Auriane. Listen to me. He is a human monster. One day he will get tired of you padding about behind you, and he'll turn round and cut you up for shark bait. I know you study him at practice. I know you spar with partners who challenge you with Aristos' favorite attacks. This will stop *at once*." Before Auriane could begin an objection, he launched a fresh assault.

"Now to the next thing: Acco says you have some strange malady you refuse to let the physicians treat. What of this, Auriane? And do not lie, because I already don't believe you."

Now she felt cold, empty panic within. She knew that if she did not concoct a plausible explanation at once, the truth would soon occur to him. She felt she fought for the life of her child as surely as if she drove a wolf away from it while it slept.

Tell him something he will believe! she shouted silently to her numbed mind. Quickly!

"I suppose I must tell you," she began, hoping her alarm would be read as fear of his wrath. "It was no true sickness, and it has passed. It was but the ill effects of a potion given me as part of the rite of initiation into a . . . a certain mystery cult which I am bound not to name. Who has not done such things at least once in this place? The draught produces visions as well. That is all." That was not even clever, she thought miserably, as she braced for an outbreak of derisive laughter.

Marcus Julianus will be slaughtered by Domitian, and our child will be forced from my body. I am accursed!

But Erato's response was far stranger than anything she could have guessed. As she watched, astonished, he slowly rose and edged his way toward her, while the dazed expression in his face rigidified into one of horror. *"What?"* he said softly. The blunt fingers of one hand dug painfully into her shoulder.

"Auriane, you did not! How could you *do* this to me?" More to himself he muttered, *"Nemesis!* The city's *crawling* with them— they're spreading like a plague of vermin ever since the Emperor's stupid cousin was caught at it!" Then he shouted into her face while the muscles of his neck strained like tautened ropes: "You simpleton! They drink children's blood! They are arsonists! They have revolting cannabalistic orgies underground that go on for days! Have you lost your wits!"

She took a nimble step back, twisting her shoulder from his grip, and managed a proud glare, though had he looked carefully he could have seen her fear. "I've no notion whatever of what you are bellowing about," she said softly. "If I have misplaced my wits, my guess is we'll find *yours* in the same place!"

"I'm not the fool you'd like me to be, Auriane. I *know* you've joined the Christiani. You're duped easily as a donkey. Don't do *anything* around here without asking my leave first. There are two kinds of religions in this city—*regular* ones that it's all right to collect as many as you want of, and wicked, foul foreign superstitions, which I won't have here, and which will turn you into panther meat. Ah, this explains much! Your refusal to kill, for one! Of course! They've no shyness about lunching on infants, but two men in a good clean fight to the death, *that* turns their stomachs! By the girdle of Medusa, how did they *get* to you in this place?"

"Erato, it's not—"

"Hold your tongue!" He stalked across the room and took down the bust of Domitian from its high shelf; the Emperor's expression suggested he had sat on a raw egg and struggled gamely to appear as though he hadn't. Erato noisily blew off the dust and slammed it down on his table so forcefully he upset a canister of styluses. Auriane looked on, mystified.

"Swear by the divinity of the Emperor that you are not a

member of the Christiani." Erato had heard it somewhere that no true member of that wretched sect would agree to do this.

"I cannot!" She shook her head, alarmed. "There is less divinity in that man than in the dogs that pick at kitchen garbage. I am a daughter of Fria and I swear only on a plait of hair."

"I knew it! Clever little whelp. It's not a religion, it's a pestilence, and you'll be quarantined until I'm satisfied you're clean of it. From this hour, you're not to speak in your own tongue—I want my guards to know every word that passes from your lips. You'll sleep with guards over you and you'll eat with guards. If this spreads, it will ruin me. We should call you *Pandora*, not Aurinia. . . . The multitude of ills you unleash! Now I've a fine, pounding headache, for which I've you to thank. Leave me!"

At noon the next day, as Sunia walked the garden stalls that choked the narrow street leading into the Cattle Market, bargaining for produce among a battalion of kitchen slaves, she found at last the herb Auriane sought: clove root. There it was, innocently obvious in its wicker basket, as if it had *not* been purposefully eluding her for a month. She slowed her steps, allowing the other kitchen girls to move ahead to the leek-and-onion stall; they paid her no mind, chattering happily as robins as they carried double baskets slung over their shoulders heavily laden with cabbages, turnips, wild asparagus, lentils, eel, and pike. Sunia winced, dropped her basket, and bent to grasp her leg, so that if the others turned to look, they would suppose she fell behind because her injured ankle gave her pain.

The herb stall was hung with bulls' hides to give shade from the morning sun; smells of anise, fennel, and mint rose from the leathery cavern. As she reached eagerly for the tied bundle, a rasping voice within demanded, "And, pray, what do you want with *that*, lambkin?"

Sunia stood still as a deer-stalker. Suddenly the crowded street seemed empty; there were only the flies, the sun, the sound of her own breathing.

"Seasoning for pigs' feet!" she said too shrilly, cursing herself for sounding intimidated.

An unpleasant-looking crone shuffled out. Her sharply down-turned mouth was thin as a razor cut; her contemptuous, faintly protruding eyes seemed capable of catching the smallest movement at her back. Her skin was like glossy leather, worn smooth from use. Sunia's fear seemed to excite the woman's natural meanness. "Ignorant trull. For pigs' feet, you need this!" She thrust a bundle of thyme into Sunia's face.

"But my master specifically ordered *this*. . . ." Sunia felt panic surge through her. Anxiously she looked round once. There, across the narrow street—between the wineshop, with its four pillars wound round with chains from which flagons were strung, and the mirror shop, with its hundreds of bronze mirrors hanging like pendants from a courtesan's ear—was a boy of Libyan countenance, with rags tied about his legs. Ice touched her heart. He watched her with insolent curiosity.

Curses. Auriane guessed rightly—Erato is having me spied on as well.

"Then your master's a benighted fool, and no cook. Tell him Phoebe at the herb market says *this* is what he needs."

"Please, I must have—" Sunia began. The woman's scrawny paw snapped round Sunia's wrist and held to it with disturbing strength. Was this an ogre in human guise? Sunia felt she had snagged her foot on a root in a treacherous river—she would be pulled under, she would drown. The crone leaned close. "Come. You don't belong to anyone *fine* enough to be eating pigs' feet. *You* need seasoning for eels caught between the Tiber bridges."

Sunia knew the boy was crossing swiftly over the cobbles. Somehow she wrenched her hand free. Then, guessing at the cost, she threw down five copper *asses* and snatched a bundle of clove root. Rapidly she limped off.

The Libyan boy approached the old woman. He picked up a bundle of the herb Sunia purchased and wagged it in her face. "What's *this* stuff used for, venerable hag?"

"Imagine, putting that on pigs' feet. Disgusting. That girl's master must be addled. It's for the sickness brought by childbearing."

The boy grinned. He did not know why he had been set to following a kitchen slave, but he guessed his own master, the first physician of the *Ludus Magnus*, would be able to make good use of this discovery.

On the final day before the start of the fourteen days of games, the Great School was thronged with people massed about the practice arena, for word had gone out at dawn that Aristos would be practicing in public. By the time Aristos finally appeared, reeking of cloying brothel scents and beautifully robed, with his dark blond hair neatly combed back, many faithful followers had waited all day for a glimpse of him. Auriane, with Sunia beside her, was being returned to her cell after a day's practice; her escort of six guards butted their way angrily through the crowd. She was disguised under a hooded cloak to spare her guards the inconvenience that might result were she recognized.

Without delay Aristos began sparring with Rodan, a hero from the first years of Domitian's reign who came from retirement to challenge Aristos' supremacy; their bout tomorrow would open the Augustan Games. Suddenly a shout rose up from the part of the throng nearest the ring: *"Murderer! Murderer of innocents!"*

A hail of fruit pits rained on Aristos. In the next moment his retainers, led by the Eel and the Acrobat, surrounded the hecklers, knocked them to the floor, and began kicking them. In an instant, violent eddies disrupted the sea of people, and soon school guards with drawn swords were rushing from every post to restore order.

Aristos heard the taunts but decided to make a show of ignoring them. The arrhythmic striking of wooden swords never slowed.

"It's over the girl," Auriane explained to Sunia. All knew the tale: Aristos had raped and murdered an eight-year-old girl whom he snatched away from her aged slave-attendant during the course of one of his day-long debauches. Because she was humbly clad and accompanied by but one slave, he took her to be no one of consequence. He naturally expected he would never hear of it again. But to his dismay the girl proved to be a ward of Musonius Geta's, and the Finance Minister promptly demanded Aristos be tried and given the most shameful punishment the law provides. Aristos then began steadfastly denying any part in the murder; he was troubled enough over the whole affair to go to the effort of having one of the witnesses poisoned and dropped into the Great Drain for safekeeping. Musonius Geta delayed for three days, waiting for Domitian to give him some sign of encouragement, for he dared not prosecute the Emperor's favorite without permission. But when Domitian was silent, Geta knew he must abandon the idea of pressing for justice. It seemed Domitian was not ready to sacrifice Aristos, not even for the family honor of his powerful Minister of Finance. But Musonius Geta's retainers and clients were outraged, and a group of them were present now, making their anger known.

"Toss him to the beasts!" they cried. "Crucify him!" Auriane's guards were forced to desert her as they ran to the rescue of one of Geta's cousins; the Acrobat was atop him, strenuously attempting to gouge out his eyes. But Auriane saw none of it; she stood rapt and still, aware only of Aristos, who was maddened as a bull stung by a bee — for he suspected that in secret even his own retainers dared believe him guilty.

"Look at him," Auriane said to Sunia. "He no longer *sees* Rodan. He sees only that man who shouted 'murderer.'" She was quiet for a time, then said with cautious excitement, "Sunia! Did you see that? There, he did it again. Meton must not see it — if he did, he would call the halt."

"What, Auriane? *I* don't see it."

"There! He stepped wide with his right foot, putting himself off balance. He does it all the time actually, but anger makes it more evident. Rodan could have struck him then with the advanced side-vertical attack, then killed him with a crosscut, had this been a real bout. This is well, Sunia. Rage distorts his sense of timing, but so slightly that Meton doesn't even see it. He's a cork tossed on the waves — he's leaving openings — small ones, but they're there. Meton sees *that*, at least. Look at Meton. He's concerned now, he's trying to wave Aristos out."

"He looks as always to me, Auriane."

"Then you've no eyes to see! He's like a pendulum, swinging off balance again and again. Praise to the Fates! *This* is what I waited so long to see." She watched on silently, rehearsing how she would take advantage of the openings Aristos left. "Rodan is a fool," she said more to herself than to Sunia. "He's intimidated by that rage. He should fear him *less* now, not more."

A drunken man reeking of tannery smells began pawing at Auriane's cloak. "What's *this*, my fine fellows? A leper?" Roughly he pulled back her hood.

"Blood of the Gorgons!" The man laughed theatrically and held Auriane at arm's length, examining her. "Look, friends, it's our own *bellissima Aurinia*, walking amongst us unknown, trying to hide!"

"Release me," she said in a low voice. When he did not, she kicked him in the ankle and wrenched herself free as he bent over in pain. Instantly a dozen more idlers swarmed round, rudely prodding her, pulling on her cloak. Those cursed guards, she thought. I drag them about everywhere, and when I truly need them, they're not here.

"Aurinia! Carissima!" came a delighted series of cries.

"Darling! Give me a kiss!" one man cried, making a clumsy attempt at embracing her from behind.

Another leaned in front of her and dramatically bared his breast. "Kill me!" he cried. "I've got to die one day, anyway—so I'd rather our beloved Aurinia ran me through!"

One of his fellows knocked him aside. "Not him! Kill *me!* That wastrel doesn't deserve such a noble death!"

Sunia fought to shield Auriane with her rangy body. By the time the guards came to rescue her from this aggressive homage, Auriane was crawling on the floor, trying to escape between their legs, holding her sword hand close to her body in a frantic effort to protect it, and wondering if she would live long enough to face Aristos.

CHAPTER LIV

On the Nones of the month of *Augustus,* **Marcus Arrius Julianus** summoned five of the principal conspirators to meet in an upper room of Matidia's brothel at the foot of the Aventine Hill. Her brothel-house, a squat structure of yellow stucco, had been built over a section of the Great Drain. Should they be bothered by unwelcome interruptions, escape was readily at hand: In the reeking alley beneath her balcony, footpads had cut a tunnel into the sewers, an exit unknown to the Vigiles.

There was little speech among the five as they waited for Senator Nerva to be brought in. Matidia turned her business rooms over to them. Through the thin walls they heard the frolics in the adjacent room—yelps, laughter, eloquent groans played to the rhythmic accompaniment of a rocking bed. Her accounts room lay in comfortable chaos: Scattered over a floor sticky from hot mulled wine were rolled papers covered with scratched-out figures, women's wigs, empty scent bottles, rusted curling irons. A clothes chest with a broken door spilled its garments onto the floor; from it drifted the gently exotic scent of cassia. Statuettes of Venus and Eros, glossy from handling, were respectfully kept in wall niches. Over Venus was nailed a fresh palm branch; Matidia changed it daily to signify her sympathy for the opposition.

At last Senator Nerva was carried in on a wooden pallet. His eyes were scummy pools; his slack mouth hung half open. He grunted in acknowledgment as they greeted him, then lapsed back into solitary torment. When all were settled, Marcus Arrius Julianus began quietly addressing the company, among whom were Petronius, one of the two Prefects of the Praetorian Guard, the Senators Senecio and Herennius, who on the fateful day would make the opening speeches proclaiming Nerva Emperor, and Apollonia, the wardrobe mistress of Domitia Longina, who came on the Empress's behalf.

"Do all who answer to you know their places?" he asked, his gaze moving from one taut face to another. Heads nodded in assent. Marcus Julianus lingered for an instant on Senecio, a Senator of the old aristocracy recently admitted to the plot; a lifetime of surly discontent had left deep furrows on the man's brow. Senecio seemed to watch the others with particular care, his chin faintly drawn in—a protective gesture that recalled a turtle half retracted into its shell. Everyone in the room was distinctly uneasy, but Senecio's nervousness had a furtive quality, as though he feared not the vengeance of Domitian, but the wrath of the men in this room.

I must be mistaken, Julianus thought. That harmless old man has been, for twenty years and more, one of Nerva's greatest friends.

"Apollonia, your lady's part has been changed," Marcus Julianus said to the wardrobe mistress, a woman of smooth, handsome features and grave demeanor. "Unfortunately, since the Festival of Neptunalia, the Underchamberlains have been inspecting the bedchamber five times a day." After lengthy deliberations at previous meetings, Domitian's bedchamber had been selected as the site for the deed. "She now *follows* Carinus. At the eighth hour, when Carinus locks the servants' entrances, *that* is her signal to remove the sword from beneath the pillow. But not before. Is that understood?"

"My lady will acquit herself with honor," Apollonia said with simple solemnity.

Petronius broke in like a restless ox.

"Are you sure he's going to be *standing* on the final day?" he said with a curt nod at Nerva. Petronius meant to speak so Nerva could not hear, but was incapable of it; that voice was made for barking orders on a parade ground. The Praetorian Prefect's brawny shoulders were permanently stooped—a result of lifelong resignation to ceilings that were too low for him—and he had a precarious temper oddly at variance with a harmless, youthful countenance. With his ruddy cheeks, adolescent pout and zealous blue eyes unclouded with the least sign of ambivalence, Marcus Julianus thought of him as a savage boy. "It won't look right, our fledgling Emperor taking over on his back," Petronius went on. "To my mind, that Greek charlatan's giving him too much of that sick-potion for a fellow in his dotage. It wouldn't surprise me if Anaxagoras was in league with the loyalists! Look at him! Life's vital juices have been squeezed out. And those don't come back."

"I'm ill, not deaf," Senator Nerva spoke up in a voice that displayed a surprising feistiness. "And, Petronius, if you want to remain Commander of the Guard after my accession, I would advise you to at least learn to *imitate* a man of manners."

Petronius sulkily withdrew. Marcus Julianus smiled in amusement. Respectfully he wiped the saliva that streaked from Nerva's mouth, then reached for his wrist to feel for the pulse. "I suppose we dare not ask you how you fare."

"I suppose you shouldn't," Nerva replied testily. "This had better be worth it."

"Be of better cheer," Marcus Julianus said amiably. "Once Anaxagoras stops poisoning you, in a mere eight days you'll go from teasing the Ferryman to sitting, hale and healthy, on top of the world. Domitian *does* seem to be taking the bait, if that makes it easier to bear. What I want you to do now is to free a quarter of your slaves—it's what a dying man would do."

"You are right. It shall be done tomorrow."

"It should be the *bath*, not the bedchamber," young Herennius interrupted. "If it's the bath, we don't need Domitia Longina. *Dice* are more reliable than that woman."

Apollonia gave him a murderous look.

"This has been settled," Marcus Julianus replied with controlled annoyance. "It *must* be the bedchamber—it's more private. The deed can be kept secret a little longer. Time is against us from the moment the deed is done. Whether we're condemned as criminals or hailed as liberators—all hangs upon whether we get Nerva confirmed before chaos erupts. We need every extra moment we can snatch, if we're to tie the loyalists' hands."

"You seem not much concerned that there's been no affirmative sign from the Syrian legions," Herennius nudged him again.

"We'll have to let it go," Marcus Julianus answered evenly. "We've got every Rhine commander, and they're much closer to Rome. When the men of the East see the way loyalties are going, they'll capitulate. It's our own Servilius who bothers me more— and all his fellow loyalists of the Guard. The man is a fanatic.

Domitian could skewer a baby before his eyes, and Servilius would say, 'Nobly done.'" Julianus looked at Petronius. "You'll have to contain him somehow. Must he be assigned to the private apartments that day?"

"Servilius' post never changes. If I moved him, it would rouse suspicions."

"Post him outside Domitia Longina's chambers then. There's an echo in that passage, and it will be difficult for him to determine the direction of any shouts he might hear. If he figures it out too quickly, your men will have to physically restrain him. I don't need to remind anyone of the horrors that will result if the deed is done halfway and Domitian somehow survives."

Marcus Julianus paused, alert once more to Senecio's behavior. Had the man been silently talking to himself a moment ago? As he continued to speak to Petronius, he watched Senecio with every sense, aware of the man's rough, irregular breathing, his fretting hands, his strained calm.

"Now, the deed is set for the ninth hour—midway through the watch of Petronius' young recruits, who are with us. Petronius, to you must fall the task of drawing Domitian off from the games— no one else would be admitted without question to the imperial box. It must be done no later than the eighth hour. This could prove difficult if he's watching thirty oiled, half-clad Chaucian maidens wrestling with panthers and trying to select one for the night's frolics—*so the method must be foolproof.* So I want you to interrupt him with the news that you've uncovered a small Palace conspiracy involving certain confidential, high-placed servants of the bedchamber."

"Are you off your head?" Petronius objected. "That runs perilously alongside the truth!"

Marcus Julianus quietly noted alarm in Herennius' face, and also in Apollonia's—but Senecio's expression remained the same.

"No, it is the best way, because it's the very sort of thing that vindicates his deepest fears. He'll not be able to resist examining the miscreants at once. Present it as a hastily arranged affair confined to a few disgruntled Palace chamberlains—he knows how they all loathe and fear him. Tell him Stephanus organized them. Domitian will believe it at once, for Stephanus has been charged with embezzlement. He hasn't a chance of life, unless he helps end Domitian's. The other three you will name are his trusted chamberlain Parthenius, whom you know is with us, and Clodianus, and Satur."

"Clodianus and Satur? You enlisted these men?" Petronius asked. "You are saying, then, these are the assassins?"

"Yes. The assassins—and the lure. Each loathes him, and for reasons Domitian does not particularly want known. Clodianus, for example, knows everything the Emperor's tried to hide of his near relatives' consorting with the Christiani. Satur knows the sad details of how he caused his niece Julia's death by forcing an abortion on her. And so on. You see, they're men Domitian's inclined to want to exterminate anyway. He'll waste no time ordering them assembled for a private questioning in the bedchamber."

"Yes. He would do that," Petronius agreed. "I've seen him miss meals and mistresses and sleep for the pleasures of grilling suspected traitors. But he'll have them heavily chained as he questions them, and he will hold the fetters himself, as always. How—"

"These fetters will be special ones I've ordered from the Palace armorer," Marcus Julianus replied. "Two links near their wrists will be nearly sawed off—they'll break when firm resistance is put on them. And, of course, you yourself, as Guard's Commander, will be charged with inspecting them right before.

"Now this is what is unresolved," Julianus went on. "We have four assassins, and we agreed no fewer than five should do the deed, if we want no mistakes. The two Chamberlains are solidly built men, but they've little experience in killing. A frightened, cornered man can perform amazing feats of strength. One assassin, at least, should know what he's doing—killing should be his trade. The gladiator called the Cyclops might come with us. He declined my last offer, but—"

"Which was?" Petronius asked.

"One million sesterces."

"A disgrace!" said Petronius. "The man's a criminal to ask so much! That's twice over enough cash for him to buy his way into the nobility. Can't you find someone who'd do it for love of country?"

"Petronius is right," Herennius agreed. "Killing's nothing to scum like that—they do it every day. And who's going to pay for all this? I sponsored a day of games last autumn and I'm drained dry. They sent Nero to Hades for nothing. Prices *have* gone up in twenty years, but this is ridiculous."

"Spoken like fools," Marcus Julianus replied, his voice hard. "The man is risking a far more horrible death than a thrust through

the heart in the arena. He deserves to be paid. You forget—we
need *him* more than he needs us, and that's the simple fact of the
matter. And as for Nero's death costing nothing, that absurdity
hardly deserves a reply. Do you call cities sacked in civil war,
legions destroyed, coastal towns raided by pirates, and the near
loss of the empire to the Gauls, not to mention thousands of
innocents murdered, costing nothing? Prices are going *down* this
time, friends. And if necessary, I'll cover the Cyclops' fee from my
own purse."

He turned then to Apollonia. "Lady, I want Stephanus to begin
wearing that bandage three days ahead of the final day. Let
Domitian get used to seeing it. Can he wind it so the dagger
doesn't show?"

"He rolls it expertly now."

"Good. And now to—" Julianus fell suddenly silent. He looked
quickly at Senecio, who once again seemed to be talking to
himself.

Committing our words to memory, Marcus Julianus realized all
at once.

Senecio met his eyes aggressively. But gradually, under Julianus'
unrelenting gaze, bravado gave way to terror; blood drained out of
him, and he seemed in the grip of a light palsy. Now everyone
turned to Senecio, their faces showing first comprehension, then
outrage, and finally animal terror.

When Julianus spoke, it was as if a trapdoor dropped open,
releasing them into nether blackness.

"Senecio," he said softly, "tell me, where do you intend to sell
what you learn here tonight?"

From Nerva came a moan.

Senecio's words of protest were never heard. The room seemed
suddenly full of baying dogs. Apollonia, Herennius and Petronius
began shouting at once as they lunged at Senecio, who fell heavily
onto his back. Apollonia was atop him, crying, *"Murderer!
Murderer of my mistress!"* while clawing at his face. Petronius
hauled her off him as if she were a sack of grain.

With the casual ease of a professional, the Prefect of the Guard
drew his sword. When Apollonia saw lamplight slithering down
the blade, she shielded her eyes. Herennius whispered, "Finish the
bastard! Like he would have finished us!"

Petronius drew back his arm, preparing to thrust the point
through Senecio's chest. Senecio shut his eyes tightly and spat a
curse, refusing to beg for his life.

Marcus Julianus came up swiftly behind Petronius and seized his arms. They struggled for long moments while he tried to force Petronius' sword arm down; Julianus felt he fought to subdue an unruly horse. Finally, unable to overpower him this way, he kicked Petronius in the back of the knee, and both men went down. The sword was driven deep into the wood of the floor; it stood upright and shuddering. Petronius attempted to snatch it, but Julianus got it first, then put the blade to Petronius' throat.

"Have you gone mad!" Julianus said through heaving breaths. "Do this thing and we'll be no better than what we replace!"

"How can you countenance a traitor!" Petronius managed through gasps for air.

Nerva spoke. A fine rage lent his voice the strength of a youth of twenty. "Sit *down*, Petronius, you rude, boorish lout. In my reign the charge of traitor shall be laid to rest, and no man shall ever be condemned unheard. And I will be *obeyed*, you wild ass in soldier's dress, or you can do your fine strutting in the festering swamps of outer Britannia as a soldier of the ranks!"

Marcus Julianus grinned. He had never heard Nerva truly roused. Until that moment he had occasional doubts about Nerva's willingness to behave imperiously when the situation demanded it.

Petronius slowly got up. Senecio struggled to a sitting position and stared vacantly at the wall.

Marcus Julianus did not wonder too long over the cause of Senecio's betrayal. All who were party to the plot felt disordered in mind by the cruelly tightening tension, and Senecio, he guessed, had just stared too long into the pit of that coming unknown and decided to make a desperate bargain with the Fates, hoping they would spare him if he shoved his fellows over the edge.

"Put him under arrest," Marcus Julianus instructed Petronius. "Matidia can give us rope until you bring shackles. We'll put out a story he had to depart suddenly for his estates. We'll keep him stowed in Matidia's wine cellars until after the assassination."

They resumed their seats. Apollonia had a savage, hopeless look in her eye. Herennius stared at Senecio with the intense but empty look of the madman.

"When next we come together," Marcus Julianus went on briskly, hoping to soothe them by bringing them back to the business at hand, "I'll have three copies of Caenis' letters; I want them read in the Senate when Nerva is affirmed. . . ."

As he spoke on, one thought hung in the air like a charnelhouse stench: *How many others are ready to betray us?*

• • •

Cleopas, First Physician of the *Ludus Magnus*, stood helplessly in the doorway of the accounts room while Erato stalked to and fro, bellowing. The physician felt trapped in a violent storm—he had no choice but to huddle under cover and pray it passed quickly.

"Is *this* how the little whelp repays all I've done for her!" Erato's eyes bulged—to Cleopas, he had the petrified stare of a fish dying on a bank. "By breeding herself to my patron? How *dare* she try and foist a litter on me behind my back! I ask you, is this a *nursery?* What in the name of Zeus am I supposed to do with a broodmare? Do you realize I am going to lose millions? Do you care? I want her brought!" He then cried out in one long, hoarse note: *"Guard!"*

Four guards appeared at once and stood at attention behind the First Physician. Erato said more quietly, "Fetch the woman Aurinia at once." If she were given abortives tonight, by tomorrow the whole sorry mess might be put to rest, before some agent of Marcus Arrius Julianus' got wind of it.

"Wait!" the physician Cleopas objected timorously, knowing that if he said nothing and the woman died, he would be blamed for it later. "My lord, if you are right about . . . the day she conceived, she very well might be too far gone. It is too dangerous."

"What? And let her *have* it? I pay you in good coin, and in return you insult me with imbecilic advice! Maybe you think her devotees would pay to see her give birth in the arena. Ass-brains! She'll be useless for half a year!"

Cleopas ventured, "I beg you, consider! It's a thing fraught with perils, done late *or* soon. Might I remind you the Emperor's own niece died trying to empty her womb, and she had the best of physicians. It's safer, really, to let her have it. Remember this is not a normal woman but a woman who is part ox. She is in the peak of condition. She has the endurance of a trained racehorse. Childbirth won't be much different for her than cat-birth. You will lose her forever, not just for a few months, if you do this thing. And perhaps you won't be deprived of her as long as you think."

"She can still fight?"

"She *has* been. And probably can continue to, for two months more."

Erato looked at the First Physician with a stupefied expression as, slowly, he absorbed this. Perhaps he was right.

"Cat-birth, you say?" he muttered softly. What did he know of such things? He had never been confronted with such a predicament. If they took Auriane off right now, tonight, or perhaps tomorrow, she might die.

He stopped abruptly in his pacing, as if a chasm opened before his feet. He had not the heart to peer into it. No, he thought. I cannot let . . . *my child* . . . die. My child! Yes, that is truly what she has become. I have no child but Auriane.

The sentiment embarrassed him and added savagery to his scowl.

"I'm not saying I agree. But say, just for the sake of argument, I do. Then *what*, by the girdle of Nemesis, am I supposed to *do* with it?"

Cleopas looked at him, mystified by the question.

"Expose it, of course."

Erato put his hands to his head and cursed. Expose it, indeed, he thought. That's easy for him to say—he doesn't know who the father is. I *could* resign my position, get my old post back, and let somebody else lose their head over this.

Finally he said, "All of you, dismissed. I will think on this and tell you my answer tomorrow."

On the following morning, the opening day of the Augustan Games, Erato came to the west yard to observe Auriane at practice. Auriane felt him watching her intently, a curiously sad expression on his face, and sensed at once that Erato *knew*. She fought down terror.

But Erato said nothing to her that day on the matter, though she knew his mind was crowded with many words.

· *Fria, let him say and do nothing for the next four days! After that, I will either be dead or ready to flee this place.*

Erato departed without a word, and she was left with a tangle of fears and troubles. The herb Sunia brought from the stalls settled her nausea, but still she struggled through days when she wanted only to sleep, and days when she felt she carried sacks of stones tied to every limb. This must pass, she thought frantically; it did, last time. She counted and recounted the days, praying to Fria to restore her strength. It is time. Why does the weakness remain?

Later in that same day, Aristos met Rodan, and wood was exchanged for steel. Auriane and Sunia listened to the bout from the training yard. Aristos saw the odds set against him for the first time since he was brought to this place. Although Rodan had been retired, he was little past thirty; in his day he had sent five champions of Aristos' rank to their graves and made himself immensely wealthy. Sunia found herself privately pleased. Aristos would be slain. Auriane would never fight him.

After a dread-filled wait during which Auriane and Sunia stood with indrawn breath, their nails digging into their hands, their ears battered senseless from the crowd's thundering, the roars at last melted into one shapeless din.

Sunia shook her fists, demanding of the sky: *"Who lives!"*

Odberht has gone to the sky, and taken our honor with him, Auriane thought. How swiftly I lose all hope when there's equal likelihood of one outcome or the other!

After a cruel stretch of time came the cry: *"Aristos Rex!"*

Sunia collapsed to the sand and cried. If Rodan cannot finish Aristos, no mortal can, she thought. Auriane doomed herself surely as if she gave herself to the spring sacrifice.

Auriane's outrush of relief was muddied with a terror too disconcerting to fully acknowledge.

Part of me wanted what Sunia wants. I am not so ready to die. Can a portion of the heart turn traitor while the rest stands firm?

That evening as the kitchen slaves washed down the dining tables and the guards herded their charges back to their cells, an odd tale circulated through the three halls. The Emperor had ordered Aristos to attend a public banquet at the Palace to celebrate his narrow victory. As Aristos swaggered through the street with his way-clearers, his retainers, and a small honor guard, he was set upon by assassins. He survived only because this honor guard carried concealed swords and mounted a vigorous, skilled resistance that caused some witnesses to claim the assault was expected. Common wisdom maintained the assassins were sent by Musonius Geta, in revenge for the murdered girl. But Geta stoutly denied it, and oddly, it was thought, Domitian believed him.

Auriane guessed the truth of it. "That was Marcus Julianus' work and none other," she insisted to Sunia. "Curses on Helle. He's discovered the identities of Antonius and Cleopatra, the gods know how. You have your wish, Sunia. Our stratagem is finished."

And so the plan Junilla presented to Veiento proved, to Veiento's surprise, an unreserved success. Once the ground was prepared, Domitian embraced eagerly all Veiento told him: Marcus Arrius

Julianus had lusted for the woman Aurinia from the start and had brazenly lied to him about the matter. Then the sly mountebank actually went on to enjoy the wench's favors right under the trusting nose of his Lord and God.

Domitian took the news with deceptive calm, and Veiento feared at first the enchantment Marcus Julianus worked on the Emperor could not be broken. But all the next day Domitian meted out savage sentences to supplicants who appealed their cases to the Emperor: A forger convicted on the barest evidence was condemned to have his hands cut off and hung round his neck; a contractor who took bribes was roasted over a slow fire. Then on the following morning Domitian summoned Petronius.

The Guard's Prefect was brought to a chamber so dimly lit that all Petronius could see of the Emperor was the smooth outline of the top of his skull, the gleam of multiple rings, the shimmer of the gold border of his toga. Later he supposed Domitian meant to conceal his face, lest anguish be too visible.

But the Emperor could not conceal his voice. That tone was so devoid of feeling Domitian might have called for an extra tunic against the cold. To Petronius, such indifference signified madness.

"I order you to arrest Marcus Arrius Julianus."

Petronius believed the conspiracy exposed. With a mammoth effort of will he maintained an air of neutrality. Then he turned on his heel and departed to see the order carried out.

The six Praetorians were uncomfortable in the atrium of Marcus Arrius Julianus' house. Ancestors were thick in this place, staring from the lintels, gazing coldly from the numinous eyes of the waxen death masks of forebears who walked the streets of Rome three centuries ago; they fought a reflexive need to incline their heads in reverence. This great-house made them feel like simple country louts; it was a solemn temple of the Muses, a citadel of knowledge that shut them out. They were barbarians sent to sack an ancient and venerable city. And the man himself was no less unsettling: Julianus watched them with a calm curiosity that roused all their superstitions about philosophers. Perhaps it was true they possessed a superhuman ability to weather ill fortune, to solace the dying, and to conquer the passions of the mind.

Their Centurion was Servilius, the loyalist. Servilius maintained his composure by evading Julianus' gaze, taking refuge in the document he carried, which bore the imperial seal. He found his voice and settled into his proud, complacent drone:

"Marcus Arrius Julianus, by the order of Domitianus Caesar you are hereby placed under arrest and are to be conducted at once to the Palace—"

At this, a baleful chorus rose up, forcing Servilius to silence. The whole of the household congregated behind Julianus; their lament was a thin, bleak, death-filled chorus. To Julianus' right stood Diocles; he looked like a nearsighted man blinking awake from an overlong sleep. Bitterly, soundlessly, Diocles began to sob.

Marcus Julianus felt like a commander of a fort under siege who has but an instant to devise a strategy to save his men.

For many, he knew he could do nothing. The household. His relations. He thought with horror of his aged aunt Arria—would she be sent into exile? Her sons, surely, would be stripped of posts and honors.

Was the conspiracy unraveled? He could not yet be certain. As he swiftly considered, he was alert to every look and gesture of the Praetorians who accompanied Servilius. Why were these five sent? These men were, strangely, all part of the plot. Had Petronius selected them to some purpose? If so, why did he send the fanatic loyalist with them? Perhaps to help silence any questions that might arise about the loyalty of the other five?

Or perhaps I suppose too much, and there is no plan or order here, and Petronius even now languishes in prison awaiting death. Curses on Charon, our final meeting was to have been tonight!

Julianus raised a hand for silence; after a time the maidservants stilled their cries, and Servilius read on.

"—to answer certain charges," Servilius intoned, then raised his eyes eagerly to meet Julianus' gaze, for he did not want to miss the effect, "and to await your trial and execution—"

"My good man, you must be reading it wrong," Marcus Julianus broke in, "for I've never heard such a frank admission from him!"

Servilius glared at him, close-set eyes glittering homicidally, thin lips pursed. Bad-tempered baboons look much like that, Marcus Julianus thought.

Servilius looked again at the document and saw with dismay that Julianus was correct: He *had* read it wrong.

"To await your *trial*," he repeated with sarcasm, as if to say: Have it your way, it makes no difference, "on charges of impiety, treasonable ingratitude, falseness to your Sovereign and Lord, refusal to do proper respect to his images, and failure to sacrifice to his Genius on his birthday last year."

Marcus Julianus suppressed a smile of relief. That odd assortment of charges assured him the conspiracy had *not* been uncovered; had it been, he would have been charged simply with high treason.

"Is that all?" Marcus Julianus asked mildly.

"Not enough for you? I can arrange to have 'gross insolence to the *servants* of our Lord and God' appended."

"Much appreciated, but I'll decline. Have I time to settle my affairs?"

"You've no affairs to settle. The court has already begun taking charge of the dispensation of your property. We did not want to nettle you with troublesome details while you're . . . indisposed." Servilius grinned, an affable baboon now; he was finally at ease.

At Servilius' last words the maidservants' wails began afresh, rising to keening pitch. An hour ago they had the most leisurely and secure of existences. With the stroke of a pen they were confiscated property. Friends would be torn from each other, house-marriages broken apart, children lost to parents. Some would be given to abusive masters or set to onerous tasks. It was a misfortune inherent in their condition accepted by them as death was accepted, a ghastly scene enacted again and again whenever a great man fell. In this household, however, it had one difference—their master genuinely sorrowed for them. Marcus Julianus closed his eyes briefly and gave silent oath to Nemesis that if he emerged alive from this situation he would trace them, every one, and do for them whatever he could.

"Step along with us now," Servilius said importantly. Diocles rushed up and seized Marcus Julianus' arm, clamping on single-mindedly as a crab fastened to a stick. Two Praetorians dragged Julianus forward; he in turn dragged Diocles. Finally Servilius cuffed the frail old man and Diocles sank to the floor. Marcus Julianus savagely fought his way round and bent to help him up.

"Leave him!" Servilius' shout was an impotent jerk on a rein.

Julianus met Servilius' eyes with calm contempt, then turned his back on him, shouldered the men aside, and helped Diocles to rise.

Servilius seethed within, but was silent, a dog brought to heel; he was a man who, without acknowledging it to himself, was always grateful for a master—though far from ready to love the man who took up that role.

As the Praetorians conducted Marcus Julianus through the streets, they fought their way through crowds of celebrants bearing gifts to the ancient horn-bearing Temple of Diana on the Aventine Hill, for this was the day of the temple's yearly rededication. It was a holiday for slaves as well, and it seemed the whole population idled, drank or diced in the streets. As Julianus' plight was seen, the rejoicing faltered; it was as if the drums of a passing funeral procession set all hearts to a more somber beat. In the small party's wake were troubled looks and exclamations of alarm, though none dared show grief too openly.

Marcus Julianus struggled with a wild sadness of his own that seemed ready to rend him in two. With his arrest he had lost all chance of rescuing Auriane from Aristos' murderous blade.

My lost child, the gods grant that there be an otherworld so I may find you in it. I once was certain there was a transcendent reason for suffering. Just now I cannot remember what I thought it was.

To Domitian there will be no appeal. I will survive only if my date of execution is set after the hour of the assassination. Given the near certainty of both our deaths, it seems safe to say, Auriane, we'll soon be together.

But whatever becomes of me, the plot must come to its conclusion. Domitian must die. Who betrayed me? *"Falseness to your Lord"* was one of the charges. *Lying.* Perhaps he learned I lied about Auriane. Who would reveal such a thing, or care? Junilla, possibly. Junilla, probably. All could be well if Domitian knows no more than this.

But there are matters I must settle with Petronius tonight.

Servilius walked behind him, to better watch him. To his left strode Arruntius, who answered directly to Petronius and knew of both Guard's Prefects involvement in the plot. Marcus Julianus considered a tactic, rejected it, then considered it again.

I must try. What choice have I? If I tread carefully, the worst that can happen is that I'll convince Arruntius that I've gone mad.

Marcus Julianus caught Arruntius' slitted eye for the barest moment, a quick gesture whose significance only Arruntius perceived. And Julianus saw a look of expectation.

Encouraged by this, he began to talk, hoping that to Servilius his words would sound like the typical desperate bargaining tactics of the accused.

"This is but a . . . a sorry misunderstanding, my friends!"

Julianus said with a hopeful smile. He spoke directly to Arruntius; Servilius could hear, but not every word. "If you let me return for but a moment, I can straighten out this silliness at once—"

Servilius cleared his throat threateningly and spat on the ground. Julianus ignored him. "I have *letters*," he said to Arruntius, "three letters, that prove my innocence—"

Arruntius concealed a start of excitement.

Petronius had cautioned him to be alert to any way that Marcus Julianus might try to communicate with him. *Letters*. He must mean Caenis' letters, which must be read before the Senate.

"They are in Apollo's keeping," Marcus Julianus went on. "I beg you, consider!"

What is that? Arruntius thought. If I can't puzzle it out, maybe someone else can. Wait—does he mean the Apollo Library? No, he must mean the library of his own house. We'll have to send our men in there when they go to seal up that house.

Arruntius said loudly for Servilius' benefit, "I'm innocent, you're innocent, we're all innocent when caught! I'm afraid you're beyond the help of evidence, my friend. Now step up the pace!"

"I can make it well worth your while. The library has two million rolls, so you must ask the librarian, a one-eyed man. Pity the innocent, that the gods will one day turn round and pity you—"

"*Silence*, you!" came Servilius' sulky shout from behind them.

Arruntius tramped on, thinking frantically. He has not yet given us the name of the fifth man. It must be concealed in those last words. Which word has meaning? A *librarian?* No. *A one-eyed man.* He's telling me the Cyclops is ready to come with us. The two million must be what he's costing us. The gods be praised! All is set in place. But two million! No one has that anymore. The richest Senators have either been murdered, exiled, or bled dry. Nerva's wealth is all in land. Where will they get it now that this man is gone?

Arruntius gave Marcus Julianus a nearly imperceptible nod to let him know the message would be passed on.

Junilla heard of Marcus Julianus' arrest when her chief steward brought her a letter from Veiento and a gift. *"I salute you. The elephant and the fox could learn from you,"* she read. *"The elephant, patience, and the fox, laudable cunning. I remain at your service."* With it came a tame fox. The elephant, she surmised, presented too much of a problem.

She sent the fox back to him, along with a letter of her own. *"You always were too quick with your gifts,"* she wrote him. *"Save them until after I receive justice. As long as that man is capable of speech, he's a menace."*

CHAPTER LV

At nightfall when Sunia was let into the cell she found Auriane examining the rune-sticks. The cell's only light came from the moon. Sunia counted this night evil; surely the disturbances she had heard all day in the streets flushed out night-riding spirits. The acrid smell of burning hung in the air, and the sounds of rioting, near and far.

"Auriane," she said, not coming too close. "You *know,* do you not?" She assumed Auriane sought to learn from the oracle whether she would live or die.

"I get riddling replies."

"Curses on you! Tell me!"

"I'm given the sign for death and rebirth, three times."

"There's no riddle there! The spirits of forest and grove concur with what common sense tells a simpleton! Death is death. Can our wretched lives get worse!" Though her voice was scolding, there was comfort in her step as she approached Auriane and knelt beside her.

Auriane met Sunia's gaze, considering whether she should reveal a thing at once too wonderful, too fragile, too odd. "Or it might signify something else," she ventured finally. "Sunia, a change comes to me, difficult to trap with words as a taste or a smell. . . . It's as if, sometimes, all things show me their hidden god-spirit . . . and this change might *also* be called death and rebirth. More and more often I've an odd, sure gathering of a sense

915

of the hidden goodness of all fates, and it lifts like a powerful wind. . . . It is what I felt so long ago, when I pried the stone from the hoof of Ramis' mare. Sometimes I feel there is—you will think me mad—*no distance* between things and beings. . . . Sometimes I feel I stand next to everyone I have known, alive or dead. I think that what a people knows as the truth of life is like some boundary line—a man or woman claimed it and drew it at the first, *but it can be redrawn.* It also brings a simple certainty that everyone, *even strange tribes,* are kinsmen."

Sunia frowned in a token effort of comprehension, then shrugged. "Ramis herself would not count these Roman wolves kinsmen. I tell you I tire of them parading you before their people as some joke."

Auriane sadly abandoned all attempts to explain—Sunia lived comfortably among what she could touch and see and had no more use for the spirit world than had a cat for a cloak.

"*Novelty* is the word Erato uses, Sunia, not joke."

"No matter. When you meet Aristos, the novelty is going to be on them."

"That's not rightly said, Sunia. It's another of their words we've no word for—" A succession of sharp shouts from the street silenced her.

"*Free him!*" came scattered cries. Bottles and bricks cracked against the school's monolithic wall. Auriane moved to the narrow window.

"All day I listened to that baying and yelping," Sunia said with a shrug. "'By Fria's necklace, these are a noisy and fretful people! They must have arrested someone important."

Auriane was suddenly alert and still, knowing the truth with her body before she knew it with her mind. A ghastly cold bit into her bones.

"I'm surprised there's anyone important left to arrest," Sunia went on, then fell into fright-filled silence as she realized what Auriane was thinking.

Auriane's heart clenched shut to avoid knowing the thing that she knew, with fatal certainty, was true. Numbly she struggled to make sense of the scene below: A group of unruly citizens with torches stormed the mounted statue of Domitian that stood in the cleared way about the Colosseum and began pelting it with offal. The city police streamed in and began herding everyone indiscriminately into the Via Sacra and on to the prisons, where she knew they would be sorted out according to social station: Those with powerful protectors would be let go, and those with no patron to bribe a magistrate would suffer punishment, whether they had a part in the rioting or not.

A single, clear cry from below jarred her from dazed denial: *"Doom to us all! They've taken the only sane and good man in the government from us!"*

Sunia heard it too; she came up beside Auriane and put her hands about her shoulders.

Auriane perceived it first as a simple fact: The precarious structure on which Marcus Arrius Julianus balanced so long had finally crashed down. It was inevitable, was it not? Then came a riot of rage and pain.

He is at the mercy of a monster. They will torture him.

She shut her eyes to escape the sight but only saw it with pulsing clarity. She wanted to scream with her whole body and dash herself against the walls until she either killed herself or brought the walls down. She wished she were a spear tearing through Domitian's body. She longed to draw together an army and sack the Palace, but only the dust motes settling on the sill were ready to move at her command.

There is no solace in this world. It is one devouring mouth. From birth to death is one long shriek.

Beloved. You have no chance.

Sunia was quietly crying, her face buried in Auriane's tunic. Auriane felt her whole mind careening toward an embrace of death. *I could twist my rune-cloth into a rope and . . .*

No. I made an oath. An oath reaches beyond this life. Even now in this school my people are mumbling poor, pitiful prayers for my victory. And I want the one within me to see the sun and moon. My people need not know I've fled the world. Aristos will do battle with a ghost.

When Domitia Longina was brought word of Marcus Arrius Julianus' arrest, she summoned Carinus and ordered him to die with her. While her maids rouged her face and softened her skin with pumice so her corpse would be beautiful, Carinus mustered the courage to defy her and secreted his own draught of aconite into one of her empty cosmetic pots. When they lay down on her silken bed for their final rest, Carinus waited until he saw her lids drop closed; then he padded quietly out of her bedchamber and found her personal physician, who administered the antidote.

When Domitian was informed that his wife lay gravely ill, he made a formal visit; one of his strongest instincts was to maintain a look of propriety. So the first sight that confronted Domitia Longina when she returned to the world was her husband's face as he bent over her, peering at her with brusque formality, examining her with the bland incuriousness of a goat. Thinking herself to be dead, Domitia Longina thought: Is this monster then lord of *this* world too, as well as the one I just left?

Domitian turned to leave, then paused and said offhandedly, "Do not imagine you've the wit to deceive me, my coy lamb. I *know* what spurred this childish fit of self-immolation—grief over the fact that I've brought Marcus Arrius Julianus to justice. Did you think I did not *know* he was your lover? A pity. . . . It seems your criminal lechery has finally outdistanced your cunning."

Marcus Arrius Julianus' house was stripped of its treasures and sealed; all was to be sold at a public auction to help pay for September's *Ludi Romani,* the next days of games. But the house itself Domitian decided to give to Veiento as a gift for his services, for without his keen-sighted Councillor he might never have known of Julianus' treachery. Veiento could not stop boasting of the irony of it: He would now take up residence in the mansion of the very scoundrel who once caused his exile. Victory was complete. Veiento was annoyed that he could not take possession at once, but the Emperor ordered him to wait until his secretaries calculated the extent of the property of the accused, which would require at least a month.

Within the day, men whom Marcus Julianus had helped to various posts dared not speak his name. His shut-up house was shunned as though it were haunted. To a foreign traveler it would have appeared as though he never was. But beneath the surface of this, he was mourned more than any man ruined before him. Offerings for his deliverance were made secretly at family altars or at street shrines under cover of night. Others prayed feverishly at the Temple of Diana, begging the ancient goddess to take her form of Nemesis and seek retribution on Domitian.

On the day after the arrest, the dawn of the Ides, the Senate was to convene for another day of prosecutions, but at the news of Marcus Arrius Julianus' arrest, the Senators stayed away in dozens, claiming a variety of ailments so they would be close to family and affairs—and swift, convenient means of suicide. By afternoon, when word got about that Julianus' arrest was the result of some private quarrel with the Emperor, hesitantly they crept out and took their seats. Petronius got word to members of the plot, one by one, that the conspiracy was intact.

Marcus Julianus was taken to the warren of passages beneath the Old Palace. As he was led deeper into the moist, earthen tunnels he felt he had been sucked down into a drain, submerged in the unspeakable foulness of the bottom of the world. Along the passages, hands stretched out to him from barred windows; slight stirrings could be heard in the darkness, but he could not tell whether they were produced by humans or outsized rats. The odor of blood and rot seemed thick enough to leave a scum on the walls. From somewhere ahead came a thin, tremulous wail that occasionally sharpened into a screech, a sound without age, gender, or humanity—the cries of a victim in the interrogation rooms.

He was given a cell opposite the torturers' rooms, whether by accident or design he was not certain. He felt he was among the ghosts of madmen: The prisoners in adjacent cells kept up a continuous droning, chanting songs and nonsense phrases to cover up the cries of the men on the rack.

His cell was hardly more than a fissure in a cave. Foul water dripped on his head. At every fresh shriek from the torturers' rooms he felt a bone crack or smelled flesh frying beneath a brand. But the sight that stayed before him steadily was that of Auriane lying torn and bleeding on the sand. In grief's delirium he thought the torturers' arts would bring relief from this agony of the mind. Night came; during the few hours when the torturers ceased their work he lapsed into lurid dreams in which he repeatedly rushed to Auriane's rescue, only to be dragged back by a river of slime. Then the cries from the interrogation rooms began anew, and a day passed unseen. He kept track of time by the distant shouts of guard changes.

On the second morning the guards pushed a new prisoner into the cell.

Marcus Julianus sat up, reality flooding round like ice water. He guessed it was the first hour of day, if once again they were bringing in prisoners. The assassination would be, the gods willing, tomorrow afternoon, a span of thirty-three hours away.

He listened for a time to the new prisoner's frantic breathing as the man cringed like a beaten hound against the opposite wall. Eventually a passing guard paused at the window, torch aloft, and Marcus Julianus saw his cellmate's face.

He felt a jolt of alarm as he recognized that lazy ferret's countenance, those hunched shoulders, that fair hair, straight as straw, combed forward so that it resembled a hastily thatched roof. The man was Petronius' secretary, Bato, whom the Guard's Commander had admitted to the upper hierarchy of the plot over his own protests. Marcus Julianus thought Bato knew far too much for safety. This secretary was one of the few who knew of the participation of both Prefects.

Curses on Charon. He's of an irresolute nature. If he was brought in for conspiracy in any form, they will torture him. He'll babble all he knows and more he doesn't know, when the interrogator so much as nods at him.

But then, Marcus Julianus reassured himself, he might be here for another reason.

He waited through two guard changes. Five more prisoners were brought in—poor plebeians arrested for rioting, he surmised from the guards' talk. Finally he attempted speech with Bato, but only got whimpers and moans in reply. He then gave Bato an edited tale of his own arrest, in order to win the man's confidence. They did not exchange names, and Julianus kept his voice at a whisper to better disguise it. He was fairly certain the secretary did not recognize him in the cavernous darkness, which was as he wished it. Finally he asked Bato why he had been taken. Bato answered eagerly, his manner that of a terrified child reaching out to the hand of an adult.

"An informer named me as one of the messengers who carried Saturninus' orders to the Rhine commanders. It is villainous absurdity! That was three plots ago!"

We are done, Marcus Julianus thought. A conspiracy charge. They will torture him for certain. I cannot believe Domitian is still dragging in men for that long-cold rebellion. As soon as Bato names Petronius and Norbanus, our plans will come apart. Some successor to myself—none of *us* will live to see it—will have to begin all over again to win, man by man, the support of enough of the Guard to eliminate Domitian without civil war.

While Bato began pummeling the naked rock, bloodying his fists, and crying out the name of someone called Calpurnia, who might have been a ladylove or a mother, Marcus Julianus considered rapidly.

I must not let the interrogators have Bato. They'll come for him soon enough—they're systematically taking in all the prisoners in this passage. Fair Nemesis, what is to be done?

I see no other solution but to somehow persuade them to take *me* instead. Yes, it must be so.

Even if I'm successful, though, I can at best only delay them—sooner or later they'll realize the mistake. For safety's sake, the assassination must be moved a day closer so they've less time to unravel what I've done.

Yes. All will play the same part, at the same hour—*but Domitian must die today.*

He moved to the window, examining the faces of passing prison guards. Somehow he must get a message through to Petronius. But the guards he saw were either completely ignorant of what was to come or men he knew to be loyalists.

Afterward many tales were told of this dawn. Some claimed that just as the sun showed its fiery head, it halted in its ascension, as if to stop the coming of day. Others maintained that at sunrise two moons shone on the west horizon. A traveler on one of the great roads leading into the city reported that a sudden wind tore an inscription plate from one of Domitian's triumphal arches and hurled it into a nearby tomb. It was commonly claimed that no child born in Rome as this evil dawn broke lived more than nine days.

It was the fourth day of the Augustan Games. Sunia awakened with an unpleasant start, remembering.

Antonius, Cleopatra. The day of deliverance.

Sunia realized she had been roused by Auriane's voice—hopeful, hesitant—as she intoned a prayer to Fria.

"You who are the red-gold crown of the sun . . . the fire of life in every eye . . ." The words caused Sunia to remember intimately the lost things: Footprints in the mud about wood images of Fria, filling rapidly with water as the rains came. The sound of the sky's water slashing through boughs of ash. The image of her own stern black-garbed mother laying lilies on Baldemar's cairn.

". . . Nourish me with your milk. Light my hearth. I know I am lost. I beg you, send me home. I am terrified of this day! Lay your hand on my brow and walk with me while the sun goes into midheaven. . . . Let me love vengeance a little longer so I can scatter the darkness that pursues my people.

"Let Baldemar know it: Today I either free him or come to him. Eastre, his death-day, will pass no more in sorrow.

"You who watch us with the eyes of sun and moon until we are

*waste . . . justice is your nature . . . your winds sing the law.
If I am brought down, let me be enfolded in your black-earth arms.
I am the wolf. Let my sword strike for the dead. Their blood cries
out from the ground . . ."*

There was a soft clink at the cell door; slowly it eased open.

"No," Sunia said, rising to her feet. "Not yet!"

Auriane turned around, startled, then moved swiftly to Sunia's
side. Their time was gone.

"Sunia, listen to me," Auriane said urgently, her voice husky
and dark. "If I fail, and if he . . . if Marcus survives . . . and
you speak to him—I think he would seek you out—do not tell
him about the child."

"I would not. Why make him suffer more?"

Two guards from the night watch peered into the cell.

"Tell him I have done this thing because I and my people are
one. Tell him I loved him more than I thought it possible for a
human creature to love. I do not remember if I told him that. And,
Sunia—"

One of the guards broke in gruffly, "Not *this* one? That's Erato's
favorite. Latius, you've made a mistake—your *last* one, I'll own."

"No mistake. Fetch her out of there and be quick about it."

"But Erato—"

"This is not Erato's business. Step quickly or answer to Plancius
and the givers of the games!"

The reluctant guard entered, then prodded Auriane's arm with
the butt of his javelin. "Step along there, Cleo. It's time to get
dressed for the day's audiences!"

Auriane pulled Sunia to her breast and held her for long
moments. "Don't grieve! Our people will be watching your face to
see how I fare. Stay near Thorgild and Coniaric. Sunia!" Auriane
drew the *aurr* from her tunic. "This is the hearth of the world. Why
was it returned to me if not to lead us back to our own ground?"

Sunia pressed the earth amulet to her lips. Then Auriane
disengaged herself from Sunia and put on the hooded cloak that
one of the guards held ready for her. Sunia saw that Auriane's
hands shook as she fastened it.

"Remember that I loved you," Auriane said, her voice pale.
"You are my sister. May we meet again on earth."

At the third hour of morning the throng in the Colosseum was
a placid sea; no one could have guessed at the titanic storm waves

to come. Though no favorites were expected to appear today, the amphitheater was filled past capacity with thousands standing in the wooden upper gallery because word had gone round that the Emperor was to appear alongside Plancius, the Praetor who was official giver of the games. Loathed as Domitian was, still he drew crowds like kites to a kill.

Erato had not slept. He had scarcely calmed himself enough to sit since the hour he was brought the news of Marcus Arrius Julianus' arrest. Before the day was done, the loss of his patron proved disastrous. He discovered Plancius had brazenly cheated him of payment for the five hundred men and twenty women he provided for the Augustan Games, paying less than half the agreed-upon price. When he raised this with Plancius' procurator, Erato found himself accused of slandering a member of the nobility, a dangerous charge difficult to fight—and Plancius fully intended to bring it to the courts. Before Julianus' fall, Erato would have laughed at Plancius' feeble attempts to cheat him. But now he stood helpless and alone against a ruthless aristocrat. Since dawn he had frenziedly gone over his figures to help prove his case, knowing the matter was hopeless, for half the judges in the city owed their positions to Plancius.

His panic was not eased when he entered his offices at dawn and discovered his bust of Domitian shattered into dust on the floor. He was dumbstruck with spirit-fright, as if he had come upon a severed hand in an alleyway, or bloodied cock-feathers. *What vileness does this portend?* As he cursed the clumsy slave who had knocked it from the shelf, a more earthly terror settled in: He had allowed an image of the Emperor to be abused. Men and women were executed for less than this. Hurriedly he swept up the pieces himself, fearing to leave the mess for a slave, who might gossip and cause word of this to reach the wrong ears.

And so when Meton came to Erato at noon to report that Aristos was missing, he found the school's Prefect too distracted to listen or care.

"Meton, if you are burdening me with this and you've not searched every tavern and brothel—"

"But they are closed. It is a festival day." Meton frowned, surprised Erato had not thought of this.

"Well then, imitate Penelope and bide patiently. I wouldn't fret overmuch—it's bad for the color and complexion."

Meton flushed; he despised references to his womanly appearance.

"But the Acrobat and the Eel don't know where he is. What if Musonius Geta made another try at packing him off to Hades—"

"The nonsense spun by idle minds! Go busy yourself with something, Meton. You're spreading laziness. Just looking at you makes me feel like taking a nap. Are all your men ready? Go curl your hair again. Leave me!"

If Acco had come just then to tell him that Auriane was missing as well, Erato's suspicions might have been roused. But Acco was struggling to keep the agitated Chattian captives quiet—they were unusually restless today, even for captives recently taken. Their behavior put him in mind of animals before an earthquake. Two had savagely attacked a guard and had to be killed. He could not afford to lose more; their full number was needed for the mock naval battle set for the eleventh hour.

And so in the guarded chambers where the school's costumers laboriously painted, combed, masked and dressed the contestants, Auriane's and Aristos' preparations continued undisturbed.

At the third hour of the morning Petronius was lost in the office work that beset every Commander of the Guard; as he reviewed the names of men he was considering for promotion, one of his senior Centurions sought an audience with him. The man greeted him, then said simply, "Today, you must sacrifice five doves to Venus."

Petronius felt the man struck him a blow across the face. These words were only known to Marcus Julianus and himself. "Five" and "doves" symbolized the freedom and peace the assassination would bring. But *today?* There was no mistaking the meaning of the words, or from whom they had come. He guessed at once that something must have gone gravely wrong down in the prisons.

Julianus has seen or heard something he fears will give us away. Today it must be, then.

He had somehow to inform, secretly and at once, the Senate and those Centurions of the Guard who were part of the plot. And they in turn needed to inform those who answered to them. And what of Nerva? Petronius wondered. He had begun with the antidote only yesterday morning. It was too soon for him—at the ninth hour he would hardly be able to stand without aid. And today it would be doubly difficult to draw Domitian off from the games. *Those absurd costume battles,* he thought. *Domitian takes perverse pleasure in them.* Petronius cursed Marcus Julianus, then silenced himself, knowing well that Julianus would never have sent this message if all their lives did not depend upon it.

At the same hour of morning the throng in the Colosseum dropped into respectful quiet, for the originator of the show that commenced then was Domitian himself. The Emperor stared glassily at the gladiators' entrance as twelve gold-helmeted sword-fighters came forth, two abreast. Domitian saw all about him as a gauzy waking dream that grew sharp and dangerous only when he thought of Marcus Arrius Julianus's arrest. In one moment, it made him powerfully anxious, as if he had offended some ineffable power, and he half expected a punishing hand from the sky to smite him down. But in the next, it made him feel he carried the scepter of Jupiter.

I am the stronger. Marcus, old truthteller, this was a truth you missed! Seer and philosopher, how is it that you failed to foretell your own fall?

The Numidian attendants removed the helmets from the twelve contestants and whisked off their scarlet cloaks. Domitian was eagerly alert. Twelve flaxen-haired barbarian women were revealed, each selected for comeliness. They were clad as Amazons, wearing short leopardskin tunics that hung from one shoulder, leaving one breast bared; all were armed with wickerwork shields and Samnite swords. Terror was quite visible on several faces. At the sound of a trumpet blast, twelve dwarfs attired as Thracian gladiators entered the arena, and they faced the women in a line. A second trumpet shriek ordered the attack.

The slaughter lasted less than a quarter hour. When ten women and eight dwarfs lay dead, the trumpet signaled a halt. The crowd broke into nervous applause in deference to the show's creator. Domitian gave the order that the two women who survived were to be sent as they were, armored and bloody, to await his pleasure at the Palace. He examined them as they were brought close to the imperial box, feeling the familiar hot, anticipatory stirrings in his loins. Yes, they were far more pleasing than the woman Aurinia. Their faces bore not a trace of her insane stubbornness. They were openly terrified of his majesty.

When I take them, they will think they have been raped by Zeus.

The herald then announced that from this hour forward, all combatants would appear in historical costume, and that wagers could only be made before identities were revealed. A man in the plebeian seats with a voice penetrating as a dog's howl called out in a moment of quiet: *"No more stupid, dull shows! Give us Aristos!"* Scuffling ensued as guards seized the offender and dragged him off.

Plancius, sponsor of the games, seated at Domitian's right, felt a covert surge of satisfaction.

You shall get him, you lowbred herd of human cattle. And my games will be remembered forever.

CHAPTER LVI

The *Ludus Magnus* was given over to the mob. They spilled into every available space and pushed against the rope corridor that stretched from the armory to the barricaded passage leading to the Colosseum. The throng's cries echoing off vaulted stone were violent to the ears as the din of a cheap bathhouse.

Sunia fought to get close to the rope. She felt like cloth in a press. This crowd was composed mostly of those citizens too poor or too late to get a seat in the amphitheater, many of whom were intent on getting a close, critical look at the costumed contestants before they laid their bets.

After a time she heard soft calls of awe—elephant handlers were coming down the passage, guiding a small Indian elephant. She saw only the top of its knobby gray head and part of a red leather harness flashing with hundreds of mirrors. Astride was a gladiator costumed as someone called Hannibal, she realized from the exclamations all about. Sunia watched in bitter quiet, hardly seeing, not wanting to comprehend. Hannibal's opponent followed close behind; he was Darius, the Persian king. Sunia saw a flash of red-and-gold-striped robe, a ludicrous false beard, and the top of a sedan chair studded with garishly colored glass meant to look like precious gems. Hannibal and Darius went on to their fates, and after a tense wait, during which fights erupted over their respective identities and abilities, word filtered back that Hannibal, despite his fine entrance, was dead. As debts were paid or promised, the crowd shifted restlessly, impatient for the next contestants.

Sunia at last gained the rope. Now she could see Acco by the school's entrance, shepherding his shackled herd of three hundred Chattian tribesmen, readying them for their chance to die at sea—the day's mock naval battle would begin directly after the costume events. To Sunia her tribesmen looked like wild animals just off the range, ready to dash their heads against the walls in blank fright. She was saddened by how remote she felt from them, and slightly shamed by the first thought that came to mind: For certain, I did not look so when I was first captured. The Chattian prisoners were kept to one side so the avenue would be clear; they huddled together like cattle protecting themselves from a storm. Sunia suspected they were poor farmers taken in a raid.

Then to her astonishment they began to call out in thin, pitiful voices: *"Daughter of the Ash! Give us vengeance!"*

Sunia flashed to attention.

Silence, fools, you'll give her away! Sunia thought, looking about nervously, not quite convinced no one understood. But to the Roman mob her tribesmen's speech was so much barbarous noise.

"Daughter of the Ash, lead us out!"

Sunia shut her eyes to stop the tears. It was soul-rending to hear the old battle-call in such timorous voices; she felt she gazed on a body once heroically strong now withered by plague.

And then a new chorus of shouts rooted Sunia to the floor.

"Cleopatra! She comes!"

"Hail, Cleopatra, Daughter of Isis, Queen of the Nile!"

Sunia threw herself against the rope, straining to see. For long moments the avenue was empty. Then four ibexes harnessed abreast came nodding into view—these sturdy goatlike creatures were crowned with magnificent black-curved horns that formed a bold C, lending an ordinary beast a sort of grandeur. Though the animal trainers had them lightly drugged, still the ibexes were unnerved by the crowd; fretfully they threw up their extravagantly horned heads and walked with tight, mincing steps. Gradually she saw that these beasts drew Cleopatra's chariot. The car was farcical, crudely painted to appear as if it were fashioned of ebony and ivory, and covered over with clumsily rendered Egyptian magical symbols. Affixed to the front were the horns of Horus, elegantly uplifted like hands in blessing.

Solemn and erect within the chariot was Cleopatra.

As the throng examined the stark, waxen face of the dreaded queen, they fell fleetingly into an uneasy quiet. Cleopatra was a more recent threat than Hannibal, who had rigidified into myth; the oldest members of the crowd had heard her described by aged parents who had actually set eyes upon the strange, fearsome queen who nearly succeeded in making the Mediterranean world her own. Yes, all seemed to agree, that is how that voracious foreign queen must have looked.

As Cleopatra moved closer, Sunia was given an unpleasant start. What had they done to Auriane? She looked bizarre. A sharp loneliness bit into Sunia's stomach. This was a cruel farewell; there was little of Auriane here to see.

Cleopatra's headdress concealed most of her face; it was fashioned of countless strands of small polished ivory beads, creating the appearance of shivering pearly hair that hung thickly to her shoulders. Atop it was a bronze circlet that became, at the front, a snake with upraised head. Laid along the sides of the heavy headdress were two fanned hawks' wings. She wore no mask, yet Sunia would hardly have known Auriane beneath that heavy red, white and black paint. Her serene, deathly-white face might have been carved in Pentelic marble; those pitiless crimson lips belonged to a stranger. But it was her eyes that disturbed Sunia most—they were coarsely outlined with a heavily drawn line of black paint that extended at the sides like a tail. It made her expression fixed, all-knowing, calm as eternity; it drew out Auriane's soul and left her a hollow image.

As Cleopatra passed by, Sunia saw the real eye within the hard black outline, shifting, liquid, struggling with grief. There at last was Auriane.

As Cleopatra wore a voluminous robe of white linen over her armor, the crowd failed to guess that a woman and not a man of slight stature was within. But gradually suspicions were roused.

Sunia heard the marbleworker pressed next to her mutter, "That's the scrawniest Cleopatra I've ever seen. Did they train the poor fellow on bread and water?"

"He's fair as Ganymede, whoever he is," responded a woman behind Sunia, a crone who reeked of the fish markets. "That's a woman, I would swear on Juno's girdle!"

"Ridiculous," the marbleworker retorted, wagging a finger in the direction of the avenue down which Cleopatra had come. "They'd never match a woman with *that* behemoth!"

Sunia saw that Marcus Antonius came close behind.

Aristos. Nausea churned up in her throat.

Marcus Antonius' chariot was drawn by four Mesopotamian lionesses—this brought murmurings of admiration for the skill of the animal trainers, for here was a beast nearly impossible to break to cart. The lionesses' backs were draped in gold netting that shimmered in their tawny fur. Their collars were inset with false rubies. They padded along with great composure, their expressions bored. Marcus Antonius' chariot seemed solid as a marble-cart beside Cleopatra's flimsy car; its bronze plating was embossed with scenes of Bacchic revels.

If little of Auriane was visible, Sunia saw nothing whatever of Aristos. He wore a garishly painted wooden mask so stylized it might have been the countenance of Jupiter; the eyes of the man were lost in the mask's large, vacant almond-shaped eyes. His long red-blond hair was dyed black. A scarlet robe embroidered with palms flowed from the brutish shoulders. Two rocklike fists clad in leather gloves clutched the reins aggressively, as if he squeezed the life out of some creature.

"Embrace her! Embrace her!" the crowd called gaily to him.

The sight of this unlikely pairing was beginning to draw comment. Why had the givers of the games pitted a bull against a gazelle? Some decided Cleopatra must have some secret advantage and quickly laid their bets on her. But most did the reasonable thing, and the wagers heavily favored Marcus Antonius.

When the two cars had moved many paces on and Sunia could see only Cleopatra's white robe brushing the travertine floor, she heard a jarringly familiar voice like a horse's whinny: *"Aurinia! Aurinia!"*

Sunia caught her breath. Thirty paces ahead along the rope, she saw Phoebe from the herb market. It was certainly she; Sunia would never forget those eyes full of playful malice, eager to worm their way into a soul and steal secrets.

We are betrayed. Somehow, through good guessing or witchcraft, the miserable toad recognized Auriane.

Auriane's face was not so completely concealed as Aristos' was, and once one person saw her through the paint, discerning the familiar curve of a cheek, the well-known line of a chin, others began to recognize her as well. It after all made a certain sort of sense—it explained why a burly giant had been set against one so small. The larger man was, no doubt, some clumsy novice whose size would do him little good against the near-magical skill of their Aurinia.

Now the cries *"Aurinia! Aurinia!"* rose jubilantly all around, like the taunt of unruly children who have uncovered something they should not have. Sunia imagined Auriane must be gripped with panic. If the people guessed Aristos' identity, all was lost—for in their unaccountable way the mob loved her and would never send her off to what they believed certain death.

The cry *"Aurinia!"* spread like a field fire in a brisk wind, and within moments the throng in the Colosseum knew she approached. As the two chariots came closer to the barricaded passage connecting the *Ludus Magnus* with the amphitheater, Sunia saw the dulled eyes of the Chattian prisoners catch fire. Many uttered charms, whose purpose, Sunia guessed, was to prevent the people from unmasking Aristos. As Auriane approached them, they stretched out their hands to her, crying in the native tongue, *"Wodan give strength to the sword of holiness!"* To the crowd they might have been baying hounds.

When the shout *"Aurinia!"* reached Erato's ears, he was in his accounts rooms, sparring cautiously with Plancius' procurator, striving to explain diplomatically to the man—in an effort to avoid arrest for libel—that both he and his master were thieves and extortionists. Erato pushed roughly past the procurator, strode to the end of the second-story colonnade, and looked down. In the distance he saw Cleopatra and Marcus Antonius creeping stiffly along like figures of gods carried in an Olympian procession. If Cleopatra was Auriane, he did not need to be told who was behind the mask of Marcus Antonius.

"Spawn of a black goat!" he swore, and threw his stylus noisily to the floor.

You impossible fool. I should have known you were too mule-minded to listen to sound, sober warnings. You too-clever whelp, it's not me you've outsmarted this time—it's yourself. Hades take this place!

He realized then that Auriane could not have deceived him without aid from the givers of the games. He turned slowly round and advanced on Plancius' procurator, whose name was Tiro.

"You knew of this thing and did not tell me!" Decorum fled; Erato might have drawn a dagger. His thick fingers dug into Tiro's shoulder.

"Unhand me, slave and son of a slave!" Tiro was a soft, pale man who had never done rougher physical work than hoisting an inkpot, and he was terrified of Erato. He scuttled backward to get away, but Erato held his grip firm.

"You slimy little cheat. That's Aristos! You skulked about behind my back and got him for the price of a novice. And what does a worm like you care if the woman Aurinia is slaughtered like a dog!" With one powerful shove he slammed Tiro against the concrete wall.

"Fiend! Murderer! Help me!" Tiro yelped. He cringed at first, then gave Erato an ineffectual kick in the shins. Erato landed a brutal blow to his ear; Tiro collapsed to his knees. Then four Vigiles sprang forth from their discreet stations behind the columns of the upper walk—Plancius had taken the precaution of having his accountant accompanied by city policemen. They seized Erato from behind and dragged him back several steps.

Tiro, seeing himself rescued, took his time getting up. With prim composure he addressed the Vigiles: "I order you to arrest this man for attempted murder—or you will answer to Plancius."

Before Julianus' fall the city policemen would have hesitated. But today the school's Prefect had no more protection than a common plebeian. One delivered a blow to Erato's stomach to render him easier to manage; another quickly shackled him.

Meton saw this disturbance and sprinted to Erato's aid. But he stopped before he reached them, assessing the situation with a stricken look; it was obvious at once that he could do nothing.

Black curses on Fortuna, Meton thought, full of a sense he looked upon a doomed man.

As Erato struggled, he managed to call out, "Meton! Stop that bout! I care not how you do it. *That is Auriane—and Aristos!*"

"Auriane and—" Meton paused, looked blankly at Cleopatra and Antonius, then back at Erato with a despairing look. Then he bolted off.

Meton could scarcely believe the swiftness with which all about him had fallen into chaos. The school, unknown to its hundreds of employees and slaves, was without a Prefect; he felt he ran on a rudderless ship pitching toward the reefs. And as if this were not catastrophe enough, one of the school's prized possessions, the woman Aurinia, was being delivered to certain destruction. The day was evil; he had felt a doomed wildness about this place ever since the arrest of Marcus Julianus.

When Meton came abreast of Cleopatra's chariot, he shouted to the guards posted along that section of the roped-off avenue: *"Erato's order, stop the bout!"* After much repetition and frantic waving of arms, at last he convinced them to take action.

Cleopatra and Marcus Antonius were by now abreast of the

chained Chattian prisoners. The guards stationed along that section of rope moved from position and fanned across the open way to block the two chariots' path. As they snatched at the reins of the beasts drawing the cars, Auriane's ibexes skittered sideways, reared, and tried to twist their way out of harness, while Aristos' lionesses stood with regal calm, as if knowing the guards were frightened of handling them.

But at that moment the Chattian prisoners gave the trilling native war cry and surged away from the rope in a single disordered mass. They ploughed into the guards, striking them with the loose ends of their chains. The guards were so taken by surprise by this fierce opposition from a group of doomed, unarmed men that they were readily distracted.

Swords were drawn. A furious, bloody struggle ensued, resembling a battle between naked men and sharks.

Auriane looked on in piteous horror, then averted her eyes. Her tribesmen's mad maneuver broke up the guards' human barricade, opening the way for the two chariots.

Her people were dying so that she and Aristos could get through.

For a moment she stood transfixed by their shrieks, her hands paralyzed on the reins. Shame scalded her heart. *I dared doubt the necessity of the holy rite of vengeance!*

They do not doubt. And I am their only instrument. My faltering resolve may well be what brought them to this horrible end.

Go on, Daughter of the Bogs. Move forward, unholy woman. There is only one route left open: into the pit of sacrifice.

With furious sadness she snapped the reins hard against the ibexes' backs. They responded with several jerking leaps, each animal moving independently of the other, and Auriane was nearly pitched out of the back of the chariot. But she managed to get well past the guards before the massacre was done. Her people's blood speckled Cleopatra's white robe.

Fria, be gentle to them in death as you were not in life.

The ibexes settled into a brisk, anxious trot, all four moving at slightly different speeds; she held desperately to the Horns of Horus as the car jerked crazily from side to side like a ball on a string. Aristos' lionesses were less responsive to the reins, but they glided smoothly behind her at a good pace.

The two chariots passed unopposed out the entranceway of the *Ludus Magnus* and into the barricaded passage leading to the Colosseum. Well behind them, Meton shouted at random to anyone who would listen, *"Halt them! That is Aristos!"* Many in the crowd smiled at him and shook their heads, thinking it some clever ploy to manipulate the betting. "And I'm Hercules!" one shouted back.

When the guards finally disentangled themselves from the slaughtered Chattian captives, two dozen started down the roped passage in pursuit.

But Cleopatra·and Marcus Antonius were passing into the shadow of the Colosseum. When the two chariots disappeared into the gladiators' entrance, the guards flanking it closed the door in the faces of those giving chase, meeting them bluntly with the objection: "Erato's order to stop the bout? Let us hear it from Erato, then."

Auriane and Aristos waited in the dim, vaulted passage terminating at the iron-bound door that opened onto the arena. Two officials dragged it open. Before them was misty emptiness, and sand.

The ibexes were half maddened by the slaughterhouse scents; they bolted forward in a lurching canter. Auriane's car sank into sand. The mob laughed heartily at the sight of Cleopatra scrambling for balance as she was nearly tossed from her chariot. Soon Aristos was driving alongside, his lionesses slinking along with a sleepy air; to carnivores who had just been fed, the dense, humid stench of blood was welcome and pleasant.

"Aurinia! Aurinia!" came the cries from the plebeian tiers, a reckless sound heavy with the scent of anarchy. Auriane felt keenly their readiness to bolt; they were like a loosely penned band of aurochs ready to make a collective rush at the fence. She allowed herself one cautious look at the face of Rome—to look longer might scatter her silence. The lower tiers of the amphitheater had been converted into a banquet hall; everywhere was a look of ease and opulent disarray. The people did not sit; they lounged on great, gaudy cushions. The crowns of rose garlands on every head made it appear a priestly hand from above had sprinkled the crowd with blood. Multitudes of silver wine cups glinted in the sun. Lègions of girls and boys—imperial servants dressed as forest sprites—capered along the aisles in scanty deerskin tunics with ivy twined in their hair; they poured the wine, handed out baskets of glazed fruit and offered gilded bowls for washing hands. Others fanned the guests with great feather fans. Kitharists walked the aisles playing and singing, their small voices scarcely audible in the din.

But this thin overlay of festiveness did little to disguise the coiled tension beneath. The people's gaiety seemed raised to a shrill pitch, as if to cover the screams from the Palace and the wails of private lamentations at home. Many were half drunk, and so more willing than usual to cry out dangerous opinions. *"Free Marcus Arrius Julianus!"* one shout vaulted above the others; guards were efficiently dispatched to remove the rebel. The sound of his name made Auriane feel her bones would collapse. Her concentration flickered and died, and fear for him flooded over her.

Shut down your ears! she commanded herself. Slam closed your heart. Let your whole mind inhabit the blade of your sword.

After a moment she felt a powerful indraft of returning strength. The arena was a high altar; she, a First Priestess, and Odberht, the sacrifice. She was fire, poised to consume. The smoke from this offering would carry to Baldemar in the sky. The cries *"Aurinia!"* and *"Cleopatra!"* broke meaninglessly over her head; neither woman was she.

Aristos turned slightly once and looked at her. She saw a flash of sharply focused eyes, smelled his lust to crush her bones.

They moved past the musicians' station; the three trumpeters sat with their circular instruments passively at their sides; the bronze-skinned woman at the water organ stood poised and still. Only the three drummers were in motion, beating with a sort of sluggish discipline on their huge skin drums, sounding the beat of a weary, dissolute heart.

The two chariots halted before the imperial box, where the armor-bearers awaited. Sunlight from the opening in the awning high above found her short sword on its vermilion cushion; light flared on the blade, and she imagined it excited by her approach.

The trumpets burst into a clashing fanfare accompanied by the water organ's shrill bays. Then all dropped into silence. The herald stepped onto the archers' catwalk and called out, "Hail, Antonius, hail, Cleopatra!"

"Unmask that trickster! Who says you're good enough for our Aurinia!" came a shout from the equestrian tier. Someone hurled a fruit basket at Aristos, who did not flinch. A broken plum slid down his massive arm.

The herald spoke in a rich, calm voice that was powerful, feminine; he sounded like a scolding mother: "Our Lord and God is gravely displeased with you today. I warn you, do not try his graciousness any further! Those of you with criminal opinions will keep them to yourselves, until such time as his justice finds you out. If anything more is thrown from the stands, these games will be canceled. How dare you answer his generosity with unlawfulness and riot!" Adroitly his voice shifted back to facile joviality. "Now, friends, all wagers shall stand, despite the fact that our Cleopatra has been found out. And no more shall be laid once they dismount. . . ."

Auriane missed his next words as she gazed up at Domitian. The Emperor withdrew with a slight jerk; Auriane realized he had been studying her face and did not want her to know. She saw him but dimly in the shaded box, but the sight jarred her to attention. It seemed a black nimbus clung about him; there was a look of death-knowledge in his face. *He is doomed, and a sleeping part of him knows it. A cataclysm comes—I feel it certainly as if it signaled its coming with sound and scent. This must be the day they have chosen for king-killing.*

The herald cried musically, "And now, let the bout begin!"

Cleopatra and Marcus Antonius stepped down from their chariots. Two Numidian boys took the animals in hand while two undertrainers presented themselves before the pair, ready to remove headdress and mask.

In the hush, Auriane heard Aristos muttering a curse against her. *"May her heart be home to worms. May this evening see her black with flies. . . ."*

She was uncomfortably conscious of his size as she saw that colossal chest heave faintly with every breath. For one fright-filled moment fighting him seemed utter madness. She sensed the three gray-cloaked Fates beneath their sovereign Ash, three judges proud and stern at their looms, weaving her in, weaving her out, and felt a tug on the strands as they sought her life, holding it apart as they debated whether it should be cut. *Fates, you are women, and so must love a child. Pity mine—do not let it die!* She made the runic sign of Fria and shut her eyes.

The undertrainers standing behind them whisked off the cloaks with a flourish. Auriane felt practiced hands remove the headdress and replace it with a helmet of embossed gold.

Then she heard a great groan of surprise, followed by scattered exclamations of outrage.

Aristos was exposed. The man who removed his mask dropped it in fright on seeing that dread face. And before Aristos could be concealed beneath the purple-plumed helmet, hundreds in the seats above the imperial box saw him. They would have known him soon enough from his style of fighting, Auriane knew, but by then it would have been too late to stop them. She cursed. This was too soon.

In moments the whole of the amphitheater knew. Those in the poorer sections climbed onto their seats and began stamping their feet.

"No bout!" came the tumultuous cry, growing steadily stronger. The rumbling chant was like a great fist shaken in rage.

"String up Plancius by his thumbs!" came a single shout, followed by a cheer. They wanted Aristos and they wanted Aurinia, but it never occurred to them they would be given both at the same time. It struck them as a sort of demented jest on the part of the givers of the games. Only the foreign ambassadors remained in formal quiet in their seats of honor opposite the imperial box. These bearded, colorfully robed envoys from Abyssinia, Anatolia, Parthia, Arabia Felix and outer Britain looked on with faintly baffled expressions that seemed to ask: In this temple of the tasteless and grotesque, what is particularly objectionable about this?

Word of the match spread rapidly beyond the amphitheater, and out to the milling mob in the streets. Smoldering frustrations caught fire, and the mob too began to chant, *"No bout!"* The woman Aurinia was gallant against all odds—they would not tolerate this release of a ruthless force against her. Justice prevailed nowhere else in these times, so the people demanded it be upheld in the mythic realm of the arena.

The ten Praetorians assigned to the imperial box gave Domitian tense, questioning looks, poised for his order to halt the bout. This was not even a clever jest. Someone had simply blundered.

But no order came. The Emperor sat passively, his eyes glassy as a carp's in a pool. The Guards were alarmed that he made no move to punish the crowd. It was a grave error of judgment to threaten the people for their unruliness, then let it go when they defied him again.

Plancius stole a look at Domitian and guessed he had not slept in many nights. The Emperor's face looked puffed and bruised, as if someone had given him a beating. Those eyes were cold, fixed, incurious as a reptile's, though they flashed occasionally with the manic light of one who swims close to delirium. The whites had soured to the color of curdled cream. His mouth was clamped tightly closed; the lines about it were etched deep enough for a man twice his age. That once well-formed body had succumbed

quite suddenly to years of overfeeding; Plancius had sat near him
at last year's games and he did not remember that protruding belly.
Domitian's legs had become so spindling that Plancius wondered
if the Emperor suffered from some wasting disease kept secret
from the world.

When at last Domitian spoke, it was not to his agitated Guards,
but to Plancius.

"Well, Marcus, you're irksomely silent, and you *know* how that
nettles me! As long-haired slaves have lice, I know you've got
some vile opinion tucked away you're waiting to torment me with.
Speak!"

A midnight cold settled upon Plancius. Was Domitian merely
exhausted, or had he gone mad as Caligula? If he thinks I'm
Julianus, then what is he going to do to me? Plancius thought as
he shifted in his seat, wanting desperately to take his leave.

The Guards looked away, quietly exasperated. The tillerman
would not steer the ship.

Domitian focused softly on the two figures below, his sleep-
starved mind remembering, then forgetting. The gauzy curtains
undulated. In the moments when clarity came, he knew his life and
death were being played out below. Auriane was a bringer of
omens—of that he was certain—and twice now she had given
him warning of violent death by the sword. Something in her fate
was entangled with his own, and he desired one last message from
her. Domitian would no more interfere with what took place below
than he would interrupt the flight of birds before the taking of an
augury. The difference this time was that he *knew* the outcome,
and the message she would give—for she had not a chance of life.
If he, in the guise of Aristos, dispatched this spawn of Nemesis
quickly, he would have a long and vigorous life ahead. If Aristos
played with her first, or had difficulty destroying her, he would
have perilous days ahead, but he would live. All had been perfectly set up for his purposes; the auspices *had* to be favorable—
and no augur could accuse him of manipulating the circumstance,
for she had arranged it herself.

While Domitian languished in his waking dreams, Meton, Acco
and four burly undertrainers armed with nets, whips and brands
burst noisily from the gladiators' entrance and sprinted toward the
pair; it had taken Meton this long to organize what he felt was a
sufficient force to separate Aristos from Auriane. They were
certain this was the imperial wish, and they feared punishment if
they did not quickly put a halt to this bout.

Simultaneously, Aristos and Auriane moved forward and seized their weapons. Auriane's hand closed eagerly around the bone grip of her sword.

As Fria lives, this weapon will not be wrested from me until one of us lies dead.

CHAPTER LVII

When Auriane saw Acco closing in upon them, she broke into measured motion, striding sideways in an attempt to draw Aristos into the arena's center. But Aristos stood poised and still, his head half turned toward the noisy intruders. She halted, realizing he waited for them.

In moments the undertrainers swarmed around the pair, shouting, cracking whips at their legs as if they sought to drive two dangerous animals apart. Auriane felt a dog pack flowed about them. She fenced lightly with them as if their brands were swords, while shifting sideways, attempting to get clear of them. Now Aristos moved with her. One of the Numidian boys was caught in the middle of this, crying.

"Aristos!" Meton shouted from just beyond the melee. He realized then that brands were far more effective for goading men to fight than they were for separating two combatants determined to fight. *"I command you! Throw down that sword! No bout! Erato's order!"* Aristos stalked along parallel to Auriane, giving no sign that he heard.

"Aristos!" Meton tried again, an edge of frenzy coming into his voice. "Are you mad! Do you hear the crowd? Drop that sword! Erato's order! I'll see you blocked from fighting for a year!"

Acco pleaded similarly with Auriane, who nearly struck him as she flowed sideways, her movement like a snake's head as it prepares to strike. A whip lashed round her shield, pulling her off balance, but she quickly regained it; another brought blood to her arm. She ignored it. The crowd was intrigued in spite of themselves as they watched this strange crab-walking procession with all its participants fighting among themselves. Laughter arose as they realized that the whole mass of them, as they moved steadily across the arena, were on a collision course with the musicians.

"Aristos, you hotheaded fool!" The steely authority in Meton's voice was giving way to the dip-and-lurch of hysteria. "You play with fire! Harm her and I'll see you lashed until you're nothing but bloody bones! I *command* you, throw down that sword!" Aristos had always listened to him, even when he listened to no one else; Meton could not accept that he had lost all control over his charge.

Until the last moment the musicians stood steadfastly by their instruments. Then their courage deserted them all at once; trumpets and drumsticks were thrown to the sand, and they scurried about to flee. But they delayed too long.

A dark, lusty roar issued from beneath Aristos' helmet—the sound of a carnivore eager to close in on its meal. For a heartbeat, all stood transfixed. Then Aristos' sword arm flashed back; there was something archaic and monstrous in his form, as if he were some horned dragon reared up against the sky.

Then he burst into furious, frenzied motion, whipping about with movements measured as a dance, yet so swift the crowd saw not the man so much as the result—a trail of bodies sinking slowly to the sand.

His first stroke knocked the brand out of an undertrainer's hand and sent it sailing; the backstroke severed half through the man's neck. His second neatly decapitated one of the Numidian boys. The third disemboweled a drummer who, in his panic, ran right into Aristos' blade. There was a hideous efficiency in his whirling and slashing; every cut, every backstroke dismembered or killed. He was a remorseless scythe leveling human wheat, clearing a path through living flesh.

"Jove's thunderbolts!" Meton shouted. *"Run for cover! He's gone berserk!"*

Meton, Acco, and a single drummer managed to get off with their lives. The rest lay in a twitching heap, their blood soaking into the sand. Aristos had accomplished his purpose. Now there was nothing living between him and Auriane.

One of the victims, an armor-bearer, struggled pathetically to rise. Aristos turned, and with the nonchalance of one who stabs flies with a stylus, thrust his sword into the man's chest. As the armor-bearer sank in death, Aristos bent on one huge knee and with several casual strokes wiped his bloody blade clean on his victim's hair. Then he lifted his visor and grinned at Auriane across the field of bodies. "Clean for you, *Aurinia!*" he called out in fine spirits, holding the sword aloft so she could examine the blade.

Horror came in a flood tide, tearing at her, ready to bear her off; she clung blindly to her resolve as if to a stout oak. Erato's words, *"Stay off from him—he is a human monster,"* pounded in her ears.

I can abide it no more. I am broken. Ramis, you are victor. Come for me. I fight you no more.

Or at least lend me a measure of your baffling indifference in the face of death.

I must turn his wrath against him, *now.* It is my best hope.

She lifted her visor and called out in a low, clear voice: "Well done, Odberht! You murdered seven unarmed men, four of them boys! Or perhaps you would deny *these* killings as well? The slaughter of innocents becomes easier with practice, does it not?"

He gave a growling grunt and replaced the visor with an angry clang. But she could not be certain: Was this only his regular foul temper, or the runaway rage that had seized him that day in the practice ring?

"Prepare to die, pestilential witch!" he responded gaily. "How would you like to be served? Diced for frying, or cut in joints for roasting?" He kicked aside a body and began his advance.

In the safety of the passage, Acco, Meton and a cluster of arena officials came close to blows as they debated the best way to halt the bout. Then a Centurion of the Guard pushed past them with angular stride and slammed closed the iron-bound door opening onto the arena.

"Off with you! Begone!" he commanded with the casual crispness of one accustomed to being obeyed.

Meton and Acco exchanged looks of bewildered desperation. Some order must have been handed down from above. The bout was to go on. There was nothing more to be done.

Meton shrugged. "The woman dies, then."

As Aristos and Auriane slowly closed in upon one another, the people rose to their feet by the thousands, ready to begin a brawl. The smoke of cataclysm seemed to hang over the vast bowl of the amphitheater; it was a caldera rumbling with angry life, ready to spew lava and flame. Aristos' fanatic devotees added a dissident note to the chaos, shouting, *"Good fellow! Brave show!"* and *"None to compare! He is the king!"* Aristos was decidedly frisky today, they agreed among themselves. As always he managed to enliven dull, predictable proceedings by inserting an entertaining caper or two all his own. Who before him ever thought of clearing off those insolent armor-bearers and pesky musicians?

But the greater part of the throng demanded the rescue of Auriane. The driving shouts: *"No bout!"* were hammer blows of sound striking the sky.

The people's voice finally pounded Domitian out of his lethargy. Bright malice returned to his eyes.

"You!" he grunted at the Guard's Centurion standing at attention beside the crimson curtains. He then gave the Guard the nod and dismissive wave of the hand that meant: "Do whatever you must to discipline those noisy miscreants." The Centurion, relieved to see the Emperor had rejoined the world, moved off quickly to carry out the imperial wish.

Within moments a detachment from the ranks of bowmen stationed on the wooden roof of the upper gallery crept down unobtrusively as footpads, until they occupied the aisles alongside the plebeian seats. They selected a dozen of the loudest protesters as targets and released their arrows.

Necks were pierced. Scattered screams rose up, followed by wails. By hundreds, people dropped to the floor in terror. In the vicinity of the carnage, they moved in furious eddies, clambering over seats, frantic as tenants trapped in a fiery building. A stream of people moved for the exits, but guards were stationed at the entrances to the stairwells. No one could leave.

As the bowmen withdrew stealthily as they had come, terror settled over the throng like a red fog, paralyzing every tongue. It was a remarkably effective maneuver. In an instant the temper of the crowd collapsed from dangerous spiritedness into whimpering submission.

Domitian smiled contentedly, eased forward on the throne, and languidly plucked a milk-fed snail from a silver bowl filled with snow. The taste was exquisite. He felt like an accomplished rider who knew how to control a difficult horse.

Aristos and Auriâne faced each other in airless stillness, their wills locked in murderous embrace. She could scarce believe the race to death was at last poised to begin. Before her, Aristos' form billowed, then grew large, as though swollen with all her terrors and imaginings; she felt she viewed him through the melting heat of a cremation ground.

The sun flashed on the gold-embossed eagle adorning his hexagonal shield, blinding her. She shifted a fraction to the left so she could better see—and he shifted as well, following her with the barest of movements, so that she was blinded still.

Her fearful respect intensified. *This is a seasoned predator on whom not one bat of the eye is lost.*

For long moments they were caught in stalemate. Neither was willing to make the opening strike—both knew the other's skill in taking advantage of an opponent who threw himself first into the attack. The tension grew oppressive; the throng felt they awaited the onset of a swift-gathering storm. Every mind was braced for the thunderclap.

Auriane began to ease around him, probing with every sense for an uncovered target, a moment of inattention. With oiled movements he turned with her, the muscles of his stout leather-laced calves tautening to thick ropes as he crouched slightly. She could hear his rasping breathing within the helmet, a sound of air rushing, then dying, like wind through sea-caves. *Monster.* The morbid smell of hate hung about him like a charnel stench. That grotesque helmet concealed no human face; that breast, no sympathies. This was a creature composed of pure, sulfurous loathing.

Suddenly he feigned an attack, pulling his arm back abruptly to the accompaniment of a torn-off growl. She deduced instantly what his intention was, and marshaled all her will to resist being thrown into a defensive position. She was certain this rapid deduction saved her life.

That ploy failing, he kicked hard with his right foot, throwing sand in her face. Again he misjudged her; she was not so easily distracted. She focused with keen singlemindedness solely on his center of balance, discarding the kick as irrelevant.

She sensed he was disconcerted slightly by her steadiness. Instinct told her this was the precise moment to attack.

She arced into the air, beginning a powerful cut in midflight. Quickly as the flash of illumination follows lightning bolt, he lunged to meet her. The amphitheater fell silent as a tomb.

At last came the thunderclap.

They crashed together like battling stags, shield to shield.

Auriane gave beneath his weight as he struck, or the impact would have broken her shield arm at the wrist. Then followed the piercing, arrhythmic clang of steel on steel.

It was the sound of pure rage.

Metallic shouts rose to the awnings, battering every mind into dazed quiet. Many looked on with superstitious dread; there was something markedly dark and ill-omened in this violent eruption that had the bestial speed and whiplike confusion of a dogfight. Sparks showered down in a fiery rain. The encounter was nerve-shredding, and interminable; there were many who sat with jaws clenched, praying for it to stop.

Sunia fought her way to the novices' viewing chamber just as the bout began and found it packed to rib-crushing capacity with arena officials and trainers. She knew she would never get close enough to see. Coniaric and Meton had somehow secured coveted places near the barred window. Occasionally she called out plaintively to Coniaric, begging him to tell her what passed, but he seemed sealed in his private prison of dread.

It was Meton who finally satisfied her craving to know; with casual authority he began addressing the chamber at large.

"*Look at him!* Charon's eyes, it takes ten blades to equal him! Nemesis, but Aristos is in fine fettle today! Now they're breaking into elementary parries. . . . Nothing remarkable, just demonstrations of speed . . . one thrust, hers . . . one attempt to entice a strike, his. . . . Now the woman's giving a step of ground . . ."

But as he spoke on, measured excitement began to creep into his voice. "Now they're doing close-blocking, first and second attacks, and—do my eyes fail?—she appears to match him, blow by blow. . . ." Meton half expected Aristos to march up and hack her in two with not much more trouble than it had cost him to dispatch the Numidian boys. He was silent for a time; then he exclaimed softly: *"Incredible!"*

"Helle's cauldron, I swear I'll murder you if you don't tell me at once!" Sunia cried.

Meton went on excitedly, "Madness! Look at her! She's moved in too close on his left, so he cannot use the full strength of his arm. A *building* is collapsing on her, and she thinks *strategy* will save her! By Venus—this is not courage, it is insanity!"

• • •

After long moments Auriane and Aristos dropped into stillness and drew apart, like armies retreating to high ground to plan the next attack. Auriane's whole soul shuddered from the repeated shocks of impact; she felt she butted herself half senseless against a stone wall. He left no openings whatever; it was as if he were protected by a net of steel. Nor did he miss the small openings that she left as she strove vainly for a strike; he actually seemed *drawn* to them, like lightning to a tree. And it was dismayingly evident she failed at the first to spur him to unthinking rage. She must find another way.

And she suspected as well he held back in this first foray, to tease her into relaxing her guard and lead her into false hope. Something in the looseness of his posture and the arrogant bobbing of his plume told her the expression behind that helmet was one of amused satisfaction.

Their next attack was simultaneous, as if they were so united in rage they knew each other's minds with lovers' accuracy. After a short, brutal volley she managed to assault his blade, then strove to pummel it down. It gave way, if barely. Strengthened by this small success, she whipped her own blade upward, enthusiastically throwing all her strength into a follow-up thrust to the throat.

But in that instant something struck her shield with the violence of a wild ass's kick, snapping her backward. Confused and amazed, she fought for balance. Too late, she put it together. It was a devious trick, beautifully played. His yielding to her first strike, real as it had seemed, was feigned; his purpose was to position her for a terrific blow with his left foot. As she wobbled backward, he charged, all his fury and strength undisguised. A rhinoceros bore down on her—his sword was its tusk.

A hollow roar came from beneath his helmet. Rage reared him up to Titan's size. Her knees gave way beneath his first blow; it crashed on her blade and seemed to loosen every joint in her body. The second blow she blocked by twisting round and catching it with her shield. Before the third fell, she managed to leap into a defensive stance. She knew then she failed utterly—for now Aristos launched the characteristic assault that brought him victory after victory: He took the lead and never lost it, battering his opponents' will, pummeling their spirits with a rapid series of uninterrupted attacks that left no room for counterploys. At the sight of it, his devotees broke into applause.

Death-panic seized her. It was *this* she had so wanted to avoid: falling beneath his strength.

The heavy arm rose and fell in relentless rhythm. Auriane had no chance to parry; her whole mind was focused on one task: stopping that blade. All her skill was a thin, precariously strained barrier, barely protecting soft flesh from a snapping, tearing tooth of steel. Her worst imaginings had not conjured the power of those blows—that bestial strength had to be felt to be truly known. Though she deflected them to avoid absorbing their full strength, still it seemed each would tear her arm from its socket and splinter her bones. This was not swordfighting—it was a vain effort to stop a bull.

With one sweeping stroke he tried to hamstring her. The backstroke nearly cut the child from her womb. The follow-through cut whistled down on her shoulder—she blocked it with her sword, certain the crash of steel on steel would shatter her skull.

And always, she gave ground. She was battered earth, hammered by the hooves of a runaway stallion. She had no ear for those in the throng who cheered her or for their cries of amazement that she preserved her life as long as this. For long moments she danced backward with manic speed, half a leap ahead of death. Even her great endurance was of little avail, for he managed it so that a mightier effort was required of her than of him. Soon she struggled against despair as hard as she struggled against him. She felt she staved off a rockslide—she might succeed for a time, but the end was inevitable.

She took nimble leaps sideways to prevent him from herding her against the barrier. Once she stumbled over a corpse, rolled over on her shield and sprang up again, only to be driven farther back. Aristos moved forward ponderously, his elephant steps contrasting strangely with the coltish grace of Auriane's light, fast leaps. There was a desperate beauty in her movements; to the crowd it had the tragic gallantry of the struggling stag falling beneath wolves.

Meton exclaimed softly, "Poor fool! She has the wit and skill, but not the power. He should stop dallying with her and end it! There must have been two moons in the sky at her birth. She is amazing! What a waste!"

Sunia's hand was frozen at her throat. She was too shocked with grief to cry.

I should not outlive her. She is dying for us. Sunia gripped the arm of Acco, who stood in back of Meton. "I beg you, let me have your dagger!"

"Silence, woman! If you want to die, it can be arranged. But not with my dagger!"

Auriane felt herself dying. Her every muscle seemed battered into quivering pulp; her every stratagem failed. She tried for a day and a night to launch an attack, and could not.

I leapt too far into the torrent and found it too strong for me. Fria, Wodan, holy earth, why have you abandoned me?

Her people, all hope, all love, seemed dim and distant as stars. Life ended as it began, full of fright and pain.

All at once she sensed an obstacle at her back. Too late she realized she had been driven up against the water organ. First she struck its bronze windchest, then she rolled onto the keys. Its multiple mechanisms were set into rollicking motion—the small bronze dolphins dropped their valves into cylinders, the air compressed within the windchest, and resonant, jangling screeches merrily piped forth.

Aristos' heaving laughter, breathless but triumphant, accompanied his soul-shredding cacophony. She had been troublesome to catch, but at last he had managed it.

A rumbling groan rippled down the vast sweep of seats, broken by scattered laughter. Wails of protest floated down from the women's gallery.

Domitian grinned at the water organ's windy howls. "Aurinia plays that thing better than all your musicians!" he remarked to Plancius. At the same time her plight roused him, and he thought eagerly of the two surviving Amazons awaiting him at the Palace. *Aristos, give me now my omen!*

Auriane felt the oak base of the water organ grinding into her back. Aristos' shadow engulfed her.

"Breathe your last, wretched father-killer!" he shouted between gasps as he lashed out with a flurry of stabbing motions, trying to catch her with his sword's point. Each strike missed by less than a finger-width as she frantically heaved from side to side, all escape blocked by the massive oaken instrument. She made an attempt to dive beneath his arm but he blocked her with a leather-encased foot, then struck her shoulder a bruising blow with the boss of his shield. She felt her will to defend herself ebbing away.

She saw with taunting clarity the arrangement of the runes upon the white cloth: the sign for death and rebirth. *Death comes first, before resurrection. I am yours, Odberht—the Fates do not want me.*

At that moment Petronius was quietly admitted to the imperial box. He halted beside the throne, feeling intensely uncomfortable as he waited for Domitian to give him a moment of attention. Petronius tried not to look at the Emperor's hands—the puffed, bluish flesh squeezed painfully between those many rings reminded him of the veal-and-fennel sausages he had seen in the market earlier that day.

Domitian's gloomy gaze halted halfway between his Guard's Commander and the struggle by the water organ.

"Shyness is no virtue in a Commander of the Guard. Out with it!"

Petronius prayed to Nemesis that his voice would stay firm as he leaned close to speak discreetly into the imperial ear. For one numbing moment he forgot entirely what he was supposed to say. His anxiety was not eased by Domitian's murderous scowl. If this interruption were not thought justified, Petronius guessed, his next audience would be in the arena with a pair of highly unsympathetic Molossian dogs.

"Your Excellency, you must accept the apology of your good servant for this unpardonable interruption," Petronius began, cursing himself for speaking in pinched, unnatural tones, "and if this matter did not concern your mortal safety—"

"Why don't you recite the whole of the *Aeneid* before you tell me! *Out with it!*" Domitian returned his full attention to the arena. Somehow the cunning witch evaded three more thrusts at close range—but surely the end was near.

"A plot has been unearthed. They plan to do you to the death within the hour, *right where you sit.*"

Domitian sat up abruptly, spine straight as a javelin, his face rigid, eyes sharpened to knives. He no longer saw the arena; all concern with Aristos and omens vanished before the announcement of a threat serious enough to be reported by his Commander of the Guard.

He signaled for Petronius to speak on in a covered voice. He had no wish for Plancius to learn any of this.

"This villainy started, apparently, among your most trusted chamberlains," Petronius went on, "—Parthenius, Stephanus, and Satur. . . . We believe they may have also seduced a few men of the lower ranks of the Guard insane enough to listen . . ."

Domitian was profoundly irritated when he heard these names. So his own household had turned upon him—just as Marcus Julianus warned him they would if he did not reduce the severity of their punishments. *Why do the gods love to embarrass me by unfailingly bringing to pass whatever that cursed man predicts?*

My household. *Minerva, I* knew *I had worms in my cupboard. An exceedingly dangerous business, this is. So many complicated, crossed loyalties. They must be skillfully questioned in order to pry out the names of all their hidden confederates. . . .*

And Domitian found himself thinking, against his will: *Marcus, you sly reprobate who thinks he knows more about my household than I do—undoubtedly you'd have some stimulating advice to give me on this matter. . . . No. It wouldn't look right to humble the man, then turn round and beg a favor of him. . . .*

"They're a pathetically inept crew of villains—laying a trap for them was like pinching a *denarius* from a blind man. I sent a man to one of their meetings and arrested them all when they tried to enlist him. I beg you, repair to some place where you can be easily protected—your own chambers in the Palace would be strategically best. The traitors are assembled now in your bedchamber. I arranged it so you can question them yourself without rousing too much curiosity, so the whole sorry matter can be disposed of before alarm spreads. If we move quickly, the whole city need not know of it."

Domitian rose and ordered the attendant Guard to draw the curtains so the populace would not see the empty throne.

"The matter's still quiet then?"

"It is so. A closed litter is ready for you in the Guard chamber."

"Well done, then! I will use your litter. Go ahead of me. And Petronius . . ." He hesitated; a fleeting sheepish look came to his face. "I go first to the prisons. Before I question those criminals, I must have a word with my former First Advisor."

Petronius suppressed a start of alarm.

He will see Marcus Julianus, now? *There is not time. In an hour my Guards will be dismissed—and that boot-licking Servilius has the next watch. If Domitian delays too long, the loyalists will destroy us all. I pray Julianus knows what time it is, and how to get rid of him!*

As they departed down the carpeted steps leading from the imperial box, the throng's cries rose into a single tumultuous roar. Both men felt they walked beneath a waterfall thundering down a mountain. Domitian smiled. That, surely, was a victory cry for

Aristos. The woman was dying. The plot would be crushed. Tomorrow would come. Life and fear would go on as always.

The door of the earthen chamber was pulled back and the harsh light of a torch invaded the blackness of the cell. Gradually Marcus Julianus discerned the faces of the two intruders: one was a young prison guard; the other wore the broad leather apron and black gloves of an interrogator.

Marcus Julianus was slow to react, for he battled his way through spirit-numbing sadness. He knew from the guards' talk that Auriane and Aristos had begun their bout; in the last quarter hour the guards had spoken of little else. He assumed that by now Auriane was dead—skilled as she was, still Aristos was Aristos. He felt his heart had been mauled by an animal; in that moment he cared for nothing and no one.

But his mind began to function, almost in spite of himself. *An interrogator. They have come for Bato as I knew they would.*

The assassination was but an hour away. He could not sit idly by while Bato exposed it.

We must set ourselves free. With the first blow of the dagger, Domitian will pay for Auriane.

When Bato saw the interrogator, he crawled toward the back of the cell, threading his way around the seated and prone forms of seventeen new prisoners—so many had been arrested for disorderly conduct in the last hour that the cell had grown crowded. Bato clawed furiously at the back wall as if he thought he could burrow into bare rock to escape the torturers.

Marcus Julianus thought rapidly. He was encouraged somewhat when he realized this guard was part of a crop of recent recruits, not long resident in the city.

Both men know me by report, of course, but how well do they know me by sight? And now my face is begrimed with soot, my cheek is cut and swollen, and my body is hung with rags. . . .

If the wrong man steps forward, will they know it?

And if they have momentary doubts, who would believe a man would volunteer for torture?

He could only pray that Servilius did not come to oversee the questioning.

"Bato," came the guard's chillingly casual command. "Come forth!"

From Bato came a canine whimper and a sob. Julianus moved swiftly to him in the dark and put a firm hand over his mouth.

"Silence," he whispered. "Calm yourself. I go in your place. Stay still, and say nothing."

Slowly Marcus Julianus rose and approached the interrogator, affecting the fragile step of one paralyzed with terror. When he came close, the guard thrust the torch in his face to examine him.

The guard saw a man of frightful, owlish appearance; glassy eyes stared with feral intensity out of a blackened face. He resembled one of the Lemures, those spectral-eyed spirits of ancestors abroad on moon-bright nights—except for the all-too-human trembling of his hands.

"You are Bato?"

"I am Bato."

The guard squinted critically. Marcus Julianus found himself silently, fervently invoking Mercury, a god who favored tricks and stratagems.

Finally the guard gathered up his chains and jerked him forward.

"Come then! We've some business with you."

CHAPTER LVIII

Aristos' blade sank deep into the oakwood of the water organ; with a curse he pulled it free. The next downstroke carved flesh from Auriane's shoulder; she bit back a cry. Pain and outrage lent her a surge of strength; she managed to beat his blade upward and gained just enough time to break past him, sliding rapidly sideways. Abruptly she felt open space at her back—she was free of the water organ.

As she collected her balance and leapt into a defensive stance, an idea flashed into mind, and with it, a calm certainty that it was wise.

She would cast aside the teachings of the school and fall back on the simpler ways of her own wild forest. Swiftly she disengaged her left hand from the strap of her shield and let its rectangular wooden bulk drop to the sand.

The action momentarily perplexed Aristos; he paused in midstep; a crosscut flailed too high. In the precious time she won, Auriane wrenched off her helmet and threw it down as well. Murmurs of bewilderment spread through the throng.

She knew there was no other way. She was tiring more quickly than he, and she could tolerate no encumbrances. She would fight as her people had always fought—with head and heart exposed to sun, sky and gods.

In the viewing chamber, heads shook and murmurs of derision arose.

"You are wrong," Meton corrected them, voice intent, his face pressed to the grate. "It's mad, yes—but for *her*, it's right. Truly, this one knows what she's about! Now he can't wear her out so quickly—she has less weight to bear, and she can block his cuts with double-holds. She's gained strength and speed—and she has the skill to take advantage of those things."

All at once Aristos began battering her continuously as a hail of javelins, pressing her newly exposed left side, slashing with playful viciousness at her unguarded head. But now she vaulted and thrust to the beat of a drum whose tempo had increased, reveling in this new lightness, feeling more of the air than of the ground. She was everywhere at once like a bee-swarm, evading him through sheer unpredictability. When Aristos had enough of this, he gave out a mastiff's growl and rammed her with his shield; all that bullish solidity struck her bloodied shoulder.

And at last she saw a chance.

She gave way on impact, then rolled aside. He hurtled past her. While his momentum carried him still, she whipped round in a full turn, then executed two quick, deep, opposing diagonal cuts at his back.

She broke through. As he pivoted about, her blade caught him twice, just beneath his sword arm. A chevron-shaped cut appeared in his leather tunic, and she knew by the feel of it that she struck a rib. Blood spread rapidly through the leather. It was quite by accident that the cut formed the shape of the dread and potent rune the Holy Ones used to invoke Fria. Aristos was aware of this at once; she saw a flash of spirit-panic in his eyes.

She marked him with some baleful witch-sign—surely, he thought, it released a poison in his blood. He touched the preserved wolf's muzzle to his forehead while angrily muttering the words of an aversive charm.

"One of them is hit!" Meton shouted feverishly. "By the whims of Nemesis! *Aristos* is hit! It cannot be!" Others in the room drove Meton aside, desperate to see.

"Is it grave?" Sunia asked, her voice low and eager.

"It's a place that bleeds," Meton responded. "It will weaken him. If enough, who knows? It's a mistake, though. Now she's really maddened him."

Aristos' followers could not understand why their hero was suffering this mettlesome menace to live so long. *"Punish her for that!"* they shouted at him. "Run her through! Skewer the bitch for roasting!"

Soon the news flew to the gates of the city—Aristos was hit.

Aristos then threw down his own great, rectangular Samnite shield and pulled off his gilded helmet, letting it fall to the sand. This brought applause sprinkled with laughter from those who loved him. *So much for her newly won advantage.*

Aristos' freshly exposed face was not pleasant to look upon. His cheeks, swollen from heat and rage, were plum-purple and blue; across his forehead was an angry helmet welt. Sweat caused the black dye to run from his hair; it hung in sodden ropes, and red-blond streaks showed through. He grinned at her, flaring his broad nose, exposing two fanged side teeth. His heavy chest heaved like the sea in a gale—it seemed it could burst chains. He opened and closed his naked hairy left fist, as if emphasizing its new freedom.

Aristos charged. Now their swords were both weapon and shield. He took the lead and manipulated an opening; his sword's point lashed out like an adder's tongue, piercing her thigh. Blood trickled freely into her laced boot. Aristos' supporters shot to their feet, laughing and clapping heartily. Her own devotees responded in a more muted way, moaning, uttering prayers to Juno—for they were still in terror of the bowmen. No one realized their Emperor and God was no longer among them, for the curtains of the imperial box were often closed, but their fear of him would have lingered after, even had they known.

Aristos paused, legs planted firmly apart, taking stock of the damage he had done; he felt he had the situation firmly in hand. That vile wound she gave him pained him and was certainly an annoyance, but it was nothing a skilled physician could not put right. He grinned at the sight of her reddened leg.

"This is a little more difficult than killing your father, is it not?" he taunted her. "But then, his arms were bound!"

To Aristos' irritation her eyes remained tranquil; she was unmoved as if he sung lines of a nonsense rhyme.

Within, she was wryly amused. *Odberht, you have not kept apace. That verbal strike requires two: one to execute it, and one to believe in it.* She felt her spirit was loose and serene as a hawk, ascending weightlessly over shame's old battleground.

And then suddenly Auriane *knew.* Why had she not guessed it before? She realized then her shame had acted as a veil, preventing her from discerning acutely the hearts of others. Now she was free to observe Odberht with a *ganna*'s gently piercing sight.

What formed in her mind first as a shrewd guess illumined to hard, luminous certainty. The crime Odberht so eagerly accused her of, again and again, *must be his own*. The shame he tried to bury, so long ago, would not stay buried, and so its ghost spurred him to fling it at her again and again.

"Odberht . . . ," she said so quietly that he had to ease closer to hear her. A guarded look came into his eye at the sound of his true name. ". . . *you* are the murderer of Wido."

Turbulent memories welled up in her mind then: *The battle of Antelope Ridge. The dark moon. The mysterious hunter's net, hurled above the fray, that fatally entangled Wido's horse, allowing Baldemar's Companions to flow over him and strike him down. . . .*

"You slew your own father," she went on softly. *"You are the one who threw that net."*

She knew instantly her spear struck its mark. His features contracted. The look in his eyes was hard, blank, final, as if stone doors were slammed closed. The word *"No!"* issued from him, half groan, half amelodic animal cry; it was laden with the horror of one who finds himself dangling over a demon-filled pit and feels a knife severing the rope.

"Oh, *yes*, I see it as I see you," Auriane continued. "What a clever murder! All close witnesses were killed soon after, then you got off free. If a father-killer can ever be said to be free."

The words were hot pincers peeling back his skin, leaving him hideously naked before the people, before the ancestors. *Witness, the perpetrator of the greatest crime of all humanity!* he heard a chorus of Wodan's battle-sylphs singing as they pointed him out to the Fates for punishment.

But she could not have seen it! he thought frantically. *No one saw!* Yet somehow this venomous sorceress, this sister of Helle, *knew.*

The chorus of denying voices in his head confused him and he imagined the whole of the amphitheater heard Auriane's words. They too were dumbstruck by his evil. He trembled as if the ground quaked beneath him.

Fierce refusal-to-know converted to fury.

"I'll cut out that lying throat!" He bore down on her.

Auriane stood tensed and ready, exultant with success. At last he was maddened blindly, helpless as a rudderless craft tossed about on a tumultuous river.

Meton announced, mystified, "He's off his step! Something's sent him into one of his frenzies!"

Aristos' followers cheered him, certain this was some amusing new game he played with her.

He lashed out at air before he reached her, putting more force than skill into every sweeping cut, slashing as if he believed he could cut out the truth with his blade. To many in the throng he did not seem much changed—more energetic, perhaps. But to Auriane he was a runaway cart bouncing downhill.

She leapt into range, missing his blade so narrowly that it ripped open the side of her tunic. Then she steadily drew him on while hardly spending herself at all, letting him drain himself in strokes that were too wide, in overstrenuous footwork, and thrusts that were vigorous but poorly timed. With every stroke he rasped, *"Die! Die!* Foul night-stalking sorceress!" and similar insults until he became short of breath. Finally, as he completed one flailing cut, she hammered his blade down, striking it at right angles. Their hilts locked for an instant while he careened sideways. She then jerked him hard in the direction he was already moving. As he staggered for balance she pulled back with a return stroke that slashed vertically up into his ribs, lodging in the breast. Black blood sprang forth. A grave hit, she knew, close to the heart. She felt a measured exhilaration.

In his shock and pain he reacted with a spasmodic jerk too fast to block, and his sword's point flashed out, inflicting a deep puncture in her shield-arm. The wound seared like fire; her eyes ran with tears.

In his rage he never slowed; he heaved after her, swaying slightly as he ran. Where the hair of his chest showed, it was matted with glistening blood. She judged his wound was taking a greater toll then hers, and knew with all her mind and body the end must come soon.

I must finish him now, or be finished. Fria, descend!

She flung herself at him in all her final, unbounded fury. The tempo of the dance flashed up to demonic speed. To the multitudes she might have been a maddened Maenad possessed by Dionysus, ready to rip out throats and rend beasts limb from limb. A massive silence descended over the flights of seats. Meton could no more follow her strokes than could a spectator at a race's finish discern the individual hoof-strikes of the winning horse as it thunders down to the rope. Her attacks seemed wholly random, but each made sense to him an eye-bat later. She seemed to keep him off balance by sheer force of mind. Though she was unconscious of herself as a vaulting gazelle, Meton recognized the terrific power of concentration in every stroke. As they progressed closer to the barred window, he saw she used even her eyes as a weapon, dropping her gaze when her target was high, or softening their focus just before she struck. Gradually Meton was able to discern how she turned his wrath to her advantage, crowding him when he overstepped, teasing him, sensing his careless openings almost before he left them.

No human agency taught her this, Meton thought. This came from the gods. He remembered hearing Erato say once: "It may never be known, perhaps, the extent of what she can do." He felt he was seeing it now.

Aristos was giving ground. A groan of disbelief came from the crowd, punctuated by shouts of outrage from Aristos' more fanatic followers. Some in the throng laughed. There was something droll in the sight of the august Aristos being battered back—it recalled the always-awkward sight of masters waiting on their slaves during the Festival of Saturnalia.

But many felt they were witness to some dread prodigy. Their hush was touched by fear of bewitchment, as if they attended the birth of a two-headed calf. Curious glances turned to the imperial box to witness the reaction of the Emperor to this humiliation of his favorite, but strangely, even before this most amazing of scenes, the curtains remained drawn.

Auriane felt this last jet of energy begin to lose its momentum. Every muscle was aflame. Now she felt death invading her limbs, pulling her slowly down. But she saw death in Odberht's eyes as well. His nostrils were gaped in pain and fury like some gored bull. His eyes were bright not with hope of victory but with the frantic light of an animal caught in a snare. He was full of mad recklessness, though, and so was in some ways more dangerous now, not less.

They sank to a final exhausted pause, glaring at each other over the landscape of corpses. It seemed that for years none had existed but herself and this enemy standing bloody and heaving before her still.

I have struggled for too long. I am beginning to forget why all this began. I want only peace, and if possible somehow, life for the one within me.

She wondered if Marcus Julianus was among the spirits already, watching her gently, awaiting her.

Then suddenly Aristos lifted one of the corpses—a slightly built Numidian boy. With his sword-hand he gently pushed the bloody hair from the boy's forehead, as if he just recognized him as one beloved and slain by accident. As Auriane moved round Aristos to find an opening—for the body made an excellent shield—he began to mutter soft words of love. Auriane began to worry that heat and fatigue had taken her mind. As she looked on, curious but sickened by the strange turn Aristos' madness was taking, he found the boy's lips with his own and kissed him.

Without realizing it, she was tricked from her intensely focused mind-state, and distracted from sensing all of him.

Aristos erupted into motion; he flung the boy's body at her with all the power at his command. She was taken wholly by surprise. The corpse struck hard against her midsection and propelled her backward onto the sand. Almost simultaneously, he lunged. As she fell, his blade came down on hers with a formidable hammer-strike.

He knocked the sword from her hand.

She scrambled quickly from beneath the boy's body, narrowly evading a stroke that would have lopped off her left arm at the shoulder. Her right hand scurried in the sand, seeking her sword. But it lay nearer to Aristos; triumphantly, he scooped it up.

Proudly he held her sword aloft for his devotees to admire.

"Behold the fate of a false-speaking, murdering kin-killer!" he proclaimed.

"Bravo!" his followers shouted back. *"Good show! Now nail her to the ground!"*

He turned and tossed Auriane's sword far behind him. It struck the sand beneath the imperial box. Half the width of the arena separated her from it.

Cries of dismay broke out sporadically up and down the steeply ascending seats.

Auriane quietly accepted that Fria deserted her. Of her own will she entered the sacred enclosure for a judgment, and the Fates ruled against her. It was the way of the heavens and the earth. She stood on waste ground. And yet she could not stop fighting, though she felt it meaningless as the last writhings of freshly killed creatures.

With slow, deliberate steps Aristos advanced upon her. She was too exhausted to feel much fear. Nimbly she backed away, traveling even farther from her sword. She knew she had no chance of reclaiming it; he could too easily block her. He had now only to herd her to the barrier and finish her. To the throng it seemed she faced one final choice: She could submit at once, or she could force him to pursue her, and gain a few extra moments of life.

Death hung about her like stagnant marsh mist. The air whistled as it was torn by his blade; a dozen times he missed her by less than a hand's width.

She made a last attempt to draw the forces of earth into her body, reaching hard for the invincible peace of Ramis' holy fire. This time she thought she felt a small subterranean pulse, then a deep drag, as though she were a dry tree and one long root touched water deep in the earth. And now she felt sustenance readily flowing in; gradually she was a well of warmth and light, generating soft, fiery strength. Praise to the land, praise to sun and moon, she thought as the luminous bewitchment buoyed her, held her, then let her go, flickering in and out like a distant torch carried through trees. No, she realized, *I have not been abandoned.*

Ramis, I sense you are *here,* definite as the draft from a wing-beat. Something excites you. You come to *take.* I suppose you come to collect my soul at death, and bear me north.

There came then the ghost of Ramis' voice from long ago: *"Never forget the power in hair. It is a shield and a birth-string connecting you to earth."*

What I must do is clear and evident. I have a weapon still—one holier and far older than the sword.

She was positioned now directly beneath the foreign ambassadors' seats. Later these dignitaries would relate that in the last moments she seemed thrown into some divine rapture, a thing that to them betokened madness. Cleopatra's black eye-paint had run with heat and perspiration. It streaked down her cheeks like some comet's tail, making her eyes appear narrowed and glowing, as though she wore some frightful cat's mask.

They watched, mystified, as Auriane pulled out the bone comb that secured her hair. She shook her head once to loosen it, and it shuddered down into a womanly mane.

Aristos' body jerked as though he tripped on a root. What foul trick did she play now? Bronze hair flowed over her shoulders and dropped like thick silk to her waist, shivering and alive with menacing magic. He had lived all his life knowing that much power for good and evil dwelled in women's hair. That was why, in their own country, if any woman other than a priestess padded about at night with hair unbound, the crime was punishable by death.

First she marked him with an evil rune. Then she divined

somehow his most abominable secret. And now she planned some witchery with her hair. Cursing, he pressed the wolf's muzzle to his heart.

His dizziness was increasing, and the weakness. Was loss of blood the cause, or was this, too, the result of her sorcery?

From his followers came amused laughter. "Clip it for her!" they shouted gaily. "Make us a wig of it!" Idiots, Aristos thought. They have no notion of what they speak.

"Lying whelp with poison in your veins!" he muttered as he started forward once more, slashing in greedy arcs. As she danced away, she felt for the particular rhythm of his thrusts and cuts, and began to shift in time with them.

The rebellious cry, *"Spare her!"* was thrown up all around, in spite of the people's terror of Domitian; it was as if they had decided suddenly that the bowmen could not slay them all.

For an imperceptible space of time she was poised, still. Then she sprang.

It appeared to those nearest as though she leaped right into Aristos' whipping blade, a quite unnecessary act of suicide since in moments he would have her against the barrier.

But Aristos' sword never struck flesh. Her lunge was precisely timed; she flung herself into an opening that lasted no longer than a bone-crack. She clung like a monkey to the front of him; together they toppled to the sand. He thrashed beneath her, struggling to get away from that hair—it was hideous, alive, and everywhere; in his madness it hissed, it burned, it stung like bees.

For long moments they struggled for his sword, fighting for holds like wrestlers in the palaestra, their hands slipping on blood. The wound she had inflicted beneath his heart weakened him more than her various lesser wounds weakened her and so their strength was nearly evenly matched. The throng rose up as one, screaming for both of them at once, their shouts rising into a massive mountain of incoherent noise.

Finally he flipped her onto her back. Her hair fanned out onto the sand, dark, lustrous, dangerous, a midnight lily pad on a moon-white pond. I'll scalp this demoness after I finish her, he thought, looming over her, teeth bared like some beast, sword poised, ready to fall on her jugular. But she kicked hard with both legs, striking his stomach. He grunted and crumpled onto his side. Swiftly she scrambled onto his wide back, slipping on oiled skin. He bucked like a horse, frantic to throw her off. Then she got a grip on his shoulder-guard and clung tightly as a bramble.

Her hair streamed down, plastering itself to his damp shoulders, lashing his face, snaking over the sand. Quickly she separated out a thick tress of it. Using it like rope, she looped it round his bullish neck and pulled, pouring the last of her waning strength into this final, desperate act.

Her arms soon became numb. And still she pulled, straining so hard she heaved for breath. The moments stretched, seeming deep and boundless as night. Once she nodded into childhood and heard Hertha's soft, cracked voice relating a winter-fire tale: *"And when the enemy was ringed all about their high-place and there was no escape, the battle-maids thought to give themselves to Fria rather than be sacrificed to the enemy's gods . . . and so they loosed their long hair . . . with it, they strangled one another. And thus they stayed free."*

The throng's cries betrayed confusion now; her masses of hair obscured them both, shrouding in mystery the last moments of struggle.

Auriane imagined the sand was a sea of foam-capped waves that would soon lap over them both. She felt lulled, washed clean, as slowly, his ponderous body began to sink beneath her. Tension ebbed out of him in one long, receding tide. Once a violent spasm passed through him; she thought it must be his maddened spirit, cursing her, fighting her still, outraged at being expelled from its earthly housing.

The sword dropped from his hand.

Odberht, you were right to fear my hair.

In the next moment she *knew* with warm certainty that one spirit animated all life, and was seized by the frightful sense she squeezed the life from her own body, *that she killed herself.* But still she pulled—the momentum of the years was too great. He must die.

Through labored breaths she managed the words of the rite:

"In the name of Fria, goddess of all creation . . . in the name of Wodan, god of the spear . . . I now claim vengeance for the crimes of Odberht. Let honor be returned to those he betrayed. Cleanse of bloodstain the hands compelled to perform this act. . . ."

She did not feel she lived in the words, as she expected to; it was as though they were spoken by a priestess of some foreign religion. *Does this death bring you comfort, you who threw yourselves on the guards' blades but an hour ago? I am not sure it gives me comfort. I do not see entry into heaven here. I see but one more corpse.*

He gave one final, blind kick; then Aristos, born Odberht, bane of her people, enemy of her whole life, breathed his last.

Auriane collapsed on top of him, exhausted, and slid into the soft blackness of a dreamless sleep. Her hair was a glossy coverlet thrown over them. An unholy quiet settled over the stands until it was so profound the awning high above could be heard snapping in the wind. Many shuddered as if an icy draft found its way in. The people of Rome had the sense dark gods hovered over this scene, shrieking bog-dwelling deities of the North, whose presence could pull down temples, undermine all laws — spirits unknown to their fair Olympians who ruled in sunlight. The Vestals would need to perform a purification rite on the spot to remove the stain of evil, lest it infect the whole city.

Those who loved Auriane stirred first. Uncertain cries came from the women's gallery. *"Aurinia! Arise!"*

Aristos' followers then found their voices. *"Aristos Rex!"* came the hesitant shout; it was almost a question. Many were certain he played some strange game. Surely he had played it long enough — why did he not arise?

Auriane heard none of this, for her spirit had fled the place. She glided like a hawk along the banks of Ramis' smoking lake. It was dusk. A resplendent moon, softly triumphant, crowned the pines. Ramis' voice seemed to issue from the abyssal darkness between the trees.

"And now you know it, Auriane. The lily opens. And so, now you must come to me."

Auriane felt Ramis' spirit wrap round her mind. She formed a mute reply: *"It does not feel like a great knowing. . . . It feels common as whisking a burning kettle off the hearth . . . or suckling a hungry child."*

"So it is with all great knowings. . . ."

"For all the sorrowing . . . what was the cause?"

"The cause was in you, even before your birth. You will know it fully only after your death. Understand it now only as your willingness to believe in your own evil. For it, you had to cause your father's death. For it, you were brought to this place. The lesson is learned. And so you are mine."

And then the priestess-state flowed over her with power and brilliance; all the world gently smoothed into benign shape. Ramis' old assurance, *"Catastrophe is fertile, it brings forth worlds,"* sounded like a dark strong hymn, its meaning eminently obvious. She sensed a vast cycle of life completed itself; war was the old life's chief rite. Now the clash of armies seemed pitiable, ghastly as the spectacle of children armed with sharp weapons and sent out to slaughter one another. The dead man beneath her was her own emanation—as she had been his. From the first they were caught in a cruel maze constructed from terror and delusion, then forced to fight as gamecocks are made to fight. There was no shame in it; it was simply the way of the world. She felt she reached out a hand of peace to the living and the dead. Had she been able to fear, she might have feared only that this state would desert her.

Again Ramis' words took soundless shape in her mind. *"This, then, is the death that was spoken in the runes: You died the serpent-death and sloughed off the old life so you could be born into this vaster one that knows the ends of the overarching sky. For this reason you were impelled to finish this last task with your hair. For at our last great Convening we named you as one of the Holy Nine, sovereign over all the tribes—and the Holy Nine are forbidden to touch iron."*

As Auriane's blood began to stir and consciousness grudgingly returned, she thought: This is some mad jest to play on me! To hand me the very fate my poor mother so feared she kept a sword in my cradle.

"You long wondered why I came at your birth and gave you a priestess-name. You questioned why you were brought to my isle at the sacred hour of midnight.

"Listen well; now I am free to tell the cause. When I die, you, Auriane, will be the Veleda after me. You, and no other, will ascend the high tower of the One Who Sees."

CHAPTER LIX

After a time the door of the gladiator's entrance was pulled open. Meton and Acco approached the pair with cautious steps, despite the fact that neither Aristos nor Auriane had stirred for some time. Five undertrainers followed in a line, walking as if they probed for quicksand. Each carried a javelin or a brand.

Meton lightly touched Auriane's shoulder with the butt of a javelin. She did not move. She seemed to be peacefully sleeping, her head resting on Aristos' shoulder. Her dark bronze hair was fanned about in a great circle, draped over both like a grave cloth.

Warily Meton moved around the bodies. This time he used the javelin's point and lifted a mass of her hair. And he saw Aristos' face.

He drew in a breath and backed into Acco. There was no doubt Aristos was dead. His face was horrible. His eyes bulged, staring at nothing with dry, fixed surprise. His cheeks were purplish-black; his mouth, loose and sagging like a deflated wineskin; the tongue protruded in some ghoulish imitation of a Gorgon's face.

"By the jowls of Cerberus!" Meton whispered, dropping Auriane's hair back over Aristos' face. *"She strangled him!"*

The undertrainers, emboldened by this news, came up and stood around the bodies in a ring. For long moments Meton stared dazedly at the man he had devoted so much time and effort to training, whose career had been his own best fortune, studying Aristos with detached sadness, as if he were some magnificent ruin. Never would there be another like him. The light coating of sand that stuck to Aristos' oiled body made him look like some giant's ghost. The powerfully muscled arm lay limp; now it had not even the power to lift itself. Meton kept a respectful distance, as if from a freshly killed serpent, for it was difficult to believe Aristos was harmless, even now. What a sad and ludicrous fate, he reflected, for one of the greatest swordsmen our School will ever house.

Acco said then, "Poor gallant creature, she's done the impossible and paid for it with her life! That is a prodigy to match all prodigies! She killed Aristos! And she was one of mine! I trained her, you know. She shall have a funeral to match Rodan's if I have to raise the money myself!"

Scattered sections of the throng started up a rousing chant: *"Who lives? Who lives?"* Aristos' devotees joined in with: *"Aristos! Enough! Get up!"* And *"He is the king!"* But the larger part of the crowd languished in confusion, unable to cheer or moan.

Meton recovered himself first and came forward to pull Auriane from the body of Aristos. Behind him a troupe of Numidian boys approached at a trot with two biers for the bodies. In the instant before he touched her, Auriane moved. Meton jerked back.

Wearily, ponderously, Auriane pulled herself up, a befuddled Aphrodite rising from a sea of hair. That simple movement might have been an earthquake for the titanic reaction it produced.

"Aurinia lives!" The storm of jubilant noise drove Meton to stop his ears. *"Long live our Aurinia!"*

She held out a blood-caked hand to Meton so he could help her rise. There was no victory-fire in her eyes, Meton saw; only an odd, bright calm, as if she had somehow found a mother's comfort after a nightmare.

Aristos' devotees began taking off their shoes and hurling them at him, in a vain effort to make him rise. Of course, he lived on. He laughed at death.

Even after they saw Aristos' face, and watched as the Numidian boys dropped him into the bier and hoisted it to their shoulders, they refused to believe their king had perished.

"Punish her! Strike her down!" they cried out, shaking their fists. The more sober members of the crowd began to laugh at them.

The belief that Aristos was not dead would persist; his was a powerful ghost that would not be put to rest. In coming days people would say they had seen him late at night, demanding a jar of wine at his favorite tavern, or insist they saw him training in secret. This was only his most elaborate trick of all. Aristos would return, if not at these games, then at the next. Even after his grand funeral, which was a mockery of a funeral of state, attended by hundreds of professional mourners, there were still those who said, "They burned another body. Aristos lives."

As Auriane struggled to her feet, she felt borne up by the crowd's surging cries. They know nothing of me, she thought, or why I performed this deed, but does the wave need to know the one it lifts?

Meton shouted to an undertrainer: "Bring a horse! It's the only way we'll get her through."

Auriane was unsettled by the draught of freedom that intoxicated her then. For so long the pursuit of Odberht had compressed her spirit and governed her every act that suddenly she felt she had no stable *shape*—she might be woman, or loping wolf, or mist rising from a lake. She sensed the quiet opening of gates whose existence she had never suspected. Even enslavement cannot touch this freedom, she realized. But this new boundlessness was not without unpleasantness: there was, too, a shock of noise and cold and rude light, as if she were a babe freshly pulled from the womb. She wanted to cry out like a wolf. She wondered in one instant if she should choose a new name.

A dark, celebratory mood full of exultant lawlessness possessed the amphitheater. To Auriane it had the spirit of a tribal victory dance. Word finally got about that Domitian had departed in haste from the imperial box; it was said he fled in terror because the Chief Augur warned him his Nemesis would be victor. Surely, all felt, this was a sign: Could the tyrant who called himself their Lord and God long survive the death of his favorite?

A sturdy gray cart-horse was brought for Auriane. The undertrainers hastily bandaged her wounds with strips of wool, then helped her onto the beast's broad back. She leaned heavily on the horse's neck while Meton steadied her to keep her from falling.

A playful voice from the plebeian seats rang out: *"The King is dead. Long live the Queen!"* This brought an eruption of catcalls from Aristos' followers, and another shower of shoes.

In response, from the highest seats a cry thundered out that seemed to come from one defiant throat: *"Aurinia Regina!"*

Had there been doubt in any part of the city who the victor was, it vanished then.

Auriane the Queen. Auriane felt a soft jolt, remembering Ramis' strange prophecy, *"You will be a queen in death."*

A queen with no queendom, she reflected, except in a few minds, and for a time brief as the blooming of a poppy. A negligible thing to the world at large, but not for the world within.

An angry retort was thrown up to the sky: *"Aristos Rex!"* Then all at once the warring factions broke into turbulent motion. As Auriane's heavy-footed cart-horse was led through the Victory Gate, the beast threw up its head and ponderously capered sideways in fright.

The amphitheater was brought once more to terrified quiet when the people saw the bowmen begin to move down from their stations with their catlike creep. But the mob milling restlessly in the open space about the Colosseum was not so easily restrained. Those who loved Aristos, who were fewer in number but more violent, began chanting his name like some war cry and took up whatever they could find in the streets that might be used as a weapon. They began roaming the city in wolf packs, breaking up and destroying the shops of anyone they believed to be disloyal to their king—for were they not common traitors? But the opposition was quick to seek revenge. They too found weapons—broken amphorae, glass jars, wheel spokes, or bull whips—and, accompanied by the cry, "Long live our Aurinia!" they energetically set upon the loyalists.

Every other street became a battleground. The City Cohorts were called out and bucket brigades were made ready to quench fires. Plancius declared the remaining contests of the day canceled, and soon discovered he was a hostage in the imperial box. Aristos' devotees held him partly responsible for their hero's death, and he knew he dared not venture into the street without a small army at his back.

When Auriane entered the barricaded passage she saw why the horse was needed. The people had broken in—but for the stolid and steady beast she rode, she might have been crushed. These crowds, at least, were mostly friendly; they called to her with outstretched hands, pulled at the bridle, and put rose garlands over the bowed neck of her mount. No one this time attacked her clothes with scissors; it was as though they felt such a great and good omen ought to be reverenced.

To the people she presented an odd sight, one that was strangely disturbing: She looked less like someone who had just quit the well-ordered confines of the arena, and more like a Bacchante who returned from some frenzied revel on a forested mountaintop. She was a vision of the wild unknown that lay in wait at civilization's edge: Her hair was in rebellious disarray, thick with blood-matted tangles; sprigs of green and scattered rose petals were caught in it like wildflowers scattered over a field. The hastily wound bandages were unraveling, as though she had torn her garments racing through the wood. Those flushed cheeks, those ardent eyes ringed with fading black paint gave her a sort of bright, savage hunting-animal beauty. Now that she had delivered her sign and heralded a tilt of the world order, hopefully she would withdraw to the haunted wilds from which she came.

To Auriane the world shimmered and glowed, as if washed clean after a rain. The air about seemed to shiver with pipe music—though she knew it played only in her own blood. Each indrawn breath filled her with the mind of Fria, and she felt lush surges of life-love that left her a stranger to nothing and fearless enough to walk an urn-field at midnight. She felt the drums of Eastre pounding deep in the earth, and imagined she saw, settled in the clouds, Fria exultant on a throne of flowers. As her gaze rested contentedly on the throng, in one moment all perception condensed, and her focus became diffuse. She felt what seemed like the pricking of an internal ear. And knowledge began to settle upon her. She sat very still, sensing it.

She wanted to cry out, but this knowledge brought with it a strange and not unpleasant numbness.

A cataclysm approached. She knew it as certainly as she knew she sat a horse. She sensed a dread hush, a great gathering for a leap.

Today the earth will shake.

She wanted to say to the people: *Calm yourselves. Still your rioting. You have come already to great good fortune. For when the earth is still again, you will have a hundred years of peace and good and decent kings.*

Then she knew that Marcus Julianus was alive, and poised at the cataclysm's center. In fact, he was its cause.

Marcus was alive. She wanted to embrace the neck of the cart-horse for joy.

But then she sensed dark savagery clinging about him like a bog-mist. She shook her head violently once, as if to fling out a nightmare. When the priestess-state left her, only her exhaustion kept her from shouting out, throwing herself to the ground and pummeling the earth in protest. She tried to assure herself he was *not* being tortured. Perhaps her sensing had been wrong. Frantically she tried to remember all the times her sensings *had* been wrong.

Fria, grant that this be one of those times! At least he is alive—and if he lives, he will fight his way out. Has he not always done so before?

But this brought little comfort.

As she approached the arched entranceway of the *Ludus Magnus*, she saw a half-dozen men of the First Hall standing in its shadow, watching her with the bored confidence and riveted attention of large carnivores. The men of the First Hall were a fiercely bonded brotherhood who felt they possessed exclusive rights to killing their own. Many regarded Aristos as a brother or son, but even those who did not felt she had dishonored and ridiculed a member of their guild. It was insult enough that she was a woman; to worsen matters, she had killed him with her hair, denying him his natural right to die by the sword. As she drew closer, one of them met her gaze, grinned, and slowly drew a hand across his throat.

They would kill her, she knew, in the arena or out, at practice or at dinner. As soon as they found a chance. If she lived on in Rome, she would not live long.

Meton shouted to her then, "We're taking you up to the Second Hall barracks. We'll have to lock you in with a guard day and night. I do not know what's to be done with you after that."

Auriane nodded; then suddenly she remembered Erato. "You might save me from Aristos' friends, for a while at least," she shouted down over the din, "but who'll save me from Erato? He must be ready to set me out as the target for javelin practice! The gods grant me time to regain strength before I must face him!"

Meton started at this, as if he expected that she knew. A flash of grief showed in his eyes, to be replaced quickly by his usual cynical distance. He grasped her arm and pulled her closer. "You'll not *have* to face him, Auriane," he said in a covered voice. "Erato's paid the Ferryman. And knowing Erato, probably wore him down on the price."

"What?" she whispered, suddenly still, as if the wind were knocked from her body. Slowly, black sadness wormed its way in. "Is this some cruel jest?" she protested hoarsely. "It *cannot* be!"

That she had not foreseen.

"It is true, Auriane. The news was brought to me near the end of the bout." He pulled Auriane still closer, glancing suspiciously to the right and left as if he feared spies. "Plancius' thugs did it. He was whipped to death in the custody of the City Police."

Tears quickly overfilled her eyes; a series of shudders passed through her as she suppressed sobs. She bowed her head and closed her eyes, trying not to envision the scene.

Erato. Not you! You were a good man, to whom I owed much. You gave me a scrap of hope when I had none, a bit of air to breathe. You were fair, when you'd no need to be. It is impossible that you are gone! How surprised you would have been to see me cry over you. I know you thought I had hardly a thought for you at all.

Fria, be kind and gentle to his soul, though he nearly forgot you and knew you only as Nemesis.

She laid a hand on her belly, and for a moment the budding life within acted as a balm. *One life is snatched, another is given. It's never equal, it's never enough, but it distracts us. Fria, you sly and merciful mother!* But the chaotic sadness returned, bringing Marcus to mind again, and now she cried silently, unashamedly for both.

Marcus, it is past bearing. Yet it is still far better than if it never was, than if I had never been joined with you.

What will become of me, and of Sunia? I want to cry out to the moon. I am weary enough to sleep through seven seasons.

As the crowd clamored after, the cart-horse and its disheveled rider melted into the darkness of the yawning entranceway of the school. A common thought hung on the air: *She could not have done what she has done.* It was easy to believe, suddenly, that she never was, that she was some collective delusion, one of the phantoms that materialize at crossroads to mark the turning of times.

CHAPTER LX

As the bout came to a close, its victor still unknown, the eighty Praetorians posted in double rows along the vaulted corridor that served the imperial bedchamber paid little attention to the bestial roars issuing from the Colosseum. What was one more victory for Aristos on a day such as this? Especially in some bizarre match with a woman? It all seemed but one more reason for ridding themselves of Domitian, who debased the honor of the games by filling the arena with women.

The ninth hour loomed close. Sweat dampened every back, plastering woolen tunics to flesh. Palms slipped on javelins. All flinched at the ringing shout of a guard change that issued from the distant peristyle courtyard at the center of the vast multistoried Palace. Their part was uncomplicated: They were to stand silent and still while the deed was done, no matter what strange sounds might come from the imperial bedchamber. They believed the plot was conceived by Petronius and went no further; this was to ensure the safety of Nerva, should one of this company of eighty prove disloyal. All were young recruits whose first loyalty was to Petronius; he had promised promotions to every one, and rich money gifts. Still it was a dread and awesome thing to defy a sacred oath to protect the Emperor. Most thought privately that were they offered a chance to back out of the affair even now, they would seize it in a moment.

As the August heat grew fiercer and the mounting tension made them feel they were being broken slowly on a wheel, the thought recurred insistently: And why should this attempt succeed? How swiftly and savagely their still-loyal colleagues would turn on them if they knew.

By tomorrow morning all of us could be in line for the block.

A hasty trumpet fanfare signaled that their Lord and God approached the Palace from the more private Forum entrance, and was moving now through the grand vestibule. Many felt a private throb of despair. They had hoped Petronius would fail to draw the Emperor away from the amphitheater, and that would be the end of it. In an hour their watch would end; they would go quietly back to their barracks and not another word would ever be spoken of this.

Then came a disciplined tramp of feet. Domitian's twenty-four lictors strutted into view, bearing the *fasces*, the ancient symbol of unlimited power on earth—and the men found themselves transfixed by the dully gleaming axes put in with each bundle of birch rods: the sign of the Emperor's power to execute. Next they saw Petronius, who walked at Domitian's side. Petronius' complexion was the color of dough; this did little to still their fears. But it was the sight of Domitian that overcame them to a man.

Somehow, perversely, never had Domitian appeared so imposing. Their fright rendered his height heroic; he seemed to move through clouds with Zeus-like indifference. That formidable brow was unforgiving as death. A direct look from those eyes could roast them to ashes. He looked neither left nor right; their presence was utterly beneath his notice—they might have been a row of columns.

Many believed the Emperor with his divine senses could smell the odor of treason on them. *This is folly and blasphemy. He cannot be killed. For Petronius' greedy ends, all of us will die.*

They felt like foolish servants tempting the wrath of the father-god. The same thought formed in many minds: We must move swiftly—we've but one hour to alert the loyalists.

But as the Emperor's entourage passed on, there came from the amphitheater a series of dull, rumbling explosions of noise, like a mountain erupting with fire. Finally the cries melted into a continuous din, and they knew the bout was ended. Strangely, they heard but several halfhearted attempts to start up the chant *"Aristos Rex,"* then nothing more. What in the name of Mars were they crying out?

Finally they heard it unmistakably: *"Aurinia Regina!"*

It could not be. This was some elaborate jest. Again and again the mob cried the woman's name, and gradually they had to believe. For long moments they were suspended in baleful confusion, not knowing whether to count this violent upset of natural law for good or ill. Then one of their number spoke up with authority, whispering loudly: "The divine will's never been clearer—this is the hour for the weak to strike down the strong!" Within moments this interpretation was passed down the line, and it had a wondrous effect. Through the victory of the barbarian woman, their god-filled universe had given them an answer and a blessing.

The plot would succeed. Those who had thought of defecting swiftly, confidently, changed their minds. Each fresh cry of *"Aurinia, Regina"* further fired them with boldness.

When Domitian heard the cry, he halted midstride. Petronius saw his features soften into an incongruous look of childish confusion.

"What do they shout?" Domitian whispered in a tone close to begging. The Emperor seemed dwarfed suddenly by the size of his Palace. Slowly his expression became one of reflective horror, as if he discovered he had been sleeping in a haunted room.

A Guard was dispatched to the streets to drag in one of the ragged boys who cry out tales of events in the city in exchange for a few copper coins.

"Horrible," Domitian whispered when he heard it all, including the strangling. "Aristos deserved a better death! She is a putrefying serpent in our midst!"

The third omen had stolen up behind him quietly as an assassin in a midnight-dark street. He felt like a condemned man who is set free—and then realizes his reprieve was a dream.

Aristos, fool, you were to give me an omen of life! And now she has killed me, surely as if she ran me through herself.

"Curses on those criminal children and their rejoicing!" Domitian sputtered, his wrath turning suddenly on the mob. "For the rest of the games they shall have no awnings. Let them roast in the sun and soak in the rain. I'll give them acrobats and monkey races until they shout themselves dead. Let them have their frolics, the vermin, the sewage—"

Servilius appeared in the vast corridor, advancing on them purposefully with his underconfident strut. At a respectful distance he halted before the imperial party.

"Your Excellency, I have a—a most strange thing to report,"

Servilius began, his head bowed as if for the convenience of an imaginary executioner. "You ordered us to bring out your former First Advisor, and we could not, at first, find him. That is, he was not in the cell to which the day guard recorded he'd been brought. I found him, finally—in the interrogation room. He apparently was taken by mistake—"

"What chicanery! Do not those idiots *know* him?"

"My question exactly! I know not how it happened—I mean to fully investigate the matter," Servilius went on, struggling with a voice that wobbled like a wheel loosened on its axle. In reality he knew precisely how the mishap occurred, but he needed desperately to cover any appearance of incompetence. The Emperor was a stern but just god who could be placated with good deeds and right action. And he had failed miserably. Feeling he awaited the thunderbolt, he ventured on, "It is unpardonable, of course. I will resign my office—"

"Stop flapping that useless tongue at me, I'll tell you when to resign. There's much you do not say. *Nothing happens with that man by accident.* If he was taken, he *wanted* to be taken. Did you ask him what sort of mischief he was involved in?"

"He would not speak to *me*, my lord. And . . . there's not much life left in him."

A glint of realization flashed in Domitian's eye. "If you lie, I'll know it—*who was the man he said he was?*"

"A—a man named Bato, your excellency."

"A plague on imbeciles! Did it occur to you that this *Bato* is the man we want? That our canny Julianus meant to stop him from spewing out under torture something he did not want revealed?"

"I—yes, I did think of it. Oh, yes, right away. As a matter of fact, just before I came to you now, I ordered Bato brought out. He—he died. Under torture."

"So *soon?* You had better explain that."

"He was so frightened. He died of fright, soon as they put him on the rack. . . . Weak heart, I think. Yes, for certain, a weak heart. . . ."

"My dear Servilius, why won't you look at me? You look like you fell into a vat of white lead. How terribly convenient for Marcus Arrius Julianus. Perhaps for *you* as well?"

Servilius vigorously shook his head. "No, my lord. Of course not!"

Servilius had actually killed Bato himself. When he learned that Marcus Julianus was shielding the man, likely explanations sprang to mind, including the correct one, but terror for his own life overwhelmed all other considerations, for he knew Bato was one of Julianus' many spies among the Guard. And Servilius had much to hide—there was the cousin he helped escape to Caledonia after he deserted the Tenth Legion, and the heavy bribes he took from his men for extra leave-time. Such things under Domitian brought much harsher penalties than loss of promotion. It had been a simple matter for Servilius to steal into the interrogation room and finish Bato with his dagger before the torturer began his work.

"I am your most loyal of servants!"

"The sad truth is, you probably are. It's an eternal pity that loyalty of canine proportions and good, common human intelligence never seem to go hand in hand. You are dismissed."

Domitian added happily to Petronius as they continued on their way to the prisons, "Perhaps Julianus will prove more sociable with me."

Curses on Nemesis, Petronius thought. If Julianus dies I will charge it to myself, for it was I who let Bato into the plot. All comes apart. We'll end taking our places beside Saturninus and all the others who tried to throw off Domitian and died for it.

In the octagonal bedchamber Domitia Longina hesitated before the imperial bed in its niche adorned with temple roof and pilastered columns of serpentine. Her heart felt like a swallow trapped in the eaves as she drew back the heavy Oriental coverlet and exposed the checkered pillow with its tassels of gold.

Coward. Do it now!

Her hand slid cautiously beneath the goose-down cushion. Her finger was nicked by steel. Startled, she withdrew it and slowly, sensuously, licked the blood, imagining it her husband's. Then she quickly drew out the short sword always concealed there.

Now, monster, you'll have no way to defend yourself. Just as I never did.

She was to conceal the sword beneath her palla, then calmly depart. The timing was close—loyalist Guards had just completed an inspection, and within the quarter hour Domitian was to be here, questioning the suspected traitors. But she found herself bewitched by the sight of that implacable blade and gently transformed by the feel of that deadly weight in her hand.

This is what has been lacking from my life. A weapon.

All at once her patched-together calm blew apart. And that rage, so long tamped down, was volcanic. Savagely she whipped back the embroidered coverlet. With the sword held clumsily in both hands, she began slashing the undercovers, making horrible wounds, imagining she mangled her husband's body.

This, for the pleasure you took in my mock execution.

This, for your bloody murder of Paris, who loved me.

This, for every time you made me watch while you depilated your concubines.

For long moments she continued her joyous mutilations. Soon undercovers and coverlet were heaped in a shredded mass at one end of the bed.

Finally the sound of fast, stuttering whispers—soft, urgent, persistent as a moth—penetrated the veils of her rage. It was Carinus.

"My lady! Stop! Please! Suspicions will be raised! Servilius is somewhere padding about, I saw him in the corridor not a moment ago!"

Domitia Longina slowed long enough for reality to overtake her, then slumped into passivity, cheeks flushed like a maiden's. Perspiration matted her amethyst silk stola to her deeply heaving breast. She surveyed the damage with dismay.

"What will we do? Carinus, I have destroyed us!"

Carinus loved her too much to condemn her, even in the privacy of his mind. His sole thoughts were of means of remedying the situation.

"I'll set it all to right. First, get safely off, and take the sword. We must make the bed look as before, that is all. Still your fears! In the Venus bedchamber off the East Garden is a tapestry made of the very same cloth and pattern. I'll fetch it."

She stared at him, her terror unabated. The Venus bedchamber was a quarter mile and a maze of passages away.

Carinus sprinted off like a youth in a footrace.

CHAPTER LXI

The torturer prostrated himself before Domitian. He was as free of fearful awe as some obedient beast, as though the long habit of numbing himself to the sight of human suffering taught him to deaden every other emotion as well. Those muscular hands had learned to operate the pulleys of the rack with the same indifference with which he fastened his sandals. Slowly his bald head came up—a barren moon in the twilight of the small torchlit chamber—and he gazed with inscrutable complacency upon nothing. He was a slave who had himself been tortured once—he had the misfortune to have been the key witness in an important murder case—and he had as a reminder six missing front teeth, prized out by an inventive interrogator. The vacant places made a checkered pattern as he smiled.

"He lives?" Domitian asked.

The torturer gave a furtive nod of assent, unwilling to meet his august visitor's eyes. He had the air of a shy nocturnal animal.

Domitian gave a soft grunt and gestured sharply toward the inner room. The torturer led him past a smoking brazier, and through a passage hung with the implements of his trade: brands of various shapes, whips of different weights, some with thongs fitted with steel balls, a row of sinister pliers in graduated sizes. There were pincers, thumbscrews, foot-crushers, and vises, all neatly cared for as if this were a carpenter's shop. On the floor at his right loomed a rack, a complicated set of ropes and pulleys set on a wooden trestle, designed to wrench bone from bone. They stepped over a rusted drain set in a depression in the passage so the chambers could be easily washed clean of blood, then they entered a second chamber where the reek of sickness prompted Domitian to whip out a cassia-scented handkerchief and hold it to his nose.

Chained to the wall was a man stripped to the waist. Domitian forced down the errant stirrings of arousal caused by the sight of that smoothly muscled, well-formed body, utterly at his mercy—he did not want this man to have even *that* power over him. The victim was unconscious; his head rolled to one side. His face was so misshapen from blows that Domitian could not have positively identified him at first. But from long experience in such matters, he knew precisely what the torturer had done. The vicious scarlet ruptures along the spine proved the brand had been applied; the purple-black welts, oozing red sap—beautiful, in their way, Domitian thought—were evidence he had been beaten with iron rods.

"Rouse him!" Domitian said softly. The torturer sloshed a bucket of scummy water into the man's face. He coughed, shook his head, and opened his eyes to glassy slits. Gradually they sharpened with recognition. It was only when Domitian saw the familiar flare of critical intelligence in those eyes that he was certain this was Marcus Arrius Julianus.

Domitian edged closer, feeling lured by everything he never wanted to know, while conflicting feelings surged in him, giving him a sort of emotional indigestion. He felt the bully's barbarous joy, mingled with a terrible pity, affecting as dreams, as if his own best self hung bleeding on that wall.

"Well, *well,* old friend!" Domitian said with attempted carelessness. "I see you moved right in, even though you weren't invited! Since you've so boorishly intruded on my torture chamber, I trust you're *enjoying* the accommodations. Are the brands hot enough? They can be heated more. This whipper is a disgrace, I'm afraid—I can see by the fact that you've still got flesh left on your back. My apologies! And I know what you're thinking . . . that rack should be replaced!—I'll wager you thought I didn't notice the wood's unpardonably warped."

Marcus Julianus regarded Domitian without realizing at first who he was; he felt he struggled up through bloody mud until, gradually, he saw diffuse light. His body's massive struggle against feeling fogged his vision; comprehension came in blunt, lumbering starts.

Who *is* this barking fool? Oh, yes. I remember.

Domitian. Curses on Nemesis. He should be in the bedchamber by now. Petronius, you played your part poorly—you let him get away from you!

Time closes in upon us! *I must make this visit a grievous torment for him so he will leave.*

Domitian shifted to a more confidential manner, his voice rich with remorse and veiled pleading: "Do you think I *want* to see you like this, old friend? It is greatly distressing to me. Sometimes I wish for a new Nero so we could be allies once more! What caused you to do it? What base humor, what unleashing of spite, what close-nursed hatred of me made you spit in my face in the matter of that barbarian woman? I'm trying to comprehend you. Are you still enjoying the sight of the spittle dripping from me, or have you already moved on to other conquests? Ah, I've not it in my heart to condemn you summarily. Marcus, I'm begging like the blind man that beds down under bridges. *Give me my half-measure of respect.* Tell me I deserve an arch or two, or *one* golden statue, or a single reverent mention in a history text. And I'll order our man here to cut you down."

Marcus Julianus closed his eyes and drew deeply on his last reserve of strength. "I will oblige you then and tell you what you deserve," he said in a voice forced from a parched throat. "But why waste the question on me alone? It would be edifying if we could ask it of *all* your victims." He felt something tighten in the air, as if Domitian seized up in alarm.

"How *would* you fare in Hades," Marcus Julianus continued, "before a court composed of the innocents you've murdered? Let me anticipate their ruling! I hear them pronouncing sentence: For wanton ruthlessness unbecoming of a bandit, let alone the highest caretaker of the state . . ." As Julianus paused for breath, he heard Domitian's angry, roughened breathing increase in tempo; with grim glee he continued on. ". . . for displays of peevish cruelty and murderous conceit that would make Nero blush . . . coupled with a nature so suspicious it skirts rank madness . . . and for exercising a justice that is no more than crude *revenge* for being told what your tyrant's soul cannot bear to hear . . . we condemn you to . . . to what? What *would* be just and fair?"

Domitian felt like a cat thrown in water. *What is this?* he screamed with every sense. In his subterranean self he always *had* believed Marcus Julianus loathed him. But Domitian now realized that, at an even deeper stratum, he entertained the faint hope that

Julianus loved him, as the good father, beneath everything, cherishes a son. An edifice of pretense that had protected him all his life began to crack apart at the foundation.

"Ah, yes, I have it," Julianus went on, "perfect justice! Your victims condemn you to—to be packed in a chest of ice!"

"What are these filthy spewings?" Domitian's hands flew to his ears.

Marcus Julianus felt Domitian's outrage as a blast of heat; the room felt like a kiln. Quietly he finished, ". . . the death you gave your own brother."

"You know nothing! Slithering viper! No! I'm *pleased* to hear this! Who can be injured by the ravings of a madman!" He advanced upon Marcus Julianus, fists clenched. "I'll pour molten steel down that lying throat!"

"And still you imagine you can obliterate truth by destroying the vessel through which it speaks. Little children believe such things. . . . Perhaps that's why it never seemed you truly came to a man's estate . . ."

Domitian gave a dark growl and struck Julianus hard across the mouth. A bright thread of blood traveled down his chin.

"You are a *scourge!*" Domitian breathed. "You *knew.* All these years. Worm in the cabinet! Fiend! Your father found a street-urchin and not his true son—this *proves* it—you've a slave's stupid, cunning, devious nature! How dare you judge! What do you know of being despised and vilely plotted against by an older brother—the world's darling, his father's pampered favorite! Who are you anyway? You'll die unknown and forgotten, *Endymion!*"

Domitian nodded to the torturer. "The weighted whip!"

The interrogator took up the seven-thonged lash fitted with steel balls and, with unthinking grace, laid it on. Seven fresh ragged cuts appeared on Julianus' back. His body contracted with each new blow—an organism's animal protest against massive insult. By the fifteenth, the flesh began to look pulverized. Marcus Julianus groaned with each stroke but would not cry out.

The sight suffused Domitian with strength until he felt power-fully engorged, while the body of his victim shrank into pulpy insignificance. *Now I am his god. He needs me more than he needs the immortal Fates, to end the pain.*

After twenty lashes Domitian signaled a halt—he remembered he had a question to put to his former advisor while there was still life left in him. The torturer lowered the whip, and Julianus' body lay still, dangling heavily as a haunch of meat.

"The scoundrel called Bato has met with a deserved end. What was he to you? Why did you scheme to prevent him from being questioned?" Domitian demanded softly.

Marcus Julianus' chest and throat felt ravaged from the strain of forcing back screams; for a moment no words would come, though he tried. His back was a raging conflagration. The pain pulsed furiously, swamping him in molten lava, slightly relaxing its hold, then engulfing him once more. Domitian was forced to repeat the question. Marcus Julianus thought that voice was an iron file, relentlessly abrading his eardrum.

"The man Bato"—Julianus managed finally in a rasping whisper—"knew . . . of a plot against your life . . . *a plot I did not want to fail. . . .*"

"You knew of this as well! You are shameless!"

"Oh, come now, you *expected* me to serve you and betray you. . . . You expect it of everyone."

"How can you look at me!"

"It's . . . not easy to look at you . . . believe me. Bato came to me for financial help, and . . . for advice, which I readily gave him. I knew the man had not the strength to withstand torture . . . so I let them take me . . . and that's all you'll know, *monster*. . . . You'll *never* get their names. . . . I would first bite off my tongue and spit it in your face."

Domitian heaved with soft, malicious laughter. "Well then, let me save that tongue for you! *Parthenius . . . Stephanus . . . Satur . . . Clodianus . . .* a gladiator called the Cyclops." Domitian lingered over the names as if they were delicacies, observing with satisfaction that each brought a fresh start of despair to Julianus' eyes. "So you see, your sad little plot is undone. These men are all in chains. I am truly *sorry* you had to subject yourself to all this for nothing."

Marcus Julianus lay silent and still. He knew he must let Domitian feel he was safe.

"Your ineptitude surprises me, Marcus Arrius Julianus. You know, I always thought that if ever *you* set your hand against me, I would be a dead man! A councillor who has lost his cleverness is rather like a concubine gone to fat, don't you think?"

Marcus Julianus thought frantically: *Why won't he leave?* He despises me, and he's won! Nemesis!

He made a last try. "Poor as my own opinion is of you, Spawn-of-Nero," Marcus Julianus whispered, "yet . . . there's still another who loathes you even more."

Domitian moved closer, his eyes afire with lust to know. "*Who*, you arrogant spewer of sophistries? Petronius? Norbanus? That shuffling old fool who gives kindliness a bad name, Senator Nerva? Tell me! What is it to you now?"

"You run too far afield, don't exert yourself so. I speak of yourself."

"Why do I waste time with a madman! What man despises himself? It is against nature. I order you not to think it!"

"It is a curious phenomenon, but it happens. In spite of the fact that you've taken your place on the world's highest throne, what you see in the glass is a mean, unlettered lout, a cross between criminal and slave. . . . You wear your ignorance like a pox. . . . You took to killing to get the respect of your betters and, too late, discovered it only strengthened their belief in your own father's assessment of your worth: that you're fit to be a mule driver, and no more."

Domitian silenced him with a murderous grunt that caused the torturer to jerk back as if struck. Then he nodded curtly, and the man laid on five more lashes.

Julianus relapsed into unconsciousness, leaving Domitian alone—and agonizingly conscious. All the words Marcus Julianus had spoken ate eagerly into Domitian's brain like so many vigorous worms into a corpse.

I defeated this man, and he's admitted to his shameless faithlessness. What is his cursed secret that he seems the victor, even as he waits by the Styx for the boatman to pick him up?

Roughly Domitian shook Julianus' shoulder. "You'll not get away from me so easily, you scorpion-in-the-coverlet. Bring him round!"

The torturer sloshed another bucket of filthy water into Julianus' face. This time he was not roused so quickly.

I could have him whipped to death, Domitian realized, and still it would not take the scorn out of that smile. I want to cripple him *inside,* as I have been.

Domitian thought of a way.

He crouched so his gaze was level with Marcus Julianus' eyes. Blandly he smiled.

"Sorry to bother you again, old friend," he said with easy joviality, "but it seems I forgot to give you the news of the day, which doubtless you've not heard, stowed away down here. Your barbarian Circe paid the price for her criminal insolence. Aristos chopped your Aurinia into cutlets, as she begged him to. She died slowly. I'm afraid he played with her a bit first. Would you like a part of your estate to go for her funeral? That is, if they saved enough of her for the pyre?"

He watched Marcus Julianus' face with a sculptor's attention to expression and soon saw that a few intelligently chosen words had succeeded where the torturer's arts had not.

Marcus Julianus at first did not seem to hear. Then slowly anguish became visible; Domitian saw something writhe, then collapse within those eyes. Greedily he drank in the sight.

That is life, fool! So much for your cursed independence from me! Know what I know—that the world is infinitely brutish and cold. Love is a tomb. And I spoke the words that taught it to you.

Domitian rose to full height, feeling himself a strutting lion with a fine mane that had just snapped its leash. *Never again will I bow down to this man, even in my secret thoughts. I've pulled down the idol; I've plowed the memory over with salt.*

"Feast on defeat, Marcus Julianus. For all your conspiracies, *I am victor at the last.*"

Domitian gifted the torturer with a newly minted gold *aureus*, graced, he thought, with an especially fine likeness of himself. The torturer accepted it with no emotion. The Emperor then nodded toward Marcus Julianus. "Let him hang there. Give him a full night to think on what I've told him. Tomorrow at dawn, he dies on the block with the rest of them."

Senator Nerva sputtered curses as the mob flowed around his litter and the powerful current of people began forcing him steadily back. It was a foul enough circumstance that he felt death lodged in every muscle and only wanted to lie down and sleep out all his remaining days. But he feared if this crowd did not soon disperse he would never reach the Curia quickly enough to ensure his confirmation. The austere columns of the Senate House rose serenely over the storming sea of people, appearing tantalizingly close, but they might as well have been far off as the shores of Africa. He sensed something alien and savage in the excitement of the mob, as though the wild blood of the barbarian woman whose name they cried infected their own.

Fools, Nerva thought. You are getting in victory's way.

Two of his eight Cappadocian bearers were knocked to their knees. The litter pitched; Nerva rolled out into the muddy street. A booted foot stepped on his hand. Three of his chair-men hastily lifted him and dragged him into a cleft between two massive tenement blocks.

This is catastrophe, Nerva thought. If I'm not there to secure the office when the deed is done, the Guard will be allowed too much time to think. They cannot be left without a master even for an hour—they might well tear the city apart in vengeance.

That is, if the deed is done at all. The odds are not with us. Too many know of this. The conspiracy had one necessary flaw from the beginning—to make it safe afterward, too many had to be let in.

His eyes watered in a gust of thick, foul smoke. From above came shrieks of terror, and a rain of poor possessions—tin vessels, patched clothing, jars of foodstuffs wrapped in rags—began dropping all about him. A mother threw a crying child into the waiting arms of a man below. The tenement that sheltered him had been fired by the mob.

Carinus' heart contracted with dread as he padded about to each of the bedchamber's five servants' entrances, bolting them from without, converting his Lord and God's bedroom into an escape-proof chamber of death.

Suddenly he heard a muffled disturbance within—a woman's bristling protestations, followed by her angry sobs.

Mother of the gods, the Emperor has walked in on my lady just as she replaces the coverlet! She will fall at his feet and confess it all. We are good as buried.

Carinus felt his heart was compressed in a vise. He put an ear to the door and caught blurred words here and there of an ugly, clumsy verbal duel. First came Domitian Longina's voice striking out in bold flurries, rising in pitch, as if she advanced with a weapon she did not want to be forced to use. Then came the Emperor's voice, sulkily defensive, pushing her off, the flatness in his tone betraying he thought her a petty annoyance rather than a true threat. Gradually Carinus put it together: The Emperor had indeed surprised Domitia Longina in the act, but Carinus guessed Juno preserved her—Domitian had *not* seen the shredded covers. The Empress, to prevent him from guessing the true reason for her panic, erupted into a fine display of jealousy, most likely over that haughty new concubine, too highborn in Carinus' opinion not to bring Domitia Longina public shame.

Wisely done, dear, clever Mother. It sounds as though he believes you. All is well.

• • •

Domitian was seated on a gold and ivory curule chair set on a dais near the east apse of the grand bedchamber. On his right rose a sturdy, maternal Minerva in Parian marble, her divine head turned to him slightly, her gracefully angled spear poised to protect. Behind him, the imperial bed appeared as formal, as unused as funerary furniture. A shaft of hazy illumination from a lightwell shrouded him in sallow light. The Emperor appeared waxen, preserved, a thing scarcely living, his eyes inflexible and remote as that of a god-figure in an Egyptian tomb painting. The imperial gaze was fixed somewhere just above the heads of the five prisoners chained before him. He had shed his prison-fouled clothes and was now freshly bathed, oiled, laurel-bedecked, and magisterially draped in a purple toga embroidered with silver stars.

He was in a fine, grand mood. The Prefect of the City Police assured him the unruly crowds would soon be brought under control. A dangerous plot had been exposed and crushed. There was still that ghastly matter of Aristos' death, but was not that sign of divine disfavor evenly counterbalanced by his bold outmaneuvering of Marcus Julianus?

Domitian had long reserved the imperial bedchamber for settling matters he preferred kept quiet—those occasional embarrassments a ruler must attend to, whose sad solution he knows will not add luster to his name. He allowed his gaze to move unhurriedly over the five wretched specimens of humanity in fetters before him.

All persons, all creatures, all nations have their heaven-appointed place, he philosophized grandly as was his habit when he felt keenly his magnificence. This is the most fundamental law. When people stray from the niche in which wise Minerva put them, this is the source of all impiety, all strife, all criminal acts.

For long moments Domitian glared punitively at the five miscreants who had crawled from their place. He saw this task as not too different from that of the Palace slave who oversees the taking of the day's garbage to the middens.

First on the left was the gladiator called the Cyclops. A peculiar scar in the midst of a broad forehead earned the man his name; it resembled a single, staring eye. His squat, powerful body, stooped shoulders and overlong arms gave him a decided resemblance to an ape; idly Domitian considered if there might be some obscure causal connection between the man's criminality and his bestial conformation. The Cyclops watched him with alert indifference, a calm Domitian surmised was the product of the discipline of the gladiatorial schools. He wanted to say: This is *certain* death, you ignorant brute—in the arena your chances were better.

Next to the Cyclops was Stephanus, a family steward, whose placid, inoffensive face was familiar to Domitian since boyhood. Stephanus' participation in this affair was to be expected: He had been caught embezzling from the household chest. Domitian looked briefly at Stephanus' heavily bandaged arm—three days ago he had broken it in a fall. He smiled at Stephanus, thinking, why bandage it at all? It won't have time to heal. Stephanus nervously smiled back.

Domitian's gaze moved hastily over the next man, Clodianus, a Centurion of the Guard, for in that soldier's active black eyes was a raw, unrepentant contempt that threatened to capsize Domitian's fine humor. Next to Clodianus was Satur, a tall Libyan with copper skin who was his wife's chamberlain. Domitian tarried over Satur's voluptuous lips and mentally caressed that lean, supple body. Domitian would have had Satur destroyed long ago because he knew his wife's blood was fevered in the man's presence; often he felt her eagerness to possess that neatly formed male body. But he himself had, almost accidentally one day, discovered Satur to be a master of the arts of the bedchamber and, until now, had not been able to bear the thought of giving him up.

Last was Parthenius, his own chief chamberlain, who until this day he had trusted more than any man. Parthenius alone of all the imperial household had been granted the right to wear a sword. He was the tallest of men, causing Domitian to wonder if that great height alone was not the cause of Parthenius' seeming awkward distance from his fellow men. The chief chamberlain had pleasantly battered features, distressed brown eyes, and a yellowed complexion physicians claimed was caused by a lingering malaise of the liver. Parthenius avoided Domitian's gaze; he seemed distinctly ashamed of himself.

What an amusing collection of criminal suspects, Domitian observed. Each embodies a quality—Loyalty, Deference, Doggedness, and so forth. They've a single trait in common, however: They're all *fine* physical specimens. They look a bit like characters in a country Satyr play, ready to fight over who'll play Priapus.

Unaccountably, a sudden unease overcame Domitian then, a sense this hour was somehow marked, that the world was slightly ajar in a way that should awaken him to danger. He recoiled in his soul, as if he heard an owl's call at midnight.

Why do I feel a sixth man is here, brooding over them all? I sense closely the presence of Marcus Julianus—in each man's face, I almost see that irksome, bemused smile, those eyes that apprehend with a cursory glance what most men won't notice until tomorrow.

Vigorously he banished the apparition from his mind.

"Come forward!" Domitian called out in sonorous voice. For a moment the Cyclops' impassiveness frightened him, but he was reassured by the slide-and-clink of the prisoners' heavy chains and by the knowledge that just beyond the anteroom was a double guard.

I could not be more secure. Why then this prickling sense of dread?

"All of you are impious scum, and you know it. The gods alone know what mix of bestial cunning, crippled intelligence and faithlessness inspires such acts of futile viciousness," he proclaimed importantly. "Now I want you to tell me in your own words *why* you tried to destroy your Lord and God. If you're honest and forthright in your replies, you'll get a quick death and a decent burial. If not, we've a variety of more entertaining deaths in our stock. Afterward I'll meet privately with each man and you'll give me the names of the others involved in this plot. The man who gives me the *fewest* names will earn the right to die on a cross."

They watched him with tense patience. Did he imagine it—or were they bunching more closely together? They almost seemed poised to spring.

In the corridor a door slammed shut with a rude clang. In a rough singsong voice a Guard cried out the ninth hour.

Carinus stood stiff and straight as a votive image while he poured a libation before the altar of the household gods set up in the antechamber. His hands shook; glistening red wine splashed down on the altar, onto the alabaster floor.

Mother of the Gods, give me the heart of a lion. . . . Now the volcano erupts! And I must stand quietly in its path.

In her own chambers Domitia Longina took an inscription plate bearing her husband's name and titles and dropped it into a burning brazier.

Fall away, prison walls, she prayed. Now, Juno! It is my life or his.

In the gloom of the *Ludus Magnus* the four guards posted before Auriane's cell looked on in puzzlement as their charge rose up purposefully, suddenly restless. Auriane dragged herself painfully to the cell's window; fresh blood appeared on the woolen bandages binding her thigh. Her eyes were excited, alive. Later they would report that at the ninth hour she looked directly at the Palace, as if she watched while the event occurred that later would be on everyone's lips.

Domitian realized Stephanus was slowly, furtively unwinding the bandage that bound his broken arm.

He leapt to his feet.

"Halt! You! What are you about?"

All five prisoners sprang forward as if a rope dropped at the start of a race. Vigorously they threw themselves against their chains, with the Cyclops slightly in the lead.

Carinus gripped the altar, shut his eyes, and muttered a jumbled prayer to Syrian Atargatis, goddess of his homeland. In the bedchamber all erupted into shrieking chaos. The earth dropped open beneath his feet.

As Domitian looked on, a frozen ghost, the prisoners' fetters snapped easily as if they had been made of lamp's horn. Amazement stifled the scream forming in his throat. In Stephanus' hand he saw a silvery flash.

Of course. The traitorous dogs. Of course, a dagger would be concealed in that bandage.

Domitian felt the bloody visions of a hundred nightmares tear through the veil of dream. *This could not be. But it was.*

"Die! Tyrant! Die!" Stephanus' voice rose above the others as they jostled each other in their eagerness to get to him. Domitian stood stiff as a pillar while the assassins flowed round him like wolves at a kill.

The Cyclops seized him from behind in a bear-grip, holding him steady for Stephanus' dagger thrust. But Domitian finally roused himself from paralysis and met them with brutish energy, striking out with fists and feet. In his fright his strength was past nature. He knocked Satur down with one frenzied kick to the chest. Then he lunged at Stephanus, struggling to gouge out his eyes. The dagger ripped harmlessly through the air while Stephanus thrashed about, evading those frantically clawing hands.

Clodianus combined his strength with the Cyclops' and gradually they managed to secure Domitian's arms. Satur, from the floor, got a vise-grip on Domitian's leg.

Carinus stopped his ears, unable to bear the torn-off howls and multiple yelps. It sounded as though a dozen dogs were being put to the torture.

Somehow Domitian managed to seize the dagger—but he caught it by the blade. Again and again he sliced his hands as he fought for a grip; the assassins' tunics and grappling hands became reddened with Domitian's blood.

It could not be, but it was. Domitian felt a perverse twist of satisfaction. This was the triumphant confirmation of all he believed to be true.

I truly *was* surrounded by wolves lusting for my blood. *The prosecutions were just.* They were, in fact, not stern enough— here now is proof.

Marcus Julianus, you were wrong.

"Guard!" Domitian's shout rose like a kite's screech over the assassins' grunts and curses, over the animal scuffling. For Domitian, all seemed to move with a peculiar, slowed-down tempo, as if the beat of the world were coming to a halt, and so at first it did not seem odd when no Guards came.

By sheer force of their weight the five assassins succeeded in holding their quarry still. Then Stephanus' knife whipped down, tearing once, then twice, into Domitian's groin. Crying out in baleful agony, their victim twisted off with superhuman strength and began struggling toward the imperial bed, dragging all five assassins along with him, toppling a fragile table, a tall urn, as he made his way. Domitian caught at one of the columns that flanked the bed, then pulled himself close; finally he managed to fling off the bedcushion.

No sword. The black dogs from Hades had it removed!

"Gua-a-rd!" came Domitian's second cry, this one more piteous and pleading than the last.

As he wrestled on with death, in one quick moment he caught sight of Domitia Longina, calmly watching from the antechamber. Her eyes glowed like an owl's; her cheeks were flushed with pleasure, and she had the witch-wise smile of Circe on her lips.

My wife. Foul bitch-dog from the sulfurous depths. You knew of this!

She let her gold-embroidered palla slip so he could see the sword.

My sword. How had you the audacity! Medusa! Clytemnestra! Wellspring of all womanly vileness! You stand out there in full view of a Century of the Guard and watch while my household murders me!

In that moment Domitian realized it fully: *The guards were not coming.*

A curse on the immortal gods. The whole of the Palace must have turned on me.

Stephanus' dagger came down in a fast, irregular series of blows, penetrating Domitian's neck, stomach, and thighs. A misplaced strike stabbed the Cyclops deeply in the shoulder; he spat a venomous curse at Stephanus but still managed to hold Domitian fast. The struggling mass of them presented such a tangle of torsos and limbs that Carinus could not tell assailant from victim.

It seemed to Carinus that thunder rattled in the eaves. Dark droplets of blood were flung all about, lurid, bright, visceral on the translucent floor, befouling Minerva, splattering the snowy columns, the frescoes along the wall. He pressed his ram's horn amulet to his heart. "Darkness, descend," the boy whispered. "Strengthen me, Mother Atargatis, or the sight will strike me blind." Somewhere in his deep self he thought: But it is right, it is ordained, and I know that Atargatis smiles. . . . The time was ripe for the sacrifice of the old god-king—his fructifying blood will fall on our fields and bring a new dawn. . . . Soon the city will know and be blessed.

Domitian fought with declining strength, bleeding from many wounds. The purple toga had come half unwound, hobbling him in its bloody length.

The whole of the Palace and the whole of the Guard. I've been seized in the jaws of a colossus. . . . Who in the name of the gods . . .

And then, suddenly, he knew.

Marcus Arrius Julianus. Who else could have turned so many minds? You fiend to end all fiends!

No. I refuse to believe it. I'll remember you always as I saw you last, broken and destroyed by my hand.

Another dagger thrust sank into flesh. Domitian knew he was dying.

And so the arena comes for me at the last, as I knew it would.

All the high barriers and archers can only hold it at bay for a decade or two. The world and its delights are a cruel distraction, concealing the brutal truth: Life is one tedious, graceless fight to the death. We spend our days struggling to forget the gods' thumbs were down at our birth.

Witness right and order overrun by the boiling, bestial mob. I was too lenient and good. *I failed to tame them with law.*

He sank to his knees, struggling reflexively now; the assassins followed him down. Dizziness came like some thick, welcome draught; the world became distant, diffuse, mythic—he might have been a warrior of ancient days dying in nameless glory on the battlements of Troy.

When Servilius heard the first shouts from the bedchamber, he was idly gaming with a fellow Guard's Centurion, awaiting his watch. He sprinted down the corridor to investigate, with ten off-duty soldiers at his back. At first he was mystified to find Petronius' recruits impassively blocking the door to the antechamber. Then came outrage and disbelief—for there was no doubt the terrible cries within were Domitian's. More loyalists poured into the corridor; Servilius drew his sword and sought to enter the bedchamber through the servants' side entrances. When he found every passage locked from inside, he rushed back to the anteroom, only to find Petronius' recruits had been quietly joined by the cohort handpicked by Norbanus; these men stealthily moved into place all along the length of the corridor, javelins crossed, faces implacable. The loyalists then tried to ram their way through, shields to the front; barked threats ricocheted throughout the corridor. The battle was bloodless, for none were willing to raise a sword against their own.

Servilius was astonished at the number of men of the Guard who barred his way. The majority of the loyalists fell into passive confusion. But Servilius would not give up the effort, continuing to bully and plead, determined to break in on the ghastly scene still progressing in the bedchamber.

Domitian lay on his back, still alive. The Cyclops wrested the dagger from Stephanus, muttering that the Emperor would see his hundredth birthday at the speed Stephanus was finishing this business. Parthenius, heaving and close to tears, used his weight to pin Domitian to the floor. In that moment Domitian's eyes sought Parthenius' and held them in a death grip.

"Parthenius! *Why?*" Domitian breathed the question. "I trusted you. . . . What did you want of me that I did not give?"

Parthenius dodged Domitian's gaze. "Forgive me!" he whispered. "It was not I who fated you to die. I'd no choice but to go along! You would know your murderer? It was Marcus Arrius Julianus."

It seemed to Parthenius that Domitian's spirit fled in that instant, as if his reply struck the death blow, and not the Cyclops' blade as it neatly cut the Emperor's throat.

Domitian did not feel the blade. For a little longer his mind went on knowing.

Marcus, old friend, so you won the palm. You are the king, I, the fool. I suppose you're exulting now that power was brought down by intelligence. Or perhaps by dumb patience. It must have taken you years, and the determination of a criminal madman, to seduce the Guard, my household, and my wife, and no doubt the Senate as well, then submit to torture to make certain your monstrous scheme did not come apart. Now *that* is hatred of epic proportions. And yet, once I had your regard, your precious, capricious regard. . . . What caused that manifold, mysterious intelligence to turn on me and kill me? If you think I understand, Marcus, know this: I do not.

Do not imagine yours is a noble victory, Marcus. I die as Aristos died, slain by base trickery.

Servilius broke in. With drawn sword, he rushed at the five men still crouched over Domitian. Stephanus had the ill fortune to be first within reach; Servilius dispatched him with one expert thrust to the heart. As Stephanus sank in death across Domitian's body, Petronius' Guards rushed in and wrestled Servilius to the floor.

The remaining assassins—Clodianus, the Cyclops, Parthenius, and Satur—were men roughly awakened from one nightmare and pitched into another. Slowly they rose up on shivering legs and began edging away from the frightful disarray of limp arms, legs, and bloody toga that was Domitian. Praetorians rapidly filled the room. The four moved unmolested to the door while the soldiers watched in a grim silence tangled with conflicting feeling: They could not help despising these men who dirtied their hands, and felt faintly shamefaced at letting them go. Who lets a murderer with fresh blood on his hands simply walk away? At the same time they felt mean and ungrateful that they did not hoist these men on their shoulders and parade them about as heroes.

The Guards in the anteroom shifted aside to let the assassins through. When the four reached the corridor, all broke into a run, two bolting east, two west. The furious staccato of their retreating footsteps was to the Guards a mocking, accusing sound: *You let us go, fools, you let us go.* Servilius began struggling and shouting. "Have all of you been struck mad! *After them!"*

To Domitian the shouting sounded like the cooing of pigeons. His many wounds were bruises—he would not feel them if he lay very still. Struggle trickled out of him and he felt a moist contentment creeping up slowly; tepid water encroached, embraced. He felt the impact of a wave-break of a sea of ghosts, heard whispering, felt affirming sea water rushing through his veins, gently disengaging his shade from his body, swiftly bearing him up; he imagined his consciousness flooded into the wise, watery mind of Minerva. With it came perceptions of such startling potency and drop-away depth that his whole life might have been held in a spring so clear he could see a hundred fathoms down.

I was mad—and did not know it. I thought I lived my life traveling along in one firm direction—*away* from my beginnings where I felt less worthy than the slave-murderer condemned to the mines. But I was instead like the blindfolded donkey that turns the millstone, treading one path all my life and *always thinking it new.* I saw everything in life as *one* thing—I never knew life's variousness. I see now my father and Marcus Julianus, *watching me with one and the same pair of eyes,* one piercing, damning gaze whose look gives the same raw bitter taste. Marcus, you said at the last I *expected* you to serve me and betray me. Well, of course. My father was first in that office of betrayer, and you but his successor. We are born tied up in cord and cursed few of us *ever* untangle ourselves. I was not one of the fortunate ones.

From the beginning my jealous hatred was fear of the great cold. *But there is no great cold.* Why did I live so? I spent my life like one born wealthy who fritters away his fortune on empty revels.

Domitian's ghost felt the frenzy in the minds of the people rushing about, those small harried animals still trapped in tight, narrow skulls. He gloried in his new freedom, not fully realizing he was dead. And when he did know it, "dead" hardly meant what it had an hour ago.

You poor insects scuttling about with such purposeful mindless-

ness, you set me free! You rush about for fifty years and more, evading in terror a thing that is not. You rear monuments to it, you worship it with your fear. I do not envy you who still possess life.

Petronius bent over Domitian's body, counting the wounds. *Twenty-seven.* As he struggled to remove the imperial ring, he felt a kind of pious fright. Those dread hands would never write another edict altering lives in a village in Baetica, or set events in motion in cities along the Nile. The body that knew every pleasure life had to give would taste no more. The last son of the Flavian dynasty, bringers of peace to the whole world, authors of the Colosseum, was reduced to corrupting flesh and a collection of spare sentences in a history text.

"You will roast in Hades for this!" Servilius shrieked at Petronius. "Traitorous, murdering swine!"

Petronius rose, walked over to Servilius, and quietly met his eye. "I'll let that pass as momentary folly, Servilius. Calm yourself. . . . Do not force me to order thirty lashes."

"No," Servilius rasped, shaking his head. "You *cannot* still be—" He meant to finish by saying, "Commander of the Guard," but he stopped, finally perceiving he was part of a dangerously small minority. A staggering number of the Guard stood quietly at attention, ready for Petronius' order.

"Lucius Servilius, look at me," Petronius said severely, putting a fist beneath Servilius' chin and forcing him to lift his head. "I warn you one last time to silence. You are speaking treason. Whether they are murderers or no, is not for *you* to say. It's a matter for Emperor Nerva to decide."

"Emperor—*who?*"

At last Servilius comprehended the enormity of the deed. If Nerva was set already in place, the whole of the Senate must have known of this. Petronius might have organized the Guard, but he had no influence over the upper aristocracy. And it was not in Senator Nerva's nature to set such a thing in motion—all knew him as a man of no grand ambition. Who authored this great crime?

All progressed, Servilius saw, like some tightly composed play. All knew their part. There was disorder, for certain—panicked servants ran through the halls, crying out in soul-shredding shouts, and fierce altercations continued among the Guards. But there was entirely too much order.

Whoever planned this was a master. He knew precisely who to bring in, and who to leave out; all was timed with a musician's precision. Civil war was neatly circumvented. The loyalists were swiftly surrounded and overcome, at the cost of but a single death, Stephanus'. The last of the Flavian dynasty was put out of the way with none to call it a crime.

CHAPTER LXII

Within the hour the city knew. The poorer streets throbbed with the driving chant: *"Death to the tyrant! Long live freedom!"* The people massed about the Senate House had a better understanding of the succession of events; they raised torches aloft as if at a victory-fest, and cried out, *"Long live Emperor Nerva!"* It was as though the news came by post that a great war had been won. Spiced wine ran in the streets. Houses were garlanded. Wine-flushed faces gleamed in the heat as citizens embraced strangers. The people clustered round the temples of Juno and Fortuna, tugging along a sheep or goat for a thanksgiving sacrifice. Before the Temple of Minerva, renegade musicians began to play; the gallop of their drums could be heard beyond the river—it was anarchy's insistent voice, pulling in every mind with its loose, careless rhythm.

Within the Palace, Petronius took matters in hand, ordering everyone from the bedchamber except for Domitian's childhood nurse, an aged Greek slave named Phyllis, the only person near to Domitian who cared to claim the body for burial. Petronius had already sent one messenger to the Senate to report that Domitian was dead; he now sent another to inform them of the feeling among the Guard. Then a Senate messenger was dispatched to him, bearing the alarming news that Nerva was missing.

Petronius knew the Guard must not learn of this; in order to settle matters decisively, he had already had his men take their oath to Emperor Nerva. Curses on this day, he thought. They had to find him quickly—otherwise city and Guard would be like oil awaiting the torch. They needed a ruler. Had Nerva fled in fright at the last moment, deciding on retirement after all? Petronius gave another brief speech to his men, declaring Nerva had been sighted on his way to the Curia, then repaired quickly to the prisons. It occurred to him that Marcus Arrius Julianus might have some better notion of what had become of their misplaced Emperor.

The Guard's Commander found Julianus still in chains in the interrogation room. One of Petronius' first orders had been for Julianus' release, but in the general confusion it was not carried out. Petronius stifled a cry of despair at the sight of him, thinking: The death-count will have to be put at *two*—surely this man's beyond any physician's help.

Petronius pressed wine on him, then assured Julianus when he thought him able to comprehend: "The tyrant has breathed his last. After the gods, we've *you* to thank for it!" The Guard's Commander was not surprised this brought faint response from a man more dead than alive. But he *was* baffled by Julianus' first coherent question: He wanted only to know if anyone claimed the body of the woman Aurinia.

"What? *Who?*" Petronius exclaimed. "How am I to know? You speak of the barbarian woman? But—she is alive. She was not even grievously wounded, they say."

Petronius saw no shift in the barren look in Marcus Julianus' eye.

"Come, let me prove it!" Petronius said then, anxious to give reassurance simply because the matter seemed to trouble Julianus greatly. With the aid of two prison guards Petronius helped him stand; then they walked with him to the guard room a half-floor above. Petronius bid Marcus Julianus look out a window, in the direction of the Aventine.

In the fierce sunlight at first Julianus saw nothing but an accumulation of red tile roofs broken by bouquets of green, and saffron haze mingled with sluggish cooking-smoke. Beyond the roof of the Palace kitchens, in the direction of the Circus, he discerned barely the white wall of the side of a small Temple of Hercules; on it, for two years now, devotees of Aristos had painted and stubbornly repainted the words *Aristos Rex*. Gradually he realized something new was painted there.

The words *Aurinia Regina* were written on the wall in tall, graceful red script.

"She lives!" His exclamation was soft, private. A potent mix of feelings welled up in him—vaulting exultation, pride in her, a sense of limitless solace. He felt he had taken an Olympian draught—his own pain shrank to insignificance. Sunlight seemed to live in everything, the darkened doorways, the sagging shops, the proud rooftops. All seemed harmonious, gentle and right.

Auriane, how you have done it the gods alone know. You fulfilled your vow. You had no chance, yet you prevailed. Impossible creature!

Petronius was awkwardly silent, not understanding what this was about. He made Julianus take another draught of wine, then went on urgently, "We've got a ticklish difficulty before us, good sir. Nerva cannot be found. Do you think he'd turn from us at the last?"

Marcus Julianus looked fully at Petronius then, eyes keen and focused. "Absolutely not. My guess is he set out exactly when he was supposed to, at the eighth hour, and got ensnared in the mob in the Via Sacra."

"Wonderful. That crowd won't thin out until tomorrow. Every man of the City Cohorts is already in the streets—they can do no more."

"We must somehow draw them off from about the Curia," Julianus said, and Petronius found himself relieved by the return of that durable confidence. "What, other than earthquake or threat of fire, would . . . I have it!—the woman Aurinia. Their curiosity of the moment. She killed Aristos, and I'll wager they haven't yet tired of gaping at her. Petronius, send someone you trust to the *Ludus Magnus* and have them accompany her to a place where she can be seen—a second-story window so she'll be safe. Tell the people that . . . that she will make a prophecy for the new reign. Yes. And Petronius . . . , make certain she knows the request comes from me—and tell her I am well. It is our one chance."

Petronius slowly grinned. "It's a moonstruck idea, and it doesn't say much for the intelligence of the mob—but what does? Let us try it."

Nerva hauled himself from his crevice and dazedly looked about. His litter had been set alight, and what the fire had not burned had been vandalized—the litter's poles were broken off for use as weapons; cushions and documents spilled out onto the street. One of his Cappadocians lay dead on the cobblestones, run through by one of the poles; the rest had fled. His toga looked like it had been used to scour the street. But the crowd, for some unknown reason, was slowly receding, leaving overturned carts, mountains of broken wares, and himself among the wreckage in its wake. Who, or what, had inspired them to move on? he considered in brief bewilderment. Then he hastened to take advantage of the situation.

His vision blurred; his stomach lurched. But he knew from the mob's cries that Domitian was dead. He must hurry. He loosened his toga and threw a portion of it over his head to conceal himself—he was ashamed to let these people who cried his name in adoration see him skulking about looking like a rag-picker. Then he rummaged about in the wreckage of his litter and, to his great relief, found the copy of the speech he was to make to the Senate. Miraculously, it was still legible.

He wondered if he should stop at a street fountain to wash the mud out of his hair. No—he could not risk taking the time. He would have to hope his colleagues maintained their sense of humor.

Perhaps I'll start a fashion. Young fops will take to slapping mud on their hair before sauntering out to their night's revels. Odder customs have begun over less.

All that night and through the next day the victory-fest continued. In every street and in the forums the people set up ladders, brought rope, and pulled down Domitian's many golden statues, as well as the votive shields engraved with his likeness. Where they found his name chiseled into monuments, they destroyed it with hammers. The people took one imperial statue graced with a particularly smug expression and used it in a playful mockery of a triumphal procession: Dressing it in rags, they set it facing backward in a debris-cart drawn by four asses, then paraded it down the Via Sacra while the people pelted it with filth.

On the eve of the second day a herald appeared on the steps of the Curia to inform them of the acts of the Senate since Domitian's death. Once Nerva was safely proclaimed, the Senators unleashed their fury on Domitian. First they handed down the *damnatio memoriae*—Domitian's memory was officially damned for all the ages. His name was not to appear on documents of state, and was to be erased from public buildings all over the Empire. Statues erected to him in the forums of every city, from Britannia to Egypt, were to be taken down. All the acts and laws of his reign were abolished. The month he renamed "Domitianus" became "October" once more. Senate and people would behave as if he had never lived.

When Nerva delivered his first speech as Emperor, he pledged that the time of bloody tyrants was done; in his reign no Senator would be put to death. All property seized by Domitian would be returned; the men and women he sent into exile would be brought home. An amnesty was declared and the prisons were thrown open. Nerva promised to impose no laws without first consulting the Senators. And he would permit no one in the Empire to deify him while he lived—not even foreign kings would be made to address him as Lord and God.

For many this peacefulness would last all their lives. Domitia Longina lived on happily for another thirty years in her quarter of the Flavian Palace, immersed in books and literary friends. She never married again—though she quietly took a succession of younger and younger lovers, plucked from the pantomime stage and theater dressing rooms. She never fully lost her adoration of this freedom that for so long seemed impossible. Carinus when he reached the ripe age of twenty-five became her chief chamberlain. Veiento was never punished for his long career of prosecuting the innocent, and Nerva was criticized in this case for not being harsh enough. But the people were gratified that at least the notorious informer was driven from public life. He dared not linger in Rome, however, for fear of being set upon by the relations of his victims, and within the month he slunk off to his villa in Praeneste, where he lived on for a time in obscurity and disgrace.

On the day following the assassination, Junilla boarded up her great house on the Viminal Hill, locked her jewelry in strongboxes, sent her slaves to her villas at Terracina and Baiae, donned pitiful rags, and then made a determined attempt to join the Christiani. It was done more from fear of Julianus' vengeance than from an attraction to this esoteric new mystery cult. She knew that, because of past persecutions, the shy, secretive Christiani had knowledge of places of concealment unknown to the City Cohorts, where she hoped she might escape Julianus' wrath. But matters became tense when Martha, the proud, grim freedwoman who was their leader, learned Junilla had arranged a predawn tryst with the Cyclops in the back of the abandoned government grain storage-tower that served as the sect's current meeting place. When it also came out that Junilla had lied and not given away all her worldly possessions, but only cleverly hid them from sight, the Christiani drove her out, fearing she was sent to spy on them.

But by that time she feared Marcus Arrius Julianus no more, for he had departed the city with great honor. Junilla observed it all with amazement and disdain. He was higher than anyone in the Emperor's esteem and could have done whatever he wished to her, but never once did he seek to make a move against her. Not only did he seem to forget or forgive all she had done to him; he also spurned the greatest offices the Emperor could bestow. The man, as ever, was a fool.

On the third day following Nerva's accession, Auriane nudged herself from a sleep that felt like a welcome death. She sat up, expectant, seized with an urgent melancholy that left her with a strong sense her time in this place was done. Dawn furtively infiltrated the chamber. She put her hands on her belly in an instinctive attempt to comfort the child within. The tumult outside had faded many hours ago. Now she heard the school guards' harsh voices, growing louder as they approached her cell.

She was up like a cat. A guard noisily slid back the bolt of the door. A secretary from the Prefect's staff stood behind him with bored formality, a rolled document in his hand. In back of them was Sunia, looking elated and a little lost. Auriane thought it odd she wore a rough weather cloak; where was Sunia going at this hour?

The secretary intoned in colorless voice, "Aurinia, greetings." As he spoke on, she felt something quietly inevitable in his words, like the quickening of dawn.

"We come to inform you that by the order of Emperor Nerva, you have been manumitted. You are granted the status of one born free—an honor not given to many. Here are your proof of status and manumission papers, signed by Emperor Nerva himself, before witnesses." He added with faintest contempt, "You, Aurinia, are now a citizen of Rome."

A citizen of Rome? She stared at him, feeling fastened to earth only by her body's pain. Sunia tried to catch her glance with a reserved smile of amusement, but Auriane kept her face impassive, suddenly not caring to let this man know what an arrogant gift she felt this was.

The secretary motioned her forward. "It is unlawful for you to be held here, and you must go."

"What of Sunia?"

Sunia answered with veiled eyes, the flicker of a conspiratorial smile. *She is hiding something,* Auriane realized. "I'm free as well. Well, not quite. At this moment I belong to Marcus Arrius Julianus, who bought me from the school in order to manumit me. It's not complete—there are papers to be written or some such thing."

"And . . . Coniaric . . . and Thorgild?"

"He has done the same for them. Thorgild comes with us. But Coniaric chose to stay—he plans to sign on as a free fighter. He thinks the arena will make him celebrated and dependent on no one. It does not surprise me." Auriane sadly nodded. She had noticed for some time that the spirits of this place filled Coniaric with a new soul.

The guard spoke then. "There's a woman here who would speak with you, sent from the Palace." He half turned and motioned for the woman to be brought forward.

"A woman?" Auriane said, perplexed. She knew no woman in this place other than Sunia. She looked questioningly at Sunia, who grinned broadly in reply.

Night shadows lurked on in the passage; as Auriane looked, the form of a woman, small and stooped, separated from the gloom.

She knew it with her subtle senses before she knew it with her mind. A hand went to her throat. Her knees suddenly felt wobbly as a newborn's. A warm amazement slowly overtook her.

"No!" A paralysis of joyous disbelief pinched her voice to a whisper. "No, it cannot be . . ."

Auriane broke into a hobbling run.

Frightful images of the past flashed before her then: *white flesh against black earth,* which was all she remembered of the attack on her mother while the hall burned. The sight of Athelinda as a sad sentinel by the edge of her fields, wrapped in unapproachable solitude after Baldemar's death. And then, Five Wells afire: yellow flame-tongues stretching into the cold blue of the morning sky, Roman soldiers swarming in like wasps, and the heart-shredding shrieks of the children her people could no longer protect. She felt Berinhard rearing steeply beneath her, Athelinda's strong pull on the rein, and its dreadful snap when she struck it with her sword blade.

Mother, if you are prey to whatever comes, then so am I. Do you forgive? I left you collapsing in the mud. What has your life been since?

Her voice was half prayer, half questioning.

"Mother?"

Two strong hands affirmatively seized her shoulders. Doubts lingered; in her memory Athelinda was taller—a proud, protective presence—and the top of *this* woman's white head only met her chin. She drew her closer to a wall sconce and saw those so-familiar eyes taking her in with gentle ferocity, that mouth that served as model for her own, except now it was corrupted by sorrow and clamped closed in the way of one forced to keep too many silences.

Athelinda examined her critically, alert to an impostor and cruel disappointment.

"Mother!"

Relief flooded into Athelinda, spilling over into her hands, which shook, and she pulled Auriane into a long, death-denying embrace. To Auriane that body felt frighteningly perishable, a brittle brown leaf. The life in those eyes, though, was green and strong.

"Mother, do you forgive!" she whispered, suddenly looking off, ashamed. "I did it to save us. . . . I had no notion they'd orders to take me alive. . . ."

"Foolish as ever you are, to think I would judge such a thing now!" She pushed Auriane back to arm's length to get a mother's appraising look at her. "You are here, we are alive together on earth. . . . Fria is compassionate and great!"

Auriane felt her heart compressed to silence. Her look betrayed she envisioned what her mother must have endured.

"Do not torment yourself," Athelinda said firmly. "Indignities do not kill. I'm old and nothing causes me to fret. You look well, more than well!"

"Well, yes, they feed you passably well here, Mother," she said, striving to sound buoyant, "and the lodgings are comfortable enough. . . . The burdensome part of it is, that in exchange, now and then they expect you to kill someone for them."

Athelinda gave a sharp wave of the hand, meant to dismiss the school, the city of Rome, and all its dominions. "Hives of nidings. Why did the gods spawn so *many?* The wide Middle-Earth *teems* with them—I had no notion! Pay them no mind, they are not important to the gods." With one hand she possessively smoothed back her daughter's hair and dropped her voice to its prophesying register: "*You* are great to the gods. I have heard it, Auriane. Joy of joy. You avenged Baldemar! The heavens parted when you squeezed the life out of that monster, and I saw Baldemar on the high-seat. Are you woman or lioness?"

"The unaccountable thing was it was but a death," Auriane whispered, "one more death, not different from yours or mine or the lark's . . ."

"Speak no unholy words! Do not rattle the tranquillity of the heavens on this day. How cunningly the prophecy at your birth was played out!" Knowledge flickered in Athelinda's eyes. She held Auriane's face in her hands. "Your soul burns doubly bright. You carry a child."

"Yes."

Athelinda looked long, slowly absorbing this, then whispered, "Blessing on blessing! This one carries Arnwulf's soul, I am certain of it. . . . Such a small soul, light as a drift of fleece, such a short life . . ."

The guard intruded then.

"Aurinia, you must make ready. We're charged to accompany you to the house of Marcus Arrius Julianus. Go and gather your possessions."

Auriane moved to collect her meager things—the basket in which they had kept the food Marcus sent, a terra-cotta water jar, a brown wool cloak heavy with grime, a tied bundle of crudely penned love poems from her devotees—then stopped. No, she decided, to take these things would be like hugging onto old, worn despair. She would bring nothing but the clothes she wore and the bundle of rune-sticks tied in white cloth at her waist; it seemed right to go into the new world empty-handed as a newborn.

As they moved off down the passage, Auriane stepped gingerly into freedom, not quite believing it. It seemed impossible that none now could bar her way, that she could go anywhere. She realized then how deeply enslavement burrowed into the bone—the simple act of walking out the front entrance of the school seemed outlandish and wrong, like a fish taking to land.

For the last time she descended the stone steps from the Second Hall. As they gained the ground floor and moved past the gaping dark emptiness of the practice arena, an evil draft seemed to gust over it, charged with darkness and pain. How many paused here on their way to death? Auriane turned once and looked back, feeling she had forgotten something. Then she realized she felt a probing gaze on her back—familiar, abrasive, but kind. She sensed Erato, lingering, watching with concern, wishing her well. He was the only one in this place whom she would sorrow over. Silently she said to his spirit, "Farewell, good friend," and walked on.

As they entered the street, the lightening sky was Fria's opening eye; the cobbles beneath her feet a lover's bed. Some otherworldly celebration seemed in progress. Elves looked on benignly from high windows. In the frail light the water gushing from the street fountains sparkled like the brazen adornments of whirling ghosts. Every cross-street seemed a path into a new world. How strangely beautiful this Middle-Earth is, she thought, with its bewildering twists and turns too swift and unexpected for the heart, which always lags, anguished, a step or two behind.

Avenahar, now no hand is raised to separate us. Do you know I come, you who are old enough now to be taught the magic of the fields? Soon we will all be planted in one soil. My fate asserts itself, like the bony structure through the flesh of one who ages. Are fates always so ironic? I who so loathed Ramis *am here to pass on her teaching*.

They climbed cracked steps that sprouted hardy weeds, up the Esquiline's slope; when they came to Marcus Arrius Julianus' house, tears flooded her eyes when she saw the doors thrown open and garlanded.

Marcus Julianus awakened to the reassuring smell of a healing fumigant made of sweet balsam, rose leaves and cassia. The dull, digging pain in his back was rendered just manageable by the heavy draught Anaxagoras gave him—a decoction of poppy juice and henbane that made him feel he nested cozily among clouds. He wrestled for clarity, then slid reluctantly back into numbing haze. Something had been patiently nuzzling his hair, and had been, he realized, for some time. Had some animal gotten in?

He thought the discipline of remembering might help chase off the fog. Vaguely he recalled being carried to this bedchamber in his own house. As to who unlocked it, made it ready, and summoned Anaxagoras, he did not know. Petronius, he supposed. He remembered advising Nerva through the second night: Nerva had sat next to him in the medicinal smoke as he lay unceremoniously on his stomach, and they had laid out strategies while Anaxagoras did his best, beginning by bathing the gaped wounds with myrrh dissolved in wine. Marcus Julianus remembered ordering the arrangements for Auriane. Was all truly done?

Somehow even now he feared some evil fate might overtake her. Why did they not bring her to him? *Then* he could rest.

Again he felt that animal nuzzling. Who—or *what*—was with him now? And who let it in? A spurt of annoyance gave him the strength to drag open his eyes.

And he saw two gray eyes looking inquisitively into his own, two sensing, touching, testing eyes full of tender impatience.

"Auriane," he said, his voice hoarse, hushed. Tears swiftly pooled in his eyes, and he had no thought of concealing them. "It is really you! Dearer than life!" He reached out unsteadily, meaning to circle a hand about her neck, claim her and draw her closer, but it was impossible while flat on his stomach; even that small movement caused multiple eruptions of pain.

She caught the extended hand and gently replaced it on the mat, while never disengaging her gaze from his; both felt intimately near to the gods, as if they witnessed some small, secret miracle in a temple.

"I am sorry," she said finally. From the huskiness of her voice he knew she recently cried. "I awakened you. I wasn't supposed to."

"Perhaps you did not. Dreams are like this; day-on-day life, never!" His smile broadened. "Look at you! You came out of this far better than I, you little scamp. I can scarcely stand. And you—you look hardly the worse for having recently rid the world of a rampaging behemoth! It scarcely shows!"

She smiled at this, basking in an exhausted tranquillity that put her in mind of the first flushed moments after the birth of Avenahar. Then she nodded once toward the door through which Anaxagoras occasionally entered and exited. "I do not like that man. Someone snatched his soul and set it in quick-lime. And it's the soul that heals—knowledge of the plants is not enough. But, praise to the Fates, he promises you will live and be strong—through Fria's grace, not his!"

He grinned at this decisive dismissal of the most celebrated physician in all the Greek provinces. "I've no choice. . . . Too many depend upon me. Anyway, I'm not eager to stand face to face with Domitian so soon. He's in Hades, I'm here—I like that distance between us!"

As he spoke, she eased toward him as if love overburdened her and she could not sit upright; delicately, gravely, she found his mouth with her own. It was a complicated kiss that balanced greeting, promise, consolation. She shivered at the fine-honed intimacy of even this small introductory touch; it made her feel the length of her naked body was stretched luxuriantly against his.

After long moments of rich, contented silence, she found herself suddenly anxious that he know everything.

"Marcus, there are two things I must tell you. . . . One is joyous—or I hope you'll find it so—and the other is . . . dark and marvelous. . . ." She paused, momentarily silenced by caution. Restlessly she took up one of Anaxagoras' stone stamps that he used for marking his myrrh-sticks and began testing its smoothness in her hand. Finally she said firmly, "I should not tell you now."

"Not fair! Now you've pricked my interest!" He smiled. "Frustrated curiosity slows healing—I think Anaxagoras wrote a treatise on it."

"It is a thing that may disturb you greatly. I do not know—"

"I cannot imagine anything you could tell me that would . . . unless—is it that you have decided not to go with me? Is it that, Auriane?"

"No! I want with all my heart and mind to go with you! But know this"—she paused, replaced the stone stamp, and carefully watched his expression—"in about five months, there are going to be three of us."

Auriane saw sharp dismay come into his eyes. Then he shut them and turned away. "Is there no end to fortune's inhumanity!" he whispered.

She felt alarm rapidly filling her heart.

"You do not want my children?"

"Do not be ridiculous. Of course, I want your children. Oh, it is too hideous to contemplate. You struggled through all those months alone . . . you fought Aristos . . . while you were with child. It is pathetic. It is appalling. You should have sent word to me."

"I would have had to let Erato know. Anyway, you would have stopped me."

"Of course, I would have stopped you. I should have been with you."

"Well, the thing is done, and all has come out well, and the gods have been given their due. Cannot we just—"

"A child," he said wonderingly. "Yours, mine . . . a fresh new life . . . a thousand more things to consider. . . ." He pulled her protectively closer.

She felt light as a hawk's feather. "It all seems uncomplicated enough to me, Marcus. The mountain cat stalked her prey and at long last brought her prey down. Now she slinks off to bear her litter. What else should one expect from a woman half beast?"

"All the sooner I must make that beast my wife."

At this, the smallest flash of unease came to her eyes.

"What?" he asked softly, smiling.

"You brought me right to the door of the next troublesome thing." She pulled away from him slightly. "I should not say *this* now, either. . . ."

"You know my opinion on that!"

"Very well then. You shall know it." She met his eye solemnly. "I can go with you. I can share a house with you. But I cannot be a wife."

"Well, *that's* a departure from the dull and commonplace! This city swarms with women desperate to be a wife, who relentlessly stalk husbands, preferably rich—women who've no intention of becoming the mother of children. Our mountain cat has it all refreshingly reversed!"

"You are not angered by this?"

"Angered? Amused and amazed is closer, and, yes, saddened a bit. What has happened? It is what we spoke of before?"

"That . . . and a bit more. Since last we saw one another I . . . I have learned that the staff of our highest Holy One will one day pass to me. Not for many years, though—our Veleda still has all her powers. But those who are one day to administer the highest rites of Fria must never throttle and bind her highest gift—earthly love. Our Old One despises the permanent shackling together of woman and man just as does your own Diana. It is a curse of newer times, you see, a thing that belongs to the age of iron—"

"Diana's whitethorn torch bursts into conflagration! The part of me that serves philosophy understands at once—what purpose can ever be set over the seeking of divine knowledge? But I do not like it, truthfully. It presents problems. With inheritance, with—"

"But it does *not* prevent me from going freely with you as one beloved, and staying with you for long times . . . leaving only to attend to sacred duties."

"Why is it that opposing you feels like a violation of natural law? As if wrenching you from your path were like trying to coax a tree to grow on bare rock, or breed a donkey to a doe? I knew a man once, a philosopher called Isodorus, who was under the spell of the time of Saturn. I believe he would have held you up as a model for man. Long ago, on the night before he went to his death, he asked me to look after his pupils. I never understood it, for he had no school—his pupils wandered from gutter to bridge. But I think now he meant *you*."

She watched him with bright, still eyes.

"I still hold out marriage as the only way of properly behaving toward a woman carrying my child. Curses on Nemesis—why is nothing in this life just *plain and simple* as it should be?"

Within two months they set out for the villa on the Rhine. Their train was impressive; Nerva sent with them a sizable staff to aid Marcus Julianus in carrying out the duties of his new office, that of provincial Minister of Public Works for the province of Upper Germania, and they brought with them the whole of the household—or as much of it as Marcus Julianus had been able to rescue. Auriane felt she traveled with a city, so great was the number of carriages.

Though she moved homeward, still she felt she rode into shifting mystery, and uncertainties thronged about. Could she thrive in a house at all, or would she feel anxious as a wild horse trapped in a paddock? Would her people, not yet recovered from Domitian's war, accept her gifts and aid, or would they despise her for living with one of the hated foreigners? When she found it needful to go off to study the ways of the priestesses, would he want her still when she returned? Strangely these questions did not trouble her; they almost seemed a delight, as though life would have been a dull porridge without them.

When they came so near her ancestors' country that she knew the names of the grasses and felt the familiar souls of the trees, often when they halted at dusk, she would climb to some high place, sometimes with Marcus, sometimes with Sunia, and look at the land's shape on the horizon, waiting patiently for it to know her. At first she sensed only bleak, chilly indifference. Gradually, with the passing of days, she began to feel an affectionate caress in the wind, to hear greetings in the autumn rattling of the leaves of elm, oak, and ash.

You remember the one who loved you.

What has changed? Little enough on the face of it; beneath the surface, countries rose and fell.

Most would say it all quite remarkable. I was brought to that city naked and chained in a cart. I leave it borne in a gilded carriage.

Nature explains nothing, expects everything, and swallows us all at death. Nature dresses us, then denudes us again, like the land endlessly passing from winter to summer. At least now I begin to know you, winter and summer, as one.

At eight, Donna Gillespie asked her parents for an archae-ology book for Christmas, and she has been fascinated with ancient history and civilizations ever since. During her exhaustive research for *The Light Bearer*, Gillespie immersed herself in books on early Roman culture and Germanic tribes, reading every book on the topics she could unearth.

Gillespie is a resident of San Francisco and her writing career is a departure from her earlier work in photography and the fine arts. *The Light Bearer* is her first novel.